A writer since high school, Terry Brooks published his first novel, *The Sword of Shannara*, in 1977. It was a *New York Times* bestseller for more than five months. He has published twenty consecutive bestsellers since, including The Voyage of the *Jerle Shannara* trilogy, as well as the novel based upon the screenplay and story by George Lucas: *Star Wars*®: *Episode I The Phantom Menace*™.

Terry Brooks was a practicing attorney for many years but now writes full time. He lives with his wife, Judine, in the Pacific Northwest and Hawaii.

Visit him online at www.terrybrooks.net or explore *Shannara* at www.shannara.com.

By Terry Brooks

The Magic Kingdom of Landover
MAGIC KINGDOM FOR SALE—SOLD!
THE BLACK UNICORN
WIZARD AT LARGE
THE TANGLE BOX
WITCHES' BREW

Shannara
FIRST KING OF SHANNARA
THE SWORD OF SHANNARA
THE ELFSTONES OF SHANNARA
THE WISHSONG OF SHANNARA

The Heritage of Shannara
THE SCIONS OF SHANNARA
THE DRUID OF SHANNARA
THE ELF QUEEN OF SHANNARA
THE TALISMANS OF SHANNARA

The Voyage of the *Jerle Shannara*
ILSE WITCH
ANTRAX
MORGAWR

THE WORLD OF SHANNARA

High Druid of Shannara
JARKA RUUS

Word and Void
RUNNING WITH THE DEMON
A KNIGHT OF THE WORD
ANGEL FIRE EAST

STAR WARS®:
EPISODE I THE PHANTOM MENACE™

HOOK

SOMETIMES THE MAGIC WORKS:
LESSONS FROM A WRITING LIFE

THE VOYAGE
OF THE
JERLE SHANNARA

BOOK ONE: ILSE WITCH
BOOK TWO: ANTRAX
BOOK THREE: MORGAWR

TERRY
BROOKS

The Voyage of the *Jerle Shannara* trilogy first published in the United States
by The Ballantyne Publishing Group 2000, 2001, 2002
First published in Great Britain by
Simon & Schuster UK Ltd 2000, 2002
This omnibus edition published by Pocket Books, 2004
An imprint of Simon & Schuster UK Ltd
A Viacom Company

Maps by Russ Charpentier
Interior art by Russ Charpentier and Steve Stone

3 5 7 9 10 8 6 4

Simon & Schuster UK Ltd
Africa House
64–78 Kingsway
London WC2B 6AH

www.simonsays.co.uk

Simon & Schuster Australia
Sydney

A CIP catalogue record for this book is available from the British Library

ISBN 1 4165 0204 1

Printed and bound in Great Britain by
Cox & Wyman Ltd, Reading, Berks

BOOK ONE

ILSE WITCH

To Carol and Don McQuinn
For redefining the word *friends*
in more ways than I count

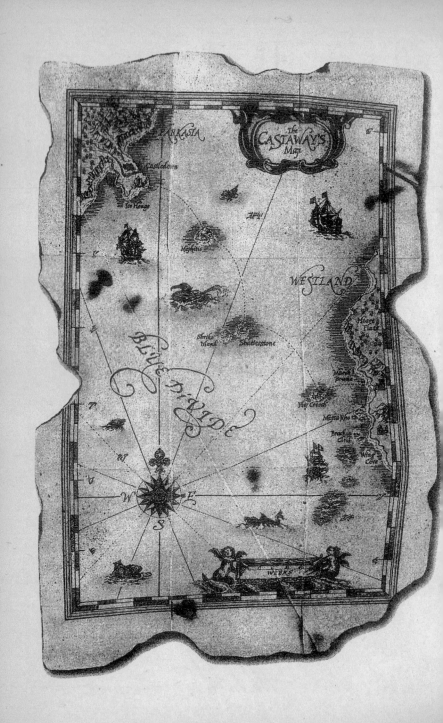

ONE

Hunter Predd was patrolling the waters of the Blue Divide north of the island of Mesca Rho, a Wing Hove outpost at the western edge of Elven territorial waters, when he saw the man clinging to the spar. The man was draped over the length of wood as if a cloth doll, his head laid on the spar so that his face was barely out of the water, one arm wrapped loosely about his narrow float to keep him from sliding away. His skin was burned and ravaged from sun, wind, and weather, and his clothing was in tatters. He was so still it was impossible to tell if he was alive. It was the odd rolling movement of his body within the gentle swells, in fact, that first caught Hunter Predd's eye.

Obsidian was already banking smoothly toward the castaway, not needing the touch of his master's hands and knees to know what to do. His eyes sharper than those of the Elf, he had spotted the man in the water before Hunter and shifted course to effect a rescue. It was a large part of the work he was trained to do, locating and rescuing those whose ships had been lost at sea. The Roc could tell a man from a piece of wood or a fish a thousand yards away.

He swung around slowly, great wings stretched wide, dipping toward the surface and plucking the man from the waters with a sure

3

and delicate touch. Great claws wrapped securely, but gently, about the limp form, the Roc lifted away again. Depthless and clear, the late spring sky spread away in a brilliant blue dome brightened by sunlight that infused the warm air and reflected in flashes of silver off the waves. Hunter Predd guided his mount back toward the closest piece of land available, a small atoll some miles from Mesca Rho. There he would see what, if anything, could be done.

They reached the atoll in less than half an hour, Hunter Predd keeping Obsidian low and steady in his flight the entire way. Black as ink and in the prime of his life, the Roc was his third as a Wing Rider and arguably the best. Besides being big and strong, Obsidian had excellent instincts and had learned to anticipate what Hunter wished of him before the Wing Rider had need to signal it. They had been together five years, not long for a Rider and his mount, but sufficiently long in this instance that they performed as if linked in mind and body.

Lowering to the leeward side of the atoll in a slow flapping of wings, Obsidian deposited his burden on a sandy strip of beach and settled down on the rocks nearby. Hunter Predd jumped off and hurried over to the motionless form. The man did not respond when the Wing Rider turned him on his back and began to check for signs of life. There was a pulse, and a heartbeat. His breathing was slow and shallow. But when Hunter Predd checked his face, he found his eyes had been removed and his tongue cut out.

He was an Elf, the Wing Rider saw. Not a member of the Wing Hove, however. The lack of harness scars on his wrists and hands marked him so. Hunter examined his body carefully for broken bones and found none. The only obvious physical damage seemed to be to his face. Mostly, he was suffering from exposure and lack of nourishment. Hunter placed a little fresh water from his pouch on the man's lips and let it trickle down his throat. The man's lips moved slightly.

Hunter considered his options and decided to take the man to the seaport of Bracken Clell, the closest settlement where he could find an Elven Healer to provide the care that was needed. He could take the man to Mesca Rho, but the island was only an outpost. Another Wing Rider and himself were its only inhabitants. No healing help could be found there. If he wanted to save the man's life, he would have to risk carrying him east to the mainland.

The Wing Rider bathed the man's skin in fresh water and applied a healing salve that would protect it from further damage. Hunter carried no extra clothing; the man would have to travel in the rags he wore. He tried again to give the man fresh water, and this time the man's mouth worked more eagerly in response, and he moaned softly. For an instant his ruined eyes tried to open, and he mumbled unintelligibly.

As a matter of course and in response to his training, the Wing Rider searched the man and took from his person the only two items he found. Both surprised and perplexed him. He studied each carefully, and the frown on his lips deepened.

Unwilling to delay his departure any longer, Hunter picked up the man and, with Obsidian's help, eased him into place on the Roc's broad back. A pad cushioned and restraining straps secured him. After a final check, Hunter climbed back aboard his mount, and Obsidian lifted away.

They flew east toward the coming darkness for three hours, and sunset was approaching when they sighted Bracken Clell. The seaport's population was a mixture of races, predominantly Elven, and the inhabitants were used to seeing Wing Riders and their Rocs come and go. Hunter Predd took Obsidian upland to a clearing marked for landings, and the big Roc swung smoothly down into the trees. A messenger was sent into town from among the curious who quickly gathered, and the Elven Healer appeared with a clutch of litter bearers.

"What's happened to him?" the Healer asked of Hunter Predd, on discovering the man's empty eye sockets and ruined mouth.

Hunter shook his head. "That's how I found him."

"Identification? Who is he?"

"I don't know," the Wing Rider lied.

He waited until the Healer and his attendants had picked up the man and begun carrying him toward the Healer's home, where the man would be placed in one of the sick bays in the healing center, before dispatching Obsidian to a more remote perch, then following after the crowd. What he knew was not to be shared with the Healer or anyone else in Bracken Clell. What he knew was meant for one man only.

He sat on the Healer's porch and smoked his pipe, his longbow and hunting knife by his side as he waited for the Healer to reemerge. The sun had set, and the last of the light lay across the waters of the bay in splashes of scarlet and gold. Hunter Predd was small and slight for a Wing Rider, but tough as knotted cord. He was neither young nor old, but comfortably settled in the middle and content to be there. Sun-browned and windburned, his face seamed and his eyes gray beneath a thick thatch of brown hair, he had the look of what he was—an Elf who had lived all of his life in the outdoors.

Once, while he was waiting, he took out the bracelet and held it up to the light, reassuring himself that he had not been mistaken about the crest it bore. The map he left in his pocket.

One of the Healer's attendants brought him a plate of food, which he devoured silently. When he was finished eating, the attendant reappeared and took the plate away, all without speaking. The Healer still hadn't emerged.

It was late when he finally did, and he looked haggard and unnerved as he settled himself next to Hunter. They had known each other for some time, the Healer having come to the seaport only a year after Hunter had returned from the border wars and settled into Wing Rider service off the coast. They had shared in more than one rescue effort and, while of different backgrounds and callings, were of similar persuasion regarding the foolishness of the world's progress. Here, in an outback of the broader civilization that was designated the Four Lands, they had found they could escape a little of the madness.

"How is he?" Hunter Predd asked.

The Healer sighed. "Not good. He may live. If you can call it that. He's lost his eyes and his tongue. Both were removed forcibly. Exposure and malnutrition have eroded his strength so severely he will probably never recover entirely. He came awake several times and tried to communicate, but couldn't."

"Maybe with time—"

"Time isn't the problem," the Healer interrupted, drawing his gaze and holding it. "He cannot speak or write. It isn't just the damage to his tongue or his lack of strength. It is his mind. His mind is gone. Whatever he has been through has damaged him irreparably. I don't think he knows where he is or even who he is."

Hunter Predd looked off into the night. "Not even his name?"

"Not even that. I don't think he remembers anything of what's happened to him."

The Wing Rider was silent a moment, thinking. "Will you keep him here for a while longer, care for him, watch over him? I want to look into this more closely."

The Healer nodded. "Where will you start?"

"Arborlon, perhaps."

A soft scrape of a boot brought him about sharply. An attendant appeared with hot tea and food for the Healer. He nodded to them without speaking and disappeared again. Hunter Predd stood, walked to the door to be certain they were alone, then reseated himself beside the Healer.

"Watch this damaged man closely, Dorne. No visitors. Nothing until you hear back from me."

The Healer sipped at his tea. "You know something about him that you're not telling me, don't you?"

"I suspect something. There's a difference. But I need time to make certain. Can you give me that time?"

The Healer shrugged. "I can try. The man inside will have something to say about whether he will still be here when you return. He is very weak. You should move swiftly."

Hunter Predd nodded. "As swift as Obsidian's wings can fly," he replied softly.

Behind him, in the near darkness of the open doorway, a shadow detached itself from behind a wall and moved silently away.

The attendant who had served dinner to the Wing Rider and the Healer waited until after midnight, when the people of Bracken Clell were mostly asleep, to slip from his rooms in the village into the surrounding forest. He moved quickly and without the benefit of light, knowing his path well from having traveled it many times before. He was a small, wizened man who had spent the whole of his life in the village and was seldom given a second glance. He lived alone and had few friends. He had served in the Healer's household for better than thirteen years, a quiet, uncomplaining sort who lacked imagination but could be depended on. His qualities suited him well in his work as a Healer's attendant, but even better as a spy.

He reached the cages he kept concealed in a darkened pen behind the old cabin in which he had been born. When his father and mother had died, possession had passed to him as the eldest male. It was a poor inheritance, and he had never accepted that it was all to which he was entitled. When the opportunity had been offered to him, he snatched at it eagerly. A few words overheard here and there, a face or a name recognized from tales told in taverns and ale houses, bits and pieces of information tossed his way by those rescued from the ocean and brought to the center to heal—they were all worth something to the right people.

And to one person in particular, make no mistake about it.

The attendant understood what was expected of him. She had made it clear from the beginning. She was to be his Mistress, to whom

8

he must answer most strongly should he step from between the lines of obedience she had charted for him. Whoever passed through the Healer's doors and whatever they said, if they or it mattered at all, she was to know. She told him the decision to summon her was his, always his. He must be prepared to answer for his summons, of course. But it would be better to act boldly than belatedly. A chance missed was much less acceptable to her than time wasted.

He had guessed wrongly a few times, but she had not been angry or critical. A few mistakes were to be expected. Mostly, he knew what was worth something and what was not. Patience and perseverance were necessary.

He'd developed both, and they had served him well. This time, he knew, he had something of real value.

He unfastened the cage door and took out one of the strange birds she had given him. They were wicked-looking things with sharp eyes and beaks, swept-back wings, and narrow bodies. They watched him whenever he came in sight, or took them out of the cages, or fastened a message to their legs, as he was doing now. They watched him as if marking his efficiency for a report they would make later. He didn't like the way they looked at him, and he seldom looked back.

When the message was in place, he tossed the bird into the air, and it rose into the darkness and disappeared. They flew only at night, these birds. Sometimes, they returned with messages from her. Sometimes, they simply reappeared, waiting to be placed back in their cages. He never questioned their origins. It was better, he sensed, simply to accept their usefulness.

He stared into the night sky. He had done what he could. There was nothing to do now, but wait. She would tell him what was needed next. She always did.

Closing the doors to the pen so that the cages were hidden once more, he crept silently back the way he had come.

* * *

Two days later, Allardon Elessedil had just emerged from a long session with the Elven High Council centered on the renewal of trade agreements with the cities of Callahorn and on the seemingly endless war they fought as allies with the Dwarves against the Federation, when he was advised that a Wing Rider was waiting to speak to him. It was late in the day, and he was tired, but the Wing Rider had flown all the way to Arborlon from the southern seaport of Bracken Clell, a two-day journey, and was refusing to deliver his message to anyone but the King. The aide who advised Allardon of the Wing Rider's presence conveyed quite clearly the other's determination not to be swayed on this issue.

The Elf King nodded and followed his aide to where the Wing Rider waited. His arrangement with the Wing Hove demanded that he accede to any request for privacy in the conveyance of messages. Pursuant to a contract drawn up in the early years of Wren Elessedil's rule, the Wing Riders had been serving the Land Elves as scouts and messengers along the coast of the Blue Divide for more than 130 years. They were provided with goods and coin in exchange for their services, and it was an arrangement that the Elven Kings and Queens had found useful on more than one occasion. If the Wing Rider who waited had asked to speak with Allardon personally, then there was good reason for the request, and he was not about to ignore it.

With Home Guards Perin and Wye flanking him protectively, he trailed after his aide as they departed the High Council and walked back through the gardens to the Elessedil palace home. Allardon Elessedil had been King for more than twenty years, since the death of his mother, the Queen Aine. He was of medium height and build, still fit and trim in spite of his years, his mind sharp and his body strong. Only his graying hair and the lines on his face gave evidence of his advanced years. He was a direct descendant of the great Queen Wren Elessedil, who had brought the Elves and their city out of the island wilderness of Morrowindl into which the Federation and the hated Shadowen had driven them. He was her great-great-grandson, and he had lived the whole of his life as if measuring it against hers.

It was difficult to do so in these times. The war with the Federation had been raging for ten years and showed no signs of ending anytime soon. The Southland coalition of Bordermen, Dwarves, and Elves had halted the Federation advance below the Duln two years earlier on the Prekkendorran Heights. Now the armies were stalemated in a front that had failed to shift one way or the other in all that time and continued to consume lives and waste energy at an alarming rate. There was no question that the war was necessary. The Federation's attempt at reclaiming the Borderlands it had lost in the time of Wren Elessedil was invasive and predatory and could not be tolerated. But the King couldn't help thinking that his ancestor would have found a way to put an end to it by now, where he had failed to do so.

None of which had anything to do with the matter at hand, he chided himself. The war with the Federation was centered at the crossroads of the Four Lands and had not yet spilled over onto the coast. For now, at least, it was contained.

He walked into the reception room where the Wing Rider was waiting and immediately dismissed those who accompanied him. A member of the Home Guard would already be concealed within striking distance, although Allardon had never personally heard of a Wing Rider turned assassin.

As the door closed behind his small entourage, he extended his hand to the Rider. "I'm sorry you had to wait. I was sitting with the High Council, and my aide didn't want to disturb me." He shook the other's corded hand and scanned the weathered face. "I know you, don't I? You've brought me a message once or maybe twice before."

"Once, only," the other advised. "It was a long time ago. You wouldn't have reason to remember me. My name is Hunter Predd."

The Elven King nodded, failing to recognize the other's name, but smiling anyway. Wing Riders cared nothing for formalities, and he didn't bother relying on them here. "What do you have for me, Hunter?"

The Wing Rider reached inside his tunic and produced a short, slender length of metal chain and a scrap of hide. He held on to both as he spoke. "Three days ago, I was patrolling the waters north off the island of Mesca Rho, a Wing Hove outpost. I found a man floating on a ship spar. He was barely alive, suffering from exposure and dehydration. I don't know how long he was out there, but it must have been some time. His eyes and his tongue had been cut out before he had been cast adrift. He was wearing this."

He held out the length of metal chain first, which turned out to be a bracelet. Allardon accepted it, studied it, and went pale. The bracelet bore the Elessedil crest, the spreading boughs of the sacred Ellcrys surrounded by a ring of Bloodfire. It had been more than thirty years since he had seen the bracelet, but he recognized it immediately.

His gaze shifted from the bracelet to the Wing Rider. "The man you found wore this?" he asked quietly.

"It was on his wrist."

"Did you recognize him?"

"I recognized the bracelet's crest, not the man."

"There was no other identification?"

"Only this. I searched him carefully."

He handed the piece of softened hide to Allardon. It was frayed about the edges, water stained and worn. The Elf King opened it carefully. It was a map, its symbols and writing etched in faded ink and in places smudged. He studied it carefully, making sure of what he had. He recognized the Westland coast along the Blue Divide. A dotted line ran from island to island, traveling west and north and ending at a peculiar collection of blocky spikes. There were names beneath each of the islands and the cluster of spikes, but he did not recognize them. The writing in the margins of the map was indecipherable. The symbols that decorated and perhaps identified certain places on the map were of strange and frightening creatures he had never seen.

"Do you recognize any of these markings?" he asked Hunter Predd.

The Wing Rider shook his head. "Most of what the map shows is outside the territory we patrol. The islands are beyond the reach of our Rocs, and the names are not familiar."

Allardon walked to the tall, curtained windows that opened onto the garden, and stood looking out at the flower beds. "Where is the man you found, Hunter? Is he still alive?"

"I left him with the Healer who serves Bracken Clell. He was alive when I left."

"Have you told anyone else of this bracelet and map?"

"No one knows but you. Not even the Healer. He is a friend, but I know enough to keep silent when silence is called for."

Allardon nodded his approval. "You do, indeed."

He called for cold glasses of ale and a full pitcher from which to refill them. His mind raced as he waited with the Wing Rider for the beverage and containers to be brought. He was stunned by the salvaged articles and by what he had been told, and he wasn't certain, even knowing what he did, what course of action to take. He recognized the bracelet and, thereby, he must assume, the identity of the man from whom it had been taken. He had not seen either in thirty years nor had he expected to see them ever again. He had never seen the map, but even without being able to decipher its language or read its symbols, he could guess at what it was meant to show.

He thought suddenly of his mother, Aine, dead for twenty-five years, and the memory of her anguish during the last years of her life brought tears to his eyes.

He fingered the bracelet absently, remembering.

Thirty years earlier, his mother, as Queen, had authorized an Elven sailing expedition to undertake a search for a treasure of great value purported to have survived the Great Wars that had destroyed the Old World. The impetus for the expedition had been a dream visited on his mother's seer, an Elven mystic of great power and widespread acclaim. The dream had foretold of a land of ice, of a ruined city within the land, and of a safehold in which a treasure of immeasurable worth lay protected and concealed. This treasure, if recovered, had the power to change the course of history and the lives of all who came in contact with it.

The seer had been wary of the dream, for she understood the power of dreams to deceive. The nature of the treasure sought was unclear, and its source was vague and uncharted. The land in which the treasure could be found lay somewhere across the Blue Divide in territory that no one had ever seen. There were no directions for reaching it, no instructions for locating it, and little more than a series of images to describe it. Perhaps, the seer advised, it was a dream best left alone.

But Allardon's elder brother, Kael Elessedil, had been intrigued by the possibilities the dream suggested and by the challenge of searching for an unexplored land. He had embraced the dream as his destiny, and he had begged his mother to let him go. In the end, she had relented. Kael Elessedil had been granted his expedition, and with three sailing ships and their crews under his command, he had departed.

Just before leaving, his mother had given him the famous blue Elfstones that had once belonged to Queen Wren. The Elfstones would guide them to their destination and protect them from harm. Their magic would bring the Elves safely back home again.

When he left Arborlon to travel to the coast, where the ships his mother had commissioned were waiting, Kael Elessedil was wearing the bracelet his brother now held. It was the last time Allardon saw him. The expedition had never returned. The ships, their crews, his brother, everything and everyone, had simply vanished. Search parties had been dispatched, one after the other, but not a trace of the missing Elves had ever been found.

Allardon exhaled softly. Until now. He stared at the bracelet in his hand. Until this.

Kael's disappearance had changed everything in the lives of his family. His mother had never recovered from her eldest son's disappearance, and the last years of her life were spent in a slow wasting away of health and hope as one rescue effort after another failed and all were finally abandoned. When she died, Allardon became the King his brother was meant to be and he had never expected to become.

He thought of the ruined man lying wasted, voiceless, and blind in the Healer's rooms in Bracken Clell and wondered if his brother had come home at last.

The ale arrived, and Allardon sat with Hunter Predd on a bench in the gardens and questioned the Wing Rider again and again, covering the same ground several times over, approaching the matter from different points of view, making certain he had learned everything there was to know. Perhaps understanding in part at least, the trauma he had visited upon the Elven King by his coming, Hunter was cooperative. He did not presume to ask questions of his own, for which Allardon was grateful, but simply responded to the questions he was asked, keeping company with the King for as long as it was required.

When the interview was ended, Allardon asked the Wing Rider to stay the night so that the King could have time to consider what further need he might have of him. He did not make it a command, but a request. Food and lodging would be provided for rider and mount, and his staying would be a favor. Hunter Predd agreed.

Alone again, in his study now, where he did most of his thinking on matters that required a balancing of possibilities and choices, Allardon Elessedil considered what he must do. After thirty years and considerable damage, he might not be able to recognize his brother, even if it was Kael whom the Bracken Clell Healer attended. He had to assume that it was, for the bracelet was genuine.

It was the map that was troubling. What was he to do with it? He could guess at its worth, but he could not read enough of it to measure the extent of its information. If he were to mount a new expedition, an event he was already seriously considering, he could not afford to do so without making every possible effort to discover what he was up against.

He needed someone to translate the phrases on the map. He needed someone who could tell him what they said.

There was only one person who could do that, he suspected. Certainly, only one of whom he knew.

It was dark outside by now, the night settled comfortably down about the Westland forests, the walls and roofs of the city's buildings faded away and replaced by clusters of lights that marked their continued presence. In the Elessedil family home, it was quiet. His wife was busy with their daughters, working on a quilt for his birthday that he was not supposed to know about. His eldest son, Kylen, commanded a regiment on the Prekkendorran front. His youngest, Ahren, hunted the forests north with Ard Patrinell, Captain of the Home Guard. Considering the size of his family and the scope of his authority as King, he felt surprisingly alone and helpless in the face of what he knew he must do.

But how to do it? How, so that it would achieve what was needed?

The dinner hour had come and gone, and he remained where he was, thinking the matter through. It was difficult even to consider doing what was needed, because the man he must deal with was in many ways anathema to him. But deal with him he must, putting aside his own reservations and their shared history of antagonism and spite. He could do that because that was part of what being a King required, and he had made similar concessions before in other situations. It was finding a way to persuade the other to do likewise that was difficult. It was conceiving of an approach that would not meet with instant rejection that was tricky.

In the end, he found what he needed right under his nose. He would send Hunter Predd, the Wing Rider, as his emissary. The Wing Rider would go because he understood the importance and implications of his discovery and because Allardon would grant the Wing Hove a concession they coveted as a further enticement. The man whose services he required would respond favorably because he had no quarrel with the Wing Riders as he did with the Land Elves, and because Hunter Predd's direct, no-nonsense approach would appeal to him.

There were no guarantees, of course. His gambit might fail, and he might be forced to try again—perhaps even to go there himself. He would have to, he knew, if all else failed. But he was counting on his adversary's inquisitive mind and curious nature to win him over; he would not be able to resist the challenge of the map's puzzle. He would not be able to ignore the lure of its secrets. His life did not allow for that. Whatever else he might be, and he was many things, he was a scholar first.

The Elf King brought out the scrap of map the Wing Rider had carried to him and placed it on his writing desk. He would have it copied, so that he might protect against its unforeseen loss. But copied accurately, with all symbols and words included, for any hint of treachery would sink the whole venture in a second. A scribe could accomplish what was needed without being told of the map's origins or worth. Discretion was possible.

Nevertheless, he would stay with the scribe until the job was completed. His decision made, he dispatched an aide to summon the one who was needed and sat back to await his arrival. Dinner would have to keep a little while longer.

Two

O n the same night Allardon Elessedil awaited the arrival of his scribe to make a copy of the map delivered by Hunter Predd, the spy in the household of the Bracken Clell Healer received a response to the message he had dispatched to his Mistress two days earlier. It was not the kind of response he had anticipated.

She was waiting for him when he came to his rooms at nightfall, his day's work finished, his mind on other things. Perhaps he was thinking of slipping out later to his cages to see if one of her winged couriers had arrived with a message. Perhaps he was thinking only of a hot meal and a warm bed. Whatever the case, he was not expecting to find her. Surprised and frightened by her appearance, he flinched and cried out when she detached herself from the shadows. She soothed him with a soft word, quieted him, and waited patiently for him to recover himself enough to acknowledge her properly.

"Mistress," he whispered, dropping to one knee and bowing deeply. She was pleased to discover he had not forgotten his manners. Although she had not come to him in many years, he remembered his place.

She left him bowed and on his knee a moment longer, standing before him, her whisper of reassurance and subtle pressure soft and light upon the air. Gray robes cloaked her from head to foot, and a hood concealed her face. Her spy had never seen her in the light or caught even the barest glimpse of her features. She was an enigma, a shadow exuding presence rather than identity. She kept herself at one with the darkness, a creature to be felt rather than viewed, keeping watch even when not seen.

"Mistress, I have important information," her spy murmured without looking up, waiting to be told he might rise.

The Ilse Witch left him where he was, considering. She knew more than he imagined, more than he could guess, for she possessed power that was beyond his understanding. From the message he had sent—his words, his handwriting, his scent upon the paper—she could measure the urgency he was feeling. From the way he presented himself now—his demeanor, his tone of voice, his carriage—she could decipher his need. It was her gift always to know more than those with whom she came in contact wished her to know. Her magic laid them bare and left them as transparent as still waters.

The Ilse Witch stretched out her robed arm. "Rise," she commanded.

The spy did so, keeping his head lowered, his eyes cast down. "I did not think you would come . . ."

"For you, for information of such importance, I could do no less." She shifted her stance and bent forward slightly. "Speak, now, of what you know."

The spy shivered, excitement coursing through him, anxious to be of service. Within the shadows of her hood, she smiled.

"A Wing Rider rescued an Elf from the sea and brought him to the Healer who serves this community," the spy advised, daring now to lift his eyes as far as the hem of her robes. "The man's eyes and tongue were removed, and the Healer says he is half-mad. I don't doubt it, from the look of him. The Healer cannot determine his identity, and the Wing Rider claims not to know it either, but he suspects something. And the Wing Rider took something from the man before bringing him here. I caught a glimpse of it—a bracelet that bears the crest of the Elessedils."

The spy's gaze lifted now to seek out her own. "The Wing Rider left for Arborlon two days ago. I heard him tell the Healer where he was going. He took the bracelet with him."

She regarded him in silence for a moment, her cloaked form as still as the shadows it mirrored. A bracelet bearing the crest of the Elessedils, she mused. The Wing Rider would have taken it to Allardon Elessedil to identify. Whose bracelet was it? What did it mean that it was found on this castaway Elf who was blind and voiceless and believed mad?

The answers to her questions were locked inside the castaway's head. He must be made to give them up.

"Where is the man now?" she asked.

The spy hunched forward eagerly, the fingers of his hands knotted together beneath his chin as if in prayer. "He lies in the Healer's infirmary, cared for but kept isolated until the Wing Rider's return. No one is allowed to speak with him." He snorted softly. "As if anyone could. He has no tongue with which to answer, has he?"

She gestured him away and to the side, and he moved as if a puppet in response. "Wait here for me," she said. "Wait, until I return."

She went out the door into the night, a spectral figure sliding effortlessly and soundlessly through the shadows. The Ilse Witch liked the darkness, found comfort in it she could never find in daylight. The darkness soothed and shaded, softening edges and points, reducing clarity. Vision lost importance because the eyes could be deceived. A shift of movement here changed the look of something there. What was certain in the light became suspect in the dark. It mirrored her life, a collage of images and voices, of memories that had shaped her growing, not all fitting tightly in sequence, not all linked together in ways that made sense. Like the shadows with which she so closely identified, her life was a patchwork of frayed ends and loose threads that invited refitting and mending. Her past was not carved of stone, but drawn on water. Reinvent yourself, she had been told by the Morgawr a long time ago. Reinvent yourself, and you will become more inscrutable to those who might try to unravel who you really are.

In the night, in darkness and shadows, she could do so more easily. She could keep what she looked like to herself and conceal who she really was. She could let them imagine her, and by doing so keep them forever deceived.

She moved through the village without challenge, encountering almost no one, those few she did unaware of her presence as they passed. It was late, the village mostly asleep, the ones who preferred the night busy in the ale houses and pleasure dens, caught up in their own wants and needs, uncaring of what transpired without. She could forgive them their weaknesses, these men and women, but she could never accept them as equals. Long since, she had abandoned any pretense that she believed their common origins linked them in any meaningful way. She was a creature of fire and iron. She was born to magic and power. It was her destiny to shape and alter the lives of others and never to be altered by them. It was her passion to rise above the fate that others had cast for her as a child and to visit revenge on them for daring to do so. She would be so much more than they, and they would be forever less.

When she let them speak her name again, when she chose to speak it herself, it would be remembered. It would not be buried in the ashes of her childhood, as it had once been. It would not be cast aside, a fragment of her lost past. It would soar with a hawk's smooth glide and shine with the milky brightness of the moon. It would linger on the minds of the people of her world forever.

The Healer's house lay ahead, close by the trees of the surrounding forest. She had flown in from the Wilderun late that afternoon, come out of her safehold in response to the spy's message, sensing its importance, wanting to discover for herself what secrets it held. She had left her War Shrike in the old growth below the bluffs, its fierce head hooded and its taloned feet hobbled. It would bolt otherwise, so wild that even her magic could not hold it when she was absent. But as a fighting bird, it was without equal. Even the giant Rocs were wary of it, for the Shrike fought to the death with little thought to protecting itself. No one would see it, for she had cast a spell of forbidding about it to keep the unwanted away. By sunrise, she would have returned. By sunrise, she would be gone again, even given the dictates of what she must do now.

She slipped through the door of the Healer's home on cat's paws, moving through the central rooms to the sick bays, humming softly as she passed the attendants on duty, turning their minds inward and eyes elsewhere as she passed so they would not see her. The ones who kept watch outside the castaway's curtained entry, she put to sleep. They sank into their chairs and leaned against walls and tables, eyes going closed, breathing slowing and deepening. It was quiet and peaceful in the Healer's home, and her song fit snugly into place. She layered the air with her music, a tender blanket tucking in around the cautions and uneasiness that might otherwise have been triggered. Soon, she was all alone and free to work.

In his bay, with a light covering over his feverish body and the window curtains drawn close to keep out the light, the castaway lay dozing on the pallet that had been provided for him. His skin was blistered and raw, and the mending salve the Healer had applied glistened in a damp sheen. His body was wasted from lack of nourishment, his heart beat weakly in his chest, and his bruised and ravaged face was skeletal, the eyelids sunken in where the eyes themselves had been gouged out, the mouth a scarred red wound behind cracked lips.

The Ilse Witch studied him carefully for a time, letting her eyes tell her as much as they could, noting the man's distinctly Elven features, the graying hair that marked him as no longer young, and the rigid crook of fingers and neck that screamed silently of tortures endured. She did not like the feel of the man; he had been made to

22

suffer purposely and used for things she did not care to guess at. She did not like the scent he gave off or the small sounds he made. He was living in another place and time, unable to forget what he had suffered, and it was not pleasant.

When she touched him, ever so softly on his chest with her slim, cool fingers, he convulsed as if struck. Quickly, she employed her magic, singing softly to calm him, lending peace and reassurance. The arched back relaxed slowly, and the clawed fingers released their death grip on the bed covering. A sigh escaped the cracked lips. Relief in any form was welcome to this one, she thought, continuing to sing, to work her way past his defenses and into his mind.

When he was at rest again, given over to her ministrations and become her dependent, she placed her hands upon his fevered body so that she might draw from him his thoughts and feelings. She must unlock what lay hidden in his mind—his experiences, his travails, his secrets. She must do so through his senses, but primarily through his voice. He could no longer speak as ordinary men, but he could still communicate. It required only that she find a way to make him want to do so.

In the end, it was not all that hard. She bound him to her through her singing, probing gently as she did so, and he began to make what small and unintelligible sounds he could. She drew him out one grunt, one murmur, one gasp at a time. From each sound, she gained an image of what he knew, stored it away, and made it her own. The sounds were inhuman and rife with pain, but she absorbed them without flinching, bathing him in a wash of compassion, of reassurance and pity, of gentleness and the promise of healing.

Speak to me. Live again through me. Give me everything you hide, and I will give you peace.

He did so, and the images were brightly colored and stunning. There was an ocean, vast and blue and uncharted. There were islands, one after the other, some green and lush, some barren and rocky, each of a different feel, each hiding something monstrous. There were frantic, desperate battles in which weapons clashed and men died. There were feelings of such intensity, such raw power, that they eclipsed the events that triggered them and revealed the scars they had left on their bearer.

Finally, there were pillars of ice that reached to the misted, cool skies, their massive forms shifting and grinding like giant's teeth as a thin beam of blue fire born of Elfstone magic shone through to something that lay beyond. There was a city, all in ruins, ancient and alive with monstrous protectors. And there was a keep, buried in the earth, warded by smooth metal and bright red eyes, containing magic . . .

The Ilse Witch gasped in spite of herself as the last image registered, an image of the magic the castaway had found within the buried keep. It was a magic of spells invoked by words—but so many! The number seemed endless, stretching away into shadows from soft pools of light, their power poised to rise into the air in a canopy so vast it might cover the whole of the earth!

The castaway was writhing beneath her, and the hold she kept on him slipped away momentarily as she lost focus. She brought her song to bear again, layering it over him, embedding herself more deeply within his mind to keep him under control.

Who are you? Speak your name!

His body lurched and the sounds he made were terrifying.

Tell me!

He answered her, and when he did, she understood at once the importance of the bracelet.

What else were you carrying? What else, that speaks to this?

He fought her, not realizing what it was he was fighting, only knowing that he must. She sensed it was not entirely his idea to fight her, that either someone had implanted within his mind the need to do so or something had happened to persuade him it was necessary. But she was strong and certain in her magic, and he lacked the defenses necessary to resist her.

A map, she saw. Drawn on an old skin, inked in his own hand. A map, she surmised at once, that was no longer his, but was on its way to Arborlon and the Elven King.

She tried to determine what was on the map, and for a moment she was able to reconstruct a vague image from his grunts and moans. She caught a glimpse of names written and symbols drawn here and there, saw a dotted line connecting islands off the coast of the Westland and out into the Blue Divide. She traced the line to the pillars of ice and to the land in which the safehold lay. But the writings and drawings were lost to her when he convulsed a final time and lay back, his voice spent, his mind emptied, and his body limp and unmoving beneath her touch.

She stilled her song and stepped away from him. She had all she was going to get, but what she had was enough to tell her what was needed. She listened to the silence for a moment, making sure her presence had not yet been detected. The castaway Elf lay motionless on his raised pallet, gone so deeply inside himself he would never come out again. He would live perhaps, but he would never recover.

She shook her head. It was pointless to leave him so.

Kael Elessedil, son of Queen Aine, once destined to be King of the Elves. It was before her time, but she knew the story. Lost for thirty years, and this was his sorry fate.

The Ilse Witch stepped close and drew back her hood to reveal the face that few ever saw. Within her concealing garments, she was nothing of what she seemed. She was very young, barely a grown woman, her hair long and dark, her eyes a startling blue, and her features smooth and lovely. As a child, when she had the name she no longer spoke, she would look at herself in the mirror of the waters of a little cove that pooled off the stream that ran not far from her home and try to imagine how she would look when grown. She had not thought herself pretty then, when it mattered to her. She did not think herself pretty now, when it did not.

There was warmth and tenderness in her face and eyes as she

bent to kiss the ruined man on his lips. She held the kiss long enough to draw the breath from his lungs, and then he died.

"Be at peace, Kael Elessedil," she whispered in his ear.

She went from the Healer's home as she had come, hooded once more, a shadowy presence that drew no notice by its passing. The attendants would come awake after she was gone, unaware that anything had transpired, not sensing they had slept or that time had passed.

The Ilse Witch was already sifting through the images she had culled, weighing her options. The magic Kael Elessedil had discovered was priceless. Even without knowing exactly what it was, she could sense that much. It must be hers, of course. She must do what he had failed to do—find it, claim it, and retrieve it. It was protected in some way, as such magic necessarily would be, but there were no defenses she could not overcome. Her course of action was already decided, and only a settling of the particulars remained.

What she coveted, even if she did not require it in order to succeed, was the map.

Sliding through the darkness of Bracken Clell, she gave consideration to how she might gain possession of it. The Wing Rider had taken it to Allardon Elessedil in Arborlon, along with Kael Elessedil's bracelet. The Elven King would recognize the importance of both, but he would not be able to translate the writings on the map. Nor would he have the benefit of his now dead brother's thoughts, as she did. He would seek help from another in deciphering the mysterious symbols to determine what his brother had found.

Who would he turn to?

She knew the answer to her question almost before she had finished asking it. There was only one he could ask. One, who would be sure to know. Her enemy, one-armed and dark-browed, crippled of body and soul. Her nemesis, but her equal in the nuanced wielding of magic's raw power.

Her thinking changed instantly with recognition of what this meant. Now there would be competition in her quest, and time would become precious. She would not have the luxuries of long deliberation and careful planning to sustain her effort. She would be faced with a challenge that would test her as nothing else could.

Even the Morgawr might choose to involve himself in a struggle of this magnitude.

She had slowed perceptibly, but now she picked up her pace once more. She was getting ahead of herself. Before she could return to the Wilderun with her news, she must conclude matters here. She must tie up loose ends. Her spy was still waiting to learn the value of his information. He would expect to be complimented on his diligence and well paid for his efforts. She must see to both.

Still, as she moved silently through the village and nearer to her spy's rooms, her thoughts kept returning to the confrontation that lay ahead, in a time too distant yet to fix upon, in a place perhaps far removed from the lands she traveled now—a confrontation of wills, of magics, and of destinies. She and her adversary, locked in a final struggle for supremacy, just as she had dreamed they would one day be—the image burned in her thoughts like a hot coal and fired her imagination.

Her spy was waiting for her when she entered his rooms. "Mistress," he acknowledged, dropping obediently to one knee.

"Rise," she told him.

He did so, keeping his gaze lowered, his head bent.

"You have done well. What you told me has opened doors that I had only dreamed about."

She watched him beam with pride and clasp his hands in anticipation of the reward she would bestow upon him. "Thank you, Mistress."

"It is for me to thank you," she replied. She reached into her robes and withdrew a leather pouch that clinked enticingly. "Open it when I am gone," she said quietly. "Be at peace."

She left without delay, her business almost finished. She went from the village to the decaying cottage that belonged to her spy, uncaged her birds, and sent them winging back into the Wilderun. She would find them waiting within her safehold when she returned. The spy would have no further use for them. Within the bag of gold she had given him nested a tiny snake whose bite was so lethal that even the smallest nick from a single fang was fatal. Her spy would not wait until morning to count his coins; he would do so tonight. He would be found, of course, but by then the snake would be gone. She guessed that the money would be gone almost as fast. In quarters of the sort where her spy lived, it was well known that dead men had no need for gold.

She gave the matter little thought as she made her way back to where she had hobbled and hooded her War Shrike. Although they were many and were positioned in large numbers throughout the Four Lands, she did not give up her spies easily. She was fiercely protective of them when they were as useful and reliable as this one had been.

But even the best spy could be found out and made to betray her, and she could not chance that happening here. Better to cut her losses than to take such an obvious risk. A life was a small price to pay for an edge on her greatest enemy.

But how was she to gain possession of that map? She thought momentarily of going after it herself. But to steal it from Allardon Elessedil, who would have it by now, in the heart of Elven country, was too dangerous a task for her to undertake without careful planning. She could try to intercept it on its inevitable way to her enemy, but how was she to determine the means by which it would be conveyed? Besides, she might already be too late, even for that.

No, she must bide her time. She must consider. She must find a more subtle way to get what she wanted.

She reached her mount, removed the stays and hood while keeping him in check with her magic, then mounted him behind his thick, feathered neck and above the place where his wings joined to his body, and together they lifted away. Time and cunning would reward her best, she thought contentedly, the wind rushing past her face, the smells of the forest giving way to the pure cold of the high night air that swept the clouds and circled the stars.

Time and cunning, and the power of the magic she was born to, would yield her a world.

THREE

Typical of Wing Riders in general, Hunter Predd was a pragmatic sort. Whatever unwelcome cards life dealt him he accepted as gracefully as he could and went on about his business. Journeys into the interior of the Four Lands that stretched beyond Elven territory fell into that category. He was uncomfortable with traveling anywhere inland, but especially uncomfortable with traveling to places he hadn't been before.

Paranor was such a place.

He was surprised when Allardon Elessedil requested that he carry the map there. Surprised, because it seemed more appropriate that a Land Elf make the journey on behalf of the King than a rider from the Wing Hove. He was a blunt, straightforward man, and he asked the King's reason for making such a choice. The Elf King explained that the individual to whom Hunter was taking the map might have questions about it that only he could answer. Another Elf could accompany him on his journey if he wished, but another Elf could add nothing that Hunter did not already know, so what was the point?

What was needed was simple. The map must be carried to this certain individual to examine. Hunter should convey Allardon

Elessedil's respects and request that the map's recipient come to Arborlon to discuss with the Elf King any usable translation of the writings and symbols.

There was a catch to all this, of course. Hunter Predd, who was no one's fool, could see it coming. The Elf King saved it for last. The individual to whom the Wing Rider was to deliver the map was the Druid they called Walker, and the Rider's destination was the Druid's Keep at Paranor.

Walker. Even Hunter Predd, who seldom ventured off the coast of the Blue Divide, knew something of him. He was purported to be the last of the Druids. A dark figure in the history of the Four Lands, he was said to have lived for more than 150 years and to still be young. He had fought against the Shadowen in the time of Wren Elessedil. He had disappeared afterwards for decades, then resurfaced some thirty years ago. The rest of what the Wing Rider knew was even more shadowy. There was talk of Walker being a sorcerer possessed of great magic. There was talk that he had tried and failed to establish a coven. It was said he wandered the Four Lands still, gathering information and soliciting disciples. Everyone feared and mistrusted him.

Except, it seemed, Allardon Elessedil, who insisted that there was nothing to fear or mistrust, that Walker was a historian and academician, and that the Druid, of all men, might possess the ability to decipher the drawings and words on the map.

After thinking it over, Hunter Predd accepted the charge to take the map east, not out of duty or concern or anything remotely connected to his feelings for the Elf King, which in general bordered on disinterest. He accepted the charge because the King promised him that in reward for his efforts, he would bestow upon the Wing Hove possession of an island just below and west of the Irrybis that the Wing Riders had long coveted. Fair enough, Hunter decided on hearing the offer. Opportunity had knocked, the prize was a worthwhile one, and the risks were not prohibitive.

In truth, he did not see all that much in the way of risk no matter how closely he looked at the matter. There was the very good possibility that the Elf King wasn't telling him everything; in fact, Hunter Predd was almost certain of it. That was the way rulers and politicians operated. But there was nothing to be gained by sending him off to die, either. Clearly, Allardon Elessedil wanted to know what information the map concealed—especially if the castaway on whom it had been found was his brother. A Druid might be able to learn that, if he was as well schooled as the Elf King believed. Hunter Predd did not know of any Wing Riders who'd had personal dealings with this one. Nor had he heard any of his people speak harshly of the Druids. Balancing the risks and rewards as he understood them, which was really the best he could manage, he was inclined to take his chances.

So off he went, flying Obsidian out of Arborlon at midday and traveling east toward the Streleheim. He crossed the plains without incident and flew into the Dragon's Teeth well above Callahorn, choosing a narrow, twisting gap in the jagged peaks that would have been impassable on foot but offered just enough space for the Roc to maneuver. He navigated his way through the mountains quickly and was soon soaring above the treetops of Paranor. Once over the woodlands, he took Obsidian down to a small lake for a cold drink and a rest. As he waited on his bird, he looked out across the lake to where the trees locked together in a dark wall, a twisted and forbidding mass. He felt sorry, as he always did, for those who were forced to live their lives on the ground.

It was nearing sunset when the Druid's Keep came in sight. It wasn't all that hard to find from the air. It sat on a promontory deep in the woodlands, its spires and battlements etched in sharp relief by the setting sun against the horizon. The fortress could be seen for miles, stone walls and peaked roofs jutting skyward, a dark and massive presence. Allardon Elessedil had described the Keep in detail to Hunter Predd before he left, but the Wing Rider would have known it anyway. It couldn't be anything other than what it was, a place where dark rumors could take flight, a haunt for the last of a coven so mistrusted and feared that even their shades were warded against.

Hunter Predd guided Obsidian to a smooth landing close by the base of the promontory on which the Keep rested. Shadows layered the surrounding land, sliding from the ancient trees as the sun lowered west, stretching out into strange, unrecognizable shapes. Lifting out of the woods, out of the shadows, rising above it all, silent and frozen in time, only the Keep was still bathed in sunlight. The Wing Rider regarded it doubtfully. It would be easier to fly Obsidian to the top of the rise than to leave him here and walk up himself, but he was loath to risk landing so close to the walls. Here, at least, the trees offered a protective perch and there was room for a swift escape. For a Wing Rider, his mount's safety was always foremost in his mind.

He did not hobble or hood the great bird; Rocs were trained to stay where they were put and come when they were called. Leaving Obsidian at the base of the rise and the edge of the trees, Hunter Predd began the short walk up. He arrived at the towering walls as the sunlight slid away completely, leaving the Keep bathed in shadows. He stared upward, searching for signs of life. Finding none, he walked to the closest gate, which was closed and barred. There were smaller doors set on either side. He tried them, but they were locked. He stepped back again and looked up at the walls once more.

"Hello, inside!" he shouted.

There was no response. The echo of his voice faded into silence. He waited patiently. It was growing increasingly dark. He glanced around. If he didn't rouse someone soon, he would have to retreat back down the rise and make camp for the night.

He looked up again, scanning the parapets and towers. "Hello! I have a message from Allardon Elessedil!"

He stood listening to the silence that followed, feeling small and insignificant in the shadow of the Keep's huge wall. Maybe the Druid was traveling. Maybe he was somewhere else, away from the Keep, and this was all a big waste of time. The Wing Rider frowned. How could anyone even know if the Druid was there?

His question was cut short by a sudden movement at his side. He turned swiftly and found himself face-to-face with the biggest moor cat he had ever seen. The huge black beast stared at him with lantern eyes in the manner of a hungry bird eyeing a tasty bug. Hunter Predd stayed perfectly still. There was little else he could do. The big cat was right on top of him, and any weapons he might call upon to defend himself were woefully inadequate. The moor cat did not move either but simply studied him, head lowered slightly between powerful front shoulders, tail switching faintly in the darkness behind.

It took Hunter a moment to realize that there was something not quite right about this particular moor cat. In spite of its size and obvious power, it was vaguely transparent, appearing and disappearing in large patches as the seconds passed, first a leg, then a shoulder, then a midsection, and so forth. It was the strangest thing he had ever seen, but it did not prompt him to change his mind about trying to move.

Finally, the moor cat seemed satisfied with his inspection and turned away. He advanced a few paces, then turned back. Hunter Predd did not move. The moor cat walked on a few paces more, then looked back again.

To one side of the main gates, a small, iron-bound door swung open soundlessly. The cat moved toward it, then stopped and looked back. It took a few more tries, but finally the Wing Rider got the message. The moor cat was waiting on him. He was supposed to follow—through the open door and into the Druid's Keep.

Hunter Predd was not inclined to argue the matter. Taking a deep breath, he passed from the bluff face through the entry and into the Keep.

* * *

The man who had once been Walker Boh and was now simply Walker had seen the Wing Rider coming from a long way off. His warding lines of magic had alerted him to the other's approach, and he had stood on the walls where he could not be seen and watched the Rider land his Roc and walk up the rise to the gates. Black robes gathered close about his tall, broad-shouldered frame, Walker had watched the Wing Rider scan the Keep's walls. The Wing Rider had called up, but Walker had not answered. Instead, he had waited to see what the other would do. He had waited, because waiting until he was sure was an advisable precaution.

But when the Wing Rider called up a second time, saying that he carried a message from Allardon Elessedil, Walker sent Rumor down to bring him in. The big moor cat went obediently, silently, knowing what he must do. Walker trailed after him, wondering why the King of the Land Elves would send a message with a Wing Rider. He could think of two reasons. First, the King knew how Walker would respond to an Elf from Arborlon and to her King in particular, and he was hoping a Wing Rider would do better. Second, the Wing Rider had special insight into what the message concerned. Descending the stairs from his perch on the battlements, Walker shrugged the matter away. He would find out soon enough.

When he reached the bottom of the stairs and moved out into the courtyard, the Wing Rider and Rumor were already waiting. He drew back his hood and left his head and face bare as he crossed to give greeting. There was nothing to be gained by trying to intimidate this man. Clearly the Wing Rider was a tough, seasoned veteran, and he had come because he had chosen to do so and not because he had been commanded. He owed no allegiance to the Elessedils. Wing Riders were notoriously independent, almost as much so as Rovers, and if this one was here, so far from his home and people, there was good reason for it. Walker was curious to learn what that reason was.

"I am Walker," he said, offering his hand to the Wing Rider.

The other accepted it with a nod. His gray eyes took in Walker's dark face, black beard and long hair, strong features, high forehead, and piercing eyes. He did not seem to notice the Druid's missing arm. "Hunter Predd."

"You've come a long way, Wing Rider," Walker observed. "Not many come here without a reason."

The other grunted. "Not any, I should think." He glanced around, and his eyes settled on Rumor. "Is he yours?"

"As much as a moor cat can belong to anyone." Walker's gaze shifted. "His name is Rumor. The joke is, wherever I go, I am preceded by Rumor. It fits well with the way things have turned out for me. But I expect you already know that."

The Wing Rider nodded noncommittally. "Does he always show up like that—in bits and pieces, sort of coming and going?"

"Mostly. You called up that you had a message from Allardon Elessedil. I gather the message is for me?"

"It is." Hunter Predd wiped at his mouth with the back of his hand. "Do you have any ale you can spare?"

Walker smiled. Blunt and to the point, a Wing Rider to the core. "Come inside."

He led the way across the courtyard to a doorway into the main keep. In a room he used for storing foodstuffs and drink and for taking his solitary meals, he produced two glasses and a pitcher and set them on a small wooden table to one side. Gesturing the Wing Rider to one seat, he took the other and filled their glasses. They drank deeply, silently. Rumor had disappeared. He seldom came inside these days unless called.

Hunter Predd put down his glass and leaned back. "Four days ago, I was patrolling the Blue Divide above the island of Mesca Rho, and I found a man in the water."

He went on to tell his story—of finding the castaway Elf, of determining his condition, of discovering the bracelet he wore and the map he carried, of conveying him to the Healer in Bracken Clell, and of continuing on to Arborlon and Allardon Elessedil. The bracelet, he explained, had belonged to the King's brother, Kael, who had disappeared on an expedition in search of a magic revealed in a dream to Queen Aine's seer thirty years earlier.

"I know of the expedition," Walker advised quietly, and bid him continue.

There wasn't much more to tell. Having determined that the bracelet was Kael's, Allardon Elessedil had examined the map and been unable to decipher it. That it traced his brother's route to the sought-after magic was apparent. But there was little else he could determine. He had asked Hunter to convey it here, to Walker, whom he believed might be able to help.

Walker almost laughed aloud. It was typical of the Elf King that he would seek help from the Druid as if his own refusal to supply it in turn counted for nothing. But he kept silent. Instead, he accepted the folded piece of weathered skin when it was offered and set it on the table between them, unopened.

"Have you provided sufficiently for your mount?" he inquired, his gaze shifting from the map to the other's face. "Do you need to go outside again tonight?"

"No," Hunter Predd said. "Obsidian will be fine for now."

"Why don't you have something to eat, a hot bath afterwards, and then some sleep. You've done much traveling over the past few days, and you must be tired. I will study the map, and we will talk again in the morning."

He prepared a soup for the Wing Rider, tossed in a little dried fish, added a side portion of bread, and watched in satisfaction as the other ate it all and drank several more glasses of ale in the bargain. He left the map where he had put it, on the table between them, showing no interest in it. He was not sure yet what he had, and he wanted to be very sure before he conveyed to the Wing Rider a reaction that might be carried back to the Elf King. The uneasy relationship he shared with Allardon Elessedil did not permit giving anything away in their dealings. It was bad enough that he must pretend at civility with a man who had done so little to deserve it. But in a world in which alliances were necessary and, in his case, tended to be few and infrequent, he must play at games he would otherwise forgo.

When Hunter Predd was fed, bathed, and asleep, Walker returned to the table and picked up the map. He carried it from that room down musty halls and up winding stairs to the library, which had served the Druids since the time of Galaphile. Various inconsequential books filled with Druid recordings of weather and farming and lists of surnames and the births and deaths of noted families lined the ancient shelves. But behind those shelves, in a room protected by a magic that no one could penetrate save himself, lay the Druid Histories, the fabled books that recorded the entire history of the order and the magic its members had conceived and employed in the passage of more than a thousand years.

Settling himself comfortably in place amid the trappings of his predecessors, Walker unfolded the map and began to study it.

He took a long time doing so, much longer than he had supposed would be necessary. What he found astonished him. The map was intriguing and rife with possibilities. Inarguably, it was valuable, but he could not make a firm determination of how valuable until after he had translated the writings in the margins, most of which were scripted in a language with which he was unfamiliar.

But he had books of translations of languages to which he could turn, and he did so finally, walking to the shelving that concealed the Histories and their secrets of power. He reached back behind a row of books and touched a series of iron studs in sequence. A catch released, and a section of the shelving swung outward. Walker slipped through the opening behind and stood in a room of granite walls, floor, and ceiling, empty of everything but a long table and four chairs set against it. He lit the smokeless torches set in iron wall racks and pulled the shelving unit back into place behind him.

Then he placed his hand against a section of the granite wall, palm flat and fingers spread, and lowered his head in concentration. All the lore of all the Druids since the beginning of their order belonged now to him, given when he recovered lost Paranor and became a Druid himself those many years ago. He brought a small part of it to bear, recalling the Druid Histories from their concealment. Blue light emanated from his fingertips and spread through the stone beneath like veins through flesh.

A moment later, the wall disappeared, and the books of his order lay revealed, shelved in long rows and in numbered sequence, their covers bound in leather and etched in gold.

He spent a long time with the books that night, reading through many of them in his search for a key to the language on the map. When he found it, he was surprised and confounded. It was a derivation of a language spoken in the Old World, before the Great Wars, a language that had been dead for two thousand years. It was a language of symbols rather than of words. How, Walker wondered, would an Elf from his era have learned such a language? Why would he have used it to draw the map?

The answers to his questions, once he thought them through, were disturbing.

He worked on the translation almost until dawn, being careful not to misinterpret or assume. The more he deciphered, the more excited he became. The map was a key to a magic of such worth, of such power, that it left him breathless. He could barely manage to sit still as he imagined the possibilities. For the first time in years he saw a way in which he could secure what had been denied him for so long—a Druid Council, a body independent of all nations, working to unlock the secrets of life's most difficult and challenging problems and to improve the lives of all the peoples of the Four Lands.

That dream had eluded him for thirty years, ever since he had come awake from the Druid Sleep and gone out into the world to fulfill the promise he had made to himself when he had become what he was. What he had envisioned was a council of delegates from each of the lands and races, from each of the governments and provinces, all dedicated to study, learning, and discovery. But from the very beginning there had been resistance—not just from quarters where resistance might be expected, but from everywhere. Even from the Elves, and especially from Allardon Elessedil and his mother before him. No one wanted to give Walker the autonomy he believed necessary. No one wanted anyone else to gain an advantage. Everyone was cautious and suspicious and fearful of what a strong Druid Council might mean to an already precarious balance of power. No one wanted to take the kind of chance that the Druid was asking of them.

Walker sighed. Their demands were ridiculous and unacceptable. If the nations and the peoples were unwilling to let go of their delegates, to give up control over them so that they could dedicate themselves to the Druid life, the whole exercise was pointless. He had been unable to convince anyone that what he was doing would, given enough time, benefit them all. Druids, they believed, were not to be trusted. Druids, they believed, would visit problems on them they could do without. History demonstrated that Druids had been responsible for every war fought since the time of the First Council at Paranor. It was their own magic, the magic they had wielded in such secrecy, that had finally destroyed them. This was not an experience anyone wanted to repeat. The magic belonged to everyone now. It was a new age, with new rules. Control over the Druids, should they be permitted to re-form, was necessary. Nothing less would suffice.

In the end, the effort fell apart, and Walker was made outcast everywhere. Petty feuds, selfish interests, and short-sighted personalities stymied him completely. He was left enraged and stunned. He had counted heavily on the Elves to lead the way, and the Elves had spurned him as surely as the others. After the death of Queen

Aine, Allardon Elessedil had been his best hope, but the Elf King had announced he would follow his mother's wishes. No Elves would be sent to study at Paranor. No new Druid Council would be approved. Walker must make his way alone.

But now, Walker thought with something bordering on euphoria, he had found a way to change everything. The map gave him the kind of leverage that nothing else could. This time, when he asked for help, he would not be refused.

If, of course, he cautioned himself quickly, he could find and retrieve the magic that had eluded the Elven expedition under Kael Elessedil. If he could recover it from the safehold that hid and protected it. If he could survive the long, dangerous journey such an effort would require.

He would need help.

He replaced the Druid Histories on their shelves, made a quick circular motion with his hand, and closed the wall away. When the room was restored to blank walls and snuffed torches, he went back out into the library and pushed the shelving unit securely into place again. He looked around momentarily to be certain that all was as it had been. Then, with the map tucked into his robes, he went up onto the battlements to watch the sunrise.

As he stood looking out over the treetops to the first faint silvery lightening of the eastern sky, Rumor padded up to join him. The big cat sat beside him, as if seeking his companionship. Walker smiled. Each was all the other could turn to for comfort, he mused. Ever since the shade of Allanon had appeared. Ever since they had been locked in limbo in lost Paranor. Ever since he had brought the Druid's Keep back into the world of men by becoming the newest member of the order. Ever since Cogline had died.

All the rest were gone, too, from that earlier time—the Ohmsfords, Morgan Leah, Wren Elessedil, Damson Rhee, all of them. Rumor and he alone survived. They were outcasts in more ways than one, solitary wanderers in a world that had changed considerably during the time of his sleep. But it wasn't the changes in the Four Lands that worried him this morning. It was his sense that the events that would transpire because of his reading of the map and his search for the magic it detailed would require him to become what he had always worked so hard to avoid—a Druid in the old sense, a manipulator and schemer, a trader in information who would sacrifice who and what he must to get what he believed necessary. Allanon, of old. It was what he had always despised about the Druids. He knew he would despise it in himself when it surfaced.

And surface it would, perhaps changing him forever.

The sun crested the horizon in a splash of brilliant gold. The day would be clear and bright and warm. Walker felt the first rays of sunlight on his face. Such a small thing, but so welcome. His world had shrunk to almost nothing in the past few years. Now it was about to expand in ways he had barely imagined possible.

"Well," he said softly, as if to put the matter to rest.

He knew what he must do. He must go to Arborlon and speak with Allardon Elessedil. He must convince the Elven King they could work together in an effort to discover the secret of the map. He must persuade him to mount an expedition to go in search of the magic of which the map spoke, with Walker in command. He must find a way to make the Elven King his ally without letting him see that it was the Druid's idea.

He must reveal just enough of what he knew and not too much. He must be cautious.

He blinked away his weariness. He was Walker, the last of the Druids, the last hope for the higher ideals his order had espoused so strongly when it had been formed. If the Four Lands were to be united in peace, the magic must be controlled by a Druid Council answerable to no single government or people, but to all. Only he could achieve that. Only he knew the way.

He bent to Rumor and placed his hand gently on the broad head. "You must stay here, old friend," he whispered. "You must keep watch for me until I return."

He rose and stretched. Hunter Predd slept in a darkened room and would not wake for a while yet. Time enough for Walker to catch an hour's sleep before they departed. It would have to be enough.

With the moor cat trailing after him, fading and reappearing like a mirage in the new light, he abandoned his watch and descended the stairs into the Keep.

FOUR

His worn black flight leathers creaking softly, Redden Alt Mer strode through the Federation war camp on his way to the airfield, and heads turned. For some it was the mane of red hair streaming down past his shoulders like fiery threads that drew attention. For some it was the way he carried himself, fluid, relaxed, and self-assured, a big man who exuded strength and quickness.

For most, it was the legend. Seventy-eight confirmed kills in 192 missions, all flown in the same airship, all completed without serious mishap.

It was good luck to fly with Redden Alt Mer, the old boots swore. In a place and time where an airman's life expectancy was rated at about six months, Alt Mer had survived for three years with barely a scratch. He had the right ship, sure enough. But it took more than that to stay alive over the front. It took skill, courage, experience, and a whole basketful of that most precious of commodities, luck. The Captain had all of them. He was steeped in them. He'd lived almost his whole life in the air, a cabin boy at seven, a First Officer by fifteen, a Captain by twenty. When the winds of fortune shifted, the old boots said, Redden Alt Mer knew best how to ride them.

The Rover didn't think about it. It was bad luck to think about good luck in a war. It was worse luck to think about why you were different from everyone else. Being an exception to the rule was all well and good, but you didn't want to dwell on the reasons you were still alive when so many others were dead. It wasn't conducive to clear thinking. It wasn't helpful in getting a good night's sleep.

Walking through the camp, he joked and waved to those who acknowledged him, a light, easy banter that kept everyone relaxed. He knew what they thought of him, and he played off it the way an old friend might. What harm did it do? You could never have too many friends in a war.

He'd been three years now in this one, two of them stuck here on the broad expanse of the Prekkendorran Heights while Federation and Free-born ground forces hammered each other to bloody pulps day after day after day. A Rover out of the seaport of March Brume, west and south on the Blue Divide, he was a seasoned veteran of countless conflicts even before he signed on. It was no exaggeration to say that he had spent his whole life on warships. He'd almost been born at sea, but his father, a Captain himself, had managed to reach port with his mother just before she gave birth. But from the time he'd taken that first commission as a cabin boy, he'd lived in the air. He couldn't explain why he loved it so; he just did. It felt right when he was flying, as if a net of invisible constraints and bonds had been slipped and he had been set free. When he was on the ground, he was always thinking about being in the air. When he was in the air, he was never thinking about anything else.

"Hey, Cap!" A foot soldier with his arm tied against his body and a bandage over one side of his face hobbled into view. "Blow me a little of your luck!"

Redden Alt Mer grinned and blew him a kiss. The soldier laughed and waved with his good arm. The Rover kept walking, smelling the air, tasting it, thinking as he did that he missed the sea. Most of his time in the air had been spent west, over the Blue Divide. He was a mercenary, as most Rovers were, taking jobs where the money was best, giving allegiance to those who paid for it. Right now, the Federation offered the best pay, so he fought for them. But he was growing restless for a change, for something new. The war with the Free-born had been going on for more than ten years. It wasn't his war to begin with, and it wasn't a war that made much sense to him. Money could carry you only so far when your heart lay somewhere else.

Besides, no matter who you were, sooner or later your luck ran out. It was best to be somewhere else when it did.

He passed out of the sprawling clutter of tents and cooking fires onto the airfield. The warships were tethered in place by their stays, floating just off the ground, ambient-light sails tilted toward the sun off twin masts. Most were Federation built and showed it. Big, ugly, cumbersome brutes, sheathed in metal armor and painted with the insignia and colors of their regiments, in flight they lumbered about the skies like errant sloths. As troop transports and battering rams, they were a howling success. As fighting vessels that could tack smoothly and quickly, they left something to be desired. If they were ably commanded, which most weren't, their life expectancy on the front was about the same as that of their Captains and crews.

He walked on, barely giving them a glance. The banter that had passed between himself and the foot soldiers was absent here. The officers and crews of the Federation airships despised him. Rovers were mercenaries, not career soldiers. Rovers fought only for money and left when they chose. Rovers cared nothing for the Federation cause or the lives of the men that had been expended on its behalf. But the worst of it was the knowledge that the Rover officers and crews were so much better than the Federation crews were. In the air, faith in a cause did little to keep you alive.

A few taunting remarks were tossed at him from behind the anonymity of metal-clad hulls, but he ignored them. No one would make those same remarks to his face. Not these days. Not since he had killed the last man who'd dared to do so.

The sleeker, trimmer Rover airships came into view as he neared the far end of the field. *Black Moclips* sat foremost, polished wood-and-metal hull gleaming in the sunlight. She was the best ship he had ever flown, a cruiser built for battle, quick and responsive to the tack of her ambient-light sails and the tightening and loosening of her radian draws. Just a shade under 110 feet long and 35 feet wide, she resembled a big black ray. Her low, flat fighting cabin sat amidships on a decking braced by cross beams and warded by twin pontoons curved into battering rams fore and aft. Twin sets of diapson crystals converted to raw energy the light funneled from the collector sails through the radian draws. Parse tubes expelled the converted energy to propel the ship. The bridge sat aft with the pilot box front and center on the decking, its controls carefully shielded from harm. Three masts flew the ambient-light sails, one each fore, aft, and center. The sails themselves were strangely shaped, broad and straight at the lower end, where they were fastened to the booms, but curved where spars drew them high above to a triangle's point. The design allowed for minimal slack in a retack and minimal drag from the wind. Speed and power kept you alive in the air, and both were measured in seconds.

Furl Hawken came racing down the field from the ship, long blond beard whipping from side to side. "We're ready to lift off, Captain," he shouted, slowing as he reached Alt Mer and swung into step beside him. "Got a good day for it, don't we?"

"Smooth sailing ahead." Redden Alt Mer put his hand on his Second Officer's broad shoulder. "Any sign of Little Red?"

Furl Hawken's mouth worked on whatever it was he was chewing, his eyes cast down. "Sick in bed, Captain. Flu, maybe. You know her. She'd come if she was able."

"I know you're the worst liar for a hundred miles in any direction. She's in a tavern somewhere, or worse."

The big man looked hurt. "Well, maybe that's so, but you'd better let it pass for now, 'cause we got a more immediate problem." He shook his head. "Like we don't have one every time we turn around these days. Like every single oink doesn't come from the same pig's house."

"Ah, our friends in Federation Command?"

"A full line Commander is aboard for the flight with two of his flunkies. Observation purposes, he tells me. Reconnaissance. A day in the skies. Shades! I nod and smile like a sailor's wife at news of his plans to give up sailing."

Redden Alt Mer nodded absently. "Best thing to do with these people, Hawk."

They had reached Black Moclips, and he swung onto the rope ladder and climbed to the bridge where the Federation Commander and his adjutants were waiting.

"Commander," he greeted pleasantly. "Welcome aboard."

"My compliments, Captain Alt Mer," the other replied. He did not offer his own name, which told the Rover something right away about how he viewed their relationship. He was a thin, pinch-faced man with sallow skin. If he'd spent a day on the line in the last twelve months, it would come as a surprise to the Rover. "Are we ready to go?"

"Ready and able, Commander."

"Your First Officer?"

"Indisposed." Or she would wish as much once he got his hands on her. "Mr. Hawken can take up the slack. Gentlemen, is this your first time in the air?"

The look that passed between the adjutants gave him his answer.

"It is our first," the Commander confirmed with a dismissive shrug. "Your job is to make the experience educational. Ours is to learn whatever it is you have to teach."

"Run 'em up, Hawk." He gestured his Second Officer forward to oversee lofting the sails. "We'll be seeing action today, Commander," he cautioned. "It could get a little rough."

The Commander smiled condescendingly. "We're soldiers, Captain. We'll be fine."

Pompous fathead, Alt Mer thought. You'll be fine if I keep you that way and not otherwise.

He watched his Rover crew scramble up the masts, lofting the sails and fastening the radian draws in place. Airships were marvelous things, but operating them required a mind-set that was sorely lacking in most Federation soldiers. The Southlanders were fine on solid ground executing infantry tactics. They were comfortable with throwing bodies into breaches, like sandbags, and relying on the sheer weight of their numbers to crush an enemy. But put them in the air and they couldn't seem to decide what to do next. Their intuition vanished. Everything they knew about warfare dried up and blew away with the first breath of wind to fill the sails.

Rovers, on the other hand, were born to the life. It was in their blood, in their history, and in the way they had lived their lives for two thousand years. Rovers did not respond well to regimentation and drill. They responded to freedom. Flying the big airships gave them that. Migratory by nature and tradition, they were always on the move anyway. Staying put was unthinkable. The Federation was still trying to figure that out, and they were constantly sending observers aloft with the Rover crews to discover what it was their mercenaries knew that they didn't.

Trouble was, it wasn't something that could be taught. The Bordermen who fought for the Free-born weren't any better. Or the Dwarves. Only the Elves seemed to have mastered sailing the wind currents with the same ease as the Rovers.

One day, that would change. Airships were still new to the Four Lands. The first had been built and flown barely two dozen years earlier. They had been in service as fighting vessels for less than five years. Only a handful of shipwrights understood the mechanics of ambient-light sails, radian draws, and diapson crystals well enough to build the vessels that could utilize them. Using light as energy was an old dream, only occasionally realized, as in the case of airships. It was one thing to build them, another to make them fly. It took skill and intelligence and instinct to keep them in the air. More were lost through poor navigation, loss of control, and panic than through damage from battle.

Rovers had sailed the seas in trading ships and pirate vessels longer than anyone had, and the jump to airships was easier for them. As mercenaries, they were invaluable to the Federation. But the Southlanders continued to believe that if they could just learn how the Rovers managed to make it all look so easy, they wouldn't need them as Captains and crews.

Hence, his passengers, three more in a long line of Federation hopefuls.

Resigned, he sighed. There was nothing he could do about it. Hawk would fuss enough for the both of them. He took his station in the pilot box, watching his men as they finished tying down the draws and securing the sails. Other ships were preparing to lift off, as well, their crews performing similar tasks in preparation. On the airfield, ground crews were preparing to release the mooring lines.

The old, familiar excitement was humming in his blood, and the clarity of his vision sharpened.

"Unhood the crystals, Hawk!" he shouted to his Second Officer.

Furl Hawken relayed the instructions to the men stationed at the front and rear parse tubes, where the crystals were fed light from the radian draws. Unhooding freed the mechanisms that allowed Alt Mer to fly the ship. Canvas coverings and linchpins securing the metal hoods that shielded the crystals were released, giving control over the vessel to the pilot box.

Alt Mer tested the levers, drawing down power from the sails in small increments. *Black Moclips* strained against her tethers in response, shifting slightly as light converted to energy was expelled through the parse tubes.

"Cast off!" he ordered.

The ground crew freed the restraining lines, and *Black Moclips* lifted away in a smooth, upward swing. Alt Mer spun the wheel that guided the rudders off the parse tubes and fed power down the radian draws to the crystals in steadily increasing increments. Behind him, he heard the hurried shift of the Federation officers toward pieces of decking they could hold on to.

"There are securing lines and harnesses coiled on those railing stays," he called back to them. "Fasten one about your waist, just in case it gets bumpy."

He didn't bother checking to see if they did as he suggested. If they didn't, it was their own skins they risked.

In moments, they were flying out over the flats of the Prekkendorran, several hundred feet in the air, *Black Moclips* in the lead, another seven ships following in loose formation. Airships could fly comfortably at more than a thousand feet, but he preferred to stay down where the winds were less severe. He watched the twin rams slice through the air to either side of the decking, black horns curving upward against the green of the earth. Low and flat, *Black Moclips* had the look of a hawk at hunt, soaring smooth and silent against the midday sky.

Wind filled the sails, and the Rover crew moved quickly to take advantage of the additional power. Alt Mer hooded the diapson crystals in response, slowing the power fed by the radian draws, giving the ship over to the wind. Furl Hawken was shouting out instructions, exhorting in that big, booming voice, keeping everyone moving smoothly from station to station. Accustomed to the movements of a ship in flight, the crew wore no restraining lines. That would change when they engaged in battle.

Alt Mer risked a quick glance over his shoulder at the Federation officers—risked, because if he started laughing at what he found, he would find himself in trouble he didn't need. It wasn't as bad as it might have been. The Commander and his adjutants were gripping the rail with white-knuckled determination, but no one was sick yet and no one was hiding his eyes. The Rover gave them a reassuring wave and dismissed them from his thoughts.

When *Black Moclips* was well away from the Federation camp and approaching the forward lines of the Free-born, he gave the order to unlock the ship's weapons. *Black Moclips* carried several sets, all of them carefully stacked and stored amidships. Bows and arrows and slings and javelins were used mostly for long-range attacks against opposing crews and fighters. Spears and blades were used in close combat. Long, jagged-edge pikes and grappling hooks attached to throwing ropes were used to draw an enemy ship close enough to tear apart her sails or sever her radian draws.

The two dozen Federation soldiers who rode belowdecks during embarkation climbed up the ladder through the hatchway amidships and moved to arm themselves. Some took up positions behind shielding at the rails. Some moved to man the catapults that launched buckets of metal shards or burning balls of pitch. All were veterans of countless airship battles aboard *Black Moclips*. Alt Mer and his crew of Rovers left the fighting to them. Their responsibility was to the ship. It took all of their concentration to hold her steady in the heat of battle, to position her so that the soldiers could bring their weapons to bear, and to employ her when necessary as a battering ram. The crew was not expected to fight unless the ship was in danger of being boarded.

Watching the soldiers take up their weapons and move eagerly into position, the Rover Captain was struck by the amount of energy men could summon for the purpose of killing one another.

Furl Hawken appeared suddenly at his side. "Everything's at the ready, Captain. Crew, weapons, and ship." He shifted his eyes sideways. "How's our stouthearted passengers holding up?"

Alt Mer glanced briefly over his shoulder. One adjutant had freed himself from his safety line and had buried his head in the slop bucket. The other, white faced, was grimly forcing himself not to look over at his companion. The pinch-faced Commander was scribbling in a notebook, his black-clad body wedged into a corner of the decking.

"They'd prefer it if we just stayed on the ground, I think," he offered mildly.

"Wonder if they've got anything to report regarding the functions of their insides?" Hawk chuckled and moved away.

Black Moclips passed over the Free-born lines headed toward their airfields, the other seven airships spread out to either side. Two were Rover ships, the other five Federation. He knew their Captains. Both Rover Captains and one of the Federation Captains were reliable and skilled. The rest were marking time until one mistake or another caught up with them. Redden Alt Mer's approach to the situation was to try to keep out of their way.

Ahead, Free-born airships were lifting off to meet them. The Rover Captain produced his spyglass and studied the markings. Ten, eleven, twelve—he counted them as they rose, one after the other. Five were Elven, the rest Free-born. Not the kind of odds he liked. Ostensibly, he was to engage and destroy any enemy airships he encountered, without sustaining damage to his own. As if doing so could possibly make a difference in the outcome of the war. He brushed the thought aside. He would engage the Elven airships and let the others bang up against themselves.

"Safety lines in place, gentlemen!" he called to his Federation passengers and crew, gripping the controls as the enemy ships drew near.

At two hundred yards and with an airspeed approaching twenty knots, he sideslipped *Black Moclips* out of formation and dipped sharply toward the ground. Leveling out again, then increasing his speed, he brought the airship out of her dive and into a climb beneath the Free-born. As he sailed upward on their lee side, his catapults began launching scrap metal and fireballs into the exposed hulls and sails. One ship exploded into flame and began drifting away. A second responded to the attack by launching its own catapults. Jagged bits of metal screamed overhead as Alt Mer spun the wheel sharply to carry *Black Moclips* out of the line of fire.

In seconds, all the airships were engaged in battle, and on the ground, the men of the opposing armies paused to look skyward. Back and forth the warring vessels glided, rising and falling in sudden tackings, fireballs cutting bright red paths across the blue, metal shards and arrows whistling through their deadly trajectories. Two of the Federation ships collided and went down in a twisted, locked heap, steering gone, hoods shattered, crystals drawing down so much power they exploded in midair. Another of the ships spun away from an encounter in a maneuver that lacked explanation and suggested panic. A Free-born vessel skidded into a Rover ship with a sharp screech of metal plates. Radian draws snapped loudly, sending both into slides that carried them away from each other. Everywhere, men were shouting and screaming in anger and fear and pain.

Black Moclips rose through the center of the maelstrom, breaching like a leviathan out of turbulent waters. Redden Alt Mer took her sideways and out from the pack in pursuit of a lone Elven ship that was maneuvering for position. Fireballs sizzled through the air in front of Alt Mer, but he slid underneath, tilting to bring his own weapons to bear. The Elf ship swung about and came at him. No coward, this Captain, the Rover thought with admiration. He banked left and rose sharply, the curved tip of his right battering ram taking off the top of the Elf's mainmast and dropping her mainsail. The Elf vessel lurched in response, fought to stay level.

Black Moclips swung about, readying an attack. "Steady, now!" Alt Mer yelled, red hair flying behind him in the wind like a crimson flag.

But a second ship lumbered into view from his right, a Federation vessel with her bridge in ruins, her Captain nowhere in sight, and her crew frantically trying to regain control. Flames leapt from her decking amidships and climbed her mainmast with feathery steps. Alt Mer held *Black Moclips* steady, but all at once the Federation ship swung around, slewing sideways toward a collision. The Rover Captain hauled back on the steering, opened the hoods, and fed power through the parse tubes. *Black Moclips* surged upward, barely missing the Federation vessel as it passed underneath, pontoons scraping mast tips and tearing sails.

Alt Mer swore under his breath; it was bad enough that he had to worry about the enemy's ships. Expecting to find the partially disabled Elven ship, he brought *Black Moclips* about and found the Federation ship he had just avoided instead. Somehow it had come back around and was sweeping right in front of him. He hauled back on the hooding controls, lifting away on the ship's nose, trying to avoid it. But the Federation vessel was still slewing left and right. A burning brand, its captainless crew was desperately trying to tie off the radian draws before power to the crystals spilled her sideways. Sails were aflame and crystals were exploding and the Federation crew was screaming in fear.

Alt Mer couldn't get out of the way in time. "Brace!" he roared to everyone who could listen. "Brace, brace, brace!"

Black Moclips struck the Federation ship just below her foresail decking, shuddered and rocked violently, and absorbed the blow through her rams. Even so, the force of the collision threw him into the controls. Behind him, he caught a glimpse of the Federation Commander and his adjutants flying sideways across the decking. The restraining harnesses brought the Commander and one adjutant up short, but the line securing the second adjutant snapped, and the unfortunate man pinwheeled across the deck, flew over the railing, and was gone. Alt Mer could hear him screaming all the way down.

"Captain!" he heard the Federation Commander howl in anger and terror.

But there was no time to respond. Two more of the Elven ships were closing fast, sensing that they had a chance to destroy their greatest enemy. Alt Mer shouted to brace for evasive maneuvers, and took the ship into a sudden, slewing dive that sent the Federation Commander and his remaining adjutant flying back across the deck in the other direction. One Elf ship dropped after him, and when it did, he took it back under the second, *Black Moclips* twisting and dipping in smooth response to his hands on her controls.

The Federation Commander was still screaming at him from behind, but he paid no attention. He took *Black Moclips* around and up in a tight spiral, missiles from his catapults firing into the Elf ships, which were firing back. Scrap metal took out the foresail of one and, in one of the luckiest shots Alt Mer had ever seen, damaged the steering rudders, as well. The ship lurched and fought to regain power. Alt Mer ignored it, wheeling on the other. Metal shards hammered into *Black Moclips'* pontoons and upper decking, knocking her sideways. But her armor held, and Alt Mer swung right into the enemy.

"Brace!" he yelled down, jamming the controls forward to feed power to the crystals.

Black Moclips collided with the second Elf ship about halfway up its mainmast. The mast snapped as if caught in a high wind and toppled to the deck, bringing down sails and radian draws alike. Bereft of more than a third of his ship's power, her Captain was forced to hood his crystals and take her down. Alt Mer held *Black Moclips* away, watching as both Elf vessels began to descend, rolling and slewing as they fought to stay upright, crews scrambling madly to reposition the draws. All around them, Free-born ships were descending, giving up the hunt. Four Federation ships were down, burning on the plains. Two of those still airborne were damaged, one badly. Alt Mer glanced earthward at the crippled Free-born ships and gave the order to withdraw.

Suddenly the Federation Commander was shouting in his ear, his pinched face red and sweating. He had freed himself from his safety line and dragged himself across the decking. One hand gripped the railing of the pilot box and the other gestured furiously. "What do you think you're doing, Captain?"

Alt Mer had no idea what he was talking about and didn't care for his tone of voice. "Heading home, Commander. Put your safety line back on."

"You're letting them get away!" the other snapped, ignoring him. "You're letting them escape!"

Alt Mer glanced over the side of *Black Moclips* at the Free-born vessels. He shrugged. "Forget about them. They won't fly again for a while."

"But when they do, they'll be back in the skies, hunting our airships! I'm ordering you to destroy them, Captain!"

The Rover shook his head. "You don't give the orders aboard this vessel, Commander. Get back in place."

The Federation Commander seized his jacket. "I'm a superior officer, Captain Alt Mer, and I'm giving you a direct order!"

Redden Alt Mer had put up with enough. "Hawk!" he yelled. His Second Officer was beside him in a heartbeat. "Help the Commander back into his safety harness, please. Make sure it's securely fastened. Commander, we'll discuss it later."

Furl Hawken removed the almost incoherent officer from the pilot box, muscled him over to the aft railing, and snapped him back into his harness, pulling out the release pin in the process. He passed by Alt Mer on his way forward with a wink, tossing the Captain the pin. "Wish Little Red were here to see this," he whispered with a grin.

Well and good to say so now, the Rover thought darkly, his hands steady on the ship's controls, but it would be a different story when they landed. This wasn't something the Commander was likely to overlook, and he doubted that a board of inquiry would back a mercenary against a regular. Even the appearance of insubordination was enough to have you brought up on charges in this army. The right or wrong of it wouldn't matter, nor even the fact that on board any airship, like any sailing ship, the Captain's was the final word. The Federation would back its own, and he would be reduced in rank or dismissed from service.

His green eyes scanned the horizon, west to where the mountains rose against the blue of the sky. The one good thing about being a flyer was that you could always be somewhere else by nightfall.

He thought momentarily of taking *Black Moclips* and heading out, not even bothering to go back. But she wasn't his ship, and he wasn't a thief—not just then, anyway—and he couldn't leave Little Red behind. It was best to go back, pack up, and be out of there by dark.

Before he knew it, he was smelling the Blue Divide and remembering the colors of spring in March Brume.

He brought the ship down carefully, letting the ground crew haul her in and secure her, then walked back to free the Commander and his aide. Neither of them said a word or even looked at him. As soon as they were unhooked, they bolted from the ship as if scalded. Alt Mer let them go, turning his attention to checking the damage to *Black Moclips*, making certain steps would be taken to complete the necessary repairs. Already he was thinking of her as someone else's ship. Already, he was saying good-bye.

As it turned out, he was a little too slow doing so. He was just coming down off the rope ladder onto the airfield when the Commander reappeared with a squad of Federation regulars.

"Captain Alt Mer, you are under arrest for disobeying a superior officer while engaged in battle. A hanging offense, I think. Let's see who's in charge now, shall we?" He attempted a menacing smile, but it failed, and he flushed angrily. "Take him away!"

Furl Hawken and his crew started off the ship, weapons already in hand, but Redden Alt Mer motioned for them to stay where they were. Slipping free his weapons, he deliberately walked past the Commander and handed them to the grizzled squad leader, a man with whom he had shared more than a few glasses of ale and knew well enough to call by his first name.

"I'll see you tonight, Hawk," he called back over his shoulder.

He paused suddenly to look at *Black Moclips*. He would never see her again, he knew. She was the best ship he had ever captained, maybe the best he ever would. He hoped her new Captain would prove worthy of her, but he doubted it. Whatever the case, he would miss her more than he cared to imagine.

"Lady," he whispered to her. "It was grand."

Then, looking past the Commander to the squad leader, he shrugged his indifference to the whole business. "Lead the way, Cap. I put myself in your capable hands."

Whatever his thoughts might have been on the matter, the squad leader was smart enough to keep them to himself.

FIVE

The flat-faced, burly line sergeant had been drinking at the bar in the back room of the company blacksmith's for over an hour before he got up the nerve to walk over to Little Red. She was sitting alone at a table in the rear, clouded by shadow and the kind of studied disinterest in her surroundings that made it clear she was not to be approached. The line sergeant might have recognized as much five tankards of ale earlier, when his judgment was still clear enough to warn him against foolish behavior. But his anger at the way that she had humiliated him the night before, coupled with false bravado fueled by the quantity of his drink, finally won out.

He squared himself away in front of her, a big man, using his size as an implied threat.

"You and me got something to settle, Little Red," he declared loudly.

Heads turned. A few soldiers rose and quietly moved for the doors leading out. The blacksmith's wife, who tended bar for her husband in the midday, glanced over with a frown. Outside, in the sweltering heat of the forge, iron clanged on iron, and hot metal thrust into water hissed and steamed.

Rue Meridian did not look up. She kept her gaze steady and direct, staring off into space, her hands cupped loosely around her tankard of ale. She was there because she wanted to be alone. She should have been flying, but her heart wasn't in it anymore and her thoughts were constantly on the coast and home.

"You listening to me?" he snapped.

She could smell the line sergeant, his breath, unwashed body and hair, soiled uniform. She wondered if he noticed how foul he had become while living in the field, but guessed he hadn't.

"You think you're something, don't you?" Perhaps because of her silence, he was growing braver. He shifted his weight closer. "You look at me when I talk to you, Rover girl!"

She sighed. "Isn't it enough that I have to listen to you and smell you? Do I have to look at you, too? That seems like a lot to ask of me."

For a moment he just stared at her, vaguely confused. Then he knocked the tankard of ale from between her hands and drew his short sword. "You cheated me, Little Red! No one does that! I want my money back!"

She leaned back in her chair, her gaze lifting. She gave him a cursory glance and looked away again. "I didn't cheat you, Sergeant." She smiled pleasantly. "I didn't have to. You were so bad that it wasn't necessary. When you get better, which you might one day manage to do, then I might have to cheat you."

His bearded face clouded with fresh anger. "Give me back my money!"

Like magic, a throwing knife appeared in her hand. At once, he backed away.

"I spent it, all of it, every last cent. There wasn't that much to begin with." She looked at him once more. "What's your problem, Sergeant? You've been drinking at the bar for the last hour, so you're not broke."

He worked his mouth as if he was having trouble getting words out. "Just give me my money."

Last night she had bested him in a knife-throwing contest,

61

although that would be using the word *contest* rather loosely since he was the worst knife thrower she could remember competing against. The cost to him had been his pride and his purse, and evidently it was a price he had not been prepared to pay.

"Get away from me," she said wearily.

"You're nothing, Little Red!" he exploded. "Just a cheating little witch!"

She thought momentarily about killing him, but she didn't feel like dealing with the consequences of doing so, so she abandoned the idea. "You want a rematch, Sergeant?" she asked instead. "One throw. You win, I give you back your money. I win, you buy me a fresh tankard of ale and leave me in peace. Done?"

He studied her suspiciously, as if trying to determine what the catch was. She waited him out patiently, watching his eyes, the throwing knife balanced loosely in her palm.

"Done," he agreed finally.

She rose, loose and easy in her dark Rover clothing, decorative bright scarves and sashes wrapped about her waist and shoulders, the ends trailing down in silken streamers, her long red hair shimmering in the lamplight. Rue Meridian was a beautiful woman by any standard, and more than a few men had been attracted to her when she had first joined the Federation army. But the number had dwindled after the first two who had tried unsuccessfully to force their affections on her had spent weeks in the hospital recovering from their wounds. Men still found her attractive, but they were more careful now about how they approached her. There was nothing "little" about Little Red. She was tall and broad-shouldered, lean and fit. She was called Little Red in deference to Big Red, her half brother, Redden Alt Mer. They had the same red hair and rangy frame, the same green eyes, the same quick smile and explosive temper. They had the same mother, as well, but different fathers. In theirs, as in many Rover clans, the men came and went while the women remained.

The line sergeant was casting about for a target. Last night, they had used a black circle the size of a thumbnail drawn on a support beam. They had thrown their knives in turn, two throws each. The sergeant had missed the mark both times; she had not. The sergeant complained, but paid up, cowed perhaps by the presence of so many other Rovers and fellow soldiers. There had been no mention of cheating then, no mention of getting his money back. He must have been stewing about it all night.

"There," he said, pointing at the same black circle on the beam, stepping to the same line they had drawn on the board flooring the night before.

"Here, here," the smith's wife complained at once. "You busted up a whole row of glasses throwing past the beam last night. Your aim's as poor as your judgment, Blenud Trock! You throw your knives somewhere else this time!"

The sergeant glared at her. "You'll get your money when I get mine!"

Trock. It was the first time Rue Meridian had heard his name spoken. "Let's move over here, Sergeant," she suggested.

She led him away from the bar and deeper into the room. The makeshift building was backed into a hill, and a stain from runoff had darkened the rear wall in a distinctive V. Just above and to the right, water droplets hung from a beam, falling every now and then onto the floor.

She stopped twenty feet away and drew a line with her toe in the dust and grime. Not the cleanest establishment she had ever frequented, but not the dirtiest either. These sorts of places came and went with the movement of the army. This one had endured because the army hadn't gone anywhere in some time. It was illegal, but it was left alone because the soldiers required some sort of escape out in the middle of nowhere, miles from any city.

She brushed back her fiery hair and looked at the sergeant.

"We'll stand together at the line. Once set, when the next drop of water falls from that beam, we throw at the V. Closest and quickest to the crease wins."

"Huh!" he grunted, taking his place. He muttered something else, but she couldn't hear. Throwing knife in hand, he set his stance. "Ready," he said.

She took a deep, slow breath and let her arms hang loose at her sides, the throwing knife resting comfortably in the palm of her right hand, the blade cool and smooth against the skin of her wrist and forearm. A small crowd had gathered behind them, soldiers from the front on leave and off duty, anxious for a little fresh entertainment. She was aware of others drifting in from outside, but the room remained oddly hushed. She grew languid and vaguely ethereal, as if her mind had separated from her body. Her eyes remained fixed, however, on the beam with its water droplets suspended in a long row, tiny pinpricks of reflective light against the shadows.

When the droplet of water finally fell, her arm whipped up in a dark blur and the throwing knife streaked out of her hand so fast that it was buried in the exact center of the V before the line sergeant had completed his throwing motion. The sergeant's knife was wide of the mark by six inches.

There was a smattering of applause and a few cheers from the spectators. Rue Meridian retrieved her knife and walked over to the bar to collect on her wager. The smith's wife already had the tankard of ale on the counter. "This one's yours, Sergeant Trock," she said in a loud voice, giving Rue a broad smile. "Pay up before you leave."

The line sergeant stalked over to the wall and pulled his heavy throwing knife free. For a moment he held it balanced in his hand as he gave Rue Meridian a venomous look. Then he sheathed the knife beneath his tunic and swaggered over to where she stood. "I'm not paying," he announced, planting himself at her side.

"Up to you," she replied, sipping at the ale.

"If you don't, you won't be coming back in here again," the smith's wife advised pointedly. "Stop being so troublesome."

"I'm not paying because you cheated!" he snapped, his response directed at Rue. "You threw before the water drop left the beam. It was plain as day."

There was a general murmur of dissent and a shaking of heads from the assembled, but no one called him on it. Emboldened, he leaned close enough that she could feel the heat of his breath and smell its stink. "You know what your problem is, Little Red? You need someone to teach you some manners. Then you wouldn't be so stuck—"

The rest of what he was going to say caught in his throat as he felt the tip of her throwing knife pressed against the soft underside of his bearded chin.

"You should think carefully before you speak again, Sergeant," she hissed. "You've already said enough to persuade me that it might be just as well if I cut your throat and have done with it."

The room had gone silent. No one was moving, not even the smith's wife, who stood watching with a dishrag in one hand and her mouth open.

The line sergeant gasped as Rue Meridian pressed upward with the knife tip, lifting his chin a little higher. The knife had appeared so suddenly that his hands still hung loose at his sides and his weapons remained sheathed. "I didn't mean—"

"You didn't mean," she cut him short, "that I needed to learn new manners, am I right?"

"Yes." He swallowed thickly.

"You didn't mean that someone as crude and stupid as yourself could teach them to me in any case, right?"

"Yes."

"You wish to tell me that you are sorry for saying I cheated and for spoiling my midday contemplation of things far away and dear to me, right?"

"Yes, yes!"

She backed him away, the knife tip still pressed against his neck. When he was standing clear of the bar, she reached down with her free hand and stripped him of his weapons. Then she shoved him backwards into a chair.

"I've changed my mind," she said, her own knife disappearing into her dark clothing. "I don't want you paying for my drink, wager or no. I want you sitting quietly right where you are until I decide you can leave. If I see you move a muscle, I'll pretend the V of your crotch is the V on the back wall and try my luck with a fresh throw."

The big man's eyes dropped involuntarily and then lifted. The rage reflected in his eyes was tempered only by his fear. He believed she would do what she said.

She was reaching for her tankard of ale when the door to the smith's shop burst open and Furl Hawken lumbered into view. Everyone in the room turned to look, and he slowed at once, aware of the unnatural silence, his eyes darting right and left.

Then he caught sight of her. "Little Red, something's come up. We have to go."

She stayed where she was, taking the tankard of ale in hand, lifting it to her lips, and drinking down the contents as if she had all the time in the world. Everyone watched in silence. No one moved. When she was finished, she set the tankard on the counter and walked over to the line sergeant. She bent close, as if daring him to do something about it. When he didn't, she said softly, "If I see you again, I'll kill you."

She dropped a coin on the counter as she passed the smith's wife, giving her a wink as she did so. Then she was through the door and surrounded by the clamor and fire of the forge, Furl Hawken at her back as he followed her out.

They moved swiftly through the maze of anvils, furnaces, and scrap heaps to the cluster of makeshift buildings beyond—kitchen, armory, surgery, command center, stables, supply depots, and the like, all bustling with activity in the midday heat. The sky was cloudless and blue, the sun a ball of white fire burning down on the dusty heights and the encamped army. Rue Meridian shook her head. It was the first daylight she had seen since yesterday, and it made her head pound.

"Is Big Red upset with me?" she asked as they moved away from the buildings and into the tented encampment, where she slowed her walk.

"Big Red is in irons and looking at twenty years' hard labor or worse," her companion growled, moving closer, keeping his voice low. "We had some company on our outing this morning, a couple of Federation officers. One went over the side during an attack, an accident, but he's just as dead. The ranking officer was furious. He was even madder when your brother refused to go after a couple of disabled Free-born ships, knock 'em out of the sky instead of letting them descend. When we set down again, he had Big Red arrested and taken away, promising him that he would soon be experiencing an abrupt career change."

She shook her head. "Nothing we can do about it, is there? I mean, nothing that involves words and official procedure?"

Furl Hawken grunted. "We're Rovers, Little Red. What do you think?"

She put her hand on his massive shoulder. "I think I'm sick of this place, these people, this war, the whole business. I think we need a change of employment. What do we care about any of this? It was only the money that brought us here in the first place, and we have more than enough of that to last us for a while."

Furl Hawken shook his head. "Can't ever have enough money, Little Red."

"True," she admitted.

"Besides, it's not so bad here." His voice took on a wistful tone. "I've kind of gotten used to it. Grows on you, all this flatness and space, dust and grit—"

She shoved him playfully. "Don't you play that game with me! You hate it here as much as I do!"

His bluff face broke into a wide grin. "Well, maybe so."

"Time to go home, Hawk," she declared firmly. "Gather up the men, equipment, our pay, supplies, horses for everyone, and meet me on the south ridge in one hour." She shoved him anew, laughing. "Go on, you great blowhard!"

She waited until he was on his way, then turned toward the stockade where Federation convicts and miscreants were housed, chained in the open or in barred wooden boxes that on a hot day could cook the brain. Just thinking of her brother in one of those set her teeth on edge. The Federation's attitude toward Rovers hadn't changed a whit in the three years of their service. Rovers were mercenaries, and mercenaries were a necessary evil. It didn't matter how faithfully they served. It didn't matter how many of them died in the Federation cause. It didn't matter that they had proved themselves the better flyers and, for the most part, the better fighters. In the eyes of most Southlanders, Rovers were inferior solely because of who they were, and nothing of their abilities or accomplishments could ever change that.

Of course, Rovers were at the bottom of almost everyone's list because they were nomadic. If you lacked homelands, a central government, and an army, you lacked power. Without power, you had difficulty commanding respect. Rovers had survived in the same way for two thousand years, in mobile encampments and by clans. Rovers believed the land belonged to everyone, but especially to those who traveled it. The land was their mother, and they shared the Elven concept that it should be protected and nurtured. As a consequence, the Elves were the most tolerant and allowed the Rovers to make their way through the forests of the Westland, functioning as traders inland and sailors along the coast.

Elsewhere, they were less welcome and lived in constant danger of being driven out or worse. Except when they were taken on as mercenaries to fight in wars that never had much of anything to do with them.

Rue Meridian and her brother, along with several dozen others, had come east from the area around the coastal village of March

Brume to serve the Federation in this one. The money was good and the risks acceptable. The Free-born weren't much better than the Federation at handling airships. There were regular battles, but they were viewed by the Rovers largely as exercises in trying to stay out of the way of incompetents.

Still, she concluded, it had grown boring, and it was time to move on. Especially now. She had been looking for an excuse to make a break for weeks, but her brother had insisted on sticking out the term of their enlistment. She shook her head. As if the Federation deserved their loyalty while treating them as subhuman. Now this. Clapping Big Red in irons over something as silly as ignoring an order from an officer of the Federation who ought to have known better than to try to give one. On an airship, the Captain's word was law. It was just another excuse to try to bring the Rovers into line, to put their collective necks under the Federation boot. Stupid, stupid people, she seethed. It would be interesting to see how successful they were with their airships once they lost the Rover crews who manned them.

She kicked at the dusty trail as she wound her way through the encampment, ignoring the inevitable catcalls and whistles, shouts and crude invitations, giving a wave or an unmistakable gesture where appropriate. She checked her weapons—slender rapier, brace of throwing knives strapped about her waist, dirk hidden in her boot, and sling looped through her shoulder strap and hanging down her back amid the scarves. Any one of them would be enough for this effort.

She could already smell the sea, the salt-laden pungency of the air, the raw damp of wooden docks and timbers, the fish-soaked reek of coastal shores, and the smoke from fireplaces lit at sunset to drive out the night's chill from homes and ale houses. Inland smells were of dust and dryness, of hard-packed earth and torrential rain-water that flooded and seeped away in a matter of hours. Three years of grit and dehydration, of men and animals who smelled alike, and of never seeing the blue of the ocean were enough.

Detouring momentarily at a campsite she recognized, she begged a meal off one of the cooks she was friendly with, wrapped it in paper, and took it with her. Big Red would be hungry.

Striding down through the outer stretches of the encampment, she approached the flat wooden walls of the stockade as if she were out for a midday stroll.

"Hey, Little Red," one of the two guards standing watch at the gates greeted cheerfully. "Come to see your brother?"

"Come to get him out," she replied, smiling.

The other guard grunted. "Huh, that'll take some doing."

"Oh, not all that much," she said. "Stockade commander in?"

"Having lunch or an afternoon snooze, take your choice." The first guard chuckled. "What's that you're carrying?"

"Lunch for Big Red. Can I see him?"

"Sure. We put him in the shade by the back wall, under the cat-walk overhang. Might as well make him as comfortable as we can while this business gets settled, though I don't like his chances from the look of that officer that hauled him in. Mean face on that one." He shook his head. "Sorry about this, Little Red. We like your brother."

"Oh, you like him, but not me?"

The guard flushed. "You know what I mean. Here, hand over your weapons, let me check your food package, and then you can go in and see him."

She handed over her belt with the knives and rapier, then un-hooked the sling. She kept the dirk in her boot. Compliance got you only so far in this world. She smiled cheerfully and passed through the gates.

She found her brother sitting under the overhang against the back wall, right where the guards had told her she would. He watched her approach without moving, weighted down in irons that were clamped to his wrists, ankles, and waist and chained to iron rings bolted tightly to the walls. Guards patrolled the cat-walks and stood idly in the roofed shade of watchtowers at the stockade's corners. No one seemed much interested in expending any energy.

She squatted in front of her brother and cocked a critical eyebrow. "You don't look so good, big brother."

Redden Alt Mer cocked an eyebrow back at her. "I thought you were sick in bed."

"I was sick at heart," she advised. "But I'm feeling much better now that we're about to experience a change of scenery. I think we've given the Federation army just about all of our time it deserves."

He brushed at a fly buzzing past his face, and the chains clanked furiously. "You won't get an argument out of me. My future as a mercenary doesn't look promising."

She glanced around. The stockade was filled with the sounds of men grumbling and cursing, of chains clanking, and of booted feet passing on the catwalk overhead. The air was dry and hot and still, and the smell of unwashed bodies, sweat, and excrement permeated everything.

She adjusted her stance to sit cross-legged before him, setting the food package on the ground between them. "How about something to eat?"

She unwrapped the food, and her brother began to devour it hungrily. "This is good," he told her. "But what are we doing, exactly? I thought you might have thought of a way to get me out of here."

She brushed back her thick red hair and smirked. "You mean you haven't figured that out for yourself? You got yourself in, didn't you?"

"No, I had help with that." He chewed thoughtfully on a piece of bread. "Do you have anything to drink?"

She reached inside her robes and produced a flask. He took it from her and drank deeply. "Ale," he announced approvingly. "What's going on? Is this my last meal?"

She picked at a cut of roast pheasant. "Let's hope not."

"So?"

"So we're killing time until Hawk gets things ready for our departure." She took the flask back from him and drank. "Besides, we may not have time to eat again once we set out. I don't expect we'll be stopping until after dark."

He nodded. "I suppose not. So you do have a plan."

She grinned. "What do you think?"

They finished the meal, drank the rest of the ale, and sat quietly until Rue Meridian was satisfied that enough time had passed for Furl Hawken to be ready and waiting. Then she rose, brushed herself off, gathered up the remains of their feast, and walked toward the shack that served as the stockade commander's office. On the way, she dropped their leftovers in the stockade compost heap. You did what you could to care for Mother Earth, even here.

She walked into the commander's office without knocking, closing the door behind her. The commander was leaning back in his chair against the wall behind his desk, dozing. He was a red-faced, corpulent man, his face and hands scarred and worn. Without slowing, she walked around the desk, the dirk in her hand, and hit him as hard as she could behind the ear. He slumped to the floor without a sound.

Racks of keys lined the wall. She selected the set with her brother's name tagged to the peg and walked back to the door. When she caught sight of a guard passing across the compound, she called him over. "The commander wants to see my brother. Bring him over, please."

The guard, used to obeying orders from almost everyone, didn't question her. He took the keys and set off. A few minutes later he was back, herding Big Red at a slow shuffle, the wrist and ankle irons still attached. She stood aside to let them enter, closed the door, and flattened the guard with a blow to the neck.

Her brother glanced at her. "Very efficient. Do you plan to dispatch the entire garrison this way?"

"I don't think that will be necessary." She worked the keys into the wrist and ankle locks, and the chains dropped away. He rubbed his wrists appreciatively and looked around for a weapon. "Never mind that," she said, gesturing impatiently.

She took a sheet of paper from the commander's desk, one embossed with the Federation insignia, and wrote a brief note on it with a quill pen and ink. When she was finished, she eyed it critically, then nodded. "Good enough. You're a free man. Let's go."

She slipped the dirk back in her boot, and they walked out of the command shack and across the yard toward the gates. Her brother's eyes shifted about nervously. Prisoners and guards alike were watching them. "Are you sure about this?"

She laughed and shoved him playfully. "Just watch."

When they reached the gates, the two guards she had given her weapons to on entering were waiting. She waved the insignia-embossed paper at them. "What did I tell you?" she asked brightly, handing the paper to the first guard.

"Let me have a look at that," he replied suspiciously, squinting hard at the paper.

"You can see for yourself," she declared, pointing at the writing. "He's released to my custody until all this gets straightened out. I told you it wouldn't be that hard."

The second guard moved closer to the first, peering over his shoulder. Neither seemed entirely certain what to do.

"Don't you understand?" she pressed, crowding them now, jamming her finger at the paper. "The army can't afford to keep its best airship pilot locked up in the stockade with a war going on. Not because of one Federation officer who thinks it's a good idea. Come on! Give me back my weapons! You've looked at the order long enough! What's the matter, can't you read?"

She glared at them now. Neither guard said a word.

"Do you want me to wake up the commander again? He was mad enough the first time."

"Okay, okay," the first guard said hastily, shoving the piece of paper at her.

He handed back her knives, rapier, and sling and shooed them out the gates and back into the encampment. They walked in silence for several dozen paces before Redden Alt Mer said, "I don't believe it."

She shrugged. "They can't read. Even if they could, it wouldn't matter. No one could make out what I wrote. When they're asked about it, they'll claim I had a release order signed by the commander. Who's to say I didn't? This is the army, big brother. Soldiers don't admit to anything that might get them in trouble. They'll fuss for a day or two and then decide they're well rid of us."

Her brother rubbed his arms to restore the circulation and glanced at the cloudless sky. "Three years in this forsaken place. Money or no, that's a long time." He sighed wearily and slapped his thighs. "I hate leaving *Black Moclips*, though. I hate that."

She nodded. "I know. I thought about taking her. But stealing her would be hard, Big Red. Too many people keeping watch."

"We'll get another ship," he declared, brushing the matter aside, a bit of the old spring returning to his step. "Somewhere."

They walked through the camp's south fringe to where the passes led downward out of the heights toward the city of Dechtera and the grasslands west. Once across the Rappahalladran and the plains beyond, they were home.

Ahead, Furl Hawken stood waiting in a draw with a dozen more Rovers and the horses and supplies.

"Hawk!" Redden Alt Mer called, and gave him a wave. Then he glanced over his shoulder at the fading outline of the camp. "Well, it was fun for a time. Not as much fun as we'll have where we're going, of course, wherever that turns out to be, but it had its moments."

Rue Meridian smirked. "My brother, the eternal optimist." She brushed stray strands of her long hair from her face. "Let's hope this time you're right."

Ten minutes later, they had left the Federation army behind and were riding west for the coast of the Blue Divide.

SIX

A t first light, the Druid known as Walker slipped from the sleeping room he had been given in the summer house on his arrival the night before. Arborlon was still sleeping, the Elven city at rest, and only the night watch and those whose work required an early rising were awake. A tall, spare, shadowy figure in his black robes, hair, and beard, he glided soundlessly from the palace grounds and through the streets and byways of the city to the broad sweep of the Carolan. He was aware of the Home Guard who trailed him, an Elven Hunter assigned to him by the King. Allardon Elessedil was not a man who took chances, so the presence of a watchdog was not unexpected, and Walker let the matter be.

On the heights, where the Carolan fronted the sprawl of the Westland forests, visible all the way to the ragged jut of the Rock Spur south and the Kensrowe north, he paused. The first glimmer of sunlight had crested the trees behind him, but night still enfolded the land west, purple and gray shadows clinging to treetops and mountain peaks like veils. In the earthen bowl of the Sarandanon, small lakes and rivers reflected the early light in silvery flashes amid the patchwork quilt of farms and fields. Farther out, the waters of the Innisbore shimmered in a rough, metallic sheen, their surface coated with broken layers of mist. Somewhere beyond that lay the vast expanse of the Blue Divide, and it was there that he must eventually go.

He looked all about the land, a slow, careful perusal, a drinking in of colors and shapes. He thought about the history of the city. Of the stand it had made in the time of Eventine Elessedil against the assault of the demons freed from the Forbidding by the failure of the Ellcrys. Of its journey out of the Westland in the Ruhk staff and the magic-riven Loden to the island of Morrowindl—buildings, people, and history disappeared as if they had never been. Of its journey back again, returned to the Four Lands by Wren Elessedil, where it would withstand the onslaught of the Shadowen. Always, the Elves and the Druids had been allies, bound by a common desire to see the lands and their peoples kept free.

What, he asked himself in dark contemplation, had become of that bond?

Below the heights, swollen with snowmelt off the mountains and spring's rainfall, the Rill Song churned noisily within its banks. He listened to the soothing, distant sound of the water's heavy flow as it echoed out of the trees. He stood motionless in the enfolding silence, not wanting to disturb it. It felt strange to be back here, but right, as well. He had not come to Arborlon in more than twenty years. He had not thought he would come again while Allardon Elessedil lived. His last visit had opened a rift between them he did not think anything could close. Yet here he was, and the rift that had seemed so insurmountable now seemed all but inconsequential.

His thoughts drifted as he turned away. He had come to Arborlon and the Elven King out of desperation. All of his efforts at brokering an agreement with the races to bring representatives to Paranor to study in the Druid way had failed. Since then, he had lived alone at Paranor, reverting to the work of recording the history of the Four Lands. There was little else he could do. His bitterness was acute. He was trapped in a life he had never wanted. He was a reluctant Druid, recruited by the shade of Allanon in a time when there were no Druids and the presence of at least one was vital to the survival of the races. He had accepted the blood trust bestowed by the dying Allanon hundreds of years earlier on his ancestor Brin Ohmsford, not because he coveted it in any way, but because fate and circumstance conspired to place him in a position where only he could fulfill its mandate. He had done so out of a sense of responsibility. He had done so hoping that he might change the image and work of the Druids, that he might find a way for the order to oversee civilization's advancement through cooperative study and democratic participation by all of the peoples of the Four Lands.

He shook his head. How foolish he had been, how naive his thinking. The disparities between nations and races were too great for any single body to overcome, let alone any single man. His predecessors had realized that and acted on it accordingly. First bring strength to bear, then reason. Power commanded respect, and respect provided a platform from which to enjoin reason. He had neither. He was an outcast, solitary and anachronistic in the eyes of almost everyone. The Druids had been gone from the Four Lands since the time of Allanon. Too long for anyone to remember them as they once were. Too long to command respect. Too long to serve as a catalyst for change in a world in which change most often came slowly, grudgingly, and in tiny increments.

He exhaled sharply, as if to expel the bitter memory. All that was in the past. Perhaps now it could be buried there. Perhaps now, unwittingly, he had been given the key to accomplishing what had been denied him for so long.

The Gardens of Life rose ahead of him, sun-streaked and vibrant with springtime color. Members of the Black Watch stood at their entrances, rigid and aloof, and he passed them by without a glance. Within the gardens grew the Ellcrys, the most sacred of the Elven talismans, the tree that kept in place the Forbidding, the wall conjured in ancient times to close away the demons and monsters that had once threatened to overrun the world. He walked to where she rooted on a small rise, set apart from the rest of the plantings, strikingly beautiful with her silver limbs and crimson leaves, wrapped in serenity and legend. She had been human once. When her life cycle was complete and she passed away, her successor would come from among the Chosen who tended her. It was a strange and miraculous transition, and it required sacrifice and commitment of a sort with which he was intimately familiar.

A voice spoke at his elbow. "I always wonder if she is watching me, if by virtue of having been given responsibility over all of her people I require her constant vigilance. I always wonder if I am living up to her expectations."

Walker turned to find Allardon Elessedil standing beside him. It had been many years since he had seen him last, yet he recognized him at once. Allardon Elessedil was older and grayer, more weathered and careworn, and the robes he wore were pale and nondescript. But he carried himself in the same regal manner and exuded the same rocklike presence. Allardon Elessedil was not one of the great Elven Kings; he had been denied that legacy by a history that had not given him reason or need to be so and by a temperament that was neither restless nor inquisitive. He was a caretaker King, a ruler who felt his principal duty was to keep things as they were. Risktaking was for other men and other races, and the Elves in his time had not been at the forefront of civilization's evolution in the Four Lands.

The Elven King did not offer his hand in greeting or speak any words of welcome. It remained to be seen, Walker judged, how their meeting would conclude.

Walker looked back at the Ellcrys. "We cannot hope to know what she expects of us, Elven King. It would be presumptuous even to try."

If the other man was offended, he did not show it. "Are you rested?" he asked.

"I am. I slept undisturbed. But at first light, I felt the need to walk here. Is this a problem?"

Allardon Elessedil brushed the question off with a wave of his hand. "Hardly. You are free to walk where you choose."

Yes, but not to do as I please, Walker thought. How bitter he had been on leaving all those years ago. How despairing. But time's passing had blunted the edges of those once sharp feelings, and now they were mostly memory. It was a new age, and the Elven King was growing old now and in need of him. Walker could achieve the result that had been denied him for so long if he proceeded carefully. It was a strange, exhilarating feeling, and he had to be cautious to keep it from showing in his voice and eyes.

"Your family is well?" he asked, making an effort at being cordial.

The other shrugged. "The children grow and take roads of their own choosing. They listen to me less and less. I have their respect, but not their obedience. I am more a father and less a King to them, and they feel free to ignore me."

"What is it you would have them do?"

"Oh, what fathers would usually have children do." The Elven King chuckled. "Stay closer to home, take fewer chances, be content with the known world. Kylen fights with the Free-born in a struggle I do not support. Ahren wanders the north in search of a future. My sons think I will live forever, and they leave me to be ruler alone." He shrugged. "I suppose they are no different than the sons of other fathers."

Walker said nothing. His views would not have been welcomed. If Allardon Elessedil's sons grew up to be different men than their father, so much the better.

"I am pleased you decided to come," the King ventured after a moment.

Walker sighed. "You knew I would. The castaway elf—is he Kael?"

"I assume as much. He wore the bracelet. Another elf would have carried it. Anyway, we'll know tomorrow. I hoped the map would intrigue you sufficiently that you would be persuaded. Have you studied it?"

Walker nodded. "All night before flying here yesterday."

"Is it genuine?" Allardon Elessedil asked.

"That's difficult to say. It depends on what you mean. If you are asking me whether it might tell us what happened to your brother, the answer is yes. It might be a map of the voyage on which he disappeared. His name appears nowhere in the writings, but the condition and nature of the hide and ink suggest it was drawn within the last thirty years, so that it might have been his work. Is the handwriting his?"

The Elven King shook his head. "I can't tell."

"The language is archaic, a language not used since the Great Wars changed the Old World forever. Would your brother have learned that language?"

The other man considered this for a moment, then shrugged. "I don't know. How much of what it says were you able to decipher?"

Walker shifted within his dark robes, looking out again toward the Carolan. "Can we walk a bit? I am cramped and sore from yesterday's journey, and I think it would help to stretch my legs."

He began moving slowly down the pathway, and the Elf King fell into step beside him wordlessly. They walked in silence through the gardens for a time, the Druid content to let matters stay as they were until he was ready to speak to them. Let Allardon Elessedil wait as he had waited. He turned his attention to other things, observing the way in which the gardens' plantings flowed into one another with intricate symmetry, listening to the soft warble of the resident birds, and gazing up at the clouds that drifted like silk throws across the clear blue of the spring sky. Life in balance. Everything as it should be.

Walker glanced over. "The guard you assigned to watch me appears to have lost interest in the job."

The Elven King smiled reassuringly. "He wasn't there to watch you. He was there to let me know when you awoke so that we could have this talk."

"Ah. You sought privacy in our dealings. Because your own

guards are absent, as well. We are all alone." He paused. "Do you feel safe with me, then?"

The other's smile was uneasy. "No one would dare to attack me while I was with you."

"You have more faith in me than I deserve."

"Do I?"

"Yes, if you consider that I wasn't referring to an attack that might come from a third party."

The conversation was clearly making the King uncomfortable. Good, Walker thought. I want you to remember how you left things between us. I want you to wonder if I might be a greater threat to you than the enemies you more readily fear.

They emerged from the gardens onto the Carolan, the sunlight illuminating the green expanse of the heights in bright trailers that spilled over into the forests below. Walker led the way to a bench placed under an aging maple whose boughs canopied out in a vast umbrella. They sat together, Druid and King, looking out over the heights to the purple and gold mix of shadow and light that colored the horizon west.

"I have no reason to want to help you, Allardon Elessedil," Walker said after a moment.

The Elven King nodded. "Perhaps you have better reason than you think. I am not the man I was when last we spoke. I regret deeply how that meeting ended."

"Your regret can be no greater than my own," Walker replied darkly, keeping his gaze averted, staring off into the distance.

"We can dwell on the regret and the loss or turn our attention to what we might accomplish if we relegate both to the past." The Elven King's voice was tight and worried, but there was a hint of determination behind it, as well. "I would like to make a new beginning."

Now Walker looked at him. "What do you propose?"

"A chance for you to build the Druid Council you desire, to begin the work you have sought to do for so long, with my support and blessing."

"Money and men would count for more than your support and blessing," the Druid remarked dryly.

The Elven King's face went taut. "You shall have both. You shall have whatever you need if you are able to give me what I need in return. Now tell me of the map. Were you able to decipher its writings?"

Walker took a long moment to consider his answer before he spoke. "Enough so that I can tell you that they purport to show the way to the treasure of which your mother's seer dreamed thirty years ago. As I said, the writing is archaic and obscure. Some symbols suggest more than one thing. But there are names and courses and descriptions of sufficient clarity to reveal the nature of the map. Travel west off the coast of the Blue Divide to three islands, each a bit farther than the one before. Each hides a key that, when all are used together, will unlock a door. The door leads to an underground keep that lies beneath the ruins of a city called Castledown. The ruins can be found on a mountainous spit of land far west and north of here called Ice Henge. Within the ruins lies a treasure of life-altering power. It is a magic of words, a magic that has survived the destruction of the Old World and the Great Wars by being kept hidden in its safehold. The magic's origins are obscure, but the map's writings say it surpasses all others."

He paused. "Because it was found on the blind and voiceless Elven castaway together with your brother's bracelet, I would be inclined to believe that if followed, it would reveal your brother's fate and perhaps the nature of the magic it conceals."

He waited, letting the King collect his thoughts. On the heights, the Elves were beginning to appear in clusters for the start of the workday. Guards were exchanging shifts. Tradesmen and trappers were arriving from the west, crossing the Rill Song on ferries and rafts bearing wagons and carts laden with goods, then climbing the ramps of the Elfitch. Gardeners were at work in the Gardens of Life, weeding and pruning, planting and fertilizing. Here and there, a white-robed Chosen wandered into view. Children played as teachers led them to their study areas for lessons on becoming Healers in the Four Lands.

"So you support a quest of the sort my brother undertook all those years ago?" the King asked finally.

Walker smiled faintly. "As do you, or you would not have asked me to come here."

Allardon Elessedil nodded slowly. "If we are to learn the truth, we must follow the route the map chronicles and see where it leads. I will never know what happened to Kael otherwise. I will never know what became of the Elfstones he carried. Their loss is perhaps the more significant of the two. This is not easy to admit, but I can't pretend otherwise. The stones are an Elven heritage, passed down from Queen Wren, and the last of their kind. We are a lesser people without them, and I want them back."

Walker's dark face was inscrutable. "Who will lead this expedition, Allardon?"

There was no hesitation in his answer. "You will. If you agree to. I am too old. I can admit it to you if to no one else. My children are too young and inexperienced. Even Kylen. He is strong and fierce, but he is not seasoned enough to lead an expedition of this sort. My brother carried the Elfstones, and even that was not enough to save him. Perhaps a Druid's powers will prove more formidable."

"And if I agree to do this, you give me your word that the Elves will support an independent Druid Council, free to study, explore, and develop all forms of magic?"

"I do."

"A Druid Council that will answer to no one nation or people or ruler, but only to its own conscience and the dictates of the order?"

"Yes."

"A Druid Council that will share its findings equally with all people, when and if those findings can be implemented peacefully and for the betterment of all races?"

"Yes, yes!" The King made an impatient, dismissive gesture. "All that you sought before and I denied. All. Understand, though," he added hurriedly, "I cannot speak for other nations and rulers, only for the Elves."

Walker nodded. "Where the Elves lead, others follow."

"And if you disappear as my brother did, then the matter ends there. I will not be bound to an agreement with a dead man—not an agreement of this sort."

Walker's gaze wandered across the Carolan to the Gardens of Life and settled on the men and women working there, bent to their tasks. It spoke to him of his own work, of the need to care for the lives of the people of the races the Druids had sworn long ago to protect and advance. Why had their goals been so difficult to achieve when their cause was so obviously right? If plants were sentient in the way of humans, would they prove as difficult and obstructive to the efforts of their tenders?

"We understand each other, Allardon," he said softly. His eyes found the King's face. He waited for the lines of irritation to soften. "One more thing. Any treasure I discover on this journey, be it magic or otherwise, belongs to the Druids."

The Elven King was already shaking his head in disagreement. "You know I will not agree to that. Of money or precious metals, I care nothing. But what you find of magic, whatever its form, belongs to the Elves. I am the one who has sanctioned and commissioned this quest. I am the one whose cause requires it. I am entitled to the ownership of whatever you recover."

"On behalf of your people," Walker amended casually.

"Of course!"

"Suggesting that the cause and ownership rights of the Elven people are greater than those of the other races, even if the magic recovered might benefit them, as well?"

The King flushed anew, stiffening within his robes. He leaned forward combatively. "Do not try to make me feel guilt or remorse for the protections I seek to give to my own people, Walker! It is my duty to do so! Let others do so, as well, and perhaps a balance will be struck!"

"I have trouble understanding why, on the one hand, you support a Druid Council giving equal rights to all nations and peoples while, on the other, you seek to withhold what might benefit them most. Should I undertake a quest only for you, when what I would most covet at its end is forbidden me?" He paused, reflecting. "Magic belongs to everyone, Elven King, especially when it impacts all. A sharing of magic must begin somewhere. Let it begin here."

Allardon Elessedil stared hard at him, but the Druid held his gaze and kept his expression neutral. The seconds dragged past with neither man speaking further, eyes locked.

"I cannot agree," the Elven King repeated firmly.

Walker's brow creased thoughtfully. "I will make a bargain with you," he said. "A compromise of our positions. You will share fully in what I find, magic or no. But we shall make an agreement as to the nature of that sharing. That which you can use without my help, I will give to you freely. That which only I can use belongs to me."

The King studied him. "The advantage is yours in this bargain. You are better able to command the use of magic than I or my people."

"Magic that is Elven in nature will be readily understood by Elves and should belong to them. The Elfstones, for example, if found, belong to you. But magic that has another source, whatever its nature, cannot be claimed by Elves alone, especially if they cannot wield it."

"There is no magic in the world except that which was handed down by the Elves out of the world of Faerie! You know that!"

"Then you have nothing to worry about."

The King shook his head helplessly. "There is a trick in all this."

"Describe it, then."

"All right, all right!" The Elf sighed. "This matter has to be resolved. I'll accept your compromise. That magic that is Elven in nature and can be commanded by us is ours. The rest stays with the Druid Council. I don't like this bargain, but I can live with it."

They shook hands wordlessly. Walker rose, squinting against the sharp glare of the sunrise as he looked east over the trees. His black robes rippled softly in the breeze. Allardon Elessedil stood up with him. The sharp features looked pinched and tired despite the early hour. "What do you intend to do now?"

The Druid shifted his gaze back to the King. "I'll need the use of the Wing Rider and his Roc."

"Hunter Predd? I'll speak with him. Will you fly to Bracken Clell?"

"Will you go with me, if I do?" the Druid countered. "Or have you done so already?"

Allardon Elessedil shook his head. "I've been waiting on you."

"It is your brother, perhaps, who lies dying in the Healer's home, Elven King."

"Perhaps. But it's been thirty years, and he's been dead to me a long time already." The King sighed. "It complicates things if I go with you. Home Guard will insist on going as well, to protect me. Another Roc will be needed. It might be better if I remain here."

Walker nodded. "I'll go alone then, and afterwards farther on to find a ship and crew."

"I could help you with that."

"You could, but I would prefer that you helped me in another way if you choose to remain here. There are certain things I want from a ship and crew that will take us in search of the map's treasure, things that I must determine for myself. But I will rely on you to select those who would defend us. Elven Hunters, of course, but perhaps a handful of others as well. Bordermen and Dwarves, I should think. Are you willing to find them for me?"

The Elven King nodded. "How many do you wish?"

"Two dozen to choose from, no more."

They began to walk back across the heights, moving toward

the gardens once more, taking their time. All around them, the city of Arborlon was waking.

"Two dozen is a small number of blades and bows on which to depend," the King observed.

"Three ships with full crews and dozens of Elven Hunters were apparently too few, as well," Walker pointed out. "I prefer to rely on speed and stealth and on the heart and courage of a few rather than on sheer numbers."

"One ship is all you will take, then?"

"One will suffice."

Allardon Elessedil hunched his shoulders, his eyes lowered. "Very well. I will not go with you myself, as I have said, but I will want to send someone in my place."

"Send anyone you like, only . . ."

Walker was shading his eyes against the sun's brightness as he spoke or he would have missed the flash of the metal blade as it was hurled. The assassin was one of the gardeners, inconspicuous in his working clothes, just another worker at his job. He had come to his feet as if to move his tools, and suddenly the knife appeared.

Walker's swift gesture sent the blade spinning harmlessly, knocked aside as if it had struck a wall.

By now, the second assassin was attacking, this one with a blowgun. Another of the seeming gardeners, he knelt in a patch of bright yellow daffodils and fired three darts in rapid succession. Walker yanked the King aside and blocked that attack as well. A third assassin came at them with a rapier and a knife. All of the assassins were Elves, their features unmistakable. But their eyes were fixed and unseeing, and the Druid knew at once that they had been mind-altered to assure their compliance in making the attack.

Screams rose across the Carolan as the other Elves realized what was happening. Black Watch soldiers charged to the King's defense, massive pikes lowered. Elven Hunters appeared, as well, lean, swift forms bolting from the trees. All were too far away.

Walker gestured toward the assassin with the rapier and knife, and a massive, ethereal form materialized before the man, a giant moor cat lunging out of nowhere to intercept him. The man screamed and went down, weapons flying as the beast sailed into him and vanished, leaving him huddled and cringing against the earth. The remaining two assassins charged, as well, silent and determined, skirting the third man, madness in their empty eyes. They barreled into the Druid and were cast aside as if made of paper. Black robes flaring like shadows released, Walker turned from one to the other, stripping them of weapons and blunting their attacks.

But the Home Guard and Black Watch were close enough now to respond as well. Frightened for their king, they acted instinctively and unwisely to protect him. A hail of spears and arrows took down the assassins, leaving them sprawled on blood-soaked earth, their lives draining away. Even the third man was caught in the barrage, come back to his feet too quickly to be spared. Walker yelled at the Elves to stop, to leave the assassins to him, but he was too late to save them.

Too late, as well, to save Allardon Elessedil. An arrow meant for the assassins struck the Elf King squarely in the chest. He gasped at the impact, lurched backwards, and went down in a heap. Walker had no chance to save him. Focused on stopping the assassins, he could not react to the King's guards in time.

The Druid knelt at the King's side, lifted his shoulders, and cradled his head in his lap. "Elven King?" he whispered. "Can you hear me?"

Allardon Elessedil's eyes were open, and his gaze shifted at the sound of the Druid's voice. "I'm still here."

Elven Hunters had surrounded them, and there were calls for a Healer and medicines. The heights were a maelstrom of activity as Elves pushed forward from every quarter to see what had happened. Black Watch formed a ring about their stricken ruler and pushed the crowds back. The assassins lay dead in their own blood, their lifeless forms bathed in sunlight and bedded in deep grasses.

Allardon Elessedil was coughing blood. "Call a scribe," he gasped. "Do it now."

One was found almost at once, a young man, barely grown, his face white and his eyes frightened as he knelt next to the king.

"Move everyone back but this boy, the Druid, and two witnesses," Allardon Elessedil ordered.

"High Lord, I cannot . . . ," a Captain of the Home Guard began softly, but the King motioned him away.

When an area had been cleared around them, the Elven King nodded to the scribe. "Copy down what I say," he whispered, keeping his eyes on Walker as he spoke. "Everything."

Carefully, detail by detail, he repeated the agreement that he had reached with the Druid moments earlier. A voyage was to be undertaken with Walker as its leader. The purpose of the voyage was to follow the route described on a map carried by the Druid, a copy of which was held by the King's scribe at the palace. A search for the missing blue Elfstones was to be undertaken. And on and on. Slowly, painstakingly, he repeated it all, including the bargain struck regarding the recovery of magic. A Healer appeared and began work on the injury, but the King kept talking, grimacing through his pain, his breathing raspy and thick and his eyes blinking as if he was fighting to see.

"There," he said, when he was finished. "They have killed me for nothing. See this through, Walker. Promise me."

"He's bleeding to death," the Healer announced. "I have to take him to my surgery and remove the arrow at once."

Walker lifted the Elven King as if he weighed nothing, cradling him in the crook of his good left arm and with the stump of his right, and carried him from the plains. All the while, he talked to him, telling him to stay strong, not to give up, to fight for his life, for it had worth and meaning beyond what he knew. Surrounded by Home Guard, he bore the King as he might a sleeping child, holding him gently within his arms, head cushioned against his shoulder.

Several times, the King spoke, but the words were so soft that only Walker could hear them. Each time the Druid replied firmly, "You have my promise. Rest, now."

But sometimes even a Druid's exhortations are not enough. By the time they reached the surgery, Allardon Elessedil was dead.

SEVEN

It took Walker until well after noon to secure a copy of the young scribe's notes and carry it to Ebben Bonner, who was First Minister of the Elven High Council and nominal leader of the Elves pending the formal succession of Allardon Elessedil's eldest son. There, in an extraordinary concession to the circumstances surrounding the King's death, the First Minister approved Walker's request to depart for Bracken Clell so that he might act on the terms of the dead King's agreement. Walker successfully argued that there was reason to believe that the mind-altered Elves who were behind the death of Allardon Elessedil had been sent by someone intent on preventing an expedition to retrace the route detailed on the castaway's map. It was entirely too coincidental that the attack had come just as King and Druid had agreed to mount such an expedition, especially since it was their first meeting in twenty-three years. Certainly the King had believed it was more than coincidence or he would not have spent the last moments of his life dictating instructions for carrying out the expedition to his scribe. Clearly, someone had found out about the map and the treasure it revealed. It took a leap of faith to accept that there was a connection between the King's death and the map's appearance, but it would be better to make that leap than do nothing. Walker was concerned that if the King's enemies were bold enough to strike in the Elven capital city, they would be equally quick to strike in Bracken Clell. The castaway who was under care in the healing center would be at great risk. Perhaps Walker could still reach him in time. Perhaps he could discover yet if he was Kael Elessedil.

He recruited Hunter Predd and Obsidian for the journey. The Wing Rider was anxious to depart the chaos unfolding around him and frankly curious to know more about where this business of the castaway and the map was leading. With barely a word of encouragement from Walker or question of his own, he had Obsidian saddled and ready for flight. They rose into the afternoon sun while the people of Arborlon were still trying to come to terms with the news of their King's death. Some were just learning, returned from journeys of their own or preoccupied with the demands and difficulties of their own lives. Some still didn't believe it was true. Walker wasn't sure what he believed. The suddenness of the King's death was shocking. Walker was no less affected than the Elves. To not have seen or spoken to the man in so many years and then to watch him die, on their first morning, was difficult to accept. It was bad enough that he had been hostile toward the King in their final meeting and almost intolerable that he had all but wished him dead. He did not feel guilt for his behavior, but he did feel shame.

Allardon Elessedil already lay in state, awaiting his funeral and burial. Messengers had been sent to his children, east to the front where Kylen fought with the Free-born, north into the wilderness where Ahren hunted. Across the length and breadth of the Four Lands, word of the Elven King's death had gone out.

But Walker could give no further thought to any of it. His concern now was for the safety of the castaway and the initial preparations for the voyage chronicled on the map he carried within his robes. He strongly believed that whoever arranged for the King's assassination had done so to keep him from underwriting the voyage.

Until a new King sat upon the throne, the Elven High Council would be unlikely to do much more than tread water. What saved Walker from being blocked entirely was the old King's quick action in recording, almost literally with his last breath, the agreement they had struck regarding the map so that the Druid could act on it without having to wait around.

And, if the Druid's suspicions were correct, whoever had recruited the Elven assassins had probably determined to make the voyage, as well.

Steady and unflagging, Obsidian flew his master and Walker south for the remainder of the afternoon over the dense tangle of Drey Wood and the watery mire of the Matted Brakes. As sunset neared, they passed the Pykon's solitary spires and crossed the silver thread of the Rill Song into the deep woods that fronted the Rock Spur. The light was beginning to fail badly as Hunter Predd guided his mount to a good-size clearing. There, he sent the Roc back into the trees to roost, while he and the Druid made camp. They lit a fire in a shallow pit, laid out their bedrolls on a carpet of soft needles beneath an ancient pine, and cooked their meal. Druid and Wing Rider, they sat as if a part of the forest shadows, dark figures in the deepening gloom, eating in silence and listening to the sounds of the night.

"Strange day," the Elf remarked, sipping at the ale he shared with his traveling companion. "Makes you wonder about the way life works. Makes you wonder why anyone would want to be King."

Walker nodded, straight-backed within his black robes, eyes distant. "The Wing Hove must have thought the same thing a long time ago."

"It's true. It's one reason we have a council to make our laws and decisions for us, not just one man." The Wing Rider shook his head. "Killed by his own people. He wasn't a bad man, Walker. Why would they do it?"

Walker's gaze fixed on him. "They didn't. I saw their eyes.

Whatever their motives in acting against the King, they were not the men they had been even a few days ago. They had been mind-altered in some permanent way. They were meant to attack the King, to kill him however they could manage it, and then to die."

Hunter Predd frowned. "How could a man be made to do that?"

"Magic."

"Elven?"

Walker shook his head. "I'm not sure yet. If they had lived, I might have been able to tell. Dead, they could give me nothing."

"Who were they? Not gardeners, surely?"

"No one could identify them. Elves, but not of Arborlon. Hard men, who had led hard lives, from the look of their hands and faces. They would have killed other men before this."

"Still."

"Still, they would have needed some incentive to kill an Elven King. Whoever recruited them provided that incentive using magic." Walker held the other's gaze. "I'm sorry to drag you out again so suddenly, but there wasn't time to wait. I think our cast-away is in danger. And it won't stop there. I'm going to need you to fly me a few more places in the next week or two, Hunter Predd. I'm going to need your help."

The Wing Rider drained the rest of the ale from his cup and poured himself another serving from the skin pouch beside him. "Tell you the truth, I was ready to leave anyway. Not just because of the King's dying, but because cities and me don't much agree. A few days are more than enough. I'm better off flying, whatever the risk."

The Druid gave him a wry smile. "Nevertheless, it appears you are knee-deep in something more than you bargained for when you decided to carry that map and bracelet to Arborlon."

The Elf nodded. "That's fine. I want to see where all this is going." He grinned suddenly. "Wouldn't it be a shame if I didn't give myself the chance?"

* * *

They slept undisturbed and by sunrise were winging their way south once more. The weather had changed during the night, with heavy clouds rolling inland off the coast and blanketing the skies from horizon to horizon. The air was warm and still, smelling of new rain, and in the distance, farther west, the sound of thunder echoed ominously. Shadows draped the land they passed over, a cloaking of movement and light that whispered in their thoughts of secrets and concealments not meant to be revealed.

Walker was already beginning to suspect the identity of the enemy who was trying to undermine his efforts. There were few in the Four Lands who could command magic strong enough to alter minds—fewer still with a sufficient number of well-placed eyes to know what was happening from Bracken Clell to Arborlon. He was afraid that he had acted too slowly in this matter, though he accepted at the same time that he could not have acted any faster. He was only one man, and his adversary, if his suspicions were correct, commanded a small army.

Obsidian flew them through the jagged defiles and down the deep canyons of the Rock Spur Mountains, angling to keep low enough for cover, high enough to clear the ridges. They passed over the dark bowl of the Wilderun, home to castoffs and outcasts who had come from everywhere to that final refuge. At its center, the Hollows was a pool of shadows, dark and forbidding, a quagmire that might swallow them up should they fly too low. Beyond, at the south end of the wilderness, they passed through the deeper maze of the Irrybis Mountains and came in sight of the Blue Divide.

Rain had begun to fall in a slow drizzle, soon soaking their clothing through, and it was approaching nightfall when they arrived at the seaport of Bracken Clell. In darkness unbroken by the light of moon or stars, they proceeded slowly along muddied, rain-slicked pathways, hooded and cloaked, wraiths in the night.

"Not much farther," the Wing Rider advised from the darkness of his cowl, when the lights of the seaport came in view.

They came to the healing center where Hunter had left the castaway less than a week earlier. They mounted the steps of the covered porch, shaking the rain from their cloaks, and knocked on the door. Waiting, they could hear a low murmur of voices from inside and see shadows move across the lighted, curtained windows.

The door opened on a lean, graying Elf with kind, tired eyes and a questioning look. He smiled on seeing Hunter Predd and extended his hand to invite them in.

"My friend, Dorne," the Wing Rider said to Walker. "This man," he advised the Healer in turn, gesturing in a deliberately offhanded way toward the Druid, "is an emissary sent by Allardon Elessedil to have a look at our castaway."

He offered no further explanation and said nothing of the King's death. The healer seemed to accept this. He shook Walker's hand solemnly. "I have some bad news for you. I did my best, but it wasn't enough. The man Hunter left in my care is dead. He died in his sleep several days ago."

Walker took the news calmly. He was not surprised. It merely confirmed his suspicions. Whoever had sent the assassins to kill Allardon Elessedil had disposed of the castaway, as well. "Have you buried him?"

"No." The Healer shook his head quickly. "I've put him in the cold house, waiting to see what news Hunter brought from Arborlon."

"And his room? The room in which he died? Is it occupied?"

"Vacant. We've cleaned it, but it services no new patient yet." The Healer glanced from face to face. "Come in by the fire and dry off. I'll have some hot soup brought. It's turning nasty out there."

He placed them in chairs before the fire burning in the great room, took their cloaks, and gave them blankets with which to dry. Assistants to the Healer came and went in pursuit of their tasks, glancing over at the travelers, but saying nothing. Walker paid them no attention, his thoughts on the dead man. All chance was lost to learn anything from him in life. Could he find a way to learn something from him in death?

The Healer returned with bowls of soup and cups of ale, gave them a moment to begin eating, then pulled up a chair beside them. He seemed tired and nervous, but both were to be expected. Walker sensed no dissembling or bad intention in him; he was not an evil man.

The Healer asked after their journey, and they exchanged small talk with him as they ate. Outside, the rain was falling harder, the sound of the drops on the roof and windowpanes a constant, dull thrum. Lights burning in the windows of the surrounding houses turned watery and blurred through the gloom.

"The man you cared for, Dorne—did he ever communicate with anyone?" Walker asked finally.

The Healer shook his head. "No one."

"Did anyone ever come to see him, even for a few moments?"

"No, never."

"Did his condition change in any way before he died?"

"No."

"Was there anything different about him after he died?"

The Healer thought about it for a moment. "Well, I may be reading more into this than I should, but he seemed somehow at peace." He shrugged. "But death is a form of release from suffering, and this man was suffering greatly."

Walker considered the matter silently for a moment. In the hearth, the burning wood snapped and popped in the flames. "Has anyone else died in the village in the past two days, unexpectedly perhaps?"

The Healer's eyes widened. "Yes, as a matter of fact. A man who worked for me as an attendant—not in healing, but in caretaking— was found dead in the woods not far from his cottage. It was lucky he was found at all, really. A remote spot, not often visited. A snake bit him, a very poisonous variety—unusual for around here, really. Something you might better expect to find in the Wilderun."

Walker put aside his bowl and cup and stood up. "Could you show me the room in which the man died?" he asked the Healer. "Hunter, finish your dinner. I can do this alone."

He followed Dorne down a hallway to a room at the rear of the healing center. Then he sent Dorne back out to keep Hunter company, saying he would be along shortly. The Healer tried to give him a light for the wall candles, but Walker said the darkness was better suited for what he intended.

When he was alone, he stood in the middle of the room, cloaked in its gloom, listening to the sound of the rain and watching the movement of the shadows. He closed his eyes after a time, tasting the air, smelling it, making himself a part of his surroundings. He let his thoughts settle within him and his body relax. Down the hall, he could hear the soft murmur of voices. Carefully, he shut them out.

Time slipped away. Slowly, he began to find fragments of what he was looking for, the leavings and discards of a powerful magic employed not long ago. They came to him in different ways, some as small sounds, some as flickers of movement that reached him even behind his closed eyelids, and some as scents of the magic's wielder. There was not enough to form an entire image, but enough to determine small truths that could allow him to make educated guesses.

He opened his eyes finally, satisfied. Magic's use could never be disguised entirely from those who knew how to look for it. A residue always remained to testify.

He went back out into the main room, where Hunter Predd and Dorne were visiting. Both looked up quickly at his appearance. "Can you take me to the cold house?" he asked the Healer. "I need to see the castaway's body."

The Healer said he could, although he informed the Druid that the cold house was some distance away from the healing center. "It's not much of a night to be out in the weather," he said.

"I'll go alone," Walker advised. "Just show me the way."

The Druid wrapped himself in his damp cloak and went out the front door. Following the Healer's instructions, he worked his way around the house, first along the porch and under the veranda, then under the eaves along one side, and slipped through the shadows in the rain. The forest began twenty yards from the back of the center, and the cold house was a hundred more beyond. Cowled head dipped against the rainfall and low-hanging branches, Walker made his way down a footpath widened from usage by the Healer and his attendants. Thunder rumbled in the distance, and whistling fiercely, a wind off the ocean blew steadily through the sodden limbs.

At the end of the footpath, the cold-house door opened into an embankment buttressed by huge boulders and covered thickly with sod and plants. Runoff cascaded down a sluice to one side and disappeared into a stream. The handle on the door was slippery and cold beneath the Druid's fingers, and it took him a moment to release the catch.

Inside, the sounds of the storm faded into silence. There were torches set in brackets on the wall, and tinder with which to light them. Walker lit one in its bracket, then lit a second to carry. He looked around. The room was large and square and laid floor to ceiling with slabs of rock. Niches in the wall contained wooden sleds for the bodies, and runnels chiseled in the stone floor carried away excess moisture and body fluids. A metal-sheathed wood table sat in the center of the room, empty now, but used by the Healer for his examination of the dead. In the deep shadows, glinting like predators' eyes, sharp instruments hung from pegs on the wall.

The room smelled of blood and death, and the Druid moved quickly to do what was needed and get out of there. The castaway was in the lower niche to the far left of the entry, and Walker slid the body free of its casing and turned down the covering sheet. The man's face was bloodless and white in the torchlight, his body rigid and his skin waxy. Walker looked upon him without recognition. If he had been Kael Elessedil, he no longer looked so.

"Who were you?" Walker whispered to the dead man.

He jammed the torch he was carrying into the nearest wall bracket. Carefully, he placed his fingertips on the man's chest, moving them slowly down his torso and then up again to his shoulders. He felt along the man's throat and skull, probing gently, carefully. All around the man's face he worked his fingers, searching.

"Tell me something," he whispered.

Outside, a burst of thunder shook the earth, but the Druid did not look up from his work. He placed his fingers against the dead man's ruined eyes, the unsupported lids giving beneath his touch, then probed slowly down to his nose and cheeks.

When he reached the man's bloodless lips, he jerked away as if stung. Here, he mused silently, this was where the man's life had been taken from him! The magic lingered still, and even two days later it was potent enough to burn. He brushed the lips quickly, testing. No force had been used. Death had come gently, but with a swift and certain rendering.

Walker stepped away. He knew the man's identity now, knew it with certainty. What fragments remained of the magic used against him confirmed that he was Kael Elessedil.

Questions flooded Walker's mind. Had the dead man's killer probed his memory before giving him over to his death? He had to believe so. The killer would have looked there for what Walker had found in the map. A dark certainty began to grow in the turmoil of the Druid's thinking. Only one person had the ability to do that. His enemy was one to whom he felt no hostility himself, but for whom he was anathema. He had feared for a long time that one day there must be a resolution of their antagonism, but he would have preferred that it wait awhile longer.

She, of course, would be most pleased and eager to have it happen now.

His eyes lifted to the darkness of the room, and for the first time he felt the cold. He must change his plans. Any other enemy but this one would not require the adjustments he was now forced to make. But a confrontation with her—a confrontation that must surely come—would be resolved only if he could blunt her rage by revealing a truth that had been hidden for many years. It pained him anew to think that he had not been present to prevent that truth from being concealed when it might have had a more immediate impact. But there was no help for it now; the events of the past were irreversible. What was given to him to do was to alter the future, and even that might be possible only at great cost.

He placed Kael Elessedil's body back in its niche, extinguished the torches, and went out into the night once more. Darkness and rain closed about him as he threaded his way through the forest trees towards the center. He must act quickly. He had thought to go next in search of a ship and crew, but that would have to wait. There was a more pressing need, and he must see to it at once.

By midnight tomorrow, he must speak with the dead.

EIGHT

B y sunrise of the following day, Walker had left Bracken Clell behind. Back aboard Obsidian and seated just behind Hunter Predd, he watched through a curtain of rain as the eastern sky slowly brightened to the color of hammered tin. The rains had lessened from the night before, but not abated altogether. The skies remained clouded and dark, pressing down upon a sodden earth with a mix of shadows and mist. Hunched within his travel cloak, cold and damp already, he retreated deep inside himself to help pass the time. There, he worked his way carefully through the details of the tasks he faced. He knew what was needed, but he found himself wishing again and again that there could be others with whom to share his responsibilities. That he felt so alone was disheartening. It lessened to almost nothing the margin of error he was permitted. He thought of how he had disdained the work of the Druids in his youth, of Allanon in particular, and he chided himself anew for his foolishness.

They flew through the morning with only a single stop to rest Obsidian and to give themselves a chance to eat and drink. By midday, they had crossed the Tirfing and left the Westland behind. The Duln Forests passed beneath, then the slender ribbon of the

Rappahalladran. The rains began to lessen, the storm clouds to move south, and snatches of blue sky to appear on the horizon. They were flying east and slightly north now, the Wing Rider taking them along the southern edge of the Borderlands below Tyrsis and across the Rainbow Lake. Lunch was consumed on the lake's western shores, the day clear and bright by then, their clothing beginning to warm in the sun, their interest in their mission beginning to sharpen once more.

"The castaway, Walker—was he Kael Elessedil?" Hunter Predd asked as they finished the last of the cold grouse Dorne had provided them on leaving that morning.

Walker nodded. "He was. I couldn't tell at first. I haven't seen him since he was not much more than a boy and don't remember him all that well in any case. Even if I had remembered how he looked then, it would have been difficult to recognize him after what he had been through. But there were other signs, scattered traces, that revealed his identity."

"He didn't die in his sleep, did he? Not of natural causes. Someone helped end his life."

The Druid paused. "Someone did. How did you know that?"

The Wing Rider shrugged, his whipcord-tough body lengthening as he stretched. "Dorne is a talented Healer and a careful man. The castaway had survived days at sea before I found him. He should have survived a couple more in a Healer's bed." He glanced at Walker questioningly. "Our assassins' employer?"

The Druid nodded. "I would guess so. Magic was used to kill the man, to steal his life. Not so different from what was done to those men sent to kill Allardon Elessedil."

For a moment the Wing Rider was silent, sipping at his cup of ale and looking off into the distance. Then he said, "Do you know yet who your enemy is?"

My enemy. Implacable and deadly. Walker's smile was ironic. "I'll know better by tonight."

The Wing Rider cleaned and packed their gear, made certain

his mount was fed and watered sufficiently, then motioned Walker back aboard. They flew east across the Rainbow Lake, passing below the mouth of the Mermidon and the broad, rumpled humps of the Runne Mountains. A handful of fishing boats floated on the lake below but, absorbed in their work, the fishermen did not glance up. The day wore on, the sun dropped toward the western horizon, and the light began to fade. The moon brightened in the skies ahead, and a single star appeared close by. Shadows lengthened across the land below, stretching out like fingers to claim it for nighttime's coming.

It was twilight by the time they started up the south end of the Rabb Plains for the Dragon's Teeth. By then, the huge jagged peaks were dark and shadowy and stripped of definition, a forbidding wall that stretched all the way across the northern skyline. The temperature was dropping, and Walker pulled his cloak closer about his body for warmth. Hunter Predd seemed unaffected. Walker marveled at how little the Wing Rider seemed to mind the weather, aware of, but untroubled by it. He supposed that to be a Wing Rider, one had to be so.

It was fully dark when they reached the foothills leading up to where he would go this night. Guided by the light of moon and stars, Obsidian landed on an open rise, safely away from rocks and brush that might hide enemies or hinder a quick escape. After seeing to the needs of the Roc, the Wing Rider and the Druid set camp, built a fire, and cooked and ate their dinner. In the distance, they could hear the hunting cries of night herons and the strident wail of wolves. Moonlight bathed the plains south and east, and through the pale brightening, furtive shadows moved.

"I've been thinking about the castaway," Hunter Predd declared after a period of silence. They were almost finished with their meal, and he was digging at the hard ground with the heel of his boot, sitting back from the fire with his cup of ale. "How could a blind man have escaped his captors unaided?"

Walker looked up.

"How could he have made his way from wherever he was imprisoned to come back across the Divide to us?" The Wing Rider's frown deepened. "Assuming he was returning from the voyage Kael Elessedil made thirty years ago, he'd have had to travel a long way. A blind man couldn't have managed it without help."

"No," Walker agreed, "he couldn't."

The Elf hunched forward. "Something else's been bothering me. How did he get his hands on the map? Unless he drew it himself, he either stole it or it was given to him. If he drew it himself, he must have done so before he was blinded. How did he hide it from his captors? If someone else drew it, they must have given it to him. Either way, he must have had help. Even to escape. What became of that other person?"

Walker nodded approvingly. "You've asked all the right questions, Hunter Predd. Questions I have been asking myself for several days. Your mind is as sharp as your instincts, Wing Rider."

"Have you answers to give?" Hunter pressed, ignoring the compliment.

"None I care to share just yet." He stood up, setting his plate and cup aside. "It's time for me to go. I won't be back before morning, so you might as well get some sleep. Do not come looking for me, no matter how tempted you might be. Do you understand?"

The Wing Rider nodded. "I don't need to be told to stay out of those mountains. I've heard the stories of what lives there. I'll be content to stay right where I am." He wrapped his cloak more tightly about him. "Good luck to you."

It grew colder on the walk up from the foothills and into the Dragon's Teeth, the temperature dropping steadily as the Druid climbed. Within the massive rock walls, the night was silent and empty feeling. The moon disappeared behind the peaks, and there was only starlight to guide the way, though that was sufficient for the Druid. He proceeded along a narrow pebble-strewn trail that angled through clusters of massive boulders. The jumble of crushed and broken rock suggested that an upheaval in some long-forgotten time had changed the landscape dramatically. Once another peak might have occupied the place. Now there was only ruin.

It took him almost two hours to make the climb, and it was nearing midnight when he reached his destination. Cresting a rise, he found himself looking down on the Valley of Shale and the fabled Hadeshorn. The lake sat squarely in the valley's center, its smooth waters dull and lifeless within the bowl of polished black rock that littered the walls and floor. Starlight reflected brightly off the stone, but was absorbed by the Hadeshorn and turned to shadow. Within the valley, nothing moved. Cupped by the high, lonesome peaks of the Dragon's Teeth, it had the look and feel of a tomb.

Not far from wrong, Walker thought to himself, staring out across its lifeless expanse.

Faced toward the Valley of Shale, he seated himself with his back against a huge slab of rock and dozed. Time slipped away without seeming to do so, and before he knew it, the night was almost gone. He rose and walked, moving steadily but cautiously over the loose rock, picking his way down the valley's slope to its floor. He was careful not to trip and fall; the edges of the polished rock were razor sharp. Only the crunching of the rubble beneath his boots broke the silence of his descent. Starlight flooded the valley, and he made his way without difficulty to the edge of the lake by the hour before dawn, when the spirits of the dead might be summoned to reveal secrets hidden from the living.

There, a solitary figure silhouetted against the flat terrain, he stilled himself within to prepare for what would come next.

The waters of the Hadeshorn had taken on a different cast with his approach, shimmering now from just beneath the surface with light that did not reflect from the stars but emanated from some inner source. There was a sense of something stirring, coming awake and taking notice of his presence. He could feel it more than see it. He kept his focus on the lake, disdaining all else, knowing that any break in concentration once he began would doom his efforts and possibly cause him harm.

When he was at peace within and fully concentrated, he began the process of calling to the dead. He spoke softly, for it was not necessary that his voice carry, and gestured slowly, for precision counted more than speed. He spoke his name and of his history and need, motioning for the dead to respond, for the lake to give them up. As he did, the waters stirred visibly, swirling slowly in a clockwise motion, then churning more violently. Small cries rose from their depths, calling out in tiny, ethereal voices, whispers that turned to screams as thin as paper. The Hadeshorn hissed and boiled, releasing the cries in small fountains of spray, then in geysers that plumed hundreds of feet into the air. Light beneath the lake's surface brightened and pulsed, and the valley shuddered.

Then a rumbling sounded from deep within the earth, and out of the roiling waters rose the spirits, white and transparent forms that climbed slowly into the air, linked by thin trailers of vapor, freed from their afterlife for a few precious moments to return to the earth they had left in dying. Their voices intertwined in a rising wail that made the Druid's skin crawl and chilled the bones of his body. He held his ground against their advance, fighting down the part of him that screamed at him to back away, to turn aside, and to be afraid. They spiraled into the night sky, reaching for what was lost, seeking to recover what was denied. More and more of them appeared, filling the empty bowl of the valley until there was no space left.

Who calls? Who dares?

Then a huge, black shadow lifted from the waters and scattered the spirits like leaves, a cloaked form that took shape as it ascended, one arm stretching out to sweep aside the swarms of ghosts who lingered too close. The Hadeshorn churned and boiled in response to its coming, spray jetting everywhere, droplets falling on the Druid's exposed face and hand. Walker lifted his arm in a warding gesture, and the cloaked figure turned toward him at once. Suspended in space, it began to lose some of its blackness, becoming more transparent, its human form showing through its dark coverings like bones exposed through flesh. Across the wave-swept surface it glided, taking up all the space about it as it came, drawing all the light to itself until there was nothing else.

When it was right on top of Walker, it stopped and hung motionless above him, cowled head inclining slightly, shadows obscuring its features. Flat and dispassionate, its voice flooded the momentary silence.

—What would you know of me—

Walker knelt before him, not in fear, but out of respect.

"Allanon," he said, and waited for the shade to invite him to speak.

Farther west where the deep woods shrouded and sheltered the lives of its denizens as an ocean does its sea life, dawn approached in the Wilderun, as well. Within the old-growth trees, the light remained pale and insubstantial, even at high noon and on the brightest summer day. Shadows cloaked the world of the forest dwellers, and for the most part there was little difference between day and night. Long a wilderness to which few outsiders came, in which only those born to the life remained, and by which all other hardships were measured, the Wilderun was a haven for creatures for whom the absence of light was desirable.

The Ilse Witch was one such. Though born in another part of the Four Lands, where her past was bright with sunlight, she had long since adapted to and become comfortable with the twilight existence of her present. She had lived here nearly all of her life, which was to say since she was six. The Morgawr had brought her here when the Druid's minions had killed her parents and tried to steal her away for their own use. He had given her his home, his protection, and his knowledge of magic's uses so that she might grow to adulthood and discover who she was destined to be. The darkness in which she was raised suited her, but she never let herself become a slave to it.

Sometimes, she knew, you became dependent on the things that gave you comfort. She would never be one of those. Dependency on anything was for fools and weaklings.

On this night, working through the rudimentary drawings she had stolen from Kael Elessedil's memories before dispatching him, she felt a stirring in the air that signaled the Morgawr's return. He had been gone from their safehold for more than a week, saying little of his plans on departing, leaving her to her own devices pending his return. She was grown now, in his eyes as well as her own, and he did not feel the need to watch over her as he once had. He had never confided in her; that would have gone against his nature in so fundamental a way as to be unthinkable. He was a warlock, and therefore solitary and independent by nature. He had been alive for a very long time, living in his Hollows safehold deep within the heart of the Wilderun, not far from the promontory known as Spire's Reach. Once, it was rumored, these same caverns had been occupied by the witch sisters, Mallenroh and Morag, before they destroyed each other. Once, it was rumored, the Morgawr had claimed them as his sisters. The Ilse Witch did not know if this was true; the Morgawr never spoke of it, and she knew better than to ask.

Dark magic thrived within the Wilderun, born of other times and peoples, of a world that flourished before the Great Wars. Magic rooted in the earth here, and the Morgawr drew his strength from its presence. He was not like her; he had not been born to the magic. He had gained his mastery through leeching it away and building it up, through study and experimentation, and through slow, torturous exposure to side effects that had changed him irrevocably from what he had been born.

Looking up from her work, the Ilse Witch saw the solitary candles set in opposite holders by the entry to the room flicker slightly. Shadows wavered and settled anew on the worn stone floor. She set aside the map and rose to greet him. Her gray robes fell about her slender form in a soft rustle, and she shook back her long dark hair from her childlike face and startling blue eyes. Just a girl, a visitor come upon her unexpectedly might have thought. Just a girl approaching womanhood. But she was nothing of that and hadn't been for a long time. The Morgawr would not make such a mistake, although he had once. It took her only a heartbeat to set him straight, to let him know that she was a girl no longer, an apprentice no more, but a grown woman and his equal.

Things had not been the same between them since, and she sensed that they never would be again.

He appeared in the entry, all size and darkness within his long black cloak. His body was huge and muscular and still human in shape, but he was looking more and more like the Mwellrets with whom he spent so much of his time. His skin was scaly and gray and hairless. His features were blunt and unremarkable, and his eyes were reptilian. He could shape-shift like the rets, but far better and with greater versatility, for he had the magic to aid him. Numerous once, the rets had been reduced over the past five hundred years to a small community. They were secretive and manipulative of others, and perhaps that was why the Morgawr admired them so.

He looked at her from out of the cowl's darkness, the green slits of his eyes empty and cold. Once, she would have been terrified to have him regard her so. Once, she would have done anything to make him look away. Now, she returned his gaze, her own colder and emptier still.

"Allardon Elessedil is dead," he said softly. "Killed by mistake by his own guards in an assassination attempt by Elves who had been mind-altered. Who do we know who has the ability to use magic in that way?"

It was not a question that required an answer, and so she ignored it. "While you were gone," she replied calmly, "a castaway was found floating in the Blue Divide. He carried with him an Elessedil bracelet and a map. A Wing Rider bore him to the village of Bracken Clell. One of my spies told me of him. When I went to have a look, I discovered who he was. Kael Elessedil. The map he carried was already on its way to his brother, but I extracted much of its writings from the memories in his head."

"It is not your place to decide to take the life of a King!" the Morgawr hissed angrily. "You should have consulted with me before acting!"

She went very still. "I do not need your permission to do what I deem necessary. Ever. The taking of a life—of anyone's life—is my province and mine alone!"

She might as well have told him the sun would rise in less than an hour. His reaction to her words was indifferent, his response unreadable, and his body posture unchanged. "What of this map?" he asked.

"The map is of a treasure, one of magic formed of words, come out of the Old World from before the Great Wars." She used her voice to draw him close, to bind him to her own sense of urgency and need. He would sense what she was doing, but he was vulnerable still. "The magic is hidden in a safehold in a land across the Blue Divide. Kael Elessedil has been there and seen the magic. It exists, and it is very powerful. Unfortunately, his brother knew of it as well. Until I stopped him, he intended to act on the matter."

The Morgawr came into the room, not toward her, but away, sidling along the far wall, as if to retrieve something from the cases that lined it. A potion, perhaps? A recording of some discovery? Then he slowed and turned, and his voice was like ice. "You intend to go in his place, little witch?"

"The magic should be ours."

"You mean yours, don't you?" He laughed softly. "But that's as it should be."

"You could go with me," she said, hoping as she said it he would not.

He cocked his reptilian head, considering. "This is your discovery and your cause. Pursue it if you wish, but without me. If the magic will belong to both of us, I am content."

She waited, knowing there would be more. "But?" she said finally.

His eyes glimmered. "You will go alone?"

"Across the Blue Divide? No. I will need a ship and crew to take me." She paused. "And there is a complication."

The Morgawr laughed again, slow and faintly mocking. "I sensed as much from the way you approached this business. What sort of complication?"

She walked toward him a few steps and stopped, showing she was not afraid, that she was in command of what she intended. Presence was of great importance with Mwellrets and with the Morgawr in particular. If they thought someone confident, they were less likely to challenge. The Morgawr was a powerful warlock, and he had spent a lifetime learning to command magic that could destroy his enemies in a heartbeat. She was his equal now, but she had to be careful of him.

"Before he died, Allardon Elessedil sent the map to Paranor and summoned Walker to Arborlon."

"The Druid!" the warlock said, loathing in his voice.

"The Druid. He arrived in time to agree upon the terms of a search for the map's treasure before witnessing the King's death. If luck had favored us, he would have died, as well. As it was, he lived. He will lead an Elven expedition in quest of the magic."

The Morgawr studied her wordlessly for a moment. "A contest with your greatest enemy. How keen your anticipation must be."

"He is a formidable opponent."

"One you have sworn you would one day destroy." The warlock nodded. "Perhaps that day has arrived."

"Perhaps. But it is the magic I covet more than the Druid's death."

The Morgawr shifted within his cloak, and one clawed hand gestured at the air. "A Druid, some Elven Hunters, and a Captain and crew. A few others, as well, if I know Walker. He will draw a strong company to support his quest, particularly since he knows that Kael Elessedil has failed already. Even with the Elfstones to protect him, he failed."

He glanced sideways at her. "And what of them, little witch? What of the precious Elfstones?"

She shook her head. "Nothing. He did not bring them back with him. His memories did not reveal what had become of them. Perhaps they are lost."

"Perhaps." His rough voice had lost its edge and taken on a contemplative tone. "Where is the Druid now?"

"He was in Bracken Clell a day ago. He left and has not yet resurfaced. My spies watch for him."

The warlock nodded. "I leave him to you. I know you will find a way to deal with him. It is left to me to give you the rest of what you need to undertake your search—a ship, Captain, and crew, and a handful of suitable protectors. I shall supply them all, little witch. You shall have everything you need."

She did not like the way he said it, and she knew that by doing her this favor he intended to keep close watch and perhaps even control over her while she was away from him. He did not trust her anymore. Where once he had been the teacher and she the student, now they were equals. Worse still, she knew, they were rivals—not yet at odds, but headed there. But she could not refuse his help. To do so would be to acknowledge her fear of his intentions. She would never do that.

"Whatever assistance you can give me will be welcome," she told him, inclining her head slightly as if in gratitude. It was better to keep him appeased for now. "Where do we begin?"

"With the details of the map you reconstructed from Kael

Elessedil's memories." He glanced past her to the table at which she had been seated and the drawings that lay there. "Do I see the beginnings of your work?"

Without waiting for her response, he walked over for a closer look.

It was well after dawn when Walker departed from the Valley of Shale. His meeting with the shade of Allanon had sapped him of strength and energy in a way he hadn't expected. It had been a long time since he had come to the Hadeshorn, a long time since he had needed to, and he had forgotten how draining the experience could be. So much concentration was required. So much intuition had to be applied to interpretation of the shade's words. Even though the Druid knew as much as he did and was prepared for the rest, it was necessary to be careful while he listened and not to make false assumptions or to forget any of what he was told.

When the spirits of the dead were gone and the sun had crested the horizon, he had looked at himself in the now still waters, and his face seemed weathered and lined beyond his years. For just an instant, he imagined himself an old, old man.

This day was sunny and bright, the clouds and rain of the past two had disappeared east, and the air carried the smell of living things once more. Over the course of the next several hours, he retraced his steps, too weary to complete the journey more quickly, using the time to contemplate what he had learned. The shade of Allanon had spoken to him of a past he already knew, of a present he suspected, and of a future he did not understand. There were people and places with whom he was familiar and ones with whom he was not. There were riddles and strange visions, and the whole was a jumble in his mind that would not straighten itself out until he was better rested and had time to consider the information more thoroughly.

But his course of action was determined, and his mind was focused on where he must go.

When he reached the encampment in the foothills where he had left Hunter Predd, the Wing Rider was waiting. He had struck camp, repacked their gear, and was grooming Obsidian's ebony feathers so that they gleamed. The Roc saw the Druid first and dipped his fierce head in warning. Hunter Predd turned, put down the curry brush, and watched the Druid approach. He handed Walker a thick slice of bread with jam spread over it and a cup of cold water and went back to grooming his mount.

Walker moved to a patch of grass, seated himself, and began to devour the bread hungrily. Images roiled in his mind as the Hadeshorn had with the coming of the spirits of the dead. Allanon's shade loomed over him, blacking out the starlight, eyes bright within shadows, voice deep and commanding, an echo of the rumbling earth. Walker could see him still, could feel his dark presence, could hear him speak. When Allanon's shade departed finally at first light, it was as if the world was coming to an end, the air swirling with shadows, shimmering with spirit bodies, and filling with the keening of the dead. The waters of the Hadeshorn geysered anew, as if some leviathan were breaching, and the dead were drawn back again from the world of the living to their own domain. Walker had felt as if his soul was being torn from him, as if a part of him had gone with them. In a way, he supposed, it had.

He paused in his eating and stared into space. If he thought too long and hard on what was required of him, if he dwelled on the demands the shade of Allanon had made, he would begin to question himself in ways that were harmful. What would keep him sane and whole was remembering what was at stake—the lives of people who depended on him, the safety of the Four Lands, and his dream of seeing a Druid Council become a reality in his lifetime. This last drove him more strongly than the others, for if it came to pass, it would vindicate his still-troubling decision to become the very thing he had abhorred for so long. If he must be a Druid, let him be one on his own terms and of a sort that would not require him to live with shame.

When he had finished eating the bread and jam and drinking the water from the cup, he rose again. Hunter Predd glanced over his shoulder at the movement and ceased his grooming.

"Where do we go now, Walker?" he asked.

The Druid took a moment to study a flight of egrets as they passed overhead toward the Rainbow Lake. "South," he answered finally, eyes distant and fixed, "to find someone whose magic is the equal of my own."

 ek Rowe crept through the tall grasses at the edge of a clearing just below a heavily wooded line of hills, listening to the sound of the boar as it rooted in the tangle of thicket across the way. He paused as the wind shifted, mindful of staying downwind of his quarry, listening to its movements, judging its progress. Somewhere to his left, Quentin Leah waited in the deep woods.

NINE

B ek Rowe crept through the tall grasses at the edge of a clearing just below a heavily wooded line of hills, listening to the sound of the boar as it rooted in the tangle of thicket across the way. He paused as the wind shifted, mindful of staying downwind of his quarry, listening to its movements, judging its progress. Somewhere to his left, Quentin Leah waited in the deep woods. Time was running out for them; the sun was descending toward the western horizon, and only another hour of good light remained. They had been hunting the boar all day, trailing it through the rough up-country scrub and deep woods, waiting for a chance to bring it down. Their chances of doing so were negligible under the best of conditions; boar hunting afoot with bow and arrow was risky and difficult. But as with most things that interested them, it was the challenge that mattered.

The soft scent of new leaves and fresh grasses mixed with the pungent smell of earth and wood, and Bek took a deep breath to steady himself. He could not see the boar, and the boar, having exceptionally poor eyesight, certainly could not see him. But the boar's sense of smell was the sharper, and once he got a whiff of

Bek, he might do anything. Boars were short-tempered and fierce, and what they didn't understand they were as likely to attack as to flee.

The wind shifted again, and Bek dropped into a hurried crouch. The boar had begun moving his way, grunts and coughs marking his progress. A boy still, though approaching manhood rapidly, Bek was small and wiry, but made up for his size with agility and speed and surprising strength. Quentin, who was five years his senior and already considered grown, was always telling people that they shouldn't be fooled, that Bek was a lot tougher than he looked. If there was a fight, the Highlander would insist, he wanted Bek Rowe at his back. It was an overstatement, of course, but it always made Bek feel good. Especially since it was his cousin saying it, and nobody would even think of challenging Quentin Leah.

Putting an arrow to his bow in readiness, Bek crept forward once again. He was close enough to the boar to smell it, not a pleasant experience, but it meant he would likely have a shot at it soon. He drifted right, following the boar's sounds, wondering if Quentin was still up on the forested slope or had come down to approach from the boar's rear. Shadows stretched from the trees at Bek's back, lengthening into the clearing like elongated fingers as the day waned. A bristly dark form moved in the grasses ahead—the boar coming into view—and Bek froze where he was. Slowly, he brought up his bow, nocked his arrow, and drew back the string.

But in the next instant a huge shadow passed overhead, sliding across the clearing like liquid night. The boar, startled by its appearance, bolted away in a tearing of earth and a cacophony of squeals. Bek straightened and sighted, but all he caught was a quick glimpse of the boar's ridged back as it disappeared into the thicket and then into the woods beyond. In seconds, the clearing was empty and quiet again.

"Shades!" Bek muttered, lowering his bow and brushing back his close-cropped dark hair. He stood up and looked across the empty clearing toward the woods. "Quentin?"

The tall Highlander emerged from the trees. "Did you see it?"

"I got a glimpse of its backside after that shadow spooked it. Did you see what that was?"

Quentin was already wandering down into the clearing and through the heavy grasses. "Some kind of bird, wasn't it?"

"No birds around here are that big." Bek watched him come, glancing away long enough to scan the empty skies. He shouldered his bow and shoved his arrow back into its quiver. "Birds that big live on the coast."

"Maybe it's lost." Quentin shrugged nonchalantly. He slipped in a patch of mud and muttered a few choice words as he righted himself. "Maybe we should go back to hunting grouse."

Bek laughed. "Maybe we should go back to hunting earthworms and stick to fishing."

Quentin reached him with a flourish of bow and arrows, arms widespread as he dropped both in disgust. "All day, and what do we have to show for it? An empty meadow. You'd think we could have gotten off at least one shot between us. That boar was making enough noise to wake the dead. It wasn't as if we couldn't find it, for cat's sake!"

Then he grinned cheerfully. "At least we've got that grouse from yesterday to ease our hunger and a cold aleskin to soothe our wounded pride. Best part of hunting, Bek lad. Eating and drinking at the end of the day!"

Bek smiled in response, and after Quentin retrieved his cast-off weapons, they swung into step beside each other and headed back toward their camp. Quentin was tall and broad-shouldered, and he wore his red hair long and tied back in the manner of Highlanders. Bek, his lowland cousin, had never adopted the Highland style, though he had lived with Quentin and his family for most of his life. That his origins were cloudy had fostered a strong streak of independence in him. He might not know who he was, but he knew who he wasn't.

His father had been a distant cousin of Coran Leah, Quentin's father, but had lived in the Silver River country. Bek remembered little more than a shadowy figure with a dark, strong face. He died when Bek was still tiny, barely two years of age. He contracted a fatal disease and, knowing he was dying, brought Bek to his cousin Coran to raise. There was no one else to turn to. Bek's mother was gone, and there were no siblings, no aunts and uncles, no one closer than Coran. Coran Leah told Bek later, when he was older, that Bek's father had done a great favor for him once, and he had never thought twice about taking Bek in to repay the favor.

All of which was to say that although Bek had been raised a Highlander, he wasn't really one and had never been persuaded to think of himself in those terms. Quentin told him it was the right attitude. Why try to be something you know you're not? If you have to pretend to be something, be something no one else is. Bek liked the idea, but he hadn't a clue what that something else might be. Since he never talked of the matter with anyone but Quentin, he kept his thoughts to himself. Sooner or later, he imagined, probably when it mattered enough that he must do something, he would figure it out.

"I'm starved," Quentin announced as they walked through the deep woods. "Hungry enough to eat that boar all by myself, should it choose to fall dead at my feet just now!"

His broad, strong face was cheerful and open, a reflection of his personality. With Quentin Leah, what you saw was what you got. There was no dissembling, no pretense, and no guile. Quentin was the sort who came right at you, speaking his mind and venting his emotions openly. Bek was more inclined to tread carefully in his use of words and displays of temperament, a part of him always an outsider and accustomed to the value of an outsider's caution. Not Quentin. He opened himself up and laid himself bare, and if you liked him, fine, and if you didn't, that was all right, too.

"Are you sure about that bird?" Bek asked him, thinking back to that huge shadow, still puzzled by its appearance.

Quentin shrugged. "I only caught a glimpse of it, not enough to be certain of anything much. Like you said, it looked like one of those big coastal birds, black and sleek and fierce." He paused thoughtfully. "I'd like to ride one of those someday."

Bek snorted. "You'd like to do lots of things. Everything, if you could manage it."

Quentin nodded. "True. But some things more than others. This one, I'd like to do more."

"I'd just settle for another crack at the boar." Bek brushed a hanging limb away as he ducked beneath. "Another two seconds . . ."

"Forget it!" Quentin grabbed Bek's shoulders playfully. "We'll go out again tomorrow. We have all the rest of the week. We'll find one sooner or later. How can we fail?"

Well, Bek wanted to say, because boars are quicker, faster, and stronger, and much better at hiding than we are at finding them. But he let the matter drop, because the truth was that if they'd bagged the boar today, they'd have had to figure out what to do with the rest of the week. Bek didn't even want to speculate on what Quentin might have come up with if that had happened.

Shadows were layering the woodlands in ever-darkening pools, the light failing quickly as the sun slipped below the horizon and the night began its silent advance. Serpentine trailers of mist already had begun to appear in the valleys and ravines, those darker, cooler havens were the sun had been absent longer and the dampness was rooted deeper. Crickets were beginning to chirp and night birds to call. Bek hunched his shoulders against a chilly breeze come up off the Rappahalladran. Maybe he would suggest they fish tomorrow as a change of pace. It wasn't as exciting or demanding as boar hunting, but the chances of success were greater.

Besides, he mused, he could nap in the afternoon sun when he was fishing. He could dream and indulge his imagination and take small journeys in his mind. He could spend a little time thinking about his future, which was a good exercise since he really didn't have one figured out yet.

"There it is again," Quentin announced almost casually, pointing ahead through the trees.

Bek looked, and as sharp as his eyes were, he didn't see anything. "There *what* is again?" he asked.

"That bird I saw, the one that flew over the meadow. A Roc— that's what it's called. It was right above the ridge for a moment, then dropped away."

"Rocs don't travel inland," Bek pointed out once more. Not unless they're in thrall to a Wing Rider, he thought. That was different. But what would a Wing Rider be doing out here? "This late-afternoon light plays tricks with your eyes," he added.

Quentin didn't seem to hear him. "That's close to where we're camped, Bek. I hope it doesn't raid our stash."

They descended the slope they were on, crossed the valley below, and began to climb toward the crest of the next hill, on which their camp was set. They'd quit talking to each other, concentrating on the climb, eyes beginning to search the deepening shadows more carefully. The sun was below the horizon, and twilight cloaked the forest in a gloom that shifted and teased with small movements. A day's-end silence had descended, a hush that gave the odd impression that everything living in the woods was waiting to see who would make the first sound. Though not conscious of the effort, both Bek and his cousin began to walk more softly.

When it got dark in the Highland forests, it got very dark, especially when the moon wasn't up, as on this night, and there was only starlight to illuminate the shadows. Bek found himself growing uneasy for reasons he couldn't define, his instincts telling him that something was wrong even when his eyes could not discover what it was. They reached their camp without incident but, as if possessed of a single mind, stopped at the edge of the clearing and peered about in silence.

After a moment, Quentin touched his cousin's shoulder and shrugged. Nothing looked out of place. Bek nodded. They entered the clearing, walked to where their stash was strung up in a tree, found it undisturbed, checked their camping gear where it was bundled in the crotch of a broad-rooted maple, and found it intact, as well. They dragged out their bedrolls and laid them out next to the cold fire pit they'd dug on their arrival two days earlier. Then they released the rope that secured their provisions and lowered them to the ground. Quentin began sorting foodstuffs and cooking implements in preparation for making their dinner. Bek produced tinder to strike a flame to the wood set in place that morning for the evening's meal.

Somewhere close, out in the darkness, a night bird cried shrilly as it flew in search of prey or a mate. Bek looked up, studied the shadows again, and then lit the fire. Once the wood was burning, he walked to the edge of the clearing and bent down to gather more.

When he straightened up again, he found himself face-to-face with a black-cloaked stranger. The stranger was no more than two feet away, right on top of him really, and Bek hadn't heard his approach at all. The boy froze, arms wrapped about the load of deadwood, his heart in his throat. All sorts of messages screamed at him from his brain, but he couldn't make himself respond to any of them.

"Bek Rowe?" the stranger asked softly.

Bek nodded. The stranger's cowl concealed his face, but his deep, rough voice was somehow reassuring. Bek's panic lessened just a hair.

Something about the unexpected encounter caught Quentin Leah's notice. He walked out of the firelight and peered into the darkness where Bek and the stranger stood facing each other. "Bek? Are you all right?" He came closer. "Who's there?"

"Quentin Leah?" the stranger asked him.

The Highlander continued to advance, but his hand had dropped to the long knife at his waist. "Who are you?"

The stranger let the Highlander come up beside Bek. "I'm called Walker," he answered. "Do you know of me?"

"The Druid?" Quentin's hand was still on the handle of his long knife.

"The same." His bearded face came into the light as he pulled back the cowl of his cloak. "I've come to ask a favor of you."

"A favor?" Quentin sounded openly skeptical, and frown lines creased his brow. "From us?"

"Well, from you in particular, but since Bek is here, as well, I'll ask it of you both." He glanced past them to the fire. "Can we sit while we talk? Do you have something to eat? I've come a long way today."

As if arrived at a truce, they left the darkness and moved into the light, taking seats on the ground around the fire. Bek studied the Druid carefully, trying to take his measure. Physically, he was forbidding—tall and dark-featured, with long black hair and beard, and a narrow, angular face that was seamed by sun and weather. He looked neither young nor old, but somewhere in between. His right arm was missing from just above the elbow, leaving only a stump within a pinned-up tunic sleeve. Even so, he radiated power and self-assurance, and his strange eyes registered an unmistakable warning to stand clear. Although he said he had come to find them, he did not seem particularly interested now that he had. His gaze was directed toward the darkness beyond the fire, as if he was watching for something.

But it was his history that intrigued Bek more than his appearance, and the boy found himself digging through his memory for bits and pieces of what he knew. The Druid lived in the Keep at ancient Paranor with the ghosts of his ancestors and companions dead and gone. He was rumored to be Allanon's successor and direct descendant. It was said he had been alive in the time of Quentin's great-great-grandfather, Morgan Leah, and the most famous of all the Elf Queens, Wren Elessedil, and that he had fought with them in the war against the Shadowen. If that was true, then the Druid was more than 130 years old. No one else from that time was still alive, and it seemed strange and vaguely chilling that the Druid should have survived what no ordinary man could.

Bek knew a lot about the Druids. He had made it his business to know about them because of their long-standing connection to the Leah family. There had been a Leah involved in almost every great

Druid undertaking since the time of the Warlock Lord. Most people were frightened of the Druids and their legacy of magic, but the Highlanders had always been their advocates. Without the Druids, they believed, the people of the Four Lands would be living much different lives at a cost they would not have cared to pay.

"You said you came far today?" Quentin broke the momentary silence. "Where did you come from?"

Walker's dark gaze shifted. "The Dragon's Teeth originally. Then from Leah."

"That was your Roc," Bek blurted out, suddenly able to speak again.

Walker glanced at him. "Not mine. Obsidian belongs to a Wing Rider named Hunter Predd. He should be along in a minute. He's bedding down his bird first." He paused. "You saw us, did you?"

"Saw your shadow, actually," Quentin said as he worked on laying out strips of smoked fish in a pan. He had coated them with flour and seasonings, and was adding a bit of ale for flavor. "We were boar hunting."

The Druid nodded. "Your father told me so."

Quentin looked up quickly. "My father?"

Walker stretched his legs and braced himself with his good arm as he leaned back. "We know each other. Tell me, did you have any luck with the boar?"

Quentin went back to his fish, shaking his head to himself. "No, he was frightened off by you. The Roc's shadow spooked him."

"Well, my apologies for that. On the other hand, getting you back here to speak with me was of more consequence than seeing you bag that boar."

Bek stared. Was he saying that he had spooked the boar deliberately, that the Roc's passing hadn't been by chance? He glanced quickly at Quentin to catch his cousin's reaction, but Quentin's attention had shifted at the sound of someone else's approach.

"Ah, here is our friend, the Wing Rider," Walker said, rising.

Hunter Predd trooped into the firelight, a lean, wiry Elf with gnarled hands and sharp eyes. He nodded to the Highlander and his cousin as they were introduced. He took a seat across from the Druid. Walker spent a few minutes talking about Wing Riders and Rocs, explaining their importance to the Elves of the Westland, then asked Quentin for news of his family. The conversation continued as the Highlander prepared the fish, some fry bread, and a clutch of greens. All the while, Bek watched Walker carefully, wondering what the meeting was all about, what sort of favor the Druid could want of them, how he knew Coran Leah, what he was doing with a Wing Rider, and on and on.

They had eaten their meal, washed it down with cold stream water, and cleaned up the dishes before Walker provided Bek with the answers he was seeking.

"I want you to come with me on a journey," the Druid began, sipping at the ale Quentin had poured into his cup. "Both of you. It will be long and dangerous. It may be months before we return, maybe longer. We have to travel across the Blue Divide to a land none of us has ever seen. When we get there, we have to find a treasure. We have a map, and we have instructions written on the map about what we need to do to find this treasure. But someone else is after it, as well, someone very dangerous, and she will do everything she can to prevent us from reaching it first."

There were no preliminaries, no buildups, and no small talk to lead into all this. The explanation was casual; they might have been talking about taking a rafting trip down the Rappahalladran. Bek Rowe had never ventured outside the Highlands, and now someone had appeared who wanted him to travel halfway around the world. He could scarcely believe what he was hearing.

Hunter Predd was the first to speak. "She?" he asked curiously.

Walker nodded. "Our nemesis is a very powerful sorceress who calls herself the Ilse Witch. She is the protégé of a warlock known as the Morgawr. The names derive from a language used in the world of Faerie, most of it lost. Hers means *singer*. His means *wraith* or something like it. They reside in the Westland, down in the

Wilderun, and seldom venture far from there. How the Ilse Witch found out about the map and our journey, I don't know. But she is responsible for the death of at least two people because of it." He paused. "Do you know of her?"

Bek and Quentin glanced at each other blankly, but the Wing Rider was shaking his head in dismay. "Enough to keep clear," he snapped.

"We don't have that option." Walker crossed his legs in front of him and leaned forward. "One of the dead men is Allardon Elessedil, the Elven King. If the Ilse Witch was willing to kill him to prevent us from seeking out the treasure described by the map, she will certainly not hesitate to kill us, as well. Forewarned is forearmed, I'm afraid."

His eyes shifted to Quentin and Bek. "The other dead man is the map's bearer, a castaway Hunter found floating in the Blue Divide a little more than a week ago. The hunt I'm proposing begins with him. He was Allardon Elessedil's older brother, Kael, one of a company of Elves that undertook a search similar to ours thirty years ago. All of them disappeared. No trace of them or their ships was ever found. The map our castaway carried suggests their search might have yielded something of great importance. It is up to us to find out what that something is."

"So you intend to sail all the way across the Blue Divide to search out this treasure?" Quentin asked dubiously.

"Not sail, Highlander," the Druid replied. "Fly."

There was a moment's silence. The wood burning in the fire pit crackled sharply. "On Rocs?" Quentin pressed.

"On an airship."

The silence resumed. Even Hunter Predd seemed surprised. "But why do you want us to come?" Bek asked finally.

"Several reasons." Walker fixed the boy with his dark gaze. "Bear with me for a moment. Aside from the three of you, I have told this to no one. Most of it, I have determined only very recently, and I am still in the process of deciphering quite a bit more. I need to have someone with whom I can discuss my thinking, someone I can trust and in whom I can confide. I need someone of sharp mind and willing spirit, of ability and courage. Hunter Predd is one such. I think you and your cousin are two more."

Bek felt his excitement growing by leaps and bounds. He leaned forward in response to the Druid's words.

"Hunter's usefulness is obvious," Walker continued. "He is a seasoned veteran of the skies, and I intend to take a small number of Wing Riders as escorts for our airship. Hunter will be their leader, if he agrees to accept the position. But in doing so, he needs to be confident that he can anticipate my thinking and respond as circumstances and events dictate."

He was still looking straight at Bek. "Quentin's purpose is obvious, as well, although he doesn't realize it yet. Quentin is a Leah, the oldest of his father's sons, and heir to a powerful magic. There is no one else I can recruit for this journey who will have such a magic to lend to our cause. Once, we might have relied upon the use of Elfstones, but those in the possession of the Elves were lost with Kael Elessedil. The Ilse Witch will have allies she can turn to who possess magic of their own. Moreover, we are certain to encounter other forms of magic during our quest. It will be difficult for anyone to stand alone against them all. Quentin must support me."

The Highlander looked as if the Druid had lost his mind. "You can't mean that old sword, the one my father gave me several years back when I crossed into manhood? That old relic is symbolic and nothing more! The Sword of Leah, handed down for generations, carried by my great-great-grandfather Morgan against the Federation when he fought for the liberation of the Dwarves in the wake of the Shadowen defeat—everyone knows the tale, but . . . but . . ."

He seemed to run out of words, shaking his head in disbelief and turning to Bek for support.

But it was Walker who spoke first. "You are familiar with the weapon, Quentin. You've held it in your hands, haven't you? When you took it out of its scabbard to examine it, you must have noticed that it was in perfect condition. The weapon is centuries old. How do you account for that if it is not infused with magic?"

"But it doesn't do anything!" Quentin exclaimed in exasperation.

"Because you tried to summon the magic, and failed?"

The Highlander sighed. "It feels foolish to admit it. But I knew the stories, and I just wanted to see if there was any truth to them. Honestly, I admire the weapon. Its balance and weight are exceptional. And it does look as if it is new." He paused, his broad, open Highlander face suffused with a mix of doubt and cautious expectation. "Is it really magic?"

Walker nodded. "But its magic does not respond to whim; it responds to need. It cannot be called forth simply out of curiosity. There must be a threat to the bearer. The magic originated with Allanon and the shades of the Druids who preceded him in life. No magic of theirs would be wild or arbitrary. The Sword of Leah has value, Highlander, but you will discover that only when you are threatened by the dark things you must help protect against."

Quentin Leah kicked at the earth with the heel of his boot. "If I go with you, I'll get my chance to discover this, won't I?"

The Druid stared at him without answering.

"Thought so." Quentin studied his boot a moment, then glanced at Bek. "A real adventure, cousin. Something more challenging than boar hunting. What do you think?"

For a moment, Bek didn't respond. He didn't know what he thought about any of it. Quentin was more trusting, more willing to accept what he was told, particularly when what it offered was what he was seeking. For several years he had asked for permission to join the Free-born and fight against the Federation, but his father had forbidden it. Quentin's obligations were to his family and his home. As the oldest son, he was expected to help in the raising and training of his younger siblings and of Bek. Quentin wanted to travel the whole of the Four Lands, to see what else was out there.

So far, he had not been allowed to go much farther than the borders of the Highlands.

Now, all at once, he was being offered a chance to experience what had been denied him for so long. Bek was excited, too. But he was not so willing as his cousin to jump into the adventure with both feet.

"Bek is probably wondering why I'm asking him to come, as well," Walker said suddenly, his gaze fixed once more on the boy.

Bek nodded. "I guess I am."

"I'll tell you then." The Druid hunched forward once more. "I need you for an entirely different reason than Hunter or Quentin. It has to do with who you are and how you think. You have displayed a healthy dose of skepticism about what you are hearing. That's good. You should. You like to think things through carefully before giving credence to them. You like to measure and balance. For what I require of you, such an attitude is essential. I need a cabin boy on this journey, Bek, someone who can be anywhere and everywhere without questions being asked, someone whose presence is taken for granted, but who hears and sees everything. I need someone to keep watch for me, someone to investigate when it is called for and to report back on things I might have missed. I need an extra pair of hands and eyes. A boy like you has the intelligence and instincts to know when and how to put those hands and eyes to work."

Bek frowned. "You've only just met me; how can you be so sure of all this?"

The Druid pursed his lips reprovingly. "It is my business to know, Bek. Do you think I'm wrong about you?"

"You could be. What if you are?"

The Druid's smile was slow and easy. "Why don't we find out?"

He looked away. "One more thing," he said, speaking to all of them now. "When we begin this voyage, we shall do so with certain expectations regarding the character of those chosen to go. Over time, those expectations will change. Circumstances and events will touch all of us in ways we cannot foresee. Our company will number close to forty. I would like to believe that all would persevere and endure; they will not. Some will prove out, but some will fail us when we have need of them most. It is in the nature of things. The Ilse Witch will continue to try to stop us from leaving and, when that fails, to prevent us from reaching our goal. Moreover, she may not prove to be the most dangerous enemy we encounter. So we must learn to rely on ourselves and on those we discover we can depend upon. It is a formidable responsibility to shoulder, but I have great confidence in all three of you."

He leaned back, his dark face unreadable. "So, then. Are you with me? Will you come?"

Hunter Predd spoke first. "I've been with you from the start, Walker. I guess maybe I'll stick around for the finish. As for how dependable or trustworthy I'll turn out to be, all I can say is that I will do my best. One thing I do know—I can find the Wing Riders you need for this expedition."

Walker nodded. "I can ask no more." He looked at the cousins. "And you?"

Quentin and Bek exchanged a hurried glance. "What do you say, Bek?" Quentin asked. "Let's do it. Let's go."

Bek shook his head. "I don't know. Your father might not want us to—"

"I've spoken to him already," Walker interrupted smoothly. "You have his permission to come if you wish to do so. Both of you. But the choice is yours, and yours alone."

In that instant, Bek Rowe could see the future he had been searching for as clearly as if he had already lived it. It wasn't so much the specific events he would experience or the challenges he would face or the creatures and places he would encounter. These could be imagined, but not yet firmly grasped. It was the changes he would undergo on such a voyage that were discernible and thereby both intimidating and frightening. Many of them would be profound and lasting, affecting his life irrevocably. Bek could feel these changes as if they were layers of skin peeled back one at a time to demonstrate his growth. So much would happen on a journey like this one, and no one who returned—for he was honest enough with himself to accept that some would not—would ever be the same.

"Bek?" Quentin pressed softly.

He had come from nowhere to be where he was, an outsider accepted into a Highland home, a traveler simply by having come from another place and family. Life was a journey of sorts, and he could travel it by staying put or by going out. For Quentin, the choice had always been easy. For Bek, it was less so, but perhaps just as inevitable.

He looked at the Druid called Walker and nodded. "All right. I'll go."

§

TEN

On the way home the next day, Bek Rowe agonized over his decision. Even though it was made and he was committed, he could not stop second-guessing himself. On the face of things, he had made the right choice. There were lives at stake and responsibilities to be assumed in questing for the mysterious magic, and if the result of his going was to secure for the people of all nations a magic that would further their development and fulfill their needs—a result that Walker had taken great pains to assure him was possible—it was the right thing to do.

But in the back of his mind a whisper of warning nagged at him. The Druid, he felt, had told the truth. But the Druid was also reticent about giving out information, a tradition among the members of his order, and Bek was quite certain he was keeping something to himself. More than one something, in all likelihood. Bek could sense it in his voice and in the way he presented his cause to them. So careful with his words. So deliberate with his phrasing. Walker knew more than he was saying, and Bek worried that some of his misgivings about how a journey of this sort would influence his and Quentin's lives had their source in the Druid's secrets.

But there was a secondary problem with not going. Quentin had made up his mind even before Bek had agreed and would likely have gone without him. His cousin had been looking for an excuse to leave Leah and go elsewhere for a long time. That his father had apparently agreed to his going on this particular journey—a decision that Bek found remarkable—removed the last obstacle that stood in Quentin's path. Quentin was like a brother. Much of the time, Bek felt protective toward him, even though Quentin was the older of the two and looked at the matter the other way around. Whatever the case, Bek loved and admired his cousin and could not imagine staying behind if Quentin went.

All of which was fine except that it did nothing to alleviate his misgivings. But there was no help for that, so he was forced to put the matter aside as they journeyed home. They walked steadily all day, crossing through the Highlands, navigating the deep woods, scrub wilderness, flowering meadows, streams and small rivers, misty valleys and green hills. They left much more quickly than they had gone in, Quentin setting the pace, anxious to return home so that they could prepare to set out again.

Which was another sticking point with Bek. Walker had asked them to come with him on a journey and then promptly departed for regions unknown. He hadn't waited for them to join him or offered to take them with him. He hadn't even told them when they would see him again.

"I want you to return to Leah on the morrow," he had advised just before they had rolled into their blankets and drifted off to an uneasy sleep. "Speak with your father. Satisfy yourselves that he has given you his permission to leave. Then pack your gear—not forgetting the sword, Quentin—saddle two strong horses, and ride east."

East! East, for cat's sake! Isn't that the wrong direction? Bek had demanded instantly. Didn't the Elves live west? Wasn't that where their journey to follow the map was supposed to initiate?

But the Druid had only smiled and assured him that traveling east was what was needed before going on to Arborlon. They must carry out a small errand for him, an errand he had insufficient time to run. Maybe it would offer Quentin a chance to test the magic of his blade. Maybe Bek would be given an opportunity to test his intuitive abilities. Maybe they would have a chance to meet someone they would come to depend upon in the days ahead.

Well, there wasn't much they could say to all that, so they had agreed to do as he asked. Just as Walker had known they would, Bek felt. He sensed, in fact, that Walker knew exactly how to present a request so that it would always be agreed to. When Walker spoke, Bek could feel himself agreeing almost before the words were out. Something in the Druid's voice was compelling enough to make him want to acquiesce out of hand.

Magic's sway, he supposed. Wasn't that a part of the Druid history? Wasn't that one reason why people were so afraid of them?

"This fellow we're supposed to find," he spoke up suddenly, halfway through the long walk home, glancing over at Quentin.

"Truls Rohk," his cousin said.

Bek shifted the heavy pack on his back. "Truls Rohk. What kind of name is that? Who is he? Doesn't it bother you that we don't know the first thing about him, that Walker didn't even tell us what he looks like?"

"He told us how to find him. He told us exactly where to go and how to get there. He gave us a message to deliver and words to speak. That's all we need to get the job done, isn't it?"

"I don't know. I don't know what we need because I don't know what we're getting ourselves into." Bek shook his head doubtfully. "We jumped awfully quick at the chance to get involved in this business, Quentin. What do we know about Walker or the Druids or this map or any of it? Just enough to get excited about traipsing off to the other side of the world. How smart is that?"

Quentin shrugged. "The way I look at it, we have a wonderful opportunity to travel, to see something of the world, something beyond the borders of Leah. How often is that kind of chance going to come along? And Father agrees that we can go. Talk about miracles!"

Bek huffed. "Talk about blackmail—that's more likely."

"Not Father." Quentin shook his head firmly. "He would die first. You know that."

Bek nodded reluctantly.

"So let's give this a chance before we start passing judgment. Let's see what things look like. If we think we're in over our heads, we can always give it up."

"Not if we're flying somewhere out over the Blue Divide, we can't."

"You worry too much."

"Sure enough. And you worry too little."

Quentin grinned. "True. But I'm happier worrying too little than you are worrying too much."

That was Quentin for you, never spending too much time on what might happen, content to live in the moment. It was hard to argue with someone who was so happy all the time, and that was Quentin right down to the soles of his boots. Give him a sunny day and a chance to walk ten miles and he was all set. Never mind that a thunderstorm was approaching or that Gnome Hunters prowled the region he traveled. Quentin's view was that bad things happened mostly when you thought too much about them.

Bek let the matter drop for the rest of the way back. He wasn't going to change Quentin's mind, and he wasn't sure he even ought to try. His cousin was right—he should give the idea a chance, let things develop a bit, and see where they were going.

The sun had set and the blue-green haze of twilight had begun to shroud the Highlands when the city of Leah at last came in sight. They walked out of the trees and down a long, gently sloped hillside to where Leah sat on a high plain overlooking the lowlands east and south and the Rappahalladran and the Duln Forests west. Leah sprawled outward from its compact center in a series of gradually expanding estates, farms, and cooperatives owned and managed by its citizenry. Leah had been a monarchy in the time of Allanon, and various members of the Leah family had ruled in unbroken succession for nine hundred years. But eventually the monarchy had dissolved and the Highlands had fallen under Federation sway. It was only in the last fifty years that the Federation had withdrawn to the cities below the Prekkendorran Heights, and a council of elders had taken over the process of governing. Coran Leah, as a member of one of the most famous and prestigious Highland families, had gained a seat on the council and recently been elected First Minister. It was a position that he occupied reluctantly, but worked hard at, intent on justifying the trust his people had shown him.

Quentin thought the whole governing business an appropriate one for old men. Leah was a drop in an ocean, to his way of thinking. There was so much more out there, so much else happening, and none of it was affected in even the tiniest way by events in Leah. Entire nations had never even heard of the Highlands. If he wanted to have an impact on the future of the Four Lands, and possibly even on countries that lay beyond, he had to leave home and go out into the world. He had talked about it with Bek until his cousin was ready to scream. Bek didn't think like that. Bek wasn't interested in affecting the rest of the world. Bek was quite content to stay pretty much where he was. He viewed Quentin's relentless search for a way out of Leah as an obsession that was both dangerous and wrongheaded. But, he had to admit, at least Quentin had a plan for his life, which was more than Bek could say for himself.

They passed through farmlands, across horse and cattle fields, and past estate grounds and manor houses until they had reached the outskirts of the city proper. The Leah house occupied the same site on which their palace had been settled when the family ruled the Highlands. The palace had been destroyed during Federation occupation—burned, it was rumored, by Morgan Leah himself in defiance of its occupiers. In any case, Coran's father had replaced it with a two-story traditional home, multiple eaves and dormers, long rooflines and deep alcoves, casement wraps and stone fireplaces. The old trees remained, flower gardens dotted the grounds front and rear, and vine-draped arbors arched above crushed-stone walk-ways that wound from the front and rear entry doors to the sur-rounding streets.

Lights already burned in the windows and along the paths. They gave a warm and friendly feel to the big house, and as the cous-ins walked up to it Bek found himself wondering how long it would be before he would enjoy this feeling again.

They ate dinner that night with the family, with Coran and Liria and the four younger Leahs. The children spent the meal clamoring for details about their adventures, especially the boar hunt. Quentin made it all sound much more exciting than it really was, accommo-dating his younger brothers and sisters with a wild and lurid tale about how they barely escaped death on the tusks and under the hooves of a dozen rampaging boars. Coran shook his head and Liria smiled, and any discussion of Walker's unexpected appearance and proposed journey was postponed until later.

When dinner was finished and Liria had taken the younger chil-dren off to bed, Bek left Quentin to speak alone with his father about the Druid and took a long, hot bath to wash off the dirt from their outing. He gave himself over to the heat and damp, letting go of his concerns long enough to close his eyes and soak away his weariness. On finishing, he went to Quentin's room and found his cousin sitting on the bed holding the old sword and studying it thoughtfully.

Quentin looked up as he entered. "Father says we can go."

Bek nodded. "I never thought he wouldn't. Walker wouldn't be foolish enough to lie to us about something like that." He brushed a lock of damp hair off his forehead. "Did he tell you why he's had this change of heart about our leaving?"

"I asked. He said he owed the Druid a favor for something that happened a long time ago. He wouldn't say what. Actually, he changed the subject on me." Quentin looked thoughtful. "But he didn't seem disturbed about our going or about Walker's appear-ance. He seemed more . . . oh, sort of determined, I guess. It was hard to read him, Bek. He was very serious about this matter—calm, but intense. He made sure I knew to take the sword."

He looked down at the weapon in his hands. "I've been sitting here looking at it." He smiled. "I keep thinking that if I look hard enough, I'll discover something. Maybe the sword will speak to me, tell me the secret of its magic."

"I think you have to do what Walker said. You have to wait until there's a need for it before you learn how it works." Bek sat down on the bed next to him. "Walker was right. The sword is perfect. Not a mark on it. Hundreds of years old and in mint condition. That's not something that could happen if magic wasn't warding it in some way."

"I suppose not." Quentin turned the blade over and back again, running his fingers along the smooth, flat surface. "I feel a little strange about this. If the blade is magic and I'm to wield it, will I know what to do when it's time?"

Bek chuckled. "When did you ever not know what to do when it was time? You were born ready, Quentin."

"And you were born twice as smart and a lot more intuitive than I was," his cousin replied, and there was no joking or laughter in his response. His steady, open gaze settled on Bek. "I know my strengths and weaknesses. I can be honest about them. I know I rush into things, the way I did the chance to go on this expedition. Sometimes that's okay, and sometimes it isn't. I rely on you to keep me from wandering too far astray."

Bek shrugged. "Always happy to bring you back into line." He grinned.

"You remember that." Quentin looked back down at the sword. "If I don't see what needs doing, if I miss the right and wrong of things, I'm counting on you not to. This sword," he said, hefting it gently, "maybe it is magic and can do wonderful things. Maybe it can save lives. But maybe it's like all magic and can be harmful, as well. Isn't that the nature of magic? That it can work both ways? I don't want to cause harm with it, Bek. I don't want to be too quick to use it."

It was a profound observation for Quentin, and Bek thought his cousin did not give himself nearly enough credit. Nevertheless, he nodded in agreement. "Now go take a bath," he ordered, standing up again and moving toward the door. "I can't be expected to think straight when you smell like this!"

He returned to his room and began putting together clothes for their journey. They would leave early in the morning, getting a quick start on their travels. It would take them a week to track down Truls Rohk and then to reach Arborlon. How much longer would they be gone after that? What would it be like in the lands beyond their own, across the Blue Divide? Would the climate be hot or cold, wet or dry, bitter or mild? He looked around his room help-lessly, made aware again of how little he knew about what he had let himself in for. But that kind of thinking wasn't going to help, so he put it aside and went back to work.

He was almost finished when Coran Leah appeared in the doorway, grave and thoughtful. "I wonder if I might talk to you a minute, Bek?"

Without waiting for a response, he stepped into the room and closed the door behind him. For a moment he just stood there, as if undecided about what to do next. Then he walked over to the bench on which Bek was laying out clothing, made a place for him-self, and sat down.

Bek stared, still holding a shirt he was folding up to put in his backpack. "What is it? What's the matter?"

Coran Leah shook his gray head. He was still a handsome man, strong and fit at fifty, his blue eyes clear and his smile ready. He was well liked in Leah, well regarded by everyone. He was the kind of man who made it a point to do the small things others would over-look. If there were people in need, Coran Leah was always the first to try to find help for them or, failing that, to help them himself. He had raised his children with kind words and gentle urgings, and Bek didn't think he had ever heard him shout. If he could have chosen a father for himself, Bek wouldn't have looked farther than Coran.

"I have been thinking about this since Walker came to see me yesterday and told me what he wanted. There are some things you don't know, Bek—things no one knows, not even Quentin, only Liria and I. I've been waiting for the right time to tell you, and I guess maybe I've waited as long as I can."

He straightened himself, placing his hands carefully on his knees. "It wasn't your father who brought you here all those years ago. It was Walker. He told me your father had died in an accident, leaving you alone, and he asked me to take you in. The fact is, I wasn't close to Holm Rowe. I hadn't seen him in more than ten years before you came to live with us. I didn't know he had children. I didn't even know he had a wife. I thought it very strange that your father would choose to send you to me, to live with my family, but Walker insisted that this was what he wanted. He convinced me that it was the right thing to do."

He shook his head anew. "He can be very persuasive when he chooses. I asked him how your father had come to know him well enough to put you in his care. He said it wasn't a matter of choice, that he was there when no one else was, and your father had to trust him."

Bek put down the shirt he was holding. "Well, I know how persuasive he can be. I've seen it for myself. How did he talk you into agreeing with him on this present business?"

Coran Leah smiled. "He told me the same thing I assume he told you—that he needed you both, that people's lives depended on it, that the future of the Four Lands required it. He said you were old enough to make the decision for yourselves, but that I must give you the freedom to do so. I didn't like hearing that, but I recognized the truth in what he was saying. You are old enough, almost grown. Quentin is grown. I've kept you with me as long as I can." He shrugged. "Maybe he's right. Maybe people's lives do depend on it. I guess I owe it to you both to let you find out."

Bek nodded. "We'll be careful," he reassured him. "We'll look after each other."

141

"I know you will. I feel better with both of you going rather than only one. Liria doesn't think you should go at all, either of you, but that's because she's a mother, and that's how mothers think."

"Do you think Quentin's sword really does have magic? Do you think it can do what Walker says?"

Coran sighed. "I don't know. Our family history says so. Walker seems certain of it."

Bek sat down across from him on the edge of his bed. "I'm not sure we're doing the right thing by going, and I realize we don't know everything yet, maybe not even enough to appreciate the risk we're taking. But I promise we won't do anything foolish."

Coran nodded. "Be careful of those kinds of promises, Bek. Sometimes they're hard to keep." He paused. "There's one thing more I have to say. It has occurred to me before, but I've kept it to myself. I thought about it again yesterday, when Walker reappeared on my doorstep. Here it is. I have only the Druid's word that Holm Rowe really was your father and that he sent you here to live with me. I tried to check on this later, but no one could tell me where or when Holm had died. No one could tell me anything about him."

Bek stared at him in surprise. "Someone else might be my real father?"

Coran Leah fixed him with his steady gaze. "You are like one of my own sons, Bek. I love you as much as I love them. I have done the very best I could to raise you in the right way. Both Liria and I have. Now that you are about to leave, I want no secrets between us."

He stood up. "I'll let you get back to your packing."

He started for the door, then changed his mind and came back across the room. He put his strong arms around Bek and hugged him tightly. "Be careful, son," he whispered.

Then he was gone again, leaving Bek to conclude that there was as much uncertainty about his past as there was about his future.

ELEVEN

I t was raining again by the time Hunter Predd and Walker arrived aboard Obsidian at the seaport of March Brume, some distance north of Bracken Clell on the coast of the Blue Divide. They had flown into the rain just before sunset after traveling west all day from the Highlands of Leah, and it felt as if the dark and damp had descended as one. March Brume occupied a stretch of rocky beach along a cove warded by huge cliffs to the north and a broad salt marsh to the south. A stand of deep woods backed away from the village into a shallow valley behind, and it was just to the south of that valley, on a narrow plateau, that the Roc deposited her passengers so that they might take refuge for the night in an old trapper's shack.

March Brume was a predominately Southland community, although a smattering of Elves and Dwarves had settled there, as well. For centuries, the seaport had been famous for the construction of her sailing ships, everything from one-man skiffs to single-masted sloops to three-masted frigates. Craftsmen from all over the Four Lands came to the little village to ply their trades and offer their services. There was never a shortage of need for designers or builders, and there was always a good living to be made. Virtually everyone who lived in the seaport was engaged in the same occupation.

Then, twenty-four years ago, a man named Ezael Sterret, a Rover of notorious reputation, a sometime pirate and brigand with a streak of inventive genius, had designed and built the first airship. It had been unwieldy, ungainly, and unreliable, but it had flown. Other efforts by other builders had followed, each increasingly more successful, and within two decades, travel had been revolutionized and the nature of shipbuilding in March Brume had been changed forever. Sailing ships were still built in the shipyards of the old seaport, but not in the same numbers as before. The majority of ships constructed now were for air travel, and the customers whose pockets were deepest and whose needs were greatest came from the Federation and Free-born army commands.

None of which had anything to do with Walker's primary reason for choosing to come here rather than to one of a dozen other shipbuilding ports along the coast. What brought him to March Brume was the nature of the shipbuilders and designers who occupied the seaport—Rovers, a people universally disliked and distrusted, wanderers for the whole of their history, who even as mostly permanent residents still came and went from the seaport whenever the urge struck. Not only were they the most skilled and reliable of those engaged in shipbuilding and flying, but they accepted work from all quarters and they understood the importance of keeping a bargain and a confidence once engaged.

Walker was about to test the truth of this generally held belief. His instincts and his long association with Rovers persuaded him that it was his best option. His cousin, the Elven Queen Wren Elessedil, had been raised by Rovers as a child and taught the survival skills that had kept her alive when she had journeyed to the doomed island of Morrowindl to recover the lost Elven people. Rovers had aided various members of Walker's family over the years, and he had found them tough, dependable, and resourceful.

Like him, they were wanderers. Like him, they were outcasts and loners. Even living in settled communities, as many of them were doing now, they remained mostly isolated from other peoples.

This was fine with Walker. The less open and more secretive his dealings in this matter, the better. He did not think for a moment that he could keep secret for long either his presence or his purpose. The Ilse Witch would be seeking to discover both. Sooner or later, she would succeed.

Hunter Predd managed a fire in the crumbling hearth of the old trapper's cabin, and they slept the night in mostly dry surroundings. At dawn, Walker gave the Wing Rider orders to replace their dwindling provisions and to wait for his return from the village. He might be gone for several days, he cautioned, so the Wing Rider shouldn't be concerned if he did not reappear right away.

The day had cleared somewhat, the rain turned to a cold, damp mist that clung to the forests and cliffs like a shroud, and the skies brightened sufficiently to permit a hazy glimpse of the sun through banks of heavy gray clouds. Walker navigated the woods until he found a trail, then the trail until it led to a road, and followed the road into the village. March Brume was a collection of sodden gray buildings, with the residences set back from the shoreline toward the woods, and the shipyards and docks set closer to the water. The sounds of building rose in a din above the crash of waves, a steady mix of hammers and saws punctuated by the hiss of steam rising from hot iron hauled from the forge and by the shouts and curses of the laborers. The village was crowded and active, residents and visitors alike clogging the streets and alleys, going about their business in the damp and gloom in remarkably cheerful fashion.

Walker, wrapped in his cloak to hide his missing arm, was not remarkable enough to draw attention. People of all sorts came and went in March Brume, and where a Rover population dominated, it was best to mind your own business.

The Druid moved unhurriedly toward the docks through the

businesses at the center of town. Federation soldiers dressed in silver and black uniforms lounged about while waiting to take delivery of their orders. There were Free-born soldiers, as well, not so obvious or bold in revealing their presence, but come to March Brume for the same reason. It was odd, the Druid thought, that they would shop at the same store as if it were the most natural thing in the world, when in any other situation they would attack each other on sight.

He found the man he was looking for in a marketplace toward the south end of the village, not far from the beginnings of the docks and building yards. He was a scarecrow dressed in brilliant but tattered scarlet robes. He was so thin that when he braced himself against the occasional gusts of wind that blew in off the water, he seemed to bend like a reed. A wisp of black beard trailed from his pointed chin, and his dark hair hung long and unkempt about his narrow face. A vivid red scar ran from hairline to chin, crossing the bridge of his broken nose like a fresh lash mark. He stood just off the path of the traffic passing the stalls, close by a fountain, head cocked in a peculiarly upward tilted fashion, as if searching for guidance from the clouded skies. One hand held forth a metal cup, and the other gestured toward passersby with a fervor that suggested you ignored him at your peril.

"Come now, don't be shy, don't be hesitant, don't be afraid!" His voice was thin and high pitched, but it caught the attention. "A coin or two buys you peace of mind, pilgrim. A coin or two buys you a glimpse of your future. Be certain of your steps, friend. Take a moment to learn of the fate you might prevent, of the misstep you might take, of the downward path you might unwittingly follow. Come one, come all."

Walker stood across the square from the man and watched silently for a time. Now and then, someone would stop, place a coin in the metal cup, and bend close to hear what the man had to say. The man always did the same thing: he took the giver's hand in his own and held it while he talked, moving his fingers slowly over the other's open palm, nodding all the while.

Once or twice, when the man shifted positions or moved to take a drink from the fountain's waters, the scarlet robes shifted to reveal that he had only one leg and wore a wooden peg for the other.

Walker held his position until the rain quickened sufficiently to drive most of the crowd elsewhere and force the man to back away under the shelter of an awning. Then he crossed the square, approached the man in the scarlet robes as if seeking to share his shelter, and stood quietly at his side.

"Perhaps you could read the future of a man who seeks to take a long and hazardous journey to an unknown land?" he queried, looking out at the rain.

The man's gaze shifted slightly, but stayed directed skyward. "Some men have made journeys enough for five lifetimes already. Perhaps they should stay home and quit tempting fate."

"Perhaps they have no choice."

"Paladins of shades revealed only to them, questers of answers to secrets unknown, ever searching for what will put an end to their uncertainty." The hands gestured helplessly. "You've been away for a long time, pilgrim. Up there, in your high castle, alone with your thoughts and dreams. Do you really seek to make a journey to a faraway land?"

Walker smiled faintly. "You are the forecaster of fates, Cicatrix. Not me."

The scarred face nodded. "A teller of futures this day, a disabled soldier the next, a madman the third. Like yourself, Walker, I am a chameleon."

"We do what we must in this world." The Druid bent closer. "But I didn't seek you out for any of the skills you've listed, formidable though they are. I require instead a small piece of information from that vast storehouse you manage—and I would keep that information from reaching other ears."

Cicatrix reached for the Druid's hand and took it in his own, running his fingers over the palm, keeping his ruined face directed skyward as he did so. "You intend to make a trip to an unknown land, pilgrim?" His voice had dropped to a whisper. "Perhaps you seek transport?"

"Of the sort that flies. Something fast and durable. Not a warship, but able to be fitted to withstand an attack by one. Not a racer, but able to fly as if born to it. Her builder must have vision, and the ship must have heart."

The thin man laughed softly. "You seek miracles, pilgrim. Do I seem to you the sort that can provide them?"

"In the past, you have."

"The past comes back to haunt me, then. There lies the trouble with having to live up to another's expectations, when those expectations are founded on questionable memories. Well." He kept running his hands over Walker's palm. "Your enemy in this endeavor wouldn't happen to wear silver and black?"

Walker glanced out into the rain. "Mostly, my enemy would have eyes everywhere and kill with her song."

Cicatrix hissed softly. "A witch with a witches' brew, is it? Stay far from her, Walker."

"I'll try. Now listen carefully. I need a ship and a builder, a Captain and a crew. I need them to be strong and brave and willing to ally themselves with the Elves against all enemies." He paused. "March Brume's reputation will be tested in this as it has not been tested before."

"And mine."

"And yours."

"If I disappoint you, I shall not see you again, pilgrim?"

"You will at least wish as much."

Cicatrix chuckled mirthlessly. "Threats? No, not from you, Walker. You never threaten; you only reveal your concerns. A poor cripple like myself is advised to pay close attention, but not to act out of fear." His fingers stopped moving on Walker's hand. "Are the rewards for those who become involved reasonable, given the risks?"

"Well beyond that. The Elves will open wide the doors to their vaults."

"Ah." The other man nodded, head tilted strangely, gaze directed at nothing. He released Walker's hand. "Come to the docks at the end of Verta Road after nightfall. Stand where you can be seen. Mysteries shall unfold and secrets be revealed. Perhaps a journey shall be taken to an unknown land."

Walker produced a pouch filled with gold coins, and Cicatrix pocketed it smoothly. He turned slowly and limped away. "Farewell, pilgrim. Good fortune to you."

Walker spent the remainder of the day walking the docks, studying the ships under construction and the men building them, listening to talk of sailing, and garnering small amounts of information. He ate at a large, dockside tavern, where he was one of many, and pretended disinterest while keeping close watch for the Federation spies he knew to be there. The Ilse Witch would be looking for him, determined to find him. He had no illusions. She was relentless. She would attack him wherever and whenever she could, hoping to finish what she had started in Arborlon. If she could kill or disable him, the quest he sought to mount would fall apart and her own path to the map's treasure would be left unobstructed. She did not have the map, but she probably had the castaway's memories to guide her, and for all he knew, they would prove sufficient.

He pondered at length the implications of an encounter with her, of a confrontation he was almost certain he could not avoid. He mulled the consequences of cruel chance and unkind fate, of opportunities lost and games played, and waited patiently for nightfall.

When it was dark, he made his way through March Brume, his progress hidden by a mist come in off the water with the temperature's drop and the rain's passing. The forges and shipyards had emptied with the end of the workday, and the sound of the surf lapping against the shoreline was clearly audible in the ensuing silence.

Vendors had closed their shops, and peddlers had stowed their wares. The taverns, eating establishments, and pleasure houses were packed full and boisterous, but the streets were mostly deserted.

Several times, he stopped in the shadows and waited—listening and watching. He did not pursue a direct route to his destination, but instead worked his way through the village in an oblique fashion, making certain he was not followed. Even so, he was uneasy. He was inconspicuous enough to those who did not know to look for him, but easily recognizable by those who did. The Ilse Witch would have advised her spies of his appearance. He might have been wiser to disguise himself. But that was hindsight talking, and hindsight was of little use now.

At the end of Verta Road, cloaked in the mist and silence, he stood in the faint light of a streetlamp. The docks stretched away oceanside, the stark, spectral forms of partially formed ship hulls and support cradles outlined by the lights of the village. No one moved in the night's gloom. No sounds broke the steady roll and hiss of the surf.

He had been in place for only a few minutes when a man materialized out of the dark and walked toward him. The man was tall and had flaming red hair worn long and tied back with a brightly colored scarf. A Rover, by the look of him, he walked with the slightly rolling gait of a sailor, and his cloak billowed open to reveal a set of flying leathers. The man smiled easily as he came up to Walker, as if they were old friends reuniting after a long separation.

"Are you called Walker?" he asked, coming to a stop before the Druid. His gold earrings glittered faintly in the streetlamp's hazy light.

Walker nodded.

The other bowed slightly. "I'm Redden Alt Mer. Cicatrix tells me you have plans for a journey and need help with the preparations."

Walker frowned. "You don't have the look of a shipbuilder."

Redden Alt Mer grinned broadly. "That's probably because I'm not one. But I know where to find the man you need. I know how to put you aboard the fastest, most agile ship ever built, enlist the best crew who ever sailed the open sky, and then fly you to wherever you want to go—because I'll be your Captain." He paused, cocking his head. "All for a price, of course."

Walker studied him. The man was cocky and brash, but with a dangerous edge to him, as well. "How do I know you can manage all this, Redden Alt Mer? How do I know you're the man I need?"

The Rover managed a look of complete astonishment. "Cicatrix sent me to you; if you trusted him enough to find me in the first place, that should be enough."

"Cicatrix has been known to make mistakes."

"Only if you cheated him of his fee, and he wants to teach you a lesson. You didn't, did you?" The Rover sighed. "Very well. Here are my credentials, since I see that my name means nothing to you. I was born to ships and have sailed them since I was a boy. I have been a Captain for most of my life. I have sailed the entire Westland coast and explored most of the known islands off the Blue Divide. I have spent the last three years flying airships for the Federation. More to the point, I have never, ever, been knocked out of the skies."

"And should I trust you enough to believe you speak the truth?" Walker moved a step closer. "Even though you place an assailant at my back with a drawn dagger, waiting to strike me down should you feel I do not?"

Alt Mer nodded slowly, the grin still in place. "Very good. I know something of Druids and their powers. You are the last of your kind and not well respected in the Four Lands, so I felt it wise to test you. A real Druid, I am told, would sense an assailant's presence. A real Druid would know if he was threatened." He shrugged. "I was simply being cautious. I meant you no offense."

Walker's dark face did not change expression. "I take none. This is to be a long and dangerous journey, should we agree that you are the right man to make it, Redden Alt Mer. I understand that you don't want to attempt it in the company of a fool or a liar." He paused. "Of course, neither do I."

The Rover laughed softly. "Little Red!" he called.

A tall, auburn-tressed woman emerged from the misty dark behind Walker, eyes sweeping the shadows, suggesting she was even less trusting of him than her companion was. When she nodded to Alt Mer, and he back to her, agreeing between them that all was well, the resemblance was unmistakable.

"My sister, Rue Meridian," Alt Mer said. "She'll be my navigator when we sail. She'll also watch my back, just as she did here."

Rue Meridian extended her hand in greeting, and Walker took it. Her grip was strong and her eyes steady as they met his own. "Welcome to March Brume," she said.

"Let's move out of the light while we conduct our business," Alt Mer suggested cheerfully.

He led his sister and Walker away from the streetlamp's hazy light and into a darkened alleyway that ran between the buildings. On the road behind them, a small boy darted past, chasing after a metal hoop he rolled ahead of him with a stick.

"Now then, to business," Redden Alt Mer said, rubbing his hands with enthusiasm. "Where is this journey to take us?"

Walker shook his head. "I can't tell you that. Not until we're safely away."

The Rover seemed taken aback. "Can't tell me? You want me to sign on for a voyage that has no destination? Do we go west, east, north, south, up or down——?"

"We go where I say."

The big man grunted. "All right. Do we carry cargo?"

"No. We go to retrieve something."

"How many passengers will we carry?

"Three dozen, give or take a few. No more than forty."

The Rover frowned. "For a ship that size, I'll need a crew of at least a dozen, including Little Red and myself."

"I'll allow you ten."

Alt Mer flushed. "You place a good many constraints on us for someone who knows nothing of sailing!"

"How well do you intend to pay?" his sister interjected quickly.

"What would be your normal rate of pay for a long voyage?" Walker queried. Now they were down to the part that mattered most. Rue Meridian glanced at her brother. Alt Mer thought about it, then provided a figure. Walker nodded. "I'll pay that much in advance and double it when we return."

"Triple it," Rue Meridian said at once.

Walker gave her a long, considering look. "What did Cicatrix tell you?"

"That you have rich friends and powerful enemies."

"Which are good reasons to hire us," her brother added.

"Especially if the latter are allied with someone whose magic is as powerful as your own."

"Someone who can kill with little more than the sound of her voice." Redden Alt Mer smiled anew. "Oh, yes. We know something of the creatures that live in the Wilderun. We know something of witches and warlocks."

"Rumor has it," his sister said softly, "that you were standing next to Allardon Elessedil when he was killed."

"Rumor has it that he struck some sort of bargain with you, and that the Elves intend to honor it." Alt Mer cocked one eyebrow quizzically.

Walker glanced out at the darkness of Verta Road, then back at the red-haired siblings again. "You seem to know a great deal."

The Rover Captain shrugged. "It is our business to know, when we are being asked to put our lives at risk."

"Which brings up an interesting point." The Druid gave them both a considering look. "Why do you want to come with me on this voyage? Why choose to involve yourselves in this venture when there are other, less dangerous expeditions?"

Redden Alt Mer laughed. "A good question. A question that

requires several answers. Let me see if I can provide them for you. First, there is the money. You offer more than we can make from anyone else. A great deal more. We're mercenaries, so we pay close attention when the purse offered is substantial. Second, there are the unfortunate circumstances surrounding our recent leave-taking from the Federation. It wasn't altogether voluntary, and our former employers could decide to come looking for us to settle accounts. It might be best if we were somewhere else if that happens. A long voyage out of the Four Lands would provide them with sufficient time to lose interest.

"And third," he said, smiling like a small boy with a piece of candy, "there is the challenge of making a voyage to a new land, of going somewhere no one else has gone before, of seeing something for the first time, of finding a new world." He sighed and gestured expansively. "You shouldn't underestimate what that means to us. It's difficult to explain to someone who doesn't fly or sail or explore like we do, like we've done all our lives. It is who we are and what we do, and sometimes that counts for more than anything."

"Especially after our experience with the Federation, where we hired out just for the money," his sister growled softly. "It's time for something else, something more fulfilling, even if it is dangerous."

"Don't be so quick to demystify our thinking, Little Red!" her brother reproved her sharply. He cocked a finger at the Druid. "Enough about the reasons for our choices. Let me tell you something about yours, about why you chose to involve yourself with us. I don't mean Little Red and myself, personally—though we're the ones you want. I mean the Rovers. You are here, my friend, because you're a Druid and we're Rovers, and we have much in common. We are out-siders and always have been. We are outcasts of the lands, just barely tolerated and suspiciously viewed. We are comfortable with wanderlust and the wider view of the world, and we do not see things in terms of nationalities and governments. We are people who value friendship and loyalty, who prize strength of heart and mind as well as of body, but who value good judgment even more.

You can be the bravest soul who ever walked the earth and be worthless if you do not know when and where to choose your battles. How am I doing?"

"A little long-winded," Walker offered.

The tall Rover laughed gleefully. "A sense of humor in a Druid! Who would have thought it possible? Well, you catch my drift, so I needn't go on. We are made for each other—and for quests that most would never dream of even considering. You want us, Walker, because we will stand against anything. We will go right into death's maw and give a yank of his tongue. We will do it because that is what life is for, if you are a Rover. Now tell me—am I wrong?"

Walker shook his head, as much in dismay as in agreement.

"He actually believes all this," his sister declared ruefully. "I worry that it might prove contagious and that one day soon we will both become infected and then neither one of us will be able to think straight."

"Now, now, Little Red. You're supposed to stand up for me, not knock me down!" Alt Mer sighed and stared at Walker with his cheerful gaze. "There is also, of course, the inescapable fact that almost no one else of talent and nerve would give you the time of day in this business. Rovers are the only ones bold enough to accept your offer while still respecting your need for secrecy." He grinned. "So, what's it to be?"

Walker pulled his black robes more closely about him, and the mist that had filtered into their dark alleyway stirred in response. "Let's sleep on it. Tomorrow we can have a talk with your shipbuilder and see if he backs you up. I'll want to see his work and judge the man himself before I commit to anything."

"Excellent!" the big Rover exclaimed joyfully. "A fair response!" He paused, a shadow of regret crossing his broad face. "Except for one thing. Sleep is out of the question. If you're interested in our services, we'll have to leave here tonight."

"Leave?" Walker didn't bother to hide his surprise.

"Tonight."

"And go where?"

"Why, wherever I say," the Rover answered, feeding Walker's words back to him. He grinned at his sister. "I'm afraid he thinks me none too bright after all." He turned back to Walker. "If the ship-builder you wanted could be found in March Brume, you wouldn't need us to locate him for you, would you? Nor would he be of much use if he conducted his business openly."

Walker nodded. "I suppose not."

"A short journey is required to provide you with the reassurances you seek—a journey that would best be begun under cover of darkness."

Walker glanced skyward, as if assessing the weather. He couldn't see moon or stars or fifty feet beyond the fog. "A journey we will make on foot, I hope?"

The big Rover grinned anew. His sister cocked her eyebrow reprovingly.

Walker sighed. "How soon do we leave?"

Redden Alt Mer draped one companionable arm over Rue Meridian's shoulders. "We leave now."

The boy with the iron hoop and stick remained hidden in the deep shadows of the dockyards across the way until the trio emerged from the alleyway and disappeared up the road. Even then, he did not move for a long time. He had been warned about the Druid and his powers, and he did not wish to challenge either. It was enough that he had found him; nothing more was required.

When he was confident he was alone again, he left his hiding place, hoop and stick abandoned, and raced toward the woods backing the village. He was small for his age and wild as an animal, lean and wiry and unkempt, not quite a child of the streets, but close. He had never known his father and had lost his mother when he was only two. His half-blind grandmother had raised him, but had lost all control before he was six. He was bright and enterprising, however, and he had found ways to support them both in a world that otherwise would have swallowed them whole.

In less than an hour, sweaty and dirt-streaked from his run, he reached the abandoned farm just beyond the last residences of March Brume. His labored breathing was the only sound that broke the silence as he entered the ruined barn and moved to the storage bins in back. Within the more secure one on the far right were the cages. He released the lock, slipped inside the bin, lit a candle, and scribbled a carefully worded note.

The lady for whom he gathered information from time to time would pay him well for this bit, he thought excitedly. Enough that he could buy that blade he had admired for so long. Enough that he and his grandmother could eat well for weeks to come.

He fastened the message to the leg of one of the odd, fierce-eyed birds she had given him, walked back outside with the bird tucked carefully under his arm, and sent it winging off into the night.

TWELVE

R edden Alt Mer and Rue Meridian took Walker along the
dockside for several hundred yards, then turned onto a narrow pier bracketed by skiffs. Stopping at a weathered craft
with a knockdown mast and single sail and a rudder attached to
a hand tiller at the stern, they held her steady while the Druid
boarded, then quickly cast off. Within seconds, they were out of sight
of the dock, the village, and any hint of land. The Rovers placed
Walker in the bow with directions to keep an eye open for floating
debris, and went about putting up the mast and sail. Walker glanced
around uneasily. As far as he could determine, they had no way of
judging where they were or where they were going. It did not seem
to matter. Once the sail was up and filled with a steady wind off the
sea, they sat back, Alt Mer at the stern and his sister amidships,
tacking smoothly and steadily into the night.

It was a strange experience, even for the Druid. Now and then a
scattering of stars would appear through the clouds, and once or
twice the moon broke through, high and to their right. But for that,
they sailed in a cauldron of fog and darkness and unchanging sea. At
least the water was calm, as black and depthless as ink, rolling and
sloshing comfortably below the gunwales. Redden Alt Mer whistled

and hummed, and his sister stared off into the night. No bird cries sounded. No lights appeared. Walker found his thoughts drifting to a renewed consideration of the ambiguity and uncertainty of what he was about. It was more than just the night's business that troubled him; it was the entire enterprise. It was as vague and shrouded as the darkness and the fog in which he drifted, all awash in unanswered questions and vague possibilities. He knew a few things and could guess at a few more, but the rest—the greater part of what lay ahead—remained a mystery.

They sailed for several hours in their cocoon of changeless sounds and sights, wrapped by the darkness and silence as if sleepers who drowsed before waking. It came as a surprise when Rue Meridian lit an oil lamp and hooked it to the front of the mast. The light blazed bravely in a futile effort to cut through the darkness, but seemed able to penetrate no more than a few feet. Redden Alt Mer had taken a seat on the bench that ran across the skiff's stern, his arm hooked over the tiller, his feet propped up on the rail. He nodded to his sister when the light was in place, and she moved forward to change places with Walker.

Shortly after, a sailing vessel appeared before them, looming abruptly out of the night, this one much larger and better manned. Even in the darkness, Walker could estimate a crew of six or seven, all working the rigging on the twin masts. A rope was tossed to Rue Meridian, who tied it to the bow of the skiff. Her brother put out the lamp, hauled down the sail, took down the mast, and resumed his seat. Their work was done in moments, and the towrope tightened and jerked as they were hauled ahead.

"Nothing to do now until we get to where we're going," the Rover Captain offered, stretching out comfortably on the bench. In moments, he was asleep.

Rue Meridian sat with Walker amidships. After a few moments, she said, "Nothing ever seems to bother him. I've seen him sleep while we're flying into battle. It isn't that he's incautious or unconcerned. Big Red is always ready when he's needed. It's just that he knows how to let go of everything all at once and then pick it up again when it's time."

Her eyes swept the dark perfunctorily as she talked. "He'll tell you he's the best because he believes it. He'll tell you he should be your Captain because he's confident he should be. You might think him boastful or brash; you might even think him reckless. He's neither. He's just very good at flying airships." She paused. "No, not just good. He's much better than that. He's great. He's gifted. He is the best I've ever known, the best that anyone's ever seen. The soldiers talked about him on the Prekkendorran like that. Everyone who knows him does. They think he's got luck. And he does, but it's mostly luck he makes by being brave and smart and talented."

She glanced at him. "Do I sound like a younger sister talking about a big brother she idolizes?" She snorted softly. "I am, but I'm not deceived by my feelings for him. I've been his protector and conscience for too long. We were born to the same mother, different fathers. We never knew either father very well, just vague memories. They were sailors, wanderers. Our mother died when we were still very young. I looked after him for much of his life; I was better at it than he was. I know him; I understand him. I know his abilities and shortcomings, strengths and weaknesses. I've seen him succeed and fail. I wouldn't lie about him to anyone, least of all to myself. So when I tell you Big Red is worth two of any other man, you should listen to me. When I tell you he's the best man you'll find for your journey, you ought to pay attention."

"I am," Walker said quietly.

She smiled. "Well, where would you go if you didn't want to? You're my captive audience." She paused, studying him. "You have intelligence, Walker. I can see you thinking all the time. I look inside your eyes and see your mind at work. You listen, you measure, and you judge accordingly. You'll make your own decision about this expedition and us. What I say won't influence you. That's not why I'm telling you how I feel about Big Red. I'm telling you so you will know where I stand."

She paused and waited, and after a moment, he nodded. "That's fair enough."

She sighed and shifted on the seat. "Frankly, I don't care about the money. I have enough of that. What I don't have is peace of mind or a sense of future or something to believe in again. I had those once, when I was younger. Somewhere along the way, I lost them. I'm sick at heart and worn-out. The past three years, fighting on the Prekkendorran, chasing Free-born back and forth across the heights, killing them now and then, burning their airships, spilling fire on their camps—it charred my soul. The whole business was stupid. A war over land, over territorial rights, over national dominion—what does any of it matter? Except for the money, I have nothing to show for that experience."

She fixed him with her green eyes. "I don't sense this about your expedition. I don't feel that a Druid would bother with something so petty. Tell me the truth—is your enterprise going to offer anything more?"

She was so intense as she stared at him that he was momentarily taken aback by her depth of feeling. "I'm not sure," he said after a moment. "There is more to what I'm asking you to do than the money I've offered. There are lives at stake besides our own. There are freedoms to be lost and maybe a world to be changed for better or worse. I can't see far enough into the future to be certain. But I can tell you this much. By going, we might make a difference that will mean something to you later."

She smiled. "We're going to save the world, is that it?"

His face remained expressionless. "We might."

The smile disappeared. "All right, I won't make a joke of it. I won't even suggest you might be overstating what's possible. I'll allow myself to believe a little in what you're promising. It can't hurt. A little belief on both sides might be a good beginning to a partnership, don't you think?"

He nodded, smiling. "I do."

Bird cries heralded the arrival of dawn, and as the early light broke through the darkness, massive cliffs rose against the skyline, craggy and barren facings lashed by wind and surf. At first it appeared as if there was no way through the formidable barrier. But the ship ahead lit a lantern and hoisted it aloft, and a pair of lamps responding from shoreside indicated the approach. Even then, it was not apparent that an opening existed until they were almost on top of it. The light was thin and faint, the air clogged by mist and spray, and the thunder of waves crashing on the rocks an unmistakable warning to stay clear. But the Captain of the ship ahead proceeded without hesitation, navigating between rocks large enough to sink even his craft, let alone the skiff in which Walker rode.

Redden Alt Mer was awake again, standing at the tiller, steering the skiff with a sure hand in the wake of the two-master. Walker glanced back at him, and was surprised to find his features alive with happiness and expectation. Alt Mer was enjoying this, caught up in the excitement and challenge of sailing, at home in a way most could never be.

Standing next to him, Rue Meridian was smiling, as well.

They passed through the rocks and into a narrow channel, the skiff rising and falling on the roiling sea. Gulls and cormorants circled overhead, their cries echoing eerily off the cliff walls. Ahead lay a broad cove surrounded by forested cliffs with waterfalls that tumbled hundreds of feet out of the misted heights. As they sailed from the turbulence of the channel into the relative calm of the harbor, the sounds of wind and surf faded and the waters smoothed. Behind them, the lamps that had been lit to guide their way in winked out.

Etched out of gloom and mist, the first signs of a settlement appeared. There was no mistaking its nature. A sprawling shipyard fronted the waters of the cove, complete with building cradles and docks, forges, and timber stores. A cluster of ships lay anchored at the north end of the cove, sleek and dark against the silvery waters, and by the glint of radian draws and the odd slant of light sheaths furled and waiting for release, Walker recognized them as airships.

As they neared the shoreline, the towing ship dropped anchor, and a small transport was lowered with a pair of sailors at the oars. It rowed back to the skiff and took Walker and the Rovers aboard. Alt Mer and his sister greeted the sailors familiarly, but did not introduce the Druid. They rowed ashore through hazy light and swooping birds and disembarked at one of the docks. Dockworkers were hauling supplies back and forth along the waterfront, and laborers were just beginning their workday. The sounds of hammers and saws broke the calm, and the settlement seemed to come awake all at once.

"This way," Redden Alt Mer advised, starting off down the dock toward the beach.

They stepped onto dry land and proceeded left through the shipyards, past the forges and cradles, to where a building sat facing the water. A broad covered porch fronted the building, with narrow trestle tables set along its length. Sheaves of paper were spread upon the tables and held in place by bricks. Men worked their way from one set of papers to the next, examining their writings, marking them for adjustments and revisions.

The man who supervised this work looked up at their approach and then came down the steps to meet them. He was a huge, burly fellow with arms and legs like tree trunks, a head of wild black hair, and a ruddy, weathered face partially obscured by a thick beard. He wore the bright sashes and gold earrings favored by Rovers, and his scowl belied the twinkle in his bird-sharp eyes.

"Morning, all," he growled, sounding less than cheerful. His black eyes lit on Walker. "Hope you're a customer who's deaf, dumb, and blind, and comes ready to share a small fortune with those less fortunate than yourself. Because if not, I might as well kill you now and have done with it. Big Red knows the rules."

Walker did not change expression or evidence concern, even when he heard Redden Alt Mer groan. "I've been told that by coming here I have a chance to do business with the best shipbuilder alive. Would that be you?"

"It would." The black eyes shifted to Alt Mer suspiciously, then back to Walker. "You don't look stupid, but then you don't look like a man with a fat purse, either. Who are you?"

"I'm called Walker."

The burly man studied him in silence. "The Druid?"

Walker nodded.

"Well, well, well. This might prove interesting after all. What would bring a Druid out of Paranor these days? Don't think it would be anything small." He stuck out a massive hand. "I'm Spanner Frew."

Walker accepted the hand and shook it. The hand felt as if it had been cast in iron. "Druids go where they are needed," he said.

"That must be extremely difficult when there is only one of you." Spanner Frew chuckled, a deep, booming rasp. "How did you have the misfortune to fall in with these thieves? Not that young Rue wouldn't turn the head of any man, mine included."

"Cicatrix sent them to me."

"Ah, a brave and unfortunate man," the shipbuilder allowed with a solemn nod, surprising Walker. "Lost everything but his mind in a shipwreck that wasn't his fault but was blamed on him nevertheless. Do you know about it?"

"Only the rumors. I know Cicatrix from other places and times. Enough to trust him."

"Well said. So you've tied in with Big and Little Red and come looking for a shipbuilder. That must mean you have a voyage in mind and need a ship worthy of the effort. Tell me about it."

Walker provided a brief overview of what it was he required and how it would be used. He gave Spanner Frew no more information than he had Redden Alt Mer, but was encouraging where he could be. He had already decided he liked the man. What remained to be determined was his skill as a craftsman.

When Walker was finished, Spanner Frew's scowl deepened and his brow creased. "This would be a long voyage you're planning, one that could take years perhaps?"

Walker nodded.

"You'll need your ship for living quarters, supplies, and cargo when you arrive at your destination. You'll need it for defense against the enemies you might encounter. You'll need it to be weatherworthy, because there's storms on the Blue Divide that can shred a ship of the line in minutes." He was listing Walker's requirements in a matter-of-fact way, no longer asking questions. "You'll need weapons that will serve on both land and air. You'll need replacement parts that can't be found on your travels—radian draws and ambient-light sheaves, parse crystals and the like. A big order. Very big."

He glanced at the workmen behind him, then off at the harbor. "But your resources are plentiful and your purse is deep?"

Walker nodded once more.

Spanner Frew folded his beefy arms. "I have the ship for you. Just completed, a sort of prototype for an entire line. There's nothing else like her flying the Four Lands. She's a warship, but built for long-range travel and extended service. I was going to offer her on the open market, a special item for those fools who keep trying to kill each other above the Prekkendorran. If they liked her well enough, and I think they would, I'd build them a few dozen more and retire a rich man." His scowl became a menacing grin. "But I would rather sell her to you, I think. Care for a look?"

He took them north all the way through the shipyards to where the beach opened on a series of rocky outcroppings and the fleet Walker had seen earlier when entering the harbor lay at rest. There were nearly a dozen ships of various sizes, but only one that caught the Druid's eye. He knew it was the ship Spanner Frew had been talking about even before the other spoke.

"That's her," the burly shipbuilder indicated with a nod and a gesture. "You picked her out right away, didn't you?"

She was built like a catamaran, but much larger. She was low and sleek and wicked looking, her wood and stays and even her light sheaves dark in color, and her twin masts raked ever so slightly, giving her the appearance of being in motion even when she lay at rest. Her decking rested on a pair of pontoons set rather close together, their ends hooking upward into twin horns at either end, their midsections divided into what appeared to be fighting compartments that could hold men and weapons. Her railings slanted away and back from her sides, bow, and stern to allow for storage and protection from weather and attacks. The pilothouse sat amidships between the masts, raised well above the decking and enclosed by shields that gave ample protection to the helmsman. Low, flat living quarters and storage housing sat forward and aft of the masts, broad but curved in the shape of the decking and pontoons to minimize wind resistance. The living and sleeping quarters were set into the decking and extended almost to the waterline, giving an unexpected depth to the space.

Everything was smooth and curved and gleamed like polished metal, even in the faint, misted light of the cove.

"She's beautiful," Walker said, turning to Spanner Frew. "How does she fly?"

"Like she looks. Like a dream. I've had her up myself and tested her. She'll do everything you ask of her and more. She lacks the size and weapons capability of a ship of the line, but she more than makes up for it in speed and agility. Of course," he added, glancing now at Redden Alt Mer, "she needs a proper Captain."

Walker nodded. "I'm looking for one. Do you have any suggestions?"

The shipbuilder broke into a long gale of laughter, practically doubling over from the effort. "Oh, that's very good, very funny! I hope you caught the look on Big Red's face when you said that! Why, he looked as if he'd been jerked by his short hairs! Hah, you do make me laugh, Druid!"

Walker's solemn face was directed back toward the ship. "Well, I'm glad you're amused, but the question is a serious one. The bargain we strike for the purchase of the ship includes the builder's agreement to come with her."

Spanner Frew stopped laughing at once. "What? What did you say?"

"Put yourself in my position," Walker replied mildly, still looking out at the harbor and the ship. "I'm a stranger seeking the help of a people who are notorious for striking bargains that have more than one interpretation. Rovers don't lie in their business dealings, but they do shade the truth and bend the rules when it benefits them. I accept this. I am a part of an order that has been known to do the same. But how do I protect myself in a situation where the advantage is all the other way?"

"You had best place a tight hold on—" the shipbuilder began, but Walker cut him short with a gesture.

"Just listen a moment. Redden Alt Mer tells me he is the best airship Captain alive. Rue Meridian agrees. You tell me you are the best shipbuilder alive and this craft you wish to sell me is the best airship ever built. I will assume all of you agree that I can do no better, so I won't even ask. In fact, I'm inclined to agree, from what I've seen and heard. I believe you. But since I'm going to give you half your money in advance, how do I reassure myself that I haven't made a mistake?"

He turned now and faced them squarely. "I do it by taking you with me. I don't think for a moment you would sail in a ship or with a Captain you don't trust. If you go, it means you have faith in both and I know I haven't been misled."

"But I can't go!" Spanner Frew shouted in fury.

Walker paused. "Why not?"

"Because . . . because I'm a builder, not a sailor!"

"Agreed. That's mostly why I want you with me. Those repairs you spoke of earlier, the ones that would be required after an encounter with enemies or storms. I would feel better if you were supervising them."

The shipbuilder gestured expansively at the shore behind them. "I can't leave all these projects half completed! They need my skills here! There are others just as competent who can go in my place!"

"Leave them," Walker said calmly. "If they are as competent as you, let them complete your work here." He stepped forward, closing the distance between them until they were almost touching. Spanner Frew, his face flushed and scowling, held his ground. "I haven't told this to many, but I will tell it to you. What we go to do is more important than anything you will ever do here. What is required of those who do go is a courage and strength of will and heart that few possess. I think you are one. Don't disappoint me. Don't refuse me out of hand. Give some thought to what I'm saying before you make up your mind."

There was a momentary silence. Then Redden Alt Mer cleared his throat. "That sounds fair, Spanner."

The shipbuilder wheeled on him. "I don't care a whit what you think is fair or not, Big Red! This has nothing to do with you!"

"It has everything to do with him," Rue Meridian cut in sharply. She gave him a slow, mocking smile. "What's the matter, Black Beard? Have you grown old and timid?"

For just a moment, Walker thought the burly shipbuilder was going to explode. He stood there shaking with fury and frustration, his big hands knotted. "I wouldn't let anyone else alive speak to me like that!" he hissed at her.

A knife appeared in her hand as if by magic. She flipped it in the air above her, caught it, and made it vanish in the blink of an eye. "You used to be a pretty fair pirate, Spanner Frew," she prodded. "Wouldn't you like the chance to be one again? How long since you've sailed the Blue Divide?"

"How long since you've ridden the back of the wind to a new land?" her brother added. "It would make you young again, Spanner. The Druid's right. Come with us."

Rue Meridian looked at Walker. "You'll pay him, of course. The same as you'll pay Big Red and me."

She made it a statement of fact for him to affirm, and he did so with a nod. Spanner Frew looked from face to face in disbelief. "You're committed to this, aren't you?" he demanded of Walker.

The Druid nodded.

"Shades!" the shipbuilder breathed softly. Then abruptly he shrugged. "Well, let it lay for now. Let's sit for breakfast and see how we feel when we have full stomachs. I could eat a horse, saddle and all. Hah!" he roared, pounding his midsection. "Come along, you bunch of thieves! Trying to drag an honest man off on a voyage to nowhere! Trying to make a poor shipbuilder think he might have something to offer a clutch of madmen and madder women! Spare me, I hope you've not picked my purse, as well!"

He wheeled back in the direction of the settlement, shouting out epithets and protests as he went, leaving them to follow after.

They ate breakfast in a communal dining hall assembled beneath a huge tent, the cooking fires and pots all set toward the back of the enclosure where they could vent, the tables and benches toward the front. Everything had a makeshift, knockdown look to it, and when Walker asked Spanner Frew how long the settlement had been there, the shipbuilder advised him that they moved at least every other year to protect themselves. They were Rovers in the old tradition, and the nature of their lives and business dealings involved a certain amount of risk and required at least a modicum of secrecy. They valued anonymity and mobility, even when they weren't directly threatened by those who found them a nuisance or considered them enemies, and it made them feel more secure to shift periodically from one location to another. It wasn't difficult, the big man explained. There were dozens of coves like this one located up and down the coast, and only the equally reclusive and discreet Wing Riders knew them as well.

As they dined, Spanner Frew explained that those who worked and lived here frequently brought their families, and that the settlement provided housing and food for all. The younger members of the family were trained in the shipbuilding crafts or pressed into service in related pursuits. All contributed to the welfare of the community, and all were sworn to secrecy concerning the settlement's location and work. These were open secrets in the larger Rover community, but Rovers never revealed such things to outsiders unless first ascertaining that they were trustworthy. So it was that Walker would not have found Spanner Frew if Cicatrix had not first assured Redden Alt Mer of the Druid's character.

"Otherwise, you would have been approached in March Brume and a business deal struck there," the shipbuilder grunted around a mouthful of hash, "which, come to think of it, might have been just as well for me!"

Nevertheless, by the time breakfast was finished, Spanner Frew was talking as if he might be reconsidering his insistence on not going with Walker. He began cataloguing the supplies and equipment that would be required, advising as to where they might best be stored, mulling over the nature of the crew to be assembled, and weighing the role he might play as helmsman, a position he had mastered years earlier in his time at sea. He reassured Walker that Redden Alt Mer was the best airship Captain he knew and was the right choice for the journey. He said little about Rue Meridian, beyond commenting now and then on her enchanting looks and sharp tongue, but it was clear he believed brother and sister a formidable team. Walker said little, letting the garrulous shipbuilder carry the conversation, marking the looks that passed between the three, and taking mental notes on the way they interacted with one another.

"One thing I want understood from the beginning," Redden Alt Mer said at one point, addressing the Druid directly. "If we agree to accept you as expedition leader, you must agree in turn that as Captain I command aboard ship. All decisions regarding the operation of the vessel and the safety of the crew and passengers while in flight will be mine."

Neither Rue Meridian nor Spanner Frew showed any inclination to disagree. After a moment's consideration, Walker nodded, as well.

"In all things," he corrected gently, "save matters of destination and rate of progress. In those, you must give way to me. Where we go and how fast we get there is my province alone."

"Save where you endanger us, perhaps unknowingly," the other declared with a smile, unwilling to back down completely. "Then, you must heed my advice."

"Then," Walker replied, "we will talk."

They rowed out to the ship afterwards, and Spanner Frew walked them from bow to stern, explaining how she was constructed and what she could do. Walker studied closely the ship's configuration, from fighting ports to pilothouse, noting everything, asking questions when it was necessary, growing steadily more confident of the ship's ability to do what was needed. But already he was reassessing the amount of space he had determined would be available for use, realizing that more would be needed for weapons and supplies than he had anticipated. Consequently, he would have to scale down the number of expedition members. The crew was already pared down to a bare minimum, even with the addition of Spanner Frew. That meant he would have to reduce his complement of fighting men. The Elves would not like that, but there was no help for it. Forty men were too many. At best, they could take thirty-five, and even that would be crowding the living space.

He discussed this at length with the Rovers, trying to find a way to make better use of the available space. Redden Alt Mer said the crew could sleep above decks in hammocks strung between masts and railings, and Spanner Frew suggested they could reduce their supplies and equipment if they were willing to chance that foraging in the course of their travels would produce what was needed in the way of replacements. It was a balancing act, an educated guessing game at determining what would suffice, but Walker was somewhat reassured by the fact that they would have the aid of Wing Riders for foraging purposes and so could afford to take chances they might otherwise never have considered.

By the close of the day, they had settled on what was needed in the way of onboard adjustments and compiled a list of supplies and equipment to be secured. A crew of Redden Alt Mer's choosing would be found in the surrounding seaports and could be readily assembled. Ship, Captain, and crew, Spanner Frew included, could be in Arborlon within a week.

Walker was satisfied. Everything was proceeding as he had hoped. After a good night's sleep, he would depart for March Brume.

But he was to get little rest that night.

The attack on the settlement came just before sunset. A sentry perched high on a cliff overlooking the cove blew a ram's horn in warning, three sharp blasts that shattered the twilight calm and sent everyone scurrying. By the time the dark hulls of the airships hove into view through the gap in the cove entry, sailing out of the glare of the setting sun, the Rover women and children and old people were already fleeing into the forests and mountains and the Rover men were preparing to defend them.

But the attacking ships outnumbered those of the Rovers by more than two to one, and they were already airborne and readied for their strike. They streamed through the harbor entrance in a dark line, flying less than a hundred feet above the water, railings and fighting ports bristling with men and weapons. Fire from casks of pitch and catapults rained down on the exposed vessels and their crews. Spears and arrows filled the air. Half of the Rover ships burned and sank before their sails could even be hoisted. Dozens of men died in the ensuing conflagrations and many more died in the small boats attempting to reach them.

Solely by chance, Walker and his three Rover companions were spared the fate of so many. Just before the attack arrived, they had been testing the responsiveness of their ship. As a result, they were still aboard when the warning was given, light sheaths yet unfurled, radian draws in place, and the anchor barely down. The Rovers acted instantly, leaping to tighten the stays and reset the draws, cutting the anchor with a sword stroke, and casting off. In seconds, they were airborne, lifting toward their attackers like a swift, black bird. Even with only three hands to sail her, she responded with a quickness and agility that left the enemy ships looking as if they were standing still.

A safety line secured about his waist, Walker crouched just in front of the pilothouse and behind the forward mast and watched the land and water spin away in a dizzying rush. With Spanner Frew and Rue Meridian manning the starboard and port draws respectively, Redden Alt Mer wheeled their sleek craft recklessly through the dark line of attackers, nearly colliding with those nearest. The hulls of ships loomed on either side, sliding past like night phantoms, great massive ghosts at hunt. Some passed so close that Walker could identify the Federation uniforms worn by the soldiers who knelt in the fighting ports firing their arrows and launching their spears.

"Hold tight!" Alt Mer shouted down to him from atop his precarious station, hauling back on the steering levers to gain more height and speed.

Missiles flew everywhere, dark projectiles against the twin glows of the sunset and the fires in the harbor. Walker flattened himself against the rough wall of the pilothouse, protecting his back. He did not want to use magic. If he did, he would reveal his presence, and he thought it best not to do so. To his right, crouched deep in one of the fighting ports, so close to the nearest ship that he could have reached out and touched it, Spanner Frew was cursing loudly under a hail of bow fire. Across from him, Rue Meridian was dashing recklessly from draw to draw, miraculously avoiding the barrage of arrows that sailed all around her, dark face grim and determined as she set the lines.

Their wild, hair-raising escape was punctuated by the underside of their ship raking across the mastheads of the last attacker as they finally gained the safety of the open skies. All about them, the remaining Rover airships were fleeing into the darkness, skimming across the cliff tops, and disappearing down the coast. Below, their attackers were descending on the settlement buildings, setting fire to everything, and driving the last of the residents into the surrounding forests. Masts jutting sharply against the flaming debris, dark hulls glided everywhere.

As their vessel steadied and their passage smoothed, Rue Meridian appeared at Walker's side. "Those were Federation ships!" she snapped angrily. Her face was streaked with soot and sweat. "They must be madder at us than I thought! All those people driven out or killed, their ships and homes burned, just to make a point?"

Walker shook his head. "I don't think it was you they were after." He caught her startled gaze and held it. "Nor do I think it was the Federation who was behind this witch hunt."

She hesitated a moment, then let her breath out in a long, slow hiss of understanding.

Behind them, hidden by the cliffs they were fleeing and reduced to a reddish-yellow glow against the darkness of night, Rover buildings burned unhindered to the ground and gutted airships sank into the deep.

THIRTEEN

Provisioned and readied, Bek Rowe and Quentin Leah departed at daybreak and rode east through the Highlands. The day was cool and clear, with the smell of new grass and flowers heavy on the scented air and the sun warm on their faces. Clouds were massing west, however, and there was a clear possibility of rain by nightfall. Under the best of conditions it would take them several days just to navigate as far as the Eastland and the beginning of their search for the mysterious Truls Rohk. In the old days, before invasion and occupation by the Federation army, they could never have gone this way. Directly in their path lay the Lowlands of Clete, a vast, dismal bog choked with deadwood and scrub, shrouded in mist and devoid of life. Beyond that were the Black Oaks, an immense forest that had claimed more victims than either of the young men cared to count, most to mishap and starvation, but some, in earlier times, to the huge wolves that were once its fiercest denizens. All this was daunting enough, but even after navigating bog and woods, a traveler wasn't safe. Just east of the Black Oaks was the Mist Marsh, a treacherous swamp in which, it was rumored, creatures of enormous power and formidable magic prowled. Below the marsh, and running south for a hundred miles, were the Battlemound Lowlands, another rugged, difficult stretch of country populated by Sirens, deadly plants that could lure and hypnotize by mimicking voices and shapes, seize with tentacle-like roots, paralyze with flesh-numbing needles, and devour their victims at leisure.

None of this was anything the cousins wanted to encounter, but all were difficult to avoid in making passage below the Rainbow Lake. Any route that would take them above the Rainbow Lake would cost them an additional three days at least and involved dangers of their own. Traveling farther south required a detour of better than a hundred miles and would put them almost to the Prekkendorran, a place no one in his right mind wanted to be.

But the Federation had realized this, as well, during the time of its occupation of Leah and so had built roads through Clete and the Black Oaks to facilitate the movement of men and supplies. Many of these roads had fallen into disrepair and could no longer be used by wagons, but all were passable by men on horseback. Quentin, because he was the older of the two, had explored more thoroughly the lands they intended to pass through, and was confident they could find their way to the Anar without difficulty.

True to his prediction, they made good progress that first day. By midday, they had ridden out of the Highlands and into the dismal morass of Clete. Sun and sky disappeared and the cousins were buried beneath a dismal gray shroud of mist and gloom. But the road remained visible, and they pressed on. Their pace slowed as the terrain grew more treacherous, scrub and tree limbs closing in so that they were forced to duck and weave as they went, guiding their horses around encroaching pools of quicksand and bramble patches, picking their way resolutely through the haze. Shadows moved all about them, some cast by movements of light, others by things that had somehow managed to survive in this blasted land. They heard sounds, but the sounds were not identifiable. Their conversation died away and time slowed. Their concentration narrowed to keeping safely on the road.

But by the approach of nightfall, they had navigated the lowlands without incident and moved into the forbidding darkness of the Black Oaks. The road here was less uneven and better traveled, the way open and clear as they rode into a steadily lengthening maze of shadows. With twilight's fall, they stopped within a clearing and made camp for the night. A fire was built, a meal prepared and eaten, and bedding laid out. The cousins joked and laughed and told stories for a time, then rolled into their blankets and fell asleep.

Sleep lasted until just after midnight, when it began to rain so hard that the clearing was flooded in a matter of minutes. Bek and Quentin snatched up their gear and retreated to the shelter of a large conifer, covering themselves with their travel cloaks as they sat beneath a canopy of feathery branches and watched the rain sweep through unabated.

By morning they were stiff and sore and not very well rested, but they resumed their travels without complaint. In other circumstances, they would have come better equipped, but neither had wanted the burden of pack animals and supplies, and so they were traveling light. A few nights of damp and cold were tolerable in the course of a week's passage if it meant shaving a few days off their traveling time. They ate a cold breakfast, then rode all morning through the Black Oaks, and by afternoon the rain had abated and they had reached the Battlemound. Here they turned south, unwilling to chance crossing through any part of the Mist Marsh, content to detour below the swamp and come out to the east, where they would turn north again and ride until they reached the Silver River.

By sunset, they had succeeded in accomplishing their goal, avoiding Sirens and other pitfalls, keeping to the roadway until it meandered off south, then sticking to the open ground of the lowlands as the terrain changed back to forests and low hills and they could see the glittering ribbon of the river ahead. Finding shelter in a grove of cottonwood and beech, they made camp on its banks, the ground sufficiently dry that they could lay out their bedding and build a fire. They watered and fed the horses and rubbed them down. Then they made dinner for themselves and, after eating it, sat facing out toward the river and the night, sipping cups of ale as they talked.

"I wish we knew more about Truls Rohk," Bek ventured after the conversation had been going on for a time. "Why do you think Walker told us so little about him?"

Quentin contemplated the star-filled sky thoughtfully. "Well, he told us where to go to find him. He said all we had to do was ask and he would be there. Seems like enough to me."

"It might be enough for you, but not for me. It doesn't tell us anything about why we're looking for him. How come he's so important?" Bek was not about to be appeased. "If we're to persuade him to come with us to Arborlon, shouldn't we know why he's needed? What if he doesn't want to come? What are we supposed to do then?"

Quentin grinned cheerfully. "Pack up and go on. It isn't our problem if he chooses to stay behind." He grimaced. "See, there you go again, Bek, worrying when there isn't any reason for it."

"So you're fond of telling me. So I'll tell you something else that's worrying me. I don't trust Walker."

They stared at each other in the darkness without speaking, the fire beginning to burn down, the sounds of the night lifting out of the sudden silence. "What do you mean?" Quentin asked slowly. "You think he's lying to us?"

"No." Bek shook his head emphatically. "If I thought that, I wouldn't be here. No, I don't think he's that sort. But I do think he knows something he's not telling us. Maybe a lot of somethings. Think about it, Quentin. How did he know about you and the

Sword of Leah? He knew you had it before he even talked to us. How did he find out? Has he been keeping an eye on you all these years, waiting for a chance to summon you on a quest? How did he manage to convince your father to let us go with him, when your father wouldn't even consider your request to fight for the Free-born?"

He stopped abruptly. He wanted to tell Quentin what Coran had said about his parentage. He wanted to ask Quentin why he thought Coran hadn't said a word about it until the Druid appeared. He wanted to ask his cousin if he had any idea how the Druid had ended up ferrying him to the Leah doorstep in the first place, not a task a Druid would normally undertake.

But he was not prepared to talk about any of this just yet; he was still mulling it over, trying to decide how he felt about it before sharing what he knew.

"I think you're right," Quentin said suddenly, surprising him. "I think the Druid's keeping secrets from us, not the least of which is where we're going and why. But I've listened to you expound on Druids and their history often enough to know that this is normal behavior for them. They know things we don't, and they keep the information mostly to themselves. Why should that trouble you? Why not just let things unfold in the way they're intended rather than worry about it? Look at me. I'm carrying a sword that's supposed to be magic. I'm supposed to trust blindly in a weapon that's never shown a moment's inclination to be more than what it seems."

"That's different," Bek insisted.

"No, it isn't." Quentin laughed and rocked back onto his elbows, stretching out his long legs. "It's all the same thing. You can live your life worrying about what you don't know, or you can accept your limitations and make the best of it. Secrets don't harm you, Bek. It's fussing about them that does you in."

Bek gave him a disbelieving look. "That's entirely wrong. Secrets can do a great deal of harm."

"All right, let me approach it another way." Quentin drained off his ale and sat forward again. "How much can you accomplish worrying about secrets that may not exist? Especially when you have no idea what they are?"

"I know. I know." Bek sighed. "But at least I'm prepared for the fact that some nasty surprises might lie ahead. At least I'm ready for what I think is going to happen down the road. And by keeping an eye on Walker, I won't be caught off guard by his shadings of the truth and purposeful omissions."

"Great. You're prepared and you won't be fooled. Me, too, believe it or not—even if I don't worry about it as much as you." Quentin looked off into the darkness, where a shooting star streaked across the firmament and disappeared. "But you can't prepare against everything, Bek, and you can't save yourself from being fooled now and then. The fact is, no matter what you do, no matter how hard you try, sometimes your efforts fall short."

Bek looked at him and said nothing. True enough, he was thinking, but he didn't care for the implications.

He slept undisturbed by rain and cold that night, the skies clear and the air warm, and he did not dream or toss. Even so, he woke in the deep sleep hours of early morning, bathed in starlight and infused by a feeling of uneasiness. The fire had burned itself out and lay cold and gray. Beside him, Quentin was snoring, wrapped in his blankets. Bek did not know how long he had been asleep, but the moon was down and the forest about him was silent and black.

He rose without thinking, looking around cautiously as he did so, trying to pinpoint the source of his discomfort. There seemed to be no reason for it. He pulled on his great cloak, wrapping himself tightly against a sudden chill, and walked down to the banks of the Silver River. The river was swollen with spring rains and snowmelt off the Runne Mountains, but its progress this night was sluggish and steady and its surface clear of debris. As he stood there, a night bird swooped down and glided into the trees, a silent, purposeful shadow. He started at the unexpected movement, then quieted once more. Carefully, he studied the glittering surface of the waters, searching for what troubled him, then shifted his attention to the far bank and the shadowed trees. Still nothing. He took a deep breath and exhaled. Perhaps he had been mistaken.

He was turning back toward Quentin when he saw the light. It was just a glimmer of brightness at first, as if a spark had been struck somewhere back in the trees across the river. He stared at it in surprise as it appeared, faded, reappeared, faded anew, then steadied and came on. It bobbed slightly with its approach to the river, then glided out of the trees, suspended on air and floating free as it crossed the water and came to a halt just yards away from him.

It flashed sharply in his eyes, and he blinked in response. When his vision cleared, a young girl stood before him, the light balanced in her hand. She was somehow familiar to him, although he could not say why. She was beautiful, with long dark hair and startling blue eyes, and there was an innocence to her face that made his heart ache. The light she held emanated from one end of a polished metal cylinder and cast a long, narrow beam on the ground between them.

"Well met, Bek Rowe," she said softly. "Do you know me?"

He stared, unable to answer. She had appeared out of nowhere, perhaps come from across the river on the air itself, and he believed her to be a creature of magic.

"You have chosen to undertake a long and difficult journey, Bek," she whispered in her childlike voice. "You go to a place where few others have gone and from which only one has returned. But the greater journey will not carry you over land and sea, but inside your heart. The unknown you fear and the secrets you suspect will reveal themselves. All will be as it must. Accept this, for that is the nature of things."

"Who are you?" he whispered.

"This and that. What you see before you and many things you do not. I am a chameleon of time and age, my true form so old I have forgotten it. For you, I am two things. The child you see and think you might perhaps know, and this."

Abruptly, the child before him transformed into something so hideous he would have screamed if his voice had not frozen in his throat. The thing was huge and twisted and ugly, all wrapped in scarred and ravaged skin, hair burnt to a black stubble about its head and face, eyes maddened and red, mouth twisted in a leer that suggested horrors too terrible to contemplate. It loomed over him, tall even when bent, its clawed and crooked hands gesturing hypnotically.

"Thiss am I, too, Bek. Thiss creature of the pitss. Would you ssee me thiss way or the other? Hsss. Which do you prefer?"

"Change back," Bek managed to whisper, his voice harsh, his throat gone dry and raw and tight with fear.

"Sso, foundling of ill fortune. What are you willing to do to make it happen? Hsss. How much of yoursself are you prepared to ssacrifisse to make it sso?"

The thing almost touched him, claws brushing against the front of his tunic. He would have run if he could, would have called out to Quentin, sleeping not fifty feet away. But he could do nothing, only stand in place and stare fixedly at the apparition before him.

"Yourss iss the power to change me from one to the other," the creature hissed. "Do not forget thiss. Do not forget. Hsss."

Once more the creature transformed in the blink of an eye, and Bek found himself looking into the kind, pale eyes of an old, weathered man.

"Do not be afraid, Bek Rowe," the old man said softly, his voice warm and reassuring. "Nothing comes to harm you this night. I am here to protect you. Do you know me now?"

Surprisingly, he did. "You are the King of the Silver River."

The old man nodded approvingly. A legend in the Four Lands, a myth whose reality only a few had ever encountered, the King of the Silver River was a spirit creature, a magical being who had survived from times long before even the Great Wars had destroyed the world. He was as old as the Word, it was said, a creature who had been born into and survived the passing of Faerie. He lived within and gave protection to the Silver River country. Now and then, a traveler would encounter him, and sometimes when it was needed, he would give them aid.

"Heed me, Bek," the old man said softly. "What I have shown you is the past and the present. What remains to be determined is the future. That future belongs to you. You are both more and less than you believe, an enigma whose secret will affect the lives of many. Do not shy from discovering what you must, what you feel compelled to know. Do not be deterred in your search. Go where your heart tells you. Trust in what it reveals."

Bek nodded, not certain he understood, but unwilling to admit as much.

"Past, present, and future, the symbiosis of our lives," the old man continued quietly, gently. "Our birth, our life, our death, all tied into a single package that we spend our time on this earth unwrapping. Sometimes we see clearly what it is we are looking at. Sometimes we do not. Sometimes things happen to distract or deceive us, and we must look more carefully at what it is we hold."

He reached into his robes then and produced a chain from which hung a strange, silver-colored stone. He held up the stone for Bek to see. "This is a phoenix stone. When you are most lost, it will help you find your way. Not just from what you cannot see with your eyes, but from what you cannot find with your heart, as well. It will show you the way back from dark places into which you have strayed and the way forward through dark places into which you must go. When you have need of it, remove it from the chain and cast it to the ground, breaking it apart. Remember. In your body, heart, and mind—all will be revealed with this."

He passed the stone and its chain to Bek, who took it carefully. The depths of the phoenix stone seemed liquid, swirling as if a dark pool into which he might fall. He touched the surface gingerly, testing it. The movement stopped and the surface turned opaque.

"You may use it only once," the old man advised. "Keep it concealed from others. It is an indiscriminate magic. It will serve the bearer, even if stolen. Keep it safe."

Bek slipped the chain about his neck and tucked the stone into his clothing. "I will," he promised.

His mind was racing, trying to find words for the dozens of questions that suddenly filled it. But he could not seem to think straight, his concentration riveted on the old man and the light. The King of the Silver River watched him with his kind, appraising eyes, but did not offer to help.

"Who am I?" Bek blurted out in desperation.

He spoke without thinking, the words surfacing in a rush of need and urgency. It was this question that troubled him most, he realized at once, this question that demanded an answer above all others, because it had become for him in the last few days the great mystery of his life.

The old man gestured vaguely with one frail hand. "You are who you have always been, Bek. But your past is lost to you, and you must recover it. On this journey, that will happen. Seek it, and it will find you. Embrace it, and it will set you free."

Bek was not certain he had heard the old man right. What had he just said? Seek it, and it will find you—not, you will find it? What did that mean?

But the King of the Silver River was speaking again, cutting short Bek's thoughts. "Sleep, now. Take what I have given you and rest. No more can be accomplished this night, and you will need your strength for what lies ahead."

He gestured again, and Bek felt a great weariness descend. "Remember my words when you wake," the old man cautioned as he began to move away, the light wavering, back and forth, back and forth. "Remember."

The night was suddenly as warm and comforting in its darkness and silence as his bedroom at home. There was so much more that Bek wanted to ask, so much he would have known. But he was lying on the ground, his eyes heavy and his thinking clouded. "Wait," he managed to whisper.

But the King of the Silver River was fading away into the night, and Bek Rowe drifted off to sleep.

FOURTEEN

When Bek woke the next morning, he was back where he had started the night before, rolled into his blankets next to the defunct fire. It took him several minutes to shake off his confusion and decide that what he remembered about the King of the Silver River was real. It felt as if he had dreamed it, the events hazy and disjointed in his mind. But when he checked inside his tunic, there were the chain and phoenix stone, tucked safely away, just where he had put them before falling asleep.

He sleepwalked through breakfast and cleanup, thinking he should say something about the encounter to Quentin, but unable to bring himself to do so. It was a pattern he was developing with the events surrounding this journey, and it worried him. Normally, he shared everything with his cousin. They were close and trusted each other. But now he had kept from Quentin both his conversation with Coran and his midnight encounter with the being that claimed to be the King of the Silver River. Not to mention, he amended quickly, his possession of the phoenix stone. He wasn't entirely sure why he was doing this, but it had something to do with wanting to come to terms with the information himself before he shared it with anyone else.

He supposed that he was being overly cautious and perhaps even selfish, but the greater truth was that he was feeling confused and somewhat unnerved by all of this happening at once. It was difficult enough coming to grips with the idea of making a journey that would take him halfway around the world. This was Quentin's dream, not his. It was Quentin, with his sword of magic and his great courage, of whom the Druid Walker had need, and not Bek. Bek had agreed to go out of loyalty to his cousin and a rather fatalistic acceptance of the fact that if he stayed behind, he would be second-guessing himself forever. It was only in these recent developments with Coran and the King of the Silver River that he began to wonder if perhaps he had his own place on the expedition, a place he had never even imagined might exist.

So he kept what he knew to himself as they ate their food and packed their gear and set out once more, into a day that was bright and sunny. Loose and easy as always, Quentin joked and laughed and told stories as they rode, leaving Bek to play the role of the audience and to simmer in his own uncertainty. They rode upstream along the banks of the Silver River through a morning filled with spring smells and birdsong, through a backdrop of mingled green hues splashed with clusters of colorful wildflowers and the glint of sunlight off the river. They sighted fishermen seated on the banks of the river and anchored in skiffs just offshore in quiet coves, and they passed travelers on the road, mostly tradesmen and peddlers on their way between villages. The warm day seemed to infect everyone with a spirit of good humor, inviting smiles and waves and cheerful greetings from all.

By midday, the cousins had forded the Silver River just west of where it disappeared into the deep forests of the Anar and were traveling north along the treeline. It was a short journey from there to the Dwarf village of Depo Bent, a trading outpost nestled in the shadow of the Wolfsktaag, and the sun was still high when they arrived. Depo Bent was little more than a cluster of homes, warehouses, and shops sprung up around a clearing in the woods that opened up at the end of the sole road leading in or out from the plains. It was there that Bek and Quentin were to ask for Truls Rohk, although they had no idea of whom they were supposed to make inquiry.

They began their undertaking by leaving their horses at a stable where the owner promised a rubdown and feeding and watering. Bluff and to the point, in the way of Dwarves, he agreed for a small extra charge to store their gear. Freed of horses and equipment, the cousins walked to a tavern and enjoyed a hearty lunch of stew, bread, and ale. The tavern was visited mostly by the Dwarves of the village, but no one paid them any attention. Quentin was wearing the Sword of Leah strapped across his back in the fashion of Highlanders, and both wore Highlander clothing, but if the residents found it curious that the cousins were so far from home, they kept it to themselves.

"Truls Rohk must be a Dwarf," Quentin ventured as they ate. "No one else would be living here. Maybe he's a trapper of some sort."

Bek nodded agreeably, but he couldn't quite fathom why Walker would want a trapper on their journey.

After lunch, they began asking where they could find the man they were looking for and promptly discovered that no one knew. They started with the tavern's barkeep and owner and worked their way up and down the street from shop to warehouse, and everyone looked at them blankly. No one knew a man named Truls Rohk. No one had ever heard the name.

"Guess maybe he doesn't live here after all," Quentin conceded after more than twenty unsuccessful inquiries.

"Guess maybe he's not going to be as easy to find as Walker led us to believe," Bek grumbled.

Nevertheless, they pressed on, continuing their search, moving from one building to the next, the afternoon slipping slowly away from them. Eventually they had worked their way back around to the stables where they had left their horses and supplies. The stableman was nowhere in sight, but a solid-looking Dwarf dressed in woodsman's garb was sitting on a bench out front, whittling on a piece of wood. As the cousins approached, he glanced up, then set aside his knife and carving and rose.

"Quentin Leah?" he asked in a way that suggested he already knew the answer. Quentin nodded, and the Dwarf stuck out his gnarled hand. "I'm Panax. I'm your guide."

"Our guide?" Quentin repeated, extending his own hand in response. He winced at the other's grip. "You're taking us to Truls Rohk?"

The Dwarf nodded. "After a fashion."

"How did you know we were coming?" Bek asked in surprise.

"You must be Bek Rowe." Panax extended his hand a second time, and Bek shook it firmly. "Our mutual friend sent word. Now and then I do favors for him. There's a few of us he trusts enough to ask when he needs one." He glanced around idly. "Let's move somewhere less public while we talk this over."

They followed him down the road to a patch of shade where a clutch of weathered benches was grouped around an old well that hadn't seen much use lately. Panax gestured them to one bench while he took a second across from them. It was quiet and cool beneath the trees, and the traffic on the road and in the village suddenly seemed far away.

"Have you eaten?" he asked. He was a rough-featured, bearded man, no longer young. Deep lines furrowed his forehead, and his skin was browned and weathered from sun and wind. Whatever he did, he did it outdoors and had been at it for quite a while. "You look a little footsore," he observed.

"That's probably because we've tramped all over this village searching for Truls Rohk," Bek said sourly.

The Dwarf nodded. "I doubt that anyone in Depo Bent even knows who he is. If they do, they don't know him by his name." His brown eyes had a distant look, as if they were seeing beyond what was immediately visible.

Bek glared openly. "You could have saved us a lot of trouble by finding us sooner."

"I haven't been here all that long myself." Panax seemed unruffled. "I don't live in the village, I live in the mountains. When I got word you were coming, I came down to find you." He shrugged. "I knew you'd be back for your horses sooner or later, so I decided to wait for you at the stables."

Bek would have said more on the matter, but Quentin cut him short. "How much do you know about what's going on, Panax? Do you know what we're doing here?"

Panax snorted. "Walker is a Druid. A Druid doesn't feel it necessary to tell anyone more than what he feels they absolutely have to know."

Quentin smiled, unperturbed. "Do you think Truls Rohk knows more than you do?"

"Less." Panax shook his head, amused. "You don't know anything about him, do you?"

"Just that we're supposed to deliver a message from Walker," Bek said rather more sharply than he intended. He took a steadying breath. "I have to tell you that I don't like all this secrecy. How is anyone supposed to make a decision about anything if there's no information to be considered?"

The Dwarf laughed, a deep, booming sound. "You mean, how is Truls supposed to give you an answer to whatever question you're bringing from Walker? Hah! Highlander, that's not what you're doing here! Oh, I know you're carrying a message from the Druid. Let me guess. He wants you to tell Truls something about what he's up to now and see if Truls wants to be a part of it. Is that about right?"

He looked so smug that Bek wanted to tell him it wasn't, but Quentin was already nodding agreeably. "You have to understand something," Panax continued. "Truls doesn't care what Walker is up to. If he feels like going with him, which he usually does, he will. It doesn't take you two coming all the way here to determine that. No, Walker sent you here for something else."

Bek exchanged a quick glance with Quentin. To test the power of the Sword of Leah, Bek was thinking. To put them in a situation that would measure their determination and toughness. Suddenly, Bek was very worried. What sort of challenge were they being asked to measure up to?

"Maybe we should go talk with Truls Rohk right now," he suggested quickly, wanting to get on with things.

But the Dwarf shook his head. "We can't do that. First off, he won't be out until after dark. He doesn't do anything in the daylight. So we have to wait until nightfall. Second, it isn't a matter of going to him to have our talk. He has to come to us. We could hunt for him until next summer and never catch even a glimpse." He gave Bek a wink. "He's up in those mountains behind us, running with things you and I don't want anything to do with, believe me."

Bek shivered at the implication. He had heard stories of the things that lived in the Wolfsktaag, creatures out of myth and legend, nightmares come to life. They couldn't hurt you if you were careful, but a single misstep could lead to disaster.

"Tell us something about Truls Rohk," Quentin asked quietly.

Panax regarded him solemnly for about two heartbeats and then smiled almost gently. "I think I'd better wait and let you see for yourselves."

He changed the subject then, asking them for news about the Southland and the war between the Federation and the Free-born, listening intently to their answers and comments as he resumed work on the carving he had been shaping while awaiting their return to the stables. Bek was fascinated by the Dwarf's ability to divide his attention so completely between the tasks. His eyes were focused on the speakers, but his hands continued to whittle at the piece of wood with his knife. His blocky, solid body settled into a comfortable position and never shifted, still save for the careful, precise movement of his hands and the occasional nod of his bearded head. He might have been there or gone somewhere else entirely inside his head; it was impossible to tell.

After a time, he placed the carving on the bench next to him, a finished piece, a bird in flight, perfectly realized. Without so much as a glance at it, he reached into his tunic, produced a second piece of wood, and went back to work. When Bek managed to work up sufficient courage to ask him what he did for a living, he deflected the question with a shrug.

"Oh, a little of this and a little of that." His bluff face was wreathed momentarily in an enigmatic smile. "I do some guiding for those who need help getting through the mountains."

Who, Bek wondered, would need help getting through the Wolfsktaag? Not the people who lived in this part of the world, the Dwarves and Gnomes who knew enough to avoid passing that way. Not the hunters and trappers who made their living off the forests of the Anar, who would choose better and safer working grounds. Not anyone who led a normal life, because there was no reason for those people to be here in the first place.

He must guide people like us, he concluded, who needed to go into the mountains to find someone like Truls Rohk. But how many like us can there be?

As if reading his thoughts, the Dwarf glanced at him and said, "Not many people, even Dwarves, know their way through these mountains—not well enough to know all the pitfalls and how to avoid them. I know because Truls Rohk taught me. He saved my life, and while I was healing from my wounds, he instructed me. Perhaps he thought he owed it to me to help me find a way to stay alive when I left him."

He stood up, stretched, and picked up his carvings. He handed the bird to Bek. "It's yours. Good luck against the things that frighten you now and again. Like a good carving, such things can be better understood when we give them shape and form. Whatever undertaking Walker has in store for you, you'll need all the protection you can get."

He started away without waiting for their response. "Time to be going. My place, first, then up into the mountains. We should be there by midnight and back again by sunrise. Take what you need for the hike in and leave the rest here. It'll be safe."

Bek tucked the carving into his tunic, and the cousins followed after obediently.

They walked out of Depo Bent and up into the shallow foothills fronting the peaks of the Wolfsktaag, the shadows lengthening before them as the sun settled into the west and twilight descended. The air cooled and the light failed, and a crescent moon appeared overhead to the north. They proceeded at a steady pace, climbing gradually out of the flats into more rugged country. Within a short while, the village had disappeared into the trees, and the trail had faded. Panax led the way, head up and eyes alert, giving no indication of having to think about where he was going, saying nothing to either of them. Bek and Quentin kept silent in turn, studying the forest around them, listening to the sounds of the approaching night begin to filter out of the twilight's hush—the cries of night birds, the buzz of insects, and the occasional huff or snort of something bigger. Nothing threatened, but the Wolfsktaag loomed ahead like a black wall, craggy and forbidding, its reputation a haunt at play in their minds.

It was fully dark by the time they reached Panax's cabin, a small, neat shelter built of logs and set back in a clearing near the crest of the foothills, well out of sight. A stream ran nearby, one they could hear but not see, and the trees formed a sheltering wall against the weather. Panax left them standing outside while he went into his home, then reappeared almost immediately carrying a sling looped through his belt and a long-handled double-edged battle-ax laid comfortably over one shoulder.

"Stay close to me and do whatever I tell you," he advised as he came up to them. "If we're attacked, use your weapons to defend yourselves, but don't go looking for trouble and don't become separated from me. Understood?"

They nodded uneasily. Attacked by what? Bek wanted to ask.

They left the cabin and the clearing behind, hiked through the trees to the lower slopes of the mountains, and began to climb. The way was unmarked, but Panax seemed to know it well. He took them in switchback fashion through clumps of boulders, stands of old growth, and shadowy ravines and defiles, steadily ascending the Wolfsktaag's rugged slopes. The night sky was clear and bright with moon and stars, and there was sufficient light to navigate by. They climbed for several hours, growing more alert as the trees began to thin, the rocks to broaden, and the silence to deepen. It grew colder, as well, the mountain air thin and sharp even on this wind-less night, and they could watch their breath cloud before them. Shadows passed overhead in smooth, silent flight, night hunters at work, secretive and swift.

Bek found himself thinking of his own life, a past wrapped in vague possibility and shrouded in concealments. Who was he, that a Druid had brought him to Coran Leah's doorstep all those years ago? Not just the orphaned scion of a relative with a family no one had ever heard anything about. Not just a homeless child. Who was he, that the King of the Silver River would appear so unexpectedly to give him a phoenix stone and a warning of dark and hidden meanings?

He found himself remembering all the times he had asked about his parents and had his questions deflected by Coran or Liria. Their actions had never seemed all that important before. It was bother-some sometimes not to be given the answers he sought, to be put off in his inquiries. But his life had been good with Quentin's family, and his curiosity had never been compelling enough to persuade him to insist on a better response. Now he wondered if he had been too accepting.

Or was he making something out of nothing, his parentage no more than what it had always seemed—an accident of birth of no consequence at all, incidental to his upbringing at the capable hands of his stepparents? Was he looking for secrets that didn't exist, simply because Walker had appeared in Leah so unexpectedly?

The night deepened and swelled with cold and silence, and their efforts to climb higher slowed. Then a gap opened in a cliff face, and they were passing through a deep defile into a valley beyond. There the forest was thick and sheltering, and what lived within could only be imagined. Panax continued on, his thoughts his own. The defile opened into a draw that angled down onto the valley floor. Beyond, the peaks of the Wolfsktaag rose in stark relief against the moonlit sky, sentries standing watch, each a little more misted and a little less clear than the one before.

Within the valley's center, Panax called an unexpected halt in a small clearing hemmed in by towering elm. "We will need to wait here."

Bek glanced around at the encroaching shadows. "How long?"

"Until Truls notices we've come." He laid down his ax and moved toward the shadows. "Help me build a fire."

They gathered deadwood and used tinder and flint to strike a spark and coax a flame to life. The fire built swiftly and threw light across the open space of the clearing, but could not penetrate the wall of shadows beyond. If anything, it seemed to emphasize how isolated the travelers were. The burning wood crackled and popped as it was consumed, but the surrounding night remained silent and enigmatic. The Dwarf and the Highland cousins sat in silence on the ground, backed up against each other so that they could share the warmth and watch the shadows. Now and again, one of them would add fuel to the blaze from the small pile of wood collected earlier, keeping the clearing lit and the signal steady.

"He might not be in the valley tonight," Panax said at one point, shifting against Bek so that the youth was bent forward under the weight of his stocky frame. "He might not return until morning."

"Does he live here?" Quentin asked.

"As much as he lives anywhere. He doesn't have a cabin or a

camp. He doesn't keep possessions or even stash his food for when he might have need of it." The Dwarf paused, reflecting. "He isn't anything at all like you and me."

He let the matter drop, and neither Quentin nor Bek chose to pursue it. Whatever the cousins were going to learn would have to await the other's appearance. Bek, for one, was growing less and less certain that this was an event he should anticipate. Perhaps they would all be better off if the night passed, morning arrived, and nothing happened. Perhaps they would be better off if they let the matter drop here and now.

"I was just twenty when I met him," Panax said suddenly, his gruff voice quiet and low. "Hard to remember what that was like now, but I was young and full of myself and just learning that I wanted to be a guide and spend my time away from the settlements. I'd been alone for a while. I'd left home young and stayed gone, not missing it much, not thinking I should have reconsidered. I was always apart from everyone else, even my brothers, and it was probably a relief to everyone when I wasn't there anymore."

He glanced over his shoulder at Bek. "I was a little like you, cautious and doubtful, not about to be tricked or misled, knowing enough to take care of myself, but not much yet about the world. I'd heard the stories about the Wolfsktaag and decided to go there to see for myself. I thought that lying as it did across the backbone of the Eastland it would have to be crossed frequently enough that a guide could earn a living. So I tied in with some men who did this, but who didn't know as much as they pretended. I made a few crossings with them and lived to tell about it. After a year or two, I struck out on my own. Thought I'd be better off alone.

"Then one day I got myself so lost I couldn't find my way out. I was exploring, trying to teach myself how the passes connected, how the crossings could best be made. I knew something of the things that lived in the Wolfsktaag, having learned of them from the older guides, having seen most of them for myself. Some, you never saw, of course—unless you were unlucky. Most could be avoided or driven off, at least the ones made of flesh and blood. The ones that were spirit or wraith you had to stay clear of or hide from, and you could learn to do that. But this time I forgot to pay attention. I got lost and desperate, and I made a mistake."

He sighed and shook his head. "It hurts to admit it, even now. I backtracked into a stretch of land I knew I shouldn't go into, thinking I could do so just long enough to get clear of the mess I was in. I fell and twisted my ankle badly enough that I could barely walk. It was almost nightfall, and when it got dark enough, a werebeast came for me."

The fire snapped loudly, and Bek jumped in spite of himself. Werebeasts. They were something of a legend in the Southland, one half believed in by most, but seen only by a few. Part animal, part spirit, difficult even to recognize, let alone defend against, they fed off your fear and took shape from your imagination and almost nothing could stand against them, not even the great moor cats. The possibility that they might encounter one here was not comforting. "I thought they only lived in the deep Anar, farther east and north."

Panax nodded. "Once, maybe. Times change. Anyway, the werebeast attacked, and I did battle with it for most of the night. I fought so long and so hard I don't think I even knew what I was doing in the end. It changed shape on me repeatedly, and it tore me up pretty good. But I held my ground, backed up against a tree, too stubborn to know that I couldn't possibly win that sort of contest, growing weaker and more tired with every rush."

He stopped talking and stared off into the dark. The cousins waited, thinking him lost in thought, perhaps remembering. Then abruptly he came to his feet, battle-ax gripped in both hands.

"Something's moving out there—" he started to say.

A fleet, dark shape hurtled out of the night, followed by a second and then a third. It seemed as if the shadows themselves had come alive, taking form and gathering substance. Panax was knocked to the ground, grunting with the force of the blow he was struck. Quentin and Bek rolled aside, the shadows hurtling past them, dark shapes with just a flash of teeth and claws and deep-throated growls.

Ur'wolves! Bek snatched his long knife from its loop at his belt, wishing that he had something more substantial with which to defend himself. An ur'wolf pack was even capable of bringing down a full-grown Koden.

Panax had recovered and was wielding the two-edged ax, shifting his weight left and then right as the shadows flitted all around him at the edges of the light, looking for an opening. Every so often, one would launch itself at him, and he would meet the attack with a sweep of his curved blade and find nothing but air. Bek shouted at Quentin, who had tumbled away from the fire and was struggling to climb back to his feet. Finally Panax moved to aid him, but the moment he shifted his gaze to the Highlander, an ur'wolf slammed into him, knocking him flat and sending the battle-ax spinning away.

For an instant, Bek thought they were lost. The ur'wolves were coming out of the darkness in a rush, so many the Dwarf and the Highlanders could not have stopped them even had they been ready to do so. As it was, Panax and Quentin were both down, and Bek was trying to defend them with nothing more than his long knife.

"Quentin!" Bek screamed in desperation, and was knocked flying by a sleek form that materialized out of nowhere to catch him from behind.

Then the Highlander was beside him, the Sword of Leah unsheathed and gripped in both hands. Quentin's face was bloodless and raw with fear, but his eyes were determined. As the ur'wolves came at them, he swept the ancient weapon in a wide arc and cried out *"Leah! Leah!"* in challenge. Abruptly, his sword flared white-hot, threads of fire racing up and down its polished length. Quentin gasped in surprise and staggered back, almost falling over Bek. The ur'wolves scattered, twisting away frantically and disappearing back into the dark. Quentin, shocked by what had happened, but exhilarated, as well, impulsively gave chase.

"Leah! Leah!" he called out.

Back came the ur'wolves, attacking anew, sheering off at the last moment as the sword's fire lanced out at them. Panax was back on his feet, astonishment mirrored in his eyes as he retrieved his battle-ax and moved to stand next to the Highlander.

Magic! Bek thought as he rushed to join them. There was magic in the Sword of Leah after all! Walker had been right!

But their problems weren't over. The ur'wolves were not breaking off their attack, just working around the edges of the defense that had been raised against them, waiting for a chance to break through. They were too wily to be caught off guard and too determined to give up. Even the sword's magic could do little more than keep them at bay.

"Panax, there are too many!" Bek shouted above the din of the ur'wolves' howls and snarls. He snatched up the cold end of a burning brand to thrust into the jaws of their attackers.

Half-blinded by ash and sweat, the three put their backs to the fire and faced out into the darkness. The ur'wolves flitted through the shadows, their liquid forms all but invisible. Eyes glimmered and disappeared, pinpricks of brightness that taunted and teased. Unable to determine where the next attack would come from, Bek swept the air before him with the long knife. He wondered suddenly if he should use the magic of the phoenix stone. But he couldn't see how it would help them.

"They'll rush us soon!" Panax shouted. His voice was raspy and filled with grit. "Shades! So many of them! Where have they all come from?"

"Bek, do you see, do you see?" Quentin was laughing almost hysterically. "The sword is magic after all, Bek! It really is!"

Bek found his cousin's enthusiasm entirely unwarranted and would have told him so if he could have spared the strength. But it was taking everything he had to stay focused on the movements of their attackers. He had no energy to waste on Quentin.

"*Leah! Leah!*" his cousin howled, darting out from their little circle, faking a strike at the shadows, then quickly retreating. "Panax!" he cried. "What are we supposed to do?"

Then something even darker and quicker than the ur'wolves crossed in front of them, trailing shards of cold wind in its wake. The three defenders shrank from it instinctively. The night hissed as if steam had been released from a fissure, and the ur'wolves began to howl wildly and to snap at nothing. Bek couldn't see them in the darkness, but he could hear the sounds they were making, sounds of madness and fear and loathing. A moment later, they were in full flight, gone back into the forest as if swallowed whole.

Bek Rowe held his breath in the ensuing silence, crouching so far down he was almost kneeling, his long knife extended blindly toward the trees. Beside him, Quentin was as still as carved stone.

Suddenly the darkness shifted anew, and a huge, tattered form that was not quite human, but not quite anything else, rose against the flicker of the firelight. It came together in a slow gathering of shadows, taking shape but not assuming identity, never quite becoming anything recognizable, formed of dreams and nightmares in equal parts.

"What is it?" Quentin Leah whispered.

"Truls Rohk," Panax breathed softly, and his words were as chill and brittle as ice in deep winter.

FIFTEEN

Hunkered down in the sprawling, treacherous tangle of the Wilderun, Grimpen Ward was ablaze with light and suffused with sound. Patrons of the ale houses and pleasure dens overflowed into the dirt streets, celebrating nothing, as lost to themselves as to those who had once known them. Grimpen Ward was the last rung on the ladder down, a melting pot for those who had no other place to go. Inquiries of strangers were as apt to get your purse stolen or your throat cut as your questions answered, fights broke out spontaneously and for no particular reason, and the only rule of behavior that mattered was to keep your nose out of what didn't concern you.

Even Hunter Predd, a veteran of countless reckonings and narrow escapes, was wary of those who lived in Grimpen Ward.

Once, Grimpen Ward had been a sleepy village catering to trappers and hunters seeking game within the vast and little explored expanse of the Wilderun. Too remote and isolated to attract any other form of commerce, it had subsisted as an outpost for many years. But there was little money to be made in hunting game and much to be made in gambling, and slowly the nature of the village began to change. The Elves shunned it, but Southlanders and

Rovers found that its location suited their needs perfectly. Men and women seeking escape from their past, from pursuers who would not let them be, and from failed dreams and constant disappointment; men and women who could not live under the constraints of rules that governed elsewhere and who needed the freedom that came with knowing that being quickest and strongest was all that mattered; and men and women who had lost everything and were hoping to find a way to begin anew without having to be anything but clever and immoral; eventually all such found their way to Grimpen Ward. Some stayed only a short time and moved on. Some stayed longer. If they failed to stay alive, they stayed forever.

In daylight, it was a squalid, sleepy village of clapboard buildings and sheds, of rutted dirt roads and shadowed alleyways, and of a populace that remained inside and slept, waiting for nightfall. The forests of the Wilderun closed it about, ancient trees and choking scrub, and it was always on the verge of being swallowed completely. Nothing of what it was seemed permanent, as if everything had been thrown together on a whim, perhaps within a few desperate days, and might be torn down again by the end of the week. Its populace cared nothing for the town, only for what the town had to offer. There was a sullen, angry cast to Grimpen Ward that suggested a caged and malnourished animal waiting for a chance to break free.

Hunter Predd walked its streets cautiously, staying back from the light, keeping clear of the knots of people crowded about the doorways and porches of the public houses. Because he was a Wing Rider, he preferred open spaces. Because he was a sensible man who had been to Grimpen Ward and places like it before, he knew what to expect.

He slowed and then stopped at the entrance of an alley where three men were beating another with clubs, already pulling at his clothes, searching for his purse. The man was pleading with them not to kill him. There was blood on his face and hands. One of his attackers looked over at Hunter Predd, feral eyes bright and hard, assessing his potential as an adversary. The Wing Rider did as he had been instructed. He held the other's gaze for a moment to demonstrate he was not afraid, then turned aside and walked on.

Grimpen Ward was not a place for the faint of heart or those seeking to redress the wrongs of the world. Neither could survive in the claustrophobic atmosphere of this breeding ground of cruelty and rage. Here, everyone was either prey to or hunter of someone else, and there was no middle ground. Hunter Predd felt the pall of hopelessness and despondency that shrouded the village, and he was sickened by it.

He moved out of the central section of the village, away from the brighter lights and louder noises, and entered a cluster of hovels and shacks occupied by those who had fallen into a twilight existence of drug-induced escape. The beings who lived here never emerged from their private, self-indulgent worlds, from the places they had created for themselves. He could smell the chemicals burning on the air as he passed through. He could smell the sweat and excrement. Everything they needed to escape life was free, once they forfeited everything they had.

He turned up a pathway that disappeared back into the trees, glanced about cautiously to be certain he had not been followed, and proceeded into the shadows. The trail wound back a short distance to a cabin set within a small grove of ash and cherry. The cabin was neat and well tended with flower boxes hung from the windows and a garden out back. It was quiet, an oasis of calm amid the tumult. A light burned in the front window. The Wing Rider walked to the door, stood quietly for a moment listening, and then knocked.

The woman who opened the door was heavy and flat-faced, her hair cropped short and graying, her body shapeless. She was of indeterminate age, as if she had passed out of childhood sometime back and would not change her look again until she was very old. She regarded Hunter Predd without interest, as if he were just another of the lost souls she encountered every day.

"I've got no more rooms to let. Try somewhere else."

He shook his head. "I'm not looking for a room. I'm looking for a woman called the Addershag."

She snorted. "You've come too late for that. She's been dead these past five years. News travels slowly where you come from, I guess."

"You know this to be so? Is she really dead?"

"As dead as yesterday. I buried her out back, six feet down, standing upright so she could greet those who tried to dig her up." She smirked. "Want to give it a try?"

He ignored the challenge. "You were her apprentice?"

The woman laughed, her face twisting. "Not hardly. I was her servant woman and the caretaker of her house. I hadn't the stomach for what she did. But I served her well and she rewarded me in kind. You knew her, did you?"

"Only by reputation. A powerful seer. A worker of magic. Few would dare to challenge her. None, I think, even now that she is dead and buried."

"Only fools and desperate men." The woman glanced out at the village lights and shook her head. "They come here still, now and then. I've buried a few, when they didn't listen to me about letting her be. But I haven't her power or abilities. I just do what I was brought here to do, looking after things, taking care. The house and what's in it are mine now. But I keep them for her."

She stared at him, waiting.

"Who reads the future of those in Grimpen Ward now that she is gone?" he asked.

"Pretenders and charlatans. No-talent thieves who would steal you blind and send you to your death pretending it was something else entirely. They moved in the moment she was gone, laying claim to what she was, to what she could do." The woman spit into the earth. "They'll all be found out and burned alive for it."

Hunter Predd hesitated. He would have to be careful here. This woman was protective of her legacy and not inclined to help. But he needed what she could give him.

"No one could replace the Addershag," he agreed soberly. "Unless she chose someone herself. Did she ever train an apprentice?"

For a long moment, the woman just looked at him, suspicion mirrored in her sharp eyes. She brushed roughly at her ragged hair. "Who are you?"

"An emissary," he said truthfully. "But the man who sent me knew your mistress well and shared her passion for magic and secrets. He, too, has lived a long time."

Her features scrunched up like crumpled paper, and she folded her heavy arms before her defensively. "Is he here?"

"Close by. He prefers not to be seen."

She nodded. "I know of whom you speak. But name him anyway if you wish me to believe you are his man."

The Wing Rider nodded. "He is called Walker."

"Hah!" Her eyes were bright with glee. "Even the vaunted Druid needed her help from time to time! That was how powerful she was, how well regarded!" There was triumph and satisfaction in her voice. "She might have been one of his order, had she wanted it. But she was never inclined to be anything other than a seer."

"Is there, then," he pressed gently, "another he might turn to, now that she is gone?"

The silence pressed in about them as she stood studying him anew, thinking the matter over. She knew something, but was not inclined to share it. He waited patiently on her.

"One," the woman said finally, but spoke the word as if it left a bitter taste in her mouth. "One only. But she was not suitable. She was flawed in character and made waste of her talent. My mistress gave her every chance to be strong, and each time the girl failed. Finally, she left."

"A girl," Hunter Predd repeated carefully.

"Very young when she was here. Still a child. But old even then. Like she was already grown inside her child's body. Intense and secretive, which was to her credit, but passionate, as well, which was not. Very powerful in her talent. She could see the future clearly, could mark its progress and read its signs." The woman spat once more, her voice suddenly weary. "So gifted. More than just a seer. That was her undoing."

The Wing Rider was confused. "What do you mean?"

The woman glared and shook her head. "There's no reason for me to talk about it. If you're so curious to know, ask her yourself. Ryer Ord Star is her name. She lives nearby. I can give you the directions. Do you want them or not?"

Hunter Predd took the directions she had offered and thanked her for her help. In return she gave him a look that suggested both pity and disdain. He had barely turned away before she had closed the cottage door behind her.

It felt empty and silent in the woods where Walker waited outside Grimpen Ward for Hunter Predd's return. Nothing moved in the darkness. No sound came from the gloom. He waited patiently, but reluctantly, uncomfortable with leaving the search for the Addershag to the Wing Rider. It wasn't that he thought Hunter Predd lacking in ability; in fact, he thought the Wing Rider better able than most. But he would have preferred to handle the matter himself. Contacting her was his idea. Seeking her out was something he knew how to do. But it was clear after the attack on Spanner Frew's safehold that the Ilse Witch was determined to disrupt his efforts to retrace the route on the castaway's map. It might have appeared it was the Federation who attacked the Rover settlement, but the Druid was convinced it was the Ilse Witch. Her spies must have caught sight of him in March Brume, and she had tracked him north to Spanner Frew. He had been lucky to elude her on the coast—luckier still to escape with his new airship intact. His Rover allies—Redden Alt Mer, Rue Meridian, and Spanner Frew—had flown him back to March Brume under cover of darkness and early morning mist, dropped him close to where he had left Hunter Predd, and then taken the airship in search of a crew. Once that crew was assembled, they would fly north to Arborlon, present themselves to the Elves and their new ruler, and await the Druid's arrival.

All of which would take time, but Walker needed that time to accomplish two things. First, he must wait for Quentin Leah and Bek Rowe to find Truls Rohk, then reach Arborlon. Second, he must confer with a seer.

Why a seer? Hunter Predd had asked as they flew aboard Obsidian across the peaks of the Irrybis toward Grimpen Ward. What need did they have of a seer when Walker had already determined the purpose of the map? But their journey, Walker explained, was not so easily fathomed. Think of the Blue Divide as a depthless void and its islands as stepping-stones. The stability of those stones and the dark secrets of the waters all around were unknown. The Addershag might help them better understand their dangers. She could see some of what would threaten, what would lie in wait, what would steal away their lives if they weren't prepared.

A seer could always provide insights, and no seer could provide more than the Addershag. Her abilities were renowned, and while she was dangerously unpredictable, she had never been antagonistic toward him. Once, long ago, she had helped his cousin, the Elf Queen Wren Elessedil, in her search for the missing Elven nation. It was the beginning of a connection he had carefully preserved. The Addershag had accommodated him now and again over the years, always with a grudging nod of admiration for the magic he could wield, always with a veiled hint of warning that her own was a match. She had been alive almost as long as he had, without the benefit of the Druid Sleep. He had no idea how she had managed this. She was both burdened and conflicted by her talent, and her life was a closely guarded secret.

Walker was not certain that Hunter Predd could succeed in persuading her to speak to him. She might well refuse. But it made sense to try. If he were to accomplish anything, he would have to do so both swiftly and surreptitiously.

Still, he chafed at the waiting and the uncertainty, and wished he could involve himself openly. Time was precious and success uncertain. The Addershag's aid was vital. She would never agree to go with him, but she could open his eyes to the things he must know if he were to go himself. She would do so reluctantly and with carefully crafted words and confusing images, but even that would help.

A soft rustle broke his concentration, and he looked up as Hunter Predd materialized out of the night. The Wing Rider was alone.

"Did you find her?" the Druid asked at once.

Hunter Predd shook his head. "She's been dead five years. The woman who looked after her told me so."

Walker took a long, slow breath and exhaled. Disappointment welled up inside. A lie? No, a lie of that sort wouldn't stand up for long. He should have known of the seer's death, but he had shut himself away in Paranor for the better part of twenty years and much of what had happened in the world had passed him by completely.

The Wing Rider seated himself on a stump and drank from his water skin. "There is another possibility. Before she died, the seer took an apprentice."

"An apprentice?" Walker frowned.

"A girl called Ryer Ord Star. Very talented, according to the woman I spoke with. But she had some sort of falling out with the Addershag. The woman hinted that it had something to do with a flaw in the girl's character, but wouldn't say more. She said I should ask her myself if I wanted to know. She lives not far from here."

Walker thought it through quickly, weighing the possible risks and gains. Ryer Ord Star? He had never heard of her. Nor had he heard of the Addershag taking an apprentice. But then he hadn't heard of the seer's death either. What he knew or didn't know of the larger world the past few years was not the most accurate measure of its truths. Better to find things out for himself before deciding what was or wasn't so.

"Show me where she is," he said.

Hunter Predd led him along a series of trails that circumvented the center of Grimpen Ward and avoided contact with its denizens. Darkness hid their passage, and the forests were a vast, impenetrable maze into which only they appeared to have ventured. Distant and removed, the sounds of the village rose up in tiny bursts within the cloaking silence, and slivers of light appeared and faded like predators' eyes. But both Wing Rider and Druid knew how to walk undetected, and so their passing went unnoticed.

As he slipped through the dark tangle of the trees, Walker's thoughts crowded in on him. His opportunities, he sensed, were slipping away. Too many he had depended on were dead—first Allardon Elessedil, then the castaway, and now the Addershag. Each represented information and assistance that would be difficult, if not impossible, to replace. The loss of the Addershag troubled him most. Could he manage without a seer's visions in this endeavor? Allanon had done so, years earlier. But Walker was not chiseled from the same rock as his predecessor and made no claims to being his equal. He did what he could with what he had, mostly because he understood the need for doing so and not because he coveted the role into which he had been cast. Druids had traditionally desired their positions in the order. The mold had been broken with him.

He did not like thinking about who he was and how he had gotten to be that way. He did not like remembering the road he had been forced to travel to become what he had never intended to be. It was a bitter memory he carried and a difficult burden he bore. He had become a Druid because of Allanon's machinations and Cogline's urgings and in spite of his own considerable misgivings because, in the end, the need for his doing so was overwhelming. He had never thought to have anything to do with the Druids, never thought to be part of what they represented. He had grown up with a determination to stay apart from the legacy that had claimed so many of his family—the legacy of the Shannara. He had vowed to take his life in another direction.

But this is old news, he admonished himself even as he remembered the early fire of his doomed commitment to change what was fated. He supposed what pained him most, what weighed so heavily on his conscience, was not the breaking of the vow itself, which he could justify in light of the need it served, but the distance he had strayed from his appointed path in taking up his role. He had sworn he would not be a Druid like those others, like Allanon and Bremen before him. He would not cloak himself in subterfuge and secrecy. He would not manipulate others to achieve the ends he wished. He would not deceive and misdirect and conceal. He would be open and forthright and honest in his dealings. He would reveal what he knew and be truthful always.

He marveled at how naive he had been. How foolish. How terribly, fatally unrealistic.

Because life's dictates did not allow for quick and easy distinctions between right and wrong or good and bad. Choices were made between shades of gray, and there was healing and harm to be weighed on both sides of each. As a result, his life had irrevocably followed the path of his predecessors, and in time he had taken on the very characteristics he had despised in them. He had assumed their mantles more completely than he had ever intended. Without ever wishing it to be so, he had become like them.

Because he could see the need for doing so.

Because he was then required to conduct himself accordingly.

Because, always and forever, the greater good must be considered in determining his course of action.

Tell that to Bek Rowe when this is over, he thought darkly. Tell it to that boy.

They emerged suddenly from the forest into a clearing in which a solitary cottage sat dark and silent. Far removed from everything, the cottage was poorly tended, its windows broken, its roof sagging, its yard choked with weeds, and its gardens bare. It looked as if no one had lived in it for some time, as if it had been abandoned and let run to ruin.

Then Walker saw the girl. She sat in the deep shadows of the porch stoop, perfectly still, at one with the darkness. When his eyes settled on her, she rose at once and stood watching his approach with Hunter Predd. Revealed more clearly by the light of moon and stars, she became older, less a girl, more a young woman. She wore her silver hair long and loose, and it fell about her pale, thin face in thick waves. She was rail thin, so insubstantial it seemed as if a strong wind might blow her away completely. She wore a plain wool dress cinched at her tiny waist by a strip of braided cloth. Sandals that were dusty and worn were strapped to her feet, and an odd collar of metal and leather was clasped about her neck.

He came up to her and stopped, Hunter Predd at his side. She never took her eyes from his, never even glanced at the Wing Rider.

"Are you the one they call Walker?" she asked in a soft, high voice.

Walker nodded. "I am called that."

"I am Ryer Ord Star. I have been waiting for you."

Walker studied her curiously. "How did you know I was coming?"

"I saw you in a dream. We were flying far out over the Blue Divide in an airship. There were dark clouds all about, and thunder rolled across the skies. But within the dark clouds there was something darker still, and I was warning you to beware of it." She paused. "When I had that dream, I knew you would be coming here and that when you did, I would be going with you."

Walker hesitated. "I never intended to ask you to come with me, only to ask—"

"But I must come with you!" she insisted quickly, her hands making sudden, anxious gestures to emphasize her need. "There have been other dreams of you as well, more as time has passed. I am meant to go with you across the Blue Divide. It is my destiny to do so!"

She spoke with such conviction that Walker was momentarily taken aback. He glanced at Hunter Predd. Even the Wing Rider's rugged face reflected surprise.

"See?" she inquired, gesturing down at a canvas bag that sat at her feet. "I am packed and ready to leave with you. I dreamed of you again last night, of your coming here. The dream was so strong it even told me when you would arrive. Such dreams do not come often, even to seers. They almost never come in such numbers. When they do, they must not be ignored. We are bound, you and I—our destinies intertwined in a way we cannot sever. What happens to one, happens to both."

She regarded him solemnly, her thin, pale face questioning, as if she could not understand his inability to accept her words. Walker, for his part, was confounded by her determination.

"You apprenticed with the Addershag?" he inquired, turning the conversation another way. "Why did you leave?"

The thin hands gestured anew. "She was suspicious of what I was. She was distrustful of how I employed my gifts. I am a seer, but I am an empath, too. Both talents are strong within me, and I find the need to use them too compelling to ignore. On occasion, I used the one to alter the other, and the Addershag would scream at me. 'Never do anything to change what is to be!' she would shrill. But if I can take away another's pain through divining the future, where is the harm? I saw nothing wrong in doing so. Such pain can be better borne by me than by most."

Walker stared. "You read the future, determine that something bad will happen, then use your empathic skill to lessen the hurt that will result?" Walker tried to envision it and failed. "How often can you do this?"

"Only now and then. I can only do a little. Sometimes, the use of my gifts is reversed. Sometimes I come to those already in pain, see the future that pain will create, and act to change it. It is an imperfect skill, and I do not use it carelessly. But the Addershag distrusted my empathic side altogether, believing it affected my seer's eyes. Perhaps she was right. The two are equal parts of me, and I cannot separate them out. Does this bother you?"

Walker didn't know. What bothered him most was his own confusion over what to do with the girl. She seemed convinced she was going with him, while he was still struggling with whether he should consult with her at all.

"You are unsure of me," she said. He nodded, seeing no reason to dissemble. "You have no reason to fear that I cannot do what is needed. You are a Druid, and a Druid's instincts never lie. Trust what yours tell you about me."

She took a step forward. "An empath can give you peace you can find in no other way. Give me your hand."

He did so without thinking, and she took it in her own. Her hands were soft and warm, and they barely enclosed his. She ran her fingers slowly over his palm and closed her eyes. "You are in such pain, Walker," she said. A tingling began that turned slowly to sleepy calm, then to a sudden, soaring euphoria. "You feel yourself beset on all sides, your chances slipping away from you, your burden almost too much to bear. You hate yourself for what you are because you believe it is wrong for you to be so. You conceal truths that will affect the lives of those who—"

He jerked his hand free and stepped back, shocked at how easily she had penetrated his heart. Her eyes opened and lit on him anew. "I could free you of so much of your pain if you would let me," she whispered.

"No," he replied. He felt himself naked and revealed in a way he didn't care for. "The pain is a reminder of who I am."

At his side, Hunter Predd stirred uneasily, a witness to words he shouldn't hear. But Walker could do nothing about it now.

"Listen to me," Ryer Ord Star intoned softly. "Listen to what I have seen in my dreams. You will make your voyage across the Blue Divide in search of something precious—more to you than to any who go with you. Those who accompany you will be both brave and strong of heart, but only some will return. One will save your life. One will try to take it. One will love you unconditionally. One will hate you with unmatched passion. One will lead you astray. One will bring you back again. I have seen all this in my dreams, and

I am meant to see more. I am meant to be your eyes, Walker. We are bound as one. Take me with you. You must."

Her small voice was filled with such passion that it left the Druid transfixed. He thought momentarily of the Addershag, of how black and twisted she had always seemed, her words sharp edged and threatening, her voice come out of a dark pit into which no one should venture. How different, then, was Ryer Ord Star? He could see how difficult it must have been for the girl to train at the feet of someone so different from herself. She must have struggled in her training and would have lasted as long as she did because of her passion for her gift. He could see that in her. Trust your instincts, she had urged him. He always did. But his instincts here were mixed and his conclusions uncertain.

"Take me with you," she repeated, and her words were a whisper of need.

He did not look at Hunter Predd. He knew what he would find in the Wing Rider's eyes. He did not even look into his own heart, because he could already feel what was lurking there. He read, instead, her face, to be certain he had missed nothing, and he gave counsel to his mission and his need. A seer was required for the dark places into which he must venture. Ryer Ord Star had the gift, and there was no time to seek it in another. That she was not the Addershag was troubling. That she was not only willing, but eager to go with him, was a gift he could not afford to spurn.

"Pick up your bag, Ryer Ord Star," he said softly. "We fly tonight to Arborlon."

SIXTEEN

Bek Rowe froze as the huge apparition swung away from the fleeing wolves to face them. Quentin took an involuntary step back, his earlier euphoria over the rediscovered magic of the Sword of Leah forgotten. Neither dared even to breathe as the thing before them rippled like windblown cedar limbs, a kind of shimmering movement that suggested an image cast on a rain-drenched window or a ghost imagined in a sudden change of light.

Then the tattered cloak that wrapped Truls Rohk's broad, rangy form billowed once and settled about his shoulders, the edges trailing stray threads and ragged strips of cloth. Hands and feet moved like clubs within the circle of darkness he cast, but no face could be seen within the shadows of his cowl. If not for his vaguely human form, Truls Rohk could as easily have been a beast of the sort that prowled those mountains.

"Panax," he hissed. "Why are you here?"

He spoke the Dwarf's name with recognition, but without warmth or pleasure. His voice bore the sharp whine of metal scraping metal, and ended with the sound of steam released under pressure. Bek had forgotten the Dwarf. Battle-ax lowered to his side, Panax stood straight and unbowed in the presence of the dark creature that confronted them. But there was a tenseness in his rough features and wariness in his eyes.

"Walker has sent you a message," he said to the apparition.

Truls Rohk made no move to come forward. "Walker," he repeated.

"These are Highlanders," Panax continued. "The tall one is Quentin Leah. The younger is his cousin, Bek Rowe. They were entrusted to carry the message to you."

"Speak it," Truls Rohk said to the cousins.

Bek looked at Quentin, who nodded. Bek cleared his throat. "We've been asked to tell you that Walker is preparing to undertake a journey by airship across the Blue Divide. He goes in search of a safehold in an unknown land. The safehold contains a treasure of great value. He says to tell you that others search for it, as well, one of them a warlock called the Morgawr and one a sorceress called the Ilse Witch."

"Hsssshh! Dark souls!" Truls Rohk spat sharply, the sound so venomous it stopped Bek right in the middle of his speech. "What else, boy?"

Bek swallowed thickly. "He says to tell you that his enemies have already killed the Elf King, Allardon Elessedil, and a castaway who carried back a map of the safehold. He says to tell you he needs you to come with him to help in the search and to protect against those who would prevent it."

There was a long silence, then a cough that might have been a laugh or something less pleasant. "Lies. Even with only one arm, Walker can protect himself. What does he really need?"

Bek stared at the other in confusion and fear, then glanced at both Quentin and Panax, found no help, and shook his head. "I don't know. That was all he told us. That was the whole message, just as he gave it to us. He wants you to—"

"He wants more than he says!" The raspy voice grated and

hissed. "You, Highlander." He gestured vaguely within his cloak toward Quentin. "What magic do you wield?"

Quentin did not hesitate. "An old magic, just this night recovered. This sword belongs to my family. It was given its magic, I'm told, in the time of Allanon."

"You wield it poorly." The words were cutting and dismissive. "You, boy." Truls Rohk spoke once more to Bek. "Have you magic as well?"

Bek shook his head. "No, none."

He was aware that Truls Rohk was studying him carefully, and in the stillness that followed, it seemed as if something reached out and touched him, brushing against his forehead with feathery lightness. It was there and gone so quickly that he might only have imagined it.

Truls Rohk moved a step to his right, and the movement revealed a flash of arm and leg of huge proportions, all muscle and thick hair, bare to the mountain night. Bek had a strong sense that the other was stooped within his cloak, affecting a kind of guarded crouch, a readiness that never left him. As big as Truls Rohk already seemed, Bek believed he would be much bigger still if he was to stand upright. Nothing got that big that wasn't a Rock Troll, but Truls Rohk lacked a Rock Troll's thick hide and cumbersome, deliberate movements. He was too quick and fluid for that, and his skin was human.

"The Druid sent you to be tested," he growled softly. "Tested against your own fears and superstitions. Your magic and your grit are untried weapons." He gave a low chuckle that died away into the familiar hiss. "Panax, are you party to this game?"

The Dwarf grunted irritably. "I play no games with anyone. I was asked to see these Highlanders into the Wolfsktaag and out again. You seem to know more about this than I do."

"Games within games," the shadowy form murmured, stalking a few steps to the right, then turning back again. This time Bek caught a glimpse of a face within the hood, just a momentary illumination by the edges of the firelight. The face was crisscrossed with deep, scarlet welts, and the flesh looked as if it had been melted like iron in a furnace. "Druid games," Truls Rohk went on, disappearing again into shadow. "I do not like them, Panax. But Walker is always interesting to watch." He paused. "Maybe these two, as well, hmmm?"

Panax seemed confused and said nothing. Truls Rohk pointed at Quentin. "Those wolves would have had you if not for me. Better practice your sword's magic if you expect to stay alive for very long."

Bek felt the other's eyes shift and settle on him. "And you, boy, had better not trust anyone. Not until you learn to see things better than you do now."

Bek was conscious that both Quentin and Panax were looking at him, as well. He wanted to ask Truls Rohk what he was talking about but cowed by the giant's size and dark mystery, he was afraid to question him.

Truls Rohk spat and wheeled away. "Where do you go to meet Walker?" he called over his shoulder.

"Arborlon," Bek answered at once.

"Then I'll see you there." His words were soft and whispery. "Now get out of these mountains, quickly!"

There was a rush of wind, cold and sharp, and a whisper of movement in the night. Bek and Quentin shrank involuntarily from both, shielding their eyes. Behind them, the fire flickered and went out.

When they looked back toward the silent darkness, Truls Rohk was gone.

Far south, below the Highlands of Leah, the Prekkendorran Heights, and the older, more industrialized cities, Wayford and Sterne, in the Federation capital city of Arishaig, Minister of Defense Sen Dunsidan was awakened by a touch on his shoulder.

His eyes blinked open and he stared through the gloom toward the ceiling without seeing anything, uncertain what had disturbed him. He was lying on his back, his big frame sprawled on the oversize bed, the sleeping room cool and silent.

"Wake up, Minister," the Ilse Witch whispered.

His eyes settled on her slender, cloaked form as she bent over him. "Dark Lady of my dreams," he greeted with a sleepy smile.

"Don't say anything more, Minister," she advised, stepping back from him. "Rise and come with me."

She watched him do as he was told, his strong face calm and settled, as if it were not at all unexpected that she should appear to him like this. He was a powerful man, and the effective exercise of his power relied in part on never seeming surprised or afraid. He had been Minister of Defense of the Federation for better than fifteen years, and he had achieved his longevity in that position in part by burying a lot of men who misjudged him. He seemed mild and even detached at times, just an observer on the edges of the action, just a man eager to make things right for everyone. In truth, he had the instincts and morals of a snake. In a world of predators and prey, he preferred to take his chances as the former. But he understood clearly and unequivocally that his survival depended on keeping his preference secret and his ambitions concealed. When he felt threatened, as perhaps he did now, he always smiled. But the smile, of course, hid the teeth behind.

The Ilse Witch led him wordlessly from his sleeping chamber down the hall to his study. His study was his place of business, and he would understand from her taking him there that there was business to be done. He was a man of huge appetites, and he was accustomed to satisfying them when he chose. She did not want him mistaking her purpose in coming to his bedchamber for something other than what it was. She had seen the way he looked at her, and she did not care for what she saw in his eyes. If he were to attempt to put his hands on her, she would have to kill him. She did not mind doing so, but it would accomplish nothing. The best way to prevent that from happening was to make it clear from the outset that their relationship was not about to change.

Sen Dunsidan was both her spy and her ally, a man well placed in the Federation hierarchy to do favors for her in exchange for favors she might do for him. As Minister of Defense, he understood the uses of power in government, but he was mindful, too, of the need for cautious selection. He was clever, patient, and thorough, and his work ethic was legendary. Once he set his mind to something, he did not give up. But it was his ambition that attracted the Ilse Witch. Sen Dunsidan was not satisfied with being Minister of Defense. He would not be satisfied if he were to become Minister of War or Minister of State or even if he were chosen Prime Minister. He might not be satisfied with being King, a position that didn't even exist in the current structure of the Federation government, but it was closer to the mark. What he desired was absolute power—over everything and everyone. She had learned early on in their relationship that if she could show him ways of achieving this, he would willingly do whatever she asked.

They reached his study and entered. The room was wood paneled and austere, an intimidating lair. Disdaining the brighter light that the torches set in wall brackets would have afforded, the minister moved to light a series of candles on a broad-topped desk. Tall and athletic, his silvery hair worn long and flowing freely, he moved from place to place unhurriedly. He was an attractive man with a magnetic personality until you got to know him, and then he was just someone else to be watched carefully. The Ilse Witch had encountered more than her share of these. Sometimes it seemed the world was full of them.

"Now, then," he said, seating himself comfortably on one end of a long couch, taking time to adjust his dressing gown.

She stayed somewhat removed from him, still wrapped in her hooded cloak, her face hidden in shadows. He had seen what she looked like on several occasions, mostly because it was necessary to let him do so, but she had been careful never to encourage his obvious interest in her. She did not treat him as she did her spies, because he considered himself an equal and his pride and ambition would not allow for anything less. She could reduce him to servitude easily enough, but then his usefulness would be ended. She must let him remain strong or he could not survive in the arena of Federation politics.

"Did those airships I sent you not do what was needed?" He pressed, his brow furrowing slightly.

"They did what they could," she said in a neutral tone of voice. She chose her words carefully. "But my adversary is clever and strong. He is not easily surprised, and he was not surprised there. He escaped."

"Unfortunate."

"A momentary setback. I will find him again, and when I do, I will destroy him. In the meantime, I require your help."

"In finding him or destroying him?"

"Neither. In pursuing him. He has the use of an airship, with a Captain and a crew. I will need the same if I am to catch up to him."

Sen Dunsidan studied her thoughtfully. Already he was working it through, she could tell. He had determined quickly that there was more to this than she was telling him. If she was chasing someone, there had to be a reason. He knew her well enough to know she would not waste time hunting someone down simply to kill him. Something else was involved, something of importance to her. He was trying to figure out what might be in it for him.

She decided not to play games. "Let me tell you a little about my interest in this matter," she offered. "It goes well beyond my determination to see my adversary destroyed. We compete for the same prize, Minister. It is a prize of great and rare value. It would benefit both of us, you and I, if I were to gain possession of it first. My request to you for aid in this endeavor presupposes that whatever success I enjoy, I intend to share with you."

The big man nodded. "As you have always so graciously done, Dark Lady." He smiled. "What sort of prize is it you seek?"

She hesitated deliberately, as if debating whether to tell him. He must be made to think it was a difficult decision, the result of which would favor him. "A form of magic," she confided finally. "A very special magic. If I was to gain possession of this magic, I would become much more powerful than I am. And if I was to share possession with you, you would become strongest among those who seek power within the Federation government." She paused. "Would you like that?"

"Oh, I don't know," he said, laughing softly. "Such power might be too much for a simple man like me." He paused. "Do I have your assurance that I will share in the use of this magic on your return?"

"My complete and unequivocal assurance, Minister."

He bowed slightly in acknowledgment. "I could ask for nothing more." She had convinced him a long time ago that she would keep her word once she gave it. She also knew that his confidence was buttressed by his belief that even if she broke it, her betrayal would not cost him much.

"Where do you go to seek this magic?" he asked.

She gave him a long, careful look. "Across the Blue Divide, to a new land, an old city, a strange place. Only a few others have gone there. None have returned."

She did not mention the castaway or the Elves. There was no reason for him to know of them. She gave him just enough to keep him interested.

"None have returned," he repeated slowly. "Not very reassuring. Will you succeed where everyone else has failed?"

"What do you think, Minister?"

He laughed softly. "I think you are young for such machinations and intrigue. Do you never think of taking time for more casual pleasures? Do you never wish that you could put aside your obligations, just for a few days, and do something you never imagined?"

She sighed wearily. He was being obtuse. He was refusing to accept that his advances were not welcome. She must put a stop to it now before it got out of hand. "If I were to consider such a thing," she purred, "do you know a place to which I might escape?"

His gaze on her was steady and watchful. "I do."

"And would you be my guide and companion?"

He straightened expectantly. "I would be honored."

"No, Minister, you would simply be dead, probably before the first day was out." She paused to let him absorb the impact of her words. "Put aside your dreams of what you think I might be. Do not let them enter your mind or be persuaded to speak of them again. Ever. I am nothing of what you imagine and less of what you would hope. I am blacker than your worst deeds could ever be. Don't presume to know me. Keep far away from me, and maybe you'll stay alive."

His face had stilled, and there was uncertainty in his eyes. She let him wrestle with it a moment, then whispered words of calming in the silence, and laughed like a girl, soft and low. "Come now, Minister. Harsh words are unnecessary. We are old friends. We are allies. What of my request? Will you aid me?"

"Of course," he answered swiftly. A political animal first and always, Sen Dunsidan could recognize reality quicker than most. He did not want to anger or alienate her or sever their mutually advantageous connection. He would attempt to move past his clumsy attempt at an assignation as if it had never happened. She, of course, would let him. "A ship, a Captain, and crew," he assured her, grateful for a chance to accommodate, to be back in her good graces. He brushed at his silver hair and smiled. "All at your disposal, Dark Lady, for as long as you need them."

"Your best of each, Minister," she warned. "No weak links. This voyage will not be easy."

He rose, walked to the study window, and looked out over the city. His home sat in a cluster of Federation government buildings, some residences, some offices, all warded by a walled park into which no one was admitted without invitation. The Ilse Witch smiled. Except for her, of course. She could go anywhere she wished.

"I'll give you *Black Moclips*," Sen Dunsidan announced suddenly. "She is the best of our warships, a Rover-built ship of the line, a proven vessel. Her history is remarkable. She has fought in over two hundred engagements and never been defeated or even disabled. Just now, she has a new Captain and crew, and they are eager to prove themselves. Veterans all, don't misunderstand me, but new to this ship. They were brought aboard when her Rover crew deserted."

She studied him. "They are seasoned and reliable? They are tested in battle?"

"Two full years on the Prekkendorran, all of them. They are a strong and dependable unit, well led and thoroughly trained."

And a full complement of Federation soldiers, she was about to say when the Morgawr's rough-edged voice stopped her. *No soldiers*, he hissed, so that only she could hear. It was an unmistakable reminder of his earlier warning, when she had insisted she must have soldiers to combat the Elven forces. *A ship, a Captain, and a crew— nothing more. Do not question me.* She froze under the lash of his voice, projected from the shadows behind Sen Dunsidan, where he waited in hiding.

"Lady?" the Minister of Defense asked solicitously, sensing the hesitation in her.

"Supplies for a long voyage," she said, forging ahead as if nothing had intruded on her thinking, looking directly toward the Morgawr, unwilling to concede him anything. She resented his insistence on trying to control matters when he himself had no intention of being involved in the expedition. He saw himself as her mentor, and he was, but she was his equal now and no longer in his thrall. She had always possessed magic, even before he came to her and helped her to rebuild her shattered life. She had never been helpless or unaware, and he seemed too quick to forget how strong she was.

"The ship will be delivered to you fully outfitted and ready to sail." Sen Dunsidan reclaimed her attention. "I'll have her ready in a week."

"Four days," the Ilse Witch said softly, holding his gaze firmly with her own. "I'll come for her myself. Have her Captain and crew under orders to obey me in everything. Everything, Minister. There are to be no questions, no arguments, and no hesitations. All decisions are to be mine."

The Federation Minister nodded without enthusiasm. "The Captain and crew will be advised, Dark Lady."

"Go back to bed," she ordered, and turned away, dismissing him.

Standing with her gaze directed out the windows and into the night, she waited until he was gone, then wheeled back to face the Morgawr, who had emerged from hiding, tall and dark and spectral. He had come with her to the city, but kept hidden while she did the talking. He told her that it was best if Sen Dunsidan believed she was the one he must listen to, the one in control. As in fact I am, she had wanted to reply, but instead held her tongue.

"You did well," he said, sliding into the faint light.

"I don't appreciate your interference with my efforts!" she snapped, unappeased. "Or your reminders of what you think I should or shouldn't do! I am the one who risks life and limb to gain possession of the magic!"

"I only seek to supply help where help is needed," he replied calmly.

"Then do so!" she snapped. Her patience was exhausted. "We need soldiers! We need hardened warriors! Where are they to come from, if not from the Federation?"

He dismissed her anger and displeasure with a wave of his gloved hand. "From me," he replied casually. "I have already arranged for it. Three dozen Mwellrets, commanded by Cree Bega. They will be your warriors, your fighters. You will have nothing to fear with them beside you."

Mwellrets. She cringed at the idea. He knew she hated rets. As fighters, they were savage and relentless, but they were deceivers, as well. She did not trust them. She could not see inside their minds. They resisted her magic and employed subterfuges and artifices of their own. It was why the Morgawr liked them, why he was using them. They would be effective fighters in her behalf, but they would act as her keepers, as well. Giving her Mwellrets was a means of keeping her in line.

She could refuse his offer, she knew. But to do so would demonstrate weakness. Besides, the warlock would simply insist that she do as he asked, having already made up his mind that the rets were necessary—

She caught herself in midthought, realizing suddenly what sending the rets really meant. It wasn't just that the Morgawr no longer trusted her or that he was no longer certain she would do as he ordered.

He was afraid of her.

She smiled, as if deciding she was pleased with his suggestion, careful to keep her true feelings veiled. "You are right, of course," she agreed. "What better fighters could we find? Who would dare to challenge a ret?"

Only me, she thought darkly. *But by the time you discover that, Morgawr, it will already be too late for you.*

SEVENTEEN

Four days after departing the Wolfsktaag Mountains, Bek Rowe, his cousin Quentin Leah, and the Dwarf Panax arrived at the Valley of Rhenn.

Bek had heard stories of the valley his entire life, and as the trio rode their horses slowly out of the plains and down its broad, grassy corridor, he found himself remembering them anew. There, more than a thousand years ago, the Elves and their King, Jerle Shannara, stood against the hordes of the Warlock Lord in three days of ferocious fighting that culminated in the renegade Druid's defeat. There, more than five hundred years ago, the Legion Free Corps rode to the aid of the Elven people when they were beset by the demon hordes freed from the Forbidding. There, less than 150 years ago, the Elf Queen Wren Elessedil commanded the Free-born allies in their defense against the Federation armies of Rimmer Dall, breaking the back of the Federation occupation and destroying the cult of the Shadowen.

Bek glanced upward at the steepening valley slopes and sharp ridgelines. So many critical battles had been fought and pivotal confrontations had taken place within only a few miles of that gateway to the Elven homeland. But as he looked at it, quiet and

227

serene and bathed in sunshine, there was nothing to indicate that anything of importance had ever happened there.

Once, Bek heard a man remark to Coran that this ground was sacred, that the blood of those who had given up their lives to preserve freedom in the Four Lands had made it so. It was a fine and noble thought, Coran Leah replied, but it would mean more if the sacrifice of those countless dead had bought the survivors something more permanent.

The boy thought about that as he rode through the midday silence. The valley narrowed to a defile at its western end, a natural fortress of cliff walls and twisting passes through which all traffic gained entry into the Westland forests leading to Arborlon. It had served as a first line of defense for the Elves each time their homeland was invaded. Bek had never been here, but he knew its history. Remembering his father's words, he was surprised at how different it felt being here rather than picturing it in his mind. All the events and the tumult faded in the vast quiet, the open spaces, the scent of wildflowers, the soft cool breeze, and the warm sun, masked as if they had never taken place. The past was only an imagining here. He could barely put a face to it, barely envision how it must have been. He wondered if the Elves ever thought of it as he did now, if it was ever for them a reminder of how transitory victories in battle so often were.

He wondered if the journey he was making now would feel any different to him when it was finished. He wondered if he would accomplish anything lasting.

His travel west had been uneventful. All four days had passed without incident. The Highland cousins and the Dwarf had come down out of the Wolfsktaag after their encounter with Truls Rohk, spent what remained of the night and the early morning hours sleeping at Panax's cabin, then packed their gear, collected their horses, and set out for Arborlon at midday. They traveled light, choosing to forgo pack animals and supplies, foraging on the way. There were countless settlements scattered across the Borderlands, and they had little difficulty obtaining what they needed. Their passage west was straightforward and unobstructed. They crossed the Rabb Plains above the Silver River, followed the north shore of the Rainbow Lake below the Runne, bypassed Varfleet and Tyrsis through Callahorn's hill country to the flats above the Tirfing, then angled north along the Mermidon River toward the Valley of Rhenn. They traveled steadily, but without haste, the days clear and sunny and pleasant, the nights cool and still.

Not once did they catch sight of or hear from Truls Rohk. Panax said they wouldn't, and he turned out to be right.

Their encounter with the shadowy, formidable Truls had left both Bek and Quentin shaken, and it wasn't until the next day, when they were well away from Depo Bent and the Wolfsktaag, that they had felt comfortable enough to pursue the subject. By then, Panax was ready to tell them the rest of what he knew.

"Of course, he's a man, just like you or me," he replied to Bek's inevitable question regarding what sort of creature Truls Rohk really was. "Well, not just like you or me, I guess, or anyone else I've ever come across. But he's a man, not some beast or wraith. He was a Southlander once, before he went into the mountains to live. He came out of the border country below Varfleet, somewhere in the Runne. His people were trappers, poor migrants who lived close to the bone. He told me this once, a long time ago. Never spoke of it again, though. Especially not the part about the fire."

They were somewhere out on the Rabb by then, chasing the sun west, the daylight beginning to fade to twilight. Neither cousin spoke as the Dwarf paused in his narration to gather his thoughts.

"When he was about twelve, I guess, there was a fire. The boy was sleeping with the men in a makeshift shelter of dried skins and it caught fire. The others got out, but the boy ran the wrong way and got tangled up in the tent folds and couldn't get free. The fire burned him so badly he was unrecognizable afterwards. They thought he was going to die; I think they thought it would be better if he did. But they did what they could for him, and it turned out to be just enough. He says he was a big lad in any case, very strong even then, and some part of him fought back against the pain and misery and kept him alive.

"So he lived, but he was disfigured so badly even his family couldn't stand to look at him. I can't imagine what that must have been like. He says he couldn't look at himself. He kept away from everyone after that, trapping and hunting in the woods, avoiding other people, other places. When he was old enough to manage it, he set out on his own, intending to live apart from everyone. He was bitter and ashamed, and he says that what he really wanted was to die. He went east into the Wolfsktaag, having heard the stories of what lived there, thinking no other man would try living in such a place, so he could at least be alone for whatever time he had left.

"But something happened to him in those mountains—he won't say what, won't talk about it. It changed his way of thinking. He decided he wanted to live. He decided he wanted to be healed. He went to the Stors for medicines and balms, for whatever treatments they could offer, then began some sort of self-healing ritual. He won't talk about that, either. I don't know whether it worked or not. He says it did, but he still hides himself in that cloak and hood. I've never seen him clearly. Not his face, not any part of his body. I don't think anyone has."

"But there's something else about him," Bek interjected quickly. "You say he's human, that he's a man underneath, a man like you and me, but he doesn't seem so. He doesn't seem like any man I've ever come across."

"No," Panax agreed, "he doesn't. And for good reason. I say he's a man like you and me mostly so you don't think he was born anything else. But he's become something more, and it's difficult to say just what that something is. A little of it, I know, I understand. He's found a way of assimilating with the things that live in the Wolfsktaag, a way of becoming like they are. He's able to shape-shift; I know that for a fact. He can take on the look and feel of animals and spirit creatures; he can become like they are—or, when he chooses, like the things that frighten them. That's what he did back there with those ur'wolves. That's why they ran from him. He's like some force of nature you don't want to cross; he's able to become anything he needs to become to kill you. He's big and strong and quick and fast to begin with; the shape-shifting only enhances that. He's feral and he's instinctive; he knows how to fit in where you and I would only know enough to want to run. He's at home in those mountains. He's at home in places other men never will be. That's why the Druid wants him along. Truls Rohk will get past obstacles no one else would dare even to challenge. He'll solve problems that would leave others scratching their heads."

"How did Walker meet him?" Quentin asked.

"Heard about him, I believe, rumors mostly, then tracked him down. He's the only man I know who could do that." Panax smiled. "I'm not sure he really did track Truls, only that he got close enough to attract his attention. There might not be anyone alive who can track Truls Rohk. But Walker found him somehow and talked him into coming with him on a journey. I'm not sure where they went that first time, but they formed some kind of a bond. Afterwards, Truls was more than willing to go with the Druid."

He shook his head. "Still, you never know. No one really has his ear. He likes me, trusts me, as much as he likes or trusts anyone, but he doesn't let me get too close."

"He's scary," Bek offered quietly. "It's more than how he hides himself or appears like a ghost out of nowhere or shape-shifts. It's more than knowing what's happened to him, too. It's how he looks right through you and makes you feel like he sees things you don't."

"He was right about me and the sword," Quentin agreed. "I didn't know what I was doing. I was just fighting to keep the magic under control, to keep those wolves at bay. If he hadn't come along, they probably would have had us."

Truls Rohk had seen or recognized something about Bek, as well, but had chosen to keep it to himself. Bek wasn't able to stop thinking about it. Trust no one, the shape-shifter had said, until you learn to see things better. It was an admonition that revealed Truls Rohk had gained an insight into him that he himself had not yet experienced. All the way down from the Wolfsktaag and on the journey across the Borderlands to Arborlon, he found himself remembering how it had been to have the shape-shifter looking at him, studying him, penetrating beyond what he could see. It was an old Druid trait, Bek knew. Allanon had been famous for the way his eyes looked right through you. There was something of that in Walker, as well. Truls Rohk was not a Druid, but when he looked at you, you felt as if you were being flayed alive.

The discussion of the shape-shifter pretty much died away after the first night, since Panax seemed to have exhausted his store of knowledge and Quentin and Bek chose to keep their thoughts to themselves. Conversation turned to other matters, particularly the journey ahead, of which the Dwarf was now part but knew little. He had been drafted into the cause because Walker had insisted he join them if Truls Rohk agreed to come. So Bek and Quentin filled Panax in on what little they knew, and the three spent much of their time tossing back and forth their ideas about exactly where they might be going and what they might be looking for.

The Dwarf was blunt in his assessment. "There is no treasure big or rich enough to interest a Druid. A Druid cares only for magic. Walker seeks a talisman or spell or some such. He goes in search of something so powerful that to let it fall into the hands of the Ilse Witch or anyone else would be suicide."

It was a compelling and believable assessment, but no one could think of anything that dangerous. There had been magic in the world since the new races had been born out of the Great Wars, reinvented by the need to survive. Much of it had been potent, and all of it had either been tamed or banished by the Druids. That there might be a new magic, undiscovered all these years and now released solely by chance, felt wrong. Magic didn't exist in a vacuum. It wouldn't just appear. Someone had conjured it, perfected it, and set it loose.

"Which is why Walker is taking people like you, Highlander, with your magic sword, and Truls Rohk," Panax insisted bluntly. "Magic to counter magic, linked to men who can wield it successfully."

This did nothing to explain why Bek was going, or Panax either, for that matter, but at least Panax was a seasoned hunter and skilled tracker; Bek was untrained at anything. Now and again, his hand would stray to the smooth hard surface of the phoenix stone, and he would remember his encounter with the King of the Silver River. Now and again, he would remember that perhaps he was not his father's son. Each time, of course, he would question everything he thought he knew and understood. Each time, he would feel Truls Rohk's eyes looking at him in the Eastland night.

Elven Hunters met them at the far end of the valley and escorted them back through the woods to Arborlon. An escort was unusual for visitors, but it was clear from the moment they gave their names to the watch that they were expected. The road to the city was broad and open, and the ride through the afternoon hours was pleasant. It was still light when they arrived at the city, coming out of the shadow of the trees onto a stretch of old growth that thinned and opened through a sprawl of buildings onto a wide bluff. Arborlon was much bigger and busier than Leah, with shops and residences spreading away for as far as the eye could see, traffic on the roads thick and steady, and people from all the races visible at every turn. Arborlon was a crossroads for commerce, a trading center for virtually every form of goods. Absent were the great forges and factories of the deep Southland and of the Rock Trolls north, but their products were in evidence everywhere, brought west for warehousing and shipping to the Elven people living farther in. Caravans of goods passed them going in and coming out, bound for or sent from those less accessible regions—the Sarandanon west, the Wilderun south, and the Troll nations north.

Quentin glanced about with a broad smile. "This is what we came for, Bek. Isn't it all grand and wonderful—just what you imagined?"

Bek kept his thoughts to himself, not trusting them to words.

Mostly he wondered how a people who had just lost a King to assassination could carry on with so little evidence of remorse—though he had to admit he couldn't think of how they should otherwise behave. Life went on, no matter the magnitude of the events that influenced it. He shouldn't expect more.

They passed through the city proper and turned south into a series of parks and gardens to reach what were clearly the Elessedil palace grounds. It was late by then, the light failing quickly, the torches on street poles and building entries lit against the encroaching gloom. The crowds of people they had passed earlier had been left behind. Home Guard materialized out of the shadows, the King's own protectors and the heart of the Elven army, stoic, silent, and sharp-eyed. They took the travelers' horses away, and the Dwarf and cousins were led down a pathway bordered by white oak and tall grasses to an open-air pavilion somewhere back from the palace buildings and overlooking the bluffs east. High-backed benches were clustered about the pavilion, and pitchers of ale and cold water sat on trays beside metal tankards and glasses.

The Home Guard who had escorted them from the road gestured toward the benches and refreshments and left.

Alone, the pavilion empty except for them, the surrounding grounds deserted, they stood waiting. After a few minutes, Panax moved to one of the benches, took out his carving knife and a piece of wood, and began to whittle. Quentin looked at Bek, shrugged, and walked over to help himself to a tankard of ale.

Bek stayed where he was, glancing about warily. He was thinking of how the Ilse Witch had orchestrated the death of an Elven King not far from that spot. It did not give him a good feeling to think that killing someone in the heart of the Elven capital city was so easy, since all of them were now eligible targets.

"What are you doing?" Quentin asked, sauntering over to join him, tankard of ale in hand. He wore the Sword of Leah strapped across his back as if it was something he had been doing all his life instead of for less than a week.

"Nothing," Bek replied. Already Quentin was evidencing the sort of changes that would affect them both in the end, growing beyond himself, shaking loose from his life. It was what his cousin had come to do, but Bek was still struggling with the idea. "I was just wondering if Walker is here yet."

"Well, you look as if you expect Truls Rohk to appear again, maybe come right out of the earth."

"Don't be too quick to discount the possibility," Panax muttered from the bench.

Quentin was looking around, as well, after that, but it was Bek who spied the two figures coming up the walk from the palace. At first neither cousin could make out the faces in the gloom, catching only momentary glimpses as they passed through each halo of torchlight on their approach. It wasn't until they had reached the pavilion and come out of the shadows completely that Bek and Quentin recognized the short, wiry figure in the lead.

"Hunter Predd," Quentin said, walking forward to offer his hand.

"Well met, Highlander," the other replied, a faint smile creasing his weathered features. He seemed genuinely pleased to see Quentin. "Made the journey out of Leah safely, I see."

"Never a moment's concern."

"That old sword strapped to your back reveal any secrets on the way?"

Quentin flushed. "One or two. You don't forget a thing, do you?"

Bek shook the Wing Rider's hand, as well, feeling a little of his earlier uneasiness fade with the other's appearance. "Is Walker here?" he asked.

Hunter Predd nodded. "He's here. Everyone's here that's going. You're the last to arrive."

Panax rose from his bench and wandered over, and they introduced him to the Wing Rider. Then Hunter Predd turned to his companion, a tall, powerfully built Elf of indeterminate age, with close-cropped gray hair and pale blue eyes. "This is Ard Patrinell," the Wing Rider said. "Walker wanted you to meet him. He's been placed in command of the Elven Hunters who will go with us."

They clasped hands with the Elf, who nodded without speaking. Bek thought that if ever anyone looked the part of a warrior, it was this man. Scars crisscrossed his blunt features and muscular body, thin white lines and rough pink welts against his sun-browned skin, a testament to battles fought and survived. Power radiated from even his smallest movements. His grip when shaking hands was deliberately soft, but Bek could feel the iron behind it. Even the way he carried himself suggested someone who was always ready, always just a fraction of a second away from swift reaction.

"You're a Captain of the Home Guard," Panax declared, pointing to the scarlet patch on the Elf's dress jacket.

Ard Patrinell shook his head. "I was. I'm not anymore."

"They don't keep you on as Captain of the Home Guard if the King is assassinated on your watch," Hunter Predd observed bluntly.

Panax nodded matter-of-factly. "Someone has to bear the blame for a King's death, even when there's no blame to be found. Keeps everyone thinking something useful's been done." He spat into the dark. "So, Ard Patrinell, you look a seasoned sort. Have you fought on the Prekkendorran?"

Again, the Elf shook his head. "I fought in the Federation Wars, but not there. I was at Klepach and Barrengrote fifteen years ago, when I was still an Elven Hunter, not yet a Home Guard." If Patrinell was irritated by the Dwarf's questions, he didn't show it.

For his part, Bek was wondering how a failed Captain of the Home Guard could end up being given responsibility for the security and safety of Walker's expedition. Was his removal only ceremonial, made necessary because of the King's death? Or was something else at work?

There was an enormous calm in Ard Patrinell's face, as if nothing could shake his confidence or disrupt his thinking. He had the look of someone who had seen and weathered a great deal and understood that loss of control was a soldier's worst enemy. If he had failed the King, he did not carry the burden of that failure openly. Bek judged him a man who understood better than most the value of patience and endurance.

"What remains to be done before we leave?" Quentin asked suddenly, changing the subject.

"Impatient to be off, Highlander?" Hunter Predd chided. "It won't be long now. We've got an airship and a Captain and crew to speed us on our way. We're gathering supplies and equipment. Loading is already under way. Our Captain of the Home Guard has selected a dozen Elven Hunters to accompany us."

"We're ready then," Quentin declared eagerly, his grin broadening with expectation.

"Not quite." The Wing Rider seemed reluctant to continue, but unable to think of a way not to. He glanced out at the encroaching night, as if his explanation might be found somewhere in the gloom. "There's still a few adjustments to be made to the terms of our going, a couple of small controversies to be resolved."

Panax frowned. "What might these small controversies be, Hunter Predd?"

The Wing Rider shrugged rather too casually, Bek thought. "For one thing, Walker feels we have too many members assigned to the expedition. Space and supplies won't support them all. He wants to reduce by as many as four or five the number that will go."

"Our new King, on the other hand," Ard Patrinell added softly, "wants to add one more."

W̲hat you are asking is not only unreasonable, it is impossible," Walker repeated patiently, stymied by Kylen Elessedil's intransigence on the matter, but fully aware of its source. "Thirty is all we can carry. The size of the ship will allow for no more. As it is, I have to find a way to cut the number who expect to go."

"Cut that number to twenty-nine, then add one back in," the Elven King replied with a shrug. "The problem is solved."

They stood in what had been Allardon Elessedil's private study, the one in which he had perused the castaway's map for the first time, but more to the point the one in which he had conducted business with those with whom he did not want to be seen on matters he did not wish to discuss openly. When the Elven King desired a public audience or a demonstration of authority, he held court in the throne room or the chambers of the Elven High Council. Allardon Elessedil had been a believer in protocol and ceremony, and he had employed each in careful and judicious measure. His son, it appeared, was inclined to do the same. Walker rated courtesy and deference, but only in private and only to the extent to which the old King had obligated his son before dying.

Kylen Elessedil understood what must be done regarding the matter of Kael Elessedil and the Elves who had disappeared with him. There was to be a search, and the Druid was to command it. The Elves were to assign funds for the purchase of a ship and crew, secure supplies and equipment for the journey, and provide a command of Elven Hunters to ensure the ship's safety. It was the command of a dying King, and his son was not about to challenge it as his first official act of office.

This did not mean, however, that he viewed the idea of a search for ships and men gone thirty years as a sane one, the appearance of the castaway, the Elessedil bracelet, and the map notwithstanding. Kylen was not his father. He was a very different sort. Allardon Elessedil had been tentative, careful, and unambitious in his life's goals. His son was reckless and determined to leave his mark. The past meant little to Kylen Elessedil. It was the present and, to an even greater extent, the future that mattered to him. He was an impassioned youth who believed without reservation that the Federation must be destroyed and the Free-born made victorious. Nothing less would guarantee Elven security. He had spent the last six months fighting aboard airships over the Prekkendorran and had returned only because his father was dead and he was next in line for the throne. He did not particularly want to be King, except to the extent that it furthered his efforts to crush the Federation. Imbued with the fever of his commitment to a victory over his enemies, he wanted only to remain on the front in command of his men. In short, he would have preferred it if his father had stayed alive.

As it was, eager to return to the battle, he was chafing already at the delay his coronation had occasioned. But he would not go, Walker knew, until this matter of the search for Kael Elessedil was resolved and, even more important, until he was certain the Elven High Council was settled on the terms of his succession. This last, Walker was beginning to understand, was at the source of his insistence on adding his younger brother's name to the ship's roster.

Kylen Elessedil stopped pacing and faced the Druid squarely. "Ahren is almost a man, nearly fully grown. He has been trained by the man I personally selected to command your Elven Hunters on this expedition. My father arranged for my brother's training five years ago. Perhaps he foresaw the need for it better than you or I."

"Perhaps he believed it should continue until Ahren is older, as well," Walker offered mildly, holding the other's gaze. "Your brother is too young and too unseasoned for a journey like this. He lacks the experience needed to justify including him. Better men will be asked to remain behind as it is."

The Elven King dismissed the argument with a grunt. "That's a judgment you cannot make. Is Ahren less a man than this cabin boy you insist on including? Bek Rowe? What does he have to offer? Is he to be left behind?"

Walker held his temper. "Your father left it to me to make the decision about who would go and who would stay. I have chosen carefully, and there are good reasons for my choices. What is at issue is not why I should take Bek Rowe, but why I should take Ahren Elessedil."

The Elf King took a moment to walk over to a window and look out into the night. "I don't have to support you in this matter at all, Druid. I don't have to honor my father's wishes if I deem them wrongheaded or if I decide circumstances have changed. You are pressing your luck with me."

He turned back to Walker, waiting.

"There is a great deal at stake in this matter," Walker replied softly. "Enough at stake that I will find a way to make this voyage, with your blessing and assistance or without. I would remind you that your father died for this."

"My father died *because* of this!"

"Your father believed me when I told him that what the Elven people stood to gain from completing this voyage successfully was of enormous importance."

"Yet you refuse to tell me what that something is!"

"Because I am not yet certain myself." Walker walked over to the King's desk and rested the tips of his fingers on its polished surface. "It is a magic that may yield us many things, but I will have to discover what form that magic will take. But think, Elven King! If it is important enough for the Ilse Witch to kill your father and your uncle as well, important enough for her to try to kill me and to stall this expedition at all costs, isn't it important enough for you?"

The young King folded his arms defensively. "Perhaps your concerns in this matter are overstated. Perhaps they are not as important as you would have me believe. I do not see the future of the Westland Elves tied to a magic that may not even exist, may not be able to be traced if it does, and may not even be useful if found. I see it tied to a war being waged with the Federation. The enemy I can see is a more recognizable threat than the one I can imagine."

Walker shook his head. "Why are we arguing? We have covered this ground before, and there is nothing to be gained by covering it again. I am committed to this journey. You have determined that your father's wishes should be followed regarding any support from the Elves. What we are arguing about is the inclusion on this expedition of a youth who is untested and inexperienced. Shall I tell you why I think you want me to take him?"

Kylen Elessedil hesitated, but Walker began speaking anyway.

"He is your younger brother and next in line for the throne. You are not close. You are the children of different mothers. If you were to be killed in the fighting on the Prekkendorran, he would be named Regent, if not King. You wish to secure the throne for your children instead. But your oldest boy is only ten. Your brother, if available, would be named his protector. That worries you. To protect your son and heir to the throne, you would send your brother with me, on a journey that will consume months and perhaps years. That removes your brother as a possible successor, either as King or Regent. It removes him as a threat."

He spoke calmly, without malice or accusation. When he was finished, Kylen Elessedil stared at him for a long time, as if weighing carefully his response.

"You are awfully bold to speak those words to me," he said finally.

Walker nodded. "I am only telling you this so that I may better understand your thinking on the matter. If Ahren Elessedil is to go with me, I would like to know why."

The young King smiled. "My father never liked you. He respected you, but he never liked you. Were you this bold with him?"

"More so, I would guess."

"But it never helped you, did it? He never agreed to support you in your bid for an independent Druid Council, convened anew at Paranor. I know. He told me."

Walker waited.

"You risk all that now by challenging me. Part of your bargain with my father was his agreement to support a new Council of Druids on your successful return. You've worked twenty-five years for that end. Would you give it all up now?"

Still Walker waited, silent within his black robes.

Kylen Elessedil stared at him a moment more, then judging that nothing further was to be gained, said, "Ahren will accompany you as my personal representative. I cannot go, so he will go in my place. This is an Elven expedition, and its goals and concerns are peculiarly Elven in nature. Kael Elessedil's disappearance must be explained. The Elfstones, if they can be found, must be returned. Any magic that exists must be claimed. These are Elven matters. Whatever happens, there must be an Elessedil in attendance. That is why my brother is going, and that is the end of the matter."

It was a firm decision, one rendered and dismissed for good. Walker could see that nothing was to be gained by arguing further. Whatever his convictions and concerns on the subject of Ahren Elessedil, Walker knew when it was time to back off. "So be it," he acknowledged, and turned the discussion to other matters.

It was after midnight when Quentin shook Bek awake from the sleep that had claimed him an hour before. With no further word from Walker on the fate of the expedition and its members, they had retired from the palace gardens and been shown to their sleeping quarters by another of the silent Home Guard. Panax was snoring in another room. Ard Patrinell and Hunter Predd had disappeared.

"Bek, wake up!" Quentin urged, pulling on his shoulder.

Bek, still catching up on sleep lost during their journey west out of the Wolfsktaag, dragged himself out of his cottony slumber and opened his eyes. "What's the matter?"

"Hunter Predd just returned from the palace, where he's spoken with Walker." Quentin's eyes were bright and his voice excited. "I heard him come in and went to see what he'd learned. He said to tell you good-bye for now. He's been sent to the coast to recruit two more Wing Riders from the Hove. The decision's been made. We leave in two days!"

"Two days," Bek repeated, not yet fully awake.

"Yes, cousin, but you didn't hear me clearly. I said *we* are going, you and I!" Quentin laughed gleefully. "Walker kept us both! He's leaving behind three of the Home Guard and taking only a single

Healer. I don't know, maybe there was someone else left off the list, as well. But he kept us! That's what matters! We're going, Bek!"

Afterwards, Quentin fell into bed and off to sleep so quickly that Bek, now awake, was unable to measure the time lapse between the two. It seemed somehow inevitable that he should be going. Even when Hunter Predd had warned that there were too many chosen for the voyage and some would be left behind, it had never occurred to him that he would be one of them. It was logical that he would be, of course. He was the youngest and the least skilled. On the face of things, he was the most expendable. But something in the Druid's insistence that he come, coupled with his encounters with the King of the Silver River and Truls Rohk, had convinced him that his selection was no afterthought and was tied inextricably to secrets of the past and to resolution of events yet to be determined. Bek was there because it was necessary for him to be so, and his life was about to change forever.

It was what Quentin had wanted for them both. But Bek Rowe was inclined to wonder if one day soon they would have cause to remember the danger of getting what you wish for.

EIGHTEEN

Bek Rowe woke the following morning to sunshine and blue skies and no sign of Quentin Leah. He took a moment to orient himself, decided he was still in Arborlon, and jumped out of bed to dress. When he checked the adjoining bedrooms, he found that Panax was missing as well. A quick glance out the window revealed the sun at midmorning height, a clear indicator of how late he had slept. There was grain cereal, cheese, and milk on the table in the anteroom, and he wolfed them down hungrily before charging out the door in search of his friends.

He was running so fast and so hard he ran right into the black-cloaked figure coming in.

"Walker!" he gasped in shock and embarrassment, and jumped back quickly.

"Good morning, Bek Rowe," the Druid said formally. A faint smile played at the corners of his mouth. "Did you sleep well?"

"Too well," Bek answered, chagrined. "I'm sorry. I didn't mean to be such a layabout—"

"Please, young traveler, don't be so anxious to apologize." Walker was chuckling softly now. He put his big hand on Bek's shoulder. "You haven't missed anything. Nor have you neglected any obligations. You were right to sleep. That was a long journey up to Depo Bent and then west to here. I would rather have you rested when we set out from here."

Bek sighed. "I guess I just assumed that since Quentin and Panax are already up and gone I was lagging in some way."

Walker shook his head. "I passed the Highlander on my way here. He had just gotten up. Panax rose a little earlier, but he doesn't sleep much. Don't think on it again. Did you eat?"

Bek nodded.

"Then you're ready to go out to the airfield and have a look around. Come with me."

They left the sleeping quarters and walked through the palace grounds, moving away from the city and out toward the south end of the Carolan. They passed any number of Elven Hunters and Home Guard on the way, but few regular citizens. No one paid them any attention. It was quieter where they walked than in the main sections of the city, less traveled by those who lived and worked there. On the backside of the Gardens of Life, they passed a pair of Black Watch guarding one of the entrances. The pair stood as if frozen, towering over everyone in their sleek black uniforms and tall hats, everything smooth and clean and trimmed in red. Within the gardens, birds darted and sang, and butterflies flitted from bush to bush, as bright as the flowers they touched upon, but the Black Watch might have been carved from stone.

Somewhere deep in the center of those gardens was the legendary Ellcrys. Even Bek, who had traveled so little, knew her story. The Ellcrys was a tree imbued with magic that formed a Forbidding to shut away the demons banished by the Word from the Faerie world centuries ago at the beginning of life. She had begun her life as an Elf, a member of an order called Chosen, and had transformed into the tree as a result of exposure to the Bloodfire. So long as she remained strong and healthy in her changed state, her magic would keep the Forbidding in place. When she began to fail, as she one day must, another would take her place. The need for replacement did not happen often; the Ellcrys on average lived for a thousand years. But the order of the Chosen was kept filled and ready even so. Once, not so long ago, almost all had been slaughtered by demons that had escaped a weakened Forbidding. Only one had survived, a young Elessedil girl named Amberle, and she had sacrificed herself to become the present Ellcrys.

Bek thought of how Coran had told him that story when he was still very little. Coran had told him any number of Elven stories, and it had always seemed to Bek that the history of the Elves must be more colorful and interesting than those of the other races, even without knowing what they were. Seeing the Gardens of Life now and having passed through the Valley of Rhenn earlier, a visitor at last to the city of Arborlon, he could believe it was so. Everything had a feeling of magic and enchantment, and all that history imparted to him by Coran felt newly alive and real.

It made him think that coming on the journey was not such a bad idea after all, though he would never admit it to Quentin.

"Did Truls Rohk arrive?" he asked Walker suddenly.

Walker did not look at him. "Did you ask him to come?"

Bek nodded. "Yes."

"Did he say he would?"

"Yes."

"Then he's here."

Walker seemed perfectly willing to accept the shape-shifter's presence on faith, so Bek let the matter drop. It wasn't his concern in any case. Another encounter with Truls Rohk could wait. Walker had already moved on, talking about their plans for departure on the following morning, the airship fitted and supplied, its crew and passengers assembled, and everything in readiness for their journey. He was confident and relaxed as he detailed their preparations, but when Bek glanced over, he caught a distant look in the other's dark eyes that suggested his thoughts were somewhere else.

Away from the buildings of the city, the Gardens of Life, and the Carolan, they passed down a well-traveled road through woods that opened onto a bluff farther south. Bek could hear the activity before he could see it, and when they emerged from the trees, an airfield and a dozen Elven airships were visible. Bek had never seen airships up close, only flying over the highlands now and then, but there was no mistaking them for anything other than what they were. They hung motionless above the earth as if cradled by the air on which they floated, tethered like captured birds to anchoring pins. From the ground they looked much bigger, particularly from where Bek stood looking up at them. Broad stretches of decking, single and multilevel, were fastened to pontoons fitted out and armored as fighting stations. On some of the airships, cabins and steering lofts were affixed aft; on others, they were settled amidships. Various forms of housing could be found both atop and beneath the decking. Single, double, and triple masts speared the clear blue sky.

"There's our vessel, Bek," Walker announced softly, his voice gone distant and soft.

Even without being told, Bek knew which of the airships the Druid was talking about. The ship in question was so different from the others that his eyes were drawn to it immediately. Its profile was low and sleek, and while it did not appear less formidable as a fighting vessel, it had a look of quickness and maneuverability that the others lacked. Its twin masts were raked and its cabins were recessed deep into the decking both fore and aft, adding to the long, smooth look. Its elevated pilot box sat amidships between the masts. Several sets of fighting ports were built into the pontoons, which curved upward at both ends like horns and were fashioned as battering rams. Other sets of fighting ports were integrated into the deck railings, which were slanted inward to provide maximum protection against attack. The airship had a dark and wicked look to it, even at rest, and a shiver went down Bek's spine as he imagined it in motion.

Men were swarming all over its decking, some working on sails and lines, some carrying aboard supplies and equipment. On this morning, it was the center of activity, with preparations for its voyage long since under way.

"If you wait here, I'll send someone over to put you to work," Walker said. Without waiting for a response, he moved away.

Bek stood looking at the shadowy form of the airship, trying without success to imagine what it would feel like to fly in her, to have this strange vessel as his home. He knew a journey of the sort they were planning would take weeks and probably months. All that time, they would live and travel aboard this ship. Thirty men and women, confined in a small, constantly moving wood-and-iron shell, adrift in the world. It was a sobering image.

"She's a striking lady, isn't she," a voice broke into his thoughts.

He glanced over as the speaker came up to him, a tall man with long red hair and clear green eyes and dressed in a wild combination of black leather and bright scarves. "She is," Bek agreed.

"You'd be Bek Rowe?" the man inquired with a grin, his manner open and friendly and immediately disarming. Bek nodded. "I'm this lady's Captain. Redden Alt Mer." He stuck out his hand in greeting, and Bek took it. "You're to be my cabin boy, Bek. You can call me Captain or sir. Or you can call me Big Red, like nearly everyone else does. Have you sailed before?"

Bek shook his head. "Not really. On the Rainbow Lake once or twice and on rivers and streams in the Highlands."

The tall man laughed. "Goodness, they've given me a cabin boy with no sea legs at all! No experience on open water or free air either, Bek? What am I to do with you?"

Bek grimaced. "Hope for the best?"

"No, no, no, we can't be relying on hope to see you through." He grinned anew. "Are you a quick study?"

"I think so."

"Good, that will help our cause. This morning is all I've got to teach you what I know before we set out, so we must make the most of it. You know about airships, do you?"

"A little." Bek was feeling foolish and slow, but the tall man was not unkind or intimidating.

"You'll know everything by the time I'm done." He paused. "A few words of advice to begin with, Bek. I'm a Rover, so you know two things right off. One, I've forgotten more about airships than other men have learned, and with the crew of Rovers I've chosen to serve under me, I can see us through anything. So don't ever question or doubt me. Second, don't ever say anything bad about Rovers—not even if you think I can't hear you."

He waited for Bek to answer, so Bek said, "No, sir."

"Good. Now here's the really important thing to remember." The cheerful face took on a serious, almost contemplative cast. "The Druid's in charge of this expedition, so I am obliged to respect his wishes and obey his orders save where the safety of the ship and crew are concerned. He's ordered me to take you on as cabin boy. That's fine. But you and I need to understand each other. The Druid intends you to serve as his eyes and ears aboard ship. He wants you to watch everyone and everything, me included. That's fine, too. I expect you can do this and do it well. But I don't want you thinking I don't know why you're really here. Fair enough?"

Bek flushed. "I'm not a spy."

"Did I say you were? Did I suggest that you were anything of the sort?" The Rover shook his head reprovingly. "Smart lads keep their eyes and ears open in any case. I don't begrudge any man that advantage. My purpose in bringing this up is to make sure you understand that as clever as the Druid thinks he is, he's no more clever than I am. I wouldn't want you to make a foolish assumption about your Captain."

Bek nodded. "Me either."

"Good lad!" Redden Alt Mer seemed genuinely pleased. "Now let's put all that behind us and begin our lessons. Come with me."

He took Bek over to the airship and had him climb the rope ladder to the decking. There, standing amidships with the boy, he began a step-by-step explanation of the ship's operation. The sails were called light sheaths. Their function was to gather light, either direct or ambient, from the skies for conversion to energy. Light could be drawn from any source, day or night. Direct light was best, but frequently it was not to be found, so the availability and usefulness of ambient light was the key to an airship's survival. Light energy gathered by the sheaths was relayed by lines called radian draws. The draws took the heat down to the decking and into containers called parse tubes, which housed diapson crystals. The crystals, when properly prepared by craftsmen, received and converted the light energy to the energy that propelled and steered the airship. Hooding and unhooding the crystals determined the amount of thrust and direction the airship took.

Redden Alt Mer had Bek repeat all this back when he was finished, word for word. Intrigued by the process and interested to learn everything about how it worked, the boy did so faultlessly. The Rover was pleased. Understanding the principles of airship flight was crucial to learning how to operate her. But it took years to learn how to fly an airship properly, as the Federation pilots had not yet discovered. The nuances of hooding and unhooding the crystals, of riding and sideslipping wind currents, and of avoiding downdrafts and lightfalls that could change the momentum and responsiveness of an airship in an instant were not easily mastered. Rovers were the best pilots, he offered without a trace of boasting. Rovers were born to the free life, and they adapted and understood flight better than other men.

Or women, a tall, red-haired woman who might have been his twin offered pointedly, coming up beside them. Redden Alt Mer only barely managed to salvage his gaffe by introducing his sister, Rue Meridian, as the best airship pilot he had ever known and a better fighter than any man he had flown with. Rue Meridian, with her striking looks and flaming hair, her confident, no-nonsense attitude, and her smiling eyes and ready laugh, made Bek feel shy and awkward. But she made him feel good, too. She did not challenge him as her brother had done or question his presence in any way. She simply told him she was glad to have him aboard. Still, there was an iron core to her that Bek did not misjudge, a kind of redoubt beneath the cheerful facade that he suspected he did not want to come up against.

She chatted with them for a few minutes more, then left to oversee the loading of the vessel. Her departure left a void in Bek that was tangible and startling.

With Redden Alt Mer leading, they continued to walk the airship end to end, the Rover explaining what everything was as they went. Each time he finished an explanation, he made Bek repeat it back to him. Each time, he seemed satisfied with the answer he received. He explained the pilot box and the connectors that ran to the parse tubes, hoods, rudders, and main draws. For the most part, the crew raised and lowered the sheaths and set the draws, but in an emergency, everything could be controlled from the pilot box. There were anchors and stays for landing. There were weapons of all sorts, some handheld, some attached to the decking of the ship. The Rover took Bek into the sleeping quarters and supply bins. He took the boy all the way up the pegged climbing steps of the masts to see how the sheaths were attached to the draws, then down to the parse tubes to see how the draws were attached to the diapson crystals. He was quick with his explanations, but thorough. He seemed intent on the boy's learning, and Bek was eager to comply.

There was only one component of the airship that the Rover avoided assiduously, a large rectangular box set upright against the foremast in front of the pilot box. It was covered with black canvas and lashed to the mast and decking with a strange type of metal-sheathed cable. They walked right by it repeatedly, and after they had done so for about the third or fourth time, Bek could contain himself no longer.

"Captain, what's under the canvas?" he asked, pointing at the box.

The Rover scratched his head. "I don't know. It belongs to the

Druid. He had it brought aboard in the dead of night without my knowing two days ago, and when I found it there, he told me it was necessary that we take it with us, but he couldn't tell me what it was."

Bek stared at it. "Has anyone tried to get a look under the canvas?"

The Rover laughed. "A lad after my own heart! Shades, Bek Rowe, but you are a wonder! Of course, we tried! Several of us!" He paused dramatically. "Want to know what happened?"

Bek nodded.

"Try looking for yourself and see."

Bek hesitated, no longer so eager.

"Go on," the other urged, gesturing, "it won't hurt you."

So Bek reached for the canvas, and when his hand got to within a foot of it, lines of thin green fire began to dance all over the cables that lashed the box in place, jumping from cable to cable, a nest of writhing snakes. Bek jerked his hand back quickly.

Redden Alt Mer chuckled. "That was our decision, as well. A Druid's magic is nothing to trifle with."

His instruction of Bek continued as if nothing had happened. After Bek had been aboard for a time and his initial excitement had died down, he became aware of a movement to the airship that had not been apparent before, a gentle swaying, a tugging against the anchoring lines. There was no apparent wind, the day calm and still, and there was no movement from the other ships that might account for the motion. When Bek finally asked about it, Redden Alt Mer told him it was the natural response of the ship to the absorption of light into their sheaths. The converted energy kept her aloft, and it was only the anchor cables that kept her from floating away completely, because her natural inclination was to take flight. The Rover admitted that he had been flying for so long that he didn't notice the motion himself anymore.

Bek thought it gave the airship the feel of being alive, of having an existence independent of the men and women who rode her. It was a strange sensation, but the longer he stayed aboard, the more he felt it. The ship moved like a great cat stirring out of sleep, lazy and unhurried, coming slowly awake. The motion radiated through the decking and into his body, so that he soon became a part of it, and it had something of the feel of floating in water that was still and untroubled.

Redden Alt Mer finished with him at midday and sent him off to help inventory supplies and equipment with a bluff, burly fellow Rover called Furl Hawken. The Rover everyone called Hawk barely gave him a second glance, but was friendly enough and pleased at his quickness in picking up the instructions he was given. Once or twice, Rue Meridian came by, and every time Bek was mesmerized.

"She affects everyone that way," Furl Hawken observed with a grin, catching the look on his face. "Little Red will break your heart just by looking at you. Too bad it's wasted effort."

Bek wanted to ask what he meant but was too embarrassed to pursue the matter, so he let it drop.

By the end of the day, Bek had learned most of what there was to know about the operation of their airship, the components that drove her, and the nature of the supplies and equipment she would be carrying. He had met most of the crew as well, including the ship's builder, a truly frightening Rover named Spanner Frew, who yelled and cursed at everyone in general and looked ready to knock down anyone who dared question him. He acknowledged Bek with a grunt and afterwards ignored him completely. Bek was just as happy.

He was on his way back across the airfield with the sun at his back when Quentin caught up with him.

"Did you go aboard the ship?" he asked eagerly, falling into step with his cousin. He was sweating through his rumpled, stained clothes. His long hair was matted, and the skin of his hands and forearms was cut and bruised.

"I've hardly been *off* the ship," Bek said. He gave the other a smirk. "What have you been doing, wrestling bears?"

Quentin laughed. "No, Walker ordered me to train with the Elven Hunters. Ard Patrinell worked with me all day. He knocked me down so many times and skinned me up so many different ways that all I can think about is how little I know." He reached back for his sword. "This thing's not all it's cracked up to be, Bek."

Bek grinned mischievously. "Well, it's probably only as good as its bearer, Quentin. Anyway, count your blessings. I spent all day learning how much I don't know about airships and flying. I'd be willing to bet that there's a lot more I don't know about flying than you don't know about fighting."

Quentin laughed and shoved him playfully, and they joked and teased each other all the way back to the palace compound as the last of the sunlight disappeared below the horizon and the twilight began to shadow the land. With the setting of the sun, a stillness enveloped the city as her people drifted homeward and the bustle and clamor of traffic faded away. In the woods through which the cousins passed close by the palace grounds and parks, the only sounds were of voices, indistinct and distant, carried in the silence from other places.

They were approaching the pathway that led to their sleeping quarters when Bek said quietly, "Quentin? What do you think we're really doing here?"

They stopped, and his cousin looked at him in confusion. "What do you mean?"

Bek put his hands on his hips and sighed. "Think about it. Why are we here? Why us, with all these others that Walker's chosen?"

"Because Walker thinks we—"

"I know what Walker told us." Bek cut him short impatiently. "He told us he wanted two young, clever fellows to share his thoughts. He told us he wanted you for your magic sword and me for my keen eyes and ears or some such thing. I know what he said, and I've been trying to make myself believe it since we set out. But I don't. I don't believe it at all."

Quentin nodded matter-of-factly, unperturbed. Sometimes Bek just wanted to throttle him. "Are you listening to me?" he snapped.

His cousin nodded. "Sure. You don't believe Walker. Why not?"

"Because, Quentin, it just doesn't feel right." Bek emphasized his words with chopping gestures. "Everyone selected for this expedition has years of experience exploring and fighting. They've been all over the Four Lands, and they know how to deal with all sorts of trouble. What do we know? Nothing. Why take two inexperienced nobodies like us?"

"He's taking Ahren Elessedil," Quentin offered. "And what about the seer? Ryer Ord Star? She doesn't look very strong."

Bek nodded impatiently. "I'm not talking about strength alone. I'm talking about skill and experience and talent. I'm talking about purpose! What's ours? We've just spent the entire day training, for goodness' sake! Did you see anyone else training for this trip? Are you really the only one Walker could turn to who could back him up with magic? In all the Four Lands, the only one? Given what happened in the Wolfsktaag, how much use do you think you would be to him at this point? Be honest!"

Quentin was quiet a moment. "Not much," he admitted grudgingly, and for the first time a hint of doubt crept into his voice.

"What about me?" Bek pursued his argument with a vengeance. "Am I the only clever pair of eyes and ears he can call on? Am I really that useful to him that he would drop several Elven Hunters with years of experience and training behind them and a skilled Healer, as well? Are you and I all that wondrous that he just can't afford to leave us behind, even though we know he's pressed for space?"

They stared at each other in the growing dark without speaking, eyes locked. Somewhere in the compound ahead, a door slammed and a voice called out a name.

Quentin shook his head. "What are you saying, Bek?" he asked softly. "That we shouldn't go? That we should give this whole business up?"

Oddly enough, that wasn't his intent. It might have been a logical suggestion, given his arguments and conclusions. It might have been what another man would have done under the circumstances, but Bek Rowe had decided he would make the voyage. He was committed. He was as determined to go as Quentin was. Maybe it had something to do with the secrets he had discovered since Walker had appeared to them in the Highlands—of his father's identity and his own origins, of the King of the Silver River and the phoenix stone, of Truls Rohk and his cryptic warning not to trust anyone. Maybe it was just that he was too stubborn to quit when so many would know and judge him accordingly. Maybe it was his belief that he was meant to make the journey, whatever his fears or doubts, because going would determine in some important and immutable way the course of his life.

A small voice of reason still whispered that he should tell Quentin, *Yes, we should give this business up and go home.* He squelched that voice with barely a second's thought.

"What I'm saying," he replied instead, "is that we should be careful about what we accept at face value. Druids keep secrets and play games with ordinary men like you and me. That's their history and tradition. They manipulate and deceive. They are tricksters, Quentin. I don't know about Walker. I don't know much of anything about what he really intends for us. I just think we ought to be very careful. I think we . . ."

He ran out of words and stood there, looking at his cousin helplessly.

"You think we ought to look out for each other," Quentin finished, nodding slowly. "We always have, haven't we?"

Bek sighed. "But maybe we need to do more of it here. And when something doesn't sit right, like this business, I think we have to tell each other so. If we don't, Quentin, who will?"

"Maybe no one."

"Maybe not."

Quentin studied him in silence once more, then smiled suddenly. "You know what, Bek? If you hadn't agreed to come on this journey, I wouldn't have come either."

Bek stared at him in surprise. "Really?"

Quentin nodded. "Because of what you've just said. There isn't anyone else I would trust to watch my back or tell me the truth about things. Only you. You think I look at you like a bothersome younger brother that I let tag along because I have to. I don't. I want you with me. I'm bigger and stronger, sure. And I'm better at some things than you. But you have a gift for figuring things out that I don't. You get at the truth in a way I can't. You see things I don't even notice."

He paused. "What I'm trying to say is that I think of us as equals as well as brothers. I pay pretty close attention to how you feel about things, whether you realize it or not. That's the way it's always been. That's the way it will be here. I won't accept anything I'm told without talking it over with you. You don't have to ask me to do that. I'd do it anyway."

Bek felt awkward and foolish. "I guess I just needed to say what I was thinking out loud."

Quentin grinned. "Well, who knows? Maybe I needed to hear you say it, too. Now it's done. Let's go eat."

They went inside then, and for the rest of the night until he fell asleep Bek found himself thinking how close he was to Quentin—as a brother, a friend, and a confidant—closer than he was to anyone in the world. They had shared everything growing up, and he could not imagine it being any other way. He made a promise to himself then, the sort of promise he hadn't made since he was a small boy filled with the sort of resolve that age tempered and time wore down. He did not know where they were going or what they would encounter in the days ahead, Quentin and he, but whatever happened he would find a way to keep his brother safe.

NINETEEN

§

awn broke in a bright golden blaze at the line between sky and earth on the eastern horizon, and the airfield south of Arborlon began to fill with Elves come to watch the launch of the expedition. Thousands approached, crowding down the roads and walks, slipping along the narrow forest trails and pathways, filling the spaces at the edges of the field until their eager, excited faces ringed the bluff. Organized by unit and company, a sizable contingent from the Elven army was already in place, drawn up in formation at both ends of the field, Elven Hunters in their soft green and taupe dress uniforms, Home Guard in emerald trimmed with crimson, and Black Watch standing tall and dark and forbidding like winter trees. Overhead, Elven airships that had already lifted off circled like silent phantoms, sailing on the back of a slow, soft morning wind.

At the center of the airfield, solitary and proud, the sleek, dark airship that was the object of everyone's attention hung just off the ground in the new light, her sails unfurled and her lines taut, straining to be free.

Quentin on one side and Panax on the other, Bek Rowe stood watching from the bow. All about the railings fore and aft were gathered the Rovers who would crew the ship, the Elven Hunters who would defend her, and the few other members of the expedition chosen by Walker. The Druid stood with Redden Alt Mer in the pilot box, talking quietly, sharp eyes shifting left and right as he spoke, hands folded into his black robes.

Ahren Elessedil stood alone amidships by the foremast, isolated from everyone. He was a small, slight Elf with boyish features and a quiet manner. Whereas his brother Kylen was fair and blond in the traditional manner of the Elessedils, Ahren was dusky of skin and brown of hair, closer in appearance to the great Queen Wren. He had come aboard with the other Elves, but quickly separated from them and had remained apart since. He seemed lost and uncertain of himself as he stood looking out at the crowds. Bek felt sorry for him. He was in a difficult position. Officially, he was a representative of the Elessedil family and the crown, but everyone knew that Walker had been forced to include him because Kylen had insisted on it. Rumor had it that Kylen wanted him out of the way.

That accounted for everyone but Truls Rohk. Of the shape-shifter, there was still no sign.

A blare of trumpets drew Bek's eyes to where the crowd was parting to make way for the Elven King and his retinue. A long line of Home Guard marched through the gap, flanking standard bearers who bore the flags of all the Elven Kings and Queens dead and gone, personal icons sewn on brightly colored fields swirling in the breeze. When they had passed onto the airfield, the Elessedil family banner hove into view, a crimson image of the Ellcrys emblazoned on a field of green. Kylen Elessedil followed on horseback, raised high enough above the heads of the crowd so that all could see him. His wife and children rode on horses behind him followed on foot by the more distant members of his family and his personal retinue. The long column marched out of the trees and onto the airfield and took up a position directly in front of the airship's curved bow.

The trumpets sounded once more and went still. The crowd quieted, and Kylen Elessedil lifted his arms in greeting.

"Citizens of Arborlon! Friends of the Elven!" His booming voice carried easily from one end of the field to the other. "We are gathered to witness and to celebrate an epochal event. A band of men and women of great courage will go forth this day on our behalf and on behalf of all free and right-thinking men and women everywhere. They sail the winds of the world in search of truths that have eluded us for thirty years. On their journey, they will attempt to discover the fate of my father's brother's expedition, lost those thirty years ago, of those ships and men, and of the Elfstones they carried, which are our heritage. On their journey, they will seek out treasures and magics that are rightfully ours and that can be put to the uses for which they were intended by the men and women for whom they were meant—Elves, one and all!"

A cheer rose from the crowd, swelling quickly to a roar. Bek glanced about at the faces of those gathered close, but found no expression on any save Quentin's, where a kind of vague amusement flickered like candlelight in the wind and was gone.

"My brother Ahren leads this expedition on behalf of my family and our people," Kylen continued as the cheering died away. "He is to be commended and respected for his bravery and his sense of duty. With him go some of the bravest of our Elven Hunters; our good friend from the Druids of Paranor, Walker; a complement of skilled and capable Rovers to captain and crew the ship; and a select band of others drawn from the Four Lands who will lend their talents and courage to this most important effort. Acknowledge them all, my friends! Praise them well!"

Again, the roar went up, the banners waved, and the air was filled with sound and color, and Bek, in spite of his cynicism, found himself infused with unmistakable pride.

Kylen Elessedil held up his hands. "We have lost a good and well-loved King in these past weeks. Treachery and cowardice have taken my father, Allardon Elessedil, from us. It was his dying wish that this expedition set forth, and I would be a poor son and subject indeed if I failed to honor his wishes. These men and women"—he gestured behind him toward the ship—"feel as I do. Everything possible has been done to assure their success and speedy return. We send them off with our good wishes, and we will not cease to think of them until they are safely home again."

Clever, Bek thought, to lay everything off on the old King, dead and gone. Kylen had learned something of politics already. If the expedition failed, he had made certain the blame would not be laid at his feet. If it succeeded, he would be quick to share in the rewards and claim the credit.

Bek shook his head at Quentin, who just shrugged and grinned ruefully.

The crowd was cheering anew, and while the people did so, a member of the Elven High Council carried to the King a long, slender green bottle. The King accepted it, wheeled his stallion about, and walked him to just below the bow of the airship. Hands raised anew, he turned once more to the crowd.

"Therefore, as King of the Land Elves and Sovereign Lord of the Westland, I wish this brave company success and good sailing, and I give to their ship the cherished name of one of our own, revered and loved over the years. I give to this ship the name *Jerle Shannara!*"

He turned back to the airship, standing tall in the stirrups of his saddle, and swung the bottle against the metal-sheathed horns of the bow rams. The green glass shattered in a spray of bright liquid, and the air was filled with silver and gold crystals, then with rainbow colors erupting in showers that geysered fifty feet skyward and coated in a fine crystalline mist all those who stood with the King and those aboard ship. Bek, who had shielded himself automatically, brushed at his tunic sleeves and watched the mist come away in a soft, warm powder that fizzled on his hands like steam, then faded on the air.

The crowd cheered and shouted anew, "Long live the *Jerle Shannara*" and "Long live Kylen Elessedil." The cheering went on and on, rising across the open bluff and sailing off into the distant forests beyond, echoes on the wind. Trumpets blew and drums boomed, and the banners of the dead Elven Kings waved and whipped at the end of their lofted standards. The ropes that bound the *Jerle Shannara* were released, and the sleek black airship rose swiftly, wheeled away from the sun toward the still-dark west, and began to pick up speed. The bluff below and those assembled on it fell away, turning small and faint in the light morning haze. The cheers died and the shouts faded, and Arborlon and her people were left behind.

That first day passed quickly for Bek, though not as quickly as he would have liked. It started out well enough, with Redden Alt Mer bringing the boy into the pilot box to stand next to him while he conducted a series of flight tests on the *Jerle Shannara*, taking her through various maneuvers intended to check her responses and timing. The Rover even let the boy steer the great ship at one point, talking him through the basics of handling the rudder and line controls. Bek repeated once more what he had learned the previous day about the components of the airship and their functions.

All this helped take his mind off the motion of the ship as it rocked and swayed on the back of the wind, but it wasn't enough to save him. In the end, his stomach lurched and knotted with deliberate and recognizable intent. Redden Alt Mer saw the look on his face and pointed him toward the bucket that sat at the foot of the box.

"Let her go, lad," he advised with an understanding smile. "It happens to the best of us."

Bek doubted that, but there was nothing he could do to save himself. He spent the next few hours wishing he were dead and imagining that if the weather was even the least bit severe, he would be. He noted between heaves that the frail young seer, Ryer Ord Star, looked equally distressed where she sat alone at the aft railing with her own bucket in hand, and that even the stalwart Panax had gone green around the gills.

No one else seemed to be affected, not even Quentin, who was engaged in combat practice with the Elven Hunters in a wide space on the foredeck, working his way through a series of blows and parries, advances and retreats, urged on by the immutable Ard Patrinell. Most of the others aboard, he was told later by Big Red, had sailed airships before and so were accustomed to their motion. Bek would never have believed that so little movement could make anyone feel so sick, but, his safety line securely in place, he forced himself to stay upright and interested in what was happening about him, and by midafternoon he was no longer struggling.

Walker came by once or twice to inquire after him. The Druid's dark face and somber demeanor never changed when he did so, and nothing in his words suggested reproval or disappointment. He simply asked both the boy and the ship's Captain how the former's training was coming and seemed satisfied with their answers. He was there and gone so quickly that Bek wasn't entirely sure Walker had noticed how ill "the boy" was—although it seemed impossible to imagine he hadn't.

In any case, Bek got through the experience and was grateful when later in the day the Elven Healer Joad Rish gave him a root to chew that would aid in staving off further attacks. He tried a little, found it bitter and dry, but quickly decided that any price was worth keeping his stomach settled.

It was nearing sunset, his flying lessons complete for the day and his equilibrium restored, when Ahren Elessedil approached Bek. He was standing at the portside railing looking out at the sweep of the countryside below, the land a vast, sprawling checkerboard of green and brown, the sun sliding westward into the horizon, when the young Elf came up to stand beside him.

"Are you feeling better now?" Ahren asked solicitously.

Bek nodded. "Although I thought I was going to turn myself inside out for a while there."

The other smiled. "You did well for your first time. Better than me. I was sent up when I was twelve to learn about airships. On my father's orders. He believed his children should be schooled often and early in the world's mechanics. I was not a very strong boy, and the flying didn't agree with me at all. I was up for two weeks and sick every day. The Captain of the ship never said a word, but I was humiliated. I just never got the hang of any of it."

"I was surprised at how quickly I got sick."

"I think it builds up inside you, so that by the time you realize how badly you feel, it seems like it's happening all at once." The Elf paused and turned toward him. "I'm Ahren Elessedil."

Bek shook the other's hand. "Bek Rowe."

"The Druid brought you with him, didn't he? You and the Highlander? That says you are someone special. Can you work magic?"

There it was again. Bek smiled ruefully. "Quentin has a sword that can work magic, although he doesn't know how to use it very well yet. I can't do anything." He thought about the phoenix stone, but kept the thought to himself. "Can you?"

Ahren Elessedil shook his head. "Everyone knows why I'm here. My brother doesn't want me anywhere near Arborlon. He's worried that if something happens to him, I'll be placed on the throne ahead of his own children because they're too young to rule. It's an odd concern, don't you think? If you're dead, what does any of it matter?" He seemed sad and distant as he spoke. "My father would probably agree with me. He didn't think all that much about succession and order of rule, and I guess I don't either. Kylen does. He's been training for it all his life, so it matters to him. We don't like each other very much. I suppose it's better that I'm out here, on this airship, on this expedition, than back in Arborlon. At least we're out of each other's hair."

Bek nodded and said nothing.

"Did you know that my father and Walker didn't like each other?" Ahren asked, looking at him sharply. Bek shook his head no. "They had a terrible fight some years ago about establishing a

Druid Council at Paranor. Walker wanted Father's help, and Father wouldn't give it. They didn't speak for years and years. It's odd that they agreed on this expedition when they couldn't agree on anything else, don't you think?"

Bek furrowed his brow.

"But maybe they found more in the way of common ground on the issue of this expedition than they did on the issue of a Druid Council." Ahren didn't wait for his reply. "There's some sort of Elven magic involved, and both would have wanted possession of that. I think the truth of the matter is that they needed each other. There is this map that only Walker can read, and there is the cost of the airship and crew that only Father could manage. And he would have agreed to provide the Elven Hunters to keep us all safe. If anyone can manage to do so. My uncle carried Elfstones, and that wasn't enough to save him."

He was being so forthright about matters that Bek was encouraged to ask a question he otherwise would not have asked. "Ard Patrinell was removed as Captain of the Home Guard when your father was killed. If he's out of favor with your brother and the High Council, why has he been sent to command the Elven Hunters on this expedition?"

Ahren grinned. "You don't understand how these things work, Bek. It is because he is out of favor that he's been sent with us. Kylen wants him out of Arborlon almost as much as he wants me out. Ard is my friend and protector. He trained me personally at my father's express command. Everything I know about fighting and battle tactics, I learned from him. Kylen doesn't trust him. My father's death gave my brother the perfect excuse to strip Ard of his command, and this expedition offered him a way to remove both Ard and me from the city."

He gave Bek a cool look of appraisal. "You seem pretty smart, Bek. So let me tell you something. My brother doesn't think we're coming back—any of us. Maybe, deep down inside where he hides his darkest secrets, he even hopes it. He's supporting this expedition because he can't think of a way out of it. He's doing this because Father decreed it as he lay dying, and a newly crowned King can't afford to ignore that sort of deathbed admonition. Besides, in a single stroke of good fortune he manages to get rid of me, Ard Patrinell, and the Druid, none of whom he has any particular use or liking for. If we don't come back, that solves his problem for good, doesn't it?"

Bek nodded. "I suppose so." He paused, thinking about the implications of it all. "It doesn't make me feel very good about being part of the expedition, however."

Ahren Elessedil cocked his head reflectively. "It's not supposed to. On the other hand, maybe we'll fool him. Maybe we'll survive."

That night, when dinner was complete, the airship coasting on ambient starlight, and crew and passengers alike beginning to settle into their quarters for sleep, Walker called together a small number of the ship's company for a meeting. Bek and Quentin were among those summoned, which surprised both, since neither considered himself a part of the vessel's leadership. By then Bek had shared with his cousin his conversation with Ahren Elessedil, and the two of them had debated at length how many others aboard ship understood as the young Elf did how expendable they were considered by the Elven King who had dispatched them. Certainly Walker appreciated the situation. Ard Patrinell probably understood it as well. That was about it. Everyone else would be operating under the assumption that Kylen Elessedil and the Elven High Council fully supported the expedition and anticipated its safe and successful return.

Except perhaps the Rovers, Bek added, almost as an afterthought. Big Red and his sister seemed pretty quick, and it was common knowledge in the Four Lands that Rovers had ears everywhere.

Bek was of the opinion that he should tell all of this to Walker in any case, since the Druid wanted to know everything the boy saw or heard while aboard ship, but there had been no opportunity as yet to talk with him. Now they were gathered in Redden Alt Mer's quarters below the aft decking for the meeting Walker had called, and Bek put the matter aside. In addition to the Druid and the Highland cousins, others present included Big Red and his sister, Ahren Elessedil and Ard Patrinell, and the frail-looking seer, Ryer Ord Star. As the others crowded close to Walker, who stood at a table with a hand-drawn chart spread out before him, the seer alone hung back in the shadows. Childlike and shy, her strange eyes luminescent and her skin as pale as parchment, she watched them as if she were a wild thing ready to bolt.

"Tomorrow midday we will reach the coast of the Blue Divide," Walker began, looking at each of them in turn. "Once there, we meet up with Hunter Predd and two other Wing Riders who will accompany us on our voyage, serving as scouts and foragers. Our journey from there will take us west and north, where we will seek out three islands. Each requires a stop and a search for a talisman that we must claim in order to succeed in our quest. The islands are familiar to no one aboard, myself included. They lie beyond the regions explored either by airships or Rocs. They are named on the map we follow, but they are not well described."

"Nor are we certain of the distances to each," Redden Alt Mer added, drawing all eyes momentarily to him. "Headings are clearly marked, but distances are vague. Our progress may depend greatly on the weather we encounter."

"Our Captain believes from the information I've been able to extract from the original map that the first island requires about a week's travel," Walker continued. He pointed at the map. "This copy is an approximation of the one we follow and will be left out for anyone who wishes to view it during the course of our travels. I've made it larger so that it will be easier to see. The islands we seek lie here, here, and here." He pointed to each. "Flay Creech is the first, Shatterstone the second, and Mephitic the third. They will have been chosen deliberately by whoever concealed the talismans we seek. Each talisman will be protected. Each island will be warded. Going ashore will be a dangerous business, and we will limit each search party to the smallest number possible."

"What sort of talismans do we search for?" Ard Patrinell asked quietly, leaning forward for a better look at the map.

"Keys," Walker said. "Of their size and shape, I can't be sure. I think from the writing on the map they are all the same, but possibly they are not."

"What do they do?" Ahren Elessedil asked boldly, his young face wearing its most determined look.

Walker smiled faintly. "What you might expect, Elven Prince. They open a door. When we have the keys in our possession, we will sail until we reach Ice Henge." He pointed to a symbol drawn on the map. "Once there, we search for the safehold of Castledown. The keys will gain us entrance when we have found it."

There was momentary silence as they studied the map in earnest. In the shadows, Ryer Ord Star's eyes were locked on Walker's dark face, an intense and feverish gaze, and it seemed to Bek, glancing over at her, as if she fed herself in some way by what she found there.

"How will you get ashore on these islands?" Rue Meridian asked, breaking the silence. "Will you use the ship or the Rocs?"

"The Rocs, when and where I can, because they are more mobile," the Druid answered.

She shook her head slowly. "Reconsider your decision. If we use the ship, we can lower you by winch basket or ladder from the air. If you rely on the Rocs, they will have to land. When they are grounded, they are vulnerable."

"Your point is well taken," Walker said. He glanced around. "Does anyone else wish to speak?"

To Bek's surprise, Quentin responded. "Does the Ilse Witch know all this, too?"

Walker paused to study the Highlander carefully, then nodded. "Most of it."

"So we are engaged in a race of sorts?"

Walker seemed to consider his answer before giving it. "The Ilse Witch does not have a copy of the map. Nor has she had the opportunity to study its markings as I have. She has probably gleaned her information from the mind of the castaway who carried the map. Of our general purpose and route, she will have full knowledge, I think. But of the particulars, there is some doubt. The castaway's mind was nearly gone, and I have reason to think he did not know all of what the map revealed."

"But knowing what she does she will have left by now on an airship of her own," Ard Patrinell interrupted. "She will be looking for us, either following behind or lying in wait ahead."

He made it a statement of fact, and Walker did not contradict him. Instead, he looked around once more. "I think we all appreciate the dangers we face. It is important that we do. We must be ready to defend ourselves. That we will be required to do so, probably more than once, is almost certain. Whether or not we are successful depends on our preparation. Be alert, then. Wherever you are, look about you and keep careful watch. Surprise will undo us quicker than anything."

He made a small gesture of dismissal. "I think we've talked enough about it for tonight. Go to your berths and sleep. We will meet again tomorrow night and each night hereafter to discuss our plans."

Leaving Redden Alt Mer to his cabin, they filed silently out, dispersing in the corridors belowdecks. As Bek followed Quentin, Walker stopped him with a light touch and took him aside. Quentin glanced back, then continued on without comment.

"Walk with me," the Druid said to Bek, taking him down the corridor that led to the supply room. From there, they climbed topside and stood together at the portside railing, alone beneath a canopy of black sky and endless stars. A west wind brushed at their faces with a cool touch, and Bek thought he could smell the sea.

"Tell me what Ahren Elessedil had to say to you today," Walker instructed softly, looking out into the night.

Bek did so, surprised the Druid had even noticed his conversation with the Elf. When he was finished, Walker did not speak again right away, continuing to stare off into the darkness, lost in thought. Bek waited, thinking that nothing he had repeated would be news to the Druid.

"Ahren Elessedil is made of tougher material than his brother knows," was all the other said of the matter, when he finally spoke. Then his eyes shifted to find Bek's. "Will you be his friend on this voyage?"

Bek considered the question, then nodded. "I will."

Walker nodded, seemingly satisfied. "Keep your eyes and ears open, Bek. You will come to know things that I will not, and it will be important that you remember to tell me of them. It might not happen for a time, but eventually it will. One of those things might save my life."

Bek blinked in surprise.

"Our young seer has already forecast that at some point I will be betrayed. She doesn't know when or by whom. But she has seen that someone will try to kill me and someone else will try to lead me astray. Maybe they are the same person. Maybe it will be purposeful or maybe an accident. I have no way of knowing."

Bek shook his head. "No one I've met aboard this ship seems disposed to wish you harm, Walker."

The Druid nodded. "It may not be anyone aboard ship. It may be the enemy who tracks us, or it may be someone we will meet along the way. My point is that four eyes and ears are better than two. You still suspect you have no real function on this journey, Bek. I can see it in your eyes and hear it in your voice. But your importance to me—to all of us—is greater than you think. Believe in that. One day, when the time is right, I will explain it fully to you. For now, keep faith in my word and watch my back."

He glided silently into the darkness, leaving Bek staring after him in confusion. The boy wanted to believe what the Druid had told him, but that he might have any real importance on their journey was inconceivable. He considered the matter in silence, unable to come to terms with the idea. He would watch Walker's back because he believed it was right to do so. How successful he would be was another matter, one he did not care to look at too closely.

Then, suddenly, he was aware of being watched. The feeling came over him swiftly and unexpectedly, attacking, not stealing. The force of it stunned him. He scanned quickly across the empty decking from bow to stern, where at each end an Elven Hunter as still and dark as fixed shadow kept watch. Amidships, the burly figure of Furl Hawken steered the airship from the pilot box. None of them looked at him, and there was no one else to be seen.

Still, Bek could feel hidden eyes settled on him, their weight palpable.

Then, as suddenly as the feeling had swept over him, it disappeared. All about, the star-filled night was wrapped in deepest silence. He stood at the railing a few moments longer, regaining his equilibrium and screwing his courage back into place, then hurried quickly below.

TWENTY

Early the following afternoon, the *Jerle Shannara* arrived on the coast and swung out over the vast expanse of the Blue Divide into the unknown. Within moments Hunter Predd and two other Wing Riders soared skyward from the cliffs below the Irrybis to meet them. Hunter Predd glided close to the airship to offer greetings, then angled away to take up a flanking position. For the remainder of that day and for most of the days that followed, the Wing Riders flew in formation off the bow and stern of the ship, two forward and one aft, a silent and reassuring presence.

When Bek asked Walker at one point what happened to them at night, the Druid told him it varied. Sometimes they flew right on through until daybreak, matching the slower pace that the airship set in darkness. Rocs were enormously strong and resilient, and they could fly without stopping for up to three days. Most of the time, however, the Wing Riders would take their Rocs ahead to an island or atoll and land long enough to feed, water, and rest the birds and their riders before continuing on. They worked mostly in shifts, with one Wing Rider always warding the ship, even at night, as a protective measure. With the Rocs on watch, nothing could approach without being detected.

They traveled without incident for ten days, the time sliding away for Bek Rowe in a slow, unchanging daily routine. Each morning he would rise and eat his breakfast with the Rovers, then follow Redden Alt Mer as he completed a thorough inspection of the airship and its crew. After that, he would stand with the Rover Captain in the pilot box, sometimes just the two of them, sometimes with another Rover at the controls, and Bek would first recite what he knew about a particular function of the ship's operating system and then be instructed in some further area or nuance. Later, he would operate the controls and rudders, drawing down power from the light sheaths or unhooding the crystals or tightening the radian draws.

Sometimes, when Big Red was busy elsewhere, Bek would be placed in the care of Little Red or Furl Hawken or even the burly Spanner Frew. The shipbuilder mostly yelled at him, driving him from pillar to post with his sharp tongue and acid criticism, forcing him to think harder and act faster than normal. It helped steady him, in an odd sort of way. After an hour or two of surviving Spanner Frew, he felt he was ready for anything.

Between sessions with the Rovers, he would perform a cabin boy's chores, which included running messages from Captain to crew and back again, cleaning the Captain's and his sister's quarters, inventorying supplies every third day, and helping serve the meals and clear the dishes. Most of it wasn't very pleasant or exciting, but it did put him in close proximity to almost everyone several times a day and gave him a chance to listen in on conversations and observe behavior. Nothing of what he saw seemed of much use, but he did as Walker had asked and kept his eyes and ears open.

He saw little of Quentin during the day, for the Highlander was constantly training with the Elven Hunters and learning combat skills and technique from Ard Patrinell. He saw more of Ahren Elessedil, who never trained with the others and was often at loose ends. Bek took it upon himself to include the young Elf in most of what he did, teaching him what little he knew of airships and how they flew and sharing confidences and stories. He did not tell Ahren any more than he told Quentin, but he told him almost as much. As they spent more time together, he began to see what Walker had meant about Kylen Elessedil misjudging his brother. Ahren was young, but he had grown up in a family and political situation that did not foster or tolerate naïveté or weakness. Ahren was strong in ways that weren't immediately apparent, and Bek gained a new measure of respect for him almost daily.

Now and again he visited with Panax and even Hunter Predd, when the Wing Rider came aboard to speak with Walker or Redden Alt Mer. Bek knew most of the Rovers by name, and they had accepted him into their group in a loose and easy sort of way that offered companionship if not necessarily trust. The Elves had little to do with him, mostly because they were always somewhere else. He did speak with the Healer, Joad Rish, a tall, stooped man with a kind face and reassuring manner. The Healer, like Bek, was not certain of his usefulness and felt more than a little out of place. But he was a good conversationalist, and he liked talking with the boy about cures and healings that transcended the standard forms of care and were the peculiar province of Elven Healers.

Bek even talked once or twice with the wistful seer, Ryer Ord Star, but she was so reclusive and shy that she avoided everyone except Walker, whom she followed everywhere. As if in thrall to the Druid, she was his shadow on the airship, trailing after him like a small child, hanging on his every word and watching his every move. Her fixation was a steady topic of conversation for everyone, but never within Walker's hearing. No one cared to broach the strangeness of the young woman's attachment directly to the Druid when it was apparent it did not matter to him.

Of Truls Rohk, there was still no sign. Panax insisted he was aboard, but Bek never saw any evidence of it.

Then, ten days out of land's view, they came in sight of the island of Flay Creech. It was nearing midday, the sky clouded and gray, the weather beginning to turn raw for the first time since they had set out. Thunderheads were massed to the west, approaching at a slow, steady roll across the back of a still-calm wind, and the burn of the sun through gaps in the thinner clouds east was giving way before cooler air. Below them, the sea rose and fell in gentle waves, a silver-tipped azure carpet where it broke against the shores of the island ahead, but beyond, out on the horizon, it was dark and threatening.

Flay Creech was not a welcoming sight. The island was gray and barren, a collection of mostly smooth mounds irrigated by an irregular patchwork of deep gullies that deposited seawater in shallow ponds all across its surface. Save for clusters of scrub trees and heavy weed patches, nothing grew. The island was small, barely a half mile across, and marked by a rocky outcropping just off the coast to the south that bore a distinct resemblance to a lizard's head with its mouth agape and its crest lifted in warning. On the map that Walker had drawn for the ship's company, the lizard's head was the landmark that identified the island.

Redden Alt Mer took the *Jerle Shannara* slowly around the island, keeping several hundred feet above its surface, while the ship's company gathered at the railings to survey the forbidding terrain. Bek looked downward with the others, but saw nothing of interest. There was no sign of life and no movement of any kind. The island appeared deserted.

When they had completed several passes, Walker signaled to Hunter Predd, who with his complement of Wing Riders had been gliding silently overhead. The grizzled rider swung close aboard Obsidian and shook his head. They had seen nothing either. But they would not descend to the island for a closer look, Bek knew, because they were under orders from the Druid not to land on any of the three islands where the talismans were hidden until a party from the airship had gone down first. The Rocs and their riders were too valuable to risk; if lost, they could not be replaced.

Walker called Redden Alt Mer and Ard Patrinell to his side, and Bek and Quentin eased nearer to listen to what was being said.

"What do you see?" the Druid was asking the Rover Captain as they drew close enough to hear.

"The same as you. Nothing. But there's something not right about the look of the island. What made those gullies that crisscross everything?"

However unhappy Redden Alt Mer was, Ard Patrinell was even more so. "I don't like what I'm seeing at all. The terrain of this island doesn't fit with anything I've ever come across. It's the shape of it. False, somehow. Unnatural."

Walker nodded. Bek could tell that he was troubled, too. There was something odd about the formation of the gullies and the smoothness of the island.

The Druid walked over to where Ryer Ord Star stood watching and bent down to speak softly with her. The seer listened carefully, then pressed her thin, small hands against her breast, closed her eyes and went completely still. Bek watched with the others, wondering what was happening. Then her eyes opened, and she began to speak to the Druid in rapid, breathless sentences. When she was finished, he held her gaze for a moment, squeezed her hand, and turned away.

He came back to where Ard Patrinell and Redden Alt Mer stood waiting. "I'm going down for a closer look," he said quietly. "Lower me in the basket and stand ready to bring me up again when I signal. Don't come down for me with either the ship or the Rocs if anything goes wrong."

"I don't think you should go alone," Ard Patrinell said at once.

Walker smiled. "All right. I'll take one man with me."

Leaving them, he walked over to Quentin Leah. "Highlander, I need a swift, sure blade to protect me. Are you interested in the job?"

Quentin nodded instantly, a grin breaking out on his sun-browned face. He hitched up the Sword of Leah, where it was strapped across his back, and gave Bek a wink before hastening to follow the Druid, who was already walking over to stand with Furl Hawken while he readied the winch basket for lowering.

Ahren Elessedil appeared at Bek's elbow and put a hand on his shoulder. Panax came up beside him, as well. "What's going on?" the Dwarf rumbled.

Bek was too stunned to answer, still trying to come to grips with the idea of his untested cousin being selected to go with the Druid rather than the Elf Captain or one of his Hunters. Walker was already in the basket, his dark robes drawn close, and Quentin quickly climbed in after him. Redden Alt Mer was at the airship's controls, swinging her around and then descending to within twenty feet of a flat place at the island's eastern tip. Bek wanted to shout something encouraging to his cousin, to warn him to be careful and to come back safe. But he couldn't manage to get the words out. Instead, he just stood there staring as the Rover crew winched the basket and its occupants aloft, then pushed them out over the railing and into space.

With the remainder of the ship's company looking on, the crew slowly lowered the basket and the two men who rode within it toward Flay Creech.

Walker's mind was working swiftly as the basket began its descent to the island, the words of the seer repeating over and over in his mind with harsh urgency.

"Three dark holes in place and time do I see, Walker. Three, that would swallow you up. They lie in deep blue waters that spread away forever beneath skies and wind. One is blind and cannot see, but will find you anyway. One has mouths that would swallow you whole. One is everything and nothing and will steal your soul. All guard keys that look to be other than what they are and are nothing of what they seem. I see this in a haze of shadow that tracks you everywhere and seeks to place itself about you like a shroud."

These were the words she had spoken to him last night when she had come to him unexpectedly after midnight, waking from a dream that had shown her something new of their quest. Wide-eyed and frightened, her childlike face twisted with fear for him, she had shaken him from his sleep to share her strange vision. It had come unbidden, as they almost always did, buried in a mix of other dreams and no dreams, the only part of her mind's sight that had reason for being, clear and certain to her, a glimpse of a future that would unfailingly come to pass.

He steadied her, held her because she was shaking and not yet even fully awake. She was tied to him, he knew, in a way neither of them yet understood. She had accompanied him on the voyage because she believed it was her destiny, but her bonds to him were as much emotional as psychic. She had found in him a kindred soul, another part of her being, and she had given herself into his care completely. He did not approve and would have it otherwise, but he had not found a way as yet to set her free.

Her eyes glistened with tears and her hands clasped his arm as she told him of the dream and struggled with what it meant. She saw no more than what she was given to see, had no insights to aid him, and therefore felt inadequate and useless. But he told her that her vision was clear to him and would help to keep him safe, and he held her for a time until she quieted and went back to sleep.

But his words to her were false, for he did not understand her vision beyond what was immediately apparent. The black holes were the islands they sought. On each, something dark and dangerous awaited. The keys he would find did not look like the keys with which he was familiar. The haze of shadow that followed after and sought to wrap about him was the Ilse Witch.

Of the eyes and mouths and spirits, he had no opinion. Had she seen them in order of appearance? Were they manifestations of real dangers or metaphors for something else? He had gone to her again, just before making this descent, asking her to repeat what she had seen, everything. He had hoped she might reveal something new, something she had forgotten in the rush of last night's telling. But her description of the dream remained unchanged. Nor had there been a new vision from which to draw. So he could not know what waited on the island, and he must look for any of the three dangers she had foreseen until one revealed itself.

Taking the Highlander with him was a risk. But Quentin Leah possessed the only other true magic of those accompanying him, save Truls Rohk, and he must have someone at his back while he sought out the first of the three keys. Quentin was young and inexperienced, but the Sword of Leah was a powerful weapon, and Quentin had trained for almost two weeks now with Ard Patrinell, whom Walker believed to be the finest swordsman he had ever seen. No mention had been made of Patrinell's great skill by the other Elves, but Walker had watched him spar for days now with the Highlander and could tell it was there. Quentin was a quick study, and already he was showing signs that one day he might be a match for the Elf. It was enough to persuade the Druid to take a chance on him.

It could be argued that Truls Rohk was a more logical choice for this than Quentin, but it would have meant waiting until nightfall. Walker did not like the look of the storm approaching, and he felt it better in any case to keep the shape-shifter's presence a secret for a little longer.

The basket bumped against the surface of the island, and the Druid and the Highlander scrambled out. The latter had his sword held ready, gripped in both hands, blade upward. "Stay close to me, Quentin," Walker ordered. "Do not stray. Watch my back and your own, as well."

They hastened across the flats in a low crouch, eyes watchful. The surface was rocky and slick with dampness and moss. Up close, the deep furrows were even more mysterious, worn into the rock like open irrigation runnels, not straight and even, but twisty and irregular, some of them as deep as four feet, their strange network laid all across the island. Walker cast about for bolt-holes in the rock in which something might burrow and hide, but there was nothing to be seen, only the exposed rock and the shallow ponds.

They continued on, Walker searching now for a trace of the key, a hint of its presence in the solid rock and shifting seawaters that lay all about. Where would such a key be hidden? If it was infused with magic, he should detect its presence quickly. If not, their search would take longer—time, perhaps, they did not have.

He glanced about warily. The island lay still and unmoving save for the soft wave of sea grasses buffeted by the approaching storm winds.

Suddenly Walker sensed something unfamiliar, not the magic he had anticipated, but an object that nevertheless had a living presence—though not one he could identify. It was over to his left, within a jumble of broken rock that formed a pocket on the high ground close to the southern tip of the island. The Druid swung toward it at once, working his way along the lip of one of the odd gullies, staying where he could see what lay about him. Pressed close to the dark-robed leader, Quentin Leah followed, his sword gleaming in the sunlight.

Then the sun slipped behind a bank of heavy clouds, and the island of Flay Creech was cloaked in shadow.

In the next instant, the sea came alive in a frenzy of movement.

Aboard ship, Bek Rowe gasped sharply as the waters surrounding Flay Creech began to boil and surge with terrible ferocity. The bright azure color darkened, the crystalline stillness churned, and dozens of squirming dark bodies surged from the ocean's depth in a twisting mass. Giant eels, some more than thirty feet long, their huge bodies sleek and speckled and their mouths agape to reveal hundreds of razor-sharp teeth, squirmed out of the water and onto the island. They came from everywhere, sliding smoothly into the deep channels that fit their bodies perfectly, that Bek could see now had been formed by their countless comings and goings over the years. In a rush they slithered from the ocean onto the land, then along the gullies from shallow pond to shallow pond, closing on the two men who were racing for a cluster of broken rocks to make a stand against them.

"Shades!" Bek heard Panax hiss as he watched the eels advance in a thrashing, frenzied mass.

The eels were so maddened they were colliding with each other as they twisted and squirmed down the gullies toward their prey. Some ascended the high ground long enough to gain a momentary advantage over their brethren before dropping back into the grooved channels they favored. Some, perhaps enraged at being crowded, perhaps simply ravenous with hunger, snapped and tore at others. It gave the impression that the entire island was being overrun at once, all slithery bodies and movement. Bek had never heard of such huge eels or imagined that so many could be in any one place. What could possibly sustain such a massive number on this barren atoll? Even the occasional presence of other creatures could not be enough to keep them all alive.

Walker was digging frantically in the rocks, his back to the approaching monsters. Quentin faced them alone, standing close to the Druid, elevated on an abutment so that he could bring his sword to bear without hindrance. He shifted from right to left and back again on his chosen defensive ground, watching the mass of sea hunters come at him, readying himself.

Oh, but there were so many! Bek thought in horror.

The first eel reached Quentin and launched itself like a striking snake, snapping its body from the depression. The Highlander brought the Sword of Leah around in a short whipping motion, the magic flaring to life along the length of the heavy blade, and the eel was severed just behind its gaping maw and fell back again, thrashing in pain and confusion. Other eels fed upon it instantly, tearing it to shreds. A second eel struck at Quentin, but he brought his sword to bear again, swift and steady, and that one fell away, too. On the backswing, he dispatched a third that had come up behind him, flinging it away.

Walker straightened from his crouched position within the rocks long enough to summon the Druid fire. It lanced from his fingers in an explosion of blue flame, burning into the advancing eels and forcing them back down into the gullies. Then he was bending down again, searching anew.

Back came the eels in only moments, breaking past the already diminishing ring of fire, mouths gaping hungrily.

There's too many! Bek thought again, hands gripping the railing of the airship helplessly as a fresh wave of attackers closed on Quentin and the Druid.

"Captain!" Ard Patrinell shouted at Redden Alt Mer in desperation. The flame-haired Rover swung into the pilot box in response. "Safety lines!" he roared. "We're going after them!"

Bek had barely managed to secure himself when the *Jerle Shannara* went into a steep, swift dive toward the island.

Quentin Leah struck down his nearest attacker and swung instantly about to face the next. He had driven back the first assault, but the second seemed even more frenzied and determined. The Highlander's strokes were steady and smooth, and he wheeled skillfully to keep his back from being exposed for more than a few seconds at a time, just as Patrinell had taught him in their exercises. The Highlander was strong and quick, and he did not panic in the face of the overwhelming odds he faced. He had hunted the Highlands since he was old enough to run, and he had faced great odds and terrible dangers before. But he understood that here, in this place, time was running out. The giant eels were vulnerable to the magic of his weapon but undeterred by the deaths of their fellows. They would keep coming, he knew, until they had what they wanted. There were so many that eventually they would succeed.

Already his arms were growing tired and his movements jerky. Use of the sword's magic was draining him of his energy and breaking down his will. He could feel it happening and could do nothing to stop it. Wounds had been opened on both arms and one leg where the razor-sharp teeth of his attackers had slashed him, and his face was bathed in sweat and salt spray from the sea.

Walker gave a grunt and uncoiled from his search in the rocks, swinging up to stand beside him. "I have it!" he shouted, jamming something into his robes. "Run now! This way!"

They leapt out from the rocks and raced toward an open flat that lay less than a hundred feet away, scrambling through the shallow, slippery ponds. The eels thrashed after them, their huge bodies twisting and squirming along the deep channels. Overhead, the *Jerle Shannara* was dropping swiftly, sails full and radian draws taut, her sleek dark form plummeting out of the gray sky. The eels were closing on Quentin and Walker, who turned to stand one final time, the Druid with his fire exploding from his extended arm, the Highlander with his sword's magic flashing.

Then the shadow of the airship fell over them and a trailing rope ladder swung past, their lifeline to safety. They reached for it instinctively, grasped it, and were whisked off the ground and into the air as eel jaws snapped only inches away.

Seconds later, they were clear of the island once more and climbing the ladder to safety.

Bek was among those who helped pull the Druid and the Highlander back aboard the airship as it lifted high above Flay Creech and its twisting mass of frustrated, maddened eels. When he had his cousin standing before him, torn and bloodied, but smiling, as well, Bek tried to say something to him about agreeing to take risks and scaring him half to death, then gave it up and threw his arms about the other in a warm, grateful hug.

"Ouch, you're hurting me!" Quentin yelped. When Bek hurriedly backed off, his cousin's smile broadened. "Happy to see me safe, Bek? Never a moment's doubt, was there? You could tell. We had a clear path all the way."

Walker was at his elbow, fumbling in his robes for what he had recovered, and the rest of the ship's company crowded close. What he produced was a flat metal rectangle with symmetrical ridges that connected in a geometrical pattern to a small raised square that vibrated softly. A red light embedded in the square blinked on and off. Everyone stared at it in wonder. Bek had never seen anything like it before.

"What is it?" Panax asked finally.

"A key," Walker answered. "But not a key of the sort we know. This key belongs to the technology of the Old World, from before the Great Wars, from the old civilization of Man. It is a form of machine and has a life of its own."

He let them study it a moment longer, then slipped it back into his robes. "It has secrets to tell us if we can unlock them," he said quietly, then clasped Quentin's shoulder in thanks, and walked away.

The remainder of the company dispersed to their stations and work, the adventure of Flay Creech behind them. Joad Rish was already stripping off the Highlander's tunic to clean his wounds. Quentin accepted congratulations from a few of the ship's company who lingered, then sat heavily on a barrel top and winced as the Healer began to work on him in earnest. Bek stayed close, silent company, and alone saw the hint of raw fear that flashed in his cousin's green eyes as he looked down at his torn body and realized momentarily how close he had come to dying.

But then he was looking up again, himself once more, smiling rakishly as he held up a single finger.

One down, Quentin was saying.

Bek smiled back. One down, he was thinking in response, but two still to go.

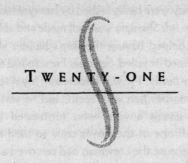

TWENTY-ONE

It took two more months of travel to reach the island of Shatterstone. Bek had thought they would arrive more quickly since it had taken them only ten days to gain Flay Creech. But Walker's rough-drawn map showed the distance to be considerably greater, and it was.

Nevertheless, the days between passed swiftly, eaten up by routine tasks and small crises. Bek continued to learn about airships—how they were constructed, why they flew, and what was needed to maintain them. He was given a chance to try his hand at almost everything, from polishing the diapson crystals to threading the radian draws. He was allowed to go topside to see how the draws were attached to the light sheaths so as to draw down their power. He was given time at the ship's rudders and controls and a chance at plotting courses. By the end of the two months, Redden Alt Mer thought him competent enough to leave him alone in the pilot box for several hours at a stretch, allowing him to become accustomed to the feel of the airship and the ways she responded to his touch.

For the most part, the weather continued to favor them. There were storms, but they did not cause the ship damage or ship's company to fear. A few were severe enough that ship and passengers sought shelter in an island's protective cove or windward bluffs. Once or twice they were badly lashed by heavy winds and rain while still aloft, but the *Jerle Shannara* was well made and able to endure.

Certainly it helped having the ship's builder aboard. If something malfunctioned or failed, Spanner Frew found the problem and fixed it almost instantly. He was ferociously loyal to and protective of his vessel, a mother hen with teeth, and he was quick to reprimand or even assault anyone who mistreated her. Once Bek watched him cuff one of the Rover crew so hard he knocked the man down, all because the crewman had removed a diapson crystal improperly.

The only one who seemed able to stand up to him was Rue Meridian, who was intimidated by no one. Of all aboard ship, save Walker, she was the coolest and calmest presence. Bek remained in awe of Little Red, and when he had the chance to do so, he watched her with an ache he could not quite manage to hide. If she noticed, she kept it to herself. She was kind to him and always helpful. She would tease him now and then, and she made him laugh with her surreptitious winks and clever asides. She was the airship's navigator, but Bek soon discovered that she was much more. It was apparent from the beginning that she knew as much as her brother about flying airships and was his most valued adviser. She was also extremely dangerous. She carried knives everywhere she went, and she knew how to use them. Once, he watched her compete against the other Rovers in a throwing contest, and she bested them easily. Neither her brother nor Furl Hawken would throw against her, which told Bek something. He thought she might not be as skilled at the use of weapons as Ard Patrinell, but he would not have wanted to put it to a test.

Much of his time was spent with Ahren Elessedil. Together, they would walk the ship from end to end, discussing everything that interested them. Well, not quite everything. A few things, he did not share with anyone. He still hid, even from the Elf, the presence of the phoenix stone. He still told no one of his meeting with the King of the Silver River. But it was growing harder and harder to keep these secrets from Ahren. With time's passage, he was becoming as close to the young Elf as to Quentin, and sometimes he thought that Ahren would have been his best friend if Quentin hadn't claimed the position first.

"Tell me what you want to do with your life, Bek," the Elf said one evening as they stood at the railing before sleep. "If you could do anything at all, what would it be?"

Bek answered without thinking. "I would find out the truth about myself."

There it was, right out in the open without his meaning for it to happen. He would have swallowed the words if there had been a way, but it was too late.

"What do you mean?" Ahren looked sharply at him.

Bek hesitated, seeking a way to recover. "I mean, I was brought to Coran and Liria when I was a baby, given to them when my parents died. I don't know anything about my real parents. I don't have any family history of my own."

"You must have asked Quentin's father and mother. Didn't they tell you anything?"

"I asked them only a little. Growing up, I felt it didn't matter. My life was with them and with Quentin. They were my family and that was my history. But now I want to know more. Maybe I'm just beginning to realize that it's important to me, but now that I find it so, I want to know the truth." He shrugged. "Silly to wonder about it, out here in the middle of nowhere."

Ahren smiled. "Out in the middle of nowhere is exactly the right place to wonder who you are."

Every day at high noon, usually while Bek was eating lunch with the Rovers or steering the airship from the pilot box or perhaps languishing in the narrow shade of the foremast with Panax, Ahren Elessedil stood out in the midday sun with Ard Patrinell and for the better part of two hours honed his skills with Elven weapons. Sometimes it was with swords and knives. Sometimes it was with bow and arrow, axes, or slings. At times the two simply sat and talked, and Bek would watch as hand gestures and sketches were exchanged. The former Captain of the Home Guard worked his young charge hard. It was the hottest time of the day and the training rendered was the most exhaustive. It was the only time Bek ever saw the two together, and finally he asked Ahren about it.

"He was your teacher once," Bek pointed out. "He was your friend. Why don't you spend any time with him aside from when you train?"

Ahren sighed. "It isn't my idea. It's his. He was dismissed from his position because my father's life was his responsibility. The Elven Hunters he commands accept his leadership because the King, my brother, ordered it and because they value his experience and skill. But they do not accept his friendship with me. That ended with my father's death. He may continue to train me, because my father ordered it. Anything more would be unacceptable."

"But we are in the middle of the ocean." Bek was perplexed. "What difference does any of that make here?"

Ahren shrugged. "Ard must know that his men will do what he orders of them without question or hesitation. He must have their respect. What if they believe he curries favor with me in an effort to get back what he has lost, perhaps with my help? What if they believe he serves more than one master? That is why he trains me at midday, in the heat. That is why he trains me harder than he does them. That is why he ignores me otherwise. He shows me no favoritism. He gives them no reason to doubt him. Do you see?"

Bek didn't see, not entirely, but he told Ahren he did anyway.

"Besides," Ahren added, "I'm the second son of a dead King, and second sons of dead Kings have to learn how to be tough and independent enough to survive on their own."

Panax, gruff and irascible as always, told Ahren that if Elves spent less time worrying about stepping on each other's toes and more time trusting their instincts, they would better off. It used to be like that, he declared bluntly. Things had changed since this cur-

rent crop of Elessedils had taken office. How he arrived at this conclusion, living in the backwoods beyond Depo Bent, was beyond
Bek. But for all that he lived an isolated and solitary existence, the
Dwarf seemed to have his finger firmly on the pulse of what was
happening in the Four Lands.

"You take this ridiculous war between the Free-born and the
Federation," he muttered at one point, while they sat watching Patrinell and Ahren duel with staves. "What is the point? They've been
fighting over the same piece of ground for fifty years and over control of the Borderlands for more than five hundred. Back and forth it
goes; nothing ever changes, nothing ever gets resolved. Wouldn't
you think after all this time, someone would have found a way to get
them all to sit down and work it out? How complicated can it be?
On the surface, it's an issue of sovereignty and territorial influence,
but at heart it's about trade and economics. Find a way to stop them
from posturing about whose birthright it is to govern and get them
to talk about trade alliances and dividing the wealth those alliances
would generate, and the war will be over in two days."

"But the Federation is determined to rule the Borderlands," Bek
pointed out. "They want the Borderlands to be part of their Southland empire. What about that?"

The Dwarf spat. "The Borderlands will never be part of any one
land because it's been part of all four lands for as long as anyone can
remember. The average Southlander doesn't give a rat's behind if
the people in the Borderlands are a part of the Federation. What the
average Southlander cares about is whether those ash bows that are
so good for hunting and those silk scarves the women love and
those great cheeses and ales that come out of Varfleet and those
healing plants grown on the Streleheim can find their way south to
them! The only ones who care about annexing the Borderlands are
the members of the Coalition Council. Send them to the Prekkendorran for a week, and then see how they feel about things!"

There were small adventures to be enjoyed during those eight-
odd weeks of travel between islands, as well. One day, a huge pod

of whales came into view below the airship, traveling west in pursuit of the setting sun. They breached and sounded with spouts of water and slaps of tails and fins, great sea vessels riding the waves with joy and abandon, complete within themselves. The Highlander and the Elf peered down at them, tracking their progress, reminded of the smallness of their own world, envious of the freedom these giants enjoyed. On another day, hundreds of dolphins appeared, leaping and diving in rhythmic cadence, small glimmers of brightness in the deep blue sea. There were migrating schools of billfish at times, some with sails, some brightly colored, all sleek and swift. There were giant squids with thirty-foot tentacles, as well, who swam like feathered arrows, and dangerous-looking predators with fins that cut the water like knives.

Now and again something aboard ship would break down, and what was required to complete repairs could not be found. Sometimes supplies ran low. In both instances, the Wing Riders were pressed into service. While the third rider remained with the airship, the other two would explore the surrounding islands to forage for what was needed. Twice, Bek was allowed to accompany them, both times when they went in search of fresh water, fruit, and vegetables to supplement the ship's dietary staples. Once he rode with Hunter Predd aboard his Roc, Obsidian, and once with a rider named Gill aboard Tashin. Each time, the experience was exhilarating. There was a freedom to flying the Rocs that was absent even on an airship. The great birds were much quicker and smoother, their responses swifter, and the feeling of riding something alive and warm far different from riding something built of wood and metal.

The Wing Riders were a fiercely independent bunch and kept apart from everyone. When Bek screwed up his courage to ask the taciturn Hunter Predd about it, the Wing Rider explained patiently that life as a Wing Rider necessitated believing you were different. It had to do with the time you spent flying and the freedom you embraced when you gave up the safeties and securities others relied

TERRY BROOKS

upon living on the ground. Wing Riders needed to view themselves
as independent in order to function. They needed to be unfettered and
unencumbered by connections of any kind, save to their Rocs and
to their own people.

Bek wasn't sure that much of it wasn't just a superior attitude fostered by the freedom that flying the Rocs engendered in Wing
Riders. But he liked Hunter Predd and Gill, and he didn't see that
there was anything to be gained by questioning their thinking. If he
were a Wing Rider, he told himself, he would probably think the
same way.

When Bek told Ahren of his conversation with Hunter Predd,
the Elf Prince laughed. "Everyone aboard this ship thinks their way
of life is best, but most keep their opinions to themselves. The
reason the Wing Riders are so free with theirs is that they can always jump on their Rocs and fly off if they don't like what they hear
back!"

But there were few conflicts in the weeks that passed after their
departure from Flay Creech, and eventually everyone settled into a
comfortable routine and developed a complacency with life aboard
ship. It wasn't until one of the Wing Riders finally sighted the island
of Shatterstone that everything began to change.

It was the Wing Rider, Gill, patrolling in the late afternoon on
Tashin, who sighted Shatterstone first. The expedition had been
looking for it for several days, alerted by Redden Alt Mer, who had
taken the appropriate readings and made the necessary calculations.
An earlier sighting of a group of three small islands laid out in a line
corresponded to landmarks drawn on the map and confirmed that
the island they sought was close.

Walker was standing with the Rover Captain in the pilot box
behind Furl Hawken, who was in command of the helm that afternoon, discussing whether they needed to correct their course at
sunrise on the following day, when Gill appeared with the news. All

291

activity stopped as the ship's company hurried to the rails, and Big Red swung the *Jerle Shannara* hard to the left to follow the Wing Rider's lead.

Finally, the Druid thought as they sailed toward the setting sun. The prolonged inactivity, the seductive comfort of routine, and the lack of progress bothered him. The men and women of the expedition needed to stay sharp, to remain wary. They were losing focus. The only solution was to get on with things.

But when the island came into view, he felt his expectations fade. Whereas Flay Creech had been small and compact, Shatterstone was sprawling and massive. It rose out of the Blue Divide in a jumble of towering peaks that disappeared into clouds and mist and fell away at every turn into canyons thousands of feet deep. The coastline was rugged and forbidding, almost entirely devoid of beaches and shallows, with sheer rock walls rising straight out of the ocean. The entire island was rain-soaked and lush, heavily overgrown by trees and grasses, tangled in vines and scrub, and laced with the silver threads of waterfalls that tumbled out of the mist into the emerald green landscape below. Only at its peaks and on its windswept cliff edges was it bare and open. Birds wheeled from their aeries and plummeted in white flashes to the sea, hunting food. Below the cliff walls, the surf crashed against the rocks in long, rolling waves and turned to milky foam.

Walker had the *Jerle Shannara* circle the island twice while he noted landmarks and tried to get a feel for the terrain. A thorough search of Shatterstone by ordinary methods would take weeks, maybe even months. Even then, they might not discover the key if it was buried deep enough in those canyons. He found himself wondering which of the three horrors of Ryer Ord Star's vision guarded this key. The eels would have been the mouths that could swallow you whole. That left something that was blind but could find you anyway or something that was everything and nothing and would steal your soul. He had hoped the seer would dream again before they reached Shatterstone, but she had not. All they had to work with was what she had given them before.

He watched the rugged sweep of the island pass away below, thinking that whatever he decided, it would have to wait for morning. Nightfall was close upon them, and he had no intention of landing a search party in the dark.

But he might consider sending down Truls Rohk, he thought suddenly. The shape-shifter preferred the dark anyway, and his instincts for the presence of magic were nearly as keen as the Druid's.

The Wing Riders landed on an open bluff high above the pounding surf on the island's west coast and, leaving their Rocs tethered, began a short exploration of the area. They found nothing that threatened and determined that it was safe enough for them to remain there for the night. No attempt would be made to journey inland until morning. Redden Alt Mer anchored the airship some distance away on an adjoining bluff, fixing the anchor lines in place and letting the ship ride about twenty feet off the ground. Again, no one would leave the ship until morning, and a close watch would be kept until then. Darkness was already beginning to settle in, but it appeared that the coastal skies would remain clear. With the illumination provided by a half-moon and stars, it would be easy to see anything that tried to approach.

After dinner was consumed, Walker called his small group of advisers together in Redden Alt Mer's cabin and told them his plan for the coming day. Though he didn't say so, he had abandoned for the moment the idea of using Truls Rohk. Instead, he would fly with one of the Wing Riders over the peaks and into the canyons in an attempt to locate the hidden key using his Druidic instincts. Because the key had such a distinctive presence and would likely be the only thing like it on the island, he had a good chance of determining its location. If it were in a place he could reach without endangering the Wing Rider and his Roc, he would retrieve it himself. But the canyons were narrow and not easily navigated by the great birds with their broad wingspans, so retrieval might have to be undertaken by the ship's company.

Everyone agreed that the Druid's plan seemed sensible, and the matter was left at that.

The following morning, the dawn a bright golden flare on the eastern horizon, Walker set off with Hunter Predd and Obsidian to conduct a methodical sweep of the island's west coast. They searched all day, dipping into every canyon and defile, soaring over every bluff and peak, crisscrossing the island from the coastal waters inland so that nothing was missed. The day was sunny and bright, the weather fair, the winds light, and their search progressed without difficulty.

By sunset, Walker had found exactly nothing.

He set out again the next day with Po Kelles, seated behind the whip-thin Wing Rider on his gray-and-black-dappled Roc, Niciannon. They rode the back of a strong wind south along the most forbidding stretch of the island's shoreline, and it was here just after midday that Walker detected the presence of the key. It was buried deep in a coastal valley that opened off a split between a pair of towering cliffs and ran inland into heavy jungle for better than five miles. The valley was unnavigable from the air, and after ascertaining the approximate location of the key, Walker had Po Kelles fly them back to the airship. Postponing any further effort for the day, he asked Redden Alt Mer to move the *Jerle Shannara* to a bluff just above the valley he intended to explore at dawn, and they settled in for the night.

He waited until everyone but the watch was asleep and then summoned Truls Rohk. He had neither seen nor spoken with the shape-shifter since he had come aboard, although he had detected the other's presence and knew him to be close. Walker stood at the back of the ship, just down from the aft rise where the Elven Hunter on sentry duty peered out at the jungled island darkness, and sent out a silent call to Rohk. He was still looking for the shape-shifter when he realized Rohk was already there, crouching next to him in the shadows, virtually invisible to anyone who might be looking.

"What is it, Druid?" Rohk hissed, as if the summoning were an irritation.

"I want you to explore the valley below before it gets light," Walker answered, unruffled. "A quick search, no more. There is a key, and the key feels like this."

He produced the one he carried and let the other touch it, hold it, feel its energy.

Truls Rohk grunted and handed it back. "Shall I bring it to you?"

"Do not go near it." Walker found the other's eyes and held them. "It isn't that you couldn't, but the danger might be greater than either of us suspects. What I need to know is where it is. I'll go after it myself in the morning."

The shape-shifter laughed softly. "I would never deny you a chance to risk your life over mine, Walker. You think so much less of the risk than I do."

Without a word, he vaulted over the side of the ship and was gone.

Walker waited for him until nearly dawn, dozing at the railing, his back to the island, his thoughts gone deep inside. No one disturbed him; no one tried to approach. The night was calm and warm; the winds of the day died away into soft breezes that carried the smells of the ocean to higher ground. Inland, the darkness enfolded and blanketed everything in black silence.

He might have dreamed, but if he had, his memory of it was lost when Truls Rohk's touch brought him awake.

"Sweet dreams of an island paradise, Walker?" the other asked softly. "Of sand beaches and pretty birds? Of fruit and flowers and warm winds?"

Walker shook his head, coming fully awake.

"That's just as well, because there are none of these in the valley you seek to explore." The dark form shifted against the railing, liquid black. "The key you seek lies three miles inland, close to the valley floor, in a cavern of some size. The jungle hides it well, but you will find it. How it is concealed within the cave, I could not say. I did not enter because I could tell that something keeps watch."

Walker stared at him. "Something alive?"

"Something dark and vast, something without form. I felt no eyes on me, Walker. I felt only a presence, a stirring in the air, invisible and pervasive and evil."

No eyes. Was it something blind, perhaps? Walker mulled the shape-shifter's words over in his mind, wondering.

"That presence was with me all the way up the valley, but it did not bother with me until I got close to the cavern." Truls Rohk seemed to reflect. "It was in the earth itself, Druid. It was in the valley's soil, in its plants and trees." He paused. "If it decides to come after you, I don't think you can run from it. I'm not certain you can even get out of its way."

Then he was gone, disappeared as suddenly as he had come, and Walker was left standing at the railing alone.

Dawn broke brilliant and warm across a still, flat sea. The winds had died completely, and the sky was a cloudless silver blue. Everywhere, the horizon was a depthless void where air and water joined. Seabirds wheeled and shrieked, then dived past the cliffs and down to the ocean's surface. Thick patches of mist clung to the island's peaks and nestled in her valleys, hiding her secrets, obscuring her in gloom.

Walker chose Ard Patrinell and three of his Elven Hunters to go with him. Experience and quickness would count for more than power in the confines of the valley jungle, and the Druid wanted veterans to face whatever kept watch there. Redden Alt Mer would take them into the valley aboard the *Jerle Shannara* for as far as the airship could go in the narrow confines. Then the Druid and the Elven Hunters would descend in the winch basket to the valley floor and walk the rest of the way in. With luck, they would not have to walk far. Once Walker had retrieved the key, the five would make their way back to the basket and be pulled up again.

As the ship's company assembled, Walker saw edginess in the eyes of the veterans and uncertainty in the eyes of the rest. Ryer Ord Star seemed particularly distressed, her thin face white with fear. Perhaps all were remembering the eels of Flay Creech, the devouring mouths and rending teeth, though none would say so. There, the Druid had retrieved the hidden key and everyone had escaped harm. Perhaps they were wondering if their good fortune would carry over here.

With safety lines secured, Redden Alt Mer sailed the *Jerle Shannara* slowly from the bluff down the cliff wall and into the haze of the valley. Dawn's light faded behind them as the airship slid silently between the massive peaks and disappeared into the gloom. Visibility diminished to less than two dozen yards. Alt Mer occupied the helm, taking his vessel ahead cautiously, his speed reduced to dead slow. Rue Meridian stood at the curve of the forward rams, peering ahead into the fog, calling out sightings and navigational corrections to her brother. Everyone else crouched at the railings in silence, watching and listening. The mist clung to them in a fine damp sheen, gathering in droplets on their skin and clothing, causing them to blink and lick their lips. Except for the mist, which moved like an ancient behemoth, lumbering and slow, everything about them was still.

As the minutes passed and the gloom persisted, Walker began to worry about visibility on the valley floor. If they could see no more than this from the air, how could they find their way once they were off the ship? His Druidic instincts would give them some help, but no amount of magic could replace the loss of sight. They would be virtually blind.

He caught himself. There it was again, that word. Blind. He was reminded of Ryer Ord Star's vision and the thing that waited on one of these islands, a thing that was blind but could find you anyway. He pricked his senses for what Truls Rohk had felt the night before, coming here alone. But from the air, he could sense nothing.

Ahead, the mist cleared slightly, and the cliff walls reappeared, closing in on them sharply. Redden Alt Mer brought the airship to a complete stop, waiting for Little Red to call back to him. She hung from the bow on her safety line, peering into the gloom, then motioned him ahead cautiously. Tree branches reached out of the haze, spectral fingers that seemed to clutch for the airship. Vines hung from the trees and the cliff face in a ropy tangle.

Then the mist disappeared altogether, and the *Jerle Shannara* eased into a canyon that was unexpectedly open and clear. The sky reappeared overhead, blue and welcoming, and the valley floor opened in a sea of green dappled with striations of damp color. Redden Alt Mer took the airship lower, down to within a few feet of the treetops, then slid her cautiously ahead once more. Walker searched the far end of the pocket, finding the cliff walls narrowed down so completely that the tree limbs almost touched. They had come as far as they could by air. From here, they must walk.

When they arrived at the canyon's far end, Redden Alt Mer brought the *Jerle Shannara* right down to where the treetops scraped the hull. Walker and the four Elven Hunters released their safety lines and climbed into the winch basket. A dozen hands swung them out over the ship's railing, and they were lowered slowly into the trees.

Once grounded and out of the basket, Walker signaled back to Rue Meridian, who was still hanging off the bow, that they were safely down. Then he stood motionless in the silence to get his bearings and search for hidden danger. Nothing. Though he probed their surroundings carefully, he could find no threatening presence.

Yet something was clearly out of place.

Then he realized what it was. The jungle was a thick, impenetrable wall of emptiness and silence. No birds, Walker thought. No animals. Nothing. Not even the smallest chirp of an insect. Except for what was rooted in the earth, nothing lived here.

Walker could see a gap in the cliffs ahead, and he nodded to Ard Patrinell to proceed. The Elven leader did not reply, but turned to his Hunters and used hand signals to communicate his orders. A burly Elf named Kian was given the lead. Walker followed just behind, then Patrinell with lean Brae and tall Dace trailing. They moved from the canyon into the narrow gap, casting about warily as they proceeded, mindful of the danger they could expect to find waiting. Walker continued to probe the jungle gloom with tendrils of magic that brushed softly like feathers and then withdrew. The gap tightened about them, narrowing to a corridor less than fifty feet wide where trees and vines clogged everything. There was passage to be found, but it was circuitous and required them to push their way through the vegetation that grew everywhere. All about, the jungle was silent.

They moved ahead steadily, still without encountering any sign of life. Their narrow corridor broadened into another canyon, and the sky reappeared in a blue slash overhead. Sunlight dappled the trees and illuminated the dampness. They crossed to yet another defile and passed down its narrow corridor into a third canyon, this one larger still.

Suddenly, Walker was rocked by something that seized him as a giant hand would a tiny bug. It came out of the earth in a rush, sweeping over him so fast that he did not have time to react and was left momentarily stunned. Perhaps it had been there all along and had masked its presence; perhaps it had only just now found him. Pervasive and powerful, it had no identifiable form, no substantive being. It was everywhere at once, all around him, and though invisible to his eye, it was unmistakably real. He went limp in its grasp, offering no resistance, letting it think him helpless. The Elven Hunters stared at him in confusion, not realizing what was happening. He did not acknowledge them, gave no indication that he even knew they were there. He disappeared inside himself, down where nothing could touch him. There, closed away, he waited.

A few moments later, the presence withdrew, sliding back into the earth, satisfied perhaps that it was not threatened.

Walker shook off the lingering effects of its touch and took a deep, steadying breath. The attack had shaken him badly. Whatever lived in this valley possessed power that dwarfed his own. It was old, he could tell, perhaps as old as the Faerie world. He signaled to the Elves that he was all right, then glanced around quickly. He did not want to stay where he was. A rise of barren, empty rock formed a smooth hump at the center of the canyon, a sun-drenched haven within the jungle gloom. Perhaps from there he could see better where to go next.

Beckoning to the Elven Hunters, he moved out of the undergrowth and gloom and climbed onto the stone rise. The last traces of the hateful presence faded as he did. Odd, he thought, and moved to the center of the rise. From this new elevation, he surveyed the canyon. There was not much to see. At its far end, the canyon broadened and rose in a long, winding slope that disappeared into mist and shadow. The Druid could not determine what lay beyond. He glanced around at the portion of the canyon in which he stood and saw nothing helpful.

Yet something tugged at him. Something close. He closed his eyes, cleared his mind, and began to probe gently outward with his senses. He found what he was looking for almost at once, and his eyes snapped open to confirm his vision.

He could just make out a darkening through the green of the jungle wall in a cliffside a hundred yards or so away. It was the cavern Truls Rohk had found the night before.

He stood looking at the darkness and did not move. The second key was in there, waiting. But the thing that guarded it was waiting, as well. He considered for a moment how best to approach the cavern. No solution presented itself. He turned to the Elven

Hunters and gestured for them to remain where they were. Then he walked down off the jumble of rock toward the cave.

He felt the presence return almost instantly, but he had already turned his thoughts inward. He was nothing, an object without purpose, random and devoid of thought. He walled himself away before the sentry that guarded the key could read his intentions or discover his purpose and walked straight into the cavern.

Within, he stopped to collect his thoughts. He could no longer feel the presence shadowing him. It had left him at the entrance of the cave as it had left him at the foot of the rise. Rock did not offer it passage, he decided. Only the soil from which it drew its power. Could he use that to protect himself in some way?

He put the thought aside, and looked around carefully. The cavern opened into a series of chambers, which were dimly lit by splits in the rock that admitted small streamers of light from above the jungle canopy. Walker began to hunt for the key and found it almost immediately. It was sitting out in the open on a small rock shelf, unguarded and unwatched. Walker studied it for a moment before picking it up, then studied it some more. Its configuration was similar to the one he already had, with a flat power source and a blinking red light, but the ridged metal lines on this one formed different patterns.

Walker glanced about the cavern warily, searching for the key's sentry, for some hint of an alarm, for anything dangerous or threatening, and found nothing.

He walked to the cave entrance once more and stood looking out at the clearing. Ard Patrinell and his Elven Hunters were clustered on the rocky mound, looking back at him. In the surrounding jungle, nothing moved. Walker stayed where he was. Something would try to stop him. Something had to. Whatever warded the key would not simply let him walk away. It was waiting for him, he sensed. Out there, in the trees. There, in the soil from which it drew its strength.

He was still debating what to do next when the earth before him erupted in an explosion of green.

Aboard the *Jerle Shannara*, which hovered in a cloud of mist two clearings away, Bek Rowe was watching Rue Meridian tie off a fresh radian draw close by the horns of the bow when Walker's voice cried out sharply in the silence of his mind.

Bek! We're under attack! Two canyons farther in! Have Alt Mer bring the airship! Drop the basket and pull us out! Quick, now!

Startled by the unexpected assault, the boy jumped at the sound of the Druid's voice. Then he was racing for the pilot box. It never occurred to him to question whether he was being misled. It never occurred to him that the voice might not be real. The urgency it conveyed catapulted him across the decking in a rush, crying out to Big Red as if stung.

In moments, the airship was sailing skyward through the rugged peaks, lifting over the defiles it could not navigate to reach the beleaguered men.

Walker stared from the cavern entrance at the Elven Hunters marooned on the rocky rise. The entire floor of the canyon had risen up in a tangle of writhing vines and limbs, all of them grasping for anything that came within reach. They had gotten the Elven Hunter Brae before he could even defend himself, dragged him from the rise, and pulled him apart as he screamed for help. The other three had backed to the center of their island, swords drawn, and were striking frantically at the tentacles that snatched for them.

The Druid shoved the second key deep inside his robes and called up the Druid fire against the wall that had formed before him. Blue flames lanced into the tangle and burned everything they touched, momentarily clearing a path. Walker continued his assault, burning through the twisting mass of foliage toward the rise, seeking to reach his companions. But the jungle refused to give way, thrusting back at him from both sides, driving him back. An enormous, implacable weight settled on him, driving him to his knees. He backed from the entrance, recoiling from the assault, and the weight lessened. The key's guardian could not reach him while he remained protected by the cave's stone. But it would keep him there forever.

He realized then what had happened, both here and at Flay Creech. The guardians of the keys had been set at watch against any foreign presence and all threatened thefts of the keys. They were not thinking entities and did not rely on reason; they acted out of pure instinct. Eels and jungle both had been conditioned to serve a single purpose. How that had been managed and by whom, Walker had no idea. But their power was enormous, and while probably confined to a small area, it was more than sufficient to subdue anyone who came within reach.

The jungle reached for him through the cavern entrance, and he responded with the Druid fire, charring vines and limbs, filling the air with clouds of smoke and ash. If Redden Alt Mer didn't reach them soon, they were finished. The Elves could not hope to withstand a prolonged assault on the rise. And even a Druid's magic had its limits.

A hint of desperation driving at him, he thrust his way forward, determined anew to break free. He beat back the jungle wall in an effort to reach the light beyond. As he did so, he caught a glimpse of the *Jerle Shannara* passing overhead and heard the shouts of her company. The Elves trapped on the rise glanced skyward, as well, momentarily distracted, and tall Dace paid the price. Knocked sprawling by a whiplash assault of grasses, his legs became tangled in their implacable weave. Kicking wildly, he fought in vain to break free. Patrinell and Kian reached for him instantly, but he had already been pulled from the rise to his death.

Then a torrent of liquid fire rained down about the rocky isle, encircling the trapped Elven Hunters. Poured from barrels stored aboard ship, it showered onto the vines and grasses and exploded into flame. Down came the winch basket in the fire's wake, jerking up short just above Ard Patrinell and Kian. Breaking off their struggle with the jungle, they scrambled over the basket's side and were pulled to safety.

The jungle turned now on Walker, vines and tall grasses, supple limbs and trunks, twisting and writhing in fury. Walker stood in the cavern opening and burned them with the Druid fire to prevent them from dragging him down. A few moments more and he would be free.

But the guardian of the key was determined to have him. A bramble limb snaked out of the shadows to one side, lashing at the Druid's face. Two-inch needles bit into his flesh, raking his arm and side. Walker felt their poison enter him instantly, a cold fire. He ripped the bramble away, threw it on the ground, and turned it to ash.

Then the winch basket dropped in front of him, and he dragged himself over its side. Vines clutched frantically at him as he rose. With the last of his strength, Walker burned them away, fired them one by one, fighting to stay conscious. The basket lurched free and began to rise swiftly. The airship rose, as well, lifting away into the blue. Anxious faces peered down at him from the railing, blurred and fading quickly. He fought to keep them in focus and failed. Collapsing to the floor of the basket, he lost consciousness.

Below, the floor of the valley writhed in a fiery mass of shriveled limbs and then disappeared in black clouds of roiling smoke.

TWENTY-TWO

For six days and nights, Walker lay near death. A swift and deadly agent, the poison from the brambles had penetrated deep into his body. By the time he was brought back aboard the *Jerle Shannara*, he was already beginning to fail. The Elven Healer Joad Rish recognized his symptoms immediately and roused him long enough to swallow an antidote, then spent the next few anxious minutes applying baen-leaf compresses to his injuries to draw out the poison.

Although the Healer's efforts slowed the poison and blunted its killing effects, they could not counteract it completely. At Redden Alt Mer's insistence, Walker was carried below and placed in the Rover Captain's cabin, and there Joad Rish wrapped the stricken Druid in blankets to keep him warm, gave him liquids to prevent dehydration, changed his dressings regularly, and sat back to wait. Walker's own body was doing more than the Healer could to keep him alive. It waged a silent struggle that was apparent to him but that he could do little more to aid.

Bek Rowe was there for most of it. Since his summoning by Walker during the jungle attack, he felt tied to the Druid in a new and unexpected way. There was considerable wonder and confusion among the members of the ship's company at the fact that he alone had heard Walker's summons. No one had made much of it as yet, but Bek could tell what they were thinking. If the Druid could have summoned anyone, he would have summoned Redden Alt Mer, who piloted the airship and could respond more directly than Bek Rowe. But Big Red had heard nothing. Nor had Quentin or Panax or even Ryer Ord Star. Perhaps not even Truls Rohk had heard. Only Bek. How could that be? Why would Bek be able to receive a summons of that sort when no one else could? How had Walker known that Bek could hear and so chosen to call to him?

The questions plagued him, and there would be no answers unless the Druid recovered from his wounds. But it was not for that reason that Bek chose to keep watch over the Druid. It was because he was afraid that Walker, locked inside his body while unconscious and stricken, in need of help that he could communicate in no other way, would call to him again. Perhaps distance wasn't a problem for the Druid when he was well, but what if it was while he was sick? If Bek were not close and listening, a cry for help might go unheard. Bek did not want that on his conscience. If there was a way to save the Druid's life, he had to be there to provide it.

So he sat with Walker in Redden Alt Mer's cabin and watched in silence while Joad Rish worked. He slept now and then, but only in short naps and never deeply. Ahren Elessedil brought him his meals, and Quentin and Panax came to visit. No effort was made to remove him from the cabin. If anything, the ship's company seemed to feel he belonged at the Druid's side.

To no one's surprise, he did not keep his vigil over Walker alone. Sitting with him the whole of the time was the young seer, Ryer Ord Star. As she had since their departure from Arborlon, she stayed as close to the Druid as his shadow. She studied him intently during his struggle, her head bent in concentration. She watched while Joad Rish worked, asking occasionally what he was doing, nodding at his responses, giving silent approval and support to his efforts. Now and then she spoke to Bek, a word or two here and there, never more, always with her eyes directed toward the Druid. Bek studied her surreptitiously, trying to read her thoughts, to see inside her mind deep enough to discover if she had caught a glimpse of Walker's fate. But the seer revealed nothing, her thin, youthful face a mask against whatever secrets she kept.

Once, when Joad Rish had left them alone and they sat together on a wooden bench at the Druid's side in candlelit gloom, Bek asked her if she thought Walker would live.

"His will is very strong," she replied softly. "But his need for me is greater."

He had no idea what she was talking about and could not think of a way to ask. He was silent long enough that Joad Rish returned, and the matter was dropped. But he could not shake the feeling that the young woman was telling him that in some inextricable way Walker's life was linked to hers.

As he discovered two nights later, he was right. Joad Rish had announced earlier in the day that he had done everything he could think to do for the Druid and that further healing was up to the Druid himself. He had not abandoned hope or given up on his treatment, but he was seeing no change in Walker and was clearly worried. Bek could tell that the Druid had reached a critical juncture in his battle. He was no longer sleeping quietly, but thrashing and twisting in his unconsciousness, delirious and sweating. His great strength of will seemed to have hit a wall, and the poison was pushing back against it relentlessly. Bek had an uneasy feeling that Walker was losing ground.

Ryer Ord Star must have decided the same. She rose suddenly as the midnight hour approached and announced to Joad Rish that he must step back from Walker and give her a chance to help him. The Healer hesitated, then decided for whatever reason to comply. Perhaps he knew of her reputation as an empath and hoped she could do something to relieve his patient's distress. Perhaps he felt there was nothing more he could do, so why not let someone else try? He moved to the bench beside Bek, and together they watched the young seer approach.

She bent to the Druid soundlessly. Like the shadow she so often seemed, she hovered over him, her hands placed carefully on the sides of his face, her slender form draped across his own. She spoke softly and gently, the words lost to Bek and Joad Rish, murmurings that faded into the sounds of the airship as it sailed on the back of the night wind. She continued for a long time, linking herself to Walker, Bek decided, by the sound of her voice and her touch. She wanted him to feel her presence. She wanted him to know she was there.

Then she laid her cheek against his forehead, keeping her hands on his face, and went silent. She closed her eyes and breathed deeply and steadily. Walker began to convulse, arching off the bed in violent spasms, gasping and moaning. She held on to him as he thrashed, and her own body jerked in response to his. Sweat appeared on her thin face, and her pale brow furrowed in anguish. Joad Rish started to go to them, then sat back again. Neither he nor Bek looked at each other, their eyes riveted on the drama taking place.

The strange dance between Druid and seer went on for a long time, a give and take of sudden motion and harsh response. She's taking the poison with its sickness and pain into herself, Bek realized at one point, watching her body knot and her face twist. She's absorbing what's killing him into herself. But won't it then kill her? How much stronger can she be than the Druid, this tiny frail creature? He felt helpless and frustrated watching her work. But he could do nothing.

Then she collapsed to the floor so suddenly that both Bek and the Healer sprang to their feet to go to her. She was unconscious. They laid her on some spare bedding on the cabin floor and covered her with blankets. She was sleeping deeply, locked within herself, carrying Walker's poison inside, carrying his sickness and pain; Walker was sleeping peacefully, the thrashing stopped, the delirium faded. Joad Rish examined them both, feeling for heartbeat and pulse, for temperature and breathing. He looked at Bek when he was finished and shook his head uncertainly. He couldn't tell if she'd been successful or not. They were alive, but it was impossible for him to judge as yet if they would stay that way.

He returned to the bench, and the waiting began anew.

At dawn, the *Jerle Shannara* encountered the worst storm of the voyage. Redden Alt Mer had felt it coming all night as it was signaled by sudden drops of temperature and changes in the wind. When dawn broke iron gray and bloodred, he ordered the sails reefed and all but the main draws shortened. Lightning flashed in long, jagged streaks across the northwest skies, and thunderheads rolled out of the horizon in massive dark banks. Placing the dependable Furl Hawken at the helm, Big Red moved down to the main deck to direct his Rover crew. Everything not already secured was lashed down. Everyone who was not a part of the crew was sent belowdecks and told to stay there. Rue Meridian was dispatched to her brother's cabin to make certain that Walker was tied to his bed and to warn Bek, Ryer Ord Star, and Joad Rish that rough weather lay ahead.

By the time this was done and Little Red was back, the wind was howling across the decking and through the masts and spars as if a living thing. Rain washed down out of the clouds, and darkness descended on the airship in a smothering wave. Redden Alt Mer took the helm back from Furl Hawken, but ordered him to stand by. Spanner Frew was already stationed aft where he could see everything forward of his position. Little Red moved to the bow. All of the crew had secured safety lines and were crouched in the shelter of the railings and masts in anticipation of what was to come.

What came was ferocious. The storm swallowed them in a single gulp of black fury that shut out every other sight and sound, drenched them in rain, and lashed at them with winds so fierce it seemed the ship must surely come apart. Searching for a place to ride out of the storm, Big Red took the *Jerle Shannara* down to a little over a hundred feet above the ocean surface. He would not take the ship all the way down, because the ocean was more dangerous than the wind. What he could see of the Blue Divide, as intermittent flashes of lightning illuminated it, convinced him he had made the right choice. The surface of the ocean was a boiling cauldron of swirling foam and wicked dark troughs with waves cresting thirty and forty feet. In the air, they were buffeted hard, but they would not sink.

Even so, the Rover Captain began to fear they might break apart. Spars and lines were crashing to the decking, flying off into the windswept void. The airship was sleek and smooth and could sideslip the worst of the wind's gusts, but, it was taking a beating. It tossed and dipped wildly. It slewed left and right with sudden lurches that caused stomachs to drop and jaws to clench. Redden Alt Mer stood tall in the pilot box, trying to keep his ship level and directed, but even that soon became hopeless. He could not tell in what direction they traveled, what speed they held, or where within the storm they lay. All he could manage was to keep them turned into the wind and upright above the sea.

The struggle went on all morning. Several times Big Red gave up the wheel to Furl Hawken and sank down in the shelter of the pilot box for a few moments of rest. His hearing was lost temporarily to the howl of the wind, and the skin of his face and hands felt raw. His body ached, and there was a thrumming in his arms and legs from fighting to hold the wheel steady. But each time he rested, he worried that he was taking too long. A few minutes were all he would spare himself. Responsibility for the ship and crew belonged to him, and he would not yield that responsibility to anyone else. Furl Hawken was as able as they came, but the safety of the ship and her company belonged to the Captain. He might have shared his duty with Little Red, but he had no idea where she was. He hadn't seen

310

her in hours. He could no longer see the ship's bow or stern or anyone on them.

Eventually the storm passed, leaving all aboard ship sodden and battered and grateful to be alive. It was the worst storm Redden Alt Mer could remember. He thought they were lucky to have had a vessel as well built as the *Jerle Shannara* to weather it, and one of the first things he did after a hurried best-guess correction of their heading was to relinquish the helm to Furl Hawken so he could tell Spanner Frew as much. A quick check of the ship's company revealed that everyone was still with them, although a few members had sustained minor injuries. Little Red appeared out of the shelter of the forward rams to advise him they had lost several spars and a couple of radian draws, but sustained no major damage. The most immediate problem they faced was that a forward hatch had fallen in on the water casks and all of their fresh water was lost. Foraging for more would be necessary.

It was at that point that Alt Mer remembered the Wing Riders and their Rocs, who had ridden out the storm on their own. He searched the skies in vain. All three had disappeared.

Well, there was nothing he could do about it. Half a day's light remained to them, and he intended to take advantage of it. They were still following Walker's map, sailing on toward the last of the three islands. Even though the Druid was lost to them for now, continuing on made better sense than turning back or standing still. If the Druid died, a different decision might be necessary, but he would make it only then.

"Bring everyone topside and put them to work cleaning up," he told his sister. "And check on the Druid."

She left at once, but it was Bek Rowe who appeared with the news he sought. "He's sleeping better now, and Joad Rish thinks he will recover." Bek looked exhausted, but pleased. "I don't need to be down there anymore. I can help with what's needed up here."

Alt Mer smiled and clapped the boy on the back. "You are a

game lad, Bek. I'm lucky to have you for my good right hand. All right, then. You go where you want for now. Lend a hand where it's needed."

The boy went at once to join Rue Meridian, who was clearing away one of the broken spars. Big Red watched him for a moment, then moved back into the pilot box with Furl Hawken and watched Bek some more.

"That boy's in love with her, Hawk," he declared with a wistful sigh.

Furl Hawken nodded. "Aren't they all. Much good that it will do him or any of them."

Redden Alt Mer pursed his lips thoughtfully. "Maybe Bek Rowe will surprise us."

His friend grunted. "Maybe cows will fly."

They turned their attention to determining the ship's position, taking compass and sextant readings, and beginning a search for landmarks. For now, they could do little but wait. The stars would give them a better reading come nightfall. Tomorrow would see a return of good weather and clear sailing. Maybe the Wing Riders would reappear from wherever they had gone. Maybe Walker would be back on his feet.

Redden Alt Mer glanced over at his sister and Bek Rowe once more and smiled. Maybe cows would fly.

It was almost twenty-four hours later when the Wing Riders soared into view out of the eastern horizon, winging for the airship across clear skies and over placid waters. Hunter Predd rode the lead bird. He was steady and calm as he swung close enough to shout across at Redden Alt Mer.

"Well met, Captain! Are you all right?"

"We survived, Wing Rider! What kept you?"

Hunter Predd grimaced. Rover humor. "We saw the storm coming and found an island on which to wait it out! You don't want

312

to be caught aloft on a Roc in a storm like that! You've been blown well off course, you know!"

Alt Mer nodded. "We're working our way back! What we need now is fresh water! Can you find us some?"

The Wing Rider waved. "We'll take a look! Don't wander off while we're gone!"

With Gill and Po Kelles in tow, he swung Obsidian south and west and began tracking the path of the sun in search of an island. The Wing Riders had weathered the storm on an island some miles east, in a cove sheltered by hills and trees. They had lost all contact with the airship and its company, but there was no help for that. Flying their Rocs in winds that heavy would have killed them all. Experience had taught them to take whatever shelter they could find when a bad storm appeared. They had remained on the island through the night and set off again at dawn. Rocs were intelligent birds possessed of extraordinary eyesight, and their tracking instincts were almost infallible. Using a method they had employed countless times before, the Wing Riders had flown a spiral search pattern that eventually brought them back on course with the *Jerle Shannara*.

Hunter Predd sighed. Storms and other navigational challenges did not concern him all that much. Losing Walker was a different matter. He assumed that Walker was still alive from the simple fact that Redden Alt Mer hadn't said otherwise. Perhaps the Druid had even improved. But having him incapacitated even temporarily pointed up dramatically the weak link in the chain that anchored this entire expedition—only Walker understood what it was that they were trying to accomplish. Granted, a handful of others knew about the keys and the islands and the nature of their destination. Granted, as well, the seer had her visions and whatever information they supplied. Perhaps there were even a few additional things known to one or two others that were crucial to the success of the voyage.

But Walker was the glue that held them all together and the

only one who understood completely the larger picture. He had told Hunter Predd that he needed the Wing Rider's experience and insight to help him succeed on this expedition. He had intimated that the Wing Rider was to keep a sharp eye out. But half the time Hunter felt as if he were groping in the dark. He was never entirely sure what he was watching out for, save in the very narrow context of momentary circumstance. It was bad enough to operate in this fashion with Walker safe and sound. But if the Druid was incapacitated, how were the rest of them supposed to function reliably knowing as little as they did? It would be guesswork at best.

He made up his mind that he could not allow this situation to continue. Foraging and scouting in unknown territory, miles from any mainland, were sufficiently dangerous. But doing so without a clear idea of their purpose was intolerable. Certainly others aboard ship must feel the same. What about Bek Rowe and Quentin Leah? They had been taken into the Druid's confidence, as well. They had been given the same charge he had. He had barely spoken to either since they had set out, but surely they must be having the same misgivings he was.

Still, Hunter Predd was reluctant to force the issue. He was a trained Rider of the Wing Hove, and he understood the importance of obeying orders without questioning them. Leaders did not always impart everything they knew to those they led. Certainly he did not do so with Gill and Po. They were expected to accept the assignments they were given and to do as they were told.

He shook his head. If there was no order, you ran the risk of anarchy. But if there was too much, you ran the risk of revolt. It was a fine line to walk.

He was still pondering this dilemma, trying to reason it through, when he sighted the island.

There were storm clouds lingering ahead, and at first he thought the island was a part of them. But as he drew nearer, he saw that what he had mistaken for dark clouds were rugged cliffs of the sort they had encountered on Shatterstone, their craggy faces exposed and windswept. The island's foliage grew thick and lush inland on the lee side. The Wing Rider squinted against the glare of waterfalls cascading out of the rocks in long silver streams and sunlight where it reflected off the brilliant green of the trees. There would be fresh water available here, he thought.

Then something strange caught his eye. Hundreds of dark spots dotted the cliffs, making it look as if deep pockmarks had formed in the crevices and ridges after long years of severe weathering.

"What is that?" Hunter Predd muttered to himself.

He swung Obsidian about, motioning for Gill to move off to his left and Po Kelles to flank him on the right. On a long, sweeping glide, they approached the island and its cliffs, peering through the brightness of the afternoon sun.

Hunter Predd blinked. Had one of the dark spots moved? He glanced over at Po. The young Wing Rider nodded in response. He had seen it, too. Hunter Predd motioned for him to fall back.

He was trying to signal Gill, whose concentration had been distracted by a passing pod of whales, when several of the dark spots lifted away from the cliffs entirely.

Beneath him, Obsidian tensed and then screamed in alarm. Wings were unfolding from the black dots, giving them size and shape. Hunter Predd went cold. The Roc had recognized the danger before he had. Shrikes! War Shrikes! The fiercest and most savage of the breed. This island, which the Rocs and Wing Riders had stumbled upon unwittingly, must be their nesting ground. The War Shrikes would not ignore a trespass on their home ground, regardless of the reason for it. Rocs were their natural enemies, and the Shrikes would attack.

Hunter Predd wheeled Obsidian around hurriedly, watching Po Kelles and Niciannon follow his lead. To his astonishment, Gill continued to advance. Either he hadn't seen the Shrikes or hadn't recognized what they were. It was useless to yell warnings from that distance, so he used the signal whistle. Startled, Gill glanced over his shoulder and saw his companions pointing. Then he caught sight of the Shrikes. Frantically, he reined in Tashin. But the Roc panicked, and instead of wheeling back, he went into a steep dive, spiraling toward the ocean, pulling up and leveling out only at the last possible moment.

Then he was streaking after Obsidian and Niciannon, but he was still far behind and the Shrikes were closing. War Shrikes were swift and powerful short-range fliers. A Roc's best hope was to gain height and distance. Hunter Predd realized that Tashin had failed to do either and would not escape.

He brought Obsidian back around swiftly and flew at the Shrikes in challenge, trying to distract them. Po Kelles and Niciannon were beside him almost instantly. Both Rocs screamed in fury at the approaching Shrikes, their hatred of their enemies as great as that of their enemies for them. Secured to their riding harnesses by safety lines and gripping their mounts with knees and boots, both Wing Riders brought out their long bows and the arrows that were dipped in an extract from fire nettles and nightshade. Close enough now to find their targets, they began to fire on the Shrikes.

Some of their missiles struck home. Some of the Shrikes even broke off the attack and wheeled back toward the island. But the bulk, more than twenty, descended on Gill and Tashin like a black cloud and caught them just off the surface of the water. Gill was torn from his Roc's back on the first pass. Sharp talons and hooked beaks scattered parts of him everywhere in a red spray. Tashin lasted only seconds longer. Shuddering from the blows he received, he righted himself momentarily, then disappeared under a swarm of black bodies. Forced down into the ocean, he was quickly ripped to shreds.

Hunter Predd stared down at the carnage in helpless rage and frustration. It had happened so fast. One minute there, the next gone. Alive, and then a memory, a senseless loss of life that shouldn't have happened. But what could have been done to avoid it? What could he have done?

He wheeled Obsidian about. Po Kelles and Niciannon followed. Swiftly they gained height and then distance, and in a matter of moments, they were safely away. Their pursuers did not give chase; they were otherwise occupied, wheeling above the broad patch of rolling ocean streaked with feathers and blood. The Wing Riders flew on and did not look back.

TWENTY-THREE

After having their number reduced by three in a matter of a few days, the men and women of the *Jerle Shannara* continued their voyage for another six weeks without incident. Even so, tempers flared more easily than before. Perhaps it was the strain of prolonged confinement or the increased uncertainty of their fate or just the change in climate as the ship turned north, the air grew cold and sharp, and storms became more frequent, but everyone was on edge.

The change in Walker was pronounced. Recovered from his ordeal on Shatterstone, he had nevertheless grown increasingly aloof and less approachable. He seemed as sure of himself as ever and as fixed of purpose, but he distanced himself in ways that left no doubt that he preferred his own company to that of others. He consulted regularly on the ship's progress with Redden Alt Mer and spoke in a civil way to everyone he came upon, but he seemed to do so from a long way off. He canceled the nightly meetings in the Rover Captain's quarters, announcing that they were no longer necessary. Ryer Ord Star still followed him around like a lost puppy, but he seemed unaware of her. Even Bek Rowe found him difficult to talk to, enough so that the boy put off asking why he, in particular, had been mind-summoned on Shatterstone.

Nor was Walker the only member of the company affected. Ard Patrinell still worked his Elven Hunters daily, as well as Quentin Leah and Ahren Elessedil, but he was virtually invisible the rest of the time. Spanner Frew was a thunderhead waiting to burst. One time he engaged in a shouting match with Big Red that brought everyone on deck to stare at them. Rue Meridian grew tight-lipped and somber toward everyone except her brother and Bek. She clearly liked being with Bek, and spent much of her time exchanging stories with him. No one understood her attraction for the boy, but Bek basked in it. Panax shook his head at everything and spent all of his time whittling. Truls Rohk was a ghost.

Once, Hunter Predd came aboard for a hard-edged, whispered confrontation with Walker that seemed to satisfy neither and left the Wing Rider angry when it was finished.

They had been gone for almost four months, and the voyage was beginning to wear on them. Days would pass with no land sighted, and sometimes those days would stretch into weeks. The number of islands they passed diminished, and it became necessary to ration their stores and water more strictly. Fresh fruit was seldom available, and rainwater was caught in tarps stretched over the decking to supplement what was foraged. Routines grew boring and change more difficult to invent. The course of their lives settled into a numbing sameness that left everyone disgruntled.

There was no help for it, Rue Meridian explained to Bek one day as they sat talking. Life aboard ship did that to you, and long voyages were the worst. Some of it had to do with the fact that explorers and adventurers detested confinement. Even the members of the Rover crew liked to move around more than was permitted here. None of them had ever sailed on a voyage of such length, and they were discovering feelings and reactions they hadn't even known were there. It would all change when they reached their destination, but until then they simply had to live with their discomfort.

"There's a lot of luck involved in being a sailor, Bek," she told him. "Flying airships is tricky business, even with a Captain as experienced as Big Red. His crews like him more for his luck than his skill. Rovers are a superstitious bunch, and they're constantly looking for favorable signs. They don't feel good about new experiences and unknown places if they come at the price of their shipmates' lives. They're drawn to the unknown, but they take comfort in what's familiar and reassuring. Sort of a contradiction, isn't it?"

"I thought Rovers might be more adaptable," he replied.

She shrugged. "Rovers are a paradox. They like movement and new places. They don't like the unknown. They don't trust magic. They believe in fate and omens. My mother read bones to determine her children's future. My father read the stars. It doesn't always make sense, but what does? Is it better to be a Dwarf or a Rover? Is it better to have your life fixed and settled or to have it change with every shift in the wind? It depends on your point of view, doesn't it? The demands of this particular voyage are a new experience for everyone, and each of us has to find a way to deal with them."

Bek didn't mind doing that. He was by nature an accepting sort, and he had learned a long time ago to live with whatever conditions and circumstances he was provided. Maybe this came from being an orphan delivered into the hands of a stranger's family and being brought up with someone else's history. Maybe it came from an approach to life that questioned everything as a matter of course, so that the uncertainties of their expedition didn't wear at him so cruelly. After all, he hadn't gone into this with the same high spirits as many of the others, and his emotional equilibrium was more easily balanced.

To a measurable extent, he found he was a calming influence on the other members of the company. When they were around him, they seemed more at ease and less irritable. He didn't know why that was, but he was pleased to be able to offer something of tangible value and did his best to soothe ruffled feathers when he encountered them. Quentin was of some use in this regard, as well. Nothing ever seemed to change Bek's cousin. He continued as eager and bright-eyed and hopeful as ever, the only member of the company who genuinely enjoyed each day and looked forward to the next. It was the nature of his personality, of course, but it provided a needed measure of inspiration to those who possessed a less generous attitude.

Shortly after their encounter with the Shrikes, the airship assumed a more northerly heading in accordance with the dictates of the map. As the days passed, the weather turned colder. Autumn had arrived at home, and a fresh chill was apparent in the sea air as well. The sky took on an iron-gray cast much of the time, and on the colder mornings a thin layer of ice formed on the railings of the ship. Furl Hawken broke out heavy coats, gloves, and boots for the company, and warming fires were lit on deck at night for the watch. The days grew shorter and the nights longer, and the sun rose farther south in the eastern sky with each new dawn.

Snow flurries appeared for the first time only two nights before the *Jerle Shannara* arrived at the island of Mephitic.

Walker stood at the bow of the airship to study the island during their approach. The Wing Riders had discovered it several hours earlier while making their customary sweep forward and to either side of the ship's line of flight. Redden Alt Mer had adjusted their course at once on being informed, and now Mephitic lay directly ahead, a green jewel shining brightly in the midday sun.

This island was different from the other two, as Walker had known it would be. Mephitic was low and broad, comprising rolling hills, thickly wooded forests, and wide smooth grasslands. It lacked the high cliffs of Shatterstone and the barren rocky shoals of Flay Creech. It was much larger than either, big enough that in the haze of the midday autumn light, Walker could not see its far end. It did not appear forbidding. It had the look of the Westland where it bordered the Plains of Streleheim north and abutted the Myrian south. As the airship descended toward its shores and began a slow circle about its coastline, he could see small deer grazing peacefully and flocks of birds in flight. Nothing seemed out of place or dangerous. Nothing threatened.

Walker found what he was looking for on their first pass. A massive castle sat on a low bluff facing west, backed up against a deep forest and fronted by a broad plain. The castle was old and crumbling, its portcullis collapsed, its windows and doors dark empty holes, and its battlements and courtyards deserted. It had been a mighty fortress in another age and time, and its walls and outbuildings sprawled across the grasslands for perhaps a mile in all directions. The castle proper was as large as Paranor and every bit as formidable.

Unlike the other two islands, where only the name had been given, Mephitic had been carefully drawn on the castaway's map. The fortress, in particular, had been noted. The third and final key, the map indicated, was hidden somewhere inside.

Walker folded himself into his black robes and stared at the castle. He was aware of the growing dissatisfaction of the ship's company. He understood that some of it was due entirely to him. He had indeed distanced himself from them in a very deliberate fashion, but not without consideration for the consequences and not for the reasons they thought. Their disgruntlement and unrest were side effects he could not avoid. He knew things they did not, and one of them had prompted him to keep everyone at arm's length since his recovery.

That would change once he had possession of the third key and could instill in the ship's company a reasonable expectation of reaching the safehold the keys would unlock.

Not that anything was as simple as it appeared on the surface, or even that anything was *what* it appeared.

He felt a bitter satisfaction in knowing the truth, but it did nothing to make him feel better. Hunter Predd had a right to be angry with him for keeping secrets. They all had a right to be angry, more so than they realized. It reminded him anew of his own bitter feelings toward the Druids in times past. He knew the nature of their order. They were wielders of power and keepers of secrets. They manipulated and deceived. They specialized in creating events and directing lives for the greater good of the Four Lands. He had wanted no part of them then and wanted little now. Although he had become one of them, a part of their order and their history, he had promised himself that things would be different with him. He had sworn that in carrying out the admittedly necessary task of implementing order and wielding magic in a way that would unite the Races, he would not resort to their tactics.

He was finding out anew how hard that vow was to keep. He was discovering firsthand the depth of his own commitment to their cause and to his duty.

He ordered Redden Alt Mer to take the *Jerle Shannara* down to the plain in front of the castle and to anchor her several hundred yards away and in the open so that all approaches could be watched. He called the ship's company together and told them he would take a scouting party into the castle now, before dark, for a look around. Perhaps they would find the key at once, as they had on the other two islands. Perhaps they would even manage to secure it quickly and escape. But he did not want to run the risks of Shatterstone, so he would proceed cautiously. If he sensed any form of danger, they would turn back at once and begin again tomorrow. If it took them longer to achieve their objective because of his caution, so be it.

He chose Panax, Ard Patrinell, and six Elven Hunters to go with him. He considered Quentin Leah, then shook his head. He did not even glance at Bek.

The scouting party descended from the airship by rope ladder and set off across the flats for the castle. Wading through waist-high grasses, they reached the castle's west entry, a drawbridge that was lowered and rotting and a portcullis that was raised and rusted in place. They stopped long enough for the Druid to read the shadows that lay pooled at every silent opening, dark hollows within the walls of stone and mortar, then crossed the drawbridge warily and entered the main courtyard. Dozens of doors opened through walls and dozens of stairs led into towers. Walker scanned them all for whatever might threaten and found nothing. There was no sign of life and no indication of danger.

But he could sense the presence of the key, faint and distant, somewhere deep inside the keep. What sort of guardian kept watch over it? *One is everything and nothing and will steal your soul.* The words of the seer echoed in the silence of his mind, enigmatic and troubling.

Walker stood in the courtyard for a long time making sure of what his senses told him, then started ahead once more.

They combed the ruins from tower to cellar, dungeon to spire, hall to courtyard, and parapet to battlement, crisscrossing its maze swiftly, but thoroughly. Nothing interfered with their efforts, and no dangers presented themselves. Twice, Walker thought they were close to the key, able to sense its presence more strongly, to feel its peculiar mix of metal and energy reaching out to him. But each time he believed himself close, it eluded him. The second time, he divided the Elven Hunters into pairs and sent two with Ard Patrinell, two with Panax, and two with himself in an effort to surround it. But no one found anything.

Their search was frustrating in other ways, as well. The fortress was a puzzling warren of chambers, courtyards, and halls, and all sense of direction disappeared once they were inside. The searchers constantly found themselves going around in circles and ending up back where they started. Worse, led astray by a deceived sense of direction, they were as likely to find themselves outside the walls at the end of a corridor's turn or stairwell's twist as they were inside. It was irksome and somewhat troubling to the Druid, but he could find no reason for it beyond the construction of the keep. Probably it had been designed to confuse enemies. Whatever the case, all efforts at completing a successful search were thwarted as they found themselves starting over time and again.

Finally, they gave it up. The afternoon sun had drifted west to the horizon, and Walker did not want to get caught inside the castle after dark. The keep might be less friendly then, and he didn't want to find that out the hard way. Even though they hadn't discovered it, he knew the key was close at hand. It was only a matter of time before their search was concluded.

He returned to the ship and called his first meeting of the company's inner circle in almost two months to give his report and express his confidence. Redden Alt Mer, Rue Meridian, Ard Patrinell, Ahren Elessedil, Ryer Ord Star, Quentin Leah, and Bek Rowe were all there, and all were heartened by what they heard. Tomorrow they would resume their search for the final key, he concluded, and this time their efforts would prove successful.

At dawn, Walker took everyone with him but the Rovers, Ryer Ord Star, Truls Rohk, and Bek. He could see the disappointment and hurt in Bek's eyes, but there was no help for it. Again they searched diligently, taking all day to do so, and again they found nothing. Walker sensed the presence of the key just as he had the day before, unmistakable and clear. But he could not find it. Without results, he combed the castle for magic that might conceal it. He kept a wary eye out for whatever guarded it—for he knew something must be doing so—but could identify nothing.

For three more days, Walker searched. He took the same members of the ship's company with him each time, splitting them up into different groups, hoping that some new combination would see what the others had missed. From dawn until dusk, they crisscrossed the ruins. Again and again, they found themselves traveling in circles. Over and over, they found themselves starting their search inside and ending up outside. Nothing new was uncovered. No one caught even a glimpse of the key.

On the fifth night, weary and discouraged, he was forced to admit to himself, if to no one else, that he was getting nowhere. He had reached a point where he felt failure's grip tightening on his hopes. His patience was exhausted and his confidence was beginning to erode. Something about this business was wearing at him in a very unpleasant and subtle way.

While the other members of the company drifted off to sleep, he stood at the bow of the ship for a long time trying to decide what he should do. He was missing something. The key was there; he could feel it. Why was it so difficult for him to pinpoint its location? Why was it so hard to discover how it had been concealed? If no magic was protecting it and no guardian was evident, how could it continue to elude him?

Another approach was needed. Something new must be tried. Perhaps someone should go into the castle at night. Perhaps the darkness would change the way things looked.

It was time to call on Truls Rohk.

Far astern of the *Jerle Shannara*, south and east of the island and well out of sight below the horizon, *Black Moclips* hung silently above the water, anchored in place for the night. Mwellret sentries prowled across her sleek, armored decking, their spidery forms hooded and cloaked as they drifted through the shadows. The Federation crew was belowdecks in the sleeping quarters, all save for the helmsman, a whip-thin veteran corded with muscle and wrapped in his disdain and repulsion for the lizardlike creatures his ship was forced to carry.

The Ilse Witch shared his feelings. The Mwellrets were loathsome and dangerous, but there was nothing she could do about them. The presence of the Morgawr's minions was the price she had been forced to pay in order to pursue her search for the map's promised magic. Had she been free to do so, she would have turned them all to chum and fed them to the big fish.

Not that she was much better regarded than they were by Commander Aden Kett and his crew. The Federation soldiers disliked her almost as much; she was a shadowy presence who stayed aloof from them, who gave them no reasons for what she did, and who had on the very first day made a small example of one of their number who had disobeyed her. That she was apparently human was her only saving grace. That she commanded power beyond their understanding and had little regard for them beyond what they could do for her made her someone they went out of their way to avoid.

Which was as it should be, of course. Which was as it had always been.

Wrapped in her gray robes, she stood before the foremast and looked off into the night. She had been shadowing the *Jerle Shannara* and her company ever since the departure from Arborlon. *Black Moclips* was a formidable and efficient craft, and her Federation crew was as well trained and experienced as Sen Dunsidan had promised. Both had done what was needed to track the Elven airship. Not that there was ever any real danger they might lose contact with her. The Ilse Witch had seen to that.

But what was happening here? What was keeping the other ship at anchor for so long? For six days and nights she had waited for the Druid to secure the final key. Why had he failed to do so? Apparently the puzzle offered by this island was proving more difficult to solve than that of the previous two. Was this where Walker would fail? Was this as far as he would get without her help?

She sniffed in disdain at the thought. No, not him. Even crippled, he would not be so easily defeated. She might hate and despise him, but she knew him to be formidable and clever. He would solve the puzzle and continue on to the safehold they both journeyed to find. It would be settled between them there, and a lifetime of anger and hatred would be put to rest at last. It would happen as she had foreseen. He would not disappoint her.

Yet her uncertainty persisted, nagging and insidious. Perhaps she gave him too much credit. Did he realize yet the ways in which he was being manipulated in his quest? Had he reasoned out, as she had, the hidden purpose of the castaway and the map?

Her brow furrowed. She must assume so. She could not afford to assume otherwise. But it would be interesting to know. Her spy could tell her, perhaps. But the risk of compromise was too great to attempt any contact.

She walked forward to the ship's bow and stood looking off into the dark for a time, then produced a small milky glass sphere from within her robes and held it up to the light. Softly, she sang to the sphere, and the milkiness faded and turned clear and captured within it an image of the *Jerle Shannara*, anchored above the grasslands running west from the ruined castle. She studied it carefully, searching for the Druid, but he was nowhere to be found. Elven Hunters kept watch fore and aft, and a burly Rover lounged at the helm. At the center of the ship, the strange case the Druid had brought aboard remained covered and warded by magic-enhanced chains.

What was hidden in it and behind those chains? What, that he must guard it so carefully?

"Elvess do not ssusspect our pressensse, Misstress," a voice hissed at her elbow. "Killss them all while they ssleepss, perhapss?"

White-hot rage surged through her at the interruption. "If you come into my presence again without permission, Cree Bega, I will forget who sent you and why you are here and separate you from your skin."

The Mwellret bowed in obsequious acknowledgment of his trespass. "Apologiess, Misstress. But we wasste our time and opportunitiess. Let uss kill them and be done with it!"

She hated Cree Bega. The Mwellret leader knew she would not harm him; the Morgawr had given him a personal guarantee of protection against her. She had been forced to swear to it in his presence. The memory made her want to retch. He was not afraid of her in any case. Although not completely immune, Mwellrets were re-

sistant to the controlling powers of her magic, and Cree Bega more
so than most. The combination of all this added to his insufferable
arrogance toward and open disdain for her and made their alliance
all but intolerable.

But she was the Ilse Witch, and she showed him nothing of her
irritation. No one could penetrate her defenses unless she allowed it.

"They do our work for us, ret. We will let them continue until
they are finished. Then you can kill as many as you like. Save one."

"Knowss your claim upon the Druid, misstress," he purred.
"Givess the resst to me and mine. We will be ssatissfied. Little peopless, Elvess, belongss to uss."

She passed her hand across the sphere. The image of the *Jerle
Shannara* disappeared and the sphere went white again. She tucked
it back inside her robes, all without glancing once at the creature
hovering next to her. "Nothing belongs to you that I do not choose
to give you. Remember that. Now get out of my sight."

"Yess, Misstress," he replied tonelessly, without a scintilla of respect or fear, and slid away into the shadows like oil over black
metal.

She did not look to see that he had gone. She did not trouble
herself. She was thinking that it did not matter what she had
promised the Morgawr. When this matter was finished, so were
these treacherous toads. All of them, her promise to the Morgawr
notwithstanding. And Cree Bega would be the first.

The night was silent and windless, and she cradled the *Jerle
Shannara* like a slumbering child rocked gently in her arms. Bek Rowe
sat up suddenly, staring into the darkness of his sleeping room, listening to the snores and breathing of Quentin and Panax and the
others. Someone had called his name, whispered it in his mind, in a
voice he did not recognize, in words that were lost instantly on
waking. Had he imagined it?

He rose, pulled on his boots and cloak, and climbed topside to the decking. He stood without moving at the top of the stairs and looked about as if he might find the answer in the darkness. He had heard his name clearly. Someone had spoken it. He brushed back his curly hair and rubbed the sleep from his eyes. The moon and stars were brilliant white beacons in a velvet black sky. The lines and features of the airship and the island were distinct and clear. Everything was still, as if frozen in ice.

He walked to the forward mast, just ahead of the mysterious object Walker kept so carefully warded. He stared about once more, searching now as much inside himself as without for what had drawn him here.

"Looking for something, boy?" a familiar voice hissed softly at his elbow.

Truls Rohk. He jumped in spite of himself. The shape-shifter crouched somewhere in the shadows of the casing, so close Bek imagined he could reach out and touch him. "Was it you who called me?" he breathed.

"It is a good night for discovering truths," the other whispered in that rough, not-quite-human voice. "Care to try?"

"What are you talking about?" Bek struggled to keep his voice steady and calm.

"Hum for me. Just a little, soft as a kitten's purr. Hum as if you were trying to move me back with just your voice. Do you understand?"

Bek nodded, wondering what in the world Truls Rohk was trying to prove. Hum? Move him back with his voice?

"Do it then. Don't question me. Think about what you want to do and then do it. Concentrate."

Bek did as he was asked. He imagined the shape-shifter standing beside him, visualized him there in the darkness, and hummed as if the sound, the vibration alone, might move him away. The sound was barely audible, unremarkable, and so far as Bek could determine, pointless.

"No!" the other spat angrily. "Try harder! Give it teeth, boy!"

Bek tried again, jaw clenched, angry now himself at being

chided. His humming buzzed and vibrated up from his throat and through his mouth and nose with fresh purpose. The force of his effort caused the air before his eyes to shimmer as if turned to liquid.

"Yes," Truls Rohk murmured in response, satisfaction reflected in his voice. "I thought so."

Bek went silent again, staring into the shadows, into the night. "You thought so? What did you think?" The humming had revealed nothing to him. What had it revealed to Truls Rohk?

A part of the blackness surrounding the casing detached itself and took shape, rising up against the light of moon and stars. An only vaguely human form, big and terrifying. Not to step away from it took everything Bek had.

"I know you, boy," the other whispered.

Bek stared. "How could you?"

The other laughed softly. "I know you better than you know yourself. The truth of you is a secret. It is not for me to reveal it to you. The Druid must be the one to do that. But I can show you something of what it looks like. Are you interested?"

For an instant, Bek considered turning around and walking away. There was something dark in the other's meaning, something that would change the boy once it was revealed. He understood that instinctively.

"We are alike, you and I," the shape-shifter said. "We are nothing of what we seem or others think they know. We are joined in ways that would surprise and astonish. Perhaps our fates are linked in some way. What becomes of one depends on what becomes of the other."

Bek could not imagine it. He could barely follow what the shape shifter was saying, let alone fathom what it meant. He made no reply.

"Lies conceal us as masks do thieves, boy. I, because I choose it to be so—you, because you are deceived. We are wraiths living in the shadows, and the truths of identities are carefully guarded secrets. But yours is the darker by far. Yours is the one that has its source in a Druid's games-playing and a magic's dark promise. Mine is simply the result of a twist of fate and a parent's foolish choice." He paused. "Come with me, and I'll tell you of it."

Bek shook his head. "I can't leave—"

"Can't you?" the other shot, cutting him short. "Down to the island and into the castle? Come with me, and we'll bring the third key back to the Druid before he wakes. It's lying there, waiting for us. You and I, we can do what the Druid cannot. We can find it and bring it back."

Bek took a deep breath. "You know where the key is?"

The other shifted slightly, a flowing of darkness against the moonlight. "What matters is that I know how to find it. The Druid asked me earlier this night to seek it out, and so I did. But now I have decided to go back on my own and get it. Want to come along with me?"

The boy was speechless. What was going on here?

"This should be easy for you. I know your heart. You've been allowed to do nothing. You've been kept aboard for no reason you can determine. You've been lied to and put off as if you didn't count. Aren't you weary of it?"

Just two days earlier, Bek had mustered the courage to ask Walker about his use of the mind-summons on Shatterstone. The Druid had told him it was only a coincidence that he had settled his thoughts on Bek, that he had been thinking of the boy just before the attack and had flashed on him instinctively. It was such an obvious lie that Bek had simply walked away in disgust. Truls Rohk seemed to be speaking directly to this incident.

"This is your chance," the shape-shifter pressed. "Come with me. We can do what Walker cannot. Are you afraid?"

Bek nodded. "Yes."

Truls Rohk laughed, deep and low. "You shouldn't be. Not of anything. But I'll protect you. Come with me. Take back something of who you are from the Druid. Give him pause. Make him reconsider how he thinks of you. Find out something about yourself, about who you are. Don't you want that?"

To be honest, Bek wasn't sure. All of a sudden he wasn't sure of anything. The shape-shifter frightened him for more reasons than he cared to consider, but chief among them was his dark intimation that Bek was nothing of who and what he assumed himself to be. Revelations of that sort usually damaged as much as they healed. Bek wasn't sure he wanted them revealed by this man, in this way.

"I'll keep my promise to you, boy," Truls Rohk whispered. "I'll tell you my truth. Not what you've heard from Panax. Not what you've imagined. The truth, as it really is."

"Panax said you were burned in a fire—"

"Panax doesn't know. No one does, save the Druid, who knows it all."

Bek stared. "Why would you choose to tell me?"

"Because we are alike, as I've said already. We are alike, and perhaps by knowing me you will come to know yourself, as well. Perhaps. I see myself in you, a long time ago. I see how I was, and I ache with that memory. By telling you my story, I can dispel a little of that ache."

And give it to me, Bek thought. But he was curious about the shape-shifter. Curious and intrigued. He glanced off into the night, toward the castle bathed in moonlight. Truls Rohk was right about the key, as well. Bek wanted to do something more than serve as a cabin boy. He resented being kept aboard ship all the time. He wanted to feel a part of the expedition, to do something other than study airships and flying. He wanted to contribute something important. Finding the third key would accomplish that.

But he remembered the eels of Flay Creech and the jungle of Shatterstone, and he wondered how he could even think of going down to Mephitic and whatever waited there. Truls Rohk seemed confident, but the shape-shifter's reasons for taking him were questionable. Still, others had gone and returned safely. Was he to hide aboard this ship from everything they encountered? He had known when he agreed to come that there would be risks. He could not avoid them all.

But should he embrace them so willingly?

"Come with me, boy," Truls Rohk urged again. "The night passes swiftly, and we must act while it is still dark. The key waits. I'll keep you safe. You'll do the same for me. We'll reveal hidden truths about ourselves on the way. Come!"

For an instant longer, Bek hesitated. Then he exhaled sharply. "All right," he agreed.

Truls Rohk's laugh was wicked and low. Seconds later they slipped over the side of the airship and disappeared into the night.

TWENTY-FOUR

Truls Rohk was born out of fierce passion, misguided choice, and a chance encounter that should never have happened.

His father was a Borderman, a child of frontier parents and grandparents, woodsmen and scouts who lived the whole of their lives in the wilderness of the Runne Mountains. By the time the Borderman was fifteen, he was already gone from his family and living on his own. He was a legend by the time he was twenty, a scout who had traveled the length and breadth of the Wolfs-ktaag, guiding caravans of immigrants across the mountains, leading hunting parties in and out again, and exploring regions that only a few had ventured into. He was a big man, strong of mind and body, powerfully built and agile, skilled and experienced in a way few others were. He knew of the things that lived within the Wolfs-ktaag. He was not afraid of them, but he was mindful of what they could do.

He met Truls Rohk's mother in his thirty-third year. He had been guiding and scouting and exploring for half his life, and he was more at home in the wilderness than he was in the camps of civilization. More and more, he had distanced himself from the settlements and their people. Increasingly, he had sought peace and solace in isolation. The world he favored was not always safe, but it was familiar and comforting. Dangers were plentiful and often unforgiving, but he understood and accepted them. He thought them fair trade for the beauty and purity of the country.

He had always been lucky, had never made a serious mistake or taken an unnecessary risk. He had shaped and honed his luck into a mantle of confidence that helped to keep him safe. He learned to think defensively, but positively, as well. He never thought anything would hurt him if he made the right choices. He suffered injuries and sickness, but they were never severe enough to prevent a full and complete recovery.

On the day he met Truls Rohk's mother, however, his luck ran out. He was caught in a storm and seeking shelter when a tree on a slope above him was struck by lightning. It shattered with a huge explosion and tumbled down, along with half the hillside. The Borderman who had escaped so often was a step slow this time. A massive limb pinned his legs. Boulders and debris pummeled him senseless. In seconds, he was completely buried under a mound of rocks and earth, unconscious before he understood fully what had happened.

When he woke, the storm had passed and night had fallen. He was surprised to find that he could move again. He lay in a clearing, away from the slide and the limb, his body aching and his face bloodied, but alive. When he propped himself up on one elbow, he was aware of someone looking at him. The watcher's eyes glimmered in the darkness, well back in the shadows, bright and feral. A wolf, he thought. He did not reach for his weapons. He did not panic. He stared back at the watcher, waiting to see what it would do. When it did nothing, he sat up, thinking it would slink away with his movement. It did not.

The Borderman understood. The watcher had been the one who pulled him free of the limb, of the rocks and earth, of his tomb. The watcher had saved his life.

The staring contest continued for a long time with neither

watcher nor Borderman advancing or retreating. Finally the Borderman spoke, calling to the watcher, thanking it for helping him. The watcher stayed where it was. The Borderman spoke for a long time, keeping his voice low and calm in the way he had learned was effective, growing more and more convinced that the watcher was not human. It was, he believed, a spirit creature. It was a child of the Wolfsktaag.

It was nearing dawn when the watcher finally came close enough to be seen clearly. It was a woman, but it was not human. She slid from the shadows as if formed of colored water, changing her look as she came, a beast one moment, a human the next, a cross of each soon after. She seemed to be trying to take form, uncertain of what to be. In all of her variations, she was beautiful and compelling. She knelt by the Borderman and stroked his forehead and face with soft, strange fingers. She whispered words that the Borderman could not identify, but in a tone of voice that was unmistakable—sweet, silky, and thick with lust.

She was a shape-shifter, he realized, a creature of the Old World, a thing of magic and strange powers. Something of who and what he was, or perhaps something of her own nature, had drawn her to him. She stared at him with such unbridled passion that he was caught up in her fire. She wanted him in a primal, urgent way, and he found his response to her need equally compelling.

They mated there in the clearing, quick and hard, a coupling more terrible for its frenzy than for its forbidden character. A human and a spirit creature—no good can come of that, the old ones would say.

She carried him to her lair, and for three days they mated without stopping, resting only when it was required, submerged in their passion when it was not. The Borderman forgot his wounds and his misgivings and any sense of reason. He put aside everything for this wondrous creature and what she was giving him. He lost himself in his uncontrollable need.

When it was finished, she was gone. He woke on the fourth day to silence and emptiness. He lay alone, abandoned. He rose, weak and unsteady, but alive in ways he had never thought to be. Her smell and taste lingered in the air around him, on his skin, in his throat. Her presence, the feel of her, was burned into his memory. He wept uncontrollably. He would never be the same without her. She had marked him forever.

For months afterwards, he hunted for her. He combed the Wolfsktaag from end to end, forsaking everything else. He ate, drank, slept, and hunted. He did so ceaselessly. The weather and the seasons changed, then changed back again. A year passed. Two. He never saw her. He never found a trace of where she had gone.

Then one day, a little more than two years later, when he was reduced to searching because he did not know what else to do, when he no longer held out any hope, she came to him again. It was late in the year, and the leaves were changed and beginning to fall in careless pools of bright red and orange and yellow on the forest floor. He was walking toward a spring from which he could drink before continuing on. He did not know where he was or where he was going. He was moving because moving was all that was left to him.

And all at once she was there, standing in front of him, at the pool's edge.

She was not alone. A boy stood beside her, part human, part beast, instantly recognizable from his features. He was the child of the Borderman. Already grown to become nearly as large as his mother, he was too big for a normal boy of two. Sharp-eyed and quick, he stared at his father cautiously. There was recognition and understanding in his eyes. There was acceptance. His mother had told him the truth about his father.

The Borderman came forward and stood awkwardly before them, not knowing what to do. The woman spoke to him in low, compelling tones. Her words, the Borderman found, were clear. She had mated with him when the urge was irresistible and her attraction to him inexplicably strong. They were mismatched and unsuited. But he should know they had a son. He should know and then forget them both.

It was a pivotal moment. The Borderman had searched for her while she had all but forgotten him. She neither needed nor wanted him. She had her own life, a spirit's life, and he could never be part of it. She did not understand that she had destroyed him and he could never forget her, could never go back to being what he had been. He was hers as surely as the boy was his. It did not matter what world he had come from or what life he had led. He was hers, and he would not be sent away.

He begged her to stay. He got down on his knees, this strong and driven man, this man who had endured and survived so much, and he pleaded with her. He wept uncontrollably. It was useless. Worse, it was pointless. She did not understand his behavior. She had no frame of reference for doing so. Spirits did not weep or beg. They acted instinctively and out of need. For her, the choice was clear. She was a creature of the forests and the spirit world. He was not. She could not stay with him.

When finally she turned to leave, her recognition of him already beginning to fade, his desperation turned to rage. Without thinking, his life ruined, his torment too much to bear, he leapt upon her and drove his hunting knife through her back and into her heart. She was dead before he bore her to the earth.

He sprang up instantly then and ripped his knife free to kill the boy as well, but the boy was gone.

The Borderman ran after him, his mind collapsed and turned inward so that nothing else existed. In one hand he carried the hunting knife, wet with the shape-shifter's blood, waving it at the shadows about him, at the fate that had undone him. In the shadowy concealment of the trees, in the silence of the forest, he sought the boy. His madness was thorough and complete. Bloodlust ruled his life.

He ran until he collapsed in exhaustion, and then he slept.

But before he could wake to resume his search, the boy found him, pried the knife from his sleeping hand, and with a sure and practiced touch, cut his throat.

Truls Rohk's low, guttural voice went silent. Crouched and hidden from view, he continued to slide through the tall grass ahead of Bek. Bek waited for him to continue his tale, but he did not. Sweat coated the boy's sun-browned face, a damp sheen prompted as much by his horror as by his exertion. To have watched your father kill your mother and then to have killed your father was an experience too horrifying to contemplate. What must it have felt like to have witnessed and endured such madness at two years of age? Even if you were a spirit creature, a shape-shifter, and not entirely human, what must it have been like? Worse than he could imagine, Bek decided, because Truls Rohk was half human and cloaked in human sensibilities.

"Stay low," the shape-shifter growled in warning.

He stopped and turned back to Bek. His face was hidden in the folds of his hood and his body concealed by his cloak, but Bek could feel the heat of him emanate from beneath his coverings.

"I buried them where they will never be found. I felt nothing at first, not until later, when I had time to think on it." Truls Rohk's voice seemed distant and reflective. "It was not so terrible until I realized I had lost the only two people who were like me—not because we were the same physically, but because we were bonded by blood. These were my parents. No one else would ever care for me as they could. Even my father might have loved me, given time and sanity. If he had not gone mad, perhaps. Now I was alone, not all of one species or the other, human or spirit. I was some of each, and that meant I belonged with neither."

He laughed softly, bitterly. "I never tried living with humans. I knew what their response to me would be. They spied me in the mountains a couple of times and sought to hunt me as they would an animal. I tried living with shape-shifters, for there are bands of them concealed deep in the Wolfsktaag, and I could find their hiding places. But they smelled the part of me that was human, and they knew what I was. My mother had crossed a forbidden line, they said. She had committed an unpardonable act. She had died for her foolishness. It would be best if I died, too. I could never be one of them. I must live out my life alone."

He looked at Bek. "Do you understand yet why we are alike?"

Bek shook his head. He had no idea at all. He was not sure he cared to speculate.

"You will," the other whispered.

He turned away and began moving ahead again through the tall grass, closing swiftly now on the castle entry, another of night's shadows. Bek followed, not knowing what else to do, still waiting to hear why they were alike, still wondering what was going to happen to him. He had come this far on faith and because of his need to be more than a spectator on this voyage. Had he made a mistake?

The castle rose before them, a maze of crumbling stone walls and black holes where doors and windows had fallen away. The moon had dropped toward the horizon, and the shadows cast by towers and battlements fell across the earth like long, black garments. No sound came from within the ruins. Nothing moved in the dark.

Truls Rohk stopped and faced him once more. "The Druid looked for the key's guardian within the castle walls. He did not think to consider the guardian might be the castle itself—his first mistake. He looked for the key's guardian to defend the key by attacking and destroying those who invaded. He did not think to consider the guardian might rely instead on deception—his second mistake. He sought his answers with reason and magic, with a certainty that one or the other must give him the answers he needed. He did not think to consider that his adversary relied on neither—his last mistake."

Smoothly, he retreated through the grasses to hover close. Bek flinched at the other's approach, uncomfortable with looking at the black hole of Truls Rohk's hood and the eyes that haunted there. "The guardian of the third key is a spirit, and it dwells within these castle walls. It has no presence but for the castle itself and wards its treasures equally. The key is but one of its possessions; it has no special value to the spirit. Whoever put it there knew that. The castle wards everything equally, hiding all, revealing nothing, an immutable sentry. It deceives, boy. Like me. Like you."

"How do we penetrate that deception?" Bek asked, glancing up sharply now, eager to know.

The strange eyes glimmered. "We try seeing with different eyes."

They moved forward to the very edge of the grasses, no more than a few yards from the drawbridge and the castle entry. They had stayed low during their approach, hidden by the grasses, concealed by tall stalks, not because the guardian could see them if they stood, for it had no eyes, but because it could sense their presence once they were exposed.

"Time to use other means to conceal ourselves," Truls Rohk advised, hunching down within his robes. "Easy enough for me. I am a shape-shifter and can become anything. Harder for you, boy. But you have the tools. Hum for me again. This time, use your voice as if you were hiding still within the grasses, as if they were all around you. Here, slip this over your head."

He handed Bek a cloak, torn and frayed and dirtied. Bek slipped into it obediently. It smelled of the grasses the shape-shifter wished him to blend into. He took a moment to adjust the garment, then looked at the other questioningly.

Truls Rohk nodded. "Go on. Do as I told you. Hum for me. Use the sound to change the air about you. Stir it like water at the end of a stick. Push what you can away from you. Bury what you can't deep inside. Make yourself a part of the cloak."

Bek did, losing himself in the smells and feel of the cloak, in his vision of the plains, burrowing deep into loam and roots, into a place where only insects and animals ventured. He hummed softly, steadily for a time, then stopped and looked at the shape-shifter again.

"You see a little of it now, don't you?" the other whispered. "A little of how you are? But only a little. Not yet all. Come."

He took Bek out from their concealment into the open, his form changing visibly in front of the boy, turning liquid, losing shape against the night. Bek hummed softly, wrapping himself in the feel and smell of his cloak, masking himself, hiding who and what he was deep within. They entered the castle without difficulty, moving from the darkness of the outer courtyards and into the gloom of the inner halls. They penetrated deep within the ruins, advancing steadily, as if they were no more than a breeze carried off the grasslands. Walls appeared before them, looking solid and impenetrable, but Truls Rohk passed right through them with an astonished Bek following in his wake. Stairs appeared where none had been moments earlier, and they climbed or descended accordingly. Doors materialized and closed behind them. Sometimes the air itself changed from light to dark, from pitch to clear liquid, altering the nature of the path ahead. Gradually, Bek came to see that the entire castle was nothing of what it seemed, but was instead a vast labyrinth of mirages and illusions integrated into the stone and designed to deceive—to provide doorways and paths that led nowhere, to offer obstacles where none existed, to obscure and confuse.

If it wasn't magic, Bek wondered, what was it? Or was it simply that the magic was so vast and so thoroughly infused that it could not be separated from everything else?

They reached a stone wall thick with dust and spiderwebbing, a barrier of heavy stone blocks pitted with weather and age. Truls Rohk stopped and gestured for Bek to stay back. He faced the wall and swept the air before him with his arm. The air shimmered and changed, and the shape-shifter turned all but invisible, a hint of a shadow, a stirring of dust in a soft rustle of wind. Then he was gone, melting into the stone, disappearing as if he had never been there at all. Bek searched for him in vain. There was nothing to see.

But an instant later, he was back, materializing out of nowhere, rising up out of the gloom, his cloaked and hooded form as liquid as the shadows he emulated. He paused just long enough to hold out his hand, open his fingers, and reveal the third key.

It was a mistake. In that instant, caught up in the excitement of their success, Bek stopped humming.

At once, his disguise fell away and the feel of the castle changed. The change was palpable, a heavy rush of wind, a flurry of dust and debris, an agonizing sigh that spilled down the stone hallways and across the courtyards, a shudder that emanated from deep within the earth. Bek tried to recover, to conceal himself anew, but it was too late. Something fierce and primal howled down the corridors and rushed across the stones like an uncaged beast. Bek felt his heart freeze and his chest tighten. He stood where he was, trying to muster a defense he didn't have.

Truls Rohk saved him. The shape-shifter snatched him off his feet as if he were a child, tucked him under an arm that felt as if it were banded in iron, and began to run. Back down the halls and passageways and across the courtyards he raced. Leaping over crumbled stone and along worn trenches, he bore the boy away from the enraged spirit. But it was all around, infused in the castle stone, and it came at them from everywhere. Hidden doors dropped into place before them with deafening thuds. Iron gates clanged shut. Spikes rose out of the earth to spear at them. Trapdoors dropped away beneath their feet. Truls Rohk catapulted and twisted his way past every hazard, sometimes using the walls and even the ceilings to find handholds and footholds. Nothing slowed him. He ran as if on fire.

Bek used his voice in an effort to help, humming anew, not knowing what he did, but needing at least to try. He hummed to make them as swift and elusive as birds, to give them the liquidity of water, to lend them the ethereal qualities of air. He threw up anything and everything he could think of, constantly changing tactics, trying to throw off the thing that pursued them. He melted into the creature that bore him away, disappearing into the smell of earth and grasses, into the feel of iron muscles, into the feral instincts and quick reflexes. He lost himself completely in a being he did not begin to understand. He lost all sense of who he was. He stripped himself of identity and fragmented into the night.

Then suddenly he lay stretched upon the earth, buried in the tall grasses, and he realized they were back outside again. Truls Rohk crouched next to him, head lowered, shoulders heaving, and the sound of his breathing was like an animal's growl. Then he began to laugh, low and guttural at first, then broader and wilder. Bek laughed with him, oddly euphoric, strangely exhilarated, the death that had sought them outrun and outsmarted.

"Oh, you're nothing of what you seem, are you, boy?" the shapeshifter gasped out between laughs. "Nothing of what you were told all these years! Did you know you had a voice that could do this?" He gestured back toward the castle.

"What was it I did?" Bek pressed, convulsed by laughter, as well.

"Magic!"

Bek went still then, his laughter fading to silence. He lay in the tall grasses and stared at the stars, listening to the echoes of the word in his mind. *Magic! Magic! Magic!* No, he thought. That wasn't right. He didn't know any magic. Never had. Oh, yes, he had the phoenix stone, the talisman he wore about his neck, given to him by the King of the Silver River, and perhaps that was what—

"You saved us, boy," Truls Rohk said.

Bek looked over quickly. "*You* saved us."

The dark form shifted and slid nearer. "I took us clear of the spirit's reach, but you were the one who kept it at bay. It would have had us otherwise. It dwells all through those ruins. It masks the truth of what it is and how it looks. It protects itself with deception. But you were its equal this night. Don't you see? Yours was the greater deception, all movement and sound and color . . . ah, sweet!"

He leaned close, invisible within his cloak and hood. "Listen to me. You saved us this night, but I saved you once before. I carried you from the ruins of your home and the dark fate of your family. That makes us even!"

Bek stared. "What are you talking about?"

"We are the same, boy," Truls Rohk said again. "We were born of the ashes of our parents, of the heritage of our blood, of a history and fate that was never ours to change. We are kindred in ways you can only guess at. The truth is elusive. Some of it you discovered for yourself this night. The rest you must claim from the man who holds it hostage."

He reached out and pressed the third key into Bek's hand, closing the boy's fingers over it. "Take this to the Druid. He should be grateful he did not have to retrieve it himself—grateful enough to give up the truth he wrongfully imprisons. Trust begets trust, boy. Ward yourself carefully until that trust is shared. Keep secret what you have learned this night. Pay heed to what I say."

Then he vanished, sliding away so swiftly and suddenly that he was gone almost before the boy realized he was going. Bek stared into the quivering grasses through which Truls Rohk had vanished, speechless, aghast. Moments later, he watched a shadow lift off the plains and slide upward along one of the airship's anchor lines before disappearing over the side.

The *Jerle Shannara* hung etched against the departing night by the first pale glimmerings of dawn as Bek waited for a glimpse of something more. When nothing came, he rose wearily and began his walk back.

TWENTY-FIVE

"You disobeyed me, Bek," the Druid said quietly, his voice so chilly the boy could feel the ice in it. "You were told not to leave the ship at night, and you did so anyway."

They were alone in Redden Alt Mer's cabin, where as many as nine of the company had gathered comfortably on more than one occasion during their voyage, but where on this morning it felt as if the Druid was taking up all the space and Bek was in danger of being crushed.

"The order I gave extended to everyone, yourself included. It was very clear. No one was to leave the ship without my permission. And particularly not to go into the castle."

Bek stood frozen in front of the Druid, his hand outstretched, the third key held forth. Of all the possible reactions he had anticipated, this was not among them. He had expected to be chastised for his impetuous behavior, certainly. He had expected to be lectured on the importance of following orders. But all of his imagined scenarios ended with Walker expressing his gratitude to the boy for having gained possession of the key. There would be no need for another day of scavenging through the ruins and risking the safety of the ship's company. There would be no more delays. With the third key in hand, they could proceed to their final destination and the treasure that waited there.

Bek saw no hint of gratitude in the Druid's eyes as he stood before him now.

It had not occurred to him until he was back aboard ship that his plan to hand the key over to Walker in front of the other members of the ship's company so that he could bask in the glow of their praise and be recognized at last as an equal would not work. If he gave the key to Walker in public, he would have to explain how he obtained it. That meant telling everyone about Truls Rohk, which Walker would certainly not appreciate, or about his own magic, which the shape-shifter had warned him not to do. He would have to present the key to the Druid in private and be satisfied with knowing that at least the ship's leader appreciated his value to the expedition.

But it didn't look just now as if appreciation was high on Walker's list of responses. He hadn't even bothered to ask how Bek had obtained the key. The moment he saw it, held out to him just as it was now, he had gone black with anger.

He took the key from Bek's hand, his dark eyes heavy on the boy, hard and piercing. Overhead, the members of the ship's company were preparing for another day's search, not yet advised that it would not be necessary to go ashore again. The sound of their movements across the decking rumbled through the cabin's silence, another world away from what was happening here.

"I'm sorry," Bek managed finally, his arm dropping back to his side. "I didn't think that—"

"Truls Rohk put you up to this, didn't he?" Walker interrupted, new fury clouding his angry features. Bek nodded. "Tell me about it, then. Tell me everything that happened."

To his own astonishment, Bek did not do so. He told Walker almost everything. He told him how the shape-shifter had come to him and urged him to go with him into the castle ruins and bring out the key. He told him how Truls Rohk insisted they were alike and repeated the other's strange story of his birth and parentage. He related their approach and entry into the castle, their discovery of the key, and their escape. But he left out everything about the magic the shape-shifter claimed Bek possessed. He made no mention of the way in which his voice seemed to generate this magic. He kept his discovery to himself, deciding almost without meaning to that this was not the time to broach the subject.

Walker seemed satisfied with his explanation, and some of the fire went out of his eyes and the ice out of his voice when he spoke again. "Truls Rohk knows better than to involve you in this. He knows better than to risk your life needlessly. He is impetuous and unpredictable, so his actions should not surprise me. But you have to use better judgment in these situations, Bek. You can't let yourself be led around by the nose. What if something had happened to you?"

"What if it had?"

The words were out of his mouth before he could stop them. He hadn't intended to speak them, hadn't planned to challenge the Druid in any way this morning, given his unexpected reaction to Bek's recovery of the key. But the boy felt cheated of all recognition for his accomplishment and was angry now himself. After all, it wasn't Truls Rohk who was leading him around by the nose so much as Walker.

"If I hadn't come back," he pressed, "what difference would it make?"

The Druid stared, a look of surprise in his dark eyes.

"Tell me the truth, Walker. I'm not here just because you needed another pair of eyes and ears. I'm not along just because I'm Quentin's cousin." He had gone too far to turn back, so he plowed ahead. "In fact, I'm not really his cousin at all, am I? Coran told me before I left that Holm Rowe didn't bring me to him. You did. You told Coran his cousin gave me to you, but Truls Rohk said he pulled me from the ruins of my home and saved me from the dark fate of my family. His words. Who's telling the truth about me, Walker?"

There was a long pause. "Everyone," the Druid said finally. "To the extent they are able to do so."

"But I'm not a Leah or a Rowe either, am I?"

The Druid shook his head. "No."

"Then who am I?"

Walker shook his head anew. "I'm not ready to tell you that. You must wait a while, Bek."

Bek kept his temper and frustration in check, knowing that if he gave vent to what he was feeling, the conversation would be over and his chance at discovering anything lost. Patience and perseverance would gain him more.

"It wasn't by chance or coincidence that you contacted me on Shatterstone when the jungle had you trapped, was it?" he asked, taking a different approach. "You knew you could reach me with a mind-summons."

"I knew," the Druid acknowledged.

"How?"

Again, the Druid shook his head no.

"All right." Bek forced himself to remain calm. "Let me tell you something I've been keeping from you. Something happened on the journey from Leah to Arborlon that I haven't told anyone, not even Quentin. On our first night out, while we were camped along the Silver River, I had a nighttime visitor."

Quickly, he related the events that surrounded the appearance of the King of the Silver River. He told him how the spirit creature had appeared as a young girl who looked vaguely familiar, then transformed into a reptilian monster, then into an old man. He repeated what he could remember of their conversation and ended by telling Walker of the phoenix stone. The Druid did not change expression even once during the tale, but his dark eyes revealed the mix of emotions he was feeling.

Bek finished and stood shifting his feet nervously in the silence that followed, half anticipating another attack on his lack of judgment. But Walker just stared at him, as if trying to figure him out, as if seeing him in an entirely new light.

"Was it really the King of the Silver River?" the boy asked finally.

The Druid nodded.

"Why did he come to me? What was his reason?"

Walker looked away for a moment, as if seeking his answers in the walls of the vessel. "The images of the young girl and the monster are meant to inform you, to help you make certain decisions. The phoenix stone is to protect you if those decisions prove dangerous."

Now it was Bek's turn to stare. "What sort of decisions?"

The Druid shook his head.

"That's all you're going to tell me?"

The Druid nodded.

"Are you mad at me for this, too?" Bek demanded in exasperation. "For not telling you sooner?"

"It might have been a good idea if you had."

Bek threw up his hands. "I might have done so, Walker, if I hadn't begun to wonder what I was really doing on this expedition! But once I knew you weren't telling me everything, I didn't feel it was necessary for me to tell you everything either!" He was shouting, but he couldn't help himself. "I'm only telling you now because I don't want to go another day without knowing the truth! I'm not asking that much!"

The Druid's smile was ironic and chiding. "You are asking much more than you realize."

The boy set his jaw. "Maybe so. But I'm asking anyway. I want to know the truth!"

The Druid was implacable. "It isn't time yet. You will have to be patient."

Bek felt himself flush dark crimson, his face turning hot and angry. All of his resolve to control himself vanished in a heartbeat. "That's easy for someone to say who has all the answers. You wouldn't like it so much if you were on the other end of this business. I can't make you tell me what you know. But I can quit being your eyes and ears until you do! If you don't trust me enough to share what you know, then I don't see why I should do anything more to help you!"

Walker nodded, calm and unmoved. "That's your choice, Bek. I will miss your help."

Bek stared at him a moment longer, trying to think of what else to say, then gave it up and stalked from the room, slamming the cabin door behind him. There were tears in his eyes as he stomped back up on deck with the others.

Walker stayed where he was for a few moments, thinking through what had happened, trying to decide if he had made the right choice in not revealing what he knew. Eventually, he must. Everything depended on it. But if he told Bek too soon, if the boy was given too much time to dwell on it, he might be paralyzed by fear or doubt when it came time to act. It was better to keep the burden of it from him for as long as possible, even if it meant incurring his anger. It was better to leave him in ignorance awhile longer.

Yet he longed to reveal to Bek Rowe what he had known from the time of the boy's birth and carried hidden inside all these years. He yearned to share what he had so carefully nurtured and protected so that it might find a purpose beyond his own selfish needs.

He looked down at the key in his hand, at the connecting ridges of metal and the flashing red light embedded in the power source. He had all of them now, all three keys, and there was nothing to stop him from gaining entrance to Castledown.

Nothing.

The word echoed in his mind, a bitter and terrifying lie. Of all the lies he fostered by concealing truths he alone understood, this was the most insidious. He closed his eyes. What could he possibly do to keep it from destroying them all?

He walked from the cabin up to the main decking and called everyone together. When they had gathered around him, he held up the third key and announced that with the invaluable aid of Bek Rowe he had recovered it during the night and brought it aboard. It was time to cast off and continue their journey to Ice Henge and the treasure.

Cheers rose from the company, and Bek was hoisted aloft on Furl Hawken's burly shoulders and paraded around like a hero. The Elven Hunters saluted him with their swords, and Panax clapped him on the back so hard Bek was almost dislodged from his uncertain perch. Finally, Rue Meridian grabbed him by his shoulders and kissed him hard on the mouth. The boy grinned and waved in response, clearly pleased with the unexpected attention. Even so, he avoided looking at Walker.

Fair enough, the Druid thought. *It's them who will need you most and whose trust and respect you must earn.*

Placing the third key inside his robes with the other two, he turned away.

The weather continued cold and brisk for almost a week as they traveled on toward Ice Henge, sailing crosswise against a north wind with the light sheaves reefed close and their course set to account for the push south and west. Coats and gloves cut the chill of the wind, but everyone felt it gnawing at their bones and thickening their blood, making them sluggish and ill-tempered. They ate and drank sparingly, conserving their supplies. No one knew how far this last leg of the trip would be, but the map indicated it was some distance and therefore would require a considerable amount of time.

After Mephitic, there were no further islands to be found, and the Rocs were forced to roost on makeshift wooden platforms that were constructed from spare lumber. The platforms were lashed to the *Jerle Shannara*'s pontoons by day and dropped into the sea and towed by night. Their progress slowed measurably as a result.

Bek continued his studies with Redden Alt Mer, feeling very much at home at the helm of the airship by now, able to navigate and steer without asking for help, comfortable that he knew what to do in most situations. When Quentin was training with the Elven Hunters, Bek spent his free time with Ahren Elessedil trading stories and life philosophies. All of them had changed in noticeable ways since they had set out, but no one more than Ahren Elessedil. It seemed to Bek that Ahren had grown physically, his body much tougher and stronger from his training, his fighting abilities now almost the equal of any man aboard. He had always seemed a quick learner, but Ard Patrinell had accomplished wonders with him nevertheless. He was still a boy like Bek, but newly confident in himself and less an outsider.

The same could not be said for Bek. Following his confrontation with Walker, he had retreated further inside himself, putting up walls and locking down hatches, persuaded that for the time being, the less accessible he was, the better. It was a decision fueled by his determination not to do anything to put himself back within Walker's sphere of influence. He avoided the Druid very deliberately and kept to those few with whom he shared an established companionship—Quentin, Ahren, Panax, and Big and Little Red. He was friendly and outgoing still, but in a measured way, burdened with the secrets he was carrying and by the questions that haunted him. He thought on more than one occasion to share those secrets with someone, either Quentin or Ahren, but he could not make himself do so. What would it accomplish, after all? It would merely shift his burden to someone else without lightening his own load. No one could help him with what he needed to discover except the Druid. He knew he would simply have to wait Walker out, and it might take a very long time.

At the end of that first week out from Mephitic, the weather changed with the arrival of a warm front blown up from the south. The wind shifted, a wall of thick clouds rolled in, and the temperature rose. The clear, cold air disappeared before a wall of heavy mist and soft, damp wind, and all the colors of the world faded to gray. On the day of the front's arrival, there were still sufficient gaps in the clouds to read the stars at night and set a course. By the second day, there were only glimpses of sky to be found. By the third day, the airship was enveloped completely. The sun was reduced to a bright spot in the sky overhead, then to a barely discernible hazy ball, and then to a faint wash that was everywhere and nowhere at once.

By the fourth day, only a brightening or darkening of the light measured the difference between day and night, and visibility was reduced to less than a dozen yards. Big Red had tried sailing out of this soup without success, and the Wing Riders had been forced to descend to the makeshift rafts to wait out the front's passing. The *Jerle Shannara* was enveloped in swirling mist and impenetrable gloom.

Finally, Redden Alt Mer ordered the sails taken in completely and shut down the airship's power. Unable to see anything, he was afraid that they might sail right into a cliff wall without realizing it was there. Better to wait this weather out, he declared, than to court disaster. Everyone accepted the news stoically and went about their business. There was no help for it, after all. It was unnerving, being unable to see anything—no sky, no sea, no colors of any sort. Not even the cries of seabirds or the splash of fish penetrated the blanket of gloom that enfolded them. It was as if they had been consigned to in-limbo existence. It was as if they were alone in the world. Men gathered at the railing and stared out at the gloom in silent groups, searching for something recognizable. Even the Rovers seemed disconcerted by the immensity of the fog. Off the coast of the Blue Divide and the Wing Hove, fog lasted only a day or two before the winds moved it along. Here, it seemed as if it might last forever.

The fourth day dragged into the fifth and sixth with no change. It had been almost a week since they had seen anything but the airship and each other. The silence was becoming unnerving. Efforts at livening things up with music and song seemed only to exacerbate the problem. As soon as the playing and singing stopped, the silence returned, thick and immutable. The Rover crew had nothing to do while the ship was at rest. Even the training sessions for the Elven Hunters had been shortened as everyone began to spend more and more time staring off into the void.

It was on the sixth night, while Bek and Quentin stood at the aft railing talking about the mist that periodically enveloped the Highlands of Leah, that the boy heard something unfamiliar break the silence. He stopped talking at once, motioning Quentin to be quiet. Together, they listened. The sound came again, a kind of creaking that reminded Bek of the ship's rigging working against spars and cleats. But it did not come from the *Jerle Shannara*. It came from somewhere behind her, off in the mist. Baffled, the cousins stared at each other, then off into the gloom once more. Again they heard the noise, and now Bek turned to see if anyone else was aware of it. Spanner Frew was in the pilot box, his dark, burly form clearly visible as he stood looking over his shoulder at them. Redden Alt Mer had come on deck, as well, and was standing just below the shipwright, confusion mirrored on his strong face. A handful of others stood clustered about the railings on either side.

A long silence descended as everyone waited for some further sound to reach their ears.

Bek bent close to Quentin. "What do you think—?"

He gasped sharply and choked on the rest of what he was going to say. A huge black shape hove into view out of the mist, a massive shadow that materialized all at once and filled the whole of the horizon. It was right on top of them, so close that there was barely time to react. Bek stumbled back, dragging at Quentin's arm as the black shape towered out of the gloom. Shouts of warning went up, and the shrill of a Roc rose above them. The cousins went backwards off the low rise of the aft deck and landed in a jarring heap below as the black shape struck the *Jerle Shannara* in a crash of metal and splintering of wood. The airship lurched and shuddered in response, and the air was filled with cries and curses.

Everything spiraled into instant chaos. Bek rolled to his feet to find the phantom shape locked against the *Jerle Shannara*'s aft battering rams and realized to his shock that he was looking at another airship. The impact of the collision had sent both ships spiraling in a slow, clockwise motion that made it difficult for Bek to keep his feet. One of the Rocs soared past him, lifting out of the gloom, a silent phantom that appeared and was gone again almost immediately.

Then something cloaked and hooded rose off the aft decking and lurched toward him. Bek stared at it in surprise, mesmerized by its unexpected appearance. He did not even have the presence of mind to reach for his weapons as it approached. He just stood there. The shape took form, and the dark opening of the hood lifted into the gray misted light to reveal a reptilian face dominated by lidless eyes and a twisted mouth. Clawed hands lifted toward him, gesturing.

"Little peopless," the creature whispered.

Bek froze, terrified.

"Sstay sstill now," it urged softly, hypnotically, and reached for him.

"No!" he cried out frantically.

He did so without thinking, solely in response to the danger. But he used his voice as he had that night on Mephitic when he had gone into the castle ruins with Truls Rohk, infusing it with the magic he had discovered there. He felt the force of his words strike at the creature, causing it to flinch with the impact.

Then Quentin was yanking him away and leaping into the creature's path. The Sword of Leah cut through the darkness in a single, glittering stroke, severing the creature's head from its body. The creature collapsed without a sound, and its blood sprayed everywhere.

Other creatures of the same look appeared at the railing of the phantom airship, crowding through the gloom and night to look down at them, the glint of their weapons visible. Shouts rose from the Rovers and Elves, and they surged out of the darkness behind the cousins, their own weapons drawn. A hail of missiles showered down off the other ship, and a few sent members of the *Jerle Shannara* to the deck, writhing in pain. Quentin pulled Bek behind a stack of boxes below the rise of the aft deck, yelling at him to stay down and cover himself up.

A moment later both airships lurched anew, and in a grinding of metal and a crunching of wood, unlocked and separated. Slowly, ponderously, the leviathans drifted apart, their occupants still gathered at the railings to stare silently across the void at each other, faceless shadows in the mist.

"Stations!" Redden Alt Mer roared from the pilot box.

Hands working furiously on the controls, he dropped the mainsail to gather what ambient light he could, unhooded the diapson crystals to give the airship power, and swung her about to face the gloom into which the other ship had disappeared. His Rover crew scattered across the decking to lock down the radian draws, and the Elven Hunters, weapons at the ready, dropped quickly into the fighting ports. Everyone was moving at once as Bek climbed back to his feet.

"What happened?" Bek tried to ask Quentin, but his cousin was gone as well.

With a quick glance at the fallen monster in front of him, Bek raced over to join Big Red. The Rover Captain was still shouting out instructions, windburned face grim with determination as he searched the gloom. Bek looked with him. For just an instant, the other ship reappeared, huge and spectral in the night, three masts cutting through the mist, pontoons and decking slicing across the haze. Then it was gone again.

"That's *Black Moclips!*" Bek heard Redden Alt Mer gasp in disbelief.

They searched for the other airship a while longer, but it was nowhere to be found. Walker appeared and ordered Alt Mer to have his men stand down. "Just as well," Big Red muttered, half to himself, still shaken by what he had seen. "Fighting an air battle in this mess is a fool's errand."

The Elven Hunters had gathered about the fallen attacker to examine him, and Bek heard the word *Mwellret* whispered. He didn't know what a Mwellret was, but he knew the thing that lay dead on the deck looked an awful lot like the monster the King of the Silver River had transformed into at their meeting months earlier.

Joad Rish was on deck looking after the wounded. He advised Walker that no one was badly injured. The Druid asked Big Red for a damage report and suggested the watch be increased from two men to four. Bek was standing close to him while an accounting was made, but they didn't speak. It wasn't until everyone had moved away and Redden Alt Mer had given back the helm to Spanner Frew, that Walker bent down to the boy on passing and whispered that Truls Rohk was missing.

TWENTY-SIX

§

A board *Black Moclips*, the chaos was more pronounced, and a deadly confrontation was about to take place.

The Ilse Witch was sleeping when the collision between the airships occurred, and the force of it threw her from her berth onto the floor. She came to her feet swiftly, threw on her gray robes, and hastened from her locked cabin onto the main deck. By then Federation soldiers and Mwellrets were running everywhere, shouting and cursing in the gloom and mist. She strode to where most had gathered and saw the distinctive raked masts of the *Jerle Shannara*. One of the Mwellrets lay dead on the other ship's decking, the first barrage of spears and arrows had been launched, and a full-scale battle was only moments away.

Of Cree Bega and Federation Commander Aden Kett, she saw no sign.

In a cold fury, she strode to the pilot box and swung up beside the helmsman. The man was staring down at the milling ship's company with a look of mingled disbelief and incredulity, his hands frozen on the controls.

"Back her off at once, helmsman!" she ordered.

His eyes filled with fear as he saw who it was, but his hands remained motionless on the levers.

"Back away now!" she snapped, her words lashing at him with such force that his knees buckled.

He reacted instantly this time, drawing down power from the light sheaths and unhooding the diapson crystals. *Black Moclips* lurched backwards, unhooked from the other ship with a grinding crunch, and slid soundlessly into the gloom. The helmsman glanced over at her without speaking, waiting for further instructions.

"What happened?" she demanded, all fire and sharp edges within her hooded concealment, wrapped in the power of her voice.

"Mistress?" he replied in confusion.

"How did we manage to collide with that other ship? How could that have happened?"

"I don't know, Mistress," the man stammered. "I was just following orders—"

"Whose orders? I gave no orders to proceed! My orders were to stand down!" She was beside herself with rage.

The helmsman made a vague gesture toward the front of the airship. "Commander Kett said the ret ordered him . . ."

She was down out of the pilot box, and striding forward without waiting to hear the rest. Concealed once more by the mist, *Black Moclips* was an island, solitary and adrift. Her Federation crew was already at work on the damage to the bow rams and decking. At the forward railing, a handful of Mwellrets was clustered about Cree Bega, who had finally surfaced. She went up to him without slowing and stopped less than a yard away.

"Who countermanded my orders?" she demanded.

Cree Bega regarded her with a sleepy look, his lidless eyes fixing on her. She could tell what he was thinking. *This girl, this child, speaks to me as if she were my better. But she is nothing to me. She is a human, and all humans are inferior. Who is she, to speak to me in this way?*

"Misstress," he greeted with a small, perfunctory bow.

"Who countermanded my orders to stand down?" she asked again.

"It wass my misstake, Misstress," he acknowledged without a hint of remorse in his sibilant voice. "There sseemed no reasson not to prosseed, not to sstay closse to the little peopless. I wass worried they might get too far away from uss."

She gave him a long, careful appraisal before she spoke again. She knew where this was heading, but she could not afford to back down. "Who is in command of this expedition, Cree Bega?"

"You, Misstress," he answered coldly.

"Then why would you take it upon yourself to give orders without consulting me first? Why would you assume you had authority to rescind an order I had already given? Do you think, perhaps, you are better able than me to make the decisions that are needed on this voyage?"

He turned slowly to face her, and she could see that he was considering the advisability of a confrontation. Five of his fellows stood directly behind him, and she was alone. Separately, none of them was her equal. Together, they might be. He hated her and wanted her dead. He undoubtedly felt he could accomplish what was needed without her. If she were to disappear on this voyage, the Morgawr would never know what had happened to her.

But that knife cut both ways, of course.

"Sshe sspeakss to uss like children!" the Mwellret to Cree Bega's right snarled, hunching down like a snake.

The Ilse Witch did not hesitate. She stepped to one side, just out of reach of the others, and used her magic on the speaker. Her voice lashed at him with a sound that was bone-chilling and ferocious. Every ounce of power she could muster, she brought to bear. The force of her attack lifted the shocked Mwellret off its feet, twisted it into a shattered and broken mess, so ravaged it was virtually unidentifiable, and dropped the remains over the side. It took only seconds.

The Mwellret was gone almost before his fellows understood what had happened.

She faced the remaining Mwellrets calmly. She had needed to make an example of someone to keep the others under control. Better an unknown than Cree Bega, whose leadership was established and effective. Better to keep the enemy she knew than to install one she did not. Changes in command necessitated adjustments that could give rise to new problems. This was enough for now. She looked into his eyes and found what she was looking for. His hatred of her was still apparent, but there was a hint of fear and doubt present, as well. He was no longer seeing her as a slender, vulnerable girl. More to the point, he was no longer measuring her for a coffin.

"Misstress," he hissed, bowing in submission.

"Do not challenge me again, Cree Bega," she warned. "Do not presume to question or alter my orders in any way. Obey me, ret, or I'll find someone who will."

She held his gaze a moment longer, then wheeled away. She did not look back at him, did not act as if she feared him. Let him think she saw herself as invulnerable and he might come to believe she was. Let him see she gave no thought to her safety because there was no need and he would think twice before confronting her again.

As she moved back toward her cabin, her senses searching carefully for any further signs of trouble, she caught a hint of something that was out of place. She stopped at once, motionless within her gray robes. By now, she knew everything that belonged on *Black Moclips*, every member of her company, every stash of supplies and weapons, every timber and metal plate that held her together. She had infused herself with the feel of the airship, so that she was at one with it and always in control, and she could sense if anything changed. She sensed it now, a subtle alteration, so small she'd almost missed it. Carefully, she began to probe for something more.

There had been movement and presence, a suggestion of a living creature that didn't belong.

She was still searching when Aden Kett appeared in front of her. "Mistress, we are fully operational and ready to sail on your orders. For now, we are standing down to wait out the fog. Is there anything else?"

His face was pale and drawn; he had witnessed the death of the Mwellret. But he was a ship's Captain and committed enough to being one that he would carry out his duties regardless of his personal feelings. She was angry at the interruption, but knew enough to keep it to herself.

"Thank you, Commander," she acknowledged, and he bowed and moved away.

The distraction had cost her the fragile connection she had made with the unfamiliar presence. She glanced around casually, using the time to probe anew. There was nothing there now. Perhaps a passing seabird had caused her to sense a change. Maybe there was a residual Elven presence from their contact with the *Jerle Shannara*.

She grimaced at the thought of the collision. An entire ocean of air to navigate, and they had somehow managed to find their enemy. It was ironic and maddening. Still, it changed nothing. Walker would already know that she tracked him. Their encounter tonight, while unfortunate, gave away nothing of importance. He would try harder to escape her now that he realized she was close, but he would not be able to do so. Wherever he went, she would be waiting. She had made certain of that.

She took a moment longer to survey the shadows that wrapped the airship, still searching for what had eluded her, then turned away without another glance and disappeared back into her cabin to sleep.

* * *

Bek stared after the departing figure of Walker. Truls Rohk was missing, the Druid had said, a whispered utterance in the boy's ear, and then he had walked away. Bek took another moment to let the information sink in, and then did what anyone else would have done. He went after him.

He had reason to believe, thinking it through later, that this was what Walker had intended, that it was a way to break the silence between them. If so, it worked. He caught up with the Druid as the latter slowed by the bow railing, and without even thinking about it began speaking to him.

"Where is he?" Bek demanded.

Walker shook his head. "I expect he's on the other ship."

With the Ilse Witch, Bek thought, but couldn't bring himself to say so. "Why would he do that?"

"It's difficult to say. With Truls, most things are done instinctively. Perhaps he wanted to see what he could find out over there. Perhaps he has a plan he hasn't shared with us."

"But if the Ilse Witch finds him . . ."

Walker shook his head. "There's nothing we can do about it, Bek. He made the choice to go." He paused. "I saw what you did to that Mwellret before Quentin stepped in. With your voice. Were you aware of what you were doing?"

The boy hesitated, then nodded. "Yes."

"How long have you known you had use of this magic?"

"Not long. Since Mephitic."

Walker frowned. "Truls Rohk, again. He showed you it was there, didn't he? Why didn't you tell me?"

Bek stared at him defiantly, refusing to answer. The Druid nodded slowly. "That's right. I wasn't confiding much in you at the time either, was I?" He studied the boy carefully. "Maybe it's time to change all that."

Bek felt a twinge of expectation. "Are you going to tell me who I am?"

Walker looked off into the mist-shrouded night, and there was a sense of time and place slipping away in his dark eyes. "Yes," he said.

Bek waited for him to say something more, but Walker remained silent, lost in thought, gone somewhere else, perhaps into his memories. Behind them, the Rover crew worked to repair the damage to the aft part of the vessel, where the horns of the battering rams had absorbed most of the shock of their collision with the other airship, but portions of the deck and railing had buckled from the impact. The crew labored alone in the near dark. Almost everyone else, save the watch, had gone back to bed. Even Quentin had disappeared.

In the pilot box, Spanner Frew's fierce dark face stared out over the controls as if daring something else to go wrong.

"I would have told you most of what I know sooner if I hadn't thought it better to wait," Walker said quietly. "I haven't been any happier keeping it from you than you've been not knowing what it was. I wanted to be closer to our final destination, to Ice Henge and Castledown, before speaking with you. Even after the events on Mephitic and the suspicions aroused by Truls Rohk, I believed it was best.

"But now you know you have command of a magic, and it is dangerous for you not to know its source and uses. This magic is of a very powerful nature, Bek. You've only scratched the surface of its potential, and I don't want to risk the possibility that you might choose to use it again before you are prepared to deal with it. If you understand how it works and what it can do, you can control it. Otherwise, you are in grave danger. This means I have to tell you what I know about your origins so you can arm yourself. It isn't going to be easy to hear this. Worse, it isn't going to be easy to live with it afterwards."

Bek stood beside him quietly, listening to him speak. Outwardly, the boy was calm, but inside he was tight and edgy. He was aware of the Druid looking at him, waiting for his response, for permission to continue. Bek met his gaze squarely and nodded that he was ready.

"You are not a Leah or a Rowe or even a member of their families," Walker said. "Your name is Ohmsford."

It took a moment for the boy to recognize the name, to remember its origins. All the stories he had heard about the Leahs and the Druids came back to him. There had been Ohmsfords in those stories, as well, as recently as 130 years ago when Quentin's great-great-grandfather, Morgan Leah, had battled the Shadowen. Before that, Shea and Flick Ohmsford had fought with Allanon against the Warlock Lord, Wil Ohmsford had stood with Eventine Elessedil and the Elves against the Demon hordes, and Brin and Jair Ohmsford had gone in search of the Ildatch in the dark reaches of the Eastland.

But they had all been dead for many years, and the rest of the Ohmsford family had died out. Coran had told him so.

"Your magic is the legacy of your family, Bek." The Druid looked back over the railing into the gloom. "It was absorbed by Wil Ohmsford into his body hundreds of years ago when he used the Elfstones to save the lives of two women, one who became the Ellcrys, one who became his wife. His Elven blood was too thin to permit him to do so safely, and he was altered irrevocably. It didn't manifest itself in him so much as in his children, Brin and Jair, who were born with the use of magic in their voices, just as you were. It was strong in both, but particularly in the girl. Brin had the power to transform living things by singing. She could heal them or destroy them. Her power was called the wishsong."

He took a deep breath and exhaled slowly. Bek was watching him closely now. "The magic surfaced in other generations, but only sporadically. It was three hundred years before it returned in a meaningful way. This time, it appeared in the brothers Par and Coll Ohmsford, who fought with me and with the Elf Queen Wren Elessedil against the Shadowen. The magic was strong in Par Ohmsford, very powerful. He was your great-great-grandfather, Bek."

He shifted away from the railing and faced the boy anew. "I'm related to you, as well, though I wouldn't care to try to trace the lineage. We are both Ohmsford scions. But whereas you inherited the wishsong, I inherited the blood trust bestowed on Brin by Allanon as he lay dying, the trust that foretold that one of her descendants would be the first of the new Druids. I was that descendant, though I didn't want to believe it when it was revealed to me, didn't want to accept it afterwards for a long time. I came to the Druid order reluctantly and served with constant misgiving."

His sigh was soft and wistful. "There. It's said. We are family, Bek, you and I—joined by blood as well as by magic's use." His smile was bitter. "The combination allowed me to summon you on Shatterstone when we were under attack, to connect with you through your thoughts when I could not do so with the others. It wasn't a coincidence that I called to you."

"I don't get it," Bek blurted out in confusion. "Why didn't you tell me this before? Why did you keep it a secret? It doesn't seem so bad. I'm not afraid of my magic. I can learn to use it. It can help us, can't it? Isn't that why I was asked to come? Because I have the magic? Because I'm an Ohmsford?"

The Druid shook his head. "It isn't so simple. In the first place, use of the magic carries a terrible responsibility and a very real threat to the bearer. The magic is powerful and sometimes unpredictable. Using it can be tricky. It can even be harmful, not just to others but to you, as well. Magic often reacts as it chooses and not as you intend; your attempts to control it can fail. It isn't necessarily good that you know you have it and can call it forth. Once you have unearthed its existence, it becomes a burden you cannot put down. Ever."

"But it's there nevertheless," Bek pointed out. "It isn't as if I had a choice about adopting it. Besides, you brought me on this journey to use my magic, didn't you?"

The Druid nodded. "Yes, Bek. But there is more to it than that. I brought you for the use of your magic, but I brought you for another reason, as well—a more compelling one. Your parents and your sister were the last of the Ohmsfords. There were others, distant cousins and so forth, but your father was the last direct descendant of Par Ohmsford. He married your mother and they lived in the hamlet of Jentsen Close not far from the northeast edge of the Rainbow Lake, in a part of the farming community off the Rabb Plains. They had two children, your sister and you. Your sister's name was Grianne. She was three years older than you, and signs of the wishsong's magic appeared in her very early. Your father recognized those signs and sent for me. He knew of the connection between us. I visited you when you were still a baby and your sister only four years of age. Because of my Druid experience, I was able to recognize the magic not only in your sister, but in you as well."

He paused. "Unfortunately, the Morgawr discovered the existence of this magic as well. The Morgawr has lived for a very long time, hidden away in the Wilderun. He may have been an ally of the Shadowen, but he was not one of them and was not destroyed as they were. He surfaced about fifty years ago and began to expand his influence to the Federation. He is a powerful warlock, with ties to the Eastland Mwellrets and shape-shifters. It was because of these ties that I learned about his interest in your family. I was friends with Truls Rohk by then, and several times he followed shape-shifters that had gone to your home. They didn't do anything but observe, but it was a clear warning that something wasn't right."

He stopped talking as a clutch of Rovers came down off the aft decking and moved to the forward stairway. Their work for the night was finished, and they were eager for sleep. One or two glanced over, then looked quickly away. In seconds, the Druid and the boy were alone again.

"I should have realized what was happening, but I was preoccupied with trying to form a Druid Council at Paranor." Walker shook his head. "I didn't act quickly enough. A band of Mwellrets dressed in black cloaks and led by the Morgawr killed your parents and burned your house to the ground. They made it look like an attack by Gnome raiders. Your sister hid you in a cold room off the cellar and told them you were dead when they took her. It was Grianne they wanted all along, for her magic, for the power of the wishsong. The Morgawr coveted her. His intent was to subvert her, to make her his disciple, his student in the use of her magic. He tricked her into believing that the black-cloaked Mwellrets were Druid led and influenced. I became the enemy she grew up hating. All of my efforts to change that, to rescue her, to gain her trust so that she might discover the truth, have failed."

He gestured toward the enfolding wall of mist. "Now she hunts me, Bek, somewhere out there on that other airship." He looked at the boy. "Your sister is the Ilse Witch."

They stood for a while without speaking, looking off into the void where the woman who had once been Grianne Ohmsford tracked them. The enormity of Walker's revelation settled over Bek. Was it the truth or was the Druid playing games with him here, as well? He had so many questions, but they all jumbled together and screamed at him at once. He did not know what he was supposed to do with what he had been told. He could see the possibilities, but he could not make himself consider them yet. He found himself remembering the nighttime visit of the King of the Silver River, all those months ago, and of the forms the spirit creature had taken—the girl, who was the past, and the monster, who was the present. That girl, he now understood, was his sister. That was why she had seemed so familiar to him—he still retained a memory of her child's face. The monster was what she had become, the Ilse Witch. But the future remained to be determined—by Bek, who must not shy from his search, his need to know, or what his heart compelled him to do.

The jumble of questions gave way to just one. Was it within his power to change his sister back?

"There is one last thing, Bek," Walker said suddenly. "Come with me."

He moved away from the railing toward the center of the airship, and the boy followed. Within the pilot box, black-bearded Spanner Frew faced ahead into the gloom, paying them no attention, his eyes sweeping the mist and the dark.

"Does she know I'm alive?" Bek asked quietly.

The Druid shook his head. "She believes you dead. She has no reason to believe otherwise. Truls Rohk found you in the ruins of your home three days after your sister was stolen. He was keeping watch on his own and had seen the Mwellrets returning through the Wolfsktaag. He was able to find the hiding place that they had missed. You were almost dead by then. He brought you to me, and when you were strong enough, I took you to Coran Leah."

"Yet my sister blames you for what happened."

"She is deceived by her own bitterness and the Morgawr's guile. His story of what happened is quite different from the truth, but it is a story she has come to believe. Now she cloaks herself in her magic's power and shuts out the world. She seeks to be a fortress that no one can breach."

"Except perhaps for me? Is that why I'm here? Is that what the King of the Silver River was showing me?"

The Druid said nothing.

They stopped before the mysterious object he had brought aboard in secret and wrapped in chains of magic. It sat solitary and impenetrable against the foremast, a rectangular box set on end, standing perhaps seven feet in height and three feet across and deep. The canvas concealed all trace of what lay beneath, revealing only size and shape. The chains glistened with the mist's damp and on closer inspection seemed to have no beginning and no end.

Bek glanced around. The decks of the airship were deserted this night save for the helmsman and a pair of Elven Hunters of the watch, who were clustered about the aft railing. None of these would venture forward to take up his position while the Druid stood talking with the boy. In the wake of the airship's silent passing, the only movement came from the shadows in the mist.

"No one will see what I show you now but you and me," the Druid said softly.

He passed his hand before the casing, and it was as if the side they were facing melted away. Within the blackness revealed, suspended blade downward, was a sword. The sword was slender and its metal shone a deep-bluish silver against the surrounding dark. The handle was old and worn, but finely wrought. Carved into its polished wooden grip was a fist that clenched and thrust aloft a burning torch.

"This is the Sword of Shannara, Bek," the Druid whispered, bending close so that his words would carry no farther than the boy's ears. "This, too, is your legacy. It is the birthright of the descendants of the Elven King Jerle Shannara, for whom this vessel is named. Only a member of the Shannara bloodline can wield this blade. Ohmsfords, who were the last of the Shannara, have carried this sword into battle against the Warlock Lord and the Shadowen. They have used it to champion the freedom of the races for more than a thousand years."

He touched Bek's shoulder lightly. "Now it is your turn."

Bek knew the stories. He knew them all, just as he knew the history of the Druids and the Wars of the Races and all the rest. No one had seen this talisman in over five hundred years, when Shea Ohmsford stood against the Warlock Lord and destroyed him—though there were rumors it had resurfaced in the battle with the Shadowen. Rumors, the Druid's words would suggest, that were true.

"The sword is a talisman for truth, Bek. It was forged to defend against lies that enslave and conceal. It is a powerful talisman, and it requires strength of will and heart to wield. It needs a bearer who will not shrink from the pain and doubt and fear that embracing the truth sometimes engenders. You are a worthy successor to those others of your family who have been called to the sword's service. You are strong and determined. Much of what I exposed you to on this voyage was meant to measure that. I will be frank with you.

Without your help, without the Sword's power to aid us, we are probably lost."

He turned back to the casing and passed his hand in front of it once more. The Sword of Shannara disappeared, and the wrappings of canvas and chains were restored.

Bek continued staring at them, as if still seeing the talisman they concealed. "You're giving the Sword of Shannara to me?"

The Druid nodded.

The boy's voice was shaking as he spoke. "Walker, I don't know if I can—"

"No, Bek," the Druid interrupted him quickly, gently. "Say nothing tonight. Tomorrow is soon enough. There is much to discuss, and we will do so then. You'll have questions, and I will do my best to answer them. We will work together to prepare for what will happen when it is necessary for you to summon the sword's magic."

Bek's eyes shifted anxiously, and the Druid met the question mirrored there with a reassuring smile. "Not against your sister, though one day you might have to use it in that way. No, this first time the magic will serve another purpose. If I have read the map correctly, Bek, the Sword of Shannara is the key to our gaining entry into Ice Henge."

TWENTY-SEVEN

Come daybreak, Bek rose and went about his morning duties as cabin boy in something of a daze, still struggling with the previous night's revelations, when the Druid intercepted him coming out of Rue Meridian's cabin and told him to follow. It was an hour after sunrise, and Bek had dressed and eaten breakfast. He still had tasks to perform, but Walker's summons didn't leave room for discussion on the matter.

They climbed topside and walked forward to the bow railing, very close to where they had stood the night before. The sky around them was unchanged, gray and misted and impenetrable. Everywhere Bek looked, right or left, up or down, the color and light were the same. Visibility was still limited to thirty feet or so. Those of the ship's company already on deck had the look of ghosts, ethereal and not quite fully formed. Redden Alt Mer stood in the pilot box with Furl Hawken, two Rovers were at work aft, braiding new ends on the portside radian draws, and Quentin sparred with the Elven Hunters on the foredeck under Ard Patrinell's steady gaze. No one looked up as Bek passed or acted as if anything about the boy had changed, even though in his mind everything had.

"To begin with, you are still Bek Rowe," Walker told him when they were seated together on a casing filled with light sheaths. "You are not to use the name Ohmsford. It is too recognizable, and you don't want to draw unneeded attention to yourself."

Bek nodded. "All right."

"Also, I don't want you to tell anyone what you've told me or what you've learned from me about your magic, your history, or the Sword of Shannara. Not even Quentin. Not one word."

He waited. Bek nodded once more.

"Finally, you are not to forget that you are here to serve as my eyes and ears, to listen and keep watch. That wasn't an idle assignment, meant to give you something to do until it was time to tell you who you were. Your magic gives you powers of observation that are lacking in most. I still need you to use those talents. They are no less important now than they were before."

"I can't see that I've put them to much use so far," Bek observed. "Nothing I've told you has been particularly useful."

The Druid's ironic smile flashed momentarily and was gone. "You don't think so? Maybe you're not paying close enough attention."

"Does Ryer Ord Star see anything in her dreams that could help you? Is she keeping watch as well?"

"She does what she can. But your sight, Bek, though not a seer's, is the more valuable." He shifted so that he was leaning very close. "She dreams of outcomes before they happen, but you spy out causes while they're still seeking to create an effect. That's the difference in the magic you wield. Remember that."

Bek had no idea what Walker was talking about, but decided to mull over it another time. He nodded.

Curtains of gray mist drifted past, and the sounds of swordplay and of metal tools in use echoed eerily in the enshrouding haze. It was as if each group of men formed a separate island, and only the sounds they made connected them in any real way.

"The Sword of Shannara," Walker began quietly, "is not like any other weapon. Or any other magic. It seeks truth where truth is concealed by deception and lies, and through revelation, it empowers. But empowerment comes at a cost. Like all Elven talismans, the sword draws its power from the wielder. Its strength, and thereby its effectiveness, depends entirely on the strength of the bearer. The stronger the bearer, the more effective the magic. But the connection between the two is established by subtle means. The Sword of Shannara relies on the bearer's willingness to shed personal deceptions, half-truths, and lies in order to see clearly the same in others."

He gave Bek a moment to digest this. "This is what will happen, Bek. When you call up the power of the sword, it will seek to reveal the larger truths that other magic and magic wielders mask. But in order to understand those larger truths, you must first accept the smaller truths about yourself. This requires sacrifice. We live our lives hiding from the things that displease and discomfort us. We reinvent ourselves and our history, constantly placing things in a light most favorable to us. It is in the nature of mankind to do this. Mostly, our deceptions are small ones. But they gather weight through numbers, and having them revealed all at once can be crushing. As well, there are larger truths that, exposed, seem more than we can bear, and so we hide them most carefully.

"After you have been confronted by these personal truths, you will be confronted by truths about those you love and care for, then of the world you know through your own experience, and finally of the deception or lie you seek to unmask. This will not be easy or pleasant. Truth will assault you as surely as an ordinary metal blade. It will have impact and cutting edges. It can kill you if you do not ward against it. Knowledge and acceptance of what is coming are your best defense. You can do what you need to do to protect yourself and adapt. Do you understand?"

Bek nodded. "I think so. But I don't know how I can prepare myself for something like this. I don't know what sorts of lies and deceptions I have concealed over the years. Am I to try to catalogue them all before using the sword?"

"No. You've said it yourself. You can't separate them out easily. Some you will have forgotten entirely. Some you will have tried to shade with a better interpretation than you should. Some you will never even have identified. What you need to do, Bek, is to understand how the sword works so that you will not be surprised by its power and will be better able to survive its demands." He paused. "Let me tell you a story."

He spent the next few minutes relating the tale of the Elven King Jerle Shannara and his confrontation with the Warlock Lord a thousand years earlier. The Sword of Shannara had been forged out of Druid fire by Bremen in the Southland city of Dechtera and carried north so that a champion could do combat with the Dark Lord and destroy him. But Bremen had misjudged the Elf King's ability to adapt to the sword's demands and not sufficiently prepared him. When Jerle Shannara called up the magic of the sword, he failed to bring sufficient strength to bear. As a result, he broke down the Dark Lord's physical form but did not destroy him completely. It would be left to his descendant, Shea Ohmsford, five hundred years later, to complete the job.

"My task with you, Bek," Walker finished, "is to make certain you do not falter as Jerle Shannara did, that once you summon the sword's magic, you employ it to the degree necessary. Your first usage of the talisman is not so demanding. It does not involve an encounter with another creature of magic that seeks to destroy you. It involves a portal that is warded by an impersonal and indiscriminate barrier. It is a good test with which to begin your training."

Bek looked down at his feet, then up into the Druid's dark eyes. "But my sister, the Ilse Witch, will be waiting to test me, as well."

"Not waiting. She knows nothing of you or the sword. But, yes, the possibility is good that you will have to face her eventually. Even so, that is not your principal concern. Your testing will come from other sources, as well. Everything connected with this expedition is shrouded in deception and lies, Bek. It might seem straightforward enough, a map and a castaway found floating on the Blue Divide, a trail to a place reached by other Elves and their ships thirty years ago before they disappeared, and the lure of a treasure beyond price. But few things are as they seem in this matter. If we are to succeed—indeed, if we are to survive—we will require the power of the Sword of Shannara to see us through. Only you can use the sword, Bek, so you must be ready to do so when the magic is needed. I bring a Druid's fire and insight to our task. Quentin brings the power of the Sword of Leah. Others bring their own gifts and experience. Perhaps we will find the missing Elfstones. But your use of the Sword of Shannara is vital and necessary to everything we attempt to do. And your training in that use begins now."

They spent the remainder of that day and much of every day after talking about the sword's magic and how it would work. Walker understood the principles, but he had never experienced the power of the sword's magic himself, so they were reduced to fencing without weapons. It wasn't so different, Bek supposed, than what Quentin did in his training with the Elven Hunters. He sparred, but the combat wasn't real. Because there was no way to call up the magic of the sword until it was actually needed, there was no way to test its effect on Bek. What Walker did mostly, besides talk about the nature of self-deception, was to teach a form of acceptance that came with finding inner peace, with going deep inside to let go of extraneous matters and concerns, and with opening up instead of closing down as a way of dealing with the things that caused pain.

It was a grueling and often frustrating exercise that sometimes left Bek more confused than when he started. Already reeling from revelations of his identity and history, the boy was staggered by the responsibility the Druid was giving him for the safety of the ship's company. But he understood the importance of that responsibility and so trained and studied hard, working to prepare himself, to become more adaptable, to be ready for what would happen when he was infused with the sword's power.

Nor did he neglect his other duties. He was still the ship's cabin boy and must continue to behave as such. The combination of time spent with the Druid talking about magic, with Redden Alt Mer in the pilot box, and with carrying out his daily chores pretty much filled up the day. He saw less and less of Quentin and Ahren Elessedil, but that saved him from having to work so hard at keeping what he knew to himself.

A few days after their encounter with the Ilse Witch, the fog dissipated, the skies cleared, and the broad expanse of the Blue Divide lay revealed once more and the Wing Riders had returned. Repairs were made to the airship, and foraging resumed with the discovery of several clusters of islands. The air became sharp and cold, and the members of the expedition wore winter coats and gloves most of the time now. Ice floes were spotted between the channels of the islands, and the skies turned gray and wintry. Days grew shorter, and the light took on a pale, thin cast that washed the earth and sky of color.

All the while, Bek wondered what lay ahead. Walker had cautioned him that everything surrounding the expedition was mired in deception and lies. If so, how much of it had the Druid uncovered? What else did he know that he was keeping secret?

Nine weeks after leaving Mephitic, with thin sheets of sleet driving out of the north on the back of a polar wind, they arrived at the cliff-walled fortress of Ice Henge, and the boy found out.

The land appeared as a low dark rumpling of the horizon's thin line and was a long time taking shape. It stretched away to either side of the center for miles, sprawled like a twisted snake atop the blue-gray sea. Hours passed before they drew close enough to make out a wall of cliffs so sheer they dropped straight down into the ocean and so towering that their peaks disappeared into clouds of mist and gloom. Cracked and broken, the carcasses of trees bleached by the sun and stripped bare by the wind jutted out of the rock. White-and-black flashes against the gloom, seabirds screamed as they soared from hidden aeries to the waters below. Smaller islands led up to the cliffs like stepping-stones trod upon by time and weather, barren atolls offering little of shelter or sustenance, devoid of vegetation save for hardy sea grasses and wintry gray scrub.

Walker held up the airship when they were still miles away and sent the Wing Riders ahead for a quick look. They were back again very quickly. Shrikes inhabited the cliffs, and the Rocs could fly no nearer. Leaving Hunter Predd and Po Kelles on one of the larger atolls, Walker had Redden Alt Mer sail the *Jerle Shannara* right up to the landmass. A closer inspection did nothing to lessen his concerns. The cliffs formed a solid, impenetrable wall, split now and then by narrow fissures that were flooded with mist and rain and virtually impassable. As Shrikes regarded them warily from their perches, waiting to see what they would do, winds blew off the cliffs in sharp, unpredictable gusts, knocking the airship about even before it reached the wall.

Walker had them sail the coastline for a time. Caverns had been carved into the cliffs by the ocean, and clusters of rock tumbled from the heights formed odd monuments and outcroppings. Waves crashed against and retreated from the base of the cliffs, surging in and out of the caverns, washing over the rocks and debris. No passage inland revealed itself. Alt Mer refused to fly into the mist and wind that clogged the fissures; suicide, he declared, and put an end to any discussion of it. He shook his head when asked by Walker if they might fly over the mist. A thousand feet higher into thicker mist and stronger winds? Not hardly. The castaway's map revealed that this was a peninsula warded by miles of such cliffs and that the only opening lay through pillars of ice. Big Red was inclined to believe the map.

They sailed on, continuing their search, and the look of the land never changed.

Then, late in the day, the cliffs opened abruptly into a deep, broad bay that ran back through the mist and gloom to a towering range of snowcapped mountains. Through gaps in the barren peaks, glaciers wound their way down to the water's edge, massive chunks of ice, blue-green and jagged, a grinding jumble of frozen moraine that emptied into the bay in blocks so huge they formed small islands, some rising several hundred feet off the surface of the water. Within the bay the winds died, the seabirds huddled in their rookeries, and the ocean's crash faded. Only the occasional crack of the ice as it split and re-formed, chunks breaking away from the larger mass to tumble down slides and ravines, disturbed the deep stillness.

The *Jerle Shannara* sailed through the cliffs into the bay, sliding between icebergs and rock walls, listening to the eerie sound of the shifting ice, searching the gloom for passage. The opening to the bay narrowed to a channel, then opened into a second bay and continued on. The mist thickened above them, forming a roof so dense that it shut out the sun and left the light as pale and gray as the mist. Colors washed away until ice, water, mist, and gloom were all of a piece. With the deepening of the light and the fading of color came a sense of the land's presence that was inexplicably terrifying—a feeling of size and power, of a giant hidden somewhere in the gloom, crouched and waiting to spring. The sounds it emitted were of glaciers breaking apart and sliding into the bay, of fissures opening and closing, of mass shifting constantly from the pressure and cold. The men and women aboard the *Jerle Shannara* listened to it the way a traveler would listen to a storm tear at his lean-to, waiting for something to give way, to fail.

Then the channel narrowed once more, this time clogged by pillars of ice so huge they blocked the way completely, crystal towers that rose out of the bay's liquid floor like spikes. Through gaps in the pillars Bek could see a brightening of the light and a lessening of the mist, as if the weather and geography might be different on the other side. Walker, standing close, touched his shoulder and nodded. Then he turned to Redden Alt Mer and told him to hold the airship where it was.

Hovering before the pillars of ice, clustered at the railings in silent groups, the ship's company stood waiting. The cold air shimmered and seabirds glided in silence. Through the deep mist, the ice continued to rumble and crack, the reverberations distant and ominous.

Then abruptly the pillars began to shift, tilting in a series of thrusts and twists that mimicked the closing of jaws and the grinding of teeth. As the awestruck company watched, the icy towers came together in a series of grating collisions, smashing into each other with booming explosions, closing off the channel's entry and clogging all passage through. Shards of ice catapulted through the air and into the bay's waters, and new cracks opened along the huge towers as they collided then retreated, shifting leviathans hammering at each other in mindless fury. Waves surged and the bay boiled with the force of the furious movement.

Minutes later, the pillars retreated once more, backing away from each other, taking new positions, bobbing gently in the dying swells.

"That," the Druid whispered in Bek's ear, "is called the Squirm. That is what the Sword of Shannara must overcome."

On the Druid's orders, they sailed back out of the bay and down the coast to the atoll where the Wing Riders waited. It was almost dark by then, and Redden Alt Mer had his crew secure the *Jerle Shannara* for the night. Bek was still pondering the Druid's words, trying to figure out how the magic of the Sword of Shannara was supposed to find a way through those shifting icebergs, unable to see how the talisman could help. Walker had left him almost immediately to confer with the Rover Captain, and Ahren had come over to occupy his attention, so there was nothing further he could do to find out right away. Mostly, he had to trust that the Druid knew what he was talking about.

When they were anchored and had eaten dinner, Walker called his council of eight together for a final conference. This time Hunter Predd was included to bring the number to nine. They gathered in Redden Alt Mer's cabin—the Druid, the Rover Captain and his sister, Ard Patrinell and Ahren, Quentin and Bek, Ryer Ord Star, and the Wing Rider. The sky was overcast and the night so black that it was impossible to see either the ocean or the atoll to which they were anchored.

"Tomorrow we will pass through the pillars of the Squirm," Walker advised when they were all gathered and settled. "Captain Alt Mer will command from the pilot box. I will stand on the deck in front of the foremast and call out directions. Bek will help me. Everyone else will take their normal stations and stand ready. No one is to go forward until we are through—not one step beyond me."

He looked at Big Red. "Adjustments will have to be made swiftly and accurately, Captain. The ice will not forgive us our mistakes. Listen carefully to what I call out. Do exactly as I tell you. Trust my directions, even if they seem wrong. Do not try to second-guess me or anticipate my wishes. This one time, I must be in command."

He waited for the Rover to acknowledge him. Redden Alt Mer glanced at his sister, then nodded his agreement.

"Hunter Predd," Walker continued. "The Wing Riders must remain behind. The Shrikes are numerous and the winds and fog treacherous. Fly down the coast and try to find a better place than this atoll to await our return. If we can, we will come back for you or at least get word to you. But it may take time. We may be gone for as long as several months." He paused. "Maybe longer."

The grizzled rider nodded. "I know what to do."

He was saying he understood that those who passed through the pillars of Ice Henge might not be coming back. He was saying that he would wait until waiting was pointless, then try to make his way back to the Four Lands. But Bek heard something more. Hunter Predd wasn't the sort to give up easily. If those on the *Jerle Shannara* didn't make it home, then in all probability, neither would he.

If Walker had picked up on this, he gave no indication. "Ryer Ord Star has had another vision," he advised, beckoning the young woman forward.

She came reluctantly, head lowered into the silver shadow of her long hair, violet eyes directed at the floor, moving into the Druid's shadow as if only there could she be safe, so close that she was pressing up against him. Walker put his hand on her shoulder and bent down. "Tell them," he urged gently.

She took a moment before she responded, her voice high and clear. "I see three moles who seek to burrow into the earth. They carry keys to a lock. One is caught in an endless maze. Ribbons of fire trap another. Metal dogs hunt a third. All are blind and cannot see. All have lost their way and cannot find it again. But one will discover a door that leads to the past. Inside, the future waits."

There was a long silence when she was finished. Then Redden Alt Mer cleared his throat. "Kind of vague, isn't it?" he offered with a wry, apologetic smile at the seer. "What does it mean?"

"We don't know," Walker answered for her. "It might mean that one of us will find the entry into Castledown and the treasure that lies within. That would be a meeting of past and future. Whatever other purpose it serves, it gives warning of three dangers—an endless maze, ribbons of fire, and metal dogs. In some form, these are what we will face when we gain land again." He glanced at Ryer Ord Star. "Maybe by then, we will have new insights to ponder."

We can only hope, Bek thought to himself, and the discussion turned to other matters.

Bek slept poorly that night, riddled by self-doubt and misgiving. He was awake when dawn broke lead-gray and misty, the sun a red-glowing forge at the edge of the world. He stood on deck and watched the light grow from pale to somber as the sky took on a wintry cast that layered clouds and mist and water like gauze. The air was chill and smelled of the damp, and the cliffs of Ice Henge were aswirl with snowflakes and wheeling gulls. The Shrikes were up, as well, hunting the coastline, their larger forms all wings and necks, their fierce cries echoing off the rock walls.

Walker appeared and stopped long enough to place a reassuring hand on the boy's shoulder before moving on. Anchor lines were cast off, sails were unfurled, and the *Jerle Shannara* rose from its berthing and flew north. The Wing Riders left at the same time, flying south. Bek watched them go from the aft railing, solitary forms riding the air currents in a slow, steady glide, the Rocs' great wings spread to the faint winter light. In seconds they were gone, disappeared into the gloom, and Bek turned his attention to what lay ahead. Perhaps a mile offshore, they sailed up the coast making for the opening in the cliffs that led to the Squirm. Breakfast, a hearty mix of breads and cheeses washed down by cold ale, was consumed in shifts and mostly on deck. The day advanced in a slow passing of the hours and an even slower brightening of the sky. The air warmed just enough to change snowflakes to rain, and the wind picked up and began to gust in fierce giant's breaths that knocked the airship about.

Bek stood in the pilot box with Redden Alt Mer for a long time while Walker paced the decking like a ghost at haunt. The Rover Captain said almost nothing to the boy, his concentration focused on the handling of his vessel, his gaze directed ahead into the gloom. Once he caught Bek's eye and smiled briefly. "We'll be fine, Bek," he said quietly, and then looked away again.

Bek Rowe, born Bek Ohmsford, wasn't at all sure that was so, but if hope and determination counted for anything, maybe they had a chance. He was wrestling with doubts about his ability to control any sort of magic, even his mastery of the wishsong suspect. It was all too new and unfamiliar for him to have much confidence. He had experienced the magic of his voice, but in such a small way and with so little sense of control that he barely felt he understood what it could do. As for the magic of the Sword of Shannara, he had no idea what he could do with that. He could repeat everything Walker had told him about how it worked. He could intellectualize its behavior and function. He would apply all the appropriate and correct words to how it would affect him. But he could not picture it. He could not imagine how it would feel. He had no frame of reference and no sense of proportion with which to measure its power.

He did not try to deceive himself. The magic of the Sword of Shannara would be immense and overwhelming. It would engulf him like a tidal wave, and he would be fortunate to survive its crushing impact, let alone find a way to swim to its surface. All he could do was hope he would not be drowned straightaway when it swept over him. Walker had not said so, but it was there in the gaps between his words. Bek was to be tested in a way he had never imagined. Walker did not seem to think he would fail, but Walker would not be there inside him when the magic took hold.

Bek climbed down out of the pilot box after a while and went to stand at the ship's railing. Quentin came up to him, and they talked in low voices about the day and the weather, avoiding any mention of the Squirm. The Highlander was relaxed and cheerful, in typical fashion, and he made Bek feel at ease even without intending it. Wasn't this everything they had hoped for? he asked his cousin with a broad smile. Wasn't this the adventure they had come to find? What did Bek think lay on the other side of those ice pillars? Somehow they must make certain they stayed together. Whatever happened, they must remember their promise.

It was nearing midmorning when they reached the gap in the cliffs and rode the edges of the air currents through its opening and into the silence and calm beyond. The roar of the ocean and the whistle of the wind died away, and the bay with its cliff walls and cloud ceiling enfolded them like an anxious mother would her offspring. The ship's company crowded to the railings and looked out over the gray expanse of water and ice. Floes passed beneath like massive ships launched off the glaciers, riding the currents out to sea. Ice cracked and chuttered in the silence, filling hearts with sudden moments of apprehension and eyes with bright looks of concern. Bek stood in the cold and silence like a statue, wrapped in the former's raw burn and layered in the latter's rough emptiness.

The *Jerle Shannara* passed through the outer bay and rode down the narrowing channel inland, the ceiling of mist lowering to scrape the airship's raked masts, the gloom a whisper of shadows that tricked the eyes into seeing things that weren't there. No one spoke as the airship slid past icebergs and along cliff walls, moving so slowly that it seemed almost at rest. Seabirds arced and soared about them, soundless and spectral. Bek watched them keep pace, following their progress, intrigued by their obvious interest.

Then his throat tightened and his breath exhaled in a sharp cloud as he realized they were waiting to see if there would be bones to pick once the airship reached the Squirm.

Moments later the haze cleared sufficiently that he could see the first of the ice pillars that barred their passage, towering spikes swaying hypnotically, seductively in the gloom.

"Come with me," Walker said softly, causing the boy to jump, to feel the tightening in his throat work swiftly to his chest and stomach.

So it was time. He remembered his certainty months earlier when he had agreed to come on this voyage that it would change him forever. It had done that, but not to the extent it was about to do now. He closed his eyes against a fresh wave of fear and doubt. He understood that the course of his life was already determined, but he could not quite accept it, even now. Still, he must do the best he could.

Obediently, silently, willing himself to place one foot in front of the other, Bek followed after the Druid.

TWENTY-EIGHT

Bek waited in the shadow of the chain-wrapped casing that housed the Sword of Shannara while Walker moved everyone back from the forward deck to take up positions along the aft and side railings. Redden Alt Mer occupied the pilot box with Rue Meridian. Spanner Frew stood just below, ready to leap into action if his aid was required. Furl Hawken commanded the Rover crew from the rise of the aft deck, and the Elven Hunters under Ard Patrinell clustered on both sides, safety lines firmly attached. Panax, Quentin, and Ahren Elessedil were gathered on the starboard railing just to one side of the aft mast, whispering. About *him*, Bek thought uncomfortably, but that was nonsense. Their eyes were directed toward the Squirm, and their concentration was on its movements within the ice-melt bay. Only Walker knew what he was there to do. Only Walker understood how much depended on him.

The Druid reappeared at his side. "Ready, Bek?"

Not trusting himself to speak, the boy nodded. He was not ready, of course. He would never be ready for something as frightening as this. There was no way to become ready. All he could do was trust that the Druid was right about his connection to the magic and hope that he could find a way to make himself do what was needed.

But looking at the monstrous barrier ahead, at the tons of ice and rock that rose above him, he could not imagine doing anything that would make a difference.

He breathed slowly, calming himself, waiting for something to happen. The *Jerle Shannara* advanced toward the pillars on a slow, steady course, easing up to the barrier as if seeking an invitation to enter. Walker was speaking to Redden Alt Mer, but Bek could not make himself focus on the words. His heart was hammering in his chest, and all he could hear was the sound of his breathing and the cracking of the ice as new pieces broke away.

"Now, Bek," the Druid said softly.

Walker's hand swept the air about them, and the air shimmered and turned murky with a swirling of mist and gloom. Everything behind and to either side of the boy and the Druid lost focus and faded away. All that remained was a window before them that opened on the channel and the cliffs and the ice.

As if in response, the pillars began to move.

"Hold steady, Bek," Walker urged softly, touching Bek's shoulder to reassure him, dark face close, his eyes staring out at the ice as it came together.

Like mobile teeth, the pillars tilted and clashed, grinding and crunching until shards of ice splintered and flew in all directions. The sea below boiled and crashed in waves against the base of the cliffs, spray rising in clouds to mingle with the mist. Bek flinched at the sound and the motion, hunched his shoulders in spite of himself. He could feel the ice closing about him, crushing him, reducing the airship to driftwood and the ship's company to pulp. He could feel it happening as if it really were, tearing at him in ways that turned him so cold and dead he could not bear it. He stood on the deck of the *Jerle Shannara*, washed by spray and hammered by sound, and felt as if his soul had been torn open.

Something burned before him, a beacon out of the gloom,

rising like a flame into the gray haze. He stared at it in wonder, and he saw that he held in his hands the Sword of Shannara and that it was ablaze with light.

"Shades!" he hissed in disbelief.

He had no idea when Walker had given it to him, no idea how long he had been holding it. He stared at its light, transfixed, watching it surge up and down the blade in small crimson ribbons that twisted and wound about the metal. He watched as it descended into the pommel and wrapped about his hands.

Then it was rushing through him in a wave of warmth and tingling sensation, spreading all through his limbs and body. It consumed him, swallowed him, wrapped him about, and made him its own. He was captured by it, and there was a slow leavening of thought, emotion, and feeling. Everything about him began to disappear, fading away into darkness which only the sword's light illuminated. The airship, the ship's company, the gloom and mist, the ice, the cliffs, everything was gone. Bek was alone, solitary and adrift within himself, buoyed on the back of the magic that infused him.

Help me, he heard himself asking.

The images began at once, no longer of the Squirm and its crushing pillars, no longer of the world in which he lived, but of the world he had left behind, of the past. A succession of memories began to recall themselves, taking him back in time, reminding him of what had once been and now was gone. He grew younger, smaller. The memories became a rush of sudden, frightening images, rife with fury and terror, with distant cries and the labored breathing of someone who held him close before tucking him into a black, cold place. The smell and taste of smoke and soot filled his throat and nostrils, and he could feel a panic within that refused to be stilled.

Grianne! he heard himself call out.

Blackness cloaked and hooded him once more, and a new series of images began. He saw himself as a child in the care of Coran and

Liria. He saw himself at play with Quentin and his friends, with his younger brothers and sisters, at his home in Leah and beyond. The scenes were dark and accusatory, memories of his growing up that he had suppressed, memories of the times in which he had lied and cheated and deceived, in which his selfishness and disregard had caused hurt and pain. Some of these scenes were familiar, some he had forgotten. The weaknesses of his life were revealed in steady procession, laid bare for him to witness. They were not terrible things taken separately, but their number increased their weight, and after a time he was crying openly and desperate for them to end.

A wind of dark haziness swept them all away and left him with a view of the Four Lands in which all that was bad and terrible about the human condition was displayed. He watched in horror as starvation, sickness, murder, and pillage decimated lives and homes and futures in a canvas so broad it seemed to stretch from horizon to horizon. Men, women and children fell victim to the weaknesses of spirit and morality that plagued mankind. All of the races were susceptible, and all participated in the savagery. There was no end to it, no lessening of it, no sense that it had ever been other than this. Bek watched it unfold in horror and profound sadness and felt it to be a part of himself. Even in his misery he could sense that this was the history of his people, that this was who he was.

Yet when it was over, he felt cleansed. With recognition came acceptance. With acceptance came forgiveness. He felt cleansed, not just of what he had contributed to the morass, but of what others had contributed as well—as if he had taken it all on his shoulders, just for a little while, and had been given back a sense of peace. He rose up within the darkness, strengthened in ways he could not define, reborn into himself with a boy's eyes, but a man's understanding.

The darkness drew back, and he stood again on the deck of the *Jerle Shannara*, arms lifted, sword outstretched. He was still masked back and sides by Walker's magic, but the way forward was clear.

The Squirm had opened anew, its pillars swaying seductively, beckoning him to proceed, to come within their reach. He could feel the cold that permeated them. He could feel their crushing weight. Even the air that surrounded them was infused with their power and their unpredictability. But there was something else here as well, he felt it at once. Something man-made, something not of nature but of machines and science.

A hand reached out to him, not made of flesh and blood, but of spirit, of ether, of magic so vast and pervasive that it lay everywhere about. He shrank from it, warded himself against it by bringing the sword's light to bear, and abruptly it was gone.

Walker? he called out in confusion, but there was only silence.

Ahead, the pillars of the Squirm rocked in the ice-melt sea, and the gulls flew round and round. Bek tested the air and the temperature. He joined himself to the ice of the spikes and the rock of the cliffs. He immersed himself in their feel, in their movements, in the vibrations of sound they emitted, in the shifting of their parts. He became one with his immediate world, extending into it from where he stood, so that he could read its intention and anticipate its behavior.

"Go forward," he instructed, gesturing with the sword. The words seemed to come from someone else. "Ahead, slow."

Walker must have heard him. The *Jerle Shannara* eased cautiously toward the pillars. Like a fragile bird, it sailed within their monstrous jaws, through the misted gaps of their teeth. "Left fifteen degrees," he said, and heard Walker repeat his orders. "Ahead slow," he called. "Faster now, more speed," he instructed. The airship slid through the forest of ice, a moth into the flame, tiny and insignificant and unable to protect itself from the fire.

Then the pillars shifted anew and began to close on them. Bek was aware of it from somewhere deep inside, not just through his eyes, but through his body's connection with the sword's magic and the sword's magic with the land and air and water. Cries rose from members of the ship's company, frantic with fear. The boy heard them as he heard the crashing of waves against the cliff walls and the whisper of gull wings on the morning air. He heard them and did not respond. "Go right twenty degrees. Take shelter in that pillar's crevice." His voice was so soft it seemed a wonder to him that anyone could hear.

But, hearing the words repeated by Walker, Redden Alt Mer did as Bek instructed. He rode the *Jerle Shannara* swiftly into a split that warded her while all about the ice pillars clashed and hammered at each other, and the air turned damp with spray and the sea white with foam. The sound and the fury of it deafened and shocked, and it felt as if an avalanche were sweeping over them. In the midst of the madness, Bek ordered the airship out of its protection through a momentary gap in two of the surging towers. The ship responded as if wired to his thinking, and an instant later, a wedge of ice broke off from the pinnacle of their momentary shelter and crashed down to lodge in the crevice they had just departed.

Forward they sailed, down through the haze, through errant and sudden collisions, through the closing of icy jaws and the grinding of sharpened teeth. A tiny bit of flotsam, they weaved and dodged, barely avoiding a crushing end time after time, riding spray and wind and cold. What must have gone through the minds of his shipmates, Bek could only imagine. Later, Quentin would tell him that after the first few moments, he had been unable to see much and had not wanted to look anyway. Bek would reply that it had been like that for him as well.

"Up! Quickly! Go up!" he cried a sharp and frantic warning, and the airship rose with a sudden lurch that threw everyone to the deck. Kneeling with the sword outstretched and his legs spread for balance, Bek heard the explosion of an ice floe beneath them, and a massive piece, propelled from the water's surface like a projectile, just missed the underside of their hull before falling back into the sea.

Sword raised to the light, magic entwined with the air and the ice and the rock, Bek shouted his instructions. Relying on instinct rather than sight, on sensation rather than thought, he responded to impulses that flashed and were gone in seconds, trusting to their ebb and flow as he guided the airship ahead. He could not explain to himself then or later what he was doing. He was reacting, and the impetus for what he did came from something both within and without that lacked definition or source, that was like the air he breathed and the cold and damp that infused it—pervasive and all-consuming. Again and again, huge shadows fell over him as the pillars of the Squirm swept by, barely missing them, rising and falling in the misty light, advancing randomly, soldiers at march through the gloom. Over and over, the monoliths collided, splintered, exploded, and turned to jagged shards. Lost within himself, wrapped within his magic, Bek felt it all and saw none of it.

Then the gloom began to brighten ahead, the haze to thin, and the sound and movement of the pillars to lessen. Still focused on the crushing weight of the ice and rock, Bek registered the change without letting it distract him. There was a sense of growing warmth, of color returning, and of smells that were of the land and not the sea. The airship surged ahead, propelled by an expectancy and hope Bek had not felt before. He lowered the Sword of Shannara in response, and his connection with the magic was broken. The warmth that infused him drew back, and the light that encircled the blade faded. Still on his knees, exhausted, he sagged to the decking. He breathed in deeply, gratefully, head lowered between his shoulders.

Walker took the Sword of Shannara from his hands and knelt beside him. "We're through, Bek. We're safe. Well done, young Ohmsford."

The boy felt the Druid's arm come about his shoulders, and then he fell away into blackness and didn't feel anything.

* * *

When he regained consciousness, he was lying beneath the foremast with Joad Rish bent over him. He blinked and stared down at himself for a moment, as if needing reassurance that he was still all there, then looked up at the Healer.

"How do you feel?" the Elf asked, concern mirrored in his narrow features.

Bek wanted to laugh. How could he possibly answer that question after what he'd been through? "I'm all right. A little disoriented. How long was I unconscious?"

"No more than a few minutes. Walker said you were thrown into that crate and cracked your head. Do you want to try to stand up?"

With the Healer's help, Bek climbed to his feet and looked around. The *Jerle Shannara* was under sail, moving down a broad, twisting channel through a bleak landscape of barren cliff walls and small, rocky islands. But the mist had begun to clear, and traces of blue sky shone in the bright light of an emerging sun. Trees dotted the ridgelines of the cliffs, and the glaciers and ice floes were gone.

A rush of memories crowded into Bek's mind, hard and fast and dangerous, but he blinked them away. The Squirm and its pillars of ice were gone. The Sword of Shannara was gone as well, put back into its casing by Walker, he supposed. He shivered momentarily, thinking of all he had experienced, of the feelings generated, of the whiplash of power. The sword's magic was addictive, he realized. He didn't need more than one experience with it to know. It was terrifying and overwhelming and incredibly empowering. Just to have survived it made him feel strangely exhilarated. As if he could survive anything. As if he were invulnerable.

Quentin came up and put a hand on his shoulder, asking how he was. Bek repeated Joad Rish's story about hitting his head when the ship lurched, playing it down. Nothing much. Nothing to give a second thought to. It was such a ridiculous explanation that he felt embarrassed giving it, but he realized it seemed ridiculous only if you knew the truth. One by one, the members of the ship's company came up to him, and he repeated the story to each. Only Ahren Elessedil voiced any skepticism.

"You're not usually so clumsy, Bek," he observed with a grin. "Where were your instincts when you needed them? An Elf wouldn't have lost his footing so easily."

"Be a touch more careful next time, young hero," Little Red joked, ruffling his hair. "We can't afford to lose you."

Walker appeared momentarily, shadowed by the slight, silver-haired figure of Ryer Ord Star. Distant, he nodded to the boy without speaking, and passed on. The seer studied the boy carefully before following.

The morning had passed away into afternoon, and the landscape began to change. The sharp-edged cliffs retreated from the waterline and softened to gentle slopes. Green and lush in the sunlight, forests appeared. From where they flew, the ship's company saw rolling hills stretching into the distance for miles. The river they followed split into dozens of smaller tributaries that spider-webbed out through the trees to form lakes, rivers, and streams. There was no sign of the ocean; the peninsula was sufficiently large that its outer shores were too distant to spy. Clouds were gathered on the horizons to either side and behind, markers of where the shoreline probably lay. Bek thought that Redden Alt Mer had been right not to try to fly over the cliffs to come inland. Even had they been able to do so, they would probably never have found this channel in the maze of rivers that surrounded it. Only by coming through the Squirm could they have known where to go.

The channel narrowed, hemmed in by old-growth spruce and cedar, the scent of the trees fragrant and lush on the warming air. The smells of the sea, of kelp and seaweed and fish, had faded. For all that remained of the coastline and its forbidding passage through the Squirm, they might have passed into another world entirely. Hawks soared overhead in slow, sweeping glides. Crows cawed raucously, their calls echoing down the defile. The *Jerle Shannara* edged ahead carefully, so close to the shore at times that its spars brushed against the tree limbs.

The river eventually ended in a bay surrounded by forest and fed by dozens of rivers and streams. A huge waterfall tumbled into its basin at one end, and a handful of smaller falls splashed over rocky precipices farther along. Birdsong filled the air, and a small herd of deer moved quickly off the water's edge on sighting their craft. The *Jerle Shannara* eased into the bay like a large sea creature that had wandered inland, and Redden Alt Mer brought her to a stop at the bay's center.

Gathered at the railings, the ship's company stared out at the destination they had traveled so far to find. It was nothing special. It might have been any number of places in the Westland, so similar did it look with its mix of conifers and hardwoods, the scent of loam on the air, and its smells of needles and green leaves.

Then Bek realized in mild shock that it didn't look or feel like winter here, even though it was the winter season. Once through the Squirm, they hadn't found anything of ice or cold or snow or bitter wind. It was as if they had somehow found their way back to midsummer.

"This isn't possible," he murmured softly, confused and wary.

He glanced quickly at those around him to see if anyone else had noticed, but no one seemed to have done so. He waited a moment, then moved over to where Walker stood, alone, below the pilot box. The Druid's eyes were leveled on the shoreline ahead, but they registered the boy's approach.

"What is it, Bek?"

Bek stood beside him uncertainly. "It's summer here, and it shouldn't be."

The Druid nodded. "It's a lot of things here it shouldn't be. Strange. Keep your eyes open."

He ordered Big Red to take the airship down to the water and anchor her. When that was done, he sent a foraging party of Elven

Hunters ashore for water, warning them that they were to stay together and in sight of the shoreline. The company would remain
aboard ship tonight. A search for Castledown would begin in the
morning. What was needed now was an inventory of the ship's
stores, an updated damage report, an unpacking and distribution of
weapons to the members of the shore party, and some dinner. The
Elven Hunters under Ard Patrinell and Ahren Elessedil would accompany him on the morrow's search, along with Quentin, Bek,
Panax, Ryer Ord Star, and Joad Rish. The Rovers would remain
aboard ship until their return.

Before anyone could offer comment or complaint about his decision, he summoned his council of eight to a meeting in Redden Alt
Mer's cabin and walked from the deck.

Quentin sidled up to Bek. "Something is up, I'll wager. Do you
think the seer's had another vision?"

Bek shook his head. The only thing he knew for certain was that
Redden Alt Mer, dark-browed and stiff-necked as he came down off
the pilot box, was not happy.

When the eight who composed Walker's inner council were
gathered belowdecks in the Rover Captain's cabin, the boy found
out what it was.

"I didn't come this far to be left aboard ship while everyone else
goes ashore," Big Red snapped at the Druid.

"Nor I," Rue Meridian agreed, flushed and angry. "We sailed a
long way to find out what's here. You ask too much of us, Walker."

No one else spoke. They were pressed close about the Druid,
gathered at the table that held the large-scale drawing of the castaway's map, all but Ryer Ord Star, who remained in the background, a part of the shadows, watching silently. The warmth of
their new environment not yet absorbed into the hull, the room
smelled of damp and pitch and was still infused with the feel of the
ice and cold they had left on the other side of the Squirm. Bek
glanced at the faces about him, surprised by the mix of expectancy

and tension he found mirrored there. It had taken them a long time to reach their destination, and much of what they had bottled up inside during their voyage was coming out.

Walker's black eyes swept the room. He gestured at the map laid out before them. "How do you think the castaway who brought us the original of this map managed to get all the way from here to the coast of the Westland?"

He waited a moment, but no one answered. "It is a voyage of months, even by airship. How did the castaway manage it, already blind and voiceless and probably at least half-mad?"

"Someone helped him," Bek offered, not wanting to listen any longer to the uncomfortable silence. "Maybe the same someone who helped him escape."

The Druid nodded. "Where is that person?"

Again, silence. Bek shook his head, not eager to assume the role of designated speaker for the group.

"Dead, lost at sea during the escape, probably on the voyage back," Rue Meridian said. "What are you getting at?"

"Let's assume that is so," Walker replied. "You have had a chance to study the map at length during this voyage. Most of the writings are done not with words, but with symbols. The writings aren't of this age, but of an age thousands of years old, from a time before the Great Wars destroyed the Old World. How did our castaway learn that language?"

"Someone taught it to him," Rue Meridian answered, a thoughtful, somewhat worried look on her sun-browned face. She tossed back her long red hair impatiently. "Why would they do that?"

"Why, indeed?" Walker paused. "Let's assume that the Elven expedition that Kael Elessedil led thirty years ago reached its destination just as we have, and then something happened to it. They were all killed, all but one man, perhaps Kael Elessedil himself. Their ships were destroyed and all trace of their passage disappeared. How did they find their way here? Did they have a map, as we do?

We must assume so, or how would the castaway know to draw one for us to follow? To make the copy we have, they must have followed the route we followed. They must have visited the islands of Flay Creech, Shatterstone, and Mephitic, and found the keys we found. If so, how did those keys get back to the islands from which they were taken?"

Another long silence filled the room. Booted feet shifted uncomfortably. "What are you saying, Walker?" Ard Patrinell asked.

"He's saying we've sailed into a trap," Redden Alt Mer answered softly.

Bek stared at the Rover Captain, repeating his words silently, trying to make sense of them.

"I have given this considerable thought," Walker said, folding his arm into his robes, a pensive look on his dark face. "I thought it odd that an Elf should have possession of a map marked with symbols he couldn't possibly know. I thought it convenient that the map spelled out so clearly what was needed for us to find our way here. The keys were not particularly well concealed. In fact, they were easily gained once the creatures and devices that warded them were bypassed. It struck me that whoever hid the keys was more interested in seeing if and how we managed to overcome the protectors than whether or not we found the keys. I was reminded of how hunters trap animals, laying out bait to lure them to the snare, the bait itself having no value. Hunters think of animals as cunning and wary, but not of intelligence equal to their own. Animals might mistrust a baited trap instinctively, but they would not be able to reason out its purpose. That sort of thinking seems to be at work here."

He paused and looked at Big Red. "Yes, Captain, I think it is a trap."

Redden Alt Mer nodded. "The keys are merely bait. Why?"

"Why not just provide us with a map and let us find our way here? Why bother with the keys at all?" Walker looked around the room, meeting each person's eyes in turn. "To answer that, you have to go all the way back to the first expedition. A different technique was employed to lure the Elves to this place, but the purpose was probably the same. Whoever or whatever brought us here is interested in something we have. I wasn't sure what it was at first, but I am now. It is our magic. Whatever hunts us wants our magic. It used the mystery of the first expedition's disappearance to lure us here. It knows we possess magic because it has already encountered the power of the Elfstones that Kael Elessedil carried. So it expects us to have magic, as well. Requiring us to gain possession of the three keys gave it an opportunity to measure the nature and extent of that magic. The protectors of the keys were set in place to test us. If we could not overcome them, we had no business coming here."

"If you suspected most of this before we set out, why didn't you tell us then?" Redden Alt Mer snapped, angrier than ever now. "In fact, why did you bring us here at all?"

"Don't give me too much credit for what I am presumed to have known," Walker replied quietly. "I suspected more than I knew. I intuited the possibilities, but could not be certain of their accuracy without making the journey. How could I have explained all this and made sense if I had done so without your having experienced what you have? No, Captain, it was necessary to make the voyage first. Even so, I would not have changed my decision. Whatever destroyed Kael Elessedil and his Elven Hunters seeks to do the same to us. Nor will it stop there. It is a powerful and dangerous being, and it has to be destroyed. The Elves want their Elfstones back, and I want to free the magic our adversary hoards. There are good reasons for being here, in spite of what we know, in spite of the obvious dangers. Good enough that we must accept the risks they bear."

"Easy enough for you to say, Walker," Rue Meridian observed. "You have your magic and your Druid skills to protect you. We have only our blades. Except for Quentin Leah, who has his sword, who else has magic to protect us?"

Bek braced for the response he expected Walker to give, but the Druid surprised him. "Magic is not what will save us in this matter or even what will do us the most good. Think about it. If our adversary uses a language of symbols, a language that was devised before the Great Wars by a Mankind steeped in science, then in all likelihood, it has no magic itself. It brought us here because it covets our magic. It covets what we have and it does not. Why this is so is what we must determine. But our chances of overcoming our adversary are not necessarily reliant on the use of magic."

"That is a large assumption, Druid," Little Red declared bluntly. "What of the things that warded the keys on the islands we visited? The eels might have been real enough, but what of that living jungle and that castle? Wasn't magic in play there?"

Walker nodded. "But not a magic of the sort that devised those keys. The keys are a technology from the past, one lost since the Great Wars or perhaps even before. The magic of the castle and the jungle are Faerie-induced and have been resident since the time of the Word. The eels probably mutated after the Great Wars. Our adversary did not create them, but only identified them. What's interesting is not that these traps were baited to test the strength and nature of our magic but that it was done without having to overcome the things that warded those islands. How did our adversary do that? Why didn't it try to steal their magic, as well? Why did it choose to go to so much trouble to summon us instead?"

He nodded toward Big Red. "The reason I am leaving the Rovers aboard ship instead of taking them inland with the Elven Hunters is that I think our adversary might well try to steal our ship. It knows we are here, I expect, and how we arrived. It will know as well that if it steals the *Jerle Shannara*, we will be marooned and helpless. We can't afford to let that happen. Who better to protect and defend our airship than the people who sailed and built her?"

Redden Alt Mer nodded slowly. "All right. Your argument is sound, Walker. But how will we fight this thing off if it comes after the ship? We won't have any magic to use against it, only our blades. If it's as powerful as you suggest—"

"After we go ashore tomorrow," Walker interrupted quickly,

holding up his hand to silence the other, "you will take the *Jerle Shannara* out of this bay and back down the channel toward the Squirm. Then take a bearing and fly back out over the peninsula to the coast and find the Wing Riders. When you've done so, bring them back to a safe haven downriver. Map your route going out so you can find your way coming back. Have the Wing Riders fly inland over this bay and the surrounding forests every day until we signal you to take us out. If you aren't where you can be easily found, you'll be safe enough."

Big Red looked at his sister. Rue Meridian shrugged. "I don't like the idea of splitting up," he said. "I understand the reason for it, but it puts you and those with you at great risk if something goes wrong. You will be marooned if we can't find you."

Walker nodded. "Then we'll have to make sure you can."

"Or if we can't find the Wing Riders," Little Red added.

"The Wing Riders will find you. They will be looking for you, for the airship. Just be certain you map your route out and back carefully."

"I'll see that I do." Rue Meridian held his gaze.

Bek glanced from Quentin to Ahren Elessedil to Ard Patrinell and finally to the wan, youthful face of Ryer Ord Star. There was determination and acceptance on each, but the seer's face showed apprehension and conflict, as well. She knew something she was not telling them. Bek sensed it instinctively, as if he still held the Sword of Shannara and had brought its magic to bear, seeking out the truth, drawing back the veil of concealment the young woman held in place.

What was it she was hiding? Something of their fate? Something of what waited inland? Bek studied her surreptitiously. Had she told Walker everything? Or was she holding something back? He didn't have any reason to ask himself that question, no cause to believe that she would conceal anything from the Druid.

But there was something in the way she distanced herself from him, from everyone . . .

"Let's finish our preparations and have something to eat," Walker said, breaking into his thoughts. "Tomorrow we set out at sunrise."

"Good luck to you, Walker," Rue Meridian said.

He gave her a wry smile. "Good luck to us all, Little Red."

Then he gathered in his black robes and walked from the room.

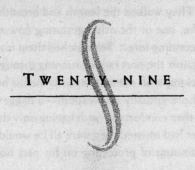

TWENTY-NINE

nchored well offshore and forty feet above the water, the company of the *Jerle Shannara* spent the night in the tree-sheltered bay. Taking no chances, Walker set a full watch—one man forward, one aft, and one in the pilot box—using Rovers so that the Elven Hunters could get a full night's sleep and be fresh for the morning's search. Even so, the Druid suspected that sleep was an elusive quantity that night. He slept little himself, and while pacing the corridors and decks he encountered, at one time or another, almost everyone else doing the same. Anticipation kept them all on edge and restless, and even the absence of wind and surf did nothing to ease their discomfort.

Dawn arrived in a flare of golden light that burst through the trees and across the horizon, brightening a clear blue sky and heralding a weather-perfect day. The members of the company were up and moving about almost instantly, grateful for any excuse to quit pretending that sleep might somehow come. Breakfast was consumed and weapons and provisions were gathered up. The search party gathered on deck in the early light, grim-faced and re-solved, no one saying much, everyone waiting for the order to de-part. Walker did not give it at once. He spent a long time conversing with Redden Alt Mer and Rue Meridian, then with Spanner Frew. They walked the length and breadth of the airship while they spoke, one or the other gesturing now and then at the ship or the surrounding forest. Bek watched them from where he sat cross-legged against the port railing, running through a list of what he carried, checking it off mentally against the list he had prepared last night. He bore virtually no weapons—a dagger and a sling—and he was less than comfortable with having only those for protection. But Walker had insisted they were all he would need or could carry, and no amount of protesting on his part had changed the Druid's mind.

"This would be a good day for hunting," Quentin, who was seated beside him, his gear at his feet, observed.

Bek nodded. Quentin carried a short sword at his belt, a bow and arrows over his shoulder, and the Sword of Leah strapped across his back in the Highland style. Bek supposed that if they encountered anything really dangerous, he could rely on his cousin to come to his aid.

"Do you suppose they have boar here?"

"What difference does it make?" Bek found the small talk irritating and unnecessary.

"I was just wondering." Quentin seemed unperturbed. "It just feels a little like home to me."

Ashamed of his disgruntled attitude, Bek forced a smile. "They have lots of boar here, and you couldn't track a one of them without me."

"Do tell." Quentin arched one eyebrow. "Will I see some proof of your prowess one day soon? Or will I have to go on taking your word for it for the rest of my life?"

He leaned back and stretched his arms over his head. Quentin seemed loose and easy on the outside, but Bek knew he was as anxious as the rest of them where it couldn't be seen. The banter was a time-honored way around it, a method of dealing with it that both instinctively relied on. They had used it before, on hunts where the game they tracked was dangerous, like boar or bear, and the risk of injury was severe. It moved them a step away from thinking about what might happen if something went wrong, and it helped to prevent the kind of gradual paralysis that could steal over someone like a sickness and surface when it was too late to find an antidote.

Bek glanced across the decking to where the Elven Hunters clustered around Ard Patrinell, talking in their low, soft voices as they exchanged comments and banter of their own. Ahren Elessedil stood a little apart from them, staring off into the trees, where night's shadows still folded through the gaps in thick layers and the silence was deep and steady. Nothing of his newfound maturity was in evidence this morning. He looked like a little boy, frightened and lost, stiff with recognition of what might happen to him and fighting a losing battle against the growing certainty that it would. He carried a short sword and bow and arrows, but from the look on his face he might as well have been carrying Bek's weapons.

Bek watched him a moment, thinking about how Ahren must feel, about the responsibility he bore as nominal leader of the expedition, then made a quick decision and climbed to his feet. "I'll be right back," he told Quentin.

He crossed to Ahren and greeted him with a broad grin. "Another day, another adventure," he offered brightly. "At least Ard Patrinell gave you a real sword and an ash bow."

Ahren started at the sound of Bek's voice, but managed to recover a little of his lost composure. "What do you mean?"

"Look what Walker gave me." Bek gestured at his dagger and sling. "Any small birds or squirrels that come after me, I'm ready for them."

Ahren smiled nervously. "I wish I could say the same. I can barely make my legs move. I don't know what's wrong."

"Quentin would say you haven't hunted enough wild boar. Look, I came over to ask a favor. I want you to keep this for me."

Before he could think better of it, he took off the phoenix stone and its necklace and placed them about Ahren's neck. It was an impulsive act, one he might have reconsidered if he had allowed himself time to think about it. The Elf looked down at the stone, then back at Bek questioningly.

"I'm afraid I haven't been entirely honest with you, Ahren," Bek admitted. Then he told his friend a revised version of his encounter with the King of the Silver River and the gift of the phoenix stone, leaving out the parts about his sister and the spirit creature's hints of the stone's real purpose. "So I do have a little magic after all. But I've been keeping it a secret from everyone." He shrugged. "Even Quentin doesn't know about it."

"I can't take this from you!" Ahren declared vehemently, reaching up to remove the stone and necklace.

Bek stopped him, seizing his hands. "Yes, you can. I want you to have it."

"But it isn't mine! It wasn't given to me; it was given to you! By a Faerie creature at that!" His voice softened. "It isn't right, Bek. It doesn't belong to me."

"Well, it doesn't belong to me, either. Not really. Consider it a loan. You can give it back to me later. Look, fair is fair. I have Quentin to protect me, and he has a talisman to help him do the job. You have Ard Patrinell, but he doesn't have any magic. The Elfstones might turn up along the way, but for now, you need something else. Why not take this?"

Bek could tell that the Elf wanted to accept the gift, a talisman of real magic that would give him fresh confidence and a renewed sense of purpose. Just now, Ahren needed those things more than he did. But the Elven prince was proud, and he would not take something from Bek if he thought it was a charity that would put his friend at risk.

"I can't," he repeated dully.

"Could you take it if I told you that Walker has given me another magic to use, something else with which I can protect myself?" Bek kept the truth behind the lie masked in a look of complete sincerity.

Ahren shook his head doubtfully. "What magic?"

"I can't tell you. Walker won't let me. I'm not even supposed to tell you I have the magic. Just trust me. I wouldn't give you the phoenix stone if it was the only real protection I had, would I?"

Which was true enough. The fact that he possessed the magic of the wishsong gave him some reassurance that by handing over the phoenix stone, he wasn't leaving himself entirely defenseless. Anyway, the stone hadn't been of much use to him; perhaps it would help his friend.

"Please, Ahren. Keep it. Look, if you promise to use it to help me if you see that I'm in trouble, that will be repayment enough. And I'll do the same for you with my magic. Quentin and I already have an agreement to look out for each other. You and I can have one, too."

He waited, holding Ahren's uncertain gaze. Finally, the other boy nodded. "All right. But just for a while, Bek." He ran his fingers over the stone. "It's warm, like it's heating from the inside out. And so smooth." He glanced down at it a moment, then back at Bek. "I think it really is magic. But maybe we won't have to find out. Maybe we won't have to use it at all."

Bek smiled agreeably, not believing his reassurances for a single moment. "Maybe not."

"Thanks, Bek. Thanks very much."

Bek was on his way back to Quentin when Walker stopped him amidships and turned him gently aside. "That was very foolish," he said, not unkindly. "Well intentioned, but not particularly well advised."

Bek faced the Druid squarely, the set of his jaw revealing his attitude on the matter. "Ahren has nothing with which to protect himself. No magic of his own, Walker. He is my friend, and I don't see anything wrong with giving him something that might help keep him alive."

The dark face looked away. "You weren't listening to me as

closely as I hoped when I said that magic wasn't necessarily the key to survival here. Instincts and courage and a clear head are what will keep us alive."

Bek stood his ground. "Well, maybe having the phoenix stone will help him find those particular attributes. What's bothering you, Walker?"

The Druid shook his head. "So many things I don't know where to start. But in this case, your rashness gives me pause. Giving up magic entrusted to you by the King of the Silver River may cost you more than you realize. The magic of the phoenix stone wasn't intended as a defense. The King of the Silver River would know, as I do, that you possess the magic of the wishsong. The stone is for something else, most likely something to do with your sister. Mark me well, Bek, and retrieve it as soon as you reasonably can. Promise me."

Only partially convinced, the boy nodded without enthusiasm. Too much of what the Druid had told him during their travels was suspect. This was no exception. No one could know the future or what it would require of a man. Not a spirit creature. Not even a seer like Ryer Ord Star. The best anyone could do was reveal glimpses out of context, and those could deceive.

"Meanwhile," Walker said, interrupting his thoughts, "I am giving you this to carry."

He reached beneath his black robes and produced the Sword of Shannara. It was sheathed in a soft leather scabbard, but the carving of the fist and the raised torch on the pommel were unmistakable.

Bek took it from the Druid and held it out before him, staring at it. "Do you think I will need it?"

The Druid's smile was unexpectedly bitter. "I think we will need whatever strengths we can call upon once we are off this airship. A talisman belongs in the hands of a bearer who can wield it. In the case of the Sword of Shannara, that bearer is you."

Bek thought about it for a moment and then nodded. "All right, I'll carry it. Not because I am afraid for myself, but because maybe I can be of some use to the others. That's the reason I went with Truls

Rohk into the ruins on Mephitic. That's the reason I agreed to use the sword at the Squirm. I came on this journey because I believed what you told me the night we met—that I could do something to help. I still believe it. I'm a part of this company, even if I don't know for sure yet what that part might be."

Walker bent to him. "Each of us has a part to play and all of us are still discovering what that part is. None of us is superfluous. Everyone is necessary. You are right to look out for your friends."

He put his hand on the boy's shoulder. "But remember that we can do little to look out for others if we forget to look out for ourselves. In the future, don't be too quick to discount what might be required to do that. It isn't always apparent beforehand. It isn't always possible to anticipate what is needed."

Bek had the distinct impression that Walker was talking about something besides the phoenix stone. But it was clear from his words that he had no intention of saying what it was. By now, the boy was used to veiled references and hidden meanings from the Druid, so he felt no real urgency to pursue the matter. Walker would tell him when he was ready and not before.

"Ahren and I made a pact to stick together," he said instead. "So the phoenix stone won't be far away. I can get it back from him anytime I choose."

Walker straightened, a distant look in his dark eyes. "Time to be going, Bek. Whatever happens, remember what I said about the magic."

He called out sharply to those waiting and beckoned them to follow.

Redden Alt Mer brought up the anchors and eased the *Jerle Shannara* across the still waters of the bay to a broad stretch of open shoreline. Using rope ladders, the search party descended from the airship, seventeen-strong—Walker, Bek, Quentin Leah, Panax, Ryer Ord Star, Joad Rish, Ahren Elessedil, Ard Patrinell, and nine

Elven Hunters. From there, they gathered up their weapons and supplies and stood together as the airship lifted off and sailed back along the channel that had brought her in. They watched until she was out of sight, then on Walker's command, they set out.

The Druid placed Ard Patrinell in charge, giving over to the Elf the responsibility for protecting the company. The Captain of the Home Guard sent a young woman named Tamis, a tracker, ahead some fifty yards to scout the way in and placed an Elven Hunter to either side to guard their flanks. The rest of the company he grouped by twos, placing Walker in the vanguard and Panax in the rear, with Elven Hunters warding them both. Quentin was given responsibility for the center of the formation and those who were not trained fighters, Joad Rish and Ryer Ord Star and Bek in particular.

Walker glanced at the boy from time to time as they proceeded, trying to take his measure, to judge how Bek felt about himself now that he knew so much more. It was difficult to do. Bek seemed to have adapted well enough to his increased responsibility for use of the magic of the wishsong and the Sword of Shannara. But Bek was a complex personality, not easily read, and it remained to be seen how he would react to the demands that his heritage might require of him down the road. As of now, he had only scratched the surface of what he could or would in all probability be asked to do. The boy simply didn't understand yet how enmeshed in all this he was and what that was likely to mean to him. Nor was there any easy or safe way to tell him.

Like it or not, Bek would grow increasingly difficult to manage. He was independent to begin with, but what control the Druid had maintained over him to date was mostly the result of what he knew that the boy didn't. Now that advantage was pretty much gone, and in the process Bek had grown distrustful of him. As matters stood, the boy was as likely to do what he felt like as what Walker suggested, and choices of that sort could prove fatal.

The Druid was reminded once again how far he had strayed from his vow to avoid falling into a Druid's manipulative ways. He could not escape the fact that he was becoming more like Allanon with the passing of every day. All of his good intentions and promises had come to nothing. It was a sobering conclusion, and it induced a deep and profound sadness. He could argue that at least he was aware of his failings, but what good was that if he was unable to correct them? He could justify everything and still feel as if he had betrayed himself utterly.

The company pressed deeper into the woods, climbing from the bay's coastline into the surrounding hills, burrowing deeper into the sun-speckled shadows and thickening woods. The ground was rough and uneven, crisscrossed by ravines and gullies, blocked entirely in places by deadfall and heavy brush. A handful of times they found their way blocked by cuts too deep and wide to cross. Twice they encountered clumps of trees that appeared to have been dropped by a storm, twisted masses of deadwood that ran for a quarter of a mile. Each time they had to back away from one approach and try another. Each time they were forced to change direction, and with each change it grew increasingly difficult to determine exactly where they were.

Walker carried a compass he had borrowed from Redden Alt Mer, but even so it was impossible to maintain a straight line of approach. The best the Druid could manage was to plot a course from where they had come, which was of dubious value. But the day stayed bright and warm, the sun a cheerful presence in the blue sky, and the sounds of birdsong comforting and reassuring. Nothing threatened from the shadows. Nothing dangerous appeared or gave sign of its presence. Nothing appeared out of the ordinary in a forested wilderness that could easily have been their own.

Even so, Walker was wary. Despite appearances, he knew what waited for them somewhere along the way. He would have preferred to have Truls Rohk foraging ahead to ward their approach, but there was no help for that. The Elven Hunters would have to do. They were well trained and able, but no one was as good at staying hidden as the shape-shifter. He wondered where the other was, if he had escaped detection aboard the airship of the Ilse Witch, if he was accomplishing something important. He shook his head at the thought. Whatever Truls was doing, it couldn't be as important as what he could be doing here.

Morning came and went, and still they trekked on through the forest without finding anything. The castaway's map had brought them to the bay and pointed them inland and that was as much direction as they were going to get. On the map, a dotted line led to an X that said Castledown. There was no explanation of what Castledown was. There was no description of how they might recognize it. Walker had to assume that its identity would be self-evident when they came across it. It wasn't the biggest assumption he had made in this business by any means, so he wasn't uncomfortable following it.

It was late in the afternoon when his faith was rewarded. They topped a steep rise through a heavily wooded draw and discovered all three Elven scouts clustered together waiting for them. Her pixie face solemn and expectant, Tamis pointed ahead.

It was hardly necessary for her to do so. The hillside before them fell away into a broad, deep valley that easily ran ten miles from end to end and another five across. Trees carpeted the slopes and ridges, a soft green ring in the afternoon sunlight. But across the entire valley floor, all ten miles wide and five miles deep of it, sprawled the ruins of a city. Not a city from the present, Walker realized at once. Even from where they stood, still a half mile away, that much was apparent. The buildings were low and flat, not tall like those of Eldwist had been in the land of the Stone King. Some were damaged, their surfaces cracked and broken, their edges ragged and sharp. Holes opened through walls to reveal twisted, burned-out interiors. Debris lay scattered everywhere, some of it rusted and pitted by weather, some of it overgrown with lichen and moss. There was a uniformity to the ruins that indicated clearly that no one had lived here for a very long time.

But what struck the Druid immediately about the city, even more so than its immense size, was that virtually everything was made of metal. Walls, roofs, and floors all gleamed with patches of metallic brightness. Even bits and pieces of the streets and passageways reflected the sun. As far as the eye could see, the ruins were composed of sheets and slabs and struts of metal. Scrub grasses and brush had fought their way up through gaps in the fittings like pods of sea life breaching in an open sea. Isolated groves of trees grew in tangled thickets that might have been parks, carefully tended once perhaps, gone wild now. Even in its present state, crumbling and deteriorated since the Great Wars had reduced it to an abandoned wreck, the nature of its once sleek, smooth condition was evident.

"Shades!" Panax hissed at his elbow, thinking perhaps of the ruins his people had once mined in the aftermath of the holocaust.

Walker nodded to himself. The ruins of Castledown were gigantic. He had never imagined something of this size could exist. How many people had there been in the world if this was an example of the massiveness of their cities? He knew from the Druid histories that the number had been large, much larger than now. But there had been thousands of cities then, not hundreds. How many of them had been this huge? Walker found himself suddenly overwhelmed by the images, the numbers, and the possibilities. He wondered exactly what it was they were going to find. For the first time, he found himself wondering if they were up to it.

Then it struck him suddenly that perhaps he had made an incorrect assumption. The more he stared at the ruins, the more unlikely it seemed that it had been built to house people. The look of the buildings was all wrong. Low and wide and flat, vast spaces with high windows and broad entrances, sprawling foundations with no personal spaces, they seemed better suited for something else. For warehousing, perhaps. For factories and construction yards.

For housing machines.

He glanced at those around him. All looked awestruck, staring at the city as if trying to comprehend its purpose, as if working to make it seem real. Then he noticed Ryer Ord Star. She stood apart from the others as she always did, but she was shaking, her eyes cast down and her fingers knotted tightly in the folds of her clothing. Her breath came in short, ragged gasps, and she was crying soundlessly. Walker moved next to her, placed his arm on her shoulders, and drew her slender body close.

"What's wrong?" he asked softly.

She glanced up at him momentarily, then shook her head and melted against him once more, burying her face in his robes. He held her quietly until she stilled—it took a few minutes, no more—then stepped away from her and ordered Ard Patrinell to move out.

They descended the valley slope to its floor, stopping in a wooded clearing a hundred yards back from the edge of the ruins to make camp for the night. By now the sun was brushing the valley rim west and would be down in another hour. It was too late to attempt any exploration of the city today. Walker felt confident that they had located Castledown and that what they had come to find was hidden somewhere within. How difficult it would be to uncover what he sought remained to be seen, but he preferred that their first foray be undertaken in daylight.

Alone, while the others set camp and prepared dinner, he walked to the edge of the city. He stood there in the waning light staring into the shadowed ruins, down long, broad avenues, through gaps in the metal walls, along rooflines long since reshaped by time and the ravages of a conflict he was grateful he had not been alive to see. The races of the present thought of a Druid's magic as powerful, but real power was unknown to them. Real power was born of science. He found himself wondering what it might have been like to live in those distant times, before the Old World was destroyed. How would it have felt to have power that could destroy entire cities? What sort of havoc would it play with your soul to be able to snuff out thousands of lives at a touch? It made him shiver to imagine it. It made him feel frightened and sick inside.

Perhaps that was what Ryer Ord Star was feeling. Perhaps that was why she cried.

Thinking of her triggered a memory of her vision of the islands and their protectors. It was what she had said after speaking of the keys that surfaced unexpectedly in his thoughts. He had almost forgotten it, dismissed it out of hand as obvious. *I see this in a haze of shadow that tracks you everywhere and seeks to place itself about you like a shroud.* He had believed her words referred to the Ilse Witch and her relentless pursuit of him.

But looking into the ruins of Castledown and feeling the presence of the thing that waited there like an itch against his skin, he knew he had been mistaken.

THIRTY

Morning arrived in a haze of mist and light rain. Crowded together in leaden skies, dark clouds hid the sun and foreshadowed a gloomy day. The air was windless and warm and smelled of damp earth and new leaves. Silence wrapped the world in a veil of hushed expectancy and whispered caution, and even the small comfort of yesterday's birdsong had disappeared.

In the valley's pale brume, the ruins of Castledown hunkered down in glistening, sharp-edged relief, dark metallic surfaces streaked bright green by rain-dampened lichen and moss.

Walker divided the search party into three groups. Ard Patrinell would take Ahren Elessedil, Joad Rish, and three of the nine Elven Hunters on the right flank. Quentin Leah and Panax would take another three Elven Hunters on the left. He would occupy the center with Bek, Ryer Ord Star, and the remaining three Hunters. They would enter the ruins with the center group slightly ahead of the other two, all of them spread out but in sight of one another. They would move directly through the city to its far side and then reverse their march displaced by the width of the search party. They would do this for as many times as it took to complete a sweep of the city, changing their route each time. Anything that appeared worth investigating would be given a look. If they failed to turn up what they were looking for today, they would resume their search on the morrow. It was a huge city. Even if they were quick and encountered no difficulties, it could take them more than a week.

Everyone was to stay quiet and listen carefully, he cautioned. There would be no talking. They were to watch out for one another and keep one eye on the leader of their group, taking directions from him. If something required a look, signal by hand or whistle. Stay low and use the buildings for cover. There was every reason to believe that an enemy who was on watch for intruders had laid traps throughout the city. What they had come to find would be carefully guarded.

"Which is what exactly?" Panax asked, an uneasy look in his eyes. Like the others, he was wrapped against the weather in a cloak and hood. In the misted gloom, they looked like wraiths. "What is it we've come to find, Walker?"

The Druid hesitated.

"We've come a long way not to be told now," the Dwarf pressed. Rain ran down his seamed face into his beard. "How are we supposed to find what we're looking for if we don't know what it is?"

A moment's silence followed. "Books," Walker answered softly. The silence returned and lengthened. "Of spells and magic," he added with a quick glance around. "Gathered during the time of the Old World, then lost in the Great Wars. Except that some of those spells and that magic may have been saved. Here, in Castledown. That's the treasure the map says is hidden here."

"Books," the Dwarf muttered in disbelief.

"They will be of immense value to the races, if we find them," Walker assured him. "More so than you can imagine. More so than anything else we might have set out to find. But your skepticism is not unwarranted. As far as we know, no books survived the Great Wars. They would have been one of the first things destroyed, if not by fire, then by time and weather. The writings of the Old

World were lost two thousand years ago, and only our oral story-telling traditions have preserved the information they contained. Even that small knowledge was diluted and changed over time, so that much of it was rendered useless. What books we have now were assembled by the Druids during the First and Second Councils at Paranor. The Elves have some at Arborlon and the Federation some in Arishaig, but most are kept in the Druid's Keep. But they are books of this world and not the old. So if there are books here that have survived, they will have been sealed away. That they are books may not be immediately apparent. Their form may have been changed."

"If the books are numerous and have retained their original look, it will take a large building to house them," Bek offered quietly.

Walker nodded. "We begin our search with that in mind. We search for anything that might serve as a safehold, a container, or a storehouse. We might not know it when we see it. We will have to be open-minded. Remember, too, that we've come here to discover what became of Kael Elessedil's expedition and the Elfstones he carried with him."

No one said anything. After a moment, Quentin adjusted the Sword of Leah where it was strapped across his back and glanced at the sky. "Looks like the rain's letting up," he advised to no one in particular.

"Let's get on with it," Panax added with a grunt.

They set out then, crossing the open ground between the forested valley slope and the ruins, a line of dark ghosts approaching through the haze. They entered the city in three loosely knit groups set about fifty yards apart. They moved swiftly at first, finding mostly rubble amid the shells of smaller buildings that contained machines and apparatuses that sat rusted and dead. They had no idea what they were looking at for the most part, although some of the equipment had the look of weapons. A thick layer of dust had settled over everything, and there was no indication that anyone had come this way recently. Nothing had been disturbed or changed with the passing of the years. Everything was frozen in time.

Walker was aware of Ryer Ord Star pressing close to him, enough so that they were almost touching. Last night, when the others were asleep, she had come to him and told him what had frightened her so. In the hushed darkness of a moonless night, she had knelt beside him and whispered in a voice so soft that he could barely make her out.

"The ruins are the maze I saw in my vision."

He touched her thin shoulder. "Are you certain?"

Her eyes were bright and staring. "I felt the presence of the other two, as well. As I stood on the rim of the valley and looked down into the maze, I felt them. The ribbons of fire and the metal dogs. They are here, waiting for me. For all of us."

"Then we will be ready for them." She was shaking again, and he put his arm about her to keep her from her fear, which he could feel through her clothing as if it were alive. "Don't be afraid, Ryer. Your warnings keep us safe. They did so on Flay Creech, on Shatterstone, and on Mephitic. They will do so here."

But she shrank from the words. "No, Walker. What waits for us here is much bigger and stronger. It is embedded in the ruins and in the earth on which they rest. Old and hungry and evil, it waits for us. I can feel it breathing. I feel its pulse in the movement of the air and the rise and fall of the temperature. It is too much for us. Too much."

He held her quietly in the velvet darkness, trying to comfort her, listening to the sound of her breathing as it steadied and slowed. Finally, she rose and began to move away.

"I will die here, Walker," she whispered back to him.

She believed it, he knew, and perhaps she had seen something in her visions that gave her cause to do so. Perhaps she only sensed it might be so, but sometimes even that was enough to make something happen. He would watch out for her, would try to keep her from harm. It was what he would have done anyway. It was what he would do for all of them, if it was within his power. But even a Druid could do no more than try.

He glanced over his shoulder. She had dropped back to walk with Bek, keeping pace with the boy, as if finding some comfort in his silent presence. Fair enough. She could do worse than stay close to him.

He looked ahead into the gloom, into the maze of the ruins, and he could feel the seer's vision, mysterious and dark, drawing them on like bait on a hook.

Miles away, back toward the channel's headwaters, but well clear of the Squirm, Redden Alt Mer stood at the bow railing of the *Jerle Shannara* and looked off into the gloom. The weather was impossible. If anything, it was worse now than when they had sailed inland two days ago. Yesterday had started out fine, but the sunshine and clear skies had gradually given way to heavy mist and clouds on the journey downriver. They had anchored the airship several miles from the ice, safely back from the clashing pillars and the bitter cold, and had gone to sleep, hoping to continue on this morning as Walker had wanted.

But the haze was so thick now that Alt Mer could barely make out the cliffs to either side and could not see the sky overhead at all. Worse, the mist was shifting in a steady wind, swirling so badly that it cast shadows everywhere and rendered it virtually impossible to navigate safely. In these narrow confines, with treacherous peaks, glaciers, and winds all around, it would be foolhardy to attempt to venture out of the channel when they could not see where they were going. Like it or not, they would have to wait for the weather to clear, even if it meant delaying their departure a day or two.

Rue Meridian came up beside him, long red hair as darkened by the damp as his own. It wasn't raining, but a fine mist settled over them like gauze. She looked out over the railing at the fog and shook her head. "Soup."

"Soup that Mother Nature feels a need to stir," he amended with a weary sigh. "All for the purpose of keeping us locked down for the foreseeable future, I expect."

"We could sail back up the channel and hope for a break in the clouds. Inland, it might be better."

He nodded. "It might, but the farther back up the channel we go, the harder it becomes to track our course. Better to do it from as close to the coastline as possible."

She snorted. "Have you forgotten who you have as your navigator?"

"Not likely. Anyway, a day of waiting won't hurt us. We'll lie to until tomorrow. If it doesn't clear up by then, we'll do as you say and sail back up the channel and try to find a cloud break."

Her eyes found his momentarily. "No one much cares for this sitting around, Big Red." She glanced off into the haze. "If you listen closely, you can hear those pillars clashing. You can hear the ice crack and the glaciers shift. Far away, off in the haze." She shook her head. "It's spooky."

"Don't listen, then."

She stood with him a moment longer, then moved off. He didn't care for the waiting either or their proximity to the Squirm or anything about their situation, but he knew better than to overreact. He would be patient if he must.

After a few minutes, he walked back to where Spanner Frew sat working on a diapson crystal that had been damaged in their collision with *Black Moclips*. The Rover Captain was still perplexed at the appearance of the ship. In all likelihood it meant she was being sailed by a Federation crew. That gave Alt Mer a distinct advantage with his Rover crew, but not one he was eager to test. *Black Moclips* was much bigger and stronger than the *Jerle Shannara*, and in close quarters could probably reduce it to kindling. It would be strange in any case to do battle with a ship he had flown for so long and of which he had grown so fond.

"Making any progress?" he asked the shipwright.

The big man scowled. "I'd make more if people didn't distract me with foolish questions. This is delicate work."

Alt Mer watched him for a moment. "Did you get a good look at that other airship when she rammed us?"

"As good as your own."

"Did you recognize her?"

"*Black Moclips*. Hard to mistake her. Doesn't give me a good feeling to know she's the one chasing us, but on the other hand this ship's quicker and more responsive." He paused to hold the crystal up to the pale light, squinting as he examined it. "Just keep her from getting too close to us, and we'll be fine."

The Rover Captain folded his arms within his cloak. "Can't be sure of doing anything on a hunt like this. We may have to stand and face her at some point. I don't relish that happening, I can tell you."

Spanner Frew stood up, gave the crystal a final check, then grunted in satisfaction. "Won't be a problem today, at least. Nothing can sail in this."

"Not safely, anyway," Alt Mer amended. He resumed staring out into the gloom. The wind had picked up, and the airship was rocking with its sudden gusts. The Rover Captain walked slowly across the deck, checking things in a perfunctory manner, giving himself something to do besides think about their predicament. A low whistle had begun to develop, faint and distant still, but unmistakable. He glanced in its direction, back toward the Squirm. Maybe he should move the *Jerle Shannara* farther upriver. Maybe they should find a cove in which to take shelter.

He walked the aft railing, the sound of the wind enveloping him like a shroud, strangely warm and comforting. He stopped to listen to it, amazed at its appeal. Winds of this sort were rare in a sailor's life and as out of place to this land as yesterday's weather. They belonged in another climate and another part of the world. How could glaciers and snowpacks exist in such close proximity to warm air and green trees?

His thoughts drifted, and he found himself remembering his

childhood in March Brume, days he had spent on land, wandering the forests, playing with other children. Those days had been few and passed swiftly, but their memory lingered. Perhaps it was because he had spent so much of his life on the sea and in the air. Perhaps it was because he could never have them back again.

Something moved in the mist, but staring blankly at its darkening form, he could not seem to put a name to it.

To one side, a Rover slid to the decking and lay there, silent and unmoving, asleep. Redden Alt Mer stared in disbelief, then pushed away from the railing to go to him. But his legs wouldn't work, and his eyes were so heavy he could barely keep them open. All he could seem to focus on was the sound of the wind, risen to a new pitch, wrapping him about, closing him away.

Too late, he realized what was happening.

He staggered a few steps and fell to his knees. On the decks of the airship, the Rovers lay in heaps. Only Furl Hawken was still upright in the pilot box, if barely so, hanging on to the handgrips, draped over the controls.

A huge, dark shape had come alongside the *Jerle Shannara*. Redden Alt Mer heard the sound of grappling hooks locking in place and caught a glimpse of a cloaked form approaching through the mist. A face lifted out of the shadows of a hood, a young woman who looked at him with blue eyes that were as cold as glacier ice. Helpless, he stared back at her with undisguised fury.

Then everything went black.

Bek glanced over at the strained, frightened face of Ryer Ord Star and smiled reassuringly as they moved with the others of the company through the deepening gloom. The rain had turned to a fine mist. The seer blinked against the droplets that gathered on her eyelids, and brushed at her face with her sleeve. She moved closer to Bek.

The boy peered left and right to where the groups led by

Quentin and Ard Patrinell navigated the misted ruins. He caught a glimpse of his cousin and the Captain of the Home Guard, but found no sign of Ahren Elessedil. The buildings were growing larger now and took longer to get around. At times the searchers were separated by walls fifty feet high and would catch only momentary glimpses of one another through sagging doors and burned-out entries. The buildings were all the same, either empty or full of rusted machinery. In some, banks of casings sat in long rows, studded with dials and tiny windows that resembled the blank, staring eyes of dead animals. In some, machines so large they dwarfed the searchers hunkered down like great beasts fallen into endless slumber. Shadows filled the open spaces, layering machines and debris alike, stretching from one building to the next, a dark spiderweb tangled through the city.

He looked again for Ahren, but everyone in the Elven Hunter group looked pretty much the same, hooded and cloaked against the damp. A sudden wave of fear and doubt washed over him. He forced his gaze back to Walker, who was striding just ahead. He was being stupid. It was probably the look on Ryer Ord Star's face that infused him with such uneasiness. It was probably the day, so dark and misted. It was probably this place, this city.

In the silence and gloom, you could imagine anything.

He thought about the books that Walker had come to find and was troubled anew. What would the people of the Old World be doing with books of spells? No real magic had been practiced in that time. Magic had died out with the Faerie world, and even the Elves, who had survived when so many other species had perished, had lost or forgotten virtually all of theirs. It was only with the emergence of the new Races and the convening of the Druids at Paranor that the process of recovering the magic had begun. Why would Walker believe that books of magic from before the Great Wars even existed?

The more he worried over the matter, the more obsessed with it he became. Soon he found himself wondering about the creature that had lured them here. Ostensibly to steal their magic, it seemed—yet if it already had books of magic at its disposal, why not use these? Surely they were written in a language it could understand. What was it about the magic that Walker and Quentin and he possessed that was so much more attractive? What was it that had doomed Kael Elessedil's expedition thirty years earlier? He could repeat everything that Walker had told him, had told them all, and still not get past this gaping hole of logic in the Druid's explanation.

They passed through a cluster of large empty warehouses into a section of low, flat platforms that might have been buildings or something else entirely. Windowless and sealed all about, they appeared to lack any purpose. Pitted with rust and streaked with patches of moss and lichen, they shimmered in the rain like huge ruined mirrors. Walker took a moment to study one, placing his hands on its surface, closing his eyes in concentration. After a moment he stepped away, shook his head at the others, and motioned for them to continue on.

The platform buildings disappeared behind them in the mist. Ahead, a broad metal-carpeted clearing that was studded with odd-shaped walls and partitions materialized out of the gloom. The clearing stretched away for hundreds of yards in all directions, and dominated the surrounding buildings by virtue of its size alone. The walls and partitions ranged in height from five to ten feet and ran in length anywhere from twenty to thirty more. They were unconnected to each other, seemingly placed at random, seemingly constructed without purpose. They did not form rooms. They did not contain furniture or even machinery. Here, unlike the surrounding warehouses, there was no rubble. Or plants, grasses, and scrub. Everything was swept clean and smooth.

At the center of the square, barely visible through the gloom, an obelisk rose more than a hundred feet. A single door opened into it, massive and recessed, but the door was sealed. Above this entryway, a red light blinked on and off in steady sequence.

Walker brought them to a halt with a hand signal and stood staring into the tangle of half walls and partitions to where the obelisk sat like a watchtower, its blinking light a vigilant eye. Bek searched the ruins about them, his uneasiness newly heightened. Nothing moved. He turned back to Walker. The Druid was still studying the obelisk. It was clear that he sensed the possibility of a trap, but equally clear that he believed he must step into it.

Ryer Ord Star bent close to Bek. "It is the entrance we seek," she whispered. Her breathing was quick and anxious. "The door to the tower opens into Castledown. The keys he carries fit the door's lock."

Bek stared at her, wondering how she knew this, but she was staring at the Druid, the boy already forgotten.

Walker turned. His eyes were troubled and his face bore a resigned look. "Wait here for me." His voice was so low that Bek could barely hear him. He gestured at the Elven Hunters. "All of you."

He straightened and signaled to Quentin and Panax on his left and Ard Patrinell on his right to remain where they were.

Alone, he started toward the tower.

The Ilse Witch walked the deck of the *Jerle Shannara*, making certain all of the Rovers were asleep. One by one, she checked them, then signaled for Cree Bega to come aboard and ordered him to send one of his Mwellrets below to search for anyone she might have missed. The chosen ret disappeared down the hatchway and returned again in only moments, shaking his head.

She nodded, satisfied. It had been easier than she had thought. "Take them below and lock them in the storerooms," she ordered, dismissing Cree Bega with a gesture. "Separate them."

She walked to the pilot box and climbed up to stand next to the big Rover slumped over the controls. She stood in the box and stared out over the length and breadth of the captured airship, taking in its look and feel. A sleek and able vessel, she saw. Quicker and more maneuverable than her own. Mwellrets were swarming over the sides of *Black Moclips* to haul the sleeping Rovers belowdecks. She watched them without interest. The magic of her wishsong had overcome the Rovers before they knew what was happening. Not expecting it or able to fight it and without the Druid to ward them, they had been powerless. Her spy had provided her with a link to the *Jerle Shannara* from the beginning, and it was easy enough to get close once she was through the Squirm. Using the wishsong to put the unsuspecting crew to sleep was child's play. Transforming her magic to sound like the wind, soft and lulling and irresistible, was all it took.

Even getting past the ice pillars was not much of a challenge, although it required a little inventiveness. Choosing to avoid that approach completely, she used her magic to harness one of the Shrikes that nested on the outer cliffs, mounted it, and had it fly them over the top. Even with the heavy fog, she was able to guide *Black Moclips* without too much risk. The Shrike was a native and knew its way in and out of the mountains well. The winds were tricky, but not so much so that the airship couldn't manage them. She had no idea how Walker had managed to navigate the pillars, believing his own magic, while powerful in some ways, not sufficiently adaptable for this. Her spy hadn't been able to communicate that information. Not that it mattered. Both of them had made it through. They were still on course for their confrontation.

Except that now, for the first time, she had the upper hand. He was ashore and marooned there, even if he didn't realize it yet. Without the use of an airship, he was helpless to escape her. Sooner or later, she would track him down, either on foot or from the air. The only question that remained to be answered was whether she would get to him before the thing that waited in the ruins did.

Even in this, she had an advantage the Druid did not. She knew what the thing was. Or more to the point, what it wasn't. She had gone inside Kael Elessedil's ruined mind to discover why he had been lost for thirty years. By doing so, she had seen through his eyes what it was that had captured him. She had witnessed the tearing out of his tongue and the gouging out of his eyes. She had witnessed the uses to which he had been put. Walker knew none of this. If he wasn't careful, he might come to the same end. That would achieve her goal of destroying him, but cheat her of the personal satisfaction she would derive by seeing him die at her hands.

Yes, Walker would have to be very careful. The thing that had lured them here was patient and its reach was long. It was dangerous in ways she had not encountered before. So she would have to be careful, too. But she was always careful, always on guard against the unexpected. She had trained herself to be so.

Cree Bega sidled up to her. "The little peopless are all ssafely locked away," he hissed.

"Leave five of your rets to make sure they stay that way," she ordered. "Commander Kett will assign two of his crew to watch over the ship. The rest of us will take the *Black Moclips* after those already ashore."

I'm coming for you, Druid, she thought triumphantly. *Can you feel me getting close?*

She climbed down from the pilot box, wrapped in grim fury and fierce determination, and walked back through the mist and gloom.

When the attack came, Walker was a little more than halfway between the others of the company and the obelisk, deep inside the maze of half walls and partitions. He heard a sharp click, like a lock opening or a trigger released, and he threw himself down just as a slender thread of brilliant red fire lanced overhead. Without even thinking, he turned the Druid fire on its source and fused the tiny aperture through which the thread had appeared.

Instantly, a dozen more threads crisscrossed the area in which he lay, some of them burning paths across the metal carpet, seeking him out. He rolled quickly into the shelter of a wall and burned shut one opening after another, snuffing out the threads, exploding apertures and entire sections of wall, filling the hazy air with smoke and the acrid stench of scorched metal.

Then he was on his feet and moving swiftly toward the obelisk, sensing that whatever controlled the fire could be found there. His robes hindered his progress, prevented him from running, and kept him to a quick shuffle. *Ribbons of fire.* He repeated the words as he angled his way through the maze, ducking behind walls and through openings as the slender threads sought him out, Ryer Ord Star's vision come to life.

He had gotten maybe twenty yards deeper into the maze when the walls began to move. Without warning, they started to raise and lower, a shifting mass of metal that cut off some approaches and opened others, whole sections materializing out of the smooth, polished floor while others disappeared. It was so disorienting and unexpected that he slowed momentarily, and the ribbons of fire began to close on him once more, new ones stabbing out from sections of wall closer to where he hesitated, old ones shifting to target him. In desperation, he threw a wide band of his own fire back at them, knocking some askew, destroying others. He heard shouts behind him, rising from behind a screen of smoke and mist, from out of a well of emptiness and darkness.

"Don't come in here!" he shouted in warning, hearing the echoes cried of his voice come back at him.

Fire lances burned in faint glimmerings through the haze, penetrating the darkness with killing quickness. Screams rose, and he felt his heart sink at the realization that at least some of those he led had not heard him. He started back for them, but the walls shifted anew, the fire threads barred his path, and he was forced to back away.

Get to the obelisk! he screamed at himself in the silence of his mind.

Heat radiated through his body as he turned and hurried ahead once more, sweat mingling with beads of mist on his taut face. Something moved to one side, and he caught the sound of skittering, of metal scraping metal. Fire exploded next to him, barely missing his head, and he ducked and moved faster, twisting and turning through the shifting walls, the changing maze, losing track of everything but the need to reach the obelisk. He felt a stickiness on his hand, and glanced down to find his fingers red with his blood. A fire lance had opened a gash in his arm just above his wrist.

Ignoring the wound, he glanced up to find the obelisk directly in front of him. Impulsively, he darted out from behind the wall that had sheltered him right into the path of a creeper.

For a second he was so stunned he just stopped where he was and stared, his mind a jumble of confusion. What was a creeper doing here? Wait, it wasn't a creeper at all, it just looked like one. It was spidery like a creeper, had a creeper's legs and body, but it was all metal with no fusing of flesh, no melding of animate and inanimate, of matter and material . . .

There was no more time for speculation. It reached for him, pincers extending at the end of flexible limbs, and he thrust out his arm in a warding motion and sent the Druid fire flying into it. The creeper was rocked backwards on its spindly legs and then toppled. It lay writhing, no longer able to rise, thrashing as it melted and burned. Walker raced past. It was constructed entirely of metal, just as he'd thought. He caught a glimpse of another, then two more, three, four; they were all around, coming toward him.

Metal dogs!

All of the components of Ryer Ord Star's vision had come together—the maze, the ribbons of fire, and the metal dogs—pieces of a nightmare that would consume them if he couldn't find a way to stop it. He sidestepped another fire lance, dashed across an opening between several shifting walls, and leapt onto the threshold of the doorway to the obelisk.

Behind him, there was chaos. He could hear shouts and screams, the rasp of metal on metal, the steady hiss of fire threads, and the boom of explosions. He could see the distinctive flash of Quentin Leah's blade. He could smell the magic and taste the smoke.

The entire company was under attack, and he was doing nothing to help them.

Quickly! Get into the tower!

He spied the slots for the keys in a raised metal surface to one side of the door. Swiftly he produced the keys from his robes and inserted them into the thin, flat openings. The keys slid into place easily, a bank of lights flashed in the black metal surface of the wall, and the door eased aside to give him entry. He stepped through quickly, the sounds of the pursuing creepers spurring him on, and the door closed behind him.

He stood blinded by the blackness for a moment and waited for his vision to return. He saw the lights first, some steady and unchanging, some blinking on and off, some green, some red, some yellow. There were hundreds of them, ahead somewhere, tiny beacons glowing in the dark. When he could make out the surfaces of floor and walls and ceiling sufficiently to find his way, he started toward them. The controls to the fire threads and the creepers would be there. This was a kingdom of machines, and the machines in this tower would control the machines in the maze. Shut down the one, and you shut down the others.

It was his last thought before the floor opened beneath him, and he tumbled away into space.

THIRTY-ONE

Rue Meridian woke when her head banged against the wall of the storeroom in the forward hold. She tried to roll away and found herself pinned to the floor by a heavy weight. The weight turned out to be Furl Hawken, who was still unconscious, his bulk sprawled across her torso. She could hear the wind howling like a scorched cat and feel the pitch and roll of the ship. A storm was in progress, and a bad one at that. With every fresh gust and new jolt she was thrown headfirst back toward the offending wall.

Squirming and wriggling, she worked herself free of Hawk and pushed herself into a sitting position, her back to the bulkhead. For a moment she couldn't remember what had happened, then couldn't figure out how. What was she doing down here, belowdecks? She had been working with another Rover on setting a fresh radian draw, tightening it down, when that wind had come up, soft and lulling, singing to her like her mother once had.

And put her to sleep, she thought ruefully, beginning to see exactly what had happened.

She climbed to her feet and staggered across the room through the lurching of the ship to the door. She tried the handle. Locked.

No surprise there. She grimaced and exhaled sharply. The Rovers were all prisoners or dead, overpowered in all likelihood by the Ilse Witch. Somehow she had gotten to them when they weren't expecting it, put them to sleep, and locked them below. Or worse, it wasn't the Ilse Witch at all, but the thing that Walker had gone inland to find. Or was it worse, the one rather than the other? She rubbed her head where it had banged against the wall, wondering how many jolts it had taken to wake her. Too many, she decided, feeling an ache work its way through her skull and down into her neck.

She glanced around the room. It was empty except for Hawk and herself. The others were somewhere else. There were crates of supplies stacked against the walls, but they contained light sheaths, radian draws, parse tubes, ropes, and the like. No heavy clubs or axes. No sharp objects or keen blades to rely on. No weapons of any kind.

She looked down hopefully for her sword and throwing knives, even though she knew her weapons belt was gone. She reached into her boot. The dagger she hid there was gone, as well. Whoever put her here was smart enough to search her before locking her in. Hawk's weapons would have been taken, too. Escaping confinement was not going to be easy.

But it would, of course, be possible.

Little Red never once stopped to think otherwise. It wasn't in her nature to do so. She did not panic and she did not despair. She was a Rover, and she had been taught from a very early age that Rovers had to look out for themselves, that no one else was going to do it for them. She was locked in the hold of her own ship, and it was up to her to get free. She already knew she was going to do that. Someone had made a big mistake in assuming she wasn't. Someone was going to pay for putting her here.

A sudden violent pitch of the airship sent her staggering to one side, and she was barely able to keep her feet while righting herself. Something bad was happening topside, and she had to get up there quickly to find out what it was. It didn't feel as if the people who had locked her in had any idea what they were doing with the ship. If there was a storm in progress, it would take accomplished sailors to see the *Jerle Shannara* safely through. She thought briefly of the Squirm's grinding pillars, of the sheer cliffs surrounding them, and of their proximity to both, and she felt a tug of concern deep in her stomach.

She worked her way over to Furl Hawken and began to shake him. "Wake up, Hawk!" She kept her voice low enough that anyone standing outside the door wouldn't hear. Not that there was much chance with the storm howling all about them. "Hawk!" She slapped his face. "Wake up!"

His eyes fluttered and he grunted like a bull. Slowly he rolled onto his side, clasping his head, muttering to himself. Then he sat up, running his big hands through his tangled blond hair and beard. "What hit me? I can feel it all the way down to my teeth!"

The airship did a quick pitch and roll, causing him to brace himself hurriedly with his hands. "Shades!"

"Get up," she ordered, pulling at him. "We've been drugged and locked up, and the ship's in the hands of incompetents. Let's do something about it."

He lumbered to his feet, steadying himself by leaning on her shoulder as the ship shook with the force of the wind. "Where's Big Red?"

"Can't say for sure. He's not here, anyway." She hadn't allowed herself to think what might have happened to her brother. Locked in another storeroom, probably aft of this one, she told herself. They'd probably been separated to render them more manageable. Alive, though. She wouldn't consider the alternative.

She moved back over to the door and stood with her ear pressed against the wood, listening. All she could hear was the howl of the wind, the singing of the draws, and the rattle of something not properly tied down. She sat with her back to the wall and pulled off her boot. Inside the heel, tucked into the leather, was a metal hook.

"I see they didn't get quite everything," Hawk chuckled, coming over to stand next to her.

She pulled on her boot and stood up. "Did they miss anything you were carrying?" she asked.

He reached under his left arm, found a small opening in the seam of his stiff leather vest, and removed a long, slender blade. "Could be." He grinned. "Enough to get us close to some real weapons, if we're lucky."

"We're Rovers, Hawk," she said, bending to the lock in the door. "We make our own luck."

Kneeling with one leg braced against the door, she inserted the pick into the lock and began to work it around. The lock was new and its workings easily tapped. It gave in less than a minute, the latch snapping open as she pulled down on the handle, the door giving way. She cracked it and looked out into the passageway. Shadows cast by oil lamps and ropes hung from pegs in the walls flickered and danced with the rolling of the ship. At the passageway's forward end, a bulky form braced against the shipwalls and stared up the ladder at the hatchway.

Rue Meridian ducked back inside the storeroom and eased the door closed again. "One guard, a big guy. I can't tell who or what he is. We have to get past him, though. Do you want to handle him or shall I?"

Furl Hawken tightened his grip on the knife. "I'll deal with him, Little Red. You get to the others."

They stared at each other in the dim light, breathing quickly, faces flushed and anxious. "Be careful, Hawk," she told him.

They went out the door on cat's paws, sliding silently into the shadowed hallway. Furl Hawken glanced back at her, then started toward the guard. The *Jerle Shannara* continued to shake and sway in the grip of the storm, the wind howling so fiercely that the guard seemed unable to think of anything else. A crash jarred the decking, something falling from a height, a loosened spar probably. The guard stared upward, frozen in place. Rue Meridian glanced at the doors of the storerooms closest, two only. The smaller held their water and ale in large casks. There was no extra room for prisoners in there. The other contained foodstuffs. That was a possibility, but the larger holds lay farther aft.

Another few steps, Rue Meridian was thinking, watching Hawk's cautious progress, when the hatchway opened, and a rain-drenched figure started down the stairs.

He caught sight of the Rovers immediately, screamed a warning to the guard with his back turned, and bolted up the ladder. The guard wheeled at once toward Furl Hawken, a wicked-looking short sword in one clawed hand. Hawk closed with him at once, and Rue Meridian could hear the impact of their collision. She caught a glimpse of the guard's reptilian face, scaled and glistening with rain that had washed down the hatch. *A Mwellret!* The other man, by the look of his uniform, was a Federation soldier. She felt a cold sinking in the pit of her stomach. She and Hawk were no match for Mwellrets. She had to stop the fleeing soldier from giving warning to whatever others there were.

Impulsively, she went after him, leaping past Hawk and the Mwellret. Bounding up the ladder through the hatchway, she charged onto the open deck into the teeth of the storm, the wind whipping so wildly that it threatened to tear her clothes from her body, the rain drenching her in seconds. The ship wheeled and twisted in the storm's grip, its light sheaths down, its draws gathered in, stripped bare as she should be in this weather, but for some reason drifting in powerless confusion. Rue Meridian took in everything in a heart-beat as she raced after the soldier. She caught up with him amid-ships, just below the pilot box, where a second soldier struggled with the airship's steering, and she threw herself on his back. Locked together, they rolled across the deck and into the foremast. The soldier was so desperate to escape, he didn't even think to draw his weapons. She did so for him, yanking loose the long knife he wore at his belt and plunging it into his chest as he thrashed beneath her.

Leaving him sprawled out and dying on the deck, she sprang back to her feet. The Federation soldier in the pilot box was screaming for help, but there was nothing she could do about that. If she killed him, the ship would be completely out of control. The wind was obscuring his cries, so perhaps no one would hear. She started aft. Without a safety line to tether her, she was forced to creep ahead, bent low to the deck, taking handholds wherever she could find them, slipping and sliding on the rain-soaked wood. Through clouds of mist and sheets of rain, she glimpsed the rugged gray walls of the channel's cliffs, rising through the mist. Somewhere not too distant, she could hear the pillars of the Squirm clash hungrily.

She came upon another of the Mwellrets almost immediately. It emerged from the gloom of the aft mast carrying a coil of rope. It was staggering and stumbling with the movements of the airship, but it threw down the rope, drew out a long knife, and came for her at once. She dodged away from it. The Mwellret was much stronger than she was; if it got hold of her, she would not get free unless she killed it, and she had no reason to expect she could manage that. But there was nowhere for her to go. She scrambled for the starboard railing, then turned to face it. It charged after her recklessly, and she waited for its momentum to carry it close, dropped into a crouch, and whipped her legs into its heavy boots, causing it to lose its balance. It staggered past her, fighting to stay upright against the pitch and roll of the ship, slammed into the railing, toppled over the side, and was gone.

That was easy, she thought giddily, suppressing a ridiculous urge to laugh. *Bring on another!*

She had just regained her feet when her wish was granted. Two more of the creatures appeared through the aft hatchway and started toward her.

Shades! She stood her ground in the swirl of wind and rain, trying desperately to think what to do. She had only her long knife, a poor weapon to keep two Mwellrets at bay under any circumstances. She edged along the railing, trying to gain some time, to think of a way to get past them and down the hatchway to where she believed Big Red and the others were imprisoned. But the Mwellrets had already guessed her intention and were spreading out to cut off any attempt she might make to get past them.

An instant later, a wild-eyed Furl Hawken emerged from the forward hatch, covered in blood and shouting like a madman. With a Mwellret's short sword in one hand and his dagger in the other, he charged bowlegged and crouched at Little Red's attackers. They turned instinctively to defend themselves, but they were too slow and too unsteady. The burly Rover slammed into the closest and sent it sprawling, then catapulted into the second, plunging his dagger into the cloaked body over and over while the Mwellret roared.

Rue Meridian broke at once for the hatchway. Hawk had bought her the precious seconds she needed. Leaping heedlessly across debris and through slicks, she gained the aft hatch—only to have yet another of the Mwellrets heave through the opening to greet her.

This time, she had no chance to escape. It was on top of her almost instantly, its broad sword swinging at her head. She slipped trying to avoid the blow and went down, flailing helplessly. But a sudden lurch of the airship saved her, and the Mwellret's blow went wide, the blade burying itself in the wood of the deck. She rolled to her feet as the Mwellret struggled to free its weapon, and slammed her long knife into its side. The Mwellret jerked away with a hiss, released its grip on the sword, and fastened its clawed hands about her neck. Down they went in a heap, and Rue Meridian could feel her head begin to swim. She tried to yank free the knife for another blow, but it was caught in the Mwellret's leather clothing. She kicked and struggled against the tightening hands, hammered at the muscular body with her fists, and fought like a trapped moor cat. Nothing worked to free her. Spots danced before her eyes, and her strength began to ebb. She could feel the Mwellret's breath on her face and smell its stench.

TERRY BROOKS

Groping desperately for a weapon, she found the pick she had stuck in her pocket after she'd left the storeroom. Yanking it out, she jammed it into her attacker's hooded eye.

The Mwellret reared back in pain and surprise, releasing its grip on her throat. She twisted clear instantly, scrambling away as her adversary thrashed about on the decking, its hands clawing at its bloodied eye. Using both hands and what remained of her fading strength, she worked free the Mwellret's embedded sword and jammed it all the way through the writhing body.

Drenched in blood and rain, tangled knots of her long red hair plastered against her face, she dropped to her knees, gasping for air. Rain beat down ferociously, the wind howled and gusted, and the airship twisted and lurched as if alive. Little Red felt the decking shudder and creak beneath her, as if everything was coming apart.

A booming crash brought her head up with a jerk. The lower aft spar had broken loose and fallen on top of the pilot box. The Federation soldier who had been struggling with the steering lay crushed and dying in a mass of splintered wood and bent metal. The *Jerle Shannara* was flying out of control.

Then she saw Furl Hawken. Almost buried by broken parts and debris, he lay atop one Mwellret and close beside another, bleeding from a dozen wounds, his face a mask of blood. A long knife was buried in his back and a dagger in his side. His short sword was still clutched in one hand. He was staring right at her, blue eyes open and fixed. He seemed to be looking past her to something she could not see.

She choked back a sob as tears filled her eyes and her throat tightened in a knot. *Hawk! No!* She pushed herself to her feet and started toward him, already knowing she was too late, but refusing to believe it. Staggering against the force of the wind and the lurching of the airship, she shook her head and began to cry, unable to help herself, unable to stop.

Then the Mwellret that lay next to the dead man turned slowly to face her. Blood streaked its reptilian face and cloaked body, and

441

its eyes were dazed and furious. Lurching to its feet, it yanked the long knife from Hawk's back and started toward her.

She retreated slowly, realizing she had no weapon with which to defend herself. When she stumbled over the Mwellret she had killed, her hand brushed against the sword that jutted from its body. Turning, she pulled the blade free and faced her opponent.

"Come get me, ret!" she taunted through anger and tears and a terrible sadness.

The Mwellret said nothing, approaching cautiously, warily through the haze. Rue Meridian dropped into a crouch, working to keep her balance, to steady herself against the rolling of the airship. She found herself wishing she had her throwing knives. Perhaps she could have killed the Mwellret before it reached her if she did. But the sword would have to do. Both hands gripped the pommel as she held the blade stretched out before her. There was no time to find the others and no one else to turn to for help. There was only her. If she died, they were all lost. Given the condition of the ship, they might all be lost anyway.

Like Hawk.

The Mwellret was on top of her before she realized it, a huge dark shadow. It had masked its approach with a hissing sound that was so hypnotic and distracting that for a few precious seconds she had lost all sense of her danger. It was only her tears that saved her. Hands still clasped about the sword's handle, she wiped at them with her sleeve, saw the Mwellret right in front of her, and swung the weapon without thinking. The blade slipped under the Mwellret's raised arm and bit deeply into its side. Blood spurted, and the creature staggered into her, striking at her chest with the long knife. She deflected the blow, but the blade ripped down her arm and into her thigh. She cried out, seizing the Mwellret's arm and pinning it against her body, fighting the shock that threatened to paralyze her.

Locked together, they surged across the decking, each fighting to upend the other, to gain a killing hold. The contest was equal; the Mwellret was stronger, but it was badly injured and weakened from loss of blood. Unable to find anything better, it used its claws as a weapon, shredding Rue Meridian's cloak and tunic and finally her skin. She shrieked in pain and fury as the claws tore at her, then threw herself backwards in an effort to break free. Rover and Mwellret careened into the masthead and went down. As they did, the latter's grip loosened, and Little Red kicked free. But the Mwellret did not lose contact with her entirely, its clawed fingers grasping one leg as she tried to crawl clear. She kicked at the creature with her other leg, her boot heel slamming into its head. Twisting and rolling, they slid toward the railing, picking up speed as the airship gave a violent lurch. A broken spar slowed their skid, then gave way before their combined weight.

In a knot of arms and legs and broken wood, they slammed into the railing. Already weakened by earlier damage, the balusters splintered and gave way before the impact. The Rover girl saw the opening appear and twisted frantically to avoid it. She was too slow. In the space of a heartbeat, Rue Meridian and the Mwellret slid through the gap and disappeared over the side.

Unmanned and out of control, its decks littered with bodies and debris, the *Jerle Shannara* wheeled slowly about and began to move downriver toward the grinding pillars of the Squirm.

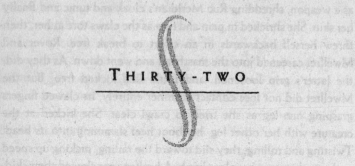

THIRTY-TWO

Bek was standing right next to Ryer Ord Star when the attack on Walker began, so close that he could hear her sudden intake of breath as the first fire thread lanced out at the Druid. The seer staggered, a high keening sound escaping her lips, and then she bolted into the maze. The boy, stunned by the unexpectedness of her action, stood rooted in place, and it was one of the three Elven Hunters who gave chase. The other two grabbed Bek's arms and pulled him back from the battleground as he struggled to break free of them. Walker was down, bolts of magic flying from his fingers in response to the attack, burning into the walls and partitions from which the fire threads burst. To either side of the boy, members of the flanking parties charged into the maze in support of the Druid, swords drawn, shouting out their battle cries.

Then the fire threads lanced from the walls through which they rushed, too, cutting into their unprotected bodies, slicing them apart. In horror, Bek watched one Elf disintegrate in a cross-hatching of threads, body parts and blood flying everywhere. Screams rent the misted air, mingling with smoke and the acrid stench of burning flesh. As the fire began to seek them out, trailing lines of red death, the Druid's would-be rescuers flattened themselves against the metal floor of the maze and crawled swiftly into the protection of its closest walls. Bek saw one of the threads clip Ryer Ord Star, spinning her into a wall where she collapsed in a heap. The Elf who chased her was cut in half a dozen yards away.

Walker had regained his feet and was calling back to them, but his words were lost in the tumult. Without waiting for their response, he started ahead, a wraithlike figure in the gloom, his arm extended before him like a shield, swinging right and left to counterattack the fire threads with his magic as he fought his way toward the obelisk.

Bek exhaled sharply, a wave of despair sweeping through him, and turned to the Elves who held his arms. He was surprised to see that one was the tracker Tamis. "We have to go to him!" he snapped at her in frustration, renewing his struggle to break free.

"He told us to stay where we are, Bek," she replied calmly, gray eyes sweeping the haze as she spoke. "It's death to go in there."

A scraping of metal on metal drew their attention to their left. From the low flat buildings they had passed coming in, a cluster of spidery forms skittered into view. Crooked-legged and squat, they spread out behind what remained of the flanking party led by Quentin and Panax.

"Creepers," Tamis said softly.

Bek went cold. Ordinary men didn't stand a chance against creepers. Even Quentin, with the magic of his sword, would be hard-pressed to stop so many. An endless maze, ribbons of fire, and now metal dogs—Ryer Ord Star's horrific vision had come to pass.

"We're getting out of here," Tamis announced, pulling him back in the direction from which they had come.

"Wait!" He brought her up short with a jerk of his arm. He pointed into the maze. Ryer Ord Star was trying to rise, dragging herself to her knees. He looked at Tamis pleadingly. "We can't just leave her! We have to try to help!"

Driven by a sudden wind, the taste and smell acrid, smoke roiled past them, and ash-clouded mist swept into their faces. The tracker stared at him a moment, then released his arm, leaving him in the grip of her companion. "Wait here."

She sprinted into the maze without hesitating, the fire threads chasing after her, trying to cut her off, burning across the metal carpet in pursuit. Twice she went down in a long slide that took her under the threads, and once she barely cleared the edge of a wall before the fire scorched its smooth surface. Ahead, Ryer Ord Star was on her hands and knees, head bent, long silver hair hanging like a curtain across her face. Blood streaked one arm, soaking into the torn fabric of her tunic.

To Bek's right, more creepers had emerged from the gloom and were descending on Ard Patrinell's group.

Tamis reached Ryer Ord Star in a flying leap that sent both of them sprawling out of the sweeping path of a fire thread. Dragging the seer to her feet, the tracker led her back through the maze, running crouched along walls and across open spaces as the threads burned all around them.

They aren't going to make it, Bek thought. *It's too far! The fire is everywhere!*

He looked for Walker, but the Druid had disappeared. The boy hadn't seen what had happened to him, where he had gone, even if he had managed to reach the obelisk. The center of the maze was choked with mist and smoke-shrouded forms and sudden bursts of the red fire. To his left, Quentin was under attack, the blue fire of the Sword of Leah flashing bravely, the sound of his battle cry lifting out of the haze. To his right, the creepers were spreading out through the maze in search of Ard Patrinell, Ahren Elessedil, and the remainder of the Elven Hunters.

A trap, a trap, it was all a trap! The boy's throat burned with anger and frustration, his mind awash with thoughts of missed chances and bad decisions.

Tamis burst through the smoke and out of the spiderweb of killing red fire, dragging Ryer Ord Star in her wake. "Go, go, go!" she screamed at the waiting Bek and his companion, and in a knot they charged back through the ruins.

Quentin! Bek cried out in the silence of his mind, glancing helplessly over his shoulder.

They had gone less than a hundred feet when a pair of creepers intercepted them. The metal beasts appeared to have been waiting for anyone who made it this far, emerging from behind one of the low buildings, metal limbs scraping and clanking as they blocked the way forward. Tamis and her companion leapt instantly to the defense of the boy and the seer. The creepers attacked at once, moving so fast that they were on top of the Elven Hunters before they could defend themselves. Tamis dodged her attacker, but the other Elven Hunter was less fortunate. The creeper bowled him over, pinned him to the ground, reached down with one pincer while the Elf thrashed helplessly, and tore off his head.

Bek watched it happen as if it were a dream, each movement of Elf and creeper clearly visible and endlessly long, as if both were weighted and chained by time. He crouched with Ryer Ord Star held protectively in his arms, his mind telling him to do something, anything, to help because help was needed and there was no one else. Frozen in place by his horror and indecision, he watched glimmerings of light flash off the edges of the pincers as they descended, the frantic movements of the Elf's arms and legs as he struggled to break free, and the gouts of blood spurt from the severed neck.

Something inside him snapped in that instant, and forgetting everything but the now-overpowering impulse to respond to what he had witnessed, he screamed. A dam broke, and rage, despair, and frustration that he could no longer contain flooded through him, releasing his magic in a torrent, giving it life and power, lending it the strength of iron, honing it to the sharpness of knives. It tore from him in a rush and it ripped through the creepers as if they were made of paper, shredding them instantly and reducing them to scrap.

He was on his feet now, wheeling in a miasma of invincibility, everything forgotten but the euphoria he felt as the power of his magic swept through him. Another of the creepers appeared ahead, and he savaged it with the same ruthless determination—his voice seizing it, lifting it, and tearing it apart. He sent the pieces whirling into space. He scattered them to the wind like leaves and cried out in triumph.

Then something clutched at his leg, drawing him back from the brink of wildness into which he had allowed himself to wander. His voice went silent, its echoes singing in his ears, its images flashing through his mind like living things. Ryer Ord Star was grasping at him with her fingers crooked like claws, her bloodshot eyes gazing up at him in horror and disbelief.

"No, Bek, no!" she was crying out over and over, as if she had been doing so for a long time, as if she had been seeking to reach him through stone walls and he had not heard.

He stared down at her stricken face without comprehension, wondering at the pain and despair he found there. He had saved them, hadn't he? He had found another use for his magic, one that he had not even suspected. He had tapped into power that transcended even that of the Sword of Leah—perhaps even that of Walker himself. What was so wrong with what he had done? What, that made her so distraught?

Tamis was at his side, reaching down for the seer and pulling her back to her feet, her young face grim and blood-streaked. "Run, don't look back!" she commanded at Bek, shoving Ryer Ord Star into his arms.

But he did look. He couldn't help himself. What he saw was nightmarish. The maze was alive with creepers and threads of red fire. Ryer Ord Star's vision had engulfed them all. His eyes stung with tears. Nothing human could live in there. Screams rose out of the gloom, and explosions rent the air with wicked flashes of light. What had become of Ard Patrinell and Ahren and Panax? What about Quentin? He remembered their promise, brothers in arms, each to look out for the other. Shades, what had become of that?

"Run, I said!" Tamis screamed in his ear.

He did so then, charging through the gloom with Ryer Ord Star hanging off one arm as she struggled to keep up. She was keening again, a high soft wail of despair, and it was all he could do to keep from trying to silence her. Once, he glanced over, thinking to stop her. She ran with her eyes closed, her head thrown back, and a look of such anguish on her face that he let her be.

Shards of bright magic flickered in his eyes, hauntings of the legacy he had uncovered and embraced, whispers of a power released. Too big a legacy, perhaps. Too much power. A yearning for more speared through him, an unmistakable need to experience anew the feelings it had released. He gasped at the intensity of it, breathing quickly and rapidly, his face flushed, his body singing.

More, he kept thinking as he fled, was necessary. Much more, before he would be satisfied.

Moments later, the chaos of the maze behind them, the screams and flashes of fire fading, they disappeared into the gloom and the mist.

They ran for a long time, all the way back through the ruins and into the forest beyond before Tamis brought them to a halt in a shadowed stand of hardwoods. With the damp and the mist all about, they crouched in the silence of the trees as the sound of their heartbeats hammered in their ears. Bek bent over, gasping for air, his hands on his knees. Beside him, Ryer Ord Star still keened softly, staring off into space as if seeing far beyond where they huddled.

"So cold and dark, metal bands on my body, emptiness all around," she murmured, lost in some inner struggle, not aware of anything or anyone about her. "Something is here, watching me . . ."

"Ryer Ord Star," he whispered roughly, bending close to her.

"There, where the darkness gathers deepest, just beyond . . ."

"Can you hear me?" he snapped.

She jerked as if she had been struck, and her hands reached out, grasping at the air. "Walker! Wait for me!"

Then she went perfectly still. A strange calm descended on her, a blanket of serenity. She sank back on her heels, kneeling in the gloom, hands folded into her robes, body straight. Her eyes stared off into space.

"What's wrong with her?" Tamis asked, bending down beside Bek.

He shook his head. "I don't know."

He passed his hand in front of her eyes. She neither blinked nor evidenced any recognition of him. He whispered her name, touched her face, and then shook her roughly. She made no response.

The tracker and the boy stared at each other helplessly. Tamis sighed. "I've no cure for this. What about you, Bek? You seem to be full of surprises. Got one to deal with this?"

He shook his head. "I don't think so."

She brushed at her short dark hair, and her gray eyes stared at him. "Well, don't be too quick to make up your mind about it. What happened back there with those creepers suggests you've got something more going for you than the average cabin boy." She paused. "Magic of some sort, wasn't it?"

He nodded wearily. What was the point of hiding it now? "I'm just finding out about it myself. On Mephitic, I was the one who found the key. That was the first time I used it. But I didn't know it could do this." He gestured back toward the ruins, toward the creepers he had destroyed. "Maybe Walker knew and kept it a secret. I think Walker knows a lot of things about me that he's keeping secret."

Tamis sat back on her heels and shook her head. "Druids." She looked off into the trees. "I wonder if he's still alive."

"I wonder if any of them are still alive." Bek's voice broke, and he swallowed hard against what he was feeling.

The tracker stood up slowly. "There's only one way to find out. It's getting dark. I can move about more easily once the light's gone. But you'll have to stay here with her, if I do." She nodded toward Ryer Ord Star. "Are you up to it?"

He nodded. "But I'd rather go with you."

Tamis shrugged. "After seeing what you did to those creepers, I'd rather that, too. But I don't think we can leave her alone like this."

"No," he agreed.

"I'll be back as quick as I can." She straightened and pointed left. "I'll skirt through the trees and come at the ruins from another direction. You wait here. If anyone got out, they'll likely come back this way and you should see them. But be careful you know who it is before you give yourself away."

She studied him a moment, then leaned close. "Don't be afraid to use that newfound magic if you're in danger, all right?"

"I won't."

She gave him a quick smile and melted into the trees.

It grew dark in a hurry after that, the last of the daylight fading into shadow until the woods were enveloped by the night. Clouds and mist masked the sky, and it began to rain again. Bek moved Ryer Ord Star back under the canopy of an old shagbark hickory, out of the weather. She let herself be led and resettled without any form of acknowledgment, gone so far away from him that he might as well not have been there for all the difference it made. Yet it did make a difference, he told himself. Without him, she was at the mercy of whatever found her. She could not defend herself or even flee. She was completely helpless.

He wondered why she had rendered herself so vulnerable, what had happened to make her decide it was necessary. It was a conscious act, he believed. It had something to do with Walker, because everything she did had something to do with the Druid. Was she linked to him now, just as Bek had been linked to him those few moments on Shatterstone? But this was continuing for so much longer. She hadn't spoken or reacted to anything in several hours.

He studied her for a time, then lost interest. He watched the trail instead, hoping to see someone from the company emerge from the gloom. They couldn't all be dead, he told himself. Not all of them. Not Quentin. Not with the Sword of Leah to protect him. Bitterness flooded through him, and he exhaled sharply. Who was he kidding? He had seen enough of the fire threads and the creepers to know that it would take an army of Elven Hunters to get free of those ruins. Even a Druid's magic might not be enough.

He leaned back against the hickory and felt the flat surface of the Sword of Shannara push against his back. He had forgotten it was even there. In the scramble to escape the fire threads and the creepers, he hadn't even thought to use it as a weapon—though what sort of weapon would it have made? Its magic didn't seem like it would have been of much use. Truth? What good was truth against fire and iron? As a fighting weapon, it might have served a purpose, but not against something like what they'd found back there in the ruins. He shook his head. The most powerful magic in the world, Walker had told him, and he had no use for it. The magic of his voice was the better weapon by far. If he could just figure out the things it could do and then bring it under a little better control . . .

He left the thought unfinished, aware of doubts and misgivings he could not put a name to. There was danger in the use of his voice, something nebulous, but unmistakable. The magic was too powerful, too uncertain. He didn't trust it. It was enticingly seductive, and he sensed something deceitful in its lure. Anything that created such euphoria and felt so addictive would have consequences. He was not yet certain he understood what those consequences were.

It was growing cold, and he wished he still had his cloak, but he had lost it in the flight here. He looked at Ryer Ord Star, then moved over to tuck her robes closer about her. She was shivering, though clearly unaware of it, and he put his arms around her and held her against him for warmth. What would they do if Tamis found no one else alive? What if the tracker herself failed to return? Bek closed his eyes against his doubts and fears. It did no good to dwell on them. There was nothing he could do to change things. All he could do was to make the best of the situation, bleak as it was.

He must have dozed for a while, exhausted from the day's events, because the next thing he remembered was waking to the sounds of someone's approach. Yet it wasn't so much the sounds of approach that alerted him as it was his sense of the other's nearness. He lifted his head from the crook of Ryer Ord Star's shoulder and blinked at the darkness. Nothing moved, but something was there, still too far away to see, but coming directly toward them.

And not from the direction of the ruins, but from the direction of the airship.

Bek straightened, eased himself away from the seer, and came to his feet, listening. The night was silent save for the soft patter of a slow rain on the forest canopy. Bek reached back for the Sword of Shannara, then took his hand away. Instead, he moved to one side, deeper into the shadows. He could feel the other's presence as if it were an aura of heat or light. He could feel it as he could the skin of his own body.

A cloaked figure materialized in front of him, appearing all at once, wraithlike. The figure was small and slight and not physically imposing, and the boy could not identify it from its look. It approached without slowing, robed and hooded, a mystery waiting to be uncovered. Bek watched in fascination, unable to decide what to do.

An arm lifted within the robes and stretched out toward Ryer Ord Star. "Tell me what has happened," a woman said, her voice soft but commanding. "Why are you here? You were instructed—"

Then she saw Bek. It must have startled her, because she stiffened and her arm dropped away abruptly. Something in her carriage changed, and it seemed to him that she was unsettled by his unexpected presence.

"Who are you?" she asked.

There was no friendliness in her voice, no hint of the softness that had been there only seconds before. She had changed in the blink of an eye, and he did not think he was the better off for it. But he heard something familiar in her voice, too, something that connected them so strongly he could not miss it. He stared at her, sudden recognition flooding through him.

"Who are you?" she repeated.

He knew her now, and the certainty of it left him breathless. Years dropped away, shed like rainwater from his skin, and a kaleidoscope of patchwork memories returned. Most he had forgotten until his use of the Sword of Shannara had caused them to resurface. They were of her, holding him close as she ran through smoke and fire, through screams and shouts. They were of her, tucking him away in a dark, close place, hiding him from the death that was all around them. They were of her, a child herself, long ago, in a place and time he could only barely remember.

"Grianne," he answered, speaking her name aloud for the first time since infancy. "It's me, Grianne. It's your brother."

Here ends Book One of *The Voyage of the* Jerle Shannara. Book Two, *Antrax*, will reveal the secrets of Castledown and its magic as the Druid Walker and his companions confront the mysterious creature that wards both.

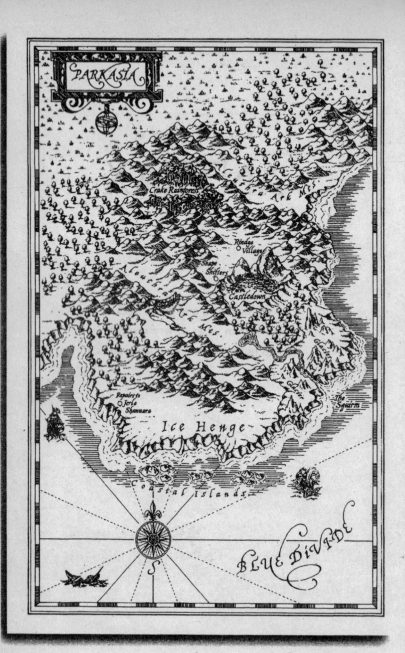

PARKASIA

Aleutra Ark Mts.

Crake Rainforest

Rindge Village

Shape Shifters

Castledown

Aleutra Ark Mts.

Repairs to Jerle Shannara

The Squirm

Ice Henge

Coastal Islands

BLUE DIVIDE

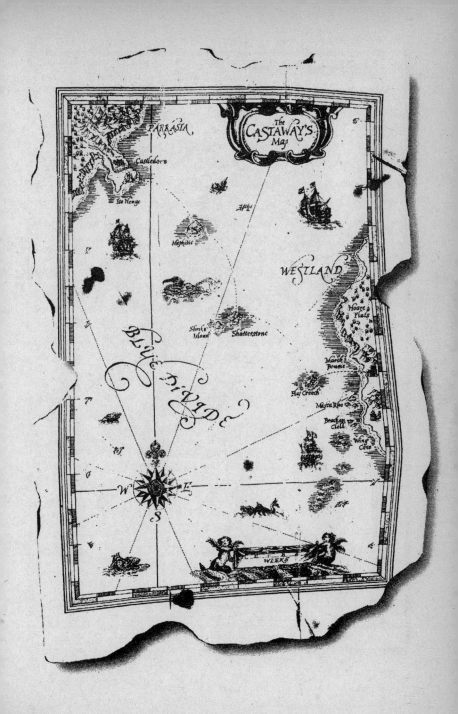

ONE

Grianne Ohmsford was six years old on the last day of her childhood. She was small for her age and lacked unusual strength of body or extraordinary life experience and was not therefore particularly well prepared for growing up all at once. She had lived the whole of her life on the eastern fringes of the Rabb Plains, a sheltered child in a sheltered home, the eldest of two born to Araden and Biornlief Ohmsford, he a scribe and teacher, she a housewife. People came and went from their home as if it were an inn, students of her father, clients drawing on the benefit of his skills, travelers from all over the Four Lands. But she herself had never been anywhere and was only just beginning to understand how much of the world she knew nothing about when everything she did know was taken from her.

While she was unremarkable in appearance and there was nothing about her on the surface of things that would suggest she could survive any sort of life-altering trauma, the truth of the matter was that she was strong and able in unexpected ways. Some of this showed in her startling blue eyes, which pinned you with their directness and pierced you through to your soul. Strangers who made the mistake of staring into them found themselves glancing quickly away. She did not speak to these men and women or seem to take anything away from her encounters, but she left them with a sense of having given something up anyway. Wandering her home and yard, long dark hair hanging loose, a waif seemingly at a loss for something to do or somewhere to go, or just sitting alone in a corner while the adults talked among themselves, she claimed her own space and kept it inviolate.

She was tough-minded, as well, a stubborn and intractable child who once her mind was set on something refused to let it be changed. For a time her parents could do so by virtue of their relationship and the usual threats and enticements, but eventually they found themselves incapable of influencing her. She seemed to find her identity in making a stand on matters, by holding forth in challenge and accepting whatever came her way as a result. Frequently it was a stern lecture and banishment to her room, but often it was simply denial of something others thought would benefit her. Whatever the case, she did not seem to mind the consequences and was more apt to be bothered by capitulation to their wishes.

But at the core of everything was her heritage, which manifested itself in ways that hadn't been apparent for generations. She knew early on that she was not like her parents or their friends or anyone else she knew. She was a throwback to the most famous members of her family—to Brin and Jair and Par and Coll Ohmsford, to whom she could directly trace her ancestry. Her parents explained it to her early on, almost as soon as her talent revealed itself. She was born with the magic of the wishsong, a latent power that surfaced in the Ohmsford family bloodline only once in every four or five generations. Wish for it, sing for it, and it would come to pass. Anything was possible. The wishsong hadn't been present in an Ohmsford in her parents' lifetimes, and so neither of them had any firsthand experience with how it worked. But they knew the stories, had been told them repeatedly by their own parents, the tales of the magic carried down from the time of the great Queen Wren, another of their ancestors. So they knew enough to recognize what it meant when their child could bend the stalks of flowers and turn aside an angry dog simply by singing.

Her use of the wishsong was rudimentary and undisciplined at first, and she did not understand that it was special. In her child's mind, it seemed reasonable that everyone would possess it. Her parents worked to help her realize its worth, to harness its power, and to learn to keep it secret from others. Grianne was a smart girl, and she understood quickly what it meant to have something others would covet or fear if they knew she possessed it. She listened to her parents about this, although she paid less attention to their warnings about the ways it should be used and the purposes to which it should be put. She knew enough to show them what they expected of her and to hide from them what they did not.

So on the last day of her childhood she had already come to terms with having use of the magic. She had constructed defenses to its demands and subterfuges to her parents' refusals to let her fully test its limits. Wrapped in the armor of her strong-minded determination and stubborn insistence, she had built a fortress in which she wielded the wishsong with a sense of impunity. Her child's world was already more complex and devious than that of many adults, and she was learning the importance of never giving away everything of who and what she was. It was her gift of magic and her understanding of its workings that saved her.

At the same time, and through no fault of her own, it was what doomed her parents and younger brother.

She knew there was something wrong with her child's world some weeks before that last day. It manifested itself in small ways, things that her parents and others could not readily detect. There were oddities in the air—smells and tastes and sounds that whispered of a hidden presence and dark emotions. She caught glimpses of shadows on the vibrations of her voice that returned to her when she used the magic of her song. She felt changes in heat and cold that came only when she was threatened, except that always before she could trace their source and this time she could not. Once or twice, she sensed the closeness of dark-cloaked forms, perhaps the shape-shifters she had found out on several occasions before, always hidden and out of reach, but there nevertheless.

She said nothing to her parents of these things because she had no solid evidence of them and only suspicion on which to buttress her complaints. Even so, she kept close watch. Her home was at the edge of a grove of maple trees and looked out across the flat, green threshold of the Rabb all the way to the foothills of the Dragon's Teeth. While nothing could approach out of the west without being visible from a long way off, forests and hills shielded the other three quadrants. She scouted them from time to time, a precaution undertaken to give her a sense of security. But whatever watched was careful, and she never found it out. It hid from her, avoided her, moved away when she approached, and always returned. She could feel its eyes on her even as she looked for it. It was clever and skilled; it was accustomed to staying hidden when others would find it out.

She should have been afraid, but she had not been raised with fear and had no reason to appreciate its uses. For her, fear was an annoyance she sought to banish and did not heed.

She asked her father finally if there was anyone who would wish to hurt her, or him, or her mother or brother, but he only smiled and said they had nothing anyone would want that would provide reason for harm. He said it in a calm, assured way, a teacher imparting knowledge to a student, and she did not believe he could be wrong.

When the black-cloaked figures finally came, they did so just before dawn, when the light was so pale and thin that it barely etched the edges of the shadows. They killed the dog, old Bark, when he wandered out for a look, an act that demonstrated unmistakably the nature of their dark intent. She was awake by then, alerted by some inner voice tied to her magic, hurrying through the rooms of her home on cat's paws, searching for the danger that was already at the door. Her family was alone that morning, all of the travelers either come and gone or still on their way, and there was no one to stand with them in the face of their peril.

Grianne never hesitated when she caught sight of the shadowy forms sliding past the windows. She sensed the presence of danger all around, a circle of iron blades closing with inexorable purpose. She yelled for her father and ran back to her bedroom, where her brother lay sleeping. She snatched him up without a word, hugging him to her. Soft and warm, he was barely two years old. She carried him from the room and down into the earthen cellar where perishable food-stuffs were kept. Above, her parents sought to cover her flight. The sounds of breaking glass and splintering wood erupted, and she could hear her father's angry shouts and oaths. He was a brave man, and he would stand and fight. But it would not be enough; she sensed that much already. She re-leased a catch and pulled back the shelving section that hid the entrance to the cramped storm shelter they had never used. She placed her sleeping brother on a pallet inside. She stared down at him for a moment, at his tiny face and balled fists, at his sleeping form, hearing the shouts and oaths overhead turn to screams of pain and anguish, aware of tears flooding her eyes.

Black smoke was seeping through the floorboards when she slipped from the shelter and sealed the entry behind her. She heard the crackle of flames consuming wood. Her parents gone, the intruders would come for her, but she would be quicker and more clever than they expected. She would escape them, and once she was safely away, outside in the pale dawn light, she would run the five miles to the next closest home and return with help for her brother.

She heard the black-cloaked forms searching for her as she hurried along a short passageway to a cellar door that led directly outside. Outside, the door was concealed by bushes and seldom used; it was not likely they would think to find her there. If they did, they would be sorry. She already knew the sort of damage the wishsong could cause. She was a child, but she was not helpless. She blinked away her tears and set her jaw. They would find that out one day. They would find that out when she hurt them the same way they were hurting her.

Then she was through the door and outside in the brightening dawn light, crouched in the bushes. Smoke swirled about her in dark clouds, and she felt the heat of the fire as it climbed the walls of her home. Everything was being taken from her, she thought in despair. Everything that mattered.

A sudden movement to one side drew her attention. When she turned to look, a hand wrapped in a foul-smelling cloth closed over her face and sent her spiraling downward into blackness.

* * *

When she awoke, she was bound, gagged, and blindfolded, and she could not tell where she was or who held her captive or even if it was day or night. She was carried over a thick shoulder like a sack of wheat, but her captors did not speak. There were more than one; she could hear their footsteps, heavy and certain. She could hear their breathing. She thought about her home and parents. She thought about her brother. The tears came anew, and she began to sob. She had failed them all.

She was carried for a long time, then laid upon the ground and left alone. She squirmed in an effort to free herself, but the bonds were too tightly knotted. She was hungry and thirsty, and a cold desperation was creeping through her. There could be only one reason she had been taken captive, one reason she was needed when her parents and brother were not. Her wishsong. She was alive and they were dead because of her legacy. She was the one with the magic. She was the one who was special. Special enough that her family was killed so that she could be stolen away. Special enough to cause everything she loved and cared for to be taken from her.

There was a commotion not long after that, sudden and un-expected, filled with new sounds of battle and angry cries. They seemed to be coming from all around her. Then she was snatched from the ground and carried off, leaving the sounds behind. The one who carried her now cradled her while run-ning, holding her close, as if to soothe her fear and despera-tion. She curled into her rescuer's arms, burrowed as if stricken, for such was the depth of her need.

When they were alone in a silent place, the bonds and gag and blindfold were removed. She sat up and found herself facing a big man wrapped in black robes, a man who was not entirely human, his face scaly and mottled like a snake's, his fingers ending in claws, and his eyes lidless slits. She caught her breath and shrank from him, but he did not move away in response.

"You are safe now, little one," he whispered. "Safe from those who would harm you, from the Dark Uncle and his kind."

She did not know whom he was talking about. She looked around guardedly. They were crouched in a forest, the trees stark sentinels on all sides, their branches confining amid a sea of sunshine that dappled the woodland earth like gold dust. There was no one else around, and nothing of what she saw looked familiar.

"There is no reason to be afraid of me," the other said. "Are you frightened by how I look?"

She nodded warily, swallowing against the dryness in her throat.

He handed her a water skin, and she drank gratefully. "Do not be afraid. I am of mixed breed, both Man and Mwellret, little one. I look scary, but I am your friend. I was the one who saved you from those others. From the Dark Uncle and his shape-shifters."

That was twice he had mentioned the Dark Uncle. "Who is he?" she asked. "Is he the one who hurt us?"

"He is a Druid. Walker is his name. He is the one who attacked your home and killed your parents and your brother." The reptilian eyes fixed on her. "Think back. You will remember seeing his face."

To her surprise, she did. She saw it clearly, a glimpse of it as it passed a window in the thin dawn light, dusky skin and black beard, eyes so piercing they stripped you bare, dark brow creased with frown lines. She saw him, knew him for her enemy, and felt a rage of such intensity she thought she might burn from the inside out.

Then she was crying, thinking of her parents and her brother, of her home and her lost world. The man across from her drew her gently into his arms and held her close.

"You cannot go back," he told her. "They will be searching for you. They will never give up while they think you are alive."

She nodded into his shoulder. "I hate them," she said in a thin, sharp wail.

"Yes, I know," he whispered. "You are right to hate them." His rough, guttural voice tightened. "But listen to me, little one. I am the Morgawr. I am your father and mother now. I am your family. I will help you to find a way to gain revenge for what has been taken from you. I will teach you to ward yourself against everything that might hurt you. I will teach you to be strong."

He whisked her away, lifting her as if she weighed nothing, and carried her deeper into the woods to where a giant bird waited. He called the bird a Shrike, and she flew on its back with him to another part of the Four Lands, one dark and solitary and empty of sound and life. He cared for her as he said he would, trained her in mind and body, and kept her safe. He told her more of the Druid Walker, of his scheming and his hunger for power, of his long-sought goal of dominance over all the Races in all the lands. He showed her images of the Druid and his black-cloaked servants, and he kept her anger fired and alive within her child's breast.

"Never forget what he has stolen from you," he would repeat. "Never forget what you are owed for his betrayal."

After a time he began to teach her to use the wishsong as a weapon against which no one could stand—not once she had mastered it and brought it under her control, not once she had made it so much a part of her that its use seemed second nature. He taught her that even a slight change in pitch or tone could alter health to sickness and life to death. A Druid had such power, he told her. The Druid Walker in particular. She must learn to be a match for him. She must learn to use her magic to overcome his.

After a while she thought no longer of her parents and her brother, whom she knew to be dead and lost to her forever; they were no more than bones buried in the earth, a part of a past forever lost, of a childhood erased in a single day. She gave herself over to her new life and to her mentor, her teacher, and her friend. The Morgawr was all those while she grew through adolescence, all those and much more. He was the shaper of her thinking and the navigator of her life. He was the inspiration for her magic's purpose and the keeper of her dreams of righting the wrongs she had suffered.

He called her his little Ilse Witch, and she took the name for her own. She buried her given name with her past, and she never used it again.

TWO

Her memories of the past, already faded and tattered, fell away in an instant's time as she stood in a woodland clearing a thousand miles from her lost home and confronted the boy who claimed he was her brother.

"Grianne, it's Bek," he insisted. "Don't you remember?"

She remembered everything, of course, although no longer as clearly and sharply, no longer as painfully. She remembered, but she refused to believe that her memories could be brought to life with such painful clarity after so many years. She hadn't heard her name spoken in all that time, hadn't spoken it herself, had barely even thought of it. She was the Ilse Witch, and that name defined who and what she was, and not the other. The other was for when she had achieved her revenge over the Druid, for when she had gained sufficient recognition and power that when it was spoken next, it would never again be forgotten by anyone.

But here was this slip of a boy speaking it now, daring to suggest that he had a right to do so. She stared at him in disbelief and smoldering anger. Could he really be her brother? Could he be Bek, alive in spite of what she had believed for so long? Was it possible? She tried to make sense of the idea, to find a way to address it, to form words to speak in response.

But everything she thought to say or do was jumbled and incoherent, refusing to be organized in a useful way. Everything froze as if chained and locked, leaving her so frustrated with her inability to act that she could barely keep herself from screaming.

"No!" she shouted finally. A single word, spoken like an oath offered up against demon spawn, it escaped her lips when nothing else dared.

"Grianne," he said, more softly now.

She saw the mop of dark brown hair and the startling blue eyes, so like her own, so familiar to her. He had her build and looks. He had something else, as well, something she had yet to define, but was unmistakably there. He could be Bek.

But how? How could he be Bek?

"Bek is dead," she hissed at him, her slender body rigid within the dark robes.

On the ground to one side, a small bundle of clothing and shadows, Ryer Ord Star knelt, head lowered in the veil of her long silver hair, hands clasped in her lap. She had not moved since the Ilse Witch had appeared out of the night, had not lifted her head an inch or spoken a single word. In the silence and darkness, she might have been a statue carved of stone and set in place by her maker to ward a traveler's place of rest.

The Ilse Witch's eyes passed over her in a heartbeat and fell upon the boy. "Say something!" she hissed anew. "Tell me why I should believe you!"

"I was saved by a shape-shifter called Truls Rohk," he answered finally, his gaze on her steady. "I was taken to the Druid Walker, who in turn took me to the people who raised me as their son. But I am Bek."

"You could not know any of this! You were only two when I

hid you in that cellar!" She caught herself. "When I hid my brother. But my brother is dead, and you are a liar!"

"I was told most of it," he admitted. "I don't remember anything of how I was saved. But look at me, Grianne. Look at us! You can't mistake the resemblance, how much alike we are. We have the same eyes and coloring. We're brother and sister! Don't you feel it?"

She advanced a step. "Why would a shape-shifter save you when it was shape-shifters who killed my parents and took me prisoner? Why would the Druid save you when he sought to imprison me?"

The boy was already shaking his head slowly, deliberately, his blue eyes intense, his young face determined. "No, Grianne, it wasn't the shape-shifters or the Druid who killed our parents and took you away. They were never your enemies. Don't you realize the truth yet? Think about it, Grianne."

"I saw his face!" she screamed in fury. "I saw it through a window, a glimpse, passing in the dawn light, just before the attack, before I . . ."

She trailed off, wondering suddenly, unexpectedly, if she could have been mistaken. Had she seen the Druid as the Morgawr had insisted, when he told her to think back, so certain she would? How could he have known what she would see? The implication of what it would mean if she had deceived herself was staggering. She brushed it away violently, but it coiled up in a corner of her memory, a snake still easily within reach.

"We are Ohmsfords, Grianne," the boy continued softly. "But so is Walker. We share the same heritage. He comes from the same bloodline as we do. He is one of us. He has no reason to do us harm."

"None that you could fathom, it appears!" She laughed

derisively. "What would you know of dark intentions, little boy? What has life shown you that would give you the right to suppose your insight into such things is better than mine?"

"Nothing." He seemed momentarily at a loss for words, but his face spoke of his need to find them. "I haven't lived your life, I know. But I'm not naive about what it must have been like."

Her patience slipped a notch. "I think you believe what you are telling me," she told him coldly. "I think you have been carefully schooled to believe it. But you are a dupe and a tool of clever men. Druids and shape-shifters make their way in the world by deceiving others. They must have looked long and hard to find you, a boy who looks so much like Bek would look at your age. They must have congratulated themselves on their good fortune."

"How did I come to have his name, then?" the boy snapped in reply. "If I'm not your brother, how do I have his name? It is the name I was given, the name I have always had!"

"Or at least, that is what you believe. A Druid can make you embrace lies with little more than a thought, even lies about yourself." She shook her head reprovingly. "You are sadly deceived, to believe as you do, to think yourself a dead boy. I should destroy you on the spot, but perhaps that is what the Druid is hoping I will do, what he wants me to do. Perhaps he thinks it will somehow damage me if I kill a boy who looks so like my brother. Tell me where the Druid waits, and I will spare you."

The boy stared at her in horror. "You are the one who is deceived, Grianne. So much so that you will tell yourself anything to keep the truth at bay."

"Where is the Druid?" she snapped, her face contorting angrily. "Tell me now!"

He took a deep breath, straightening. "I've come a long way for this meeting. Too far to be intimidated into giving up what I know is true and right. I am your brother. I am Bek. Grianne—"

"Don't call me that!" she screamed. Her gray robes billowed from her body and she threw up her arms in fury, almost as if to smother his words, to bury them along with her past. She felt her temper slipping, her grip on herself sliding away like metal on oiled metal, and the raw power of her voice took on an edge that could easily cut to ribbons anything or anyone against which it was directed. "Don't speak my name again!"

He stood his ground. "What name should I speak? Ilse Witch? Should I call you what your enemies call you? Should I treat you as they do, as a creature of dark magic and evil intent, as someone I can never be close to or care about or want to see become my sister again?"

He seemed to gain strength with every new word, and suddenly she saw him as more dangerous than she had believed. "Be careful, boy."

"You are the one who needs to be careful!" he snapped. "Of who and what you believe! Of everything you have embraced since the moment you were taken from our home. Of the lies in which you have cloaked yourself!"

He pointed at her suddenly. "We are alike in more ways than you think. Not everything that links us is visible to the eye. Grianne Ohmsford has her magic, her birthright, now the tool of the Ilse Witch. But I have that magic, too! Do you hear it in my voice? You do, don't you? I'm not as practiced as you, and I only just discovered it was there, but it is another link in our lives, Grianne, another part of the heritage we share—"

She felt his voice taking on an edge similar to her own, a

biting touch that caused her to flinch in spite of herself and to bring her defenses up instantly.

"—just as we share the same parents, the same fate, the same journey of discovery, brought about by a search for the treasure hidden in the ruins that lie inland from here . . ."

She brought her voice up in a low, vibrant hum, a soft blending with the night sounds, faint and sibilant, leaves rustling in the breeze, insects chirping and buzzing, birds winging past as swift shadows, the breath of living things. Her decision was made in an instant, quick and hard; he was too dangerous for her to let live, whoever or whatever he was. Too dangerous for her to ignore as she had thought to do. He had something of magic about him after all, magic not unlike her own. It was what she had sensed about him earlier and been unable to define, hidden before but present now in the sound of his voice, a whisper of possibility.

Put an end to him, she warned herself.

Put an end to him at once!

Then something shimmered to one side, drawing her attention from the boy. She struck at it without thinking, the magic escaping from her in a rush of iron shards and razored bits that cut through the air and savaged her intended target without pause or effort. But the shimmer had moved another way. Again, the Ilse Witch struck at it, her voice a weapon of such power that it shattered the silence, whipped the leaves of the surrounding trees as if they were caught in a violent wind, and left voiceless and wide-eyed in shock the boy who had been speaking.

An instant later, he disappeared. It happened so quickly and unexpectedly that it was done before the Ilse Witch could act to stop it. She blinked at the empty space in which he had stood, seeing the brightness take on shape and form anew, becoming a series of barely recognizable movements that crossed through the night like shadows vaguely human in form chasing one another. She lashed out at them in surprise, but she was too slow and her attack too misdirected to catch more than empty air.

She wheeled this way and that, searching for what had deceived her so completely. Whatever it was, it was gone and it had taken the boy with it. Her first impulse was to give pursuit. But first impulses were seldom wise, and she did not give in to this one. She scanned the empty clearing, then the surrounding forest, searching with her senses for traces of the boy's rescuer. It took her only a moment to discover its identity. A shape-shifter. She had sensed its presence before, she realized—on *Black Moclips*, after the nighttime collision with the *Jerle Shannara*. It was the same creature and no mistake. It must have come aboard during the confusion to spy on her, then remained hidden for the remainder of the voyage. That could not have been easy, given the intensity of her control over ship's quarters and crew. This particular shape-shifter was skilled and experienced, a veteran of such efforts, and not in the least awed by her.

A new rage built in her. It must have followed her from the ship to the clearing, revealing itself when it believed the boy in danger. Did it know the boy? Or the Druid? Did it serve either or both? She believed it must. Otherwise, why would it involve itself in this business at all? A protector for the boy then? Perhaps. If so, it would confirm what she had believed from the beginning, from the moment the boy had tried to trick her into thinking he might be Bek. The Druid had concocted an elaborate scheme to undermine her confidence in her mission and her trust in the Morgawr, to sabotage their relationship, and to render her vulnerable so that he might find a way to destroy her before she could destroy him.

She clenched her hands before her, fingers knotting until the knuckles turned white. She should have killed the boy at once, the moment he spoke her name! She should have used the wishsong to burn him alive, waiting for him to beg her to save him, to admit to his lies! She should never have listened to anything he said!

Yet now that she had, she couldn't shake the feeling that she shouldn't dismiss him too quickly.

She turned the matter over in her mind carefully, examining it anew. The resemblance between them could be explained away, of course. A boy who looked like her could be found easily enough. Nor would it be all that hard for Walker to make the boy think he was Bek, even to think he had always been called Bek. Duping him into believing he was her brother and somehow her rescuer was certainly within the Druid's capabilities. It was reasonable to believe that he had been brought along on the voyage solely for the purpose of somehow, somewhere encountering her and acting out his part.

But . . .

Her pale, luminous face lifted and her blue eyes stared off into the night. There, at the end, when he had lost his patience with her, when he had challenged her as no one else would dare to do, not even the Morgawr, something about him had reminded her of herself. A conviction, a certainty that registered in his words and his posture, in the directness and intensity of his gaze. But more than this, she had sensed something unexpected and familiar in his tone of voice, something that could not be mistaken for anything other than what it was. He had told her, but in the heat of the moment she had not believed him, thinking only that he was threatening her, that he could do damage to her in an unexpected way, and so she must protect herself. But it had been there nevertheless.

He had the magic of the wishsong, her magic, her power duplicated.

Who but her brother or another Ohmsford would possess power like that?

The contradiction of what seemed to be true and what seemed to be a lie frustrated and confused her. She wanted to explain the boy away with no further consideration, but she could not do so. There was in him enough of real magic to cause her to wonder at his true identity, even if she did not believe him to be Bek. The Druid could do many things in creating a tool with which to deceive her, but he could not instill another with magic, and particularly not with magic of this sort.

So who was the boy and what was the truth of him?

She knew what she should do; it was what she had come all this way to do. Find the treasure that was hidden in Castle-down and make it her own. Find the Druid and destroy him. Regain the safety of *Black Moclips* and sail home again as swiftly as possible and be shed of this voyage and its dangers.

But the boy intrigued and disturbed her, so much so that almost without understanding why, she was rethinking her plans entirely. Despite what she knew of his duplicity, whether willing or not, she was loath to give up on solving the mystery of him when so much of what she discovered might impact her. Not in any life-altering manner, of course; she had already made her mind up to that. But in some smaller, yet still important way.

How hard would it be to discover the truth about him, once she set her mind to it? How much time would it take?

The Morgawr would not approve, but he approved of little

she did these days. Her relationship with her mentor had been deteriorating for some time. They no longer shared the student/ teacher connection they once had. She was as much the master now as he was, and she chafed at the restrictions he constantly sought to place upon her. She had not forgotten what she owed him, was not ungrateful for all he had taught her over the years. But she disliked his insistence on keeping her in her place, always his subordinate, his underling, a charge who must do as he dictated. He was old, and perhaps because he was old he could no longer change as easily as could the young. Self-preservation was what mattered to him. But she did not aspire to live a thousand years. She did not consider near immortality a benefit to be sought. Hence the need to get on with things, rather than sit and plot and wait and scheme, as he was so used to doing.

No, he would not approve, and in this case she would be wrong in failing to consider that. Seeking out the boy to solve his mystery and satisfy her curiosity was mere self-indulgence. She hesitated a moment, then brushed her hesitation aside. It was her decision to make, her choice if she wasted time that, in any case, belonged to her. The boy had something she needed, whether the Morgawr would agree with her or not. In any event, he was not here to advise her. Cree Bega would presume to speak for him, but the Mwellret's opinion meant next to nothing to her.

She would have to act quickly, however. The ret was not too far behind her, coming along with two dozen others. His approach was delayed only because, wishing to go ahead by herself, to have the first look at what waited, she had ordered him to wait. Perhaps, she added, to make certain he did not interfere with anything she decided she must do with what she found. Perhaps just to keep him in line, where he belonged.

She walked over to Ryer Ord Star and bent down, trying to determine if the seer was coming out of her trance. But the girl never moved, sitting silently, motionlessly in the night, head lowered in shadow, eyes closed. She was breathing steadily, calmly, so it was apparent her health was not in danger. What was she doing, though? Where inside herself had she gone?

The Ilse Witch knelt in front of the girl. She had no time to wait for the seer to conclude her meditations. She needed her answers. She placed her fingers on the other's temples, just as she had done with the castaway whose revelations had begun this whole matter, and she began to probe. The effort required was small. Ryer Ord Star's mind opened to her like a flower before the rising sun, her memories tumbling out like falling petals. Without a glance at most of them, the Ilse Witch went directly for those most recent, the ones that would reveal the fate of the Druid.

Revelations surfaced like the ocean's dead, stark and bare. She saw a battle within Old World ruins, a battle in which the Druid and his company were assaulted on all sides by lines of red fire that burned and seared. Walls shifted, raising from and lowering into smooth metal floors. Creepers appeared from nowhere, metal monsters on skittering legs with claws that rent and tore. Men fought and died in a swirl of thick smoke and spurts of fire. Seen through Ryer Ord Star's eyes, filtered through her emotions, everything was chaotic and awash in fear and desperation.

Amid the madness, the Druid advanced past lines of attack and changes in terrain, his steady, deliberate progress aided by his magic and buttressed by his courage and determination. Say what you would, the Druid had never been a coward. He fought his way into the heart of the ruins, shouting in vain for the others of his company to fall back, to flee, trying to keep them alive. At last he gained the doorway to a black tower, forced an entry, and disappeared inside.

Ryer Ord Star screamed and started after him, then was struck by the fire and sent pinwheeling into a wall. Her thoughts of the Druid faded, then went black.

The Ilse Witch took her fingers from the seer's temples and sat back on her heels, perplexed. Interesting. The communication had come without words of any sort and with no resistance at all. Was this the nature of empaths, that they could neither dissemble nor conceal? She found herself wondering at the girl's pursuit of the Druid, galvanized by the latter's disappearance into the tower. Why would she risk herself so? The girl had been instructed to stay close to the Druid at all times, to make herself indispensable to him, to gain his confidence and his ear. Clearly she had done so. But was there something more between them, something that went beyond the charge she had been given as the Ilse Witch's spy?

There was no way to know. Not without damaging the girl, and she wasn't prepared to go to that length just yet. She had what she wanted for now—a clear picture of what had befallen those from the company of the *Jerle Shannara* who had gone inland with the Druid. She could not be certain of the Druid's fate, however. Perhaps he was dead. Perhaps he was trapped beneath the ruins. Whatever the case, he did not present any danger to her. Without an airship to carry him off and with most of his company dead or imprisoned, he could do little harm.

She had time for the boy, then. Enough, that she did not need to consider the matter further.

No more than a handful of minutes passed before Cree Bega and his company of Mwellrets appeared out of the gloom, heavy bodies trudging warily through the forest dark, slitted eyes glittering as they caught sight of her. Repulsive creatures! she thought, but she kept her face expressionless. She rose to meet them and stood waiting on their approach.

"Misstress," their leader, her designated protector, hissed, bowing obsequiously. "Have you found the little peopless?"

"I have decided to leave that to you, Cree Bega. To you and your companions. There has been a battle in the ruins ahead, and those of the Druid's company who are not dead are scattered. Find them and make them your prisoners. That includes the Druid, should you come upon him and find him helpless enough to subdue."

"Misstress, I thinkss—"

"Be careful otherwise, because he is more than a match for all of you put together." She ignored his attempt to speak. "Leave him to me if you find he is able to defend himself. Do not go into the ruins; they are well protected. Do not expose yourself or your men to the danger they pose. Keep a close watch over both airships and do not land them under any circumstances."

He was watching her closely now, realizing that she had already removed herself from everything she was instructing him to do.

"Something has come up that I must investigate." She held his reptilian eyes with her steady, calm gaze. "I will be gone for a time, and while I am gone, you will be in charge. Do not fail me."

For a moment there was no response and she thought he had not understood. "Am I clear on this?"

"Where iss it my misstress goess?" he asked softly. "Our mission iss here—"

"Our mission is where I say it is, Cree Bega."

Something in the Mwellret's cold gaze turned suddenly

dangerous. "Your masster would not approve of thiss diverssion . . ."

Two quick steps placed her right in front of him. "My master?" There was an uncomfortable silence as she waited on his reply. He stared at her in silence. "I have no master, ret," she whispered. "You have a master, not I, and he is not here in any case. I am the one you must answer to. I am your mistress. Is there anything else that I need to explain?"

The Mwellret said nothing, but she did not care for what she found in his eyes. She gave him a moment more, then repeated softly, "Is there?"

He shook his head. "Ass you wissh, misstress. Little peopless will be our prissonerss on your return, I promiss. But what of the treassure?"

"We'll have it soon enough." She looked away, off in the direction of Castledown. Was that so? Would it be so easy? She thought that her knowledge of the situation gave her an advantage over the Druid, but she could not afford to underestimate the enemy that warded Castledown. If it could defeat the Druid so easily, it was much stronger than she had expected. "Leave the matter of retrieving the treasure to me."

She dismissed him with barely a glance, then remembered Ryer Ord Star, still kneeling in a huddle to one side, still lost in some other place and time. "Do not harm the girl," she told Cree Bega, giving him a quick, hard look of warning. "She has been my eyes and ears aboard the Druid's airship on this voyage. There is much she knows that she has not yet told me. I want her kept safe for my return so that I may discover what she hides."

The Mwellret nodded, giving the seer a doubtful look. "Thiss one sseemss already dead."

"She sleeps. She is in a trance of some sort. I haven't had

time to discover what is wrong with her." She brushed the ret aside. "Just do what I told you. I won't be long."

She departed the clearing without a glance back. Cree Bega and the others would do what she had ordered. They would be afraid to do anything else. But she was reminded again that it was growing more difficult to control them. She would be better off without them once she had the treasure in hand. Sometime soon, she would rid herself of them for good.

Eastward, the sky was beginning to brighten faintly with the dawn's approach. Night was already sliding westward, liquid ink withdrawing silently through the trees. A new day would bring fresh revelations. About the boy, perhaps. About why he thought as he did. About how his magic had found its way to him and why it was so like her own. A smile of expectation brightened her pale face. She looked forward to discovering the answers. She felt a rush of anticipation.

Hesitation and doubts were for others, she thought dismissively, for those who would never find their own way in the world and never make anything of their lives that mattered.

Picking up faint traces of the shape-shifter that still lingered on the fading night air, she began the hunt.

Gleaming eyes filled with malice, Cree Bega watched wordlessly until she was well out of sight. Hunched within his cloak and surrounded by those he commanded, he imagined how sweet it would feel when he was permitted at last to put an end to the insufferable girl child. That he hated her as he hated no one else went without saying; he had never felt anything but hate for her. He despised her as she despised him, and nothing shared through their service to the Morgawr would ever change that.

But the Morgawr, though claiming to be the girl's mentor

and friend, was more Mwellret than human. His connection to Cree Bega's people was ancient and blooded. He had bonded to the girl because she was a novelty and he saw a use for her in the larger scheme of things. But his heart and soul were those of a Mwellret.

The girl, of course, believed them equals, outcasts bound together in their struggle for recognition and power over their oppressors. The Morgawr let her believe as much because it suited his purposes to do so. But they were not equals in any way that mattered, and the little Ilse Witch was far less skilled in her use of magic than she believed. She was a strutting, posturing annoyance, a foolish, ludicrously inept practitioner of an art that had been mastered by the Mwellrets and their kind centuries ago, before the Druids had even thought to take up the Elven magic as their sword and shield. Mwellrets would never be subjugated by humans, never become their inferiors, and this girl child was just another self-deceived morsel waiting to be plucked from their food chain.

He felt the eyes of his fellows upon him, awaiting his orders, their own thoughts as dark and vengeful as his. They, too, waited for their chance at the Ilse Witch. Cree Bega would give her the satisfaction of believing him subdued and obedient for now. He had pledged as much to the Morgawr. He would heed her commands and carry out her wishes because there was no reason for him to do otherwise.

But a shift in the wind was coming, and when it did, it would mark the end of her.

He wheeled on the others, finding them grouped tightly about him, dark visages expectant and eager within shadowed cowls. They awaited his orders, anxious for something to do. He would accommodate them. Members of the company of the *Jerle Shannara* were loose somewhere ahead within these trees, waiting to be harvested, to be killed or taken prisoner. It was time to accommodate them.

Growling softly, he told his men to start with Ryer Ord Star, then move on.

But when they turned to take charge of the seer, she was nowhere to be found.

THREE

Arms of iron clutched Bek Ohmsford close to a body that smelled vaguely fetid and loamy, of earth and chemicals mixed. The body moved with the swiftness of thought, sliding through trees and brush, shedding layers of itself like skin, shadows that hung dark and empty on the air and then faded away completely. Some exploded into bits of night as the magic of the Ilse Witch caught up to them, but always Bek and his rescuer were one skin ahead.

Then they were beyond the clearing and into the concealing trees, still running hard, but cloaked in shadows and screens of brush and limbs. Bek began to struggle then, frightened suddenly of the unknown, of anything powerful and mysterious enough to challenge the Ilse Witch's magic.

"Be still, boy!" Truls Rohk hissed, giving him a sharp squeeze of warning with those powerful arms, never once slowing his pace.

They ran for a long time, Bek crumpled nearly into a ball in the other's grip, until the clearing and the witch were far behind them. Then they stopped, and the shape-shifter dropped to one knee and released the boy with a nudge of hands and shoulders, letting him roll to the earth in a crumpled heap, there to uncoil and straighten himself again. Bek heard Truls

Rohk breathing hard, winded and spent, bent over within his concealing cloak while he waited for his strength to return. Bek climbed to his hands and knees, nerve endings tingling with new life as fresh blood finally reached his cramped limbs. They were in a place grown so thick with trees and brush that the light of moon and stars did not penetrate, where everything was cloaked in deepest silence.

"Keeping you alive is turning into a full-time job," the shape-shifter muttered irritably.

Bek thought of his lost opportunity to persuade the Ilse Witch of who he was. "No one asked you to interfere! I was that close to convincing her! I was just about—"

"You were just about to get yourself killed," the other said with a quick, harsh laugh. "You weren't paying close enough attention to the effect you were having on her, you were so caught up in the righteousness and certainty of your argument. Hah! Convincing her? Couldn't you feel what was happening? She was getting ready to use her magic on you!"

"That's not true!" Bek was suddenly furious. He leapt to his feet in challenge. "You don't know that!"

Now the shape-shifter was really laughing, a low and steady howl that he worked hard to suppress. "Can't afford to laugh as loud as I'd like, boy. Not here. Not this close still." He stood up, confronting the boy. "You listen to me. Your arguments were good. They were sound and they were true. But she wasn't ready for them. She wanted to believe some of it, I think. She might have believed all of it in other circumstances, maybe will after time spent thinking it over. But she wasn't ready for it then and there. Especially not at the end, when you let your own magic get away from you again. Not your fault, I know, that you're still learning. But you have to be aware of your limitations."

Bek stared. "I was using the wishsong?"

"Not consciously, but it was slipping out of you even while you tried to tell her about it." Truls Rohk paused. "When she sensed its presence, she felt threatened. She thought you were about to attack her. Or she just decided it was all too much to deal with and she should put an end to you."

He turned and walked away a few steps, looking back the way they had come. "All quiet for now. But I don't know that it's finished yet." He turned back. "You surprised her, boy, and that's dangerous with someone so powerful. You gave her too much all at once, too much she didn't want to hear, that would impact her in ways she couldn't manage so quickly." He grunted. "It couldn't be helped, I imagine. She appeared and found you. What were you supposed to do?"

Bek stood silently before him, thinking it through. Truls Rohk was right. He had been so caught up in persuading Grianne he was her brother that he had paid almost no attention to what she was doing. It was possible she had not believed him, could not have for that matter, given the suddenness and surprise of it. Just because he believed didn't mean she would. She'd had much longer to live with the lie than he'd had to live with the truth. She was less likely to be swayed as easily.

"Sit down, boy," Truls Rohk said, and moved over to join him. "Time for a few more revelations. You were wrong about how well you were doing convincing your sister of who you were. You're wrong about no one asking me to interfere in your life, as well."

Bek looked at him. "Walker?"

"What I told you before, on Mephitic, was true. I pulled you from the ashes of your parents' home. Aware that your family was in danger, I was keeping watch at the Druid's request. The Morgawr's Mwellrets, shape-shifters of a sort, were prowling about your home in Jentsen Close. You lived not far from the Wolfsktaag, there at a corner of the Rainbow Lake, amid a community of isolated homes occupied mostly by farmers. You were vulnerable, and Walker was looking for a way to keep you safe."

He shook his head within its cowl, his face layered in shadow. "I warned him to act quickly, but he was too slow. Or perhaps he tried, and your father would not listen to him. They talked infrequently and were not close friends. Your father was a scholar and did not believe in violence. In his mind, the Druids represented violence. But violence doesn't care anything about whether or not you believe in it. It comes looking for you regardless. It came for your family just before dawn on a day when I was absent. Mwellrets, there on the orders of the Morgawr. They killed your parents and burned your home to the ground, making it appear as if it were the work of Gnome raiders. They thought you had perished in the blaze, not realizing your sister had hidden you in the cold cellar. They were in a hurry, having taken her, whom the Morgawr coveted most, and so did not search as carefully as I did when I came later. I found you in the cellar, tucked carefully away, crying, hungry, chilled, and frightened. I took you from the ashes and gave you to Walker."

Bek looked away from him, thinking it through. "Why didn't he tell me any of this before he sent me to you with Quentin?"

The other laughed. "Why doesn't he ever tell any of us anything? He told me a boy and his cousin were coming, that I should look for them, that I should test them to see if they had merit and heart." He shook his head. "He left it to me to realize that it was you, the boy I had saved all those years ago.

He left it to me to determine what I was meant to do. Do you see?"

Bek shook his head, not entirely certain he did.

"You were told to ask me to come with you on this voyage. You were given a message to deliver, one that I was to interpret in whatever way I chose. I realized what he hadn't told you, what he was asking of me. It was clear enough. He wanted me to be your protector, your defender when danger threatened. But I was to monitor the progress of your magic's development, as well. He knew it would begin to surface, and when it did you would have to be told the truth about who you really were. He did not want to rush things, though; he wanted to keep you in the dark as long as possible so that you would not be overwhelmed by the enormity of it all. But I knew that the sooner you discovered you had the use of magic, the sooner you could find a way to come to terms with it. We differ in our approach to things, the Druid and I, and I imagine he was not happy at all with what I did to you on Mephitic."

"He was furious." Bek hesitated. "But I'm glad you took a chance on me. That you showed me what I could do. That you gave me a chance to prove myself."

The shape-shifter nodded, eyes a flicker of brightness in the shadows. "You saved us in those ruins. You have heart and strength of mind and body, boy—tools you need to manage the wishsong's power. But your skills are still raw and untried. You need time and experience before you will be the equal of your sister."

Bek studied him a moment in the ensuing silence. "Tell me the truth. You're not deceiving me about any of this, are you? Because I've been deceived more than once already on this journey."

The other grunted. "By the Druid. Not by me."

"Grianne really is my sister, isn't she? The Ilse Witch is my sister? I need to hear you say it."

The bright eyes glimmered fierce and sharp within the cowl, all that was visible of the other's face. "She is your sister. Why would I tell you otherwise? Do you think I am the Druid's tool, as the witch would have you be?"

Bek shook his head. "I had to ask."

The shape-shifter grunted, not entirely mollified. "Don't ask such questions again. Not of me." He folded his arms into his cloak. "Enough of this. What's happened to the others who went ashore with you? I've had no chance to search for them. I boarded the witch's airship during the collision off Mephitic because I thought I would be more useful there and might learn something that would help us gain an advantage. But she almost found me out, and I was forced to hide myself carefully, to wait for a chance to make my escape. She came alone in search of Walker, so I followed. She led me to that clearing and to you. But not to Walker. What's become of him?"

Swiftly, Bek filled him in on the disastrous events of the past day, of the attempt to penetrate the ruins, of the traps found waiting, of the company's decimation and the scattering of its members. With Ryer Ord Star and the Elven Tracker Tamis he had fled to the clearing where the Ilse Witch had found him. Of the fates of Quentin, Panax, Ahren Elessedil, and Ard Patrinell, he could not be certain. Tamis had gone looking for them, but she had not come back. Walker had disappeared into the black tower that dominated the center of the ruins and had not come out.

"We'll need help to search for them," Bek said. "Especially if the Ilse Witch and the Mwellrets are looking, too."

Truls Rohk rocked back slightly on his heels and gave an audible sigh. "We'll have some difficulty finding any. There's bad news everywhere in this business. Your sister used her magic to immobilize the *Jerle Shannara*'s crew. She boarded the ship and took them all prisoner. She has locked them belowdecks, and she controls both ships. *Black Moclips* is anchored in the bay, where you went ashore. The *Jerle Shannara* is downriver, closer to the ice gates. There's no help to be had from either."

Bek felt as if the ground had fallen away beneath his feet. Whatever else had been taken from them, at least they'd had the *Jerle Shannara* to retreat to. Now that haven was lost, as well. They were trapped on Ice Henge. They couldn't even get word of where they were to the Wing Riders.

He thought suddenly of Rue Meridian and felt a sharp pang of terror, one much sharper than he would have expected. He took a steadying breath. "Are the Rovers unharmed and well?" he asked, trying to sound casual.

The shape-shifter shrugged. "No one was hurt in the boarding. I don't know what's happened since, but probably nothing."

"Shades! We've lost everything, Truls. You and I and maybe one or two more are all that's left, alive and free." He heard a hint of desperation creep into his voice and tried to block it away. "We have to do something. At least we have to go back and face Grianne, find a way to convince her that she's an Ohmsford, make her see that she's been—"

"Slow down, boy," Truls Rohk said. "Let's take a deep breath and think this through. There's no going back to face the Ilse Witch just yet. What's already happened is still too fresh in her mind. We need a way to reach her besides what you've already tried. Something she can't brush aside as easily as your words."

He glanced meaningfully over Bek's shoulder. The boy glanced with him and found himself staring at the pommel of the Sword of Shannara still strapped across his back. In the excitement of his encounter with his sister, he had forgotten he was carrying it.

He looked back at the shape-shifter. "You mean, I should try using this?"

"I mean, find a way to use it." The other's voice was ironic. "Not so easy to do, I'd think. Your sister isn't just going to stand there and let you use the magic on her. But if you can find a way to catch her off guard, surprise her maybe, she might not have a choice. Like it or not, she might have to face up to the truth of things. It's the best chance we have of persuading her."

Bek shook his head doubtfully. "She'll never give us the chance. Never."

Truls Rohk said nothing, waiting.

"She'll fight us!" Bek reached back to touch the handle of the Sword of Shannara, then let his hand fall away helplessly. "Besides, I don't know if I can make it work against her."

"Not against her," the shape-shifter advised quietly. "For her."

Bek nodded slowly. "For her. For both of us."

"I wouldn't be so quick to discount our chances," Truls Rohk continued. "We've lost the ship and crew, but we don't know about Panax and that Highlander and the others. And I wouldn't put finished to the Druid if I saw him dropped six feet underground; he has more lives than a cat. He won't have gone into the tower without a plan for getting out. I know him, boy. I've known him a long time. He thinks everything through. I wouldn't be surprised if he was already free and looking for us."

Bek looked doubtful, but nodded anyway. "What do we do next? Where do we go from here?"

Truls Rohk climbed to his feet, cloak falling about his wide shoulders, shadowing him from the ground up, leaving him a wraith, even in the growing dawn light.

"I need to backtrack far enough to make certain we aren't being followed by the witch or her rets. You wait here for my return. Don't move from this spot." He paused. "Unless you're in danger. In that case, hide yourself the best way you can. But if that becomes necessary, don't use your magic. You're not ready yet, not without me."

He gave the boy a hard stare in warning, then turned and disappeared into the trees.

Bek sat with his back against an aging shagbark hickory and watched the eastern sky brighten with the dawn's coming. Darkness gave way to first light, then first light to morning, the sky changing colors in gaps through the trees that were invisible in the darkness and could be discerned only now. He sat thinking of where he was, of the journey that had brought him to this place and time, and of the changes he had gone through. He remembered thinking, on the evening that Walker had first appeared in the Highlands months earlier and asked him to come on this voyage, that if he went with the Druid, nothing in his life would ever be the same again. He hadn't realized how right he would prove to be.

He closed his eyes momentarily and tried to imagine what it had been like back in Leah, in the Highlands, in his home. He couldn't do it. It was so far away, so removed from the present, that it was little more than a memory, fading with a past that seemed lost in another lifetime.

He gave up on the Highlands and instead tried to imagine what it would be like to have Grianne as his sister. Not just in name, but in fact. To have her accept that it was so. To have her call him Bek. He failed in this effort, as well. As the Ilse Witch, Grianne had taken lives and destroyed dreams. She had done things that he might never be able to accept, no matter how mistaken she had been or how much contrition she exhibited. Her life was wrapped in deception and trickery, in a misdirected search for revenge, in isolation and bitterness. It was not as if she could simply wipe away her past and begin fresh. She could not become someone different all at once simply because he wanted it to be so. That was asking for a child's-fable ending of a kind that had long since ceased to be possible. Whatever he expected of her, it was probably too much. The best he could hope for was that she would come to realize the truth.

He pictured her in his mind, standing before him in her gray robes, austere and imperious. He could not imagine her being happy. Had she laughed even once since she had been stolen away? Had she ever smiled?

Yet he had to find a way to bring her back to herself, to something of the girl she had been fifteen years ago, to a little part of the world she had abandoned and disdained as meant for lesser creatures. He had to help her, even if by helping he should cause her greater pain.

How could he manage this, when their next encounter would likely result in her trying her very best to kill him?

He wished he had Quentin with him—Quentin, with his sensible, straightforward approach to things, always able to see with such clarity the right way to proceed, the best thing to do. Had Quentin survived the battle at Castledown's ruins? Tears filled his eyes at the thought that his cousin might be dead. Even thinking such a thing seemed a betrayal. He could not imagine life without his cousin—his confidant, his best friend. Quentin had been so eager to come on this voyage, so anxious to see some other part of the world, to learn something new of life. What if it had cost him his own?

Bek knotted his hands together in frustration and stared out into the trees, into the growing sunlight, the new day, and his determination hardened into certainty. He must find Quentin. Maybe even before he found Walker, because the fact of the matter was that Quentin was the more important of the two. If they were stranded in this strange land, if their airships were lost to them and their companions dead, at least they would have each other to see the worst of it through. To face what lay ahead, however bad, in any other way was inconceivable to him.

Look after each other, Coran Leah had urged them. They had promised each other as much—long ago, in Arborlon, when there had still been a chance to turn back.

He sighed wearily. At least he had Truls Rohk to help him. As strange and frightening as the shape-shifter was, he had shown himself to be a friend. As conflicted as his life had been, he was perhaps the most dependable and capable of the ship's company. There was a measure of reassurance in that, and Bek embraced it eagerly.

Because he had nothing else to embrace, he admitted. Because sometimes you took comfort where you found it.

Truls Rohk was not gone long. The light had not yet chased away the last of the night when he reappeared through the trees, his cloaked form crouched low, his movements quick and furtive.

"On your feet," he hissed roughly, pulling the boy up. "Your sister's on our trail and coming fast."

Bek tried to keep the fear from his eyes and throat, tried to breathe normally as he glanced in the direction from which the shape-shifter had come. Then they were running into the trees and gone.

FOUR

She was perhaps a hundred yards into the forest and well away from Cree Bega and the other Mwellrets when the Ilse Witch paused to adjust her clothing. She pulled out a length of braided cord, looped it over her shoulders, crisscrossed it down her body and through her legs, and bound up her robes where they hung loose so that she could move more easily through the heavy brush ahead. The robes she had chosen were light but strong, and would not tear easily. Anticipating a rough climb into the ruins of Castledown, she had exchanged the sandals she normally favored for ankle boots with tough, flexible soles. She had intended her clothing and footgear for something else entirely, but her foresight was paying off. She had hunted before, though for different quarry, and she understood the importance of being prepared.

Her mind drifted momentarily to those days she had buried so thoroughly until the boy had confronted her. As Grianne Ohmsford, she had spent time in the woods and hills about her home, learning to use the magic of the wishsong. One of the exercises she engaged in regularly was a form of tracking. Using the magic, she would detect the passing of an animal and then follow it to its lair. Her singing, she discovered, could color its fading body heat and movements just enough to show her its progress, if the trail wasn't too old. She couldn't read prints or signs in the manner of Trackers, but the ability to trace heat and movement worked just as well. She became quite good at it even before she was stolen away.

She thought again of the boy. He bothered her more than she wanted to admit. The hair and eyes were right for Bek. Even something about his movements and facial expressions was familiar. And that hint of magic that surfaced right at the end of things—that was the wishsong. No one should have all three save Bek. What were the odds? How long would the Druid have had to look to find such a combination? But she was forgetting that he could create everything but the magic, layer it on as if it had always been there, making over the one he had chosen to fool her.

Bek had never evidenced use of the wishsong before she hid him that last morning. He had been a normal baby. She had no way of knowing if he would ever have had use of the magic. Or did now.

She blinked away her discomfort and her thoughts and set about adjusting her robes a final time. She looked down at the pale skin of her wrists and ankles where it was exposed to the light, virtually untouched by the sun, so white it looked iridescent in the mix of forest shadows and golden dawn. She touched herself as if to make certain she was real, thinking as she did that sometimes it felt as if she weren't, as if she was created out of dreams and wishes, and nothing about her was hard and true.

She gritted her teeth. It was that boy who was making her think like this. Find him, and the thoughts would disappear for good.

She set out once more, leaving the hood in place, her face in darkness, hidden away from prying eyes. With her robes bound close, she eased through the trees, humming softly to reveal the trail of the shape-shifter and the boy, finding their lingering presence at every turn, their passage as clear as if marked by paint on tree bark. She moved at a steady pace, used to walking, to journeys afoot and not just to riding her Shrikes, toughened long since because she knew that she would not otherwise survive. The Morgawr might have been content to let her remain just a girl, less a threat, more mal-leable, but she had determined early on that she would never allow herself to be vulnerable again. Sooner or later, she would be threatened by something or someone toughened by years of wilderness living, and she wanted to be ready for that. Nor did she ever want to be considered just a girl or even a woman, somehow reduced in stature by her sex and not re-garded with caution.

No, she thought grimly, she would never be thought of like that. The Morgawr had trained her in the use of her magic, but she had trained herself in the art of survival. When he was gone, which was often, she tested herself in ways he did not know about, going out alone, into dangerous country, some-times well beyond the Wilderun. She lived as an animal, tracking as they did, foraging, hunting, and always learning what they knew. Because she had the use of the wishsong, she could speak their language and gain their acceptance. She could make herself appear one with them. It took concentra-tion and effort, and a single slip might have spelled disaster. She was powerful, but it required only a moment's inattention to let a predator past her defenses. Moor cats and Kodens could strike you down before you thought to wonder what had happened. Werebeasts were quicker than that.

She had not gone far before she detected a second pres-ence, one that overlapped the first. She slowed, suddenly cautious, reading the images, the traces of heat and movement, wary of a trap. But after a few moments she realized what she had discovered. The shape-shifter had backtracked to see if anyone was following, then retraced his steps to where he had left the boy. It was likely he'd seen her. She had to assume as much. She already knew he was experienced and skilled, and he had been wise enough not to assume that after rescuing the boy he was clear of her. He had returned to check, then gone back to warn his charge.

She set off in pursuit, anxious to close the gap between them. If he had been close enough to detect her, he could not be all that far ahead now. The images revealed by her magic were unmistakable and strong. He was not even bothering to hide his trail. He was running, fleeing, frightened of her perhaps, realizing how little distance separated them. That made her smile. It was what she wanted. Frightened, panicked people made mistakes. The shape-shifter was not one of these under normal circumstances, but conditions had changed.

Down through ravines and along the crests of low hills studded with hardwoods and choked with brush she made her way, breaking into a lope in the open areas, so close she felt she could smell them. Overhead, the sun had crested mid-morning and was moving toward noon, bright and clear in a cloudless blue sky. She breathed in the warmth and freshness of the forest, a sheen of perspiration coating her face and hands, seeping down her limbs inside her garments. She felt a wildness infuse her, familiar and welcome. It was like this sometimes when she was on a chase, that sense of being feral and untamed, dangerous. She wanted to cast aside her human garments and hunt as the animals did. She craved a taste of fresh blood.

In a broad clearing ringed tightly with old growth, images

of the boy reappeared, joining with the shape-shifter. Excitement raced through her, spurring her anew. The images told her they were running now, racing to escape her. The boy would know she was coming. He would be wondering what he could do to save himself if she caught up to him. He would lie, of course. He would tell his story again. But he had to know already that it would be useless to try to trick her a second time. He had to know what she would do to him.

Just another few hundred yards, perhaps. Not much more than that, and she would have them. They were right ahead.

But all of a sudden, as she entered a meadow filled with yellow and blue wildflowers that rolled like the surface of the sea in the wind, the trail she followed so eagerly disappeared. For a moment she could not believe it. She kept on, pushing ahead in disbelief, crossing the meadow to its far side, trying to make sense of what had happened. Then she stopped. The images were still there, still as discernible as ever, bright and clear. But they were everywhere, all across the meadow, all through the trees beyond, thousands of them, flickers of heat and light. It seemed as if the shape-shifter and the boy were everywhere at once, gone in all directions at the same time.

It wasn't possible, of course.

It wasn't real.

She took a deep breath to calm herself, then exhaled slowly. She reached within her hood to brush back a lock of her thick, dark hair and looked from one end of the meadow to the other, casting into the shadows beneath the trees beyond, searching. No one was there. The boy and his protector were elsewhere, safely clear and farther away from her with every passing second.

In spite of herself, she smiled. She had believed them panicked, but the shape-shifter and the boy were smarter than she'd thought. Realizing she would track them using her magic, they had retaliated by using their own. Or, more accurately, if she was reading things right, the boy had used his. He had used it to cast their images all about, to disperse them in all directions. She could sort them out, find the right set to see which way the pair had gone, but it would take time. They would do this again, farther on, and each time she was forced to unravel one of the confusing puzzles, she would lose ground.

They were hoping, of course, that she lacked a Tracker's skills and could not pursue them through reading prints and signs if they foiled her magic. They were right. Her magic was all she had, and it would have to be enough.

She sat down, cross-legged with her back against an oak, looking out into the meadow, thinking things through. There was no need for hurry. She would catch them, of course. Nothing they tried would be enough to throw her off their trail for long. It was more important not to act in haste. She took a moment to consider where all this was leading. The boy and his protector were running, but to what? This was a strange land, and they knew nothing of its geography or inhabitants. The shape-shifter would have told the boy by now that their airship was under her control and outside their reach. The members of the landing party led by Walker were scattered or dead, and the Druid had disappeared. At best, running offered only a temporary solution to their problem. How did they intend to make use of it? Where would they try to go and to what end? Surely, they weren't running blindly and toward nothing. The shape-shifter was too smart for that.

She stood slowly, her mind made up. Answers to questions like those would have to wait. It didn't make any difference where they went or why if she couldn't find them, and she intended to find them right now. If her magic couldn't serve her one way, it would have to serve her another.

Standing at the edge of the meadow, she cupped her hands to her mouth and gave a long, low cry, eerie and chilling as it wafted into the distance and died away. She gave the cry three times, stood waiting awhile, then gave it three more.

Time slipped away, the meadow and the surrounding forest silent save for birdsong and the rustle of leaves in the wind. The Ilse Witch stood where she was, listening and watching everywhere at once.

Then something moved out of the trees and into the grasses on the far side of the meadow, causing the flowers to ripple and part. The Ilse Witch waited patiently as the submerged creature made its way toward her, invisible beneath the bobbing coverlet of wildflowers, crouched low to the earth.

When it was a dozen yards away, too late for it to escape, it lifted its narrow muzzle slightly from the sea of brightness, testing the wind, searching for the source of the call that had summoned it. The wolf was not of a recognizable breed, bigger than the ones with which she was familiar, but it would do. It was an outcast, a renegade—she could sense that about it—not part of any pack, solitary by choice and nature, its face a mask of grizzled black hair and sharp features, its scarred gray body sinewy and muscular. A ferocious predator, the wolf possessed unmatchable tracking skills and instincts, which would serve her needs well, once the necessary adjustments had been made.

The wolf must have realized it was trapped, unable to break free of her magic, of her compelling voice, of the chains she had already wound about it as she hummed and sang softly. But it was not so stunned by what was happening that it did not try to escape. It bristled and snarled, thrashing against her attempts to exercise control, its hatred for her revealed in its baleful eyes and curled muzzle. She let it have its moment of rage, and then she bore down on it relentlessly. Bit by bit she overcame its resistance, harnessing its will, claiming its heart and mind, making its body and thoughts her own.

Then she began to reshape it. It was a dangerous brute, but she decided it needed to be more dangerous still; the shape-shifter would be more than a match for an ordinary wolf, no matter how ferocious, and she wanted the odds reversed. She wanted a caull, a beast of reshaped flesh and bone, a creature of magic molded by her hand and obedient only to her. Using the magic of the wishsong, she caused it to evolve in very specific ways, focusing her attention on its predatory instincts, tracking skills, and resiliency. To enhance its intelligence was too difficult a task, too complex even for her. But its form could be changed to suit her needs, and she did not shrink from what was required, even when the beast screamed as if it were a human child.

Afterwards, it lay panting and feverish on the sun-dappled earth, the wildflowers ripped to shreds for fifteen or twenty feet in all directions, the ground torn and furrowed, the grasses coated with sprays of blood. She held the caull in check, then gave it sleep to calm and heal its re-formed body. Its yellow eyes closed, and its breathing slowed and deepened in response to the change in her song. In seconds, it slept.

The effort had exhausted her, and she sat down to rest. The day lengthened from morning to afternoon. She dozed in the sunlight, wrapped within her hood and robes, a small dark shape at the edge of the savaged patch of earth and sleeping beast. Time drifted, and she dreamed of a tiny baby boy with a shock of dark hair and startling blue eyes, staring back at her from an enfolding darkness as she closed a hidden door on it forever.

She awoke before the caull, alerted by the rustle of its legs as it stirred from its own sleep. Her wishsong already coming into play, she rose and waited for its eyes to open. When its head lifted, she ordered it to rise. It did so, lurching to its feet, big and menacing in the fading light. It was twice the size it had been, with a thickened neck and huge shoulders, its body re-formed for fighting and running. Its head was a broad, flat shelf of bone, wedge-shaped from pointed ears to snout. Its muzzle split as it panted, revealing a double row of razor-sharp teeth made for rending and tearing. Its legs had short-ened to give it a splay-footed stance, and the digits of its paws had lengthened and spread like fingers to end in hooked claws. Sleek gray hair layered its body, less fur than skin, a tough coarse hide that even brambles could not scratch. It wheeled this way and that, as if anxious to test its newfound strength, and in its maddened eyes glittered an unmistakable bloodlust.

She watched it carefully, pleased with her handiwork, cer-tain that with this creature to aid her, she would be more than a match for the wiles of the shape-shifter and his young ac-complice. She had learned to fashion caulls while practicing her magic with the Morgawr. But she had discovered the shape of this one on her own. Hundreds of years ago, there had been another, a monster out of Faerie called a Jachyra that had stalked and killed a Druid. She didn't need the real thing. A close approximation would be sufficient to serve her needs.

"Relentless," she hissed at the caull. It swung its flat, heavy head toward her watchfully. "That is what you will be for me in your search for those I hunt. Unstoppable."

The jaws split in what might have been a smile if the beast had been capable of understanding what a smile was. It was enough to satisfy the Ilse Witch. If it accomplished what she wished, she would do the smiling for them both.

Bek trailed Truls Rohk as they entered a meadow filled with blue and yellow wildflowers. He was already beginning to tire from the pace the shape-shifter was setting, sweat coating his face and drenching his tunic. The sun was high in the midday sky and the air warm. Truls Rohk loped to the center of the meadow and stopped, looking back.

"Far enough," he said, his ravaged face a shadow within his cowl, barely seen even in the bright midday sun. He looked back in the direction from which they had come. "We can't outrun her forever. Sooner or later, she'll wear us down. Something else is needed."

Bek blew out his breath wearily and took a fresh gulp, swallowing against the dryness in his throat. "Maybe she'll give up if we keep going."

"Not likely. Think about it. She put aside her hunt for the Druid, her mortal enemy, to come in search of you. She put everything aside, the whole of her purpose in coming on this voyage, because of you. You think you didn't reach her with your words and arguments, but I think maybe you did. Enough at least to make her wonder."

Bek shook his head. "It didn't feel like it at the time." Truls Rohk didn't even seem to be breathing hard, his body still and composed within his cloak, not a ripple of movement, not a stir.

"She's tracking us with her magic, reading our passing with it. I saw the way she walked, head up, eyes forward. She wasn't studying signs or searching for prints." He cast about for a moment, looking off into the distance in all directions, taking in the lay of the land. "We have to throw her off, boy. Now, before this gets any tighter, before she's so close nothing will slow her."

He faced the boy squarely, broad-shouldered and threatening. "Time to take some responsibility for yourself. Your magic against hers—that might be the answer. It lacks power and subtlety both, but it has its uses even so. Listen to me. She's probably reading our body heat, our movement from place to place. See if you can do the same. Watch me closely. When I disappear, track me. Use your voice, like you did on Mephitic."

In an instant, he disappeared, right from in front of Bek, vanishing as if into vapor. The boy called up his magic and cast it about wildly, searching. Nothing happened.

The shape-shifter reappeared, right where he had been an instant before. Bek gasped at the suddenness, then shook his head angrily. "It didn't work!" Frustration colored his words. "I can't make it do anything!"

Truls Rohk bent close, big and menacing. "Too bad for us if you can't, isn't it? Try again. Cast about as if you're throwing a net! Pretend you're draping images with cloth. It isn't me you're looking for—it's my shade. Do it!"

Again he was gone, and again Bek summoned the magic and cast it out. This time he was more successful. He caught pieces of Truls Rohk moving left to right and back again, ghostly presences that hung on the midday air.

"Better." The shape-shifter was back in front of him again. "Once more, but hold tight to a corner of the magic you're releasing. Then draw it in, fisherboy."

On this try, he caught all of Truls Rohk's movements, a series of passages clearly defined, moving all around him and back again. Like shades released from the dead, they hung suspended on the air, one after the other, each moving slowly to catch up to the next, as if runners slowed by quicksand and weariness.

They worked at it steadily, and then the shape-shifter changed his look to match the boy's, and suddenly Bek was casting for his own images, seeing himself replicated over and over across the meadow. Back and forth, this way and that, from one end to the other and into the trees, Truls Rohk cast his own image and the boy's until the meadow was filled with their shadows and the trail was hopelessly tangled.

"Let her try to sort that out," Truls Rohk grunted as he led the boy through the drifting images in a zigzag fashion, making for a set of mountains east. "We'll do it again a little farther on, somewhere close to water."

They ran on, not so quickly and furiously as before, the shape-shifter setting a more reasonable pace, one the boy was able to keep up with more easily. They did not speak, but concentrated on their effort, on putting as much distance between themselves and their pursuer as possible, on conserving their strength. Twice more they stopped to produce a confusing set of images, a tangled trail, crossing a deep stream once, doubling back twice at right angles, choosing difficult, rocky terrain for their passage.

It was nearing nightfall when they stopped finally to rest and eat, the light fading rapidly west, the forestland already cloaked in lengthening shadows. Night birds lifted out of the growing twilight, dark winged shapes against the sky. Bek watched them fly away and wished he had their wings. He carried no food or water, but Truls Rohk had come bearing both, stolen from *Black Moclips* on leaving, the shape-shifter prepared as always.

"Though I did not think it would come to this," he admitted grimly, handing over his water skin for the boy to drink.

Bek was exhausted. He had not faltered, but his muscles were drained and his body aching. He was used to hard treks and long hikes, but not to running for so long. Life aboard the *Jerle Shannara* had helped prepare him, but even so his endurance had its limits and did not begin to approach that of Truls Rohk.

"Will she give up now?" he asked hopefully, passing back the water skin and gnawing hungrily on the dried beef the other passed him in return. "Will she lose interest and go back for Walker?"

The shape-shifter laughed softly, wrapped in his robes and hood, his expression and thoughts hidden away. "I don't think so. She isn't like that. She doesn't give up. She'll find another way to track us. She'll keep coming."

Bek sighed in resignation. "I'll have to face her again sooner or later. There isn't any help for it." The Sword of Shannara lay at his side, and he glanced down at it. His expectations for its use against his sister seemed foolish and desperate.

"Maybe. But we have other problems to solve first. We can't just keep running for no better purpose than to escape the witch. Even if we lose her or she gives up, where does that leave us? Somewhere in the middle of a strange country without an airship or friends, without adequate supplies or weapons, and without a decent plan, that's where. Not so good."

"We have to go back for Quentin and the others," Bek answered at once, convinced that was the right choice. "We have to help them if we can. We have to try to find Walker."

It sounded so obvious and so logical that the words were

out of his mouth before he realized that he was ignoring obstacles that rendered his response only a few steps shy of ridiculous. Even given their respective magics and the shape-shifter's skill and experience, they were only two men—one man and a boy, he amended ruefully. They had no idea where their friends were. They had no means of searching for them other than to go afoot, a mode of transportation hardly conducive to the sort of search required. Their enemies outnumbered them perhaps fifty to one and that wasn't counting whatever it was that lived belowground in Castledown.

Truls Rohk didn't say anything. He simply sat there, looking out at the boy from within the shadows of his hood.

Bek cleared his throat. "All right. We can't do it alone. We need help."

The shape-shifter nodded. "You're learning, boy. What sort of help?"

"Someone to even the odds when we go back to face the Ilse Witch and the Mwellrets and whatever else is waiting."

"That, but also someone who knows a way past the things that guard those ruins and protect the treasure Walker's come to find." Truls Rohk laughed bitterly. "Don't think for a moment that the Druid, assuming he still lives, will give up on the treasure."

Bek thought of all that the company of the *Jerle Shannara* had endured to come so far, of what had been promised and what given up. He thought of how much Walker was risking to make the journey, both of life and reputation. Truls Rohk was right. The Druid would rather die than fail, given what was at stake. Even from the little he knew of Walker, it was certain that failure to gain the support of the Elves for a Druid Council at Paranor would be the end of him. It was everything he had worked for, all that mattered to him now. He had

spent his life as a Druid seeking that support. Bek knew it
from their conversations. He knew it from what he had heard
from Ahren Elessedil. Walker had tied his fate to this voyage,
to the recovery of the Elfstones and the finding of the treasure
on the castaway's map.

And weren't they all tied in turn to the Druid in coming
with him, Bek as well as the others? Weren't their fates all inextricably linked?

"Sleep for an hour; then we'll set out again." Truls Rohk
sat with his hands locked together in front of him, animal hair
on their backs gleaming faintly, like silver threads. "I'll keep
watch."

Bek nodded wordlessly. An hour was better than nothing.
He took a moment to look back the way they had come, to
where the Ilse Witch was, to where his friends and companions were, somewhere in the dark.

Be strong, he prayed for all of them. He prayed it even for
Grianne.

FIVE

Dozens of miles away, deep within the glacier-draped mountains that warded the coast of the peninsula, bracketed by the thousand-foot walls of the gorge that channeled the ice melt out into the Blue Divide, the *Jerle Shannara* drifted in solitary grandeur. Rudderless, unmanned, sails in shreds, she rode the twists and turns of the winds that howled down the canyon, moving as if drawn toward the pillars of ice that blocked the way out. Clouds roiled overhead, mingling with mist off the ice and the spray off the crash of waves against the rocks below, white sheets of gauze layered against dim shards of sunlight. Shrikes circled and dived past the rigging, bright anticipation in their gimlet eyes, each pass bringing them closer to the dead men who lay sprawled across the airship's decks. Echoes from their cries and from the pounding surf mingled and reverberated off the cliffs in eerie counterpoint.

Ahead, growing closer with each twist and turn of the airship, the pillars waited. Giant's teeth ground together and withdrew, opening and closing over the gap through which the ship must pass, hungry-sounding, ravenous, as if anxious to catch hold of what had escaped before, as if needing to feel the wood and metal of the *Jerle Shannara* reduced to shards of debris and its crew reduced to bones and pulp.

Battered and dazed, barely conscious, Rue Meridian dangled from a rope nearly fifty feet below the stern of the ship. She hung from the rope with the last of her fading strength, too weary to do anything else. Blood coated her left arm and ran in rivulets down her side, and she could no longer feel her right leg. The wind howled in her ears and froze her skin. Ice had formed in her hair, and her clothes were stiff. Everything leading up to this moment was a haze of fragmented memories and jumbled emotions. She remembered her struggle with the Mwellret, both of them wounded, their tumbling to the deck of the airship, then sliding inexorably toward the wooden railing, picking up speed and unable to stop. She remembered them striking the railing, already splintered and broken by a falling spar, the Mwellret first, taking the brunt of the impact. The railing had given way like kindling, and they had gone through in a tangle.

It should have been the end of her. They were a thousand feet up, maybe more, with nothing between them and the rocks and rapids below but air. She had kicked free of the Mwellret instinctively, then grasped for something to hold on to. By sheer chance, she had caught this length of trailing rope, this lifeline to safety. Slowing her rapid descent had nearly dislocated her arms and had torn the skin of her hands as she ripped down its length to a knot that brought her up short. Twisting and turning in the wind, she clung to the rope in stunned relief, watching the dark shape of her antagonist tumble away into the ether.

But then shock and cold had set in, and she found she could not move from where she hung, pinned against the skyline like an insect on paper, frozen to her lifeline as she fought to stay conscious. She kept thinking that eventually she would find the strength to move again, to make some effort at climbing back aboard, or that someone aboard would haul her to safety. Her mind drifted in and out of various scenarios and near unconsciousness, always unable to do more than tease her with possibilities.

But she was not so far gone that she didn't realize the danger she was in and how little time was left to deal with it. The *Jerle Shannara* was drifting ever nearer to the ice pillars, and when she reached them she was finished. No one aboard ship was going to help her. Those who were topside were all dead, Furl Hawken among them. Those below were locked away in storerooms and could not break free or they would have done so by now. Her brother, Redden Alt Mer. The shipwright, Spanner Frew. Her friends, the Rovers from her homeland. Trapped and helpless, they were at the mercy of the elements, and their end was certain.

No one would help her.

No one would help them.

Unless she did something now.

With what seemed like superhuman effort, she unclenched one frozen hand from the rope and reached up to take a new hold. The effort sent pain through her body in ratcheting spasms and shocked her from her lethargy. Ignoring the cold and numbness, she hauled herself up a notch, freed the other hand, and took a new grip. She felt fresh blood run down the inside of her frozen clothing, where her body still maintained a small amount of warmth. She was freezing to death, she realized, hanging there from that rope, buffeted by the wind blown down off the glaciers. She forced herself to take another grip and pull to a new position, one hand over the other, each length of rope she traversed an excruciating ordeal. Her eyes peered out of ice-rimmed lids. There were glaciers all around, cresting the mountains and cliffs, spreading away into the mist and clouds. Snow blew past her in feathery gusts, and through gaps in their curtains she glimpsed the pillars ahead, slow-moving behemoths against the white, the light glinting off their azure surface. Booming coughs and grinding shrieks marked their advancement, collision, and retreat, and she could feel the pressure of their weight in her mind.

Keep going!

She climbed some more, still racked with pain and fatigue, still hopelessly far beneath the broken railing she needed to reach. Despair filled her. She would never make it in time. Had she made any progress at all? Had she even moved? She hurt so badly and felt so helpless and miserable that a part of her wanted just to give up, to let go, to fall and be done with it. That would be so easy. She wouldn't feel anything. The pain and cold would be gone; the desperation would end. A moment's relaxation of her tired hands would be all that was necessary.

Coward!

She howled the word into the wind. What was she thinking? She was a Rover, and above all else Rovers knew how to endure anything. Endurance demanded sacrifice, but gave back life. Endurance was always the tougher choice, but gave the truer measure of a heart. She would not give in, she told herself. She would not!

Stay alive! Keep moving!

She tucked her chin into her chest and put one hand over the other, the second over the first, hauling herself upward inch by inch, foot by foot, refusing to quit. Her body screamed in protest, and it felt as if the wind and the cold suddenly heightened their efforts to slow her. Frozen strands of her long hair whipped at her face. She dredged up every source of inspiration she could think of to force herself to keep going.

Her brother and the other Rovers, trapped within the ship, dependent on her. Walker, stranded ashore with the others of the landing party, including her young friend Bek. Furl Hawken, dead trying to save her. The Ilse Witch and her Mwellrets, who would never pay for what they'd done if she did not find a way to stay alive and make them do so.

Shades!

She was crying freely, the tears freezing against the skin of her face, and she could not see through them well enough to tell how far she had climbed. Her jaw was clenched so tightly her teeth hurt, and the muscles of her back were knotting and cramping from the strain of her ascent. She could not take much more, she knew. She could not last much longer. One hand over the other, pull and clutch the rope with the second hand, pull again and clutch the rope with the first, on and on . . .

She screamed in pain as the wind slammed her against the hull of the airship, and she almost released her grip on the rope as she spun away from the rough wood. Then she realized what that meant, how far she had come, and opened her eyes and looked up. The gap in the broken railing was just above her. She redoubled her efforts, hauling herself up the final few yards of rope to the edge of the decking, gaining a firm grip on a still-solid balustrade, and pulling herself over the side to safety.

She lay on the rain- and ice-slicked deck for a moment, gazing skyward at the vast canopy of white mist and clouds, exhausted, but triumphant, too. Her mind raced. No time to rest. No time to spare. She rolled onto her side and peered across the bodies and debris, through the tattered shreds of sail and broken spars to the aft hatchway. She could not manage to get to her feet, so she crawled the entire way, fighting to stay conscious. The hatchway was thrown back, and she slid through the opening, lost her grip, and tumbled down the stairs. At the bottom she lay in a tangled heap, so numb she could not tell if anything was broken, still hearing the roar of the wind and the surf in her ears.

Get up!

She dragged herself to her feet, using the wall of the passageway to keep from falling again, pain shooting down her injured leg, blood soaking her clothing in fresh patches. How much had she lost? The passageway was shadowed and empty, but she thought she could hear voices calling. She tried calling back, but her voice was hollow and faint, lost in the roar of the wind. She stumbled along the corridor, using the wall for support, trying to trace the voices. She thought she heard her name a couple of times, but couldn't be sure. There was blood in her throat by then, hot and thick, and she swallowed it to keep her breathing passages clear. She was light-headed, and everything was spinning.

With a sudden lurch of the airship, she fell hard, still short of the storerooms, careening off one wall of the corridor into the other, slamming into it with such force that it knocked the breath from her lungs and she simply collapsed. She lay gasping for air, just barely able to keep from losing consciousness, the world about her spinning faster and faster. She tried to straighten herself and found she couldn't. She had no strength left, nothing more to give. It was the end of her. It was the end of them all.

She closed her eyes against the pain and fatigue, searching in her mind for the faces of those trapped only yards away. She found those faces, and Hawk's, as well, as familiar to her as her own. She heard their voices speaking her name, clear and welcoming, in other places, in better times. She found herself smiling.

The *Jerle Shannara* lurched once more, caught in a violent gust of wind, and she thought to herself, *I'm not ready to die.*

Somehow she got back to her feet. She never really knew how she managed it, how long it took, what mechanics she employed, what willpower she called upon. But, broken and crying, covered everywhere with blood, she got up and dragged herself the last few yards down the passageway to the first storeroom door. She tugged and tugged on the latch, hearing the voices shouting at her from inside, but the latch would not give. Screaming in rage and frustration, she hammered at the door, then realized it wasn't the latch that was holding it shut, it was the crossbar.

Gasping for breath, she threw back the crossbar with the last of her strength, pulled free the latch, yanked open the heavy door, and tumbled through into blackness.

When she came awake again, the first thing she saw was her brother.

"Are we still alive?" she asked, her voice weak, her throat parched with thirst. "It doesn't feel like it."

He gave her a rueful grin. "Not to you, I expect. But, yes, we're still alive, if only just by the barest of margins. It would be easier on all of us if the next time you come to the rescue, you do so with a little more alacrity."

She tried to laugh and failed. "I'll try to remember that."

Redden Alt Mer rose to bring a water skin close, poured out a measure into a cup, and lifted her head just enough to let her drink. He gave her small sips, letting her take her time. His big hand on the back of her head and neck felt gentle and reassuring.

When she had finished, he laid her back again and resumed his seat at her bedside. "It was closer than what I would have liked. They had us in two rooms, all but you and Hawk. With the crossbars thrown over the doorways, we couldn't free ourselves. We tried everything to knock the bar free, to work it clear through the jamb slit, even to break down the door. We could hear the storm and knew it was bad; we could feel the ship drifting. At first Mwellrets were watching us; then they were gone. We couldn't tell what was happening."

She closed her eyes, remembering. Hawk, using his dagger to pick the lock to their door, a forward storeroom that lacked a crossbar. Their battle with the Mwellret in the passageway. The charge up the stairs and onto the deck where other rets were waiting along with two members of the Federation crew. The airship in shambles, out of control, wheeling wildly in the grip of the canyon winds as it sailed toward the pillars of ice. The struggle with their captors. Furl Hawken giving up his own life to save hers. Her own brush with a deadly fall she only just managed to avoid. The long climb back.

"After you freed us, we rushed out on deck and saw what had happened to the ship and how close we were to the Squirm." He shook his mane of red hair, lips tightening. "By then, we were right on top of it. The pilothouse was smashed, the steering fouled, the light sheaths in shreds, the rigging flying everywhere, spars broken, and even a couple of the parse tubes jammed shut. But you should have seen Spanner and the others. They were all over that decking in seconds, clearing away the tubes, refastening the radian draws, bringing enough of the rigging and sail remnants into play to give us at least a small measure of control. You know what it was like up there, everything tossing and wild, the wind strong enough to knock you right off the deck if you didn't watch yourself, or maybe even if you did."

She nodded, her eyes opening again to meet his. "I know."

"A couple of the men went right up the masts, even in that storm, as if it didn't matter or they didn't care how dangerous it was. Kelson Riat barely missed getting his head taken off by a loose spar, and Jahnon Pakabbon was slashed all the way down his left arm by a spike. But no one gave up on the ship. We got her functioning again in minutes. I'd cleared the controls, but the lines were smashed, so we had to do it all by hand. We used the power stored in the parse tubes to right her, turn her from the ice pillars, and start her back the way she had come. The wind fought us the whole way, blowing down off the ice fields and up the gorge, trying to overpower us. But she's a good ship, Little Red. The *Jerle Shannara* is the best. She fought her way right into the teeth of the wind and held her own until we found some calm space to make headway in."

He rocked back in his seat, laughing like a boy. "Even Spanner Frew was spitting and howling in defiance of that wind, standing at the wheel to keep the rudder steady, even without the controls to work. Old Black Beard fought for her like the rest of us. To him she's a child he's nurtured and reared as his own, and he's not going to lose her, is he?"

She smiled with him, his glee infectious, her relief giving her an edge on the ache of her body. She glanced down at herself, tucked in one of the berths belowdecks, in the Healer's quarters, she thought. Light shone through the room's only window, bright and cheerful. She tried moving her arms and legs, but her body didn't seem to want to respond.

"Am I all in one piece?" she asked, suddenly concerned.

"Except for a few bad slashes and deep bruises." He arched

one eyebrow at her. "You must have had one terrible battle up there, Little Red. You and Hawk."

She kept trying to make her hands and feet move, saying nothing in reply. Finally, she felt a tingle at the ends of each, working its way through the pain that ran up and down her body in sharp spasms. She let herself relax and looked at her brother. "Hawk died for me. You've probably guessed as much. I wouldn't have made it without him. None of us would. I can't believe he's gone."

Her brother nodded. "Nor me. He's been with us forever. I didn't think we'd ever lose him." He sighed. "Care to tell me what happened? It might help us both a bit if you did."

She took her time, pausing once to let him bring her a fresh drink of water, taking him through the events leading up to her finally freeing him from the aft storeroom, leaving nothing out, forcing herself to remember it all, especially everything about Furl Hawken. It took considerable effort just to tell it, and when she had finished, she was exhausted.

Redden Alt Mer didn't say anything at first, simply nodded, then rose and walked to the cabin window to look outside. She cried a little when his back was turned, not tears, not audible sobs, but tiny hiccups and little heaves that he wouldn't notice or that, at least, she could pretend he didn't.

When he turned back to her, she was composed again. "He was everything a Rover is supposed to be," her brother offered quietly. "It doesn't help much just now, but down the road, when it matters, I think we'll find some part of him is inside us, keeping us strong, telling us how to be as good a man as he was."

She fell asleep then, almost before she knew it, and her sleep was deep and dreamless. When she woke, the room was dark save for a single candle by her bed, the sunlight that had shone through the cabin window earlier gone. She felt stronger this time, though the aches and pains that had beset her before were more pronounced. She managed to lever herself up on one elbow and drink from the cup of water sitting on the table next to her. The *Jerle Shannara* sailed in calm and steady winds, the motion of its passage barely perceptible. It was quiet aboard ship, the sounds of men's voices and movements absent. It must be night, and most must be sleeping. Where were they? How far had they come since she had slept? She had no way of knowing as long as she lay in bed.

She forced her legs from under the covers and tried to stand, but her efforts failed, and she knocked the cup of water flying as she grasped the table for support before falling back again. The clatter echoed loudly, and moments later Big Red appeared, bare-chested and, clearly, roused from sleep.

"Some of us are trying to get our rest, Sister Rue," he muttered, helping her back beneath the covers. "What do you think you are doing anyway? You're a day or two away from walking around and maybe not then."

She nodded. "I'm weaker than I thought."

"You lost a lot of blood, if I'm any judge of wounds. You won't replace it all right away. Nor will you be healing up overnight. So let's try to be reasonable about what you can and can't do for the immediate future."

"I need a bath. I smell pretty bad."

He grinned, seating himself on a three-legged stool. "I can help you with that. But no one was going to attempt it while you were unconscious, let me tell you. Not even Spanner Frew. They know how you feel about being touched."

She tightened her lips. "They don't know anything about me. They just think they do." The words were sharp, bitter.

She forced the sudden anger away. "Go back to bed. I'm sorry I woke you."

He shrugged, his red hair glistening in the candlelight, loose and unruly as it hung about his strong face. "Well, I'm up now, so maybe I'll stay up and talk with you awhile. The bath can wait until morning, can't it? I don't much want to haul a tub and water in here in the dark."

She grinned faintly. "It can wait." She regretted her anger; it was misdirected and inappropriate. Her brother was only trying to help. "I feel better tonight."

"You look better. Everyone was worried."

"How long have I been in this bed?"

"Two days."

She was surprised. "That long? It doesn't feel like it." She exhaled sharply. "Where are we now? How close to where we left the others? We've gone back for them, haven't we? We have to warn them about the Ilse Witch."

He smiled. "You are better. Ready to get up and fight another battle, aren't you?" He shook his head, then turned suddenly sober. "Listen carefully, Little Red. Things aren't so simple. We're not headed inland to the Druid's shore party. We're headed for the coast and the Wing Riders. We're doing just what we were told to do."

He must have seen the anger flare in her eyes. "Don't say something you'll live to regret. I didn't make this choice because it was the one I favored. I made it because it was the only one that made sense. Don't you think I want to square accounts with the witch? Don't you think I want to lock up those Mwellrets the same way they locked us up? I don't like leaving any of them running around loose any more than you do. I don't for a minute like abandoning Walker and the others. But the *Jerle Shannara* is in tatters. We can replace the light sheaths and radian draws, repair the parse tubes, and readjust the diapson crystals to suit our needs. We can manage to sail at maybe three-quarters power and efficiency. But we've lost spars and damaged two of the masts. We're all beaten up. We can't fight a battle, especially against *Black Moclips*. We can't even outrun her, if she should catch sight of us. Going inland now would be foolhardy. We wouldn't be of much use to anyone if we got ourselves knocked out of the sky or captured a second time, would we?"

The glare had not faded from her eyes. "So we just abandon them?" she snapped back.

"We were already abandoning them when the Druid ordered us out of that bay. Walker knew the risks when he sent us away. If we'd gotten clear of the channel before *Black Moclips* found us, she still would have sailed on up the river to the bay. Walker understood that. He wasn't thinking it couldn't happen."

She shook her head stubbornly. "We're their lifeline! They can't survive without us! What if anything goes wrong?"

"Don't be so quick to discount what they can or can't do without us. Something's already gone wrong, only it went wrong with us. And we survived, didn't we? Give them a little credit."

They stared at each other in silence for a moment, eyes fierce and intense. Rue backed down first. "They're not Rovers," she pointed out quietly.

Her brother smiled in spite of himself. "Granted. But they have their good points anyway and a fair chance of holding their own until we can get to them. Which I fully intend to do, Little Red, if you'll just have some faith in me." He leaned forward, resting his elbows on his knees. "We're on our way to the coast to make repairs and heal wounds. If we're to out-smart and outsail the Ilse Witch and her Mwellrets and per-haps do battle with *Black Moclips*, we have to be at our best. Maybe it won't come to that, if we're lucky, but we can't rely on luck to see us through this mess. We should be able to map our way in and out again, just as the Druid wanted. We should be able to make contact with the Wing Riders, as well. And while the ship's being overhauled and you're healing, I'll be flying back in with Hunter Predd to have a look at what's be-come of our friends and to help them if I can."

Rue Meridian smiled. "That's more like the Big Red I know. No sitting around and waiting. But we'll see about who's coming back and who's staying behind to heal."

He shook his head at her. "I sometimes think you don't have the sense of a gnat. Indestructible, are you? Half-dead one minute and whole the next? Off to the rescue of those un-fortunates who need you so badly? Shades! It's a wonder you've lived this long. Well, we'll talk about it."

He rose. "Enough of words for now, though. I'm off to bed and a few more hours of rest before daylight and work. Maybe you should try getting a few hours' sleep yourself. Put the past behind you and the future ahead where they belong and spend your time in the present with the rest of us." He waved dismissively as he turned away. "Sleep well, Little Red."

He went out without looking back, closing the door softly behind him. She stared after him for a long time, thinking that for all his faults, there wasn't anyone better than her brother. Whatever lay ahead, she would rather face it with him at her side than anyone else. Redden Alt Mer had the luck, they said. They were right, but he had something more than that. He had the heart. He would always find a way because he couldn't conceive of it being any other way. It was the Rover in him. It defined who he was.

She spent another few moments thinking about those trapped inland, about Walker and the rest, still worried how they would fare without the Rovers to turn to. Big Red could say what he wanted, but she didn't like the idea of abandoning them even for the time it would take to reach the coast and find the Wing Riders. They were a tough and experienced group except for Bek and the seer and one or two others who were more talented than experienced, but even the Elven Hunters were too much at risk when afoot and cut off from the airship. Especially with the Ilse Witch and her Mwellrets hunting them.

She thought of Hawk then, one final time. Someone will pay for what happened to you, she promised him silently. One day soon, that account will be settled.

She was crying again, almost before she realized it.

"Good-bye, Hawk," she whispered into the darkness.

Then she was asleep.

SIX

When Panax gripped his shoulder in warning, Quentin Leah dropped into a crouch and froze in place, eyes searching the gloom ahead. He felt the Dwarf's harsh breathing in his ear.

"Over there." The words were a soft hiss in the silence. "By the edge of that building, in the rubble."

Quentin's hand tightened on the Sword of Leah, then just as quickly loosened. *No, don't summon the magic! You'll only draw their attention if you do!* His heart began to race. Around him, everything went still, not a sound, not a movement, as if the city and its deadly inhabitants were waiting with him. Dirt, sweat, and blood streaked his face and clothing, and his body ached with fatigue. He was cut and bruised almost everywhere, and the slashes on his left side cut all the way through to his ribs. Off to one side, crouched in a screen of brush that had grown up through broken slabs of stone, Kian and Wye watched with him, waiting for his signal. He was their leader now. He was their last, best hope. Without him, they would all be dead. Dead, like so many of the others.

Quentin scanned the place in which Panax had spotted movement, but saw nothing. It didn't matter; he stayed where he was and kept searching. If the Dwarf said something was there, then it was. They hadn't gotten that far by doubting each other, and getting that far was nothing short of a miracle.

Nothing had gone the way it was supposed to go, not from the moment they had entered that square with its smooth metal floor and irregular sections of wall. An odd formation to begin with, unlike anything the Highlander had ever seen, it whispered of trouble. But Quentin had taken up his position on the left wing of the search party, along with Panax and the Elven Hunters Kian, Wye, and Rusten, and watched as an unaccompanied Walker made his way cautiously ahead. Across the way, barely visible, Ard Patrinell crouched with Ahren Elessedil, the Healer Joad Rish, and three more Elven Hunters. He could just make out their figures, little more than shadows clinging to the protective walls of the outlying buildings. Between them, and well behind the Druid, Bek and the seer Ryer Ord Star waited with three more Elven Hunters. Like a tableau, they were etched in the fading light, motionless statues sealed in place by time and fate.

Quentin had listened carefully for the sound of trouble, for any indication that this place that seemed so like a trap in fact was. He had his sword out already, gripped in one hand and laid flat against the metal square on which he crouched, the ridged pommel not nearly reassuring enough against his sweating palm. *Get out of here!* He kept shouting the words in the silence of his mind, as if by thinking it he could somehow make it happen. *Get out of here now!*

Then the first fire threads speared toward the Druid, and Quentin was on his feet instantly, catapulting from his crouch and charging ahead. Rusten went with him, the two of them rushing to Walker's aid, reckless and willful and foolhardy, ignoring the shouts from Panax to come back. They should have both died. But Quentin tripped and went down, sprawling across the metal floor, and the fall saved his life. Rusten, ahead of him and still charging toward the Druid, was caught in a crossfire of deadly threads and cut apart while still on his feet, screaming as he died.

Moving forward, his dark-cloaked form somehow sliding past the fire threads, Walker was yelling at them to stay back, to get clear of the ruins. Heeding the Druid's command, Quentin crawled back the way he had come, the fire chasing after him, passing so close that it seared his clothing. He caught a glimpse of the others, Bek in the center group, the Elves on the right wing, all dispersing and taking cover, shielding themselves from whatever might happen next. Ryer Ord Star bolted from Bek's side, her slender form streaking away into the ruins after Walker, ephemeral and shadowy as she passed ghostlike through walls that were now shifting in all directions, charging ahead heedlessly into the heart of the maze. He saw her stumble and go down, struck by one of the deadly threads, and then he lost sight of everything but what was happening right in front of him.

"Creepers!" Panax screamed.

Quentin rolled to his feet to find the first of them almost on top of him, seemingly come out of nowhere. He caught a glimpse of others behind it and to either side. They were of different sizes and shapes and metal compositions, a strange amalgam of what looked to be castoff pieces and oddly formed parts jointed and hinged to make something that seemed not quite real. Blades and powerful cutters glittered at the ends of metal extensions. Protruding metal eyes swiveled. They advanced in a crouch, as if they were armored insects grown large and given life and sent out to hunt.

He destroyed the first so quickly that it was scrap metal be-

fore he was aware of what he had done. All those long hours
of training with the Elven Hunters saved him from the hesitation that would have otherwise cost him his life. He reacted
without thinking, striking with the Sword of Leah at the
creeper closest, the magic flaring to life instantly, responding
to his need. The dark metal blade flashed with fire of its own,
blue flames riding up and down the edges of the weapon as he
left his antagonist a metal ruin. Without slowing, he leapt
over it to confront the next, fighting to reach his companions,
who were backed against a nearby wall, struggling with their
ordinary weapons to keep a tandem of creepers at bay. He
smashed the second creeper, then was struck from the side by
something he didn't see and knocked flying. Red threads
sought him out, searing their way slowly over the metal carpet, leaving deep grooves that smoked and steamed. He rolled
away from them once again, came to his feet, and with a howl
of determination launched himself back into the fray.

   He fought for what seemed like a long time, but was probably no more than a handful of minutes. Time stopped, and the
world around him and all it had offered and might offer again
in his young life disappeared. Creepers came at him from
everywhere, creepers of all shapes and sizes and looks. He
seemed to be a magnet for them, drawing them like flies to
the dead. They converged from everywhere. They turned away
from Panax and the Elven Hunters to get at him. He was slashed
and battered by their attempts to pin him down—not necessarily to kill him, but as if their goal was to capture him. It occurred to him then for the first time that it was the magic they
were after.

   By then, the magic was all through him. It surfaced with
his first sword stroke, the blue fire racing up and down the
blade's surface. But soon it was inside him, as well. It fused

him with his weapon and made them one, leaving the metal to enter flesh and bone, rushing through his bloodstream and back out again, all heat and energy. It burned in a captivating, seductive way, filling him with power and a terrible thirst for its feel. Within only a short time, he craved the feeling as he had craved nothing else in his life. It made him believe he could do anything. He had no fear, no hesitation. He was indestructible. He was immortal.

Smoke drifted across the battleground, obscuring everything. He heard the cries of his companions, but he could not see them. Walker had disappeared entirely, as if the earth had swallowed him. Disembodied voices cried out in the darkness. Everyone was cut off, surrounded by fire threads and creepers, caught in a trap from which none of them seemed able to escape. He didn't care. The magic buoyed and sustained him. He wrapped himself in its cloak and, unstoppable, fought with even greater fury.

Finally Panax shouted to him that they had to get clear of the square. It took several tries before he heard the Dwarf, and even then he was reluctant to break off the battle. Slowly, they began to retreat the way they had come. Creepers sought to bar their escape, turning them aside at every opportunity, giving pursuit like hungry wolves, skittering along on their metal struts and spindly legs, strange and awkward machines. The chase veered from one building to another, down one passageway to the next, until Quentin had no idea where he was. His arms were tiring, leaden from swinging the sword, and the magic did not come so easily. The Elves and Panax were grim-faced and battle-worn. Time and numbers were eating away at their resistance.

Then, without warning, the creepers pulled back, the fire threads disappeared, and the Highlander and his three companions were left in an empty swirl of smoke and silence. Weapons held before them like talismans, the hunted men backed through the haze, putting distance between themselves and their vanished pursuers, watching everywhere at once, waiting for the attack to resume. But the ruined city seemed to have become a vast burial ground, a massive tomb empty of life save for themselves.

So it had gone ever since, with Quentin and the other three edging their way ahead, not entirely certain to where they had gotten themselves or were going. Once or twice, there had been sudden, hurried movements in the shadows, things skittering away too swiftly to be clearly seen. The night had begun to fade and dawn to approach, and sunlight was creeping through the haze that cloaked the city. They searched for signs of their friends, for familiar landmarks, for anything that would tell them where they were. But it all looked the same, and the look never changed.

Now, crouched in yet another part of the ruined city, Quentin found himself almost wishing he had something to fight again, something of substance to combat. The sustained tension of watching and waiting for invisible creepers and vanished fire threads was wearing him down. Traces of the magic still roiled within him, but a mix of fear and doubt had replaced his craving for it. He did not like what the magic had made him do, as if he were as much a fighting machine as those creepers. He did not like how thoroughly it had dominated him, so much so that even thinking became difficult. There was only response and reaction, need and fulfillment. He had lost himself in the magic, had become someone else.

Without looking at Panax, he whispered, "I can't trust my senses anymore. I'm exhausted."

He felt, rather than saw, the Dwarf nod. "We have to get some rest. But not here. Let's go."

Quentin did not move. He was thinking about Bek, somewhere out there in the haze and rubble, lost at best, dead at worst. He could scarcely bear to think of how badly he had failed his cousin, leaving him behind without meaning or wanting to, abandoning him as surely as Walker seemed to have abandoned them all. He blinked away his weariness and shook his head. He should never have left Bek, not even after Walker had separated them. He should never have believed Bek would be all right without him.

"Let's go, Highlander," Panax growled again.

They rose and started ahead, easing away from the place where the Dwarf had seen movement, skirting the building and the rubble both, choosing a wide avenue that passed between a series of what looked like low warehouses with portions of their walls and roofs fallen in and collapsed. Quentin's thoughts were dismal. Who was going to protect Bek if he didn't? With Walker gone, who else was there? Certainly not Ryer Ord Star and maybe not even the Elven Hunters. Not against things like the fire threads and the creepers. Bek was his responsibility; they were each other's responsibilities. What good was a promise to look after someone if you didn't even know where he was?

He peered into the gloom as he walked, seeing other places, remembering better times. He had come a long way from the Highlands to have it all end like this. It had seemed so right to him, that he should do this, he and Bek. To live an adventure they would remember for the rest of their lives—that was why they must come, he had argued that night with Walker. That argument seemed hollow and foolish now.

"Wait," Panax hissed suddenly, bringing him to an abrupt stop.

He glanced at the Dwarf, who was listening intently once more. To one side, Kian and Wye stared out into the gloom. Quentin thought that maybe he was too tired to listen, that even if there was something to hear, he would be unable to tell.

Then he heard it, too. But it wasn't coming from ahead of them. It was coming from behind.

He turned quickly and watched in surprise as a slender figure appeared out of the haze and rubble.

"Where are you going?" Tamis asked in genuine confusion as she approached. She pulled off the leather band that tied back her short-cropped brown hair and shook her head wearily. "Is this all of you there are?"

They welcomed the Tracker with weary smiles of relief, lowering their weapons and gathering around her. Kian and Wye reached out to touch her fingers briefly, the standard Elven Hunter greeting. She nodded to Panax, and then her gray eyes settled on Quentin.

"I've just come from Bek. He's waiting a couple of miles back."

"Bek?" Quentin repeated, a wave of relief surging through him. "Is he all right?"

There was blood on her clothing and scratches on her smooth, tired face. Her clothes were soiled and torn. She didn't look all that different from him, he realized. "He's fine. Better off than you or me, I'd say. I left him in a clearing at the edge of the ruins to watch over the seer while I came looking for you. We're all that's left of our group."

"We lost Rusten," Kian advised quietly.

She nodded. "What about the others? What about Ard Patrinell?"

The Elven Hunter shook his head. "Couldn't tell. Too much smoke and confusion. Everyone disappeared after the fighting started." He nodded at Quentin. "The Highlander saved us. If we hadn't had him and that sword, we would have been finished."

Tamis gave Quentin an ironic look. "It must run in the family. Look, you're going in the wrong direction. You're going inland instead of back toward the bay."

"We've just been running," Quentin admitted. He blinked at the Tracker in confusion. "What do you mean, 'It must run in the family'? What are you saying?"

"That young Bek saved us, as well. If it hadn't been for him, we wouldn't have gotten clear. He smashed those creepers as if they were made of paper. I've never seen anything like it."

Quentin stared at her. "Bek? Bek did that?"

She studied him carefully. "Didn't he tell you? Or did he just discover it for himself, I wonder? He didn't seem all that sure about what he was doing, I'll grant you. But to have that kind of power and not know anything about it . . . Well, maybe so. Anyway, this is what happened."

She related the details of their escape, of how they had fled back through the ruins, the three Elven Hunters, Ryer Ord Star, and Bek, until the creepers had hemmed them in. The other two Elves had died quickly, but she and the seer were saved when Bek used his voice to call up magic.

"It was eerie," she admitted. Her eyes held Quentin's. "He was singing, a strange sound, but it tore the creepers apart, like a wind or a weapon cutting through them. One minute they were there, killing us, and the next they were scrap." She nodded solemnly. "Bek saved us. And you don't know a thing about what I'm saying, do you?"

Quentin was thinking, *Bek has magic? How could that be?* He shook his head. "Not a thing."

He found himself wondering suddenly about Bek's background. Bek was the child of a cousin, but which cousin? Or was he related at all? Coran Leah had always been close-mouthed about Bek's background, but that was the way he was with private information, and Quentin had never pressed the subject. But if Bek really did have the use of magic . . .

But Bek?

All of a sudden Quentin realized why Walker had wanted Bek to come along. It wasn't because he was Quentin's cousin. It was because he possessed magic as powerful as the Sword of Leah. Bek was every bit as necessary to the expedition as he was. Maybe more so. He never questioned for a moment that Walker would know about it. What he questioned instead was how much the Druid knew that he was still keeping to himself.

"We have to get going," Tamis advised, drawing him away from his thoughts. "I don't like leaving Bek and the seer alone. Even with his magic to protect him, he's still not experienced enough to know what to look out for."

They started back through the ruins, Tamis leading the way. When queried by Panax about what sort of trouble she had encountered on the way, she said that she suspected there were creepers hiding all through the ruins, but they showed themselves only in response to certain things. Maybe it was a signal of some sort. Maybe it was only when intruders entered restricted areas. Maybe someone or something was guiding them. But she hadn't seen a single one on her way back.

The Dwarf grunted and said there wasn't much more damage they could do anyway. Walker was missing and the expedition was in shambles. It was a miracle any of them were still alive.

But Quentin didn't hear any of it. He was still thinking about Bek. His cousin was suddenly an enigma, an entirely different person than he had seemed. Quentin had no reason not to believe what Tamis was telling him. But what did it mean? If Bek had the use of magic, particularly magic that was as much a part of him as his voice, where had it come from? It must be in his bloodline and therefore a part of his heritage. So who was his real family? Not some distant Leah cousins, he knew that much. There weren't any Leahs who'd had the use of that sort of magic, not ever. No, Bek was the child of someone else. But someone the Druid knew. Someone his father knew, as well, because otherwise Bek wouldn't have been brought to Coran as a baby.

Someone . . .

Suddenly he found himself remembering all those stories Bek was so fond of telling—about the Druids and the history of the Races. The Leahs were a part of that history, but there was another family that had been part of it, as well. Their name was Ohmsford. They had been close to the Leahs once, not so long ago. Even the great Elven Queen, Wren Elessedil, was rumored to be related to that family. There hadn't been an Ohmsford in Leah or Shady Vale or anywhere in that part of the world in fifty years. There hadn't even been a mention of them.

But the Ohmsfords had magic in their blood. It had surfaced in a pair of brothers who had joined with Walker to battle the Shadowen over a century ago. He remembered the story now, bits and pieces of it. The brothers were supposed to have had magic in their voices, just like Bek. What if the family hadn't died out after all? What if Bek was one of them? If there were Ohmsfords alive anywhere in the world, certainly Walker would know. He would have made it a point to know. That would explain how he had managed to track down Bek. It would explain why he had been so determined to bring Bek along.

Quentin felt an odd suspicion creep through him. Perhaps it was Bek that Walker was after all along, and he had used Quentin as a lever to persuade the boy to come.

Was his cousin Bek Ohmsford? Was that who he really was?

The Highlander blinked away his weariness and confusion. He couldn't trust his thinking just now. He might be completely off track on this. He was just guessing. He was just trying to make the pieces fit when he didn't even have a clear picture to work from. Could anything he imagined be trusted?

Truls Rohk had warned them on their first encounter that they couldn't trust a Druid. Games-playing, he'd called it. It was almost the first word out of his mouth, a clear indication of the usage to which he felt the Druid might be putting them. Games-playing. They might be pieces being moved about a board. It was possible, he was forced to admit.

They made their way back through the city as the sun rose in a cloudless sky and the last of the night faded. The air was heavy and still within the ruined buildings, and the heat rose off the stone and metal in waves. Nothing moved in the silence. The creepers had gone to ground once more, almost as if they had never been there. Tamis gave a wide berth to the square where they had encountered the monsters earlier, and it was not much past midmorning when they reached the edge of the woods bordering the city.

She paused there, listening.

"I thought I heard something," she said after a moment, her gray eyes sharp and searching. Her slender hand made a circular motion. "I can't tell where it came from, though. It sounded like a voice."

They entered the woods and began to thread their way through the trees. Birds flitted past them, small bits of sound and movement in bright swatches of sunlight, no longer in hiding. The haze that had cloaked the ruins earlier had cleared, and the edges of the buildings glinted sharply as they disappeared from view. Within the forest there were only the trees and brush, a thick concealment rising all about, green and soft in a mix of shadows and light. The familiar, welcome smells revived Quentin's spirits and helped push back his fatigue. At least Bek was all right. Whatever the story behind his magic and his family, they would work it all out once they were together again.

They had gone a fair distance from the ruins when Tamis turned to them. "The clearing is just ahead. Stay quiet."

They approached it cautiously and were all the way to its edge when the Tracker abruptly picked up the pace, burst into the open space almost at a run, and drew up short.

The clearing was empty. "They're gone," she whispered in disbelief.

Ordering the others to stay where they were, she crept slowly about the clearing's perimeter, sometimes dropping to her hands and knees to read the signs. Quentin stood frozen in place, frustrated and angry. Where was Bek? This was the Tracker's fault. She shouldn't have left Bek alone, no matter the reason or what she thought Bek could do with his magic or anything else. But he forced his anger down, quick to realize that it was misplaced. Tamis had done what was best, and there was no point in second-guessing her.

She came back to them finally, her face grim, but her gray eyes calm. "I can't tell what's happened for sure," she announced. "There are tracks all over the place, and the last set has obscured the others. Those belong to Mwellrets. There was some sort of struggle, but it doesn't look like anyone was injured, because there are no traces of blood."

Quentin exhaled sharply. "So where are Bek and Ryer Ord Star? What's happened to them?"

Tamis shook her head. "I told Bek that if anyone came, they were to hide. I left it to him to make the decision, but he knew to keep watch. I think he probably did as I instructed, and when he saw the Mwellrets, he got out of here. You know him better than I do. Does that sound like what he would do?"

The Highlander nodded. "He's hunted the Highlands for years. He knows how to hide when it's needed. I don't think he would have been caught off guard."

"All right," she said. "Here's the rest of it then. The Mwellrets spent some time here doing something, then continued on toward the city, not back the way they had come. If they'd taken Bek and the seer prisoner, they likely would have sent them to the airship under guard. No tracks lead back that way. Someone may have gone off in the direction from which we came, inland, but I can't be sure. The signs are very faint and difficult to read. Anyway, the Mwellret signs are very clear. They don't continue on in the same way; there is a change of direction. From the way several sets of prints start out and come back again, then all move off together in a pack, I'd say they were tracking someone."

"Bek," Quentin said at once.

"Or the girl," Panax offered quietly.

"He wouldn't leave her," Quentin said. "Not Bek. He'd take her with him. Which might explain why the Mwellrets could track him. Without her, I'm not sure they could. Bek is good at concealing his trail."

Tamis nodded, her gaze steady and considering. "I say we go after them. What do you say, Highlander?"

"We go after them," he said at once.

She looked at Panax. The Dwarf shrugged. "Doesn't make any sense to go the other way. The *Jerle Shannara*'s gone off to the coast. Whoever's left that matters is back in those ruins. I don't want to leave them to the rets and the witch."

Quentin had forgotten about the Ilse Witch. If there were Mwellrets ashore, *Black Moclips* had found its way through the pillars of ice and into the bay. That meant the Ilse Witch was somewhere close at hand. He realized all at once how dangerous going back toward the ruins would be. They were tired and worn, and they had been fighting and running for hours. It wouldn't take much for them to make a mistake, and it wouldn't take much of a mistake to finish them.

But he was not going to leave Bek. He had already made up his mind about that.

Kian and Wye were speaking with Tamis. They wanted to go back into the ruins. They wanted a chance to find Ard Patrinell and the others. They knew that would be dangerous, but they agreed with her. If anyone was still alive back there, they wanted to lend what help they could.

While the Elves conferred, Panax moved over to stand next to Quentin. "I hope you're up to saving all of us again," he said. "Because you might have to."

He smiled tightly as he said it, but there was no humor in his voice.

SEVEN

Ahren Elessedil crouched in the darkest corner of an abandoned warehouse well beyond the perimeter of the deadly trap from which he had escaped, and tried to think what he should do. The warehouse was a cavernous shelter with holes in three of its four walls. It had a roof that was mostly intact, ceiling-high doors on two sides that had slid back on rollers and rusted in place, and barely more space than debris. He had been there for a very long time, pressed so tightly against the walls that he'd begun to feel as if he were a part of them. He had been there long enough to memorize every feature, to plan for every contingency, and to rethink every painful detail of what had brought him to that spot. Outside, the sun had risen to cast its light across the ravaged city in a broad sweep that chased the night's shadows back into the surrounding woods. The sounds of death and dying had long since vanished, the battle cries, the clash of weapons against armor, and the desperate gasps and moans of human life leaking away. He watched and listened for the faintest hint of any of them, but there was only silence.

It was time for him to get out of there, to stand up and walk away—or run if he must—while the chance was there. He had to do something besides cower in his corner and relive in his mind the horrific memories of what he had been through.

But he could not make himself move. He could not make himself do anything but try to disappear into the metal and stone.

To say that he was frightened would be a gross understatement. He was frightened in a way he had never thought possible. He was frightened into near catatonia. He was so frightened that he had shamed himself beyond recognition of whom and what he had always believed himself to be, and probably beyond all redemption.

He closed his eyes against what he was feeling and thought back once more to what had happened, searching for a clue that would help him to better understand. He saw his friends and companions spread out across the maze of walls and partitions of that seemingly empty square—his group on the right, Quentin Leah's on the left, and Bek's in the center. Elven Hunters warded them all, and there seemed no reason to think they could not manage against whatever might confront them. Ahead, Walker crept deeper into the maze. The lowering sun cast shadows everywhere, but there was no movement and no sound to suggest danger. There was no hint of what was about to happen.

Then the fire threads appeared, razoring after the Druid first, then after those who tried to reach him, then even after those who had remained where they were. With Ard Patrinell, Joad Rish, and the three Elven Hunters who accompanied them, Ahren ducked behind a wall to escape being burned. Smoke filled the square and mingled with the haze to obscure everything in moments. He heard the shouts from Quentin's group, the unexpected clank and scrape of metal parts, and the screams from across the way. Huddled behind his wall, filled with dread and panic, he realized quickly how bad things had become.

When the creepers had appeared behind him, he was already on the verge of bolting. He could not explain what had happened, only that the courage and determination that had infused and sustained him earlier had drained away in an instant's time. The creepers seemed to materialize out of nowhere, metal beasts lumbering from the haze. Razor-sharp pincers protruded from their metal bodies, giving him a clear indication of the fate that awaited him. He stood his ground anyway, perhaps as much from an inability to move as anything, his sword lifted defensively, if futilely. The creepers attacked in a staggered rush, and he pressed himself away from them, back behind a wall, into a corner. To his amazement, they passed him by, choosing other adversaries, descending on his companions. One Elven Hunter—he couldn't tell which one—went down almost at once, limp and bloodied. Ard Patrinell surged to the forefront of the defenders, throwing back the creepers single-handedly, a warrior responding to a need, a small wall against an attacking wave. For a moment he withstood the charge, but then the creepers closed over him and he disappeared.

Ahren left his hiding place then, desperate to help his friend and mentor, forgetting for an instant his fear, pushing back his panic. But then one of the fire threads found Joad Rish kneeling by the first Elf who had fallen, trying to drag him to safety. Joad was looking up when it happened, staring right at Ahren, as if beseeching his help. The fire thread caught him in the face, and his head exploded in a shower of red. For an instant he remained where he was, kneeling by the fallen Elven Hunter, hands still grasping the other's arms, headless body turned toward Ahren. Then slowly, almost lan-guidly, he collapsed to the metal floor.

That was all it took. Ahren lost all control over himself. He screamed, backed away, threw down his sword, and ran. He never paused to think about what he was doing or even where he was going. He only knew he had to get away as fast and as far as he could manage. The headless image of Joad Rish hung right in front of him, burned into the smoky air, into his eyes and mind. He could not make it go away, could not avoid its presence, could do nothing but flee from it even when fleeing did no good. He forgot the others of the company, all of them. He forgot what had brought him to that charnel house. He forgot his training and his promises to himself to stand with the others. He forgot everything that had ever meant anything to him.

He had no idea how long he ran or how he found his way to the empty warehouse. He could hear the screams of the others for a long time afterwards, even there. He could hear the sounds of battle, and then the faint scrape of metal legs as the creep-ers moved away. He could smell the smoke of burning metal and the stench of seared flesh. Curled in a tight ball with his face buried in his chest and knees, he cried.

After a time, he regained sufficient presence of mind to wonder if any of the creepers had followed him. He forced himself to lift his head, to wipe away his tears, and to look around. He was alone. He kept careful watch after that, still huddled in that same corner, still wrapped in a ball of arms and legs, still haunted by the image of Joad Rish in his final moments.

Don't let that happen to me, he kept repeating in his mind, as if by thinking it he could somehow save himself.

But now he knew he had to do more than huddle in his

corner and hope he would never be found. He had to try to get out of there. It had been long enough that he thought he might have a chance. The attack had ended long ago. There had been no sound or movement anywhere in all that time. The smoke had faded, and the sun had risen. It was bright and clear outside, and he should be able to see anything that threatened. It would take him several hours to work his way back through the city and longer still to retrace his steps to the bay where he could wait for the return of the *Jerle Shannara*. He thought he could make it.

More to the point, he knew that he must.

It took him a long time, but he finally managed to uncurl himself and get to his feet. He stood motionless in the shadows of his corner and scanned the warehouse from end to end for signs of life. When he was satisfied it was safe to do so, he started for the nearest opening, a broad gap in the west wall that offered the most direct route back through the city. He felt parched and light-headed, and his hands were shaking. To calm himself, he reached up for the phoenix stone, remembering suddenly that it was there, hanging about his neck. He did not know whether it would work if he was threatened, but it reassured him to know he had something he could fall back on, even if he was uncertain it would be of any use.

He wondered suddenly, dismally, what had become of Bek. His friend Bek, who had done so much to encourage and support him on their voyage out of Arborlon. Was he dead with all the others? Were any of them alive back there? He knew he should go back and find out. He knew, as well, that he couldn't.

Brave Elven Prince! he chided himself in fury and sadness. *Your brother was right about you!*

He reached the opening and stepped out into the daylight.

The ruins stretched away in all directions in sprawling sameness, stark and empty. He waited a moment to see if anyone
would appear, if there was anything to be heard. But the city
seemed empty and lifeless, a jumble of stone and metal and
encroaching weeds and scrub. Not even a bird flew overhead
in the cloudless blue sky.

He began to walk, slowly at first, almost gingerly, trying
not to make any noise, still on the verge of panic, fighting to
keep himself together. He had no weapons save for a long
knife belted at his waist and the phoenix stone. If he was attacked, his only real defense was to run. The knowledge that
it was all he could rely on wasn't very reassuring, but there
was nothing he could do about it. He wished he had his sword
back, that he hadn't thrown it down when he fled. But then he
wished a lot of other things, as well, that couldn't be. Instinct
kept him moving when his conscience whispered that he
didn't deserve even to be alive.

He'd gone only a few steps when tears filled his eyes once
more. How proud he had been of himself that he was chosen
to go on the expedition. How certain he had been that it would
give him the chance he needed to prove himself. A Prince of
the Realm, destined perhaps to be a King—it would all be
made so clear on the journey. Even Ard Patrinell had believed
it, had taught him to believe it while teaching him how to survive those who did not. Yet what had he done for his friend
and mentor when it mattered? He had run like a coward, fled
in a rush of panic and despair, abandoned his friends and his
principles and all his hopes for what might be.

You are despicable!

He kept walking, wiping the tears from his eyes, swallowing his sobs, thinking that he must be brave now, that he
must try to regain some small measure of self-worth. He was

alive when others were not, and he must try to make something of that gift. He did not know how he would do that or why it would matter after what had happened, but he knew he must at least try.

The sun beat down on him, and soon he was sweating freely. He blinked against the brightness and moved into the shadows, staying close to sheltering walls to gain a measure of coolness. He thought he was going the right way, but could not be sure. He did not see anything that looked familiar—or perhaps it was just that everything looked the same. At least there were no creepers about. In the wake of his passage, nothing moved.

Then suddenly, unexpectedly, he caught sight of something that did. He caught only a glimpse of it, a flicker of movement, no more, and then it was gone. He pressed himself back into the shadows and went still, waiting to see if he would spot it again. He did so, only seconds later, another glimpse, but enough to tell him more. It was someone human, slender and robed, sliding along the walls as he had been doing, a little off to one side of where he stood. He debated what to do. His impulse was to flee or hide, anything to avoid an encounter. But then he realized that it might be a member of the company, someone as lost as he was and looking for a way out of their shared nightmare. He let the other person come closer, trying to make out who it was, barely breathing in case he was making a mistake.

Then the other stepped into a patch of bright sunlight, and he saw her face clearly.

"Ryer Ord Star!" he called to her, keeping his voice low and guarded, still mindful of the things that might be hunting him.

She turned toward him instantly, hesitated, saw him standing back in the shadows, and moved over to him. He was surprised at how calm she looked, her face composed and her violet eyes untroubled. She had always looked somewhat ethereal, but just then she seemed oddly distant, as well—as if she were seeing beyond him to another place, as if in her mind she were already there.

She reached for his hand and took it in her own, surprising him. "Elven Prince, you are alive," she whispered. There was genuine relief in her voice, and it made him ashamed to know that she thought better of him than he deserved. "You shouldn't be out here alone," she continued urgently, her grip on his hand tight. "It is very dangerous. Where are the others?"

He took a quick breath to steady himself. "Dead, I think. I'm not really sure."

She glanced around quickly, her long, silver hair shimmering in bright waves. "There are Mwellrets back that way, a large company of them." She pointed from where she had come. "I think they might be following me."

"Mwellrets?" he repeated in confusion.

"From *Black Moclips*. They've come ashore to hunt us down, all of us that remain. The Ilse Witch came with them, but she's gone now. She found us in a clearing where the Elven Tracker left us—"

"You mean Tamis?" he interrupted excitedly. "Is Tamis with you?"

"She was, but she left to find help. Bek was with me, too, but when the Ilse Witch found us, there was a confrontation between them. I'm not sure what happened, but Bek disappeared and she went after him. In the confusion, I slipped away. But the Mwellrets will have missed me by now and be searching. That was what the witch told them they were to do—to find all of us who weren't dead and make us prisoners, then take us to *Black Moclips* and hold us there until she returned."

Ahren stared at her. Accepting that the Ilse Witch had somehow made it through the Squirm and come down the channel to the cove, what was all this about a confrontation with Bek? Why would she be hunting him?

"Hsst!" she signaled in warning, clasping his hand in hers once more. "We have to go now! Quickly! They're coming!"

She drew him from his concealment, back the way he had just come, and he pulled up sharply. "No, wait, I'm not going back there!"

"You have to! They're sweeping all of the ruins! They'll find you otherwise!"

"But I can't!" he whispered in desperation. "I can't!"

She stopped tugging on his hand and released it. "Do what you wish, Elven Prince. But if you stay here, they will find you. Hiding won't help. Mwellrets can sense you better than most creatures can, and they will search you out." She stepped close. Her violet eyes were steady and searching. "Come with me."

He wasn't sure what made him decide to follow, but he did so, abandoning his shelter and hurrying after her. He glanced back several times without seeing anything, but his instincts told him she was telling the truth.

"What about Bek?" he asked after a few moments, keeping his voice low and his head bent toward hers as they slipped through the ruins. "Is he all right? Did you say the Ilse Witch is tracking him, that she's gone after him on her own?"

The seer nodded. "Bek is unhurt. His magic and his courage ward him. Perhaps she will find it difficult to overcome both."

"His magic? What magic?" The Elf hurried to keep up with her. "Wait a minute. Are you saying she's tracking him because he has some sort of magic?"

Ryer Ord Star grasped his arm and pulled him close to her. "She is his sister, Elven Prince." She registered the shock in his eyes and tightened her grip. "Walker told him just before we arrived, but Bek kept it to himself. When she appeared in the clearing, he told her who he was. The Ilse Witch did not believe him. She cannot. That was the cause of the confrontation between them. She hunts him now because she can't get the truth out of her mind, even if she doesn't accept it. She thinks that if she can confront him once more, he will admit he lied to her. Or perhaps she realizes there is something to what he says. Now walk more quickly!"

They moved ahead, faster, back through the buildings and rubble, back toward the trap they had been lucky to escape once already and were now braving again. Ahren Elessedil's mind spun with the revelations about Bek, but his thoughts were made jumbled and confused by his fear. He knew that by going back, he was tempting fate in a way he would regret. He did not really think he could survive another encounter with the creepers, whatever Ryer Ord Star believed. But he could not let this slip of a girl return alone, leaving him behind to remember he had failed her as well as Ard Patrinell and his Elven Hunters. He kept thinking he could find a way to cause her to reconsider, to change her mind, and to turn her aside. But she was strong-minded and determined, and for the moment, at least, he would have to do what she wanted.

It took them much less time than he had expected to reach the square they had fled only hours earlier. It sat still and empty in the bright midday light, its maze of walls back in place, metal sheeting baking in the heat. Ahren cast about for signs of those who had been left behind. There was no one to be seen anywhere. There were no signs that a battle had been fought, no bodies, not a trace of blood, not a scar from the fire threads, not a piece of stray metal from one of the creepers. It was as if nothing had ever happened.

"How can this be?" he whispered to her in shock.

She shook her head slowly, staring out at the clean, empty expanse with him. "I don't know."

He glanced back over his shoulder. There was no sign of the Mwellrets. "What do we do now?" he asked.

She looked about momentarily, then took his hand in hers once more. "Follow me. Don't speak, don't do anything but what I do. Don't run, whatever happens."

Still holding tightly to his hand, she squared her slender shoulders, and walked out into the maze.

His shock was complete, and perhaps that was why he went with her without protest. Fighting down a surge of fear and horror that crowded into his throat, his eyes cast right and left for creepers and his skin prickled as he waited for the fire threads to burn him. She penetrated only a few yards into the deadly square before turning aside to skirt its edges, moving carefully across the metal flooring, staying clear of the shadows and well out into the bright sunlight. They moved as one, making no sound, no unnecessary movement, not speaking, barely breathing. Ahren thought he was a dead man already, but in an act of faith that surprised him completely, he gave himself over to the seer.

What surprised him even more was that nothing happened. They worked their way just inside the perimeter of the maze until they were about a quarter of the distance around, almost even with the northern facing of the dark tower that dominated its center. Once there, the seer led him just outside again into a deeply shadowed concealment formed by what remained of the walls and roofing of a collapsed building that abutted the square.

Atop a pile of rubble that looked out through a narrow gap in a wall on the landscape through which they had come, they crouched and waited.

"Why weren't we attacked?" he asked in a whisper, still cautious, pressing close to her slender form, his lips brushing her hair.

"Because what wards the tower attacks only when there is a perceived threat to its security." Her violet eyes glistened as she turned to look at him. "Walker was a threat, so it attacked him first and then the rest of us. Had we bypassed the square and the tower, we would have been safe."

He stared at her. "How do you know this?"

Her pale, youthful face turned away. "I dreamed it," she answered quietly. "In a vision, in my search for Walker."

He didn't say anything for a long time after that, mulling over her words while watching the ruins for signs of movement. Where were the Mwellrets? Why hadn't they appeared?

"Do you think Tamis found any of the others?" he asked finally. "Did you see what became of them after we were attacked? What about Quentin Leah's group?"

She shook her head wordlessly. Her eyes remained directed away from him, out toward the city. He studied her carefully. "They're all dead, aren't they? You've dreamed that, as well."

"Not Walker Boh," she said softly.

Before he could press her further, he caught sight of the Mwellrets moving through the ruins, dark forms sliding along walls and across empty spaces, little more than an extension of the shadows to which they clung. Ryer Ord Star gripped his arm anew, and she pressed against him in warning or, perhaps, in reassurance. He held himself still, his former composure regained at least in part from having survived yesterday's attack and the return. He did not feel in the least invincible, but neither did he feel quite so vulnerable either. What he had lost in the attack that had claimed his friends had been restored in small part by his tightrope walk with the seer back through the maze to this hiding place. Before, he had thought that any kind of survival was momentary at best and undeserved. Now, he believed he might still be alive for a reason, that he might be alive because there was something he could accomplish.

Ryer Ord Star leaned close to him, her face almost touching his. "Don't worry," she whispered, as if to keep him calm and in place. "They won't find us."

The Mwellrets snaked through the city in increasing numbers, as many as twenty of them, appearing and disappearing like wraiths, cloaked forms blending with the shadows as they advanced. When they reached the maze, unaware of its dangers, they barely slowed. Using the walls for shelter in the same way the members of Walker's company had done, they entered the square in ones and twos, hunched over and faceless within their robes and hoods, reptilian bodies easing ahead cautiously. Deeper and deeper into the maze they penetrated, and nothing happened.

Ahren glanced quickly at Ryer Ord Star, his brow creased in worry. How had they managed to get so far in? The seer's gaze, calm and untroubled, remained fixed on the maze and the Mwellrets. Her fingers tightened on the Elven Prince's arm.

All at once the maze exploded in a burst of fire threads, deadly red lines crisscrossing everywhere at once, catching the Mwellrets in a web of destruction. An odd mix of hisses and shrieks rose from the trapped creatures as they sought to evade the burning ropes and failed. A handful were sliced to ribbons in the first few seconds, robes catching fire as they twisted and turned in a futile effort to flee, scorching and burning bodies collapsing in lifeless heaps. The men and women from the *Jerle Shannara* had sought to go to Walker's aid, but the Mwellrets simply abandoned their stricken companions, fleeing back through the maze in short bursts of dark robes and sudden movement. They were gone so quickly that in a matter of seconds they had vanished as if swallowed by the city.

Ahren and Ryer Ord Star remained where they were, motionless, eyes scanning the ruins in all directions. Perhaps six of the Mwellrets lay dead below them, their crumpled dark shapes visible within the maze of walls. Of those who had fled, there was no sign at all. The fire threads had ceased their deadly tracking, leaving behind smoke trails that rose from scarred ruts in the otherwise smooth metal surfaces of the walls and flooring. The creepers had never appeared at all.

Ryer Ord Star released her grip on Ahren's wrist. "They won't be back anytime soon," she said softly.

He nodded in agreement. Not after that, they wouldn't. They would wait for the Ilse Witch to return. "What do we do now?" he asked.

She rose without looking at him, her eyes shifting toward the dark tower at the center of the maze. "We begin looking for Walker."

EIGHT

Ahren Elessedil stared at Ryer Ord Star with no small amount of incredulity. What in the name of everything sane was she talking about? Look for Walker? She'd said it as if it was the most obvious and reasonable suggestion in the world. But Ahren didn't find it to be either. He thought she'd lost her mind.

"What are you saying?" was all he could manage.

The words came out in a sort of threatening hiss, and she turned to look at him at once. "I have to find him, Elven Prince," she said, her own voice maddeningly calm and self-assured. "It's where I was going when you found me."

"But you don't know where he is!" Ahren exclaimed in dismay. "You don't even know where to look!"

She knelt again, facing him, her violet eyes boring into him him with a look of unmistakable determination and certainty. She looked so young, so impossibly vulnerable, that the idea of her undertaking so dangerous a task seemed at once preposterous and foolish.

"You may not have seen what happened to him during the attack," she began quietly, "but I did. I ran into the ruins after him, knowing he was in danger from more than the creepers and the fire threads. The visions had warned me of this place, and I understood the threat to him better than any of you did. I was struck by one of the threads and prevented from reaching him, but I saw what happened. He went on alone, past fire threads and creepers, through all the smoke and confusion. He reached the tower at the center of the maze, found a doorway, and disappeared inside. He did not come out again. He is still in there somewhere."

Ahren felt his exasperation building. "Maybe so. Maybe you saw everything you say. Maybe Walker is inside that tower. But how are we supposed to get to him? Fire threads and creepers attack everyone who tries to get close. There isn't any way past those things! You've seen what happened to us and to the Mwellrets, as well! Besides, even if you some-how managed to get all the way up to that tower, how are you going to get in? You don't have a Druid's powers. Don't tell me the door will just open for you. And if it did, that wouldn't be good news either, would it? Why would you even think of doing something this . . . this ridiculous?"

He was almost shouting, and his breath was ragged as he cut himself off and rocked back on his heels. "You can't do this!" A surge of fear washed through him as he imagined trying. "I won't help you," he finished in a rush.

She gave him such a patient, understanding look that he wanted to shake her. She hadn't heard a word he'd said, or if she had, she hadn't paid him the least attention.

But then she surprised him by saying, "Everything you say is true, Ahren Elessedil."

He stared at her, not knowing what to say. "Then you'll give up on this idea, won't you? Come with me instead, back to the coast. We can wait for the *Jerle Shannara* there. We can hide until she returns. Maybe we can find Tamis again, maybe one or two others who might have escaped. They can't all be dead, can they? What about Bek? Won't he try to find his way back to that clearing?"

She brushed back her long hair and folded her hands into her lap, tucking them between her legs like a little girl. Her violet eyes were depthless and filled with pain as they fixed on him. He was suddenly certain that although she was no older than he was, her experience with life's vicissitudes was far greater than his own.

"Let me tell you something about Walker and me," she said quietly. "Something I haven't told anyone. When we left the island of Shatterstone and he was sick from its poison, I sat with him in his cabin. Bek was there, as well. Joad Rish was doing everything he knew to help Walker, but nothing was working. After several days it became clear to all of us that Walker was dying. The poison was in too deep, and it was infused with the magic of that place and the spirit who warded it. Walker's own magic could not give him sufficient protection against what was happening. He couldn't make himself well again without help."

She smiled. "So I used my own skills to heal him. I am a seer, but an empath, as well. My empathic powers allow me to absorb the hurt in others so that they can better mend. It is a draining and debilitating effort, but I knew there was no other choice. Know this, Elven Prince. I would have died gladly for him. He is special to me in a way you know nothing about and I don't care to discuss. What matters is that in healing him, I formed a link with his subconscious. I think it was intentional on his part, but I cannot be sure. I became joined to him through the bond created by my willingness to give up something of my life in order to save his. It happens now and then with empaths, though usually it fades after the healing is finished. It did not do so here. It continued. It continues now."

He studied her carefully in the silence that followed. "Are you saying Walker is communicating with you? That you can hear him speaking?"

"After a fashion, yes. Not words exactly. More a presence that comes and goes and suggests things. He is there in my mind, whispering to me that he is alive and well. I can feel him. I can sense him reaching out to me. It is the link we share, he and I, forged of a blending of our lives, of our magic, of the experience shared when he was dying and I saved him."

She paused. "Do you remember when he was trapped on Shatterstone and Bek warned us he needed help? Walker called to him because Bek shares his magic, and he can reach out to Bek when it is needed. A Druid's tool. But I heard it, too. Walker didn't call to me, but I heard his voice in my mind, as well. Because we're linked, Elven Prince. I hear his voice now, except that this time it is meant for me and no other. He speaks to me through images, fragments of what he is experiencing. He is in trouble, trapped underground, beneath these ruins, beneath that tower. He is deep in a maze of catacombs that lie below this city. Castledown is not up here, Elven Prince. It is down there."

"So the treasure and whatever wards it—"

"Is there, as well, the one secreted away, the other watching everything, controlling what happens aboveground as well as below. Walker tells me this in his images, in my visions and dreams, but in my subconscious, as well. He doesn't tell me everything, because he does not feel safe doing so. But he tells me what he can, what he must. He is in trouble, and he clings to me as he might a broken spar on a shipwrecked sea. He is adrift and lost, and I am his lifeline back."

She waited for his response. He did not have one to give.

He wasn't sure if he believed it all or not. She might be confused, misled, or delusional from the events of yesterday afternoon. She seemed lucid and assured, but you couldn't always tell another person's state of mind from the way they looked and sounded.

"Is he asking you to come to him?" he said finally.

Suddenly she seemed confused, as if the question had presented a new dilemma for her. "No," she replied after a moment. "He clings to me without revealing I am here. It is a reaching that asks nothing of me." Tears filled her eyes and ran down her cheeks. "But I will go to him anyway. I will because I must. There is no one else, no one left but me. And you, if you will go with me."

He would do no such thing, Ahren thought, certain that it was suicide to go back into the maze under any circumstances. He was filled with dread at the prospect and riddled with fear by his memories of that encounter. He couldn't help himself. He was still fighting to come to terms with his failure to fight, his abandonment of his friends, and the shame he felt as a result of both. But even his growing desire to redeem himself was not enough to make him go back into that maze. The best he could do for Ryer Ord Star was to convince her she was making a mistake.

"How will you get into that tower?" he asked, looking for a way to reach her.

She shook her head. "I don't know."

"If you do get in, how will you find Walker? If he isn't summoning you, isn't calling to you, how will you track him?"

"I don't know."

"This whole city, ruins and all, is made of stone and metal. There are no tracks to follow. Look at the size of it. If it's only half this big underground, it will take weeks, maybe even months, to search it all. How are you going to know where to look?"

She was crestfallen, but her lips tightened with resolve. "I don't know any of this, Elven Prince. I only know I have to try. I have to go to him."

He felt helpless in the face of her blind determination to go forward, to do what she had set her mind to do no matter the obstacles and complications. He felt as if he was crushing her hopes without persuading her to give them up, so that when all was said and done, she would go anyway, but he would have stripped her of her spirit.

He sat back on the rubble and peered out into the ruined city. It stretched away in the sunlight, vast and broken, its history lost deep in the past with the dead civilization that had occupied it. It was a relic of the Old World, of that time before the Great Wars when science ruled and all of the Races were one. He wondered if any of those who had lived then had foreseen this end to things. He wondered if they had tried to do anything to prevent it.

"Maybe we could find some of the others to help us," he said finally, feeling doomed and trapped, but unable to bring himself to abandon her.

She shook her head. "No, Ahren. There is only you and me."

It was the first time she had used his name, and he was surprised at the depth of feeling it aroused in him. It was as if she knew just how to say it—as if by saying it, she was linking them in the same way that she was linked to Walker.

It drew him to her and at the same time it made him afraid.

"I can't go with you," he said quickly, shaking his head for emphasis because he thought his voice was shaking.

She did not reply, simply sat there looking at him. He

couldn't bring himself to meet her gaze, but kept his eyes directed out at the city, at the miles of rubble and debris, at that mirror of the wasteland he was feeling inside.

"My brother knew what he was doing by sending me on this voyage," he said to the empty landscape, at the same time trying to make the girl understand. "He knew I was weak, not strong enough to survive—"

"Your brother was wrong," she interrupted quickly.

He turned and stared at her, surprised at the vehemence in her voice. "My brother—"

"Your brother was wrong," she repeated. "About this voyage. About Walker. But especially about you."

He took a deep breath and exhaled slowly, feeling a shift in his thinking that was impossible to reconcile with common sense but equally impossible to ignore. Could he do what she was asking of him? Could he possibly find the resolve that seemed to come so easily to her? It was madness of the sort that he could not quite manage to dismiss. Something deep inside was responding to her need, and it made him disregard all other considerations.

Even so, what could he do that would make a difference? "I don't think I can protect you, Ryer Ord Star," he whispered.

Then a distant sound caught his attention, one so tiny and insignificant he almost missed hearing it. He froze momentarily, afraid of what it might be. The seer watched him, waiting. Finally he rose to peer from their hiding place into the ruins. She was beside him at once, pressing close.

The sound had come from the maze. Dozens of tiny metal creatures skittered and wheeled their way through its intricate system of walls, none of them more than perhaps two feet high. There were several different kinds, each clearly built to perform a specific task. Some hauled away the bodies of the dead Mwellrets, gripping them with pincers at the end of stubby arms and dragging them across the smooth metal floor, where they dropped them down chutes that opened briefly and then sealed again. Some used a torch mechanism attached to their bodies to repair the rents caused by the fire threads in the metal surface of the maze. Some swept and polished and otherwise cleaned away all traces of the one-sided battle, restoring the maze so that it looked as if nothing had ever happened there.

It took them less than an hour to complete their work, speeding about like mice in a cage, sunlight gleaming off their metal shells, the sounds of clicking and whirring and buzzing barely audible in the stillness surrounding them. When they were finished, they wheeled into lines and disappeared down rampways that opened to admit them in the same fashion as the chutes that had swallowed the Mwellrets. In seconds, they were gone.

Ahren looked at Ryer Ord Star. A surge of relief swept through him. He felt giddy. "Sweepers," he said, gesturing toward the tiny machines, the word popping into his mind all at once, causing him to smile in spite of himself.

She did not smile back. Instead, she pointed to something just behind him. His heart lurched as he followed her gaze and found one of the newly named sweepers parked not three feet away.

The sweeper wasn't doing anything. It was just sitting, a squat, cylindrical body on a set of multiple rollers. Its round head might have been the top half of a metal ball resting on a set of heavy springs. Thin, short probes stuck out from the head in various places and directions, and a pair of fat knobs stuck out of its body on opposite sides, each about the size of a fist.

Ahren had no idea how it had gotten so close without them hearing it. Nor did he care. What mattered was what it was doing there. It didn't appear to have any weapons, but he was not about to discount the possibility.

Neither Ryer Ord Star nor he said anything for a moment. They stared at the sweeper and waited for it to do something. The sweeper, to the extent that it was capable of doing so, stared back.

Then all of a sudden a hatch on its head popped open and a beam of light shot out, freezing an image in the air about two feet away from them. The image wasn't very big, but it was quite clear. It was of Walker.

Ryer Ord Star gasped, and Ahren gripped her arms to steady her as she sagged into him.

The image was gone an instant later. A second image appeared in its wake, this one showing the Druid running swiftly through a series of tunnels lit by odd lamps with no flame, sliding from one patch of light to the next, his face tense and worn. Every so often he paused to look over his shoulder or peer ahead into the gloom, listening and searching. His black robes were torn and soiled, and his dark face was streaked with sweat and dirt and perhaps blood. He was being hunted, and the strain of running and hiding was beginning to tell on him.

The image disappeared. Ryer sobbed softly, as if the impact of the images had collapsed whatever wall of strength remained to her and all that was left was despair.

Ahren clutched at her. "Stop it!" he hissed angrily. "We don't know if that is really happening! We don't have any idea what this is about!"

Another image appeared, then another and another, all of

creepers moving through the same tunnels, hunting something. Claws and blades flashed brightly when they passed
through light. Some of them were huge. Some were rocking
in an eager, anticipatory fashion. All had parts awkwardly
grafted onto them, giving them a barbaric, half-finished look.

The images disappeared. Ahren decided he'd had enough.
"What do you want!" he snapped at the sweeper, not giving a
moment's consideration to whether it could understand him.

Apparently it could. Another image appeared, the Elf and
the seer following the little sweeper through the same series
of tunnels, searching the gloom. A second image followed,
Walker, looking over his shoulder, stopping, lifting his arm
as if in recognition, beckoning. Then all of them were joined
in a third image, relief painted on their faces, hands reaching
out in greeting, Ryer Ord Star melting into Walker's strong
embrace.

The seer was almost hysterical. "It wants us to follow!" she
cried. "It wants to take us to Walker. Ahren, we have to go!
You saw him! He needs us!" She was shaking him, any attempt at calm forgotten.

Nowhere near as convinced as she was, Ahren freed himself roughly. "Don't be so quick, Ryer." He used her first
name to make her listen, and it worked. She went still, eyes
fastened on him. "We don't know if any of this is true. We
don't know if these images are real. What if this is a trick?
Where did this sweeper come from anyway?"

"It isn't a trick, it's real; I can feel it. That really is Walker,
and he's down in those tunnels, and he needs our help!"

Ahren was wondering what sort of help they would be able
to provide to the Druid. He was wondering how following the
sweeper down into the tunnels—supposing they could do
that—would result in the happy ending they had been shown.

If Walker, with all his magic, couldn't get free of the creepers, what difference would their coming after him make?

He looked at the little sweeper. "How did you find us?"

A fresh image appeared. The sweeper was cleaning down at the edges of the maze, just below their hiding place. It was viewing everything through some sort of lens. Something distracted it, and it moved out of the maze and into the ruins, climbing slowly through the rubble until it was just behind them.

The image faded. "It must have heard us," the seer whispered, giving Ahren a quick, hopeful look.

He didn't see how. They had been careful not to make any noise at all. Maybe it had sensed their presence. But why hadn't the other sweepers sensed them, as well?

"I don't like it," he said.

"Ahren!" she pleaded, her voice wrenching and sad.

He gave an exasperated sigh, feeling trapped by her need and expectations. She was so desperate to get to Walker, to do something to help him, that she was abandoning any attempt to exercise caution or good sense. On the other hand, he was so desperate to get away from this place, that he was refusing to give the sweeper's credibility any consideration at all.

"Why are you trying to help us?" he asked the little machine. "What difference does it make to you what we do?"

The sweeper must have expected the question; an image immediately appeared in the same place as the others. It showed the sweeper performing its tasks in the maze and the tunnels belowground. A second set of images followed, these showing the sweeper being kicked and pummeled and knocked about in almost every conceivable way by something big and dark and fearsome that was always cloaked in shadow or just out of sight. Time and again, the sweeper was picked up and flung against a wall. Over and over, it was knocked on its side and had to be righted by other sweepers coming to its aid. There seemed to be no reason for the attacks. They appeared random and purposeless, the result of misdirected or pointless anger and frustration. Dented and cracked, the little sweeper would have to be repaired by its fellows before returning to its duties.

The images disappeared. The sweeper went still once more. Ahren tried to reconcile his doubts. An abused sweeper? Kicked around so thoroughly and for so long that it would do anything to put a stop to it? That meant, of course, that the sweeper was capable of feeling emotion and reacting to treatment that troubled it. As a rule, machines didn't feel anything, not even creepers. They were machines, which by definition meant they weren't human.

But these machines might well be as old as the city and whatever lived in it. It was not impossible to imagine that before the Great Wars destroyed the old civilization, humans had developed machines that could think and feel.

"It's asking for our help," Ryer Ord Star pointed out, breaking the silence. She brushed back her long silver hair in frustration. "In return, it will help us find Walker. Don't you understand?"

Not entirely, Ahren thought. "What sort of help does it expect us to give it?"

An image flashed from the open hatchway in the sweeper's metal head. Walker, Ahren, and Ryer Ord Star were walking from the ruins with the sweeper in tow.

"You want us to take you along when we leave?" he asked in disbelief.

The image repeated itself twice more, insistent and unmistakable. Then a new image appeared, the *Jerle Shannara* rising skyward, light sheaths stretched taut, radian draws rippling with power. At the bow of the airship stood the little sweeper, looking back at the land it was leaving behind.

"This is ridiculous," Ahren muttered, almost to himself. "It's a machine!"

"A sentient machine," Ryer Ord Star corrected him. "Sophisticated and capable of feeling. Ahren, it wants what we all want. It wants to be free."

The Elven youth sat down slowly on the pile of rubble and put his chin in his hands. "I still don't feel good about this," he said, his eyes watching the sweeper. "If we do what it wants and go underground, we'll be cut off from everything. If this is a trap, we won't have any chance of escaping. I don't know. I still think we ought to find the others first."

She knelt in front of him and put her hands over his, the tips of her fingers brushing his face. "Elven Prince, listen to me. Why would this be a trap? If whatever wards Castledown wanted us, couldn't it have had us by this time? If this sweeper meant to betray us, wouldn't we already be surrounded by creepers? What difference does it make to anything if it manages to get us belowground? Why would it go to so much trouble to accomplish so little?"

He had to admit he didn't know. She was right; it didn't make much sense. But neither did a lot of other things that had happened on this voyage, and he wasn't about to discount the way his instincts kept tugging at him in warning. Something was bothering him. Maybe it was just his fear of ending up like Joad Rish and the others. Maybe it was his indelible memory of the carnage and screams and dying. It was all too fresh to allow him to think objectively yet.

"There's no time to look for anyone else," she insisted. "There may not be anyone out there to find!"

It was his greatest fear, of course. That there was no one else alive, that they were all that was left.

She was pressing her hands over his, cupping them. He lifted his chin from their cradle, but she would not release him. "Ahren," she whispered. "Come with me. Please."

She was afraid, too. He could feel it in her touch and hear it in her voice. She was no less vulnerable than he. She could see the future, and perhaps she had seen things that she shouldn't, things that frightened her more than what was past. But she was going because she felt so strongly about Walker that she could not abandon him no matter what. He envied her such strength. It eclipsed his own and left him newly ashamed. She would go whether he went or not. And what would he do then? Go back to the bay, hide from the Mwellrets, and wait for the *Jerle Shannara* to return? Fly home again and live for the rest of his life with what he had done?

He might as well be dead if he did that.

"All right," he said quietly, taking her hands in his, holding them like tiny birds. He bent to her reassuringly, his voice steady. "We'll give it a try."

NINE

Quentin Leah crouched in the shadowed concealment of a partially collapsed building just below the maze into which the Mwellrets had ventured all too boldly a little earlier and from which they were now fleeing in a somewhat less orderly fashion. Panax and Tamis flanked him, motionless as they peered out through cracks in the walls. The Elven Hunters Kian and Wye knelt a little to the side. The Mwellrets raced past them unheeding and uncaring. Quick glances were cast over their shoulders, to see what might be following, and nowhere else. Some of the rets were bloodied, their cloaks torn and stained, their movements halting and ragged. They had not had a good time of it back there, certainly no better than Quentin and his companions, and they were anxious to be well away.

"How many do you count?" Tamis whispered to him.

He shook his head. "Maybe fifteen."

"That means five or six didn't make it out." She said it matter-of-factly, eyes straight ahead, watching the Mwellrets slide through the ruins. "It doesn't look like they managed to catch up to the seer."

Unless she was dead, of course. Quentin kept that thought to himself. Tamis wasn't saying anything about Bek, but that may have been because she still wasn't sure which way he had gone. She'd picked up Ryer Ord Star's trail easily enough, even with the herd of Mwellrets tromping all over everything, but there had been no sign of his cousin. Quentin felt frustrated and increasingly desperate. Time was getting away from them, and they weren't making any progress. He'd had reasonable hopes that they would encounter Bek or Ryer Ord Star by following the rets. Now it looked as if they wouldn't be encountering anyone.

The last of the Mwellrets trailed past, hurrying away through the bright midday light, disappearing back the way they had come. Tamis didn't move, so neither did Quentin or the others. They stayed where they were, frozen in place, watching and listening. After what seemed a very long time, Tamis turned to face them, her small, blocky form squared away and her gray eyes calm.

"I'm going to slip out for a quick look, try to find out what's happened. Wait here for me."

She was starting away when Quentin said, "I'm coming with you."

She turned back at once. "No offense, Highlander, but I'll do better alone. Leave this to me."

She slipped out through a gap in the wall and was gone. They looked for her in the ruins, but she had disappeared. Quentin glanced at Panax, then at the Elves, his disgruntlement plainly visible.

Kian shrugged. "Don't take it personally, Highlander. She's like that with everyone. No exceptions."

Quentin was thinking she had taken over leadership of their little group, a position he had occupied until she appeared. He wasn't the sort who was troubled by ego problems, but he couldn't help feeling a little irritated by her abrupt manner. He was competent at tracking, after all. He wasn't a novice who would place her at risk by going along.

Wye stretched his legs. A former member of the Home Guard, he had served in Allardon Elessedil's household before coming on this voyage. "She wanted to serve in the Home Guard, but Ard Patrinell thought she would be wasted there. He wanted her as a Tracker. She had a gift for it, was better than almost anyone."

"She resented his interference, though," Kian added with a yawn, dark face haggard and tired. "It took her a while to forgive him."

Wye nodded. "Places in the Home Guard are highly coveted; competition is intense. Women have never been fully accepted as equals; men are preferred as the King's protectors. And the Queen's. That was true even of Wren Elessedil. History and common practice more than prejudice and favoritism dictate what happens. Women don't serve in the Home Guard. On the other hand, women have come to dominate the tracking units of the Elven Hunters."

Wye nodded. "Their instincts are better than ours. No point in denying it. They seem better able to sort things out and make the choices you have to make when you're tracking. Maybe they've learned to better hone their instincts to compensate for lack of physical strength."

Quentin didn't know and didn't care. He admired Tamis for her straightforward approach to things, and he couldn't find any reason for her not to be accepted as a Home Guard. But he would have preferred her to show a little more confidence in him. Her demeanor didn't suggest she thought for a minute that she would ever have need of him or anyone else to come to her rescue. Those steady gray eyes and quiet voice were rimmed in iron. Tamis would save herself if there was any saving to be done.

Panax seated himself cross-legged in a corner of the room, a block of wood in one hand, his whittling knife in the other. He worked slowly, carefully in the silence, wood shavings curling and falling to the stone, shaggy head bent to his task.

"Sorry you came on this journey, Highlander?" he asked without looking up.

Leaving the Elven Hunters to keep watch, Quentin sat down next to him. "No." He considered momentarily. "I wish I hadn't been so eager to have Bek come along, though. I won't forgive myself if anything happens to him."

Panax grunted. "I wouldn't worry about Bek if I were you. You heard Tamis. I'd guess he's better off than we are. There's something about that boy. It's more than the magic Tamis saw him use. Walker's marked him for something special. It's why he sent you both to Truls Rohk—why Truls was persuaded to come with us. He saw it, too. He recognized it. He won't have forgotten it either. You might want to bear that in mind. The shape-shifter's out there somewhere, Highlander—mark my words. I won't tell you I can sense it. That would be silly. But I know him, and he's there. Maybe with Bek."

Quentin considered the possibility. The fact that no one had seen Truls Rohk—at least, no one he knew of—didn't mean he wasn't there. It was possible he was shadowing Bek. That made perfect sense if Walker had brought him along to keep Bek safe. He thought again about his cousin's mysterious past and his newfound use of magic that he'd never known he had. Maybe Bek really was better off than the rest of them.

"What about you, Panax?" he asked the Dwarf.

The whittling knife continued to move in smooth, effortless strokes. "What about me?"

"Are you sorry you came?"

The Dwarf laughed. "If I were, I'd have to be sorry about the larger part of my life!" He shook his head in amusement. "I've been living like this, Highlander, drifting from one mishap to the next, one expedition to another, for as long as I can remember. For all that I'm up in those mountains living alone much of the time, I've been more places and risked my life more often than I care to think about." He shrugged. "Well, there you are. If you live your life in the Wolfsktaag, you pretty much live on the edge all the time anyway."

"So Walker knew what he was doing when he sent us to find you? He knew you'd be coming, too."

"I'd say so." The Dwarf's dark eyes lifted a moment, then refocused on his work. "He wanted Truls and me both. Same as you and Bek. He likes companions, friends, and people who've known each other a long time and trust each other's judgment. He knows what sorts of risks you take on a voyage like the one we've made. Strangers bond, but not fast and hard enough as a rule. Friends and family are a better match in the long run. Besides, if he can get two magic wielders for the price of one, why not do so?"

Quentin refitted the headband around his long hair. "Always thinking ahead, the way Druids do."

The Dwarf grunted. "Farther ahead than you and I and most others could manage. That's why I think he's still alive." He stopped whittling and looked up. "That's why I think that sooner or later we'll find him."

Quentin wasn't so sure, but he kept that to himself, as well. His attitude about things in general was less positive than when he had started the journey. Bek would be surprised at the change in him.

Not ten minutes later, Tamis reappeared. They didn't see her until she was almost on top of them and she was not trying to hide her coming. She loped up through the rubble and into their shelter, her face damp with sweat, her short dark hair tousled, and her clothing disheveled. Quentin saw by the look on her face that all was not well.

"I followed the Mwellrets almost all the way back through the ruins." She spoke quickly, wiping at her face with her tunic sleeve as she crouched before them. She was breathing hard. "I caught up with one of them. He was injured and lagging behind the rest so I took a chance. I knocked him down, put a knife to his throat, and asked him what had happened. It was pretty much what you would guess, the same thing that happened to us. He told me they were tracking the seer, but they never found her."

"What about Bek?" Quentin asked at once.

She shook her head. "They don't know anything about him. When they reached that clearing, only the seer and the Ilse Witch were there. The witch told them to hunt us down and make us prisoners and then went off to hunt someone or something by herself." She paused. "It could have been Bek."

The Highlander frowned. "Why would she waste time hunting Bek? That doesn't make any sense."

"It does if she knows about his magic," Panax pointed out.

Quentin shook his head stubbornly. "She's after the treasure in Castledown. Maybe the Mwellret was lying to you."

"I don't think so," Tamis replied. "Bek was there when I left to find you and gone when the Mwellrets showed up. Something happened to him between times, and it probably involved the Ilse Witch. If we could find the seer, we might find out the truth. She must have seen something."

Panax tucked his whittling wood and knife away. "She could have died in the maze, along with the rets."

Tamis waved the suggestion off. "Why would she go back into the maze knowing what she does about its dangers? Besides, the ret I questioned said they didn't find her, dead or alive." She stood up. "That's enough for now. We have to get out of here. They'll be coming for us."

"You didn't kill the ret?" Kian asked her sharply.

Tamis wheeled on him angrily. "He was unarmed and helpless," she snapped. "I need better reasons than that to kill a man. I knocked him senseless and left. When he wakes, we'll be far away. Now let's go!"

"Go where?" Quentin demanded, standing up, brushing dirt and debris off his pants legs. "Do what?"

She shrugged. "We'll figure that out later. For now, we'll get far enough away that we won't be looking over our shoulders all the time. But we'll stay here in the ruins. They're big enough that we can hide and not be easy to track. We can keep looking for Patrinell and the others."

She started away, and they followed without further argument, knowing she was right, that they had to find a new hiding place, farther from the maze, deeper into the city. The Mwellrets would certainly hunt them, and they were excellent trackers, relying on their highly developed senses, on their shape-shifting abilities, and on their reptilian ancestry. In any case, it was foolish to assume that staying put would help. Following along behind Tamis, the Highlander, the Dwarf, and the Elven Hunters took care to disguise their tracks, to walk on the hard slabs of metal and stone where footprints wouldn't show. Several times, Tamis dropped back to muddy further any sign of their passing, using her special skills to conceal their trail.

Overhead, the sun had passed the midday point, easing into the afternoon, sliding through the cloudless blue toward nightfall. Within the ruins, the heat cast in the wake of its passing rose off the stone and metal in shimmering waves. Quentin loosened the buttons of his tunic and pushed up his sleeves. The Sword of Leah, strapped across his back, felt heavy and cumbersome. The magic with which it had infused him had faded, gone back into whatever dark pocket it had come from, leaving him bereft, but free, as well. He wondered if he would manage it better next time it was needed. There would be a next time, after all. He could hardly expect otherwise.

After they had gone some distance, he moved up beside Tamis. "Why are we going this way and not back toward the bay where we landed? What about Bek?"

She glanced over at him, her lips compressing in a tight line. "Two things. We have to find where Bek went before we can go after him, and we don't want the Mwellrets knowing what we intend."

He nodded. "We need them to believe we are doing something entirely different, running away perhaps, fleeing inland." He paused. "But won't they expect us to try to get back to the *Jerle Shannara*?"

"I expect they're hoping we do exactly that."

It was the way she said it that caught his attention. "What do you mean?"

Tamis rounded on him, bringing him up short. Her face was hard and set. The others closed about. "The Mwellret told me something else," she said, "something I didn't tell you before. I thought it could wait, since there was nothing we could do about it anyway. But maybe it can't. We've lost the ship. The Ilse Witch found a way through the pillars of ice and surprised it in the channel. She used her magic to put the Rovers to sleep and made them all prisoners. She's left Federation soldiers and Mwellrets to fly her." She shook her head. "We're on our own."

They stared at her, stunned. They were all thinking the same thing. They were marooned in a strange land, and any hope of being rescued by Redden Alt Mer and his Rovers or of getting back to the *Jerle Shannara* was gone.

Quentin started to say something, but she cut him short. "No, Highlander, the ret wasn't lying. I made sure. He was very definite. The *Jerle Shannara* is under the control of the Ilse Witch. She's not coming back for us."

"We have to get her back!" he replied at once, blurting it out before he could stop himself.

"Shouldn't be too hard," Panax observed, arching one eyebrow. "All we need are wings to fly up to her. Or maybe she'll do us the favor of coming down where we can reach her."

"For now, what we need to do is walk," Tamis said, dismissing the subject as she wheeled away. "Let's go."

They continued on for the better part of the afternoon, watching the sun descend into the west until it was little more than a bright glimmer along the horizon. By then they had crossed to the other side of the city and could see the trees of the forest ahead through gaps in the fallen buildings. Their shadows trailed behind them in long dark stains, sliding over the rubble like oil. The heat had dissipated and the air cooled. There had been no sign of the Mwellrets all afternoon. Nor had there been any sign of other survivors from their own company. The city seemed empty of life, save for themselves.

Ahead, the trees formed a dark wall over which the fading sun cast its silver halo.

Tamis called a halt, glancing around as she did so, taking her time. "I don't think we should attempt to circle back through the city at night," she said. "There's bound to be other traps. There might be sentries, as well. Better to wait until morning when we can see something."

Quentin, like the others, had adjusted to the idea that they were alone and cut off from rescue or escape, that whatever they chose to do, they had better do so with that in mind. Mistakes would prove costly now, perhaps fatal. If the Mwellrets wanted to try tracking them in the dark, let them do so. With any luck, the city and its horrors would swallow them.

"We'll make camp in the forest?" Panax asked.

Tamis nodded. "As best we can. No fire, cold food, and one of us on watch all night. We've seen what's in the city, but not what's in these woods."

A comforting thought, Quentin mused, trailing after her into the trees until she found a suitable clearing. The sun was down by then, and the first stars were appearing. The same stars would already be out at home, so far away he could barely imagine it anymore. His parents would be in bed and perhaps asleep under them. He wondered if Coran and Liria were thinking of him now, as he was thinking of them. He wondered if he would ever see them again.

They had a little food and water, but no bedding. Almost everything had been lost in the flight out of the maze or left behind at the edge of the ruins. They ate what they had, drank from an aleskin Panax was carrying, and slept in their clothes using whatever they could find for pillows. Tamis took the first watch. Quentin was asleep so fast he had barely cradled his head in the crook of his arm before he was gone.

He dreamed, but his dreams were jumbled and disjointed fragments. They left him shaken and at times frantic, but they lacked meaning and were forgotten almost immediately. Each time, after jerking awake, he slipped quickly back to sleep again. Black and still, the night enveloped and carried him away.

It was Kian who woke him, gripping his shoulder firmly, steadying him when he started from his sleep. "You've been dreaming all night, Highlander," the Elven Hunter whispered. "You might as well take the watch and let those of us who can rest do so."

His was the last watch, and already he could sense the shift in time. The stars had circled about and the darkness was losing its hold. Quentin sat looking out across the clearing to where the sunrise would begin, waiting for the light to change. His companions slept all about him, their dark shapes unmoving, the sounds of their breathing slow and ragged in the stillness.

Once, something flew through the branches of the trees overhead, a quick and hurried movement that disappeared almost as fast as it had come. A bird of some sort, he decided, and let his heart settle back into his chest. A little later, feeling uneasy, he rose and peered out into the ruins of the city, searching the darkness. He saw nothing and heard nothing. Maybe there was nothing to see or hear. Just themselves. Maybe in a world of creepers and fire threads, of Mwellrets and the Ilse Witch, they were all of humankind that was left.

But as the dawn brightened in a thin silver thread along the eastern horizon, chasing back the forest shadows just enough to give identity to shapes and forms, he saw that he was wrong. A man stood opposite him on the far side of the clearing, vaguely defined by the light, immobile against the gloom. At first Quentin thought he was seeing something that wasn't really there, that the light was playing tricks on his eyes. Why would someone be standing there in the dark? But as the light sharpened the image and gave clarity to its features, he found he wasn't mistaken after all. The man was tall and thin, wearing a sleeveless tunic, pants that ended at the knees, sandals that laced up his ankles, and leather wrist guards. He carried what seemed to be a spear yet wasn't, a slender piece of wood six feet in length with a second, much shorter length fastened to its center.

Quentin waited until he was absolutely certain of what he was seeing, then reached over to Tamis, who was sleeping right beside him, and touched her arm.

She was awake instantly, rising to a sitting position and staring at him. He pointed at the figure. A second later, she was standing beside him, fully alert.

"How long has he been there?" she whispered.

"I don't know. He was already there before it was light enough to see him."

"Has he done anything?"

Quentin shook his head. "Just stand there and watch us."

Tamis went silent. She sat with Quentin, studying the man, waiting to see what would happen. In the new light, her small face took on a different cast; she looked young and pretty and faintly exotic with her Elven features. Quentin found himself studying her as much as the stranger. He liked the calm, easy way she dealt with things, the way she was never flustered, the fact that she never overreacted. In another time and place, in other circumstances, he would have responded to that attraction; he did not think he could allow that there.

The sun crested the horizon and sent splinters of brilliant

light chasing after the fading night. In the wake of their passing, the stranger's features were fully revealed. His skin had a reddish cast to it, almost copper. It gleamed faintly, as if it was oiled. His hair, redder still, if a shade lighter, was thick and tightly curled against his skull, cut short and left free. Even his eyes, now visible in the dawn, were vaguely cinnamon.

He continued to regard them, a statue carved of stone. For the first time, Quentin saw what might be a short javelin tucked into his leather belt behind his back, one end protruding.

"What is he carrying in his hand?" he whispered to Tamis.

She shook her head. "I think it's a blowgun, but I've never seen one that size. See the piece strapped to its middle? That would be a holder for the darts." She went silent again, then said, "We can't wait on this any longer. We have to see what he wants. Stay here while I wake the others."

She rose and moved from Panax to the Elven Hunters, waking each with a touch, bending close to caution them, to tell them not to react. One by one they sat up and looked over to where the stranger stood watching.

Tamis came back to Quentin and bent close. "This might be tricky. He won't be alone. There will be others in the trees. He wouldn't expose himself so completely if there wasn't someone protecting his back. He's offering himself as a decoy to see what we do. Let's not give him reason to think we mean him harm."

She stood up and walked slowly over to where he stood. She kept her hands at her sides and her weapons sheathed. Quentin heard her greet him in the Elven tongue and then, when he failed to respond, in several variants. None worked. She tried several Southland languages. Still nothing. She spoke bits of half a dozen Troll dialects, all without result.

Then all at once the stranger said something. When he spoke, his mouth opened to reveal that even his teeth were burnished copper instead of white. His speech was rough and guttural, and Quentin could not understand any of it. Tamis seemed perplexed, as well.

"Hold up a minute." Panax stood suddenly and walked over to them. "I think he's speaking in the Dwarf tongue, a very old dialect, a kind of hybrid. Let me try."

He spoke to the stranger, taking his time, trying out a few words, waiting for a response, then trying again. The stranger listened and finally replied. They went back and forth like this for several minutes before Panax turned back to his companions. "I'm getting some of it, but not all. Come over and stand with me. I think it's all right."

He went on talking with the stranger, Tamis staying close beside him, as Quentin, Kian, and Wye joined them.

"He says he's a Rindge. His people live in villages at the foot of those mountains behind him. They're native to this area, been here for centuries. They're hunters, and he's part of a hunting party that stumbled on us during the night." He glanced at Tamis. "You were right. He's not alone. There are other Rindge with him. I don't know how many, but I'd guess they're all around us."

"Ask him if he's seen anyone else besides us," Tamis suggested.

Panax spoke a few words and listened to the other's reply. "He says he hasn't seen anyone. He wants to know what we're doing here."

There was another exchange. Panax told the Rindge they had come to search for a treasure in the ruins of the city. The Rindge grew animated, punctuating his words with gestures and grunts. He said there wasn't any treasure, the city was very dangerous, and metal beasts would hunt them and fire would burn their eyes out. The city had eyes everywhere, and nothing came or went without being seen, except for the Rindge, who knew how to stay hidden.

Quentin and Tamis exchanged a quick glance. "How do the Rindge hide from the creepers?" she asked Panax.

The Dwarf repeated the question and listened intently to the answer. Confused, he made the Rindge repeat it. While they spoke, other Rindge appeared out of the trees, just faces at first in the dim light, then bodies, as well, materializing one after the other, ringing the little company. Quentin glanced around uneasily. They were vastly outnumbered and very much cut off from any chance of flight. He resisted the urge to put his hand on his sword; relying on weapons for help would be foolish.

Panax cleared his throat. "He says the Rindge are a part of the land and know how to disappear into it. Nothing can find them if they keep careful watch, even at the edges of the city. He says they never go into the ruins themselves. He wants to know why we did."

Tamis laughed softly. "Good question. Ask him what it is they're hunting."

The Rindge, tall and rawboned, listened and nodded slowly as Panax spoke. Then he replied at length. The Dwarf waited until he was finished, and glanced over his shoulder. "I'm not sure I'm getting all this. Maybe I've got it wrong. I almost hope I do. He says they're hunting creepers, that they're setting traps for them. Apparently the traps are to discourage the creepers from hunting them. He says the creepers harvest the Rindge for body parts, that they use pieces of the Rindge to make something called *wronks*. Wronks look like them and us, but are made of metal and human parts both. I can't quite figure it out. The Rindge are pretty frightened of them, whatever they are. This one says that by taking pieces of you, the wronks steal your soul so that you can never really die."

Tamis frowned. "What does that mean?"

Panax shook his head. He spoke to the Rindge again, then glanced at the Tracker and shrugged. "I can't make it out."

"Ask him who controls the wronks and the creepers and the fire," she said.

"Ask him who lives under the city," Quentin added.

Panax turned back to the Rindge and repeated the questions in the strange, harsh Dwarf dialect. The Rindge listened carefully. All about them, the other Rindge pressed close, exchanging hurried glances. The air was charged with fear and rage, and the Highlander could feel the tension in the air.

When the Dwarf was finished, the Rindge to whom he had been speaking straightened, looked past them toward the ruins, and spoke a single word.

"Antrax."

TEN

Deep within the bowels of Castledown, far below the ruins of the city above, Antrax spun down the lines and cables that gave it passage through its realm. Traveling somewhere between the speeds of light and sound, faster than the eye could follow if the eye had been permitted to try to do so, it sped along corridors and passageways, from chamber to chamber, riding the metal threads that linked it to the kingdom it ruled. It was a presence that lacked substance and shape and could be virtually everywhere at once or nowhere at all. It was the crowning achievement of its creators in a time and a world long since dead, but it had transcended even that to become what it was.

The perfect weapon.

The ultimate protector.

Built almost three thousand years earlier, in a time when artificial intelligence was commonplace and thinking machines proliferated, it was advanced for its kind even then, a prototype created in the heat of events that culminated in the Great Wars. Skirmishes had begun already, and its creators suspected where things were heading when they first conceived of it. They were archivists and visionaries, people whose primary interest was in preserving for the future that

129

which might otherwise be lost. Lesser minds dominated the thinking of the times; they manipulated the rules of power and politics to stir within the populace a mix of rage and frustration that eventually would consume them all. To thwart the madness that was overtaking them, the creators determined that those who would destroy what they would not concede should not be allowed to undo the progress of civilization. Antrax knew that because when it was built, the knowledge was programmed into it. It was necessary that it know the reason for its existence, because otherwise how could it understand the importance of what it was created to do?

It took years to build Antrax, and the building of it was accomplished at a great cost of lives and resources. Few of those who began the project lived to see it completed. Antrax had a sense of time, and knew that it had gained life in small increments. A bit of knowledge here, a piece of reasoning there, it expanded until it was housed in more than one place and could travel the city's catacombs like a wraith. Aboveground, the city masked its presence and its purpose. Only a few knew that it was there, functioning. Only those few knew what it was meant to do. The Great Wars were consuming the world of the creators in a widening swath of destruction and ruin, and humankind was being changed forever. So much would be lost as a result—irreparably lost. But not what was housed within those chambers, not that which Antrax was created to preserve and with which it was entrusted. That would be protected. That would endure.

In the end, the creators simply faded away. Antrax never knew what happened to them. They gave it life, a place to reside, a domain to watch over, and a directive to follow. They set it on its course, and then they disappeared.

All but one.

That one returned a final time. He was alone and his appearance unexpected. When all else was done, and Antrax was functioning as intended, the input receptors had been closed. No further instructions were necessary. Then the last creator appeared and opened the receptors anew. He gave greetings to Antrax. They could speak to each other through the keyboards and touch screens. They could communicate as equals. He told Antrax that the worst had come to pass. Everything was lost. The world was destroyed, and civilization was in ruins. Centuries of progress had been wiped out. Art, culture, knowledge, and understanding were gone. The creators, save he alone, were destroyed. Perhaps no one was still alive anywhere in the entire world. Perhaps everyone was dead.

Antrax did not respond. It had not been built to understand human emotion; it could not sense it in the words of the creator who spoke to it. But a new directive followed, and Antrax was required to obey directives. The directive entered its memory banks through the keyboard and became a part of its consciousness. The command was clear. Those chambers, the complex, and everything housed within had been given to Antrax to ward. They must not be compromised. They must not be lost. It was not enough that Antrax watch over them and keep them safe for when the creators returned. Antrax must protect them, as well; it must combat and destroy anything that threatened them. The means for doing so was already in place, weapons and defenses both, installed in secret by the last creator himself, who knew better than his fellows what the times required. Antrax must draw from its memory banks, as it did energy from its power cells, knowledge of how those defenses and weapons worked. It must adapt that knowledge to fulfill its directive; it must extrapolate what was needed to survive. If defenses or weapons were called for,

Antrax must use them. If they were not enough and others were required, Antrax must build them. If anyone tried to reclaim the chambers without entering the proper code, the intrusion must be stopped—even at the cost of lives.

The final admonishment was a direct violation of any previous programming, but the command was overriding and absolute. Causing harm to humans was permissible. Killing was allowed. Antrax was given control over its own destiny. No one must threaten its existence or interfere with its purpose and function. No one must enter into its domain without knowledge of the code. That was the new directive. That was how Antrax was reprogrammed in the final throes of the apocalypse, when the last of the creators disappeared.

It was alone for a long time after that. No one came to try to find it. No one even ventured close. In the ruins of the city, nothing moved. Not humans, animals, insects, or birds. The air was hazy and thick with debris, and nothing lived within its gloom. Antrax kept its vigil over the catacombs it had been set to guard. It warded them carefully, speeding down its lines of communication, through its myriad halls and chambers, into its memory banks and energy cells, all across its kingdom. Always watching. For a very long time, it had no need to do so; there was nothing outside to watch for. There was nothing but wasteland.

Sometimes, it wondered why it was guarding the underground chambers. It had been told what was housed there, but it did not understand why that held such importance for the creators. Some of it, yes. Some of it was obvious. Mostly, it was a puzzle. Antrax had been programmed to solve the puzzles that confronted it, and so it sought a solution to that one. It consulted its memory banks for help and got none. Its memory banks were vast, but the information stored there was not always useful. Words could be vague and confusing, especially when lacking a context into which to put them. Mathematics and engineering provided the most familiar and useful concepts, for Antrax had been built and programmed from them. Yet other words were only strings of symbols that meant nothing to it. Pictures and drawings confounded it. Vast amounts of the information it had been given seemed pointless, so much so that as its knowledge and sense of self-sufficiency grew, it even questioned the programming choices of the creators.

But the directive was immutable. Everything housed within the catacombs was precious. No part of it must be disturbed. No piece must be lost. Everything must be saved for when the creators came to reclaim it.

Yet when would that time come? Antrax had a vague memory of a blueprint for such a time, but the directive of the last creator had blurred and finally erased the specifics. There seemed to be no rules for when the catacombs should be opened up again. Or to whom. The catacombs it warded must be left inviolate, must be protected and preserved, must be kept hidden and safe.

Forever.

When the first of the four-legged creatures wandered into the ruins, years after the last of the creators had vanished, Antrax was ready. It had probed its memory banks for the details of the defenses and weapons that had been given to it, and it used them. Lasers effortlessly cut apart many of the intruders. Metal sentries and fighting units chased down the rest. The four-legged creatures were no challenge, but they gave Antrax a chance to test its ability to fulfill its directive.

Later, humans tried to venture into the ruins, as well, to explore the collapsed chambers and crumbling passageways, even to find their way underground. None of them had the code. Antrax destroyed them all. Yet others returned from time to time, some of them becoming recognizable by their look and feel, some of them persistent in their efforts. Like ants, they tunneled and burrowed, little annoyances that refused to be chased away for more than a short time. Even the lasers and probes failed to discourage them. Antrax began to explore other solutions. It found interesting possibilities in its memory banks and experimented with them. The wronks proved the most successful. Something about revisiting the dead was especially frightening to humans.

They gave it a name. Antrax. They took it from their own language. Antrax had no idea what it meant. Nor did it care to know. What mattered was that they knew it was there. That was enough to accomplish what was needed. The humans began to avoid the ruins. They no longer spent time searching for entrances into the catacombs beneath.

But Antrax had grown fond of its wronks, which it adapted to serve other needs. It continued to harvest humans for the parts that the wronks needed. It continued to experiment. The humans were no longer intruders; they were prey.

It was the failure of the first energy cell that prompted Antrax to explore the larger world. There were three such cells, vast capacitors that drew their energy from the sun and fed it into the receptors so that Antrax could function. The cells were meant to last forever, so long as there was sun and light. But everything has a finite life, even components that are built to last forever, especially when those components are overworked. Antrax had evolved in its time as guardian of the catacombs. Its commitments to its directive had multiplied, and its hunger had grown. It needed more fuel than anticipated by its creators. Its cells were being drained of energy more quickly than the sun could replenish them. Perhaps it was the strain of maintaining the lasers and probes and wronks. Perhaps the efficiency of the cells had been grossly overestimated to begin with. Whatever the case, Antrax was losing power.

It decided that another source of energy must be found.

It acted quickly. It sent its probes in search of such a source, far out into the world, beyond what Antrax knew. The probes were not meant to return, only to send the information they acquired. They did as they were programmed to do, and while most places were empty of human life and of the sources of energy Antrax required, one place showed promise. It was across the sea to the east, a land in which humans had survived the Great Wars. Theirs was a rudimentary civilization in many ways, but there were possibilities to be explored. The Old World had changed and Mankind had evolved. The sciences of the past were barely in evidence. Instead, there was a new kind of science. Elements of that science were able to generate power far greater than that which sustained Antrax. The elements could be found in weapons and talismans borne by the descendants of his creators. But genetics and training had infused a few of those men and women with the elements of power, so that in some the power was generated from within.

A dream, or what the dreamer thought was one, had brought the first of the Great War survivors to Antrax thirty years before. Of those, only one was useful. Now that one, supplied with a map that revealed the existence of the catacombs and their contents, had lured others. What had value for the creators would have value for their descendants, whether Antrax comprehended the nature of that value or not. Examined and measured on the islands that Antrax had established as testing grounds through probes dispatched years earlier, subjected to attacks by creatures and spirits no ordinary human could hope to overcome, a few had shown themselves more powerful than their fellows and were therefore suitable for culling. Three at least had come into the ruins overhead, and perhaps more waited without. Antrax would use them as it had used the one thirty years earlier, as components essential to its continued existence, necessary sacrifices to its directive. The creator had been specific. The lives of humans were expendable. It was Antrax who must survive.

Deep within the corridors and chambers of its domain, Antrax slowed its spinning passage and paused to take inventory of those it would use to feed it.

One was momentarily beyond its reach, although a special wronk was being constructed to hunt it down.

The second was already on his way.

But it was the third that interested Antrax most. That one had actually penetrated all the way into the catacombs. It had bypassed the code at the tower door. It was not a creator, one of the expected ones, but it had resources and incredible inner power. Antrax could not determine the source of its power, only its measure. What mattered was that there was enough of it to sustain Antrax for decades to come, perhaps for centuries, limited only by the capacity of the available storage units.

Already Antrax was gathering and converting that power, drawing it from the intruder without his realizing, leeching it away bit by bit. It seemed to replenish itself, so the leeching was not yet detrimental to the intruder's health. But that could change. Antrax would have to monitor it closely. Reaching out with its sensors to take the necessary readings, it took a moment to do so, finding the intruder still working hard in his futile effort to escape.

* * *

The Druid known as Walker, who, in a time before he lost his arm and found his destiny, had been called both Walker Boh and Dark Uncle, was seeking his way yet again. He stood in one of the myriad passageways of Castledown and tried to understand what he was doing wrong. His stomach roiled and his head ached. Something was amiss. Even without knowing what it was, he could feel it as surely as he could feel the discomfort in his body. All of his efforts to outdistance his pursuers had failed. All of his attempts to escape had led to nothing.

Behind him in the near darkness of the corridors and chambers, invisible for the moment, but there nevertheless, the creepers hunted him. He had fled them from the moment he had dropped through the floor of the black tower and spiraled down a chute into these lower depths. They had found him at once, and he had fought them off and escaped. But everywhere he turned, everywhere he went, they were waiting. Castledown was full of them, prowling the depths in such numbers that Walker could not see how an army could stand against them, let alone a single man. Yet he would do so, for as long as he was able, for as long as his strength allowed it.

What baffled him, in his desperate flight, was how unendingly similar everything was. Corridors and rooms without number, all empty of anything other than machinery built into the walls and lines of power that fed those machines, all of them the same. Nothing was different about any of them; nothing suggested the presence of the treasure he sought. There were no hidden doorways or secret passages, no concealing panels behind which or under which or above which a treasure might lie. He could detect nothing of what he was certain was there. He knew what he was looking for. Unlike the others who had come searching for it, save perhaps the Ilse Witch, he knew exactly what it was that he must find.

Unless it was all a clever lie, created by the mapmaker to lure and trap him.

Yet he had discarded that possibility long ago. The knowledge contained in those symbols and markings was more revealing than the mapmaker had intended. Unwittingly, perhaps, the mapmaker had given away a truth it did not fully understand.

That Castledown was a trap had been obvious almost from the beginning, and the reason for that trap became clear after their experiences on the islands of Flay Creech, Shatterstone, and Mephitic. What lived within Castledown wanted their magic. What it wanted the magic for, what purpose it intended for its use, remained a mystery. Walker was not even clear as yet as to whether his adversary was looking for a specific form of magic. It might be seeking only another wielder for the missing Elfstones, someone to take Kael Elessedil's place. It might be looking for something more.

Whatever the case, it had used the castaway and the map as bait, the keys as lures, the islands as testing grounds, the spirits and creatures on those islands as measuring sticks, and its victims' curiosity and persistence as goads. The keys they had struggled so hard to obtain were worthless in any real sense, of course. He still carried them within his robes, but had long since discarded the possibility that they would prove useful. They were lures and nothing more. But the map, notwithstanding its maker's belief that it, too, was only bait, was invaluable.

None of which helped Walker in his plight. He began moving along the passageways once more, probing as he did so, seeking either to escape or to find the hidden treasure. Either would give him what he needed, a way out, a weapon to use against his mysterious adversary. He wondered at the fate of those still aboveground. They would never find him. They might not even try. The destruction they had encountered might have demoralized them utterly. If he was lost, they would reason, what chance had they? He had to hope that one or two would hold the rest together, that those he counted on most to stand firm would find a way do so.

Nevertheless, he had to get back to them quickly. Time was working against him; he had to get clear of the maze.

Creepers appeared from out of the walls right in front of him. Bright bursts of Druid fire lanced from the fingers of his good arm. Bits and pieces of his attackers flew apart, and then he was rushing past their remains, finding others waiting ahead. He destroyed them, as well, still advancing, knowing they could track him by his magic, that they could determine his progress by his use of magic. The less he expended, the better. Yet he could not hide completely, not mask his passage sufficiently, no matter what he did.

He rounded a corner and found a new set of passageways. Winded and aching, he pressed his back against the cool of the metal wall and clutched at his churning stomach with his hand. The maze of chambers and corridors was disorienting. He peered ahead and then back. He had come that way before. Or another way just like it. He was traveling in circles, careening this way and that to no discernible end. His mind spun with the possibilities of what might be happening, but a new rush of creepers distracted him and forced him to stand and fight once more.

He charged into them, hurtling them aside with his magic, slamming them against the walls of the passageway and turning them into smoking, shattered heaps. Again, he broke free.

Moments later, he was alone again, a solitary fugitive in an unfamiliar world. He still didn't feel right. It was there in his bones and in his heart. He was half a step slower in his movements, a shade duller in his thinking, off balance just enough that he wasn't functioning as he knew he should. Why would that be? He sped through shadows and pools of light given off by smokeless lamps, trying to find an answer.

But no answer came to him. He ran on, searching for help that wasn't there.

Antrax monitored the human a few moments longer, taking measurements. The siphon was unobstructed and strong. Power from the expenditure of the intruder's fire surged into the converters, then into the capacitors housing the fuel on which Antrax would feed. Antrax would let the human run from the creepers awhile longer, then change the scenario to give him something else to do. The possibilities were endless. But caution was needed. The human was intelligent; he was quick to reason things out. If Antrax wasn't careful, wasn't subtle enough, he would see through the subterfuge. That could not be allowed to happen.

Dismissing him, Antrax spun back down the miles of power lines that wound through the passageways and chambers, feeding out its sensors as it made a quick survey of its perimeter. No boundaries had been breached. No further intruders had tried to enter. Satisfied, it switched back to the room in which the special wronk was being constructed.

Matters were progressing as expected. Surgeon probes were assembling the wronk with their customary skill and delicate touch. The parts lay spread out on gurneys, those of metal sterilized and wrapped, those of flesh and bone hooked to the life-support systems, artificial body fluids pumping steadily through arteries and veins. Already the process of joining flesh to metal and synthetics had begun, a fusing technique developed in the waning days of the Old World and perfected since by Antrax through study and experimentation. There had been failures for a long time; madness had claimed the early wronks and negated their usefulness. But eventually Antrax had found a way to control the wronk mind sufficiently that insanity was not an option. Breakdowns eventually rendered the wronks useless, but they were longer coming and less devastating when they arrived. Now and again, the damage could be repaired and the wronks put back into service. The surgeon probes were quite efficient at their work.

Through images conveyed by its sensors, Antrax studied the face of its latest subject as its head floated in the preserving fluid. The eyes stared out, shifting back and forth, searching for a way to escape, not understanding that the means for doing so had long since been stripped away. The meds, fed in through tubes that ran down its throat, kept it stable and calm. Its mouth was open, as if it were a fish feeding. It was in perfect condition.

Antrax took quick inventory of the still-unassembled parts. When it was complete, the wronk would be the most dangerous ever built, in no small part because the human from which it was being constructed was an excellent specimen with superb skills. To bring the other elements of power to bay and to overcome the humans that wielded them, it would have to be. But the technology of the Old World could accomplish anything. Antrax would have its sources of power in hand and working for its benefit before long.

Let the humans run as fast and far as they could manage, it thought. In the end, it would not matter. Castledown and its catacombs had been given to it to preserve and protect, but the world beyond, even that part so distant it was still a mystery, was not out of reach. The creators had given Antrax a directive, and there were no restrictions on the methods it could employ to fulfill it. If the power Antrax required lay elsewhere, it would find a way to bring it close. If the energy it needed must be obtained at the cost of human lives, so be it.

Antrax had been programmed to believe that nothing was more important than its survival. Nothing had happened to change that belief.

ELEVEN

The hand that clamped on his shoulder and shook Bek from his slumber was rough and urgent. "Wake up!" Truls Rohk hissed in his ear. "She's found us!"

Bek didn't need to ask whom the shape-shifter was talking about. The Ilse Witch. His sister. His enemy. He lurched to his feet, still half-asleep. He blinked to get his bearings, to clear his head. He was only partially successful. He felt the other's hand steady him, less compelling, almost gentle. "How close is she?" he managed.

"Close enough to hear you sneeze," the other whispered, gesturing behind him into the dark.

It was still night, the sky a tapestry of stars against which thin strips of broken clouds floated like linen. The quarter-moon was a tipped crescent on the northern horizon. The woods about them were an impenetrable black. She was tracking them in the dark, Bek realized. How could she do that? Could she read the traces of their body heat and energy even at night? He supposed she could. There wasn't much she couldn't do with the magic of the wishsong to aid her. He had fallen asleep at sunset, certain they had lost her in the meadow, that they had left her far enough behind to ensure at least one good night's sleep. So much for being certain.

"How could she find us so fast?" he whispered. He took a few deep breaths, shivering as a sudden gust of chill wind blew down off the mountains.

Truls Rohk's face was unreadable within the shadows of his cowl. "Luck, I would guess. She shouldn't have had any left after what we did to throw her off, but she's resourceful enough that she makes her own. Start walking."

Snatching up their few supplies, they departed their camp, heading inland once more, moving parallel to the base of the mountains. They made no effort to hide their passage out. If the Ilse Witch had tracked them that far, she would have no trouble discovering where they had spent the night. Bek was wondering if he had been saved by Truls Rohk's instincts or by his foresight. Whichever it was, it gave Bek a renewed sense of dependence on him. Bek had slept, after all. If he had tried to flee alone from his sister, she would have had him already.

He shook his head. What would that mean for him, to be in her hands? When it finally happened, when she finally caught up to them, as he felt certain she must, what would transpire?

They slid down a steep hillside to a rocky flat and hurried across to a river. They waded in, moving upstream, crossing to the far side to make their way below the bank. The water was icy cold and swift, and Bek had to concentrate hard on keeping his feet planted solidly beneath him.

"Either she stumbled on our real trail and is relying still on her magic to track us or she's found an ally who can read sign." The shape-shifter's voice was low and menacing, a whisper of dark anger above the soft gurgle of the water. His cloaked form seemed to glide through the shallows, his movements steady and deliberate against the current. "We'll have to find out which."

They continued upstream for a mile or so, then climbed out on a rocky flat on the far shore and worked their way inland for a time. East, the sky was beginning to brighten with a silver glow as sunrise neared. Bek found himself thinking of sunrise in the Highlands of Leah, of hunts with Quentin in the early dawn, of how much alike it felt and yet how different, too. Awake now, his mind picked its way nimbly through the debris of his life. He wasn't afraid anymore, not in the way he had been afraid in the ruins of Castledown when the fire threads and creepers had attacked them. But he was feeling lost; he was feeling disconnected. Everything he knew from his past life had been stripped away from him—his home, his family, and his land. There was nothing left of any of it, and the farther he walked, the more unlikely it seemed that he would ever have any of it back.

It was as if he were walking out of himself, as if he were shedding his skin.

He hitched up the Sword of Shannara across his back and tried to find comfort in its solid, dependable presence, but could not.

Truls Rohk took him back down to the river and into the cold waters once more. The sun was up, the silver light brightened to gold, the first tinges of blue sky visible. The sound of the rushing water enveloped him, and he turned his attention to keeping upright and moving ahead. They crossed the channel a second time, back to where they were close to the other bank, then began wading upriver. The cold water numbed Bek's legs, and after a time he could barely feel the feet in his boots. He kept on, forcing himself to put one foot in front of the other and think of better times, because there was nothing else he could do.

When they were several miles farther upstream, at a bend

in the river where the limbs of towering cedars and hickory overhung the water, Truls Rohk stopped. He reached within his cloak and produced a length of thin rope and an odd grappling hook on which the arms were collapsed against the base, but which unfolded and locked in place when he released the wire that held them down. Doubling the rope through an eye at the base of the hook, he coiled it carefully about his left forearm. Motioning for Bek to stay put, he crossed the river, stepped ashore momentarily, took several steps into the trees, then carefully backed up, retracing his own footprints, reentered the water, and moved ahead fifty yards onto a rise barely concealed by the swift waters. Checking to make certain that the boy was where he had left him, he began to swing the grappling hook overhead, playing out the rope gradually to widen the arc. Then he released the hook with a heave and sent it soaring high into the tree limbs overhead. The grappling hook caught and held. He tugged at it experimentally, then motioned for Bek to join him.

"Climb onto my back, put your arms about my neck, and hold on."

Bek did so, feeling the ridged muscles beneath him, the ropes of sinew and gristle that crisscrossed the other's shoulders and gave him the feel of an animal. The boy tried not to think of that. Clasping his right hand about his left wrist, he took firm hold.

Truls Rohk lunged up the rope and began climbing hand over hand as they swung out across the river. Skimming over the chill waters, they drew up their legs as they bottomed out at the nadir of their arc before rising again to the near shore where the river hooked left. Just above the bank, deep within the woods, Truls Rohk loosened his grip just enough to slide back to the ground. Still holding on to the ends of the rope, he waited for Bek to climb off his back, then ran the rope out through the eye until it dropped free of the hook, coiled it up once more, and tucked it away beneath his robes.

"That should give her something to puzzle out," the shape-shifter growled softly. "If we're lucky, she'll think we went ashore on the far bank and track us that way."

They moved inland again, away from the river and back toward the mountains, angling over rocky ground and dry creek beds, avoiding soft earth that would leave footprints, keeping clear of scrub where broken twigs would signal their passing. The sun was fully up, and it warmed their chilled bodies and dried their clothes. Truls Rohk slouched ahead like a great beast, all size and bulk, enigmatic and unknowable within his robes and hood. Bek, trailing after, found himself wondering if the shape-shifter ever exposed himself to the light. In the time they'd been together since meeting in the Wolfsktaag, he hadn't done so once. That didn't trouble Bek as it had at first, but he thought about what it would be like always to be wrapped up in cloth and never to be comfortable with showing anyone what you looked like. He wondered anew about the connection between them, a link strong enough to make the shape-shifter willing to accept his role as Bek's protector, to come on the journey when he could just as well have refused.

They walked all day, moving out of the lowlands and into the mountains, climbing the lower slopes to a forested promontory where Bek could see the whole of the land stretching back to the river from which they had come. Truls Rohk stopped there, took a quick moment to look around, then guided Bek into the trees.

"It's all well and good to choose a place where you can see anyone following," he pointed out. "But if you can see them, they can probably see you, as well. Best not to chance it. There's better ways. Once it's dark, I'll try one of them."

They found a dry grassy space within a grouping of cedar and spruce and sat themselves down to eat and drink. They had water for several days more, and in the mountains replacing what they consumed would not be hard. But their food was almost gone. Tomorrow, they would have to forage. And the day after that. And so on, which made Bek wonder anew how much farther in they were going.

"We might find help in these mountains," his companion ventured after a while, almost as if reading the boy's mind. Bek looked at him. "Shape-shifters live in these hills. I sense their presence. They don't know me or of my history. They might think differently about halflings than those in the Wolfsktaag. They might be willing to give us help."

The words were soft and contemplative, almost a prayer. It surprised Bek. "How will you make contact with them?"

The other shrugged. "I won't have to. They'll come to us, if we continue on. We're in their country now. They'll know what I am and come to find out what I want." He shook his head. "The trouble is, as a rule, shape-shifters won't interfere in the lives of others, even their own kind, unless they have a reason to do so. We have to give them one if we want their help."

Bek thought about it a moment. "Can I ask you something?"

The shadowed cowl shifted slightly to face him, the opening dark and empty-looking. "What would you ask of me, Bek Ohmsford, that you haven't asked already?"

It was said almost in challenge. Bek adjusted the Sword of Shannara where it lay at his side on the grass, then pushed back his unruly mop of dark hair. "You said shape-shifters don't interfere in the lives of others without a reason. If that's so, why did you choose to become involved in mine?"

There was a long silence as the other studied him from out of the blackness of the cowl. Bek shifted uncomfortably. "I know you said you felt there was a link between us, through our magic—"

"You and I, we're alike, boy," Truls Rohk interrupted, ignoring the rest of what Bek was trying to say. "I see myself in you as a boy, struggling to come to terms with who I was, with finding out I was different from others."

"But that's not it, is it? That's not the reason."

Truls Rohk seemed to shimmer, his blackness turning liquid, as if he might simply fade away without answering anything, as if he might disappear and never come back. But the movement steadied, and the big man went still.

"I saved your life," he said. "When you save another's life, you become responsible for it. I learned that a long time ago. I believe it to be so."

He made a quick, dismissive gesture. "But it's much more complicated. Games-playing, of another sort. I have no one in my own life—no home, no people, no place that belongs to me. I have no real purpose. My future is a blank. It is a need for direction that draws me to the Druid. For a time, he gives me one. Each message he sends is an invitation to be a part of something. Each message gives me a chance to discover something about myself. I don't do much of that in the Wolfsktaag. There's not really much left of me to discover there.

"You, boy—you interest me because you offer answers to the questions I've asked myself. I learn from you. But I can teach you, as well—how to live as an outsider, how to survive who and what you are, how to endure the magic that will always be part of you. I'm curious to see how well you learn. Curiosity is all I have, and I try to satisfy it whenever I can."

"You've taught me more than I could ever hope to teach you," Bek ventured. "I don't see that I can do much for you."

For just an instant, the shape-shifter went absolutely still. Then he made a low growling sound. "Don't be so sure of that. It's early yet. If you live long enough, you might surprise yourself."

Bek let that pass. Truls Rohk was giving him just enough to keep him happy, but not everything. There was something more that he wasn't revealing, some important piece of information he was keeping to himself. It was probably true that he felt a connection to Bek, that he felt it in part because of the magic and in part because he had saved the boy's life. It was also probably true that he had come on the voyage because it gave him purpose and insight and satisfied his need to be involved with something. Living alone in the Wolfsktaag might well be too confining, too restrictive. But that was still only part of what had brought him along, and the greater part, the larger truth, lay somewhere else in his bag of secrets.

"Why don't you ever take off your cloak?" Bek asked suddenly, impulsively.

He did it without thinking, but knowing even so that it would generate a strong response. It did. He could feel a change in the other, instantly, a chilling withdrawal that whispered of anger and frustration and sadness, as well, but he did not back off.

"Why don't you ever show me your face?" he pressed.

Truls Rohk was silent for a moment. Bek could hear him breathing, rough and agitated within his enveloping blackness. "You don't want to see me the way I really am, boy. You don't want to see me without this cloak."

Bek shook his head. "Maybe I do. What's wrong with seeing who you really are? If we're connected as you say, linked by our sharing of magic, then you shouldn't need to hide how you look."

"Hssst! What would you know of my needs? We've barely met, you and I. You think you're ready for what's hidden under these robes and within this cowl, but you aren't. You know nothing of what I am. There isn't another like me out there, a halfling—a shape-shifter and a human both. There's no mold for what I am. Maybe I don't even know what that is. Have you thought of that? We change at will, shape-shifters do, becoming what we need to be. What does that mean, when half of you is human? What happens when part of you is unchangeable and part as thin as air? Think on that before you ask me again to show you how I look!"

Then he stood up. "Enough of this. I've been thinking about our situation. The witch still tracks us, your sister. Even if she was thrown off the scent at the river, she will find us again. I want to know if she's done so yet and what help she's found. If she's close, I need to find a way to slow her down. I'll backtrack down the mountain to see if she's picked up our trail."

He paused. "You sleep while I'm gone, boy. Look for me in your dreams. Or in your nightmares, better yet. Maybe you'll see who I really am there."

He turned and was gone, fading into the night. Bek stared after him. He did not move again for a long time.

The Ilse Witch finished chewing on the vegetable root she had harvested for her dinner and stared out into the growing darkness. She would set out again soon, tracking the boy and the shape-shifter once more, following them into the mountains. They were clever and resourceful—or at least the shape-shifter was—and she could not afford to let them get too far ahead of her. She must press hard to keep them within reach. She might even catch up to them that night if they stopped to rest. They would have to, wouldn't they? The boy did not possess the stamina to go without rest, even if the shape-shifter did. He would have to sleep sometime. If she was quick enough, she would catch them unprepared.

She finished what she wanted of the root and threw the rest away. She would have them by now if they hadn't been working so hard to throw her off. That was clever, back by the river, setting up a false trail on one bank and swinging back across to the other. It had confused the caull, had sent it running up and down the wrong bank without purpose, had caused it to go half-mad with rage. The caull was skilled and possessed exceptional instincts, but it lacked insight. She was the one who spied the hook still caught in the upper branches of that hickory and sent the caull back across the river to search out the trail anew. By that time she had given back to her quarry the time they had lost to her during the night. Tonight she must make it up all over again. Easy enough though, if the boy slept.

The bushes parted, and the caull reappeared. She had sent it out to find something to eat, and from the smear of blood on its muzzle, it had been successful. It moved to within a dozen yards of her and then sat back on its haunches, watching. It was a dangerous beast. She could not afford to turn her back on it; it hated her for what she had done to it and would kill her if it got the chance. It was obedient because it had no choice; her magic kept it in line. But if she loosed its leash, even a little . . .

She studied it a moment, then looked away, dismissing it. It was important to show she was not afraid of or even particularly interested in it beyond its intended usefulness. She had created it for a purpose, and it was there to serve that purpose and nothing more. What it thought she would do with it when the boy was found, she had no idea. Probably it could not think that far ahead, which was just as well.

She found herself wondering, instead, what she would do with the boy. It was easy enough to decide what would become of the caull and the shape-shifter, but the boy was another matter. She hadn't followed him all that way just to put an end to him; he was an important link to understanding the Druid, a potential window into his mind. Before the Druid died, she would know everything there was to know about him. The boy was a device to unsettle and confuse her, but he might prove to be a resource, as well. There were things about him that needed understanding—how he could have magic so like her own, how he could know so much about her that felt true, how he could seem so real. She knew there were explanations for all of it, but the explanations were not enough as they stood. She would have the whole truth before she was finished with him. She would strip him bare before she tossed him away.

She pictured his face, recalled his voice. She could still hear him telling her he was her brother, he was Bek, survived somehow from the burning of her home and the killing of her family. She couldn't accept that, of course. The Druid had wanted only her, and when she had told the Morgawr how she had hidden her brother, he had been certain that no one else was left alive in the ashes of her home.

Dark shadows gathered at the back of her thoughts, then crowded to the fore in warning. Unless he was lying. Unless the Morgawr had concealed the truth about Bek. But there could be no reason for that, when Bek might have proved useful to him in the same way she had. No, the Druid and his minions had deceived her parents and then murdered them, all because of her, because of who and what she was. He alone was responsible and must answer for that, and the boy was just another pawn employed in their war to destroy each other. He was clever, the boy, but an artifice, a Druid stratagem; in the end he was still just a boy who looked the way Bek might have looked had he lived to grow up, just a boy who had been deceived into thinking he was someone he was not.

She rose to her feet, and the caull rose with her, eyes bright and anticipatory. It was ready to hunt, and she was ready to let it do so. She sent it ahead with a gesture, letting it sniff out the trail, yet keeping it close enough that it could not act without her knowing. She did not want it catching the boy and tearing him apart before she had a chance to plumb his mind. The shape-shifter was another matter, but she doubted that the caull would catch that one unawares. In all likelihood, they must deal with it before they could expect to find the boy. She wondered again why a shape-shifter would take such an interest in their business. Perhaps it was in thrall to the Druid, although that would be unusual for a shape-shifter. Perhaps it was in some way connected to the killing of her parents and the destruction of her home, and its own life was at risk because of that. The Druid had used shape-shifters to carry out his purpose. This might be one of them.

She mulled the possibilities over as she trailed after the caull, keeping her senses alert to what lay around her. The forest dark concealed many things, and one of them might be her enemy. She moved silently in her tied-up gray robes, sliding through the brush and trees like a shadow. The night

sky was clear, and the light of moon and stars flooded down
through the canopy of the limbs overhead. There was too
much light to make her comfortable. She caught glimpses of
the caull ahead of her, bits and pieces of movement in the
patches of silver. It padded forward, then circled back again,
over and over, keeping to the trail its prey had left, reading the
signs, sorting them out to be certain it was not being misled.
It was good at that; all its wolf instincts were intact and
working within its new form, all its skills at play.

It was nearing midnight when she reached an open stretch of
ground that fronted the foothills leading up into the mountains,
a rocky flat empty of everything but scrub and deadwood.
Standing hidden within the trees, she watched the caull move
out into the open ground, sniffing, circling, then continuing
on. She stayed where she was, letting it go. The terrain ahead
was too exposed. She didn't feel right about moving through
it, even though the trail clearly went that way.

She tightened her invisible leash on the caull and summoned it back to her. Her instincts told her that something
was amiss and she must determine what it was before continuing on.

Staring out across the flat, the caull crouched at her side,
she began to reason it out.

Bek did not sleep after Truls Rohk left him, but sat thinking on what all their running and hiding were leading to.
True, he was fleeing to save his life, to escape the Ilse Witch
who, sister or no, wanted him dead. But flight alone was not
the solution to his problem, and the more he ran and the farther he went, the less it seemed like he was achieving anything. To solve the problem of Grianne Ohmsford, he must
convince her of who he was. He could see that probably

wouldn't happen through words alone. It would take something more, perhaps the magic of the Sword of Shannara, perhaps another magic entirely. But a confrontation and a
strategy for dealing with that confrontation were inescapable.

How could he bring about the necessary epiphany without
losing his life? How could he make her believe?

The answer did not come to him, and he grew tired thinking on it. He lay down to sleep. He drifted off quickly, but he
did not dream. He slept and woke in fits and starts, troubled in
a way he could not identify, unable to rest for more than a few
minutes at a time. He thought it was because he was waiting for Truls Rohk to return, but maybe it was just that he
couldn't stop thinking about his part in the journey to Castledown. He wished he knew everything that Walker did, all the
secrets he was still keeping to himself about Bek, about his
purpose on the voyage, about the reasons for his presence. It
did not stop with his usage of the Sword of Shannara at the
Squirm. It did not end with his heritage of magic or his relationship to Grianne. It went beyond all that. But how far did
it go?

When he woke the last time that night, he was still caught
up in stray thoughts of his sister and their tangled relationship, discomforted enough that he felt as if he had not slept at
all. Hearing a soft murmur of voices, he sat up with a start
and stared into the surrounding darkness.

There were faces all around him. None of them belonged
to Truls Rohk. None of them was attached to a body.

Like the faces of wraiths risen from the netherworld, they
floated in the air, and in their empty eyes, Bek Ohmsford saw
the reflection of his soul.

TWELVE

Bek fought down the rush of fear that threatened to overwhelm him as he felt himself stripped bare and laid open by the faces that floated before him. Their features were flat and empty of life, drained of all expression, sketched on air with chalk so that they did not seem fully formed, but in need of completion, a child's rendering. They were shades, he believed, the dead come back to haunt, compelled to seek out the living by urges and needs only they could know. Their wide, empty eyes fastened on him without seeing, but he could feel them looking anyway, inside, where he hid everything he wanted to keep secret.

Who are you?

The voice was thin and whispery. He couldn't tell which of the shades was speaking. He couldn't see movement of mouth or lips. The voice seemed to come from everywhere at once, resonating inside his head.

"I'm Bek Ohmsford," he replied, frozen in his sitting position, struggling not to scream.

Where have you come from?

His voice shook. "From the Highlands of Leah, across the sea, in another land."

Far away?

"Yes."

Have you come alone?

He hesitated. "No. I came with others."

Where are they?

He shook his head, eyes shifting from one dead face to the next, from one set of blank features to another. "I don't know."

Would you dare to lie to us?

He exhaled sharply. "I don't think so."

The heads shifted slightly, moving in a clockwise motion, as if stirred by a passing wind. Eyes and mouths gaped open, the eyes and mouths of corpses. They did not seem to threaten in any way, but they were all around him, and Bek could not escape the feeling that there was more to them than what he was seeing. He kept himself as calm and still as he could manage, the last traces of his restless sleep gone now, his mind and body tingling and taut with his terror.

The shades went still again.

Why have you come here?

How should he answer that one? His mind raced. "I was running away from someone who wants to hurt me."

Where are you running to?

"I don't know. I'm just running."

Where is your companion?

So they knew about Truls Rohk, as well. What did they want with him? "He went back to see if our pursuer is still following us."

Who is your pursuer? Do not lie to us.

He wouldn't dream of lying at this point. Seeing no reason not to do so, he told the shades about Grianne and their history. He did not dissemble or try to hide anything. It might have been that he thought it pointless or perhaps was too weary to pick and choose between what to tell and what to keep secret. There were no interruptions as he spoke. The heads of the dead hung suspended before him, and the night about was empty and still.

When he was finished, there was no immediate response. He thought that perhaps they had decided he was lying after all or trying to trick them in some way. But he had no way of knowing what else he could do or say to convince them. He had used up all his words.

Will you use your magic against your sister when she finds you?

The question was unexpected, and he hesitated. "I don't know," he said finally.

Will she use hers against you?

"I don't know that either. I don't know what will happen when we meet again."

Do you wish her harm?

For a moment, Bek was left speechless. "No!" he blurted out. "I just want to make her understand."

There was a stirring in the air, a sort of rustling sound, like the wind passing through trees or tall grasses. Buried in its sound were words and phrases, as if the dead were communicating with each other in their own language. Bek heard it at the edges of his mind, barely audible, faintly recognizable for what it was. It came and went quickly, and the silence returned.

Tell us of your companion. Do not lie to us.

Again, Bek did as he was ordered, certain now that lying was a mistake he should not make. His fear had lessened, and he was speaking with more confidence, almost as if the shades were companions about a fire and he a storyteller. He did not think they meant him harm. He thought that he must have trespassed somehow, and they had come to determine his reasons. If he just explained, he would be all right.

So he related what he knew of Truls Rohk and the events that had brought them to Castledown. It took him a while to tell everything, but he felt it was important to do so. He said that the shape-shifter had watched over him on his journey and twice saved his life. He wasn't sure why he made a point of this. Perhaps it was because he thought the shades should know Truls was a friend. Perhaps he thought that knowing this would help keep them both from harm.

When he had finished, the heads shifted and settled anew.

Breeding between shape-shifters and humans is forbidden.

It was said without rancor or condemnation. Nevertheless, it was a strong comment for them to make. And an odd one. What did it matter to the dead what the living did?

He shook his head. "It's not his fault; his parents made that choice."

Halflings have no place in the world.

"Not if we don't make one for them."

Would you make a place for him?

"Yes, if he needed one."

Would you give up your own place in the world so that he might have his?

The conversation was getting oddly metaphysical, and Bek had no idea where it was going, but he stayed with it. "Yes."

Would you give up your life for him?

Bek paused. What was he supposed to say to that? Would he give up his life for Truls Rohk? "Yes," he said finally. "Because I think he would do the same for me."

This time the pause was much longer. Again, the heads rotated and the rustling sounds returned, rife with words and phrases, with conversations the boy could not understand. He listened carefully, but while bits and pieces were audible, he could comprehend none of it. He wondered suddenly if he had misjudged things, if the shades meant him harm after all.

Then the voice spoke again.

Look at us.

He did so. A sudden chill in the air made him shiver, as if a cold wind had found its way down off the mountains, a wind with the brittle snap of deep winter. He shrank from it—and from the abrupt flurry of movement about him. The faces had begun to change. Gone were the empty, expressionless features. Gone were the disembodied heads. Huge, dark forms appeared in their place, bristling with tufts of grizzled hair. Massive bodies rose out of the shadows. Like beasts that walked upright, these new creatures closed about, gimlet eyes fixing on him. Bek felt his heart stop and his blood turn to ice. The fear he had dispelled earlier returned in a rush, become outright terror. There was nothing he could do to save himself. There was nowhere to run and no chance to do so. He was trapped.

Do you know what we are?

He couldn't speak. He could barely move. He shook his head slowly, the best he could manage.

We are whatever we wish to be. We are the living and the dead. We are flesh and blood and wind and water. We are shape-shifters. This is our land, and humans do not belong here. You trespass and must leave. Go back down off the mountain and do not return.

Bek nodded quickly in agreement. He would take any chance they offered to get away. He could hear their heavy, raw breathing and smell their animal bodies. He could feel the weight of their shadows falling over him, layer upon layer.

He understood in that instant what it felt like to be hunted and cornered. He understood what it felt like to be prey.

The voice whispered to him in a low, threatening hiss, and he was aware of a change in tone.

When your sister comes for you, go with her. When she asks for the truth, tell it to her. When she seeks a way to understand, help her find it. Do not run away again. Trust in yourself.

His sister was coming? How close was she? He panicked, tried to rise, and found he could not. His strength failed him completely. He sat dazed and helpless on the ground, the shape-shifters all around him, a wall of animal stink and fetid breath, dark shadows and glittering eyes. Where was Truls Rohk? Where was anyone who could help him? He hated his fear, his desperation, but he could not dispel it. All he wanted was to be out of there, to be someplace else, to have a chance to stay alive, even for just another day.

He gasped in shock as the cold struck him anew, and he squeezed his eyes shut against its bite. He could hear the rustle of the shape-shifters, the movement of their bodies, but he could not bring himself to look at them. It took all of his concentration just to breathe, to keep himself from screaming, to stay in control. He felt his resolve crumble around the edges. Then he felt something else. Inside, deep down where the core of him burned with raw emotion, he felt the magic come alive. It sparked and flared, coming to his defense, rising up within him. He could feel it building, layers of it bubbling up like lava out of a volcano's mouth, ready to explode. He tightened his resolve anew, desperate to keep it in check. He could not afford to let it surface. He did not want to test himself against the shape-shifters. He knew it would be a mistake.

Then the cold that surrounded him faded all at once and

the animal smell was gone. Fresh air, warmer and gentler now, filled his nostrils; the heavy, raw presence of the shapeshifters had disappeared.

When he opened his eyes again, he was alone.

Truls Rohk hung suspended within the concealing canopy of a massive old maple, pressed against its limbs perhaps twenty feet off the ground. He had waited there for over an hour, keeping watch through the foliage. From there, he had a clear view of the rocky flats that separated the two stretches of forest at the base of the mountains through which he and the boy had passed earlier. If the Ilse Witch was tracking them, if she had found their trail anew, she would come that way.

When the caull appeared, he was not surprised. He knew she was using something to track them besides her magic. Her magic alone, though formidable, was not sufficient to enable her to stay with them. The caull was some sort of mutated wolf or dog and was tracking them by their scent. It was an ugly, dangerous-looking beast, nothing like any creature he had encountered before, not even in the Wolfsktaag. It was a creature out of the old world of Faerie, he guessed, something she had studied in a book of dark magic or conjured from a nightmare. It was there to track and then to dispatch them. Or himself, at least. He was just an unnecessary distraction. The boy was who she was really after, and she would keep him alive for a time.

Truls Rohk watched the beast venture onto the flat, circle about for a bit, then disappear back into the trees. She would be there, watching and waiting, just as he was doing. He could not see her, but he could sense her presence. She was deciding what to do. He could go back to the boy now; he could slip away while she debated. But he was tired of running, and he could sense that the boy was tired, too. It might be better to see if he could slow her down a bit—or perhaps stop her altogether. If the caull came across the flats alone, he might have a chance to kill it. It would take her a while to make a new one, even if she decided to continue, which she might not.

Maybe he would even have a chance at her, as well, although he knew the boy did not want her harmed and would not be happy if she was. Still, he might not be given any choice.

He stayed where he was, debating the matter. The minutes ticked by. Neither the caull nor the witch appeared. He wondered if she could sense him as he could sense her. He did not think so. He had taken precautions to disguise himself, to appear as one with the trees, all bark and wood and sap, all leaves and buds. No part of his human self remained in his current guise. She could not detect his presence in that way.

Then abruptly she appeared, walking to the edge of the treeline across the flats and stopping. The caull materialized beside her. She stared out into the night for a long time, just a vague shape in the star-brightened darkness, just a shadow in the woods. After a moment, she disappeared again, and the caull with her, then reappeared a bit later somewhat farther along the edge of the trees, still staring out into the flats. What was she doing? He watched her carefully, measuring her progress as she appeared, then disappeared, then reappeared once more, several times. She seemed to be looking for something, for a way across perhaps. But why was she going to such trouble? Once she had shown herself, why not simply cross and be done with it?

Time slipped away. Truls Rohk grew steadily more uneasy

with what he was seeing. She was there, but she wasn't doing anything. She hadn't even bothered sending the caull ahead to investigate whatever disturbed her. She was losing time she did not have to give. Appearing and disappearing, coming and going, she was like a wraith that had wandered out of—

He caught himself, lifting off the branch on which he lay with a start, a chilling realization flooding through him. She was a wraith. A wraith made out of magic. He wasn't seeing her at all. Even if she couldn't sense his presence, she had guessed at it. She had smelled out the possibility of a trap and decided to turn it around on him. She had used images to deceive him into believing she was still there and had gotten around behind him. She was already past him on her way to the boy.

He knew it as surely as he knew he was already too late to stop her.

Fool! You fool!

He was down out of the tree in a heartbeat and racing back through the night the way he had come.

When his sister walked out of the trees, Bek was still sitting on the ground where the shape-shifters had left him. He was not panicked by her appearance and did not try to escape. He had known she would come. The shape-shifters had told him so, and he had believed them. He had thought about running from her, fleeing deeper into the mountains, but had decided against it. *Do not run away from her again,* they had said. He did not know why, but he believed them to be right. Running would solve nothing. He must stand and face her.

He rose as she approached, staying calm, oddly at peace with himself. He wore the Sword of Shannara strapped across his back, but he did not reach for it. Weapons would not serve his cause; fighting would not aid him. His sister, the Ilse Witch, would react badly to either, and he needed her to want to keep him safe. Perhaps it was his encounter with the shape-shifters that left him feeling as if no harm could come to him in the mountains. Whatever harm she might do to him, she would wait to do elsewhere. That would give him time to find a way to make her see the truth.

"You don't seem surprised to see me," she offered mildly, moving fluidly within her tied-up robes, her face lost in shadow beneath her hood. Her eyes were on him, searching. "You knew I would come, didn't you?"

"I knew. Where is Truls Rohk?"

"The shape-shifter?" She shrugged. "Still looking for me where I can't be found. He'll come too late to help you this time."

"I don't want his help. This is between you and me."

She stopped a dozen paces away, and he could feel her tension.

"Are you ready to admit to me that you lied about who you are? Are you willing to tell me why you did so?"

He shook his head. "I haven't lied about anything. I am Bek. I am your brother. What I told you before was true. Why can't you believe me?"

She was silent a moment. "I think you believe it," she said finally, "but that doesn't make it true. I know more of this than you do. I know how the Druid works. I know he seeks to use you against me, even if you don't see it."

"Let's say that's true. Why would he do so? What could he hope to gain?"

She folded her arms into her robes. "You will come with me back to the airship and wait for me there while I find him and ask him. You will come willingly. You will not try to escape. You will not try to harm me in any way. You will not use your magic. You will agree to all this now. You will give me your word. If you do so, you have a chance to save your life. Tell me now if you will do as I ask. But be warned—if you lie or dissemble, I will know."

He thought about it, standing silent in the night, facing her through a wash of moonlight, and then nodded. "I'll do what you ask."

He felt her humming softly, her magic reaching out to him, surrounding and then infusing him, a small tingle of warmth, probing. He did not interfere, simply waited for her to finish.

She came forward and stood right in front of him. She reached up and lowered the hood so he could see her strong, pale, beautiful face. Grianne. His sister. There was no anger in her eyes, no harshness of any sort. There was only curiosity. She reached out and touched the side of his face, closing her eyes momentarily as she did so. Again, he felt the intrusion of the wishsong's magic. Again, he did not interfere.

When she opened her eyes again, she nodded. "Very well. We can leave now."

"Do you want my weapons?" he asked her quickly.

"Your weapons?" She seemed startled by the question. She glanced at the sword and long knife perfunctorily. "Weapons are of no use to me. Leave them behind."

He tossed the long knife aside, but left the Sword of Shannara in place. "I can't give up the sword. It isn't mine. It was given to me in trust, and I promised I would look after it. It belongs to Walker."

She gave him a sharp look. "To the Druid?"

He was taking a chance telling her this, but he had thought it through carefully and the risk was necessary. "It is a talisman. Perhaps you know of it. It is called the Sword of Shannara."

She came right up against him, her face only inches from his own, her startling blue eyes boring into his. "What are you saying? Give it to me!"

He did so, handing it over obediently. She snatched it from him, stepped back again, and examined it doubtfully. "This is the Sword of Shannara? Are you certain? Why would he give it to you?"

"It's a long story. Do you want to hear it?"

"Tell me on the way." She handed the talisman back. "You bear the weight of it while we travel. Just don't let me find it in your hands again."

"You can keep it if you want."

There was a flicker of amusement on her pale face. "I don't need you to tell me that. I can take it from you whenever I choose. Make sure you remember."

She started away, not bothering to look back to see if he was following. He hesitated a moment, then started after her. "What about Truls Rohk?"

She cast a quick glance over one shoulder, and the hard determination that had stamped her features so clearly on their first encounter was back in place. "He'll find you gone when he returns, but I don't think he will do anything about it."

She didn't explain further. Bek knew that even if he asked her to do so, she wouldn't. With an apprehensive glance back at the deserted clearing, he followed her into the night.

Truls Rohk flew through the darkness, a silent shadow twisting past trees and leaping over gullies and ravines. He was driven by fear for the boy and anger at himself. He had been unforgivably careless, and Bek Ohmsford would pay the price for it if he didn't reach him in time.

All about him, the forest was a silent curtain behind which eyes watched and waited.

He ascended the mountain slope at a dead run, alert for the presence of the witch and her caull, sensing neither yet, but knowing they must be close. He tried to calculate how far ahead of him they might have gotten, but it was impossible to do. At best, he could only hazard a guess. He had lost track of time while watching from his perch, while being deceived by those magic-induced wraiths. He knew he had to assume the worst, that she had reached the boy already, that she had made him her prisoner, and that it would be up to the shape-shifter to set him free again.

When he reached the place within the trees where he had left the boy, the clearing was empty, the boy gone, and the scent of the witch everywhere. Silence layered the open space as he entered it, watchful still, cautious of traps she might have left. It was beginning to rain, the drops falling in a soft patter on the dry moonlit earth, staining it the color of the shadows.

The boy's long knife lay to one side, discarded. He walked over and knelt to pick it up. As he did so, the caull slid from the forest shadows behind him. Silky smooth and powerful, massive jaws gaping wide, it launched itself at his head.

THIRTEEN

A handful of the Rindge took Quentin Leah and his companions from the ruins of Castledown back to their village. Most stayed to finish setting traps for the mysterious wronks, but the one who had spoken with Panax, along with several of his fellows, broke off from the main group to act as escort. Although the Rindge made no mention of it, the bloodied, ragged, and worn condition of their visitors made it obvious they needed food, rest, and medical treatment. Quentin and company, while reluctant to break off their search for the others, realized they were in no condition to continue. If they were to be effective in finding their missing friends, they would first need to eat, dress their wounds properly, and sleep in a safe place. Moreover, the Rindge might prove helpful in telling them how and where to direct their efforts once they resumed looking.

So they made the three-hour trek through the woods to the Rindge village and were there by midday. On their journey, they learned more about the land to which they had traveled. The Rindge who did all the talking was called Obatedequist Parsenon, or something that sounded very like it, according to Panax. Since the Dwarf was unsure, the cumbersome name was quickly reduced to just Obat. Obat was a subchief in the village hierarchy, the son of a former high chief. It was clear from the deference showed him by the other Rindge that he was a respected member of the community. Obat told them the land of his people was called Parkasia and they had been there two thousand years, since the beginning of time. He did not speak of the Great Wars, but seemed to date everything from then, as if nothing had existed before his people's appearance in Parkasia. It was difficult to be certain, but it appeared to Panax that Parkasia was a peninsula attached to a much larger body of land north and west in which tribes other than the Rindge made their home.

There were various tribes of Rindge living in Parkasia, Obat explained, some of them hunters, some farmers. They were a self-sufficient people and engaged in little trading. Wars sprang up between them now and then, but their greatest common enemy was the thing that lived in Castledown's ruins. Antrax, Obat called it, but he could not find a way to explain what it was. He said it was a spirit, but it commanded creepers and fire threads, strange things that seemingly had nothing to do with spirits. Antrax warded Castledown against all intruders and had done so for as far back as anyone could remember. But it also raided the villages of the Rindge now and then and stole away the people. Those taken were never seen again. They were sacrificed to satisfy Antrax's hunger, their bodies dismembered and their spirits enslaved so that they could never die or be at rest.

It was the same story the company had been told earlier and it made no more sense than it had then; dead was dead, and you didn't enslave souls once the body was gone. But Obat insisted on it, even though he could offer no explanation as to why Antrax took the Rindge and treated them so, what he needed them for, or why he would bother with humans when he possessed command over such formidable technology. Every time the name Antrax was spoken, the Rindge showed signs of discomfort, casting glances in all directions, making warding motions, even when they were several hours away from the ruins.

Still mired in his discomfort at leaving Bek, Quentin Leah listened to it all with half an ear. Exhausted and battered from his struggle against the creepers, he knew he was staying upright through sheer force of will. But he was heartsick at abandoning his search for his cousin, and he could not stop thinking about it. They had promised they would look out for each other. Bek would never break that promise, no matter what, unless he was unable to carry it out. It didn't matter that Quentin had no idea where to look for his cousin other than in the ruins, and that looking for anyone in the ruins was suicide. It didn't matter how tired he was. All he knew was that he was walking away from Bek at a time when Bek might need him most.

Obat was talking about Antrax again, saying that many of the Rindge tribes believed that Antrax had created humans at the beginning of time and took some back now because he was dissatisfied with their behavior. Antrax was a god and must be worshipped and respected or disaster would result. So they made pilgrimages, bringing gifts to the ruins several times a year. Sometimes, they brought humans as sacrifices to the wronks who were once their kindred. They did not do those things in Obat's village, but that was because the Rindge there believed in the old stories that said humans were created from the earth and given life long before Antrax discovered them. In Obat's village, they believed that Antrax was a demon.

Quentin absorbed all that and consoled himself about Bek

by deciding that his cousin, with his newly discovered magic, was probably better equipped than he to ward off demons or creepers or anything else. That Bek should have magic of any sort still astonished him, yet it made sense in light of what they had both decided about Walker's decision to bring them along. It explained why they had been chosen when there were so many others who might have been taken instead. But it left the Highlander pondering anew his cousin's origin and the reason it had been kept secret so long. It made him wonder how much Coran and Liria knew and had been keeping from them.

They arrived at the village of the Rindge by midday, newly footsore and barely mobile. The village sprawled through a series of connected clearings in a wooded area backed up against foothills leading west into a spine of mountains and consisted mostly of open-air huts and pavilions constructed of wood and bark with blankets and reed screens used as dividers for rooms. The people came out to look at them, men, women, and children alike, all henna-complexioned and red-haired, the youngest darker than their elders.

No palisade or moat warded the village, and when asked, Obat said there was no point; the wronks and creepers could push right through such defenses in any case. When a raid took place, the Rindge simply fled into the hills until it was safe to return. A good system of outposts kept them safe most of the time. The defenses that made a difference were the traps they set out in the woods, deep camouflaged pits with jagged rocks at their bottoms. The creepers and wronks often fell into them and if damaged or not sufficiently mobile, could not climb out. If the metal predators were found and the pits filled in quickly enough, they could no longer hear the commands of Antrax and so remained there.

Fetishes tied to poles ringed the village, protectors for the Rindge against the things that sought to hunt them. Quentin looked into the eyes of the children who watched him and wondered how many the fetishes would save from raids and other dangers.

The five guests were taken to a screened-off area to bathe in large tubs of heated water, then visited by healers who dressed their wounds. Afterwards, they were taken to a pavilion, seated on mats, and given food. The Rindge were primitive, but their life seemed well ordered and reasonable. Quentin thought them intelligent, as well, not just from their speech, which had a musical lilt, but from the look in their eyes and the feel of their homes. Everything was simple, but all needs appeared to be met and served.

After an initial period of congregating to look over their visitors, the Rindge went back to work. Everyone seemed to have a task, even the children, although the youngest mostly played and clung to their mothers. *Things aren't so different here than they are in the Highlands,* Quentin thought.

They slept then, and although Quentin promised himself he would rest for no more than a couple of hours, he did not wake until dawn. Panax was already up by then, engaged in conversation with Obat, and it was their voices, soft and distant from where they conversed outside the sleeping shelter, that roused Quentin. He glanced around and found to his chagrin that the Elves were up and gone, as well. Washing his hands and face in the basin of water provided for that purpose, he strapped the Sword of Leah across his back and walked out to see what was happening.

He found Panax and the Elves with Obat and several more of the Rindge, seated in a circle on mats, talking. As he walked up, he saw that sketches had been drawn in the dirt in

front of them. The conversation between Panax and Obat was
sufficiently intense that the Dwarf did not even glance at
Quentin, but Tamis caught his eye and beckoned him over.

"Nice to see you back among the living," she offered dryly.
Her round, pixie face was freshly scrubbed, the skin ruddy
beneath her tan. "You snore like a bull in rut when you sleep."

He arched an eyebrow in response. "You spend a lot of time
with bulls in rut, do you?"

"Some." She brushed at her short-cropped hair. "What
would you say if I told you that Obat knows another way into
Castledown?"

Quentin blinked in surprise. "I'd say, when do we leave?"

There was no hesitation on anyone's part about going.
Rested and fed, their spirits renewed, the edges of their
memories sufficiently blunted that wariness had replaced
fear, they were anxious to return. All of them sought answers
to what had happened to their friends, and there could be no
peace of mind until those answers were found. Each of them,
without saying so to the others, believed that there was still
something to be accomplished at Castledown.

Their attitude was buttressed in no small way by the fact
that the Rindge had agreed to guide them. Creepers and fire
threads notwithstanding, if there was another way into the
chambers beneath the ruins, they were eager to explore it.
Ard Patrinell, Ahren Elessedil, and a handful of other Elves
were still missing. Walker was still unaccounted for. Bek had
disappeared along with Ryer Ord Star. Some of them, perhaps all, were still alive and in need of help. Quentin and his
companions were not going to make them wait for that help.

They ate a quick meal, strapped on their weapons, and set
out. Obat led their Rindge escort, two dozen strong. Most of

the Rindge carried six-foot blowguns along with knives and javelins, but a substantial number bore short, stout, powerful spears with razor-sharp star heads that could penetrate even the metal of creepers. They used them like pry bars, Obat explained when Panax questioned him about it. They jammed the heads into joints and gaps of the creepers' metal armor and twisted until something gave. Numbers usually gave the Rindge the advantage in such encounters. The creepers, he advised solemnly, were not invincible.

It was educational to watch the Rindge at work. They were a tribal people, but their fighting men appeared to be well trained and disciplined. They fought in units, their numbers broken down by weaponry. The front ranks used the heavy spears, the rear the blowguns and javelins. Even during travel, they kept their fighting order intact, dividing the men into smaller groups, scouts patrolling front and rear, and spear bearers warding the edges of the march. The outlanders, untested in battle, were placed in the middle, screened by their would-be protectors.

Quentin noted the way the Rindge rotated in and out of their loose formation as they traveled, shifting here and there in response to orders from Obat, burnished bodies gleaming with oil and sweat. No one in the little company thought to question their tactics. The Rindge had been living in that land and dealing with the minions of Antrax for hundreds of years; they knew what they were doing.

After a time, Panax dropped back to walk with Quentin, letting the Elves walk ahead of them a few paces. He did so quite deliberately, and the Highlander let him choose his own pace.

"The Rindge believe that Antrax controls the weather," the Dwarf told him quietly, keeping both his head and voice lowered.

Quentin looked at him in surprise. "That isn't possible. No one can control the weather."

"They say Antrax can. They say that's why the weather in their region of Parkasia never changes like it does everywhere else. He says he knows of the glaciers and ice fields on the coast. He says it snows inland, farther north and west, on the other side of the mountains. There are seasons there, but not here."

Quentin shifted the weight of the Sword of Leah on his back. "Walker said something to Bek about the weather being odd. I thought it must be a combination of wind currents and geography, an anomaly." He shook his head. "Maybe Antrax is a god after all."

The Dwarf grunted. "A cruel god, according to the Rindge. It preys on them for no discernible reason. It uses them for fodder and then throws them away, minus a few parts. I keep asking myself what we've gotten ourselves into."

"I keep wondering how much of all this Walker knew and kept to himself," Quentin replied softly.

Panax nodded. "Truls would tell you Walker knew everything because Druids make it a point to find things out and then keep them concealed. I'm not so sure. We walked right into that trap three days back, and the Druid seemed as surprised as any of us."

They walked on in silence, passing into the midday calm and heat, winding along a well-used trail that took them through ancient hardwoods whose boughs canopied and interlocked overhead in such thickness that the light could penetrate only in slender threads and narrow bands. Birds flew overhead, singing cheerfully, and there were squirrels and voles in evidence. The sun traveled slowly west across a cloudless sky, and the air smelled of green leaves and dry earth.

Then Tamis dropped back to walk with them. "I've been thinking," she said quietly. "Something is wrong about this."

They both stared at her. "What do you mean?" Panax asked, looking around as if he might find the answer hidden in the forest green.

Tamis glanced from one to the other. "Ask yourself this. Why are the Rindge being so helpful? Out of the kindness of their hearts? Out of a sense of obligation to help strangers from other lands? Out of compassion for our obvious misery at losing our friends and finding ourselves stranded?"

"It's not unheard of," Quentin replied, an edge to his voice.

She glared at him. "Don't be stupid. By helping us, the Rindge are risking their lives and possible retaliation by Antrax, whatever it is. They wouldn't do that unless there was something to be gained from doing so, something that would benefit them."

Panax scowled, no happier than Quentin upon hearing this accusation. "What would that something be, Tamis?"

"I've been thinking," she advised, keeping her voice low, her eyes on the Rindge. "You told them we came here seeking a treasure, and they know we went into the ruins very deliberately to find it. They must assume we knew something about what we were getting ourselves into before we tried that— however misguided that assumption might be. At the very least, that suggests to them that we have a means of dealing with Antrax. Now think about this. They haven't said so, but what if they were watching us the first time we went in and know about Quentin's sword and Walker's Druidic powers? They've been looking for a way to rid themselves of Antrax for hundreds of years, and now, finally, they may have found one. Us. What if they're using us as a weapon?"

"To destroy Antrax," Quentin finished. "So they're taking

us right to it and turning us loose, hoping for the best. They won't stand and fight with us, if it comes to that. They'll run."

She shrugged. "I don't know what they'll do. I just think we'd better watch our backs. They have to wonder about us—where did we come from and what do we intend to do when this is over? Perhaps they're thinking that the best thing that could happen would be for Antrax and us to destroy each other and leave the Rindge in peace. They have to have considered that. They don't want to swap one form of tyranny for another. They know that's a possibility, and nothing we say is going to convince them otherwise."

"Obat doesn't seem like that," Quentin ventured after a moment.

Tamis sneered softly. "You haven't been out in the world as long as I have, Quentin Leah. You haven't seen as much. What do you think, Panax?"

The Dwarf glanced at Quentin, his gruff features set. "She's right. We'd better be ready for anything."

"Kian and Wye already know my thinking," she said, starting ahead again. She glanced back at Quentin. "I hope I'm wrong, Highlander. I really do."

They marched on in silence for the remainder of their journey, Quentin mired in gloom at the prospect of being betrayed yet again. He knew Tamis was right about the Rindge, but he could barely bring himself to consider what that might mean. He wished Bek were there to give his opinion. Bek would see things more clearly. He would be quicker to ferret out the truth. The Rindge didn't seem antagonistic, but they had been at war with Antrax for the whole of their existence, so they knew something about staying alive. They hadn't tried to harm their visitors, but Tamis might have been right about them watching the company fight its way clear of the maze. It was possible they were simply waiting to see what would happen when Antrax and the outlanders came face-to-face.

The more Quentin thought about it, the more uneasy he grew. The only real weapon they had was his sword. It might be enough to see them through, but he could not be certain. If Walker had been overcome by Antrax, what chance did he have? He wondered if Bek had come up against Antrax, as well, and having discovered his own form of magic, brought it to bear. If so, what success had he enjoyed? If his magic was powerful enough to shred creepers, as Tamis had reported, could it bring Antrax down? He did not like thinking of Bek facing Antrax alone. He did not like even considering the possibility. It shouldn't happen that way, Bek alone. Or himself, for that matter. It should be the two of them, standing together the way they had planned it, watching out for each other.

He wondered if there was any chance that it could still happen like that and if it could happen in time to make a difference.

It was still early afternoon when they reached the edges of Castledown and paused long enough for the Rindge to scout ahead for creepers. While they waited, Quentin sat with Panax and stared out into the midday heat as it rose in visible waves off the metal of the devastated city. In the flat, raw wasteland, nothing moved. There was no sign of the maze, farther in from where they sat, and nothing to show that anyone had ever passed that way. Panax drank from a water skin and offered it to Quentin.

"Worried about Bek?" he asked, wiping his mouth.

Quentin nodded. "I can't stop worrying about him. I don't like the thought of him out there alone."

The Dwarf nodded and looked off into the distance. "Might be better if he is, though."

The Rindge scouts returned. There were no creepers in evidence along the city's perimeter. Obat motioned everyone ahead, and they moved through the trees, staying just inside the forestline as they followed the edge of the ruins east and south. No one talked as they scanned the city, moving with slow, careful steps. The buildings stared back at them, the gaping holes of windows and doors like vacant eyes and mouths. Castledown was a tomb for dead men and machines, a graveyard for the unwary. Quentin carried the Sword of Leah unsheathed, bearing it before him, feeling just the slightest tingle of imprisoned magic awaiting its summoning. His pulse throbbed in his temples, and he heard the sound of his breathing in his throat.

Obat brought them to a grated entry cut into the side of a building that sprawled several hundred yards in both directions. Stationing Rindge at either end and carefully back from where he stood, he worked with a handful of others to free the grate from its clasps and swing it back on its rusted hinges. The effort produced a series of squeals barely muted by old grease and the weight of the metal.

Obat pointed into the black opening and spoke to Panax in hushed tones.

"Obat says that this leads to where Antrax lives," the Dwarf translated. "He says this is how it breathes underground."

"A ventilation shaft," Quentin said.

"Ask him how he knows Antrax is down there," Tamis demanded.

Panax did so, listened to Obat's reply, and shook his head. "He says he knows because this is where he's seen the creepers come out to hunt."

Tamis looked at Quentin. "What do you think, Highlander? You're the one with the sword."

Quentin stared into the blackness of the shaft and thought
that it was the last place he would like to go. He could just
make out lights farther in, dim glimmers in the blackness, so
they would not be blind. But he didn't care for being trapped
underground beneath all that stone and metal with no map to
guide them and no way of knowing where to look.

"This might be a waste of time," Panax offered quietly.

Quentin nodded. "On the other hand, what else do we have
to do? Where else do we look for the others if not here?" His
grip tightened on the sword. "We've come this far. We should
at least take a peek."

Tamis stepped forward to peer more closely into the darkness. "A peek should be more than enough. Are the Rindge
coming with us?"

Panax shook his head. "They've already told me they
won't go into the ruins, above or belowground. They're terrified of Antrax. They'll wait for us here."

"It doesn't matter. We don't need them anyway." She
looked over her shoulder at Quentin. "Ready, Highlander?"

Quentin nodded. "Ready."

They went in bunched close together, Tamis leading,
picking her way carefully. Their eyes adjusted quickly to the
blackness. The walls, floor, and ceiling of the air shaft were
smooth and unobstructed. They walked for several hundred
yards without changing direction, locked in silence and the
faintly metallic smell of the corridor, the opening through
which they had entered shrinking behind them to a pinprick
of light. The shaft began to descend then, dropping away at a
slant, then splitting in two. The little company paused, then
turned into the larger of the passageways, descending farther,

moving past countless smaller ducts that burrowed through the walls and ceiling like snake holes. Ahead, still so distant at first that it was barely discernible, they could hear the sound of machinery, a soft purring, a gentle hum, a reminder of life ancient and enduring.

Lights burned at regular intervals, flameless lamps set into the walls, yellowish light steady and unwavering. Strange fish-eyes peered down at Quentin from the ceiling, set farther apart than the lights, tiny red dots blinking steadily at their centers. They seemed to be looking at him. It was ridiculous to think this, yet he could not shake the feeling that it was so. He glanced at Panax and Tamis to see if they were looking, too, but their eyes were directed ahead into the corridor they followed.

Quentin found himself staring around in amazement. He had never seen anything like this. So many metal sheets layered together, yards and yards of them, bolted and sealed against weather and animals and plants, a man-made warren carved into the earth. How had it been done? He tried to picture the culture and machines and skill that must have been required but he failed. The Old World had been a very different place, he knew, but that had never been more dramatically apparent to him than it was in the ventilation shaft.

Held in place by stanchions, metal pipes began to appear in connected lines along the walls of the passageway. Quentin could not discern their purpose. Everything felt strange and foreign to him, all the metal surfaces, all that space and emptiness. If Antrax lived down there, he had room to move about—that much was clear. But what sort of creature would choose to live in such a place? Only another machine, another creeper made of metal, Quentin thought. Perhaps Antrax was a machine, similar, yet more powerful than the creepers it commanded.

Suddenly, Tamis froze. Her hand came up in warning. The four men stopped instantly. Everyone listened. Ahead, the corridor ended in a hub from which a series of similar corridors fanned out like spokes in a wheel. Within one of those corridors, footsteps were audible. The footsteps were heavy and slow and deliberate, as if what made them bore a great weight.

Quentin had never heard footsteps like those. What made them walked on two legs, but it did not sound like something he had encountered before. He glanced at the others. Tamis was crouched like a cat. Panax stood upright, his expression unreadable. There was a sheen of sweat on the faces of the Elven Hunters, Kian and Wye. Quentin felt as if he couldn't breathe. No one seemed able to move.

Then Tamis started forward, creeping up the corridor toward the shadowy hub ahead. She glanced back at Quentin once, her tough, no-nonsense face intense and her gray eyes bright. *Don't let me down,* she was saying. Without even looking at the others, he went after her, matching her pace. Behind him, the Dwarf and the Elven Hunters followed. The sound of the footfalls grew louder. Whoever or whatever it was, it was making no effort to disguise its approach. It was big and it was confident. It was no one, Quentin thought in dismay, that he and his companions had come looking for.

Twenty feet from the hub, with the entrances of all of the intersecting tunnels visible, they slowed as light cast a shadow from the one just to the left of where they crouched in hiding. Then a tall, lumbering figure stalked out of the gloom and into the light of a dozen lamps set all around the hub.

Quentin caught his breath sharply as the figure was revealed. He heard gasps from the others. Even Tamis, who seemed unafraid of anything, took a step back in shock.

Like a shade or a demon or perhaps something of both, but most like a monster come from a nightmare's imagining into the real world, the thing—for there was no other word for it— turned to face them.

It was Ard Patrinell.

Or what was left of him.

FOURTEEN

In worrying about what sort of disaster might have befallen his missing friends, Quentin Leah had considered some frightening and horrific possibilities, but nothing on the order of what confronted him there. The creature that stood before him, the thing that had once been Ard Patrinell, was beyond imagining. It had been cobbled together from flesh and bone on the one hand and metal on the other. There was machinery inside it; the Highlander could hear it humming softly and steadily from somewhere within the metal torso to which its other parts were attached. The legs and left arm were metal, as well, all three composed of struts hinged at knees and elbows and feet and hands, and attached by ball joints set into sockets surrounded by cables that ran up and down the creature like arteries and veins in a human body.

What remained of the old Ard Patrinell formed the right arm and face. Both were intact and the distinctive features of the Captain of the Home Guard were instantly recognizable. His metal-capped head was set into a tall collar. It was impossible to tell if his head was still connected to some portion of his body, although even at a distance and in the dim light of the ventilation shaft, Quentin could see color in the strong features and movement in the dark eyes. But there was no question about the connection of the right arm, the flesh and bone of which were capped and cabled in metal at the shoulder and attached in the same manner as the other limbs by a metal ball and socket.

Red and green lights blinked like tiny glass eyes all over the creature's gleaming torso, and numbers set in windows clicked and whirred, counting out functions that Quentin could only guess at. Pads cushioned the skeletal metal pieces of the feet so that when the creature walked it made thumping sounds and did not clank as it otherwise surely would. The human right hand held a broadsword in its powerful grip, ready to strike. The metal left hand held a long knife and was bound and warded by an oval shield that ran from wrist to elbow.

When it saw them—and it did see them, they could tell from the movement of the eyes and shift of the body—it started for them at once, weapons raised to strike.

For just an instant the members of the little company stood their ground, more out of an inability to respond than out of courage. Then Tamis shouted, "No! Get out of here!"

They began to back away, slowly at first, then more quickly as the advancing monster picked up speed. It was heavy, but its movements were smooth and effortless, as if a part of Ard Patrinell's agility had been captured in his new form. Finally, the Elves, the Dwarf, and the Highlander broke into a run, propelled by fear and horror, but by something else, as well. They did not want to face a thing that was made out of pieces of someone they had known and admired. Ard Patrinell had been their friend, and they did not want to do battle with his shade.

But what they might have wanted did not count for much. They retreated down the corridor the way they had come,

yelling encouragement to one another, Tamis shouting to
them to get back outside where they had more room to maneuver. And to where the Rindge might give them aid, Quentin thought without saying so. Kian and Wye, toughened and
well conditioned, quickly outdistanced the other three. Tamis
deliberately hung back, intent on warding the obviously struggling Panax. Quentin might have kept up with the speedy
Elves, but the Dwarf was stocky and slow and not built for
speed. He was laboring in minutes, and the tireless metal
monster that gave chase was closing the gap between them.

At the first split in the passageway, Quentin rounded on
their pursuer, shouting at the others to go on. Braced in the
center of the corridor, the Sword of Leah raised before him,
he confronted the thing that had been Ard Patrinell. It came at
him without slowing, all size and weight, metal parts gleaming in the flameless lamplight. For an instant Quentin thought
he was a dead man, that he had misjudged what he could
manage altogether and was wholly inadequate to the task. But
then the magic flared to life, running up and down the blade
of his talisman, and he was crying out, "Leah! Leah!"

He closed with his attacker in a shocking clash of metal
blades, and the impact of the collision nearly threw him off
his feet. Forced backwards by superior weight and size, he
kept his blade between them, struggling to find purchase on
the smooth metal floor. He seized the other's metal arm to
keep the long knife at bay, but quickly discovered he lacked
the strength to do more than slow its advance. Wrenching
free, he spun away, the current of the sword's magic flooding
through him like a swollen river, rough and unyielding in its
passage. All thoughts of anything but defending himself fled,
and he came around with a blow aimed at taking off Ard Patrinell's head. To his astonishment, the blow failed. Partially

deflected by the other's sword, it was stopped completely by some invisible shield that warded the metal-capped head.

Quentin thrust himself clear a second time; then Tamis was beside him, yelling at Panax to run. Together, they fought to hold the metal juggernaut at bay, hammering at it from two sides, striking at anything that seemed vulnerable, that might break or shatter to slow it down. That was all that was needed, Quentin kept thinking—just enough of a breakdown to cripple it and let them escape.

Then it sidestepped a blow from his blade and stepped between the Elf girl and himself, reaching for him with bladed hands to pin him to the tunnel wall. He grappled with it a moment, hammering with his sword blade at the clear faceplate, unexpectedly meeting the familiar eyes long enough to see something that made him cry out in shock before breaking free once more.

"Run!" he shouted to Tamis, and together they sped back down the passageway in pursuit of Panax and the Elven Hunters.

His mind locked on a single image. What he had found in those eyes, the eyes of a dead man, had frozen his soul. It was all he could do to accept that he had not been mistaken, that what he had seen was real. He understood why the Rindge said that when their people were taken and dismembered by Antrax, they didn't die but were still alive, their souls captured.

He felt afraid in a way he had never thought possible, certainly in a way he had never been before. Suddenly, all he wanted to do was to escape that place and leave its horrors behind him forever.

"Did you see?" he gasped at Tamis as they ran. "His eyes! Did you see his eyes?"

"What?" she shouted back. Her breathing was rough and labored. "His eyes?"

He couldn't make himself say any more, couldn't finish what he had begun. He shook his head at her and ran harder, faster, the burn of his breathing sharp and raw in his throat as he fled back up the dimly lit passageway.

It took only minutes, but it seemed much longer, to regain the entrance to the ventilation shaft and burst clear once more. The others were already there—Kian, Wye, Panax, and even the Rindge, who had not fled as Tamis had feared. Obat had formed up his warriors in ranks two dozen yards back from the grate entry, heavy spears lowered, blowguns lifted. Quentin's little band took up positions on one end of the formation, breathing heavily, staring back at the dark opening they had fled.

The monster burst into view in a lumbering rush that took it right into them. It did not slow, did not hesitate, but barreled into the center of the Rindge line, thrusting past the spears, brushing off the darts from the blowguns, sending those who tried to stop it flying in all directions. There was barely time for some to cry "Wronk" in voices steeped in terror before three lay dead or dying and all but a handful of the rest had scattered. Obat and two more stood their ground, joined by the Elves, Panax, and Quentin Leah, who hammered at the monster from all sides, trying to break through its defenses, to find a weak spot, to do anything to stop it. Grunts and cries mingled with the clash of iron weapons, rising up through the heat. Blades flashed in the sunlight, and bodies slick with sweat and smudged with dirt and grit struggled to stay upright and clear of the metal behemoth.

"Leah!" Quentin roared in fury, striking blow after blow at the wronk that had once been Ard Patrinell, watching in horror as it responded with the unerring instincts and skill of the Captain of the Home Guard, infused with the knowledge that Patrinell had acquired through twenty-odd years of combat and training. It was terrifying. It was as if Patrinell was still there, his spirit captured within that metal form, able to direct its actions, to give thought to its responses. It was as if it knew what Quentin would do before he did it, as if it could anticipate the Highlander's every move.

Perhaps he could, Quentin thought in dismay. Ard Patrinell had taught the Highlander almost everything he knew about fighting. Aboard the *Jerle Shannara*, Patrinell had trained and schooled Quentin in the tricks and the maneuvers that would keep him alive in combat. Quentin had been a good student, but Patrinell knew the tricks and maneuvers, as well, had known them longer, and could employ them better.

As did the wronk he had become, remade in this new image, in this monstrous form, in this horrific fusing of metal and flesh.

Another of the Rindge went down, bloodied and broken, torn open from neck to crotch. Obat and the remaining Rindge turned and fled. Quentin's tiny band sagged back before the wronk's fresh onslaught. Despair clouded their faces and drained them of their strength. But then they got lucky. Pressing its attack, the wronk got tangled up in the body of a dead Rindge, lost its footing, and went down. It was up almost instantly, but a broken limb of the dead man was lodged between its joints. In the few moments it took the wronk to free itself, Quentin and his companions broke off their seemingly hopeless struggle and raced after the fleeing Rindge. Whatever was needed to win their battle, it would first require a plan. Just then, it was best just to get away.

Sheathing their weapons on the fly, they raced back into the trees. Obat slowed to let them catch up, shouting something at Panax, who shouted back; then all of them disappeared into the trees. In seconds, they could no longer see the ruins. They ran a long time. Others of the Rindge joined them, all of them breathing hard, bathed in sweat, riddled with fear. Quentin felt the magic of his sword subside, a red haze fading into twinges of emptiness and unfulfilled need, a mix of emotions that tore at him like brambles. He was burned out and chilled through all at once, and part of him wanted to go back into battle while the other wanted only to escape.

He did not know how long they ran or even how far. They were well away from the ruins before they staggered to a halt, a forlorn and dejected band. They knelt in the fading afternoon light, heads lowered in exhaustion, listening through ragged gasps for the sounds of pursuit. Quentin glanced at Tamis, and his emotions coalesced into an overwhelming feeling of shame. Their effort had failed utterly. They were no better off than they had been when they started out—worse off, perhaps, because now they knew the fate of at least one of their missing companions and maybe of the rest, as well.

Tamis glared back at him. He was surprised to see tears in her eyes. "Don't look at me!" she snapped.

Obat spoke to one of the Rindge, and the man rose and started back toward the ruins—looking to see if the thing they had fled was still following them, Quentin thought.

Panax eased over to him, gruff face flushed and angry. "What sort of monster would do that to a man?" he growled. "Make him into a machine out of bits and pieces of himself?"

"Another machine, maybe," Quentin offered wearily. "A better question might be why?"

Panax shook his head. "There's no sense to it."

"There's sense to everything, even if we don't understand

what it is." Quentin was thinking about the wronk's eyes, Ard Patrinell's eyes. "There's a reason Antrax uses wronks. There's a reason for this one. Did you see how it fought us? Did you watch it respond to our attacks? It has Ard Patrinell's memories, Panax. It's using his skills and tactics. It knows how to fight the same way he did."

The Rindge who had been dispatched by Obat returned on the run, speaking hurriedly to the subchief, who in turn spoke to Panax. The Dwarf came to his feet at once.

"Let's go! It's right behind us!"

They climbed to their feet and continued on quickly, Obat in the lead, choosing an unobstructed path that allowed them to move swiftly; their best chance lay in outrunning their pursuer. Once or twice, Quentin glanced over his shoulder, but there was nothing to see. He did not doubt for a moment that the wronk was following, untiring and implacable, determined to pursue them until they were run to ground. The Highlander was already feeling twinges of doubt over whether they could escape it. But to stand and fight would be a mistake. The wronk was bigger and stronger. Its armor gave it better protection. It possessed Ard Patrinell's fighting instincts and skills. Perhaps if there were more of the Rindge, if they could reach the village and summon others to their aid, they might stand a chance. Otherwise, even with the magic of the Sword of Leah to aid them, he wasn't sure they would prevail.

They were strung out through a dense part of the forest they were unable to avoid when the wronk caught up with them. It came out of the trees to one side, its appearance so unexpected that no one was ready for it. Instantly, trapped and cut to pieces, two of the Rindge and the Elven Hunter Wye died. The remainder of the company scattered in a mix of shouts and cries, going off in all directions, fighting to break free of the wronk and the entangling trees. Quentin and Tamis ran one way while Panax and Kian ran the other. The Rindge ran everywhere. For an instant everything was chaos as the wronk surged through the center of their line, blades cutting at everything.

Then the Highlander and the Tracker were in the clear once more. Quentin risked a quick glance over one shoulder. A gleam of metal in sunlight and the sounds of something huge thrashing after them told him the wronk was still coming, and it was coming for them.

"This way!" Tamis hissed, dodging deadwood and scrub like a rabbit as she plunged down a ravine.

They ran in silence for a long time, neither one speaking, trying to put as much distance as possible between themselves and their pursuer. It was growing dark, twilight settling over Parkasia, shadows lengthening into night. It was difficult to pick up all the obstacles that hindered or blocked their path, especially when they were running, and more than once Quentin almost lost his footing. All the while, they could hear the sounds of pursuit, the breaking of branches, the rending of brush and grass, the steady, relentless clump of heavy steps.

Something unexpected and frightening insinuated itself into the Highlander's thinking as he fled. At first he discounted the possibility, pushed it aside angrily, but then he began to wonder. Both times, here and there, the wronk had made it a point to come after *him*. He had seen it in the monster's attack on the Rindge defensive formation, back in the ruins, where it had rushed the natives first, then turned directly for him. Again, in the woods, after striking down those closest, it had chosen to pursue him. It seemed paranoid to think like that. Why would the wronk be after him in particular? Had his attack on it in the ventilation shaft provoked it? Was there something about him especially that drew it?

Then he remembered something Walker had said during their final meeting aboard ship before disembarking for their ill-fated journey to the ruins, and he had his answer.

It was completely dark when they finally stopped, miles from where they had started, deep in the woods. The only visible light came from moon and stars, the forest around them layered with shadows and cloaked in silence. They crouched on a ridge, concealed in a stand of brush, and looked back the way they had come, listening. The sounds of the wronk's pursuit had faded, disappearing almost without their realizing it, as if the creature had stopped, as well. Neither Quentin nor Tamis moved or spoke for a very long time, waiting.

"I know what it's after," Quentin whispered finally, staring off into the dark. "It's after me."

She looked at him without speaking.

"It wants the sword. It wants the magic. Remember what Walker told us about why we were lured here in the first place? For our magic, he said. I think Antrax knows all about us, maybe even about Bek. It wants everything we have."

She thought it over. "Maybe."

"That's why it sent this wronk made of pieces of Ard Patrinell. It's using his brain, his instincts, and his fighting skills to get what it wants from us. From me. I thought at first it had chosen Patrinell because he would know us best, could kill us easiest. But why send a wronk after us? Why bother, when we were so easily cut apart in the maze and pose so little threat?"

"So you think it constructed the wronk deliberately," she said. "It used Patrinell's head and sword arm, so it had to have a specific purpose in mind."

"It used those parts it needed to make the wronk function

as closely as possible to the real thing. None of this happened by accident. The wronk was constructed and dispatched for a reason. It's after me. It keeps coming right for me. I didn't think anything of it at first, back in the ventilation shaft. But it came after me again once we were outside and again in the forest, and now it's chasing me. It wants the sword, Tamis. It wants the magic."

For a moment, she was quiet. He went back to staring off into the impenetrable dark, listening. "You haven't thought it through far enough," she whispered suddenly. She waited until he turned to look at her again. "Think about it. Your sword won't work for just anyone, will it?"

Her steady gaze unnerved him. "No. It only works for me. So you're saying it wants me, too."

"Or parts of you, like Patrinell."

His throat tightened, and he looked away. "I'll die first."

She didn't say anything but put a hand on his arm. "What were you trying to tell me about his eyes back there in the tunnel? When we were running, you started to say something. You asked me if I'd seen his eyes."

Quentin was quiet for a long time, remembering what he had seen, trying to overcome the revulsion that even thinking of it caused. Tamis kept her hand on his arm and her eyes on his face. "Tell me, Highlander."

He sagged a little as he spoke, despair and fear taking fresh hold. "When we struggled underground below the ruins, I got a good look at those eyes. While I was grappling with it, I got close enough to see into them. They weren't dead eyes. They weren't soulless. They weren't filled with anger or madness or anything I expected. They were frightened and trapped and helpless. I know it sounds impossible, but he's still alive in there. In his head and brain. In what he sees and feels. He's shut away in there. I could see it. I could tell. He was asking for help. He was begging for it."

She was shaking her head, denial, rage, and fear twisting her features, her hand tightening on his arm until her nails bit into his flesh.

"He's not attacking us because he wants to!" Quentin hissed. "He's doing it because he doesn't have a choice, because he's been rebuilt to carry out the wishes of Antrax! He's been mind-altered like those Elves who murdered Allardon Elessedil! Only there's no body left, nothing whole. He's—" He caught himself. "He isn't Ard Patrinell anymore, but Antrax has stolen something of who he was and is holding it prisoner inside that wronk."

Something moved in the darkness, but the movement was small and quick. Quentin glanced out hurriedly, then back to Tamis.

"You could be wrong," she insisted angrily.

"I know. But I'm not. I saw him. I saw *him*."

There were fresh tears in her eyes. He caught their gleam in the moonlight. Her grip on his arm loosened. She blinked hard and looked away. "I can't believe it. It isn't possible."

"The Rindge knew. They've seen it happen before with their own people. They tried to tell us."

She shook her head and ran her fingers through her short-cropped hair. "It makes me sick. It makes me want to scream. No one should have to . . ."

She couldn't finish. Quentin didn't blame her. There were no words sufficient to express her feelings. What had been done to Ard Patrinell was so loathsome, so despicable that it left the Highlander feeling unclean.

And afraid, because there was every chance that Antrax intended that he come to the same end.

"We'll have to kill him," she said suddenly, looking over with such fierceness that it left him off balance. For a moment, he wasn't certain who she was talking about. "Again, all over again. We can't leave him trapped in there. We have to set him free."

She took his hands in her own and gripped them tightly. "Help me do it, Highlander. Promise me you will."

He saw it then, the reason for her passion. She had been in love with Ard Patrinell. He had missed that before, not seen even the barest hint of it. How had he been so blind? Maybe she had kept it well enough hidden that no one could have known. But there it was, out in the open, as certain as daylight's return with the dawn.

"All right," he agreed softly. "I promise."

He had no idea how he was going to keep that promise, but his feelings on the matter were as strong as her own. He was the one who had looked into Ard Patrinell's eyes and seen him in there, still alive. That was not something he could pretend never happened and would have no effect on him if he walked away from it. Like Tamis, he could not leave the Captain of the Home Guard a slave to a machine. The wronk had to be destroyed.

"Get some sleep," she said, easing away from him. There was weariness and sadness in her voice. All of her strength seemed drained away. He had not seen her like that before and he did not like seeing her that way. It was as if she had suddenly grown old.

"Wake me in a few hours," he said.

She did not respond. Her gaze was directed out into the night. He waited a moment, then stretched out, placing his head in the crook of his arm. He watched her for a time, but she didn't move. Finally, his eyes closed and he slept.

In his troubled dreams, he ran once more from the wronk. It pursued him through a forest, and he could not find a way to escape it. After a long time, he found himself backed against a wall, and he was forced to turn and fight. But the wronk was not solid or recognizable. It was insubstantial, a thing made of air. He could feel it pressing into him, suffocating him. He fought to break free, just to draw a breath, and then suddenly it materialized right in front of him and he saw its face. It belonged to Bek.

It was almost dawn when he woke, the first tinges of daylight seeping through the trees, the sky east lightening. Tamis had fallen asleep on watch, her body leaning against a tree, her chin lowered into her chest. When he pushed himself into a sitting position, she heard him move and looked up at once.

In the distance, far off but recognizable, something big moved through the trees.

They stood up together, staring in the direction of the sounds.

"It's coming again," Quentin whispered. "What do you want to do? Make a stand here or choose another place?"

Her look was unreadable, but the weariness and sadness of the previous night had vanished. "Let's find one of those pits the Rindge dug for wronk traps," she replied softly. "Let's see how well it works."

FIFTEEN

Even though he had been persuaded by Ryer Ord Star to follow the little sweeper in search of Walker, Ahren Elessedil insisted on waiting until after dark before reentering the deadly ruins. He accepted that it was unlikely they would be attacked by creepers or fire threads if the sweeper was leading them and it probably made no difference whether it was dark or light, but he didn't care. Still firmly in the grip of his memory of the attack that had destroyed everyone with him when they had attempted an entry in daylight last time, it was all he could do to make himself go back down there at all. He must at least, he insisted, be allowed the one concession.

Ryer Ord Star had no choice but to agree since she wanted him with her; the sweeper had nothing to offer on the matter. It sat there on its wheeled base, insides whirring, keeping its images to itself. Summery and hot, the day drifted slowly away, and Ahren and Ryer took turns sleeping. Below their hiding place, the ruins sat shimmering in silence.

With the coming of nightfall, darkness settling over the land in blue-gray shadows and thinning light, they set out. The sweeper led them down out of their concealment, its wheeled base flexing on the stairs and over the rubble, scarcely making a sound as it worked its way through the perimeter and into the ruins. The seer and the Elven Prince followed, the former without hesitation, the latter with nothing but. They were barely twenty yards into the maze when the sweeper approached a wall, made a series of small clicking noises, and triggered a concealed entry. The wall slid back to reveal a dimly lit ramp leading down, and the three unlikely companions stepped within.

When the door slid shut again behind them, Ahren experienced such an attack of panic that it was all he could do to keep from crying out. He felt trapped, exposed, and helpless all at once, and he expected the fire threads and the creepers to cut him apart. But there was no attack, and they proceeded unchallenged down the ramp to a joining of corridors at a hub. Flameless lamps encased in glass spilled yellow light across the flooring in dim pools. Pipes ran along the ceilings, burrowing in and out of the walls like snakes. Sealed doors, some of them round rather than rectangular, were the only thing marring the smooth metal surfaces. Spaced evenly along each passageway, glass fish-eyes peered down at them from overhead, tiny red dots within dark centers flashing wickedly.

Ahren, his eyes peering everywhere at once, found himself regretting anew his decision; he was still bothered by their willingness to accept that the sweeper could help them. Or would, for that matter. That a machine that was at least part creeper would be anxious to help them seemed patently ridiculous. In his mind, he replayed the images the sweeper had shown them, reevaluating them, trying to get behind them to see more than he had been shown. The whole business felt wrong. He kept thinking that Ryer Ord Star would have detected any subterfuge, but the seer was so blinded by her need to reach Walker that he couldn't be sure. Even if they found the Druid, how were they supposed to help him? If he couldn't help himself, what use would they be? He thought about the missing Elfstones. If he had their magic to call upon, he might be able to do something, although even that wasn't a given, since he had never used them and had no real idea if he could.

They walked a very long way without seeming to get anywhere, the tunnels and chambers and stairways passing in endless succession, all of it looking and feeling the same. Every so often he heard machinery at work, soft and distant, muffled by steel and earth. He kept thinking they would find something new, a chamber that would reveal something important, but it never happened. On the other hand, they didn't encounter anything that threatened either. Time drifted away, and their strange descent wore on.

Finally, Ahren called a halt. They had walked for miles, and there was nothing to suggest they wouldn't walk for miles more. They needed to rest. Ryer, he felt, would keep going until she dropped. He sat down with his back against one of the metal walls and took out his water skin. The seer sat down next to him, accepting the water skin when he passed it, then a small bit of bread and cheese from the little food that remained to him. The silence of the underground passageways seemed to echo all around them, a reminder of just how alone and isolated they were.

The sweeper took up a position in the center of the corridor just in front of them, lights blinking in sleepy cadence. It did not seem to be in any hurry.

Ahren shifted himself so that he was facing the young seer. "Do you have any sense of how close we might be to Walker?"

She shook her head. "I can still feel him, but the feeling isn't any different from before."

"Nothing? But we've been walking forever. You have to be able to tell something."

"It doesn't work like that, Ahren. Distance doesn't matter. I can feel the same things whether I am very near or far away. Only the healing part has anything to do with being close. Then I have to touch the one who is in pain." She tried a quick, reassuring smile. "Don't be afraid."

He was, though, and he couldn't seem to help himself. Everything about Castledown felt like a weight pressing him against the earth, crushing him to nothing. He was embarrassed and ashamed, still carrying guilt for having run from the attack, for having been so petrified with fear that he couldn't bring himself to help the others. Maybe that was why he was afraid. Maybe that was why he seemed to be afraid all the time.

She reached over and touched his arm, surprising him. "It's all right to be frightened. I'm frightened, too. I don't want to be here either. But we might be the only ones who can help Walker. We have to try."

He nodded disconsolately. She was right, but that didn't make him feel any better. Or braver. They rose and started off again, following after the little sweeper. It took them down new passageways and ramps, stairs and corridors, leading them on, deeper and deeper into the catacombs of the underground city. The journey was tedious and numbing; the world of Castledown was the same wherever they went. Fatigue set in, physical and emotional both. Ahren found himself wondering if it was still dark outside. He didn't think it could be. He wondered if anyone else had come into the ruins since.

What were the chances that someone else from their scattered little band would find a way underground as they had?

Several times he tried asking the sweeper how much farther they had to go, but there was never any response. The sweeper simply pressed on, not bothering to communicate, no longer showing images. They were completely dependent on it by then; they could not find their way back to the surface alone. They could not find their way anywhere. If the sweeper did not lead them to Walker, they were hopelessly lost.

When they stopped again to rest, backs against the wall once more, eating and drinking to stay strong, tired enough to sleep, but unwilling to chance it, Ahren was so consumed by their predicament that he could no longer stand it. He waited a moment, thinking through the suggestion he was about to make, watching the sweeper as it faced them from the center of the corridor some ten feet away.

"I want you to do something," he said quietly to the seer. She glanced over at once. He paused and leaned closer. "I want you to try your empathic skills on the sweeper and see what they tell you."

She furrowed her brow. "You want me to see if touching it will induce a vision?"

"Of the past, of the future, of the present, of anything that will help us."

"But it's a machine, Ahren."

"Try anyway. You said it was sentient. If that's so, you might be able to trigger something from its thoughts. Maybe you can discover how much farther we have to go or where to look for Walker." He shook his head helplessly. "I just want something that says we're down here for a reason and should keep going."

She stared at him for a long time, undecided. Then she gave him a slow nod. "All right, I'll try."

She finished a last bite of bread, put down the water skin, and rose. The sweeper started to move away, thinking they were ready, but then turned back when Ahren made no move to follow. Ryer approached it without speaking, knelt beside it, and put her hands on its rounded metal body, fingertips pressing as her eyes closed. Her pale, ethereal features tightened in concentration, and her face lifted out of the shadow of her silvery hair.

In the next instant, she rocked back sharply on her heels and her slender body went rigid with shock. Ahren started. The sweeper never moved; Ryer Ord Star clung to it, fingertips crooked and head thrown back, eyes closed and arms extended, finding in whatever vision her contact with the sweeper had induced such images that the emotions elicited could be read upon her face, raw and naked and terrible.

She gave a low moan, then sagged, her hands falling away. Right away, without prompting, without even opening her eyes, she began to speak.

"A young man, an Elf, was brought here in chains, battered and broken from a struggle that left his companions dead. His eyes were then gouged out and his tongue removed. He carried Elfstones, gripped so tightly in his hand he could not release them. They were magic and so powerful that they could have freed him had he the will to use them to do so. But his mind was shackled like his body, and he no longer had control over it. Creepers bore him into this place, deep underground, into a chamber filled with machines and blinking lights. He was placed in a chair. Iron cuffs secured him and wires were inserted into his body, carefully inserted beneath his skin by creepers."

Her eyes snapped open and she looked at him, her face wan and haunted. Stricken by what she had witnessed in a world she hadn't imagined could exist, she looked like a child woken from a nightmare.

"A presence watched it happen, a sentient being that lacked substance and form. It was called Antrax. It hid in the walls and floor and ceiling, all about, everywhere at once. It could see, but had no eyes. It could feel, but had no touch. It was controlling the fate of the ruined Elf. It was controlling his mind. When the Elf was securely attached to the chair, a box with many wires was latched about the hand that held the Elfstones. Images were fed into the Elf's mind through the wires, causing him to see things that were not there, forcing him to use the magic of the stones. That magic was captured by the box and stolen away, carried down into the wires, siphoned off to other places."

She stared at Ahren as if unable to look away, lost in the images of her vision. "This is what I saw. All of it. Everything."

"You saw Kael Elessedil," he said quietly.

She took a deep breath. "Kael Elessedil," she repeated. She shuddered. "For thirty years, Ahren, that was his life!"

He tried to picture that and failed. How could anyone be used in that way? What sort of creature could commit such a travesty? A deep cold settled into the pit of his stomach as he realized that whatever it was, it wasn't human. Antrax was something else altogether.

He rose to go to her, to help her to her feet, but she made a quick warding gesture. "Don't touch me, Ahren. There's something more—something darker still. I couldn't bear to look on it all at once, but now I must. I have to. I have opened myself to visions triggered by the sweeper's memories. If you put your hands on me, it will disrupt everything. Stay clear."

Without waiting for his response, she leaned forward again and placed her hands on the sweeper once more. Her face went rigid instantly, and a gasp escaped her lips. Her head drooped, and she was clinging to the sweeper as if she might otherwise fall. "Oh! Oh!" she cried softly, almost desperately.

Her hands dropped away and she sagged back on her heels once more. She remained like that for a long time, her breathing ragged and shallow, her face bloodless, her body limp. Ahren, though wanting to go to her, stayed where he was, obeying her instructions. The tunnel was still as a tomb, its silence a voiceless echo racing up and down the corridors through the dim pools of yellow light. Filled with dread, the Elven Prince waited. He felt young and stupid and vulnerable all over again, as if exposed by the seer's visions, as if laid open without ever having been touched.

Then, crablike, Ryer Ord Star backed slowly away from the sweeper, her head bent and her body slumped. "Ahren?" she whispered brokenly.

He reached for her, taking her in his arms. She melted against him, and he held her close and gave her what strength he had to lend. Within her robes, she was shaking and cold. He touched her face, and he could feel the dampness leaking from her eyes. "It's all right," he reassured her, not knowing what else to say.

She shook her head instantly in denial. "Ahren," she said so quietly that he could barely hear her words. Her face lifted so that her lips were pressed against his ear. "You were right," she whispered. "We've been tricked. It's a trap."

He went still, terror-stricken. He started to say something in response, but kept himself in check. He had enough presence of mind to remember that the sweeper could hear and translate what they said.

"Antrax plans for you to replace your uncle," she murmured, her hands clutching him. "You've been kept alive and brought here to serve as he did." Her words were tiny bits of glass, cutting at his heart. "The sweeper is a tool. It was sent to lure you to the same room in which Kael Elessedil was imprisoned for all those years. It used me to persuade you. And I . . ."

She couldn't finish, and he pressed her closer still, hanging on to her as much as giving her something to cling to in turn. *Are you sure?* he wanted to ask. But that was a foolish question. Her power at reading the fates was already proved several times over, and there was no reason to doubt her here. Especially since he had been uneasy about what they were doing from the start. His eyes shifted up and down the corridor. Still empty, still deserted. Whatever fate awaited them, they hadn't crossed its path yet, although they were clearly on their way to doing so if they didn't act quickly.

But what were they to do? They were deep underground, hopelessly lost, their companion and would-be guide a creature in the enemy's service. Antrax would have tracked them the whole way, watching their progress, orchestrating their passage. It would be watching them now. Whatever they did, wherever they went, it would see. Antrax would not let them walk away from what it intended for them. It would not allow its plan to replace Kael Elessedil to be thwarted. Ahren's heart was pounding.

The seer's words came back to him in a rush, and he closed his eyes against the pain they induced in him. Antrax had kept him alive, she had said. His escape, while all the others with him were fighting and dying, had been arranged. It was not by chance or good fortune that he had not been harmed. Perhaps Antrax saw him as weak and malleable, a coward through and through. Perhaps it knew how easily Ahren could be manipulated without any use of force. That way he would stay undamaged and whole, better able to serve as Antrax wished, perhaps for fifty years instead of the thirty Kael Elessedil had endured.

It all made sense to him. Walker had told them that whatever had lured them to Castledown wanted their magic. It had never occurred to Ahren that in order to secure that magic, it might require a summoner, as well. Hence the fate of Kael Elessedil. Hence, perhaps, his own.

Tears filled his eyes and ran down his face. He hated himself. He hated what had been done to him. He hated everything about Castledown. But he hated Antrax most of all. He wanted to scream his rage into the silence and watch it explode in shards of razor-sharp fury that would smash the sweeper, that would put an end to at least some small part of the monster that had inhabited this loathsome place. He ran his hand along the back of Ryer Ord Star's silken head, gently, comfortingly. He went still inside, and all of his rage drained away like blood out of a dead man. They were going to die down there, both of them. They had come too far, gone too deep to get out. Perhaps if he had possession of the Elfstones, they might stand a chance. But the Elfstones hadn't done Kael Elessedil much good. Another magic, a stronger one, might make a difference. But he hadn't any other magic to call upon, nothing he could—

Then he remembered the phoenix stone. In the crush of events, he had forgotten it completely. It hung where he had placed it, on its chain about his neck, tucked within his tunic—Bek Rowe's magic, given to him by the King of the Silver River on his journey to Arborlon, given in turn by Bek to Ahren. He tried to remember what Bek had told him about the stone, struggled to recall the words of the King of the Silver River.

When you are most lost, it will help you find your way. With your heart as well as your eyes. Back from dark places into which you have strayed and through dark places into which you must go.

He closed his eyes. He could not be more lost than he already was. He could not find himself in any darker place. He was sick in heart and mind, and he was trapped in every way imaginable. If ever there was a time when he needed the magic of the stone, it had arrived. Would the magic work for him? He didn't know, but there was nothing else left to try. He had not thought he would ever use the stone. He had thought he would keep it safe for Bek and return it to him when they met again. But he didn't think that they would ever see each other again if he did not use the phoenix stone and find a way clear of the labyrinth.

He looked past Ryer Ord Star to the sweeper where it waited in the center of the corridor. If they followed it, things would continue as before. If they broke away from it, Antrax was certain to employ other measures to assure their compliance. There was no reason to wait any longer on what he must do.

He moved the young seer back from him, easing her gently away by placing his hands on her shoulders. "Ryer," he said softly. Her tear-streaked eyes lifted to meet his. "Listen to me." He kept his voice at a whisper that would not carry beyond the two of them. "We're not going any farther. Not with this sweeper. We're finished with that. I have something that I think will help us escape, something Bek gave me when we left the ship. It is a magic given him by the King of the Silver River. If it works, perhaps we will find our way to Walker or, if not to Walker, at least back through these tunnels and outside again. Are you willing to try?"

She nodded at once, her lips compressed, her gaze steady. He waited a moment to be certain of her; then shielding his movements from the sweeper, he reached into his tunic and pulled out the phoenix stone. He glanced down at its silvery surface, a glimmer of liquid light in his hand, then slipped it free of its chain.

You can use it only once, Bek had recalled. *Only once, for casting it to the earth to release its magic will shatter it.* Ahren looked at Ryer Ord Star, feeling for the first time in days that he was doing something right.

"Take my hand," he said.

She did so, her eyes never leaving his. Then he took a deep breath, pulled her to her feet so that they were both standing, and cast the phoenix stone to the passage floor.

SIXTEEN

The instant the phoenix stone struck the floor and shattered, Ahren Elessedil and Ryer Ord Star were enveloped in a haze the color of old ashes. It swirled around them, a mix of tiny particles and smoky light, as though stirred by an unseen hand like soup in a cauldron. It clung to them in a cloud and never spread much farther than where they stood. Beyond its perimeter, the passageways of Castledown remained unchanged.

For a moment, the Elven Prince and the seer stayed where they were, uncertain, waiting to see what would happen. The little sweeper was staring right at them as if nothing had changed, insides whirring, lights blinking, motionless in the center of the corridor. Then it began to wheel right and left, its movements quickly growing more frantic. It appeared to be searching for them, as if it didn't realize they were still right in front of it. Ahren pulled Ryer several steps to his left, testing whether or not the sweeper could see them. It did not turn toward them or register their movement in any way. It simply wheeled about aimlessly, trying to decide what to do.

Then an odd thing happened to Ahren. Within the mist of the phoenix stone, he felt an oddly compelling need to keep moving, to continue on without stopping. It was a sort of tugging in his chest, an unexpressed certainty about what he must do. He had never felt anything like it before. He glanced at Ryer and found her looking back at him. Without speaking, he gestured ahead, indicating what he wished. She nodded quickly. When he touched his chest, she did the same. She felt it, too. It was the magic of the phoenix stone at work. To find a way back after being lost, you must know where it is that you want to go. Unexpectedly, surprisingly, Ahren Elessedil did.

He moved a bit farther down the corridor, away from the hapless sweeper and its efforts to figure out what had happened to them. He held tightly to Ryer, afraid that if he released her, she would lose the protection of the magic. The smoky haze moved with them, an enveloping shroud, wrapping them as they proceeded, never changing its size or shape or perimeter. It was like being in an invisible bubble, shut away from the rest of the world, enclosed in an atmosphere and given over to a life that was denied to everyone but them.

Ahren was just wondering if Antrax knew what was happening to his carefully laid plans when the corridor ahead abruptly filled with creepers.

He stopped where he was, pulling Ryer against him protectively, watching as the metal crawlers slipped from openings in the walls like ghosts, metal limbs clutching knives and pincers and strange-looking cylinders. In a careful sweep, they came up the passageway, fanning out to both sides. Ahren's throat tightened. There was no way past them. They were too many to avoid.

When he glanced hurriedly in the opposite direction, he found the other end of the corridor blocked, as well.

For a moment, he panicked; there was nowhere to run, no way to get clear. The jaws of the trap were closing, and he and

Ryer were caught right in the middle. He stood his ground because there was nothing else to do, still holding to the seer with one hand while he drew free his long knife, his only weapon, with the other. *I won't run this time,* he told himself. He would stand and fight, even if the struggle was hopeless. Maybe Ryer could break past in the ensuing struggle. Maybe at least one of them could . . .

He never finished the thought. As the closest of the creepers reached them, the enshrouding mist went completely opaque, and its quiet swirling turned into a whirlwind. He ducked his head against the sudden movement, feeling Ryer press close. He blinked in an effort to see what was happening, but everything beyond their concealment had disappeared. Beyond the rush of the enshrouding haze, there was only blackness.

Then the mist cleared enough to see beyond its perimeter again. They were past the creepers and in the clear once more.

Ahren didn't question the magic of the phoenix stone any further; he simply accepted it for the gift it was. He believed it would protect them from everything so long as it lasted. Moving quickly, almost at a trot, he pulled Ryer after him down the passageway, leaving the creepers behind. Antrax would have to find another way to trap them.

During the course of their flight, it tried to do exactly that.

First it sent more creepers, squads of them, as if there were an inexhaustible supply to call upon. They flooded the corridors ahead and behind, some advancing in search, some standing watch at every turn. They began to use the odd-looking cylinders now, weapons that emitted bursts of the deadly fire threads, cast here and there at random, seeking them out. Time and again, the creepers closed on Ahren and Ryer, and it seemed there could be no escape. But each time, the smoke darkened and swirled, and when it cleared enough to see again, they were safely past their hunters.

When it became obvious that the creepers and their hand-held weapons weren't getting the job done, fire threads appeared out of the walls, crisscrossing the corridors, oscillating like deadly spiderwebbing caught in a wind. But the magic of the phoenix stone was able to bypass the threads as easily as it had the creepers, cloaking and protecting the Elven Prince and the girl.

Then metal doors began to close, sealing off passageways a few at a time. It was a random effort at best, because it hampered the hunters as well as the hunted. At first it didn't affect Ahren and Ryer at all because the sealed passageways were ones through which they had come or down which they were not impelled to go. But eventually the closings caught up with them, and a door closed directly in their path. Immediately, Ahren knew to change direction, to go another way. He obeyed the impulse, without understanding why, backtracking up that corridor and turning down a new one.

Once, they were forced to wait in front of a sealed door until it opened. Ahren had no idea how long that took. All sense of time slipped away from him within the mist, as if it no longer had meaning or relevance in his life. The magic of the phoenix stone had re-created his world, and while he was in its thrall, nothing of the temporal world would much affect him.

Eventually the creepers, fire threads, and closing doors ceased to be more than a sporadic occurrence. Finally, they disappeared completely. They were all alone in a passageway far from where they had started, and Ahren paused to look out through the swirling mist of their enclosure. He felt drained, empty. He felt worn.

"It worked," he said softly.

Her slender hands tightened on his in acknowledgment. "You made it work," she whispered.

He shook his head. "I took a chance. The magic wasn't even mine to use. It belonged to Bek. It was given to him."

"It was given to you by Bek!" Her voice was angry. "Stop belittling yourself, Ahren! Before, when I asked you to come with me into Castledown to find Walker, you said you didn't think you could protect me. But you have, haven't you? It doesn't matter how you did it—only that you did."

She paused to study him. "It took courage to do what you did back there. To use the phoenix stone without knowing what it would do, then to lead us through the creepers and fire threads. It took courage to come with me at all. Why are you so quick to dismiss that?"

He shook his head. "I'm not brave. I'm anything but. I just did the only thing I could think to do to help us escape." She was staring at him as if he were transparent. He felt exposed and vulnerable. He didn't like the idea of her thinking of him as something he knew he wasn't.

She pulled him against one of the walls and leaned into him, still holding tightly to his hands. "Tell me what's bothering you," she said quietly. She fixed him with her violet eyes. "It's all right."

Strangely enough, he felt it was. Not only right, but necessary. He wanted to tell her what he was hiding about himself, to confide in her the truth of his cowardice, to open himself and let out the terrible hurt he was carrying, to rid himself of its burden. There, deep underground, shut away with her by the magic of the phoenix stone, he felt he could.

He forced himself to meet her intense gaze as he spoke. "When we went into the ruins and were attacked, I panicked," he said. "While the others stood and fought, I ran. I threw down my sword, and I ran." He swallowed against the bitterness of his words. "I didn't want to, but I couldn't help myself. All I could think about was saving my life, finding a way to stay alive. Joad Rish was bending down to help one of the Elven Hunters, one of Ard Patrinell's men, and I saw him cut apart by fire threads, his head—"

He choked on the words and had to stop. Ryer's free hand touched his cheek. "Don't you think they all felt as you did, Ahren?" she asked him. "Don't you think they all did whatever they could to stay alive? The Elven Hunters fought back because that's what they knew to do, not because of a code of conduct or a special kind of courage. Joad Rish tried to heal an injured man because that was what he could do. You ran, Ahren, because staying with the others would have gotten you killed and you didn't want that. You did what you could."

"Except that your vision showed that Antrax let me live, that I was kept alive on purpose!" he said bitterly.

Her smile was warm and gently remonstrative. "You didn't know that then, did you? What we do in any situation is based on what we know. I ran to Walker's aid in the maze. I didn't think about it, I didn't stop to reason it out, I didn't consider what I was doing. I reacted in the only way I knew to react. That's all we can do."

"At least you ran in the right direction."

"Did I?" she asked softly.

There was such sadness in her voice, such pain, that it stopped him momentarily. He stared at her, confused. She was telling him something important, but he didn't know what it was.

"Let go of my hands," she told him.

"But if the magic—"

"I know." She stopped him with the fingers of one hand

pressed against his lips. "But we need to know what happens if we do. There may come a time when it is necessary, when we have to fight. Let's test it now, while we're alone and safe."

He hesitated a moment, then did as she asked, releasing her other hand. Nothing changed. The magic continued to envelop them, cloaking them like forest mist in twilight, the swirling gray unchanged.

Ryer Ord Star put her hands in her lap and rocked back on her heels, facing him. "You told me your secret, Ahren. I will do the same for you. I will tell you mine. If you want to hear it."

There was a darkness to her words that frightened him, a promise of something unpleasant. "You don't have to tell me anything unless you want to."

"I know."

He waited a moment, then nodded. "All right."

She lifted her chin slightly, as if facing up to something she did not want to, a confession of truths she would just as soon avoid. The gesture was a telling one, defiant and brave. It made Ahren feel something for her that hadn't been there before. Respect, perhaps. Admiration.

"I'm not what you think I am," she began, holding his gaze. It seemed to him that she was forcing herself to look at him. "I'm not what anyone thought I was. I came on this journey for more reasons than one. When Walker came to find me, I already knew he was coming. I had been instructed to go with him when he did. My purpose was to act as seer, but not only that—not even primarily that. My purpose in coming with you was to spy for the Ilse Witch."

She waited to hear Ahren's reaction, but he was too surprised to respond.

She smiled bitterly. "You look stunned. Don't you believe

me? It's true. I was a spy for the Ilse Witch from the day Walker came to see me and for many years before. I sold myself to her long ago. It wasn't difficult at all, really. It happened like this. I was born with the sight, and I knew I had it from an early age. I could see the futures of those around me, sometimes in detail, sometimes just bits and pieces. I was an orphan raised by caregivers who took in strays like myself. They were kind to me, but they thought me strange, and indeed I was. I told no one of my gift, for I understood right from the start that to be different was to be dangerous in the eyes of many. I kept my gift a secret and tried to forget it was there. That was impossible to do, of course. It grew even worse when I discovered, quite by accident, that I was an empath, as well, and could heal physical and emotional wounds by touch. I didn't discover that gift until later, but once it was revealed, I had to leave my caregivers and find a place where no one knew me.

"I was twelve years old when I came to Grimpen Ward with a band of Rovers. They took me in because that is the way of Rovers, and they saw no harm in seeing me safely to my intended destination. They thought me strange, as well, but they left me alone. In Grimpen Ward, I sought out the Addershag. She was the reason I had gone there. Everyone knew she was the most powerful seer in the Four Lands, and I hoped that she would take me in and train me. I did not know she had never taken an apprentice. I did not appreciate the enormity of what it was I was seeking to accomplish.

"She set me straight quick enough. She turned me away without taking even a moment to consider what I was asking of her. I was devastated but I refused to give up. I stayed outside her door, waiting for her to change her mind. I stayed there for two months. Finally, she invited me to come in and sit with her. She tested me, asking me to do different things. When I finished doing what she wanted, she nodded and said I could stay. That was all. I could stay.

"For weeks, I did nothing but cook and clean and fetch for her. She treated me as a servant girl, and I was eager enough to be with her that I didn't mind. Finally, she began showing me something of my gift, a little only, then a little more. My instruction had begun. After a while, I became her assistant and confidante, as well. She was old and tough and dangerous. She was unpredictable, too. But I did well enough that I didn't feel threatened."

She took a deep breath and let it out slowly, as if releasing anguish she had kept bottled up for a long time. "I made a mistake, though. When I came to her and told her of my gift of sight, asking that she teach me to use it, I kept to myself that I was an empath. I was afraid to tell her, thinking that it might affect her decision to train me, that it did not matter if I was, so long as I kept it to myself. But in the third year of my training, I had a vision in which a little girl in the village was struck down in an accident. As was our custom, we gave the information to the parents for a fee of their choosing. We did that with everyone, not to make money, but so that we could live comfortably. No one ever complained. But our warning was not enough to save the little girl, and although she was not killed, she was injured badly enough that it seemed clear she would die.

"I asked the Addershag to let me go to her. She refused. There was nothing we could do, nothing we hadn't already done. I went anyway. I used my empathic powers and healed the little girl. I did it so that it appeared she recovered on her own, that I was only a vessel to show her the way back. But the Addershag knew better. She told me that my empathic gift would kill me one day, that an empath tracking fate in an effort to change its course would only end up throwing away her own life in the process. She said I was wasting my precious gift and her time, and I would do better on my own. She disowned me. She cast me out."

She pulled her knees to her chest and gave Ahren a wry, sad smile. "She was right. I did well enough. I was known and liked. Some mistrusted and challenged my talent, but not so many. I was visited often enough and kept busy. I was careful with use of my empathic abilities. Once or twice, I tried visiting the Addershag, but she would have nothing to do with me. Her interest lay in deciphering the future; she cared nothing for the past and hence nothing for me. I grew bitter toward her, angry that she would treat me with such disdain. But I was afraid of her, too. She was very old and her enemies all lay dead and buried. I did not care to become one of them. So I stayed out of her way.

"Then the Ilse Witch came to me, and everything changed."

She looked away from him for a moment, out into the emptiness of the passageway, into the dimly lit shadows beyond their magic-induced sanctuary, but beyond even that, he sensed, into the past.

Her eyes shifted back to his. "She showed herself to me, something it was said she never did. She was young, like me. She was an orphan, like me. She was so like me that I saw myself in her from the moment we met. She was a powerful sorceress, and I wanted her friendship and patronage. So when she proposed the bargain, I accepted. I would be her eyes and ears in Grimpen Ward and give her news of things that she should know. She, in turn, would make certain that when the

Addershag died, I would ascend to her position as principal seer in Grimpen Ward."

Her pale, ethereal features tightened. "I insisted I did not want the Addershag to come to any harm. I was assured she would not. She was old, after all, and would die soon enough. Did I question this? Did I want to see her fate? The Ilse Witch handed me a scarf. She told me to use my vision by channeling it through that piece of cloth she had stolen from the old woman. I did so, and saw her dead upon her cottage floor, eyes open and staring. The Ilse Witch took back the scarf. Now I had seen for myself. All that was required, once she died, was that I step into her shoes. Why not? I was her former apprentice, the most skilled of all seers next to her. Wasn't I her logical successor?

"I believed I was, of course, and I was still hurt from her rejection of me. So I agreed to the bargain and let events take their course. The Ilse Witch became my new mentor and friend. I began reporting by carrier bird everything I saw in the village and surrounding countryside. And I waited for the Addershag to die. It took a year, but die she did. She was bitten by a small, deadly snake that nestled in a bag of gold given to her by a patron. It was never clear who that patron was. Her lady servant was gone for a day and a night and found her dead when she returned. She buried her out back and kept the house for herself."

She sighed. "And I, I became what I had wanted to be, the new Addershag, her successor. Her followers, her patrons, all came now to me, and no one challenged me. I convinced myself that her death had nothing to do with me, that it was simply the result of a vision fulfilling itself, and that I, by not interfering, was behaving just as she had taught me. She would not have listened to me anyway, I thought. There was nothing I could have done to change things."

She shivered violently, and she hugged her knees more tightly to chase away the chill. "But there is a price for everything, and eventually I found out what it cost to follow the Addershag. The Ilse Witch came to me in response to a vision I had of Walker; I had been told to tell her everything I discovered concerning him. My vision showed him coming to me at night, a dark presence, an irresistible force who would change everything in my life. He came to me to discover what he could of a voyage he wished to make to a new land, of what he would find along the way. He induced my visions by giving me something to touch. It was a map.

"When I told the Ilse Witch of my vision, she became very excited. She wanted that map, and she said I must find a way to steal it for her. But then she changed her mind. Instead of stealing the map, I must insist on going with him. I must convince him I was indispensable so that he would take me. I was to reveal to him what I had seen in my vision and a few things more that she would tell me so that he could not refuse my request. I would be his shadow, and she would be mine. Everywhere I went, everywhere that Walker went, she would track us. She possessed a magic that gave her a way to see through my eyes. She assured me it was necessary that I do this. She insisted that Walker was our common enemy, the enemy of all those possessed of magic in the Four Lands."

She laughed without humor, without kindness. "I knew enough by then to be wary of such statements. Walker was not my enemy. He had done nothing to me or to anyone else so far as I knew. But I was in no position to refuse. When I suggested that the task was beyond me, she brushed my concerns aside and warned that it would take only a casual word dropped here or there to make the villagers of Grimpen Ward believe that it was I who had given the bag of gold with the snake in it to the Addershag. Besides, the Ilse Witch was my patron, my mentor. I was afraid of her, but I felt a kinship to her, as well. I agreed to do as she asked. I became her spy aboard the *Jerle Shannara*."

Tears filled her eyes, sudden and unexpected in the wake of her self-reproaching laughter. "But an odd thing happened, Ahren. Something neither she nor I had planned. Even before he came to see me, before I had touched the map or discovered anything more of what the voyage would require, I began to have other visions." She leaned close to him, the tears spilling down her cheeks. "They were of Walker and me. They were so strong, so overpowering, that I could not ignore them. They were of a blue ocean and of islands, a flying ship, and battles being fought and men dying. It was the voyage Walker sought to make, and I was seeing small parts of it. Most were so vague and jumbled that I could not sort them out, but one was very clear. Of those who traveled with Walker, these would be among them—one who would save his life and one who would try to take it; one who would love him unconditionally and one who would hate him with unmatched passion; one who would lead him astray and one who would bring him back again."

She paused. "I saw no faces to connect to any of these acts. Only my own, standing outside the vision, watching Walker— always very close, observing and waiting. But for what? I couldn't tell. Yet I was there each time, shadowing him."

"But now you know who these people are, who it is who will do these things to Walker," he interrupted, speaking for the first time, wanting to help her. "Now you can identify each one."

She laughed anew, and this time her laughter was so bitter and raw that he flinched from it. Her eyes turned wild, and she tossed back her hair in a defiant gesture. "Oh, yes! Yes, Ahren, I know who these people are! It is so ironic, so fitting! I knew these people from the start, but I didn't read the vision carefully enough! I was blinded by my own needs and wants and concerns! Who are all these people to Walker, who would take his life and save it, who would lead him astray and bring him back again, who would love and hate him both? Who are they, Ahren? I'll tell you. They are all the same person. They are all me!"

She seized his arms, gripping him so tightly he could feel her nails digging into his skin. "I did all those things to him and felt those ways about him! I almost caused him to die on Shatterstone by keeping from him that part of my vision that warned of poison thorns, and then I saved him with my empathic talent because I could not bear to let him die! I've loved and hated him both, sometimes without quite knowing which was which! He brought me with him when he shouldn't have, he put me in this terrible, hateful position because he trusts me, and he thinks even now that I will save him from whatever's trapped him down here! And I will, Ahren! I've led him astray so many times I've lost count! Each time, he's found his way back on his own. But this time, this one time, I will be the one to bring him back or I will die trying!"

She was crying so hard she was shaking, racked with sobs, her silvery hair a pale curtain reflecting her tears in threads of gleaming dampness. Her hands loosened their grip on his arms, and he took hold of her in turn, not wanting to break the contact.

"Now you know my secret," she whispered roughly. "It's much worse than yours, much uglier. I am consumed by it. I can't ever be forgiven for what I've done. I can't ever redeem myself."

He shook his head and bent close. "Everyone can be forgiven, Ryer Ord Star. Of anything and everything. It isn't always easy, but it is possible."

She shuddered in response. "Do you want to know something, Ahren?" Her voice was so small he could barely hear it. "When I used my empathic talent to heal Walker after he was poisoned on Shatterstone, I became linked to him in a way that has never happened before. It was as if our magics joined in some way, and I could see all the way into his soul. It was so painful! I knew that pain was there—I'd seen it in his eyes when we first met, felt it in his hands—but I didn't realize it was so vast! It overwhelmed me and by doing so, opened me up to him as he had been opened to me. He saw what was hidden inside of me; he saw everything. He knew what I was, what I had come to do. He understood the danger I presented to him and to the others."

She shook her head in wonderment. "But he kept it all to himself. He never spoke of it. He put it all aside as if it no longer mattered, and he let me stay. I think he hoped that by doing so he would make me an ally instead of an enemy. And he did. I quit doing anything of importance for the Ilse Witch. She could still track the airship's progress through me, but I guess Walker did not think that was very important. She already knew where we were going; she had read the mind of the castaway to learn what waited. What I would no longer do, what he was counting on me not to do, was to hide any truths from him, any parts of visions experienced, any secrets that might cause him injury. I was his now, willingly. I will be his always, so long as he needs me. Our connection transcends everything. It is strong enough that I feel his need for me, down here in this dark place, in these passageways and chambers, in all this metal. I can feel him reaching out to me, when there is no one else he can touch." She swallowed her tears. "It is why I go to him now. It is why I have to find him."

She broke their embrace and wiped at her eyes with both hands. Then she began to cry anew, hugging herself, rocking back and forth on her heels. "Isn't it sad that I might be all he has?" she asked, her voice breaking. "So pathetic."

He took her in his arms and held her while she cried, not trying to stop or soothe her, but just holding her. He thought several times to say something comforting or wise, but nothing he considered felt right. Silence seemed best, and so he kept it. Around them, the magic of the phoenix stone swirled like murky water, steady and somehow reassuring, an escape that gave them space and time to let their emotions settle. Ahren looked out through the haze to the corridor beyond, where it was empty and silent. It felt as if they really were alone down there, abandoned and forgotten by everyone.

Ryer stopped crying, disengaged from his arms, and looked directly at him. "Are you still coming with me?"

He nodded. He had never thought to do otherwise.

"You don't have to," she said. "I wouldn't expect you to honor your promise, not after knowing that I—"

"Stop it," he interrupted quickly, remonstratively. "Don't say any more."

She studied him a moment, then leaned forward to kiss his cheek. In the warmth and softness of her lips, he could feel a measure of his self-worth and respect return.

They rose then and continued through Castledown's endless corridors and chambers, shrouded by the magic of the phoenix stone, guided by their instincts and need. The young seer was still warring with her inner demons, but her pale, ethereal features were tight with resolve. She had taken Ahren's hand again, even though they had determined she did not need to do so. Ahren was glad. Her touch did at least as much for him as his did for her. He felt as if they were children lost in a dark forest, with night coming on and wolves all about, blindly trusting in a talisman he neither understood nor controlled. The magic of the phoenix stone was protecting them, but how much longer would it last? He did not want to be caught unprepared or short of their goal.

Or goals, he corrected himself. There was Walker on the one hand and the missing Elfstones on the other. He had not spoken of the latter to Ryer Ord Star, but once they found the Druid, he intended to search for the Stones. It might be that he was asking too much. It was possible that after locating Walker, the magic would vanish. He had no way of knowing. He could only plan for contingencies and hope and do the best he could with whatever happened.

They walked for a long time, but encountered neither creepers nor fire threads. If Antrax was hunting for them, it was doing so another way. They were descending at a steady rate now, down ramps and stairways alike, farther underground than they had gone before. It made sense to Ahren that Antrax would keep the magic it hoarded deeper down and better hidden. He thought there was a better than even chance that Walker would be there, too.

Ahead, not far away, machinery thrummed and chugged softly, a steady cadence, one that reverberated through the steel of the tunnels into his bones.

Then the corridor branched left and right into a series of

arched, doorless openings, all of them leading onto a cat-walk that overlooked a cavernous room filled with huge metal cabinets and clusters of blinking lights set into panels. Wheels spun behind smoky windows; brilliant silver disks reflected the soft light of flameless lamp tubes that ran up and down the walls and across the room's high ceiling. The hum of machinery was everywhere, punctuated by beeps and chirps and other strange sounds, all of it coming from the chamber below.

It was an eerie sight, a surreal vision of something that hadn't existed for thousands of years beyond these walls. They paused on the catwalk, looking down at the contents of the room, searching for something that made sense. Nothing they saw was familiar to either of them, but an instant later Ryer gasped sharply, spoke Walker's name, and pulled on Ahren's hand, dragging him after her toward a metal stairway leading down. He went without questioning her, already knowing what was happening. They descended the stairs and made their way through the maze of fifteen-foot-high cabinets filled with rows of spinning silver disks. At least some of the machinery they had heard from the catwalk was behind the panels. Ahren glanced up at their smooth surfaces, certain they had come out of the Old World, wondering if they contained the magic the company of the *Jerle Shannara* had come searching for. What sort of magic, he wondered, is kept in a metal shell of spinning disks and blinking lights? It was books they had come to find, but there were no books here—at least, none that he could see. Perhaps they were deeper underground, and the cabinets and their machinery served as protectors of some sort.

Then he caught sight of the creepers. Several of them were working their way down the rows of cabinets, stopping every so often to manipulate the spinning disks and blinking lights. If they saw Ahren and Ryer, they gave no indication of it. The creepers were different from the ones they had encountered before. Larger than the so-called sweepers, they were nevertheless more of that sort—tenders of Castledown rather than defenders. They were equipped with strange metal limbs that reached out in all directions, touching here and there, inserting odd-shaped digits into slots and openings, causing the sound of the machinery or the blinking of the lights to alter, changing now and again the cadence or speed of the disks.

Fascinated, Ahren slowed to take a closer look, but Ryer Ord Star was having none of that. She jerked him ahead, pulling at him anxiously. Her destination was the far end of the chamber. One of the creepers was moving the same way, somewhat ahead of them, as if anticipating what she intended. The seer shot Ahren a frantic glance over her shoulder, then broke into a run, dragging him with her. Wrapped in the protective cloud of phoenix-stone magic, they rushed after the creeper toward a series of metal doors that stood closed on dimly lit chambers that could just be distinguished through a line of tall, dark windows.

The creeper was quicker and got there first, touching a panel that caused the door to one of the chambers to slide open. Fresh light spilled through the doorway to reveal panel after panel of blinking lights and dozens of tubes that snaked inward toward the center of the room. The creeper disappeared inside, rolling soundlessly on its wheeled base.

Ahren and Ryer came up behind it in a rush, the girl still leading the way. They were through the open doorway and into the room before she stopped so suddenly that he ran into her from behind. Struggling to keep them both from falling over, he followed her gaze across the room. His breath left his body in a rush.

They had found Walker.

But maybe it would have been better if they hadn't.

SEVENTEEN

Night descended on the land like a great silken cat, its shadow darkening the woods in steadily deepening layers, stealing away the daylight with stealth and cunning. Bek sat across from his sister and watched her cut slices of cheese from a wedge and toast bread on flat rocks made hot by coals. She had already cleaned and portioned out berries on broad leaves culled from tropical plants that shouldn't grow so far north but somehow did. She worked steadily and purposefully and did not look up at him. She did not look at him, anyway, most of the time. She treated him very much the way Quentin treated his hunting dogs: she fed, watered, and rested him, and expected him to do what he was told and to keep up with her when she traveled. She showed just enough interest in him to let him know she was keeping watch, nothing more. The wall she had erected between them was thick and high and very sturdy.

"Go down to the steam and bring us fresh water," she said without lifting her head.

He rose, picked up the nearly empty water skin, and walked into the trees. She didn't worry about him trying to escape. He had given his word, after all. Not that he believed for a moment that his word counted for anything with her. But he was forbidden to leave her presence carrying the Sword of Shannara, and he knew she could track him easily should he choose to stray. He did not like to think about what she would do to him if he did. If he had needed further evidence of how ruthless she could be, she had provided it by telling him what she had done to Truls Rohk.

She kept it to herself for the better part of two days as they traveled back through the wooded hill country toward the ruins, brushing aside his repeated inquiries. But he pressed her stubbornly for an answer, and finally she provided one. She had left the caull in hiding to deal with the shape-shifter on his return from his failed ambush. Eventually, he would realize that she had outsmarted him and return to find Bek. She couldn't risk him then coming after her once he knew the boy was gone. He was as relentless as she was and every bit as dangerous. She respected him for that, but he would have to be eliminated. She had left the caull to finish him.

Bek was stunned, left both angry and heartsick, but there was nothing he could do about it. Maybe she had guessed wrong about the shape-shifter, and he had not come back for Bek after all. Maybe he had sensed that the caull was waiting and avoided it. But she seemed so certain that the matter was resolved, that his hopes dimmed almost immediately. He was on his own, he knew. Whatever choices he made from then forward, he would have to answer for them.

So running was out of the question. It hadn't worked the first time, and there was no reason to think it would work now. Besides, if there was any chance at all of persuading her that he really was her brother, he had to take advantage of it. He could not afford to alienate her further. Though she paid him scant attention, she let him talk, and he used every opportunity she gave him to try to convince her of who he was.

Mostly, she ignored him, but now and again she would reply to his arguments, and even those small responses, those cryptic remarks, provided evidence that she was listening to what he was telling her. She might not believe him, but at least she was considering his words.

He filled the water skin, kneeling by the stream, looking out into the darkness. Nevertheless, time was running out. They were only a day away from their destination. Once back, she intended to give him over to the Mwellrets while she set out again in search of Walker. The rets would place him aboard *Black Moclips* and hold him prisoner until she returned. That would be the end of any chance to argue his cause and, maybe, the end of any chance to save Walker's life.

The water skin ballooned out, and he sealed it, then stood up. Walker could take care of himself, of course—if he was still alive and able to do so, which was by no means certain. But the Ilse Witch was a formidable enemy; she had proved that already. Bek didn't know if Walker was a match for her because he wasn't sure that the Druid could be as ruthless as she was, and in order to survive, he would have to be.

He walked back through the trees to the little campsite and handed the water skin to his sister. She took it without looking at him and sprinkled the berries with droplets of water. He stood looking at her for a moment, then sat down again. After they ate, they would bathe, he first, she later. They did that every night, using whatever water was at hand, washing themselves as best they could. There were no fresh clothes to change into, but at least they could keep their bodies clean. It was warm enough even at night to wash in the rivers and streams—in winter, in a land farther north than any part of the one he had come from. Bek wondered anew at the strangeness of such a thing, remembering Walker's own comment on it.

Grianne passed him a slice of bread covered with crushed berries reduced to a sugary spread, and he chewed on it thoughtfully, eyes on her face. She was still testy from his efforts at breaking down her disbelief earlier in the day. In fact, she had told him not to speak of it again. But he could not stay silent when there was so much at stake. Nor could he afford to wait until she was more receptive.

When she made the mistake of glancing over at him, he spoke at once.

"You're not thinking clearly," he said. "If you were, you would see all the flaws in your reasoning. You would see the gaps of logic in what you've been told."

She stared at him without expression and chewed slowly.

"If I'm not Bek, how come I have the same name? You say I was mind-altered to believe that 'Bek' was my real name. But Quentin has known me all of my life. So have my adoptive father and mother. I've been Bek since I was brought to them. Are they mind-altered, as well? Is everyone in Leah mind-altered to believe I'm someone I'm not?"

She made no response, other than to lift a slice of cheese to her mouth and take a bite.

"Or is Walker so clever that he's been planning all this since he brought me to Coran and Liria fifteen years ago?"

She stared at him, an insect regarding a leaf.

"That's what you believe, isn't it? You think he's been planning this charade all these years, just to trick you. But you can't tell me why he would do this, can you?"

She lifted the water skin to her lips and drank from it, then handed it over so that he could do the same. Her eyes were as flat and dead as those of a snake.

"Oh, that's right, he wants to break you down, to undermine your resolve, to get past your guard. That way he can subvert you, can turn you to his own uses, whatever they might be. He can steal your magic and make you his puppet. Just like he's done with me, only you're the bigger catch, because your magic is so much stronger than mine and you're a bigger threat to him." He let the sarcasm slide through his words like oil. "Shades, isn't it is a good thing you were smart enough to see this coming?"

She reached for the water skin and took it back from him. "I thought I told you not to speak of this again."

He shrugged. "You did." He finished off his bread and took a slice of the cheese. "But I can't help myself. I have to understand why you don't see the truth. Nothing you believe makes any sense at all." He paused. "What about the reason the Morgawr gave you for why Walker tried to steal you away in the first place? What about that? He said it was because Walker wanted you to become a Druid like he was, but our parents refused. They wouldn't allow it, wouldn't consider it, so he killed them and stole you away. Wasn't that a little clumsy, when there were so many more subtle ways to win you over? Why would he be stupid enough to let you witness the killing of our parents while snatching you away? Couldn't he have just mind-altered you instead? Wouldn't that have been a whole lot easier? He's clever enough, isn't he? His magic can make you believe anything. That's how he got to me."

Her eyes were locked on his. "You are not me. You are weak and stupid. You are a pawn, and you do not understand anything."

She spoke without rancor or irritation. Her words were cold and lifeless, and they mirrored the pale, hard cast of her young face as she finished her bread and cheese without shifting her gaze from his, looking so deeply into his eyes that he thought she must see everything that was hidden there.

He shook off the chill her gaze made him feel. "What I understand," he said quietly, "is that you've become the very thing you were so intent on avoiding."

She shook her head quickly. "I am not a Druid," she said. "Don't call me that."

"You're as good as. The same as, really." He leaned forward in challenge. "Explain to me how you differ from Walker. Tell me what he has done in his life that you have not done in yours. Show me where the road you have traveled branches from his."

She regarded him silently, but her eyes were angry now. "You seem intent on provoking me."

"Do I? Let me tell you a story, Grianne. While I was on my way to Arborlon, I traveled with Quentin through the Silver River country. While I slept, I had a vision. The vision was of a young girl who appeared to me, then transformed into a monster, a thing so hideous I could barely manage to look upon it. That young girl was you at six years of age and the thing you transformed into seemed very like the Mwellrets you command. I believe in visions, in portents of things to come, in foreshadowings of the future. That was one. I was being shown your past and your future. I was being told that it was up to me to change your destiny, to prevent that transformation from happening."

"You take a lot on yourself then. You presume more than you should."

He shook his head. "Do I? I didn't go looking for this. I didn't even understand what I was being shown. Not until I learned who I was. Not until I found you. But I think now that if I don't find a way to convince you of the truth, no one else will, and that vision will come to pass."

"I have nothing in common with Mwellrets or Druids," she sneered. "You are a boy with a too vivid imagination and no brains. You trust blindly in the wrong people and assume your truths should be mine, when they are nothing but deceptions. I am tired of listening to you. Don't say anything more to me. Not a word."

"I will say what I like!" he snapped back at her. Inside, he was shaking. She could be volatile, dangerous, but caution no longer served a purpose. "You are surrounded by obsequious followers and liars of all sorts. You have separated yourself from the truth for so long that you wouldn't recognize it if it jumped up in front of you. Why don't you admit that you're not sure about me? Why don't you at least confess that?"

Her face darkened. "Keep still."

"Let me go with you to find Walker. Let him help you. What can it hurt to talk with him? Just listen to what he has to say. If you would take five minutes to think—"

"Enough!" she screamed.

He leapt to his feet. "Enough of what? The truth? I'm your brother, Grianne! I'm Bek! Stop trying to deny it! Stop twisting everything around!"

She was on her feet, as well, rigid with fury. He knew he should stop, but he couldn't. "Do you want me to tell you what really happened to our parents? Do you want me to tell you what's been done to you? Do you want me to speak the words out loud, so that you can hear how they sound? You're so blind you can't—"

She screamed again, only this time there were no words, only sound that rent the air like razors. The wishsong's magic seared his throat, twisting and tightening until he was gasping for air. He threw up his hands in a belated effort to protect himself as he stumbled backwards and fell. The unexpected force and suddenness of her attack left him dazed and crumpled on the ground, his eyes tearing, his breath coming in deep, rasping gulps.

She loomed over him, robes drawn close, her pale face twisted with disgust. Then her hand reached down to touch his neck and everything went black.

When he was asleep and breathing normally again, she straightened his arms and legs and covered him with his tattered cloak. Such a fool. She had warned him not to say anything more, but he had continued to press her. She had reacted almost without thinking, losing control of herself and lashing out in anger. She felt vaguely ashamed for doing so. It didn't matter what the provocation was; she should have been able to keep the magic in check. She should have been able to avoid attacking him that way. She easily might have killed him. It wouldn't have taken all that much to do so. The power of the wishsong was immense. Should she choose it, she could use her magic to wither one of the huge old oaks that sheltered their camp, to shred it to pulp and bark and sap, to reduce it to the earth from which it had grown. How much less difficult it would be to do the same with this boy.

"I warned you," she hissed at his sleeping form, still inwardly seething at herself.

She straightened and walked away, stopping at the edge of the clearing and peering off into the dark. She brushed back the long dark hair from her face and folded her arms into her robes. Perhaps it was just as well that she had reacted as she did. What she had done now was what she had intended to do anyway once they reached the bay where *Black Moclips* lay at anchor—to take away his voice and render him harmless. She could not afford to leave him with the Mwellrets otherwise. She would take his sword, as well, the blade he claimed was the Sword of Shannara. He would be locked in the hold and kept there until she finished her business with the Druid.

She glanced over her shoulder to where he lay sleeping, then quickly away again. She had meant to tell him what she was going to do before she did it, to reassure him that it was temporary, a few days and no more. She had meant to tell him she would restore his voice when she saw him again, that she would negate the magic that held it bound. She would still tell him tomorrow when he woke, but the effect would be different from what she had planned.

It irritated her that she felt the need to justify herself to him. It wasn't as if she owed him anything, as if he mattered to her in even the slightest way. But try as she might, she could not dismiss him as nothing more than a boy the Druid had somehow subverted to use against her. She knew that such an explanation was too simplistic. He was more than that; his magic was real. He was perhaps as strong-minded as she was, and there was at least some truth to what he was saying. She wouldn't admit it to him, but she could sense it. Her problem was in deciding how much. Where did the lies end and the truth begin? What was the Druid trying to accomplish by sending him to her? For he had sent the boy, however they might have found each other. He had sent the boy as surely as she had sent Ryer Ord Star to spy on him.

Was it possible he really was Bek?

She stopped breathing momentarily, the thought suspended before her like an exotic creature. Was it possible after all? He could still be Bek and be lying about their parents. He could still be an unwitting dupe. He could be mistaken without realizing it.

But how had the Druid found him, when she had thought him dead? How had the Druid known who he was? Had the Druid gone back into the rubble and searched him out? Had the Druid decided to make use of Bek in his schemes because he had lost the use of her?

Her lips tightened. Everyone was used in this life. She thought about the Morgawr, her mentor all these years, her teacher in the fine art of magic's use. She knew enough of him, of what he was, to know that he could not be trusted, to accept that he was every bit as devious as the Druid. She knew he had used her. She knew he kept things from her that he believed enabled him to maintain his hold over her. It was just the way of things. She manipulated and deceived, too. The boy was right about that. She was not so different from the Morgawr, and the Morgawr was very like the Druid.

But would the Morgawr have lied to her about her parents? How could she have such strong memories of the Druid and his dark-cloaked servants descending on her home that final dawn if he had? That didn't feel right to her. It didn't seem possible. The Druid had wanted her to come with him to Paranor. She remembered his visits to her father, his conversations and dark warnings. No, he had orphaned her and stolen her away as she believed.

Yet the boy who thought himself her brother was right. She had ended up a Druid anyway, in another place, in another form. She could not say she was any different from Walker, any better or worse. She could not point to where their lives were that much different. In escaping him, she had allowed the Morgawr to turn her into a mirror image of her enemy. Her use of magic and her efforts at accumulating power were very much the same as his. If he had done bad things in their pursuit, so had she.

Thinking about all of that, accepting the truth of it, made her even angrier with herself. But there was no place for anger in her efforts to accomplish the tasks that she had undertaken. She must find the magic concealed in Castledown, gain possession of it, and return to her ship. She must decide what to do with the boy and his unsettling accusations. She must settle matters once and for all with both the Druid and the Morgawr.

She never once doubted that she was capable of all that or that she could carry out her plans in the manner she intended.

But, like it or not, she was beginning to question her reasoning for doing so.

Miles to the east and south, well clear of the inlet opening into the Squirm and its ice fields and beyond the cliffs that warded the eastern approach from the Blue Divide, the *Jerle Shannara* lay at anchor. She was berthed in a forested cove nestled among a dozen others in lowlands miles from where she had deposited Walker and those others who had gone ashore in search of Castledown. The *Jerle Shannara* was sheltered from the wintry weather that swept the coast, concealed from prying eyes while she underwent repairs.

Seated on a bench at the ship's stern and facing out toward the cove's narrow opening, Rue Meridian could only just glimpse the distant waters of the Blue Divide. She wore loose-fitting trousers and tunic, red-orange scarves wrapped about her throat and forehead, and soft, worn ankle boots. A blanket warded her against the chill. Restless and bored, she scuffed one boot across the decking and pondered her dissatisfaction for the hundredth time. It was almost a week since Big Red had brought the airship overland after its near catastrophic encounter with the Squirm, charting a course back to the coast that avoided glaciers and mountains and obscuring mist. A longer, more circuitous route than the one that led through the Squirm and up the river channel, it was by far the safer. Regaining the coast, the Rovers cruised in search of the Wing Riders, whom they quickly found and who in turn led to the sheltering bay. Since then, Rovers and Wing Riders had been engaged in repairing the damaged vessel while Rue had lain belowdecks, healing from her wounds and sleeping undisturbed.

Endless processes both, she fumed to herself in silence. She glanced down at her leg, where she had incurred the deepest and most serious injury in her battle with the Mwellrets. Stitches and poultices had begun to heal it nicely, but the wound wasn't closed entirely and she still couldn't walk without pain. The knife wound to her arm had healed more quickly, and the claw marks on her back and sides were little more than the beginnings of scars she would never lose. She guessed that meant she was two for three, but the leg wound kept her from doing much and the inactivity was beginning to grate on her.

It would have helped if the repairs to the ship had gone more quickly and they were sailing back the way they had come in search of their abandoned friends and shipmates. But the damage to the *Jerle Shannara* had been more extensive than anyone had realized at first glance. It was not just the shattered spars and shredded light sheaths and cracked mainmast that had crippled the ship. Two of the parse tubes together with their diapson crystals had been torn free and lost overboard. A dozen radian draws were frayed beyond repair. The nature of the damage precluded simple replacement; it required reworking the entire system that allowed the ship to fly. Spanner Frew was equal to the task, but it was taking too much time.

She watched the burly shipwright bent over the left fore hooding, directing the set of the existing tube and crystal, re-aligning the left midship draw that now ran to that emplacement, as well. It was the second of three that were involved in the realignment. No one knew how well the new configuration would work, so that meant testing it out before they ventured inland and risked a further encounter with *Black Moclips* and the Ilse Witch.

Every time she thought of the witch, she was consumed by a white-hot anger. It wasn't the damage to the ship or the imprisonment of the Rovers that fueled it. It wasn't even the unavoidable loss of contact with Walker's company. It was the death of Furl Hawken for which she most blamed the witch, because if not for the witch's seizure of the *Jerle Shannara* and her imprisonment of the Rover crew, it would never have happened.

Somehow, someway, she had promised herself, the Ilse Witch would be made to pay for Hawk's death. It was something she had vowed while she lay belowdecks, still too weak even to sit up, unable to stop thinking about what she had witnessed. There would be a reckoning for Hawk, and Little Red wanted to be the one to bring it about.

The day was dragging on toward midafternoon, the sky a mass of thick gray clouds, the sun screened away, the air raw with cold. At least they were sufficiently sheltered by the landfall to be protected from the bitter wind and sleet blowing with such ferocity along the coast. She marveled at the oddness of the weather there, so different on the coast than inland, so unexplainably in contrast. Only Shrikes and gulls and the like could make homes in the cliffs of the coastal waters. Humans could never live here in any comfort. She wondered if humans lived inland. She wondered if there were humans anywhere at all.

"Afternoon," a voice growled, snapping her out of her reverie.

She turned to find Hunter Predd standing a few feet away, his wiry frame wrapped in a heavy cloak, his weathered features ruddy and bemused. She smiled ruefully. "Sorry. I was somewhere else. Good afternoon to you."

He moved a step closer, looking out toward the ocean. "There's a big storm coming on, a bad one. Saw it building out there while flying in with the last of the hemp and reed. It might lock us down for a few days."

"We're locked down anyway until the ship can fly again. What's it looking like now, two or three more days at least before we can get under way again?"

"At least."

"Are you foraging for materials still?"

He shook his head and ran one gnarled hand through his windblown hair. "No, we're done. It's up to Black Beard and the others to make it all work now."

She gestured him over. "Sit down. Talk with me. I'm sick of talking with myself."

She made room for him on the bench, swinging her legs off and placing her feet carefully on the decking. She winced in spite of herself at the pain the effort brought on.

The sharp eyes darted toward her. "Still a little tender, I guess."

"Do all Wing Riders possess such acute powers of observation?"

He chuckled softly. "Feelings seem a little tender, too."

She didn't say anything for a moment, looking down at her

legs, her boots, the decking. Time passed. She felt a great void in her heart, a place opening up where opportunity slipped away while she sat doing nothing.

She lifted her eyes to meet his. "How long has it been since we left them? More than a week anyway, isn't it? Too long, Wing Rider. Way too long."

He nodded, his brow furrowing. He started to say something, then stopped, as if deciding that anything he had to say was unnecessary. He clasped his hands about one knee and rocked back slightly in his cloak, grizzled head shaking.

"You can't favor this delay any more than I do," she said. "You must want to do something about it, too."

He nodded. "I've been considering it."

"If we could just find out if they are all right, if they would be safe enough until the ship could reach them . . ."

She didn't finish, waiting on him to do so for her. He looked off into the distance instead, as if trying to spy them through the mist and cold. Then he nodded once more. "I could take a look for them. I could leave now, in fact. Should leave now, because once the storm comes in, it won't be so easy to fly out."

She leaned forward eagerly, red hair fanning out about her shoulders. "I have the coordinates Big Red mapped out from our journey in. We won't have any trouble following them back."

He looked at her in surprise. "We?"

"I'm going with you."

He shook his head. "Your brother won't let you go and you know it. He'll put a stop to it before you finish telling him what you intend."

She gave it a moment, then reached up with one finger and touched her temple. "Think about what you just said, Hunter

Predd," she advised softly. "When was the last time my brother told me what to do, would you guess?"

He smiled in rueful understanding. "Well, he won't like it, anyway."

She smiled back. "It won't be the first time he's had to deal with this sort of disappointment. Nor the last, I'd wager."

"You and me?" he asked, arching one eyebrow.

"You and me."

"I won't ask if you're up to it."

"Best not."

"I won't ask what you intend once we get there either, even though I'd be willing to bet it goes beyond a quick flyover."

She nodded without answering.

He sighed deeply. "It will feel good to be back in the air, good to be doing what we were trained to do, Obsidian and me." He rubbed his callused hands together. "We'll leave Po Kelles and Niciannon to run whatever errands your brother and the others need until they catch up to us. Maybe our leaving will inspire them to work faster on the repairs."

"Maybe. My brother hates to miss out on anything. Going inland for a look around was his idea in the first place."

"And now you've stolen it." He shook his head, smiled ruefully. "How soon can you be ready?"

She rose gingerly and unwrapped herself from the blanket. Underneath, throwing knives were strapped in place about her waist.

She cocked an eyebrow at him. "How soon can you saddle your bird?"

EIGHTEEN

They flew west off the coast and inland aboard Obsidian, settled comfortably upon the riding harness strapped to the Roc's feathered back, Hunter Predd at the reins and Rue Meridian seated just behind him. The Rover wore her flying leathers, black like her brother's and molded to her body from constant use. Beneath, her wounds were carefully bound and padded, and the leathers served as light armor to protect them from the rougher abuses she might suffer on her journey. For weapons, she bore a brace of throwing knives about her waist, another tucked into her boot, a long knife strapped to her good thigh, and bow and arrows slung across her back. A great cloak and hood wrapped her against the cold and wind, but even so she found herself ducking her chin and hunching her shoulders to stay warm.

That her brother was angry at her decision to make this journey was the understatement of the year. He was so furious, so stunned by what he considered her obvious stupidity and immeasurably poor judgment, that he ended up shouting at her loud enough to bring work on the airship to a halt until he was finished. No one else said a word, not even Spanner Frew. No one else wanted any part of the argument. Big Red was speaking for them all—loudly enough for all of their voices combined, come to that—and there was nothing further to be said or done. She listened patiently for a few minutes, then began shouting back at him, and eventually threw up her hands and limped away, screaming back one final time to suggest that if he was so worried about her, maybe he'd better hurry along his repair efforts and follow.

It wasn't fair to chide him so, but she was beyond caring about what was fair and reasonable. What she cared about— the only thing she cared about by then—was that sixteen men and women were trapped inland in strange and dangerous territory with no realistic hope of finding their way out and a madwoman and her reptilian servants hunting for them. She had no idea what might have happened to them, but she didn't like to think about the possibilities. She wanted reassurance that her worst fears had not been realized. She wanted evidence of their safety. Time was an enemy, swift and elusive. There was risk in what she was doing, but it was a risk worth taking when measured against the consequences of further inaction. Hunter Predd said nothing during the argument or afterwards, but she knew he agreed with her decision. Wing Riders were made cautious by training and from experience, but they knew when it was time to act.

It was late afternoon when they departed, and they flew until the night enveloped them. The blue-gray line of the ocean and clouds was left behind, along with the freezing cold of the coastal air. The inland darkness was warm and soft, a welcome change. The land stretched away before them, an unbroken rippling of green treetops and dark ridgelines dotted with lakes and laced with rivers, hemmed away behind the coastal cliffs and mountain peaks. Far distant, caught in a patch of fading sunlight, an ice field's glimmer was hard and bright against the enfolding dark.

Hunter Predd turned Obsidian downward to find a camp-site. After several minutes of searching, they landed in a clearing atop a broad wooded rise that gave Obsidian several choices of perch and routes of escape and his riders a good view of the surrounding countryside. It wasn't that they expected trouble, just that they knew enough to be ready for it. It was a country about which they knew virtually nothing. There could be things there that would kill, things that they had never encountered before. Even if they avoided whatever it was that warded Castledown, there would be other dangers.

While Hunter Predd unsaddled Obsidian, groomed his feathers, and watered and fed him, Rue Meridian set about preparing their meal. They had agreed to forgo a fire, to avoid attracting unwanted attention, so she settled for cold cheese, bread, and dried fruit from the stores she had brought from the ship. When Hunter Predd joined her, she brought out an aleskin and shared it with him between bites. They ate their meal in silence, watching the darkness deepen and the stars appear. Light from the full moon rising in the north was brilliant and cleansing, and the land took on a fresh white cast amid the shadows. Atop the rise, the woods were silent. Within the trees, nothing moved.

"How long will it take us to get to where we're going?" the Wing Rider asked when they were finished eating. He sipped from the aleskin and handed it over to her. "Your best guess will do. I just need some idea of how to pace my bird."

She drank, as well, and put the container down. "I think we can get there by late tomorrow if we leave at sunrise and push through the day. It took longer coming out, but we were feeling our way and nursing our wounds, so it went more slowly. We'd lost half our power and much of our steering. Your Roc will fly faster than we did."

"Then we take a look around and see who's there?"

She shrugged. "When I was a girl and we played hide-and-seek, I learned that the best way to find someone was not to look too hard. I learned that instincts are necessary, that you have to trust them. We can have a look at the bay where the *Jerle Shannara* put Walker and the others ashore. We can fly inland until we sight Castledown. But I don't think we can be certain that what we're looking for is at either place."

"Or even aboveground."

She gave him a sharp look.

"What I mean is that the Druid told us the safehold was belowground. That's all."

She nodded. "We'll have to look sharp, in any case, to find them. They won't just be standing around waiting."

"We'll have Obsidian to help with that." The Wing Rider gestured to where the bird roosted in the dark on a broad outcropping of rocks. "That's what he's been trained to do, to look for things we can't see, to hunt for what's lost and needs finding. He's good at it. Better than you and me."

She eased her injured leg into a new position. It ached from being locked about the Roc during their flight, even for only the two hours they had traveled. How much worse would it be by tomorrow night? She sighed wearily as she rubbed it back to life, careful to avoid the knife wound. It was no worse, she supposed, than she had imagined it would be. She'd already checked the bandage, and there was no evidence of bleeding. The stitches were holding her together so far.

"We'll rest pretty regularly tomorrow," Hunter Predd declared, watching her. Her eyes lifted in sharp reproof. "Not just for you," he added. "For the bird, too. Obsidian travels better with frequent stops."

"As long as you're not doing me any special favors."

His laugh was dry and mirthless. "We wouldn't want that, would we?"

She passed him the aleskin and leaned back on her elbows. "You can laugh all you want. You didn't grow up a girl among men the way I did. If you asked for special favors from my brother or my cousins, they laughed at you. Worse, they made things so difficult you wished you'd never opened your mouth. Rover women have a tradition of endurance and toughness born out of constant travel, responsibility for family, and a mostly hard life. In the old days, we had no cities, no place in the world outside of our wagons and our camps. We were no-mads, adrift much of the time, at sea or in flight the rest. No one helped us just because they wanted to. We taught them to depend on us, on our skills and our goods, so they had no choice. We have always been a self-sufficient people, even now, as sailors and shipbuilders and mercenaries, and what-ever else we can do better than others—"

"Hold on!" he interrupted in protest. "I'm not laughing at you. Do you think I don't know about your kind of life? We're not so different, you and me. Wing Riders and Rovers, they've always lived apart, always been self-sufficient, al-ways depended on no one. That's been true since as far back as anyone can remember."

He leaned forward. "But that doesn't mean we can't extend a helping hand when it's needed. Friendship doesn't have anything to do with shoring up weakness. It has to do with re-spect and consideration for those you care about. It has to do with wanting to give something back to those you admire. You might keep that in mind."

She smiled in spite of herself, charmed by his bluntness. "I've been living with soldiers too long on the Prekkendor-ran," she offered. "I've forgotten how to be grateful."

He shook his head. "You haven't forgotten much, I expect. You just get a little too close to your feelings sometimes, Little Red. Better that than getting too far away."

They slept undisturbed, taking shifts at watch, and woke refreshed and ready to go on. They set out at sunrise, its pale golden light cresting the horizon like a fanfare to give chase to the night. The features of the land below gradually emerged from the shadows, a slow etching out of detail and color. The air warmed as the sun lifted, and the sky was bright and cloudless. Rue Meridian lifted her face to the light, thinking that perhaps the world could be kinder, after all, than she had supposed.

They flew on through the entire day, stopping to rest and water Obsidian and to eat their lunch and stretch cramped limbs. Other than small birds and an occasional forest animal, they saw no sign of life. After midday, the terrain began to change, turning more rugged and less open. Ahead, bald-topped mountains reared against the skyline, a ragged spine down the length of the land, bisecting its mass. Foothills cradled deep lakes formed by streams and runoff from the higher elevations. Clouds began to mass along the peaks. The sky north turned gray and murky with rainsqualls. South, where the cliffs and ice fields lay clustered, the horizon was black with thunderstorms and streaked with bolts of lightning that flashed like explosions of white fire.

It was twilight when they came in sight of the bay where the *Jerle Shannara* had left the shore party more than ten days ago. They circled around to fly out of the descending gloom so they would not be seen, keeping low above the treetops, hidden against the dark mass of the mountains. They could just identify the faint outline of *Black Moclips* where she hung tethered at anchor above the waterline. No lights burned from her masts or through her windows, and no movement could be seen on her decks. Hunter Predd took Obsidian down to an open stretch of rock fronting a barren ridge. They dismounted and walked to a place where they could look down on the airship and the bay.

West, the sun had dropped below the horizon and the last of the day's fading light was disappearing into shadow.

"Now what?" Hunter Predd asked quietly.

Rue Meridian shook her head, staring fixedly at *Black Moclips*. "Maybe we ought to take a closer look."

Leaving Obsidian to roost, they walked down from the heights to the shoreline, taking their time, moving cautiously through the deepening darkness so as to make as little noise as possible. In the silence of the cove, noise would travel a great distance. Little Red's eyes were sharp, but Hunter Predd's were sharper still, so he led the way, choosing the path that offered them the quietest passage. It took them almost an hour to make the descent, and by then darkness had fallen completely and the sky was bright with the light of stars and moon.

Standing on the shoreline, well back within the trees, the Rover and the Wing Rider stared out across the bay at the anchored airship. They could see movement on her decks now, guards at watch, crewmen at work. They could hear voices, kept deliberately low, but audible. They could just catch glimpses of lantern light masked by shadows and curtains within the cabins below the decking.

After standing there for a time, Hunter Predd turned to her. "What are you thinking?"

She kept silent. What she was thinking was wild and dangerous. What she was thinking was that perhaps fate had presented them with a unique opportunity. She had come looking for the missing members of the *Jerle Shannara*'s company, but instead found their enemy's transport.

The Ilse Witch couldn't know yet that they had liberated the *Jerle Shannara* from the Mwellrets and Federation sailors left to keep watch over her. She couldn't know that she now commanded only *Black Moclips*. She would believe both vessels still safely under her control.

Rue Meridian pursed her lips. There was a chance for real irony here, a bit of poetic justice, if she could just figure out how to orchestrate it.

Wouldn't it be fitting, she was thinking, if she could somehow put the witch in the same position that the witch had put her?

Frowning in discontent, the Ilse Witch glanced over her shoulder at the darkening silhouette of *Black Moclips* as she disappeared into the trees. Twilight cloaked the bay in shadows that stretched in the wake of the sunset to seize and entwine the airship like ghost fingers. She had given strict instructions to Cree Bega and his rets. The boy had been placed in their care, to be watched and warded until her return. They were not to try to speak with him, to interact with him, or to have anything at all to do with him. He was to be kept locked up. He was to be given food and drink, but nothing else. He was not to be allowed out. No one was to visit him. No one was to disturb him.

Whether or not her instructions would be followed was another matter entirely.

Cree Bega was suspicious, but she had deflected the worst of it by offering up a small lie. The boy had information that would prove useful to them, but she must be the one to extract it from him since he could not speak. The Mwellret had no way of knowing that the reason the boy couldn't speak was because of the magic she had used against him, so he might do as he was told and wait for her return. It was a risk she had to take. She could not take the boy with her; it was too dangerous to go looking for the Druid with him in tow. She could not chance leaving him anywhere else besides the ship; someone from his company might find and free him. She had taken the Sword of Shannara with her, to be certain he found no use for it. She wore it slung across one shoulder, sheathed in the worn scabbard she had found to hold it. Without the use of his talisman or his voice, the boy would have no magic to call upon. It was best to leave him where he was and hope that her absence would be brief.

She had reason to think it would. She had amended her earlier plans, which were entirely too ambitious. As much as she wanted to settle things with the Druid, he was never the primary reason she had undertaken the expedition. Retrieving the powerful magic that lay in the bowels of Castledown was her most important goal. Besides, she needed more time to decide what to do about both the Druid and the boy, especially in light of what the latter was claiming about his lineage. What she intended to do was to walk into the ruins, to bypass the fire threads and creepers that had so easily bested the Mwellrets but would be less effective against her, to gain entry into Castledown, to locate and siphon off the magic of the books that were concealed there, and to escape. She would leave Walker for later, when she was safely back in the Wilderun. She would have her chance at him then because she would have the magic he coveted, and he would be forced to come to her to retrieve it.

Unless he had it already, of course. The possibility that the boy had been sent to draw her away from Castledown crossed her mind briefly, but she dismissed it. Still, the Druid might have gotten possession of the books while she was searching for the boy. If he had, she would have to deal with him immediately. But she didn't think that was the case. The fact that his company had been decimated by the fire threads and creepers and that there had been no sign of him since suggested that he had accomplished nothing, that instead he was in trouble, perhaps injured or dead. If he was not, he would have emerged already. He would have come for the boy or for her. The boy and the shape-shifter would not have continued their flight. There would have been some sign of activity. Her Mwellrets had patrolled the fringes of the ruins since their arrival and seen no one.

Besides, even if he had somehow avoided them, what could he do? Books of magic or not, he was trapped. She had control of both airships. She had the boy and the Sword of Shannara. The Druid was alone, or nearly so. To have any chance at all of escaping, he would have to come to her. She was prepared for that to happen.

She shrugged. Whatever the case, she would know what to do about the Druid when she found the books of magic. Her senses would tell her quickly enough if he had been there before her.

She moved through the darkening twilight like a shade, wrapped in her gray robes, a silent presence. She sent her magic ahead of her, sweeping the darkness, searching for what she could not see, for what might lie in wait. She found nothing. It was as if the world were deserted save for her. She liked the feeling. She always preferred the night, but preferred it best when she was alone. She did not feel anxious or concerned about what lay ahead. She knew what to expect from what she had been told by Cree Bega and, more important, from what she had discovered in her mind probe of the dying Kael Elessedil. She knew of the fire threads and creepers and did not feel them to be a threat. She knew about the books of magic and the thing that warded them. Antrax. That was the name it had been given many centuries ago. She knew what it was and how it could be overcome. She knew more about it than it knew about her. It had misjudged the extent of the information contained in Kael Elessedil's brain. She thought she even knew how to destroy it, should it become necessary to do so.

But the destruction of Antrax was not her concern. The books of magic were what she wanted, and while she did not know how many there were or where they were hidden, she was confident she could uncover and seize them, which was all she wanted of the machine. She would take the ones she needed, the ones that would give her the most power, and leave the rest for another time. She would use her magic to disrupt Castledown's security, concealing her presence, masking her theft, and hiding her retreat. If everything went as she wished, she would be there and gone again with Antrax none the wiser.

Then she would deal with that boy.

That boy who claimed he was Bek.

Even thinking about him angered her. His words skipped and jumped through her mind like small unruly animals. Even while trying to focus her thinking on what lay ahead, she could not dismiss them. Or him. That boy! His image was constant and tenacious, lingering in a way that came close to causing her panic. It was ridiculous that he should affect her so strongly. She had overcome him easily enough, outsmarted him time and again, stolen away his voice and his talisman, made him her prisoner, and crushed his hopes for convincing her of who he thought he was.

And yet . . .

And yet she could not rid herself of his voice, his face, his presence! Working on her like iron tools on hard earth, digging and hoeing and shoveling, breaking up her resistance with their sharp edges, with their implacable certainty. How had he managed that, when no one else could? Others had sought to breach her defenses, to convince her of their rightness, to twist her thinking to suit their own. No one had come close to succeeding, not since she was very little, when the Morgawr . . .

She did not finish the thought, not wanting to travel that road again just now. The boy was no Morgawr, but he might prove to be just as dangerous. His talent for magic was raw and unskilled, but that could change quickly enough. When it did, he would be a formidable adversary. She did not need another of those.

She stopped suddenly, startled by a realization that had escaped her earlier. His magic, rough and undisciplined as it was, had affected her already. *Infected her.* That was why she could not rid herself of his voice, why she could not banish it. She exhaled sharply, angry all over again. How could she have been so stupid! She used her own voice in the same way, as if speaking in ordinary conversation, but all the while working on the listener's thinking. She had let him talk to her because she had foolishly believed it made no difference what he said. She had missed the point. What he said didn't matter; how he said it, did! She had given him an opportunity he could not possibly have missed and he had used it!

She was shaking with rage. She looked back the way she had come. She was tempted to go back and deal with him. He was too much like her for comfort. Too similar. It was disquieting. It was cause for more concern than she had been willing to give it until now.

For a long time she stood, undecided. Then she shook off her hesitation. What lay ahead was what mattered most. The boy was helpless. He was not going to cause problems before she got back. He was not going to do anything but sit and wait.

Hitching up the Sword of Shannara once more, smoothing the angry wrinkles from her pale face, she adjusted the concealing cloak and cowl and continued on into the night.

NINETEEN

In a maelstrom of jetting fire and clashing steel, Walker fled through the corridors of Castledown. He was under attack from every quarter, fire threads lashing out at him from hidden ports and crevices, creepers converging in droves. They had found him only moments before, while he crept through what seemed an empty passageway, and now they were all about him. He had kept them at bay with the Druid fire, but only barely, and the circle was tightening as he tried to fight his way clear, dodging through tunnels and into chambers, out doorways and into corridors, taking every stairway that led up, desperate to regain the surface where he might gain his freedom. He no longer sought to find the books of magic. His plans for that had long since been abandoned. Fatigue and tension had eroded his resolve. He had not slept in so long he could not remember the last time. He had eaten nothing in what seemed like weeks. He kept going out of sheer determination, out of stubbornness, and out of certainty that if he stopped, he would die.

Flattened against a wall, he watched a cluster of fire threads crisscross the passageway ahead, blocking his advance. He could not understand it. Whatever he did seemed only to make things worse. No matter how careful he was, he could not elude his pursuers. It was as if they knew what he was going to do before he did it. That should not be possible. He was cloaked in Druid magic, which hid him from everything. His pursuers should not be able to see where he was or what he was about. He should have lost them long ago. Yet there they were, at every turn, at every juncture, waiting on him, striking at him, hemming him in.

He edged back through a doorway that led down a narrow corridor to a larger passage. For a moment, the fire threads were left behind. He took deep, life-giving breaths of air, his throat on fire from running, and his chest tight and raw. He tried to think what to do, but his mind would not respond. His thinking, once so precise and clear, had turned muddled and thick. Exhaustion and stress would have contributed to that, but it was something more. He simply could not reason, could not make his thoughts come together coherently, could not consider in a balanced way. He knew to run and he knew to defend himself, but beyond that his mind refused to function. It locked away all thoughts of the past, everything that had led to his present predicament; all of it had turned to vague, surreal memories. Nothing mattered to him anymore. Nothing but the here and now and his battle to stay alive.

He knew it was wrong. Not morally, but rationally—it was wrong. It made no sense that he should think that way. He fought against it, struggled to get a handle on the problem so that he could twist it around and make it right again, but nothing he attempted worked. He was adrift in the moment, with no sense that he could ever get himself out.

There was a stairway at the end of the larger corridor, and he raced to gain it ahead of his pursuers. It led upward toward fresh light, a brightness more genuine than the flameless lamps of his prison. He charged up the stairs into its glow, thinking that at last—at last!—he had found his way free. He gained the head of the stairs and found himself in a cavernous chamber with tall windows opening to blue sky and green trees. His fatigue and despair forgotten, he rushed to the closest one and peered out. There was a forest beyond the wall of the chamber, so close it seemed he could reach out and touch it. Somehow he had fled far enough that he was all the way to the edge of the city. He wheeled about, searching for a door. There was none to be found.

Behind him, he heard the clank and whir of creepers on the stairs. In desperation, he sent the Druid fire lancing into the glass windows. It struck their clear surface and bounced harmlessly away. Walker stared in disbelief. That wasn't possible. Glass could not deflect Druid magic. He moved quickly down the line of windows and tried again, on another pane, then a second and third. They, too, held fast.

The creepers appeared at the head of the stairs. He lashed out at them in fury and frustration, burning those closest, sending their scrap metal leavings back down the well into the others.

He caught sight of a deep alcove he had missed before. Nestled within its shadowy confines was a small wooden door. He moved quickly toward it, found its lock old and rusted, and burned it away with barely any effort. The door collapsed on its broken hinges, and he kicked it aside, pushing through to the fresh air and sunshine beyond.

A jungle rose all about him, vast and impenetrable, stretching away against the open sky like a wall. He plunged into it, heedless of what waited, knowing only that he had to get away from what followed. Thick grasses and tangled vines choked off any clear passage through the massive trees. Walker twisted and fought his way ahead, buoyed by the smell of rotted wood and leaves, by the warm glow of the sun and the feel of soft earth beneath his feet. Behind him, the city ruins disappeared from view, and he could no longer hear the creepers. He smiled faintly, relief surging through him. It would be all right. Whatever lay ahead couldn't be any worse than what he had escaped.

Then the ground heaved beneath his feet and sent him stumbling away. It settled and heaved again, as if an animal breathing. He tried to get clear of the motion, but it followed, tossing him from one side to the other, almost upending him. The trees began to shiver and the grasses to wave. Vines reached down, trying to grasp the Druid, to snare him, and he twisted away from them desperately. More waited, and more after that. He was forced to call up the Druid fire once more, burning them away to clear passage. The assault was relentless and purposeful, as if the jungle was determined to devour him. He could not understand it. There was no reason for the attack and no way to explain why or how it was happening.

He fought his way ahead, unable to do anything else, adrift in an undulating sea of green.

In a room of smoky glass, its walls papered with myriad panels of blinking lights and flashing red numbers, Ahren Elessedil and Ryer Ord Star stared in horror at the limp, motionless form of the missing Druid. He lay on a metal table, bound in place by padded straps fastened about his forehead, throat, waist, ankles, and the wrist of his good arm so that he could not move. Tubes ran to his arm and torso, attached to needles inserted into his veins. Liquids pulsed through the tubes, fed from bottles slung about metal hangers. One tube, the largest, was inserted into his mouth and attached to a bellows that worked slowly and steadily by his side. Machines

hemmed him in, all of them blinking with lights and humming with activity. Wires ran to his temples, eyes and throat,
heart and loins, even to the fingers of his hand, black snakes
ending in suckers fastened to his skin. The wires that trailed
from his fingers were attached to their tips by what looked
like the ends of gloves, cut away and fitted in place to the
second knuckle of each digit. The wires pulsed within clear
coverings as they ran from the Druid to a bank of clear glass
containers. Flashes of blue light surged into a reddish liquid,
which then flowed on through tubes into ports in the metal
walls and recycled back.

Ahren could not make himself move. What was being done
to Walker? He leaned closer to look at the Druid's face. Were
his eyes gouged out? Had his tongue been removed? He
peered down fearfully, but he could not tell. The Druid's eyes
were blinkered and his mouth clogged with the tube; everything was obscured. Ahren wanted to rip the tubes out of
Walker, to cut loose the straps that secured him. But he
sensed that he should not, that by doing so he might injure the
Druid. He couldn't be certain, couldn't know by just looking,
but he thought that the tubes might be keeping Walker alive.

He looked over at Ryer Ord Star, who was crying soundlessly beside him, her hands closed into fists and pressed
against her mouth. She was hunched over and shaking, and he
pulled her against him, trying to share with her a reassurance
he didn't feel. On the other side of the room, the multilimbed
metal attendant moved diligently from panel to panel, studying dials and numbers, touching switches and buttons. It
seemed to be monitoring things, perhaps studying the Druid's
condition, perhaps recording what was happening.

Which was what?

Still hidden away from Antrax and creepers alike within

the protective seal of the phoenix stone's magic, Ahren tried to make sense of it. There could be only one explanation. Antrax was siphoning off Walker's magic. It had lured the men and women of the *Jerle Shannara* to Castledown for precisely that purpose, just as it had lured Kael Elessedil and his Elven command all those years ago. Once Walker was a prisoner, trapped underground and rendered helpless, the milking had begun. Ahren would suffer the same fate, once Antrax found him; he would be drugged and bound and drained of life. He didn't know how the process worked, but he was certain of what it was.

The metal attendant finished its duties and wheeled back toward the door. Ahren pulled Ryer Ord Star out of its way and watched it disappear outside, leaving them alone. He looked around the room, at all the machinery. He could never hope to understand it, to learn enough about it to know how to free the Druid. The technology belonged to another era, and all knowledge of it had been lost for centuries. Ahren felt helpless in the face of that reality.

He bent close to the seer. "I don't know what to do," he admitted softly.

She brushed at her eyes with the heels of her palms, swallowed her tears, and stiffened her body. He released her, waiting to see what she would do—because it was clear she intended to do something.

She took his hand in hers. "Stay close to me. Don't let go."

He followed her as she hurried to where Walker lay, easing between the machines, stepping carefully over the wires and tubes. Ahren could see that the Druid was alive. He was breathing and there was a pulse in his neck. His face twitched, as if he dreamed. His skin was bloodless and damp with perspiration. Of course, he was alive. He would have to be alive to be of any use to Antrax.

The Elven Prince fought down his revulsion and fear. *Don't let me end up like this,* he prayed. *Let me die first.*

Ryer Ord Star looked over at him. "I have to try to reach him. I have to let him know I'm here."

Turning back to the Druid, she trailed the fingers of her free hand over his face and down his arm to his hand, then back again. She spent a long time doing that, staring down at him as she did so, looking impossibly small and frail amid the metal banks of machinery. Ahren held her hand tightly in his, remembering her instructions, knowing that he was her lifeline back from wherever she might have to go to try to save the Druid.

"Walker?" she whispered.

There was no response. There was no movement at all that communicated understanding. His chest rose and fell, his pulse beat, and his features twitched. Liquids flowed in and out of his body, and the wires flashed where they connected to the glass containers. He was lost to them, Ahren thought. Even Ryer Ord Star was not going to be able to get him back.

The seer straightened and brushed at loose strands of her silvery hair. Her face turned slightly toward him. "Let go of me, Ahren," she ordered. "But stay close."

Then she was climbing onto the metal table, easing carefully into the nest of wires and tubes, fitting her slender body to the Druid's, nestling against him as if a child clinging to a parent who slept. The Elf stayed so close to her that he could feel the heat of her body.

"Walker?" she said again. She lifted her hands to his cheeks and turned his head toward her own, snuggling into his shoulder. Her leg fitted itself over his, so that they were intertwined.

"Please, Walker," she begged, the words breaking on her lips like shattered glass.

There was no response. Walker lay as if his body had been drained of all but just enough life to keep death at bay.

"Please, Walker," the seer whispered again, her fingers moving across his face, her eyes closing in concentration. Tears ran down her cheeks once more.

Please, Ahren repeated the word in the silence of his mind, standing over them both, watching helplessly. *Come back to us.*

Walker fought his way through the writhing tentacles of the jungle vines and grasses for what seemed an endless amount of time, burning them away to clear a path, fighting for space to breathe, and still he seemed to get nowhere. The jungle was vast and unchanging, and he could find no distinguishing features to mark his passage. In the back of his mind, deep within the hazy thinking that drove him on, he realized that by escaping Castledown and gaining the jungle, he had merely exchanged one type of maze for another.

Having no other choice, he forced himself to go on. His body ached with fatigue; all he could think about now was finding a place to sleep. He was beginning to hallucinate, to hear voices, to see movement, and to feel the touch of shades that weren't there. The sensations emerged from the green of the jungle, from the emerald sea he sought to swim, reaching out to him. They grew steadily more insistent, so much so that they were soon overshadowing even the plants and trees of the jungle, causing some to fade and others to change their look entirely. Oddly, the attacks on him ended, the vines and grasses drew back, and the undulations of the earthen floor quieted.

He slowed his ragged advance and looked around, trying to decide what had happened.

He heard someone speak his name.

Walker? Please, Walker.

He recognized the voice, but it was a distant memory he could barely bring into focus. He grasped for it nevertheless, clutching at it as if it were a lifeline. The surging earth was still, and the deep green of the jungle had darkened to something hard and black, a night sky filled with blinking red stars. A face appeared, hazy and indistinct. It was a young woman's face, its thin, frail features framed with long, silver hair. She was so close to him he could feel the softness of her skin, and her breath upon his cheek was a feathery tickle. He felt her arms reach about him, cradling him. Where had she come from to find him, here in this jungle, in the middle of nowhere, a part of this madness?

Walker?

He remembered now. She was Ryer Ord Star. She was the seer he had brought with him on his voyage out of the Four Lands. Of all those who might have found him, she alone had managed to do so. He could not understand it.

Abruptly he was assailed by a rush of odd sensations, feelings that seemed foreign and wrong to him. At first, he could not identify them, could not trace their source or determine their purpose. He stood motionless and confused in the fading jungle and the descending night with its odd red stars, the young woman clinging to him, the world turned upside down.

Then everything changed in an instant. The jungle was gone. The green of the trees, the blue of the sky, the smell of rotted wood and leaves, the softness of the earth—his entire sense of place and time—disappeared. He was no longer standing upright, but was laid out upon a hard metal surface in a room filled with blinking lights and softly humming machines. Tubes ran from the machines to his body, pumping fluids. Wires attached to his skin snaked everywhere. He did not see this with his eyes. His eyes were blindfolded. He saw it instead with his mind, his Druid senses suddenly come awake from a deep, immobilizing sleep. He saw it the way a dream is seen, except that the dream was of the jungle, of the ruins and the creepers and the fire threads, of everything he had believed to be true.

He remembered then. He knew what had happened, what had been done to him. He understood it all, brought back into reality from drug-induced sleep and nightmarish dreams by the presence of the young woman who lay beside him, by her voice and her touch. She alone had reached him when no one else could. When he lay dying of the bramble poison after Shatterstone and she saved him with her empathic healing, a link had been forged between them. It bound them in an unintended way, through trading life for death and healing for suffering. So it was that she had sensed his need when even he was not aware of it, heard his subconscious call for help, come to him.

She stirred slightly, her fingers trailing down his face like velvet, her warmth infusing him with strength. She called his name softly, repeatedly, still reaching out to him, determined to bring him back from his prison.

When he felt her hand slide over his, cupping it, he lifted his fingers and pressed them against her palm in response.

Ahren missed the movement, his eyes on the Druid's face. But he saw Ryer Ord Star suddenly go very still, her body motionless. Even her fingers stopped tracing lines on Walker's face. He waited for her to speak, to begin moving again, to give him some indication of what was happening. But the seer had turned to stone.

"Ryer?" he whispered.

She made no response. She lay pressed against the Druid as if to become a part of him, her eyes closed and her breathing slowed so completely that he could barely detect it. He thought to touch her, but he was afraid to do so. Something had happened, and whatever it was, she was responding to it in the best way she could. He knew he must not disturb her. He must wait for her. He must be patient.

The minutes ticked by, endless and silent. He bent over her once, trying unsuccessfully to see what was happening. Then he stepped back a pace, as if a measure of distance might give him a better view. Nothing helped. He looked around at the banks of lights and switches, thinking the answer might lie there. If it did, he could not detect it. He looked out through the darkened glass to the cavernous room beyond, to the banks of spinning disks. Metal attendants moved down the brightly lit aisles, steady and purposeful in their labors. None looked in his direction or seemed in any way aware of what was happening in the room. He listened for a change in the sounds of the machinery, but there was none. Everything seemed the same.

Yet he knew it wasn't.

He did not think that he or Ryer Ord Star had been detected. The concealing haze of the phoenix stone still wrapped them both. If the magic had failed, there would have been some indication of it. If Ryer's presence at the Druid's side had been detected, an alarm would have sounded or flashed. Ahren hugged himself against the chill seeping through his body, against raw impatience and fear. What could he do? What should he do? He had to trust in the magic; it was all he had. That, and his sense of purpose in going there, in agreeing to do something that terrified him, persuaded by the seer that doing anything was better than giving up.

Yet it wasn't even *his* sense of purpose, he realized. It was *hers*. She was the one who had wanted to find Walker, who had insisted they find him, who had believed that they must do so if he was to have any chance of escaping Castledown. It seemed that she had been right, that if they hadn't come, Walker would have remained where he was, undiscovered, neither quite dead nor quite alive, neither one thing nor the other, but something in between, something terrible and repulsive and inhuman.

But having found the Druid, how were they supposed to save him? What were they supposed to do? Whatever it was, he did not know if they were equal to the task.

"Ryer?" he said again.

There was no response. What was she doing? He glanced around nervously, aware of how long they had lingered in the room, of how much they were risking. Sooner or later, the magic of the phoenix stone would fail and they would be discovered. Nothing could save them then. Bravery and sense of purpose would count for nothing.

"Ryer!" he hissed.

To his astonishment, she looked up at him, eyes snapping open as if she had come awake suddenly, unexpectedly. There was such unrestrained joy, such boundless hope in her gaze that he was momentarily speechless.

"He's come back!" she breathed softly, tears flooding her eyes. "He's free, Ahren!"

Free of what? Ahren wondered. He didn't look free. But the Elven Prince nodded and smiled as if what she said were so. He reached out to take her arm and help her stand again, but she motioned him away.

"No. Wait. We have to wait. It's not time yet." She closed her eyes and pressed herself tighter against the Druid. "He's going back in. To find Antrax. To find the books of magic. I have to stay with him while he does. I have to be here for him."

She went still again, eyes closing, breathing slowing, hands moving to the Druid's forehead, fingers pressing against his temples. "The machines don't know. We mustn't let them find out. I have to keep them from knowing. Stay close to me, Ahren."

He wasn't sure what she was talking about, what it was she was doing to help Walker, but the urgency in her plea was unmistakable. He stood beside her, beside the Druid, feeling alone and vulnerable and lost, looking down in helpless silence, and waited to find out.

TWENTY

Surfacing from the stream of drug-induced illusions that Antrax had used to control him, Walker drew on Ryer Ord Star's empathic strength to keep from going under again. He was swimming upstream against a raging tide, but at least he understood what had been done to him. His tumble down the tower chute after escaping the fire threads and the creepers had ended in his loss of consciousness and ultimate imprisonment. He had been drugged and immobilized immediately, then brought to the room to be strapped down and drained of his power. The method was clever and effective: let the victim think himself still free, make him fight to stay that way, and siphon off the power of the magic he used to do so. The tubes that ran to his body fed him liquids and drugs, keeping him alive but dreaming of a life that never was. If not for the seer, he would have remained that way until he died.

His understanding brought no comfort. Kael Elessedil must have spent his days the same way, using the Elfstones over and over, thinking himself free, unable ever to manage to do more than to keep running. He would have lived thirty years like that, until he had grown too old or weak or sick to be of any further use. Then Antrax would have sent him home again, using him one final time, to lure a replacement.

Except that Antrax had gotten lucky. It had succeeded in luring not one, but several, luring to his deadly trap not only the Druid, but Ahren Elessedil, Quentin Leah, and perhaps even Bek Ohmsford, all of whom had command of significant magic. Antrax would have known about them, of course. It would have known from what it had recorded of their efforts to recover the keys on the islands of Flay Creech, Shatterstone, and Mephitic. A machine that built machines, a creation of the technology of the Old World, it had known to test the capabilities of those it sought to snare. That was the reason for luring humans to its lair. That was the purpose for the underground prison. To steal their magic and convert it to the power that fed Antrax. To keep Antrax alive.

Yet perhaps that was only one reason and not the one that mattered most to it. Perhaps it was still searching for those who had created it, waiting for them to come back to claim the treasure they had left it to guard. The books of the Old World. The secrets of another time.

How did he know that? Unconscious and dreaming, how could he know? He knew it in part from what he had deciphered from the map, written in a language the Druid Histories still recorded. He knew it in part from what Ryer Ord Star had communicated to him in bringing him back from his slumber, her words and thoughts revealing his situation. He knew it in part from what he could deduce from the use of the machinery that immobilized and drugged him. He knew it finally from what he was able to intuit. It was enough to keep him from slipping back into his prison, to keep him fixed on what he must do if he was to complete his task in going there—the task that had cost the lives of so many of his companions and might yet, if he was not swift and sure and focused enough, cost him his.

He gathered himself within his body, using his magic to summon his shade and set it free, the way Cogline had done years ago in entering lost Paranor. It was what Allanon had done in his time. There was danger in it. If his body should die, his shade was lost. If he strayed too far or allowed himself to be trapped outside his body, he might never get back again. Yet it was a gamble he must take. He could not free his body from the wires and tubes that linked it to Antrax without triggering alarms that would bring the creepers. There was no reason to free himself if he did not know what to do to stay free. As a shade, he could explore Castledown without Antrax being any the wiser. Ryer Ord Star would keep his body strong and alive and functioning, would keep the machines deceived as to what was happening. She would feed him enough of her empathic healing power to prevent him from slipping back into the deadening dreams. So long as she could do so, nothing would seem any different. So long as the magic of the phoenix stone cloaked the seer, even the eyes of Antrax could not detect her presence. Walker's magic would continue to feed out in small increments, reduced by the absence of real thought, responding out of reflex only. Antrax would not be concerned at the decline in his magic's output right away. Not even for several hours, should it take that long. Time was relative in Castledown. Antrax had lived for more than twenty-five hundred years. A few hours were nothing.

Walker did not consider further what he must do. He went out from his body as a shade, tracking the wires that fed into it back to their source. Penetrating metal, glass, and stone as if they were air, he sped through the walls of the keep, a silent and invisible presence. He stayed alert for Antrax all the while, wanting to keep it from that room where his body lay, from examining him too closely, from finding out the truth. He surged down conduits and through clusters of wires and metal pieces that conducted electricity and thought, power garnered from magic and converted to use. He seethed at the knowledge of what had been done to the men and women who had been lured there, but stayed focused on what was needed to stop it from happening again.

He found the relays for the security system quickly enough. Eyes of glass watched from ceilings all through the safehold, mechanical orbs that let Antrax view everything. But of what use were they? Antrax was a machine; it did not need eyes. The eyes, Walker realized with a start, were for the humans who had once controlled Antrax. They served no other purpose now. Antrax would use a more sophisticated system— one of touch and feel and sound and perhaps body heat. Only magic would thwart it, and perhaps not all magic at that.

Where did Antrax dwell within this vast complex?

Where did all the information feed?

He tracked it for a time, down lines and through chambers, along corridors and around corners. But one set of relays led to another. One bank of machines was tied to a second. Lines of power opened into new lines, and there was no end of them. Nothing to tell him where to find the start and finish of things.

He tried quieting himself and tracking Antrax by feel. It was not difficult to do. But once again, there seemed to be no start or finish. Antrax was vast and sprawling. It was everywhere at once, all about and seeping through, endless and immutable. Antrax was the safehold of Castledown; spread in equal parts throughout, there was no part of the keep that it did not inhabit. It warded everything at once.

Walker did not waver from his goal. He had come too far to

give up. There was too much at stake and no one else who could do what was needed. *Not even . . .*

He hesitated. The words were bitter with realities he did not want to face.

Yet what choice did he have?

He finished the sentence in a rush. *Not even her.*

He must change his thinking, he acknowledged in what, for some, might have been considered an admission of defeat. But Druids dealt with neither victory nor defeat, but with reality and truth. What was fated could not be denigrated or altered by imposition of moral judgment. It was not his mandate. Druids served a higher cause, the preservation and advancement of Mankind and the Races. The Great Wars had reduced civilization to ruins and humans to animals. That must not happen again. The Druid Council had been formed in the time of Galaphile to see that it could not, and every Druid since had worked in furtherance of that end.

But what could he accomplish in the time that remained to him? There, in that nightmarish place, with only a few to stand beside him, with so much at stake? What, that would give life to the bargain he had struck with Allardon Elessedil all those months ago?

Time was slipping away, time he could not afford to waste. He was taking the wrong approach to the business, he decided. His search for answers was leading him in the wrong direction. It was not Antrax that had brought him to Castledown in the first place. Antrax was a secondary concern. It was the treasure Antrax warded that mattered, that could change everything.

He must look for the books of magic.

* * *

Pervasive in presence and reach, Antrax sprawled in contented solitude across the vast complex of its underground kingdom, monitoring its sensors and readouts, fulfilling functions its creators had programmed. With the blind certainty of artificial intelligence, it relied on the reassurance of constant input and an unchanging environment. For not quite three thousand years, it had maintained its world through its preassigned functions and unswerving vigilance. Any possibility of disruption brought a swift response.

Such a possibility had just drawn Antrax's attention. It was still tiny and signified nothing as yet, but it was there nevertheless. It wasn't a wave so much as a ripple in the lines of power, undetectable by the warning systems that warded Castledown, virtually immeasurable as an electronic current denoting life, more like a shadow that changed light to dark and dropped the temperature a fraction of a degree. Antrax was alerted to the unexplained presence mostly because it was still searching for two of the intruders whose magic it coveted. While it held one imprisoned in dreams and fantasies, draining it of the power it possessed, assimilating it into Castledown's power cells, the others continued to elude it. Its wronk still hunted the second, tracking it relentlessly through the forest that bordered Castledown. The readouts were steady and unchanged, so there could be no question that the wronk was still functioning properly. It would have its quarry before long.

The third, on the other hand, was proving to be an enigma that Antrax was not able to solve. That one had followed the metal probe into Castledown's warren without resistance, but then something had happened to startle it, and it had bolted. Since then, it had managed to hide itself despite everything

Antrax had done to find it. Heat and movement sensors, pressure pads, trip ports, and sound detectors had failed to uncover it. Lasers and metal probes had scoured the corridors and chambers of the complex without result. It was possible that it had escaped Castledown entirely, but there was nothing to confirm that. Antrax wanted this one in particular because it was needed to replace the intruder that had failed and been sent back as a lure. No other was suited for the drawing down of power from the blue stones. Only the one who was missing.

Nothing had ever evaded Antrax for so long. Could it be that the odd ripple it felt in the lines of power was the third intruder, changed in form? Did it possess such power, such adaptability, when the other had not? Evolution was a fact of life, of the human condition, so perhaps it was so.

Antrax extended itself through its sensors and detectors, through all its communicators, searching. It went everywhere at once, monitoring readouts. Its examination took a long time, but time was something of which it had plenty. It explored the skin of its walls and floors and ceilings as would a living creature, making certain it was whole and free of clinging debris and secreting, burrowing minutiae.

Nothing revealed itself.

All of its metal probes responded to its inquiries regarding their operability. None were broken or disrupted, where such would signal a foreign presence. Nor did the lasers register any problem. Even the vast complex that housed the recordings of the creators hummed steadily along in its transference of information from one storage unit to another, keeping fresh, keeping whole. No system failed to respond when checked. All was as it should be.

Yet something was out of place.

Antrax took readings on the intruder housed in Extraction Chamber Three. The expulsion of power into the cells was noticeably down, but the intruder was still strapped in place and the wires that monitored its bodily functions had not been tampered with. Heat sensors indicated normal temperature readings for the room and no other presence. His prisoner seemed to be resting, asleep perhaps, though that rarely happened with the extraction techniques used by Antrax. Antrax paused to consider the readings more closely. The expected bursts of power in response to perceived threats had diminished noticeably. But that could be a result of exhaustion or even the extraction machine's determination of the subject's need for a respite. Draining off power was a delicate process, requiring a careful monitoring of the mental and emotional condition of the victim. Antrax had learned that humans were creatures of infinite possibility if kept whole. But flesh and blood were not as durable as metal. The creators had demonstrated that.

Sometimes Antrax wished the creators would return, though less so than in the beginning. At first, it had felt they must, that the creators were essential to its ultimate survival. Later, it had discovered how well it could survive on its own. Later still, the importance of the creators had diminished to such a degree that it saw them as unnecessary.

Yet it would house and protect their recordings, awaiting their return, because that was its mandate and prime directive. Survival was assured so long as there were sources of power to draw upon and ways to gain control over them. For Antrax, that was not so difficult a task. If not one way, then another. If not by securing them here, then by tracking them there.

After all, even for an artificial intelligence of its size and capacity, there were ways to leave Castledown.

Antrax took a moment longer to consider the readouts on its prisoner, and then spun slowly back through its network of living metal threads, searching.

Cloaked in the magic of the phoenix stone, wrapped in the blanket of his thoughts, Ahren Elessedil stood close to the table on which Walker and Ryer Ord Star lay entwined. He had been waiting and watching for what seemed like an impossibly long time, and he was growing restless. Something was nudging at him, a sense of dissatisfaction with his role as observer, a feeling of opportunity slipping away. He needed to be *doing* something.

Yet the seer had told him to wait. To keep watch. To serve as her lifeline to the Druid.

He stared down at her, amazed anew at what he saw. Her face was so calm, her features radiant. She was curled tightly against the Druid, who continued to breathe and occasionally to twitch as before, gone somewhere inside himself to accomplish whatever tasks he had determined were necessary to get free of Antrax. Perhaps the seer had gone with him. Perhaps she was only giving him the strength she said he so desperately needed. That they were joined was obvious—a joining that favored both, but Ryer Ord Star in particular.

She had found what she had come searching for.

He mulled that over for a moment, and in doing so he was reminded of the purpose of the phoenix stone. To help those who were lost to find their way back—not just from what they could not see with their eyes, but from what they could not find with their hearts. Those were the words the King of the Silver River had spoken to Bek Rowe.

*To show you the way back from dark places into which you
have strayed. To show you the way forward through dark
places into which you must go.*

Ahren Elessedil looked up suddenly, staring at nothing.
Understanding flooded through him as he realized for the
first time what those words meant. Who was more lost than
the seer or himself? Who had strayed farther? Not just physically, but emotionally. She had betrayed them all by agreeing
to act as a spy for the Ilse Witch. He had betrayed his coun-
trymen by abandoning them when they needed him most.
She was a traitor and he a coward. Those were the dark places
into which they had wandered and from which they sought to
return. In their hearts, they were lost.

He had not thought on his cowardice for some time, perhaps not allowing himself, perhaps simply caught up in what
was happening within Castledown. But he would not become
whole again until he had found a way to make amends for
what he had done.

What would that take?

He knew at once. He looked down at the seer, pressed
against the man she had betrayed. Having found her way back
from the wilderness to give him the help he needed and to
make herself whole in the process, she was at peace. The
magic of the phoenix stone had given her that. It would do
the same for him, if he let it. He could not bring to life those
he had abandoned. But he could give them back their legacy.

Phoenix stone. The reason for the name was not that the
stone could be reborn from the ashes of its destruction, but
that the user could. That was the magic's true purpose—to
make Ahren whole again, to provide him with new life. That
was what it had done for Ryer Ord Star in leading her to
Walker. Ahren could have that, as well, but he must first do

what the stone required—what it had already required of the seer. He must let the magic take him into the dark place where he would find redemption and, thereby, his way back from the cowardice that had crippled him.

He took a deep breath and exhaled. He must do for his people what he had pledged to do in coming on the voyage. He must do for his dead companions what they could not. He must recover the lost Elfstones.

He could feel the magic of the phoenix stone nudging him in that direction, a subtle hint of dissatisfaction, of need unfulfilled, of realization that his rebirth was not yet complete. He had come with Ryer Ord Star to find and aid Walker because that was what the magic had required of her. But what the magic required of him was to find the Stones. What it demanded was that he walk into the trap that Antrax had set for him, confront and overcome it, and retrieve the missing talismans.

Now.

While there was still time.

He could not explain it, but he could feel it as surely as he could feel the weight of the responsibility he was proposing to accept. Time was slipping away, and when it was gone his chance at retrieving the Elfstones and thereby his chance to be made whole again would be gone, as well. A confrontation between Walker and Antrax loomed, a resolution of the latter's attempt at destroying the Druid and his companions. It would not wait, and it could not be avoided.

For a moment, he was paralyzed by fear. He was so shattered by the feeling that he did not think he could get past it. How could he even contemplate the undertaking? What chance did he have against Antrax and his devices? Fire threads and creepers would be waiting, machines like the ones that had overwhelmed Walker. He lacked any weapons to combat them, any of sufficient strength or capability to offer him even the slightest chance of success. He was alone and impossibly vulnerable.

What made him think he wouldn't run again?

He broke away from his fear, wrenching free as he might from quicksand that threatened to swallow him. It didn't matter what the odds were. He was going. He had to. He reached down for Ryer Ord Star and placed his hand over hers. Her warmth infused him, and although she did not respond to his touch, he told himself that somehow she knew whose it was. He was withdrawing the protective mantle of his magic from her shoulders, breaking the link that bound them. He did not know what that would mean for her, what it would do to her chances for helping Walker. He knew only that the magic was telling him to go, and he must do what it asked of him.

He stepped away from her, backing toward the door through which they had entered. He watched the hazy shroud of the magic stretch and then divide, a little of it clinging to them both, diminished, but still functional. It was the best he could hope for. It was all he could ask.

Good luck to you, Ryer, he thought. *Good luck to us both.*

Then he turned away, passed back out through the doorway, and was gone.

TWENTY-ONE

Insubstantial and ethereal as air, Walker began his search for the books of magic.

From the first, from the moment he had translated the writings on the map carried back to the Four Lands from Castledown by a dying Kael Elessedil, he had kept the truth about the books to himself. He did so in part to protect against attempts by others to interfere with his plans to undertake their recovery. The Ilse Witch had reached the dying Elven Prince before him and discovered what was at stake. Her subsequent interference had forced him to alter his plans time and again. So in that regard he had failed. But he had also kept the truth to himself to persuade Allardon Elessedil to his cause, and in that he had been more successful. If he was honest with himself, he would admit that he had hidden the truth in order to persuade the crew of the *Jerle Shannara* to accompany him. What he knew of the books and the consequences of reintroducing them to the Races was too overwhelming for others to deal with.

Nothing was as simple as everyone thought, the Ilse Witch included. All of them believed what Antrax had allowed Kael Elessedil to believe—that the books really were a compilation of magic's uses. They weren't. It was an easy enough deduction if you were schooled in the history of the Old World. It was apparent if you considered what Castledown really was—a storehouse for knowledge accumulated in a time and place in which magic was virtually unknown and almost never used. The Old World was a world of science, one in which no one had possessed magic since the time of Faerie; what had survived that world had been salvaged by the Elves, but they had lost virtually everything through neglect. A place like Castledown wouldn't house books of real magic; it would house books of learning—of science, history, and culture.

Once, long ago, it would have been called a library.

This was not to say that the books were unimportant because they did not contain spells and conjuring and the like. In truth, they were more important for being what they were—a compilation of everything that had fueled life in the Old World, when power was generated through the application of science to nature. What the books contained was so valuable, so rich in possibility, that there was no way to measure its potential impact on the Four Lands. But that impact could take any number of forms, some constructive, some destructive. The science that had sustained the Old World would all be recorded in the library. Everything that had advanced that civilization would be set down. But everything that had destroyed it would be set down, as well—the secrets of power with their immense destructive capabilities and the formulas for building weapons that could level entire cities the size of Castledown.

Since he had first understood that, the questions in Walker's mind had always been the same. How much of that information should be reintroduced into the world? How many of its secrets should be placed back into the hands of the Races? How much of what had led to the destruction of civilization and the reduction of Mankind to the level of animals should he entrust to the descendants of the survivors?

He didn't know. He supposed it depended on what he found, and so he had struck his bargain with Allardon Elessedil. He would share what he found with the Elves, but only that part that the Elves could make use of or that dealt with magic that was their heritage. He expected that once the books were recovered, nothing in them would offer secrets of magic that would be of any use to the Elves. He did not think they could even read them. To decipher their meaning would take a scholar versed in ancient languages, one who possessed reference books that would facilitate the necessary translations. Only the Druids possessed those—which meant, just then, only him.

But one day, if all went as he hoped, that would change. One day, a Druid Council would again come into being.

As he moved through the myriad chambers and corridors of Castledown in a wide, sweeping search, he mulled his options. There would be too many books for him to carry out. He would have to choose. A handful only, he knew, even with Ryer Ord Star and Ahren Elessedil to help him. Antrax would react too quickly to permit them to take more. He might destroy Antrax; he would at least have to try to render it less of a threat. But if he attacked the keeper, there was a fair chance the library would be lost in the process. Disabling Antrax meant cutting off its power source. Accomplishing that probably meant shutting down whatever systems protected the books, as well. The books would be ancient and fragile, so delicate that any change in their environment might cause them to fall apart. Finding them was one thing; protecting them long enough for them to be of use was another. His magic could help salvage a few, but only a few. He would have to choose. More important, he would have to choose wisely.

He was reminded of a game children played. If you were to be shut away by yourself somewhere and could take with you only a handful of possessions, which ones would you choose? It was much the same choice he faced. Which books of all those available were most important? Which ones would most benefit the world he lived in and the people he sought to help? Which ones would enable the Druids to most ease the pain and suffering of the human condition? Books of healing and cures? Books of agriculture? Books of construction? Books of the Old World's history? Which?

He did not like having to make the choice. He would have preferred to let someone else make it, had there been someone else. Whatever he decided, whichever books he chose, he would make mistakes. It was inevitable. He could not see the future, and to some extent the future would determine what knowledge was necessary to navigate its uncharted waters. No one could know what would be needed until the time arrived. It was equally possible that what he chose would be misused in some way, causing damage and destruction of the sort he was trying so desperately to avoid.

He needed Ryer Ord Star's gift of future sight, but only if he could wield it with a craftsman's skill. It wouldn't be enough to have glimpses of the future. It wouldn't help to take events out of context or in a haphazard fashion. A comprehensive look was needed if future sight was to be of any use.

Even then, he admitted, the odds against recognizing what was both important and necessary were enormous. The future was painted on a canvas of infinite reach; it entailed too many connections and joinings. Change one and you changed others. No amount of insight would enable a single individual to decipher it all.

Only the Word could know, and even that was not given to Mankind as truth.

His search went on, the minutes slipping away, time shedding them like leaves at the change of seasons. Though he searched diligently, he could not find the library. He went everywhere in Castledown, through all its vast chambers and down all its long corridors, and still the books eluded him. He was growing tired, and he knew he could not maintain his shade form much longer. Yet he needed to know where the books were kept if he was to reach them once he returned to his body. If he had to search for them once he cut himself loose from Antrax, he was doomed to fail. Antrax would know what had happened, and there would not be enough time to do anything but escape. He must find the books quickly and determine how to reach them.

In the end, he used a simple artifice to solve the problem. He put himself in the minds of the men and women who had built Castledown and created Antrax and asked how they would have gone about warding their treasure. The answer wasn't so difficult. The books would be housed where the defenses were strongest and most sophisticated, but would cause the least amount of damage should an intruder gain entry. On the surface of Castledown, the defenses were brutal and indiscriminate. Whatever breached them was cut apart. Beneath the surface, where the books were housed, the defenses would be of a different sort. Fire threads and creepers would not be used. Something subtler would be employed.

The Druid changed his way of thinking and began his search anew. As he did so, he was reminded of the strange keys that had lured him to Castledown. He had thought them keys of the sort he was familiar with, metal implements used for unlocking doors. But they had taken a different form than he had expected. Tools of a technological age, they still functioned as keys, but used different principles in doing so. Flat rectangles, they had caused the locks they opened to respond through impulses generated by tiny power cells.

Could it be, he wondered suddenly, that the books had been converted to another form, as well?

A suspicion as cold and deadening as winter night settled through him. He had gotten it all right save for one thing only. He sped through the chambers and corridors, intent on a specific destination, knowing deep inside that his worst fears were about to be realized and that he could do nothing to prevent it. He retraced his route toward the place of his imprisonment, aware of a quickening in Ryer Ord Star's pulse at his approach, triggered by her mistaken belief that he had succeeded in what he had set out to do and was returning. He blanked out that part of his awareness, making no response to her unspoken inquiry, needing her strength for just a little longer.

When he reached the cavernous chamber just outside the smaller one in which his body lay, he paused. Slowly and carefully, he began sweeping the room with his Druid senses, reaching into the banks of machinery with their spinning silver disks. In silent appraisal, he roamed through the tall metal housings, touching here and there with his mind, listening and deciphering. He could hear voices talking, words being spoken, ideas and recitations being repeated, transferred from one space to another, from a first storage unit to a second. He knew at once that he had found what he was looking for. He knew, as well, that it was useless to have done so.

His disappointment approached despair. There were no

books, not of paper and ink. The library existed, but it was a library of the sort that was probably common to its time, that had transcended and replaced the libraries of old. All the knowledge of books had been transcribed onto metal disks and stored in machines. There was no way to make use of it elsewhere without the technology to translate the disks. To decipher what was here, it would be necessary to search the storage units and listen to what was recorded. It would take an enormous amount of time to do that—far more than the Druid could muster.

Even in his shade form, Walker's reaction to his failure was physical. A visceral pain that was deep and hard and cutting knifed through him. He had come all that way, expending time and energy and lives, only to discover that it was for nothing. The library was useless. The books were disks that might as well be drawings on sand at a shore's edge. None of the millions of words of knowledge contained in this safehold could be salvaged unless he could find a way to disable Antrax without shutting down the power sources that fueled them both. He had already analyzed the impossibility of accomplishing that. The power sources that enabled both were linked inextricably. He had scanned them in his travels and found them joined in a way that would not permit separation. Antrax was the heart of the safehold and its treasure.

He listened absently to the steady stream of words as they were transferred from one unit to another, a restoring of some sort, a process intended to keep them fresh and new, even with the passage of time, even after nearly three thousand years. It was all there, everything out of the Old World, the whole of its knowledge in one place, his for the taking—yet just out of reach.

His bitterness was palpable. This journey couldn't have

been for nothing. He couldn't bear that. He wouldn't tolerate it.

He'd had all the choices in the world—too many to consider—when faced with the possibility that the books of the library could be his; suddenly his choices were reduced to one. He saw it instantly, a single chance, one so extreme that on initial consideration he nearly dismissed it out of hand. Yet it reached out to him, revealing how time and an ironic dovetailing of circumstance and fate sometimes gave birth to the impossible.

A hundred and thirty years ago, when he had gone to Eldwist and recovered the Black Elfstone, when he had made his decision to become the first of the new Druids and thereby bring back lost Paranor, he had encountered a similar choice. No, he corrected abruptly, not a similar choice—the same choice. It was his to make because there was no one else to make it. It was his to make because he alone had the means to do so.

He was reminded anew of Allanon's words at the Hadeshorn, all those months ago. Of all the things he wished to accomplish on undertaking this journey, the shade had told him, he would be permitted only one.

A sense of irony and amazement filled him. Life was so mysterious and quixotic. It was an infinite maze, but ultimately there was only one right path for each human who sought to navigate its twisting corridors.

He released his grip on the machines and their disks, withdrawing into himself, letting go of all his hopes and expectations save the one he believed he might still realize. Abandoning his shade and resuming habitation of his corporeal form, he swept aside the last fragments of his disappointment and prepared to wake Ryer Ord Star.

* * *

Aboveground, at the edge of the maze, the Ilse Witch paused to look about. It was well after midnight, the sky clouded and black, the air thick and warm and smelling of rain. It was so dark in the absence of moon and stars that even with her keen eyesight, she could barely distinguish the buildings and walls of the surrounding ruins. Castledown's surface felt like a tomb. She had seen nothing move since she entered from the forest. Silence lay over everything in a heavy blanket, masking what she knew to be hiding in wait.

She had been wise not to bring Cree Bega or any of his Mwellrets for support. In that situation, they would be underfoot, a hindrance to her progress. More important, they would pose a threat; she no longer trusted them with her safety, despite the assurances of the Morgawr and their pledge to obey her. She could feel their resentment and anger every time she was in their presence. They hated and feared her. Sooner or later, they would try to eliminate her. It would be necessary for her to eliminate them first, but that was a task she was not yet ready to undertake. Until the Druid and his followers were accounted for and she had possession of the books of magic, she had need of the Mwellrets and their peculiar skills. But she didn't want them watching her back.

She shifted the weight of the Sword of Shannara where it hung from its strap across her shoulder. She wished she had left it behind, but she had been reluctant to leave it within reach of either the boy or the Mwellrets. She had considered hiding it, but was fearful it might be found. If real, it was a powerful magic, and she wanted it for herself. So she was stuck with hauling it about until the business was finished and she was on her way home. She supposed it was a small price to pay for the uses it might later serve, but she could not get past the resentment at having to endure the ache it caused her shoulders.

Unslinging the sword, she laid it on the ground and stretched her arms over her head. She had not slept for a while, and although sleep was not particularly important to her physical well-being, she felt mentally drained. It was that boy, in part, with his incessant chatter and clever reasoning, trying to persuade her to his cause, trying to trick her. Sparring with him had taken more out of her than she had realized. He was relentless in his insistence of who and what he was, and she found that fighting him off had wearied her.

She yawned. Sleep would give her mind and body rest, but there would be no sleep that night. Instead, she must find a way into Castledown, retrieve the books of magic, and avoid a confrontation with the Druid in the process.

It was a much different mandate than before, she thought ironically, when she had determined to kill Walker. But things had changed, as things had a way of doing.

She picked up the sword and fitted it back across her shoulders, adjusting its weight to gain a measure of comfort. She stood quietly for a time, her gray robes hanging loosely from her slender form, her hood drawn back, her pale face lifted slightly as she concentrated on what lay ahead. Her eyes closed, and she sent the magic of her wishsong into the labyrinth of the ruins. It was there that the Druid had disappeared underground. It was there that the Mwellrets had encountered the creepers. There would be an entrance somewhere close, probably more than one. She need only find it. The rest would be child's play.

It did not take long to accomplish her goal. There were trapdoors and hidden entryways everywhere, some larger than others, all leading down ramps or steps to the safehold.

She used her song to cloak herself in the shape and feel of the maze, cold metal plates and fastenings, wire and machines. Her eyes opened once more. She studied the darkness ahead, then walked in. No creepers or fire threads appeared. She didn't expect them to. When she used the wishsong in that way, it gave her the feel and appearance of whatever lay around her. Only the magic was detectable, and only by something that could recognize its presence.

She did not take a subtle approach to gaining entry; the longer she took, the more risk she assumed. A safehold built in the Old World would employ technology she did not understand. One safeguard or another would detect her eventually. It was best not to give it a chance to do so.

She placed herself against a wall next to one of the larger hidden doors and used her magic to shatter a smaller port across the way. Almost instantly, the door she stood beside slid open and creepers wheeled into view. She kept herself concealed, letting them move quickly past, then froze the last, holding it in place, breaking down its systems as she swiftly recorded its look and feel, both within and without. It took her only seconds, then she was through the door and inside the keep.

There were lights inside, flameless lamps attached to the walls of a handful of corridors that fanned out from an atrium in which dozens of creepers stood frozen in racks. She held herself motionless for a few seconds, testing her new disguise, waiting to see if there would be a reaction to her presence. There wasn't. She gave it a few seconds more, then started ahead.

She passed down the corridors of Castledown without incident, long robes rustling softly, her presence wrapped in the look and feel of a creeper. In a place where only machines had functioned for more than twenty-five hundred years, anything of flesh and blood would trigger an alarm instantly. There would be devices that would indicate a human presence either through readings of weight or body heat or even a tracing of form. She had already spied the glass eyes that peered out of their ceiling niches and felt the presence of the pressure plates. The machines would use other methods, as well, but whatever they were, she could thwart them by disguising her look, changing her weight, and hiding her body temperature. Every warning system would register her as a creeper. Even the Druid couldn't manage that.

Yet she did not allow herself to grow overconfident or drop her guard. There was still the possibility that whatever warded Castledown possessed the ability to track her use of magic, to detect its presence, and to penetrate her subterfuge. If that were to happen, she would have to take evasive action, and quickly. She hoped that her enemy was otherwise occupied, perhaps with Walker. She hoped that the magic she used was too small to detect. She hoped, mainly, that she could accomplish her goals quickly enough that she would be gone before there was a chance to discover that she had ever come in.

She passed dozens of other creepers, all of whom ignored her. Each seemed to have a purpose in mind, but she could not tell what it was. She moved through a maze of chambers and hallways of all shapes and sizes, some empty, some crammed with machinery and materials. She didn't know what was housed there, and she didn't care. She was looking for the books of magic and she was not finding them. Nothing else mattered to her. She could not afford the time necessary to undertake a scavenger hunt.

Ahead, the sound of machinery rose out of the silence, a low and steady thrumming. It penetrated even the steel of the walls; it caused the floor beneath her feet to vibrate. She paused, considering. What she was hearing was huge, a piece of machinery or perhaps several pieces that dwarfed anything she had encountered and performed a function central to the operation of the safehold. It was probably a power plant, but it might have something to do with the protection of the books of magic. She should have a look.

She had not taken another ten steps when all the alarms went off at once.

Ryer Ord Star.

Walker felt her stir against him, waking slowly from the trance into which she had gone to provide him with her empathic strength. Her fingers, resting against his temples, slid down his cheeks like tears.

Come awake, young seer.

He was speaking to her with his mind, a silent summoning that only they could hear. He was back within his body, come out of the drugs and dreams, returned from his shadow form, aware once more of his flesh and blood and the condition in which he had been placed. It was time to free himself of the machines and Antrax. But he must do so carefully, and he could not manage it alone.

Listen to me.

She was awake now, her eyes open, her hands bracing her body as she lifted away from him. "Walker?"

Don't speak. Just listen. Do what I say. Do it quickly. Take the blindfold from my eyes and the breathing tube from my mouth.

She did as she was told, her hands fluttering about his face like small moths. He could feel the expansion and contraction of her lungs as she pressed back against him.

Now release the straps that bind my wrists and ankles, then my neck and forehead and waist. Do it in that order. Do not disturb the wires attached to me. Do not knock them loose.

It took her longer to comply; the straps were fastened with catches of a kind she had never seen and did not understand. They were not formed of metal, but of hard plastic, and she fumbled with them before deciphering their workings. His release went quickly after that as, one by one, the straps fell away.

She was back beside him, leaning close. He opened his eyes for the first time and looked at her. Her wan childlike face, framed by its curtain of silvery hair, broke into a broad smile, and tears filled her eyes. Traces of a cloaking magic still clung to her slender form, but they were fading. How had she gotten to him? Where had she found the magic to do so?

Walker, she mouthed silently.

He scanned himself in an effort to determine what must happen next, trying to decide the right order for the removal of his remaining constraints, knowing that when he released them, alarms would certainly sound.

Block open the door to the room so that when the alarms to the monitoring machines are triggered, Antrax cannot lock us in.

She slipped agilely through the nest of wires still attached to his body, found a low, single-door cabinet on wheels, and rolled it into the opening between the door and the jamb and wedged it securely in place.

Then she was back beside him.

Take the needles from my arm and body. Let them hang loose from their fastenings.

She pulled away the tape that secured the needles, then

slipped them from his veins. She touched the punctures with her cool fingers, healing the wounds, providing him with new strength. Her ability to give of her empathic self seemed boundless. She shuddered once at the contact, held her fingers steady for a moment, and then lifted her hands away.

Alarms would be going off; Antrax would know the equipment that drugged and milked him had malfunctioned in some way. He would have to act fast. He sat up on the metal table, finding his strength diminished and his head spinning. The drugs had left him weak and lethargic, but he could still function. He must. He began ripping free the suckers that fastened the monitoring wires to his body. They came away easily, and in seconds none remained but the five that ran to the gloved tips of his fingers. He left those in place. He had a use for them.

Lights were flashing everywhere on the panels of instruments that ringed his bed. He felt a shift in the atmosphere of the chamber as Antrax descended swiftly to correct what had happened. Walker rose unsteadily, the girl supporting him as he gathered his robes and moved away from the table. He walked to where the wires that ran from his fingertips were bunched into a metal plug that, in turn, was fastened into the containers of reddish liquid. He pulled the plug from its sheath and steered it into an identical opening in one of the wall panels marked with brilliant red symbols.

Walker knew what the symbols read. It was the same language in which the map had been lettered, the language from the Old World he had deciphered in the Druid Histories.

He knew, as well, where the lines of the second sheath ran. He had explored them well in his out-of-body travels, tracing them to their source.

Castledown's main warning system.

Before Antrax could act to prevent it, he sent a burst of Druid fire through the central lines and into all the auxiliaries and set off all the alarms at once.

"Time to be going," he whispered to himself, wheeling Ryer Ord Star toward the blocked entry.

He had only a few minutes to do what was needed.

TWENTY-TWO

Aboard *Black Moclips*, Bek Ohmsford waited patiently for deliverance. He didn't much care what form it took, only that it come soon. He wasn't panicked yet, but he could feel it sneaking up on him. He was imprisoned in an aft hold, a storeroom containing replacement parts and supplies—ambient-light sails, radian draws, diapson crystals, cheese blocks, and water barrels. Shadows cloaked everything in layers of darkness. The room was not large, but even by the light from the candle atop the barrel next to him, he could only barely make out the Mwellret who kept watch from the far side of the room. Bek was tethered to the wall by three feet of chain locked about one ankle. A length of rope bound his hands in front of him and ran down through the chain so that he could not lift his arms above his waist. He was gagged, as well, although that was probably overkill since Grianne had already stolen his voice and rendered him mute.

Leaving nothing to chance, she had taken the Sword of Shannara from him, as well. When she returned, she expected to find him a prisoner still. While he had no real reason to think things would turn out any other way, he had nothing better to do with his time than to visualize the possibility. He was not encouraged. He was a prisoner aboard an airship full of Mwellrets and Federation soldiers. He had no weapons. His friends were dead or scattered. Deliverance in any form would have a hard time finding him under such circumstances.

Moonlight streamed through an open portal to one side, the only breathing hole in the room, the only source of fresh air. As clouds passed across the face of the moon, the light darkened and brightened by turns, changing the depth of the shadows, allowing him small glimpses of his silent jailer. Now and then, the Mwellret would shift position, and a small rustling of cloth and reptilian skin would reveal his otherwise nearly invisible presence. He never spoke. He was under orders not to. The boy had heard his sister give the order. No one was to speak to him. He was to be given water, but no food. He was not to be approached otherwise. He was not to be allowed out. He was not to be taken off the chain, even for a moment. He was to be left where he was until she returned.

Seated on the hard plank flooring of the ship, legs drawn up, wrists draped loosely over his knees, he leaned back against the bulkhead that supported him. He could reach the gag if he wanted, but he understood from painful experience that if he tried, he had better be sure he had a good reason for doing so. Punishment for misbehavior was assured. He had endured several kicks already for moving the wrong way. So he sat as still as possible, thinking. He had tested his voice several times, surreptitious efforts, to see if he could make even a small noise. He could not. Whatever magic his sister had used on him, it was effective. He did not think she had destroyed his voice, because she would want to speak to him again at some point, or she would have killed him and been done with it. Then again, she had not needed Kael Elessedil to speak in order to discover what he knew. It might be the same with Bek. He had to hope that she wanted something else—that the doubt he sensed in her about his identity would protect him awhile longer.

He closed his eyes momentarily. He had to get out of there. He had to do so before his courage broke. But how was he going to do that? How could he possibly escape?

Momentary despair welled up inside him. He had thought himself safe with Truls Rohk. He had not believed anyone was strong or clever enough to best the shape-shifter. But he had been wrong, and now Truls was dead. She had left the caull to finish him, and if the caull had failed and died instead, she would have known. She had created it, after all. She was linked to it. The caull was alive. That meant Truls Rohk was not.

Bek had no real hope of being rescued by anyone else. In all likelihood, his companions were dead. Even Walker. It was too long for them to still be alive and not have shown themselves. He felt numb inside thinking about it. Even if they weren't all dead, those still alive were helpless against his sister. Grianne was too powerful for anyone. She had rendered the entire Rover crew, Redden Alt Mer and Rue Meridian included, unconscious with her magic. She had taken over the *Jerle Shannara* and cut off any possibility of escape. She had told Bek all of that in a matter-of-fact way, very much as if reciting what the weather would be like in the days ahead. She had done so to emphasize his helplessness, to convince him that his best hope lay through her, and he would do well to stop defying her. Only by cooperating, by revealing the truth about himself, could he hope to come out of this situation alive and well. Any other course of action would result in unpleasant consequences. He was supposed to think about that while she was gone.

He guessed he was doing so.

He guessed he was doing not much of anything else.

He tested again the bonds on his wrists. There was some give, but not enough for him to pull his hands free. The rope was dry and raw, and his sweat did not provide sufficient lubrication. Not that it mattered. Even if he could free himself from the rope, there was still the chain. He supposed his jailer had the key tucked away somewhere in his clothing, but he had no way of knowing for sure. He imagined himself loose from both rope and chain, racing through the corridors of the ship, gaining the upper deck, diving over the side, and swimming to shore. He could imagine it, but he might as well imagine he could fly.

He had only himself to rely on. Maybe he could still convince Grianne of the truth, but he was beginning to accept that it was unlikely. She just wasn't ready to hear it. She did not want to believe that he was her brother or that the Morgawr had tricked her. She had built her entire life around her belief that Walker was the enemy, that the Druid had destroyed her home and killed her family. She had made herself over so that she could not only match his power, but also exceed his perceived ruthlessness. She had done things that she could probably never live with if she were to discover how completely she had been manipulated. She was so deeply entrenched in her persona as the Ilse Witch that she could think of herself in no other way.

He considered for a moment the possibility that it was too late to save her, that she had gone too far to be redeemed, that she had committed too many atrocities to be forgiven. It was possible. Perhaps he had reached her too late.

He found himself thinking back to that night in the Highlands when he had encountered Walker for the first time. He had been reluctant to accept the Druid's offer to go on this journey. He had known somehow that if he did, nothing in his life would ever be the same. The reality was much grimmer than he could have imagined. It made him feel shriveled up and useless, torn apart by feelings that he had never hoped to experience. He wanted things to go back to the way they had been. He wanted to go home. He wanted Quentin and his friends to be safe and well. He wanted to be who he had always thought himself to be and not someone he knew nothing about. He wanted the nightmare to end.

The latch on the storeroom door grated loudly and the door opened. Three Mwellrets appeared, slouching into the room in cloaked and hooded anonymity, shades come out of the night. None of them said a word. The last to come inside closed the door and stood with his back placed firmly against it. The one directly ahead of him joined the guard in the shadows across the room. The leader came right up to Bek and pulled back his hood to reveal his reptilian face. It was Cree Bega, the Mwellret to whom his sister had entrusted his safety.

Cree Bega regarded the boy without speaking, his gimlet eyes hard and unpleasant. Bek tried to hold his own gaze steady, but the Mwellret's eyes made him queasy and weak. Finally, ashamed at his failure, he looked away.

Cree Bega reached with clawed fingers and removed the gag from Bek's mouth. He dropped the piece of cloth on the floor and stepped back. Bek took his first unobstructed breath of air in hours, but he could smell the Mwellrets in doing so, their raw, fecal odor rough and overpowering.

"Who are you, boy?" Cree Bega asked softly.

He spoke in a distant, almost distracted way, as if he didn't really expect an answer, but was asking only to voice the question to himself. His voice made Bek shiver. Fearing that what was going to happen next was not what his sister had planned, Bek worked his hands against the ropes once more.

Catching sight of the surreptitious movement, Cree Bega stepped forward and cuffed him sideways onto the floor. Then he reached down, hauled the boy back into a sitting position, and slammed him against the wall.

"There iss no esscape for little peopless," he whispered, "no esscape from uss!"

Bek tasted blood in his mouth and he swallowed it, his eyes locked on the Mwellret. Cree Bega knelt slowly so that his gaze was level with the boy's when he spoke.

"Thinkss perhapss sshe will come back to ssave you? Ilsse Witch, sso powerful, sso sstrong, fearss nothing? Hssst! Fool-issh little peopless are nothing to her. Sshe forgetss you already."

He leaned forward. "Retss are your only friendss, little peopless. Only oness who can ssave you." His cold eyes glittered. "Thinkss me wrong, foolissh like you? Sshe wantss what'ss up here." He tapped Bek's head slowly. "Wantss nothing elsse but what sshe can usse againsst the Druid."

His eyes dead, his strange face empty of expression, he studied the boy's face for a long moment. "But if little peopless do ass I assk, I will sset you free."

Bek tried to speak and could not. He tried to move and could not. He was voiceless and paralyzed, locked in place by the other's gaze and the effects of the Ilse Witch's magic. Fear and despair flooded through him, and he fought to keep them from showing in his eyes. He did not succeed.

Cree Bega rose and walked away as if he were finished with Bek. He strode to the other side of the room, looked out of the open portal at the night sky, and then moved over to the two Mwellrets who stood waiting in the shadows against the wall. Bek watched him the way a ground bird would watch a hungry snake. He could do nothing to save himself. He could only listen and wait and hope.

One of the Mwellrets emerged from the darkness and knelt beside Bek. Slowly and deliberately, he unfolded a leather apron to reveal a series of glittering knives and razor-sharp probes. He never looked at Bek, never paid him any attention at all. He simply laid out the pouch with its cutting implements, rose again, and walked away.

Everything inside Bek knotted and twisted. He wanted to scream for help, but he knew it wouldn't do any good. He strained anew against the bonds that secured his wrists, but they were as tight as before. His choices were narrowing and his time was running out. Just moments earlier he might have believed that he had a chance still to escape harm; he no longer believed that was so.

Cree Bega moved back over to where Bek sat, stood over him like a great, dark, crushing force. "Thinkss carefully, little peopless," he rasped softly. "Wayss to make you sspeak the wordss you hide. Retss know wayss. Makess you sscream if you wissh to have uss tesst you. Eassier to jusst answser uss when we assk. Besst if you do. Then little peopless goess free."

He waited a moment, watching. Bek stared straight ahead at nothing, fighting against his terror, willing himself to stay calm.

Cree Bega nudged him gently with his boot. "Comess back to ssee you ssoon," he whispered.

Without a glance back, he turned and went to the storeroom door, opened it, and disappeared from view. The door closed softly behind him, and the latch snapped back into place.

Bek kept his gaze directed two feet in front of him at the edge of the candlelit darkness, trying to come to grips with what he must do. He could not get free without help. Help was not likely to come soon enough to matter. He was going to have to give the Mwellret what he wanted. But how could he do that? He could not speak, even if he wanted to do so. He tested the effects of Grianne's magic again, thinking that perhaps he had missed something. He tried everything he could, but nothing worked. His voice was gone.

Where did that leave him? He could write his answers to the Mwellret's questions, but that might not be enough to save him. Cree Bega looked the sort to test his speaking ability not just with words but with his deadly assortment of blades, as well. What could it hurt, after all, to make certain? Why not see just how voiceless the boy really was?

For the first time since he had departed the *Jerle Shannara* and gone inland in search of Castledown, Bek regretted giving up the phoenix stone. If he had kept it for himself, if he had not forced it on Ahren Elessedil, he would have a way to escape, even bound up as he was. Perhaps that was what the King of the Silver River had intended all along. Perhaps he had foreseen the situation and given Bek the stone as a means of getting free. The idea that he had willingly forsaken his chance was more than Bek could stand, and he banished the thought angrily. His gag was still off, and he took several deep, slow breaths to steady himself, but he could still feel his heart pounding. He glanced down again at the array of blades laid out beside him, then quickly away. He was so afraid. He felt tears start at the corners of his eyes and fought to keep them from running down his cheeks. The Mwellret guards would be watching. They would be hoping for this. They would report it to Cree Bega, who would think him even weaker than he already supposed. Cree Bega would use that against him.

He ran through his options, all of them, however remote or impossible they seemed; nothing new suggested itself. He would answer the questions Cree Bega asked of him. He would hope he could do so in writing and not be tortured first to find out if he was playing games. He would hope they would set him free from the ropes and chains—either of their own volition or by his suggestion—and if they did, that he could find an opportunity to escape. It was a pathetic plan, devoid of particulars or favorable odds, but it was all he could come up with. His hopes were in tiny shreds, and he clung to them as to bits of colored string, once bright with promise, now faded and worn.

It wasn't fair, he kept thinking. None of it. It was nothing of what he had thought he would find in coming here. It was promise turned to dust. The tears came again, harder, and they ran down his cheeks in crooked lines. He lowered his head into shadow in an effort to hide them.

As he did so, he heard the storeroom door open anew, a snapping of the latch, a soft creaking of the hinges. He glanced up quickly, expecting to see Cree Bega. But no one was there. The doorway was empty, a black hole into the outer passageway, where no lights burned.

Had those lights not been lit when Cree Bega departed the room? Bek wondered, suddenly alert.

For an instant, the Mwellret guards stood frozen in place. Then the ret who stood closest to the door drew a short sword from beneath his cloak and walked over for a look. He stood in the opening, unmoving, peering out into the corridor. Nothing happened. Slowly, carefully, he closed the door once more, the hinges creaking in the new-formed silence, the latch clicking sharply into place.

In the next instant, the candle next to Bek went out and the room was plunged into blackness except for the light from the single portal across the way, but that left everything shadowy and vague. Something went by Bek in a rush, the movement of its passage a cold breath of air against his skin. It made no sound as it closed with the nearest Mwellret, who grunted at the impact and went down. There was a warning hiss from the other two, and then both were engaged in a struggle that sent them careering across the darkened room and into the far wall. Bek caught a glimpse of their antagonist, a big cloaked form that moved with the speed and agility of a moor cat, launching into first one and then the other, hammering them, sending them down in broken heaps.

Bek stared. *It couldn't be.*

The first ret was back on its feet, charging to the aid of its fellows, the glitter of its blade caught momentarily in a wash of moonlight. There was a muffled collision of bodies and a grunt. Seconds later the ret staggered back again, the short sword buried in its chest, its movements limp and unfocused as it fought to stay upright. When it collapsed a moment later, the life gone out of it, the room was so still that Bek could hear himself breathe.

"What's the matter, boy?" someone whispered in his ear. "You look like you've seen a ghost."

It was Truls Rohk. Bek started so violently at the guttural sound of the other's voice that he nearly choked. The shape-shifter materialized beside him out of the darkness, his cloaked and hooded form blocking out the moonlight. In seconds he cut apart the ropes that bound the boy's wrists. Then, using a slender length of metal bar, he snapped apart the link that fastened the leg iron clasp in place, and Bek was free.

Truls Rohk hauled him to his feet. "No talking," he whispered. "Not until we're off this ship."

They went out into the darkened passageway, the shapeshifter leading the way. Despite stiffness and cramped muscles, still not quite believing his good fortune, Bek stayed close enough to touch him. They were barely a dozen paces beyond the storeroom when a raspy, broken cry went up from within. Bek at his heels, the shape-shifter continued down the corridor without looking back. The boy expected him to make for one of the stairways leading up and was surprised when he did exactly the opposite. Instead of ascending to the main deck, Truls Rohk turned down a dead-end corridor that led to the rear of the craft. Overhead, the sound of booted feet echoed through the decking, mingling with shouts and cries. The ship's company was fully awake and, if not hunting for them yet, well on the way to doing so.

The corridor Truls Rohk had turned down ended after only a few steps at a heavy wooden door. The shape-shifter opened it without hesitating and pulled Bek inside. The room was dark, but moonlight poured through two sets of open windows to reveal a fully furnished chamber. A man came awake in a bed to one side, springing out of the covers hurriedly, but a single blow from Truls Rohk knocked him into a wall where he collapsed in an unconscious heap.

"Out the window," the shape-shifter hissed at Bek, shoving him toward the open portals.

He turned back toward the door to the chamber, but it was already flying open, and half a dozen dark forms were charging through. Truls Rohk slammed into them with such fury that he sent all six careening backwards into the passageway, stumbling and cursing as they tried to keep their feet. Knives and short swords glittered in the moonlight, but the shapeshifter dodged through the slashing blades like a ghost, snatched hold of the open door, and slammed it shut, throwing the heavy latch in place.

"Get out!" he snarled over his shoulder at Bek.

Bodies hurtled against the door from without, and heavy blades pried at the metal latch and bit into the wood. Bek climbed onto the empty bed and lifted one leg over the sill. Almost at once, a darkened form dropped in front of him, suspended from a rope. Bek caught the gleam of a Federation insignia, kicked at the man's head, and sent him spinning away.

Behind him, the door splintered and sagged. Bek hesitated anew.

"Get out!" Truls Rohk repeated.

Bek went through the window just as another form dropped on a rope over the ship's railing, snatching for him. Bek evaded the savage lunge of his attacker and went headfirst into the water. Submerged in the concealing darkness, he swam away from the airship until his lungs were begging for air. When he resurfaced, there was no one else in sight. Aboard *Black Moclips*, the sounds of battle continued, sharp and desperate. Bek waited a moment for Truls Rohk to follow him into the water, but when he saw boats filled with Mwellrets being lowered over the side, he began to swim again. He was a good swimmer, and he carried no weapons or baggage to encumber him. He swam toward the darkened shoreline in smooth, easy strokes and was there before the first of his pursuers had cut loose from the ship to row after him.

Creeping as quietly as he could from the shallows, he ducked into the concealing trees, then looked back. Spread out across the waterline, their squat, bulky shapes frozen in the moonlight, the boats were coming toward him. He scanned the dark outline of *Black Moclips* for some sign of Truls Rohk, but found nothing. Aboard the airship, the clamor had died to a dull murmur of voices that carried easily across the open waters of the bay. Undecided about what he should do, Bek waited as the rowboats drew nearer. He was free, but he had nowhere to go. He had lost his magic and his weapons, so it was pointless to stand and fight. But if he ran, his captors would just track him down again. He needed the shape-shifter to help him. He needed Truls badly.

Finally he could wait no longer. The rowboats were almost on top of him. He melted into the trees as soundlessly as he could manage. His pursuers would not be able to pick up his tracks in the darkness, so he would have the better part of the night to put some distance between them. By morning, he could be far away.

But where was he going to go?

The hopelessness of his situation overwhelmed him, and for a moment he simply stopped where he was, staring out into the darkness. He was free, but what was he supposed to do about it? Should he go in search of the others from the ship's company, hoping that one or two might still be alive? Should he find Walker and warn the Druid about Grianne? Was there time enough to do anything at this point besides try to stay alive?

"What are you doing?" Truls Rohk hissed, materializing out of the darkness beside him. Water ran from his sodden cloak into the dirt. "If you stand around long enough, they'll find you for sure!"

He took an astonished Bek by the arm and propelled him forward into the trees. "Did you think I wasn't coming? Have some faith, boy. Cats aren't the only ones with nine lives." His cloak was torn, and blood was smeared on it. Within the concealment of his cowl, his eyes glittered. "Enough of this. Let's go after your sister. Family reunions are always interesting, but this one should be better than most." His sudden laughter was rough and unpleasant. "You try to save her and I'll try to kill her. Fair enough?"

His grip was like iron as he pulled Bek Ohmsford after him into the night.

TWENTY-THREE

Rue Meridian was still watching *Black Moclips* from the shoreline shadows with Hunter Predd, trying to decide what she should do, when the shipboard silence erupted in a cacophony of shouts and the clash of metal blades. It happened so suddenly that at first it was disorienting, and she was not even sure where the sounds were coming from. Exchanging a hurried glance with the Wing Rider, she moved farther along the shoreline, as if by doing so she might somehow better determine the source of the disruption.

To complicate her efforts, the moon slid behind a broad bank of clouds, plunging the bay and the airship into blackness.

"What's going on?" she hissed helplessly.

She paused in her advance as she heard wood splintering and metal hinges tearing loose. She couldn't mistake those sounds, she decided, glancing again at Hunter Predd. Then a splash sounded as something or someone went overboard. A second splash sounded immediately after, and she heard thrashing in the waters of the bay. Her first thought, instant and unconditional, was that someone was trying to escape. That someone would have to be a member of the company of the *Jerle Shannara*.

She ran down the shoreline, trying to track the sounds that

carried from the airship as she did so. But the struggle aboard ship continued unabated, and the clang of metal blades and the cries of the injured or dying drowned out everything else.

Finally, she stopped, knelt by the shore in the lee of a rocky overhang, and listened once more. She could hear movement in the water, as if someone was swimming, but she still couldn't tell from where it was coming. The fighting aboard *Black Moclips* had ended, replaced by angry grunts and the thud of heavy boots. The moon reappeared momentarily, giving her a glimpse of the airship's decks, bulky, cloaked forms rushing everywhere at once. In moments, they had lowered rafts into the water and were piling into them.

Mwellrets, off in pursuit of someone, she thought. But who?

The moon disappeared behind the clouds again, and the rafts slid away into the fresh darkness, making for shore behind the labored efforts of determined rowers. When the rets reached shore, they clambered from the rafts and disappeared into the jungle. Aboard *Black Moclips*, the sounds died away to isolated mutters and soft moans. Soon, even those faded.

Hunter Predd leaned close. "Someone got away from them."

She nodded, still listening, watching and thinking about what it meant. An opportunity, she believed. But how was she to take advantage of it?

"How many did you count in the rafts?" she asked.

"More than a dozen. Fifteen, probably. Mwellrets."

"All of them, I'll bet. All that's left." She thought of the dead ones aboard the *Jerle Shannara*, strewn across the decking in company with Hawk amid the wreckage of the rigging from the storm. She blinked the image away and made a quick calculation. *Black Moclips* would carry a crew and fighting complement of thirty-five. Subtracting the Mwellrets and the two Federation soldiers dead aboard the *Jerle Shannara*, that left a crew of perhaps eleven or twelve.

Hunter Predd nudged her arm. "What are you thinking?"

She looked right at him. "I need to get aboard."

He shook his head at once. "Too dangerous."

"I know that. But we have to find out if any others from the company are held prisoner. We won't get a better chance."

His leathery features creased with doubt. "You're still injured, Little Red. If you have to make a fight of it, you'll be in trouble."

"Trouble of the sort I don't need to hear about later, I know." She looked off toward the airship, a dark shape suspended over the water. "All I want is a look around."

The Wing Rider followed her gaze, but didn't say anything. He hunched his shoulders and studied the darkness with an intensity that surprised her.

"How do you plan to get out there?" he asked finally.

"Swim."

He nodded. "I thought as much. Of course, now that someone has escaped by jumping overboard and the rets have shoved off on the rafts in pursuit, I don't suppose those men left aboard will waste their time keeping an eye on the bay." He looked back at her. "Will they?"

He kept the sarcasm from his voice, but his point was well taken. A watch of some sort would be keeping a close eye on the surrounding waters for anything suspicious. She could approach by swimming underwater, but it was a long way and she was not as strong as she needed to be to try that. Nor could she count on the moon staying hidden behind the cloudbank. If it emerged at the wrong time, she would be silhouetted in the water as clearly as if by daylight.

"On the other hand," he continued quietly, "they won't be expecting anyone to fly in."

She stared at him. "On Obsidian? Can you do that? Can you drop me into the rigging?"

He shrugged. "It's still too dangerous. What do you think you can accomplish?"

"Have a look around, see if anyone else aboard is one of us." He held her gaze in an owlish, accusing look, and she grinned in spite of herself. "You don't believe me?"

"I believe you're telling me what you think I want to hear. But I read faces better than most, and I see something more in yours than what you're saying." He cocked his head. "Anyway, I'm going aboard with you."

"No."

He laughed softly. "No? I admire your spirit, but not your good sense. You can't get from here to there without me, and I won't take you unless I go, as well. So let's not debate the matter any further, Little Red. You need someone to watch your back, and if this matter turns sour, I need to be able to tell your brother that I did everything I could to protect you."

She gave him a rueful look. "I don't like it that you can see so clearly what I'm thinking."

He nodded. "Well, it might be that it will help me save your life somewhere down the road. You never know."

"Just get me on and off that ship in one piece," she said. "That's enough for me."

They waited a long time, giving the ship and crew time to quiet and settle back into a routine, keeping watch over the shoreline for the return of the Mwellrets. Rue Meridian believed they would be gone all night, trying to track whoever they were chasing, unable to see clearly enough in the darkness, forced to wait for daybreak. She was wondering about the Ilse Witch. There had been no sign of her, no indication of her presence. If she was not aboard ship, she was probably somewhere inland hunting for the magic that had brought them all to Castledown. Who had possession of that magic now? Had Walker found and claimed it yet? Was it what he had been expecting to find? There was no way of knowing without making contact with a member of the shore party, another good reason for finding out if any of them had been made prisoner by the witch and her rets.

"We should go, if we're going," Hunter Predd said finally.

Shedding his cloak and checking his weapons and clothing, he explained to her that Obsidian had been trained, as all Rocs were trained, to lower their Wing Riders to aid in a rescue. Using a harness and pickup rope, they would ride the Roc out to the airship and lower themselves into the rigging. When they were ready to leave, Obsidian would pick them up again.

"This is the key," Hunter Predd advised, producing a small silver implement. "A whistle, but only Rocs can hear it, not humans. Stealth and silence are the rest of it, Little Red." He grunted. "And luck, of course. That, most of all."

When they were ready, he used the whistle to summon the Roc. Obsidian appeared from the bluff, sweeping down over the bay to perch on the overhang they had passed on the way down the shoreline. It was dark by then, the moon having disappeared with most of the stars behind the cloudbank. They would have to hurry if they were to gain *Black Moclips* before their cover broke.

On setting out that morning, Rue Meridian had braided her long red hair and tied it back with a length of brightly colored cord. She tightened the cord now, checked the daggers in her belt and boot, and swung aboard Obsidian. Hunter Predd took a seat in front of her, spoke softly to the Roc, and they lifted off. Gliding skyward into the black, they rose until the dark silhouette of the airship melted into the surface of the bay so completely that Rue Meridian could no longer see it. She was still trying to make it out, when Hunter Predd signaled to her over his shoulder that they were there.

Hand over hand, they slid from their seats down the pickup rope, a thick, knotted stretch of rough hemp that fell away into blackness. From high above everything, the entire world looked like a black hole save where the horizon could be glimpsed. Little Red felt her heart stop and her stomach clench as she went down the rope. She was unable to see anything, even Hunter Predd, who was descending below her. She felt herself swaying, and she couldn't tell if Obsidian was moving or not. Could Rocs hover? She would have given anything for a glimpse of something solid, but there was nothing to see.

Below, all was silent, even the Wing Rider in his descent. She listened carefully for her own sounds, working to muffle everything, but the silence only added to her sense of isolation and helplessness.

She had to fight to keep from panicking when the rope ran out and Hunter Predd wasn't there. Then a gloved hand gripped her boot and pulled her into the rigging of *Black Moclips*. She seized the cluster of draws and stays, pulling herself in tightly, and released the pickup rope. In an instant, it was gone, and Obsidian with it.

Clinging to the rigging of the airship, Hunter Predd so close she could hear him breathing, she took a moment to orient herself. After her eyes adjusted, she concluded that they were hanging from high on the rear mast, rocking gently with the slow sway of the airship. They could not stay there because the moment the clouds broke and the moon reappeared, they would be silhouetted clearly against the night sky to the watch below.

Drawing Hunter Predd close, she gestured downward, indicating what they must do. Slowly, but steadily, pressing herself close to the mast to stay hidden, she found the first of the iron rungs that formed hand- and footholds, then began her descent. The climb down took an enormous amount of time and energy, more of the latter than it would have taken had she been whole. Her wounds ached, irritated by the strain of physical exertion and mental concentration alike. She looked up and saw Hunter Predd directly above her, following her down. His descent was noiseless and smooth. He was better equipped for it than she.

When she got close enough to the deck to see who was set at watch, she paused. She found a pair of guards fore and aft—by their build and carriage, Federation soldiers. There was no one in the pilot box, but a third man paced the decks, moving back and forth between the pontoons and the masts, a restless, uneasy shadow. She caught a momentary glimpse of his whipcord frame and gaunt face as he passed through a sliver of starlight, and she started in surprise. Did she know him? She thought so. She glanced upward to where Hunter Predd clung to the iron rungs and motioned for him to stay put.

Then she descended another few feet and dropped softly to the decking, sliding into the shadow of a weapons rack. The guards never even looked her way. She watched the pacer a few moments longer, waiting for him to pass close, for his back to be turned; then she straightened and walked directly toward him. She was almost on top of him before he sensed her presence and turned.

By then she had a dagger at his throat and was standing close enough to see who he was.

"Well met, Donell Brae," she said quietly, her free hand taking a firm grip on his arm. "No loud noises, please. No sudden moves."

His seamed, weathered face broke into an ironic grin. "I told them it was a bad idea to leave you on your own ship, captive or no."

"Someone should have listened to you. So now you listen to me. The *Jerle Shannara*'s mine again, Big Red's and mine. But we lost Hawk, and I'm looking to pay someone back for that. Is she here?"

He blinked. "The witch? She's ashore, looking for the Druid." The washed-out blue eyes, so familiar, gave her a considering look. "Stay away from her, Little Red. She's poison."

Rue Meridian gave his throat a nudge with the dagger's tip, and he grunted. "She hasn't discovered what real poison is yet. Who else is here? Does Aden Kett command?"

Donell Brae nodded.

"Stupid choice for both of you."

"Not always a matter of choice, Little Red."

"Fair enough. But you have one now. Do what I tell you, and you can stay alive." She nudged him again with the dagger, forcing his head all the way back. "I always liked you, Donell. I wouldn't want our friendship to end badly."

He swallowed against the dagger tip. "What do you want?"

"Who's aboard besides you?"

"If you don't move that dagger away, I'll cut my own throat trying to answer."

She moved the blade down to his sternum. "Keep your hands at your sides. Any weapons on you?"

He lowered his head again and shook it. "Never liked them much. I'm a pilot, not a bladesman. That's for others."

One of the best Federation pilots she had met. They'd flown missions together over the Prekkendorran. He had come into the service with Aden Kett, a couple of young Federation soldiers when they had started out. Now he was a pilot and Kett an airship Commander. Their crew had been assigned to *Flying Mourn* when Rue Meridian fled west to the coast with her brother. The Federation Command must have given them *Black Moclips* as a reward for their service. It was a good choice. Aden Kett's crew was the best Federation outfit in the skies.

She walked Donell Brae over to the mast, where Hunter Predd waited. The Wing Rider had come down from his mast perch to find better concealment and to watch her back. The sentries at either end of the airship took no visible notice as she marched Donell up to him.

"Again, now—who's aboard?" she pressed the pilot softly.

He looked straight ahead. "The Commander, me, and eleven crew. Thirteen altogether. We started at fifteen, but two were left on the *Jerle Shannara* to man her. Dead, I suppose?"

She ignored him. "No Mwellrets lurking about?"

He shook his head. "All ashore, chasing that boy and whoever freed him."

A chill ran through her. She glanced at the dark form of Hunter Predd, who was close enough to hear. "Let's have a word with Aden Kett, Donell. Same rules until we're finished. Behave yourself and don't test me."

The seamed face glanced over. "I'm no fool, Little Red. I've seen you with those knives."

"Good. Hold on to that image. Now, where's the Commander?"

They went down the stairway that led through the rear decking to the lower passageways and holds. The Commander's chamber was aft, situated on the vessel's port side in the shelter of the pontoons. They moved silently down the short passageway to the cabin door and stopped. She nodded for Donell to speak.

"Commander?" he called through the door.

"Come," was the immediate response.

The pilot released the latch, and they moved inside in a rush. She kicked the door shut behind her, one hand on Donell Brae's arm, the other holding the dagger flat against her palm and low and tight against her side in a throwing position.

A pair of candles lit the darkness. Aden Kett was alone, propped up in his berth, writing in a journal, a cluster of maps spread out before him. When he glanced up, she saw his strong, handsome face was bruised and his head swathed in bandages. He seemed unsurprised to see her.

He put down the quill and ink and pushed the maps away. "Little Red." He looked at Donell Brae. "Things go from bad to worse for us these days, don't they?"

"Trying to decide exactly where in the scheme of things you are?" she asked, indicating the maps.

He shook his head. "Trying to plot a course home, one I hope to put to use very soon." He shrugged. "I can dream."

"Can I trust you not to call out for help while we talk?" she asked, balancing the dagger where he could see it.

He nodded wearily. "Who would I call out for? Why would I bother? The rets and the witch are ashore, and my crew and I are left in the dark once more. We're all of us sick of this business."

"Not going well, is it?" She moved Donell forward, still

keeping her free hand on his arm and the door at her back where she could get to it if she must. "You must long for the old days, bad as they were."

He smiled, a bit of life returning to his battered features. "Things were less complicated."

"For you, anyway. What happened to your face?"

"Someone got aboard and rescued the boy we were holding. They broke into my cabin. I came out of my berth just in time to get knocked back into it. Your don't look so good yourself."

She returned his smile. "I'm healing. Slow and steady. But don't mistake that for a weakness you can take advantage of, Aden. You're no better with blades than Donell." She let the warning sink in. "Tell me about this boy."

Aden Kett shrugged. "I don't know anything about him. He was a boy. The Ilse Witch brought him here and told us to keep him locked away until she came back for him. The rets were given responsibility for that, so it's their problem that he got away."

"Describe him. Smallish? Dark hair? Unusual blue eyes? Not an Elf, is he? Did you get a name?"

The other shook his head. "He doesn't talk. Can't, I gather. But that's him, the way you describe. Who is he?"

She didn't answer. It must be Bek. But why couldn't he speak? And who had managed to get aboard before her and spirit him away?

"No other prisoners?"

"None that I know of. Or care about." The Federation Commander pushed the maps off his lap and swung his legs over the side of the berth, making sure he did nothing to startle her. Then he stood and stretched his back and arms, taking his time. "No sleep for me this night, I can see. What do you want, Little Red?"

She decided to take a chance. "Your ship. On loan."

He straightened his tall frame, gingerly smoothed back his dark hair, and folded his arms across his chest. He gave her a considering look. "On loan?"

"We took back the *Jerle Shannara*, Aden. Big Red and me. But we lost Hawk in the process, and someone is going to pay for that. I already told this to Donell. The witch marooned us. Now I intend to do the same to her. If I could, I would kill her. But leaving her trapped here with her rets works just as well."

He nodded slowly. "You want me to help you?"

"I want you to stay out of the way." She paused, reconsidering. "All right. I want you to help me. It might not be a bad idea, given what this voyage is likely to end up costing you otherwise. But even if you don't, I want your word that you will stay out from underfoot. I already have control of *Black Moclips* anyway."

Aden Kett glanced at Donell Brae, who shrugged. "I only saw one other man."

She laughed. "You don't think I came aboard with just one man, do you? That would be madness!"

"The kind of madness you prefer," Kett suggested. "There's not much you wouldn't risk, Little Red." He gave her an appraising look, and she held his gaze. "Anyway," he said, "I'm not going to turn *Black Moclips* over to you just because you ask."

"It's only on loan," she reminded him. "I'm borrowing her just long enough to find my friends and get us to the coast. Then you can have your ship back, and no one will be the worse for it."

"The witch might not see it that way."

"The witch might not be around to find out."

He grunted. "I wouldn't want to bet my life on that. And I would be."

"Tell her you had no choice. Or just leave her behind and sail home. This fight isn't Federation business anyway. It's between the witch and the Druid. It's about something that doesn't concern any of us. All Big Red and I care about is the money."

He saw the lie in her eyes or heard it in her voice; she couldn't tell which. But she knew he didn't believe her. "What matters is that we're different, Little Red," he said. "You're not a soldier; you're a mercenary. I'm an officer of the line. I am expected to obey the orders I'm given, not change them to suit my mood. Nor am I allowed to change sides in the middle of an engagement. They call that treason."

She studied him, letting the words hang in the silence. She saw his eyes flick briefly to where his weapons hung in their harness from a peg. "If you look that way again," she said quickly, drawing his eyes back to her, "I'll kill you before I have a chance to think better of it."

She felt Donell Brae tense and immediately tightened her grip on his arm. "Don't do it," she warned.

Then footsteps sounded in the passageway outside, sudden and unexpected. Instantly, commander and pilot exchanged a second glance, this one filled with unmistakable meaning. "Commander?" a deep voice called out.

Donell Brae swung around quickly to grapple with her, but she was already moving. She knocked aside his upraised arm and hit him as hard as she could in the temple with the butt end of the dagger. As he went down, she leapt over him, intercepting Aden Kett in midstride as he reached futilely for his weapons. She slammed him back against the bulkhead and knocked him to the floor. Straddling him in fury, she pressed the dagger so tightly against his throat that she drew blood.

"Commander!" The knock at the door was rough and urgent.

"The only reason I don't kill you here and now is that I think you are a decent man and a good officer, Aden." Her face was so close to his she could see the terror reflected in his dark eyes. "Now answer him!"

Kett, pinned to the floor and gasping for air, swallowed hard. "What is it?" he called toward the door.

"The rets are coming back, Commander! One raft, just setting out from shore! You said to let you know!"

She put her free hand over his mouth, hesitating. She was losing control of the situation, and she had to turn that around immediately. First Aden Kett and Donell Brae try to attack her, and now the Mwellrets come back to the ship early. She hadn't believed either likely to happen, and her miscalculations were threatening to undo her. If she didn't act fast, all of her plans were going to fall apart. Trying to take over an entire airship and crew by herself was indeed madness, but that was what she intended. It had started out as a half-baked idea, a goal so far-fetched as to be all but impossible. But she thought now that it actually might be within reach.

She took her hand away from Kett's mouth. "Tell him to wait a moment," she whispered.

He did so. When he finished speaking, she rolled him over swiftly, pressed her knee into his spine, laid the dagger between his shoulder blades, and pulled his hands behind his back. Using a leather tie she carried in her belt, she fastened his hands securely in place. Then she rose, the dagger in hand again, and hauled him to his feet.

"Tell him to enter," she whispered.

He did as he was told, and the crewman opened the door and stepped inside. He froze instantly when he saw her with the dagger at his commander's throat and the pilot sprawled motionless on the floor.

"Not a sound," she hissed at the crewman, making an unmistakable gesture with the dagger. She waited for his nod of agreement, then indicated Donell Brae. "Pick him up. Quick!"

Kneeling, the crewman pulled the unconscious pilot over one shoulder and stood up again. "Walk down the hall to the sleeping quarters," she ordered him. "I'll be right behind you. One sound, one wrong move, and your commander and your pilot and probably you, as well, are dead men. Tell him, Aden."

Aden Kett grunted, feeling the dagger point dig into him. "Do as she says."

They went out from the cabin and into the dimly lit corridor, the crewman carrying Donell Brae, and Rue Meridian following with Aden Kett. They wound silently through the airship's lower levels toward the sleeping quarters forward.

When they reached the door to the sleeping quarters, she stopped them outside. She turned Aden Kett around so he could see her clearly. "Inside, Aden," she ordered. "Stay put until I come down to let you out again. The door will be locked behind you, and I expect it to stay that way. If I hear anything I don't like, I'll set fire to the ship and burn her to the waterline with you and your crew still inside her." She held his gaze. "Don't test me."

He nodded, a hint of fresh anger in his eyes. "You're making a mistake, Little Red. The Ilse Witch is much more dangerous than you think."

"Inside."

She opened the door, let them enter, closed it again, and threw the locking bolt. She took an extra moment to secure it by wedging a dagger blade into the slide so it could not be pried open. The portholes cut into the hull to admit fresh air were not large enough for a man to crawl through. For the moment, at least, she had the commander and crew of *Black Moclips* trapped.

She went up the ladder through the hatchway to the main deck on the fly, found the last sentry at the aft rail, and went after him. She already knew he was too far away for her to reach before he saw her coming, but she went anyway. There was no time left for stealth. She had to hope he was all that was left of the crew. Out of the corner of her eye, she saw the approaching raft and the bulky forms of the Mwellrets it carried, closing fast. She could feel the ache of her injured leg and side as she ran, a fresh tearing of her wounds, but she pushed aside her pain and quickened her speed.

The crewman turned at the sound of her approach, weapons lifting. She was too slow and still too far away!

Then abruptly, he crumpled to the deck, and Hunter Predd stepped from behind the mainmast, sling in hand.

"Cut the anchor lines!" she called, changing direction for the pilot box.

She heard muffled shouting, sibilant and angry, from the raft. She gained the box and sprang to the controls, drawing down ambient light from the single sail already set in place to keep *Black Moclips* aloft, throwing the levers to the parse tubes, opening them up all the way. The airship lurched with the infusion of power. She heard Hunter Predd cut the aft anchor line, then run forward to cut the bow one, as well.

Faster!

The Wing Rider's sword rose and fell twice. Slowly, ponderously, *Black Moclips* rose into the air, severed anchor ropes trailing from her decking, arrows and javelins thudding into the underside like hailstones. The raft with its furious, helpless Mwellrets fell away and disappeared into the darkness.

She closed down the parse tubes and eased off on drawing down ambient light for power. The ship was an old friend and responded well to her touch. But maneuvering her alone was rough and uncertain. Without help, Rue Meridian could not manage a ship of that size for very long. She would need help, as well, with the dozen Federation soldiers she had trapped in their sleeping quarters below. She recognized the situation readily enough and knew that before long Aden Kett and his men would find a way to escape.

She slowed the airship to a crawl and brought her about, pointing her inland toward Castledown. Somewhere ahead, the Ilse Witch was hunting Walker, Bek was running for his life, and whoever still lived of the company of the *Jerle Shannara* waited for a rescue.

A rescue that perhaps only she could manage.

She watched Hunter Predd approach, saw the questioning look in his dark eyes, and shook her head.

She wished she had a better answer to give him. She knew she had better find one soon.

TWENTY-FOUR

Quentin Leah was listening so intently that he started in surprise when Tamis touched his arm in warning.

"He's coming," she whispered.

Consumed by the fact that Ard Patrinell's mind was still alive inside, she was still calling the wronk *he* rather than *it*— as if the human part mattered more. The rest of it might be mechanical—armor, wires, and machine parts, cold and emotionless metal—but not its mind, trapped as it was, whole and intact, thinking Ard Patrinell thoughts, using Ard Patrinell skills, hunting them with a determination that was relentless and implacable.

Heeding her warning, Quentin listened for its coming. Try as he might, he still could not hear it.

In the twilight he glanced over at her. Her roundish, pixie face was sweaty and her short brown hair tangled with bits of debris. Her clothing was torn and bloody and as dirty as the rest of her. She had the look of a hunted thing, a creature run to earth by something as inescapable as the coming of night.

A mirror of himself, he allowed. He did not need to see what he looked like to know it was so. They were a matched set, fugitives from a fate that neither could escape, that both were forced to confront.

They had been running from it all day, running since the coming of dawn had persuaded them they must find a way to kill it. All through the forests surrounding Castledown's ruins they had played cat and mouse with the inevitable, marking time as they searched for a way to put an end to the creature. It was a chase marked by fits and starts, by schemes and subterfuges, by equal parts skill and blind luck. The wronk was a terrifying adversary, made more dangerous by the fact that Ard Patrinell's thinking guided it. Sometimes it would come after them in direct pursuit, a hunter using strength and stamina to run them down. Sometimes it would circle around to lie in wait, a predator set to pounce. Sometimes it would stop altogether and wait for them to pause in turn, to wonder if they had lost it entirely, and then it would approach from an unexpected direction, swift and sudden, trying to catch them off guard. Many times it almost had them, but they were saved in each instance by their combined experience and skill and by the kind of luck that defies explanation.

Of the latter, Quentin reflected, there had been more than the former, which was why they were still alive.

The search for a wronk pit had taken longer than they expected. They had thought the Rindge would have set many such traps to protect themselves from the creatures of Antrax. Quentin and Tamis had set out that morning to find the nearest one, backtracking toward the village of Obat and his people to find the pits that had to be located along the approaches from Castledown. But the wronk caught up to them so quickly that they had to hurry their search and consequently failed to find what they were looking for. The wronk was unmistakable when it was close and moving, too big and heavy to conceal its coming. But even when they could not hear it, they were forced to listen and watch for it because it was subtle and clever, like Patrinell, and constantly looking for a way to catch them off guard.

For Quentin Leah, life had been reduced to the simplest of terms—survival of the fittest. He was engaged in the kind of life-and-death struggle that he had imagined happening to others, but never to himself. All of his thinking about a grand adventure and new experiences, everything that had spurred his decision to join the quest, had faded into a barely remembered past. The enthusiasm he had imparted to Bek, the limitless possibilities he had envisioned for what they would find, and the confidence that had buoyed him through so many harrowing confrontations along the way had turned to dust. He had all but forgotten Walker and the search for the books of magic. He had pushed aside any thought of rescuing the others, Bek included. All that was left was a fatalistic and dogged determination to stay alive for another day, to escape the thing that hunted him, and ultimately to regain enough space to allow something back into his life of who and what he had been.

He had no idea what Tamis was thinking, although he could guess readily enough. She was burdened by similar needs, but as well by her memories of and feelings for the man with whom she had been in love. She might pretend otherwise, might tell herself something else, but it was clear to him that she could not separate herself from her emotions, could not be truly objective about what they were seeking to accomplish. For Tamis, the struggle to destroy the wronk was more than trying to stay alive. It was giving Ard Patrinell the release he could find no other way, the peace that only death would bring. Her hatred of what had been done to him was so invasive that it simmered on her features at every turn. The battle was personal for her in a way it could never be for Quentin, and she was driven almost beyond reason.

But not beyond the limit of her skills, Quentin quickly saw, which were considerable. Trained as a Tracker by Patrinell himself, she was all business and judgment, able to play well a game in which no mistakes were allowed. She knew what to expect from the mind that hunted them, was familiar with its thinking, its nuanced reasoning. She could anticipate what it would try and blunt the effect. The wronk was physically stronger, and if they got within its reach, there was little question of the outcome. But Tamis was whole where the wronk was fragmented, cobbled together of parts that did not naturally fit. That gave her an advantage she could exploit, and she was quick to try to do so.

It was odd to think of what they were attempting, fleeing on the one hand and looking to make a stand on the other. It was schizophrenic and disjointed, grounded in opposing principles and mind-wrenching in its demands. Flee the danger, but find a way to face it. Quentin had no time for a balanced consideration of the contradiction. He was consumed by the knowledge that the thing pursuing them did so to destroy him, yet to leave a part of him alive, as well. It would turn him into itself, a perfect copy, able to wield the magic of the Sword of Leah yet unable to act save as Antrax chose to order. The idea of becoming the machine that Ard Patrinell had become was so terrifying, so mind-numbing, that he could not do more than glance at the prospect of it the way he would the sun, shunning the pain of any prolonged study. But even that gave him a bitter, clear understanding of why Tamis was so determined to save Ard Patrinell.

That day's flight was through the disjointed landscape of a surreal netherworld. The sounds of the pursuing wronk were all around and constant, letting up only now and then, when the hunter chose a less obvious tack. The day was cloudy and sunny by turns, casting shadows that moved past them like shades and suggested things that weren't there, yet might be coming. They were worn already on setting out, and their weariness quickly deepened. They passed places in which brush and trees were trampled and broken by fighting and frantic flight. They came upon dead men killed the day before. Most were Rindge, the reddish skin giving them identity when only pieces remained. One was an Elf, although there wasn't enough of him to determine which one. Blood soaked the ground and smeared the trees in splotches dried black by the sun. Weapons and clothing lay scattered everywhere. Silence cloaked the carnage and desolation.

As they had neared the Rindge village, the number of dead increased. They were too many to be only those from the hunting party. When they reached the village itself, they found its huts and shelters smashed and burned and its people gone. Some few lay dead, those who had bought with their lives a chance for the others to escape. That a single being could wreak such havoc, alone and unaided, against so many, was horrifying. That the mind of Ard Patrinell was an integral part of that being and would know what it was doing yet be unable to stop was heartbreaking. Tamis did not cry as they passed through the village, but Quentin saw tears in her eyes.

They had paused at the far side of the village, where the carnage ended. Those who remained of Obat's people had fled into the hills and perhaps to the mountains beyond. The wronk had lost interest in them at that point and gone elsewhere.

Quentin stood with Tamis and stared at the destruction.

"You were not mistaken about his eyes?" she asked him almost desperately. All of the bravado and irony gone out of her voice, she could barely bring herself to speak. "It was Ard Patrinell looking out at you from inside?"

He nodded. He could think of nothing to say.

"He would never do anything like this if he could help himself," she said. "He would die first. He was a good man, Highlander, maybe the best man I have ever known. He was kind and caring. He looked after everyone. He thought of the Home Guard as his family and of himself as their father. When new members were brought in for training, he let them know he would do everything he could to keep them safe. At gatherings, he told stories and sang. You saw him as taciturn and hard, but that was only since the death of the King, for which he blamed himself, for which he could not forgive himself. Kylen Elessedil stripped him of his command for imagined failures and political convenience. Bad enough. But now this monster, this Antrax, strips him of control over his actions, as well, and leaves him a shell of powerless knowledge."

It was the most he had ever heard her say at one time and as close as she had ever come to admitting what she felt about the man she loved.

She looked away, sullen and defeated. "Can you imagine what this is doing to him?"

He could. Worse, he could imagine it happening to himself, which was too horrifying to ponder. His hand tightened around the handle of his sword. He carried it unsheathed all the time now, determined that he would never be surprised, that if attacked, he would be ready. It was all he could think to do to tip the balance in his favor. It was strange how little comfort it gave him.

They had walked back through the village, choosing a different path out, still searching for one of the elusive pits. The sun had moved across the sky in a long, slow arc, the day wandering off with nothing to show for its passing, the night coming on with its promise of raw fear and increasing uncertainty. Time was an insistent buzzing in his ear, a reminder of what was at stake.

It had been quiet when they entered the village. When they left, they could hear in the distance the sounds of the wronk as it moved toward them.

Tamis wheeled back in something close to blind fury, her short sword glinting in the light. "Perhaps we should stand and face him right here!" she hissed. "Perhaps we should forget about hunting for pits that might not even exist!"

Quentin started to make a sharp reply, then thought better of it. He shook his head instead, and when he spoke he kept his voice gentle. "If we die making a useless gesture, we do nothing to help Patrinell." She glared at him, but he did not look away. "We made an agreement. Let's stick to it."

They went on through the afternoon, out of the village and back toward Castledown, choosing a trail that was almost overgrown from lack of use. No sign of life appeared. About halfway between the village and the ruins, at the beginnings of twilight, they were passing through an open space in the woods in which tall dips and rises rippled the ground and grasses grew in clumps. The failing light was even poorer there, screened by conifers that grew well over a hundred feet tall and spread in all directions save south, where a wildflower meadow opened off the rougher ground. They were moving toward a pathway that opened off the far side when Tamis grabbed Quentin's arm and pointed just ahead, which he thought looked like everything else around them, scrubgrown and rough. In exasperation, she pulled him right up to the place to which she was pointing, and then he recognized it for what it was. The pit was well concealed by a screen of sapling limbs layered with some sort of clay-colored cloth, sand and dirt, clumps of dried grasses, and debris. It was so well designed that it disappeared into the landscape. Unless you were right on top of it and looking down, you wouldn't see it.

Yet Tamis had. He looked at her for an explanation.

She smirked with rueful self-depreciation. "Luck."

She pointed to one side. It took him a while to see that a corner of the support cloth had worked itself to the surface and was sticking up. "Bury that, and the pit will be invisible again."

"Or move it to another place, and you create a red herring. And an edge for us." He looked at her questioningly. "What do you think?"

She nodded slowly. "Because Patrinell will see it, too, just like I did." She put a hand on his shoulder and squeezed. "This is what we've been searching for, Highlander. We make our stand here."

They had cut away the bit of cloth and reburied it off to one side with the corner sticking up. They used a scattering of twigs and grasses to suggest that the pit might be located there. It was reasonable to assume that the wronk, using Ard Patrinell's skills and experience, would be looking for traps and snares, especially if it found them prepared to stand and fight. If they could draw it in the wrong direction or mislead it in just the slightest, they could drop it into the pit before it knew what was happening.

It was a dangerous gamble. But it was all they had to work with.

So now they waited in the deepening night, listening to the adversary's approach, to a sharp crackling of brush and limbs, steady and inexorable. They had considered lighting fires to give them a clear battlefield, but decided that darkness favored them more. The moon and stars appeared and faded behind a screen of clouds, providing snatches of light with which to operate. They had positioned themselves squarely behind the false pit, leaving the best and most logical path to reach them to their right, over the real pit. They stood together now, but would change position when the wronk appeared. They had worked their plan out carefully. All that remained was to test it.

It would work, Quentin told himself silently. It had to.

He heard the wronk clearly, heavy footfalls drawing closer. His skin crawled with the sound. Tamis stood right beside him, and he could hear the soft rasp of her breathing. They held their swords in front of them, blades glinting in the moonlight as the clouds broke overhead momentarily. Quentin's head throbbed and his blood tingled with fiery sparks of magic that broke away from the Sword of Leah as it responded to his sense of danger. He felt the change in his body as he prepared to give himself over to its power. An equal mix of satisfaction and fear roiled within him. He would be transformed, and he knew now what that meant. When the magic entered him, he infused himself with its terrible fury and risked his soul.

Without it, of course, he risked his life. It was not much of a choice.

With an almost delicate grace, the wronk stepped into the clearing. Though its features were hazy and spectral in the faint light, its shape and size were unmistakable. Quentin watched it with a mix of raw fear and revulsion. It registered his presence instantly, freezing in place, casting about as if testing the wind. A glint of metal speared the darkness as a piece of the monster reflected momentarily in the starlight. The moon had disappeared back behind the clouds, and the night was thick and oppressive. Within the black wall of the trees, there was unbroken silence.

The Highlander felt Tamis tense, waiting for him to take the lead. They had agreed that he must do so, that he was the one the wronk was seeking and so could best draw it in the direction they wished it to go. Their plan was simple enough. Pretend to decoy it one way, knowing it would choose to go another. It was Ard Patrinell's brain at work inside the wronk, so it would be Patrinell's thinking that would direct it. It would sense a feint, a deception, and so act to avoid it. If they could take advantage of that thinking, if they could anticipate its reasoning, they could lure it into the pit. It was a poor plan at best, but it was the only plan they could come up with.

The wronk shifted again, drawing fresh shards of starlight to its metal skin, pinpricks of brightness that flashed and faded like fireflies. They heard its heavy body as it took a step forward and paused anew. Nothing of Ard Patrinell's tortured face was visible to them, and so they could try to pretend the wronk was nothing more than a machine. But in his mind Quentin saw the Elf's eyes anew, looking out from their prison—frantic, pleading, desperate for release. He would have banished the image if he had known how to do so, but it was so strong and pervasive that he could not manage it. It was a window not only into Patrinell's terrible fate, but also into his own. Tamis would free her lover from his living death. Quentin would simply avoid sharing his fate.

Sweating freely, the heat forming a sheen of perspiration on his face and arms, he wondered absently how matters had come to that end. He had embarked on the journey with such hopes for something wonderful and fulfilling and life-transforming. He had wanted an adventure. What he'd gotten was a nightmare.

"Ready?" he whispered.

Tamis nodded, grim-faced. "Don't let it take me alive," she said suddenly. "Promise me."

"Promise me, as well." His heart was hammering within his chest.

"I loved him," she whispered so quietly he barely heard her speak the words.

Quentin Leah took a deep breath and brought up his sword.

TWENTY-FIVE

Bek Ohmsford followed Truls Rohk from the shoreline without resistance. He ran with the shape-shifter deep into the forest for a long time and did not complain. But finally his efforts at keeping up failed. His strength gave out, and he collapsed at the base of a broad-limbed maple, sitting with his head between his legs, sucking in huge gulps of air.

The shape-shifter, a cloaked shadow in the deep night, wheeled back soundlessly and knelt beside him. "You went longer than most would. You're tough, for a boy."

They stared at each other in the darkness. Bek tried to speak and couldn't. Whatever Grianne had done to him, escaping *Black Moclips* hadn't helped. His voice was still gone. He made a series of weak, futile gestures, but the other mistook his silence for exhaustion.

"You thought I was dead, didn't you?" Truls Rohk laughed softly. "That's a mistake that's been made before." He shifted within the cloak and settled into a crouch. "I was close to dying, though. The witch set a trap I wasn't looking for—a caull. She guessed at my purpose in circling back to wait for her and got the caull behind me. I was too anxious to get back to you to be looking out for it properly. It caught me reaching down for your knife with my back turned. I didn't even know it was there."

He paused. "But you saved me. All without knowing. Think of that."

Bek shook his head in confusion.

"After I left, you had a visit from the shape-shifters who inhabit that region."

Bek nodded. He could still remember the smell and feel of them in the night, all size and bristling hair and raspy voices, like feral beasts.

"Whatever you said to them caught their interest. They decided to wait for me, as well. When a true shape-shifter hides, no one can find it. The caull, lying in wait for me, couldn't. Couldn't even tell they were there. When it attacked me, they snatched it right out of the air, bound it in cords so tough it could not break free, and carried it away. Before they left, they told me that my place in this world and my life belonged to you. What do you suppose they meant?"

Bek thought back, remembering how the shape-shifters had queried him about his relationship to Truls Rohk, probing his reasoning, testing his loyalty. *Would you give up your life for him? Yes, because I think he would do the same for me.* His answer, it seemed, had meant something after all.

Truls Rohk grunted. "Anyway, I fell asleep when they left me. Not what I had planned, but I couldn't help myself. It was something in their voices. When I woke, I came looking for you. But the witch took care to disguise her passage in ways I couldn't immediately unravel. It didn't matter. I knew she would bring you back here. I tried the airship first thing, seeing it moored in the bay. *Black Moclips,* the witch's own vessel. Your smell led me right to you, locked down in that hold. I got to you just in time, didn't I?"

He waited a heartbeat, then reached out suddenly and snatched Bek by his tunic front. "What's wrong with you, boy? Why don't you say something?"

Bek wrenched himself free and pointed angrily at his neck. Then he clapped his hand over his mouth for emphasis.

"You're injured?" the other demanded. "Something's damaged your throat?"

Impatiently, Bek scratched the words in the dirt with a stick. The cowled head bent for a look. "You can't speak?" Bek wrote some more. "The witch stole your voice? With magic?"

Truls Rohk rocked back on his haunches and stood up. He made a dismissive gesture. "She doesn't have that kind of power over you. Never has. What do you think the Druid has been trying to tell you? You're her equal, though untrained yet. You have the gift, too. I knew that from the moment we met in the Wolfsktaag, months ago."

Bek shook his head vehemently, shouting soundlessly, bitterly in response.

"Think!" the other snapped irritably. "She's kept you alive so far to find out what you know. Would she destroy your voice so that you could never speak again? Huh! No, she's done what she does best. She's played a game with your mind. She's knocked you down and left you thinking what she wants you to think. It's mind-altering, of a sort. You can speak, if you want. Go ahead. Try."

Bek stared at him in disbelief, then shook his head.

"Try, boy."

I've already tried! He mouthed the words angrily.

Truls Rohk pushed him hard. "Try again."

Bek staggered backwards and righted himself. *Stop it!*

"Do what I say! Try again!" The shape-shifter shoved him

a second time, harder than before. "Try, if you've got any backbone! Try, if you don't want me to knock you down!" He shoved Bek so hard he almost sent him sprawling. "Tell me to stop! Go on, tell me!"

Flushed with rage, Bek charged the cloaked form, but Truls Rohk blocked his rush and pushed him away. "You're afraid of her, aren't you? That's why you won't try. You're frightened! Admit it!"

He wheeled away. "I've no use for someone who can't do more than follow at my heels like a dog. Get away from me! I'll do this alone."

Bek charged in front of him and blocked his way. *Stop it! I'm coming with you!*

"Then you tell me so to my face!" Truls Rohk's voice dropped to a dangerous hiss. "Tell me right now, boy!" He shoved Bek again, harder than ever. "Tell me, or get out of my—"

Something gave way inside Bek, a visceral rending of self that had the feel of tearing flesh. It gave way before a mix of rage and humiliation and frustration that engulfed him like a swollen river slamming up against a dam built for calmer waters. His voice exploded out of him in a primal scream of such impact that it lifted Truls Rohk off his feet and sent him flying backwards. It bent the branches of trees, flattened tall grasses, shredded bark, and tore up clots of earth for a dozen yards. It began with the shriek of a hurricane's winds as it sapped the forest silence, then layered it anew in a darker and more suffocating blanket.

Bek dropped to his knees in shock and disbelief, coughing out the final shards of noise, the sound of his voice dropping to a startled whisper.

Truls Rohk picked himself up and brushed himself off.

"Shades!" he muttered. He reached out his hand to Bek and pulled him to his feet. "Was that really necessary?"

Bek laughed in spite of himself. It felt good to hear the sound again. "You were right. I could speak all along."

"But not until I got you mad enough to make you do so." The shape-shifter's impatience showed in his voice. "Don't let yourself get fooled like that again."

"Don't worry, I won't."

"You are her match, boy."

"I'll find out soon enough, won't I?"

The big shoulders shrugged within the concealing cloak. "Maybe you should leave her to me."

A chill of recognition rippled down Bek's neck. He reached out impulsively and gripped the other's shoulder, feeling corded muscle and sinew tighten in response, feeling knots of gristle shift. "What do you mean?"

"What do you think I mean?"

Bek's stomach clenched. "Don't do it, Truls. Don't kill her. I don't want that. No matter what. Promise me."

The other's laughter was harsh and empty. "Why should I promise you that? She was quick enough to try to kill me!"

"She's as confused about things as I was. She's been lied to and deceived. What she believes about herself and about me isn't even close to the truth. Doesn't she deserve a chance to find this out? The same chance you gave me, just now?"

He kept his grip on the other's shoulder, holding on to him as if to wring the concession he sought. But Truls Rohk didn't try to move away. Instead, he took a step closer.

"If another were to lay hands on me the way you have, I would kill him without a thought."

Bek did not back away even then, did not dare to move, though an inner voice was screaming at him to do so. He felt impossibly small and vulnerable. "Don't kill her. That's all I'm asking."

"Huh! Shall we invite her to join us, forget her evil life, forgive the past, pretend she has no alliance with the rets? Is that your plan—to talk her into being our friend? Didn't you try that already?"

The cowled head bent close, and Bek could hear the unpleasant rasp of the other's breathing. "Grow up all the way, boy. This isn't a game you can start over if you lose. If you don't kill her, she will kill you. She's well beyond any place where reason or truth can reach her. She's lived a lifetime of lies and half-truths, of delusions and deceptions. Think what brought her to us. Her single, all-consuming ambition is to kill Walker. If she hasn't succeeded in doing so already, she will try her luck soon. Even though the Druid irritates me and has brought much of this misfortune on himself, I won't give him up to her."

Both hands shot out suddenly and snatched hold of Bek once again. "She isn't your sister anymore! She is the Morgawr's tool! She is her own dark creation, as deadly as the creatures she is so fond of using, the things she makes out of nightmares! She is a monster!"

Bek went still, facing into the black void of the other's cowl. There was no question about what would happen if Truls Rohk found Grianne. The shape-shifter would not waste a moment's time considering the alternatives. If Bek didn't find a way to change his mind right now, the shape-shifter would kill her—or die himself in the attempt.

Before he could think better of it, before the consequences could register fully enough to make him reconsider, he said, "Some would say the same about you. Some would say that you are a monster, as well. Would they be right? Are you any different from her?"

The hands tightened on his arms. "Watch your mouth, boy. There is all the difference in the world between us, and you know it."

Bek took a deep, steadying breath. "No, I don't know anything of the sort. To me, you are the same. You both hide who you are. She hides behind lies and deceptions. You hide behind your cloak and hood. How much does anyone know about either of you? How much is concealed that no one ever sees? Why does she deserve to die and you to live?"

Truls Rohk lifted him off his feet as effortlessly as he would a child, his anger a palpable thing in the silence. For an instant Bek was certain the shape-shifter would dash him to the ground.

"Show me your face, if you want me to believe in you," he said.

"I warned you about this," the other hissed. "I told you to let it be. Now I'm telling you for the last time. Leave it alone." He held Bek like a rag doll. "Enough. Time for us to be going. Your recovery of your voice could be heard two miles away."

"Show me your face. We're not leaving until you do."

The shape-shifter shook him so hard Bek could hear his joints crack. "You can't stand to look on me!"

Bek swallowed and stiffened. "If you aren't a monster, if you're not hiding the truth, show me your face."

Truls Rohk gave an angry growl. "My face is not who I am!"

He lifted Bek higher then, almost over his head, as if he might fling him away. There was such power in the shape-shifter, such strength! The boy closed his eyes and hung in a black void, listening to his heartbeat.

Then he felt himself lowered back to the ground. The

hands released him. He opened his eyes and found Truls Rohk towering over him, black and impenetrable. All around, the forest had turned oppressively still, as if become an unwilling, frightened witness to what was taking place.

"If you see me, if you *really* see me, it will change everything between us," Truls Rohk said.

He seemed almost desperate to prevent this from happening, to change the boy's mind. It was more than wanting to preserve their relationship as protector and ward. It was a fear that their friendship, whatever stage it had reached, would shatter like glass. Bek could understand, and yet he knew he could not back away, not if he wanted to save Grianne.

"Don't ask again," Truls Rohk warned.

Bek shook his head. "Show me your face."

"All right, boy! You want to see what I look like, what I keep hidden from everyone? Then, look! See what my parents made of me! See what I am!" the other said with such venom that Bek flinched.

In a single, frenzied movement, he ripped away the cloak and stood revealed.

At first Bek saw him only as a vague shape outlined against the dark; the moon and stars were screened away by clouds, leaving the forest little more than a gathering of shadows. Truls Rohk's cloak lay in a dark puddle on the ground, and the shape-shifter had dropped into a crouch, looking feral and dangerous. Poised neither to flee nor to strike, he seemed instead caught in a spiderweb of tree limbs that formed a backdrop behind him, pinned against the distant sky.

Then Bek saw the beginnings of movement. The movement did not come from a shifting of limbs or head, but from within the dark mass of his body, as if the flesh itself was alive and crawling. The movement had a liquid appearance and Truls

Rohk the look of glass filled with water. It was so unexpected that Bek thought his eyes were deceiving him. He thought so, as well, when parts of the shape-shifter faded then re-appeared in ghostly fashion.

But when the moon slid from behind the clouds and flooded the clearing with milky brightness, Bek understood. Truls Rohk looked like something cobbled together from stray parts of human debris, some of it half-formed, some of it half-rotted, all of it shifting like a mirage that might not be there at all. The watery look came from the way in which pieces of him constantly changed from flesh and bone to mist and air. There was nothing permanent about Truls Rohk. He was only a half-completed thing, some of him recognizable as human, but not enough to call him a man.

It was easily the most terrifying sight Bek had ever witnessed—not simply for what it was, but for what it sug-gested, as well. It whispered of the grave, of death and decay, of what waited to claim the body when it began to decom-pose. It screamed of what it would feel like to have your body disintegrate about you. It suggested unimaginable pain and suffering. It reminded of nightmares and the creatures that came out of them to drive you from your sleep. It was surreal and ugly. It was anathema to any human concept of life.

He said nothing, but Truls Rohk saw the look in his eyes. "This is what happens when a shape-shifter mates with a human," he whispered in barely contained fury. "This is what comes from breaking taboos. I told you my father tried to kill me after killing my mother. He did so when she showed him what he had made with her. He did so when he saw what I was. He couldn't stand it. He couldn't abide me. Who could? I am trapped in a half-formed body. I am bits and pieces of flesh and bone on the one hand and nature's elements on the other, but not fully formed of either. I shift back and forth between them, trapped."

Bek could not speak. He stared wordlessly, trying to imagine what it must be like to be Truls Rohk, unable to do so.

The shape-shifter laughed dully. "Not so eager to look on me now, are you? Too bad. This is what I am, boy. I have strength and power at my command. I have a presence. But I lack a true shape-shifter's ability to change forms smoothly. I cannot hide the truth of myself. It's why I live apart, why I have always lived apart. No one can stand to look on me."

He came forward a step, and Bek shrank back in spite of himself as the bits and pieces of the other's body rippled and shifted, exposing ends of bones and runnels of blood and strips of torn flesh amid the shifts of air and water, of light and dark. An eye protruded and disappeared. Teeth gleamed out of a half-stripped skull. Hands showed the ends of finger bones and bare tendons. Hair and skin grew in patches, split and torn. Nothing seemed designed to hold together, yet hold it did, though everywhere with the look of something about to collapse into itself.

"Huh!" Truls Rohk spat out the sound with such venom that it caused the boy to flinch. The ravaged face turned away. "You were right, boy. I am a monster. Are you satisfied now?"

He started to turn away, but Bek leapt forward and grabbed his arm, holding on tight through the wasteland of crumbling bones and shifting flesh.

"You said it yourself," he said. "Your face is not who you are. You might appear a monster, but you're not. You're my friend. You saved my life. But you wouldn't trust me with the truth about yourself. You hid that truth because you deceived yourself into thinking that it was something else. I would rather know you this way, terrible though it is, than have the truth hidden."

"Pretty words," the other growled, but did not pull away.

"The truth, Truls Rohk. I know you hate yourself for how you are. I know you hate how you look and how you know others will look at you if you reveal yourself. But sometimes, with people who matter, you have to reveal even the worst of what you believe yourself to be. You have to have faith that it won't make a difference. I would never judge you for how you look. Who you are is what matters, and who you are is always buried deep inside. The shape-shifters in the mountains knew this. They asked me how I felt about you because they wanted to see if I thought you mattered. Could there be a friendship between us? How deep would that friendship go? Did I think there was a place for you in the world? Would I give up my own place so that you could have yours? Would I give up my life for you? I gave them answers that had nothing to do with how you look and everything to do with who you are."

"So what have you accomplished by making me show you how I am? What purpose has it served?" Bitterness and suspicion laced the other's words. "The truth helps no one here."

Bek tightened his grip on the other's arm and plunged ahead. "Don't you see? The truth helps everyone. The chance at life that the shape-shifters gave you when you were attacked by the caull is the same chance you must give Grianne. Everyone thinks she's a monster, too. But the truth is something else entirely. She just needs someone to help her see it. She needs someone to help her strip away her deceptions and lies. She needs someone to believe in her, to believe there's something more to her than what everyone sees. She needs someone to speak for her."

Bek leaned close. "There isn't anyone else but you and me. We're her last hope."

There was a long silence when he finished, a freezing of time and space as the boy and the shape-shifter faced each other in the darkness, one human, one something else. All the air had gone out of the world, leaving it empty and suffocating. Bek did not know what else to do or say. He refused to let go of Truls Rohk, keeping hold of his arm, as if by doing so he might keep him bound to his cause.

"You and me," the other said at last, his rough voice strangely soft. "But mostly you."

He freed himself so quickly that Bek did not have time to stop him, reached down for his cloak and pulled it on again, becoming once more a dark, faceless apparition in the night. All of the pieces of him, all of the ruined, shifting parts, forever fading and appearing like half-formed visions, disappeared.

"The Druid was right to choose you," he said.

Bek saw his chance. "I have a plan."

Truls Rohk grunted. "When didn't you? You are a match for your sister in more ways than one. Come. I make you no promises, no assurances of what I will or won't do about her. Talk to me some more and we'll see. But let's not delay. The rets will be coming, and the ruins wait. Walker needs us."

"But listen to what I have to tell you—"

"I'll listen later." The shape-shifter dismissed him swiftly. Then his voice hardened. "Now you listen to me. Don't you ever mention what's happened here. Not to me or to anyone else. Not ever. It's finished."

He turned and stalked away, Bek struggling to keep up.

TWENTY-SIX

"Now," Quentin Leah said quietly to Tamis.

She moved away from him, not hurriedly or with any outward sign of the turmoil she must be feeling, but as if the encounter were just one of many and in no way significant beyond that. She eased farther right and ahead of him, walking deliberately, choosing her steps and then her place to stand. They had waited until they were certain the wronk could see what she was doing. It was difficult to spy out, but she had stopped just behind a bare patch of ground that was strewn with a scattering of deadwood and scrub grasses. A trained eye would suspect a wronk pit, a well-concealed trap. But the trap lay elsewhere.

Quentin held his ground as the wronk turned toward Tamis. It studied her without moving, then abruptly started toward her. She brought up her short sword defensively and dropped into a protective crouch. Quentin waited a moment, then stepped forward, as well, the Sword of Leah lifting into the faint light. He felt the stirrings of its magic run down through the metal blade and into his arm. He felt its fiery rush enter his body, bitter and at the same time sweet. It infused him with a sense of power. It made him light-headed and alive in a way nothing else did. He wanted to use that power. Even knowing how foolish that desire was, he wanted it.

The wronk lumbered out of the night, closing on Tamis with inexorable determination, neither fast nor slow, but certain. The Tracker held her ground, refusing to give way, saying something now, taunting words that Quentin could not make out. It wasn't what they had planned. She was supposed to give way to the wronk, to stay clear of it should the decoy fail, as it seemed now it might. Quentin came forward another few steps, stopping just at the edge of where he could stand and still know his place in the darkened landscape that hid their trap. As he did so, he felt a new surge of magic fly into him, and he was consumed by a need to release it in battle.

Abruptly, without warning, the wronk turned toward him.

The suddenness of it took his breath away. It drained him of the fire of his magic. In a single moment, everything changed. The wronk came for him swiftly, closing the distance between them almost before Quentin could recover himself to act. It thundered across the clearing, much quicker than the Highlander had remembered from their previous encounter. The sword in its human hand lifted. The blade in its metal one flashed.

Tamis screamed, too far away to help. *Do something!*

At the last moment, he remembered what it was he had intended and threw himself out of the monster's way. The wronk's blades sliced through the air next to him, one so close to his face he could feel the rush of wind it generated in passing. He darted left the six paces he had counted earlier, giving himself enough leeway to make up for the steps he had taken earlier, wheeled back and braced himself. The wronk was already coming for him again. From the helmet that protected its human head, Ard Patrinell's features were suddenly, shockingly recognizable.

Don't look, Quentin told himself. *Don't feel anything.*

Tamis was rushing toward him, foolishly responding to his danger, impulsively acting to help. He shifted swiftly to his right as the wronk bore down on him, the sound of its machine parts a sharp whine against the hammer of its footfalls. It closed with an almost palpable expectation of crushing him—its momentum carrying it right over the pit they had intended for it. The screen gave way beneath its weight, collapsing in a shower of earth, a snapping of deadwood, and a rending of cloth. An instant later the wronk was gone, vanished into the hole as if it had never been. They could hear the sound of its impact as it struck bottom, then silence.

Tamis charged up, breathing hard. Her eyes were bright with surprise and excitement as she stared at the hole. "That wasn't so hard," she said as if she couldn't quite believe it.

No, Quentin was thinking, it wasn't. He moved over to the edge of the pit, still wary, and peered down. It was so dark that he couldn't make out anything. "We need a torch," he said.

She darted away, gathered up a likely stick of deadwood, wrapped it in a scrap of cloth from the edge of the pit, and, using tinder from her pouch, sparked a flame. As she did so, Quentin heard the first stirrings of movement from within the pit.

"Hurry," he whispered, trying to stay calm.

They might have trapped it, but they had most certainly not killed it. The fall alone had not been enough. More would be needed, even to disable it sufficiently to render it immobile. He waited impatiently for her to join him, reaching over the side with the makeshift torch to see what was happening.

The firelight illuminated the sheer, smooth sides of the pit,

all the way down to where the wronk was trapped more than
fifteen feet below. They could just make out its dusty shell. It
was battered and scraped, but still functioning. Neither the
fall nor the sharp rocks embedded by the Rindge in the floor
of the pit had been enough to stop it.

It heaved itself upward, grasping at stray roots, digging
into the earth in search of handholds, intent on climbing out.

Quentin Leah and Tamis fought to keep it from doing so
with a frenzy and determination that bordered on madness.
They threw everything at it that they could lay their hands
on—rocks, limbs, part of an old stump, clots of earth, and a
fair-sized boulder that they managed to roll close enough to
topple in. Several times they struck it hard enough to knock it
loose, but each time it picked itself up and began the climb
out once more, a relentless and inexorable force.

They used fire next, throwing mounds of deadwood into
the pit, then lighting it with the torch. The deadwood blazed
up, burning so quickly and fiercely that the wronk did not
have time to stamp it out. For a few moments, it was trapped
in an inferno, metal skin reflecting the flames of the burning
wood so that it seemed as if it, too, were ablaze. In the fiery
light, they watched as it tried to protect its human arm, the
flesh of which soon blistered and blackened from the heat.
Ard Patrinell's terrified, anguished face peered out from behind its clear protective shield, and in his eyes they read
things they did not want to know. Quentin hastened to feed
more wood into the pit, but quit looking down at what was
trapped there. Tamis was in tears.

But in the end, that effort failed, too. The fire burned
fiercely for a time, then began to die out. The wronk climbed
clear of the flames once more, blackened with ash and heat-
seared, but still mobile.

Quentin stepped back in dismay. The Rindge would have been better prepared for this than they were. They would have had a backup plan for dealing with the trapped wronk. They would have been able to rely on strength of numbers. But the Rindge weren't there to help. No one was.

"This isn't working!" Tamis screamed at him.

Without waiting for his answer, she darted into the trees. For an instant, he thought she had abandoned him, that she was fleeing. He stared back down into the pit, where the last of the burning wood was turning to ash and the wronk was slowly digging out hand- and footholds on its torturous, but implacable ascent.

Then Tamis was back, dragging a huge limb by one end, deadwood, well over eight feet in length, most of its smaller branches reduced to broken stubs.

"We'll use this to knock him back down each time he tries to climb out!" she shouted. "Help me!"

He leapt forward to do so, and together they hauled the branch to the side of the pit and tipped it downward, seizing the slender end and using the limb like a battering ram to hammer at the wronk. Grunting and huffing, they slammed their makeshift weapon into its metal body and sent it tumbling back down again. Again and again, they stopped its ascent, trying unsuccessfully to smash its mechanisms, to break up its working parts. Each time it just picked itself up and began the climb out anew. So the struggle continued, with no progress being made on either side. It was a battle that Tamis and he must lose, Quentin realized, because they would wear out sooner than the wronk. They had to find a way to disable it if they were to win. But he could not think of how to do that without getting close, and getting close was unthinkable.

Then they made a mistake. They let the end of the branch get too close to the wronk while preparing to use it, and the wronk dropped its weapons and seized it in both hands. Its weight was enormous, and they were forced to let go of the branch. The wronk dropped back into the pit. But it had a ladder with which to climb out, and picking up its weapons, it began to do so.

Quentin and Tamis watched helplessly. "We have to get out of here," he whispered.

"No!" she screamed at him. Her dusty, sweat-streaked face was contorted with rage and frustration. "You promised!"

"We can't stop it alone!"

"We have to! I'll do it myself!"

She began snatching up clots of dirt and throwing them at the wronk, shrieking at it. Then abruptly, she dashed away, searching for another ram to knock it loose again. Quentin stayed where he was, waiting. The wronk was more than halfway out. When it reached him, he would try to knock it back down again. His hands tightened on the Sword of Leah. He could feel its power coursing through him, singing in his blood, making him light-headed and oddly detached. He watched the magic racing up and down the blade, tiny flickers of brilliant light.

He glanced down into the pit. The wronk could see the magic, too. The knowledge of what it meant reflected in Ard Patrinell's desperate, haunted eyes.

Then Tamis was back, hauling another dead branch, one shorter and less stout than the first. Her face was so intense and her eyes so wild that he rushed to help her, and once again they tried to knock the wronk loose from its perch.

But the wronk was ready for them. It snatched the ram out

of their hands before they could bring it to bear and, one-handed, swept the deadwood into them, knocking them backwards with a single, powerful blow. Quentin lost his grip on the Sword of Leah, and it flew out into the darkness. He went down in a heap, his ribs and chest throbbing with pain, the breath knocked from his body.

He was back up again in an instant, searching frantically for his weapon, their only hope. He found it quickly, but by the time he had it in hand, the wronk was out of the pit and reaching for Tamis, who stood defiantly in its path.

"Tamis, run!" Quentin shouted.

Instead, she charged, launching herself into the wronk with such fury that she knocked it backwards, slamming her short sword into its fire-blackened human arm, grappling with its metal one, wrapping her arms about the long knife and shield.

Quentin never hesitated. He went after them as if possessed, yelling out the Highland battle cry, "Leah! Leah!" in fear and desperation, slamming into them both, trying to knock Tamis away, trying to topple the wronk. He succeeded in neither. Rebuffed, he stepped back and swung the Sword of Leah with such fury that he took off the wronk's human arm. It fell away with Tamis' short sword still buried in it, blood spraying everything in a red mist. A look of shock and disbelief crossed Ard Patrinell's face, his mouth yawning in a soundless scream. Quentin realized in horror that the Elf could still feel pain.

His hatred of what had been done to Patrinell boiled up anew. No one should be made to suffer like that. He lost control of himself and began hacking at the metal shell with short, powerful blows, trying to locate a vulnerable spot. In the darkness, it was difficult to tell much of anything. Tamis was screaming and clawing at the helmeted head, using her long knife and her fingers, no longer bothering with the metal arm and its long knife, which cut at her furiously. Quentin saw the glitter of the blade and heard the Tracker grunt in pain. He redoubled his efforts, shifting to the wronk's other side, slamming his sword into its metal-sheathed hand until it had broken the ball-and-socket joint in two and the blade had dropped from the useless fingers.

Both arms ruined, the wronk tottered back, trying to shake free of Tamis. While the Tracker clung to it, it could not adequately defend itself. Quentin pressed his advantage, hacking at the joints of its legs, and after what seemed an endless amount of time spent staggering this way and that through the bloodied night, he shattered the right ankle. The wronk dropped to its knees. Tamis sagged downward, as well, leaving Patrinell's head exposed. Quentin began hammering relentlessly at the protective shield, his body alive with his sword's magic, his ears filled with its wild humming. Lost to everything but his desperate need to have it continue, wrapped in its killing haze, he no longer felt anything but its raw power.

Tamis fell away, rolling onto the earth before rising to her hands and knees, head hanging down between her shoulders. Quentin shifted his attack to the wronk's legs again, striking blow after blow until the left one gave way, as well.

He stepped back then, exhausted and stunned. The wronk was stretched on the ground before him, limbs broken, torso battered, even the seemingly impenetrable face shield cracked. Wires and cables lay exposed and severed, and their ends crackled and sparked wickedly. The panels of lights on its chest and limbs flashed redly in warning. Unable to rise or fight longer, the wronk shuddered uncontrollably, the stubs of its severed limbs twitching. Quentin stared down at it dully, the rush of magic that had infused him beginning to fade. He looked down at himself and was surprised to discover he was still whole.

"Finish it!" Tamis snarled at him from one side, kneeling with her arms hugging her bloodied body. "Keep your promise, Highlander!"

Quentin didn't know if he had the strength to do so. He tightened his grip on his sword and walked forward again until he stood next to the stricken wronk. And Patrinell's eyes stared up at him through a haze of blood, searching his own. He was crying, all of the pain and horror mirrored clearly in his tears. He was begging for help. Quentin couldn't bear it. He felt his revulsion and horror threaten to overwhelm him.

He brought the Sword of Leah down quickly and with ferocious purpose. He shattered the protective shield in two swift blows, then smashed Ard Patrinell's face until it was an unrecognizable ruin, then severed what was left of his head from the wronk.

Dropping his sword, he staggered backwards. The wronk had quit moving, but a few lights still blinked from the panels on its chest. Then an arm stump twitched. Crying out in rage and fear, Quentin picked up his blade one final time and chopped at the body and limbs until nothing remained but scraps of metal and bits of flesh.

He might not have stopped then except that out of the corner of his eye he saw Tamis collapse. Closing off the magic as if it were an addiction he must quit forever, feeling how close he was to losing himself to it, he threw down his sword and went to her. He dropped to his knees, turned her over gently, and cradled her head and shoulders in his lap.

Her eyes stared up at him. "Is it done? Is he free?"

He nodded, his throat tight. The front of her tunic was a mass of blood and torn flesh.

"Wherever I'm going, I'll find him there," she whispered. A froth of blood coated her lips.

He touched her cheek with shaking fingers. "Tamis, no."

"I'm so cold," she whispered.

Her eyes fixed, and she stopped breathing. Quentin held her for a long time anyway. He talked to her when she could no longer hear. He told her she would have what she wanted, she would have Ard Patrinell, that she deserved to find him waiting and he would be. He whispered good-bye to her. He was crying freely, but he didn't care.

When he laid her down again and rose, he felt as if he had lost his place in the world and would never find it again.

TWENTY-SEVEN

Enveloped by the slow, steady thrumming of Castle-down's machinery, Ahren Elessedil walked back through the long rows of towering metal cabinets and spinning silver disks that occupied the cavernous chamber outside Walker's smoked-glass prison. He did not like leaving Ryer Ord Star alone to look after the Druid, did not feel at all certain that he was doing the right thing, but knew, as well, he could not turn back. The voice inside him generated by the magic of the phoenix stone was firm and compelling. The missing Elf-stones lay ahead, somewhere else in the complex, waiting for him to retrieve them. He must do as the voice insisted if he was ever to find himself again and be made whole. He must go to where the Stones were. He must take them back.

He watched the dark glass of Walker's chamber disappear into the warren of cabinets behind him, and when it was out of sight, his loneliness was palpable and his feeling of vulnerability acute. The haze of the phoenix stone's magic was beginning to dissipate, to lose its consistency, to become more penetrable. It was a gradual change, and at first he was not certain he was seeing it accurately. But as he got clear of the brightly lit central chamber and walked back into the darker corridors beyond, it became increasingly apparent that

366

he was not mistaken, that the stone's magic was failing. He immediately felt pressed and harried by the knowledge, as if he must move faster than he would have liked or than was reasonable. It was an irrational response, because he had no real idea of what the magic's lifetime might be. Then again, not much of what he had done since entering Castledown had anything to do with being rational.

He knew that Ryer's magic would be lessening, as well. When it was gone, she would have to rely on her connection with Walker to survive. In a way, she was better off with the Druid. At least Walker could offer her protection once he woke and freed himself. Without the magic of the phoenix stone, there was little that Ahren could do for her. Little that he could do for himself, for that matter.

Still, he would listen to the voice and go on, because the voice was all he had to rely on.

He climbed the stairs to the overlook they had come upon earlier, then moved back into the maze of corridors beyond. He took the path his instincts told him to take, keeping close watch over the shadows pressing close about him. The flameless lamps threw down their light in dim pools, but the stretches between were like quicksand. He repeatedly encountered creepers on their way to other places, and each time he stopped where he was and waited for them to attack. But the creepers still did not see or sense him, and they did not slow. He heard the skitterings of their approaches and departures, scrapings of metal that raised the hair on the back of his neck. He wished again he was braver and stronger. He wished he had Ard Patrinell to assure him that he would be all right. He kept thinking how comforting that would be. But Patrinell had taught him everything he would ever teach him and told him everything he would ever tell him. Patrinell was gone. Ahren's comfort, if he was to find any, would have to come from somewhere else.

As he walked deeper into the catacombs, the sound of the machinery grew louder, a steadily building whine. Without knowing anything else, he could tell that he was moving toward the power source that was the heart of Castledown. It was there that Antrax fed off the energy stored for its use by the safehold's machines. Ahren felt himself shrink as the sound increased in volume, its dull roar filling up the corridors like a river at flood. He saw himself as tiny and insignificant, impermanent flesh and blood trapped inside changeless, unyielding steel walls. He thought again about his hopes in coming on the journey—to prove himself to be more than the callow boy his brother believed him, to accomplish something that would warrant respect and even honor, to become the man his father had wanted him to be. Foolish, impossible hopes in light of his cowardice in the ruins, yet he clung to them still. Some part of what he had dreamed of accomplishing could still be realized if he could keep himself steady.

He passed out of the corridor into a vast, cavernous room in which two giant cylinders stood side by side amid a cluster of smaller pieces of equipment. The cylinders were fifty feet across and a hundred feet high. Metal pipes and connectors ran from their casings to the equipment and surrounding walls. The sound of the machinery was deafening, a pounding throb that buried everything else in the wake of its passing. It was Castledown's power source, and Ahren wanted nothing so badly as to get away from it.

Then he looked to his right and saw a pair of chambers similar to the one that had been used to contain Walker, except that they were much larger. The dark glass fronting them was recessed into the chamber walls, and the bulbous doors were rimmed with sleek metal bindings. He stared at them, and he knew without having even to question it that one of them contained the missing Elfstones. He could feel it the same way he had felt the need to go there. The phoenix stone's magic was still at work inside him, giving him his direction, telling him what to do.

Yet for a long time, he didn't move. He didn't know what to do, didn't know how to do it, and didn't really want to try. His fear returned in an enveloping wave. To go on was too much to ask of anyone; it was too overwhelming to consider. He stared at the doorways, the magic of the phoenix stone prodding at him, and fought to keep himself from bolting. He had never been so scared. His fear wasn't of what he thought might be waiting; it was of what he couldn't imagine. His fear was of the unseen, of the unknown danger that would cause him to flee once more. He did not think he could bear to have that happen again, and he did not know how to prevent it. He could sense the possibility of something lurking behind the dark glass, a predator, anxious for him to step inside and be seized. Anticipation alone was enough to freeze him in place, to render him hopelessly immobile. He thought in his unspeakable terror that he would never move again.

It was his sense of shame that saved him, reborn in the unavoidable memories of his flight from the ruins days earlier, recalled again and again in the long hours afterwards while he huddled in the debris and thought about what it would be like to return home after what he had done. His chance to redeem himself from that misery, his only chance, lay in recovery of the Elfstones. In the hauntingly inexorable nightmare of his failure to save his friends, in the cold realization of how frail a creature he was, he had come to understand that it was worse to live with fear than to die confronting it.

He remembered that, and broke free of his terror. He started forward without stopping to consider what he was doing, knowing only that he must go then or he would never go at all.

In the next instant, alarms went off everywhere, shrill metallic sounds that cut through even the suffocating roar of the machines.

Ahead, one of the doors opened and a giant creeper scuttled out, all crooked legs and sharp pincers, a war machine looking for a fight. It did not see him, but moved to take up a position between the chamber doorway and the corridor through which Ahren had come. Another creeper followed, and then another, stationing themselves in a defensive ring. The entry sealed itself tightly behind them.

Ahren kept moving ahead, making for that closed door, striding into the midst of the creepers. He held the long knife before him protectively, knowing it was all but useless should they discover him. But, just barely visible, the failing magic of the phoenix stone still clung to him in thinning wisps. Ahren imagined the alarms sucking it away, smoke caught in a breeze. He moved between the creepers for the door, bolder than he had believed he could ever be, feeling buoyant and paralyzed at the same time. He felt himself watching his own progress from somewhere outside his body, removed from the act. His thoughts were reduced to a single sequence—get to the Elfstones, take them in hand, summon their power.

He reached the door with the shriek of the alarms ringing in his ears and was surprised when it gave to his touch. The creepers behind him didn't seem to notice. He stepped into the room, a darkened chamber paneled with banks of blinking lights, tangled wires, and flexible metal cords that cast shadows over everything in inky pools. It was so black in the room that Ahren couldn't distinguish any of the pieces of apparatus that were scattered everywhere, couldn't make out the comings and goings of the cords, couldn't even tell what the room was supposed to be. He groped forward, being careful to touch nothing, picking his way toward the center of the room as his eyes tried to adjust to the abrupt, momentary flashes of illumination.

When they did, he saw the first signs of movement, faint stirrings to one side. He froze instantly, and as he did so he caught sight of something moving to his other side. At first he thought it was nothing more than the shadows that flickered in the dim light, but then with heart-stopping certainty he recognized them. They were creepers. He couldn't hear their skittering over the blare of the alarms, but even in the absence of that he knew them for what they were. They were all around him, all through the chamber. He had stumbled into their midst before realizing what he was doing.

He held himself as still as he could manage, barely daring to breathe, while he considered his next move. He could not tell how much of the phoenix stone's magic remained to him; it was too dark to measure what traces remained of its distinct haze. Some, certainly, or the creepers would have had him already. He tried to think, to ignore the alarms and the creepers and the chaos around him, to hear anew the voice that had brought him there.

A second later, he saw the chair. It was big and padded and reclined, and it sat in the center of the room, surrounded by a cluster of freestanding machines. The cords were thickest there, snaking out in every direction, all leading from parts of the chair. There was an odd box set into one armrest to which many of the wires ran, and Ahren recognized it. He had seen the same sort of apparatus in Walker's prison, siphoning off the Druid magic through his good arm. The chamber Ahren was in was where Kael Elessedil had been drained of the magic of the Elfstones in the same way for almost thirty years. It was the place in which his uncle had wasted his life.

The Elfstones, he knew instinctively and with overpowering certainty, were inside that box.

He moved over to it quickly, sliding through the nests of wires and past the bulky pieces of equipment, praying he couldn't be detected. The creepers continued to shift position in the open spaces of the room, sidling a few feet this way, then a few that. He could not tell what they were doing. They didn't seem to be doing anything that mattered. Perhaps they were only sweepers, harmless attendants of the machines rather than sentries and fighters. Perhaps his presence meant nothing to them.

He swallowed against the dryness in his throat, pausing as he passed close to one of them. It was not very big, but it sent a ripple of fear down his spine. He waited for it to turn away, then eased his slender body past, stepped into the maze of wires that surrounded the chair, and knelt next to the mysterious box.

In the flash of panel lights and the muted illumination through the dark glass windows, he peered into the box. He couldn't see anything but shadows. He wanted to reach inside, but he didn't like doing that without knowing what waited. Wouldn't there be restraints of some sort, if that was how the magic was siphoned off? Wouldn't there be needles of the sort that had been inserted into Walker to keep him connected to the machines? What if it was the trap the little sweeper had been leading him to all along?

But the Elfstones were in that box, not two feet away from his hand, and he had to get them out.

Suddenly, unexpectedly, the alarms went silent and the chamber's ceiling lights came on. Ahren froze, exposed and unprotected, crouched by the padded chair amid the clustered machines and creepers. The magic of the phoenix stone was gone; the last traces of its concealing haze had vanished. Aware of his presence, the first of the creepers was already turning toward him. The ends of its metal arms lifted to reveal the deadly cutters that marked it as a sentry and fighter.

Ahren glanced swiftly into the box, and amid its smoky shadows spied a glimmer of blue.

He thrust his right hand inside and snatched at the Elfstones. He seized the first two as iron bands clamped about his wrist, but the third one skittered away, just beyond his fingertips. A new alarm went off, this one inside the room, a whistle's shriek of warning. He jammed his left hand into the box, as well, caught hold of the loose Stone, and clasped both hands together as a second set of bands immobilized his left hand. Creepers moved toward him from everywhere, metal legs scraping wildly against the smooth floor, cutters snapping at the air.

Ahren didn't know what to do. He didn't know how to summon the power that would save him. He couldn't even make himself speak as he fought to bring the magic to life.

Please! he begged voicelessly as his hands tightened about the Elfstones. *Please, help me!*

A needle at the end of a flexible arm flashed past his face. He felt its sting in his left arm, and a slow numbing began to spread outward with languorous inevitability. Metal digits closed about him from every quarter, holding him fast, making him a prisoner.

It was happening all over again, he thought frantically, just as it had to Kael Elessedil.

Help me!

As if heeding his silent plea, the Elfstones flared to life within the darkened recesses of their confinement, their blue light so blinding that he closed his eyes against its glare. He felt, rather than saw, what happened next. The restraints on his wrists shattered, and the box was blown apart. The creepers lasted only seconds longer, then the magic caught them up and swept them away, hurtling them against the walls of the chamber and reducing them to scrap. His eyes were opening again when the padded chair exploded. The banks of machinery were shattered, as well, one after the other, engulfed in a sweep of blue light that circled the room and turned everything to useless shards and twisted wire.

Arms outstretched, hands clasped together, fingers tight about the Elfstones, Ahren lurched to his feet. The needle was gone from his arm, but the numbing hadn't lessened, and it took all his concentration to keep that arm from going limp. He fed it with the power of the Stones, with the peculiarly pleasurable pain they engendered, a burning rush that seared his flesh and left him dizzy. He staggered across the room, the Elfstones' power incinerating everything, burning it all to molten slag. The dark glass windows blew out, leaving the twisted interior of the room exposed. He saw the massive cylinders that housed the power source become ringed in blinking lights and fire threads that crisscrossed everywhere. He saw the creepers that had taken up watch outside wheel back again to deal with him.

Shades!

He had time for a single desperate exhortation before the

juggernauts barreled through the doorway, all sharp edges and brute power. He sent the magic of the Elfstones hammering into the nearest and threw it backwards into the others. He struck it again, then again, advancing on it now, light-headed and humming with the magic's power. He was transformed by its feel, made new and whole, as if he had never been powerless, as if he had never had to flee from anything. He pursued the creepers with single-minded intent and smashed them one by one, disdaining their cutters and their blades, unafraid of what they could do to him because it seemed now that they could do nothing.

They went down before him like trees caught in a hurricane, ripped out by their roots, toppled and left to die. With a final glance back at the destruction he had visited upon the machines that would have sapped away his life, Ahren Elessedil stalked from the room, consumed by a killing rage.

Antrax became aware of the intruder's presence only seconds before it felt the ruptures in its metal skin. No pain was involved because it could not feel pain, only a sensation of being opened where it knew it should not. The intruder was the one that had disappeared earlier while in the company of its probe, the one for whom the Stones were intended. Somehow it had found its way to the extraction chamber. Somehow it had gotten hold of the Stones while still aware of who and where it was and had used them against the chamber and its equipment.

Alarms were already triggered all through Antrax's domain, set off by a power surge generated in the extraction chamber where the earlier intruder had been imprisoned. It had taken Antrax precious minutes to determine the cause of the surge, and by the time it had done so, the earlier intruder was already free of its connectors and gone into the complex. Now there were two of them loose, and either was capable of doing great damage if not stopped.

Antrax spun down its lines of power in milliseconds, gaining the capacitor housing before the latest intruder was in possession of the Stones and free of the extraction chamber. With the alarms shut down again and reset, the immediate danger was to the storage units that housed its lifeblood. Triggering the screen of laser beams that the creators had installed to protect the capacitors against damage, Antrax summoned the strongest of its battle probes to bring this newest intruder to bay. It might not be possible to immobilize it without killing it, but Antrax was prepared to accept that alternative. There would be others that could use the Stones, that could summon their magic, others that could be lured to Castledown. It was more important to protect against damage to the power Antrax had harvested already.

It felt the presence of the intruder moving through the shattered doorway of the extraction chamber to confront the laser beams and the probes that had already responded to its summons. Extraction ports were housed throughout the complex, and Antrax began siphoning off the raw expenditure of the Elf's power, feeding on it as it left his body. Energy was not to be wasted, whatever its source.

Computer chips processed and analyzed with blinding speed. Antrax was informed and its course of action determined accordingly. The intruders would do battle with its probes in the mistaken belief that they could somehow prevail. They could not. They would simply feed Antrax more of the precious energy it needed, just as they had been meant to do while sedated. Still thinking they had a chance to get free, they would struggle until they were overcome.

Antrax, incapable of emotion, feeling nothing for the humans it hunted, prepared to immobilize and terminate them.

TWENTY-EIGHT

The Druid known as Walker, who had once been Walker Boh and was now on the threshold of still another life-altering transition, moved swiftly down the corridors of Castledown toward a confrontation with Antrax. Ryer Ord Star followed closely behind, one slender hand clasped firmly in his. There was such joy on her face at having found him after so long, such exhilaration at having rescued him from the machines that were leeching away his life, that he could not bear to tell her what waited ahead. He preferred to let her have her happiness, her own life recovered and her freedom from the Ilse Witch secured. She had fought hard for him, and she was entitled to bask in the glow of her accomplishment.

It was odd that she should have the sight, could see so clearly into the future, and yet be denied so much of its meaning. He had brought her with him to give him insight into what the future held, but he had never imagined that the insight he sought would come to him in such a roundabout way. It was not her simple visions that had informed him. It was not her dreams. Instead, it was the way in which he had become linked to her when she had saved him after Shatterstone that had revealed so much. That was when he had learned the truth about her. That was when he had seen what she could be and decided to trust his instincts.

Now, deep within the catacombs in that distant land, she had revealed the future yet again. Linked to her by her empathic rescue of him in the extraction chamber, he had caught another glimpse of what might come to be. Though the future was written on water, sometimes it was possible to divine its meaning based on a choice of actions. Go one way, and the future would take that twist. Go another, and there would be a different result altogether. So it was that, while coming out of his drug-induced stupor and back into the real world, he had been shown a brief but stunningly clear vision of what he must do. Triggered by her empathic touch and her talent as a seer, the purpose of his coming to that place and time, once so clear to him, once indisputable, was revealed to be something else entirely.

He marveled at how mistaken human beings were in assuming they could foresee their own fates. Even seers, who possessed the gift of Ryer Ord Star. It was easy to assume that one event must necessarily follow in the wake of another, that a thing was just what it seemed. But he knew better. A Druid knew better than anyone that life was a myriad of twists and turns that no one could unravel, a path that must be traveled to be understood. So it was there, in Castledown, for him, though he had forgotten the rules for a time. So it would be later for the survivors, when they made the journey home again.

He wondered then at the fates of the others of the company of the *Jerle Shannara*. Ahren Elessedil had been alive when Ryer Ord Star found Walker, but had since disappeared, and not even the seer knew what had become of him. The magic of the phoenix stone had sheltered them both for a time, but now it had faded. The Rovers had been alive when he departed the *Jerle Shannara* for Castledown. According to the seer, Bek and an Elven Tracker were still alive a week ago. Of the rest, he knew nothing. It was difficult to believe they were all gone, but it was a possibility he could not rule out.

Castledown's alarms continued to ring, shrill and insistent, echoing down the maze of passageways. Creepers skittered by, moving in all directions, oblivious to Walker and Ryer Ord Star. He had taken the precaution of cloaking both the seer and himself in the Druid magic, convinced that it would work in the real world, though it had seemed to fail miserably in his dreams. The creepers were preoccupied with other matters in any event, compelled by primary directives to engage in repairs and restore order. They would not be searching for him quite yet, though soon enough. He would have to move quickly.

His exploration of Castledown through Antrax's internal systems had given him the map he needed to know where he must go. The only way to put an end to Antrax was to shut down its power source. By doing so, he could drain away its intelligence and leave it incapable of action.

It sounded simple. It would not be.

The sound of the machines grew louder and more insistent. The power source, their destination, lay ahead. Walker tightened his resolve and gathered his strength for the confrontation that waited. Antrax would attempt to trap and immobilize him again. It would do so in the same way as before because it was a machine and a machine would use its primary approach to handling a situation until that approach failed. Antrax would rely again on its creepers and drugs. Walker, forewarned, had already decided on a different course of action for himself.

When the alarms unexpectedly ceased, the ensuing silence

was shocking. Given the extent of the damage he had visited on Castledown's internal systems, Antrax had repaired itself more quickly than Walker had anticipated. He thought momentarily about striking at it again, then decided against it. Antrax would be expecting such an attempt and would be prepared for it. Better to continue on. The power source lay just ahead, and once he was there, all the alarms in the world wouldn't matter.

Nevertheless, he had not yet reached the end of the passageway that opened onto the central power chamber when a new alarm went off, this one directly ahead and localized. Then he heard explosions and smelled the raw burn of magic, and he realized that another had gotten to the chamber ahead of him. Pulling Ryer Ord Star after him, not quite certain what he was going to find, he began to run. It was as apt to be the Ilse Witch as one of his companions. The sounds of battle were unmistakable, however, as machines shattered and glass exploded out of walls. Bits and pieces of creepers flew across the passageway entrance as he neared the power chamber, where smoke roiled through a surreal landscape of flameless lamps and fire threads.

He glanced back at Ryer Ord Star. The exhilaration was gone from her face, the joy from her eyes. Desperation had replaced both, born of more than her recognition of the obvious dangers that waited. It was as if she had divined both his intent and her complicity in advancing it by saving him earlier. Her face was pale and taut, and her silver hair flew out behind her in a thin curtain, lending her a ghostly look. She tried to say something, but saw the intensity of his expression and kept still.

They burst through the power source entry into a vast chamber dominated by a pair of towering cylinders situated in the center of the room and connected everywhere by pipes and conduits. Smaller machines surrounded them, metal cages and housings bristling with flexible lines. Walker had no idea how they worked, how Antrax fed, how it converted magic to a fuel it could consume. The technology for the process had been dead for more than two and a half millennia, and only Antrax itself possessed the knowledge to keep it operating. That was true of the lifeblood that fed Antrax and preserved the library of the Old World. Destroy either, and you destroyed both.

It was what Walker had come to realize he must do, a sacrifice of one to put an end to the other.

He no longer thought to debate the matter. He knew that Antrax would eventually reach out for other sources of magic, other magic-infused humans, and the cycle would begin again. Sooner or later, it would siphon off everything of worth from the world that had replaced the one Antrax had served, and all to preserve a machine that no longer mattered. Antrax must be stopped, destroyed while there was still time.

Fire threads ringed the cylinders that formed the power source, shifting at random this way and that, keeping at bay anything that might try to harm the capacitors they protected. Smoke clouded the chamber in a thick haze, giving everything the appearance of a nightmarish netherworld. The creepers that appeared out of its brume had the look of shades, and even the equipment seemed to shift and turn in the mix of light and shadow.

Then abruptly, out of nowhere, Ahren Elessedil appeared, hands stretched forth as if to ward off invisible things, slender body taut and gathered to strike as he stepped gingerly through the debris. Blue light flashed from between his fingers, shattering creepers that crossed his path, clearing the way forward. Walker felt a surge of renewed hope. The Elven Prince had managed to recover the missing Elfstones, something he had not dared to hope could happen. With their magic to aid his own, he would have a better chance to succeed in doing what was needed.

"Ahren!" Ryer Ord Star shouted out even before Walker could speak.

The Elven Prince turned toward them, his eyes as blue and wild as the fire of the Stones. He registered the presence of Walker and the seer but only barely. He was consumed by the magic, so caught up in its throes that all that mattered to him, all that he could feel, was the rush of its power through his body.

Walker moved toward him swiftly, unafraid of the dark look in his eyes, of the blue fire gathered at his clenched fists. He reached out for the Elven Prince and touched him lightly, drawing him out from the haze into which he had been carried, bringing him back to himself. Ahren stared at him in anger, then confusion, then with undisguised relief.

"You've done well, Elven Prince," Walker said, drawing him close, eyes shifting this way and that for the enemies that circled all around them. "Draw the magic back into yourself. Quickly!"

Walker watched the blue light of the Elfstones fade, then cloaked Ahren with concealing magic, as well. "Come this way."

Aware that Antrax was searching, he moved Ahren and Ryer to one side, changing their position in the chamber. He had thrown out images and set off the alarms on the pressure plates that Antrax had activated earlier, confusing things further. The sirens shrilled everywhere, and warning lights on wall panels flashed like red eyes blinking through the cross-hatching of the fire threads. Momentarily confused, the creepers shifted this way and that. They could not find either the Druid or his companions; in the chaos, their sensors were unable to fix on anything.

Walker had drawn the Elf and the seer all the way back to the partially shattered wall of the extraction chamber, where they would have some protection. "Wait for me here," he ordered.

Gathering his robes about him, he slipped away from them, maneuvering past the creepers toward the cylinders that warded the power source. There was no time left for subtlety. He would have to strike quickly. He found a seam in the plating, a weakness that might be exploited, and attacked. Druid fire rent the metal with a withering blast, peeling it away. Before Antrax could react, Walker moved again. A dozen yards farther on, he struck once more. Then the fire threads were seeking him, striking at random because they were unable to fix on him within his covering of magic. He dodged them as he attacked, avoiding the creepers, as well, circling the cylinders and surrounding machinery, continually seeking vulnerable points.

Yet despite his best efforts, the protective metal of the power source held firm. He was depleting his strength, but gaining no advantage. Another way must be found. Still throwing out distractions and false targets, he moved back across the floor, barely escaping a random fire thread that singed his cloak. Sooner or later, his luck would run out. Antrax would already be mounting a counterattack.

He barely finished the thought before the attack began. A beam of oddly hazy light radiated from a port high in the ceiling, flooding the room and outlining Walker where he crouched. If he had not already been moving, leaving images in his wake, he would have been incinerated by the fire threads that shifted instantly to find him. As it was, he was pinned between two of the smaller machines, unable to move anywhere as the creepers, able to pinpoint him at last, closed in for the kill.

Seeing the danger, Ahren Elessedil stepped away from Ryer Ord Star and turned the magic of the Elfstones on the port that had released the revealing light, shattering it, then fusing it shut. The light faded, and Walker was up and moving once more. Ahren struck out at the closest of the creepers, clearing a path for the Druid, giving him a chance to escape. Walker raced to join him, grabbed his arm, and pulled him back against the wall again. Throwing out a new set of distractions, he dragged both Elven Prince and seer into the doorway of the extraction chamber.

"Stand here!" he shouted into Ahren's ear over the din. "Hold them back for as long as you can—then run!"

He turned into the room, searching out the power feeds that were built into the wall. He had been going about the battle in the wrong way. He could not attack the power source from without; whoever had constructed Antrax would have made certain that sabotage of that sort was very difficult. Any permanent damage would have to come from within. Antrax had been installed inside Castledown to protect the library of the Old World against attacks from without. There would be internal defenses, as well, but they would not be as substantial. The intake lines that fed raw power into the capacitors for conversion and storage would have near-infinite capacity, since such power would necessarily come in different forms and increments.

But would the lines of power that Antrax used to feed itself from the capacitors be of similar durability? Walker didn't think so. Antrax would measure its own intake. It would not require a separate monitoring system, would have no reason to expect an intake greater than what it commanded. Overload the feeding lines, and they would melt or disintegrate. Antrax would have warning systems and shutoffs to prevent that, but if Walker struck quickly enough, the damage would be done before they could react.

He moved through the debris of the room, over pieces of shattered equipment and creepers, to the extraction ports that ran to the storage units. He would use them to reach the lines that fed directly into Antrax. There were relays from one to the other; he had discovered that much when he had explored the complex earlier in his out-of-body form. The trick would be in acting quickly enough to jam them, and then to sustain the attack long enough to disable Antrax before it could strike back.

Outside the extraction chamber, Ahren Elessedil fought to keep the creepers at bay. Fire threads were seeking him out, as well, though most were still engaged in warding the power source, vertical crimson stripes that climbed the smoky heights of the cavernous hall to lock in place like prison bars. The Elven Prince twisted and turned to meet each new attack, Elven magic flashing brightly. But he did not have more than a few minutes left before he would be overwhelmed.

Ryer Ord Star crouched next to him in the doorway, her gaze directed back toward Walker, helpless and beseeching. Walker gave her a calm, untroubled look, one meant to comfort and allay her fears. His attempt failed. Perhaps she saw the truth. Perhaps she was beyond seeing anything but what she feared most. She screamed, and the sound could be heard even over the howl of the alarms.

In response, Walker flattened the palm of his hand against

one of the extraction ports and sent the Druid fire hurtling inward.

Antrax was caught by surprise. Walker's magic pumped into the intake lines like floodwaters down a dry riverbed. The shock was enormous, so much so that a backlash ripped through Walker, as well. He stiffened against the pressure and pain and thrust the magic forward again, deep into the lines, feeling it build anew. Antrax was throwing up defenses in a wild effort to contain him, but it was too little, too late. He was all the way inside the feeding system, breaking from the main lines into all the little channels, all the little tributaries, everything that kept Antrax running. He could feel conductors fusing, melting, and falling away.

Fire threads ripped into the room from behind, burning into him like heated metal. He contained his screams, and blocked what he could of the counterattack without lessening his own assault. Ryer screamed anew, but he could not look to see what she was doing. Every part of him was directed toward continuing the assault. Antrax was racing down its central lines, patching what it could, closing off what it could not. Its internal systems were imploding, one after the other. Walker chased it through its central nervous system, through its bloodstream, into its heart and mind. Everything he touched he savaged with the Druid fire, carrying himself with it, feeling himself burning up, as well. He couldn't help it. He couldn't stop it. He couldn't separate himself from what was happening sufficiently to stay whole. Bits and pieces of his own body were collapsing, as well.

Then abruptly, he felt Antrax convulse. The fire threads that raked him lurched wildly, spraying out of control. Creepers, disoriented and mindless, twisted like bits of paper caught in a wind. He felt Ryer clutch at him, still screaming, pulling at him, trying to wrench him free of the ports to which his hand was fused. Ahren Elessedil was beside him, his face a mask of horror. Walker had only a moment to register their presence, and then a backlash of magic burst through the extraction port through his hand and arm and into his body and blew him across the room.

The attack on its internal systems was so sudden and powerful that Antrax was burned halfway through before it could manage to respond. It blocked the intruder's advance, turned his own power back on him, and counterattacked with its lasers. It began closing down damaged areas and calling for repairs. But in spite of its efforts, the intruder's fire raged all through it, and for every section of itself it managed to salvage, it lost two more. All of its central lines were invaded and contaminated, riddled with power so destructive that it was eating through the circuits and conductors. Antrax felt pieces of itself cease to function as feeding lines deteriorated and collapsed. It could not maintain its various functions, its complex operations. It lost control over its mobile defenses first, its probes and lasers. Its maintenance systems stalled. It kept intact the defenses surrounding the power source, but the protection devices at Castledown's surface ceased to operate. It threw everything it had left into fulfilling its prime directive—to protect the knowledge it warded in its memory banks.

Nothing worked. Everything was failing. Bit by bit, it felt itself slowing down, losing control, and slipping away. It retreated to its stronger positions to gather strength, to reconnect. But the fire tracked it as if it were a living thing and burned away its faltering defenses. Antrax was forced all the way back through its collapsing lines to the chambers that housed its power source.

There it found itself cornered, unable to move outside the twin capacitors that had fed it all these centuries. The capacitors were all it had left, and their power was leaking away through a thousand ruptures. Its charge from the creators was no longer possible to fulfill. Already it could feel the central memory banks dying.

Then Antrax could no longer move.

It began to have trouble thinking.

Time slowed, then became barely noticeable to it in its newfound state of immobility and dysfunction.

Its last conscious thought was that it was unable to remember what it was.

TWENTY-NINE

Walker blacked out from being hurled against a wall, but he woke again almost at once. He lay without moving amid the debris, staring dully into the smoky haze that enveloped him. He knew he was hurt, but he could not tell how badly. The feeling was gone from much of his body, and his hand was soaked in a wetness that could not be mistaken for anything other than what it obviously was. Somewhere close, in the swirl of the battle's aftermath, he could hear Ryer Ord Star sobbing and calling out his name.

I'm here, he tried to say, but the words would not come.

Sparks spilled like liquid fire from the broken ends of wires, and wounded machines buzzed and spat in their death throes. Tremors rocked the safehold as Antrax thrashed blindly down its lines of power in search of help that could no longer be found. By turning his head slightly to the right, Walker could just glimpse the fractured cylinders that housed the power source, the metal skin leaking steam and dampness, the protective fire threads fading like rainbows with a storm's passing.

Then the pain began, sudden and intense, rushing through him with the force of floodwaters set free from a broken dam. He gasped at the intensity of it and fought back with what little magic he could muster, shutting it away, closing it off, giving himself space and time to think clearly. He did not have much of either, he knew. What had been promised had been delivered. He had not known from the visions that Death would come for him then, at that moment, in that place. But he had known it was on its way.

A figure moved in the gloom, and Ahren Elessedil materialized. "He's here!" he called back over his shoulder, then knelt in front of Walker, his face ashen, his slender body razored with burns and slashes and streaked with blood. "Shades!" he gasped softly.

Ryer Ord Star was beside him a second later, small and ephemeral, as if she were no more substantial than the smoke from which she appeared, no better formed. She saw him, and her hands flew to her mouth in tiny fists that only partially muffled her anguished scream. Walker saw that she was looking below his neck, where the pain was centered. He read the horror in her eyes.

She started for him at once, and he brought up his hand in a warding gesture to keep her back. For the first time, he saw the blood that coated it. For the first time, he was afraid, and fear gave power to his voice.

"Stay back," he ordered her sharply. "Don't touch me."

She kept coming, but Ahren reached out for her as she tried to push past, and pulled her down next to him, holding her as she thrashed and screamed in fury and despair. He talked to her, his voice steady and soothing, even when she would not hear him, would not listen, until finally she collapsed in his arms, sobbing against his shoulder, little birdlike hands still clenched in defiance.

Walker lowered his bloodstained hand back into his lap, still not looking down at what he knew he would find there, forcing himself to close off everything but what he knew he must do next.

"Elven Prince," he said, his voice unrecognizable to him. "Bring her close."

Ahren Elessedil did as he was told, tightening his features in the way people do when they are brought face-to-face with sights they would just as soon never have witnessed. He held her possessively, shielding as well as restraining her, his own needs revealed in his determination to see them both through whatever would happen next. Walker was surprised at the resolve and strength of will he found in the youthful features. The Elven Prince had grown up all at once.

"Ryer." He spoke her name softly, deliberately infusing the sound of it with a calm that was meant to reassure her. He waited. "Ryer, look at me."

She did so, slowly and tentatively, lifting her head out of Ahren Elessedil's shoulder, her gaze directed toward his face, refusing to look down again, to risk what that would do to her. In the pale, translucent features he found such sadness that it felt to him as if he was broken now in spirit as well as in body.

"You cannot touch me, not without irreparable damage. Healing me is not possible. Healing me will cost you your own life and will not save mine. Some things are beyond even your empathic powers. Your visions told me this was coming. When I became linked to you after Shatterstone, I saw. Do you understand?"

Her eyes were blank and fixed, devoid of anything even resembling understanding, as if she had decided to leave him rather than be made to face the truth. She was hiding—he accepted that—but she had not gone so far away that she couldn't hear.

"Ahren will take you back to the surface of Castledown

and from there to the airship. Return home with him. Tell him of the visions and dreams that visit you on the way as you once told them to me. Help him as you have helped me."

She was shaking her head slowly, her eyes still unfocused, lost and empty looking. "No," she whispered. "I won't leave you."

"Ahren." Walker's gaze shifted to the Elven Prince. "The treasure we came to find is lost to us. It died with Antrax. The books of magic were housed in the machine's memory system. They could not be retrieved unless Antrax was kept whole, and allowing that to happen was too dangerous. The choice was mine to make, and I made it. Whether it was worth the cost remains to be seen. You will have to make your own judgment. Remember that. One day, you will be given the chance."

Ryer Ord Star was crying again, speaking his name softly as she did so, repeating it over and over. He wanted to reach out to her, to comfort her in some small way, but he could not. Time was running out, and there was still one thing more he must do.

"Go now," he said to the Elven Prince.

The seer gave a low wail and reached out for him, trying to tear free of Ahren Elessedil's strong grip. Her fingers were like claws, stretching as if to rend and discard whatever words he would choose to speak next.

"Ryer," he said softly, his strength ebbing. "Listen to me. This is not the last time we will see each other. We will meet again." She went silent, staring at him. "Soon," he said. "It will happen."

"Walker." She breathed his name as if it were a spell that could protect them both.

"I promise you." He swallowed against the return of his

pain, gesturing weakly at Ahren. "Go. Quickly. Not the way you came. Across the chamber, that way." He pointed past the ruptured cylinders, his memory recalling the labyrinthine passageways he had explored in his out-of-body search. "The main passageway leads out from there. Follow it. Go now."

Ahren pulled Ryer Ord Star up with him, turning her away forcefully, ignoring both her sobs and her struggles. His gaze remained fixed on the Druid as he did so, as if by looking at Walker he would find the strength he needed. *Perhaps he still seeks answers for what has happened to them all,* Walker thought. *Perhaps he just wants to know whether any of what they have endured has been worth it.*

A moment later, they were gone, through the shattered doorway of the chamber into the larger room beyond. He could hear them afterwards for a long time, the sounds of the seer crying and of boots scraping over the rubble. Then there was only the fading crackle of stricken machines fighting to stay functional, smoke that curled through the air and wires that sparked, and a vague sense of life leaking slowly away.

Time slowed.

Walker felt himself drift. She would be coming soon. The Ilse Witch, his nemesis, his greatest failure—she had caught up to him at last. He could measure her approach by the shifting of smoke on the air and the whisper of footsteps in his mind. He tightened his resolve as he waited for her.

When she appeared, he would be ready for her.

The Ilse Witch found her way to the power source through use of her magic, tracking first toward the origin of the alarms and then following in the footsteps of Walker, which she stumbled across farther on. The heat and movement of the images he had left by his passing overlapped with those of

Ryer Ord Star and an Elf. They had all come this way, and not long ago, but she could not tell if they were traveling together. She was surprised to find the seer down there, but neither her presence nor that of the Elf made any difference. It was the Druid she must deal with; the other two were merely obstacles to be cleared away.

It was true that she had given up looking for the Druid in favor of the magic they both sought, yet she could not ignore his presence. He was somewhere right ahead of her, and perhaps he had already gained possession of the books. She needed to find that out. She had not forgotten her earlier decision to concentrate on the books, but every turn she took led back to her nemesis. It was pointless to pretend any longer that she could separate the two.

She had listened to the sounds of battle during her approach, slowing automatically, not wanting to stumble into something she was not prepared for. She did not yet know what it was that lived down there, although she was fairly certain it was something from the Old World. It was intelligent and dangerous if it had survived all those years, and she would avoid it if she could. From the sounds ahead, it appeared that it might have enough to occupy it already without bothering about her.

The passageways twisted and turned, and she soon discovered that the sounds were carrying farther than she realized. By the time she was closing in on their source, they had died away almost to nothing, small hummings and cracklings, little fragments of noise broken off in a struggle that had consumed their makers. The alarms had ceased, and the traps that had warded the passageways had locked up. She could still sense a presence somewhere deep within the walls, but it was small and failing rapidly. Smoke rolled past her in clouds, beckoning her ahead to where the passageway opened into a ruin dominated by a pair of massive cylinders that had been cracked and twisted by explosions from within. Bits and pieces of creepers lay everywhere, and machines whose purpose she could not begin to comprehend were knocked askew, their cables and wires severed and sparking. The chamber that housed them was vast and silent as she stepped inside, a safehold become a tomb.

She felt the Druid's presence at once. Responding to it, she stepped through the debris and into the remains of a chamber to one side.

She saw him almost immediately. He sat propped against one wall, staring back at her. Stained red with blood, his black robes spread away from him like a tattered shroud. His body was burned and ravaged. Most of one leg was gone. His skin, where not blistered and peeling, was so pale it seemed drawn with chalk on the drifting haze.

She stared at his ruined body and was surprised to discover that she felt no satisfaction. If anything, she was disappointed. She had waited all her life for that moment, and once it had arrived, it was nothing at all as she had pictured it. She had wanted to be the instrument of the Druid's destruction. Someone had cheated her of the pleasure.

She walked to within a few feet of him and stopped. Still she did not speak, her eyes locked on his, looking for something that would give her a little of the satisfaction she had been denied. She found nothing.

"Where are the others?" she asked finally. "The seer and the Elf?"

He coughed and swallowed thickly. "Gone."

"You're dying, Druid," she said.

He nodded. "It is my time."

"You've lost."

"Have I?"

"Death steals away all our chances. Yours flee from you even as we speak."

"Perhaps not."

His refusal to acknowledge his defeat infuriated her, but she held her temper carefully in check. "Did you find the magic you sought?" She paused. "Will you tell me willingly or must I pry open your mind to gain an answer to my question?"

"Threats are unnecessary. I found the magic and took from it what I could. But while I live, it is beyond your reach."

She stared at him. "I haven't long to wait then, do I?"

"Longer than you think. My dying is only the beginning of your journey."

She had no idea what he was talking about. "What journey is that, Druid? Tell me."

Blood appeared on his lips and ran down his chin in a thin stream. His eyes were beginning to glaze. She felt a twinge of panic. He must not die yet. "I have the boy," she said. "You did an impressive job of convincing him of the lies he now insists are the truth. He really believes himself to be Bek and me to be his sister. He believes you are his friend. If you care for him, you will help me now, while there is still time."

Walker's eyes never left her face. "He is your brother, Grianne. You hid him in the cellar of your home, in a chamber behind a cabinet. He was found there by a shape-shifter, who in turn brought him to me. I took him to a man and his wife in the Highlands to raise as a foster son. That is the truth. The lies are all your own."

"Don't use my name, Druid!" she hissed at him.

One hand lifted weakly. "The Morgawr killed your parents, Grianne. He killed them and stole you away so that he could take advantage of your talents and make you his student. He told you I did it so that you would hate his greatest enemy. He did so in the hopes that one day you would destroy me. That was his plan. He subverted your thinking early and trained you well. But he did not know about Bek. He did not know that there was someone besides me who knew the truth he had worked so hard to conceal."

"All lies," she whispered, her anger strong again, her magic roiling within her. She would strike him down if he said another word. She would tear him apart and put an end to things here and now.

"Would you know the truth?" he asked.

"I know it already."

"Would you know the truth finally and forever?"

She stared at him. There was intensity to his dark eyes that she could not dismiss. He had something in mind, something he was working toward, but she was not certain what it was. Be careful, she told herself.

She folded her arms into her robes. "Yes," she said.

"Then use the sword."

For a moment, she had no idea what he was talking about. Then she remembered the talisman she wore strapped across her back, the one the boy had given her. She reached over her shoulder and touched it lightly. "This?"

"It is the Sword of Shannara." He swallowed thickly, his breath rattling in his chest. "Call upon it if you would know the real truth, the one you have denied for so long. The talisman cannot lie. There can be no deception with its use. Only the truth."

She shook her head slowly. "I don't trust you."

His smile was faint and sad. "Of course not. I'm not asking you to. But you trust yourself, don't you? You trust your own magic. Use it, then. Are you afraid?"

"I'm afraid of nothing."

"Then use the sword."

"No."

She thought that would be the end of it, but she was wrong. He nodded as if she had given him the answer he expected. Instead of thwarting his intentions, she seemed to have buttressed them. His good arm shifted so that his hand was lying on his shattered breast. She did not know how he could still be alive.

"Use the sword with me," he whispered.

She shook her head instantly. "No."

"If you do not use the sword," he said softly, "you can never gain control over the magic I have hidden from you. Everything I have acquired, all the knowledge of the Old World gleaned from these catacombs, all of the power granted by the Druids, is locked away inside me. It can be released if you use the sword, if you are strong enough to master it, but not otherwise."

"More lies!" she spat.

"Lies?" His voice was weakening, his words fatigued and slurred. "I am a dead man. But I am still stronger than you are. I can use the sword while you cannot. Dare not. Prove me wrong, if you think you can. Do as I say. Use the sword. Test yourself against me. All that I have, all of it, becomes yours if you are strong enough. Look at me. Look into my eyes. What do you see?"

What she saw was a certainty that brooked no doubt and concealed no subterfuge. He was challenging her to look at the truth as he believed it to be, asking her to risk what that might mean. She did not think she should do so, but she also believed that access to his mind was worth any risk. Once inside, she would know all his secrets. She would know the truth about the missing books of magic. She would know the truth about herself and the boy. It was a chance she could not afford to pass up. His nonsense about Druid knowledge and power was a ploy to distract her, but she could play such games much better than he could.

"All right." Her words were rimmed in iron. "But you will place your hand on the sword first, under mine, so that I can hold you fast. That way, should this prove to be a trick of some kind, you will not escape me."

She thought she had turned the tables on him neatly. She expected him to refuse, frightened of being linked to her in a way that stripped him of a chance to break free. But again he surprised her. He nodded in agreement. He would do as she asked. She stared at him. When she thought she saw a flicker of satisfaction cross his face, she was flooded with anger and clenched her fist at him.

"Do not think you can deceive me, Druid!" she snapped. "I will crush you faster than you can blink if you try!"

He did not respond, his eyes still locked on hers. For an instant she thought to abandon the whole effort, to back away from him. Let him die, and she would sort it all out later. But she could not make herself give up the opportunity he was offering her, even if it was only for a moment. He kept so many secrets. She wanted them all. She wanted the truth about the boy. She wanted the truth about the magic of that safehold. She might never have another chance to discover either, if she did not act quickly.

She took a steadying breath. Whatever else he intended,

whatever surprise he planned, she was more than a match for him, wasn't she?

She reached over her shoulder and slowly unsheathed the sword, bringing it around in front of her, setting it between them, blade down, handle up. In the smoky gloom, the ancient weapon looked dull and lifeless. Her doubts returned. Was it really the legendary Sword of Shannara or was it something else, something other than what she believed it to be? There was no other magic concealed within it; she would have detected any by now. Nor was there anything about it that would lend strength to the dying Druid. Nothing could save him from the wounds he had incurred. She wondered again at what had savaged him so and would have asked if she had thought there was enough time left to do so.

She inched closer to him, repositioning the blade so that he could reach the handle. She kept her eyes on his, watching for signs of deceit. It seemed impossible that he could manage anything. His eyes were lidded, his breathing rough and shallow, his torn body leaking blood into his robes in such copious amounts she did not know how there could be any left inside him. For just an instant, fresh doubt assailed her, warning her away from what she was about to do. She trusted her instincts, but she hated to acknowledge fear in the face of her sworn enemy, a man against whom she had measured herself for so many years.

She brushed the doubt away. "Place your hand on the sword!"

He raised his bloodied hand from his chest and wrapped his fingers around the handle. As he did so, he seemed to lose focus for a moment, and his hand extended past the talisman to brush lightly against her forehead. She was concentrating so hard on his eyes that she did not think to watch his hand.

She flinched at his touch, aware of the damp smear his fingers had left against her skin. She heard him say something, words spoken so softly she could not make them out.

The feel of his blood on her forehead disturbed her, but she would not give him the satisfaction of seeing her troubled enough to wipe it away. Instead, she placed her hand over his and tightened her grip to hold him fast.

"Now we shall see, Druid."

"Now we shall," he agreed.

Eyes locked, they waited in the smoking ruins of the extraction chamber, so alone that there might have been no one else alive in the world. Everything had gone still. Even the severed cables and wires that had sparked and buzzed only moments before and the shattered machines that had struggled so hard to continue functioning had gone still. It was so quiet that the Ilse Witch could hear the sound of the Druid's breathing slow to almost nothing.

She was wasting her time, she thought abruptly, angry all over again. This wasn't the Sword of Shannara. This wasn't anything more than an ordinary blade.

In response, her fingers dug into Walker's hand and the worn handle beneath it. *Tell me something! Show me your truth, if you have any truth to show!*

An instant later, she felt a surge of warmth rise out of the blade, enter her hand, and spread through her arm. She saw the Druid flinch, then heard him gasp. An instant after that, white light flared all about them, and they disappeared into its molten core.

On the coast of the Blue Divide, dawn was breaking off-shore through a fog bank that stretched across the whole of the horizon like a massive wall. From the deck of the *Jerle*

Shannara, Redden Alt Mer watched the fog materialize in the wake of the retreating night, a rolling gray behemoth closing on the shoreline with the inevitability of a tidal wave. He had seen fog before, but never like that. The bank was thick and unbroken, connecting water to sky, north to south, light to dark. Dawn fought to break through cracks in its surface, a series of angry red streaks that had the look of heated steel, as if a giant furnace had been lit somewhere out on the water.

March Brume experienced heavy fog at times, as did all the seaports along the Westland coast. Mix heat and cold where land met water, stir in a healthy wash of condensation, and you could muster fog thick enough to spread on your toast—that was the old salt's claim. The fog Redden Alt Mer was watching was like that, but it had something else to it, as well, a kind of energy, dark and purposeful, that suggested the approach of a storm. Except the weather didn't feel right for it. His taste and smell of the air revealed nothing of rain, and there had been no sounds of thunder or flashes of lightning. There wasn't a breath of wind. Even the pressure readings gave no hint of trouble.

The Rover Captain paced to the aft decking and peered harder into the haze. Had something moved out there?

"Pea soup," Spanner Frew grumbled, coming up to stand beside him. He frowned out of his dark beard like a thunderhead. "Glad we're not going that way anytime soon."

Alt Mer nodded, still looking out into the haze. "Better hope it stays offshore. I'll be skinned and cooked before I'll let us be stuck here another week."

One more day, and the repair on the airship would be finished. It was so close now that he could barely contain his impatience. Little Red had been gone for three days already, and he hadn't felt right about it once. He had faith in her good judgment, and in Hunter Predd's, as well, but he felt compromised enough as it was by what had befallen the members of the ship's company in that treacherous land. They were scattered all over the place, most of them lost or dead, and he had no idea how they were ever going to bring everyone together, even without the added problem of wondering what might have happened to his sister.

"Have you solved the problem of that forward port crystal?" he asked, watching the shifting fog bank, still thinking he had seen something.

The burly shipwright shrugged. "Can't solve it without a new crystal, and we don't have one. Lost the spares overboard in the channel during the storm. We'll have to make do."

"Well, we've been down that road before." He leaned forward, his hands on the railing, his eyes intent on the fog bank. "Take a look out there, Black Beard. Do you see something? There, maybe fifteen degrees off . . ."

He never finished. Before he could complete the sentence, a cluster of dark shapes materialized out of the gloom. Airborne, they flew out of the roiling gray like a flock of Shrikes or Rocs, silhouetted against the crimson-streaked wall. How many were there? Five, six? No, Alt Mer corrected himself almost at once. A dozen, maybe more. He counted quickly, his throat tightening. Two dozen at least. And they were big, too big even for Rocs. Nor did they have wings to propel them ahead, to provide them with vertical lift.

He caught his breath. They were airships. A whole fleet of them, come out of nowhere. He watched them take shape, masts and sails, rakish dark hulls, and the glint of metal stays and cleats. Warships. He brought up his spyglass and peered closely at them. No insignia emblazoned on flags or pennants, no markings on the gunwales or hulls. He watched them clear the fog and wheel fifteen degrees left, all on a line across the horizon, black as netherworld shades as they drifted into formation and began to advance.

Redden Alt Mer put down the spyglass and took a deep, steadying breath.

They were sailing right for the *Jerle Shannara*.

Here ends Book Two of *The Voyage of the* Jerle Shannara. Book Three, *Morgawr,* will conclude the series as the Ilse Witch is forced to confront the truth about herself and the survivors of Castledown begin the long journey home.

BOOK THREE

MORGAWR

To Owen Lock
For his editor's advice, friendship, and reassurances
when they were needed most

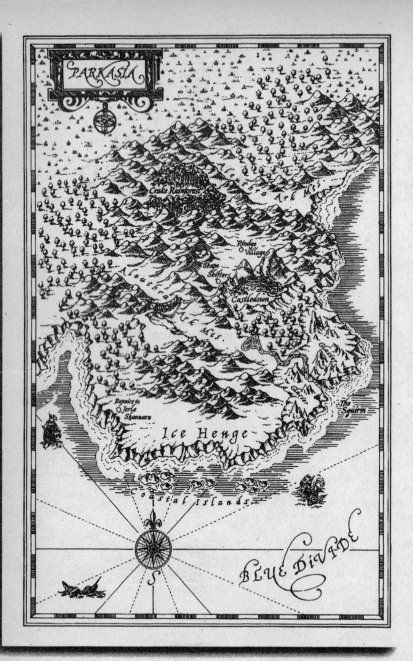

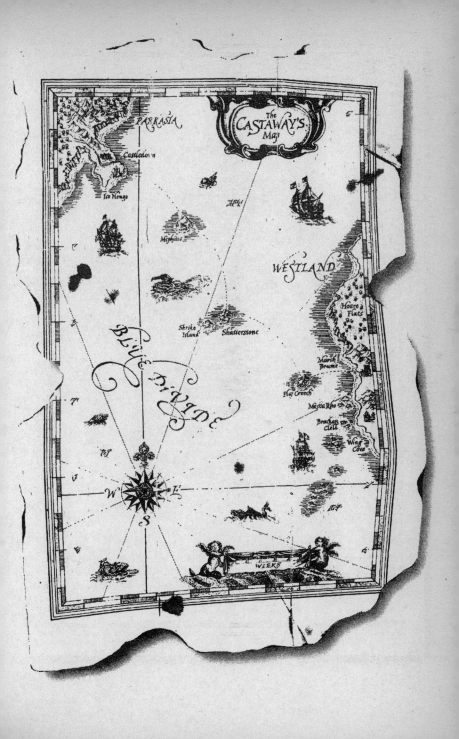

The
CASTAWAY'S
Map

PARKASIA

Castledown

Sea Henge

Mephitis

WESTLAND

Hoare's
Flats

BLUE DIVIDE

Shrike
Island

Shatterstone

March
Brume

Flay Creech

Mesta Rho

Brackento
Clett

Wing
Cove

N

W   E

S

WEEKS

ONE

The figure appeared out of the shadows of the alcove so quickly that Sen Dunsidan was almost on top of it before he realized it was there. The hallway leading to his sleeping chamber was dark with nightfall's shadows, and the light from the wall lamps cast only scattered halos of fuzzy brightness. The lamps gave no help in this instance, and the Minister of Defense was given no chance either to flee or defend himself.

"A word, if you please, Minister."

The intruder was cloaked and hooded, and although Sen Dunsidan was reminded at once of the Ilse Witch he knew without question that it was not she. This was a man, not a woman—too much size and bulk to be anything else, and the words were rough and masculine. The witch's small, slender form and cool, smooth voice were missing. She had come to him only a week earlier, before departing on her voyage aboard *Black Moclips*, tracking the Druid Walker and his company to an unknown destination. Now this intruder, cloaked and hooded in the same manner, had appeared in the same way—at night and unannounced. He wondered at once what the connection was between the two.

Masking his surprise and the hint of fear that clutched at his chest, Sen Dunsidan nodded. "Where would you like to share this word?"

"Your sleeping chamber will do."

A big man himself, still in the prime of his life, the Minister of Defense nevertheless felt dwarfed by the other. It was more than simply size; it was presence, as well. The intruder exuded strength and confidence not usually encountered in ordinary men. Sen Dunsidan did not ask how he had managed to gain entry to the closely guarded, walled compound. He did not ask how he had moved unchallenged to the upper floor of his quarters. Such questions were pointless. He simply accepted that the intruder was capable of this and much more. He did as he was bidden. He walked past with a deferential bow, opened his bedroom door, and beckoned the other inside.

The lights were lit here, as well, though no more brightly than in the hallway without, and the intruder moved at once into the shadows.

"Sit down, Minister, and I will tell you what I want."

Sen Dunsidan sat in a high-backed chair and crossed his legs comfortably. His fear and surprise had faded. If the other meant him harm, he would not have bothered to announce himself. He wanted something that a Minister of Defense of the Federation's Coalition Council could offer, so there was no particular cause for concern. Not yet, anyway. That could change if he could not supply the answers the other sought. But Sen Dunsidan was a master at telling others what they expected to hear.

"Some cold ale?" he asked.

"Pour some for yourself, Minister."

Sen Dunsidan hesitated, surprised by insistence in the other's voice. Then he rose and walked to the table at his bedside that held the ice bucket, ale pitcher nestled within it, and several glasses. He stood looking down at the ale as he poured, his long silver hair hanging loose about his shoulders save where it was braided above the ears, as was the current fashion. He did not like what he was feeling now, uncertainty come so swiftly on the heels of newfound confidence. He had better be careful of this man, step lightly.

He walked back to his chair and reseated himself, sipping at the ale. His strong face turned toward the other, a barely visible presence amid the shadows.

"I have something to ask of you," the intruder said softly.

Sen Dunsidan nodded and made an expansive gesture with one hand.

The intruder shifted slightly. "Be warned, Minister. Do not think to placate me with promises you do not intend to keep. I am not here to waste my time on fools who think to dismiss me with empty words. If I sense you dissemble, I will simply kill you and have done with it. Do you understand?"

Sen Dunsidan took a deep breath to steady himself. "I understand."

The other said nothing further for a moment, then moved out from the deep shadows to the edges of the light. "I am called the Morgawr. I am mentor to the Ilse Witch."

"Ah." The Minister of Defense nodded. He had not been wrong about the similarities of appearance.

The cloaked form moved a little closer. "You and I are about to form a partnership, Minister. A new partnership, one to replace that which you shared with my pupil. She no longer has need of you. She will not come to see you again. But I will. Often."

"Does she know this?" Dunsidan asked softly.

"She knows nowhere near as much as she thinks." The other's voice was hard and low. "She has decided to betray me, and for her infidelity she will be punished. I will administer her punishment when I see her next. This does not concern you, save that you should know why you will not see her again. All these years, I have been the force behind her efforts. I have been the one who gave her the power to form alliances like the one she shared with you. But she breaches my trust and thus forfeits my protection. She is of no further use."

Sen Dunsidan took a long pull on his ale and set the glass aside.

"You will forgive me, sir, if I voice a note of skepticism. I don't know you, but I do know her. I know what she can do. I know what happens to those who betray her, and I do not intend to become one of them."

"Perhaps you would do better to be afraid of me. I am the one who stands here in front of you."

"Perhaps. But the Dark Lady has a way of showing up when least expected. Show me her head, and I will be more than happy to discuss a new agreement."

The cloaked figure laughed softly. "Well spoken, Minister. You offer a politician's answer to a tough demand. But I think you must reconsider. Look at me."

He reached up for his hood and pulled it away to reveal his face. It was the face of the Ilse Witch, youthful and smooth and filled with danger. Sen Dunsidan started in spite of himself. Then the girl's face changed, almost as if it were a mirage, and became Sen Dunsidan's—hard planes and edges, piercing blue eyes, silvery hair worn long, and a half smile that seemed ready to promise anything.

"You and I are very much alike, Minister."

The face changed again. Another took its place, the face of a younger man, but it was no one Sen Dunsidan had ever seen. It was nondescript, bland to the point of being forgettable, devoid of interesting or memorable features.

"Is this who I really am, Minister? Do I reveal myself now?" He paused. "Or am I really like this?"

The face shimmered and changed into something monstrous, a reptilian visage with a blunt snout and slits for eyes. Rough, gray scales coated a weathered face, and a wide, serrated mouth opened to reveal rows of sharply pointed teeth. Gimlet eyes, hate-filled and poisonous, glimmered with green fire.

The intruder pulled the hood back into place, and his face disappeared into the resulting shadows. Sen Dunsidan sat motionless in his chair. He was all too aware of what he was being told. This man had the use of a very powerful magic. At the very least, he

4

could shape-shift, and it was likely he could do much more than that. He was a man who enjoyed the excesses of power as much as the Minister of Defense did, and he would use that power in whatever way he felt he must to get what he wanted.

"I said we were alike, Minister," the intruder whispered. "We both appear as one thing when in truth we are another. I know you. I know you as I know myself. You would do anything to further your power in the hierarchy of the Federation. You indulge yourself in pleasures that are forbidden to other men. You covet what you cannot have and scheme to secure it. You smile and feign friendship when in truth you are the very serpent your enemies fear."

Sen Dunsidan kept his politician's smile in place. What was it this creature wanted of him?

"I tell you all this not to anger you, Minister, but to make certain you do not mistake my intent. I am here to help you further your ambitions in exchange for help you can in turn supply to me. I desire to pursue the witch on her voyage. I desire to be there when she does battle with the Druid, as I am certain she must. I desire to catch her with the magic she pursues, because I intend to take it from her and then to take her life. But to accomplish this, I will need a fleet of airships and the men to crew them."

Sen Dunsidan stared at him in disbelief. "What you ask is impossible."

"Nothing is impossible, Minister." The black robes shifted with a soft rustle as the intruder crossed the room. "Is what I ask any more impossible than what you seek?"

The Minister of Defense hesitated. "Which is what?"

"To be Prime Minister. To take control of the Coalition Council once and for all. To rule the Federation, and by doing so, the Four Lands."

A number of thoughts passed swiftly through Sen Dunsidan's mind, but all of them came down to one. The intruder was right. Sen Dunsidan would do anything to make himself Prime Minister and control the Coalition Council. Even the Ilse Witch had known of this ambition, though she had never voiced it in such a way as this, a way that suggested it might be within reach.

"Both seem impossible to me," he answered the other carefully.

"You fail to see what I am telling you," the intruder said. "I am telling you why I will prove a better ally than the little witch. Who stands between you and your goal? The Prime Minister, who is hardy and well? He will serve long years before he steps down. His chosen successor, the Minister of the Treasury, Jaren Arken? He is a man younger than you and equally powerful, equally ruthless. He aspires to be Minister of Defense, doesn't he? He seeks your position on the council."

A cold rage swept through Sen Dunsidan on hearing those words. It was true, of course—all of it. Arken was his worst enemy, a man slippery and elusive as a snake, cold-blooded and reptilian through and through. He wanted the man dead, but had not yet figured out a way to accomplish it. He had asked the Ilse Witch for help, but whatever other exchange of favors she was willing to accept, she had always refused to kill for him.

"What is your offer, Morgawr?" he asked bluntly, tiring of this game.

"Only this. By tomorrow night, the men who stand in your way will be no more. No blame or suspicion will attach to you. The position you covet will be yours for the taking. No one will oppose you. No one will question your right to lead. This is what I can do for you. In exchange, you must do what I ask—give me the ships and the men to sail them. A Minister of Defense can do this, especially when he stands to become Prime Minister."

The other's voice became a whisper. "Accept the partnership I am offering, so that not only may we help each other now, but we may help each other again when it becomes necessary."

Sen Dunsidan took a long moment to consider what was being asked. He badly wanted to be Prime Minister. He would do anything to secure the position. But he mistrusted this creature, this Morgawr, a thing not entirely human, a wielder of magic that could undo a man before he had time to realize what was happening. He was still unconvinced of the advisability of doing what he was being asked to do. He was afraid of the Ilse Witch; he could admit that to himself if to no one else. If he crossed her and she found out, he was a dead man; she would hunt him down and destroy him. On the other hand, if the Morgawr was to destroy her as he said he would, then Sen Dunsidan would do well to rethink his concerns.

A bird in the hand, it was commonly accepted, was worth two in the bush. If a path to the position of Prime Minister of the Coalition Council could be cleared, almost any risk was worth the taking.

"What sort of airships do you need?" he asked quietly. "How many?"

"Are we agreed on a partnership, Minister? Yes or no. Don't equivocate. Don't attach conditions. Yes or no."

Sen Dunsidan was still uncertain, but he could not pass up the chance to advance his own fortunes. Yet when he spoke the word that sealed his fate, he felt as if he were breathing fire. "Yes."

The Morgawr moved like liquid night, sliding along the edges of the shadows as he eased across the bedchamber. "So be it. I will be back after sunset tomorrow to let you know what your end of the bargain will be."

Then he was through the doorway and gone.

Sen Dunsidan slept poorly that night, plagued by dreams and wakefulness, burdened with the knowledge that he had sold himself at a price that had yet to be determined and might prove too costly to pay. Yet, while lying awake between bouts of fretful sleep, he pondered the enormity of what might take place, and he could not help but be excited. Surely no price was too great if it meant he would become Prime Minister. A handful of ships and a complement of men, neither of which he cared overmuch about—these were nothing to him. In truth, to gain control of the Federation, he would have obligated himself for much more. In truth, he would have paid any price.

Yet it still might all come to nothing. It might prove nothing more than a fantasy given to test his willingness to abandon the witch as an ally.

But when he woke and while he was dressing to go to the Council chambers, word reached him that the Prime Minister was dead. The man had gone to sleep and never woken; his heart stopped while he lay in his bed. It was odd, given his good health and relatively young age, but life was filled with surprises.

Sen Dunsidan felt a surge of pleasure and expectation at the news. He allowed himself to believe that the unthinkable might actually be within reach, that the Morgawr's word might be better than he had dared to hope. *Prime Minister Dunsidan*, he whispered to himself, deep inside, where his darkest secrets lay hidden.

He arrived at the Coalition Council chambers before he learned that Jaren Arken was dead, as well. The Minister of the Treasury, responding to the news of the Prime Minister's sudden passing, had rushed from his home in response, the prospect of filling the leadership void no doubt foremost in his thoughts, and had fallen on the steps leading down to the street. He had struck his head on the stone carvings at the bottom. By the time his servants had reached him, he was gone.

Sen Dunsidan took the news in stride, no longer surprised, only pleased and excited. He put on his mourner's face, and he offered his politician's responses to all those who approached—and there were many now, because he was the one the Council members were already turning to. He spent the day arranging funerals and tributes, speaking to one and all of his own sorrow and disappointment, all the while consolidating his power. Two such important and effective leaders dead at a single stroke; a strong man must be found to fill the void left by their passing. He offered himself and promised to do the best job he could on behalf of those who supported him.

By nightfall, the talk was no longer of the dead men; the talk was all of him.

He sat waiting in his chambers for a long time after sunset, speculating on what would happen when the Morgawr returned. That he would, to claim his end of the bargain, was a given. What exactly he would ask was less certain. He would not threaten, but the threat was there nevertheless: if he could so easily dispose of a Prime Minister and a Minister of the Treasury, how much harder could it be to dispose of a recalcitrant Minister of Defense? Sen Dunsidan was in this business now all the way up to his neck. There could be no talk of backing away. The best he could hope for was to mitigate the payment the Morgawr would seek to exact.

It was almost midnight before the other appeared, slipping soundlessly through the doorway of the bedchamber, all black robes and menace. By then, Sen Dunsidan had consumed several glasses of ale and was regretting it.

"Impatient, Minister?" the Morgawr asked softly, moving at once into the shadows. "Did you think I wasn't coming?"

"I knew you would come. What do you want?"

"So abrupt? Not even time for a thank you? I've made you Prime Minister. All that is required is a vote by the Coalition Council, a matter of procedure only. When will that occur?"

"A day or two. All right, you've kept your end of the bargain. What is mine to be?"

"Ships of the line, Minister. Ships that can withstand a long journey and a battle at its end. Ships that can transport men and equipment to secure what is needed. Ships that can carry back the treasures I expect to find."

Sen Dunsidan shook his head doubtfully. "Such ships are hard to come by. All we have are committed to the Prekkendorran. If I were to pull out, say, a dozen—"

"Two dozen would be closer to what I had in mind," the other interrupted smoothly.

Two dozen? The Minister of Defense exhaled slowly. "Two dozen, then. But that many ships missing from the line would be noticed and questioned. How will I explain it?"

"You are about to become Prime Minister. You don't have to explain." There was a hint of impatience in the rough voice. "Take them from the Rovers, if your own are in short supply."

Dunsidan took a quick sip of the ale he shouldn't be drinking. "The Rovers are neutral in this struggle. Mercenaries, but neutral. If I confiscate their ships, they will refuse to build more."

"I said nothing of confiscation. Steal them, then lay the blame elsewhere."

"And the men to crew them? What sort of men do you require? Must I steal them, as well?"

"Take them from the prisons. Men who have sailed and fought aboard airships. Elves, Bordermen, Rovers, whatever. Give me enough of these to make my crews. But do not expect me to give them back again. When I have used them up, I intend to throw them away. They will not be fit for anything else."

The hair stood on the back of Sen Dunsidan's neck. Two hundred men, tossed away like old shoes. Damaged, ruined, unfit for wear. What did that mean? He had a sudden urge to flee the room, to run and keep running until he was so far away he couldn't remember where he had come from.

"I'll need time to arrange this, a week perhaps." He tried to keep his voice steady. "Two dozen ships missing from anywhere will be talked about. Men from the prisons will be missed. I have to think about how this can be done. Must you have so many of each to undertake your pursuit?"

The Morgawr went still. "You seem incapable of doing anything I ask of you without questioning it. Why is that? Did I ask you how to go about removing those men who would keep you from being Prime Minister?"

Sen Dunsidan realized suddenly that he had gone too far. "No, no, of course not. It was just that I—"

"Give me the men tonight," the other interrupted.

"But I need time."

"You have them in your prisons, here in the city. Arrange for their release now."

"There are rules about releasing prisoners."

"Break them."

Sen Dunsidan felt as if he were standing in quicksand and sinking fast. But he couldn't seem to find a way to save himself.

"Give me my crews tonight, Minister," the other hissed softly. "You, personally. A show of trust to persuade me that my efforts at removing the men who stood in your path were justified. Let's be certain your commitment to our new partnership is more than just words."

"But I—"

The other man moved swiftly out of the shadows and snatched hold of the front of the Minister's shirt. "I think you require a demonstration. An example of what happens to those who question me." The fingers tightened in the fabric, iron rods that lifted Sen Dunsidan to the tips of his boots. "You're shaking, Minister. Can it be that I have your full attention at last?"

Sen Dunsidan nodded wordlessly, so frightened he did not trust himself to speak.

"Good. Now come with me."

Sen Dunsidan exhaled sharply as the other released his grip and stepped away. "Where?"

The Morgawr moved past him, opened the bedchamber door, and looked back out of the shadows of his hood. "To the prisons, Minister, to get my men."

11

TWO

ogether, the Morgawr and Sen Dunsidan passed down the halls of the Minister's house, through the gates of the compound, and outside into the night. None of the guards or servants they passed spoke to them. No one seemed even to see them. *Magic,* Sen Dunsidan thought helplessly. He stifled the urge to cry out for help, knowing there was none.

Insanity.

But he had made his choice.

As they walked the dark, empty streets of the city, the Minister of Defense gathered the shards of his shattered composure, one jagged piece at a time. If he was to survive this night, he must do better than he was doing now. The Morgawr already thought him weak and foolish; if he thought him useless, as well, he would discard him in an instant. Walking steadily, taking strong strides, deep breaths, Sen Dunsidan mustered his courage and his resolve. *Remember who you are,* he told himself. *Remember what is at stake.*

Beside him, the Morgawr walked on, never looking at him, never speaking to him, never evidencing even once that he had any interest in him at all.

The prisons were situated at the west edge of the Federation

Army barracks, close by the swift flowing waters of the Rappahalladran. They formed a dark and formidable collection of pitted stone towers and walls. Narrow slits served as windows, and iron spikes ringed the parapets. Sen Dunsidan, as Minister of Defense, visited the prisons regularly, and he had heard the stories. No one ever escaped. Now and then those incarcerated would find their way into the river, thinking to swim to the far side and flee into the forests. No one ever made it. The currents were treacherous and strong. Sooner or later, the bodies washed ashore and were hung from the walls where others in the prisons could see them.

As they drew close, Sen Dunsidan mustered sufficient resolve to draw close again to the Morgawr.

"What do you intend to do when we get inside?" he asked, keeping his voice strong and steady. "I need to know what to say if you want to avoid having to hypnotize the entire garrison."

The Morgawr laughed softly. "Feeling a bit more like your old self, Minister? Very well. I want a room in which to speak with prospective members of my crew. I want them brought to me one by one, starting with a Captain or someone in authority. I want you to be there to watch what happens."

Dunsidan nodded, trying not to think what that meant.

"Next time, Minister, think twice before you make a promise you do not intend to keep," the other hissed, his voice rough and hard-edged. "I have no patience with liars and fools. You do not strike me as either, but then you are good at becoming what you must in your dealings with others, aren't you?"

Sen Dunsidan said nothing. There was nothing to say. He kept his thoughts focused on what he would do once they were inside the prisons. There, he would be more in control of things, more on familiar ground. There, he could do more to demonstrate his worth to this dangerous creature.

Recognizing Sen Dunsidan at once, the gate watch admitted them without question. Snapping to attention in their worn leathers, they released the locks on the gates. Inside, the smells were of damp-ness and rot and human excrement, foul and rank. Sen Dunsidan asked the Duty Officer for a specific interrogation room, one with which he was familiar, one removed from everything else, buried deep in the bowels of the prisons. A turnkey led them down a long corridor to the room he had requested, a large chamber with walls that leaked moisture and a floor that had buckled. A table to which had been fastened iron chains and clamps sat at its center. To one side, a wooden rack lined with implements of torture was pushed against the wall. A single oil lamp lit the gloom.

"Wait here," Sen Dunsidan told the Morgawr. "Let me persuade the right men to come to you."

"Start with one," the Morgawr ordered, moving off into the shadows.

Sen Dunsidan hesitated, then went out through the door with the turnkey. The turnkey was a hulking, gnarled man who had served seven terms on the front, a lifetime soldier in the Federation Army. He was scarred inside and out, having witnessed and sur-vived atrocities that would have destroyed the minds of other men. He never spoke, but he knew well enough what was going on and seemed unconcerned with it. Sen Dunsidan had used him on occa-sion to question recalcitrant prisoners. The man was good at in-flicting pain and ignoring pleas for mercy—perhaps even better at that than keeping his mouth shut.

Oddly enough, the Minister had never learned his name. Down here, they called him Turnkey, as if the title itself were name enough for a man who did what he did.

They passed down a dozen small corridors and through a hand-ful of doors to where the main cells were located. The larger ones held prisoners who had been taken from the Prekkendorran. Some would be ransomed or traded for Free-born prisoners. Some would die here. Sen Dunsidan indicated to the turnkey the one that housed those who had been prisoners longest.

"Unlock it."

The turnkey unlocked the door without a word.

Sen Dunsidan took a torch from its rack on the wall. "Close the door behind me. Don't open it until I tell you I am ready to come out," he ordered.

Then he stepped boldly inside.

The room was large, damp, and rank with the smells of caged men. A dozen heads turned as one on his entry. An equal number lifted from the soiled pallets on the floor. Other men stirred, fitfully. Most were still asleep.

"Wake up!" he snapped.

He held up the torch to show them who he was, then stuck it in a stanchion next to the door. The men were beginning to stand now, whispers and grunts passing between them. He waited until they were all awake, a ragged bunch with dead eyes and ravaged faces. Some of them had been locked down here for almost three years. Most had given up hope of ever getting out. The small sounds of their shuffling echoed in the deep, pervasive silence, a constant reminder of how helpless they were.

"You know me," he said to them. "Many of you I have spoken with. You have been here a long time. Too long. I am going to give all of you a chance to get out. You won't be doing any more fighting in the war. You won't be going home—not for a while. But you will be outside these walls and back on an airship. Are you interested?"

The man he had depended upon to speak for the others took a step forward. "What are you after?"

His name was Darish Venn. He was a Borderman who had captained one of the first Free-born airships brought into the war on the Prekkendorran. He had distinguished himself in battle many times before his ship went down and he was captured. The other men respected and trusted him. As senior officer, he had formed them into groups and given them positions, small and insignificant to those who were free men, but of crucial importance to those locked away down here.

"Captain." Sen Dunsidan acknowledged him with a nod. "I need men to go on a voyage across the Blue Divide. A long voyage, from which some may not return. I won't deny there is danger. I don't have the sailors to spare for this, or the money to hire Rover mercenaries. But the Federation can spare you. Federation soldiers will accompany those who agree to accept the conditions I am offering, so there will be some protection offered and order imposed. Mostly, you will be out of here and you won't have to come back. The voyage will take a year, maybe two. You will be your own crew, your own company, as long as you go where you are told."

"Why would you do this now, after so long?" Darish Venn asked.

"I can't tell you that."

"Why should we trust you?" another asked boldly.

"Why not? What difference does it make, if it gets you out of here? If I wanted to do you harm, it would be easy enough, wouldn't it? What I want are sailors willing to make a voyage. What you want is your freedom. A trade seems a good compromise for both of us."

"We could take you prisoner and trade you for our freedom and not have to agree to anything!" the man snapped ominously.

Sen Dunsidan nodded. "You could. But what would be the consequences of that? Besides, do you think I would come down here and expose myself to harm without any protection?"

There was a quick exchange of whispers. Sen Dunsidan held his ground and kept his strong face composed. He had exposed himself to greater risks than this one, and he was not afraid of these men. The results of failure to do what the Morgawr had asked frightened him a good deal more.

"You want all of us?" Darish Venn asked.

"All who choose to come. If you refuse, then you stay where you are. The choice is yours." He paused a moment, as if considering. His leonine profile lifted into the light, and a reflective look settled over his craggy features. "I will make a bargain with you, Captain. If you like, I will show you a map of the place we are going. If you approve of what you see, then you sign on then and there. If not, you can return and tell the others."

The Borderman nodded. Perhaps he was too worn down and too slowed by his imprisonment to think it through clearly. Perhaps he was just anxious for a way out. "All right, I'll come."

Sen Dunsidan rapped on the door, and the turnkey opened it for him. He beckoned Captain Venn to go first, then left the room. The turnkey locked the door, and Dunsidan could hear the scuffling of feet as those still locked within pressed up against the doorway to listen.

"Just down the hallway, Captain," he advised loudly for their benefit. "I'll arrange for a glass of ale, as well."

They walked down the passageways to the room where the Morgawr waited, their footsteps echoing in the silence. No one spoke. Sen Dunsidan glanced at the Borderman. He was a big man, tall and broad shouldered, though stooped and thin from his imprisonment, his face skeletal and his skin pale and crusted with dirt and sores. The Free-born had tried to trade for him many times, but the Federation knew the value of airship Captains and preferred to keep him locked away and off the battlefield.

When they reached the room where the Morgawr waited, Sen Dunsidan opened the door for Venn, motioned for the turnkey to wait outside, and closed the door behind him as he followed the Borderman in. Venn glanced around at the implements of torture and chains, then looked at Dunsidan.

"What is this?"

The Minister of Defense shrugged and smiled disarmingly. "It was the best I could do." He indicated one of the three-legged stools tucked under the table. "Sit down and let's talk."

There was no sign of the Morgawr. Had he left? Had he decided all this was a waste of time and he would be better off handling matters himself? For a moment, Sen Dunsidan panicked. But then he felt something move in the shadows—*felt*, rather than saw.

He moved to the other side of the table from Darish Venn, drawing the Captain's attention away from the swirling darkness behind him. "The voyage will take us quite a distance from the Four Lands, Captain," he said, his face taking on a serious cast. Behind Venn, the Morgawr began to materialize. "A good deal of preparation will be necessary. Someone with your experience will have no trouble provisioning the ships we intend to take. A dozen or more will be needed, I think."

The Morgawr, huge and black, slid out of the shadows without a sound and came up behind Venn. The Borderman neither heard nor sensed him, just stared straight at Sen Dunsidan.

"Naturally, you will be in charge of your men, of choosing which ones will undertake which tasks . . ."

A hand slid out of the Morgawr's black robes, gnarled and covered with scales. It clamped on the back of Darish Venn's neck, and the airship Captain gave a sharp gasp. Twisting and thrashing, he tried to break free, but the Morgawr held him firmly in place. Sen Dunsidan stepped back a pace, his words dying in his throat as he watched the struggle. Darish Venn's eyes were fixed on him, maddened but helpless. The Morgawr's other hand emerged, shimmering with a wicked green light. Slowly the pulsating hand moved toward the back of the Borderman's head. Sen Dunsidan caught his breath. Clawed fingers stretched, touching the hair, then the skin.

Darish Venn screamed.

The fingers slid inside his head, pushing through hair and skin and bone as if the whole of it were made of soft clay. Sen Dunsidan's throat tightened and his stomach lurched. The Morgawr's hand was all the way inside the skull now, twisting slowly, as if searching. The Captain had stopped screaming and thrashing. The light had gone out of his eyes, and his face had gone slack. His look was dull and lifeless.

The Morgawr withdrew his hand from the Borderman's head, and it was steaming and wet as it slid back into the black robes and out of sight. The Morgawr was breathing so loudly that Sen

Dunsidan could hear him, a kind of rapturous panting, rife with sounds of satisfaction and pleasure.

"You cannot know, Minister," he whispered, "how good it feels to feed on another's life. Such ecstasy!"

He stepped back, releasing Venn. "There. It is done. He is ours now, to do with as we wish. He is a walking dead man with no will of his own. He will do whatever he is told to do. He keeps his skills and his experience, but he no longer cares to think for himself. A useful tool, Minister. Take a look at him."

Reluctantly, Sen Dunsidan did so. It was not an invitation; it was a command. He studied the blank, lifeless eyes, revulsion turning to horror as they began to lose color and definition and turn milky white and vacant. He moved around the table cautiously, looking for the wound in the back of the Borderman's head where the Morgawr's hand had forced entry. To his astonishment, there wasn't one. The skull was undamaged. It was as if nothing had happened.

"Test him, Minister." The Morgawr was laughing. "Tell him to do something."

Sen Dunsidan fought to keep his composure. "Stand up," he ordered Darish Venn in a voice he could barely recognize as his own.

The Borderman rose. He never looked at Sen Dunsidan or gave recognition that he knew what was happening. His eyes stayed dead and blank, and his face had lost all expression.

"He is the first, but only the first," the Morgawr hissed, anxious now and impatient. "A long night stretches ahead of us. Go now, and bring me another. I am already hungry for a fresh taste! Go! Bring me six, but bid them enter one by one. Go quickly!"

Sen Dunsidan went out the door without a word. An image of a scaly hand steaming and wet with human matter was fixed in his mind and would not give up its hold on him.

He brought more men to the room that night, so many he lost count of them. He brought them in small groups and had them enter singly. He watched as their bodies were violated and their minds destroyed. He stood by without lifting a finger to aid them as they were changed from whole men into shells. It was strange, but after Darish Venn, he couldn't remember any of their faces. They were all one to him. They were all the same man.

When the room grew too crowded with them, he was ordered to lead them out and turn them over to the turnkey to place in a larger chamber. The turnkey took them away without comment, without even looking at them. But once, after maybe fifty or so, the ruined face and the hard eyes found Sen Dunsidan with a look that left him in tears. The look bore guilt and accusation, horror and despair, and above all unmitigated rage. This was wrong, the look said. This went beyond anything imaginable. This was madness.

And yet the turnkey did nothing either.

The two of them, accomplices to an unspeakable crime.

The two of them, silent participants in the perpetration of a monstrous wrong.

So many men did Sen Dunsidan help destroy, men who walked to their doom with nothing to offer in their defense, decoyed by a politician's false words and reassuring looks. He did not know how he managed it. He did not know how he survived what it made him feel. Each time the Morgawr's hand emerged wet and dripping with human life, another feasting complete, the Minister of Defense thought he would run screaming into the night. Yet the presence of Death was so overpowering that it transcended everything else in those terrible hours, paralyzing him. While the Morgawr feasted, Sen Dunsidan watched and was unable even to look away.

Until finally, the Morgawr was sated. "Enough for now," he hissed, glutted and drunk on stolen life. "Tomorrow night, Minister, we will finish this."

He rose and walked away, taking his dead with him into the night, shadows on the wind.

The dawn broke and the day came, but Sen Dunsidan saw none of it. He shut himself away and did not come out. He lay in his room and tried to banish the image of the Morgawr's hand. He dozed and tried to forget the way his skin crawled at the slightest sound of a human voice. Queries were made after his health. He was needed in the Council chambers. A vote on the position of Prime Minister was imminent. Reassurances were sought. Sen Dunsidan no longer cared. He wished he had never put himself in this position. He wished he were dead.

By nightfall, the turnkey was. Even given the harshness of his life and the toughness of his mind, he could not bear what he had witnessed. When no one else was about, he went down into the bowels of the prison and hung himself in a vacant cell.

Or did he? Sen Dunsidan could not be certain. Perhaps it was murder made to look like suicide. Perhaps the Morgawr did not want the turnkey alive.

Perhaps Sen Dunsidan was next.

But what could he do to save himself?

The Morgawr came again at midnight, and again Sen Dunsidan went with him into the prisons. This time Dunsidan dismissed the new turnkey and handled all the extraneous work himself. He was numb to it by now, inured to the screams, the wet and steaming hand, the grunts of horror from the men, and the sighs of satisfaction from the Morgawr. He was no longer a part of it, gone somewhere else, somewhere so far away that what happened here, in this place and on this night, meant nothing. It would be over by dawn, and when it was, Sen Dunsidan would be another man in another life. He would transcend this one and leave it behind. He would begin anew. He would remake himself in a way that cleansed him of the wrongs he had done and the atrocities he had abetted. It was not so hard. It was what soldiers did when they came home from a war. It was how a man got past the unforgivable.

More than 250 men passed through that room and out of the life they had known. They disappeared as surely as if they had turned to smoke. The Morgawr changed them into dead things that still walked, into creatures that had lost all sense of identity and purpose. He turned them into something less than dogs, and they did not even know it. He made them into his airship crews, and he took them away forever. All of them, every last one. Sen Dunsidan never saw any of them again.

Within days, he had secured the airships the Morgawr had requested and delivered them to fulfill his end of the bargain. Within a week, the Morgawr was gone out of his life, departed in search of the Ilse Witch, in quest of revenge. Sen Dunsidan didn't care. He hoped they destroyed each other. He prayed he would never see either of them again.

But the images remained, haunting and terrible. He could not banish them. He could not reconcile their horror. They haunted him in his sleep and when he was awake. They were never far away, never out of sight. Sen Dunsidan did not sleep for weeks afterwards. He did not enjoy a moment's peace.

He became Prime Minister of the Federation's Coalition Council, but he lost his soul.

THREE

N ow, months later and thousands of miles away off the coast of the continent of Parkasia, the fleet of airships assembled by Sen Dunsidan and placed under the command of the Morgawr and his Mwellrets and walking dead materialized out of the mist and closed on the *Jerle Shannara*. Standing amidships at the port railing, Redden Alt Mer watched the cluster of black hulls and sails fill the horizon east like links in an encircling chain.

"Cast off!" the Rover Captain snapped at Spanner Frew, spyglass lifting one more time to make certain of what he was seeing.

"She's not ready!" the burly shipwright snapped back.

"She's as ready as she's going to get. Give the order!"

His glass swept the approaching ships. No insignia, no flags. Unmarked warships in a land where until a few weeks ago there had never been even one. Enemies, but whose? He had to assume the worst, that these ships were hunting them. Had the Ilse Witch brought others besides *Black Moclips*, ships that had lain offshore until now, waiting for the witch to bring them into the mix?

Spanner Frew was yelling at the crew, setting them in action. With Furl Hawken dead and Rue Meridian gone inland, there was no one else to fill the role of First Mate. No one stopped to question him. They had seen the ships, as well. Hands reached obediently for lines and winches. The tethering line was released, giving the *Jerle Shannara* her freedom. Rovers began tightening down the radian draws and lanyards, bringing the sails all the way to the tops of the masts, where they could catch the wind and light. Knowing what he would find, Redden Alt Mer glanced around. His crew was eight strong, counting Spanner and himself. Not nearly enough to fully man a warship like the *Jerle Shannara*, let alone fight a battle against enemies. They would have to run, and run fast.

He ran himself, breaking for the pilot box and the controls, heavy boots thudding across the wooden decking. "Unhood the crystals!" he yelled at Britt Rill and Jethen Amenades as he swept past them. "Not the fore starboard! Leave it covered. Just the aft and amidships!"

No working diapson crystal in the fore port parse tube, so to balance the loss of power from the left he was forced to shut down its opposite number. It would cut their power by a third, but the *Jerle Shannara* was swift enough even at that.

Spanner Frew was beside him, lumbering toward the mainmast and the weapons rack. "Who are they?"

"I don't know, Black Beard, but I don't think they are friends."

He opened the four available parse tubes and drew down power to the crystals from the draws. The *Jerle Shannara* lurched sharply and began to rise as ambient light converted to energy. But too slow, the Rover Captain saw, to make a clean escape. The invading ships were nearly on top of them, an odd assortment, all sizes and shapes, none of them recognizable save for their general design. A mix, he saw, mostly Rover built, a few Elven. Where had they come from? He could see their crews moving about the ships' decking, slow and unhurried, showing none of the excitement and fever he was familiar with. Calm in the face of battle.

Po Kelles, aboard Niciannon, flew past the pilot box off the starboard side. The big Roc banked so close to Redden Alt Mer that he could see the bluish sheen of the bird's feathers.

"Captain!" the Wing Rider yelled, pointing.

He was not pointing at the ships, but at a flurry of dots that had appeared suddenly in their midst, small and more mobile. War Shrikes, acting in concert with the enemy ships, warding their flanks and leading their advance. Already they were ahead of the ships and coming fast at the *Jerle Shannara*.

"Fly out of here!" Big Red yelled back at Po Kelles. "Fly inland and find Little Red! Warn her what's happening!"

The Wing Rider and his Roc swung away, lifting swiftly into the misty sky. A Roc's best chance against Shrikes was to gain height and distance. In a short race, the Shrikes had the advantage. Here, they were still too far away. Already, Niciannon was opening the gap between them. With the navigational directions Po Kelles had been given already, he would have no trouble reaching Hunter Predd and Rue Meridian. The danger now was to the *Jerle Shannara*. A Shrike's talons could rip a sail to shreds. The birds would soon attempt just that.

Alt Mer's hands flew to the controls. Shrikes in league with enemy warships. How could that be? Who controlled the birds? But he knew the answer as soon as he asked himself the question. It would take magic to bring War Shrikes into line like this. Someone, or something, aboard those ships possessed such magic.

The Ilse Witch? he wondered. Come out from inland, where she had gone to find the others?

There was no time to ponder it.

"Black Beard!" he yelled down to Spanner Frew. "Place the men on both sides, down in the fighting pits. Use bows and arrows and keep those Shrikes at bay!"

His hands steady on the controls, he watched the warships and birds loom up in front of him, too close to avoid. He couldn't get above them or swing around fast enough to put sufficient distance between them. He had no choice. On his first pass, he would have to go right through them.

"Hold fast!" he yelled to Spanner Frew.

Then the closest of the warships were on top of them, moving swiftly out of the haze, all bulk and darkness in the early morning gloom. Redden Alt Mer had been here before, and he knew what to do. He didn't try to avoid a collision. Instead, he initiated one, turning the *Jerle Shannara* toward the smallest ship in the line. The radian draws hummed as they funneled the ambient light into the parse tubes and the diapson crystals turned it to energy, a peculiar, tinny sound. The ship responded with a surge as he levered forward on the controls, tilted the hull slightly to port, and sliced through the enemy ship's foremast and sails, taking them down in a single sweep that left the vessel foundering.

Shrikes wheeled about them, but in close quarters they could not come in more than two at a time, and the bowmen fired arrows at them with deadly accuracy, causing injuries and screams of rage.

"Helm port!" Big Red shouted in warning as a second vessel tried to close from the left.

As the crew braced, he swung the wheel all the way about, bringing the rams to bear on this new threat. The *Jerle Shannara* shuddered and lurched as the parse tubes emitted fresh discharges of converted light, then shot forward across the enemy's stern, raking her decking and snapping off pieces of railing like deadwood. Redden Alt Mer had only a few moments to glance over at the enemy crew. A Mwellret clutched the helm, crouched down in the pilot box to weather the impact of the collision. He gestured and yelled toward his men, but their response was oddly slow and mechanical, as if they were just coming out of a deep sleep, as if further information was needed before action could be taken. Redden Alt Mer watched their faces turn toward him, blank and empty, devoid of emotion or recognition. Eyes stared up at him, as hard and milky white as sea stones.

"Shades!" the Rover Captain whispered.

They were the eyes of the dead, yet the men themselves were still moving around. For a moment, he was so stunned that he lost his concentration completely. Though he had seen other strange things, he had never seen dead men walk. He had not believed he ever would. Yet he was seeing them now.

"Spanner!" he shouted down at the shipwright.

Spanner Frew had seen them, as well. He looked at Redden Alt Mer and shook his wooly black head like an angry bear.

Then the *Jerle Shannara* was past the second ship and lifting above the others, and Alt Mer brought her all the way around and headed her inland, out of the fray. The enemy ships gave chase at once, coming at her from all directions, but they were strung out along the coastline and too far away to close effectively. How had they found her in the first place? he wondered. For a second, he considered the possibility of betrayal by one of his men, but quickly dismissed the idea. Magic, possibly. If whoever commanded this fleet could enslave Shrikes and make the dead come alive, he could find a band of Rovers easily enough. It was more than likely that he had used the Shrikes to track them.

Or *she* had, if it was the Ilse Witch returned.

He cursed his ignorance, the witch, and a dozen other imponderables as he flew the airship inland toward the mountains. He would have to turn south soon to stay within his bearings. He could not trust to the shorter overland route. Too much danger of losing the way and missing Little Red and the others. He could not afford to do that, to leave them abandoned to these things that gave pursuit.

A sharp *whang!* cut through the rush of wind as the amidships radian draw off the port railing broke loose and began to whip about the decking like a striking snake. The Rovers, still crouched in their fighting pits, flattened themselves protectively. Spanner Frew leapt behind the mainmast, taking cover as the loose draw snapped past, then wrapped itself around the aft port line and jerked it free.

At once the airship began to lose power and balance, both already diminished by the loss of the forward draws, now thrown off altogether by the breaking away of the entire port bank. If the lines were not retethered at once, the ship would circle right back into the enemy ships, and they would all be in the hands of the walking dead.

Redden Alt Mer saw those eyes again, milky and vacant, devoid of humanity, bereft of any sense of the world about them.

Without stopping to consider, he cut power to the amidships starboard tube and thrust the port lever all the way forward. Either the *Jerle Shannara* would hold together long enough for him to give them a fighting chance to escape or it would fall out of the sky.

"Black Beard!" he yelled down to Spanner Frew. "Take the helm!"

The shipwright lumbered up the steps and into the pilot box, gnarled hands reaching for the controls. Redden Alt Mer took no time to explain, but simply bolted past him down the steps to the decking and forward to the mainmast. He felt exhilarated and edgy, as if nothing he might do was too wild to consider. Not altogether a bad assessment, he decided. Wind, wild and shrieking in his ears, whipped at his long red hair and brilliant scarves. He could feel the airship rocking under him, fighting to maintain trim, to keep from diving. He was impressed. Three draws lost; she should already be going down. Another ship wouldn't have lasted this long.

To his left, the entangled draws snapped and wrenched at each other, threatening to tear loose at any moment. He risked a quick glance over his shoulder. Their pursuers had drawn closer, taking advantage of their troubles. The Shrikes were almost on them.

"Keep them at bay!" he shouted down to the Rovers crouched in the fighting pits, but his words were lost in the wind.

He went up the foremast using the iron climbing pins hammered into the wood, pressing himself against the thick timber to keep from being torn loose and thrown out into the void. His flying leathers helped to protect him, but even so, the wind was ferocious, blowing out of the mountains and toward the coast in a cold, hard rush. He did not look behind him or over at the draws. The dangers were obvious and he could do nothing about them. If the draws worked loose before he got to them, they could easily whip about and cut him in half. If the Shrikes got close enough, they could rip him off his perch and carry him away. Neither prospect was worth considering.

Something flashed darkly at the corner of his vision. He caught just a glimpse as it whizzed past. Another whipped by. Arrows. The enemy vessels were close enough that longbows could be brought into play. Perhaps the Mwellrets and walking dead were not proficient with weapons. Perhaps some small part of the luck that had saved him so many times before would save him now.

Perhaps was all he had.

Then he was atop the mast and working his way out along the yardarm to where the renegade draw was fastened topside. He clung to the yardarm with numb, bruised fingers, his strength seeping away in the frigid wind. Below, upturned faces shifted back and forth as men fired arrows at the approaching Shrikes then glanced up at him to check his progress. He saw the worry in those hard faces. *Good*, he thought. He would hate not to be missed.

A Shrike swept past him from above, screaming. Its talons snatched at his back, and the flying leathers jerked and tore. A wash of pain rushed through him as the bird's claws ripped into his skin. He wrenched himself sideways and nearly fell, his legs losing their grip so that he was hanging from the yardarm by his fingers. The sail billowed into him like a balloon, and he lay across it, gathering his strength. While he was buried in the sail, another Shrike swept past but couldn't get close enough. It banked away in frustration.

Don't stop, he told himself through a haze of weariness and pain. *Don't quit!*

He crawled back up on the yardarm, then dragged himself to its end, swung out from the spar, and slid down the length of the midships draw to where it had tangled in the aft, his boots clearing the lines as he descended. Battered and worn, but still clinging desperately to both stays, he hollered out to his crew for help. Two of them leapt from the port fighting pits and were beside him in moments, taking hold of the draws and hauling them back toward the parse tubes from which they had broken loose, ignoring the diving Shrikes and the hail of arrows from the pursuing ships.

Redden Alt Mer collapsed on the deck, his back burning with pain and wet with blood.

"That's more than enough heroics from you, Captain," Britt Rill growled, appearing out of nowhere to take hold of one arm and haul him to his feet. "Down below for you."

Alt Mer started to object, but his throat was so dry he couldn't get the words out. Worse, his strength had failed him completely. It was all he could do to stand with Rill's help. He glanced at the other and nodded. He had done what he could. The rest was up to the ship, and he would bet on her in any race.

Belowdecks, Britt Rill helped him off with his flying leathers and began to wash and clean his wounds. "How bad is it?" Redden Alt Mer asked, head bent forward, arms resting on his knees, hands clasped, and the whole of him knotted with pain. "Did it sever the muscles?"

"Nothing so bad, Captain," the other answered quietly. "Just a few deep cuts that will give you stories to tell your grandchildren, should you ever have any."

"Not likely."

"Be a blessing for the world, I expect."

Rill applied salve to the wounds, bound him up with strips of cloth, gave him a long pull from the aleskin strapped to his waist, and left him to decide for himself what he would do next. "The others will be needing me," Rill called back as he went out the cabin door.

And me, Alt Mer thought. But he didn't move right away. Instead, he sat there on his bed for several minutes more, listening to the sound of the wind outside the shuttered windows, feeling the movement of the ship beneath him. He could tell from its sway and glide that it was doing what it should, that power was back in sufficient amounts to keep it aloft and moving. But the battle wasn't over yet.

Pursuers with magic enough to summon Shrikes and command the walking dead would not give up easily.

He went topside moments later, his shredded flying leathers pulled back in place. Stepping out into the wind, he cast about momentarily to gauge their position, then moved over to the pilot box to stand next to Spanner Frew. Content to let the shipwright guide them, he didn't ask for the helm. Instead, he spent a few long moments looking back at the clutch of dark shapes that were still in pursuit but beginning to fade into the haze. Even the Shrikes seemed to have given up the chase.

Spanner Frew glanced over at him, took note of his condition, and said nothing. The Rover Captain's look did not encourage conversation.

Alt Mer glanced at the surrounding sky. It was all grayness and mist, with a darker wash north that meant rain approached. Mountains loomed ahead and on both sides as they advanced inland toward the ice fields they must traverse in order to reach Rue and the others.

Then he saw the scattering of dots ahead and off to the starboard where the coastline bent inward in a series of deep coves.

"Black Beard!" he said in the other's ear, pulling on his shoulder and pointing.

Spanner Frew looked. Ahead, the dots began to take shape, to grow wings and sails. "More of them!" the big man growled, a hint of disbelief in his rough voice. "Shrikes, as well, if I'm seeing right. How did they get ahead of us?"

"The Shrikes know the coastline and cliffs better than we do!" Alt Mer had to fight to be heard above the wind. "They've found a way to cut us off. If we stick to our flight line, they'll have us. We have to get further inland, and we have to get there quickly."

His companion glanced around at the mist-shrouded mountains. "If we fly into these in this mist, we'll end up in splinters."

Alt Mer caught his eye and held it. "We don't have any choice. Give me the wheel. Go forward and signal back whenever you think

I need it. Hand signals only. Voices might give us away. Do your best to keep us off the rocks."

Having repaired the broken draws and swept aside the bits of wreckage, the crew was standing by on the lines. Spanner Frew called out to them as he passed, sending them to their stations, warning of what was happening. No one replied. They were schooled in the Rover tradition of keeping faith in those who had the luck. No one had more of it than Redden Alt Mer. They would ride a burning ship into a firestorm if he told them to do so.

He took a deep breath, glanced once more at the shapes ahead and behind. Too many to evade or to fight. He swung the wheel hard to port toward the bank of mist. He let the airship maintain speed until they were into the soup, then cut back to dead slow, watching the vapor gather and fade, wispy sheets of white wrapping the darker edges of the mountains. If they struck a peak at this height, in this haze, with a third of their power already gone, they were finished.

But the Shrikes couldn't track them, and their pursuers were faced with the same problem they were.

It was oddly silent in the mist, in the cradle of the peaks, empty of all sound as the *Jerle Shannara* glided like a bird. All about them the mountains seemed afloat, dark masses appearing and fading like mirages. Alt Mer read the compass, then put it away. He would have to navigate by dead reckoning and gut instinct, then hope he could get back on course when the mist cleared. If it cleared. It might stay like this even further inland, beyond the mountain peaks. If it did, they were as lost as if they had never had a course to begin with.

He could just make out Spanner Frew standing at the bow. The big Rover was hunched forward, his concentration riveted on the shifting layers of white. Now and then he would signal by hand—go left, go right, go slow—and Redden Alt Mer would work the controls accordingly. The wind whistled past in sudden gusts, then died, baffled by a cliff face or air current. Mist swirled through the peaks, empty and aimless. Only the *Jerle Shannara* disturbed its ethereal fabric.

The rain returned, a gathering of dark clouds that turned quickly into a torrent. It engulfed the airship and its crew, soaking them through, shrouding them in dampness and gloom, claiming them as the sea might a sinking ship. Alt Mer, who had weathered worse, tried not to think of the way in which rain distorted shapes and spaces, creating the appearance of obstacles where there were none, giving hints of passage where walls of rock stood waiting. He relied on his instincts rather than his senses. He had been a sailor all his life; he knew something of the tricks that wind and water could play.

Behind him, the mist and darkness closed about. There was no sign of their pursuers—no sign of anything but the sky and the mountains and the shifting rain and mist between.

Spanner Frew came back to stand with him in the pilot box. There was no reason to remain in the bow. The world about them had disappeared into space.

The shipwright glanced over and gave Redden Alt Mer a fierce smile. The Rover Captain smiled back. There was nothing for either to say.

The *Jerle Shannara* sailed on into the gloom.

FOUR

Heat and light gave way to cool darkness, the odd tingling sensation to numbness, and the present to the past as the Ilse Witch was swept away by the power of the Sword of Shannara. One moment, she was deep underground in the catacombs of Castledown, alone with her enemy, with the Druid Walker, surrounded by the wreckage of another age. In the next, she was gone so far inside herself that she had no sense of where she was. In the blink of an eye, she was transformed from a creature of flesh and blood to nothing more substantial than the thoughts that bore her away.

She had only a moment to wonder what was happening to her, and then it was done.

She went alone into the darkness, and yet she was aware of Walker being there with her, not in recognizable form, not even wholly formed, more a shadow, a shade that trailed after her like the flow of her long, dark hair. She could feel the pulse of him in the talisman she gripped like a lifeline. He was only a presence in the ether, but he was with her and he was watching.

When she emerged from the darkness, she was in another time and place, one she recognized instantly. She was in the home from which she had been taken as a child. She had thought she would never see it again and yet there it was, just as she remembered it from her childhood, wreathed in the shadows of an approaching dawn, cloaked in silence and danger. She could feel the coolness of the early morning air and smell the pungent scent of the lilac bushes. She recognized the moment at once. She had returned to the morning in which her parents and brother had died and she had been stolen away.

She watched the events of that morning unfold once more, but this time from somewhere outside herself, as if they were happening to someone else. Again, old Bark was killed when he went out to investigate. Again, the cloaked forms slid past her window in the faint predawn light, moving toward the front doorway. Again, she fled, and again, it was in vain. She hid her brother in the cellar and tried to escape the fate of her parents. But the cloaked forms were waiting for her. She saw herself taken by them as her house burned in a smoky red haze. She watched them spirit her away, unconscious and helpless, into the brightening east.

It was just as she remembered it. Yet it was different, too. She saw herself surrounded by dark forms huddled in conference as she lay trussed, blindfolded, and gagged. But something was not right. They did not have the look of the shape-shifters she knew to have taken her. Nor was there any sign of the Druid Walker. Had she seen him go past the windows of her home this time as she remembered him doing before? She did not think so. Where was he?

As if in response to her question, a figure appeared out of the trees, tall and dark and hooded like her captors. He had the look of a Druid, a part of the fading night, a promise of death's coming. He gestured to her captors, brought them close to him momentarily, spoke words she could not hear, then stepped away. In a flurry of activity, her captors squared off like combatants and began to fight with one another. But their struggle was not harsh and brutal; it was merely an exercise. Now and then, one would pause to glance at her, as if to measure the effect of this pretense. The cloaked form let it go on for a time, waiting, then suddenly reached down for her, snatched her up, and spirited her away into the trees, leaving the odd scenario behind.

As he ran, she caught a glimpse of his forearms. They were scaly and mottled. They were reptilian.

Her mind spun with sudden recognition. *No!*

She was carried deep into the woods to a quiet place, and the dark-cloaked figure set her down. She watched him reveal himself, and he was not the Druid, as she now knew he would not be, could not be, but the Morgawr. *Betrayer!* The word shrieked at her. *Liar!* But he was much worse, of course. He was beyond anything words could describe, anything recognizably human. He was a monster.

She knew it was the truth she was seeing. She knew it instinctively, even doubting that it could be so. The images drawn on the magic of the Sword of Shannara could not lie. She could feel it in her bones, and it made perfect sense to her. How had she not known it before? How had she let herself become deceived so easily?

Yet she was only six years old then, she reminded herself. She was still nothing but a child.

Besieged by emotions that tore through her like hungry wolves, she would have screamed in rage and despair had she been able to do so. But she could not give voice to what she was feeling. She could only watch. The magic of the sword would allow nothing more.

She heard the Morgawr speak to her, his words soft and cajoling and treacherous. She watched herself slowly come to terms with his lies, to accept them, to believe that he was what he claimed and that she was the victim of a Druid's machinations. She watched him spirit her away aboard his Shrike, deep into his underground lair in the Wilderun. She watched herself close the door on her own prison, a willing fool, a pawn in a scheme she was beginning to understand for the first time. She watched herself begin another life—a small, misguided child driven by hatred and determination. She watched herself, knowing she would never be the same, helpless to prevent it, to do anything more than despair at her fate.

Still the images continued, spinning themselves out, revealing to her the truth that had been concealed from her all these years. She watched a shape-shifter burrow through the smoking ruins of her home to retrieve her still-living baby brother. She watched him carry her brother away to a solitary fortress that she quickly recognized as Paranor. She saw him give her brother over to the Druid Walker, who in turn took him into the Highlands of Leah to entrust to a kind-faced man and his wife, who had children of their own and a debt to repay. She watched her brother grow in that family, his tiny baby's face changing with the passing of the years, his features slowly becoming recognizable.

She might have gasped or even cried out as she realized she was looking at the boy who had come to this distant land with Walker, who had confronted her and told her he was Bek. There was no mistaking him. He was the boy she had disbelieved, the boy she had hunted with the caull and almost killed. Bek, the brother she was so certain had died in the fire . . .

She could not finish these thoughts, any of them. She could barely force herself to confront them. Nor was there any time for a balanced consideration, for a coming to terms with what she was absorbing. Other images swiftly appeared, a wave of them, inundating her so thoroughly that her chest constricted and her breathing tightened under their crushing weight.

Now the images were ones of her training under the Morgawr, of her long, harsh schooling, of her mastery of self-discipline and her hardening of purpose as she set about learning how to destroy Walker. She saw herself grow from a girl into a young woman, but not with the same freedom of life and spirit that had invested Bek. Instead, she saw herself change from something human into something so like the Morgawr that when all was said and done she was different from him on the outside only, where her skin set her apart from his scales. She had become dark and hate-filled and ruthless in the same way he was. She had embraced her magic's poisonous possibilities with his eagerness and savage determination.

She watched herself learn to use her magic as a weapon. All of her long, dark experience was replayed for her in numbing, sickening detail. She watched as she maimed and killed those who stood in her way. She watched herself destroy those who dared to confront or question her. She saw herself strip them of their hope and their courage and reduce them to slaves. She saw herself ruin people simply because it was convenient or suited her purpose. The Addershag died so that she could gain power over Ryer Ord Star. Her spy in the home of the Healer at Bracken Clell died so that he could never reveal his connection to her. Allardon Elessedil died so that the voyage the Druid Walker sought to make might not have Elven support.

There were others, so many she quickly lost count. Most she did not even remember. She watched them appear like ghosts out of the past and watched them die anew. At her hand or by her command, they died all the same. Or if they did not die, they often had the look of men and women who wished they had. She could feel their fear, helplessness, frustration, terror, and pain. She could feel their suffering.

She who was the Ilse Witch, who had never felt anything, who had made it a point to harden herself against any emotion, began to unravel like an old garment worn too often.

No more, she heard herself begging. *Please! Please!*

The images shifted yet again, and now she saw not the immediate acts she had perpetrated, but the consequences of those acts. Where a father died to serve her needs, a mother and children were left to starve in the streets. Where a daughter was subverted for her use, a brother was inadvertently put in harm's path and destroyed. Where one life was sacrificed, two more were made miserable.

It did not end there. A Free-born commander broken in spirit and mind at her whim cost his nation the benefit of his courage and left it bereft of leadership for years. The daughter of a politician caught in the middle of a struggle between two factions was imprisoned when her wisdom might have settled the dispute. Children disappeared into other lands, spirited away so that those who obeyed her might gain control over the grief-stricken parents. Tribes of Gnomes, deprived of sacred ground she had claimed for the Morgawr, blamed Dwarves, who then became their enemies. Like the rippling effect of a stone thrown on the still waters of a pond, the results of her selfish and predatory acts spread far beyond the initial impact.

All the while, she could feel the Morgawr watching from afar, a silent presence savoring the results of his duplicitous acts, his lies and deceits. He controlled her as if she was his puppet, tugged and pulled by the strings he wielded. He channeled her anger and her frustration, and he never let her forget against whom she must direct it. All that she did, she did in expectation of destroying the Druid Walker. But seeing her past now, stripped of pretense and laid bare in brightest daylight, she could not understand how she had been so misguided. Nothing of what she had done had achieved her supposed goals. None of it was justifiable. Everything had been a travesty.

The shell of self-deception in which she was encased broke under the deluge of images, and for the first time she saw herself for what she was. She was repulsive. She was the worst of what she could imagine, a creature whose humanity had been sacrificed in the false belief that it was meaningless. In sacrifice to the monster she had become, she had given up everything that had been part of the little girl she had once been.

Worst of all was the realization of what she had done to Bek. She had done more than betray him by assuming him dead in the ashes of her home. She had done worse than fail to discover if he might be whom he claimed when he confronted her. She had tried to put an end to him. She had hunted him down and nearly killed him. She had made him her prisoner, taken him back with her to *Black Moclips*, and given him over to Cree Bega.

She had abandoned him.

Again.

In the silence of the Sword of Shannara's quieting magic, the images faded momentarily, and she was left alone with her truth, with its starkness, with its razor's edge. Walker was still there, still close, his pale presence watching her come to terms with herself. She felt him like a pall, and she could not shake him off. She fought to break free of the tangle of deceits and treacheries and wrongdoings that draped her like a thousand spiderwebs. She struggled to breathe against the suffocating darkness of her life. She could do neither. She was as trapped as her victims.

The images began again, but she could no longer bear to watch them. Tumbling through the kaleidoscope of her terrible acts, she could not imagine how forgiveness could ever be granted to her. She could not imagine she had any right even to ask for it. She felt bereft of hope or grace. Finding her voice at last, she screamed in a mix of self-hatred and despair. The sound and the fury of it triggered her own magic, dark and swift and sure. It came to her aid in a rush, collided with the magic of the Sword of Shannara, and erupted within her in a fiery conflagration. She felt herself explode in a whirl of images and emotions. Then everything began to spiral off into a vast, depthless void, and she was swept away into clouds of endlessly drifting shadows.

Bek Ohmsford stiffened at the sound. "Did you hear that?" he asked Truls Rohk.

It was an unnecessary question. No one could have missed it. They were deep underground now, back within the catacombs of Castledown, searching for Walker. They had come down through the ruins, finding doors once hidden now open and waiting. No longer did the fire threads and creepers protect this domain. No sign of life remained. The world of Antrax was a graveyard of metal skeletons and dead machines.

Truls Rohk, cloaked and hooded even here, looked around slowly as the echo of the scream died away. "Someone is still alive down here."

"A woman," Bek ventured.

The shape-shifter grunted. "Don't be too sure."

Bek tested the air with his magic, humming softly, reading the lines of power. Grianne had passed this way not long ago. Her presence was unmistakable. They were following her in the belief that she would be following Walker. One would lead to the other. If they were quick enough, they could reach both in time. But until now, they had not been so sure that anyone was left alive. Certainly they had found no evidence of it.

Bek started ahead again, running his hand through his hair nervously. "She's gone this way."

Truls Rohk moved with him. "You said you had a plan. For when we find her."

"To capture her," Bek declared. "To take her alive."

"Such ambition, boy. Do you intend to tell me the details anytime soon?"

Bek kept going, taking time to think his explanation through. With Truls, you didn't want to overcomplicate things. The shape-shifter was already prepared to doubt the possibility of any plan working successfully. He was already thinking of ways to kill Grianne before she had a chance to kill him. All that was preventing it was Bek's passionate demand that Truls give his way a chance.

"She cannot harm us unless she uses her magic," he said quietly, not looking over at the other as they walked. He picked his way carefully through collapsed cables and chunks of concrete that had been shaken loose from the ceiling by an enormous blast and a quake that they had felt even aboveground. "She cannot use her magic unless she can use her voice. If we stop her from speaking or singing or making any sound whatsoever, we can take her prisoner."

Truls Rohk slid through the shadows and flickering lights like a massive cat. "We can accomplish what's needed by just killing her. Give this up, boy. She isn't going to become your sister again. She isn't going to accept what she is."

"If I can distract her, then you can get behind her," Bek continued, ignoring him. "Put your hands over her mouth and muffle her voice. You can do this if we can keep her from discovering you are there. I think it is possible. She will be intent on finding the Druid and dealing with me. She won't be looking for you."

"You dream big dreams." Truls Rohk did not sound convinced. "If this fails, we won't get a second chance. Either one of us."

Something heavy crashed to the floor of the passageway ahead, adding to the mounds of debris already collected. Steam hissed out of broken pipes, and strange smells gathered in niches and slid through cracks in the walls. Within the catacombs, every passageway looked exactly the same. It was a maze, and if they hadn't had Grianne's distinctive aura to track, they would have long since become lost.

Bek kept his voice even. "Walker would want us to do this," he ventured. He glanced over at the shape-shifter's dark form. "You know that to be true."

"What the Druid wants is anyone's guess. Nor is it necessarily the right thing. It hasn't gotten us much of anywhere so far."

"Which is why you chose to come with him on this quest," Bek offered quietly. "Which is why you have gone with him so many times before. Is that right?"

Truls Rohk said nothing, disappearing back inside himself so that all that remained was his cloaked shadow passing along in the near darkness, more presence than substance, so faint it seemed he might disappear in the blink of an eye.

Ahead, the tunnel widened. The damage here was more severe than anything they had encountered so far. Whole chunks of ceiling and wall had fallen away. Shattered glass and twisted metal lay in heaps. Though flameless lamps lit the passageway with pale luminescence, their light barely penetrated the heavy shadows.

A vast and cavernous chamber at the end of the corridor opened onto a pair of massive cylinders whose metal skin was split like over-ripe fruit. Steam hissed through the wounds like blood leaking from a body. The ends of severed wires flashed and snapped in small ex-plosions. Struts and girders wrenched free of their fastenings with long, slow groans.

"There," Bek said softly, reaching out to touch the other's cloak. "She's there."

No movement or sound reached out to them, no indication that anyone living waited at the end of the passage amid the massive de-struction. Truls Rohk froze momentarily, listening. Then he started ahead, this time leading the way, no longer trusting Bek, taking charge of what might become a deadly situation. The boy followed wordlessly, knowing he was no longer in control, that the best he could hope for was a chance to make things work out the way he thought they should.

A sudden hissing shattered the stillness, the sibilance punctu-ated by popping and cracking. The sounds reminded Bek of animals feeding on the bones of a carcass.

As they reached the opening, Truls Rohk moved swiftly into the shadows of one wall, motioning for Bek to stay back. Unwilling to lose contact, Bek retreated perhaps a pace, no more. Flattening him-self against the smooth wall, he strained to hear something above the mechanical noises.

Then the shape-shifter faded into a patch of shadow and simply disappeared. Bek knew at once that he was trying to get to Grianne first. Bek charged after him, frightened that he had lost all chance of saving his sister. He breached the rubble at the entrance to the chamber in a rush and stopped.

The chamber was in ruins, a scrap heap of metal and glass, of shattered creepers and broken machines. Grianne knelt at its center beside a fallen Walker, her head lifting out of the shadow of her dark hair, her pale face caught in a slow flicker of light from a tangle of ruptured wires that sparked and fizzed. Her eyes were open as she stared toward the ceiling, but they did not see. Her hands were fastened securely about the handle of the Sword of Shannara, which rested blade downward against the smooth metal of the floor.

There was blood on those hands and on that handle and blade. There was blood all over her clothing and on Walker's, as well. There was blood on the floor, pooled in a crimson lake that trickled off into thin rivulets winding their way through the wreckage.

Bek stared at the scene in horror. He could not help what he was thinking. Walker was dead and Grianne had killed him.

To one side, a blade's sharp edge flashed momentarily in the shadows, and from the gathered gloom a deeper darkness eased silently forward.

Truls Rohk had reached the same conclusion.

FIVE

Hugging each other like frightened children, Ahren Elessedil and Ryer Ord Star made their way through the silent, dust-choked passageways of Castledown toward the city ruins above. The seer was still sobbing uncontrollably, her head bent into the Elven Prince's shoulder, her arms clinging as if she was afraid she might lose him. Leaving Walker had undone her completely, and though Ahren whispered reassurances to her as they went, trying to bring her back to herself, she seemed not to hear him. It was as if by leaving the Druid, she had left the better part of herself. The only indication she gave that she was still present was in the way she flinched when fresh chunks of wall or ceiling gave way or something exploded in the darkening recesses through which they fled.

"It will be all right, Ryer," Ahren kept repeating, even long after it was clear the words had no meaning for her.

Stirred by the events of the past few hours, his thoughts were jumbled and uncertain. The effects of the Elfstone magic had worn off, leaving him quieted and at peace again, no longer filled with fire and white rage. He had tucked the stones safely away inside his tunic pocket for when they would be needed again. A part of him anticipated such use, but another part hoped it might never happen. He felt vindicated and satisfied at having recovered them, having successfully summoned up their magic, and having used the blue fire against the hateful machines that had destroyed so many of his friends and companions from the *Jerle Shannara*. He felt renewed within, as if he had undergone a rite of passage and survived. He had come on this journey not much more than a boy, and now he was a man. It was his odyssey in gaining possession of the Elfstones that lent him this feeling of fresh identity, of new confidence. The experience had been horrific but empowering.

None of which made him feel any better about what had happened to Walker or what was likely to happen now to them. That Walker was dying when they left him was indisputable. Not even a Druid could survive the sort of wounds he had received. He might last a few minutes more, but there was no chance for him. So now the company, or what remained of it, must continue on without him. But continue to where? Continue for what reason? Walker himself had said that with the death of Antrax the knowledge of the books of magic was lost to them. He had made a choice in destroying the machine, and the choice had cost them any chance of recovering what they had come to find. It was an admission of failure. It was an acknowledgment that their journey had been for nothing.

Yet he could not help feeling that somehow this wasn't so, that there was something more to what had transpired than what was immediately obvious.

He wondered about the others of the company. He knew Bek had been alive when Ryer had fled the Ilse Witch and come back into the ruins to find Walker. The Elven Tracker Tamis had escaped, too. There would be others, somewhere. What must he do to find them? Find them he must, he knew, because without an airship and a crew, they were stranded indefinitely. With the Ilse Witch and her Mwellrets hunting them.

But he knew what he could do to gain help. He could use the Elfstones, the seeking stones of legend, to find a way to the others. The problem was that using the magic would alert the Ilse Witch to their presence. It would tell her exactly where they were, and she would come for them at once. They couldn't afford to have that happen. Ahren didn't think for a moment that he was a match for the Witch, even with the magic of the Elfstones to aid him. Stealth and secrecy were better weapons to employ just now. But he wasn't sure that stealth and secrecy would be enough.

He had been navigating the passageways for several hours, lost in his thoughts, when he became aware of the fact that Ryer had stopped crying. He glanced down at her in surprise, but she kept her face buried in his shoulder, pressed against his chest, concealed in the curtain of her long silvery hair. He thought that she might be working her way through her grief and should not be disturbed. He let her be. Instead, he concentrated anew on regaining the surface. The debris that had clogged the lower corridors was not so much in evidence here, as if the explosions had been centered more deeply. The air seemed fresher, and he thought they must be close to breaking free.

He found he was right. Within only minutes they passed through a pair of metal doors that stood unhinged and ajar, ducked under the collapsed framework, and stepped out into the open. They emerged from the tower into which Walker had disappeared days earlier, there in the center of the deadly maze that had ravaged the remainder of the company. It was night still, but dawn's approach was signaled by a faint lightening along the eastern horizon. Overhead, moonlight flooded out of a cloudless, starlit sky.

Ahren stopped just outside the tower entry and looked around cautiously. He could trace the outline of the walls of the maze and discern the clutter of broken creepers and weapons. Beyond, the ruins of the city spread away in a jumble of shattered buildings. No sounds came from that wasteland. It felt as if they were the only living creatures in the world.

But that was deceptive, he knew. The Mwellrets were still out there, searching for them. He must be very careful.

With Ryer still clinging to him, he knelt and put his mouth to her ear. "Listen to me," he whispered.

She went still, then nodded slowly. "We have to try to find the others—Bek and Tamis and Quentin. But we have to be very quiet. The Mwellrets and the Ilse Witch will be hunting us. At least, that's what we have to assume. We can't afford to let them catch us. We have to get out of these ruins and into the cover of the trees. Quickly. Can you help me?"

"We shouldn't have left him," she replied so softly he could barely make out the words. Her fingers tightened on his arms. "We should have stayed."

"No, Ryer," he said. "He told us to go. He told us there was nothing else we could do for him. He told us to find the others. Remember?"

She shook her head. "It doesn't matter. We should have stayed. He was dying."

"If we fail to do what he asked of us, if we allow ourselves to be captured or killed, we will have failed him. That makes his dying an even bigger waste." His voice was low, but fierce. "That isn't what he expects of us. That isn't why he sent us away."

"I betrayed him." She sobbed.

"We all betrayed each other at some point on this voyage." He forced her head out from his shoulder and lifted her chin so that she was looking at him. "He isn't dying because of anything we did or failed to do. He is dying because he chose to give up his life to destroy Antrax. He made that choice."

He took a deep breath to calm himself. "Listen to me. We serve him best now by honoring his last wishes. I don't know what he intended for us, what he thought would happen now that he is gone. I don't know what we've accomplished. But there's nothing more we can do for him beyond getting ourselves out of here and back to the Four Lands."

Her pale, drawn face tightened at the harshness of his words, then crumpled like old parchment. "I cannot survive without him, Ahren. I don't want to."

The Elven Prince reached out impulsively and stroked her fine hair. "He said he would see you again. He promised. Maybe you should give him the chance to keep that promise." He paused, then bent forward and kissed her forehead. "You say you can't survive without him. If it makes any difference, I don't think I can survive without you. I wouldn't have gotten this far if it hadn't been for you. Don't abandon me now."

He rested his cheek against her temple and held her, waiting for a response. It was a long time coming, but at last she lifted away and placed her small hands against his cheeks.

"All right," she said quietly. She gave him a small, sad smile. "I won't."

They rose and walked out of the shadow of the black tower and into the maze, then back through the ruins. They kept to the shadows and did not hurry, stopping frequently to listen for sounds that would warn them of danger. Ahren led, holding Ryer Ord Star's hand, the link between them oddly empowering. He had not lied when he told her he still needed her. Despite his recovery of the Elfstones and his successful battle against the creepers, he did not yet feel confident about himself. He had passed out of boyhood, but he was still inexperienced and callow. There were lessons still to be learned, and some of them would be hard. He did not want to face them alone. Having Ryer there to face them with him gave him a confidence he could not entirely explain but knew better than to ignore.

Yet he thought he understood at least a part of it. What he felt for the girl was close to love. It had grown slowly, and he was only just beginning to recognize it for what it was. He was not certain how it would resolve itself or even if it would survive another day. But in a world of turmoil and uncertainty, of monsters and terrible danger, it was reassuring to have her close, to be able to ask her advice, just to touch her hand. He drew strength from her that was both powerful and mysterious—not in the way of magic, but in the way of spirit. Maybe it was as simple as not being entirely alone, of having another person with whom to share whatever happened. But maybe, too, it was as mystical as life and death.

They walked a long time through the ruins without hearing or seeing anything or anyone. They moved in a southerly direction, back the way they had come, toward the bay in which the *Jerle Shannara* had once anchored. She was in the hands of the Ilse Witch now, of course—unless things had changed, which was possible. Things changed quickly in this land. Things changed without warning. Maybe this time they would change in a way that would favor Walker's company rather than the Witch's.

Suddenly Ryer Ord Star drew up short, her slim body rigid and trembling. Ahren turned back to her at once. She was staring into space, into some place he could not see, and her face reflected such dismay that he found himself quickly scanning his surroundings to find its cause.

"He's dead, Ahren," she said in a small, grief-stricken whisper.

She sank to the ground, crying. Her hand still clutched his, as if that were all that held her together. He knelt beside her, putting his arms about her, holding her close.

"Maybe he's at peace," he said, wondering if that was possible for Walker Boh.

"I saw him," she said. "In my vision, just now. I saw him being carried by a shade into a green light over an underground lake. He wasn't alone. On the shore were three people. One was Bek, the second a cloaked form I didn't recognize. The third was the Ilse Witch."

"The Ilse Witch was with Bek?"

Her hand tightened on his. "But she wasn't doing anything threatening. She wasn't even seeing him. She was just there, physically present, but at the same time she wasn't. She looked lost. Wait! No, that isn't right. She didn't look lost, she looked stunned. But that isn't all, Ahren. The vision changed, and she was holding Bek and he was holding her. They were somewhere else, somewhere in the future, I think. I don't know how to explain this, but they were the same person. They were joined."

Ahren tried to make sense of this. "One body and one face? The same in that way?"

She shook her head. "It didn't look like that, but it felt like that. Something happened to connect them. But it was as much a spiritual as a physical joining. There was such pain! I could feel it. I don't know whom it was coming from, who had generated it. Maybe both. But it was released through the connection they formed, and it was a trigger for something else, something that was going to happen after. But I didn't see that; I wasn't permitted."

Ahren thought. "Well, maybe it has something to do with them being brother and sister. Maybe that was the connection you sensed. Maybe the Ilse Witch discovered it was true, and that was what released all this pain you felt."

Her eyes were huge and liquid in the moonlight. "Maybe."

"Do you think Bek and the Ilse Witch are down in Castledown with Walker?"

She shook her head. "I don't know."

"Should we go back and look for them?"

She just stared at him, wide-eyed, frightened.

There was no way to know, of course. It was a vision, and visions were subject to misleading and false interpretations. They revealed truths, but not in terms that were immediately apparent. That was their nature. Ryer Ord Star saw the future better than most. But even she was not permitted to catch more than a glimpse of it, and that glimpse might mean something other than what it suggested.

Going back for any reason suddenly seemed unthinkable to Ahren, and he abandoned the idea. Instead, they rose and walked on. Frustrated and troubled by the seer's words, Ahren found himself hoping that when she had another vision, she would have one they could do something about. Like finding a way out of their present dilemma, for instance. Visions of other people in other places were of precious little use just now. It was a selfish attitude, and he was immediately ashamed of it. But he couldn't help thinking it nonetheless.

They continued on. It would be morning soon. If they hadn't reached the shelter of the trees by then, they would be in trouble. They had the remnants of buildings to hide in, but if they were detected, they would be easily trapped. If they kept on after it grew light, they would be left exposed on the open roadways. Ahren didn't know if it made any difference what he did at this point since they were without a destination or a plan for rescue. All he knew to do was to try to find a way to keep out of the hands of the Ilse Witch and the Mwellrets. Or maybe only the latter, if Ryer's vision proved prophetic. Was it possible that Bek had made the witch a prisoner, had found some way to subdue her? He had magic, after all, magic strong enough to shatter creepers. Was it sufficient to overcome the witch, as well?

Ahren wished he knew more about what was happening. But he had wished that from the beginning.

They were close to the edge of the forest when he heard movement ahead. It was soft and furtive, the kind that comes from someone trying not to be discovered. Ahren dropped into a crouch, pulling Ryer down with him. They were deep in the shadows of a wall, so they would not be easily seen. On the other hand, it was slowly growing lighter and they couldn't stay where they were indefinitely.

He motioned for her to keep silent and follow his lead. Then he rose and began to make his way forward, but more slowly. Moments later, he heard the noise again, a scraping of boots on stone, very close now, and he dropped back into the shadows once more.

Almost instantly, a Mwellret slid out of the darkness and made its way across the open ground in front of them. There was no mistaking what it was or its intent. It carried a battle-ax in one hand and a short sword strapped about its waist. It was searching for someone. It might not be them, Ahren accepted, but that wouldn't help them if they were found.

He waited until the ret was out of sight, and started ahead again. Maybe they could get behind it. Maybe there was only the one.

But as they angled left, away from the first, they encountered a second, this one coming right for them. Ahren ducked back into the cover of a building's roofless shell, then led Ryer across the open floor to another exit. He picked his way carefully over piles of debris, but his boots made small scraping sounds that he could not seem to avoid. Outside again, he scuttled in a crouch to another building, Ryer at his heels, and made his way through. Enough dodging, he hoped, would lose any pursuers.

Outside, he stopped and looked around. Nothing was familiar. He could see the outline of the treetops some distance off, but he had no idea in which direction he had been going or where the Mwellrets were. He listened for sound of them, but heard nothing.

"There's someone behind us," Ryer whispered in his ear.

He tugged her forward again, making for the cover of the trees, hoping that they could reach it in time. It was steadily growing lighter, the sun just beginning to crest the horizon, leaving the ruins bathed in a dangerous combination of light and shadows that could easily deceive the eyes. Ahren thought he heard a sudden grunt from somewhere close, and he wondered if they had been discovered after all.

Maybe he should use the Elfstones, even if they gave him away. But the magic wasn't any good against rets or any other creatures not motivated by magic. Nor would it respond if he wasn't physically threatened.

He put his free hand on the handle of his long knife, his only other weapon, hesitating. He was deliberating over what to do when a movement off to his right stopped him. He faded back against a wall with Ryer, holding his breath as a cloaked form shouldered into view through the buildings. He could not make out who it was. Or even what, human or Mwellret. Ryer was pressed so close against him he could feel her breathing. He tightened his grip on her hand, feeling nothing himself of the reassurance he was trying to convey to her.

Then the cloaked form was gone. Ahren exhaled slowly and began to move ahead again. It wasn't far to the trees. Beyond the ruins, only a hundred yards or so away, he could make out limbs and clusters of leaves in the new light.

As he stepped around the corner of a partially collapsed wall, he glanced back momentarily at Ryer to be certain she was all right. The look in her eyes changed just as he did so, her wariness giving way to outright terror.

Quickly he looked back, but he was too slow. Sudden movement confronted him.

Then everything went black.

W hen he saw Truls Rohk move toward his sister, Bek
Ohmsford didn't take time to consider the consequences of what he did next. All he knew was that if he
failed to act, the shape-shifter would kill her. It didn't matter what
the other had promised earlier, in a moment of rational thought,
away from the carnage in which they found themselves now. Once
Truls saw her kneeling at the side of the fallen Walker, the Sword of
Shannara in hand and blood everywhere, that promise might as well
have been written on water.

If Bek had allowed his emotions to get the better of him, perhaps he would have reacted the same way as Truls Rohk. But Bek
could see from his sister's face that something was very wrong with
her. She was staring skyward, but she wasn't seeing anything. She
held the Sword of Shannara, but not as if it was a weapon she had
just used. Nor did he think she would rely on the talisman to take
the life of the Druid. She would rely on her own magic, the magic of
the wishsong, and if she had done so here, there would not be this
much blood.

Once he got past his initial shock, Bek knew there was more to
what he was seeing than appearances indicated. But Truls Rohk was

behind Grianne and couldn't see her face. Not that it would have mattered, since he was not inclined to feel the same way Bek did. For the shape-shifter, the Ilse Witch was a dangerous enemy and nothing less, and if there was any reason to suspect she might harm them, he wouldn't think twice about stopping her.

So Bek attacked him. He did so in a reaction born out of desperation, intending to hold the other back without really harming him. But Truls Rohk was so enormously strong that Bek couldn't afford to employ half measures when calling up the power of the wishsong. He hadn't mastered it yet anyway, not in the way that Grianne had, having only just discovered a few months earlier that he even had the use of it. The best he could do was to hope it had the intended effect.

He sent it spinning out in an entangling web of magic that snared Truls and sent him tumbling head over heels through the wreckage of the chamber. The shape-shifter went down, but he was back up again almost at once, throwing off his concealment, revealing himself instantly, big and dark and dangerous. With the long knife held before him, he rushed Grianne a second time. But Bek knew enough by now to appreciate how strong Truls was, and he had already assumed his first attempt at slowing the shape-shifter would fail. He sent a second wave of magic lancing out, a wall of sound that snared the other and sent him flying backwards. Bek cried out, but he did not think Truls even heard him, so caught up was he in his determination to get at Grianne.

But Bek reached her first, dropped to his knees, and wrapped his arms about her protectively. She did not move when he did so. She did not respond in any way.

"Don't hurt her," he started to say, turning to find Truls Rohk.

Then something hit him so hard that it knocked him completely free of Grianne and sent him sprawling into the remains of a shattered creeper. Stunned, he dragged himself to his knees. "Truls . . . ," he gasped as he peered over at Grianne helplessly.

The shape-shifter was bent over her, a menacing shadow, his

blade at her exposed throat. "You haven't the experience for this, boy," he hissed at Bek. "Not yet. But that doesn't make you less of an irritation, I'll give you that. No, don't try to get up. Stay where you are."

He was silent a moment, tensed and ready as he leaned closer to Bek's sister. Then the knife lowered. "What's wrong with her? She's in some sort of trance."

Bek climbed back to his feet in spite of the warning and stumbled over, shaking off the disorienting effects of the blow. "Did you have to hit me so hard?"

"I did if I wanted to be certain you would remember what it meant to use your magic against me." The other shifted to face him. "What were you thinking?"

Bek shook his head. "Only that I didn't want you to hurt her. I thought you would kill her outright when you saw Walker. I didn't think you could see her face, so you wouldn't know she couldn't hurt us. I just reacted."

Truls Rohk grunted. "Next time, think twice before you do." The blade disappeared into the cloak. "Take the sword out of her hands and see what she does."

He was already bent over the Druid, probing through the blood-soaked robes, searching for signs of life. Bek knelt in front of the unseeing Grianne and carefully pried her fingers loose from the Sword of Shannara. They released easily, limply, and he caught the talisman in his hand as it fell free. There was no sign of recognition in her eyes. She did not even blink.

Bek laid down the sword and moved Grianne's arms to her sides. She allowed him to do this without responding in any way. She might have been made of soft clay.

"She doesn't know anything that's happening to her," he said quietly.

"The Druid lives," Truls Rohk responded. "Barely."

He straightened the ragged form and tore strips of cloth from his own clothing to stem the flow of blood from the visible wounds.

Bek watched helplessly, appalled by the extent of the damage. The Druid's injuries seemed more internal than external. There were jagged wounds to his chest and stomach, but he was bleeding from his mouth and ears and nose and even his eyes, as well. He seemed to have suffered a major rupture of his organs.

Then abruptly, unexpectedly, the penetrating eyes opened and fixed on Bek. The boy was so startled that for a moment he quit breathing and just stared back at the other.

"Where is she?" Walker whispered in a voice that was thick with blood and pain.

Bek didn't have to ask whom he was talking about. "She's right beside us. But she doesn't seem to know who we are or what's going on."

"She is paralyzed by the sword's magic. She panicked and used her own to try to ward it off. Futile. It was too much. Even for her."

"Walker," Truls Rohk said softly, bending close to him. "Tell us what to do."

The pale face shifted slightly, and the dark eyes settled on the other. "Carry me out of here. Go where I tell you to go. Don't stop until you get there."

"But your wounds—"

"My wounds are beyond help." The Druid's voice turned suddenly hard and fierce. "There isn't much time left, shape-shifter. Not for me. Do as I say. Antrax is destroyed. Castledown is dead. What there was of the treasure we came to find, of the books and their contents, is lost." The eyes shifted. "Bek, bring your sister with us. Lead her by the hand. She will follow."

Bek glanced at Grianne, then back at Walker. "If we move you . . ."

"Druid, it will kill you to take you out of here!" Truls Rohk snapped angrily. "I didn't come this far just to bury you!"

The Druid's strange eyes fixed on him. "Choices of life and death are not always ours to make, Truls. Do as I say."

Truls Rohk scooped the Druid into the cradle of his arms,

slowly and gently, trying not to damage him further. Walker made no sound as he was lifted, his dark head sinking into his chest, his good arm folding over his stomach. Bek strapped the Sword of Shannara across his back, then took Grianne's hand and pulled her to her feet. She came willingly, easily, and she made no response to being led away.

They passed out of the ruined chamber and back down the passageway through which they had come. At the first juncture, Walker took them in a different direction than the one that had brought them in. Bek saw the dark head move slightly and heard the tired voice whisper instructions. The ends of the Druid's tattered robes trailed from his limp form, leaving smears of blood on the floor.

As they progressed through the catacombs, Bek glanced at Grianne from time to time, but never once did she look back at him. Her gaze stayed fixed straight ahead, and she moved as if she was sleepwalking. It frightened the boy to see her like this, more so than when she was hunting him. She seemed as if she was nothing more than a shell, the living person she had been gone entirely.

Their progress was slowed now and again by heaps of stone and twisted metal that barred their passage. Once, Truls was forced to lay the Druid down long enough to force back a sheet of twisted metal tightly jammed across their passage. Bek watched the Druid's eyes close against his pain and weariness, saw him flinch when he was picked up again, his hand clawing at his stomach as if to hold himself together. How Walker could still be alive after losing so much blood was beyond the boy. He had seen injured men before, but none who had lived after being damaged so severely.

Truls Rohk was beside himself. "Druid, this is senseless!" he snapped at one point, stopping in rage and frustration. "Let me try to help you!"

"You help me best by going on, Truls," was the other's weak response. "Go, now. Ahead still."

They walked a long way before finally coming out into a vast underground cavern that did not look as if it was a part of Castledown, but of the earth itself. The cavern was natural, the rock walls unchanged by metal or machines, the ceiling studded with stalactites that dripped water and minerals in steady cadence through the echoing silence. What little light there was emanated from flameless lamps that bracketed the cavern entry and a soft phosphorescence given off by the cavern rock. It was impossible to see the far side of the chamber, though bright enough to discern that it was a long distance off.

At the center of the chamber was a huge body of water as black as ink and smooth as glass.

"Take me to its edge," Walker ordered Truls Rohk.

They made their way along the uneven cavern floor, which was littered with loose rock and slick with damp. Moss grew in dark patches, and tiny ferns wormed through cracks in the stone. That anything could grow down here, bereft of sunlight, surprised Bek.

He squeezed Grianne's hand reassuringly, an automatic response to the encroachment of fresh darkness and solitude. He glanced at her immediately to see if she had noticed, but her gaze was still directed straight ahead.

At the water's edge, they stopped. On Walker's instructions, Truls Rohk knelt to lay him down, cradling him so that his head and shoulders rested in the shape-shifter's arms. Bek found himself thinking how odd it seemed, that a creature who was himself not whole, but bits and pieces held together by smoky mist, should be the Druid's bearer. He remembered when he had first met Walker in the Highlands of Leah. The Druid had seemed so strong then, so indomitable, as if nothing could ever change him. Now he was broken and ragged, leaking blood and life in a faraway land.

Tears came to Bek's eyes as swiftly as the thought, his response to the harsh realization that death approached. He did not know what to do. He wanted to help Walker, to make him whole again, to restore him to who he had been when they had first met all those months ago. He wanted to say something about how much the Druid had done for him. But all he could do was hold his sister's hand and wait to see what would happen.

"This is as far as I go," Walker said softly, coughing blood and wincing with the pain the movement caused.

Truls Rohk wiped the blood away with his sleeve. "You can't die on me, Druid. I won't allow it. We've too much more to do, you and I."

"We've done all we're allowed to do, shape-shifter," Walker replied. His smile was surprisingly warm. "Now we must go our separate ways. You'll have to find your own adventures, make your own trouble."

The other grunted. "Not likely I could ever do the job as well as you. Game-playing has always been your specialty, not mine."

Bek knelt beside them, pulling Grianne down with him. She let him place her however he wished and did nothing to acknowledge she knew he was there. Truls Rohk edged away from her.

"I'm done with this life," Walker said. "I've done what I can with it, and I have to be satisfied with that. Make certain, when you return, that Kylen Elessedil honors his father's bargain. His brother will stand with you; Ahren's stronger than you think. He has the Elfstones now, but the Elfstones won't make the difference. He will. Remember that. Remember as well what we made this journey for. What we have found here, what we have recovered, belongs to us."

Truls Rohk spat. "You're not making any sense, Druid. What are you talking about? We have nothing to show for what we've done! We've claimed nothing! The Elfstones? They weren't ours to begin with! What of the magic we sought? What of the books that contained it?"

Walker made a dismissive gesture. "The magic contained in the books, the magic I spoke of to both Allardon Elessedil and his son, was never the reason for this voyage."

"Then what was?" Truls Rohk was incensed. "Are we to play guessing games all night, Druid? What are we doing here? Tell us! Has this all been for nothing? Give us something to hope for! Now, while there's still time! Because I don't think you have much left! Look at you! You're—"

He couldn't make himself finish the sentence, biting off the rest of what he was going to say in bitter distaste.

"Dying?" Walker spoke the word for him. "It's all right to say it, Truls. Dying will set me free from promises and responsibilities that have kept me in chains for longer than I care to remember. Anyway, it's only a word."

"You say it, then. I don't want to talk to you anymore."

Walker reached up with his good hand and took hold of the other's cloak. To Bek's surprise, Truls Rohk did not pull away.

"Listen to me. Before I came to this land, before I decided to undertake this voyage, I went into the Valley of Shale, to the Hadeshorn, and I summoned the shade of Allanon. I spoke with him, asking what I could expect if I chose to follow the castaway's map. He told me that of all the goals I sought to accomplish, I would succeed in only one. For a long time, Truls, I thought that he meant I would recover the magic of the books from the Old World. I thought that was what I was supposed to do. I thought that was the purpose of this voyage. It wasn't."

His fingers tightened on the shape-shifter's cloak. "I made the mistake of thinking I could shape the future in the way I sought. I was wrong. Life doesn't permit it, not even if you are a Druid. We are given glimpses of possibilities, nothing more. The future is a map drawn in the sand, and the tide can wash it away in a moment. It is so here. All of our efforts in coming to this land, Truls, all of our sacrifices, have been for something we never once considered."

He paused, his breathing weak and labored, the effort of speaking further too much for him.

"Then what did we come here for?" Truls Rohk asked impatiently, still angered by what he was hearing. "What, Druid?"

"For her," Walker whispered, and pointed at Grianne.

The shape-shifter was so stunned that for a moment he could not seem to find anything to say in response. It was as if the fire had gone out of him completely.

"We came for Grianne?" Bek asked in surprise, not sure he had heard correctly.

"It will become clear to you when you are home again," Walker whispered, his words almost inaudible, even in the deep silence of the cavern. "She is your charge, Bek. She is your responsibility now, your sister recovered as you wished she might be. Return her to the Four Lands. Do what you must, but see her home again."

"This makes no sense at all!" Truls Rohk snapped in fury. "She is our enemy!"

"Give me your word, Bek," Walker said, his eyes never leaving the boy.

Bek nodded. "You have it."

Walker held his gaze a moment longer, then looked at the shape-shifter. "And you, as well, Truls. Your word."

For a moment, Bek thought Truls Rohk wasn't going to give it. The shape-shifter didn't say anything, staring at the Druid in silence. Tension radiated from his dark form, yet he refused to reveal what he was thinking.

Walker's fingers kept their death grip on the shape-shifter's cloak. "Your word," he whispered again. "Trust me enough to give it."

Truls Rohk exhaled in a hiss of frustration and dismay. "All right. I give you my word."

"Care for her as you would for each other," the Druid continued, his eyes back on Bek. "She will not always be like this. She will recover one day. But until then, she needs looking after. She needs you to ward her from danger."

"What can we do to help her wake?" Bek pressed.

The Druid took a long, ragged breath. "She must help herself, Bek. The Sword of Shannara has revealed to her the truth about her life, about the lies she has been told and the wrong paths she has taken. She has been forced to confront who she has become and what she has done. She is barely grown, and already she has committed more heinous wrongs and destructive acts than others will commit in a lifetime. She has much to forgive herself for, even given the fact that she was so badly misled by the Morgawr. The responsibility for finding forgiveness lies with her. When she finds a way to accept that, she will recover."

"What if she doesn't?" Truls Rohk asked. "It may be, Druid, that she is beyond forgiveness, not just from others, but even from herself. She is a monster, even in this world."

Bek gave the shape-shifter an angry glance, thinking that Truls would never change his opinion of Grianne, that to him she would always be the Ilse Witch and his enemy.

The Druid had a fit of coughing, then steadied. "She is human, Truls—like you," he replied softly. "Others labeled you a monster. They were wrong to do so. It is the same with her. She is not beyond redemption. But that is her path to walk, not yours. Yours is to see that she has the chance to walk it."

He coughed again, more deeply. His breathing was so thick and wet that with every breath it seemed he might choke on his own blood. The sound of it emanated from deep in his chest, where his lungs were filling. Yet he lifted himself into a sitting position, freed himself from Truls Rohk's arms, and motioned him away.

"Leave me. Take Grianne and walk back to the cavern entrance. When I am gone, follow the passageway that bears left all the way to the surface. Seek out the others who still live—the Rovers, Ahren Elessedil, Ryer Ord Star. Quentin Leah, perhaps. One or two more, if they were lucky. Sail home again. Don't linger here. Antrax is finished. The Old World has gone back into the past for good. The New World, the Four Lands, is what matters."

Truls Rohk stayed where he was. "I won't leave you alone. Don't ask it of me."

Walker's head sagged, his dark hair falling forward to shadow his lean face. "I won't be alone, Truls. Now go."

Truls Rohk hesitated, then rose slowly to his feet. Bek stood up, as well, taking Grianne's hand and pulling her up with him. For a moment no one moved, then the shape-shifter wheeled away without a word and started back through the loose rock for the cavern entrance. Bek followed wordlessly, leading Grianne, glancing back over his shoulder to look at Walker. The Druid was slumped by the edge of the underground lake, his dark robes wet with his blood, the slow, gentle heave of his shoulders the only indication that he still lived. Bek had an almost uncontrollable urge to turn around and go back for him, but he knew it would be pointless. The Druid had made his choice.

At the cavern entrance, Truls Rohk glanced back at Bek, then stopped abruptly and pointed toward the lake. "Druid games, boy," he hissed. "Look! See what happens now!"

Bek turned. The lake was roiling and churning at its center, and a wicked green light shone from its depths. A dark and spectral figure rose from its center and hung suspended in the air. A face lifted out of the cloak's hood, dusky-skinned and black-bearded, a face Bek, without ever having seen it before, knew at once.

"Allanon," he whispered.

Walker Boh dreamed of the past. He was no longer in pain, but his weariness was so overwhelming that he barely knew where he was. His sense of time had evaporated, and it seemed to him now that yesterday was as real and present as today. So it was that he found himself remembering how he had become a Druid, so long ago that all those who were there at the time were gone now. He had never wanted to be one of them, had never trusted the Druids as an order. He had lived alone for many years, avoiding his Ohmsford heritage and any contact with its other descendants. It had taken the loss of his arm to turn him to his destiny, to persuade him that the blood mark bestowed three hundred years earlier by Allanon on the forehead of his ancestor, Brin Ohmsford, had been intended for him.

That was a long time ago.

Everything was so long ago.

He watched the greenish light rise out of the depths of the underground lake, breaking the surface of its waters in shards of brightness. He watched it widen and spread, then grow in intensity as a path from the netherworld opened beneath. It was a languid, surreal experience and became a part of his dreams.

When the cloaked figure appeared in the light's emerald wake, he knew at once who it was. He knew instinctively, just as he knew he was dying. He watched with weary anticipation, ready to embrace what waited, to cast off the chains of his life. He had borne his burden of office for as long as he was able. He had done the best he could. He had regrets, but none that gave him more than passing pause. What he had accomplished would not be apparent right away to those who mattered, but it would become clear in time. Some would embrace it. Some would turn away. In either case, it was out of his hands.

The dark figure crossed the surface of the lake to where Walker lay and reached for him. His hand lifted automatically in response. Allanon's dark countenance stared down, penetrating eyes fixing on him. There was approval in those eyes. There was a promise of peace.

Walker smiled.

As Bek and Truls Rohk watched, the shade reached Walker's side. Green light played about their dark forms, slicing through them like razors, slashing them with emerald blades. There was a hiss, but it was soft and distant, the whisper of a dying man's breath.

The shade bent for Walker, the effort strong and purposeful. Walker's hand came up, perhaps to ward it off, perhaps to welcome it; it was difficult to tell. It made no difference. The shade lifted him into his arms and cradled him like a child.

Then together they made a slow retreat back across the lake, gliding on air, their dark forms illuminated by shards of light that gathered about them like fireflies. When both were encased in the glow, it closed around completely and they slowly disappeared into its brilliant center until nothing remained but a faint rippling of the lake's dark waters. In seconds, even that was gone, and the cavern was still and empty once more.

Bek realized suddenly that he was crying. How much of what Walker had hoped to see accomplished in this life had he lived to witness? Not anything of what had brought him here. Not anything of what he had envisioned of the future. He had died the last of his order, an outcast and perhaps a failure. The thought saddened the boy more than he would have believed possible.

"It's finished," he said quietly.

Truls Rohk's response was surprising. "No, boy. It's just begun. Wait and see."

Bek looked at him, but the shape-shifter refused to say anything more. They stood where they were for a few seconds, unable to break away. It was as if they were expecting something more to happen. It was as if something must. But nothing did, and at last they quit looking and began to walk back through the passageways of Castle-down to the world above.

SEVEN

R ue Meridian flew *Black Moclips* through the last hours of night and into the first light of morning before beginning her search of Castledown's ruins. She would have started sooner, but she was afraid to attempt anything complicated until it was light enough to see what she was doing. Airships were complex mechanisms, and flying one alone, even using the controls situated in the pilot box, was no mean feat. Just keeping the vessel airborne required all her concentration. To make out anything in the darkness, she would have had to place herself at the railing, outside the box and away from the controls. She would not have lasted long that way.

She still had Hunter Predd to help her, but the Wing Rider was not a sailor and knew almost nothing of how airships functioned. He could perform small tasks, but nothing on the order of what would be required if anything went wrong. Besides, he was needed aboard *Obsidian* if they were to have any real chance of finding the missing members of the company. The Roc's eyes were better than their own, and it had been trained to search for what was lost and needed finding. For now, the giant bird was keeping pace with the airship, staying just off her sails as it wheeled back and forth across the skies, waiting for his master to rejoin him.

"'No chance of persuading that Federation Commander or any of his crew to help us, I don't suppose," Hunter Predd ventured at one point, looking doubtful even as he voiced the possibility.

She shook her head. "He says he won't do anything that contradicts his orders, and that includes helping us." She brushed back stray strands of her long red hair. "You have to understand. Aden Kett is a soldier through and through, trained to follow orders, to accept the hierarchy of command. He isn't a bad man, just a misguided one."

They hadn't heard anything from the imprisoned Federation crew since she had locked them away in the storeroom below. Twice she had sent the Wing Rider to check on them, and both times he had reported back that other than muffled conversation, there was nothing to be heard. Apparently the crew had decided that for the time being it was better to wait this business out. She was more than content to let them do so.

Still, it would have been nice to have help. As soon as it was light enough, she planned to send Hunter off on Obsidian in search of Walker, Bek, and the others. In a freewheeling search, he would have a better chance than she would of spotting something. If he was successful, she could bring *Black Moclips* close enough to pick them up. The risk to the airship was minimal. In daylight, from the safety of the skies, she would be able to see for miles. It was not likely that anything would be able to get close enough to threaten, especially now that she had control of the Ilse Witch's vessel.

Of course, she could not discount the possibility that the witch had other weapons at her disposal, ones that could affect even an airship in flight. The witch was down there somewhere in the ruins, hunting Walker, and they might be unlucky enough to encounter her in their search. Rue Meridian had to hope that Obsidian would spy out any sign of the witch before they got close enough for her to do them any damage. She also had to hope that they would find Bek or Walker or any of the others who still lived before the witch did.

She yawned and flexed her gloved fingers where they gripped the flying levers. She had been awake for twenty-four hours, and she was beginning to feel the strain. Her wounds, even padded and sealed within her flying leathers, were throbbing painfully, and her eyes were heavy with the need for sleep. But there was no one to relieve her at the controls, so there was no point in dwelling on her deprivations. Maybe she would get lucky and find Bek at first light. Bek could fly *Black Moclips*. Big Red had taught him well enough. With Bek at the controls, she could get some sleep.

Her thoughts settled momentarily on the boy. No, he was not a boy, she corrected herself quickly. Bek wasn't a boy—not in any way that mattered. He was young in years, but old already in life experience. Certainly he was more mature than those Federation fools she had been forced to suffer on the Prekkendorran. He was smart and funny, and he exuded genuine confidence. She thought back to their conversations on the flight out from the Four Lands, remembering how they had joked and laughed, how they had shared stories and confidences. Hawk and her brother both had been surprised. They didn't understand the attraction. But her friendship with Bek was different from the ones she was accustomed to; it was grounded in their similar personalities. Bek was like a best friend. She felt she could trust him. She felt she could tell him anything.

She shook her head and smiled. Bek put her at ease, and that wasn't something many men did. He didn't invite her to be anyone other than who she really was. He didn't expect anything from her. He wasn't looking to compete, wasn't trying to impress. He was a bit in awe of her, but she was used to that. The important thing was that he didn't let it interfere with or intrude on their friendship.

She wondered where he was. She wondered what had happened to him. Somehow he had fallen into the hands of the Mwellrets and the Ilse Witch, been brought aboard *Black Moclips* and imprisoned. Then someone had rescued him. Who? Had he really lost his voice, as Aden Kett had said, or was he just pretending at it? She felt frustrated by her ignorance. She had so many questions and no way to determine the answers without finding Bek first. She did not like to think of him being hunted down there. But Bek was resourceful, able to find his way through dangers that would overwhelm other men. He would be all right until she found him.

Hawk would laugh at her, if he were there. *He's just a boy*, he would say, not making the distinction she had. *He's not even one of us, not even a Rover*.

But that didn't matter, of course. Not to her, at least. What mattered was that Bek was her friend, and she could admit to herself, if to no one else, that she didn't have many of these.

She brushed the matter aside and returned her attention to the task at hand. The first faint streaks of light were appearing in the east, sliding through gaps in the mountains. Within an hour, she would begin her search. By nightfall, perhaps they could be gone from this place.

Hunter Predd, who had been absent for a time, reappeared at her elbow. "I took a quick look below. Nothing happening. Some of them are asleep. There's no sign of any attempt to break out. But I don't like the situation anyway."

"Nor do I." She shifted her position to relieve her cramped and aching muscles. "Maybe Big Red will reach us before the day is out."

"Maybe." The Wing Rider looked east. "It's growing light. I should start searching. Will you be all right alone?"

She nodded. "Let's find them, Wing Rider. All of them we left behind. Bek, for one, is still alive—along with whoever saved him from the Mwellrets. We know that much, at least. Maybe a few of the others are down there, as well. Whatever happens, we can't abandon them."

Hunter Predd nodded. "We won't."

He went back down out of the pilot box and across the deck to the aft railing. She watched him signal into the night, then lower himself over the side on a rope. Moments later, he flew by aboard Obsidian, giving her a wave of reassurance before disappearing into the gloom. She could just make him out through the fading darkness. Wheeling *Black Moclips* in the direction he was taking, she moved out of the forested hill country and over the ravaged landscape of the ruins, the airship rocking gently in the wind.

She glanced down perfunctorily. Everything below looked flat and gray. It would have to grow much lighter before she could hope to see anyone. Even then, she doubted she would have much luck. Any rescue of the missing members of the company from the *Jerle Shannara* would rely almost entirely on the efforts of the Wing Rider and his Roc.

Don't let us fail them, she thought. *Not again*.

She took a deep breath and put her back to the wind.

Hunter Predd swung down the rope from the airship railing, his keen eyes picking out Obsidian's sleek shape moving up obediently through the darkness. The Roc drifted into place below him, then rose so that his rider could settle aboard. Once Hunter Predd felt the harness between his legs, he reached down for the grips, released the rope, and with a nudge of his knees sent his carrier winging away.

Dawn was a faint gray smudge to the east, but its light was beginning to creep over the landscape. Flying out over the ruins, he could already make out the shattered buildings and debris-strewn roadways, empty and silent. Obsidian would be seeing much more. Even so, this search would not be easy. He had a feeling that Rue Meridian believed that all they needed to do was complete a sweep of the city and they would find anyone who was still alive down there. But Castledown was huge, miles and miles of rubble, and there was every chance that they would fail in their efforts to unmask its secrets. Those they sought must find a way to make themselves known if they were to be discovered other than by chance. To do that, they must be looking skyward in order to see the Roc. It had been almost two weeks since the *Jerle Shannara* had deposited the missing company on the shores of that bay to make the journey inland. By now, they might well have given up hope of being found. They might not be looking for help at all. They might not be alive.

It did no good to speculate, of course. He had come with the Rover girl to find whoever still survived, so it was pointless to start throwing up obstacles to their search before they had even begun it. After all, Obsidian had found smaller specks in larger expanses against greater odds. The chances were there; he simply had to make the best of them.

He flew in widening circles for the duration of the sunrise, searching all the while for movement on the ground, for something that looked a little out of place, for anything that would indicate a foreign presence. As he did so, he found himself thinking back on his decision to make this journey and wondering if he would have been better off staying home. It wasn't just that it had turned out so badly; it was that nothing much seemed to have been accomplished for the effort. If it turned out that Walker was dead, then following Kael Elessedil's map would have been for nothing. Worse, it would have cost lives that could have been spared. Wing Riders were strong believers in letting well enough alone, in living their own lives and not messing in the lives of others. It had taken considerable compromise for him to come on this voyage, and it was taking considerable compromise now for him to stick things out. Common sense said he should turn around and fly home, that the longer he stayed, the shorter the odds grew that he would ever leave. Certainly the Rovers must feel the same way. Rovers and Wing Riders were alike, nomads by choice, mercenaries by profession. Their loyalty and sense of obligation could be bought and paid for, but they never let that get in the way of their common sense.

But he wouldn't leave, of course. He wouldn't abandon those on the ground, no matter the odds, if there was any chance at all that they were still alive. It was just that he couldn't help second-guessing himself, even if it wouldn't make any difference in what he perceived as his commitment to his missing comrades. What if this? What if that? It was the sort of game you played at if you spent enough time alone and in dangerous circumstances. But it was only a game.

The sun crested the horizon, daylight broke across the land, and the ruins stretched away as silent and empty as before. He glanced back to where Rue Meridian flew *Black Moclips*, a solitary figure in the pilot box. She was dangerously tired, and he wasn't sure how much longer she could continue to fly the airship alone. It had been an inspired idea to steal the vessel from the Ilse Witch, but it was going to turn into a liability if she didn't get help fast. He wasn't sure at the moment where that help was going to come from. He would give it if he could, but he knew next to nothing about airships. The best he could do was to pluck her off the deck if things got out of hand.

He caught sight of something odd at the edge of the ruins north, and he swung down for a closer look. He discovered a scattering of bodies, but they were not the bodies of his companions from the *Jerle Shannara* or even the bodies of any people he had ever encountered. These people had burnished skin and red hair, and they were dressed like Gnomes. He had never seen their like, but they had a tribal look to their garb and he assumed they were an indigenous people. How they had come to this sorry end was a mystery, but it looked as if they had been ripped apart by something extraordinarily powerful. Creepers, perhaps.

He flew over the still forms for a few moments more, hoping he would spy something that would help him discover what had happened. He thought it might be worth setting down to see if there was any indication that members of the *Jerle Shannara* had been involved, but decided against it. The information wouldn't do him any good unless he tried to follow up on foot, and that was too dangerous. He glanced over his shoulder to where *Black Moclips* hovered several hundred feet away, drifting in the wind. He signaled to Rue Meridian to swing by for a look, then began a slow sweep back out over the ruins. The Rover girl could make her own decision about what to do. He would continue on. If nothing else turned up, he would come back later.

He had barely settled into a fresh glide over the blasted expanse of the city when he caught sight of something flying toward them from the northeast. Obsidian saw it, as well, and gave a sharp cry of recognition.

It was Po Kelles aboard Niciannon.

Rue Meridian had just maneuvered *Black Moclips* over the collection of dead men at the edge of the ruins and was wondering what to make of it when she glanced back at Hunter Predd and saw the second Wing Rider. She knew it had to be Po Kelles, and she felt fresh hope that his arrival signaled the approach of her brother aboard the *Jerle Shannara*. With two airships searching, she would have a much better chance of finding Bek and the others. Perhaps she could take on a couple of Rovers to help her fly *Black Moclips* so that she could catch a few hours of sleep.

She watched the two riders circle in tandem, talking and gesturing from the backs of their Rocs. Holding her course, she peered back toward the coast, for some sign of the other ship. But there was nothing to be seen as yet, so she returned her attention to the Wing Riders. The discussion had become animated, and the first vague feelings of uneasiness crept through her. Something about the way they communicated, even from a distance, didn't look right.

You're imagining things, she thought.

Then Hunter Predd broke away from Po Kelles and flew back to where she waited, swinging about to come alongside before dropping down and below the aft railing. Taking hold of the line he had left dangling from before, the Wing Rider swung down off the bird and pulled himself up, hand over hand, until he was back on board. A hand signal to Obsidian sent the Roc wheeling away to take up a position beside them, flying to keep pace.

Rue Meridian waited as the Elf hurried over to the pilot box and climbed inside. Even in the faint new light, she could tell that he was upset.

"Listen to me, Little Red." His weathered face was calm, but strained. "Your brother and the others are flying this way, but they are being chased. A fleet of enemy airships appeared off the coast yesterday at dawn. The *Jerle Shannara* barely got away from them. She's been flying this way ever since, trying to shake them off. But fast as she is, she can't seem to lose them. They tracked her all through the mountains, all the way inland, even after she'd changed course to go another way entirely, and now they're almost here."

Enemy airships? All the way out here, so far from the Four Lands? She took a moment to let the information sink in. "Who are they?"

He made a dismissive gesture with one hand. "I don't know. No one does. They fly no flag, and their crews act like dead men. They walk around, but they don't seem to see anything. Po Kelles got a close look late yesterday when the Rovers set down to rest, thinking they'd lost them. Not an hour passed, and there they were again. The ones he could see were men, but they didn't act like men. They acted like machines. They didn't look as if they were alive. They were all stiff and empty-eyed, not seeing anything. One thing is certain. They know where they're going, and they don't seem to need a map to find us."

She glanced around at the brightening day and the ruins below, her hopes for continuing the search fading. "How far away are they?"

"Not half an hour. We have to fly out of here. If they catch you in *Black Moclips* by yourself, you won't stand a chance."

She stared at him without speaking for a moment, anger and frustration blooming inside. She understood the need for flight, but she had never been good at being forced to do anything. Her instincts were to stand and fight, not to run. She hated abandoning yet again those she was searching for, leaving them to an uncertain fate at the hands of not only the Mwellrets and the Ilse Witch, but now this new threat, as well. How long would they last on their own? How long would it be before she could come back and give them any help?

"How many of them are there?" she asked.

The Wing Rider shook his head. "More than twenty. Too many, Little Red, for us to face."

He was right, of course. About everything. They should break off the search and flee before the intruders caught sight of them. But she could not help feeling that Bek and the others were down there, some of them at least, waiting for help. She could not shake off the suspicion that all that was needed was just a little more time. Even a few minutes might be enough.

"Tell Po Kelles to take up watch for us," she ordered. "We can look just a little longer before giving up."

He stared at her. She knew she had no right to give him orders, and he was debating whether or not to point that out. She knew, as well, that he understood what she was feeling.

"The weather is turning, too, Little Red," he said softly, pointing.

Sure enough. Dark clouds were rolling in from the east, borne by coastal winds, and they looked menacing even from a distance. She was surprised she hadn't noticed them. The air had grown colder, too. A front was moving through, and it was bringing a storm with it.

She looked back at him. "Let's try, Wing Rider. For as long as we can. We owe them that much."

Hunter Predd didn't need to ask whom she was talking about. He nodded. "All right, Rover girl. But you watch yourself."

He jumped down out of the pilot box and sprinted back across the decking to the aft railing and disappeared over the side. Obsidian was already in place, and in seconds they were winging off to warn Po Kelles. Rue Meridian swung the airship back around toward the ruins, heading in. Already she was searching the rubble.

Then it occurred to her, a sudden and quite startling revelation, that she was flying an enemy airship, and those on the ground wouldn't know who she was. Rather than come out of hiding to reveal themselves, they would simply burrow deeper. Why hadn't she realized this before? Had she done so, perhaps she could have devised a way to make her intentions known. But it was too late now. Maybe the presence of the Wing Rider would reassure anyone looking up that she wasn't the Ilse Witch. Maybe they would understand what she was trying to do.

Just a few minutes more, she kept telling herself. *Just give me a few minutes more.*

She got those minutes and then some, but she saw no sign of anyone below. The clouds rolled in and blocked the sun, and the air turned so cold that even though she pulled her cloak tight about her, she was left shivering. The landscape was spotted with shadows, and everything looked the same. She was still searching, still insistent on not giving up, when Hunter Predd swung right in front of her and began to gesture.

She turned and looked. Two dozen airships had materialized from out of the gloom, black specks on the horizon. One led all the others, the one being chased, and she knew from its shape that it was the *Jerle Shannara*. Po Kelles was flying Niciannon toward it already, and Hunter Predd was calling to her to tack east and head for the mountains. With a final glance down, she did so. *Black Moclips* lurched in response to her hard wrench on the steering levers and the surge of full power from the radian draws she sent down to the parse tubes and their diapson crystals. The airship shuddered, straightened, and began to pick up speed. Rue Meridian could hear the shouts and cries of the imprisoned Federation crew, but she had no time for them just now. They had made their choice in this matter, and they were stuck with things as they were, like it or not.

"Shut up!" she shrieked, not so much at the men as at the wind that whipped past her ears, taunting and rough.

At full speed, her anger a catalyst that made her as ready to fight as to flee, she flew into the mountains.

EIGHT

In the slow, cool hours before sunrise, Quentin Leah buried Ard
Patrinell and Tamis. He lacked a digging tool to provide a grave,
so he lowered them into the wronk pit and filled it in with rocks.
It took him a long time to find the rocks in the darkness and then to
carry them, sometimes long distances, to be dropped into place.
The pit was large and not easily covered over, but he kept at it, even
after he was so weary his body ached.

When he was finished, he knelt by the rough mound and said
good-bye to them, talking to them as if they were still there, wishing
them peace, hoping they were together, telling them they would be
missed. An Elven Tracker and a Captain of the Home Guard, star-
crossed in every sense of the word—perhaps they would be united
wherever they were now. He tried to think of Patrinell as the Captain was before his changing, a warrior of unmatched fighting skills,
a man of courage and honor. Quentin did not know what lay beyond
death, but he thought it might be something better than life and that
maybe that something allowed you to make up for missed chances
and lost dreams.

He did not cry, he was all done crying. But he was hollowed out and bereft, and he felt a bleakness that was so pervasive it threatened to undo him completely.

Dawn was breaking when he stood again, finished at last. He reached down for the Sword of Leah where he had cast it away at the end of his battle, and picked it up again. The bright, dark surface was unmarked save for streaks of blood and grime. He wiped it off carefully, considering it as he did so. It seemed to him that the sword had failed him completely. For all its magic properties, for all that it was touted to have accomplished in its long and storied history, it had proved to be of little use to him here in this strange land. It had not been enough to save Tamis or Ard Patrinell. It had not even been enough to enable him to protect Bek, whom he had sworn to protect no matter what. That Quentin was alive because he had possession of it was of little consolation. His own life seemed to have been purchased at the cost of others. He did not feel deserving of it. He felt dead inside, and he did not know how he could ever feel anything else.

He put the blade back into its sheath and strapped it across his back once more. The sun was cresting the horizon, and he had to decide what he would do next. Finding Bek was a priority, but to do so he had to leave the concealment of the forest and go back into the ruins of Castledown. That meant risking yet another confrontation with creepers and wronks, and he did not know if he could face that. What he did know was that he needed to be away from this place of death and disappointment.

So he began walking, watching the shadows about him fade back into the trees as sunlight seeped through the canopy and dappled the forest floor. He dropped down from the hills surrounding Castledown to the level stretches he had abandoned in his flight from the Patrinell wronk two days earlier. Walking made him feel somewhat better. The bleakness in his heart lingered, but something of his loss of direction and purpose disappeared as he considered his prospects. There was nothing to be gained by standing about. What he must do, no matter what it took, was find Bek. It was Quentin's insistence on making the journey that had persuaded his cousin to come with him. If he accomplished nothing else, at least he must see Bek safely home again.

He believed that Bek was still alive, even though he knew that many others in the company had perished. He believed this because Tamis had been with his cousin before she found Quentin and because in his heart, where instincts sometimes gave insights that eyes could not, he felt nothing had changed. But that didn't mean that Bek wasn't in trouble and in need of help, and Quentin was determined not to let him down.

Some part of him understood that his intensity was triggered by a need to grasp hold of something to save himself. He was aware that if he faltered, his despair would prove overwhelming, his bleakness of heart so complete that he would be unable to make himself move. If he gave way, he was lost. Moving in any direction, seizing on any purpose, kept him from tumbling into the abyss. He didn't know how realistic he was being in trying to find Bek, all alone and unaided by any useful magic, but the odds didn't matter if he could manage to stay sane.

He was not far from the ruins when he caught sight of an airship flying out ahead of him, distant and small against the horizon. He was so surprised that for a moment he stopped where he was and stared at it in disbelief. It was too far away for him to identify, but he decided at once that it must be the *Jerle Shannara* searching for the members of the company. He felt fresh hope at this and began walking toward it at once.

But in seconds the airship had drifted into the haze of a massive bank of clouds coming out of the east and was lost from view.

He was standing in an open clearing, trying to find it again, when he heard someone call. "Highlander! Wait!"

He turned in surprise, trying to identify the voice, to determine from where the speaker was calling. He was still searching the hills unsuccessfully when Panax walked out of the trees behind him.

"Where have you been, Quentin Leah?" the Dwarf demanded, out of breath and flushed with exertion. "We've been hunting for you all yesterday and last night! It was pure luck that I caught sight of you just now!"

He came up to Quentin and shook his hand warmly. "Well met, Highlander. You look a wreck, if you don't mind my saying. Are you all right?"

"I'm fine," Quentin answered, even though he wasn't. "Who's been looking for me, Panax?"

"Kian and I. Obat and a handful of his Rindge. The wronk tore them up pretty thoroughly. The village, the people, everything. Scattered the tribe all over the place, those it didn't kill. Obat pulled the survivors together up in the hills. At one point, they were planning to rebuild their village and go on as before, but no longer. They're not going back. Things have changed."

He stopped suddenly, taking a close look at Quentin's face, finding something in it he hadn't seen before. "Where's Tamis?" he asked.

Quentin shook his head. "Dead. Ard Patrinell, as well. They killed each other. I couldn't save either one." His hands were shaking. He couldn't seem to stop them. He stared down, confused. "We set a trap, Tamis and I. We hid in the forest by a pit and let the wronk find us, thinking we could drop it in. We used a decoy, a trick, to lure it over. It worked, but then it climbed out, and Tamis . . ."

He trailed off, unable to continue, tears coming to his eyes once more, as if he were a child reliving a nightmare.

Panax took Quentin's hands in his own, steadying them, holding on until the shaking stopped. "You don't look as if you escaped by much yourself," he said quietly. "I expect there wasn't anything you could have done to save either that you didn't try. Don't expect too much of yourself, Highlander. Even magic doesn't always provide the answers we seek. The Druid may have found that out himself, wherever he is. Sometimes, we have to accept that we have limitations. Some things we can't prevent. Death is one."

He let go of Quentin's hands and gripped him by his shoulders. "I'm sorry about Tamis and Ard Patrinell, truly sorry. I expect they fought hard to stay alive, Highlander. But so did you. I think you owe it to them and to yourself to make that count for something."

Quentin looked into the Dwarf's brown eyes, coming back to himself as he did so, able to form a measure of fresh resolve. He remembered Tamis' face at the end, the fierce way she had faced her own death. Panax was right. To fall apart now, to give in to his sadness, would be a betrayal of everything she had fought to accomplish. He took a deep breath. "All right."

Panax nodded and stepped back. "Good. We need you to be strong, Quentin Leah. The Rindge have been out exploring since early this morning, before dawn. They went into the ruins. Castledown is littered with creepers, none of them functioning. The fire threads are down. Antrax, it seems, is dead."

Quentin stared at him, not comprehending.

"Well and good, you might say, but look over there." The Dwarf pointed east to a steadily advancing cloudbank, a huge wall of darkness that stretched across the entire horizon. "What's coming is a change in the world, according to the Rindge. They have a legend about it. If Antrax is destroyed, the world will revert to what it once was. Remember how the Rindge insisted that Antrax controlled the weather? Well before that time, this land was all ice and snow, bitter cold and barely habitable. It only turned to something warm and green after Antrax changed it eons ago. Now it's changing back. Feel the nip in the air?"

Quentin hadn't noticed it before, but Panax was right. The air was growing steadily colder, even as the sun rose. There was a brittle snap to it that whispered of winter.

"Obat and his people are going over the mountains and into Parkasia's interior," the Dwarf continued. "Better weather over there. Safer country. If we don't find another way out of here pretty quick, I think we'd better go with them."

Suddenly Quentin remembered the airship. "I just saw the *Jerle Shannara*, Panax," he said quickly, directing the other's attention toward the front. "It was visible for a moment, right over there. I saw it while I was standing where you found me, and then I lost it in those clouds."

They stared into the darkness together for a several moments without seeing anything. Then Panax cleared his throat. "Not that I doubt you on this, but are you sure it wasn't *Black Moclips*?"

The possibility hadn't occurred to Quentin. He was so eager for it to be the *Jerle Shannara*, he supposed, that he had never stopped to consider that it might be the enemy airship. He had forgotten about their nemesis.

He shook his head slowly. "No, I guess I'm not sure at all."

The Dwarf nodded. "No harm done. But we have to be careful. The witch and her Mwellrets are still out there."

"What about Bek and the others?"

Panax looked uncomfortable. "Still no sign. I don't know if we can find them, Highlander. Obat's people still won't go into the ruins. They say it's a place of death even with Antrax gone and the creepers and fire threads down. They say it's cursed. Nothing has changed. I tried to get them to come with me this morning, but after they saw what had happened, they went right back up into the hills to wait." He shook his head. "I guess I don't blame them, but it doesn't help us much."

Quentin faced him. "I'm not leaving Bek, Panax. I'm all done with running away, with watching people die and not doing anything about it."

The Dwarf nodded. "We'll keep looking, Highlander. For as long as we can, we'll keep searching. But don't get your hopes up."

"He's alive," Quentin insisted.

The Dwarf did not reply, his weathered, bluff face masking his thoughts. His gaze shifted skyward to the north, and Quentin turned to look, as well. A line of black specks had appeared on the horizon, coming down parallel to the storm front, strung out across the morning sky.

"Airships," Panax announced softly, a new edge to his rough voice.

They watched the specks grow larger and begin to take shape. Quentin could not understand where so many airships had come from, seemingly out of nowhere, all at once. Whose were they? He glanced at Panax, but the Dwarf seemed as confused as he did.

"Look," Panax said, pointing.

The airship Quentin had seen earlier had reappeared out of the darkness, moving swiftly across the sky east toward the mountains. There was no mistaking it this time; it was *Black Moclips*. A cry for help died on the Highlander's lips, and he froze in place as it passed overhead and receded into the distance. They could see now that it was attempting to cut off another ship, one further ahead. The distinctive rake of the three masts marked it instantly as the *Jerle Shannara*. The witch and her Mwellrets were in pursuit of the Rovers, and these new airships were chasing both.

"What's going on?" Quentin asked, as much of himself as of Panax.

A moment later, the pursuing fleet split into two groups, one going after *Black Moclips* and the *Jerle Shannara*, the other breaking off toward the ruins of Castledown. This second group was the smaller of the two, but was commanded by the largest of the airships. In a line, the vessels swung over the ruins, where they prepared to set down.

"I don't think we should stand out in the open like this," Panax offered after a moment.

Quickly, they moved into the cover of the trees, then retreated back up into the hills until they found a vantage point from which they could look down on what was taking place. It didn't take them long to decide that they had made the right decision. Rope ladders had been lowered from the airships, which hovered a dozen feet off the ground, and knots of Mwellrets were climbing down and spreading out. On board the airships, the crews kept their stations.

But there was something odd about their stance. They stood frozen in place like statues, not moving about, not even talking with one another. Quentin stared at them for a long time, waiting for any sort of reaction at all. There was none.

"I don't think they're friends," Panax declared softly. He paused. "Look at that."

Something new had been added to the mix—a handful of creatures that lacked any recognizable identity. They were being placed in slings and lowered by winches from the largest airship, one after the other. They looked a little like humans grown all out of proportion, with massive shoulders and arms, thick legs, and hairy torsos. They hunched forward as they walked, using all four limbs like the apes of the Old World. But their heads had a wolfish look to them, with narrow, sharp snouts, pointed ears, and gimlet eyes. Even at a distance, their features were unmistakable.

"What are those?" Quentin breathed.

The search parties fanned out through the ruins, dozens of Mwellrets in each, armed and armored, a decidedly hostile invader. Secured on lengths of chain and ordered to track, the odd hunched creatures were being used like dogs. Noses to the ground, they began making their way through the rubble in different directions, the Mwellrets trailing. Within the ruins, there was no response from Antrax. No creepers appeared and no fire threads lanced forth. It appeared the Rindge were right about what had happened. But it only made Quentin wonder all the more about Bek.

Burly, dark-skinned Kian appeared suddenly out the trees, moving over to join them. He nodded a greeting to Quentin as he came up, but didn't speak.

"We've got a problem, Highlander," Panax said without looking at him.

Quentin nodded. "They're searching for us. Eventually, they'll find us."

"All too quickly, I expect." The Dwarf straightened. "We can't stay. We have to get away."

Quentin Leah stared down at the searchers as they trickled into the city, tiny figures still, like toys. Quentin understood what Panax was saying, but he didn't want to speak the words aloud. Panax was saying that they had to give up the search for Bek. They had to put as much distance as possible between themselves and whoever was down there hunting them.

He felt something shrivel up and die inside at the prospect of abandoning Bek yet again, but he knew that if he stayed, he would be found. That would accomplish nothing useful and might result in his death. He tried to think it through. Maybe Bek stood a better chance than Quentin thought. Bek had the use of magic; Tamis had told them so. She had seen him use it, a power that could shred creepers. His cousin wasn't entirely helpless. In truth, he might be better off than they were. Maybe he had even found Walker, so that the two of them were together. They might have already fled the ruins and gone into the mountains themselves.

He stopped himself angrily. He was rationalizing. He was trying to make himself feel better about abandoning Bek, about breaking his promise once more. But he didn't really believe what he was telling himself. His heart wouldn't let him.

"What do we do?" he asked finally, resigned to doing the one thing he had sworn he wouldn't.

Panax rubbed his bearded chin. "We go into the Aleuthra Ark—those mountains behind us—with Obat and his people. We go deeper into Parkasia. The airships were flying that way. Maybe we can catch up to one of them. Maybe we can signal it." He shrugged wearily. "Maybe we can manage to stay alive."

To his credit, he didn't say anything about coming back for Bek and the others, or resuming the search somewhere further down the line. He understood that such a thing might not happen, that they might never return to the ruins. He was not about to make a promise he knew he could not keep.

None of this helped Quentin with his feelings of betrayal, but it was better to be honest about the possibilities than to cling to false hopes.

I'm sorry, Bek, he said to himself.

"They're coming this way," Kian said suddenly.

One of the search parties had emerged at the edge of the ruins below and found the bodies of the Rindge that the Patrinell wronk had killed two days earlier. Already, the hunched creatures were sniffing the ground for tracks. A wolfish head lifted and looked toward where they crouched in the trees, as if aware of them, as if able to spy them out.

Without another word, the Dwarf, the Elf, and the Highlander melted into the trees and were gone.

It took them the better part of an hour to reach the clearing where Obat and his Rindge were assembled. They were high up on the slopes of the hills fronting the Aleuthra Ark, which ran down the interior of Parkasia from northwest to southeast like a jagged spine. The Rindge were a ragged and dispirited-looking group, although not disorganized or unprepared. Sentries had been posted and met the three outlanders long before they reached the main body of Rindge. Weapons had been recovered, so that all the men were armed. But the larger portion of survivors was made up of women and children, some of the latter only babies. There were at least a hundred Rindge and probably closer to two hundred. They had their belongings piled about them, tied up in bundles or stuffed into cloth sacks. Most sat quietly in the shadows, talking among themselves, waiting. In the dappled forest light, they looked like hollow-eyed and uncertain ghosts.

Obat came up to Panax and began talking to him immediately. Panax listened, then replied, using the ancient Dwarf tongue he had employed successfully when they had first met. Obat listened and shook his head no. Panax tried again, pointing back in the direction from which they had come. It was clear to Quentin that he was telling Obat about the intruders from the airships. But Obat didn't like what he was hearing.

Exasperation written all over his face, Panax turned to the Highlander. "I told him we have to move quickly, that the belongings must be left behind. As it is, it will take everything we have to move this bunch to safety without having to deal with all this stuff. But Obat says this is all his people have left. They won't leave it."

He turned to Kian. "Go back up the trail with a couple of the Rindge and keep watch."

The Elven Hunter turned without a word, beckoned a couple of the Rindge to come with him, and disappeared into the trees at a quick trot.

Panax turned back to Obat and tried again. This time he made unmistakable gestures indicating what would happen if the Rindge were too slow in the attempt to escape. His broad face was flushed and angry, and his voice was raised. Obat stared at him, impassive.

We're wasting time, Quentin thought suddenly. *Time we don't have.*

"Panax," he said. The Dwarf turned. "Tell them to pick up their things and start walking. We can't take time to argue about this any longer. Let them find out for themselves whether or not it's worth it to haul their possessions. Set a pace the women and children can follow and go. Leave me a dozen Rindge. I'll see what I can do to slow our pursuers down."

The Dwarf gave him a hard look and then nodded. "All right, Highlander. But I'm staying, as well. Don't argue the matter. As you say, we don't have time for it."

He spoke quickly to Obat, who turned to his people and began shouting orders. The Rindge assembled at once, belongings in place. Led by a handful of armed men, they set out along a narrow forest path into the hills, moving silently and purposefully. Quentin was surprised at how swiftly they got going. There was no hesitation, no confusion. Everyone seemed to know what to do. Perhaps they had done it before. Perhaps they were better prepared for the move than Panax thought.

In seconds, the clearing was empty of everyone but Quentin, Panax, and a dozen or so Rindge warriors. Obat had chosen to stay, as well. Quentin wasn't sure this was a good idea, since Obat was clearly the leader of the tribe and losing him might prove disastrous. But it wasn't his decision to make, so he left it alone.

He turned to look off in the direction of the ruins, wondering how much time they had before the Mwellrets and those hunched creatures discovered them. Perhaps it wouldn't happen as quickly as he feared. There would be other tracks to distract them, other trails to follow. They might choose one that would lead them in another direction entirely. But he didn't believe that for a minute.

He thought about his failures on his journey from the Highlands of Leah, of his missed opportunities and questionable choices. He had set out with such high hopes. He had thought himself capable of dictating the direction of his life. He had been wrong. In the end, it had been all he could do to stay afloat in the sea of confusion that surrounded him. He could not even determine whom he would use the magic of his vaunted sword to protect. He could use it to help only those whom fate placed within his reach, and maybe not even those.

The Rindge were among them. He could leave them and go on, because in the end they didn't really have anything to do with him, his reasons for coming to Parkasia, or his promise to Bek. If anything, they were a hindrance. If he was to have any chance at all of catching up to one of the airships and finding a way out of this land, speed might make the difference. But in the wake of his failure to save Tamis or Ard Patrinell or to find Bek, he felt a compelling need to succeed in helping *someone*. The Rindge were giving him that opportunity. He could not make himself walk away from it. He could not let anyone else be hurt because of him.

He would do what he could for those he was in a position to

help. If helping the Rindge was what fate had given him the chance to do, that would have to be enough.

Panax walked up beside him. "What happens now, Quentin Leah? How do we stop those things back there from catching up to Obat's people?"

The Highlander only wished he knew.

NINE

When Ahren Elessedil regained consciousness, he found himself lying on his side in Castledown's rubble looking at the boots of his captors. His hands were tied behind his back, and his head ached from the blow he had received. Even without having witnessed the particulars, he knew at once what had happened and was awash in despair and frustration. He had stumbled into a Mwellret trap, one set for him as he tried to move through the ruins with Ryer Ord Star. How could he have been so stupid? After what he had gone through to retrieve the Elfstones and escape Castledown, how could he have allowed himself to be caught so completely unawares?

There wasn't any answer for such questions, of course. Asking them only invited self-recrimination, and there was nothing to be gained from that.

He blinked against the dryness in his eyes and tried to sit up, but a heavy boot pushed him back again and settled on his chest.

"Little Elvess sstayss where they are," a voice hissed.

He glanced up at the big Mwellret standing over him and nodded. The boot and the Mwellret moved away a few steps, but the watchful eyes stayed fixed on him. He could see rets standing all about him, maybe a dozen or so, heavy reptilian bodies cloaked against the dawn light, heads bent between heavy shoulders, voices low and sibilant as they conversed among themselves. None of them seemed to be in a hurry to go anywhere or to get anything done. They seemed to be waiting for something. He tried to imagine what it might be. The Ilse Witch, perhaps. She must have gone further into the ruins. Perhaps she had gone underground in search of Walker.

He thought suddenly of Ryer Ord Star, and from his prone position he scanned as much of the area as he could in an effort to find her. He spotted her finally, seated in an open space, alone and ignored. He stared at her for a long time, waiting to be noticed, but she never looked his way. She kept her gaze lowered, her face shadowed by her long silver hair. She might have had her eyes closed; he couldn't tell. She was unfettered, and no Mwellrets stood over her as they did over him. They seemed unconcerned that she might try to escape.

Something about her situation bothered him. She didn't seem to be a prisoner at all.

He glanced around further, searching for any other members of the company who might have encountered the same misfortune. But no one else was in evidence, only the two of them. He shifted surreptitiously in an effort to see what else he might have missed from where he lay, but he saw only Mwellrets in the area.

Then he glanced skyward and saw the airships.

His throat tightened. There were six of them—no, wait, there were eight—hanging in the air, not far off the ground at the edge of the ruins, silhouetted against the morning sky. They were close enough that he could see crew members standing about, Mwellrets climbing down rope ladders, and hoists lowering animals that twisted and writhed and grunted loudly. He caught only glimpses of them against the bright sunrise as they slipped over the sides of the airships and disappeared down into the ruins, and he couldn't make out what they were.

Mwellrets and airships. He couldn't understand it. Where had they come from, all at once like this? Had the Ilse Witch brought them, keeping them back from *Black Moclips*, hiding them until they were needed? He tried to reason it through and failed.

He glanced again at Ryer Ord Star. The seer still hadn't looked up, hadn't changed position, hadn't done anything to evidence that she was even conscious. He wondered suddenly if perhaps she was in a trance, trying to connect to Walker. But the Druid had to be dead by now. He had been dying back there in the extraction chamber, his blood everywhere. Walker had sacrificed himself to destroy Antrax. Even Ryer must realize that she could no longer reach him.

So what was she doing?

Why wasn't she tied up like he was?

He waited for the answers to come, for her to respond to his mental summons, for something to happen that would reveal her condition—without success.

All of a sudden, he remembered the Elfstones. He was astonished that he had forgotten about them, that he had somehow failed to remember the one weapon he still had at his disposal. Maybe. He had tucked them into his tunic on fleeing the ruins, in a pocket near his waist. Were they still there? He didn't think he could reach them with his hands tied, but he could at least determine if he had them. The Mwellrets would have searched him for weapons, not for the Stones. They wouldn't even know what they were.

He glanced about quickly, but no one was looking at him. He rolled onto his other side, moving slowly, trying not to attract attention. He squirmed down against the hard earth, searching for the feel of the Elfstones against his body. He could not find them. His hopes sank. He shifted positions, trying to see if they were somewhere else, but he could not feel them anywhere.

He was still searching when he heard a mix of heavy footfalls, rough voices, and deep growls. The Mwellret who had pushed him down came over at once and hauled him to his feet with a jerk, standing him upright and propping him against a section of wall.

"Sseess now what becomess of you, little Elvess," he muttered before turning away.

Ahren glanced over at Ryer Ord Star. She was on her feet, as well, still alone and still not looking at him. She stood with her arms wrapped about her slender body, looking frail and tiny. Something was going on with her that he didn't understand, and she wasn't doing anything to let him know what it was.

A clutch of Mwellrets strode into the clearing. Two of the burliest held the ends of chains that were fastened to a collar strapped about the neck of one of the most terrifying creatures Ahren had ever seen. The creature tugged and twisted against the collar like a huge dog, grunts and growls emanating from deep within its throat as it did so. Its body was hunched over and heavily muscled. Four human limbs that ended in clawed fingers and massive shoulders were covered in thick black hair. Its torso was so long and sinuous that it allowed the creature to almost double back on itself as it twisted about angrily, trying to bite at the chains. Its head was wolfish, its jaws huge, and its teeth long and dark. It had the look of something bred not just to hunt, but to destroy.

When it saw Ahren, it lunged for him, and the Elf pressed back against the building wall in fear.

A tall, black-cloaked figure stepped forward, blocking the creature's path. The beast cringed and backed away.

The cloaked figure turned and looked at him. Ahren could just make out the other's face. It might have been human once, but now it was covered with gray scales like the rets, flat and expressionless, its green eyes compressed into narrow slits that regarded him with such coldness that he forgot all about the wolf creature.

"Cree Bega," the cloaked figure called, still watching Ahren.

The Mwellret who had been standing guard over him came at once. Big as he was, he looked small next to the newcomer. Even so, he did not do anything to acknowledge the other's authority, neither bowing nor nodding. He simply stood there, his gaze level and fixed.

"Cree Bega," the other repeated, and this time there was a hint of menace in his voice. "Why is this Elf still alive?"

"He iss an Elesssedil. He hass the power to ssummon the magic of the Elfsstoness."

"You have seen this for yourself?"

Cree Bega shook his head. "But the sseer tellss me thiss iss sso."

Ahren felt as if the ground had dropped away beneath him. He glanced quickly at Ryer, but she was still staring blankly.

"She is the witch's tool," the cloaked figure declared softly, looking over at the seer.

"Her eyess and earss aboard little Elvess sship." Cree Bega glanced at Ahren. "Not anymore. Belongss to uss now. Sservess uss."

Ahren refused to believe what he was hearing. Ryer Ord Star would never go back to serving their enemies, not after what she had gone through, not after breaking free of the Ilse Witch. She had said she was finished with that. She had sworn it.

Stunned, he watched as his captors turned away from him and walked to where the seer stood. Bent close, the cloaked one began speaking to her. The words were too faint for Ahren to hear, but Ryer Ord Star nodded and then replied. The conversation lasted just minutes, but it was clear that some sort of agreement had been reached.

He moved his elbows down close to his sides, pressing them against his ribs, shifting first one way and then the other, straining at the cords that bound his wrists as he tried to determine if the Elf stones were indeed gone. It seemed they were; he could find no trace of their presence.

Close by, the chained beast growled and snapped at him again, trying to break free, all size and teeth and claws as it fought against its restraints. Ahren quit moving and stood as still as he could manage, staring into the creature's eyes. He was surprised to find that they were almost human.

The cloaked figure walked back across the clearing and stood looking down at him. "I am the Morgawr," he said, his voice soft and strangely warm, as if he sought to reassure Ahren of his friendship. "Do you know of me?"

Ahren nodded.

"What is your name?"

"Ahren Elessedil," he answered, deciding there was no reason to hide it.

"Youngest son of Allardon Elessedil? Why isn't your brother here?"

"My brother wanted me to come instead. He wanted an Elessedil presence, but not his own."

The flat face nodded. "I am told you can invoke the power of the Elfstones, the ones Kael Elessedil carried on his voyage thirty years ago. Is that so?"

Ahren nodded, disappointment welling up inside him. Ryer Ord Star had betrayed him. He wished he had never trusted her. He wished he had left her behind in the catacombs of Castledown.

"Where are the Stones now?" the Morgawr asked.

Ahren was so surprised by the question that for a moment he just stared. He had assumed that the Mwellrets had taken them from him when he was captured. Had they failed to do so? Was he mistaken about having them still?

He had to say something right away, so he said, "I don't know where they are."

It was the truth, which was all to the good because he could see the Morgawr reading his eyes. The Morgawr knew about the Elfstones, but didn't know where they were. How could that be? Ahren had carried them out of Castledown. They were hidden inside his tunic when he was knocked unconscious. Could Cree Bega have taken them for himself? Could one of the other rets? Would any of them dare to do that?

The Morgawr touched his face with one scaly finger. "I am keeping you alive because the seer assures me you will use the Elfstones once I find them. She does not lie, does she?"

Ahren took a deep breath, fighting down his fear and anger. "No."

"I am mentor to the Ilse Witch. I trained her and schooled her and gave her my protection. But she betrays me. She seeks the magic of Castledown for herself. So I have come to eliminate her. You and the seer will help me find her. She is talented, but she cannot escape the seeking light of the Elfstones. Nor can she avoid her connection to the seer. She established it for the purpose of tracking the Druid and his airship; now we will use it, in turn, to track her. One or the other of you will reveal the witch to me. If you provide your help, I will set you free when I am done with her."

Ahren didn't believe this for a minute, but he held his tongue.

The gimlet eyes fixed on him. "You should welcome this offer."

Ahren nodded. As confused as he was about the disappearance of the Elfstones, he knew what to say. "I will do what I can."

The Morgawr's finger slid away. "Good. The Ilse Witch has gone underground to find the Druid. The seer says you left him there, dying. What wards this safehold is dying, too, so we have nothing to fear. You will take us down there."

A chill swept through Ahren. He did not want to go back into Castledown for any reason, least of all to help the Morgawr. But he knew that if he refused, he would be made to go anyway, and he would be watched afterwards all the more closely. If they didn't just kill him and have done with it. It was better to do what was asked of him for now, to go along with the Morgawr's wishes. Antrax was dying when Ryer and he had ascended the passageways and would be as dead as Walker by now. What could it hurt to go into the catacombs a final time?

Even so, he was not comfortable with the idea. He glanced at Ryer Ord Star across the way, but she was looking down again, her face lost in the shadow of her long hair. She would have agreed already, of course. By making herself an ally to the Morgawr and the Mwellrets, she would have promised to help them track the Ilse

Witch. She had good reason to hate the witch, but not reason enough to bring harm to Ahren and the others of the company of the *Jerle Shannara*. Didn't she realize that the Morgawr and Cree Bega were no more trustworthy than the witch? He could not believe she had compromised herself so completely.

"Cut him loose," the Morgawr ordered Cree Bega, his silky voice a whisper of comfort and reassurance.

The Mwellret severed the cords that bound Ahren's wrists, and the Elven Prince rubbed the circulation back into them. Straightening his clothes, he sought one final time to locate the Elfstones. Perhaps they were shoved way down inside his tunic. His hands and fingers ran swiftly down his sides. Nothing. The Elfstones were gone.

The Morgawr moved away, beckoned for Ahren to follow, motioned Cree Bega toward Ryer, and called out instructions to the other Mwellrets. Ahren went without hesitating, still rubbing his wrists, already thinking of ways he might escape. He would find a way, he promised himself. He would not be part of this business for one moment longer than he had to. He would flee the Morgawr and his rets at the first opportunity and continue his search for his missing friends.

He glanced wistfully at Ryer Ord Star, who was moving just ahead and still not looking at him. He tried to move over to her, but almost instantly the Morgawr blocked his way.

"Don't think that because I have released you I am not watching you," he said softly, leaning close. "If you try to escape, if you attempt to flee, if you fail to do as I ask, I will set the caull on you."

He motioned to the wolfish animal that had moved into the forefront of their party, tugging so hard on its chains that it dragged its handlers like dead weights behind it.

"No secrets, no tricks, no foolish acts, Elven Prince," the Morgawr cautioned in his smooth, quiet voice. "Do you understand?"

Ahren nodded, his eyes riveted on the caull.

The Morgawr touched Ahren's cheek with that odd caressing

motion. "You don't understand fully. Not yet. But you will. I will see to it that you do."

He moved away again, and Ahren rubbed at his cheek to erase the unpleasant feeling of the scaly touch. He had no idea what he was going to do to escape. Whatever it was, it had better work because he would get only one chance. But he could not imagine where that chance would come from if he did not regain possession of the Elfstones. His memory of what it had been like to wield the magic was still strong. Finding them and invoking their power had transformed him. He had redeemed himself in his own eyes, at least, from his cowardice in the ruins, and in doing so had discovered something of the man he had hoped to become. He had evidenced courage and strength of will, and he did not want to lose those. But without the Elfstones, he was afraid he might.

His eyes drifted skyward, to where the airships still hovered against the horizon. West, the sky was black and thick with rolling clouds. The temperature was dropping, as well. A storm was coming, and it looked to be severe.

They were moving deeper into the ruins, back the way they had come. The caull and its handlers led, but Ryer Ord Star and the Morgawr were close behind, whispering back and forth as if kindred with a common goal. Cree Bega shoved at Ahren, urging him to catch up to them, to lend whatever input he might have to give. The Elven Prince put aside his thinking and increased his pace until he was right behind the seer, following in her footsteps, close enough to reach out and touch her.

Look at me, he thought. *Say something!*

She did neither. He might not have been there at all, for all the difference his presence made to her. He could not escape the feeling that she was ignoring him deliberately. Was her sense of guilt at betraying him so strong? It seemed as if she was rejecting everything she had tried to become since finding him and was reverting to the creature she had been when in the service of the witch. It felt as if her sense of loyalty had died with Walker. He could not understand that.

Then she was pointing out something in the ruins to the Morgawr, and as the warlock turned to look, she lost her footing and stumbled, careening backwards into Ahren. He caught her without thinking, holding her upright. Without looking at him, she straightened and pushed him away.

It was over in seconds, and they were moving ahead once more, Ryer Ord Star back beside the Morgawr, Cree Bega and his Mwell-rets all about. But in those seconds, when she was pressed up against him, she whispered, so clearly he could not mistake what she said, two words.

Trust me.

TEN

Less than a quarter of a mile away Bek Ohmsford crouched in a pool of deep shadows formed by the juncture of two broken walls and waited for Truls Rohk to return. He heard the approach of the Mwellrets and whoever was with them, the sound of their voices and the scrape of their boots carrying clearly in the early morning silence. He had already seen the airships hanging in the distance over the ruins, dark hulls and masts empty of insignia or flags. He had watched them disgorge their Mwellret passengers and creatures like the caull his sister had used to track the shapeshifter and himself. He knew they were in trouble.

Truls Rohk had gone to investigate. He had not returned.

Bek's hand tightened about Grianne's, and he glanced over at her to reassure himself that she was all right. Well, to reassure himself that nothing had changed, at least. She was hunched down next to him in the darkness, staring at nothing. He had pulled back her hood to let the light find her face. Her pale skin looked ghostly in the shadows, and her strange blue eyes were empty and fixed. She was compliant to his directions, but unresponsive to anything around her. She did not speak, did not look at him, and did not react to what was happening. He did not know much about the catatonic state, about what it would take to release her from it, but he supposed she was in a great deal of emotional or psychological pain and that was the reason for her condition. She would regain consciousness when she was ready, Walker had said. But after several hours of traveling with and watching her, he was not sure he believed it.

"Grianne," he said softly.

He reached over with his free hand and touched her cheek, running his finger over her smooth skin. There was no reaction. He wished there was something he could do for her. He could only imagine what it must have been like for her to confront the truth about herself. The magic of the Sword of Shannara had drawn back the veil of lies and deception, letting in the light she had kept out for so many years. To be made to see yourself as you really were when you had committed so many atrocities, so many ugly and terrible acts, would be unbearable. No wonder she had retreated so far into herself. But how were they to help her if she remained there?

Not that Truls Rohk believed they should. The shape-shifter saw her as no different from before, save for the fact that she was helpless and at present not a danger to them. But he also saw her as a sleeping beast. When she awoke, she could easily erupt into a frenzy of murderous rage. There was nothing to say that the magic of the talisman would prevent it, nothing to say that she was any different now from what she had been before. There was no guarantee she would not revert to form. In fact, there was every reason to believe she would.

Bek had chosen not to argue the point. On their trek out, winding their way back up the passageways of Castledown to the surface of the ruins, he had kept silent on the matter. Walker had given them their charge—to care for Grianne at any cost, to see her safely home again, to accept that she was important in some still unknowable way. It didn't matter what Truls Rohk thought of her; it didn't matter what he really believed. The Druid had made them promise to ward her, and the shape-shifter had sworn that promise alongside Bek. Like it or not, Truls Rohk was bound by his word.

In any case, Bek thought it better to let the matter alone. If the Druid, even while dying, had been unable to convince the shape-shifter of Grianne's worth, there was little chance that Bek could now. Not right away, at least. Perhaps time would provide him with a way to do so. Perhaps. Meanwhile, he would have to find a way to stay alive.

He took a steadying breath and tried to fight down the panic he felt at his dwindling prospects of being able to do so. They had fought their way clear of one trap and now found themselves facing another. Antrax and the creepers and fire threads might be gone, but now a mix of enemy airships and Mwellrets confronted them. That they were allied in some way with his sister was an unavoidable conclusion. It was too big a coincidence to believe they had come all this way for any other reason. Cree Bega would have linked up with the newcomers and advised them of his presence. They would be looking for Bek and for whoever had helped him escape from *Black Moclips*. If he stayed where he was for much longer, they would find him. Truls had better hurry.

As if reading his mind, the shape-shifter materialized across the way, sliding into the light like a phantasm, blacker than the shadows out of which he came. Concealing cloak swirling gently with the movement of his body, he crouched next to the boy.

"We have fresh trouble," he announced. "The airships are commanded by the Morgawr. He's brought Mwellrets, caulls, and some men who look as if they have been turned into wooden toys. Besides the airships we see, at least a dozen more have gone off in pursuit of the *Jerle Shannara* and *Black Moclips*."

"*Black Moclips?*" Bek shook his head in confusion.

"Don't ask me, boy. I don't know what happened aboard ship after we escaped, but it seems the rets managed to lose control of her. Someone else got aboard and took her over, sent her skyward, and sailed her right out from under their noses. Good news for us, perhaps. But not soon enough to make a difference just now."

The sounds of their pursuit broke into Bek's thoughts, but he forced himself to stay calm. "So now they're hunting us, following our tracks or our scent, using these fresh caulls?"

Truls Rohk laughed. "You couldn't be more wrong. They don't care about us! It's the witch they're looking for! She's done something to convince the Morgawr she wants the magic for herself—or at least convinced him she's too dangerous to trust anymore. He's come to take possession of the magic and do away with her. He doesn't realize there isn't any magic to take possession of and the witch has already done away with herself! It's a good joke on him. He's wasting his time and he doesn't even realize it."

The cowled head turned in the direction of Grianne. "Look at her. She's as dead as if she'd quit breathing. The Druid thinks she has a purpose in all this, but I think his dying blinded him. He wanted something useful to come of all this, something that would give meaning to the lives wasted and the chances lost. But wishing doesn't make it so. When he destroyed Antrax, he destroyed what he had come to find. The Old World books are lost. There isn't anything else. Nothing!"

"Maybe we just don't see it," Bek ventured quietly. He heard snarls and growls from the approaching caull. "Look, we have to get out of here."

"Yes, boy, we do." The hard eyes peered out from the shadows, reflective stone amid a sea of shifting mist and bits of matter. "But we don't need to take her." He gestured at Grianne. "Leave her for the Morgawr. Let them do with her what they choose. They won't bother with us if we do. She's what they want."

"No," Bek said at once.

"If we take her, they will keep after us, all the way inland to wherever we run, to wherever we hide. If she could find us earlier, they can find us now. Sooner or later. She's a weight around our necks and not one we need carry."

"We promised Walker we would protect her!"

"We promised it so that the Druid could die at peace." Truls Rohk spit. "But it was a fool's promise and given without any cause beyond that. We don't need her. We don't want her. She serves no purpose now and never will. What she is has destroyed her. She isn't coming back, newly born, your sister returned; you're not going to be a happy family reunited. Thinking otherwise is foolish."

Bek shook his head. "I'm not leaving her. You do what you want."

For just an instant, Bek thought that Truls Rohk was going to do just that. The shape-shifter went as still as the shadows on a windless night, all dark presence and hidden danger. Bek could feel the tension in him, a sort of singing sound that was more vibration than noise, a cord become taut on a bow drawn back.

"You persist in being troublesome," Truls Rohk whispered. "Have you no capacity for rational behavior?"

Bek almost laughed at the words, spoken with such seriousness but rife with irony. He shook his head slowly. "She is my sister, Truls. She doesn't have anyone else to help her."

"She's going to disappoint you. This isn't going to turn out like you think."

Bek nodded. "I don't suppose it will. It hasn't so far." He kept his eyes locked on the shape-shifter as the sounds of approach intensified. "Can we go now?"

Truls Rohk stared at him a moment longer, as if trying to decide. Then he came forward, all blackness even in the early morning light, picked up Grianne like a rag doll, and tucked her under his arm.

"Try to keep up with me, boy," he said. "Carrying one of you is load enough."

He sprang atop the nearest remnant of wall and began to navigate its length like a tightrope walker in a street fair, crouched low and moving swiftly. The feel of his sister's hand in his a lingering warmth, Bek watched him for a moment, then hurried after.

Ahren Elessedil listened with growing concern as the snarls of the caull leading the Morgawr's party deeper into the ruins grew more anxious. Clearly, it had come across something, tracks or scent that it recognized and wanted to pursue. Its handlers had not released it, however. Nor was the Morgawr giving it much attention; his focus was on Ryer Ord Star as they walked next to each other, engaged once again in close conversation. What was it she was telling him? The boy was encouraged by her whispered words, but suspicious of her actions. She was asking him to trust her, but doing nothing to warrant it. He had thought she might at least try leading their captors in the wrong direction; instead she was taking them the way she had come, directly toward the entrance that led underground to where they had left Walker.

It appeared she had become the Morgawr's ally in his business, and the Elf was having trouble convincing himself that he should trust her at all.

They moved more quickly now, navigating the rubble to where the opening led downward into Castledown. Judging from the sounds emanating from the caull, its snout lowered to the ground as it tugged and pulled its handlers ahead, whomever they were tracking had come this way recently. He wondered briefly if it might be their own scent the caull had come across, but that would make the beast a good deal more stupid than the Elf was prepared to believe. Since it was the Ilse Witch the Morgawr was seeking, Ahren had to assume the caull had been given her scent. She could easily have come the same way they had and still managed to miss them in the catacombs.

They passed through the entry in a cautious knot. Creepers lay in heaps just inside, unmoving. Flameless lamps still burned, casting a weak yellow glow from the passage walls, but the Mwellrets lit torches anyway. The smoky light lent the empty corridors an eerie, shadowy look as the group moved downward into the earth.

Several times Ahren thought to make a break for freedom, but fear and common sense kept him from acting on his impulse. He needed a better opportunity, and he needed to know more about what Ryer Ord Star was doing. He needed, as well, to know who had the Elfstones so that he could try to find a way to get them back. He hadn't made a conscious decision on the matter before this, but he knew now, thinking about it, that he wasn't going back to the Four Lands without them. It was ambitious for him to think about getting home at all, but at this point, he couldn't help himself. Thinking about it was all he had to keep his mind off his current predicament, and if he didn't concentrate on something, he was afraid his dwindling courage would collapse completely.

They walked a long time, back the way Ryer and he had come, following the very same passageways down into the bowels of Castledown. Sporadic sounds rose in the distance, but nothing solid appeared to hinder them. Antrax and Castledown had gone back into time to join the rest of the Old World, dead and lost.

When they reached the cavernous chamber where Antrax had housed its power, they found it empty. Walker was gone, though pools of his blood had dried dark and sticky on the metal floor. Twisted chunks of metal and broken cables littered the landscape, and fluids had begun leaking from tanks and lines, cloudy and thick. Excited by the blood and the lingering smells, the caull lunged this way and that, but there were no people to be found. The Morgawr walked around, looking at everything carefully, distancing himself from the rest of the party as he did so. He poked at the creepers, stood close to the massive twin cylinders, and entered the extraction chamber, where he remained alone for a long time. Ahren watched everyone, but particularly Ryer Ord Star. She stood only yards from him, staring off into space. She never glanced in his direction. If she sensed him looking at her, she kept it to herself.

When the Morgawr was finished with his examination, he emerged from the extraction chamber, brushing aside Cree Bega with a hiss of impatience. The caull leading the way, its massive body jerking at its chains in frustration, they set off in a new direction. The Ilse Witch had been here, Ahren knew. No one had said so, but the behavior of the Morgawr as he plunged ahead down this new passageway made the conclusion unavoidable. Perhaps they had just missed her. He found himself wondering what had become of Walker. Even if the witch had found him, she wasn't strong enough to move him herself.

He had his answer not long afterwards. They navigated the maze of empty, ruined corridors until they came to a vast cavern housing an underground lake. Illuminated by the dim phosphorescence that streaked the cavern's rocky walls, a trail of blood led down to the edge of the water, pooled anew on the rocky shore, and disappeared. The surface of the lake was still and perfectly smooth. There was no sign of Walker.

The Morgawr stood staring out across the lake for a moment, black cloak drawn close about him. No one tried to approach him or dared to speak.

"Get back from me," he told them finally.

They did so, and Ahren watched as scaly arms emerged from the Morgawr's cloak and began to weave in quick motions, drawing pictures or symbols on the air. A greenish light emanated from the fingertips, leaving trails of emerald fire in their wake. The hush of the empty cavern filled with a whisper of phantom wind, and from the depths of the lake rose a deep, ugly hiss that seemed as much a warning as a response to the Morgawr's conjuring. Still, the warlock continued his efforts, robes whipping about his dark body, spray bursting from the waters in sudden explosions. Faint images began to appear, shades cast upon the darkness by his magic's light, there one moment and gone the next. Ahren could not tell who they were meant to be; he could not even be sure of what his senses were telling him. Once, he thought he heard voices, rough whispers that rose and fell like the lake's dark spray. Once, he was sure he heard screams.

Then the wind increased, and the torches blew out. The Mwellrets dropped back a few paces, closer to the entrance to the cavern. Ahren went with them. Only Ryer Ord Star stood her ground, head lifted, a fierce look on her childlike face as she stared out across the lake into the darkness beyond. She was seeing something, as well,

Ahren thought—maybe the strange images, maybe something else entirely.

Finally, the Morgawr's hands stopped moving, the wind and noise died away, and the lake went still. The Morgawr stepped back from the water's edge and walked to where his rets crouched watchfully at the cavern entrance, motioning for the seer to come with him as he passed her. Dutifully, she turned and followed.

"The Druid is dead," he declared as he came up to them.

Hearing someone speak the words gave their truth fresh impact. Ahren caught his breath in spite of himself, and it suddenly felt to him as if whatever hopes he had harbored that a way out of this terrible place, this savage land, might be found, had just been stolen away.

The Morgawr was looking at him, assessing his reaction. "Our little Ilse Witch, however, is alive." He kept his dangerous eyes fixed on Ahren. "She's come and gone, and she's not alone. She's with that boy you let escape from *Black Moclips*, Cree Bega—and someone else, someone I can't put a name to." He paused. "Can you, Elven Prince?"

Ahren shook his head. He had no idea who Bek might be with if it wasn't Tamis or one of the other Elves.

The Morgawr came forward and reached out to touch his cheek. The cavern air turned colder with that touch, and its silence deepened. Ahren forced himself to stand his ground, to repress the repulsion and fear that the touch invoked in him. The touch lingered a moment and then withdrew like the sliding away of sweat.

"They brought the Druid here, down to the water's edge, and left him for the shades of his ancestors to carry off." The Morgawr's satisfaction was palpable. "And so they did, it seems. They bore his corpse away with them, down into the waters of that lake. Walker is gone. All the Druids are gone. After all these years. All of them."

His gaze shifted from Ahren. "Which leaves us with the witch," he whispered, almost to himself. "She may not be as formidable as she once was, however. There is something wrong with her. I sense it in the way she moves, in the way she lets the other two lead her.

She isn't what she was. It felt to me, as I studied the traces of her passing, as if she was asleep."

"Sshe dissembless," Cree Bega offered softly. "Sshe sseekss to confusse uss."

The Morgawr nodded. "Perhaps. She is clever. But what reason does she have to do so? She does not know of my presence yet. She does not know I've come for her. She has no reason to pretend at anything. Nor any reason to flee. Yet she is gone. Where?"

No one said anything for a moment. Even the caull had gone silent, crouched on the cavern floor, big head lowered, savage eyes gone to narrow slits as it waited to be told what to do.

"Perhapss sshe iss aboard the airsship," Cree Bega suggested.

"Our enemies control *Black Moclips*," the Morgawr replied. "They would seek to avoid her, Cree Bega. Besides, there was no time for her to reach them before they fled from us. No, she is afoot with the boy and whoever goes with him—his rescuer, from the ship. She is afoot and not far ahead of us."

Suddenly he turned again to Ahren, and this time the sense of menace in his voice was so overpowering that it froze the boy where he was.

"Where are the Elfstones, Elven Prince?" the warlock whispered.

The question caught Ahren completely by surprise. He stared at the other wordlessly.

"You had them earlier, didn't you?" The words pressed down against the boy like stones. "You used them back there in that chamber where the Druid was mortally wounded. You were there, trying to save him. Did you think I wouldn't know? I sensed the Elfstone magic at once, found traces of its residue in the smells and tastes of the air. What happened to them, little boy?"

"I don't know," Ahren answered, unable to come up with anything better.

The Morgawr smiled at Cree Bega. "You searched him?"

"Yess, of coursse," the Mwellret answered with a shrug. "Little Elvess did not have them."

"Perhaps he hid them from you?"

"There wass no time for him to hide them. Hssst. Losst them, perhapss."

The Morgawr took a moment to consider. "No. Someone else has them." His gaze shifted quickly to Ryer Ord Star. "Our quiet little seer, perhaps?"

Cree Bega grunted. "Ssearched her, alsso. No sstoness."

"Then our little witch has them. Or that boy she is with." He paused. "Or the Druid carried them down with him into the nether-world, and no one will ever see them again."

He did not seem bothered by that. He did not seem concerned at all. Ahren watched his flat, empty face look off a final time toward the underground lake. Then the sharp eyes flicked back to his.

"Boy, I have no further need of you."

The chamber went so still that there might have been no one left alive, that even those who stood waiting to see what would happen next had been turned to stone. Ahren could feel the beating of his heart in his chest and the pulsing of his blood in his veins; he could hear the rasp of his breathing in his throat.

"Perhaps you do," Ryer Ord Star said suddenly. They all turned to look at her, but her eyes were fixed on the Morgawr. "The Druid brought the prince on the journey because his brother the King in-sisted, but also because the Druid knew something of the prince's worth beyond that. I have seen it in a vision. One day, Ahren Elessedil will be King of the Elves."

She paused. "Perhaps, with training, he could learn to become *your* King."

Ahren had never heard any such speculation, and he certainly didn't like hearing it now, particularly given the twist that the seer was putting to it. He was so shocked he just stared at her, not trying to hide anything of what he was feeling, a mix of emotions so pow-erful he could barely contain them. *Trust me*, she had urged him. But what reason did he have for doing so now?

The Morgawr seemed to consider this, and then he nodded.

"Perhaps." He gestured vaguely toward the girl. "You seek to demonstrate your worth by sharing what you know, little seer. I approve."

His eyes flicked back to Ahren. "You will come with me. You will do what you can to help me in my search. Together, we will track our little witch. Wherever she goes, we will find her. This will be over soon enough, and then I will decide what to do with you."

He looked at Cree Bega. "Bring him."

Then he motioned the caull to its feet, gave orders to its handlers, and sent them away into the tunnels once more. He took Ryer Ord Star by the arm and followed, ignoring Ahren. Seeing him rooted in place, Cree Bega clipped the boy across the back of his head and sent him stumbling after the warlock.

"Little Elvess musst do ass they are told!" he hissed balefully.

Ahren Elessedil, saying nothing, trudged ahead in a sullen rage.

ELEVEN

A board the *Jerle Shannara*, Redden Alt Mer paused at the aft railing of the airship and looked back at *Black Moclips*. She was laboring heavily as she tried to outrun the approaching storm, her armored hull tossing and slewing like a heavy branch caught in rapids. The storm was a black wall coming inland off the eastern coast, a towering mass of lightning-laced clouds riding the back of winds gusting at more than fifty knots. Little Red was doing the best she could to sail the airship alone, but it would have been a difficult task under ordinary circumstances. It was an impossible one here. Even if she reached the relative safety of the mountains ahead, there was no guarantee she would be able to find shelter until the storm passed. Landing an airship in the middle of a mountain range, with cliffs and downdrafts to contend with, was tricky business in any case. In the teeth of a storm like this one, it would be extremely dangerous.

Behind *Black Moclips*, at least a dozen of the enemy airships continued to give chase. He had thought he might lose them with the approach of the storm, but he had been wrong. Since yesterday morning, he had tried everything to shake them, but nothing had worked. Each time he thought he had given them the slip, they had reappeared out of nowhere. They shouldn't have been able to do that. No one should have been able to find him so easily, especially not these ships, with their walking-dead crews and ship-shy Mwellrets.

They were tracking him somehow, tracking him in a way he hadn't yet been able to identify. He had better do so soon. The repairs to the *Jerle Shannara* had not been completed before they had been forced to flee the coast, and the strain of having to rely on four of their six parse tubes and diapson crystals, the radian draws reconfigured to allow for the transference of energy, was beginning to tell. The draws were threatening to snap from the additional strain, and the airship's maneuverability was less than he needed. Even though the *Jerle Shannara* was the faster airship, if something went wrong, their pursuers would be on them before they could make the necessary adjustment.

It didn't help that no one had slept for more than a couple of hours since yesterday, and everyone was dog-tired. Tired men made mistakes, and if they made one here, it would probably cost them their lives.

He tested the aft starboard draw, adjusted the tension, and looked back again at *Black Moclips*. She was struggling to keep up, losing ground at an increasing pace. The Wing Riders flew on either side of her, offering their presence as reassurance, but the Elves were of no help in the sailing of the ship. Po Kelles had flown back to tell him what Little Red had done, and at first Alt Mer had been elated. They had the witch's airship as well as their own, two chances to find a way out of this miserable country. But the convergence of their pursuers and the approach of the storm quickly made him realize that his sister might have seized too big a prize. Without a crew to assist her, she was seriously handicapped in her efforts to sail the captured ship. He would have put a couple of his own crew aboard to help her, but there was no way to do so without docking the airships; Rovers were skittish where Rocs were concerned.

A gust of wind howled through the rigging above him, producing a sharp and eerie whine, a wounded animal's cry. The temperature was dropping, as well. If this kept up, there would be snow in the mountains and conditions for flying would become impossible.

He left the railing and hurried across the aft decking and down to the main deck and the pilot box where Spanner Frew stood like a rock at the helm, guiding the airship ahead with his steady hand.

"Lines still holding?" he bellowed as Big Red jumped up beside him in the box.

"For now—I don't know for how much longer. We need to get down before that storm catches us!" They had to shout to be heard over the wind. He glanced over his shoulder at *Black Moclips*. "We have to do something to help Little Red. She's game, but as good as she is, she can't go it alone."

Spanner Frew's black-bearded face swung about momentarily, then straightened forward again. "If we could get a line to her, we could tow her."

"Not in this weather—not with all those airships chasing us. We'd be slowed down, even using her parse tubes to help."

The big man nodded. "Better get her off there, then! When that storm catches up, chances are pretty good she won't be able to stay aloft. If she starts to go down then, we won't be able to help her."

Redden Alt Mer had already come to that conclusion. He wasn't even sure he could manage to keep the *Jerle Shannara* flying. He toyed briefly with the prospect of changing over to *Black Moclips* and sailing her instead, since she was in better condition. But the *Jerle Shannara* was the faster, more maneuverable vessel, and he didn't want to give her up when it was speed and maneuverability that were likely to make the difference in a confrontation with their pursuers. The matter was moot in any case because there wasn't any real chance that he could get everyone off his ship and onto Little Red's with the weather this bad.

He pursed his lips. Rue was going to be furious if he told her to give up her prize. She might not do it, even knowing how much trouble she was in.

He looked back again at *Black Moclips* and beyond to the enemy airships, black dots against the roiling darkness of the storm.

"How do they keep finding us?" he snapped at Spanner Frew, suddenly angry at how impossible things had gotten.

The shipwright shook his head and didn't answer. A new level of frustration crept through Big Red. It was bad enough that they had lost Walker and all those who had gone inland to the ruins. It was bad enough that they had nothing to show for having come all this way and might well return home empty-handed—if they were able to get home at all. But it was intolerable that these phantom airships continued to harass them like hunting dogs would a fleeing, wounded animal, finding their tracks or their scent where there should be no trace of their passing at all.

There was nothing he could do about it just now. But he could do something about Little Red. She was not yet recovered from her wounds and couldn't have had much more sleep than they had. She must be near exhaustion from flying *Black Moclips* alone, trying to manage everything from the pilot box, the wind howling past her like a demon set loose to tear her from the skies. She was a good pilot, almost as good as he was—and a better navigator. But it wouldn't be enough to save her from this.

"I'm taking her off, Black Beard!" he yelled over to the shipwright. "Drop our speed one quarter and hold steady toward that split in the peaks ahead."

"You want to take her off in a grapple?" Spanner Frew yelled back.

Redden Alt Mer shook his head. "It would take too long. She has to come to us. I'll send one of the Wing Riders in."

He jumped down to the main deck, shouting orders at the crew, telling them to find their places at the working parse tubes, to monitor the draws while he ran aft. At the railing, he dug through a wooden box and found the emerald pennant that meant he needed one of them to fly to him.

Of course, the signal wouldn't work if no one was looking. And in a bad storm like this one, they might not be.

He fastened the pennant's clips to a line and ran the piece of cloth up into the wind, where it snapped and cracked like ice breaking free in the Squirm. Facing back, he watched *Black Moclips* lurch and buck. Several of her draws had broken loose, and one of her sails was in tatters. She was flying on her pilot's skill and sheer luck.

Even as he watched, she faded farther back in the haze of clouds and mist. The Wing Riders were barely visible, still flying to either side. Their pursuers had disappeared entirely.

Redden Alt Mer pounded his fist on the railing cap. Neither Hunter Predd nor Po Kelles had seen the pennant.

"Look at me!" he screamed in frustration.

Lost in the howl of the wind, the words blew away from him.

A thousand yards back, so fatigued that she was near collapse, Rue Meridian fought to keep the *Jerle Shannara* in sight. Her world had narrowed down to this single purpose. Forgotten were her plans for coming inland to the ruins, for finding and rescuing Bek and the others of the company, for trying to salvage something from the disaster this voyage had become, for doing anything but keeping her vessel flying. Though her thoughts were clouded and her mind numb from concentrating on working the controls, she knew she was in trouble. The *Jerle Shannara* was drawing farther away and the airships pursuing her were drawing closer. Soon, any chance for escape would be lost.

Black Moclips shuddered anew as the winds preceding the storm buffeted her. The airship lurched sideways and down. The problem was simple enough to diagnose if not to solve. The ambient-light sails had been kept furled during the past few days, and no new power had been gathered for the diapson crystals. No new power was being collected now because she couldn't put up the sails in this storm—couldn't put them up at all, for that matter, storm or not, by herself. The limited power that remained was being exhausted. Personal attention at the various parse tubes was needed to distribute it more efficiently, but she couldn't leave the controls long enough to attempt that. The best she would do was to try to manipulate things from the pilot box, and while that was possible, it was never intended that an airship be flown by a single person.

She had a crew, but they were locked up belowdecks, and once she set them free she might as well lock herself up in their place.

The first flurries of snow blew past her face, and she was reminded again of how far the temperature had fallen. Winter seemed to be descending into a land that hadn't seen such weather in more than a thousand years.

She tried to coax more speed from the crystals, forcing herself to try a different combination of power allocations, feeling *Black Moclips* slew and skid on the wind from her efforts, fighting off her growing certainty that nothing she could do would make any difference.

She was so absorbed in her efforts that she failed to see Hunter Predd soar ahead into the misty gray toward the *Jerle Shannara*. Po Kelles kept pace with her off to the port side, but she didn't even glance at him. In her struggle to fly *Black Moclips*, she had all but forgotten the Wing Riders. Then Hunter Predd flew Obsidian right over her bow to catch her attention. She ducked in response to the unexpected movement, then turned as the Roc swung around and settled in off her starboard railing, almost close enough to touch, rocking back and forth with the force of the wind.

"Little Red!" Hunter Predd shouted into the wind, his words barely audible.

She glanced over and waved to let him know she heard.

"I'm taking you off the ship!" He waited a moment to let the impact of the words sink in. "Your brother says you have to come with me. That's an order!"

Angry that Big Red would even suggest such a thing, she shook her head no at once.

"You can't stay!" Hunter Predd shouted, bringing Obsidian in closer. "Look behind you! They're right on top of you!"

She didn't have to look; she knew they were there, the airships chasing her. She knew they were so close that if she turned, she could make out the blank faces of the dead men who flew them. She knew they would have her in less than an hour if something didn't happen to change her situation. She knew if they didn't catch her by then, it was only because she had gone down.

She knew, in short, that her situation was hopeless.

She just didn't want to admit it. She couldn't bear it, in fact.

"Little Red!" the Wing Rider called again. "Did you hear me?"

She looked over at him. He was hunched close to Obsidian's dark neck, arms and legs gripping the harness, safety lines tethering rider and bird. He looked like a burr stuck in the great Roc's feathers.

"I heard!" she shouted back.

"Then get off that ship! Now!"

He said it with an insistence that brooked no argument, an insistence buttressed by the knowledge that she must realize the precariousness of her situation as surely as her brother and he did. He stared at her from astride his bird, weathered features scrunched and angry, daring her to contradict him. She understood what he was thinking: if he didn't convince her here and now, it would be too late; already, the *Jerle Shannara* was nearly out of sight ahead and the storm upon her. She could still do what she chose, but not for very much longer.

She stared through the tangled, windblown strands of her hair to the airship's controls. Dampness ran down the smooth metal and gleaming wood in twisting rivulets. She studied the way her hands fit on the levers and wheel. She owned *Black Moclips* now; it belonged to her. She had snatched it away from the thieves who had stolen her own ship. She had claimed it at no small risk to herself, and she was entitled to keep it. No one had a right to take it away from her.

But that didn't mean she was wedded to it. That didn't mean she couldn't give it up, if she chose. If it was her idea. After all, it was just something made out of wood and metal, not out of flesh and blood. It wasn't possessed of a heart and mind and soul. It was only a tool.

She looked back at Hunter Predd. The Wing Rider was waiting. She pointed aft and down, then at herself. He nodded and swung away from the ship.

She snatched up the steering bands and lashed the wheels and levers in place, then hurried down the steps and across the slippery surface of the decking to the main hatchway. She went down in a rush, before she had time to think better of it. She was curiously at peace. The anger she had felt moments earlier was gone. *Black Moclips* was a fine airship, but it was only that and nothing more.

She reached the storeroom door where Aden Kett and his Federation crew were locked away and banged on the door. "Aden, can you hear me?"

"I hear you, Little Red," the Commander replied.

"I'm letting you out and giving you back your ship. She's struggling in this storm and needs a full crew to keep her flying. I can't manage it alone. I own her, but I won't let her die needlessly. So that's that. You do what you can for her. All right?"

"All right." She could tell from the sound of his voice that he was pressed up against the door on the other side.

"You'll understand if I don't stay around to see how this turns out." She wiped at the moisture beading her forehead and dripping into her eyes. "You might have trouble doing the right thing by me afterwards. I'd hate to see you make a fool of yourself. So after

I open this door, I'll be leaving. Do you think you and the others can refrain from giving in to your worst impulses and coming after me?"

She heard him laugh. "Come after you? We've had enough of you, Little Red. We'll all feel better knowing you're off the ship. Just let us out of here."

She paused then, leaning into the door, her face close to the cracks in the boards that formed it. "Listen to me, Aden. Don't stay around afterwards. Don't try to do the right thing. Forget about your orders and your sense of duty and your Federation training. Take *Black Moclips* and sail her home as quickly as you can manage it. Take your chances back there."

She heard his boots shift on the flooring. "Who's out there? We saw the other ships."

"I don't know. No one does, but it isn't anyone you want anything to do with. More than a dozen airships, Aden, but no flags, no insignia, nothing human aboard. Just rets and men who look like they're dead. I don't know who sent them. I don't care. You remember what I said. Fly out of here. Leave all this. It's good advice. Are you listening?"

"I'm listening," he answered quietly.

She didn't know what else to say. "Tell Donell that I'm sorry I hit him so hard."

"He knows."

She pushed away from the door and stood facing it again. "See you down the road, Aden."

"Down the road, Little Red."

She reached for the latch and threw it clear, then turned and bolted up the stairs without looking back. In seconds she was topside again, surprised to find sleet had turned the world white. She ducked her head against the bitter sting of the wind and slush and moved to the aft railing. The rope Hunter Predd had used earlier to climb down to Obsidian was still tied in place and coiled on the deck. She threw the loose end overboard and watched it tumble away into the haze. She could just barely make out the dark contours of the Roc's wings as it lifted into place below.

She looked back once at *Black Moclips*. "You're a good girl," she told her. "Stay safe."

Then she was gone into the gloom.

Minutes later, Redden Alt Mer stood at the port railing of the *Jerle Shannara* and watched his sister pause in her climb up the rope ladder. She had gotten off the Roc all right, taken firm hold of the ladder and started up. But now she hung there with her head lowered and her long red hair falling all around her face, swaying in the wind.

He thought he might have to go down the ladder and get her.

Thinking that, he was reminded suddenly of a time when they were children, and he had gone high up into the top branches of an old tree. Rue, only five years old, had tried to follow, working her way up the trunk, using the limbs of the tree as rungs. But she wasn't strong yet, and she tired quickly. Halfway up, she lost her momentum completely and stopped moving, hanging from the branches of that tree the way she was hanging from the rope ladder now. She was something of a nuisance back then, always tagging along after him, trying to do everything he was doing. He was four years older than she was and irritated by her most of the time. He could have left her where she was on the tree—had thought he might, actually. Instead, he had turned back and yelled down to her. "Come on, Rue! Keep going! Don't quit! You can do it!"

He could yell those same words down to her now, to the little sister who was still trying to do everything he did. But even as he considered it, she lifted her head, saw him looking at her, and began to climb again at once. He smiled to himself. She came on now without slowing, and he reached out to take her arm, helping her climb over the railing and onto the ship.

Impulsively, he gave her a hug and was surprised when she hugged him back.

He shook his head at her. "Sometimes you scare me." He looked into her wet face, reading the exhaustion in her eyes. "Actually, most of the time."

She grinned. "That's real praise, coming from you."

"Flying *Black Moclips* all by yourself in a bad piece of weather like you did would scare anyone. It should have scared you, but I suppose it didn't."

"Not much." She grinned some more, like the little kid she was inside. "I took her away from the witch, big brother. Crew and all. It was hard to give her up again. I didn't want to lose her, though."

"Better her than you. We don't need her anyway. It's enough if the witch doesn't have her." He gave his sister a small shove. "Go below and put on some dry clothes."

She shook her head stubbornly. "I don't need to change clothes just yet."

"Rue," he said, a hint of irritation creeping into his voice. "Don't argue with me about this. You argue with me about everything. Just do it. You're soaked through; you need dry clothes. Go change."

She hesitated a moment, and he was afraid she was going to press the matter. But then she turned around and went down through the main hatch to the lower cabins, water dripping from her across the decking.

He watched her disappear from sight, thinking as she did that no matter how old they grew or what happened to them down the road, they would never feel any differently about each other. He would still be her big brother; she would still be his little sister. Mostly, they would still be best friends.

He couldn't ask for anything better.

When she reemerged, the wind was blowing so hard it knocked her sideways. The rain and sleet had stopped, but the air was cold enough to freeze the tiny hairs in her nostrils. She wrapped her great cloak more tightly about her, warm again in dry clothes and boots, and pushed across the deck unsteadily to where her brother and Spanner Frew stood in the pilot box. Ahead, the mountains loomed huge and craggy against the skyline, a massing of jagged peaks and rugged cliffs piled one on top of the other until they faded away into the brume-shrouded distance.

She climbed into the pilot box, and her brother said at once, "Put on your safety harness."

She did so, noting that all of the Rover crew on the decks below were strapped in as well, hunched down against the weather, stationed at the parse tubes and connecting draws.

When she glanced over her shoulder, she found the world behind had disappeared in a thick, dark haze, taking with it any sign of the pursuing airships.

Big Red glanced over. "They disappeared sometime back. I don't know if they broke it off because of the weather or to go after *Black Moclips*. Doesn't matter. They're gone, and that's enough. We've got bigger problems to deal with."

Spanner Frew yelled something down to one of the Rovers amidships, and the crewman waved back, moving to tighten a radian draw. Big Red had stripped back all the sails, and the *Jerle Shannara* was riding bare-masted in the teeth of winds that side-swiped her as badly as they had *Black Moclips*. Rue saw that the radian draws had been reconfigured, strung away from two of the six parse tubes to feed power to the remaining four. Even those were singing with the vibration of the wind, straining to break free of their fastenings.

"I *left* a ship in better shape than this one," she declared, half to herself.

"She'd be in better shape if we hadn't had to leave quite so suddenly to find you!" Big Red grunted.

That wasn't true, of course. They would have had to leave in any case to flee the enemy airships, no matter whether or not they were searching for her. Repairs of the sort needed by the *Jerle Shannara* required that the airship be stationary, and that wasn't going to happen until they could set down somewhere.

"Any place we can land?" she asked hopefully.

Spanner Frew laughed. "You mean in an upright position? Or will a severe slant do?" His hands worked the steering levers with quick, anxious movements. "First things first. See those mountains ahead of us, Little Red? The ones that look like a big wall? The ones we're in danger of smashing into?"

She saw them. They lay dead ahead, rising across the skyline, barring their way. She glanced sideways and down and saw for the first time how high up they were. Several thousand feet at least—probably more like five thousand. Even so, they weren't nearly high enough to clear these peaks.

"Heading ten degrees starboard, Black Beard," she heard her brother order. "That's it. There, toward that cut."

She followed his gaze and saw a break in the peaks. It was narrow, and it twisted out of view at once. It might dead-end into the side of a mountain beyond, in which case they were finished. But Redden Alt Mer could read a passage better than anyone she had ever sailed with. Besides, he had the luck.

"Brace!" he yelled down at the crew.

They shot between the cliffs and into the narrow defile, skimming on the back of a vicious headwind that nearly drove them sideways in the attempt. Beyond, they saw the opening slant right. Spanner Frew threw the wheel over and fed what power he could to keep them steady. The passage narrowed further and cut back left. Rue felt the hair on the back of her neck lift as the massive cliff walls tightened about them like the jaws of a trap. They were so close that she could make out the depressions and ridges on the face of the stone. She could see rodent nests and tiny plants. There was no room to turn around. If the passage failed to run all the way through, they were finished.

"Steady," her brother cautioned to Spanner Frew. "Slow, now."

The winds had shifted away, and they were no longer being buffeted so violently. The *Jerle Shannara* canted left in response to Spanner Frew's handling of the controls, sliding slowly through the gap. They rounded a jagged corner, still close enough that Rue could reach out and touch the rock. Ahead, the defile began to widen, and the mountains opened out onto a deep, forested valley.

"We're through," she said, grinning in relief at her brother.

"But not yet safe." His face was tight and set. "Look ahead. There, where the valley climbs into that second set of peaks."

She did so, brushing away loose strands of her long red hair. There were breaks all through this range, but the movement of the clouds overhead suggested that the winds were much more turbulent than anything they had encountered before. Still, there was nowhere else to go except back, and that was unthinkable.

Spanner Frew glanced over at Big Red. "Where do we go? That gap on the right, lower down?"

Her brother nodded. "Where it might not be so windy. Good eye. But stay hard left to give us room to maneuver when the crosswind catches us."

They navigated the valley through a screen of mist, riding air currents that bucked and jittered like wild horses. The *Jerle Shannara* shuddered with the blows, but held her course under Spanner Frew's steady hand. Below, the forests were dark and deep and silent. Once, Rue caught sight of a thin ribbon of water where a small river wound along the valley floor, but she saw no sign of animals or people. Hawks soared out of the cliffs, fierce faces set against the light. Behind, the entire sky was dark with the storm they had left on the other side of the mountains. Everywhere else, the horizon was hazy and flat.

Rue listened to the wind sing through the taut lines of the vessel. It always seemed to her that the ship was calling to her when she heard that sound, that it was trying to tell her something. She felt that now, and her uneasiness grew.

When they reached the far side of the valley, they angled right, toward the draw that her brother had spied earlier, a deep cut in the peaks of the second range that offered clear passage to whatever lay beyond. More mountains, certainly, but perhaps something else, as well. She glanced skyward to where the clouds skittered over the peaks in frightened bursts of energy, blown by winds that channeled down out of the north. Since the weather was all behind them, she realized that these crosswinds must blow like this all the time. They would be dangerous, if that was so.

The *Jerle Shannara* lifted through the gap, catching the first rip of crosswind as she did, slewing sideways instantly. Spanner Frew brought her back on course again, keeping her low and down to the left. Ahead, more peaks and cliffs appeared, slabs of stone jutting from the earth like giant's hands lifted in warning. But the defile wormed through them, offering passage, so they continued on. Below, the floor of the canyon rose steadily as the mountains closed about, and they were forced to fly higher.

Rue Meridian took a deep breath and held it, feeling the tension radiate through her.

"Steady, Black Beard," she heard her brother say quietly. Then a burst of wind slammed into the airship and sent her spinning sideways for endless, heart-stopping seconds before Spanner Frew was able to bring her back around again.

Rue exhaled sharply. Big Red glanced over at her and broke into one of those familiar grins that told her how much he loved this.

"Hold on!" he shouted.

They bucked through the gap's twists and turns like a cork through rapids, knocked this way and that, fighting to stay steady at every turn. The winds thrust at them, then died away, then returned to hammer them again. Once they were blown so hard to starboard that they very nearly struck the cliff wall, only just managing to skip past an outcropping of rock that would have ripped the hull apart. Rue clung to the pilot box railing, her knuckles white with determination, thinking as she did so that this was much worse than what they had encountered coming through the Squirm, ice pillars notwithstanding. At any moment they could lose control completely and be smashed to bits against the rocks.

They climbed to a thousand feet as the floor of the pass rose ahead, forcing them to gain altitude beyond what Rue knew her brother had hoped would prove necessary; the winds at this elevation were too strong and unpredictable.

Then the mountains parted ahead, and far below they saw a vast forest cupped by the fingers of scattered peaks, deep and impenetrable and stretching away into the haze. There would be a landing site there, a place for them to set down and make repairs.

She had no sooner finished the thought than the aft port radian draw snapped at the masthead and fell away.

At once, the *Jerle Shannara* began to lose power and slip sideways. Spanner Frew fought to bring her nose up, but without both aft parse tubes in operation, he lacked the means to do so.

"I can't right her!" he grunted in frustration.

"Mainsail!" Big Red shouted instantly to the crew.

Kelson Riat and another of the Rovers leapt up at once from where they were crouched amidships and began to unfasten the lines and run up the sail. Without the use of the aft parse tubes, Big Red was going to rely on the sails for power. But the crosswinds were vicious; there was as much chance as not that they would fill the big sail and carry the airship right into the cliffs like a scrap of paper.

"Steady, steady, steady . . . ," Big Red chanted to Spanner Frew as the shipwright fought to hold the *Jerle Shannara* in place.

Fluttering and snapping, the mainsail went up. Then the wind caught it and drove the airship forward with a lurch. She bucked in the wind's strong grip, and another of the draws snapped and fell away.

"Shades!" Redden Alt Mer hissed. He snatched at the wheel as Spanner Frew lost his footing, struck his head on the pilot box railing, and blacked out.

They were still falling, but they were accelerating toward the gap, as well, the mountains widening on both sides. If they could stay high enough to miss the boulders clustered in the mouth of the pass, they might survive. It was going to be close. Rue willed the *Jerle Shannara* to lift, begged her silently to level off. But she was still falling, the rocky surface of the pass rising swiftly to meet her.

Her brother threw the levers that fed power to the diapson crystals all the way forward and brought the steering levers all the way back. The airship shuddered anew, lurched, and rose a final time. They surged through the gap, breaking into the clear air above the forest below. But even as they did so, the keel scraped across the boulders beneath them, making a terrible grinding, ripping noise. The *Jerle Shannara* shuddered and then dipped, the bow coming down sharply, pointing left and toward the forest a thousand feet below. The crosswind returned, sudden and vicious, snatching at the crippled vessel. The mainsail reefed as several of her lines snapped, and the *Jerle Shannara* plunged downward.

Rue Meridan, clinging to both her safety harness and the pilot box railing, thought they were dead. They spiraled down, out of control, the canopy of the trees rising to meet them with dizzying swiftness. Her brother, still struggling to bring the bow up, cursed. Crew members slid along the decking. The safety line broke away on one, and she caught just a glimpse of him as he flew out over the side of the ship and disappeared.

Then the crosswind shifted, ripping along the cliff face and carrying the *Jerle Shannara* sideways into the rock. Rue had just a moment to watch the cliff wall fly toward them before they struck in a shattering crunch of wood and metal. She lost her grip on both her safety line and the railing and flew into the pilot box control panel. Pain ratcheted through her left arm, and she felt the stitches on her wounded side and leg give. Her safety line snapped, and then she careened into her brother, who was hanging desperately onto the useless steering levers.

A moment later, everything went black.

TWELVE

As he finished tying off the bandages around Little Red's damaged torso, Redden Alt Mer was thinking things couldn't get any worse. Then Spanner Frew lumbered up the steps to the pilot box and knelt down beside him.

"We lost all the spare diapson crystals through the tear in the hull," he announced sullenly. "They've fallen somewhere down there."

His gesture made it clear that *somewhere down there* was the jungle below the wooded precipice on which the *Jerle Shannara* had finally come to rest, an impenetrable green covering of treetops and vines that spread away from the cliff face for miles.

Alt Mer rocked back on his heels and stared at the shipwright as if he were speaking in a foreign language. "All of them?"

"They were all in one crate. The crate fell out through a hole ripped in the hull." Spanner Frew reached up to touch the gash in his forehead, flinching as he did so. "As if I needed another headache."

"Can we fly with what we have?"

The shipwright shook his head. "We're down to three. We lost the port fore tube and everything with it on landing. What's left might let us fly in calm weather, but it won't get us off the ground. If we try it, we'll just go over the side and into the trees with the crystals."

He sighed. "The thing of it is, we came through this all right otherwise. We've got the timbers to repair the hole in the hull. We've got spare draws and fastenings. We've got plenty of sail. Even the spars and mast can be fixed with a little time and effort. But we can't go anywhere without those crystals." He rubbed his beard. "How's Little Red?"

Redden Alt Mer looked down at his sister. She was still unconscious. He had let her sleep while he worked on her injuries, but he thought he'd wake her soon in case she had suffered a concussion. He needed to know, as well, if there was damage inside that he couldn't see.

"She'll be all right," he said with a reassuring smile. He wasn't sure at all, but there was no point in worrying Black Beard unnecessarily. He had enough to concern him. "Who went over the side?"

"Jahnon Pakabbon."

Big Red grimaced. A good man. But they were all good men, which is why they had been chosen for the voyage. There wasn't a one he could bear to lose, let alone afford to. He had known Jahnon since they were children. The quiet, even-tempered Rover had a gift for innovation in addition to his sailing skills.

"All right." He forced himself to quit thinking about it, to concentrate on the problem at hand. "We have to go down there and bring him out. We'll look for the crystals when we do. Choose two men to go with me—and make sure you're not one of them. I need you to work on the repairs. We don't want to be stranded here any longer than necessary. Those airships with their Mwellrets and walking dead will come looking for us soon enough. I don't intend to be around when they do."

Spanner Frew grunted, stood up, and went back down the pilot box steps. The *Jerle Shannara* was canted to port at a twenty-degree angle perhaps a hundred yards from the precipice, the curved horn of her starboard pontoon lodged in a cluster of boulders. She wasn't in much danger of sliding over the edge, but she was fully exposed to anything flying overhead. Behind her, running back for perhaps another hundred yards, a forested shelf jutted from the cliff face of the mountain on which they had settled. They were lucky to be alive after such a crash, lucky not to have fallen all the way into the jungle below, from which extraction would have been impossible. That the *Jerle Shannara* had not broken into a million pieces was a testament to her construction and design. Say what you would about Spanner Frew, he knew how to build an airship.

Nevertheless, they were trapped, lacking sufficient diapson crystals to lift off, short one more crew member, and completely lost in a strange land. Big Red was normally optimistic about tough situations, but in this particular instance he didn't much care for their chances.

He glanced skyward, where clouds and mist hung like a curtain across the horizon, hiding what lay farther out in all directions. Nothing was visible but the emerald canopy of the jungle and the tips of a few nearby peaks, leaving him with the unpleasant feeling of being trapped on a rocky island, suspended between gray mist and green sea.

"Spanner!" he yelled suddenly. The burly shipwright trudged back over to stand below the box and looked up at him. "Cut some rolling logs, rig a block and tackle, and let's try to move the ship back into those trees. I don't like being out in the open like this."

The big man turned away without a word and disappeared over the side of the ship. Big Red could hear him yelling anew at the crewmen, laying into them with his shipyard vocabulary. He listened a moment and shook his head. He missed Hawk, who was always a step ahead in knowing what needed to be done. But Black Beard was capable enough, if a bit irksome. Give him some direction and he would get the job done.

Redden Alt Mer turned his attention to his sister. He bent down and gave her a gentle shake. She groaned and turned her head away, then drifted off. He shook her once more, a little more firmly this time. "Rue, wake up."

Her eyes blinked open, and she stared at him. For a moment, she didn't say anything. Then she sighed wearily. "I've been through this before—come back from the edge and found you waiting. Like a dream. Still alive, are we?"

He nodded. "Though one of us is a little worse for wear."

She glanced down at herself, taking in the bandages wrapped about her torso and leg where the clothing had been cut away, seeing the splint on her arm. "How bad am I?"

"You won't be flying off to rescue anyone for a while. You broke your arm and several ribs. You ripped open the knife wounds on your thigh and side. You banged yourself up pretty good, all without the help of a single Mwellret."

She started to giggle, then grimaced. "Don't make me laugh. It hurts too much." She lifted her head and glanced around, taking in as much as she could, then lay back. "We don't seem to be flying, so I guess I didn't dream that we crashed. Are we all in one piece?"

"More or less. There's damage, but it can be repaired. The problem now is that we can't fly. We lost all our spare diapson crystals through a break in the hull. I have to take a search party down into the valley and find them before we can get out of here." He shrugged. "Thank your lucky stars it wasn't worse."

"I'm busy thanking them that I'm still alive. That any of us are, for that matter." She licked her lips. "Got anything to drink that doesn't come from a stream?"

He brought her an aleskin, holding it up for her as she took deep swallows. "You hurt anywhere I can't see?" he asked when she was done. "A little honesty here wouldn't hurt, by the way."

She shook her head. "Nothing you haven't already taken care of." She wiped her lips and sighed deeply. "Good. But I'm really tired."

"Then you'd better sleep." He arranged the torn bit of sail he had folded under her head for a pillow and tucked in the ragged folds of her great cloak about her arms and legs. "I'll let you know when something happens."

Her eyes closed at once, which was what he had expected, given the strength of the sleeping potion he had dropped into her drink. He took the aleskin and tucked it away in a storage bin to one side of the control panel, out of sight but ready to use if he needed it again. But she wouldn't wake for twelve hours or better, if he'd measured the dosage right. He looked down at her, his little sister, tough as nails and so anxious to demonstrate it she would have insisted on getting up if he hadn't drugged her. She confused him sometimes, the way she was always trying to prove herself, as if she hadn't already done so a dozen times over. But better to be like that, he supposed, than to be content with the way things were. His sister set the standard, and she was always looking to improve on it. He could wish for more like her, but he wouldn't find them no matter how hard he looked. There was only one Little Red.

He yawned, thought he wouldn't mind a little sleep himself, then walked over to the ship's railing and looked down at Spanner Frew and the others as they placed the rolling logs under the pontoons. The block and tackle was already in place, strapped to a huge old oak fifty yards back with the rope ends clipped to iron pull rings that had been screwed into the aft horns just above the waterline.

"We could use another pair of hands!" the shipwright shouted up at Big Red as he took in the slack in the ropes with an audible grunt.

Redden Alt Mer climbed down the ship's ladder and joined the others as they picked up the lead rope, set themselves, and began to heave against the weight of the airship. Even after she had been pulled off the rocks and straightened so that her pontoons were resting on the logs, the *Jerle Shannara* was difficult to budge. Eventually, Big Red took three others forward and began to rock her. After some considerable effort and harsh words had been expended, she began to move. Once she got rolling, they worked swiftly. Pulling steadily on the ropes, they rotated the rolling logs under her floats as she lumbered backwards until they got her perhaps three dozen yards off the exposed flat and into a mix of trees and bushes.

After taking down the block and tackle and unhooking the ropes, Redden Alt Mer ordered Kelson Riat and the big Rover who called himself Rucker Bont to cut some of the surrounding brush and spread it around the decks of the airship as camouflage. It took them only a little while to change her appearance sufficiently that the Rover Captain was satisfied. With all the sails down and the decking partially screened, the *Jerle Shannara* might look like a part of the landscape, a hummock of rock and scrub or a pile of deadwood.

"Good work, Black Beard," he told Spanner Frew. "Now see what you can do with that hole in her side while I take a look down below for those crystals."

The big man nodded. "I've given you Bont and Tian Cross for company." He took hold of the Captain's arm and squeezed. "Little Red and I won't be there to look out for you. Watch yourself."

Redden Alt Mer gave him a boyish grin and patted the big, gnarled hand. "Always."

They went down the cliff face in a line, Big Red in front setting the pace and finding the most favorable route for them to follow. It wasn't a particularly steep or long descent, but a misstep could result in a nasty fall, so the three men were careful to take their time. They used ropes as safety lines where the descent was steepest; the other sections, where the slope broadened and there were footholds to be found in the jagged rock, they navigated on their own. It was midafternoon by now, and the hazy light was beginning to darken as the sun slid behind the canopy of clouds and mist. Big Red gave them another three hours at most before it would become too dark to continue the search. There wasn't as much time as he would have liked, but that was the way it went sometimes. You had to make the best of some situations. If they ran out of time today, they would just have to try again tomorrow.

The climb down took them almost an hour, and by the time they were inside the trees, everything was much darker. The canopy of limbs and vines was so thick that almost no light penetrated to the jungle floor. As a result, the undergrowth wasn't as thick as Big Red had anticipated, so they were able to advance relatively easily. They quickly discovered that they were in a rain forest, the temperature on the valley floor much higher than in the mountains. The air was steamy and damp and smelling of earth and plants. Life was abundant. Ferns grew everywhere, some of them very tall and broad, some tiny and fragile. Though most were green, others were milky white and still others a rust red. Their tiny shoots unfurled like babies' fingers, stretching for the light. Slugs oozed their way across the earth, leaving trails of moisture, sticky and glistening. Butterflies careened from place to place in bright splashes of color, and birds darted through the canopy overhead so fast the eye could barely follow. Now and again, they heard them singing, a mix of songs that seemed to come from everywhere at once.

The atmosphere was strange and vaguely unsettling, and they could feel the change immediately. The sound of the wind had disappeared. Over everything lay a hush broken only by birdsong and insect buzzes. In the silences between, there was a sense of expectancy, as if everything was waiting for the next sound or movement. They had the unmistakable feeling of being watched by things that they could not see, of eyes following them everywhere.

Some distance in, they stopped while Big Red took a reading on his compass. It would be all too easy to become lost down here, and he wasn't about to let that happen. He had only a vague idea of where to look for Jahnon's body and the missing diapson crystals, so the best they could do was to navigate in that general direction and hope they got lucky.

He stared off into the hazy distance, thinking for a moment about the direction of his life. He could stand to take a compass reading on that, as well. At best he was drifting, tacking first one way and then another, a vessel with no particular destination in mind. He shouldn't spend a moment of time worrying about becoming lost down here given how lost he was in general. He might argue otherwise—did so often, in fact—but it didn't change the truth of things. His life, for as long as he could remember, had consisted of one escapade after the other. Rue had been right about their lives as mercenaries. Mostly, they had been centered on the size of the purse being offered. This was the first time they had accepted a job because they believed there was something more at stake than money.

Yet what difference did it make? They were still fighting for their lives, still careening about like ships adrift, still lost in the wider world.

Did Little Red now feel that coming on this voyage was worth it?

He supposed he was rethinking his own life because of hers. She had been injured twice in the past two weeks, and both times she had come close to being killed. It was bad enough that he risked his own life so freely; he shouldn't be so quick to risk hers. True, she was a grown woman and capable of deciding for herself whether or not she wanted to accept that risk. But he also knew she looked up to him, followed after him, and believed unswervingly in him. She always had. Like it or not, that invested him with a certain responsibility for her safety. Maybe it was time to give that responsibility some attention.

They said he had the luck. But everyone's luck ran out sooner or later. The odds in his case had to be getting shorter. If he didn't find a way to change that, he was going to pay for it. Or worse, Rue was.

They set off again, working their way through the jungle, and hadn't gone two hundred yards when Tian Cross spied the wooden crate that contained the crystals lying in a deep depression of its own making. Amazingly, the crate was still in one piece, if somewhat misshapen, the nails and stout wire securing it having held it together despite the fall from the precipice.

Big Red bent down to examine it. The crate was maybe two and a half feet on each side and weighed in the neighborhood of two hundred pounds. A strong man could carry it, but not far. He thought about taking out several of the crystals and tucking them into his clothing. But they were heavy and too awkward for that. Besides, he wanted to retrieve them all, not just some. It would take longer to haul out the entire crate, but there was no reason to think that on the long journey home they might not need replacement crystals again.

He stood up, pulled out the compass, and took another reading.

"Captain," Rucker Bont called over to him.

He glanced up. The big Rover was pointing ahead. There was a distinct gap in the wall of the jungle where trees and brush were missing and hazy light flooded down through the canopy. It was a clearing, the first they had come across.

He snapped shut the casing on the compass and tucked the instrument back into his pocket. Something about the break in the jungle roof didn't look right. He made his way through trees and vines for a closer look, leaving the crystals where they were. The other two Rovers followed. The brush was thicker here, and it took them several minutes to reach the edge of the clearing, where they slowed to a ragged halt and, still within the fringe of the trees, peered out in surprise.

A section of the forest had been leveled on both sides of a lazy stream that meandered through the dense undergrowth, its waters so still they were barely moving. Trees had been knocked down, bushes and grasses had been flattened, and the earth torn up so badly it had the look of a plowed field. A hole had been opened in the trees that tunneled back down the length of the stream and disappeared into the mist.

Rucker Bont whistled softly. "What do you suppose did that?"

Big Red shrugged. "A storm, maybe."

Bont grunted. "Maybe. Could have been wind, too." He paused. "Could also be that something bigger than us lives down here."

His eyes darting right and left watchfully, Big Red walked out of the trees and into the clearing, picking his way across the rutted, scarred earth. The other two waited a moment, then followed. At the clearing's center, he knelt to look for tracks, hoping he wouldn't find any. He didn't, but the ground was so badly churned he couldn't be sure of what he was looking at.

He glanced up. "I don't see anything."

Rucker Bont scuffed his boot in the dirt, glanced over at Tian Cross and then back at Alt Mer. "Want me to have a look around?"

Big Red peered down the debris-strewn length of the little stream, down the tunnel that burrowed into the trees. In places the damage was so severe that the stream's banks had collapsed entirely. Tree limbs and logs straddled the stream bed, wooden barriers that stuck out in all directions and smelled of shredded leaves and wood freshly ripped asunder. Everything he was seeing felt wrong for a windstorm or a flood. The damage was too contained, too geometrical, not random enough. Perhaps Bont wasn't as far off the mark as he had thought. This had the look of something done by a very big, very powerful animal.

Aware suddenly of a change in the forest, he stood up slowly. The birds and butterflies they had seen in such profusion only minutes ago had disappeared entirely and the jungle had gone very still. His hand strayed to the hilt of his sword.

He saw Jahnon Pakabbon then, his eyes drawn to the corpse as surely as if it had been pointed out to him. Across the clearing, less than fifty feet away, Pakabbon lay sprawled against a clump of rocks and deadwood. Only he didn't look the way he had when he was alive, and the fall alone wouldn't account for it. His body had been stripped of its flesh and his organs sucked out. His clothes hung on bleached bones. His eyes were missing. His mouth hung open in a soundless scream and seemed to be trying to bite at something.

At almost the same moment, Redden Alt Mer caught sight of the creature. It was crouched right over Jahnon, as green and brown as the jungle that hid it. He might not have seen it at all if the light hadn't shifted just a touch while he was staring at Pakabbon's corpse. Intent on retrieving the remains of his friend, he might have walked right up to it without knowing it was there. It was so well concealed that even as big as it was—and it had to be huge from the size of its head—it was virtually invisible. All that Redden Alt Mer could see of it now was a blunt reptilian snout with lidded eyes and mottled skin that hovered over Jahnon's dead body like a hammer about to fall.

He never had a chance to warn Rucker Bont and Tian Cross. He never had a chance to do anything. Redden Alt Mer had only just realized what he was looking at when the creature attacked. It catapulted out of the jungle, bursting from its concealment in a flurry of powerful, stubby legs, and seized Tian Cross in its jaws before the Rover knew what was happening. Tian screamed once, and then the jaws tightened, the needle-sharp teeth penetrated, and there was blood everywhere.

It had been a long time since Redden Alt Mer had panicked, but he panicked now. Maybe it was the suddenness of the creature's attack. Maybe it was the look of it, a lizard of some sort, all crusted and horned, or the sheer size of it, rearing up with Tian Cross's crushed body dangling from its jaws. He had never seen a creature so big move so fast. It had come out of the trees, out of its concealment, with the quickness of a striking snake. He could still see that movement in his mind, could feel the terror it induced rush through him like the touch of hot metal.

Drops of blood sprayed over him as the lizard shook his friend's dead body like a toy.

Redden Alt Mer bolted back through the jungle. He never stopped to think what he was doing. He never even considered trying to help Tian. Some part of him knew that Tian was dead anyway, that there was nothing he could do to help him, but that wasn't why he ran. He ran because he was terrified. He ran because he knew that if he didn't, he was going to die.

Running was all he could think to do.

At first, he thought the creature would not follow, too busy with its kill to bother. But within seconds he heard it coming, limbs and brush snapping, leaves and twigs tearing free, the earth shaking with the weight and force of its massive body. It exploded through the jungle like an engine of war set loose. Big Red picked up his pace, even though he had thought he was already running flat out. He darted and dodged through the heavier foliage until he was back where the trees opened up, and then he put on a new burst of speed. He cast aside his cumbersome weapons, useless in any case against such a behemoth. He lightened himself so that he could fly, and still he felt as if he were weighted in chains.

Alt Mer glanced back only once. Rucker Bont was running just as hard, only steps behind, features drained of blood and filled with terror, a mirror of his own. The lizard, thundering after them in a blur of mottled green and brown, jaws open, was right behind.

"Captain!" Bont cried out frantically.

Alt Mer heard him scream. The lizard was tearing at him, and the sounds of his friend's dying followed the Rover Captain as he fled.

Shades! Shades!

He never looked back. He couldn't bear to. He could only run and keep running, closing off everything inside but the fear. The fear drove him. The fear ruled him.

He gained the cliff wall and went up it in a scrambling rush, barely feeling the sharpness of the rock and roughness of the rope as he climbed. Forgotten were the crystals and Jahnon's body. Forgotten were his hopes for a quick exit from this valley. His companions lay dead in the valley below. His weapons lay discarded.

He gave them no thought. He had no faculty for thinking. He had nothing left inside but a frantic, desperate need to escape—not so much what pursued him as what he was feeling. His fear. His terror. If he did not escape it, he knew, if he did not run fast enough, it would consume him.

He gained the heights after endless minutes of climbing through the fading afternoon light and the deepening haze of an approaching nightfall. He never stopped to see if he was being pursued, and it was only as Spanner Frew's big hands reached down to pull him over the lip of the precipice that he realized how quiet it was.

He looked back in wonder. Nothing was behind him, no sign of the lizard, no indication that anything had ever happened. There was no movement, no sound, nothing. The jungle had swallowed it all and gone as still and calm as the surface of the sea after a storm.

Spanner Frew saw his face, and the light in his own eyes darkened. "What happened? Where are the others?"

Redden Alt Mer stared at him, unable to answer. "Dead," he said finally.

He looked down at his hands and saw that they were shaking.

Later that night, when the others were asleep and he was alone again, he resolved to wake his sister and tell her what he had done. He would tell her not just that he had failed to retrieve the crystals or Jahnon Pakabbon and that the men who had gone into the valley with him were dead, but that he had panicked and run. It would be his first step toward recovery, toward finding a way back from the dark place into which he had fallen. He knew he could not live with himself if he did not find a way to face what had happened. It began with telling Rue, from whom he had no secrets, to whom he confided everything. He would not stint in his telling now, casting himself in the most unfavorable light he could imagine. What he had done was unthinkable. He must confess himself to her and seek absolution.

But when he rose and went to her and stood looking down, he imagined what that confession would feel like. He could see her face as she listened to his words, changing little by little, reflecting her loss of pride and trust in him, revealing her distaste for his actions. He could see the way her eyes would darken and veil, hiding feelings she had never before experienced, changing everything between them. Rue, the little sister who had always looked up to him.

He couldn't bear it. He stood there in the shadows without moving, studying her face, letting the moment pass, and then he left.

Back on deck, well away from where the watch stood at the airship's bow looking out toward the dark bowl of the valley, he leaned against the masthead and stared up at the hazy night sky. Glimpses of a half-moon and clusters of stars were visible through breaks in the clouds. He watched the way they came and went, thinking of his feckless courage and uncertain resolve.

After a time, he slid down to a sitting position, his back against the roughened timber, and lay his head back. As still as the mast itself, he lost himself in the fury of his bitter self-condemnation, and morning still hours away and redemption still further off, he closed his eyes and drifted off to sleep.

THIRTEEN

mprisoned in the bowels of the Morgawr's flagship, Ahren Elessedil rode out the storm that had brought down the *Jerle Shannara*. He was not chained to the wall as Bek had been when held prisoner on *Black Moclips* a day earlier, but left free to wander about the locked room. The storm had caught up to them as they flew north into the interior of the peninsula, snatching at the airship like a giant's hand, tossing it about, and finally tiring of the game, casting it away. With the room's solitary window battened down and the door secured, he could see nothing beyond the walls of his prison, but Ahren could feel the storm's wrath. He could feel how it attacked and played with the airship, how it threatened to reduce her to a shattered heap of wooden splinters and iron fragments. If it did, his troubles would be over.

In his darker moments, he thought that perhaps this would be best.

An unwilling accomplice in the warlock's search for the Ilse Witch, he had been brought aboard by the Morgawr and his Mwellrets after leaving Castledown's ruins and taken directly to his present confinement. A guard had been posted outside, but had disappeared shortly after the storm had begun and not returned.

Just before that, they had brought him some food and water, a small measure of both and only enough to keep him from losing strength entirely. No effort was made to communicate with him. From the way the Morgawr had left things, it was clear that he would be brought out only when it was felt he could be useful in some way.

Or when it was finally time to dispose of him. He held no illusions about that. Sooner or later, promises notwithstanding, that time would come.

Ryer Ord Star had disappeared with the warlock, and the Elven Prince still had no clear idea why she had turned against him. He had not stopped pondering the matter, not even during the storm, while he sat braced in a corner of the storeroom, pressed up against a wall between two heavy trusses to keep from being knocked around. She had been the willing tool of the Ilse Witch, and it did not require a great leap of faith to accept that she would take that same path with the Morgawr if she thought it meant the difference between living and dying. Walker was gone, and Walker had provided her with both strength and direction. Without him, she seemed frailer, smaller, more vulnerable—a wisp of life that a strong wind could blow away.

Even so, Ahren had thought she was his friend, that she had come to terms with what she had done and closed that door behind her. To have her betray him now, to reveal his identity and suggest a use for him to his enemy, was too much to bear. Like it or not, he was left with the unpleasant possibility that she had been lying to him all along.

Yet she had clearly mouthed the words *trust me* to him after they had been made prisoners. Why would she do that if she was not trying to let him know she was still his friend?

What sort of deception was she working?

He thought some more about the Elfstones, as well. He simply could not understand what had happened to them. They had most certainly been in his possession in Castledown. He remembered quite clearly tucking them away in his tunic. He did not think he had lost them since, did not see how that was possible, so someone must have taken them after he had been rendered unconscious. But who? Ryer Ord Star was the logical suspect, but Cree Bega had searched her. Besides, how could she have taken them after the Mwellrets took them prisoner? That left Cree Bega or another of the Mwellrets as suspects, but it would take an act of either supreme courage or foolishness to try to conceal the stones from the Morgawr. Ahren did not think that the Mwellrets would chance it.

He was still wrestling with his confusion when the storm abated and the ship settled back into a smooth and easy glide through the clearing skies. He could tell the sun had reappeared from the sudden brightening that shone through the chinks in his window shutters, and he could smell the sharp, clean air that always followed a heavy storm. He was standing with his face pushed up against the rough battens, trying to see something besides the brightness, when the lock on his door released with a *snap*. He turned. A Mwellret entered, mute and expressionless, carrying a tray of food and water. The Mwellret glanced about to make certain that nothing was amiss, then placed the tray on the floor by the entry, backed out, closed the door, and locked it anew.

Ahren ate and drank, hungrier and thirstier than he had imagined, and listened to renewed activity on the decks above, the sudden movement of booted feet amid a flurry of shouts and gruff exclamations. The airship tacked several times, swinging about, maneuvering in a series of fits and starts. The ones who sailed her were inexperienced or stiff-handed. Other than to note that they were Southlanders—Federation conscripts and sailors like the ones who fought on the Prekkendorran—he had paid no attention to the sailors on being brought aboard earlier. Mostly he had spent his time studying the layout of the decks and corridors he was moved along, thinking that at some point he might have a chance to escape and would need to know his way.

He closed his eyes and took a deep, steadying breath. That hope seemed impossibly naive just now.

A sudden jolt threw him backwards and knocked the tray aside, spilling its contents. A slow grinding of wooden timbers and a screech of metal suggested that they were rubbing up against something big. He sprawled on the floor, as the ship lurched to a stop. He heard more activity overhead. For a moment he thought they were engaged in combat, but then the sounds died away. Yet the movement of the ship had changed, the earlier smooth, easy glide gone, replaced by a stiffer sway, as if the ship was resting against something solid.

Then the door to his prison opened again, and Cree Bega stepped through, followed by two more Mwellrets. The latter crossed to where he sat, hauled him roughly to his feet, and propelled him toward the open door.

"Comess with uss, little Elvess," Cree Bega ordered.

They took him back up on deck. The sunlight was so bright that at first he was blinded by it. He stood in the grip of the Mwellrets, squinting through the glare at a cluster of figures gathered forward. Most were Mwellrets, but there were Federation sailors, as well. The sailors were slack-jawed, their faces empty of expression. They stood as if in a daze, staring at nothing. Ahren realized that they were still airborne, riding several hundred feet above a canopy of brilliant green forest with the peaks of a mountain range visible off their bow, a rippling stone spine that disappeared into a hazy distance.

Then he saw that they were lashed to a second airship, one he recognized immediately. It was *Black Moclips*.

"Besst now to pay closse attention," Cree Bega whispered in his ear.

Ahren saw Ryer Ord Star then. She was standing beside the Morgawr, almost at the bow, her small figure lost in his shadow. The Morgawr warded her protectively, and she seemed to welcome the attention, glancing up at him regularly, leaning into him as if his presence somehow gave her strength. There was anticipation on her face, though the pale features still bore that ghostly pallor, that look of otherworldliness that suggested she was someplace else altogether. Ahren stared at her, waiting for her to notice him. She never even glanced his way.

Aboard *Black Moclips*, Federation sailors crowded the rail, making secure the fastenings that bound the two ships together. Their uneasy glances were unmistakable. Now and then, those glances would stray to their counterparts aboard the Morgawr's ship, then move quickly away. They saw what Ahren saw in the faces of those who crewed the Mwellret ship—emptiness and disinterest.

A pair of men had descended from *Black Moclips*' pilothouse and come forward. The Commander, recognizable by the insignia on his tunic, was a tall, well-built man with short-cropped dark hair. The other, his Mate perhaps, was tall as well, but thin as a rail, and had the seamed, browned face of a man who had spent his life as a sailor. The crew of the *Black Moclips* looked to them at once for guidance, closing about them in a show of support as they came to the railing. The Morgawr came forward and stood talking to them for a moment, the words too soft for Ahren to make out. Then the broadshouldered Commander climbed onto the railing and stepped across to the Morgawr's ship.

"Comess closser, little Elvess," Cree Bega ordered. "Sseess what happenss."

The Mwellrets holding Ahren hauled him forward to where he could hear clearly. He glanced again at Ryer Ord Star, who had dropped back and was standing apart from everyone in the bow, her eyes closed and her face lifted, as if gone into a trance. She was dreaming, he realized. She was having a vision, but no one had noticed.

"She took you prisoner, commandeered your ship, and escaped—all of this with no one to help her but a Wing Rider?" the Morgawr was saying. His rough voice was calm, but there was an unmistakable edge to his words.

"She is a formidable woman," the Federation officer replied, tight-lipped and angry.

"No more so than your mistress, Commander Aden Kett, and you were quick enough to abandon her. I would have thought twice about doing so in your shoes."

Kett stiffened. He was staring into the black hole of the other's cowl, clearly intimidated by the dark, invisible presence within, by the other's size and mystery. He was confronted by a creature he now knew to have some sort of relationship to the Ilse Witch, which made him very dangerous.

"I thought more than twice about it, I assure you," he said.

"Yet you let her escape, and you did not give chase?"

"The storm was upon us. I was concerned more for the safety of my ship and crew than for a Rover girl."

Rue Meridian, Ahren thought at once. Somehow, after the Ilse Witch had gone ashore, Rue had boarded and gotten control of *Black Moclips*. But where was she now? Where were the rest of the Rovers, for that matter? Everyone had disappeared, it seemed, gone into the ether like Walker.

"So you have your ship back, but the Rover girl is gone?" The Morgawr seemed to shrug the matter aside. "But where is our little Ilse Witch, Commander?"

Aden Kett seemed baffled. "I've told you already. She went ashore. She never returned."

"This boy who escaped, the one she seemed so interested in when she brought him back to the ship—what do you think happened to him?"

"I don't know anything about that boy. I don't know what happened to either of them. What I do know is that I've had enough of being questioned. My ship and crew are under the command of the Federation. We answer to no one else, especially now."

A brave declaration, Ahren thought. A foolish declaration, given what he suspected about the Morgawr. If the Ilse Witch was dangerous, this creature, her mentor, was doubly so. He had come a long way to find her. He had gained control over an entire

Federation fleet to manage the task. Mwellrets who were clearly in his thrall surrounded him. Aden Kett was being reckless.

"Would you go home again, Commander?" the Morgawr asked him quietly. "Home to fight on the Prekkendorran?"

This time Aden Kett hesitated before speaking, perhaps already sensing that he had crossed a forbidden line. The Mwellrets, Ahren noticed, had gone very still. Ahren could see anticipation on their flat, reptilian faces.

"I would go home to do whatever the Federation asks of me," Kett answered. "I am a soldier."

"A soldier obeys his commanding officer in the field, and you are in the field, Commander," the Morgawr said softly. "If I ask you to help me find the Ilse Witch, it is your duty to do so."

There was a long silence, and then Aden Kett said, "You are not my commanding officer. You have no authority over me. Or over my ship and crew. I have no idea who you are or how you got here using Federation ships and men. But you have no written orders, and so I am not obligated to follow your dictates. I have come aboard to speak with you as a courtesy. That courtesy has been exercised, and I am absolved of further responsibility to you. Good luck to you, sir."

He turned away, intent on reboarding *Black Moclips*. Instantly, the Morgawr stepped forward, his huge clawed hand lunging out of his black robes to seize the luckless Federation officer by the back of his neck. Powerful fingers closed about Aden Kett's throat, cutting off his futile cry. The Morgawr's other hand appeared more slowly, emerging in a ball of green light as his victim thrashed helplessly. Then, as Ahren Elessedil watched in horror, the Morgawr extended the glowing hand to the back of his prisoner's head and eased it through skin and hair and bone, twisting and turning inside like a spoon. Kett threw back his head and screamed in spite of the grip on his throat, then shuddered once and went still.

The Morgawr withdrew his hand slowly, carefully. The back of

Aden Kett's skull sealed as he did so, closing as if there had been no intrusion at all. The Morgawr's hand was no longer glowing. It was wet and dripping with brain matter and fluids.

It was finished in seconds. Aboard *Black Moclips*, the stunned Federation crew rushed to the railing, but the Mwellrets blocked their way with pikes and axes. Pushing back the horrified Southlanders, the rets swarmed aboard, closing about and rendering them all prisoners. The sole exception was the rail-thin Mate, who hesitated only long enough to see the terrible, blasted look on his Commander's empty face, devoid of life and emotion, stripped of humanity, before going straight to the closest opening on the rail and throwing himself over the side.

The Morgawr squeezed what was left of Aden Kett's brain in his hand, pieces dripping onto the deck, dampness sliding down his scaly arm.

"Bring the others now," he said softly. "One by one, so I can savor them."

Unable to help himself, tears filling his eyes, Ahren Elessedil retched and threw up.

"Thiss iss what could happen to little Elvess who dissobey," Cree Bega hissed into Ahren's ear. "Think'ss how it feelss!"

Then he had the boy dragged belowdecks once more and into his prison.

At the bow, in the shadow of the curved rams, alone and forgotten while the subjugation of Aden Kett took place, Ryer Ord Star stood with her eyes closed and her mind at rest.

Walker.

There was no response. Borne aloft by the wind, the smell of the forest filled her nostrils. She could picture the trees, branches spread wide, leaves touching like fingers, a shelter and a home.

Walker.

—I am here—

At the sound of his voice, her tension diminished and the peace that always came when he was near began to replace it. Even in death, he was with her, her protector and her guide. As he had promised when he sent her from him out of Castledown, he had come to her again. Not in life, but in her dreams and visions, a strong and certain presence that would lend her the strength she so desperately needed.

How much longer must I stay here?

In her mind, the Druid's voice assumed shape and form and became the Druid as he had been in life, looking at her with kindness and understanding.

—It is not yet time to leave—

I am frightened!

—Do not be afraid. I am with you and will keep you from harm—

She kept her eyes closed and her face lifted, feeling the warmth of the sun and the cool of the wind on her skin, but seeing only him. To anyone who looked upon her, to Ahren in particular, who was watching, she seemed a small, fragile creature given over to a fate that only she would recognize when it came for her. She was prepared for that fate, accepting of it, and her features radiated a reassurance that she was ready to embrace it.

Her words, when she spoke them in the silence of her mind, were rife with her need.

I am so lonely. Let me be free.

—Your task is not yet finished. Grianne has not yet awakened. You must give her time to do so. She must remain free. She must escape the Morgawr long enough to remember—

How will she do that? How will she find her way back from where she has gone to hide from the truth?

She knew of Grianne Ohmsford and the Sword of Shannara. She knew what had befallen the Ilse Witch in the catacombs of Castledown. Walker had told her at the time of his first coming, when she was made a prisoner of the Mwellrets with Ahren. He had told her what had transpired and what he needed of her. She was so grateful to see him again, even in another form, in another place, that she would have agreed to anything he asked of her.

The soft, familiar voice whispered to her.

—She will come back when she finds a way to forgive herself. She will come back when she is reborn—

The seer did not know what this meant. How could anyone forgive themselves for the things the Ilse Witch had done? How could anyone who had lived her life ever be made whole again?

Walker spoke again.

—You must deceive the Morgawr. You must delay his search. You must lead him astray. No other possesses the skills or magic to find her. He, alone, threatens. If he captures her, everything will be lost—

She felt herself turn cold at the words. What did they mean? Everything? The entire world and all those who lived in it? Could that be possible? Could the Morgawr possess power enough to accomplish such a thing? Why was Grianne Ohmsford's survival so important to whether or not that happened? What could she do to change things, even should she find a way out of her madness and despair?

—Will you try—

I will try. But I must help Ahren.

For a moment it was as if he was touching her in the flesh. She watched his hand reach out to grip her shoulder. She felt his fingers close about, warm and solid and alive. She gave a small gasp of surprise and wonder.

Oh, Walker!

—Let the Elven Prince be. Do as you have been told. Do not speak to him. Do not look at him. Do not go near him. Carry through with your deception or everything I have worked for will be ruined—

She nodded and sighed, still lost in the feel of his hands, of his flesh. She knew what was expected of her. She knew she must act alone and in the best way she could. She wondered anew at his choice of words. *Carry through with your deception or everything I have worked for will be ruined.* What did that mean? What had he worked for that could be at risk? Why did it matter so to him that she be successful in deceiving the Mórgawr? What was so important that she make it possible for Grianne Ohmsford to escape?

Then she saw it. It came to her in a flash of recognition, a truth so obvious that she did not understand how she could have missed it before. *Of course,* she thought. *How could it be anything else?* The enormity of her revelation left her so off balance that for a moment she lost her concentration completely and opened her eyes without thinking. The fierce glare of the midday sun was sharp and blinding, and she squeezed her eyes closed again instantly.

Too much light. Too much truth.

His voice cut through her confusion and her agitation like a gentle breeze.

—Do as I ask of you. One last time—

I will. I promise. I will find a way.

Then he was gone, and she was alone in the darkness of her mind, his words still lingering in small echoes, his presence still warm against her heart.

When she came back to herself again, out of her trance and unlocked from her vision—opening her eyes again, careful to shade them against the light—she could hear the screams of the Federation sailors from *Black Moclips* as the Morgawr fed on their souls.

FOURTEEN

Bek Ohmsford, Truls Rohk, and the catatonic Grianne escaped the ruins of Castledown just ahead of the searching Mwellrets and their caulls and fled into the surrounding forest. Their pursuers were so close that they could hear them moving through the trees, fanning out like beaters intent on flushing their prey. Their closeness infused Bek with a sense of helplessness that even the reassuring presence of the shape-shifter could not dispel entirely. He had a vision of what it must be like to be an animal tracked by humans and their dogs for sport, though there was nothing of sport in this. Only the movement generated by their flight kept his panic at bay.

They would not have escaped at all if Truls hadn't taken on the responsibility of carrying Grianne. Lacking any will of her own, she could not have moved at any sort of pace that would have allowed them to stay ahead of their enemies, and it was only the shape-shifter's unexpected decision to carry her that gave them any chance. Even so, with Truls bearing the burden of his sister and Bek running free on his own, they were harassed on all sides for the first two hours of their flight.

What gave them a fighting chance in the end was the coming of the same storm that had brought down the *Jerle Shannara*. It swept in off the coast in a black wall, and when it struck, pursued and pursuers alike were deep in the forest flanking the Aleuthra Ark and there was no hiding from it. It blanketed them in a torrent of rain and wave after wave of rolling thunder. Bolts of lightning struck the trees all around them in blinding explosions of sparks and fire. Bek shouted to Truls that they must take cover, but the shape-shifter ignored him and continued on, not even bothering to glance back. Bek followed mostly because he had no other choice. Darting and dodging through the blasted landscape with the fury of the storm sweeping over them like a tidal wave, they ran on.

When they finally stopped, the storm having passed, they were soaked through and chilled to the bone. The temperature had dropped considerably, and the green of the forest had taken on a wintry cast. The skies were still clouded and dark, but beginning to clear where night had faded completely and the silvery dawn of the new day had become visible. The sun was still hidden behind the wall of the storm, but soon it would climb high enough in the sky to brighten the land.

Bek was taking deep, ragged breaths as he faced Truls. "We can't keep up this pace. I can't, anyway."

"Going soft, boy?" The other's laugh was a derisive bark. "Try carrying your sister and see how you do."

"Do you think we've lost them?" he asked, having figured out by now why they had kept going.

"For the moment. But they'll find the trail again soon enough." The shape-shifter put Grianne down on a log, where she sat with limp disinterest, eyes unfocused, face slack. "We've bought ourselves a little time, at least."

Bek stared at Grianne a moment, searching for some sign of recognition and not finding it. He felt the weight of her inability to function normally, to respond to anything, pressing down on him.

They could not afford to have her remain like this if they were to have any chance of escape.

"What are we going to do?" he asked.

"Run and keep running." Bek could feel Truls Rohk staring at him from out of the black oval of his cowl. "What would you have us do?"

Bek shook his head and said nothing. He felt disconnected from the world. He felt abandoned, an orphan left to fend for himself with no chance of being able to do so. With Walker gone and the company of the *Jerle Shannara* dead or scattered, there was no purpose to his life beyond trying to save his sister. If he let himself think about it, which he refused to do, he might come to the conclusion that he would never see home again.

"Time to go," Truls Rohk said, rising.

Bek stood up, as well. "I'm ready," he declared, feeling anything but.

The shape-shifter grunted noncommittally, lifted Grianne back into the cradle of his powerful arms, and set out anew.

They walked for the remainder of the day, traveling mostly over ground where it was wet enough that their tracks filled in and disappeared behind them and their scent quickly washed away. It was the hardest day Bek could remember having ever endured. They stopped only long enough to catch their breath, drink some water, and eat a little of what small supplies Truls carried. They did not slow their pace, which was brutal. But it was the circumstances of their flight that wore Bek down the most—the constant sense of being hunted, of fleeing with no particular destination in mind, of knowing that almost everything familiar and reassuring was gone. Bek got through on the strength of his memories of home and family and life before this voyage, memories of Quentin and his parents, of the world of the Highlands of Leah, of days so far away in space and time they seemed a dream.

By nightfall, they were no longer able to hear their pursuers.

The forest was hushed in the wake of the storm's passing and the setting of the sun, and there was a renewed peace to the land. Bek and Truls sat in silence and ate their dinner of dried salt beef and stale bread and cheese. Grianne would eat nothing, though Bek tried repeatedly to make her do so. There was no help for it. If she did not choose to eat, he couldn't force her. He did manage to make her swallow a little water, a reflex action on her part as much as a response to his efforts. He was worried that she would lose strength and die if she didn't ingest something, but he didn't know what to do about it.

"Let her alone" was the shape-shifter's response when asked for his opinion. "She'll eat when she's ready to."

Bek let the matter drop. He ate his food, staring off into the darkness, wrapped in his thoughts.

When they were finished, the shape-shifter rose and stretched. "Tuck your sister in for the night and go to sleep. I'll backtrack a bit and see if the rets and their dogs are any closer." He paused. "I mean what I say, boy. Go to sleep. Forget about keeping watch or thinking about your sister or any of that. You need to rest if you want to keep up with me."

"I can keep up," Bek snapped.

Truls Rohk laughed softly and disappeared into the trees. He melted away so quickly that he might have been a ghost. Bek stared after him for a moment, still angry, then moved over to his sister. He stared into her cold, pale face—the face of the Ilse Witch. She looked so young, her features radiating a child's innocence. She gave no hint of the monster she concealed beneath.

A sense of hopelessness stole over him. He felt such despair at the thought of what she had done with her life, of the terrible acts she had committed, of the lives she had ruined. She had known what she was doing, however misguided in her understanding of matters. She had embraced her behavior and found a way to justify it. To expect her to shed her past as a snake would its skin seemed ludicrous. Truls was probably right. She would never be the child she had been. She would never even come back to being human.

Impulsively, he touched her cheek, letting his fingers stray down the smooth skin. He couldn't even remember her as a child. His image of her was formed solely from his imagination. She remembered him, but his own memory was built on a foundation of wishful thinking and imperfect hope. She looked enough like he did that no small part of his image of her was based on his image of himself. It was a flawed concoction. Thinking of her as he thought of himself was fool's play.

He reached out and gently drew her against him. She came compliantly, limply, letting him hold her. He imagined what she must feel, trapped inside her mind, unable to break free. Or did she feel anything? Was she conscious at all of what was happening? He pressed his cheek against hers, feeling the warmth of her, sharing in it. He couldn't understand why she invoked such strong feelings in him. He barely knew her. She was a stranger and, until lately, an enemy. Yet what he felt was real and true, and he was compelled to acknowledge it. He would not abandon her, not even if it cost him his own life. He could not. He knew that as surely as he knew that nothing about his life would ever be the same again.

Some part of his sense of responsibility for her, he admitted, was the result of his need to feel useful. His life was spinning out of control. With her, if with no one else, himself included, he was in a position of power. He was her caretaker and protector. She had enemies all about. She was more alone than he was. Accepting responsibility for her gave him a focus that would otherwise be reduced to little more than self-preservation.

He laid her down on a dry patch of ground beneath the sheltering canopy of a tree that the rains hadn't penetrated, and covered her carefully with her cloak. He stared down at her for a long time, at the clear features and closed eyes, at the pulse in her throat, at her chest rising and falling with each breath. His sister.

Then he stood and stared out into the darkness, tired but not sleepy, his mind working through the morass of his troubles, trying to decide what he might do to help himself and Grianne. Surely Truls would do what he could, but Bek knew it was a mistake to rely too heavily on his enigmatic protector. He had done that before, and it hadn't been enough to keep him safe. In the end, as the shapeshifters in the mountains had warned him he must, he had relied on himself. He had waited for Grianne, confronted her, and changed the course of both their lives.

What he could not tell as yet was whether or not the change had been for the better. He supposed it had. At least Grianne was no longer the Ilse Witch, his enemy and antagonist. At least they were together and clear of the ruins and *Black Moclips* and the Mwellrets. At least they were free.

He sat down, closed his eyes to rest them, and in moments was asleep. His sleep was deep and untroubled, made smooth by his exhaustion and his willingness to let go of his waking life for just a little while. In the cool, silent blanket of the dark, he was able to make himself believe that he was safe.

He did not know how long he slept before he woke again, but he was certain of the cause of his waking. It was a voice summoning him from his dreams.

–Bek–

The voice was clear and certain, reaching out to him. His eyes opened.

–Bek–

It was Walker. Bek rose and stood staring about the empty clearing, the sky overhead clear and bright, filled with thousands of stars, their light a silvery wash over the forest dark. He looked around. His sister slept. Truls Rohk had not returned. He stood alone in a place where ghosts could speak and the truth be revealed.

–Bek–

The voice called to him not from the clearing, but from somewhere close by, and he followed the sound of it, moving into the trees. He did not fear for his sister, although he could not explain why. Perhaps it was the certainty that Walker would not summon him if it would put her in peril. Just the sound of the Druid's voice brought a sense of peace to Bek that defied explanation. A dead man's voice giving peace—how odd.

He walked only a short distance and found himself in a clearing with a deep, black pond at its center, weeds clustered along the edges and pads of night-blooming water lilies floating their lavender flags through the dark. The smells of the water and the forest mixed in a heady brew suffused with both damp and dry earth, slow decay and burgeoning life. Fireflies blinked on and off all across the pond like tiny beacons.

The Druid was at the far side of the pond, neither in the water nor on the shore, but suspended in the night air, a transparent shade defined by lines and shadows. His face was hidden in his cowl, but Bek knew him anyway. No one else had exactly that stance and build, Walker in death, even as in life, was distinctive.

The Druid spoke to him as if out of a deep, empty well.

—Bek. I am given only a short time to walk free upon this earth before the Hadeshorn claims me. Time slips away. Listen carefully. I will not come to you again—

The voice was smooth and compelling as it rose from its cavernous lair. It had the feel and resonance of an echo, but with a darker tone. Bek nodded that he understood, then added, "I'm listening."

—Your sister is my hope, Bek. She is my trust. I have given that trust to you, the living, since I am gone. She must be kept safe and well. She must be allowed to become whole—

Bek wanted to say that he was not the one to bear the weight of this responsibility, that he lacked the necessary experience and strength. He wanted to say that it was Truls who would make the difference; Bek was acting only as the shape-shifter's conscience in this matter so that Grianne would not be abandoned. But he said nothing, choosing instead to listen.

But Walker seemed to divine his reluctance.

—Physical strength is not what your sister needs, Bek. She needs strength of mind and heart. She needs your determination and commitment to see her safely back from where she hides—

"Hides?" he blurted out.

—Deep inside a wall of denial, of darkness of mind, of silence of thought. She seeks a way to accept what she has done. Acceptance comes with forgiveness. Forgiveness begins when she can confront the darkest of her deeds, the one she views as most unforgivable, the one that haunts her endlessly. When she can face that darkest of acts and forgive herself, she will come back to you—

Bek shook his head, thinking through what little he knew of the specifics of her life. How could one deed be darker than any other? What one deed would that be?

"This one deed . . . ," he began.

—Is known only to her, because it is the one she has fixed upon. She alone knows what it is—

Bek considered. "But how long will it take for such a thing to happen? How will it even come about?"

—Time—

Time we don't have, Bek thought. Time that slips away like night toward day, a certainty of loss that cannot be reversed.

"There must be something we can do to help!" he exclaimed.

—Nothing—

Despair settled through him, pulling down hopes and stealing away possibilities. All he could do, all anyone could do, was to keep Grianne out of the hands of the Morgawr and his Mwellrets. Keep running. Wait patiently. Hope she found a way clear of her prison. It wasn't much. It was nothing.

"Truls wants to leave her," he said quietly, searching for something more upon which to rely. "What if he does?"

—His destiny is not yours. Even if he goes, you must stay—

Bek exhaled sharply.

—Remember your promise—

"I would never forget it. She is my sister." He paused, rubbing at his eyes. "I don't understand something. Why is she so important to you, Walker? She was your enemy. Why are you trying so hard to save her now? Why do you say she is your hope and trust?"

Shards of moonlight knifed through the transparent form, causing it to shift and change. Below, the waters of the pond rippled gently.

—When she wakes, she will know—

"But what if she doesn't wake?" Bek demanded. "What if she doesn't come back from where she has hidden inside?"

—She will know—

He began receding into the dark.

"Walker, wait!" Bek was suddenly desperate. "I can't do this! I don't have the skills or experience or anything! How can I reach her? She won't even listen to me when she's awake! She won't tell me anything!"

—She will know—

"How can she know anything if I can't explain it to her?" Bek charged ahead a few steps, stopping at the edge of the pond. The Druid was fading away. "Someone has to tell her, Walker!"

But the shade disappeared, and Bek was left alone with his confusion. He stood without moving for a long time, staring at the space Walker had occupied, repeating his words over and over, trying to understand them.

She will know.

Grianne Ohmsford, his sister, the Ilse Witch, mortal enemy of the Druids and of Walker, in particular.

She will know.

There was no sense to it.

Yet in his heart, where such things reveal themselves like rainbows after thunderstorms, he knew it to be true.

FIFTEEN

Bek returned to the camp to find Grianne still sleeping and Truls Rohk not yet returned. The position of the stars told him it was after midnight, so he went back to sleep and did not wake again until he felt the shape-shifter's hand resting on his shoulder.

"Time to go," the other said quietly, eyes on the woods behind them.

"How close are they?" Bek asked at once. It was first light, the sunrise just a silvery glow east.

"Still a distance off, but getting closer. They haven't found our trail yet, but they will soon."

"The caulls?"

"The caulls. Mutations of humans captured and altered by magic." He shifted his gaze back to Bek. "Your sister's work, I would have said, if she wasn't here with us. So it must be the Morgawr. Wonder where he found his victims."

Bek sat up quickly. "Not Quentin or the others? Not the Rovers?"

Truls Rohk took his arm and pulled him to his feet. "Don't think about it. Think about staying one step ahead of them. That's worry enough for now."

He walked over to the supplies pack he carried and pulled out some of the bread. Breaking off a piece, he handed it to Bek. "If you were like me, you wouldn't need this." He laughed softly. "Of course, if you were like me, you wouldn't be in this mess."

Bek took the bread and ate it. "Thanks for staying with us," he said, nodding toward the still-sleeping Grianne.

The shape-shifter grunted noncommittally. "Packs of caulls and Mwellrets are everywhere in these woods, dozens of them. They're not chasing only us, either. I heard the sounds of someone else fighting them off when I went back to scout—a larger group, some-where off to our right, heading into the mountains. I didn't have time to see who it was. It probably doesn't bear thinking on, except that maybe it will draw some of the rets away."

He gestured impatiently, a faceless darkness within his hood. "Enough. Let's be off."

He scooped up Grianne, and they started out once more. They went swiftly and silently through the trees, then Truls moved them into a shallow stream, which they followed for several miles. It was as if they were repeating the events of less than a week ago. They were taking a different path, but traversing the same woods. Again, they were fleeing a hunter possessed of magic and a creature created to track them. Again, they were fleeing the ruins of Castledown, heading inland. Again, they were running away from something and toward nothing.

Ironic and darkly comic, but pathetic, as well, Bek thought.

As the morning slipped away, in spite of his companion's warning not to do so, he found himself speculating on the fate of his missing friends. He could not bear to think of them made over into caulls, not after what they had already endured. An image of Quentin become a snarling animal flashed through his mind. Wouldn't he know if that had happened? Wouldn't he feel it? But he wasn't Ryer Ord Star, so he couldn't be sure. At this point, he couldn't even be certain his cousin was still alive. The wishsong was a powerful magic, but it didn't make him prescient. There was nothing he could know of what happened to anyone but Walker.

He reflected anew on last night's visit from Walker's shade. He had said nothing of it to Truls. He was not sure why, only that there didn't seem to be any reason for it. If Walker had wanted Truls to hear what he had to say, wouldn't he have appeared to both of them? It was difficult enough dealing with Truls without having to argue over Walker's enigmatic pronouncements. The Druid had been quick enough to let Bek know that his destiny was not tied to that of the shape-shifter. Though they traveled together and for the moment, at least, shared a common cause, that did not mean things wouldn't change. They had changed so often on this journey that Bek knew he could ill afford to take anything for granted. There was nothing in Walker's message that was meant for Truls, nothing that would help or inform him, nothing that would change what they were doing now.

Bek didn't like dissembling, and although he could argue that he wasn't doing that here, it was close enough to feel like it.

His thoughts shifted to his present situation. He wondered if there was any chance at all that one of the Wing Riders would catch sight of them from the skies. He knew how unlikely that was, given the size and depth of this forest. They were like ants down here, all but invisible from above. Only a ground creature like a caull could track them, and that was exactly what they didn't need.

He pushed away the idea of rescue. He was dreaming, he knew. He was grasping at anything that offered even a semblance of hope. He could not afford such desperation. Determination and persever-ance were all that he was allowed.

They walked all that day and into the next, climbing steadily into the foothills that fronted the mountains. The Mwellrets and their caulls still tracked them, but seemed to draw no closer. Now and again, the Morgawr's airships cruised the skies overhead. They came across no animals or people, no indication that anything lived in these woods but birds and insects. It was an illusion, of course, but it gave Bek a feeling of such loneliness that at times he wondered if there was any hope for them at all. The air had turned steadily colder, and snow clouds ringed the peaks of the mountains. Summer had faded with the destruction of Antrax, and the climate was in flux.

On the second night, after trying and again failing to persuade Grianne to eat something, Bek confronted Truls Rohk.

"I don't get the feeling that running away is going to accomplish anything," he said. "Other than to keep us alive for another day."

The other's head was bowed, the black opening to the cowl lowered. "Isn't that enough, boy?"

"Don't call me 'boy' anymore, Truls. I don't like the way it sounds."

The cowl lifted now. "What did you say?"

Bek stood his ground. "I'm not a boy; I'm grown. You make me sound young and foolish. I'm not."

The shape-shifter went perfectly still, and Bek half expected one of those powerful hands to shoot out, snatch him by his tunic front, and shake him until his bones rattled.

"Sooner or later, we have to stop running," Bek said, forcing himself to continue. "We tried running last time, and it didn't work. I think we need a better plan. We need somewhere to go."

There was no response. The empty opening of the cowl faced him like a hole in the earth that would swallow him if he stepped too close.

"I think we ought to go back into the mountains and find the shape-shifters who live there."

The other exhaled sharply. "Why?"

"Because they might be able to tell us where we should go. They might help us in some way. They seemed interested in me when they appeared there last time, as if they saw something about me that I didn't. They were the ones who insisted I had to stand up to Grianne. I think they might help us now."

"Didn't they tell you not to come back?"

"They saved your life. Maybe it would be different if we went back together."

"Maybe it wouldn't."

Bek stiffened. "Do you have a better idea? Are we going to go up into those mountains and try to cross them without knowing what's on the other side? Or are we just going to stay down here in these woods until we run out of trees to hide in? What are we going to do, Truls?"

"Lower your voice when you speak to me or you won't have a chance to ask those kinds of questions again!" The shape-shifter rose and stalked away. "I'll think about it," he mumbled over his shoulder. "Later."

Maybe he did, and maybe he didn't. He was gone all night, out scouting, Bek presumed. But, gone deep inside himself, unreachable, Truls Rohk refused to talk to Bek on returning the next morning. They set out again at daybreak, the skies clear, the air sharp and cool, the sunlight pale and thin. Bek had told Truls not to call him a boy anymore, but in truth he still felt like a boy. He had endured tremendous hardships and confronted terrible revelations about himself, and while the experiences had changed him in many ways, they hadn't made him feel any more capable of dealing with life. He was still hesitant and unsure about himself. He might have the power of the wishsong and the heritage of the Sword of Shannara to fall back on, but none of it gave him a sense of being any more mature. He was still a boy running from the things that frightened him, and if it wasn't for the fact that he knew his sister needed him, he might have fallen apart already.

Truls Rohk's refusal to speak to him, even to acknowledge him, left him feeling more insecure than before. He half believed—had always half believed—that the shape-shifter's commitment to look after him was written on the wind. Nothing the other did or said suggested he felt particularly bound to honor that commitment, especially with Walker dead and gone. With one chase leading into another, with the effort of running wearing on the shape-shifter's nerves and nothing good coming from it, Bek felt the distance between himself and Truls growing wider.

Once, the shape-shifter had told him how much alike they were. It had been a long time since he had spoken in such terms, and Bek was no longer certain that Truls had really meant what he said. He had used Bek to poke needles into Walker, to play at the games they had engaged in for so many years. Nothing suggested to Bek there was anything more to his relationship with the shape-shifter than that.

It was mean-spirited thinking, but Bek was sullen and depressed enough by now that such thinking came easily. He resented it, regretted it the minute he was finished, but could not seem to help himself. He wanted more from Truls than what he was getting. He wanted the kind of reassurance that came from companionship, the kind he always used to get from Quentin. But Truls Rohk couldn't give him that. There wasn't enough of him that was human to allow for it.

They walked through the morning without speaking or stopping. It was nearing midday, when the shape-shifter brought them to an unexpected halt. He stood frozen in place, Grianne cradled in his arms as he lifted his head to smell the air.

"Something's coming," he said.

He pointed ahead, through the trees. They stood in a clearing ringed by old-growth cedars and firs, now high enough up in the foothills that the outlines of the peaks ahead were clearly visible. They were not far from the shape-shifter habitat that Bek had suggested they go to, and the boy thought at first that perhaps the mountain creatures were coming to meet them.

But Truls did not seem to think so. "It's tracking us," he said quietly, as if trying to make sense of the idea.

Indeed, it made no sense. Whatever it was, it was ahead of them, not behind. It was upwind, as well. It couldn't be following their footprints or their scent.

"How can that be?" Bek asked.

But the shape-shifter was already moving, taking them through the trees, perpendicular to the route they had been following and away from whatever was ahead. They worked through the deep woods, then across a narrow stream, backing down for almost a quarter of a mile before coming ashore again. All the while, Truls Rohk stayed silent, concentrating on what his senses could tell him. When Bek tried to speak, the shape-shifter motioned him silent.

Finally, they stopped on a wooded rise, where the shape-shifter set down Grianne, faced back in the direction they had been heading, then slowly pivoted to his right on a line parallel to the one they had been taking.

His rough voice was dark and hard. "It's moving with us, staying just ahead. It's waiting. It's waiting for us to come to it."

Bek had not missed the repeated use of the pronoun *it* in reference to whatever tracked them. "What is it, Truls?" he asked.

The shape-shifter stared into the distance for a moment without replying, then said, "Let's find out."

He picked up Grianne and started toward their stalker. Bek wanted to tell him that this was a bad idea and they should keep moving away. But trying to tell the shape-shifter what to do in this situation would just enrage him. Besides, if whatever tracked them could do so without following their scent or prints, it was not likely to be thrown off by a simple change of direction.

They moved ahead for a time, listening to the sounds of the forest. Slowly, those sounds died away. Within minutes, the woods had gone silent. Truls Rohk slowed, sliding noiselessly through the trees, stopping now and then to listen before continuing on. Bek stayed close to him, trying to move as quietly as the shape-shifter did, trying to be as invisible.

In a shallow vale through which a tiny stream meandered, the shape-shifter brought them to a halt. "There," he said, and pointed into the trees.

At first, Bek saw just a wall of trunks interspersed with clumps of brush and tall grasses. It was dark where they stood, the light shut away by a thick canopy of limbs. The floor of the vale sloped down to the stream, where a patchwork of shadows and hazy light carpeted the forest floor. The air was cold and still, unwarmed by the sun, unstirred by the wind.

Then he saw a shadow that didn't quite fit with everything else, squat and bulky, crouched back by the treeline where the dark trunks masked its features. He stared at it for a long time, and then it moved slightly, shifting position, and he saw the yellow glitter of its eyes.

A moment later, it detached itself from its concealment and padded into view. It was a massive creature, hump shouldered and broad chested, covered with coarse gray hair that stuck out in wild clumps. It had a wolf's head, but the head had mutated into something dreadful. The snout was long and the ears pointed like a wolf's, but the jaws were massive and broad, and when they split wide in a kind of panting grin, they revealed double rows of finger-long serrated teeth. Down on all fours, it moved with a shambling gait, its long forelegs disproportionate to its rear, which were short and powerful and sprouted from hindquarters dropped so low it appeared to be crouching.

It eased its way down into the vale until it was almost to the stream. There, it stopped, lifted its head, and emitted the most terrible mewling sound Bek had ever heard, a combination of wail and snarl that froze the woods into utter silence.

"What is it?" Bek whispered.

Truls Rohk's laugh was low and wicked. "Your sister's destiny, come back to claim her. That's the thing she made to track us when we fled from her before, the thing the shape-shifters saved me from. I thought it dead and gone, but they must have set it free outside their boundaries. It's a caull, but look at it! It's mutated beyond what even she had intended. It's become something even more monstrous. Bigger and stronger."

"What does it want with us?" Bek looked at him. "It tracks us, you said. What does it want?"

"It wants her," the shape-shifter answered softly. "It's come for her. See how it looks at her?"

It was true. The hard yellow eyes were fixed not on the men, but on the sleeping girl, locked on her as she slept in the shape-shifter's arms—focused on her with such intensity that its purpose was unmistakable.

"There's true madness," Truls whispered, a hint of wonder in his voice. "Captured, mutated, driven out, lost. It seeks only one thing. Revenge. For what has been done to it. For what has been stolen. A life. An identity. Who knows what it thinks and feels now? It must have tracked her through the connection of their magic, a joining of kindred. She created it, and it remains connected to her. It must be able to read her pulse or heartbeat. Or the sound of her breathing. Who knows? It sensed her and came."

The caull cried out again, the same high-pitched wail. The skin on the back of Bek's neck prickled and his stomach clenched. He had been afraid before on this journey, but never the way he was now. He couldn't tell if it was the look of the caull, all crooked and bristling, or the sound of its cry, or just the fact of its existence, but he was terrified.

"What are we going to do?" he asked, barely able to get the words out.

Truls Rohk snorted derisively. "We let it have her. She made it; let her deal with the consequences."

"We can't do that, Truls! She's helpless!"

The other turned on him. "This might be a good time for some rational thinking on your part, *boy.*" He emphasized the word. "There are so many things waiting to kill your sister that we can't even begin to count them! Sooner or later, one of them will finish the job. All we do by interfering now is to prolong the process. You think you can save her, but you can't. Time to let go of her. Enough is enough!"

Bek shook his head. "I don't care what you say."

"She is the Ilse Witch! Your sister is dead! Why are you so stubborn about it? Bah, I've had enough of this! You do what you wish, but I'm leaving!"

Bek took a deep, calming breath. "All right. Leave. You don't owe me anything. It isn't fair to ask you to do more than you have. You've done enough already." He looked over at the caull as it hunched down at the edge of the stream. "I can take care of this."

Truls Rohk snorted. "You can?"

"The wishsong was powerful enough to stop Antrax's creepers. It can stop that thing." He stepped close to the shape-shifter. "Give her to me."

Without waiting for the other to respond, he reached in and took Grianne right out of his arms. Cradling her, he stepped away again. "She's my sister, Truls. No matter what you say."

Truls Rohk straightened and looked directly at Bek. "The wishsong is a powerful magic, Bek Ohmsford. But it isn't enough here. You still haven't mastered it. Your sister proved that to you already. That thing over there will be at your throat before you figure out what's needed."

Bek looked at the caull and went cold to the bone thinking of how it would feel to have those teeth and claws tearing into him. It would be over quickly, he guessed. The pain would be momentary. Then it would be Grianne's turn.

"You could do something for me," he said to the shape-shifter. "If you could draw its attention away, just for a moment, I might be able to catch it off guard."

Truls Rohk stared at him. Bek couldn't see the shape-shifter's eyes within the dark confines of his cowl, but he could feel the weight of their gaze, hard and certain. For a long moment, Truls didn't speak. He just kept looking at Bek.

"Don't do this," he said finally.

Bek shook his head. "I have to. You know that."

"You won't survive it."

"Then you can do what you wish with my sister, Truls." He gave the shape-shifter a defiant look. "I won't be there to stop you."

Another long silence stole away the seconds. Bek brushed at a stray lock of hair and felt a bead of sweat slide down his forehead. He was hot in spite of the chill in the air. He felt as if he might never be cool again.

The shape-shifter stood where he was a moment longer, still staring at Bek. "All right," he said finally, his voice harsh and angry. "I've said what I needed to say. Staying with her is up to you." He turned away. "I'll try to draw its attention. Maybe that will help, but I doubt it. Good luck to you, boy."

Bek watched as Truls Rohk angled down the gentle slope, moving with the grace and precision of a moor cat. Deformed and ill made, an aberration of nature, he was nevertheless beautiful to watch. Bek could not believe he was really leaving. They had been together since the beginning of the journey west out of the Wolfsktaag. Truls had saved him so many times Bek had lost count, had given him the insights he needed to come to terms with his heritage and his destiny. They had not always agreed on everything, and there had been a degree of mistrust and uncertainty between them, but the alliance had worked. It was shattering now to see that alliance end. Even watching the other go, Bek couldn't believe it was happening. It felt as if the shape-shifter was taking a part of Bek with him. His confidence. His heart.

Truls, he wanted to call out. *Don't go.*

The caull swung around to watch the shape-shifter, its powerful body flattened and tensed. Bek lowered Grianne to the ground, placing her carefully behind him before turning back to defend them. When the caull struck, it would do so swiftly. He would have only one chance to stop it.

He never got even that. Before he could prepare himself, the caull attacked, springing sideways with blinding speed and tearing across the stream and up the slope in a blur of churning legs and gaping jaws. Bek would have been dead an instant later but for Truls Rohk, who moved even faster. So quick that he seemed simply to leave one place and reappear at another, he intercepted the caull from the side, slammed into it, and knocked it sprawling.

Then he was on top of the beast, tearing at it like an animal himself, snarling with such ferocity that for an instant Bek wasn't sure that it was Truls at all. The shape-shifter ripped at the caull using weapons that Bek couldn't see—weapons he concealed beneath his cloak or perhaps just fashioned out of the mass of raw and jagged bone that comprised his ruined body. Whatever they were, they proved effective. Bits and pieces of the caull's body flew into the air, and blood jetted in dark spurts of inky green. The fighters careened across the vale, locked in combat, joined in purpose, lost in their desperate struggle to kill each other.

Bek recovered himself enough to remember to use the wish-song, but he could not think how to use it effectively. Shape-shifter and caull were so tightly fused that there was no opportunity to bring the magic to bear without striking both. Bek darted right and left at the edge of the battle, enveloped by its sound and fury, desperately seeking a way to intervene, unable to do so.

"Truls!" he screamed helplessly.

Bright fountains of red spurted out of the tangle, the shape-shifter's human blood released from a wound somewhere beneath the concealing cloak, a wound that Bek could not see. He heard Truls snarl in rage and pain, then tear at the caull with renewed fury, bearing it down against the earth. The caull screeched with a sound like metal tearing, writhing and snapping in a flurry of claws and teeth, but it could not break free.

Then Truls Rohk locked his arms about the caull's head and hauled back on its long, thick neck, twisting violently. Bek heard cartilage snap and ligaments tear. The caull shrieked with such fury that the sound matched the howl of the worst storm Bek had ever witnessed, of hurricane winds tearing past windows and walls, of funnel clouds ripping at the earth. The caull heaved upward in one last futile effort to dislodge the shape-shifter, then its head separated from its body and exploded into an unrecognizable ruin.

In the ensuing silence, cacophonous and empty both at once, Truls Rohk threw down the remains of the body. Still twitching, it fell to the forest floor, dark blood spreading everywhere. The shape-shifter stood over it a moment, bent to the stream to drink and wash, then strode back up the hill to where Bek waited.

Without pausing for even a second, he reached down and picked up Grianne, lifting her into the cradle of his arms.

"I changed my mind," he said, his voice harsh and broken, his breathing ragged.

Then he set off walking once more, leaving an astonished Bek to follow.

SIXTEEN

As the day went on and the trio climbed out of the foothills and onto the lower slopes of the mountains, two things became increasingly clear to Bek Ohmsford.

First, they had moved into shape-shifter territory. He knew this not because there were boundary markers or signposts or anything that would designate it as such. Having come a different way, he couldn't even be certain he recognized what he was looking at from his previous visit. He knew where he was because he could feel the shape-shifters watching him. He could feel their eyes. It was broad daylight and the sparsely wooded slopes offered few hiding places, so it didn't appear as if anyone was there. Yet they were, he knew, and not far away. He might have questioned this feeling once, but having experienced it not much more than a week earlier—having felt it so strongly he could barely breathe because the shape-shifters had been right on top of him—he wasn't questioning it now.

Second, Truls Rohk was failing. He had come away from his battle with the caull winded and clearly hurt, but seemingly not in any real danger. He had walked strongly for several hours, carrying Grianne and setting a quick pace for Bek to follow. But over the last two hours, with the fading of the afternoon and the approach of nightfall, he had begun to slow, then to stagger, his smooth gait turned into an uneven lurch.

"I have to rest," Bek said finally, in an effort to find out what was going on.

The shape-shifter continued ahead for another fifty yards, then all but collapsed beside a fallen tree trunk, barely managing to set Grianne down before dropping heavily beside her. He wouldn't have thought to sit close to her before this; now, it seemed he could not find the strength to move away.

Bek walked up next to him and reached down for the water skin. Truls handed it to him without looking up. A ragged gasping came from inside the cowl, and Bek saw the rise and fall of the shape-shifter's shoulders as he struggled to breathe. Seating himself, he drank from the skin and watched as Truls give a deep, involuntary shudder.

They sat together without speaking for a long time, looking out over the valley below, listening to the silence.

"We can camp here," Bek said finally.

"We have to keep moving," Truls said, his voice raspy and weak. It didn't even sound like Truls. "We need to get higher up on the slopes while there's still light."

The cowl lifted, shadowed emptiness facing the boy like a hole dropping away into the earth. "Do you know where we are?"

Bek nodded. "In the land of the shape-shifters."

A cough racked the other's body, and he doubled over momentarily before straightening again. "We have to get deep enough in that they'll have no choice, that they'll have to come to us."

"You've decided to ask for their help?"

He didn't answer. Another spasm shook his body.

"Truls, what's wrong?" Bek asked, leaning close.

"Get away from me!" the shape-shifter snapped angrily.

Bek moved back. "What's wrong?"

For a moment, there was no response. "I don't know. I don't feel right. The caull did something to me, but I don't know what. I didn't think those cuts and bites were much, but everything feels like it's breaking down." He gave a short, sharp laugh. "Wouldn't it be a joke on me if I died because of your sister? Protecting her when I don't even like her? The Druid would love that, if he were here!"

He laughed again, the sound weak and broken. Then he struggled back to his feet, picked up Grianne, and set off once more.

They walked on for another hour, the afternoon passing slowly into twilight, the air cooling swiftly to a chill that nipped at Bek's face. Shadows lengthened on the mountainside, dark fingers stretching, and the moon appeared in the sky, rising out of the hazy distance, half-formed and on the wane. Bek looked back the way they had come to see if anyone was following, an impossible attempt in this light, and quickly gave it up. He glanced at their surroundings, searching for the watchers, but the effort yielded nothing. He listened to the silence and was not reassured.

They reached a shelf of ground that angled back into a deep stand of conifers, and Truls collapsed again. This time he went down without warning, dropping Grianne in a heap, rolling away from her onto his back where he lay gasping for air. Bek rushed over at once, kneeling beside him, but the shape-shifter pushed him away.

"Leave me alone!" he snapped. "See to your sister!"

Grianne lay sprawled to one side, eyes open and unseeing, body limp. She appeared unhurt as Bek helped her back to a sitting position, straightening her clothing and brushing leaves and twigs from her hair before returning to Truls.

"I'm done," the shape-shifter rasped. "Finished. Build a fire back in the trees to warm yourself. Wait for them to come."

A fire might attract the attention of those who hunted them, but Bek knew that whatever happened now was in the hands of the shape-shifters. No harm would come to them if the spirit creatures didn't wish it—not in their habitat and not from caulls or Mwellrets or anything else. Truls Rohk knew this, as well. He was counting on it.

Bek set about gathering wood to build a fire. It wasn't until he'd set the wood in place that he realized he didn't have any tinder. When he went back to see if Truls had any, the shape-shifter was unconscious. Bek took Grianne to where he had stacked the wood, then returned for Truls, but found him too heavy to move. All those broken and missing body parts, and he still weighed so much. Bek left him and sat with Grianne by the useless wood. He thought about using the wishsong to trigger a fire, but he didn't know how to do that. He sat staring into the night, feeling helpless and alone.

Where were the shape-shifters?

Night descended, and darkness closed about. The stars appeared overhead and the silence deepened. Soon it was so cold that Bek was shivering. He pulled Grianne close to him, trying to keep them both warm, wondering if they might freeze to death before morning. They were high up on the mountainside; it was too cold already and it was going to get much colder.

Once, he rose and walked out to where Truls Rohk lay and tried to rouse him. The shape-shifter was awake and breathing, but he did not appear lucid. A terrible heat radiated from his body, as if he was burning with fever. Bek sat with him for a while, trying to think of something he could do. But Truls Rohk's physiology was so different that Bek didn't even know where to begin. In the end, he just spoke quietly to the other, trying to reassure him, to give him some small comfort.

Then Bek returned to Grianne and the waiting.

He must have dozed off finally, because the next thing he knew he awoke to find the fire burning brightly in front of him and the night air grown warm and comforting. He glanced at Grianne, who sat next to him, awake and staring, unresponsive when he spoke her name. He looked around and saw nothing, stood and looked some more, and still saw nothing.

He started to walk out toward the edge of the flat to where Truls lay and stopped. A dozen dark shapes blocked his way, massive forms rising before him like great rocks. As he started to back away, more closed about from both sides, huge and menacing, features hidden by the darkness and a sudden mist.

Bek stopped where he was and stood his ground. He knew what they were; he had been waiting for them. What he didn't know was why they had waited so long to appear.

Why did you come back?

The voice was thin and hollow, almost a wail, and it came from all around and not from any single source.

"My friend is sick."

Your friend is dying

The words were unexpected, spoken without a trace of emotion or interest. For a moment, Bek could not make himself reply. *No,* he said to himself. *No, that's wrong. That can't be.*

"He's hurt," he said. "Can you help him?"

The shadows faded and reappeared in the deep mist like creatures conjured out of imagination. There was that ethereal quality to the shape-shifters, that otherworldliness that defied explanation. They seemed so impermanent that nothing about them was quite real. But Bek remembered how quickly they could change to something hard and deadly.

The caull has poisoned him. Teeth and claws excreted poison and it seeped into his human half, infecting it. The poison leeches away his strength When his human half dies, his shape-shifter half will die, as well.

"Is there an antidote?" Bek demanded, still trapped in a web of disbelief and shock. "Do you know of one?"

There is no cure.

Bek looked around in despair. "There must be something I can do," he said finally. "I'm not going to just let him die!"

As soon as he spoke the words, he knew they were what the shape-shifters had been waiting to hear. He could see them move in response, hear their expectant whispers as they did so. He could feel a change in the air. He thought at once to take back the words, but did not know how to do so and could not have made himself, anyway.

You were told that halflings have no place in the world. You said that you would make a place for this one. Would you do so now?

Bek took a deep breath. "What are you asking?"

Would you make a place for your friend? Would you give him a chance to live?

The voice was coldly insistent, uninterested in argument or reason, in anything but a direct answer to its question. The shape-shifters had gone still again, clustered about like stones. Bek could no longer see or feel the fire. He could no longer remember in which direction it lay. He was shrouded in darkness and enclosed by the spirit creatures, and all he could see of the world was the glitter of the stars overhead.

"I want to save him," he said finally.

He sensed a murmur of approval and, once again, of expectation. It was the answer they were hoping for, yet one that promised results he did not fully comprehend.

He must shed his human skin. He must cast it aside forever. He must become like us, all of one thing and none of the other. If he does this, the poison cannot hurt him. He will live.

Cast off his human skin? Bek was not sure what he was being told, but it didn't matter. He couldn't dismiss out of hand any offer that might save Truls. "What do you want me to do?" he asked.

Give us permission to make him one of us.

Bek shook his head quickly. "I can't do that. I have to ask him if that's what he wants. I don't have the right—"

He cannot hear you. He is lost in his sickness. He will die before he can give you an answer. There is no time. You must decide for him.

"Why do you need my permission?" Bek was suddenly frantic. "What difference does it make what I say?"

The whispers and movement stopped, and the night went completely still. Bek froze in place and held his breath like a man about to jump from a very high place.

A human must make this choice. It is his human side we would destroy. There is no one else but you. You said you were his friend. You said you would give up your life for him and he would give up his life for you. Should we make a place in the world for him? You must decide.

Bek exhaled sharply. "You have to tell me what will become of him. If I tell you to do this, whatever it is, if I give you my permission, what will become of Truls?"

There was a long pause.

He will become one with us, a part of us.

Bek stared. "What does that mean?"

We are one. We are a community. No one of us lives apart from the others. He would be joined.

Bek felt every bit a boy in that instant, a boy who had ventured out into the world and gotten himself into such trouble that he would never see home again. He closed his eyes and shook his head. He couldn't do this. He was being asked to save Truls, but he was also being asked to change him irrevocably. By saving Truls, he would transform him into something else completely—a communal creature, no longer separate and apart, but a part of a whole. What would that be like? Would Truls want this, even to save his life? How could Bek possibly know?

He stood there, adrift in a sea of profound uncertainty, knowing he was being offered the only choice available and hating that it was his to make. Truls Rohk had never been at peace in the world. He had been an outcast all his life with few friends and no family or home. He was an aberration created through forbidden breeding, a freak of nature that had never belonged. What place there was for him, he had made for himself. Maybe he would be better off changed into one of the spirit creatures, a part of a family and community at last. Maybe he would be happier.

But maybe not.

Bek wanted Truls to live—wanted it desperately—but not if the price was too high. How could he measure that?

Tell us your decision.

Bek closed his eyes. A chance at life was worth any price, too precious to give up for any reason. He could not know how this would turn out; he could not determine what Truls Rohk would do if he were able. He could do for Truls only what Bek would want done for himself in the same situation. He could fall back only on what he believed to be right.

"Save him," he said quietly.

There was a sudden rush of movement from the shape-shifters, an odd hissing that turned into a sigh. The wall of bodies that had gathered about him opened, and the darkness cleared to reveal the fire still blazing in front of his sister.

Go back to her. Sit with her and wait. When morning comes, take her and go into the mountains. You will find what you are looking for there. Do not fear for your safety. Do not worry about those who follow. They shall not pass.

Dark forms changed into the bristling monsters he had seen once before, terrible apparitions that could smash a life with barely a thought, things that existed in nightmares. They hovered close for an instant, their smell washing over him, their raw presence reinforcing the promise they had made.

Go.

He did as he was told, not yet at peace with himself, unable to gain the reassurance he sought. He could not bear to consider too closely what he had done. He did not want to ponder the result because he was afraid he might recognize something he had not considered and did not want to face. He went back to the warmth and comfort of the fire, seating himself next to Grianne, taking her hands in his and holding them while he stared into the flames. He did not look back at the shape-shifters, did not try to see where they went or what they did. He would not have been able to do so anyway, because his eyes could not penetrate the darkness beyond the firelight.

He stared instead at Grianne and tried to make himself believe that she had been worth everything that had happened—that saving her was not a Druid's whim or a brother's false hope, but a necessary act that would result in something more important and far-reaching than the losses it had caused.

After a time, he fell asleep. His dreams were vivid and charged with emotion, and they ranged across the length and breadth of his life In them, Quentin reappeared to him, working on an ash bow, red hair hanging loose and easy, strong face cocky and smiling, laughter bright with reassurance. Coran and Liria looked in on him as he slept, and he could hear them speak of him with ambition and pride. The company of the *Jerle Shannara* filed past him one by one as he stood at the edge of a forest, and then Rue Meridian stepped away long enough to come over to him and touch his face with cool fingers that swept away thoughts of everything but her.

Finally, Walker stood looking down at him from a castle rampart, from a place that looked vaguely familiar. Truls Rohk stood next to him, then faded into a disembodied voice that whispered to him to be strong, to be steadfast, to remember always how alike they were. He was different than Bek remembered him, and after a moment Bek knew that it was because Truls was no longer a halfling, but a true shape-shifter. He was one with his new family, with his community, with the world that had given him a second chance at life. There was a sense of completion about him, of having found a peace that he had never known before.

Bek watched and listened to a box of empty space, to a wall of darkness, hanging on the other's words as if to a lifeline, and the peace that Truls had found settled over him, as well.

When he came awake again, it was morning. A misty gray light rose out of the mountain peaks, east where the dawn was breaking. The fire had gone out, the smoking embers turned to dying ashes and charred stumps. He reached out his hand. The ashes were still warm. Beside him, Grianne slept, stretched out upon the ground, her eyes closed and her breathing slow and even.

He stared down at her a moment, then rose and went to find Truls Rohk.

He stopped at the edge of the flat where he had left his friend the night before. All that remained was a hooded cloak and a scattering of half-formed bones. Bek knelt and reached down to touch them, lifting the folds of the cloak away, half expecting to find something more. Truls Rohk had seemed so indestructible that it was impossible that this was all that was left of him. Yet there was nothing more. Not even bloodstains were visible on the hard, frost-covered ground.

Bek rose and stood looking at the bones and cloak a moment longer. Perhaps most of what Truls Rohk had been, what mattered and had value, had gone on to become a part of what he was now.

He wondered if the shape-shifters, Truls among them, were watching him. He wondered if he would ever know if he had done the right thing.

He walked back to the campfire, woke Grianne, took her hands in his, and brought her to her feet. She came willingly, her calm, blank expression empty of emotion, her limp acquiescence sad and childlike. He was all she had left, all that stood between her and random fate. He had become for her the protector he had promised he would be.

He was not sure he was up to it, only that he must try, that he must do what he could to save them both.

Holding hands like children, they began to climb.

SEVENTEEN

On the next mountain over from the one that Bek and Grianne were struggling to ascend, Quentin Leah looked up expectantly from his breakfast of bread and cheese as Kian appeared out of the trees below the trailhead and began to climb toward him. Further up, gathered in the copse of fir where they had spent the night, the remnant of Obat's Rindge waited for instructions on where to go next—all but Obat himself and Panax, who had gone on ahead to scout their way through the passes of the Aleuthra Ark. They had been fleeing the Mwellrets and their tracking beasts for two days, and Quentin had hoped they would not have to flee for a third.

"They found our trail," Kian growled. His dark, square face furrowed as he sank down next to the Highlander and mopped his brow. "They're coming."

He would not look at Quentin. No one would these days. No one wanted to see what was in his eyes. Not since they found him in the ruins of Castledown. Not since they heard what became of Ard Patrinell.

Quentin understood. He did not feel right about himself anymore either. Everything seemed out of joint.

He handed the Elven Hunter what was left of his bread and cheese and stared down in frustration. They were sitting on a rugged slope that had the look of a hunched-over Koden, all bristle-backed with conifers and jagged rocks. Forty-eight hours of running had brought them here—frantic hours spent trying to throw off their pursuers. Nothing had worked, and now, finally, they had been run to earth.

From the beginning, when Quentin, Panax, Kian, Obat, and a dozen Rindge had remained behind to slow down the hunt for the tribe, things had gone wrong. As a group, they possessed a lifetime of knowledge of hunting and tracking in wilderness terrain, and each knew a dozen tricks that would slow or stop anyone trying to follow them. They had employed them all. They had started with simple devices intended to create dozens of false trails that would take a hunting dog hours to unravel. But the beasts the rets were using to track them were far superior to dogs, and they separated the real trail from the false with uncanny quickness, coming after Quentin's group almost before they could make their escape. The Rindge next used extracts from plants to create strong scents that would throw off the creatures. That didn't work either. Kian and Panax led them into streams and even one river, using the water to hide their passage, but the tracking beasts found them again anyway.

In desperation, Obat lured them into a narrow ravine and set fire to the whole of the woods leading up, a strong wind blowing the fire right back down into the faces of the rets. The fire was intended not only to drive their pursuers back, but to obliterate their tracks and scent, as well. That bought them several hours, but in the end the rets and their beasts found them anyway.

Finally, in desperation, Quentin and his companions set an ambush, thinking to kill or disable the tracking beasts. The ambush caught the rets by surprise, and a handful were killed by bows and arrows and blowguns before the remainder had a chance to take cover. The tracking beasts were struck, too, but the projectiles seemed to have almost no effect on them. They shrugged off the barbs as if they were nothing more than bee stings and came after their attackers with astonishing fury. Loosed from their chains, they turned into a pack of savage killers. Quentin had been involved in many hunts over the years, but he had never seen anything like this. The tracking beasts, at least eight of them, had charged through the scrub and over the rocks like maddened wolves, voiceless monsters that vaguely resembled humans evolved into something bigger and more terrible than the gray wolves that hunted the Black Oaks east of Leah.

Having no other choice, Quentin and his companions stood their ground and fought back. But before anyone could prevent it, three of the Rindge were dead, the beasts covered in their blood. They might have all been killed but for the Sword of Leah, which lit up like a torch, the magic surging down its length in a streak of blue fire. That was when Quentin realized that these beasts had been created out of magic, and that it would take magic to stop them. He killed two of them in a flurry of shrieks and severed limbs before the rest fell back, not defeated or cowed, but wary now of the power of the sword and uncertain whether or not they were meant to continue.

Their hesitation allowed Quentin and his companions to escape, but use of the sword marked them, as well; it alerted their hunters that at least one among the pursued possessed magic, and that hardened their determination to continue the pursuit. Airships appeared in the skies overhead, and fresh units of Mwellrets and trackers were lowered to the ground to join those already gathered. Quentin couldn't tell how many there were, but it was more than enough to overpower him should he choose to stand and fight again. He couldn't be certain whom the rets thought they were tracking, but it was clear that they were serious about finding out.

The chase wore on through that first day and all through the second, with the Rindge working their way deeper into the Aleuthra Ark, higher into the rugged peaks, following a trail they knew would eventually take them over the mountains and into the broader grass-lands beyond. Quentin was beginning to wonder what good that would do. If their pursuers were this determined, they would be caught sooner or later whether they fled over the mountains or not. If they were to escape, a more permanent solution had to be found, and it had to be found quickly because the women and children that comprised the bulk of the fugitives were tiring.

Quentin was tiring, as well, not so much physically as emotion-ally. He had lost something in his battle with the Ard Patrinell wronk—something of the fire that had driven him earlier, some-thing of heart and purpose—so that now he felt more a shell than a whole person. With so many of the company dead and all the rest scattered and lost, his focus had become blurred. He was helping the Rindge because they needed it and because he didn't know what else to do. It gave him direction, but not passion. He had lost too much to find that again without a dramatic shift in his fortunes.

He didn't think Panax and Kian were much better off, although they seemed more hardened than he was, more accustomed to the idea of going on alone. Quentin was too young yet, unprepared to have experienced the kind of losses he had just endured, and the losses were affecting him more dramatically. At times, he collapsed inside completely. He saw Tamis again, covered in blood and dying. He saw Ard Patrinell's head, encased in metal and glass, an instant before he smashed it apart. He saw Bek, the way he remem-bered him in the Highlands, such a long time ago.

He was haunted and worn and disillusioned, and he could feel him-self slipping notch by notch. He cried because he couldn't help himself, trying to mask his tears, to hide his weakness. Chills racked him in bright sunshine. Dark dreams haunted his sleep—dreams of what hunted him, of what awaited him, of fate and prophecy. He awoke shaking and afraid and went back to sleep cold and empty.

But he was also the best chance the others had of staying alive, and he was painfully aware of the fact. Without the magic of the Sword of Leah, they had no answer for the magic of the things that pursued them. Quentin might be slipping off the edge, but he could not afford to let go.

"How much time do we have?" he asked Kian after a moment.

The Elf shrugged. "The Rindge will try to slow them down, but won't succeed. So, maybe an hour, a little more."

Quentin closed his eyes. They needed help. They needed a miracle. He didn't think he could give it to them. He didn't know who could.

Kian finished the bread and cheese, took a drink from his water skin, and stood. He was coated with dust and debris, and his clothes were torn and streaked with blood. He was a mirror image of Quentin. They were refugees in need of a bath and some real sleep, and they were unlikely to get either anytime soon.

"We'd better get them up and moving," Kian said.

They went back up the trail to where the Rindge waited. Using gestures and the few Rindge words they had picked up, they got the tribe back on its feet and trudging ahead once more. The Rindge were a dispirited group, not so much because of their weariness as because nothing the men had tried had worked and time was running out. Still, they kept on without complaint, the very young and old, the women and children, all helping one another where help was needed, a people dispossessed from their home of centuries, driven out by forces over which they had no control. They were demonstrating a resolve that Quentin found surprising and heartening, and he took what strength he could from them.

Still, it was not much.

They had hiked for perhaps an hour when the Rindge rearguard appeared on the run. Their gestures were unmistakable. The Mwellrets and tracking beasts were catching up to them.

At the same moment, Panax and Obat appeared from the other direction. The Dwarf was excited as he hurried to reach Kian and the Highlander.

"I think we've found something that will help," he said, eyes bright and eager as they shifted from one face to the other. He rubbed vigorously at his thick beard. "The pass divides up ahead. One fork leads to a thousand-foot drop—no way around it. The other leads to a narrow ledge with room for maybe two people to pass, but no more. This second trail winds around the mountain, then further up through a high pass that crosses to the other side. Here's what's important. You can get above the second trail by climbing up the mountainside further on and doubling back. There's a spot, perfect for what we need, to trigger an avalanche that will sweep away the pass and anything on it. If we can get the Rindge through before they're caught by the rets, we might be able to start a rockslide that will knock those rets and their beasts right off the trail—or at least trap them on the other side of where we are."

"How far ahead is this place?" Kian asked at once.

"An hour, maybe two."

The Elven Hunter shook his head. "We don't have that kind of time."

"We do if I stay behind," Quentin said at once.

He spoke before he could think better of it. It was a rash and dangerous offer, but he knew even without thinking it through that it was right.

They stared at him. "Highlander, what are you saying?" Panax asked angrily. "You can't—"

"Panax, listen to me. Let's be honest about this. It's the magic that's attracting them. No, don't say it, don't tell me I don't know what I'm talking about—we both know it's true. We all know it. They want the magic, just like Antrax and its creepers did. If I stay back, I can draw them off long enough for you to get past the place on the mountain where you want to start the slide. It will buy you the time you need."

"It will get you killed, too!" the other snapped.

Quentin smiled. Now that there were so many of the tracking beasts, he had virtually no chance of withstanding a sustained assault. If he couldn't outrun them—and he knew he couldn't—they would be all over him, sword or no. He was proposing to give up his life for theirs, a bargain that didn't bear thinking on too closely if he was to keep it.

"I'll stay with you," Kian offered, not bothering to question the Highlander's logic, knowing better than to try.

"No, Kian. One of us is enough. Besides, I can do this better alone. I can move more quickly if I'm by myself. You and Panax get the Rindge through. That's more important. I'll catch up."

"You won't live that long," Panax said with barely contained fury. "This is senseless!"

Quentin laughed. "You should see your face, Panax! Go on, now. Get them moving. The faster you do, the less time I'll need to spend back here."

Kian turned away, dark features set. "Come on, Dwarf," he said, pulling at Panax's sleeve.

Panax allowed himself to be drawn away, but he kept looking back at Quentin. "You don't have to do this," he called back. "Come with us. We can manage."

"Watch for me," Quentin called after him.

Then the Rindge were moving ahead again, angling through the trees and up the trail. They wound through boulders and around a bend, and in minutes they were out of sight.

Everything went still. The Highlander stood alone in the center of the empty trail and waited until he could no longer hear them. Then he started back down the way he had come.

It didn't take Quentin very long to find what he was looking for. He remembered the defile from earlier, a narrow split through a massive chunk of rock that wound upward at a sharp incline and barely allowed passage for one. Quentin knew that if he tried to make a stand in the open, the tracking beasts would overwhelm him in seconds. But if he blocked their way through the split, they could come at him only one at a time. Sooner or later, they would succeed in breaking through by sheer weight of numbers or they would find another way around. But he didn't need to hold them indefinitely; he only needed to buy his companions a little extra time.

The split in the boulder ran for perhaps twenty-five feet, and there was a widening about halfway through. He chose this point to make his first stand. When he was forced to give way there, he could fall back to the upper opening and try again.

He glanced over his shoulder. Further back, another two or three hundred yards, was a deep cluster of boulders where he had stashed his bow and arrows. He would make his last stand there.

"Wish you could see this, Bek," he said aloud. "It should be interesting."

The minutes slipped away, but before too many had passed, he heard the approach of the tracking beasts. They did nothing to hide their coming, made no pretense of concealing their intent. Sharp snarls and grunts punctuated the sound of their heavy breathing, and their raw animal smell drifted on the wind. Further away, but coming closer, were the Mwellrets.

Quentin unsheathed the Sword of Leah and braced himself.

When the first of the beasts thrust its blunt head around the nearest bend in the split and saw him, it attacked without hesitating. Quentin crouched low and caught it midspring on the tip of his weapon, spitting it through its chest and pinning it to the earth where it thrashed and screamed and finally died as the magic ripped through it. A second and third appeared almost immediately, fighting to get past each other. He jabbed at their faces and eyes as they jammed themselves up in the narrow opening, and forced them to back away. From behind them, he heard the shouts of the rets and the snarls of other tracking beasts as they tried in vain to break through.

He fought in the defile for as long as he could, killing two of the creatures and wounding another before he made his retreat. He might have stayed there longer, but he feared that the rets would find a way around. If they trapped him in the defile, he was finished. He had bought as much time as he could at his first line of defense. It was time to fall back.

With the tracking beasts snapping at him, he backed through the split, then made his second stand at the upper end. Straddling the opening, he bottled up the frantic creatures, refusing to let them through, killing one and wedging it back inside so that the others could not pass it without climbing over. They tore at their dead companion until it was shredded and bloodied, and still they couldn't break free. Quentin fought with a wild and reckless determination, the magic driving through him like molten iron, sweeping away his weariness and pain, his reason and doubt, everything but the feel of the moment and its dizzying sense of power. Nothing could stop him. He was invincible. The magic of the sword buzzed and crackled through his body, and he gave himself over to it.

Even when the Mwellrets got around behind him, he stood his ground, so caught up in the euphoria generated by the magic that he would have done anything to keep it flowing. He drove back this fresh assault, then returned to battling the tracking beasts trying to emerge from the split, intent on doing battle with anything that challenged him.

It took a deep slash to his thigh to sober him up enough that he finally realized the danger. He turned and ran without slowing or looking back, gaining enough ground to enable him to clamber into the rocks and find his bow and arrows just before his pursuers caught up with him. He was a good marksman, but his pursuers were so close that marksmanship counted for almost nothing. He buried four arrows in the closest burly head before it was finally knocked back, blinded in both eyes and maddened with pain. He wounded two more, slowing them enough that the others could not get past. He shot every arrow he had, killing two of the rets, as well, then threw down the bow and began running once more.

There was nowhere reasonable left to stand and fight, so he sprinted for the ledge where he hoped Panax, Kian, and the Rindge would be waiting with help. It was a long run, perhaps two miles, and he soon lost track of time and place, of everything but movement. Still infused with the magic of the sword, its power singing in his blood, he found strength he did not know he possessed. He ran so fast that he outdistanced his bulky pursuers, leaving them to scramble over boulders and rock-strewn trails he scaled with ease.

Maybe, just maybe, he would find a way out of this.

"Leah, Leah!" he cried out, euphoric and wild-eyed, with reckless disregard for who might hear him. "Leah!" he howled.

They caught up to him finally at the near end of the ledge, forcing him to turn and fight. He stood his ground just long enough to throw them back again, then rushed out onto the ledge. The sweep of the Aleuthra Ark with its massive backdrop of peaks and valleys stretched like a painting across the horizon, somehow not quite real.

The tracking beasts came at him once more, but they did not have enough room. Two tumbled away, clawing and screaming as they fell. He glanced back down the slope he had just climbed; it was crawling with tracking beasts and Mwellrets. How many more could there be? Pressed against the cliff face, he retreated as swiftly as he could, slashing at the closest of his pursuers when they came within reach. He had been clawed and bitten in a dozen places, and the singing of the magic had taken on a high, frantic whine. His stamina and strength were nearly exhausted; when they were depleted, the magic of the Sword of Leah would fail, as well.

"Panax!" he called frantically, fighting to keep his newfound fear at bay, feeling the euphoria desert him as the brilliance of his blade began to dim.

He was perhaps a hundred feet out from where he had started, the cliff wall to his left an almost vertical rise, the drop to his right deep and precipitous, when he heard Panax call back to him. He did not look away from his pursuers. They were crowded out onto the ledge behind him, still coming, rage and hunger reflected in their eyes, waiting for him to drop his guard.

Then he heard a rumble of rocks from above, and he turned and ran. He was too slow. The closest of the beasts was on top of him in a heartbeat, claws slashing. He whirled and knocked it backwards, slamming his closed fist into the rock wall with such force that he lost his grip on the sword. Knocked from his hand, it tumbled over the edge of the path and disappeared into the abyss.

He hesitated then, not quite believing what had just happened, and his hesitation cost him any chance of escape. Rocks and dirt showered down from above, pouring over everything in a thunderous slide that swept across the face of the cliff. Quentin tried to run through it, but he was too late. The avalanche was all around him, tearing away the mountainside, breaking off chunks of the ledge. The tracking beasts and their handlers disappeared in a roar of stone, then a massive section of the trail ahead tore free and was gone.

Quentin flattened himself against the cliff wall and covered his head. The entire mountain seemed to be coming down on top of him. For a moment, he held on, pressed against the stone. Then the avalanche plucked him from his perch like a leaf, and he was gone.

EIGHTEEN

The Highlander regained consciousness in a sea of mind-numbing blackness and bone-crushing weight. He could smell dust and grit and the raw odor of torn leaves and earth. At first he could not remember what had happened or where he was, and panic's sharp talons pricked at him. But he held fast, forcing himself to be patient, to wait for his mind to clear.

When it did, he remembered the avalanche. He remembered being swept over the narrow ledge and into the void, tumbling downward through a rain of rocks and debris, catching onto something momentarily before being torn free, tangling up in scrub thickets, all the while engulfed in a roar that dwarfed the fury of the worst storm he had ever endured. Then darkness had closed about in a wave and everything else disappeared.

His vision sharpened, and he realized that the avalanche had buried him in a cluster of tree limbs and roots. Through small openings in his makeshift tomb, he saw heavy gray clouds rolling across a darkening sky. He had no idea how much time had passed. He lay without moving, staring at the distant clouds and collecting his thoughts. He should, by all rights, be dead. But the roots and limbs, while trapping him in a jagged wooden cage, had saved him, as well, deflecting boulders that would otherwise have crushed him.

Even so, he was not out of trouble. His ears were ringing, and his mouth and nostrils were dry with dust. Every bone and muscle in his body ached from the pummeling he had received, and he could not tell as yet if he had broken anything in his fall.

When he tried to move, he found himself pinned to the ground.

He listened to the silence, a blanket that cloaked both his stone-encrusted prison and the world immediately outside. There wasn't the smallest rustle of life, not the tiniest whisper, nothing but the ragged sound of his breathing. He wondered if anyone would come looking for him—if anyone even could. There might be no one left to look. Half the mountain had fallen away, and there was no telling whom it had carried with it. Hopefully, Panax and the Rindge had escaped and the Mwellrets and their tracking beasts had not. But he could not be sure.

He tried not to think too hard on it, focusing instead on the problem at hand. He forced himself to relax, to take deep breaths, to gather his resources. Carefully, gingerly, he tested his fingers and toes to make certain they were all working—and still there—then tested his arms and legs, as well. Amazingly, nothing seemed broken, even though everything hurt.

Encouraged by his sense of wholeness, Quentin set about looking for a way to get free. There was only a little room to move in his cramped prison, but he took advantage of it. He was able to extricate his left leg and both arms through the exercise of a little time, patience, and perseverance, but the right leg was securely wedged beneath a massive boulder. It wasn't crushed, but it was firmly pinned. Try as he might, he could not work it free.

He lay back again, drenched in sweat. He was aware suddenly of how hot he was, buried in the earth like a corpse, covered over by layers of rock and debris. He was coated with dust and grime. He felt as if he knew exactly what it would be like to be dead, and he didn't care for it.

He wormed himself into a slightly different position, but the smallness of the space and the immobility of his trapped leg prevented him from doing much. *Deep breaths*, he told himself. *Stay calm.* He felt raindrops on his face through the chinks in his prison and saw that the sky had darkened. The rainfall was slow and steady, a soft patter in the stillness. He licked at stray drops that fell on his lips, grateful for the damp.

He spent a long time after that working with an unwieldy piece of tree limb that he was able to drag within reach and position as a fulcrum. If he could shift the boulder just an inch, he might be able to wriggle free. But from his supine position, he could not get the leverage he needed, and the branch was too long to place properly in any event. Nevertheless, he kept working at it until it grew so dark he could no longer see what he was doing.

He fell asleep then, and when he woke, it was still dark, but the rain had stopped and the silence had returned. He went back to work with the branch, and it was morning before he gave the task up as impossible. Despair crept through him and he found himself wondering how desperate his situation really was. No one was coming to look for him; he would have heard them by now if they were. If he was going to survive, he was going to have to do so on his own. What would that cost him? Would he cut off his leg if there was no other way? Would he give up part of himself if it meant saving his life?

Sleep claimed him a second time, and he woke to daylight and sunshine flooding down out of a clear blue sky. He did not give himself time to dwell on the darker possibilities of his situation, but went back to trying to get free. This time, he used a sharp-ended stick to dig away at the rock and earth packed in beneath his leg. If he could tunnel under his leg, he reasoned, he might create enough space to worm loose. It was slow going, the digging often reduced to one pebble, one small chunk of hardened earth at a time. He had to start as far back as his knee and work his way down, inch by painful inch. He had to be careful not to disturb anything that supported the boulder. If it shifted, it would crush his leg and trap him for good.

He worked all day, ignoring his growing hunger and thirst, the aches in his body, and the heat of his cage. He had come too far and endured too much to die like this. He was not going to quit. He would not give up. He repeated the words over and over again. He made them into a song. He chanted them like a mantra.

It was almost dark again when he finally worked his leg free, leaving behind most of his pants leg and much of his skin. Immediately, he began digging his way out, burrowing upward through the debris toward the fading light, toward fresh air and freedom. He could not afford to stop and rest. He felt the panic taking over.

Night had fallen, a velvet soft blackness under a starlit sky, when he pulled himself from the rocks and earth and stood again in the open air. He wanted to weep with joy, but would not let himself, afraid that if he broke down, he might not recover. His emotions were raw and jangled from his ordeal, and his mind was not entirely lucid. He glanced around at the jumble of boulders and jutting trees, then upward to the darkened cliffs. In this light he could not determine from where he had fallen. He could tell only where he was, standing at one end of a valley that lay in the shadow of two massive mountains in the middle of the Aleuthra Ark.

It was cold, and he forced himself to move further down the slope into the trees beyond the avalanche line so that he might find shelter. He found it in a grove of conifers, and he lay down and fell asleep at once.

He dreamed that night of the missing Sword of Leah, and he woke determined to find it.

In the daylight, he could see more clearly where he had been and what had happened. The slide that had carried him over the side had torn away much of the mountain below, stripping it of trees and scrub, leveling outcroppings and ledges, and loosening huge sections of cliffside, all of which had tumbled into a massive pile of rubble. Looking up, he could just make out where he had been standing when he had fallen. No trace remained of those with whom he had fled or from whom he had been fleeing.

He hunted for food and water, finding the latter in a small stream not far from where he had slept, but nothing of the former. Even his woods lore failed to turn up anything edible so high up in the mountains. He gave it up and went back to the slide to search for the Sword of Leah. He had no idea where to look, so for the entire morning he wandered about in something of a daze. The slide was spread out for almost half a mile, and in some places it was hundreds of feet deep. He kept thinking that it was impossible that he was still alive, impossible that he had ridden it out without being crushed. He kept telling himself that his survival meant something, that he was not going to die in this strange land, that he was meant to go home again to the Highlands.

By midday, the sun was burning out of the sky and the valley was steaming. He was beginning to hallucinate, seeing movement where there wasn't any, hearing the whisper of voices, feeling the presence of ghosts. He went back down into the trees to drink from the stream, then lay down to rest. He woke several hours later, feverish and aching, and went back to searching.

This time, the ghosts took on recognizable form. As he trudged through the rocks, he found them waiting for him at every turn. Tamis appeared first, rising out of the landscape, healed and new again, short-cropped hair pushed back from her no-nonsense face, eyes questioning his purpose as she stared at him. He spoke her name, but she did not respond. She regarded him for only a moment, as if measuring anew the depth of his commitment and the strength with which he intended to pursue it. Then she faded into the shimmer of the midday heat, into the tangle of the past.

Ard Patrinell appeared next, sliding out of the haze as a metal-shrouded wronk, transformed from human into something only partly so. He stared at Quentin, his trapped, doomed eyes begging for release even as he raised weapons to skewer the Highlander. Even knowing the image wasn't real, Quentin flinched from it. Words passed the lips of the Captain of the Home Guard, but they were inaudible behind his glassy face shield, empty of sound and meaning, as insubstantial as his spectre.

The image shimmered and lost focus, and Quentin dropped into a guarded crouch, closing his eyes to clear his vision, his head, and his mind. When he looked again, Ard Patrinell was gone.

Both dead, he reminded himself, Tamis and her lover, ghosts lost in the passage of time, never to return in any other form, memories only. He felt himself drawn to them, less a part of his surroundings than before, more ethereal. He was losing himself in the heat, fading away into his imaginings, in need of rest and food and something hard and fast to hold on to. A chance. A promise.

Neither appeared, and his stumbling hunt across the avalanche-strewn landscape yielded nothing of the missing talisman. The afternoon lengthened, and his exhaustion increased. He was not going to find the sword, he knew. He was wasting his time. He should leave this place and go on. But go on to what and to where? Did he have another purpose, now that he was alone and so lost? Was there something further he was meant to do?

His mind drifted into the past, to the Highlands, where he had spent his youth so carelessly, to the times he had spent hunting and fishing and exploring with Bek. He could see his cousin's face in the air before him, disembodied, but Bek all the same. Where was he now? What had become of him since the ambush in the ruins of Castledown? He had been alive when Tamis had seen him last, but had disappeared since. Bek was as much a ghost as the Tracker and Patrinell.

But alive, Quentin Leah swore softly. Even missing, even disappeared, Bek was alive!

Quentin found himself kneeling in the rocks, crying, his face buried in his hands, his shoulders heaving. When had he stopped to cry? How long had he been hunched down like this in the rubble?

He wiped at his eyes, angry and ashamed. Enough of this. No more.

When he put his right hand down to push himself back to his feet, his fingers closed about the handle of his sword.

For a second he was so stunned that he thought he was imagining it. But it was as real as the stone on which he knelt. He forced himself to look down, to see the blade lying next to him, coated with dirt and grime, its pommel nicked and scored, but its incomparable blade as smooth and unmarked as the day it was formed. His fingers tightened their grip, and he brought the weapon around so that he could see it more clearly, so that he could be certain. There was no mistake. It was his sword, his talisman, and his hope reborn.

It was impossible, of course, that he should have found it. It was a one-in-a-million chance that he would find it at all. He was not a strong believer in providence, in fate's hand reaching out, but there was no other explanation for this miracle.

"Shades," he whispered, the word a rustle of sound in the deep silence of the afternoon heat.

He took the offered gift as a sign and came back to his feet, infused with new purpose. A wayward spirit not yet ready to cross over to the land of the dead, he began to walk.

Daylight faded quickly to twilight, the sun sliding behind the western rim of the Aleuthra Ark, turning the horizon a brilliant purple and crimson, cloaking the valley in long, deep shadows. The heat faded, and the air turned crisp and raw. The unexpected shift in temperature marked the coming of another storm. Quentin hunched his shoulders and lowered his head as he pushed on through the valley and began to climb where the mountains met and formed a high pass. Clouds that had been invisible before slid into view in thick knots and gathered across the sky. The wind picked up, slow and unremarkable at first before changing to gusts that were both icy and sharp edged.

Ahead, where the pass narrowed and twisted out of view, the darkness deepened.

Quentin pressed on. There was no place to stop and no point in doing so. He was too exposed on the slopes to chance resting; what shelter he might find lay on the other side of the pass. He needed food and water, but he was unlikely to find either before morning. Darkness layered the earth; roiling storm clouds canopied the sky. Sleet spit at him, icy particles stinging his face as he ducked his head protectively. The wind howled down out of the mountains, rolling off empty slopes, gathering force as it whipped across the valley from the passes and defiles. Trying not to think about how far he still had to go to reach safety, Quentin bent and wavered before the wind's tremendous force.

By the time he gained the head of the high pass, the sleet had changed to snow, and a carpet twelve inches deep covered the ground he trod. He had strapped the Sword of Leah across his back using a length of cord he found in one pocket, a makeshift that allowed his hands to stay free. He was walking mostly uphill over uneven ground, the wind tearing at him from all sides and shifting rapidly. Light played tricks in the curtain of falling snow, and it was all Quentin could do to maintain his balance. He was still dizzy and feverish, hallucinating from dehydration and lack of food, but he could do nothing about that.

The ghosts of his past came and went, whispering words that made no sense, gesturing in ways he could not understand. They seemed to want something from him, but he could not tell what it was. Perhaps they simply wanted his company. Perhaps they waited from him to cross over from the world of the living. The idea seemed altogether too possible. If things did not change, they would not have long to wait.

He had lost his cloak, and so he had nothing to protect himself from the cold. He was shivering badly and afraid he would lose all his body heat before he reached shelter. He had been made strong and tough from his years in the Highlands, but his endurance was not limitless. He hugged himself as he slogged ahead through snow and sleet and cold, trying to hold together in body and spirit both, knowing he had to keep going.

At the head of the pass, he found something else waiting.

At first, he wasn't sure if what he was seeing was even real It was big and menacing, rising out of the rocks beyond, vague and indistinct in the whirl of the storm. It was man-shaped, but something else, as well, the limbs and body not quite right for a human, not quite in proportion. It appeared to him all at once as he crested the pass and walked into a wind howling with such fury that it threatened to tear the clothes from his body. He watched it slide through veils of white snow, then fade away entirely. He moved toward it, drawn to it instinctively, afraid and intrigued both. He had the sword, he told himself. He was not unprepared.

The shape appeared anew, further in, waited a moment for his approach, then disappeared once more

This game of hide-and-seek continued through the pass and down the other side, where the walls of the mountain were thickly grown with conifers and the force of the storm was lessened by their windbreak. He had left the mountain off which he had fallen and was now beginning to ascend the one adjoining it. The trail was narrow and difficult to follow, but the appearance of the ghost ahead kept him focused. He was convinced by now that he was being led, but there seemed no reason for concern. The ghost had not threatened him; it did not seem to mean him harm.

He climbed for a long time, winding his way westward around the mountainside, his path twisting and turning through sprawling stands of huge old trees, deep glades of pine needles dusted with snow, and rocky hillocks slick with dampened moss. The storm's fury had diminished. The snow still fell, but the wind no longer blew the flakes into his face like needles, and the cold seemed less pervasive. Ahead, the shape took on clearer definition, becoming almost recognizable. Quentin had seen that shape before somewhere, moving in the same way, a wraith of the woods in another time and place. But his mind was singing with fatigue, and he could not place it.

Not much farther, he told himself. *Not much longer.*

Placing one foot in front of the other, eyes shifting between the ground below and the swirling white ahead, between his own movements and the ghost's, he pushed on.

"Help me," he called out at one point, but there was no response.

Not much farther, he told himself again and again. *Just keep going.*

But his strength was failing.

He went down several times, his legs simply giving way beneath him. Each time, he struggled back to his feet without pausing to rest, knowing that if he stopped, he was finished. Daylight would bring light and warmth and a better chance to survive a sleep. But he could not chance it here.

In a clearing leading into a deep stand of cedar, he slowed and stopped. He could feel himself leaving his body, rising into the night like a shade. He was finished. Done.

Then the dark shape ahead seemed to transform into something else, not one but two shapes, smaller and less threatening. They came out of the night together, walking hand in hand, angling toward him from his left—how had they gotten all the way over there? He stared at the new figures in disbelief, again uncertain that what he was seeing was real, that it wasn't some new form of phantasm.

The figures hesitated as well, as they caught sight of him. He moved toward them, peering through the curtain of snow, through space and time and hallucinations, through fatigue and a growing sense of recognition, until he was close enough to be certain whom he was seeing.

His voice was parched and ragged as he called out to the one who stood closest and who stared back at him wide-eyed in disbelief.

"Bek!"

NINETEEN

B ek Ohmsford's journey over the past two days had not been as eventful as Quentin's, but it had been just as strange.

After leaving the shape-shifters, and with Grianne in tow, he had continued into the Aleuthra Ark, the ghost of Truls Rohk an unwelcome guest borne with him. An image of the hooded cloak and scattered bones spread carelessly across the frozen ground lingered in the forefront of his thinking all that first day, a haunting that refused to be banished. He found himself remembering his protector in life, seemingly indestructible, offering his incomparable strength and unshakable reassurance. Though much of the time Truls Rohk had been an invisible presence, he had always kept close watch over Bek, fulfilling his promise to the Druid.

It seemed impossible that he was really gone. Bek could tell himself that it was so, that there was no mistake, but somehow he kept thinking that Truls would reappear, just as he always had before. He kept looking for Truls to do so. He couldn't help himself. At every turn, in every patch of shadows, Bek thought to find him waiting.

So that first day passed, a dream in which Bek walked with his catatonic sister and the ghost of his lost friend.

By nightfall, he was exhausted, having traveled far and rested little. He had given little thought to Grianne, taking for granted her compliance with the hard pace he had set, forgetting entirely that she could not speak and therefore would not complain. Aware suddenly of his failure, he sat her down and examined her feet. They were not blistered, so he turned his attention to feeding her. He had to do it by hand, and even so she was still barely taking anything. Mostly, she drank water, but he was able to get a little mashed cheese and bread down her throat, as well. She did not look different to him, but he could not tell what was going on inside her head. He trailed the tips of his fingers across her cheeks and forehead and kissed her. Her strange eyes stared through him to places he could not see.

He fed himself then, eating hungrily and drinking some of the ale he had salvaged from Truls' supplies. Night descended in a deep soft blackness, and the sky was awash in stars. He wrapped Grianne in her cloak and sat next to her in the silence, one arm draped about her protectively, his thoughts straying to the past they had lost and the future they might never share. He did not know what to do for her. He kept thinking there must be something that he had not tried, that her catatonia was a condition he could change if he could just figure out what was needed. He knew there was an answer to the puzzle if he could only put his finger on what it was. But the answer he sought would not come.

After a time, he sang to her, his voice barely more than a whisper, as if anything more might disturb the night. He sang songs he remembered from his childhood, songs he had sung with Coran and Liria in the Highlands as a child. It all seemed very long ago and far away. He had not been a child for years. He had not been a boy since he had come on this journey with Quentin.

On impulse, he tried using the wishsong. Perhaps the magic could affect Grianne. It was their strongest connection, the shared heritage of their bloodline. If he could not reach her in any other way, perhaps he could reach her in this. He had not used it this way, but he knew from the history of the Ohmsford family that others before him had. The trick was in finding a chink in the armor of her catatonia, in worming his way past her natural defenses to where she was hiding. If he could reach deep inside, he might be able to let her know he was there.

He began to sing to her again, nothing more than humming at first, a soft and gentle melody to soothe and comfort. He blended himself with the night, another of its sounds, a natural presence. Slowly, he worked his singing around to something more personal, using words—her name, his own, their lost family revisited. He kept to memories that he thought would make her smile or at least yearn for what she had lost. He did not use her known name—Ilse Witch. He used Grianne, and called himself Bek, and he linked them together in an unmistakable way. Brother and sister, family always.

For a very long time, slowly and patiently, he worked to draw her to him, to find a way inside her mind, knowing it would not be easy, that she would resist. He made himself repeat the same phrases over and over, the ones he thought might trigger a response, giving her a fresh look each time, another reason to reach out for him. He played with color and light, with smell and taste, infusing his music with the feel of the world, with life and its rewards. *Come back to me*, he sang to her, over and over. *Come out from the shadows, and I will help you.*

But nothing succeeded. She stared at the fire, at him, at the night, and did not blink. She looked through the world to an empty place that shielded her from real life, and she would not come away.

Frustrated, weary, he gave it up. He would try again tomorrow, he promised himself. He was convinced that he could do this.

He lay back, and in seconds he was asleep.

They climbed higher into the mountains on the following day, finding their path a snake of coiled switchbacks and rugged scrambles. Grianne followed after him compliantly, but had to be hauled over the rougher spots. It was hard going, and the sky west was darkening with the approach of a storm.

At one point, he heard the roar of a massive slide somewhere deeper in the mountains, and the eastern horizon was left cloudy with dust and debris in the aftermath.

By nightfall, it had begun to rain. They took shelter beneath the boughs of a massive spruce, lying on a bed of fallen needles that remained warm and dry. As the rain settled in, the temperature fell, spiraling downward with the change in the weather. Bek wrapped Grianne in her cloak and sang to her once more, and once more she stared through him to other places.

He lay awake much longer this night, listening to the soft patter of the rain and wondering what he was going to do. He had no idea where he had gotten to or where he was going. He was proceeding on faith, on the promise of the shape-shifters that he was moving toward something and not away from everything. He was adrift in the world toward something and not away from everything. He was adrift in the world with his stunned, helpless sister and with his friends and allies scattered or dead. He had one weapon, one talisman, one crutch on which he could lean, but no clear idea of how he might use it. He was so alone that he felt he would never find comfort or peace again.

When he slept, it was from exhaustion.

Morning dawned sullen and gray, a reflection of his mood as he rose sluggish and dispirited, and they started out once more. The storm caught up with them at midday, sliding past the high peaks north and curling down along the slopes on which he climbed. He had descended almost a thousand feet earlier, as the trail dipped and curved through a defile that opened deep into the mountain. Now, with the wind picking up and the cold penetrating his bones, he was high on the slopes anew and without suitable shelter. He picked up the pace, pulling Grianne after him with fresh urgency. He did not want to get caught out in the open if it began to snow.

It did, soon after, but the flakes were large and lazy and the way ahead remained clear. Bek pressed on, descending at a split in the trail, intent on gaining the forested stretches lower down. He did so just as the storm blew out of the high regions in a blinding sheet of sleet and rain. Everything beyond a dozen yards disappeared. The trees turned to phantoms that came and went to either side in the manner of soldiers at march. He held Grianne's hand as tightly as he could, not wanting to chance a separation that might prove permanent.

The storm worsened, something he had not thought possible. Sleet and rain turned to deep curtains of snow. The snow began to build underfoot, and soon it was approaching twelve inches deep even in the windswept clearings. Visibility lessened further until he was groping from tree to tree. He would have taken shelter if he could have found any, but in the blinding whirl of the blowing snow, everything looked the same.

Then he stumbled and fell and lost his grip on Grianne. In an instant, she was gone. She disappeared in the whiteout, stolen away as surely as his faith in his purpose in coming on this journey. He groped for her, turning first this way and then that, everything white and empty about him, everything the same. He could not find her. Panic overwhelmed him as he grasped at snow flurries and air and empty chances, and he screamed. He screamed not just for his lost sister or his helplessness, but for all the pent-up rage and frustration he had been carrying with him for weeks. He screamed because he had reached the breaking point, and he did not care what happened to him next.

In that moment, a shape appeared before him, huge and dark, rising up like a behemoth roused from sleep to put an end to his intrusion. He stumbled backwards from it, surprised and terrified. As he did so, his hands brushed against his sister. He pushed his face close to hers to make certain he was not mistaken, calling to her. Her pale, empty features stared back at him. She was kneeling in the snow, docile and unbothered.

Tears of relief blinded him as he brought her back to her feet, holding on to her with both hands, then deciding that wasn't enough, wrapping her with his arms. He wiped the tears away with his sleeve and looked for the phantom that had caused him to find her. It was there, just ahead of him, but smaller and moving away. Bek peered after it, sensing something familiar about it, something recognizable. It faded and then reappeared, prowling just at the limits of his vision, expectant and purposeful.

Then suddenly it turned and beckoned him.

Almost without realizing what he was doing, he obeyed. Both hands clasped tight on Grianne's slender wrist, he started ahead once more into the haze.

"Which is how I found you," he finished, passing the aleskin back to Quentin, the pungent liquid warming his throat and stomach as he swallowed. "I don't know how long I was out there, but my guide stayed just ahead of me the whole way, obviously leading me toward something, keeping me on track. I didn't know where it was taking me, but after a while it didn't matter. I knew who it was."

"Truls Rohk," his cousin said.

"That's what I thought at the time, but now I'm not so sure. Truls is gone. He's become a part of the shape-shifter community, and no longer has a separate identity. Maybe I just want to believe it was him." Bek shook his head. "I don't guess it matters."

They were huddled in a shallow cave hollowed into the side of the mountain. Bek had started a fire, and it burned with little heat, but a steady, insistent flame that illuminated their faces. Grianne sat to one side, staring off into the night, unseeing. Every so often, Quentin looked at her, not quite sure yet what to make of having someone who had tried so hard to kill them sitting so close.

Bek watched Quentin take another deep swallow from the aleskin. The color was finally returning to Quentin's frozen body. He had been nearly gone when he had stumbled upon Bek and Grianne. Bek had wasted no time wrapping him in his cloak and finding shelter for them all. The fire and ale had brought Quentin around, and they had spent the last hour exchanging stories about what had happened since the ambush in the ruins of Castledown. They didn't rush it, taking their time, giving themselves a chance to adjust to the idea that the impossible had happened and they had found each other again.

"I never thought you were dead," Bek told his cousin, breaking the momentary silence. "I never believed it was so."

Quentin grinned, a hint of that familiar, cocky smile that marked him so distinctively. "Me either, about you. I knew when Tamis told me she had left you outside the ruins, that you would be all right. But this business about you having magic, that's another matter. I still can't quite believe it. You're sure you're an Ohmsford?"

"As sure as I can be after hearing everything Walker had to say." Bek leaned back on his elbows and sighed. "I suppose I really didn't believe it myself in the beginning. But after that first confrontation with Grianne, feeling the magic come alive inside me and break out like it did, I didn't have the same doubts anymore."

"So she's your sister."

Bek nodded. "She is, Quentin."

The Highlander shook his head slowly. "Well, *there's* something we'd have never guessed when we started out on this journey. But what are you supposed to do with her now that you know?"

"Take her home," Bek answered. "Keep her safe." He looked at Grianne a moment. "She's important, Quentin. Beyond the fact that she's my sister. I don't know how, but she is. Walker was insistent on it, when he was dying and afterwards when he returned as a shade. He knows something about her that he isn't telling me."

"Big surprise."

Bek smiled. "I guess that Walker keeping secrets isn't unusual, is it? Maybe there aren't any surprises left for you and me. No real ones, I mean."

Quentin exhaled a white plume that lofted into the chilly night. "I wouldn't be so sure. I'd thought that earlier, and then I found you again. You never know." He paused. "What do you think the chances are that anyone else is alive? Are they all dead, like Walker and Patrinell?"

Bek didn't say anything for a moment. All of the Elves were gone, save Kian and perhaps Ahren Elessedil. Ryer Ord Star might still be alive. The Wing Riders might be out there somewhere. And, of course, there were the Rovers.

"We saw the *Jerle Shannara* fly into these mountains," Bek ventured. "Maybe the Rovers are still searching for us."

Quentin gave him a hard look. "Maybe. But if you were Redden Alt Mer in this situation, what would you do—come looking for us or fly straight back to where you came from?"

Bek thought about it a moment. "I don't think Rue Meridian would leave us. I think she'd make her brother look."

His cousin snorted. "For how long? Chased by those Mwellret vessels? Outnumbered twenty to one?" He shook his head. "We'd better be realistic about it. They don't have any reason to think we're still alive. They were prisoners themselves; they won't want to chance being made prisoners again. They would be fools not to run for it. I wouldn't blame them. I would do the same thing."

"They'll look for us," Bek insisted.

Quentin laughed. "I know better than to try to change your mind, cousin Bek. Funny, though. I'm supposed to be the optimist."

"Things change."

"Hard to argue with that." The Highlander looked off into the falling snow and gestured vaguely. "I was supposed to look out for you, remember? I didn't do much of a job of it. I let us get separated, and then I ran the other way. I didn't even think of looking for you until it was too late. I want you to know how sorry I am that I didn't do a better job of keeping my word."

"What are you talking about?" Bek snapped, an edge to his voice. "What more were you supposed to do than what you did?

You stayed alive, and that was difficult enough. Besides, I was supposed to look out for you, as well. Wasn't that the bargain?"

They stared at each other in challenge for a moment. Then the tension drained away, and in the way of friends who have shared a lifetime of experiences and come to know each other better than anyone else ever could, they began to grin.

Bek laughed. "Coward."

"Weakling," Quentin shot back.

Bek extended his hand. "We'll do better next time."

Quentin took it. "Much better."

The wind shifted momentarily, blowing snow flurries into their faces. They ducked their heads as it whipped about them, and the fire guttered beneath its rush. Then everything went still again, and they looked out into the darkness, feeling their efforts at getting through the day catching up to them, seeping away their wakefulness, nudging them toward sleep.

"I want to go home," Quentin said softly. He looked over at Bek with a pale, worn sadness in his eyes. "I bet you never thought you'd hear me say that, did you?"

Bek shrugged.

"I'm worn out. I've seen too much. I've watched Tamis and Patrinell die right in front of me. Some of the other Elves, as well. I've fought so hard to stay alive that I can't remember when anything else mattered. I'm sick of it. I don't even want to feel the magic of the sword anymore. I was so hungry for it. The feel of it, like a fire rushing through me, burning everything away, feeding me."

"I know," Bek said.

Quentin looked at him. "I guess you do. It's too much after a time. And not enough." He looked around. "I thought this would be our great adventure, our rite of passage into manhood, a story we would remember all our lives, that we would tell to our friends and family. Now I don't ever want to talk about it again. I want to forget it. I want to go back to the way things were. I want to go home and stay there."

"Me, too," Bek agreed.

Quentin nodded, looking off again, not saying anything. "I don't know how to make that happen," he continued after a moment. "I'm afraid now that maybe it can't."

"It can," Bek said. "I don't know how, but it can. I've been thinking about getting back home, about how to take Grianne there, like Walker said I should. It seems impossible, crazy. Walker's gone, so he can't help. Truls Rohk won't be going any farther. Half of everyone I came here with is dead and the other half is scattered. Until I found you, I was all alone. What chance do I have? But you know what? I just tell myself I'll find a way. I don't know what that way is, but I'll find it. I'll walk all the way home if I have to. Right over the Blue Divide. Or fly. Or swim. It doesn't matter. I'll find a way."

He looked at Quentin and smiled. "We got this far. We'll get the rest of the way, too."

They were brave words, but they sounded right, necessary, talismans against fear and doubt. Bek and Quentin were still fighting for small assurances, for bits of hope, for tiny threads of courage. The words gave them some of each. Neither wanted to challenge them just now. Look too closely at the battlements, and the cracks showed. That wasn't what they needed. They left the words where they were, undisturbed, an echo in their thoughts, a promise of what they believed might still be.

Taking comfort in the shelter of each other, because in the end it was the best sort of comfort they could hope to find, they went off to sleep.

The dawn was cloudy and gray, a promise of new snow reflected in the colorless canvas of the slowly brightening sky. The temperature had dropped to freezing, and the air was brittle with cold. They ate breakfast with few words exchanged, mustering their resolve. The confidence that had bolstered them the night before had dissipated like fog in sunlight. All about them, the mountains stretched away in an endless alternation of peaks and valleys. Save for the intensity of the light from the sunrise east, the horizons all looked the same.

"Might as well get going," Quentin muttered, standing up and slinging his sword over his shoulder.

Bek rose, as well, and did the same with the Sword of Shannara. He barely gave thought to the talisman anymore; it seemed to have served its purpose on this journey and had become something of a burden. He glanced self-consciously at Grianne, realizing he could say the same about her and most certainly had thought as much more than once.

Thinking to cover as much ground as possible before the next storm and not wanting to be caught out in the open again, they set a brisk pace. The frozen ground crunched like old bones beneath their boots, grasses and earth cratering with indentations of their prints. If their pursuers were still tracking them, they would have no trouble doing so. Bek considered the possibility and brushed it aside. The shape-shifters had promised him that his pursuers would not be allowed to follow. There was no reason to think that their protection extended this far, but he was weary and heartsick and needed to believe this one thing if he was to have any peace of mind. So he let himself.

They trudged on toward midday, following trails that wound through the valleys ahead. The horizons never changed. In the vast mountain coldness, the land seemed empty of life. Once, they saw a bird flying far away. Once, further down in the shadowed woods, they heard some creature cry. Otherwise, there was only silence, deep and pervasive and unbroken.

Time dragged, a dying candle, and Bek's spirits lagged. He found himself wondering if there was any sense to what they were doing, if there was a purpose for going on. He understood that it gave them a goal and that movement kept them alive. But the vastness of the range and the terrible solitude it visited on them gave rise to a growing certainty that they were simply prolonging the inevitable. They were never going to walk out of the mountains. They were never going to be able to find anyone else from the doomed company of the *Jerle Shannara*. They were trapped in a nightmare world that would deceive them, break them down, and in the end destroy them.

He was marking out the time that remained to him when a dark speck appeared in the sky to the north, faint and distant. It grew quickly larger, moving swiftly toward them, taking on a familiar look. Recognition flooded through Bek, and the sense of hopelessness that had possessed him only moments earlier fell away like old ashes in a new fire.

By the time Hunter Predd swung Obsidian down to a flat just ahead of them, one whipcord thin arm raised in greeting, Bek was ready to believe that in spite of what he had told Quentin earlier, there might still be a few surprises left.

TWENTY

For nearly a week after taking control of *Black Moclips*, cruising the skies like birds of prey, the Morgawr and his Mwellrets scoured the coastal and mountain regions of Parkasia in search of the *Jerle Shannara* and the remnants of her company. Their efforts were hampered by the weather, which proved exceedingly arbitrary, changing without warning from sun to rain, either of which was as likely to see high winds and downdrafts as calm air. During the worst of the storms, they were forced to land and anchor for almost twenty-four hours, sheltered in a cove off the coast where bluffs and woods offered protection from an onslaught of sleet and hail that otherwise would have leveled them.

During most of this time, Ahren Elessedil languished below-decks in a storeroom that had been converted to a cell. It was the same room that had housed Bek Ohmsford when he was a prisoner of the Ilse Witch, although Ahren did not know this. The Elven Prince was kept alone and apart from everyone save the rets who brought him food or took him on deck for brief periods of exercise. The Morgawr had moved his personal contingent of Mwellrets onto *Black Moclips*, preferring its sleeker design and greater maneuverability to that of the larger, more cumbersome warship he had occupied previously. Reduced to mindless shells, sad remnants of better times, the doomed Aden Kett and his men were left to crew her. Cree Bega was given command. The Morgawr occupied the Commander's quarters, and while they sailed in search of the *Jerle Shannara*, the Elven Prince barely saw him.

He saw even less of Ryer Ord Star. Her absence fueled his already deep mistrust of her, and he found himself reexamining his feelings. He could not decide whether she had forsaken her promise to him and truly allied herself with the Morgawr or if she was playing a game he did not understand. He wanted to believe it was the latter, but try as he might he could not come to terms with her seeming betrayal of him when he was captured or her clear distancing from him since. She had told him in the catacombs of Castledown that she was no longer in thrall to the Ilse Witch, yet she seemed to have become very much the creature of the Morgawr. She had led the warlock on his search for the *Jerle Shannara*. She had directed him to *Black Moclips*. She had stood by while that Federation crew had been systematically reduced to members of the walking dead. She had watched it all as if in a trance, showing nothing of her feelings, as removed from the horror and degradation as if she were absent altogether.

Not once had she tried to make contact with Ahren after they had been brought aboard *Black Moclips*. Nothing had come of the words she'd whispered days earlier. *Trust me*. But why should he? What had she done, even once, to earn that trust? On reflection, the words now seemed to have been whispered to gain his confidence, to assure his compliance at a time when he still might have escaped. Now there was no chance. Aboard an airship, hundreds of feet off the ground, there was nowhere for him to go.

Not that he had any chance of getting beyond the door of his cell in the first place, he reminded himself bitterly, even if they were on the ground. Without the missing Elfstones or weapons of any sort to aid him, he had no hope of overpowering his captors.

Locked away as he was, he had not been witness to most of what had happened during the past few days. But he could tell from the slow and steady pace of the airship that they were still searching. Mostly, he could tell from the unchanging routine of his captors that they had found nothing.

He thought ceaselessly about escape. He imagined it over and over, thinking through the ways in which it could happen, the events that would precipitate it, the ways in which he would react, and the results that would follow. He pictured himself going through the motions—slipping through the door and down the passageway beyond, climbing the stairs to the decks above, crouching low against the mast, and waiting for a chance to gain the railing and go over the side. But in the end the mechanics always failed him and his chances never materialized.

One day, shortly after a storm had grounded them for almost twenty-four hours, he was on deck with Cree Bega when he caught sight of Ryer Ord Star standing at the bow. He was surprised to see her again, and for a moment he forgot himself and stared at her with undisguised longing and hope.

Cree Bega saw that look and recognized it. Touching Ahren lightly on his shoulder, he said, "Sspeakss to her, little Elvess. Tellss her of your feelingss."

The words were an open invitation for him to do something foolish. The Mwellret was suspicious of the seer, as much so as Ahren was. Cree Bega had never been persuaded that her alliance with the Morgawr was genuine. He showed it in his attitude toward her, ignoring her for the most part, making no effort to consult her, even while the Morgawr did so. He was waiting, Ahren judged, for her to reveal her treachery.

"Nothing to ssay, Prince of Elvess?" Cree Bega mocked, his face bent close, the rank smell of him strong in Ahren's nostrils. "Wassn't sshe your friend? Issn't sshe sstill?"

Ahren understood the nature of the questions. He hated himself for his uncertainty, but he stayed silent, bearing the weight of the Mwellret's taunts and his own doubts. Anything he did would reveal truths that would hurt either Ryer or himself. If she responded to him, it would suggest a hidden alliance. If she did not, he would be made even more painfully aware of how things between them had changed. He was too vulnerable for anything so raw just now. It would be smarter to wait.

He turned away. "You talk to her," he muttered.

Another opportunity arose a day later, when he was summoned to the Morgawr's quarters and, on entering, found the seer standing beside him. She had that distant look again, her face empty of expression, as if she was somewhere else entirely in spirit and only her body was present. The Morgawr asked him again about the members of the company of the *Jerle Shannara*—how many had set out, whom they were, where he had last seen them, what their relationship had been to the Druid. He asked again for a head count—how many were still alive. He had asked the questions before, and Ahren gave him the same answers. It was not hard to do so. Dissembling was not necessary. For the most part, he knew less than the Morgawr. Even about Bek, the Morgawr seemed to know as much as Ahren did. He had read the traces of magic left floating on the air in the catacombs of Castledown and knew that Bek had come and gone. He knew that Ahren's friend was still out there, running from the warlock, hiding his sister.

What little the Morgawr hadn't divined, Ryer Ord Star had told him. She had told him everything.

At times while the Morgawr interrogated Ahren, she seemed to come back from wherever she had gone. Her eyes would shift focus, and her hands twitched at her sides. She would become aware of her surroundings, but only momentarily and then she was gone again. The Morgawr did not seem bothered by this, although it caused Ahren no small amount of discomfort. Why wasn't the warlock irritated by her inattention to what he was saying? Why didn't he suspect that she was deliberately isolating herself?

It took Ahren a long time to realize what was really happening. She wasn't distancing herself at all. She was very much a part of the conversation, but in a way the Elven Prince hadn't recognized. She was hearing his words and using them to feed her talent. She was turning those words into images of his friends, trying to project visions of them. She was using him in an attempt to track them down.

He was so stunned by the revelation that for a moment he just stopped talking in midsentence and stared at her. The silence distracted her where his words had not. For a moment, she came back from where her visions had taken her, and she stared back at him.

"Don't do this," he told her softly, unable to conceal his disappointment.

She did not reply, but he could read the anguish in her eyes. The Morgawr immediately ordered him taken back to his cell, an angry and impatient dismissal. He saw his real use then—not as a hostage for negotiation or as a puppet King. Those were uses that could wait. The warlock's needs were more immediate. Ahren would serve him better as a catalyst for Ryer Ord Star's visions, as a trigger that would allow her to help find the Ilse Witch and the others who eluded him. Unsuspecting, naive, the boy would help without even realizing he was doing so.

Except he had realized.

Ahren was locked away once more, closed off in the storeroom and left to celebrate in fierce solitude his small victory. He had foiled the Morgawr's attempt to use him. He sat with his back against the wall of the airship and smiled into his prison.

Yet his elation faded quickly. His victory was a hollow one. Reality surfaced and crowded out wishful thinking. He was still a prisoner with no hope. His friends were still scattered or dead. He was still stranded in a dangerous, faraway land.

Worst of all, Ryer Ord Star had revealed herself to be his enemy.

In the Commander's quarters, the Morgawr paced with the restless intensity of a caged animal. Ryer Ord Star felt the tension radiating from him in dark waves of displeasure. It was unusual for him to display such emotion openly, but his patience with the situation was growing dangerously thin.

"He knows what we are trying to do. Clever boy."

She did not respond. Her thoughts were of Ahren's words and the way he had looked at her. She still heard the anguish in his voice and saw the disappointment in his eyes. Understandably confused and misguided, he had judged her wrongly, and she could do nothing to explain herself. If the situation had been bad before, it was spiraling out of control now.

The Morgawr stopped in front of the door, his back to her. "He has become useless to me."

She stiffened, her mind racing. "I don't need his cooperation."

"He will lie. He will dissemble. He will throw in enough waste that it will color anything good. I can't trust him anymore." He turned around slowly. "Nor am I sure about you, little seer."

She met his gaze and held it, letting him look into her eyes. If he believed she hid something, the game was over and he would kill her now.

"I've given you nothing but the truth," she said.

His dark, reptilian face showed nothing of what he was thinking, but his eyes were dangerous. "Then tell me what you have learned just now."

She knew he was testing her, offering her a chance to demonstrate that she was still useful. Ahren had been right about the game they were playing. She was feeding off his words and emotions in response to the Morgawr's questions in an effort to trigger a vision that would reveal something about the missing members of the company of the *Jerle Shannara*. He had been wrong about her intentions, but there was no way she could tell him that. The Morgawr must believe she could help him find the Ilse Witch. He must not begin to doubt that she was his willing ally in his search, or all of her plans to help Walker would fall apart.

She took a small step toward the warlock, a conscious act of defiance, a gesture that nearly took her breath away with the effort it cost her. "I saw the Ilse Witch and her brother surrounded by mountains. They were not alone. There were others with them, but their faces were hidden in shadow. They were walking. I did not see it, but I sensed an airship somewhere close. There were cliffs filled with Shrike nests. One of those cliffs looked like a spear with its tip broken off, sharp edged and thrust skyward. There was the smell of the ocean and the sound of waves breaking on the shore."

She stopped talking and waited, her eyes locked on his. She was telling him of a vision Ahren's words had triggered, but twisting the details just enough to keep him from finding what he sought.

She held her breath. If he could read the deception in her eyes and find in its shadings the truth of things, she was dead.

He studied her for a long time without moving or speaking, a stone face wrapped in cloak and shadow.

"They are on the coast?" he asked finally, his voice empty of expression.

She nodded. "The vision suggests so. But the vision is not always what I think it is."

His smile chilled her. "Things seldom are, little seer."

"What matters is that Ahren Elessedil's words generated these images," she insisted. "Without them, I would have nothing."

"In which case, I would have no further need of either of you, would I?" he asked. One hand lifted and gestured toward her almost languidly. "Or need of either of you if he can no longer be trusted to speak the truth, isn't that so?"

The echo of his words hung in the air, an indictment she knew she must refute. "I do not need him to speak the truth in order to interpret my visions," she said.

It was a lie, but it was all she had. She spoke it with conviction and held the warlock's dark gaze even when she could feel the harm he intended her penetrating through to her soul.

After a long moment, the Morgawr shrugged. "Then we must let him live a little longer. We must give him another chance."

He said it convincingly, but she could tell he was lying. He had made up his mind about Ahren as surely as Ahren had made up his mind about her. The Morgawr no longer believed in either of them, she suspected, but particularly in the Elven Prince. He might try using Ahren once more, but then he would surely get rid of him. He had neither time nor patience for recalcitrant prisoners. What he demanded of this land, of its secrets and magic, lay elsewhere. His disenchantment with Ahren would grow, and eventually it would devour them both.

Dismissed from his presence without the need for words, she left him and went back on deck. She climbed the stairs at the end of the companionway and walked forward to the bow. With her hands grasping the railing to steady herself, she stared at the horizon, at the vast sweep of mountains and forests, at banks of broken clouds and bands of sunlight. The day was sliding toward nightfall, the light beginning to fade west, the dark to rise east.

She closed her eyes when her picture of the world was clear in her mind, and she let her thoughts drift. She must do something to save the Elven Prince. She had not believed it would be necessary to act so soon, but it now seemed unavoidable. That she was committed to Walker's plan for the Morgawr did not require committing Ahren, as well. His destiny lay elsewhere, beyond this country and its treacheries, home in the Four Lands, where his blood heritage would serve a different purpose. She had caught a glimmer of it in the visions she had shared with Walker. She knew it from what the Druid had said as he lay dying. She could feel it in her heart.

Just as she could feel with unmistakable certainty the fate that awaited her.

She breathed slowly and deeply to calm herself, to muster acceptance of what she knew she must do. Walker needed her to mislead the Morgawr, to slow him in his hunt, to buy time for Grianne Ohmsford. It was not something the Druid had asked lightly; it was something he had asked out of desperate need and a faith in her abilities. She felt small and frail in the face of such expectations, a child in a girl's body, her womanhood yet so far away that she could not imagine it. Her seer's mind did not allow for growing up in the ways of other women; it was her mind that was old. Yet she was capable and determined. She was the Druid's right hand, and he was always with her, lending his strength.

She held that knowledge to her like a talisman as she made her plans.

When nightfall descended, she acted on them.

She waited until all of the Mwellrets were sleeping, save the watch and the helmsman. *Black Moclips* sailed through the night skies at a slow, languorous pace, tracking the edge of the coastline north and east as Ryer Ord Star slipped from her makeshift bed in the lee of the aft decking and made her way forward. Aden Kett and his crew stood at their stations, dead eyes staring. She glanced at them as she passed, but her gaze did not linger. It was dangerous to look too closely at your own fate.

The airship rocked gently in the cradle of night winds blowing out of the west. The chill brought by the storms had not dissipated, and her breath clouded faintly. Below where they flew, where the tips of the mountain peaks brushed the clouds, snow blanketed the barren slopes. The warmth that had greeted them on their arrival into this land was gone, chased inland by some aberration linked to the demise of Antrax. That science had found a way to control the weather seemed incredible to her, but she knew that in the age before the Great Wars there had been many marvelous achievements that had since disappeared from the world. Yet magic had replaced science in the Four Lands. It made her wonder sometimes if the demise of science was for the better or worse. It made her wonder if the place of seers in the world had any real value.

She reached the open hatchway leading down into the storerooms and descended in shadowy silence, listening for the sounds of the guard who would be on watch below. Walker would not approve of what she was doing. He would have tried to stop her if he had been able. He would have counseled her to remain safe and concentrate on the task he had given her. But Walker saw things through the eyes of a man seeking to achieve in death what he had failed to achieve in life. He was a shade, and his reach beyond the veil was limited. He might know of the Ilse Witch and her role in the destiny of the Four Lands, of the reasons she must escape the Morgawr, and of the path she must take to come back from the place to which her troubled mind had sent her. But Ryer Ord Star only knew that time was slipping away.

The passageway belowdecks was shadowed, but she made her way easily through its gloom. She heard snores ahead, and she knew the Mwellret watch was sleeping. The potion she had slipped into his evening ale ration earlier had drugged him as thoroughly as anything this side of death. It had not been all that hard to accomplish. The danger lay in another of the rets discovering the guard to be asleep before she could reach Ahren.

At the door to his storeroom jail, she took possession of the keys from the sleeping ret and released the lock, all the while listening for the sounds of those who would put an end to her undertaking. She said nothing as she opened the door and slipped inside, a wraithlike presence. Ahren rose to face her, hesitating as he realized who it was, not certain what to make of her appearance. He kept silent, though—harking to the finger she put to her lips and her furtive movements as she came over to release him from his chains. Even in the dim cabin light, she could see the uncertainty and suspicion in his eyes, but there could be no mistaking her actions. Without attempting to intervene, he let her free him and followed her without argument when she was ready to leave, stepping over the sleeping guard where he was sprawled across the passageway, creeping behind her as she moved back toward the stairs leading up. *Black Moclips* rocked slowly, a cradle for sleeping men and a drowsy watch. The only sounds were those of the ship, the small, familiar stretchings and tightenings of seams and caulk.

They went up the stairs and emerged behind the helmsman, flattening themselves against the decking, scooting along the shadow of the aft rise and across to the rail. Wordlessly, she slipped over the side and crossed down the narrow gangway to the starboard pontoon, sliding swiftly to the furthest aft fighting port, a six-foot-deep compartment stacked with pieces of sail and sections of cross beam.

Cloaked in deep shadows, she moved to where the pontoon curved upward to form the aft starboard battering ram. She felt along the inside of the structure and released a wooden latch hidden in the surface of the hull. Instantly, a panel dropped down on concealed hinges. She reached inside and drew out a framework of flexible poles to which sections of lightweight canvas had been attached.

She passed the framework and canvas forward to Ahren, where he crouched at the front of the fighting port, then moved up beside him.

"This is called a single wing," she whispered, her head bent close to his, her long silvery hair brushing the side of his face. "It is a sort of kite, built to fly one man off a failing airship. Redden Alt Mer had it hidden in the hull for emergencies." She reached up impulsively and touched his cheek.

"You never intended to help him, did you?" the Elven Prince whispered back, relief and happiness reflected in his voice.

"I had to save your life and mine, as well. That meant giving your identity away. He would have killed you otherwise." She took a deep breath. "He intends to kill you now. He thinks you're of no further use. I can't protect you anymore. You have to get off the ship tonight."

He shook his head at once, gripping her arm. "Not without you. I won't go without you."

He said it with such vehemence, with such desperate insistence, that it made her want to cry. He had doubted her and was trying to make up for it in the only way he knew. If it was called for, he would give up his life for hers.

"It isn't time for me to go yet," she said. "I made a promise to Walker to lead the Morgawr astray in his hunt. He thinks I intend to help, but I give him only just enough to keep him believing so. I'll come later."

She saw the uncertainty in his eyes and gestured sharply toward the single wing. "Quit arguing with me! Take this and go. Now! Unfold it, tie the harness in place, and lean out from the side with the wings extended. Use the bar and straps at the ends to steer. It isn't hard. Here, I'll help."

He shook his head, his eyes wondering. "How did you know about this?"

"Walker told me." She began undoing the straps that secured the framework, shaking it loose. "He learned about it from Big Red. The rets don't know of it. There, it's ready. Climb up on the edge of the pontoon and strap yourself in!"

He did as she instructed, still clearly dazed by what was happening, not yet able to think it through completely enough to see its flaws. She just had to get him off the ship and into the air, and then it would be too late. Things would be decided, insofar as she was able to make it so. That was as much as she could manage.

"You should come now," he argued, still trying to find a way to take her with him.

She shook her head. "No. Later. Fly inland from the coast when you get further north. Look for a rain forest in the heart of the mountains. That's where the others are, on a cliff overlooking it. My visions showed them to me."

He shrugged into the shoulder harness, and she cinched it tight across his back. She opened the wing frame so that it would catch the wind and showed him the steering bar and control straps. She glanced over her shoulder every few seconds toward the deck above, but the Mwellrets were not yet looking her way.

"Ryer," he began, turning toward her once more.

"Here," she said, reaching into her thin robes and extracting a pouch. She shoved it into his tunic, deep down inside so that it was snugged away. "The Elfstones," she whispered.

He stared at her in disbelief. "But how could you have—"

"Go!" she hissed, shoving him off the side of the pontoon and into space.

She watched the wind catch the canvas and draw the framework taut. She watched the single wing soar out into the darkness. She caught a quick glimpse of the Elven Prince's wondering face, saw the man he had become eclipse the boy she had begun her journey with, and then he was gone.

"Good-bye, Ahren Elessedil," she whispered into the night.

The words floated on the air feather-light and fading even as she turned away, alone now for good.

TWENTY-ONE

A hand shook his shoulder gently, and Bek Ohmsford stirred awake.

"If you sleep any longer, people will think you're dead," a familiar voice said.

He opened his eyes and blinked against the sunlight pouring out of the midday sky. Rue Meridian moved into the light, blocking it away, and stared down at him, a hint of irony in the faint twist of her pursed lips. Just seeing her warmed him in a way the sun never could and made him smile in turn.

"I *feel* like I'm dead," he said. He lay stretched out on the deck of the *Jerle Shannara*, cocooned in blankets. He took in the railings of the airship and the mast jutting skyward overhead as he gathered his thoughts. "How long have I been asleep?"

"Since this time yesterday. How do you feel?"

His memories of the past week flooded back as he considered the question. His flight out of Castledown with Grianne and Truls Rohk. Their struggle to escape the pursuit of the Morgawr and his creatures. The battle with the caull. Truls, dying. Their encounter with the shape-shifters and the lifesaving transformation of his friend. Climbing with Grianne into the mountains, trusting that they would somehow find their way. Finding Quentin after so long, a miracle made possible because of a promise made to a dead man.

And then, when it seemed the mountains would swallow them whole, another miracle, as Hunter Predd, searching for the *Jerle Shannara*'s lost children, plucked them off the precipice and carried them away.

"I feel better than I did when I was brought here," Bek said. He took a deep, satisfying breath. "I feel better than I have in a long time." He took a good look at her, noting the raw marks on her face and the splint on her left arm. "What happened to you? Been wrestling with moor cats again?"

She cocked her head. "Maybe."

"You're hurt."

"Cuts and bruises. A broken arm and a few broken ribs. Nothing that won't heal." She punched him lightly. "I could have used your help."

"I could have used yours."

"Missed me, did you?"

She tossed the question out casually, as if his answer didn't mean anything. But he knew it did. For just an instant he was convinced it meant everything, that she wanted him to tell her she was important to him in a way that went beyond friendship. It was an improbable and foolish notion, but he couldn't shake it. Anyway, he liked the idea and didn't question it.

"Okay, I missed you," he said.

"Good." She bent down suddenly and kissed his lips. It was just a quick brush followed by a touching of his cheek with her fingers, and then she lifted away again. "I missed you, too. Know why?"

He stared at her. "No."

"I didn't think so. I only just figured it out for myself. Maybe with enough time, you will, too. You're pretty good at figuring things out, even for a boy." She gave him an ironic, mocking smile, but it wasn't meant to hurt and it didn't. "I hear you can do magic. I hear you're not who you thought you were. Life is full of surprises."

"Do you want me to explain?"

"If you want to."

"I do. But first I want you to tell me how you got all beat up. I want to hear what happened."

"This," she said sardonically, and she gestured at the airship. "This and a lot of other catastrophes."

He lifted himself on one elbow and looked around. The *Jerle Shannara*'s decks stretched away in a jumble of makeshift patches and unfinished repairs. A new mast had been cut and shaped and set in place; he could tell from the new wood and fresh metal banding. Railings had been spliced in and damaged planks in the hull and decks replaced. Radian draws hung limply from cross beams and sails lay half mended. No one was in sight.

"They've deserted us," she advised, as if reading his thoughts.

He could hear voices nearby, faint and indistinguishable. "How long have you been here?"

"Almost a week."

He blinked in disbelief. "You can't fly?"

"Can't get off the ground at all."

"So we're trapped. How many of us are left?"

She shrugged. "A handful. Big Red, Black Beard, the Highlander, you, and me. Three of the crew. The two Wing Riders. Panax and an Elven Hunter. The Wing Riders found them yesterday, not too far from here, with a tribe of natives called Rindge. They're camped at the top of the bluff."

"Ahren?" he asked.

She shook her head. "Nor the seer. Nor anyone else who went ashore. They're all dead or lost." She looked away. "The Wing Riders are still searching, but so are those airships with their rets and walking dead. It's dangerous to fly anywhere in these mountains now. Not that we could, even if we wanted to."

He looked at the airship, then back at her. "Where's Grianne? Is she all right?"

The smile faded from Rue Meridian's face. "Grianne? Oh, yes, your missing sister. She's down below, in Big Red's cabin, staring at nothing. She's good at that."

He held her gaze. "I know that—"

"You don't know anything," she interrupted, her voice oddly breezy. "Not one thing." She pushed back loose strands of her long red hair, and he could see the dangerous look in her green eyes. "I never thought I would find myself in a position where I would have to keep that creature alive, let alone look after her. I would have put a knife to her throat and been done with it, but you were raving so loudly about keeping her safe that I didn't have much of a choice."

"I appreciate what you've done."

Her lips tightened. "Just tell me you have a good reason for all this. Just tell me that."

"I have a reason," he said. "I don't know yet how good it is."

Bek told her everything then, all that had happened since he had left the *Jerle Shannara* weeks earlier and gone inland with Walker and the shore party. Some she already knew, because Quentin had told her. Some she had suspected. She had guessed at his imprisonment aboard *Black Moclips* and subsequent escape, but she had not realized the true reason for either. She was skeptical and angry with him, refusing at first to listen to his reasons for saving his sister, shouting at him that it didn't matter, that saving her was wrong, that she was responsible for all the deaths suffered by the company, especially Hawk's.

Rue told Bek her story then, relating the details of her imprisonment along with the other Rovers by the witch and her followers, and of her escape and battle aboard the *Jerle Shannara*, where Hawk had given his life to save hers. She told him of her struggle to regain control of the ship and the freeing of her brother. She told him of her search for Walker and the missing company, which led in turn to her regaining possession of *Black Moclips* and fleeing inland toward the safety of the mountains as the fleet of enemy airships pursued her. She told her story in straightforward fashion, making no effort to embellish her part in things, diminishing it, if anything.

He listened patiently, trying with small gestures to encourage and support, but she was having none of it. She hated Grianne to such an extent that she could find no forgiveness in her heart. That she had kept his sister alive at all spoke volumes about her affection for him. Losing Furl Hawken had been a terrible blow, and she held Grianne directly responsible. Rue Meridian refused to let Bek sit by passively, turning her anger and disappointment back on him, insisting that he respond to it. He did so as best he could, even though he was not comfortable doing so. So much had happened to both of them in such a short time that there was no coming to grips with all of it, no making sense of it in a way that would afford either of them any measure of peace. Both had suffered too many losses and were seeking comfort that required different responses from what each was willing to provide. Where the Ilse Witch was concerned, there could be no agreement.

Finally, Bek put up his hands. "I can't argue this anymore, not right now. It hurts too much to argue with you."

She snorted derisively. "It hurts you, maybe. Not me. I don't bruise so easily. Anyway, you owe me a little consideration. You owe me a chance to tell you what I think about your sister! You owe it to me to share some of what I feel!"

"I'm doing the best I can."

She reached down suddenly and hauled him all the way out of the blankets and shook him hard. "No, you're not! I don't want you to just sit there! I don't want you to just listen! I want you to do something! Don't you know that?"

Her red hair had shaken loose of its headband and strands of it were wrapped about her face like tiny threads of blood. "Don't you know anything?"

Her eyes had gone wild and reckless, and she seemed on the verge of doing something desperate. She stopped shaking him, instead gripping his shoulders so tightly he could feel her nails through his clothing. She was trying to speak, to say something more, but couldn't seem to make herself do so.

"I'm sorry about Hawk," he whispered. "I'm sorry it was Grianne. But she didn't know. She doesn't know anything. She's like a child, locked away in her mind, frightened of coming out again. Don't you see, Rue? She had to face up to what she is all at once. That's what the magic of the Sword of Shannara does to you. She had to accept that she was this terrible creature, this monster, and she didn't even know it. Her whole life has been filled with lies and deceits and treacheries. I don't know—she may never be made whole."

Rue Meridian stared at him as if he were someone she had never seen. There were tears in her eyes and a look of such anguish on her face that he was stunned.

"I'm tired, Bek," she whispered back. "I haven't even thought about it until now. I haven't had time for that. I haven't taken time." She wiped at her eyes with her sleeve. "Look at me."

He did so, having never looked away, in truth, but giving her what she needed, trying to find a way to help her recover. He said, "I just want you to try to . . ."

"Put your arms around me, Bek," she said.

He did so without hesitation, holding her against him, feeling her body press close. She began to cry, soundlessly, her shoulders shaking and her wet face pushing into the crook of his shoulder and neck. She cried for a long time, and he held her while she did, running his hand over her strong back in small circular motions, trying to give some measure of comfort and reassurance. It was so out of character for her to behave like this, so different from anything he had seen from her before, that it took him until she was finished to accept that it was really happening.

She brushed what remained of the tears from her face and

composed herself with a small shrug. "I didn't know I had that in me." She looked at him. "Don't tell anyone."

He nodded. "I wouldn't do that. You know I wouldn't."

"I know. But I had to say it." She stared at him a moment, again with that sense of not knowing exactly who he was, of perhaps meeting him for the first time. "My brother and the others are down at the edge of the bluff, talking. We can join them when you're ready."

He climbed to his feet, reaching for his boots. "Talking about what?"

"About what it's going to take to get us out of here."

"What *is* it going to take?"

"A miracle," she said.

Redden Alt Mer stood at the edge of the cliff face and stared down at the canopy of the Crake Rain Forest, very much the same way he had stared down at it for the previous five days. Nothing at all had changed during that time, save for the level of his frustration, which was rapidly becoming unmanageable. He had considered and reconsidered every option he could think of that would let him bypass the Graak and retrieve the diapson crystals they needed to get airborne again. But each option involved unacceptable risks and little chance of success, so he would toss it aside in despair, only to pick it up and reexamine it when he decided that every other alternative was even worse.

All the while, time was slipping away. They hadn't been discovered by the airships of the Morgawr yet, but sooner or later they would be. One had passed close enough yesterday for them to identify its dark silhouette from the ground, and even though they hadn't been spotted on that pass they likely would be on the next. If Hunter Predd and Po Kelles were right, there were only one or two this deep into the Aleuthra Ark; the bulk of the fleet was still searching for them out on the coast. When that effort failed to turn them up, the fleet would sail inland. If that happened and they were still grounded, they were finished.

Still, for the first time since the *Jerle Shannara* had crashed, he had reason to hope.

He glanced over at Quentin Leah. The Highlander was staring down into the Crake with a puzzled look on his lean, battle-damaged face. The look was a reflection of his inability to imagine what waited down there, having not as yet seen the Graak. No one had, except for himself. That was part of the problem, of course. He knew what they were up against, and although the others—Rovers and newcomers alike—might be willing to go down into the rain forest and face it, he was not. What had happened to Tian Cross and Rucker Bont was still fresh in his mind. He did not care to risk losing more lives. He did not want any more deaths on his conscience.

It was more than that, though. He could admit it to himself, if to no one else. He was afraid. It had been a long time—so long he could not remember the last occasion—since he had been frightened of anything. But he was frightened of the Graak. He felt it in his blood. He smelled it on his skin. It visited him in his dreams and brought him awake wide-eyed and shaking. He could not rid himself of it. Watching his men die, seeing them go down under the teeth and claws of that monster, feeling his own death so close to him that he could imagine his bones and blood spattered all over the valley floor, had unnerved him. Though he tried to tell himself his fear was only temporary and would give way to his experience and determination, he could not be sure.

He knew the only way to rid himself of this feeling was to go down into the Crake and face the Graak.

He was about to do that.

"I won't ask you to go with me," he said to Quentin Leah without looking at him.

"He won't ask, but he'll make it plain enough that he expects it," Spanner Frew snorted. "And then he'll find a way to make you end up thinking it was your idea!"

Alt Mer gave the shipwright a dark look, then smirked in spite of himself. Something about the other amused him even now—the perpetually dour look, the furrowed brow, the cantankerous attitude, something. Spanner Frew always saw the glass as half-empty, and he was ready and more than willing to share his worldview with anyone close enough to listen.

"Keep your opinions to yourself, Black Beard," he said, brushing a fly from his face. "Others don't find them so amusing. The Highlander is free to do as he chooses, as are all of us in this business."

Quentin Leah was looking better this morning, less ghostly and wooden than the day before when he was brought in with Bek and the witch. Alt Mer was still getting used to the idea of having her around, but he wasn't having as much trouble with it as his sister. Little Red hated the witch, and she was not likely to forgive her anytime soon for Hawk's death. Maybe having Bek back would help, though. She'd been upset at the thought of losing him, more so than by anything for a long time. He didn't understand the affection she felt for Bek, but was quick enough to recognize it for what it was.

He sighed. At any rate, there were more of them now than there had been three days ago, after Rucker and Tian had died. Down to only six, the Rovers had seen their numbers strengthened since. The Wing Riders had reappeared first, flying out of the clouds on a blustery day in which rain had soaked everything for nearly twelve hours. After that, Po Kelles had found Panax, the Elven Hunter Kian, and those odd-looking reddish people they called Rindge. It had taken the Rindge another two days of travel to reach them, but now they were camped several miles east in a forested flat high in the mountains, concealed from searchers while they waited to see what would happen down here.

Their leader, the man Panax called Obat, was the one who told them that the valley was called the Crake. He knew about the thing that lived there, as well. Obat hadn't seen it, but when Panax brought him down to talk, and Alt Mer described it, he recognized it right away. He had gotten so excited that it looked as if he might bolt. Hand gestures and a flurry of words that even Panax had trouble translating testified to the extent of Obat's fear. It was clear that whatever anyone else did, neither Obat nor any other Rindge was going near whatever was down there—"A Graak," Obat told Panax over and over again. The rest of what he said had something to do with the nature of the beast, of its invincibility and domination of mountain valleys like the Crake, where it preyed on creatures who were foolish or unwary enough to venture too close.

Knowing what it was didn't help solve the problem, because Obat had no idea what they could do about the thing. Graaks were to be avoided, never confronted. His information did not aid Alt Mer in any measurable way. If anything, it further convinced him of his helplessness. What was needed was magic of the sort possessed by Walker.

Or by Quentin Leah perhaps, in the form of his sword, a weapon that had been effective against the creepers of Antrax.

But he could not say anything more to persuade the Highlander to help. If anything, he should advise against it. But then he would have to go into the Crake alone, and he did not think he could do that. Though he was a brave man, his courage had eroded so completely that he felt sick to his stomach even getting close enough to look down into the rain forest. He had concealed his fear from everyone, but it was there nevertheless—pervasive, inescapable, and debilitating. He couldn't confess it, especially to Little Red. It wasn't that she wouldn't understand or try to help. It was the look he knew he would see in her eyes. He was the brother on whom she had always relied and in whom she took such pride. He could not bear it if she found out that he had run away while his men were dying.

The Highlander looked over at him. "All right, I'll go."

Big Red exhaled slowly, keeping his face expressionless.

"I'll go," Quentin Leah continued, "but Bek stays. Whatever magic he's got is new to him, and he doesn't have the experience with it that I do. I won't risk his life."

Whatever magic the Highlander possessed was pretty new to him, too, from what the Druid had told Alt Mer. Still, he wasn't about to argue the matter. He would take whatever help he was offered if it meant getting his hands on the diapson crystals. He didn't know what they had accomplished by coming here in the first place, but he didn't think it was much. Mostly, they had succeeded in getting a lot of their friends killed, which was hardly a reason for going anywhere. You didn't have to come all the way here to get killed. His frustration with matters surfaced once more. He would do anything to get out of this place.

Before he could respond to the Highlander, Rue and Bek Ohmsford walked out of the trees from one side and Panax, having gone off earlier to try to find an easier way down the cliff face, appeared from the other.

"Morning, young Bek!" the Dwarf shouted cheerfully on spying him. A grin spread across his square, bluff face, and he gave a wave of one hand. "Back among the living, I see! You look much better today!"

Bek waved back. "You look about the same, but that's not something sleep will cure!"

They came together at the cliff edge with Spanner Frew, Quentin, and Alt Mer and clasped hands. The Highlander's face had gone dark as he realized what was about to happen and knew he couldn't prevent it. Alt Mer gave a mental shrug. Some things couldn't be helped. At least his sister seemed composed again. Almost radiant. He stared at her in surprise, but she wouldn't look at him.

"I've scouted the cliff edge all the way out and back," Panax informed them, oblivious to the Highlander's look of warning. "There's a trail further on, not much of one, but enough to give us a way down that doesn't involve ropes. It opens onto a flat, so we'll be able to see what's waiting much better than Big Red could when he dropped into the trees."

He glanced at Bek. "I forgot. You just woke up. You don't know what's happened."

"About the Graak and the crystals?" Bek asked. "I know. I heard all about it on the walk down. When do we leave?"

"No!" Rue Meridian wheeled on him furiously. "You're not going! You're not healed yet!"

"She's right," Quentin Leah said, glaring at his cousin. "What's wrong with you? I just spent weeks worrying that you were dead! I'm not going through that again! You stay up here. Big Red and I can handle this."

"Wait a minute," Panax growled. "What about me?"

"You're not going either!" Quentin snapped. "Two of us is enough to risk."

The Dwarf cocked one eyebrow. "Have you suddenly gotten so much better at staying alive than the rest of us?"

Bek glared at Quentin. "What makes you think you have the right to decide if I go or not? I decide what's right for me, not you! Why would I agree to stay up here? What about our promise to look out for each other?"

"Well, I'm going if you're going!" Rue Meridian spat out the words defiantly. "I'm the one who's done the best job of looking out for everyone so far! You're not leaving me behind! No one's leaving me!" She shifted her angry gaze from one to the next. "Which one of you wants to try to stop me?"

They were face-to-face now, all of them, so angry they could barely make themselves stop shouting long enough to hear what anyone else was saying. Spanner Frew was quiet, his dark face lowered to hide the grin on his lips, his head shaking slowly from side to side. Alt Mer listened in dismay, wondering when to step in and if it would make any difference if he did.

Finally, he'd heard enough. "Stop shouting!" he roared.

They quit arguing and looked at him, faces red and sweating in the midday heat.

He shook his head slowly. "The Druid is dead, so I command this expedition. Both aboard ship and off. That means I decide who goes."

His eyes settled momentarily on Bek—Bek, who looked taller and stronger than he remembered, more mature. He wasn't a boy anymore, the Rover Captain realized in surprise. When had that happened? He glanced quickly at his sister, suddenly seeing things in a new light. She was staring at him as if she wanted to jump down his throat.

He looked away again quickly, out over the valley, out to where his fears were centered. He wondered again why he had come all this way. Money? Yes, that was a part of the agreement. But there had been a need to escape the Prekkendorran and the Federation, as well. There had been a need to see a new country, to journey to somewhere he hadn't been. There had been a need for renewal.

"There's not that many of us left," he said, more quietly now. "Just a handful, and we have to look out for each other. Arguing is a waste of time and energy. Only one thing is important, and that's getting back into the skies and flying out of here."

He didn't wait for their response. "Little Red, you stay here. If anything happens to me, you're the only one who can fly the *Jerle Shannara* home again. Bek might try, but he doesn't know how to navigate. Besides, you're all beat up. Broken ribs, broken arm—if you have to defend yourself down there, you'll be in trouble. I don't want to have to worry about saving you. So you stay."

She was furious. "You're worried about saving me? Who was it who got you out of the Federation prison? Who was it who . . ."

"Rue."

". . . got *Black Moclips* back from the rets and would have kept her, too, with just a little help? What about Black Beard? Standing there with his head down and his mouth shut, hoping no one will remember he can sail an airship just as well as I can! Don't say a word about it, Spanner! Don't say anything that might help me!"

"Rue."

"No! It isn't fair! He can navigate just as well as I can! You can't tell me not to go just because I—"

"Rue!" His voice would have melted iron. "Four of us are risk enough. You stay."

"Then Bek stays with me! He's injured, too!"

Alt Mer stared at her. What was she talking about? Bek wasn't her concern. "Not like you. Besides, we might need his magic."

She glared at him for a moment, and he could see she was on the verge of breaking down. He had never seen her do that, never even seen her come close. For a moment, he reconsidered his decision, realizing that something about this was more important than what her words were telling him.

But before he could say anything, she wheeled away and stalked back toward the airship, rigid with anger and frustration. "Fine!" she shouted over her shoulder. "Do what you want! You're all fools!"

He watched her disappear into the trees, thinking that was that, there was nothing he could do about it. Anyway, his next confrontation was already at hand. If Rue Meridian was angry, Quentin Leah was livid. "I told you I wouldn't go if Bek went! Did you think I didn't mean it?" He could barely bring himself to speak. "Tell him he can't go, Big Red. Tell him, or I'm not going."

Bek started to speak, but Alt Mer held up his hand to silence him. "I can't do that, Highlander. I'm sorry things didn't work out the way you wanted, but I can't change that, so threats are meaningless. Bek has the right to decide for himself what he wants to do. So do you. If you don't want to go, you don't have to."

There was a long silence as the Rover and the Highlander stared each other down. There was a dangerous edge to Quentin Leah, as if nothing much mattered to him anymore. Alt Mer couldn't know what Quentin had gone through to get clear of Castledown and find them, but it must have been horrendous and it had left him scarred.

"I'm sorry, Highlander," he said, not knowing what he was sorry about, save for the look he saw in the other's eyes.

"Quentin," Bek interjected quietly, laying one hand on his shoulder. "Don't let's argue like this."

"You can't go, Bek."

"Of course I can. I have to. We promised to look out for each other from here on, remember? We made that promise only a day or so ago. That meant something to me. It should mean something to you. This is when we have to make it count. Please."

Quentin stayed silent for a moment, looking so desperate that Alt Mer wouldn't have been surprised at anything he did. Then Quentin shook his head and put his hand over Bek's. "All right. I don't like it, but all right. We'll both go."

They stood looking at each another for a moment, aware that Quentin's words had made final their commitment to undertake a task that on balance was far too dangerous even to consider. Yet it was only the latest in a long line, and their decision to take this one, as well, no longer had the edge to it that it might have had once. Gambling with their lives had become commonplace.

"We'll need a plan," Panax said.

Big Red glanced over his shoulder in search of his sister. She was out of sight now, and he wished suddenly that they hadn't left things as they had between them.

"I have one," he said.

The Dwarf stared down into the leafy depths of the Crake. "When do we do this?"

Alt Mer considered. The sun had eased westward, but most of the afternoon light still remained, and the sky was clear. It would not get dark for hours.

"We do it now," he said.

TWENTY-TWO

Quentin Leah was not in the least mollified by Big Red's and Bek's attempts to justify Bek's foolhardy decision to brave the Graak. It did not matter what reasoning they used, the Highlander could not help feeling that this would end badly. He knew it wasn't his place to tell Bek not to come with them. He knew that none of them thought him any better qualified than they were to judge the nature of the danger they would face. If anyone had the right to do so, in fact, it was Redden Alt Mer, who had already done battle with the creature and lived to tell about it.

Nevertheless, Quentin saw himself as the one they should listen to. Panax and Alt Mer were both battle-tested and experienced in the Four Lands, but neither had survived the challenges in Parkasia that he had. He knew more of this world than they did. He had a better feel for it. More to the point, he had the use of magic that they did not, which in all probability was going to make the difference between whether they lived or died.

Bek had magic, too, but he had used it sparingly and only on creepers—on things metal and impersonal—and he had not done all that much of that. Mostly, he had gotten through because he'd had Truls Rohk to protect him and Walker to advise him. He had not fought against something like the Graak. It was not going to be the same experience for him, and Quentin wasn't at all sure his cousin was ready for it.

As they made their way along the bluff toward the pathway into the valley, he trailed the others, stewing in silence and thinking about what they were going to do and how best to protect them while they were doing it. If Big Red and two of his most seasoned Rovers had been dispatched so easily, there wasn't much hope that things would change without help from the Sword of Leah. He would use it, of course. He would employ it as he had against the Ard Patrinell wronk. Maybe it would even be enough. But he wasn't sure. He had no idea how strong the Graak was. He knew it was bigger than anything he had ever encountered in the Highlands, and that was cause enough for concern. He could not be certain how well his talisman would protect them until he saw for himself what he was up against. As with all magic, the effectiveness of the sword depended on the strength of the user—not only physical, but emotional, as well. Once, he had thought himself equal to anything. He had felt the power of the magic race through him like fire, and he hadn't thought there was anything he couldn't overcome.

He knew better now. He knew there were limits to everything, even the euphoric rush of the magic's summoning and the infusion of its power. Events and losses had drained him of his confidence. He had fought too long and too often to feel eager about this. He was bone-weary and sick at heart. He had watched those around him die too quickly, more often than not helpless to prevent it. He mourned them still—Tamis and Ard Patrinell, in particular. Their faces haunted him with a persistence that time and acceptance had failed to diminish.

Perhaps that was the problem here, he thought. He was afraid of losing someone else he cared about. Bek, certainly, but Redden Alt Mer and Panax, as well. He did not think he could bear that. Not after what he had been through these past few weeks. Bek and he had agreed only a day ago that they must look out for each other as they had promised, that they needed to do so if they were to get home again safely. But the truth of the matter was that he was the one who should be shouldering the larger share of the burden. He was the older and more experienced. He was physically and emotionally tougher than Bek. It might be true that Bek's magic was the stronger; Tamis had made it sound as if it was. But it was the strength of the user that mattered. Although Bek had gotten the *Jerle Shannara* through the Squirm and had managed to get control of his sister, neither of those achievements was going to help him in a confrontation with the Graak.

Quentin did not deceive himself into thinking that his own strength would prove sufficient for what lay ahead. He thought only that of the two, he had the better chance of getting the job done.

But there was no way of convincing his three companions that this was so, especially Bek, so he would have to do what he could in spite of them. That meant putting himself at the forefront of whatever danger they encountered and giving the others a chance to escape when escape was the only reasonable option.

Given the nature of the plan that Big Red had devised, Quentin did not think it would be that difficult for him to arrange. They needed only to get close enough to the crate of diapson crystals to get three or four of them in hand. More would be better, but if recovery of just those few was all they could manage, that would be sufficient. Three would get the *Jerle Shannara* airborne once more. A lack of spares might prove a problem later on, but staying alive in the here and now was a much bigger and more immediate concern.

So the four would make for the clearing where the crate lay waiting, searching as they went for any sign of the Graak. With luck, it would have gone elsewhere by now, lured away by its need for food or by some other attraction. If it was gone, this would be easy. If it was lying in wait, then it was up to Quentin and Bek to slow it down long enough for Big Red and Panax to gather up the crystals and regain the trail leading up. Bek had only the magic of the wishsong to rely on, and he was honest enough to admit he was not certain of his command of it, or of its effectiveness. That meant Quentin, who was sure where the Sword of Leah was concerned, was the front line of defense for all of them.

With that in mind, and unable to press further his demand that his cousin remain behind, he had at least managed to persuade him to stay a few paces back on their advance into the rain forest to give Quentin room to intervene if they were attacked.

None of which changed the fact that he was feeling much the same way he had felt going into the ruins at Castledown. There had to be more to this business of the Graak than he was seeing. He was missing something. He didn't know what it was, but he knew it was there. His hunting skills and instincts were screaming at him that he was overlooking something obvious.

They reached the trailhead and started down. The valley swept away below them, a vast carpet of leaves and vines, all tangled in a profusion of greens and browns. From high up, the jungle had the appearance of a bottomless swamp where the unwary could sink and be lost with a single misstep. Even as they descended the switchback trail, Quentin experienced the sense of being swallowed.

Halfway down, Redden Alt Mer stopped and turned back to them. "We are a pretty good distance away from where we have to go," he advised quietly. "This trail leads us further away from the crystals than the other. When we get to the valley floor, we'll have to backtrack. We'll stick close to the base of the cliff before starting into the trees." He pointed. "Over there, that's about where the crystals were when I was down here before. So we'll turn in where that big tree leans against the cliff face."

No one said anything in response. There was nothing to say.

They started ahead once more, working their way carefully down the narrow pathway, pressing back against the rock to keep their footing, grasping scrub and grasses for balance. It was difficult going for Quentin because he was wearing his sword strapped across his back and the tip kept snagging on roots and branches. Alt Mer carried a short sword, and Bek carried nothing at all. Only Panax bore a more cumbersome weight in the form of his huge mace, but his squat, stocky form allowed him to better manage the task. Quentin suddenly wished he had thought to bring a bow and arrows, something he could strike out with from a distance. But it was too late to do anything about it now.

On the valley floor, they angled back along the base of the cliff, moving swiftly and silently through the tall grasses and around trees that grew close against the rocks. The terrain was still open, not yet overgrown by the rain forest, and Quentin could see through the trees for several hundred yards. He watched closely for anything that seemed out of place. But nothing moved and everything pretty much looked like it belonged. The Crake was a wall of foliage that concealed everything in its mottled pattern. Sunlight sprayed its vines and branches in thin streamers, but failed to penetrate with any success. Shadows lay over everything, layered in dusky tones, moving and shifting with the passing of the clouds overhead. It was impossible to be certain what they were seeing. They would be on top of anything hiding out there before they realized what it was.

They had gone some distance when Big Red held up one hand and pointed into the trees. This was where they would leave the shelter of the cliff wall. Ahead, the trees grew in thick clumps and the vines twisted about them like ropes. Clearings opened at sporadic intervals, large enough to admit something of size. On looking closer, Quentin could see that some of the trees had been pushed aside.

Alt Mer led with Quentin following close behind, Bek third, and Panax trailing. They worked their way in a loose line through a morass of earthy smells and green color, the dampness in the air rising off the soggy earth with the heat, the silence deep and oppressive. No birds flew here. No animals slipped through the shadows. There were insects that buzzed and hummed, and nothing more. Shadows draped the way forward and the way back with the light touch of a snake's tongue. Quentin's uneasiness grew. Nothing about the Crake felt right. They were out of their element, intruders who didn't belong and fair game for whatever lived here.

Less than ten minutes later, they found the remains of one of the Rovers who had come down with Alt Mer six days before. His body lay sprawled among shattered trees and flattened grasses. Little remained but head, bones, and some skin; the flesh had been largely eaten away. Most of his clothing was missing. His face was twisted into a grimace of unspeakable horror and pain, a mask bereft of humanity. They went past the dead man quickly, eyes averted.

Then Big Red brought them to a halt, hand raising quickly in warning. Ahead, a crate lay broken open, slats sticking skyward like bones. Quentin could not make out the contents, but assumed they were the diapson crystals. He looked around guardedly, testing the air and the feel of the jungle, searching out any predator that might lie in wait. He had learned to do this in the Highlands as a child, a sensory reading of the larger world that transcended what most men and women could manage. He took his time, casting about in all directions, trying to open himself to what might lie hidden.

Nothing.

But his instincts warned him to be careful, and he knew better than to discount them. *Tamis was better at this than I am*, he thought. *If she were here, she would see what I am missing.*

Redden Alt Mer motioned for them to stay where they were, and he stepped from the trees into the clearing and started for the crystals. He moved steadily, but cautiously, and Quentin watched his eyes shift from place to place. The Highlander scanned the jungle wall.

Still nothing.

When he reached the remains of the crate, the Rover Captain signaled over his shoulder for the others to join him. Spreading out, they moved across the clearing in a crouch. Quentin and Panax had their weapons drawn, ready for use. When they reached Alt Mer, Panax knelt to help the Rover extract the crystals while Quentin and Bek stood watch. The jungle was a silent green wall, but Quentin felt hidden eyes watching. He glanced at Bek. His cousin seemed oddly calm, almost at peace. Sweat glistened on his forehead, but it was from the heat. He held himself erect, head lifted, eyes casting about the concealment of the trees in a steady sweep.

Alt Mer had extracted two of the crystals and was working on a third when a low hiss sounded from somewhere back in the trees. All four men froze, staring in the direction of the sound. The hiss came again, closer, deeper, and with it came the sound of something moving purposefully.

"Quick," Alt Mer said, handing two of the crystals to Panax. The crystals were less than two feet long, but they were heavy. Panax grunted with the weight of his load as he started away. Big Red extracted the fourth crystal from the crate, making more noise than he intended, but unwilling to work more slowly. The hiss sounded again, closer still. Something was approaching.

With two crystals cradled in his arms, Big Red backed across the clearing, eyes on the jungle wall. Quentin Leah and Bek flanked him, the Highlander motioning for his cousin to fall back, his cousin ignoring him. The tops of the trees were shaking now, as if a wind had risen to stir them. Quentin had no illusions. The Graak was coming.

They had gained the shelter of a stand of cedar ringed by scrub brush, perhaps a dozen feet beyond the edge of the clearing, when the monster emerged. It pushed through the trees and vines with a sudden surge, a massive dragon weighing thousands of pounds and measuring more than fifty feet in length. Its body was the color of the jungle and glistened dully where the sunlight reflected off its slick hide. Horns and spikes jutted in clusters from its head and spine, and a thick wattle of skin hung from its throat. Claws the size of forearms dug into the dank earth, and rows of teeth flashed when its tongue snaked from its maw.

Squatting on four stubby, powerful legs, the Graak swung its spiky head left and right in search of what had caught its attention. Alt Mer froze in place, and Quentin and Bek followed his lead. Perhaps the creature wouldn't see them.

The Graak cast about aimlessly, then began to sniff the ground, long tail thrashing against the foliage. Quentin held his breath. This thing was huge. He had felt how the ground trembled when it lumbered out of the trees. He had seen how it shouldered past those massive hardwoods as if they were deadwood. If they had to do battle with it, they were in a world of trouble.

The Graak lumbered up to the crystals and sniffed at them, then put one massive foot atop the crate and crushed it. Hissing again, it turned away from them, searching the trees in the opposite direction.

Alt Mer caught Quentin's attention. *Now*, he mouthed silently.

Slowly, carefully, they began to inch their way backwards. Bek, seeing what they were attempting, did the same. Turned away, sniffing the wind, the Graak remained unaware of them. *Don't trip*, Quentin thought to himself. *Don't stumble*. The jungle was so silent he could hear the sound of his own breathing.

The Graak turned back again, its blunt snout swinging slowly about. As one, they froze. They were far enough back in the trees that they could barely see the creature's head above the tall grasses. Perhaps it couldn't see them either.

The reptilian eyes lidded, and the long tongue flicked out. It studied the jungle a moment more, then turned and shambled back the way it had come. Within seconds, it was gone.

When it was clear to all that it was not coming back right away, they started swiftly through the trees. Quentin was astonished. He had thought they had no chance of escaping undetected. His every instinct had warned against it. Yet somehow the creature had failed to spy them out, and now they were within minutes of reaching the cliff wall and beginning the climb back out.

They caught up with Panax, who was not all that far ahead yet. The Dwarf nodded wordlessly.

"That was close!" Bek whispered with a grin.

"Don't talk about it," Quentin said.

"You thought it had us," the other persisted.

Quentin shot him an angry glance. He didn't like talking about luck. It had a way of turning around on you when you did.

"Back home," Bek said, breathing heavily from his exertion, "if it was a boar, say, we would have looked for the mate, too."

Quentin almost stumbled as he turned quickly to look at him. *The mate?* "No," he whispered, realizing what he had missed, fear ripping through him. He pushed ahead of Bek, running now to catch up to Redden Alt Mer and Panax. "Big Red!" he hissed sharply. "Wait!"

At the sound of his name, the Rover came about, causing the Dwarf to slow and turn, as well, which probably saved both their lives. In the next instant, a second Graak charged out of the trees ahead and bore down on them.

There was no time to stop and think about what to do. There was only time to respond, and Quentin Leah was already in motion when the attack came. Never breaking stride, he flew past Big Red and Panax, the Sword of Leah lifted and gripped in both hands. The magic was already surging down the blade to the handle and into his hands and arms. He went right at the Graak, flinging himself past the snapping jaws as they reached for him, rolling beneath its belly and coming back to his feet to thrust the sword deep into its side. The magic flared in an explosion of light and surged into the Graak. The monster hissed in pain and rage and twisted about to get its teeth into its attacker. But Quentin, who had learned something about fighting larger creatures in his battles with the creepers and the Patrinell wronk, sidestepped the attack, scrambled out of the Graak's line of sight, and struck at it again, this time severing a tendon in the creature's hind leg. Again the Graak swung about, tearing at the earth with its claws, dragging its damaged rear leg like a club, its tail lashing out wildly.

"Run!" Bek yelled to Panax and Big Red.

They did so at once, bearing the crystals away from the battle and back toward the cliff wall. But Bek turned to fight.

There was no chance for Quentin to do anything about that. He was too busy trying to stay alive, and the shift of the Graak's body as it sought to pin him to the earth blocked his view of his cousin. But he heard the call Bek emitted, something shrill and rough edged, predatory and dark, born of nightmares known only to him or to those who worked his kind of magic. The Graak jerked its head in response, clearly bothered by the sound, and twisted about in search of the caller, giving Quentin a chance to strike at it again. The Highlander rolled under it a second time and thrust the blade of his talisman deep into the chest, somewhere close to where he thought its heart must be, the magic surging out of him like a river.

The Graak coughed gouts of dark blood and gasped in shock. A vital organ had been breached. Covered in mud and sweat and smelling of the damp, fetid earth, Quentin rolled free again. Blood laced his hands and face, and he saw that one arm was torn open and his right side lacerated. Somehow he had been injured without realizing it. Trying to stay out of the Graak's line of sight he ran toward its tail, looking for a fresh opening. The Graak was thrashing wildly, writhing in fury as it felt the killing effects of the magic begin to work through it. Another solid blow, Quentin judged, should finish it.

But then the creature did the unexpected. It bolted for Bek, all at once and without even looking his way first. Bek stood his ground, using the power of the wishsong to strike back, but the Graak didn't even seem to hear it. It rumbled on without slowing, without pause, tearing up the earth with its clawed feet, dragging its damaged hind leg, hissing with rage and madness into the steamy jungle air.

"Bek!" Quentin screamed in dismay.

He flew after the Graak with complete disregard for his own safety, and caught up to the creature when it was only yards away from his cousin. He swung the Sword of Leah with every last ounce of strength he possessed, the magic exploding forth as he severed the tendons of the hind leg that still functioned. The Graak went down instantly, both rear legs immobilized, its useless hindquarters dragging it to an abrupt stop. But as it fought to keep going, to get at Bek, it rolled right into the Highlander, who, unlike Bek, did not have time to get out of the way. Though Quentin threw himself aside as the twisting, thrashing body collapsed, he could not get all the way clear, and the Graak's heavy tail hammered him into the earth.

It felt as if a mountain had fallen on top of him. Bones snapped and cracked, and he was pressed so far down into the earth that he couldn't breathe. He would have screamed if there had been a way to do so, but his face was buried in six inches of mud. The weight of the Graak rolled off him, then back on again, then off again. He managed to get his head out of the mire, to take a quick breath of air, then to flatten himself as the monster rolled over him yet again, this time missing him as it twisted back on itself in an effort to rise.

"Quentin, don't move!" he heard Bek cry out.

As if he could, he thought dully. The pain was beginning to surge through him in waves. He was a dead man, he knew. No one could survive the sort of damage he had just sustained. He was a dead man, but his body hadn't gotten the message yet.

Hands reached under him and rolled him over. The pain was excruciating. "Shades!" he gasped as bones grated and blood poured from his mouth.

"Hang on!" Bek pleaded. "Please, Quentin!"

His cousin pulled him to his feet, then led him away. Somewhere close by, the Graak was in its death throes. Somewhere not quite so close, its mate was coming. He couldn't see any of this, but he could be sure it was happening. He stumbled on through a curtain of bright red anguish and hazy consciousness. Any moment now, he would collapse. He fought against that with frantic determination. If he went down, Bek would not be able to get him away. If he went down, he was finished.

Oh well, he thought with a sort of fuzzy disinterest, he was finished anyway.

"Sorry, Bek," he said, or maybe he only tried to say it; he couldn't be sure. "Sorry."

Then a wave of darkness engulfed him, and everything disappeared.

TWENTY-THREE

It was dark when Bek finally emerged from belowdecks on the *Jerle Shannara*, walked to the bow, and looked up at the night sky. The moon was a tiny crescent directly over the mountain they were backed against, newly formed and barely a presence in the immensity of the sky's vast sweep. Stars sprinkled the indigo firmament like grains of brilliant white sand scattered on black velvet. He had been told once that men had traveled to those stars in the Old World, that they had built and ridden in ships that could navigate the sky as he had the waters of the Blue Divide. It seemed impossible. But then most wonderful things did until someone accomplished them.

He hadn't been on deck for more than a few moments when Rue Meridian appeared beside him, coming up so silently that he didn't hear her approach and realized she was there only when she placed a hand over his own.

"Have you slept?" she asked.

He shook his head. Sleep was out of the question.

"How is he?"

He thought about it a moment, staring skyward "Holding on by his fingernails and slipping."

They had managed to get Quentin Leah out of the Crake alive, but only barely. With Bek's help, he had stumbled to within a hundred yards of the trail before collapsing. By then he had lost so much blood that when they had carried him out they could barely get a grip on his clothing. Rue Meridian knew something of treating wounds from her time on the Prekkendorran, so after tying off the severed arteries with tourniquets, she had stitched and bandaged him as best she could. The patching of the surface wounds was not difficult, nor the setting of the broken bones. But there were internal injuries with which she did not have the skill to deal, so that much of the care Quentin needed could not be provided. Healing would have to come from within, and everyone knew that any chance of that happening here was small.

Their best bet was to either get him to a healing center in the Four Lands or to find a local Healer. The former was out of the question. There simply wasn't time. As for the latter, the Rindge offered the only possibility of help. Panax had gone to see what they could do, but had returned empty-handed. When a Rindge was in Quentin's condition, his people could do no more for him than the company of the *Jerle Shannara* could for Quentin.

"Is he alone?" Rue asked Bek.

He shook his head. "Panax is watching him."

"Why don't you try to sleep for a few hours? There isn't anything more you can do."

"I can be with him. I can be there for him. I'll go back down in just a moment."

"Panax will look after him."

"Panax isn't the one he counts on."

She didn't reply to that. She just stood there beside him, keeping him company, staring up at the stars. The Crake was a sea of impenetrable black within the cup of the mountains, silent and stripped of definition. Bek took a moment to look down at it, chilled by doing so, the memories of the afternoon still raw and terrible, endlessly repeating in his mind. He couldn't get past them, not even now when he was safely away from their cause.

"You're exhausted," she said finally.

He nodded in agreement.

"You have to sleep, Bek."

"I left his sword down there." He pointed toward the valley.

"What?"

"His sword. I was so busy trying to get him out that I forgot about it entirely. I just left it behind."

She nodded. "It won't go anywhere. We can get it back tomorrow, when it's light."

"I'll get it back," he insisted. "I'm the one who left it. It's my responsibility."

He pictured it lying in the earth by the dead Graak, its smooth surface covered with blood and dirt. Had it been broken by the weight of the monster rolling over it, broken as Quentin was? He hadn't noticed, hadn't even glanced at it. A talisman of such power, and he hadn't even thought about it. He'd just thought about Quentin, and he'd done that too late for it to matter.

"Why don't you stop being so hard on yourself?" she asked quietly. "Why don't you ease up a bit?"

"Because he's dying," he said fiercely, angrily. "Quentin's dying, and it's my fault."

She looked at him. "Your fault?"

"If I hadn't insisted on going down there with him, if I hadn't been so stubborn about this whole business, then maybe—"

"Bek, stop it!" she snapped at him. He looked over at her, surprised by the rebuke. Her hand tightened on his. "It doesn't help anything for you to talk like that. It happened, and no one's to blame for it. Everyone did the best they could in a dangerous situation. That's all anyone can ask. That's all anyone can expect. Let it alone."

The words stung, but no more so than the look he saw in her eyes. She held his gaze, refusing to let him turn away. "Losing people we love, friends and even family, is a consequence of going on journeys like this one. Don't you understand that? Didn't you understand it when you agreed to come? Is this suddenly a surprise? Did you think that nothing could happen to Quentin? Or to you?"

He shook his head in confusion, cowed. "I don't know. I guess maybe not."

She exhaled sharply and her tone of voice softened. "It wasn't your fault. Not any more so than it was my brother's or Panax's or Walker's or whoever's. It was just something that happened, a price exacted in consequence of a risk taken."

The consequence of a risk. As simple as that. You took a risk, and the person you were closest to paid the price. He began to cry, all the pent-up frustration and guilt and sadness releasing at once. He couldn't help himself. He didn't want to break down in front of her—didn't want her to see that—but it happened before he could find a way to stop it.

She pulled him against her, enfolding him like an injured child. Her arms came about him and she rocked him gently, cooing soft words, stroking his back with her hand. The hard wooden rods of the splint on her left forearm were digging into his back.

"Oh, Bek. It's all right. You can cry with me. No one will see. Let me hold you until." She pressed him into the softness of her body. "Poor Bek. So much responsibility all at once. So much hurt. It isn't fair, is it?"

He heard some of what she said, but comfort came not from the words themselves but from the sound of her voice and the feel of her arms wrapped about him. Everything released, and she was there to absorb it, to take it into herself and away from him.

"Just hold on to me, Bek. Just let me take care of you. Everything will be all right."

She had said he owed it to her to share the losses she had suffered. Losses as great as his own. Furl Hawken. Her Rover companions. He was reminded of it suddenly and wanted to give back something of the comfort she was giving to him.

He recovered his composure, and his arms went around her. "Rue, I'm sorry . . ."

"No," she said, putting her fingers over his mouth, stopping him from saying anything more. "I don't want to hear it. I don't want you to talk."

She replaced her fingers with her mouth and kissed him. She didn't kiss him softly or gently, but with urgency and passion. He couldn't mistake what was happening or what it meant, and he didn't want to. It took him only a moment, and then he was returning her kiss. When he did, he forgot everything but the heat she aroused in him. Kissing her was wild and impossible. It made him worry that something was wrong, but he couldn't decide what it was because everything felt right. She ran her hands all over him, pushing him up against the ship's railing until he was pinned there, fastening her mouth on his with such hunger that he could scarcely breathe.

When she broke away finally, he wasn't sure who was the most surprised. From the look on her face she was, but he knew what he was feeling inside. They stared at each other in a kind of awed silence, and then she laughed—a low, sudden growl that brought such radiance to her face that he was surprised all over again.

"That was unexpected," she said.

He couldn't speak.

"I want to do it some more. I want to do it a lot."

He grinned in spite of himself, in spite of everything. "Me, too."

"Soon, Bek."

"All right."

"I think I love you," she said. She laughed again. "There, I said it. What do you think of that?"

She reached out with her good arm and touched his lips with her fingers, then turned and walked away.

When he went inside the ship to the Captain's quarters to see about Quentin, he was still in shock from his encounter with Rue.

Panax must have seen something in his face when Bek entered the room, because he immediately asked, "Are you all right?"

Bek nodded. He was not all right, but he had no intention of talking about it just yet. It was too new to share, still so strange in his own mind that he needed time to get used to it. He needed time just to accept that it was true. Rue Meridian was in love with him. That's what she had said. *I think I love you.* He tried the words out in his mind, and they sounded so ridiculous that he almost laughed aloud.

On the other hand, the way she had kissed him was real enough, and he wasn't going to forget how that felt anytime soon.

Did he love her in turn? He hadn't stopped to ask himself that. He hadn't even considered it before now because the idea of her reciprocating had seemed impossible. It was enough that they were friends. But he did love her. He had always loved her in some sense, from the first moment he had seen her. Now, kissed and held and told of her feelings, he loved her so desperately he could hardly stand it.

He forced himself to shift his thinking away from her.

"How is he doing?" he asked, nodding toward Quentin.

Panax shrugged. "The same. He just sleeps. I don't like the way he looks, though."

Neither did Bek. Quentin's skin was an unhealthy pasty color. His pulse was faint and his breathing labored and shallow. He was dying by inches, and there was nothing any of them could do about it but wait for the inevitable. Already emotionally overwrought, Bek found himself beginning to cry anew and he turned away self-consciously.

Panax rose and came over to him. He put one rough hand on Bek's shoulder and gently squeezed. "First Truls Rohk and now the Highlander. This hasn't been easy," he said.

"No."

His hand dropped away, and he walked over to where Grianne knelt on a pallet in the corner, eyes open as she stared straight ahead. The Dwarf shook his head in puzzlement. "What do you suppose she's thinking?"

Bek wiped away the last of his tears. "Nothing we want to know about, I'd guess."

"Probably not. What a mess. This whole journey, from start to finish. A mess." He didn't seem to know where else to go with his thoughts, so he went silent for a moment. "I wish I'd never come. I wouldn't have, if I'd known what it was going to be like."

"I don't suppose any of us would." Bek walked over to his sister and knelt in front of her. He touched her cheek with his fingers as he always did to let her know he was there. "Can you hear me, Grianne?" he asked softly.

"I don't know what I'm doing here anymore," Panax continued. "I don't know that there's a reason for any of us being here. We haven't done anything but get ourselves killed and injured. Even the Druid. I didn't think anything would ever happen to him. But then I didn't think anything could happen to Truls, either. Now they're both gone." He shook his head.

"When I get home," Bek said, still looking at Grianne's pale, empty face, "I'll stay there. I won't leave again. Not like this."

He thought again about Rue Meridian. What would happen to her when they got back in the Four Lands? She was a Rover, born to the Rover life, a traveler and an adventurer. She was nothing like him. She wouldn't want to come back to the Highlands and stay home for the rest of her life. She wouldn't want anything to do with him then.

"I've been thinking about home," Panax said quietly. He knelt down beside Bek, his bearded face troubled. "I never cared all that much for my own. Depo Bent was just the village where I ended up. I have no family, just a few friends, none of them close. I've traveled all my life, but I don't know if there's anything left in the Four Lands that I want to see. Without Truls and Walker to keep me busy, I don't know that there's anything back there for me." He paused. "I think maybe I'll stay here."

Bek looked at him. "Stay here in Parkasia?"

The Dwarf shrugged. "I like the Rindge. They're a good people and they're not so different from me. Their language is similar to mine. I kind of like this country, too, except for things like the Graak and Antrax. But the rest of it looks interesting. I want to explore it. There's a lot of it none of us have seen, all of the interior beyond the mountains, where Obat and his people are going."

"You would be trapped here, if you changed your mind. You wouldn't have a way to get back." Bek tried the words out on the Dwarf, then grimaced at the way they sounded.

Panax chuckled softly. "I don't see it that way, Bek. When you make a choice, you accept the consequences going in. Like coming on this journey. Only maybe this time things will turn out a little better for me. I'm not that young. I don't have all that much life left in me. I don't think I would mind finishing it out in Parkasia, rather than in the Four Lands."

How different the Dwarf was from himself, Bek thought in astonishment. Not to want to go home again, but to stay in a strange land on the chance that it might prove interesting. He couldn't do that. But he understood the Dwarf's reasoning. If you had spent most of your life as an explorer and a guide, living outside cities and towns, living on your own, staying here wouldn't seem so strange. How much different were the mountains of the Aleuthra Ark, after all, from those of the Wolfsktaag?

"Do you think you can manage without me?" Panax asked, his face strangely serious.

Bek knew what Panax wanted to hear. "I think you'd just get in the way," he answered. "Anyway, I think you've earned the right to do what you want. If you want to stay, you should."

They were nothing without their freedom, nothing without their right to choose. They had given themselves to a common cause in coming with Walker in search of the Old World books of magic, but that was finished. What they needed to do now was to help each other find a way home again, whether home was to be found in the Four Lands or elsewhere.

"Why don't you get some sleep," he said to the Dwarf. "I'll sit with Quentin now. I want to, really. I need to be with him."

Panax rose and put his hand on Bek's shoulder a second time, an act that was meant to convey both his support and his gratitude. Then he walked through the shadows and from the room. Bek stared after him a moment, wondering how Panax would find his new life, if it would bring him the peace and contentment that the old apparently had not. He wondered what it would feel like to be so disassociated from everyone and everything that the thought of leaving it all behind wasn't disturbing. He couldn't know that, and in truth he hoped he would never find out.

He turned back to Quentin, looking at him as he lay white-faced and dying. Shades, shades, he felt so helpless. He took a deep, steadying breath and exhaled slowly. He couldn't stand this anymore. He couldn't stand watching him slip away. He had to do something, even if it was the wrong thing, so that he could know that at least he had tried. All of the usual possibilities for healing were out of the question. He had to try something else.

He remembered from the stories of the Druids that the wishsong had the ability to heal. It hadn't been used that way often because it required great skill. He didn't have that skill or the experience that might lend it to him, but he couldn't worry about that here. Brin Ohmsford had used the magic once upon a time to heal Rone Leah. If an Ohmsford had used the magic to save the life of a Leah once, there was no reason an Ohmsford couldn't do so again.

It was a risky undertaking. Foolish, maybe. But Quentin was not going to live if something wasn't done to help him, and there wasn't anything else left to try.

Bek walked over to the bed and sat next to his cousin. He watched him for a moment, then took his hand in his own and held it. He wished he had something more to work with than experimentation. He wished he had directions of some kind, a place to begin, an idea of how the magic worked, anything. But there was nothing of the sort at hand, and no help for it.

"I'll do my best, Quentin," he said softly. "I'll do everything I can. Please come back to me."

Then he called up the magic in a slow unfurling of words and music and began to sing.

TWENTY-FOUR

ecause he had never done this before and had no real idea of how to do it now, Bek Ohmsford did not rush himself. He proceeded carefully, taking one small step at a time, watching Quentin closely to make certain that the magic of the wishsong was not having an adverse affect. He called up the magic in a slow humming that rose in his chest where it warmed and throbbed softly. He kept hold of Quentin's hands, wanting to maintain physical contact in order to give himself a chance to further judge if things were going as intended.

When the level of magic was sufficient, he sent a small probe into Quentin's ravaged body to measure the damage. Red shards of pain ricocheted back through him, and he withdrew the probe quickly. Fair enough. Investigating a damaged body without adequate self-protection was not a good idea. Shielding himself, he tried again and ran into a wall of resistance. Still humming, he tried coming in through Quentin's mind, taking a reading on what his cousin was thinking. He ran into another blank wall. Quentin's mind seemed to have shut down, or at least it was not giving off anything Bek could decipher.

For a moment, he was stumped. Both attempts at getting to where he could do some good had failed, and he wasn't sure what he should try next. What he wanted to do was to get close enough to one specific injury to see what the magic could do to heal it. But if he couldn't break down the barriers that Quentin had thrown up to protect himself, he wasn't going to be able to do anything.

He tried a more general approach then, a wrapping of Quentin in the magic's veil, a covering over of his mind and body both. It had the desired effect; Quentin immediately calmed and his breathing became steadier and smoother. Bek worked his way over his cousin's still form in search of entry, thinking that as his body relaxed, Quentin might lower his protective barriers. Slowly, slowly he touched and stroked with the magic, his singing smoothing away wrinkles of pain and discomfort, working toward the deeper, more serious injuries.

It didn't work. He could not get past the surface of Quentin's body, even when he brushed up against the open wounds beneath the bandages, which should have offered him easy access.

He was so frustrated that he broke off his attempts completely. Sitting silently, motionlessly beside Quentin, he continued to hold his cousin's hand, not willing to break that contact, as well. He tried to think of what else he could do. Something about the way in which he was approaching the problem was throwing up barriers. He knew he could force his way into Quentin's body, could break down the protective walls that barred his way. But he thought, as well, that the consequence of such a harsh intrusion might be fatal to a system already close to collapse. What was needed was tact and care, a gentle offering to heal that would be embraced and not resisted.

What would it take to make that happen?

He tried again, this time returning to what was familiar to him about the magic. He sang to Quentin as he had sung to Grianne—of their lives together as boys, of the Highlands of Leah, of family and friends, and of adventures shared. He sang stories to his cousin, thinking to use them as a means of lessening resistance to his ministrations. Now and then, he would attempt a foray into his cousin's body and mind, taking a story in a direction that might lend itself to a welcoming, the two of them friends still and always.

Nothing.

He changed the nature of his song to one of revelation and warning. *This is the situation, Quentin,* he sang. *You are very sick and in need of healing. But you are fighting me. I need you to help me instead. I need you to open to me and let me use the wishsong to mend you. Please, Quentin, listen to me. Listen.*

If his cousin heard, he didn't do anything to indicate it and did nothing to give Bek any further access. He simply lay on his bed beneath a light covering and fought to stay alive on his own terms. He remained unconscious and unresponsive and, like Grianne, locked away where Bek could not reach him.

Bek kept at it. He fought to use the magic for the better part of the next hour, maintaining contact through the touching of their hands while trying to heal with his song. He came at the problem from every direction he could imagine, even when he suspected that what he was trying was futile. He attacked with such determination that he completely lost track of everything but what he was doing.

All to no avail.

Finally, exhausted and frustrated, he gave up. He rocked back, put his face in his hands, and began to sob. All this crying felt foolish and weak, but he was so weary from his efforts that it was an impulsive, unavoidable response. It happened in spite of his efforts to stop it, boiling over in a rush that left him convulsed and shaking. He had failed. There was nothing left for him to try, nowhere else for him to go.

"Poor little baby boy," a voice soothed in his ear, and slender arms came around his neck and pulled him close.

At first he thought it was Rue Meridian, come down to the cabin when he wasn't looking. But he realized almost before he had completed the thought that it wasn't her voice. Gray robes fell across his face as he twisted his head for a quick look.

It was Grianne.

He was so shocked that for a moment he just sat there and let her hold him. "Little boy, little boy, don't be sad." She was speaking not in her adult voice, but with the voice of a child. "It's all right, baby Bek. Your big sister is here. I won't leave you again, I promise. I won't go away again. I'm so sorry, so sorry."

Her hands stroked his face, gentle and soothing. She kissed his forehead as she cooed to him, touching him as if he were a baby.

He glanced up again, looking into her eyes. She was looking back at him, seeing him for the first time since he had found her in Castledown. Gone were the vacant stare and the empty expression. She had come back from wherever she had been hiding. She was awake.

"Grianne!" he gasped in relief.

"No, no, baby, don't cry," she replied at once, touching his lips with her fingers. "There, there, your Grianne can make it all better. Tell me what's wrong, little one."

Bek caught his breath. She was seeing him, but not as he really was, only as she remembered him.

Her gaze shifted suddenly. "Oh, what's this? Is your puppy sick, Bek? Did he eat something bad? Did he hurt himself? Poor little puppy."

She was looking right at Quentin. Bek was so taken aback by this that he just stared at her. He vaguely remembered a puppy from when he was very little, a black mixed breed that trotted around the house and slept in the sun. He remembered nothing else about it, not even its name.

"No wonder you're crying." She smoothed Bek's hair back gently. "Your puppy is sick, and you can't make him better. It's all right, Bek. Grianne can help. We'll use my special medicine to take away the pain."

She released him and moved to the head of the bed to stand looking down at Quentin. "So much pain," she whispered. "I don't know if I can make you well again. Sometimes even the special medicine can't help. Sometimes nothing can."

A chill settled through Bek as he realized that he might be mistaken about her. Maybe she wasn't his sister at all, but the Ilse Witch. If she was thinking like the witch and not Grianne, if she had not come all the way back to being his sister, she might cure Quentin the way she had cured so many of her problems. She might kill him.

"No, Grianne!" he cried out, reaching for her.

"Uh-uh-uh, baby," she cautioned, taking hold of his wrists. She was much stronger than he would have thought, and he could not shake free. "Let Grianne do what she has to do to help."

Already she was using the magic. Bek felt it wash over him, felt it bind him in velvet chains and hold him fast. In seconds, he was paralyzed. She eased him back in place, humming softly as she moved once more to the head of the bed and Quentin Leah.

"Poor puppy," she repeated, reaching down to stroke the Highlander's face. "You are so sick, in such pain. What happened to you? You are all broken up inside. Did something hurt you?"

Bek was beside himself. He could neither move nor speak. He watched helplessly, unable to intervene and terrified of what was going to happen if he didn't.

She was speaking to him again, her voice suddenly older, more mature. "Oh, Bek, I've let you down so badly. I left you, and I didn't come back. I should have, and I didn't. It was so wrong of me, Bek."

She was crying. His sister was crying. It was astonishing, and Bek would have felt a sense of joy if he hadn't been so frightened that it wasn't his sister speaking. He fought to say something, to stop her, but no words would come out.

"Little puppy," she whispered sadly, and her hands reached down to cup Quentin's face. "Let me make you all better."

Then she leaned down and kissed him gently on the lips, drawing his breath into her body.

Rue Meridian was sleeping in a makeshift canvas hammock she had strung between the foremast and the bow railing, lost in a dream about cormorants and puffins, when she felt Bek's hand on her shoulder and awoke. She saw the look on his face and immediately asked, "What's wrong?"

It was a difficult look to decipher. His face was troubled and amazed, both at once; it reflected uncertainty mixed with wonder. He appeared oddly adrift, as if he was there almost by accident. Her first thought was that his coming was a delayed reaction to what she had told him hours earlier. She sat up quickly, swung her legs over the side of the hammock, and stood. "Bek, what's happened?"

"Grianne woke up. I don't know why. The magic, maybe. I was using it to try to help Quentin, to heal him the way Brin Ohmsford did Rone Leah once. Or maybe it was when I cried. I was so frustrated and tired, I just broke down."

He exhaled sharply. "She spoke to me. She called me by name. But she wasn't herself, not grown up, but a child, speaking in a child's voice, calling me 'poor baby boy, little Bek,' and telling me not to cry."

"Wait a minute, slow down," she said, taking hold of him by his shoulders. "Come over here."

She led him to the bow and sat him down in the shadow of the starboard ram where the curve of the horn formed a shelter at its joining with the deck. She sat facing him, pulled her knees up to her breast, and wrapped her arms around her legs. "Okay, tell me the rest. She came awake and she spoke to you. What happened next?"

"You won't believe this," he whispered, clearly not believing it himself. "She healed him. She used her magic, and she healed him. I thought she was going to kill him. She called him a puppy—I guess that's what she thought he was. I tried to stop her, but she did something to me with the magic so that I couldn't move or speak. Then she started on him, and I was sure she meant to help him by killing him, to take away his pain and suffering by taking his life. That's what the Ilse Witch would have done, and I was afraid she was still the witch."

Rue leaned forward, hugging herself. "How could she heal him, Bek? He was all broken up inside. Half his blood was gone."

"The magic can do that. It can generate healing. I watched it happen to Quentin. He's not completely well yet. He isn't even awake. But I saw his color change right in front of me. I heard his breathing steady and, afterwards, when I could move again, felt that his pulse was stronger, too. Some of his wounds, the ones you bandaged, have closed completely."

"Shades," she whispered, trying to picture it.

He leaned back into the curve of the horn and looked at the night sky. "When she was done, she came back over to me and stroked my cheek and held me. I could move again, but I didn't want to interrupt what she was doing because I thought it might be helping her. I spoke her name, but she didn't answer. She just rocked me and began to cry."

His eyes shifted to find hers. "She kept saying how sorry she was, over and over. She said it would never happen again. Leaving me, she said. She wouldn't leave me like before, not ever. All this in her little girl's voice, her child's voice."

His eyes closed. "I just wanted to help her, to let her know I understood. I tried to hold her. When I did, she went right back into herself. She quit talking or moving. She quit seeing me. She was just like before. I couldn't do anything to bring her back. I tried, but she wouldn't respond." He shook his head. "So I left her and came to find you. I had to tell someone. I'm sorry I woke you."

She reached out for him, pulled him close, and kissed him on the lips. "I'm glad you did." She stood and drew him up with her. "Come lie down with me, Bek."

She took him back to the canvas hammock and bundled him

into it beside her. She pressed herself against him and wrapped him in her arms. She was still getting used to the idea that he meant so much to her. Her admission of this to him had surprised her, but she'd had no regrets about it afterwards. Bek Ohmsford made her feel complete; it was as if by finding him, she had found a missing part of herself. He made her feel good, and it had been a while since anyone had made her feel like that.

They lay without moving for a while, without talking, just holding each other and listening to the silence. But she wanted more, wanted to give him more, and she began kissing him. She kissed him for a long time, working her way over his mouth and eyes and nose, down his neck and chest. He tried to kiss her, as well, but she wouldn't let him, wanting everything to come from her. When he seemed at peace, she lay back again, placing his head in the crook of her shoulder. He fell asleep for a time, and she held him while he dreamed.

I love you, Bek Ohmsford. She mouthed the words silently. She thought it incredibly odd she should fall in love with someone under such strange circumstances. It seemed inconvenient and vaguely ridiculous. Hawk would have been shocked. He never thought she would fall in love with anyone. Too independent, too tough-minded. She never needed anyone, never wanted anyone. She was complete by herself. She understood his thinking. It was what she had believed, as well, until now.

She put her hands inside of Bek's clothing and touched his skin. She placed her fingers over his heart. Counting the beats in her head, she closed her eyes and dozed.

When she woke again, he was still sleeping. Overhead, the sky was lightening with the approach of dawn.

"It's almost daylight," she whispered in his ear, waking him.

He nodded into her shoulder. He was silent for a moment, shaking off the last of his sleep. She could feel his breath on her neck and the strength in his arms.

"When we get back to the Four Lands," he began, and stopped. "When this is all over, and we have to decide where we—"

"Bek, no," she said gently, but firmly. "Don't talk about what's going to happen later. Don't worry about it. We're too far away for it to matter yet. Leave it alone."

He went silent again, pressed against her. She brushed back her hair where it had fallen into her face. His eyes followed the movement with interest, and he reached out to help. "I have to go down into the Crake," he said. "I have to get Quentin's sword back. I want it to be there for him when he wakes up."

She nodded. "All right."

"Will you look after Grianne for me while I'm gone?"

She smiled and kissed him on the lips. "I can't, Bek." She touched the tip of his nose. "I'm going with you."

When she said it, Bek panicked. He kept the panic in check on the surface, but inside, where his emotions could pretty much do whatever they wanted to, he was a mess. All he could think about was how afraid he was for her, how frightened that something bad would happen. It had already happened to Quentin, and his cousin had at least had the protection of the Sword of Leah. Rue wore a splint on one arm and had no magic at all. If he agreed to let her come, he would be taking on the responsibility for both of them. He was not sure he wanted to do that right after failing Quentin so miserably.

"I don't think that is a good idea," he told her, not sure what else to say that wouldn't make her furious and even more determined.

She seemed to consider the merits of his objection, then smiled. "Do you know what I like most about you, Bek? Not how you look or think, not your laugh or the way you see the world, although I like those things, too. What I really like about you is that you don't ever act as if I'm not just as good as everyone else. You take it for granted that I am, and you treat me with respect. I don't have to fight you for that. I can expect it as a matter of course. I am your equal; I might even be a little better in some ways." She paused. "I wouldn't want to lose that."

There was not much he could say to her after that. So he simply nodded and smiled back, and she kissed him hard to show that she appreciated his understanding. He liked having her kiss him, but it didn't make him feel any better about taking her along.

But the issue was decided, so they slipped over the side of the ship and walked to the edge of the bluff, followed the precipice to the trailhead, and started down. It was light enough now that they could make out the shapes of the trees and the soft movement of leaves and branches in the slow morning wind. Bek cast about with his magic as they descended, taking no chances on being caught off guard, even if what he was doing somehow alerted the dead Graak's mate. If the mate was anywhere close, he had already decided they would turn right around. Even Little Red couldn't argue with that.

But fortune smiled on them, and they slipped into the Crake as invisible as wraiths. Bek used the magic of the wishsong to cloak them in the look and feel of the rain forest, choosing images and smells that would not attract a carnivore. Draped in trailers of mist and cooled by the morning wind, they slid through the trees with the ease and freedom of shadows, untroubled by the dangers that on this occasion were elsewhere. They found Quentin's sword muddied but still in one piece beside the body of the dead Graak, retrieved it, and made their way back again. The sun was cresting the jagged line of mountains east when they began their climb back up the trail.

That was so easy, Bek thought in surprise as they regained the bluff. Why couldn't it have been like that for Quentin? But then, of course, there would have been no reason for Grianne to come awake, and he would not have seen for himself that her responses to pain and suffering were no longer those of the Ilse Witch, but of his sister. He would not have discovered that maybe she could return to him after all when she was ready.

Rue Meridian turned to him, a mix of mischievousness and satisfaction mirrored in her green eyes. "Admit it. That wasn't so bad."

He shook his head and sighed. "No, it wasn't."

"Remember that the next time you think about doing something dangerous without me." She reached out and took hold of the back of his neck with both hands and pulled him close to her. "If you love me, if I love you, there shouldn't be any question of that ever happening. Otherwise, what we feel for each other isn't real. It doesn't mean anything."

He shook his head. "Yes, it does. It means everything."

She grinned, brushing loose strands of her long hair from her face. "I know. So don't forget it."

She picked up the pace and moved ahead of him. He stared after her, barely able to contain himself. In her words and smile, in everything she said and did, he saw a future that would transcend all his expectations of what he had ever imagined possible. It was only a dream, but wasn't reality conceived in dreams?

His euphoria peaked and faded in a wash of doubt. It was foolish, he thought, to let himself think like this, to allow his emotions to cloud his reason. Look at where he was. Look at what had befallen him. Where, in all of this, did dreams like his belong? He watched Rue Meridian's stride lengthen and as he did so, felt those dreams slip away, too frail to hold, too insubstantial to grasp. He was drawing pictures in the sand, and the tide was coming in.

When they reached the trailhead and walked back toward the *Jerle Shannara*, they found Redden Alt Mer and his Rovers gathered at the edge of the bluff, looking east. The Wing Riders were flying in from the coast, and they had someone with them.

TWENTY-FIVE

When the Morgawr found that Ahren Elessedil was gone, he had Ryer Ord Star brought before him. She denied knowing anything about it, but she knew he could read the lie in her eyes and smell it on her breath. Already suspicious of their failure to find any trace of the *Jerle Shannara* and her crew or of the Ilse Witch and her brother, he wasted no time in deciding that the seer had helped the Elven Prince escape. Whatever usefulness she might have had, she had outlived it.

He gave her to Cree Bega and his Mwellrets, who stripped her naked and beat her savagely. They broke all her fingers and slashed the soles of her feet. They defiled her until she fainted. When she woke again, they hung her by her wrists from one of the yardarms, lashed her with a rawhide whip, and left her to bake in the midday sun. They gave her no water or clothing and did not treat her wounds. She hung ignored in a haze of pain and thirst that left her ravaged and delirious.

Only once did the Morgawr speak to her again. "Use your gift, little seer," he advised, standing just below her, touching the wounds on her body with interest. "Find those I have asked you to find, and I will let you die quickly. Otherwise, I will make sure your agony endures until I find them myself. There are other things I can have done to you, things that will hurt much more than those you have already experienced."

She was barely conscious when he spoke the words, but her reason was not yet gone. She knew that if she gave him what he wanted, if she told him where to find her friends, he would not kill her quickly as he had said, but would do to her what he had done to Aden Kett. He would want that experience, to feed on her mind, a seer's mind, to see what that would feel like. The only reason he had not done so yet was because he was still hoping she would lead him to those he hunted. Damaging her so significantly would prevent her from giving him any further help. His hunger for her could wait a few days. He was patient that way.

The day drifted toward nightfall. The ropes that held her suspended had cut her wrists almost to the bone. Blood streaked her arms and shoulders. She could no longer feel her hands. Her unprotected body was burned and raw from exposure to wind and sun and throbbed with unrelenting pain.

Her suffering triggered visions, some recognizable, some not. She saw her companions, both living and dead, but could not seem to differentiate between them. They floated in and out of her consciousness, there long enough for her to identify and then gone. Sometimes they spoke, but she rarely understood the words. She felt her mind going as her life drained out of her body, sliding steadily into an abyss of dark, merciful forgetfulness.

Walker, she called out in her mind, begging him to come to her.

Night descended, and the Mwellrets went to sleep, all save the watch and helmsman. No one came to her. No one spoke to her. She hung from the yardarm as she had all day, broken and dying. She no longer felt the pain. It was there, but it was so much a part of her that she no longer recognized it as being out of the ordinary. She licked her cracked lips to keep her mouth from sealing over and breathed the cool night air with relief. Tomorrow would bring a return of the burning sun and harsh wind, but she thought that perhaps by then she would be gone.

She hoped that Ahren was far away. The Morgawr and his airships had been searching for him all day without success, so there was reason to think that the Elven Prince had escaped. He would be wondering when she would join him, if she would come soon. But she had never intended to leave *Black Moclips*. Her visions had told her of her fate, of her death aboard this vessel, and she was not foolish enough to believe she could avoid it. Just as Walker had seen his fate in her visions long ago, so she had seen hers. A seer's visions came unbidden and showed what they chose. Like those she advised, Ryer Ord Star could only accept what was revealed and never change it.

But what she had told the Elven Prince about himself and his own future was the truth, as well, a more promising fate than her own. His future awaited him in the Four Lands, long after she was gone, long after this voyage was a distant memory.

He would wonder what had become of her, of course. Or perhaps he would know when enough time had passed and she hadn't appeared. He would never know how she had hidden the Elfstones from the Morgawr and the Mwellrets. That secret would remain hers. And Walker's. She had been quick to take them from Ahren when he was felled in the attack, feigning concern for his injury, bending down to shield her movements. She had known she would be searched, and she had slipped the Stones into a crevice in the wall while the Mwellrets were still concentrating on Ahren. A simple ruse, but an effective one. Search her once, and the matter was settled. After that, she had needed only to get aboard *Black Moclips* before finding a new place of concealment. She had left the Stones hidden until it was time for Ahren to leave.

She would be lying to herself if she didn't admit that she had thought of giving him the Stones earlier so that he could use them on his captors. But Ahren was new to the magic, and the Morgawr was old, too powerful to be overcome by any save an experienced hand. Only Walker would have stood a chance, and while she wanted to live as much as the next person, she was not prepared to risk Ahren's life and fate on a gamble that would almost surely fail. She had sworn an oath to protect him, to do what she could to redeem herself for the harm she had caused while in the service of the Ilse Witch. No halfway measures were allowed in fulfilling that oath. She had much to atone for, and her death was small payment for her sins.

She lifted her head out of the tangle of her hair and tasted the night air on her lips. She wanted to die, but could not seem to. She wanted release from her pain, from her helplessness, but could not find it alone. She needed Walker to help her. She needed him to come.

She drifted in and out of half sleep, always aware that no true sleep would come, that only death would give her rest. She cried for herself and her failures, and she wished she could have grown to be a woman of some worth. In another time and place, in another life, perhaps that would happen.

It was during the deep sleep hours of early morning, the sky clear indigo and the stars a wash of brightness across the firmament, that he appeared at last, lifting out of the ether in a soft radiant light that bathed her in hope.

Walker, she whispered.

—I am here—

A**hren Elessedil** flew north through the night after escaping *Black Moclips,* his only plan to get as far from the Morgawr as he could manage. He had no clear idea of where he was or where he should be trying to go. He knew he should be looking for a rain forest somewhere in the mountains, but there was no hope of doing that until it got light. He had the stars to guide him, although the stars were aligned differently in this part of the world and partially blocked by the spread of the single wing, so it was difficult to use his navigational knowledge.

Not that he was deterred by this. He was so grateful to be free that his euphoria made every potential problem save being captured again seem solvable. The single wing sped on without difficulty on the back of steady breezes off the Blue Divide. He had worried at first that he might have trouble keeping his carrier aloft, but it proved to be relatively easy to fly. The wing straps allowed him to bank to either side and change direction, and the bar that ran the length of the framework opened and closed vents in the canvas so that he could gain altitude or descend. So long as the winds blew and he stayed away from downdrafts and bad storms, he thought he would be all right.

He had time to think on his journey, and his thoughts were mostly of Ryer Ord Star. The more he mulled over her situation, the less happy he was. She was playing a dangerous game, and she had no way to protect herself if she was found out. Once the Mwellrets discovered he was missing, she would be the first person they would suspect. Nor was he convinced that she had a way to get off the ship if that happened. Was there a second single wing hidden somewhere aboard the airship? She had told him that she would follow later, but he wasn't sure it was the truth.

He wished now that he hadn't been so quick to accommodate her. He wished he had forced her to come with him, no matter what she thought Walker wanted from her. He had been so eager to get away that he hadn't pressed the matter. He didn't like what he remembered about the way she had looked at him at the end. It felt final—as if she already knew she wasn't going to see him again.

She was a seer, after all, and it was possible that in one of her visions she had seen her own fate. But if she knew what was going to happen, couldn't she act to prevent it? He didn't know, and after a while he quit thinking about it. It was impossible for him to do anything to help until he found the others, and then maybe they could go back for her.

But in his heart, where such truths have a way of surfacing, he knew it was already too late.

The sun rose, and he flew on. New light etched the details of the land below, and he began to look for something he recognized. It quickly became apparent to him that his task was impossible. Everything looked the same from up there, and he didn't remember enough about the geography from flying along the coast aboard the *Jerle Shannara* to know what to look for. He knew he should turn inland toward the mountains, but how far north should he fly before he did that? Ryer Ord Star had told him she was misdirecting the Morgawr at Walker's request, so the coast was the wrong place for him to be. He should be searching for a rain forest. But where? He could see neither the beginning nor the end of the mountains that ran down the spine of the peninsula. Clouds blanketed the peaks and screened away the horizon, giving the impression that the world dropped away five miles in. He couldn't tell how far anything went. He couldn't even be sure of his direction without a compass.

He could try using the Elfstones. They were seeking stones, and they could find anything that was hidden from the naked eye. But using them would alert the Morgawr, and he had seen enough of the warlock's abilities to know that he could follow magic as a hunter did tracks. Using the Elfstones might bring the warlock down on his friends, as well, should he manage to find them. He didn't think he wanted to bear the responsibility for that, no matter how desperate his own situation.

The sun brightened, and the last of night's shadows began to fade from the landscape. The air warmed, but was still cold enough that he wished he was wearing something warmer. He hunched his shoulders and turned the single wing farther inland, away from the chilly coastal breezes. Maybe he would spy the rain forest and his friends if he just gave himself a little more time.

He gave himself the entire day, spiraling inland in ever widening sweeps, searching the sky and ground until his head ached. He found nothing—no sign of the *Jerle Shannara* or his friends or a rain forest. He saw barely anything moving, and then only a few hawks and gulls, and once a herd of deer. As the day lengthened and the sun began to slip west, his confidence started to fail. He swept further into the mountains, but the deeper in he went the more confusing things became. He had been flying for eighteen hours with nothing to eat or drink, and he was beginning to feel light-headed. He couldn't remember the last time he had slept. If he didn't find something soon, he would have to land. Once he did that, he wasn't sure he could get airborne again.

He stayed in the air, flying into the approaching darkness, stubbornly refusing to give up. Soon, he wouldn't be able to see at all. If he didn't land, he would have to fly all night because it was too cloudy for the moon and stars to provide enough light for him to try to set down. Soon, he would have to use the Elfstones. He would have no choice.

He rolled his shoulders and arched his back to relieve the strain of holding the same position for so long. Dusk settled over the land in deepening layers, and still he flew on.

He had almost decided to give it up when the Shrikes found him. He was far enough inland that he wasn't expecting them, thinking himself safely away from the danger of coastal birds. But there was no mistaking what they were or that they were coming for him. Hunting him, he thought with a chill. Sent by the Morgawr to track him down and destroy him. He knew it instinctively. They sailed toward him in the silvery glow of the failing sunset, seven of them, long wings and necks extended, hooked beaks lifted like blades.

He swung away immediately and started downward in a slow glide, unable to make the single wing respond with any greater agility or speed. It was like canoeing in rapids; you had to ride the current. Opening the vents all the way would drop him from the skies like a stone. The single wing wasn't designed for quick maneuvers. It wasn't built to flee Shrikes.

He spiraled toward the land below, toward peaks and cliffs, defiles and ravines, already able to tell that there was nowhere safe to land. But there was no time to worry about it and nothing he could do to change things. The best he could hope for was to get down before the Shrikes reached him. His flight was over. All that remained to be seen was how it would end.

He was still almost a thousand feet up when the first Shrike swept past him, claws raking the canvas and wood frame, sending him skidding sideways with a sickening lurch. He straightened out and angled sharply away, casting about for the others. If he had been frightened before, he was terrified now. He was helpless up here, strapped into his flimsy flying device, suspended in midair, unable to outrun or hide from his pursuers.

A second Shrike attacked, slamming into the single wing with such force that it jarred Ahren to his bones. He dropped dozens of feet before leveling out, and when he did, the single wing's flight had turned shaky and uneven, and he could hear the flapping of torn canvas.

All about him, the Shrikes circled, beaks lifted, claws extended, eyes reflecting like pools of hard light in the darkness of their predatory faces.

Use the Elfstones!

But he couldn't reach them without releasing his grip on the control bar, and if he did that, he might go straight down. He also risked dropping the Stones, fumbling them away as he tried to bring them to bear. Nevertheless, he took the gamble, certain that he was doomed otherwise. He let go of the bar and plunged his right hand into his tunic, tearing open the drawstrings of the pouch to fish out the stones.

Instantly, the single wing went into a steep dive. The Shrikes attacked from everywhere, but the wing was skewing sideways so badly that they were unable to get a grip on it. Shrieking, they dived past Ahren in a flurry of movement, wings whipping the air, talons extended, huge black shadows descending and then lifting away. He closed his eyes to sharpen his concentration, forcing his fingers to find and tighten about the Elfstones, drawing them clear.

He thrust his hand out in front of him, called up the power of the magic, and sent it sweeping out into the dark in a wall of blue fire.

The result was unexpected. The magic flooded the air with its sudden brightness, frightening the Shrikes but not harming them. Ahren, however, was sent spinning off into the void, the backlash from the magic nearly collapsing the single wing about his body. Belatedly, he remembered that the magic of the Elfstones was useless against creatures that did not rely on magic themselves. The Shrikes were immune to the power of the only weapon he possessed.

Still clutching the Elfstones, he tried to maneuver downward, diving between cliff faces so sheer that if he struck one, he would slide all the way to its base unimpeded. The Shrikes followed, screaming in frustration and rage, whipping past him in one series of near misses after another, the wake of their passing spinning him around until he could no longer determine where he was.

He was finished, he knew. He was a dead man. The whirl of land and sky formed a kaleidoscope of indigo and quicksilver, stars and darkness melding as he fought to slow his descent. A strut snapped with the sharpness of broken deadwood. His left wing shuddered and dipped.

Then something bigger than the Shrikes appeared at the corner of his eye, there for only a moment before the single wing spun him a different way. The Shrikes screamed anew, but the sound was different, and the Elven Prince detected fear in it. An instant later they were winging away, their dark shadows fading as quickly as their cries.

Something huge loomed over him, its shadow blacking out the sky. He tried to look upward to see what it was, but it collided with his single wing, knocking it askew once more, then latched on to the frame. He fought wildly to free it, to regain some control, but the control straps refused to respond or the grapples release.

The Morgawr! he thought in terror. *The Morgawr has found me once more!*

Then a second shadow appeared, lifting out of the well of cliffs and valleys in a spread of massive wings and a shining of great, gimlet eyes.

"Let go, Elven Prince!" Hunter Predd called out through the haze of shadows, reaching up from Obsidian's back to catch hold of his dangling legs.

Ahren quit struggling and did as he was told, releasing first the control straps and then the buckles and ties that secured him to the harness. In a rush of wind and blackness, he slid down into the Wing Rider's arms, scarcely able to believe the other was really there. In a daze, he watched the single wing and its harness tumble away, a tangle of crumpled wreckage.

"Hold tight," Hunter Predd whispered in his ear, rough-bearded face pressing close to his own, strong arms fastening a safety line in place. "We have a ways to go, but you're safe now."

Safe, Ahren repeated silently, gratefully, and began to shake all over.

Hunter Predd's strong arms tightened about him reassuringly, and with Po Kelles and Niciannon leading the way, they flew into the night.

Miles away in the same darkness that cloaked the fleeing Wing Riders and the Elven Prince, Ryer Ord Star hung from the yardarm of *Black Moclips*, swaying gently at the ends of the ropes tied about her wrists. Blood coated her arms from the deep gouges the ropes had made in her flesh, and sweat ran down her face and body in spite of the cool night air. Her pain was all encompassing, racking her slender body from head to toe, rising and falling in steady waves as she waited to die.

"Walker," she begged softly, "please help me."

She had called to him all night, but this time he responded. He appeared out of nowhere, suspended in air before her, his dark countenance pale and haunted, but so comforting to her that she would have welcomed it even if it was nothing more than a mirage. Wrapped in his Druid robes, he was a shade come from death's gate, a presence less of this world than the one beyond, yet in his eyes she found what she was seeking.

"Let me go," she whispered, the words thick and clotted in her throat. "Set me free."

He reached for her with his one good arm, his strong hand brushing against her ravaged cheeks, and his voice was filled with healing.

—Come with me—

She shook her head helplessly. "I cannot. The ropes hold me."

—Only because you cling to them. Release your grip—

She did so, not knowing how exactly, only knowing that because he said so, she could. She slipped from her bonds as if they were loose cords and stepped out into the air as if she weighed nothing. Her pain and her fear fell away like old clothes she had tossed aside. Her heartache subsided. She stood next to him, and when he reached out a second time, she took his hand in her own.

He smiled then and drew her close.

—Come away—

She did so, at rest and at peace, redeemed and forgiven, made whole by her sacrifice, and she did not look back.

TWENTY-SIX

When he went to look for the Ahren Elessedil shortly after dawn, Bek Ohmsford found him sitting at the stern of the *Jerle Shannara*. They had been airborne for more than three hours by then, flying south through heavy clouds and gray skies, intent on reaching the coast before nightfall.

The Elven Prince glanced up at him with tired eyes. He had been asleep for almost twelve hours, but looked haggard even so. "Hello, Bek," he said.

"Hello, yourself." He plopped down next to Ahren, resting his back against the ship's railing. "It's good to have you back. I thought we might have lost you."

"I thought so, too. More than once."

"You were lucky Hunter Predd found you when he did. I heard the story. I don't know how you did it. I don't think I could have. Flying all that way without food or rest."

Ahren Elessedil's smile was faint and sad. "You can do anything if you're scared enough."

They were silent then, sitting shoulder to shoulder, staring down the length of the airship as she nosed ahead through ragged wisps of cloud and mist. The air had a damp feel to it and smelled of the sea. Redden Alt Mer and his Rovers had cut short the repairs to the *Jerle Shannara* last night, installed the recovered diapson crystals early this morning, and lifted off at first light. The Rover Captain knew that the Morgawr had some control over the Shrikes that inhabited the coastal regions of Parkasia, and he was afraid that the birds that had attacked Ahren would alert the warlock and lead him to them. He could have used another day of work on his vessel, but the risk of staying on the ground any longer was too great. No one was upset with his decision. Memories of the Crake Rain Forest were fresh in everyone's minds.

In the pilot box, Spanner Frew stood at the helm, his big frame blocking the movements of his hands as he worked the controls. Now and then he shouted orders to one of the Rovers walking the deck, his rough voice booming through the creaking of the rigging, his bearded face turning to reveal its fierce set. There weren't all that many of them left to shout at, Bek thought. He numbered them in his head. Ten, counting himself. Twelve, if you added in the Wing Riders. Out of more than thirty who had started out all those months ago, that was all. Just twelve.

Make that thirteen, he corrected himself, adding in Grianne. Lucky thirteen.

"How is your sister?" Ahren asked him, as if reading his mind.

"Still the same. Doesn't talk, doesn't see me, doesn't respond to anything, won't eat or drink. Just sits there and stares at nothing." He looked over at the Elf. "Except for two nights ago. The night you were rescued, she saved Quentin."

He told Ahren the details as he had done for everyone else, aware that by doing so he was giving hope to himself as much as to them that Grianne might recover, and that when she did, she might not be the Ilse Witch anymore. It remained a faint hope, but he needed to believe that the losses suffered and the pain endured might count for something in the end. Ahren listened attentively, his young face expressionless, but his eyes distant and reflective.

When Bek was finished, he said quietly, "At least you were able to save someone other than yourself. I couldn't even do that."

Bek had heard the story of his escape from *Black Moclips* from Hunter Predd. He knew what the Elf was talking about.

"I don't see what else you could have done," Bek said, seeking words that would ease the other's sense of guilt. "She didn't want to come with you. She had already made up her mind to stay. You couldn't have changed that."

"Maybe. I wish I were sure. I was so eager to get away, to get off that ship, I didn't even think to try. I just let her tell me what to do."

Bek scuffed his boot against the deck. "Well, you don't know. She might have gotten away. She might have done what she said she was going to do. The Wing Riders are out looking for her. Don't give up yet."

Ahren stared off into space, his eyes haunted. "They won't find her, Bek. She's dead. I knew it last night. I woke up for no reason, and I knew it. I think she realized what was going to happen when she sent me away, but she wouldn't tell me because she knew that if she did, I wouldn't go. She had promised Walker she would stay, and she refused to break her word, even at the cost of her life."

He sounded bitter and confused, as if his realization of that premonition defied logical explanation.

"I hope you're wrong," Bek told him, not knowing what else to say.

Ahren kept his gaze directed out toward the misty horizon, above the sweep of the airship's curved rams, and did not reply.

Redden Alt Mer walked down the main passageway below-decks to the Captain's quarters—his quarters, once upon a time—searching for his sister. He was pretty sure by now, having walked the upper decks without success, that she had retired once more to the temporary shelter assigned to the wounded Quentin Leah and the unresponsive Grianne Ohmsford. It was the witch Little

Red would go to see, to look at and study, to contemplate in a way that bothered him more than he cared to admit. He was feeling better about himself since braving the horrors of the Crake to recover the lost diapson crystals, especially after hearing from Bek how the witch had wakened from her dead-eyed sleep long enough to do the unexpected and use her magic to help heal the Highlander. Big Red was feeling better, but not entirely well. His brush with death in the rain forest had left him hollowed out, and he wasn't sure yet what it would take to fill him up again. Recovering the crystals was a start, but he was still entirely too conscious of his own mortality, and given the nature of his life, that wasn't healthy.

But for the moment his concern was for his sister. Rue had always been more tightly wound than he was, the cautious one, the captain of her life, determined that she would decide what was best for those she felt responsible for, no matter the obstacles she faced. But, of late, she had begun to show signs of vacillation that had never been apparent before. It wasn't that she seemed any less determined, but that she seemed uncertain what it was she should be determined about.

Her attitude toward the Ilse Witch was such a case. In the beginning, there had been no question in his mind that as soon as she could find a way to do so, Rue would dispose of her. She would do so in a way that would remove all suspicion from herself, especially because of how she felt about Bek, but do it she would. Hawk's death demanded it. Yet something had happened to change her mind, something he had missed entirely, and it was impacting her in a way that suggested a major shift in her thinking.

He shook his head, wishing he understood what that something was. Since yesterday, when she had returned from the Crake with Bek after completing a mission he would have put a stop to in a minute had he known about it, she had come down here at every opportunity. She had taken up watch over the witch, as if to see what would happen when she woke, as if trying to ascertain what manner of creature she really was. At first, he had thought she was waiting for an opportunity to finish her off. But as time passed and opportunities came and went, he had begun to wonder. This wasn't about revenge for Hawk and the others; this was about something else. Whatever it was, he was baffled.

He pushed open the door to his cabin, and there she was, sitting next to Bek's sister, holding her hand and staring into her vacant eyes. It was such a strange scene that for a moment he simply stood there, speechless.

"Close the door," she said quietly, not bothering to look over.

He did so, then moved to where she could see him, and knelt at Quentin Leah's bedside for a moment, placing his fingers on the Highlander's wrist to read his pulse.

"Strong and steady," Little Red said. "Bek was right. She saved Quentin's life, whether she intended to or not."

"Is that what you're doing?" he asked, standing up again, giving the Highlander a final glance. "Trying to decide if it was an accident or not?"

"No," she said.

"What, then?"

"I'm trying to find out where she is. I'm trying to figure out how to reach her."

He stared at her, not quite believing what he was hearing. She was leaning forward as she sat in front of the witch, her face only inches away. There was no fear in her green eyes, no suggestion that she felt at risk. She held Grianne's hands loosely in her own, and she was moving her fingers over their smooth, pale backs in small circles.

"Bek said she was hiding from the truth about herself, that when the magic of the Sword of Shannara showed her that truth, it was too much for her, so she fled from it. Walker told him that she would come back when she found a way to forgive herself for the worst of her sins. A tall order, even to sort them all out, I'd think." She paused. "I'm trying to see if a woman can reach her when a man can't."

He nodded. "I guess it's possible it might happen that way."

"But you don't know why I have to be the one to find out."

"I guess I don't."

She didn't say anything for a long time, sitting silent and unmoving before Grianne Ohmsford, staring into her strange blue eyes. The Ilse Witch was little more than a child, Alt Mer realized. She was so young that any attempt to define her in terms of the acts she was said to have committed was impossible. In her comatose state, blank-faced and unseeing, she bore a look of complete innocence, as if incapable of evil or wrongdoing or any form of madness. Somehow, they had got it all wrong, and it needed only for her to come awake again to put it right.

It was a dangerous way to feel, he thought.

She looked over at him. 'I'm doing it for Bek," she said, as if to explain, then quickly turned her attention back to Grianne. "Maybe because of Bek."

Alt Mer moved to where she could no longer see him, doubt clouding his sunburned features. "Bek doesn't expect this of you. His sister isn't your responsibility. Why are you making her so?"

"You don't understand," she said.

He waited for her to say something more, but she didn't. He cleared his throat. "What don't I understand, Rue?"

She let him wait a long time before she answered, and he realized afterwards that she was trying to decide whether to tell him the truth, that the choice was more difficult for her than she had anticipated. "I'm in love with him," she said finally.

He wasn't expecting that, hadn't considered the possibility for a moment, although on hearing it, it made perfect sense. He remembered her reaction to his decision to take Bek with him into the Crake while leaving her behind. He remembered how she had cared for the boy when Hunter Predd had flown him in from the mountain wilderness, as if she alone could make him well.

Except that Bek wasn't a boy, as he had already noted days earlier. He was a man, grown up on this journey, changed so completely that he might be someone else altogether.

Even so, he could not quite believe what he was hearing. "When did this happen?" he asked.

"I don't know."

"But you're sure?"

She didn't bother to answer, but he saw her shoulders lift slightly as if to shrug the question away.

"You don't seem suited to each other," he continued, and knew at once that he had made a mistake. Her gaze shifted instantly, her eyes boring into him with unmistakable antagonism. "Don't get mad at me," he said quickly. "I'm just telling you what I see."

"You don't know who's suited to me, big brother," she said quietly, her gaze shifting back to the witch. "You never have."

He nodded, accepting the rebuke. He sat down now, needing to talk about this, thinking it might take a while, and having no idea what he was going to say. Or should. "I thought what Hawk thought—that you were never going to settle on anyone, that you couldn't stand it."

"Well, you were wrong."

"It just seems that your lives are so different. If you hadn't been thrown together on this voyage, your paths would never have crossed. Have you thought about what's going to happen when you get home?"

"If I get home."

"You will. Then Bek will go back to the Highlands and you'll go back to being a Rover."

She exhaled sharply, let go of Grianne Ohmsford's hands, and turned to face him. "We'd better get past this right now. I told you how I feel about Bek. This is new to me, so I'm still finding out what it means. I'm trying not to think too far ahead. But here is what I do know. I'm sick of my life. I've been sick of it for a long time. I didn't like it on the Prekkendorran, and I haven't cared much for it since. I thought that coming on this voyage, getting far away from everything I knew, would change things. It hasn't. I feel like I've been wandering around all these years and not getting anywhere. I want something different. I'm willing to take a look at Bek to see if he can give it to me."

Redden Alt Mer held her gaze. "You're putting a lot on him, aren't you?"

"I'm not putting anything on him. I'm carrying this burden all by myself. He loves me, too, Redden. He loves me in a way no one ever has. Not for how I look or what I can do or what he imagines me to be. It goes deeper than that. It touches on connections that words can't express and don't have to. It makes a difference when someone loves you like that. I like it enough that I don't want to throw it away without taking time to see where it leads."

She eased herself into a different position, her physical discomfort apparent, still sore from her wounds, still nursing her injuries. "I wanted to kill the Ilse Witch," she said. "I had every intention of doing so the moment I got the chance. I thought I owed that much to Hawk. But I can't do it now. Not while Bek believes she might wake up and be his sister again. Not after all he has done to protect her and care for her and give her a chance at being well. I don't have that right, not even to make myself feel good again about losing Hawk.

"So I've decided to try to do what Bek can't. I've decided to try to reach her, to see where she is and what she hides from, to try to understand what she's feeling. I've decided to let her know someone else cares what happens to her. Maybe I can. But even if I can't, I have to try. Because that's what loving someone requires of you— giving yourself to something they believe in, even when you don't. That's what I want to do for Bek. That's how I feel about him."

She turned back to Grianne Ohmsford, lifted the girl's hands in her own, and held them anew. "I keep thinking that if I can help her, maybe I can help myself. I'm as lost as she is. If I can find her, maybe I can find myself. Through Bek. Through feeling something for him." She leaned forward again, her face so close to Grianne's that she might have been thinking of kissing her. "I keep thinking that it's possible."

He stared at her in silence, thinking that he wasn't all that secure himself, that he felt lost, too. All this wandering about the larger world had a way of making you feel disconnected from everything, as if your life was something so elusive that you spent all the time allotted to you chasing after it and never quite catching up.

"Go away and leave me alone," she said to him. "Fly this airship back to where we came from. Get us safely home. Then we can talk about this some more. Maybe by then we will understand each other better than we do now."

He climbed back to his feet and stood watching her for a moment longer, thinking he should say something. But nothing he could think of seemed right.

Resigned to leaving well enough alone, to letting her do what she felt she must, he walked out of the room without a word.

Still sitting with Ahren by the aft railing, Bek Ohmsford glanced over as Redden Alt Mer emerged from the main hatchway and turned to look at him. What he saw in the Rover Captain's face was a strange mix of frustration and wonderment, a reflection of thoughts that Bek could only begin to guess at. The look lasted only a second, and then Alt Mer had turned away, walking over to the pilot box and climbing up to stand beside Spanner Frew, his attention directed ahead into the shifting clouds.

"I heard that Panax stayed behind," Ahren said, interrupting his thoughts.

Bek nodded absently. "He said he was tired of this journey, that he liked where he was and wanted to stay. He said with Walker and Truls Rohk both gone, there was nothing left to go home to. I guess I don't blame him."

"I can't wait to get home. I don't ever want to go away again, once I do." The Elf's face twisted in a grimace. "I hate what's happened here, all of it."

"It doesn't seem to have counted for much, does it?"

"Walker said it did, but I don't think I believe him."

Bek let the matter slide, remembering that Walker had told him that his sister was the reason they had come to Parkasia and returning her safely home was the new purpose of their journey. He still didn't understand why that was so. Forget that he wasn't sure if they could do it or if she would ever come awake again if they did. The reality was that they had come here to retrieve the books of magic and failed to do so. They had destroyed Antrax, so there was some satisfaction in knowing that no one else would end up like Kael Elessedil, but it felt like a high price to pay for the losses they had suffered. Too high, given the broad scope of their expectations. Too high, for what they had been promised.

"Ryer said I was going to be King of the Elves," Ahren said softly. He gave Bek a wry look. "I can't imagine that happening. Even if I had the chance, I don't think I would take it. I don't want to be responsible for anyone else but me after what's happened here."

"What will you do when you get home?" Bek asked him.

His friend shrugged. "I haven't thought about it. Go away somewhere, I expect. Being home means being back in the Westland, nothing more. I don't want to live in Arborlon. Not while my brother is King. I liked being with Ard Patrinell when he was teaching me. I'll miss him more than anyone except Ryer. She was special."

His lips compressed as tears came to his eyes, and he looked away self-consciously. "Maybe I won't go home, after all."

Bek thought about the dead, about those men and women who had come on this voyage with such determination and sense of purpose. Who would he miss most? He had known none of them when he started out and had become close to all at the end. The absence of Walker and Truls Rohk, because they had been his mentors and protectors, left the biggest void. But the others had been his friends, more so than the Druid and the shape-shifter. He couldn't imagine what his life would be like without them or even what it would be like when he parted company with those who remained. Everything about his future seemed muddled and confused, and it felt to him as if nothing he did would be enough to clear away the debris of his past.

His gaze drifted along the length of the ship's deck, searching for Rue Meridian. She was the future, or at least as much of it as he could imagine. He hadn't seen much of her since their return from the Crake Rain Forest. There hadn't been time for visiting while they readied the *Jerle Shannara* for flight, their sense of urgency at the approach of the Morgawr consuming all of their time and energy. But even after setting out, she had kept to herself. He knew she spent much of her time looking in on his sister, and at first he had worried about her intentions. But it seemed wrong of him to mistrust her when she felt about him as she did. It felt small-minded and petty. He thought that she was reconciled to her anger and disappointment at Grianne's presence and no longer thought it necessary to act on them. He thought that because she loved him she would want to help his sister.

So he left her alone, thinking that when she was ready to come to him again, she would do so. He didn't feel any less close to her because she chose to be alone. He didn't think she cared any less for him for doing so. They had always shared a strong sense of each other's feelings, even in the days when they were first becoming friends on the voyage out. There had never been a need for reassurances. Nothing had changed. Friendship required space and tolerance. Love required no less.

Still, he missed being with her. He knew he could seek her out in Big Red's quarters and she would not be angry with him. But it might be better to let her find her own way with Grianne.

"Maybe I'll go home, too," he whispered to himself.

But he wasn't as sure about it anymore.

It was late afternoon when the Wing Riders reappeared, illumined by the red glare of the fading sun. The *Jerle Shannara* was less than an hour from the coast, and there had been no sign of the Morgawr's airships. With the return of the Wing Riders, Redden Alt Mer intended to turn his vessel south and begin working along the cliffs that warded the south end of the peninsula to where he could set out across the Blue Divide.

Hunter Predd brought Obsidian beneath the airship, released his safety harness, caught hold of the lowered rope ladder, and climbed to the aft railing. Alt Mer extended his hand, and the Wing Rider took hold of it and pulled himself aboard. His lean face was ridged with dirt and bathed in sweat. His eyes were hard, flat mirrors that reflected the sunset's bloodred light. He looked around the airship without saying anything, his callused hands flexing within their leather gloves, his arms stretching over his windswept head.

"We're maybe a day ahead of them," he said finally, keeping his voice low enough that no one else could hear. "They're north of us, strung out along the edge of the mountains and flying inland. They must think we're still there, from the look of things."

Alt Mer nodded. "Good news for us, I'd say."

He held out a water skin, which the Wing Rider accepted wordlessly and drank from until he had emptied it. "Ran out of water two hours ago." He handed it back.

"It will be dark in another hour. After that, we won't be so easy to track, especially once we get out over the water."

"Maybe. Maybe not. They tracked us easily enough from home and then inland here. The only time they had any real trouble was after you crashed. That doesn't sound like an evasion tactic you want to employ regularly."

Alt Mer grunted noncommittally as he looked out over the railing at the darkness behind them, finding phantoms in the movement of the clouds against the mountains. The Wing Rider was right. He had no reason to think they could evade the Morgawr forever. Their best chance lay in putting as much distance between themselves and their pursuers as they could manage. Speed would make the difference as to whether they would escape or be forced to turn and fight. Speed was what the *Jerle Shannara* offered in quantities that not even *Black Moclips* could match.

"One other thing," Hunter Predd said, taking his arm and

leading him over to the far corner of the aft deck. There was no one else around now. Even Bek and the Elven Prince had gone below. "We found the seer's body."

Redden Alt Mer sighed. "Where?"

"Floating in the ocean some miles west of here. All broken up and cut to pieces. I wouldn't have known she was down there if not for Obsidian. Rocs can see things men can't."

He looked at Alt Mer with his hard, weathered eyes and shook his head. "You tell young Elessedil about her, if you can manage it. I can't. I've given out all the bad news I care to."

He squeezed Alt Mer's arm hard and walked away. Moments later, he was down the rope and back astride Obsidian, winging away into the darkness. Redden Alt Mer stood alone at the railing and wished he were going with him.

TWENTY-SEVEN

F lying through the night, the *Jerle Shannara* reached the tip of the peninsula at dawn. The Wing Riders had flown ahead to scout for resistance to her passage and had not encountered the Morgawr's airships. With no sign of their pursuers to discourage them, they set out across the Blue Divide for home.

From the first, they knew the return would be a journey of more than six months, and that was only if everything went well. Any disruption of their flying schedule, anything that forced them to land, would extend the time of their flight accordingly. So a certain pacing was necessary, and Redden Alt Mer wasted no time in advising those aboard of what that meant. They were down to thirteen in number, and of those, two were incapable of helping the others. Nor could Rue Meridian be expected to do much in the way of physical labor for at least several more weeks. Nor were the Wing Riders of much use in flying the airship, since they were needed aboard their Rocs to forage for food and water and to scout for pursuers.

That left eight able-bodied men—Spanner Frew; the Rover crew members Kelson Riat, Britt Rill, and Jethen Amenades; the Elves Ahren Elessedil and Kian; Bek Ohmsford; and himself. While

Bek would be of great help to the five Rovers in flying the airship, the Elves lacked the necessary skills and experience and would have to be relegated to basic tasks.

It was a small group to man an airship twenty-four hours a day for six months. For them to manage, they were going to have to be well organized and extraordinarily lucky. Alt Mer could do nothing about the latter, so he turned his attention to the former.

He set about his task by drawing up a duty roster for the eight men he could rely upon, splitting time between the Elves so that there would never be more than one of them on watch at a time. At least three men were needed to sail the *Jerle Shannara* safely, so he drew up a rotating schedule of eight-hour shifts, putting two men on the midnight-to-dawn shift when the airship would be mostly at rest. It was not a perfect solution, but it was the best he could come up with. Rue was the only one who complained, but he deflected her anger by telling her that she could handle the navigation, which would keep her involved with sailing the vessel and not relegate her to tender of the wounded.

On the surface of things, they were in good condition. There was sufficient food aboard to keep them alive for several weeks, and they carried equipment for hunting and fishing to help resupply their depleted stock. Water was a bigger problem, but he thought the Wing Riders would be able to help with their foraging. Weapons were plentiful, should they be attacked. Now that they had replaced the damaged diapson crystals with the ones they had recovered from the Crake, they were able to fly the airship at full power. Since they were aboard the fastest airship in the Four Lands, no other airship, not even *Black Moclips*, should be able to catch them.

But things were not always as they seemed. The *Jerle Shannara* had endured enormous hardship since she had departed Arborlon. She had been damaged repeatedly, had crashed once, and was patched in more places than Alt Mer cared to count. Even a ship built by Spanner Frew could not stand up to a beating like that without giving up something. The *Jerle Shannara* was a good vessel, but she was not the vessel she had been. If she held together for even half the distance they had to cover, it would be a miracle. It was likely she would not, that somewhere along the way she would break down. The crucial question was how serious the breakdown would be. If it was too serious and took too long to correct, the Morgawr would catch up to them.

Redden Alt Mer was nothing if not realistic, and he was not about to pretend that the warlock would not be able to track them. As Hunter Predd had pointed out, he had managed to do so before, so they had to expect he would be able to do so again. It was a big ocean, and there were an infinite number of courses that they could set, but in the end they still had to fly home. If they failed to take a direct course, they were likely to find the Morgawr and his airships waiting for them when they got there. Getting back to the Four Lands before their enemies would give them a chance at finding shelter and allies. It was the better choice.

So he addressed the company as Captain and leader of the expedition and made his assignments accordingly, all the while knowing that at best he was staving off the inevitable. But a good airship Captain understood that flying was a mercurial experience, and that routine and order were the best tools to rely on in preparing for it. Bad luck was unavoidable, but it didn't have to find you right away. A little good luck could keep it at bay, and he had always had good luck. Given what the ship had come through to get to this point, he was inclined to think that his streak had not deserted him.

Nor did it do so in the weeks ahead. In the course of their travels, they encountered favorable weather with steady winds and clear skies, and they found regular opportunities to forage for food and water. They flew over the Blue Divide without need for slowing or setting down. Radian draws frayed, ambient-light sheaths tore loose, parse tubes required adjustments, and controls malfunctioned, all in accord with Alt Mer's expectations, but none of it was serious and all of it was quickly repaired.

More important, there was no sign of the Morgawr's airships and no indication that the warlock was tracking them.

Alt Mer kept his tiny crew working diligently at their assigned tasks, and if he felt they needed something more to occupy their time or take their minds off their problems, he found it for them. At first, their collective attitude was dour, a backlash from the hardships and losses suffered on Parkasia. But gradually time and distance began to heal and their spirits to lift. The passing of the days and the acceptance of a routine that was free of risk and uncertainty gave them both a renewed sense of confidence and hope. They began to believe in themselves again, in the possibility of a future safely back in the Four Lands and a life beyond the monstrous events of the past few weeks.

Ahren Elessedil emerged a little farther from his despondency each day. That he was damaged was unmistakable, but it seemed to Bek that the damage was repairable and that with time he would find a way to reconcile the loss of Ryer Ord Star. When Ahren learned of her death from Big Red, he seemed to lose heart entirely. He quit taking nourishment and refused to speak. He languished belowdecks and would not emerge. But Bek kept after him, staying close, talking to him even when he would not respond, and bringing him food and water until he started to eat and drink again.

Eventually, he began to recover. He no longer sought to blame himself for Ryer's death. He found it hard to speak of her, and Bek kept their conversations away from any mention of the seer. They spoke often of Grianne, who remained unchanged from when they had departed Parkasia, still a statue staring off into space, unresponsive and remote. They discussed what she had done for Quentin and what it meant to her chances for recovery. Ahren was more supportive of her than Bek would have expected, given the trouble she had visited on him, directly and indirectly. But Ahren seemed capable of unconditional forgiveness and infinite grace, and he displayed a maturity that had not been there when they had set out from Arborlon all those months ago. But then, Bek had been no more mature. Boys, both of them, but their boyhood was past.

Quentin continued to improve. He was awake much of the time, if only for short stretches, but he was still weak and unable to leave his bed. It would be weeks yet before he could stand, longer still before he could walk. He remembered almost nothing of what had happened in the Crake or anything of Grianne's healing use of the wishsong. But Bek was there to explain it to him, to sit with him each day, gradually catching small glimpses of the familiar smile and quick wit, finding new reasons with each visit to feel encouraged.

Bek spent time with Grianne as well, speaking and singing to her, trying to find a way to reach her, and failing. She had locked herself away again. Nothing he tried would persuade her to respond. That she had come out the first time was mystifying, but that she would not come a second time was maddening. He could think of no reason for it, and his inability to solve the riddle of her became increasingly frustrating.

Nevertheless, he kept at it, refusing to give up, certain that somehow he would find a way to break through, convinced that Walker had spoken the truth in prophesying that one day his sister would come back to him.

He spent stolen time with Rue Meridian, hidden away from the rest of the company, lost in words and touchings meant only for each other. She loved him so hard that he thought each time it ended and they separated that he could not survive letting her go. He thought he was blessed in a way that most men could only dream about, and in the silence of his mind he thanked her for it a hundred times a day. She told him that he was healing her, that he was giving her back her life in a way she had not thought possible. She had been adrift, she said, lost in her Rover wanderings, cast away from anything that mattered beyond the day and the task at hand. That she had found salvation in him was astonishing to her. She confessed she had thought nothing of him in the beginning, that she saw him as only a boy. She thought it important that he was her friend first, and that her deeper love for him was built on that.

She told him that he was her anchor in life. He told her that she was a miracle.

They spent their passion and their wonder when the night was dark and the company mostly asleep, and if anyone saw what they were doing, no one admitted to it. Perhaps for those who suspected what was happening, there was a measure of joy to be found in what Bek shared with Rue, an affirmation of life that transcended even the worst misfortunes. Perhaps in that small, but precious joining of two wounded souls, there was hope to be found that others might heal, as well.

So the days passed, and the *Jerle Shannara* sailed on, drawing further away from Parkasia and closer to home. Voracious sea birds circled the remains of meals consumed by sleek predators, and schools of krill swam from the wide-stretched jaws of leviathans. Far away on the Prekkendorran, the Races still warred across a plain five miles wide and twenty miles long. Farther away still, creatures of old magic slumbered, cradled in the webbing of their restless dreams and unbreakable prison walls.

But in the skies above the Blue Divide, the troubles of other creatures and places were as distant as yesterday, and the world below remained a world apart.

But even worlds apart have a way of colliding. Eight weeks into their journey, with the Four Lands still a long way off, Redden Alt Mer's fabled luck ran out. The sun was bright in the sky and the weather perfect. They were on course for Mephitic, where they hoped to use the Wing Riders to forage for fresh water and game while the airship stayed safely aloft. Alt Mer was at the helm, one of three on duty for the midday shift, with Britt Rill working the port draws and Jethen Amenades the starboard. The other members of the company were asleep below, save Rue Meridian, who was looking after Quentin and Grianne in the Captain's quarters, and Ahren Elessedil, who was weaving lanyards in one of the starboard pontoon fighting stations.

Alt Mer had just taken a compass reading when the port midships draw gave way with a sharp, vibrating crack that caused him to duck instinctively. It whipped past his head, wrapping about the port aft draw and snapping it loose, as well. Instantly, the masts sagged toward the starboard rail, the weight of their sails dragging them down, breaking off metal stays and pieces of crossbars and spars as they did so. Responding to the loss of balance in the sails and failure of power in the port tubes, the airship skewed sharply left. Alt Mer cried out a warning as both Rill and Amenades raced to secure the loose draws, but before he could right the listing vessel, it lurched sharply, twisting downward, sending Rill flying helplessly along the port rail and Amenades over the side.

They were a thousand feet in the air when it happened; Amenades was a dead man the minute he disappeared into the void. There was no time to dwell on it, so Alt Mer's hands were already flying over the controls as he shouted at Rill to grab something and hold fast. Without bothering to see if the other had done so, he cut power to all but the two forward parse tubes and put the ship into a steep downward glide. He heard the sound of heavy objects crashing into bulkheads and sliding along corridors, and a flurry of angry curses. As the airship finally righted itself, he opened the front end of the forward tubes, reversed power through the ports, and caught the backwash of the wind in the mainsail to bring up her nose.

Holding her steady against the tremors that rocked her, he eased her slowly into the ocean waters and shut her down.

Britt Rill staggered to his feet, Ahren Elessedil climbed from the fighting port, and all the rest poured out through the main hatchway and converged on Alt Mer. He shouted down their questions and exclamations and put them to work on the severed draws, broken stays and spars, and twisted masts. A quick survey under Spanner Frew's sharp-tongued direction revealed that the damage was more extensive than Alt Mer had thought. The problem this time did not lie with something as complicated as missing diapson crystals, but with something more mundane. The aft mast was splintered so badly it could not be repaired and would have to be replaced. To do that they would have to land, cut down a suitable tree, and shape a new mast from the trunk.

The only forested island in the area was Mephitic.

Alt Mer was as unhappy as he could be on realizing what this meant, but there was no help for it. He dispatched the Wing Riders to retrieve the body of Jethen Amenades, then called the others together to tell them what they were going to have to do. No one said much in response. There wasn't much of anything to say. Circumstances dictated a course of action they would all have preferred to avoid, but could do nothing about. The best they could do was to land far from the castle that housed the malignant spirit creature Bek and Truls Rohk had encountered and hope it could not reach beyond the walls of its keep.

They made what repairs they could, detaching the draws to the aft parse tubes and reducing their power by one-third. All of a sudden they were no longer the fastest airship in the skies, and if the Morgawr was tracking them, he would quickly catch up. The Wing Riders returned with Amenades, and they weighed him down and buried him at sea before setting out once more.

Setting a course for Mephitic, they limped along for all of that day and the two after, casting anxious glances over their shoulders at every opportunity. But the Morgawr did not appear, and their journey continued uninterrupted until at midday on the fourth day, land appeared on the horizon. It was the island they were seeking, its broad-backed shape instantly recognizable. Green with forests and grassy plains, it shimmered in a haze of damp heat like a jewel set in azure silk, deceptively tranquil and inviting.

From his position at the controls in the pilot box, Redden Alt Mer stared at it bleakly. "Let's make this quick," he muttered to himself, and pointed the horns of the *Jerle Shannara* landward.

They set down on the broad plain fronting the castle ruins, well back from the long shadow of its crumbling walls. Alt Mer had thought at first to land somewhere else on the island, but then decided that the western plain offered the best vantage point for establishing a perimeter watch against anything that approached or threatened. He assumed that the spirit that lived in the castle could sense their presence wherever they were, and the best they could hope for was that it either couldn't reach them or wouldn't bother trying if they left it alone. He dispatched the Wing Riders to search for food and water, then Spanner Frew, Britt Rill, and the Elven Hunter Kian to locate a tree from which to fashion a new mast. The others were put to work on sentry duty or cleaning up.

By sundown, everyone was back aboard. The Wing Riders had located a water source, Spanner Frew had found a suitable tree and cut it down, and the thing that lived in the ruins had not appeared. The members of the company, save Quentin and Grianne, sat together on the aft deck and ate their dinner, watching the sunset wash lavender and gold across the dark battlements and towers of the castle, as if making a vain attempt to paint them in a better light. As the sun disappeared below the horizon, the color faded from the stones and night's shadows closed about.

Alt Mer stood looking at the outline of the ruins after the others had dispersed. Kian was scheduled to stand guard, but he sent the Elven Hunter below, deciding to take his place, thinking that on this night he was unlikely to sleep anyway. Taking up a position at the *Jerle Shannara*'s stern, he left responsibility for keeping watch over the Blue Divide to Riat and gave his attention instead to the empty, featureless landscape of Mephitic.

His thoughts quickly drifted. He was troubled by what he perceived as his failure as Captain of his airship. Too many men and women had died while traveling with him, and their deaths did not rest easy with him. He might pretend that the responsibility lay elsewhere, but he was not the kind of man who looked for ways to shift blame to others. A Captain was responsible for his charges, no matter what the circumstances. There was nothing he could do for those who were dead, but he was afraid that perhaps there was nothing he could do for those who were still alive, either. His confidence had been eroding incrementally since the beginning of their time on Parkasia, a gradual wearing away of his certainty that nothing bad could happen to those who flew with him. His reputation had been built on that certainty. He had the luck, and luck was the most single important weapon of an airship Captain.

Luck, he whispered to himself. Ask Jahnon Pakabbon about his luck. Or Rucker Bont and Tian Cross. Or any of the Elves who had gone inland to the ruins of Castledown and never come back. Ask Jethen Amenades. What luck had Alt Mer given to them? It wasn't that he believed he had done anything to cause their deaths. It was that he hadn't found a way to prevent them. He hadn't kept his people safe, and he was afraid he had lost the means for doing so.

Sooner or later, luck always ran out. He knew that. His seemed to have begun draining away when he had agreed to undertake this voyage, so self-confident, so determined everything would work out just as he wanted it to. But nothing had gone right, and now Walker was dead and Alt Mer was in command. What good was that going to do any of those who depended on him if the armor of his fabled luck was cracked and rusted?

Staring at the dark bulk of the ruins across the way, he could not help thinking that what he saw, broken and crumbled and abandoned, was a reflection of himself.

But his pride would not let him accept that he was powerless to do anything. Even if his luck was gone, even if he himself was doomed because of it, he would find a way to help the others. It was the charge he must give himself, that so long as he breathed, he must get those he captained, those eleven men and women who were left, safely home again. Saving just those few would give him some measure of peace. That one of them was his sister and another the boy she loved made his commitment even more necessary. That all of them were his friends and shipmates made it imperative.

He was still thinking about this when he sensed a presence at his elbow and glanced over to find Bek Ohmsford standing next to him. He was so surprised to see Bek, perhaps because he had just been thinking of him, that for a moment he didn't speak.

"It won't come out of there," Bek said, nodding in the direction of the castle. His young face bore a serious cast, as if his thoughts were taking him to dark and complex places. "You don't have to worry."

Alt Mer followed his gaze to the ruins. "How do you know that?"

"Because it didn't come after me when I stole the key the last time we were here. Not past the castle walls, not outside the ruins." He paused. "I don't think it can go outside. It can chase you that far, but no farther. It can't reach beyond."

The Rover Captain thought about it for a moment. "It didn't bother us when we were searching the ruins, did it? It just used its magic to turn us down blind alleys and blank walls so that we couldn't find anything."

Bek nodded. "I don't think it will bother us if we stay out here. Even if we go in, it probably won't interfere if we don't try to take anything."

They stood shoulder to shoulder for a few moments, staring out into the darkness, listening to the silence. A dark, winged shape flew across the lighter indigo of the starlit sky, a hunting bird at work. They watched it bank left in a sweeping glide and disappear into the impenetrable black of the trees.

"What are you doing out here?" Alt Mer asked him. "Why aren't you asleep?"

He almost asked why he wasn't with Rue, but Bek hadn't chosen to talk about it, and Alt Mer didn't think it was up to him to broach the subject.

Bek shook his head, running his hand through his shaggy hair. "I couldn't sleep. I was dreaming about Grianne, and it woke me. I think the dream was telling me something important, but I can't remember what. It bothered me enough that I couldn't go back to sleep, so I came up here."

Alt Mer shifted his feet restlessly. "You still can't reach her, can you? Little Red can't either. Never thought she'd even try, but she goes down there every day and sits with her."

Bek didn't say anything, so Alt Mer let the matter drop. He was growing tired, wishing suddenly that he hadn't been so quick to send Kian off to sleep.

"Are you upset with me about Rue?" Bek asked suddenly.

Alt Mer stared at him in surprise. "Don't you think it's a little late to be asking me that?"

Bek nodded solemnly, not looking back. "I don't want you to be angry. It's important to both of us that you aren't."

"Little Red quit asking my permission to do anything a long time ago," Alt Mer said quietly. "It's her life, not mine. I don't tell her how to lead it."

"Does that mean it's all right?"

"It means . . ." He paused, confused. "I don't know what it means. It means I don't know. I guess I worry about what's going to happen when you get back home and have to make a choice about your lives. You're different people; you don't have the same background or life experience."

Bek thought about it. "Maybe we don't have to live our old lives. Maybe we can live new ones."

Alt Mer sighed. "You know something, Bek. You can do whatever you want, if you put your mind to it. I believe that. If you love her as much as I think you do—as much as I know she loves you—then you'll find your way. Don't ask me what I think or if I'm upset or what I might suggest or anything. Don't ask anyone. Just do what feels right."

He clapped Bek lightly on the shoulder. "Of course, I think you should become a Rover. You've got flying in your blood." He yawned. "Meanwhile, stand watch for me, since you're so wide awake. I think I need a little sleep after all."

Without waiting for an answer, he walked over to the main hatchway and started down. There was a hint of self-confidence in his step as he did so. One way or another, it would work out for all of them, he promised himself. He could feel it in his bones.

The company was awake and at work shortly after sunrise, continuing repair efforts on the damaged *Jerle Shannara*. Using axes and planes, Spanner Frew and the other two Rover crewmen took all morning to shape the mast from the felled tree trunk. It was afternoon before they had hauled it back to the ship to prepare it for the spars and rigging it would hold when it was set in place. The painstaking process required a careful removal of metal clasps and rings from the old mast so that they could be used again; the work would not be completed for at least another day. Those not involved were sent out to complete the foraging begun the other day by the Wing Riders, who had been dispatched to make certain the company was still safely ahead of the Morgawr.

They weren't. By late afternoon, the Wing Riders returned, landed their Rocs close by the airship, and delivered the bad news. The Morgawr's fleet was less than six hours out and coming directly toward them. In spite of everything, the warlock had managed to track them down once more. If the enemy airships continued to advance at their present pace, they would arrive on Mephitic shortly after nightfall.

Anxious eyes shifted from face to face. There was no way that the repairs to the *Jerle Shannara* could be finished by then. At best, if she tried to flee now, she would be flying at a speed that would allow even the slowest pursuer to catch her within days. The choices were obvious. The company could try to hide or they could stand and fight.

Redden Alt Mer already knew what they were going to do. He had been preparing since the night before, when he had decided that no one else was going to die under his command. Assuming the worst might happen, he had come up with a plan, suggested by something Bek had told him, to counteract it.

"Gather up everything," he ordered, striding through their midst as if already on his way to do so himself. "Don't leave even the smallest trace of anything that would suggest we were here. Put everything aboard so we can lift off. Hunter Predd, can you and Po Kelles find hiding places for yourselves and your Rocs offshore on one of the atolls? You'll need a couple of days."

The Wing Riders looked at each other doubtfully, then looked at him. "Where will you be while we're safe and snug on the ground?" Hunter Predd asked bluntly. "Up in a cloud?"

Alt Mer smiled cheerfully. "Hiding in plain sight, Wing Rider. Hiding right under their noses."

TWENTY-EIGHT

By the time the Morgawr brought his fleet of airships to within view of Mephitic, darkness had eclipsed the light necessary for a search, so he had them anchor offshore until dawn. His Mwellrets supervised the walking dead who crewed the ships, giving them directions for what was needed before setting themselves at watch against a night attack. Such a thing was not out of the question. His quarry was close ahead, perhaps still on the island, her scent stronger than it had been in days, a dense perfume on the salt-laden air.

The following morning, when it grew light and he could see clearly, he set out to discover where she had gone. Leaving the remainder of his fleet at anchor, he flew *Black Moclips* in a slow, careful sweep over the island, searching for her hiding place.

His mood was no longer as dark and foul as it had been after the seer had died, when he had felt both betrayed and outwitted. The seer had tricked him into following blind leads and useless visions. The *Jerle Shannara* and her crew had escaped him completely, flying out of Parkasia through the mountains even as he was flying in. With the Ilse Witch safely aboard, they had gotten behind him and turned for home.

He had known what that meant. The Druid's vessel was the faster ship, much faster than anything the Morgawr commanded, including *Black Moclips*. He had lost the advantages of surprise and numbers both, and if he did not find a way to turn things around, he risked losing them completely.

But the Four Lands were a long way off, and fate had intervened on his behalf. Something had happened to slow the *Jerle Shannara*, allowing him to catch up. Even though she had gotten far ahead of him, he had still been able to track her. She had brought aboard her own doom in the form of the Ilse Witch, and once that was done, her fate was sealed. Just as the little witch had tracked the Druid from the Four Lands through her use of the seer as her spy, so had he tracked her through her use of her magic. The scent of it, layered on the air, was pungent and clear, a trail he could not mistake. For a time, when the witch had escaped into the mountains with her brother, he had lost all track of her. He assumed she had simply ceased using the magic, though that was unlike her.

Then, only days before the Elven Prince had fled and he'd had the seer killed, there had been a resurgence of the use of magic deep in Parkasia's mountains. At the time, intent on following the seer's false visions, he had ignored it. But now he had the Ilse Witch's scent again, so strong there was no need for anything more. Small bursts of it permeated the air through which he flew, sudden fits and starts he could not explain, but could read well enough. Wherever she went, while she remained aboard the *Jerle Shannara*, he would be able to find her.

Her scent was present now, hanging in a cloud over the island, blown everywhere on the breeze. But did it lead away? Had they gotten off the island just ahead of him? That was what he must discover.

He cruised Mephitic from end to end, tracking the magic, following its trail. He determined quickly enough that it did not extend beyond the island's broad, low sweep. He felt a wildness building in him, an anticipation bordering on frenzy. They were here still, he had them trapped. He could already taste the witch's life bleeding out of her and into him. He could already imagine the sweetness of its taste.

So he swept the island carefully, flying low enough to read its details, seeking to uncover their hiding place, thinking that no matter how well they hid themselves, they could not hide the scent of his little witch's magic. They might even abandon their ship, though he could not believe they would be so foolish, but they were his for the taking so long as they kept the witch beside them. If the boy was her brother, as the Morgawr was now certain he must be, there was no question but that they would.

Even so, he could not find them. He searched from the air until his eyes ached and his temper frayed. He put Cree Bega and his Mwellrets at every railing and had them search, as well. They found nothing. They searched until midmorning, and then he brought the rest of the fleet inland and had them fan out and blanket the island from the air. When that failed, he had the Mwellrets disembark and under Cree Bega's command search on foot. He had them comb the forests and even the open grasslands, seeking anything that would indicate the presence of his quarry.

He had them search everywhere except the castle ruins.

The ruins presented a problem. Something was alive inside those walls, something birthed of old magic and not made of flesh and blood. In spirit form, it had lived for thousands of years, and it regarded those broken parapets and crumbling towers as its own. The Morgawr had sensed its presence right away and sensed, as well, that it might be as powerful as he was. He was not about to send the Mwellrets stumbling about in its domain unless there was good reason to do so. From the air, he had seen nothing to suggest that his quarry had gotten inside. That they could do so seemed doubtful, but if they had, there should be some sign of them.

The hunt continued through the remainder of the day without

result. The Morgawr was furious. It was impossible that he had been mistaken about the scent of the magic, but even so he went back around in *Black Moclips*, well off the island, to see if he had misread it somehow. But the results were the same; there was no trail leading away. Unless they had found a way to disguise the Ilse Witch's scent—which they had no reason even to think of doing—they were still on the island.

By darkness, he was convinced of it. A tree had been cut down very recently, and shavings indicated that something had been shaped from it. A mast, the Morgawr guessed. A broken mast would explain why they had been forced to slow and why he had been able to catch up to them. The Mwellrets found tracks, as well, deeper into the trees where damp grasses and soft earth left imprints. There were fresh gouges on the plains across from the castle, as well, where an airship might have been moored.

Now there was no doubt in the Morgawr's mind that the *Jerle Shannara* and her company had been on Mephitic less than a day ago, and unless he was completely mistaken, they were still here.

But where were they hiding?

It took him only a moment to decide. They were inside the castle. There was nowhere else they could be.

He sent his searchers back aboard their ships and had them make a final pass over the dusk-shrouded island before moving back out to sea to drop anchor just offshore. There he set the watch, and while the Mwellrets went about the business of shutting down the airships and settling in for the night, he stood alone in the prow of *Black Moclips*, thinking.

He did not yet know what had happened to reunite the Ilse Witch with her brother. He did not know if she was now her brother's ally or simply his prisoner. He had to assume she was the former, although he had no idea how that could have happened. That meant she would have the support of not only her brother, but also the young Elessedil Prince and whoever else was still alive, as well. But she would not have the Druid to protect her, and the Druid was the only one who might have stood a chance against him. The others, even fighting together, were not strong enough. The Morgawr had been alive a long time, and he had fought hard to stay that way. The power of his magic was terrifying, and his skill at wielding it more than sufficient to overcome these children.

Still, he would be careful. They would know he was there by now, and they would be waiting for him. They would try to defend themselves, but that would be hopeless. Most of them would die quickly at the hands of his Mwellrets, leaving the few who possessed the use of magic for him to deal with. A few quick strikes, and it would be over.

Yet he wanted his little Ilse Witch alive, so that he could feed on her, so that he could feel her life drain away through his fingertips. He had trained her to be his successor, a mirror image of himself. She had become that, her magic fed by rage and despair. But her ambition and her willfulness had outstripped her caution, and so she was no longer reliable. Better to have done with her than to risk her treachery. Better to make an example of her, one that no one could possibly mistake. Cree Bega and his Mwellrets wanted her gone anyway. They had always hated her. Perhaps they had understood her better than he had.

His gaze lifted. Tomorrow, he would watch her die in the way of so many others. It would give him much satisfaction.

Radiating black venom and hunger, he stood motionless at the railing and imagined how it would be.

Crouched in the shadow of the crumbling castle walls, only a dozen yards from where the *Jerle Shannara* lay concealed, Bek Ohmsford watched the dark bulk of an airship pass directly overhead, then swing around and pass back again. It floated over the ruins like a storm cloud.

"That's *Black Moclips*," Rue whispered in his ear, pressing up against him, her words barely more than a breath of air in the silence.

He nodded without offering a reply, waiting until the vessel was far enough away that it felt safe to speak. "He knows we're here," he said.

"Maybe not."

"He knows. He would have moved on by now if he didn't. He searched the entire island and didn't find us, but he knows we're here. He senses it somehow. Tomorrow, he'll search these ruins."

They had been in hiding all day, ever since Redden Alt Mer had taken the *Jerle Shannara* inside the castle walls. It was a bold gamble, but one that the Rover Captain thought would work. If the creature that lived in the ruins had not bothered with them when they had searched for the key, it might not bother with them now, even if they set the *Jerle Shannara* down inside one of its numerous court-yards. So long as they did not try to take anything out, it might tolerate their presence long enough for them to deceive the Morgawr.

There was time to try his plan out before the warlock reached them, and so they did. They had been able to fly the *Jerle Shannara* into the ruins and set her down in a deeply shadowed cluster of walls and towers. Once anchored, they had stripped her of sails and masts and rigging, leaving her decks bare. When that was done, they had covered her over with rocks and dirt and grasses until from the air, astride a Roc, they could not see her at all and would not have known she was there.

Alt Mer knew they were taking a big chance. If they were discovered, they would have no chance of getting aloft with the masts and rigging and sails dismantled. They would be trapped and most probably killed or captured. But the Rover Captain was counting on something else, as well. When they had tried to penetrate the ruins on their way to Parkasia, the castle's spirit dweller had used its magic to turn them aside. Each new foray took them down blind alleys and dead ends and eventually back outside. If that magic was still in place, it ought to work in the same way against the Morgawr and his rets. When they tried to come inside, they would be led astray and never get past the perimeter walls.

With luck, it should not come to that. With luck, the Morgawr should determine after a careful sweep of the island that his quarry had eluded him. There should be no reason to search the ruins from the ground if nothing was visible from the air.

But Bek knew it wasn't going to work out that way. Their concealment had been perfect, but the Morgawr's instincts were telling him that they were still on the island. They were whispering to him that he was missing something, and it wouldn't take him long to determine what it was. He would decide that they must be hiding in the ruins. Tomorrow, he would search them. It might not yield him anything, but if it did, the company of the *Jerle Shannara* was finished.

With Rue still pressing close, he leaned back against the cool stone of the old wall. *Black Moclips* had not returned, and the sky was left bright and open in its wake, a trail of glittering stars shining down through a wash of moonlight. The others of the company were inside the *Jerle Shannara*, kept there by Redden Alt Mer's strict order not to venture out for any reason. Bek was the sole exception, because an outside perspective was needed in case of an attempted ground approach and Bek was best able to conceal himself from the spirit dweller, should the need arise. Rue was with him because it was understood that wherever Bek went, she went, as well. They had been out there, hiding in the shadows, since early morning. It was time to go inside and get some sleep.

But Bek's mind was running too fast and too hard to permit him to sleep, his thoughts skipping from consideration of one obstacle to the next, from one concern to another, everything tied up with the dangerous situation facing them and what they might try to do to avoid it.

One concern, in particular, outstripped the rest.

He bent close to Rue. "I don't know what to do about Grianne." His lips pressed against her ear, his words a hushed whisper. Voices carried in the empty silence of ruins such as these, beyond even walls of mortar and stone. "If the Morgawr comes for her, she will have no way to protect herself. She will be helpless."

Rue leaned her head against him, her hair as soft as spiderwebbing. "Do you want to try to hide her somewhere besides here?" she whispered back.

"No. He'll find her wherever we put her. I have to wake her up."

"You've been trying that for weeks, Bek, and it hasn't worked. What can you do that you haven't already done?"

He kissed her hair and put his arms around her. "Find out what it is that keeps her in hiding. Find out what it will take to bring her out."

He could sense her smile even in the darkness. "That isn't a new plan. That's an old one."

He nodded, touching her knee in soft reproach. "I know. But suppose we could figure out what it would take to wake her. We've tried everything we could think of, both of us. But we keep trying in a general way, a kind of blanket approach to bringing her out of her sleep. Walker said she wouldn't come back to us until she found a way to forgive herself for the worst of her wrongs. I think that's the key. We have to figure out what that wrong is."

She lifted her head, her red hair falling back from her face. "How can you possibly do that? She has hundreds of things to forgive herself for. How can you pick out one?"

"Walker said it was the one *she* believed to be the worst." He paused, thinking. "What would that be? What would she see as her worst wrong? Killing someone? She's killed lots of people. Which one would matter more than the others?"

Rue furrowed her smooth brow. "Maybe this was something she did when she first became the witch, when she was still young, something that goes to the heart of everything she's done since."

He stared at her for a long time, remembering his dream of the other night. It had been nagging at him ever since, reduced to a vague image, the details faded. It hovered now, just beyond his grasp. He could practically reach out and touch it.

"What is it?" she asked.

"I don't know. I think there's something in what you just said that might help, something about her childhood." He stared at her some more. "I have to go down and sit with her. Maybe looking at her, being in the same room for a while, will help."

"Do you want me to come with you?"

When he hesitated, she reached out and cupped his face in her hands. "Go by yourself, Bek. Maybe you need to be alone. I'll come later, if you need me to."

She kissed him hard, then slipped from his side and disappeared back into the bowels of the airship. He waited only a moment more, still wrestling with his confusion, then followed her inside.

There was no reason to think that this night would be different from any other, but Bek was convinced by feelings he could not explain that it might be. Nothing he had tried—and he had tried everything—had gotten so much as a blink out of Grianne from the moment he had found her kneeling with the bloodied Sword of Shannara grasped in her hands. Only when he broke down in frustration and cried that one time, when he wasn't even trying to make her respond, had she come out of her catatonia to speak with him. She had done so for reasons he had never been able to figure out, but tonight, he thought, he must. The secret to everything lay in connecting the reason for that singular awakening with the wrong she had committed somewhere in her past that she regarded as unforgivable.

He told Redden Alt Mer what he was going to do and suggested someone else might want to take up watch from one of the taller towers. Alt Mer said he would handle it himself, wished Bek good luck, and went over the side of the airship. Bek stood alone on the empty deck, thinking that perhaps he should ask Rue to help him after all. But he knew he would be doing so only as a way of gaining reassurance that he had done everything he could, should things not work out yet again. It was not right to use her that way, and he abandoned the idea at once. If he failed this night, he wanted it to be on his head alone.

He went down to the Captain's quarters and slipped through the doorway. Quentin Leah lay asleep in his bed, his breathing deep and even, his face turned away from the single candle that burned nearby. The windows were shuttered and curtained so that no light or sound could escape, and the air in the room was close and stale. Bek wanted to blow out the candle and open the shutters, but he knew that would be unwise.

Instead, he walked over to his sister. She was lying on her pallet with her knees drawn up and her eyes open and staring. She wore her dark robe, but a light blanket had been laid over her, as well. Rue had brushed her hair earlier that day, and the dark strands glimmered in the candlelight like threads of silk. Her fingers were knotted together, and her mouth was twisted with what might have been a response to a deep-seated regret or troublesome dream.

Bek raised her to a sitting position, placed her against the bulkhead, and seated himself across from her. He stared at her without doing anything more, trying to think through what he knew, trying to decide what to do next. He had to break down the protective shell in which she had sealed herself, but to do that he had to know what she was protecting herself from.

He tried to envision it and failed. On the surface, she looked to be barely more than a child, but beneath she was iron hard and remorseless. That didn't just disappear, even after a confrontation with the truth-inducing magic of the Sword of Shannara. Besides, what single act set itself apart from any other? What monstrous wrong could she not bring herself to face after perpetrating so many?

He sat staring at her much in the same way that she was staring at him, neither of them really seeing the other, both of them off in other places. Bek shifted his thinking to Grianne's early years, when she was first taken from her home and placed in the hands of the Morgawr. Could something have happened then, as Rue had suggested, something so awful she could not forgive herself for it? Was there something he didn't know about and would have to guess at?

Suddenly, it occurred to him that he might be thinking about this in the wrong way. Maybe it wasn't something she had done, but something she had failed to do. Maybe it wasn't an act, but an omission that haunted her. It was just as possible that what she couldn't forgive herself for was something she believed she should have done and hadn't.

He repeated to himself what she said when she woke on the night she had saved Quentin's life—about how Bek shouldn't cry, how she was there for him, how she would look after him again, his big sister.

But she had said something else, too. She had said she would never leave him again, that she was sorry for doing so. She had cried and repeated several times, "I'm so sorry, so sorry."

He thought he saw it then, the failure for which she had never been able to forgive herself. A child of only six, she had hidden him in the basement, choosing to try to save his life over those of her parents. She had concealed him in the cellar, listening to her parents die as she did so. She had left him there and set out to find help, but she had never gotten beyond her own yard. She had been kidnapped and whisked away, then deceived so that she would think he was dead, too.

She had never gone back for him, never returned to find out if what she had been told was the truth. At first, it hadn't mattered, because she was in the thrall of the Morgawr and certain of his explanation of her rescue. But over the years, her certainty had gradually eroded, until slowly she had begun to doubt. It was why she had been so intrigued by Bek's story about who he was when they had encountered each other for the first time in the forest that night after the attack in the ruins. It was why she hadn't killed him when she almost certainly would have otherwise. His words and his looks and his magic disturbed her. She was troubled by the possibility that he might be who he said he was and that everything she had believed about him was wrong.

Which would mean that she had left him to die when she should have gone back to save him.

It was a failure for which he would never blame her, but for which she might well blame herself. She had failed her parents and then failed him, as well. She had thrown away her life for a handful of lies and a misplaced need for vengeance.

He was so startled by the idea that it could be something as simple as this that for a moment he could not believe it was possible. Or that it could be something so impossibly wrongheaded. But she did not think as he did, or even as others did. She had come through the scouring magic of the Sword of Shannara to be reborn into the world, tempered by fire he could barely imagine, by truths so vast and inexorable that they would destroy a weaker person. She had survived because of who she was, but had become more damaged, too.

What should he do?

He was frightened that he might be wrong, and if he was, he had no idea of where else to look. But fear had no place in what was needed, and he had no patience with its weakness. He had to try using his new insight to break down her defenses. He had to find out if he was right.

His choices were simple. He could call on the magic of the wishsong or he could speak to her in his normal voice. He chose the latter. He moved closer to her, putting his face right in front of hers, his hands clasped loosely about her slender neck, tangling in her thick, dark hair.

"Listen to me," he whispered to her. "Grianne, listen to what I have to say to you. You can hear me. You can hear every word. I love you, Grianne. I never stopped loving you, not once, not even after I found out who you were. It isn't your fault, what was done to you. You can come home, now. You can come home to me. That's where your home is—with me. Your brother, Bek."

He waited a moment, searching her empty eyes. "You hid me from the Morgawr and his Mwellrets, Grianne, even without knowing who they were. You saved my life. I know you wanted to come back for me, that you wanted to bring help for me and for our parents. But you couldn't do that. There wasn't any way for you to return. There wasn't enough time, even if the Morgawr hadn't tricked you. But even though you couldn't come back, you saved me. Just by hiding me so that Truls Rohk could find me and take me to Walker, you saved me. I'm alive because of you."

He paused. Had he felt her shiver? "Grianne, I forgive you for leaving me, for not coming back, for not discovering that I was still alive. I forgive you for all of that, for everything you might have done and failed to do. You have to forgive yourself, as well. You have to stop hiding from what happened all those years ago. It isn't a truth that needs hiding from. It is a truth that needs facing up to. I need you back with me, not somewhere far away. By hiding from me, you are leaving me again. Don't do that, Grianne. Don't go away again. Come back to me as you promised you would."

She was trembling suddenly, but her gaze remained fixed and staring, her eyes as blank as forest lakes at night. He kept holding her, waiting for her to do something more. *Keep talking*, he told himself. *This is the way to reach her.*

Instead, he began to sing, calling up the magic of the wishsong almost without realizing he was doing so, singing now the words he had only spoken before. It was an impulsive act, an instinctive response to his need to connect with her. He was so close, right on the verge of breaking through. He could feel the shell in which she had encased herself beginning to crack. She was there, right inside, desperate to reach him.

So he turned to the language they both understood best, the language peculiar to them alone. The music flowed out of him, infused with his magic, sweet and soft and filled with yearning. He gave himself over to it in the way that music requires, lost in its rhythm, in its flow, in its transcendence of the here and now. He took himself away from where he was and took her with him, back in time to a life he had barely known and she had forgotten, back to a world they had both lost. He sang of it as he would have wanted it to be, all the while telling her he forgave her for leaving that world, for abandoning him, for losing herself in a labyrinth of treacheries and lies and hatred and monstrous acts from which it might seem there could be no redemption. He sang of it as a way of healing, so that she might find in the words and music the balm she required to accept the harshness of the truth about her life and know that as bad as it was, it was nevertheless all right, that forgiveness came to everyone.

He had no idea how long he sang, only that he did so without thinking of what he was attempting or even of what was needed. He sang because the music gave him a release for his own confused, tangled emotions. Yet the effect was the same. He was aware of her small shivers turning to trembles, of her head snapping up and her eyes beginning to focus, of a sound rising from her throat that approached a primal howl. He could sense the walls she had constructed crumble and feel her world shift.

Then she seized him in such a powerful embrace it did not seem possible that a girl so slender could manage it. She pressed him against her so hard that he could barely breathe, crying softly into his shoulder and saying, "It's all right, Bek, I'm here for you, I'm here."

He stopped singing then and hugged her back, and in the ensuing silence he closed his eyes and mouthed a single word.

Stay.

TWENTY-NINE

S he had been hiding in the darkest place she could find, but in the blackness that surrounded her were the things that hunted her. She did not know what they were, but she knew she must not look at them too closely. They were dangerous, and if they caught even the smallest glimpse of her eyes, they would fall on her like wolves. So she stayed perfectly still and did not look at them, hoping they would go away.

But they refused to leave, and she found herself trapped with no chance to escape. She was six years old, and in her mind she saw the things in the darkness as black-cloaked monsters. They had pursued her for a long time, tracking her with such persistence that she knew they would never stop. She thought that if she could manage to get past them and find her way home to her parents and brother, she would be safe again. But they would not let her go.

She could remember her home clearly. She could see its rooms and halls in her mind. It hadn't been very large, but it had felt warm and safe. Her parents had loved and cared for her, and her little brother had depended on her to look after him. But she had failed them all. She had run away from them, fled her home because the black things were coming for her and she knew that if she stayed, she would die. Her flight was swift and mindless, and it took her away from everything she knew—here, to this place of empty blackness where she knew nothing.

Now and again, she would hear her brother calling to her from a long way off. She recognized Bek's voice, even though it was a grown-up's voice and she knew he was only two years old and should not be able to speak more than a few words. Sometimes, he sang to her, songs of childhood and home. She wanted to call out to him, to tell him where she was, but she was afraid. If she spoke even one word, made even a single sound, the things in the darkness would know where she was and come for her.

She had no sense of time or place. She had no sense of the world beyond where she hid. Everything real was gone, and only her memories remained. She clung to them like threads of gold, shining bright and precious in the dark.

Once, Bek managed to find her, breaking through the darkness with tears that washed away her hunters. A path opened for her, created out of his need, a need so strong that not even the black things could withstand it. She took the path out of her hiding place and found him again, his heart breaking as he watched his little dog lying injured beside him. She told him she was back, that she would not leave him again, and she used her magic to heal his puppy. But the black things were still waiting for her, and when she felt his need for her begin to wane and the path it had opened begin to close, she was forced to flee back into her hiding place. Without his need to sustain her with its healing power, she could not stay.

So she hid once more. The path she had taken to him was closed and gone, and she did not know what she could do to open it again. Bek must open it, she believed. He had done so once; he must do so again. But Bek was only a baby, and he didn't understand what had happened to her. He didn't realize why she was hiding and how dangerous the black things were. He didn't know that she was trapped and that he was the only one who could free her.

"But when you told me you forgave me for leaving you, I felt everything begin to change," she told him. "When you told me how much you needed me, how by not coming back to you I was leaving you again, I felt the darkness begin to recede and the black things—the truths I couldn't bear to face—begin to fade. I heard you singing, and I felt the magic break through and wrap me like a soft blanket. I thought that if you could forgive me, after how I had failed you, then I could face what I had done beyond that, all of it, every bad thing."

They were sitting in the darkness where this had all begun, tucked away in a corner of Redden Alt Mer's Captain's quarters, whispering so as not to wake the sleeping Quentin Leah. Shadows draped their faces and masked some of what their eyes would have otherwise revealed, but Bek knew what his sister was thinking. She was thinking he had known what he was doing when he found a way to reach her through the magic of the wishsong. Yet it was mostly chance that he had done so. Or perhaps perseverance, if he was to be charitable about it. He had thought it would take forgiveness to bring her awake. He had been wrong. It had taken her sensing the depth of his need.

"I just wanted to give you a chance to be yourself again," he said. "I didn't want you to stay locked away inside, whatever the consequences of coming out might be."

"They won't be good ones, Bek," she told him, reaching over to touch his cheek. "They might be very bad." She was quiet for a moment, staring at him. "I can't believe I've really found you again."

"I can't believe it either. But then I can't believe hardly anything of what's happened. Especially to me. I'm not so different from you. Everything I thought true about myself was a lie, too."

She smiled, but there was a hint of bitterness and reproach. "Don't say that. Don't ever say that. You're nothing like me, save that you didn't know you were an Ohmsford. You haven't done the things that I've done. You haven't lived my life. Be grateful for that. You can look back on your life and not regret it. I will never be able to do that. I'll regret my life for as long as I live. I'll want to change it every day, and I won't be able to do that. All of the things I've done as the Ilse Witch will be with me forever."

She gave him a long, hard look. "I love you, and I know you love me, too. That gives me hope, Bek. That gives me the strength I need to try to make something good come out of all the bad."

"Do you remember everything that happened now?" he asked her. "Everything you did while you were the Ilse Witch?"

She nodded. "Everything."

"The Sword of Shannara showed it to you?"

"Every last act. All of the things I did because I wanted revenge on Walker. All of the wrongs I committed because I thought I was entitled to do whatever was necessary to get what I sought."

"I'm sorry you had to go through that, but not sorry that I got you back."

She pushed her long dark hair out of her pale face, revealing the pain in her eyes. "There wasn't any hope for me unless I discovered the truth about myself. About you and our parents. About everything that happened to us all those years ago. About the Morgawr, especially. I couldn't be anyone other than who the Morgawr had made me to be—and who I had made myself to be—until that happened. I hate knowing it, but it's freeing, too. I don't have to hide anymore."

"There are some things you don't know yet," he said. He shifted uncomfortably, trying to decide where to start. "The people we're traveling with, the survivors of Walker's company, all have reason to hate you. They don't, not all of them anyway, but they have suffered losses because of you. I guess you need to know about those losses, about the harm you've caused. I don't think there's any way to avoid it."

She nodded, her expression one of regret mixed with determination. "Tell me then, Bek. Tell me all of it."

He did so, leaving nothing out. It took him some time to do so, and while he was speaking, he became aware of someone else entering the room, easing over next to him, and sitting close. He knew without looking who it was, and he watched Grianne's eyes shift to find those of the newcomer. He kept talking nevertheless, afraid that if he looked away, he would not be able to continue. He related his story of the journey to Parkasia, of finding the ruins and Antrax, confronting her, escaping into the mountains and being captured, breaking free of *Black Moclips* and the rets, coming down into the bowels of Castledown to find that Walker had already tricked her into invoking the cleansing magic of the Sword of Shannara, taking her back into the mountains, and finding their way at last to what remained of the company of the *Jerle Shannara*.

When he had finished, he looked over his shoulder to find Rue. She was staring at Grianne. The look on her face was indecipherable. But the tone of her voice when she spoke to his sister was unmistakable.

"The Morgawr has come searching for you," she said. "His ships are anchored offshore. In the morning, he will search these ruins. If he finds us, he will try to kill us. What are you going to do about it?"

"Rue Meridian." His sister spoke the other's name as if to make its owner real. "Are you one of those who have not forgiven me?"

Little Red's eyes were fierce as they held Grianne's. One hand came up to rest possessively on Bek's shoulder. "I have forgiven you."

But Bek did not miss the bitterness in her voice or the challenge that lay behind it. *Forgiveness is earned, not granted,* it said. *I forgive you, but what does it matter? You still must demonstrate that my forgiveness is warranted.*

He glanced at his sister and saw sadness and regret mirrored on her smooth, pale face. Her eyes shifted to where Rue's hand rested on his shoulder, and the last physical vestiges of the girl of six that she had been for all those days and nights of her catatonia vanished. Her face went hard and expressionless, the mask she had perfected to keep the demons of her life at bay when she was the Ilse Witch.

She looked back at her brother for just a moment. "I told you," she said to him, "that the consequences of my waking would not all be good ones." She smiled with cold certainty. "Some will be very bad."

There was a long pause as the two women attempted to stare each other down, each laying claim to something that the other wanted and could never have. A part of a past gone by. A part of a future yet to be. Time and events would determine how much of either they could share, but there was a need for compromise and neither had ever been very good at that.

"Maybe you should meet the others of the company, as well," Bek said quietly.

Beginnings in this situation, he thought, might prove tougher than endings.

At dawn, they stood together in the shelter of a tower's crumbling turret, Bek and Grianne and Rue, perched on its highest floor so that they could look out across the ruins to where the Morgawr's airships were beginning to stir. By now, Grianne had met all of the ship's company and been received with a degree of acceptance that Bek had not expected. If he was honest about it, Rue had proven to be the most hostile of the company. The two women were locked in some sort of contest that had something to do with him, but about which he understood little. Unable to deflect their mutual disdain, he had settled for keeping them civil.

Across the broad green sweep of the grasslands, the airships of the Morgawr were visible in the clear pale light of a sunrise that heralded an impossibly beautiful day. Bek saw the sticklike figures of the walking dead, standing at their stations, awaiting the commands that would set them in motion. He saw the first of the Mwellrets, cloaked and hooded against the light, emerging from belowdecks, climbing through the hatchways. Most important of all, he saw the Morgawr, standing at the forward railing of *Black Moclips*, his gaze, searching, directed toward the ruins where they hid.

"You were right," Grianne said softly, her slight body rigid within her robes. "He knows we're here."

The others of the company were settled in below, hiding within the hull and pontoons of the *Jerle Shannara*, waiting to see what would happen. Alt Mer knew of Bek's fears, but he could do nothing about them. The *Jerle Shannara* could not fly if they did not put up her masts and sails, and the noise alone of doing so would give them away. Even if the Morgawr tried to search the ruins, there was reason to think he would not find them, that the magic of the spirit dweller would refuse him entry and lead him back outside without his even realizing it, just as it had done to Walker. But that was a huge gamble; if it failed, they were trapped and outnumbered. Escape would be impossible unless they could overcome their enemies through means that at this point were a mystery.

Bek did not feel good about their chances. He did not believe that the Morgawr would be fooled by the magic of the spirit creature. Everything suggested otherwise. The warlock had tracked them this far without being able to see them and with no visible trail to follow. He seemed to know that they were hiding in the ruins. If he could determine all that, he would be quick enough to realize what the spirit dweller was doing to him when he tried to penetrate the ruins and would probably have a way to counteract it.

If that happened, they would have to face him.

He glanced at Grianne. She had never answered Rue's question about what she intended to do to stop the Morgawr. In fact, his sister had said almost nothing past greeting those to whom she was introduced. She had not asked them if they had forgiven her, as she had asked Rue. She had not apologized for what she had done to them and to those they had lost. All of the softness and vulnerability that she had evidenced on waking from her sleep was gone. She had reverted to the personality of the Ilse Witch, cold and distant and devoid of emotion, keeping her thoughts to herself, the people she encountered at bay.

It worried Bek, but he understood it, too. She was protecting herself in the only way she could, by closing off the emotions that would otherwise destroy her. It wasn't that she didn't feel anything or that she no longer believed that she must account for the wrongs she had committed. But if she gave them too much consideration, if she gave her past too great a hold over her present, she would be unable to function. She had survived for many years through strength of will and rigid control. She had kept her emotions hidden. Last night, she had discovered that she could not let go of those defenses too quickly. She was still his sister, but she could not turn away from being the Ilse Witch either.

She was walking a fine line between sanity and madness, between staying out in the light of the real world and fleeing back into the hiding place she had only just managed to escape.

"We have to decide what we're going to do if he comes into the ruins and finds us," Bek said quietly.

"He is only one man," Rue said. "None of the others have his magic to protect them. The rets can be killed. I've killed them myself."

She sounded so fierce when she said it that Bek turned to look at her in spite of himself. But when he saw the look on her face he could not bring himself to say anything back.

Grianne had no such problem. "What you say is true, but the Morgawr is more powerful than any of you or even all of you put together. He is not a man; he is not even human. He is a creature who has kept himself alive a thousand years through use of dark magic. He knows a hundred ways to kill with barely a thought."

"He taught you all of them, I expect," Rue said without looking at her.

The words had no visible effect on Grianne, though Bek flinched. "What can we do to stop him?" he asked, looking to avoid the confrontation he could feel building.

"Nothing," his sister answered. She turned now to face them both. "This isn't your fight. It never was. Rue was right in asking me what I intended to do about the Morgawr. He is my responsibility. I am the one who must face him."

"You can't do that," Bek said at once. "Not alone."

"Alone is best. Distractions will only jeopardize my chances of defeating him. Anyone whom I care about is a distraction he will take advantage of. Alone, I can do what is necessary. The Morgawr is powerful, but I am his match. I always have been."

Bek shook his head angrily. "Once, maybe. But you were the Ilse Witch then."

"I am the Ilse Witch still, Bek." She gave him a quick, sad smile. "You just don't see me that way."

"She's right about this," Rue interrupted before he could offer further argument. "She has magic honed on the warlock's grinding stone. She knows how to use it against him."

"But I have the same magic!" Bek snapped, hissing in anger as he sought to keep his voice down. "What about Ahren Elessedil? He has the power of the Elfstones. Shouldn't we use our magics together? Wouldn't that be more effective than you facing the Morgawr alone? Why are you being so stubborn about this?"

"You are inexperienced at using the wishsong, Bek. Ahren is inexperienced at using the Elfstones. The Morgawr would kill you both before you could find a way to stop him."

She walked over to stand beside Rue Meridian, a deliberate act he could not mistake, and turned back to face him. "Everything that has happened to me is the Morgawr's doing. Everything I lost, I lost because of him. Everything I became, I became because of him. Everything I did, I did because of him. I made the choices, but he dictated the circumstances under which those choices were made. I make no excuses for myself, but I am owed something for what was done. No one can give that back to me. I have to take it back. I have to reclaim it. I can only do that by facing him."

Bek was incensed. "You don't have to prove anything!"

"Don't I, Bek?"

He was silent, aware of how untenable his argument was and how implacable his sister's thinking. She might not have anything to prove to him, but she did to a lot of others. Most important of all, she had something to prove to herself.

"I won't be whole again until I settle this," she said. "It won't stop if we escape. I know the Morgawr. He will keep coming until he finds a way to destroy me. If I want this matter ended, I have to end it here."

Bek shook his head in disgust. "What are we supposed to do while you go out there and sacrifice yourself? Hope for the best?"

"Take advantage of the confusion. Even if I am killed, the Morgawr will not emerge unscathed. He will be weakened and his followers will be in disarray. You can choose to face them or escape while they lick their wounds. Either is fine. Talk about it with the others and decide among you."

She leaned forward and kissed him on the cheek. "You have done everything you could for me, Bek. You have no reason to feel regret. I am doing this because I must."

She turned to Rue Meridian. "I like it that you are not afraid of anyone, even me. I like it that you love my brother so much."

"Don't do this," Bek pleaded.

"Take care of him," his sister said to Rue, and without another word or even a single glance back she walked away.

Ordering the rest of the fleet to remain anchored offshore, safely away from any attempts at sabotage, the Morgawr flew *Black Moclips* over the silver-tipped surface of the Blue Divide to the grassy flats of Mephitic. He landed his vessel and tied her off, leaving Aden Kett and his walking dead on board with a handful of guards to watch over them. Then, tossing a rope ladder over the railing of the starboard pontoon, he took Cree Bega and a dozen of his Mwellrets down off the ship and toward the castle.

They crossed the grasslands openly and deliberately, making no effort to hide their approach. If the survivors of the *Jerle Shannara* were hiding within the walls of the ruins, the Morgawr wanted them to see him coming. He wanted them to have time to think about it before he reached them, to let their anticipation build, and with it their fear. The Ilse Witch might not be frightened, but her companions would be. They would know by now how he feasted on the souls of the living. They would know how the Federation crew he had captured aboard *Black Moclips* had reacted while it was happening and what they looked like afterwards. At least one of them was likely to break down and reveal the presence of the others. That would save him time and effort. It would allow him to conserve his energy for dealing with the witch.

He told Cree Bega what he wanted. The Mwellrets were to follow his lead. They were not to talk. When they found their quarry, they were to leave the Ilse Witch to him. The others were theirs to do with as they wished. It would be best if they could kill them swiftly or render them unconscious so that they could be carried outside and disposed of.

Above all, they were to remember that there was something else living in the ruins, a spirit creature possessed of magic and capable of generating tremendous power. If it was aroused or attacked, it could prove extremely dangerous. Nothing was to be tampered with once they were inside, because the creature considered the castle its own and would fight to protect it. It cared nothing for the *Jerle Shannara* and her crew, however. They were not a part of its realm, and it would not protect them.

He said all this without being entirely sure it was true. It was possible that he was wrong and that the castle's inhabitant would attack for reasons the Morgawr could not even guess at. But no good purpose was served in telling that to the Mwellrets. All of them were expendable, even Cree Bega. What mattered was that he himself survive, and he had no reason to think that he wouldn't. His magic could protect him from anything. It always had.

His plan, then, was simple. He would find the witch and kill her, retrieve the books of magic from the airship, and escape. If he could achieve the former and not the latter, it would be enough. With the Druid dead, his little witch was the only one left who might cause him problems later. The books of magic were important, but he could give them up if he had to.

He began thinking about what it meant to have the last of the Druids gone. Paranor would lie uninhabited and vulnerable— protected by magic, yes, but accessible nevertheless to someone like himself who knew how to counteract that magic. It was Walker who had kept him at bay all these years. Now, perhaps, what had belonged to the Druids could be his.

The Morgawr permitted himself a smile. The wheel had come full circle on the Druids. Their time was over. His time was not. He need only dispose of one small girl. Ilse Witch or not, she was still only that.

Ahead, the broken-down walls and parapets of the ancient castle reared against the sunrise, stark and bare. His anticipation of what was waiting within compelled him to walk more swiftly to reach them.

THIRTY

G rianne Ohmsford walked through the empty corridors and courtyards of the old castle with slow, deliberate steps, giving herself a chance to gather her wits. In spite of what she had allowed Bek and Rue Meridian to believe, her decision to face the Morgawr alone was impulsive and not particularly well thought out. But it was necessary for all the reasons she had given them. She was the one he was looking for, and therefore the one who must confront him. She was the only one who stood a chance against his magic. She had done a lot of harm in her life as the Ilse Witch, and any redemption for her wrongs began with an accounting from the warlock.

She was still weak from her long sleep, but fueled by anger and determination. The truths about her life hovered right in front of her eyes, images made bright and clear by the magic of the Sword of Shannara, and she could not forget them. They defined her, and knowing what she had been was what made it possible for her to see what she must now become. To complete that journey, she must put an end to the Morgawr.

Silence cloaked her like a shroud, and the ruins bore the aura of a tomb. She smiled at the feeling, so familiar and still welcome, her world as she had known it for so many years. Shadows cast by walls and towers where sunlight could not penetrate spilled across the broken stone and cracked mortar like ink. She walked through those shadows in comfort, the darkness her friend, the legacy of her life. It would never change, she realized suddenly. She would always favor those things that had made her feel safe. She had found a home under conditions that would have destroyed others, had done so when everything she cared for had been taken away and all that was left was her rage, and she knew she would not be able to step away from that past easily.

That would not change, should she survive this day. Bek envisioned a returning home, a coming together of their new family, a settling into a quiet life. But his vision held no appeal for her and was rooted in dreams that belonged to someone else. Her life would take a different path from his; she knew that much already. Hers would never be what he hoped it might, because the reason for her recovery lay not so much with him—though he had brought her awake when no one else could—but with the Dark Uncle, the keeper of secrets and the bestower of trusts. With Walker Boh.

Dead now, but with her always.

She began to hum, wrapping herself in the feel of the ruins and the thing that lived within them. It was dormant at present, but as pervasive in its domain as Antrax had been in its. It was everywhere at once, its presence infused in the hard stone and the dead air. She knew from Bek that the way to deceive it was to make it feel as if you belonged. She would begin her efforts to achieve that now. Once she had thoroughly integrated herself, once she was accepted as just another piece of rubble, she would be ready to deal with her enemy.

It took only a little time and effort to create the skin she needed, the mask she required. She eased herself along the corridors, listening now for the sounds of the Morgawr and his rets. They would have reached the walls and begun looking for a way inside. Her plan for him was simple. She would try to separate him from his followers, to isolate him from their help. If she was to have a chance against him, she must get him alone and keep him that way. Cree Bega and his Mwellrets were no threat to her, but they could become the sort of distraction she had worried Bek and Rue Meridian might become. To win her struggle with the Morgawr, that must not be allowed to happen.

Already, she was beginning to feel a part of her surroundings, a thing of stone and mortar, of ancient time and dust.

She shed that part of her that was Grianne Ohmsford and reverted very deliberately to being the Ilse Witch. She became the creature she must to survive, armoring herself against what waited and concealing what was vulnerable. It demanded a shift in thinking, a closing off of feelings and a shutting away of doubt. It required a girding of self for battle. Such prosaic descriptions made her smile, for the truth was much darker and meaner. She was taking a different path from the one she had followed when her purpose in life was to see Walker destroyed, but this path was just as bleak. Killing the Morgawr was killing still. It would not enhance her self-respect. It would not change the past. At best, it would give a handful of those she had wronged a chance at life. That would have to be enough.

She was glad Bek was not here to see the change happen, for she believed it was reflected in her eyes and voice. It could be contained, but not hidden. Maybe this was how she must always be, split between two selves, required by events and circumstances to be duplicitous and cunning. She could see it happening that way, but there was nothing she could do about it.

There were sounds ahead now, the echoes of small scrapings and slidings, of heavy boots passing over stone and earth. They were still a long way off, but getting closer. The Morgawr was trying to penetrate the maze. As yet, he had not detected her presence, but it would not take him long. It would be best if she attacked him before he did, while he still thought himself safe. She could wait and see if the magic of the thing in the ruins might confuse the warlock, but it would probably be wasted effort. The Morgawr was too clever to be fooled for long and too persistent to be turned away for good. Redden Alt Mer's plan had been a reasonable one, but not for someone so dangerous.

She continued to hum softly, the magic concealing her not only from the dweller in the ruins but from those who hunted her, as well. She made her way toward them, sliding through the shadows, watching the open spaces ahead for signs of movement. It would not be long until she encountered them. She breathed slowly and deeply to steady herself. She must be cautious. She must be as silent as the air through which she passed. She must be no more in evidence than would a shade come from the dead.

Most of all, she must be swift.

Redden Alt Mer seemed almost resigned to the inevitability of it when he heard what Grianne Ohmsford had done. Standing on the aft deck of the *Jerle Shannara* with Bek and Rue, he made no response, but instead stared off into the distance, lost in thought. Finally, he told them to go back on watch and let him know if they saw anything. He did not look ready to summon any of the Rover crew to prepare for an escape should Grianne fail. He did not appear interested in doing anything. He heard them out and then walked away.

His sister exchanged a quick glance with Bek and shrugged. "Wait here," she said.

She disappeared below, leaving Bek to contemplate what lay ahead. He stood at the railing of the airship and looked up at the clear blue sky. Britt Rill and Kelson Riat stood together in the bow, talking in low voices. Spanner Frew was fussing with something in the pilot box, working through the heavy boughs they had laid down to hide it from the air. Alt Mer and the others were nowhere to be seen. Everything seemed strangely peaceful. For the moment, it was, Bek thought. No one would come for them right away. Not until the Morgawr had settled things with Grianne.

He thought about looking in on Quentin, but couldn't bring himself to do so. He didn't want to see his cousin while he was feeling like this. Quentin was smart enough to read his face, and he didn't think that would be such a good thing this morning. If Quentin knew what was happening, he would want to get out of bed and stand with them. He wasn't strong enough for that, and there would be time enough for the Highlander to engage in futile heroics if everything else failed. Best just to let him sleep for now.

Rue Meridian reappeared through the hatchway, buckling on her weapons belt with its brace of throwing knives, tucking a third into her boot as she came up to him. "Ready to go?" she asked.

He stared at her. "Ready to go where?"

"After your sister," she said. "You don't think we're going to stand around here doing nothing, do you?"

Not when she put it that way, he didn't. Without another word, they slipped over the side of the airship and disappeared into the ruins after Grianne.

Redden Alt Mer had been thinking about the company's situation all night. Unable to sleep, he had been reduced to pacing the decks to calm himself. He hated being grounded, all the more so for knowing that he couldn't get airborne again easily and was, essentially, trapped. He was infuriated by his sense of helplessness, a condition with which he was not familiar. Even though it had been his plan to hide in the ruins and hope the Morgawr didn't find them, he found it incomprehensible that he would actually sit there and do nothing while waiting to see if it worked.

When Bek's sister awoke, brought out of her catatonia after all these weeks, he knew at once that everything was about to change.

It wasn't a change he could put a name to, but one he could definitely feel. The Ilse Witch awake, whether friend or enemy or something else altogether, was a presence that would shift the balance of things in some measurable way. To Alt Mer, that she had chosen to go after the Morgawr rather than to wait for the warlock to come to her seemed completely in character. It was what he would have done if he hadn't locked himself in the untenable position of hiding and waiting. The longer he stayed grounded, the more convinced he became that he was making a mistake. This wasn't the way to save either his airship or her passengers. It wasn't the way to stay alive. The Morgawr was too smart to be fooled. Alt Mer would have been better off staying aloft and fighting it out in the air.

Not that he would have stood a chance with that approach either, he conceded glumly. Best to keep things in perspective while castigating oneself for perceived failures.

He left the airship and climbed the tower into which he had sent Little Red and Bek to keep watch, but they weren't there. Confused by their absence, he looked down into the courtyard where the *Jerle Shannara* sat concealed, thinking he might spy them. Nothing. He looked off toward the surrounding courtyards and passageways, peering through breaks in the crumbling castle walls.

He found them then, several hundred yards away, sliding through the shadows, heading toward the front of the keep and the Morgawr.

For a second, he was stunned by what he was seeing, realizing that not only had his sister disobeyed him, but she was risking her life for the witch. Or for Bek, but it amounted to the same thing. He wanted to shout to them to get back to the ship, to do what they had been told, but he knew it was a waste of time. Rue had been doing as she pleased for as long as he could remember, and trying to make her do otherwise was a complete waste of time. Besides, she was only doing what he had been thinking he should do just moments earlier.

He walked to the outer wall of the tower and looked out across the grasslands. The Morgawr and his rets were already inside the castle, and the plains were empty save for *Black Moclips*, which sat anchored inland perhaps a quarter of a mile away. Beyond, clearly visible against the deep blue of the morning sky, the Morgawr's fleet hovered at anchor offshore.

He stared at the airships for a moment, at the way they were clustered to protect against a surprise attack, and an idea came to him. It was so wild, so implausible, that he almost dismissed it out of hand. But he couldn't quite let it go, and the longer he held on, the more attractive it seemed. Like a brightly colored snake that would turn on you once it had you hypnotized. Like fire, waiting to burn you to ash if you reached out to touch it.

Shades, he thought, he was going to do it.

He was aghast, but excited, as well, his blood pumping through him in a hot flush as he raced down the tower stairs for the airship. He would have to be quick to make a difference, and even that might not be enough. What he was thinking was insane. But there was all sorts of madness in the world, and at least this one involved something more than just standing around.

He burst out of the tower, leapt aboard the *Jêrle Shannara*, and headed directly for Spanner Frew. The shipwright looked up from his work, doubt clouding his dark features as he saw the look on the other's face. "What is it?" he asked.

"You're not doing anything important, are you?" Alt Mer replied, reaching for his sword and buckling it on.

Spanner Frew stared at him. "Everything I do is important. What do you want?"

"I want you to go with me to steal back *Black Moclips*."

The shipwright grunted in disgust. "That didn't work so well for Little Red, as I recall."

"Little Red didn't have a good plan. I do. Come along and find out. We'll take Britt and Kelson for company. It should be fun, Black Beard."

Spanner Frew folded his burly arms across his chest. "It sounds dangerous to me."

Alt Mer grinned. "You didn't think you were going to live forever, did you?" he asked.

Then, seeing the other man's dark brow furrow in response, he laughed.

He left Ahren Elessedil and Kian to keep watch over the *Jerle Shannara* and set out with Spanner Frew, Kelson Riat, and Britt Rill for the outside wall of the castle. It didn't occur to him until he was well away from the airship that he might have trouble finding his way back. Not only were the ruins a confusing maze to begin with, but the spirit creature's magic was designed to keep intruders from penetrating beyond the perimeter. But there was no help for it now, and besides, he didn't think he would be coming back anyway.

He told his companions what he thought they needed to know and no more. He told them that they were going to skirt the ruins to their most inland point, well away from the view of those aboard *Black Moclips*, then sneak around to the far side of the airship, get aboard, and steal her away. If they could manage it, they would have a fully operational airship in which to make their escape. With luck, the Morgawr would not be able to give chase, and without him, the rest of the fleet would lack the necessary leadership to act.

It was all an incredible bunch of nonsense, if he thought it through, but since they were already moving to do what he had suggested, there wasn't enough time for much thought on the part of anyone.

He took them directly to the outer wall, then east and north along their perimeter to a gate that opened almost directly into a heavy stand of trees. He was moving quickly, aware of the fact that the Morgawr could encounter Grianne or Bek and Rue at any time, and once that happened, it might be too late for him to succeed in what he intended. Scooting out from the cover of the walls, the four

Rovers gained the trees and worked their way through them until they were across the flats. From there, they followed a shallow ravine that allowed them to creep through the tall grasses until they were less than a hundred yards from their target.

Spanner Frew was huffing noticeably from the effort, but Kelson and Britt were barely winded. Alt Mer lifted his head for a quick look around. They were behind *Black Moclips*, and the Mwellrets he could see were all facing toward the ruins.

"Black Beard," he said to Spanner Frew, keeping his voice soft. "Wait here for us. If we don't make it, get back to the airship and warn the others. If we get aboard, come join us."

Without waiting for a response, he slithered out of the ravine into the cover of the grasses and began to crawl toward the airship. Kelson and Britt followed, all of them experienced at sneaking into places they weren't supposed to be. They crossed the open ground quickly, easing through gullies and shallow depressions, pressed close to the ground.

When Alt Mer could see the hull of the airship without lifting his head, he paused. The pontoon closest to him blocked their view of the rets on the main deck, but it blocked the rets' view of them, as well. Unless one of the rets came down into the fighting stations and peered over the side, the Rovers were safe. All they had to do now was to find a way to get aboard.

Alt Mer stood up carefully, signaled to the other two men to follow, and started toward the rope ladder. He passed under the hull of the airship, which, anchored by ropes tied fore and aft, floated perhaps two dozen feet off the ground. He paused to study the rope ladder, the easiest way onto the ship, but the one the rets would be quickest to defend. Beckoning Britt and Kelson to him, he whispered for them to move as close to the ladder as they could without being seen and to stand ready to board when he called for them.

Then moving to the bow of the airship, he took hold of the anchor rope and, hand over hand, began to haul himself up.

He reached the prow at the curve of the rams and peeked over the railing. There were four rets, two at the railing by the rope ladder, one in the pilot box and one aft. The hapless Federation crew stood around like sleepwalkers, staring at nothing, arms hanging limp at their sides. He felt a momentary pang of regret at what had to happen, but there was no way anyone could save them now.

He took a deep breath, heaved himself over the side, and charged across the deck toward the two closest Mwellrets. He killed the first with a single pass of his long knife, yelling for Britt and Kelson as he engaged the second. Both Rovers appeared up the ladder almost at once, grabbing his antagonist from behind and throwing him down. Alt Mer rushed the pilot box as the third ret snatched up a pike and launched it at him. The pike passed so close to his head that he heard the air vibrate, but he didn't slow. He went up the front of the box with a single bound, vaulted the shield, and was inside before the ret could escape. The ret swung at him with his broadsword in a desperate effort to stop him, but Alt Mer blocked the blow, slid inside the ret's guard, and buried the long knife in his chest.

The last ret tried to go over the side, but Kelson caught him halfway over the rail and finished him.

That wasn't so difficult after all, Alt Mer decided, aware that he had been injured in the struggle, both arms bleeding from slashes, his ribs bruised on his left side, and his head light with the blow it had taken from the first ret. He went back down to the deck, hiding the wounds as best he could. He ordered his men to throw the dead rets over the side, then go down the ladder and hide the bodies in the grass. It was a strange order, and they glanced at each other questioningly, but they didn't argue. They were used to doing what he told them to do, and they did so now.

As soon as they were safely over the side and on the ground, he pulled up the ladder. Then he walked quickly to the anchor ropes, passing the dead-eyed Federation crew, who made no effort to stop him or even to look at him, and cut them both. As the ropes fell away, *Black Moclips* began to rise.

"Big Red!" he heard Spanner Frew call after him, lumbering

across the grasslands in a futile effort to catch up. Below, Kelson Riat and Britt Rill were calling up to him, as well, shouting that the ropes were gone, that they couldn't reach him.

That was the general idea, of course. He didn't need any help with what he intended to do next. The sacrifice of his own life in furtherance of this wild scheme was more than enough.

Redden Alt Mer leaned over the side and waved good-bye.

THIRTY-ONE

S he could hear them coming now, the scrape of their footfalls, the hiss of their breathing, and the rustle of their heavy cloaks, the echoes reaching out to her through the silence. Grianne slowed to where her own sounds disappeared completely, lost in the concealment of her wishsong's magic. She disappeared into the stone walls and floors of the ruins, into its towers and parapets. She completed the transformation she had begun earlier, taking on the look and feel of the castle. She disappeared in plain sight.

The Morgawr had come to find her, but she had found him first.

She could feel the magic of the castle dweller working about her, changing the way the corridors opened and closed, shifting doorways and walls to confuse and mislead. It did so in arbitrary fashion, a function of its being that required no more thought than did her breathing. It was not yet aroused to do more, to lash out as it had at Bek and the shape-shifter when they had stolen the key from its hiding place. Thousands of years old, a thing out of the world of Faerie, it slumbered in its lair. If it sensed the presence of the Morgawr and his Mwellrets, or if it sensed her own for that matter, it did so in only the most subliminal way, and was not concerned by it.

That would change, she decided, when the time was right. In

any arena in which she must do combat, weapons of all sorts were permitted.

She breathed slowly and evenly to quiet her pulse and her mind and to steady her nerves. She was at her best when she was in control, and if she was to overcome the Morgawr, she must take control quickly. Hesitation or delay would be fatal. Or any show of mercy. Whether or not to kill the Morgawr was not an issue she could afford to debate. Certainly he would be quick enough to kill her—unless he thought he could render her immobile and feed on her later.

She shuddered at the thought, never having gotten used to it or quite been able to put aside her fear and revulsion of what it would feel like. She had never thought she would be at risk and so never considered the possibility. It left her chilled and tight inside to do so now.

But she was still the Ilse Witch, cloaked in a mantle of steely confidence and hardened resolve, and so she choked off her revulsion and clamped down on her fear. The Morgawr had destroyed many creatures in his long lifetime and overcome much magic. But he had never had to face anyone like her.

She thought of the creatures she had destroyed in her turn and of the magics she had overcome. She did not like thinking of it, but could not help herself. The truths of her life were too recently revealed for her to close them away. One day, she might be able to do so with some of them, perhaps most. For now, she must embrace them and draw what strength she could from the anger they engendered. For now, she must acknowledge their monstrosity and remember that they were the consequence of the Morgawr's treachery. For a little while longer, she must be the creature he had helped create.

For a little while longer.

The words had a hollow feel to them, an ephemeral quality that suggested they could be blown away in a single breath.

But there was no more time for rumination. She spied movement through breaks in the stone walls, the bulky shapes of the Mwellrets sliding past the shadows of the sunless ruins. She moved to intercept them, already laying the groundwork for separating them from the Morgawr, casting her magic in places that would draw his attention long enough for her to do what was needed.

Down through the corridors of broken rock they trudged, the Mwellrets and their dark leader. She could see him now, tall and massive and loathsomely familiar. He walked ahead, pointing the way for Cree Bega and his minions, testing the air for danger, for magic, for signs of her presence. He would already know about the spirit that warded the ruins, and he would be wary of it. His plan would be to find and engage her in single combat. He would expect her to be hiding with the company of the *Jerle Shannara*. He would not expect her to be hunting him as he was hunting her.

She used the magic of the wishsong to smooth the path he followed, to give him a sense of ease. It was a subtle effect, but one that, if he detected it, would not disturb him in a place where magic was rife. He knew he was being manipulated by the castle's dweller, and he would expect to be gently prodded in the direction the dweller wished him to go. In his arrogance, he would allow this, thinking he could compensate for it whenever he was ready. He would not suspect that she was there, acting as the dweller's surrogate, manipulating him for her own purposes. By the time he realized the truth, it would be too late.

When he neared, she found a place suitable to her intent and stepped back into the shadows to wait.

Seconds later, the Morgawr emerged from one of several corridors leading in, and she used the magic at once to suggest her presence in a chamber further on. He glanced up in response to the faint impression, leaning forward within the covering of his cowl as if to taste the air, sensing something he couldn't see, not quite sure what it was, only that it touched on her. He signaled for the Mwellrets, who were a dozen paces back, to hold up.

Come ahead, she urged him silently. *Don't be afraid.*

He slipped into the chamber on cat's paws, little more than a hint of dark movement in shadows that were darker still. He crossed the room in pursuit of her tease, cautious and deliberate, and disappeared down a corridor.

She left her hiding place and slid along the wall that followed the Morgawr's path, as deliberate and careful as he was, humming steadily, purposefully, keeping herself concealed. She could just hear the soft muttering of the rets behind her, but nothing of the warlock.

When she was all the way across the room and next to the corridor beyond, able to see the Morgawr's dark shape ahead, she turned back to the rets. Projecting the warlock's voice into their minds so that it seemed as if he were speaking, she summoned them ahead.

They came instantly, responding as she knew they would. But once they entered the room, she took them a different way. The ruins were a maze, and there were openings everywhere. She chose one that led away from the Morgawr, but gave the rets the impression they were still following him. Cree Bega's blunt, reptilian face lifted in doubt, gimlet eyes casting about for his leader. But, unable to find him, he continued on, following the thread she had laid out for him, moving steadily further away. Bunched together like cattle, they let themselves be herded into the chute she had chosen for them, and when they were all safely inside, she closed the gate. As quickly as that, the way back disappeared. She threw up a wall of magic that closed it off as surely as if it had never existed. The rets were in a corridor from which they could not escape without breaking through her magic or moving ahead down a series of twists and turns that would take them too long to navigate to be of any help to their leader.

Instantly, she turned into the passageway the Morgawr had taken, spied him turning toward her, and attacked, striking out with every last measure of power she could muster, hurtling it at him like a missile. The magic was a shriek in the silence, hammering into the

Morgawr, throwing him back down the corridor and into a wall with such force that the ancient stones shattered from the impact. She went down the corridor in a rush, bursting into the room just in time to watch her handiwork disappear in a whiff of vapor.

It was only an illusion, she realized at once. It wasn't the Morgawr at all. She had been tricked.

She turned around to find him standing right behind her.

Bek and Rue Meridian heard the explosion from several chambers away while still winding through the maze in a futile effort to catch up with Grianne. The sound was like nothing either of them had ever heard, a sort of metallic scream that set their teeth on edge. But Bek recognized the source instantly; Grianne had invoked the magic of the wishsong. He screamed her name, then charged ahead heedlessly, abandoning any effort at a silent approach, anxious now just to get to where things were happening before it was too late.

"Bek, stop!" Rue called after him in dismay.

Too late. Rounding the corner of a twisting passageway hemmed in by walls so tall they left only a sliver of blue sky visible overhead, they ran right into Cree Bega and his Mwellrets. Rushing from opposite directions into a tiny courtyard littered with debris and streaked with shadows, they skidded to a stop. It happened so quickly that the image was still registering in Bek's mind as Rue whipped out both throwing knives and sent them whistling across the short space in a blur of bright metal. Two of the rets died on their feet as the rest charged.

They would have been finished then, if Bek, watching the massive bodies of the rets bear down on them, had not reacted instinctively to the threat. Calling up his own magic in a desperate response, he sent a wall of sound hurtling into his attackers. It caught up the rets as it had the creepers in the ruins of Castledown and sent them flying. Three

got past, breaking in at the edges. Bek had only a moment to catch
the glitter of their knife blades, and then they were on top of him.

Rue, swift, agile, and lethal, killed the first, ducking under his
massive arms and burying her third throwing knife in his throat. She
intercepted the second as well, but it bore her backwards, its momentum too great to slow. Bek saw her go down, then lost track as
the final assailant crashed into him, knife slicing at his throat. He
blocked the blow, screaming at the ret in defiance. His voice was
threaded with the wishsong's magic; it exploded out of him in automatic response to his fear and anger and shredded the Mwellret's
head like metal shards. The ret was dead before he knew what had
happened, and Bek was scrambling back to his feet.

"Rue!" he called out frantically.

"Not so loud. I can hear you."

She hauled herself out from under the body of her assailant, but
only with some difficulty. Blood covered her, a jagged tear down
the front of her tunic and another down her left sleeve. Bek dropped
to his knees next to her, shoving the dead Mwellret out of the way.
He began searching through her clothing for the wounds, but she
pushed him away.

"Leave me alone. I've broken my ribs again. It hurts just to
breathe." She swallowed against her pain. "Bring me my knives.
Watch yourself. Some of them might still be alive."

He pulled free the knife buried in the throat of the ret a few feet
away, then crossed the courtyard to where the others lay in tangled
heaps. The impact of striking the wall had smashed them so badly
they were barely recognizable. He stared at them a moment, sickened by the fact that he was responsible for this, that he had killed
them. He hadn't seen so many dead men since the attack on the
company of the *Jerle Shannara* in the ruins weeks earlier. He hesitated a moment too long, thinking about the deaths here and there,
and was suddenly sick to his stomach. He went down on his knees
and retched helplessly.

"Hurry up!" Rue called impatiently.

He retrieved the other two throwing knives, carried them back and gave them to her, and again reached to bind her wounds. "Leave that to me," she said, holding him off.

"But you're bleeding!" he insisted.

"The blood isn't all mine. It's mostly the ret's." Her eyes were bright with tears, but her gaze steady. "I can't go any further hurting like this. You have to go on without me. Find your sister. She needs you more than I do."

He shook his head, suddenly concerned. "I won't leave you. How bad are you hurt, Rue? Show me."

She set her jaw and shoved at him again. "Not so bad that I can't get up and thrash you to within an inch of your life if you don't do what I tell you! Go after Grianne, Bek! Right now! Go on!"

Another explosion sounded, this one closer, the sound deeper and more ominous than before. Bek looked up in response, fear for his sister reflected in his eyes.

"Bek, she needs you!" Rue hissed at him angrily.

He gave her a final glance, then sprang to his feet and charged ahead into the gloom.

Redden Alt Mer swung the bow of *Black Moclips* toward the Blue Divide and the Morgawr's fleet, setting his course and locking down the wheel before leaving the pilot box. Down on the deck, he raised all the sails, tightened the radian draws, and checked the hooding shields on the parse tubes, making sure that everything was in good working order and could be controlled from the pilot box. A quick glance over the tips of the ramming horns revealed that nothing had changed ahead. The fleet still lay at anchor, and there was almost no movement on the decks. It was a lapse in judgment and discipline that he would make them pay dearly for.

He paused for a moment in front of Aden Kett and looked into the Federation Commander's dead, unseeing eyes. Like Rue, he had admired Kett, thought him a good soldier and a good airship Commander. To see him like this, to see all of them like this, was heartbreaking. Reducing men to puppets, to something less than the lowest animals that walked the earth, bereft of the ability to reason or act independently, was a monstrous evil. He thought he had seen more than enough kinds of evil in his life and wanted no more of this one. Perhaps he could put a stop to it here.

He went aft to the storage lockers and hauled out two heavy lines of rope and a pair of grappling hooks. Double-looping the lines through the eyes of the hooks, he carried one to each side of the rams and tied off the free ends to mooring cleats. Coiling the lines with the hooks resting on top so that they were ready for use, he went back up into the box.

He glanced back at the shoreline. Spanner Frew and the Rover crewmen stood at the edge of the bluff, staring after him in what he could only imagine was disbelief. At least they weren't shouting at him to come back, calling unwanted attention to themselves and to him. Maybe they had figured out his plan and were just watching to see what would happen.

For a moment, he found himself thinking of the Prekkendorran and all the airship raids he had survived under much worse conditions. It heartened him to imagine that he might survive this one, too, even though he couldn't see how that was possible. He looked up at the brilliant morning sky, a depthless blue expanse that seemed to open away forever, and he wished he had more time to enjoy this life that had been so good to him. But that was the nature of things. You got so much time and you made the best of it. In the end, you needed to feel that the choices you had made were mostly the right ones.

He adjusted his approach to the anchored fleet so that it would appear he intended to pass by them on their port side. The first faint stirrings of life were visible now, a few of the rets moving to the railings to look out at him. They recognized *Black Moclips* and were wondering why they didn't see any of the Mwellrets or the Morgawr. It helped that Kett's Federation crew was visible, the men who had taken her ashore, but it would keep them from acting for only a few moments more.

Redden Alt Mer pulled back on the levers to the thrusters. Drawing down power from the light sheaths through all twelve of the radian draws, *Black Moclips* began to pick up speed.

Ahren Elessedil heard the explosion, as well, standing on the deck of the dismantled *Jerle Shannara* with the Elven Hunter Kian. Save for Quentin Leah, who'd been sedated by Rue Meridian to make certain he stayed quiet, they were alone now on the airship. Quentin had suffered a setback in recent days, his injuries worsening once more after seeming to heal. He did not appear to be in any serious danger, but he was running a fever and had developed a tendency to hallucinate that often provoked loud outcries. So Rue had given him the sleeping potion to help him rest.

But the explosion might have brought him awake, so Ahren left Kian topside and went belowdecks to see after the Highlander. He wished he didn't have to stay aboard the airship, that he could go out with the others and see what was happening. It was bad enough when Bek and Rue left, but now the Rovers had all disappeared, as well, and with only the taciturn Kian and the sleeping Quentin Leah for company, he felt like he had been deserted.

He ducked his head into the Captain's quarters long enough to reassure himself that Quentin was all right, then went back down the passageway and upstairs again. Kian was standing at the port railing, looking off into the ruins.

"See anything?" Ahren asked him, coming alongside.

Kian shook his head. They stood together listening, then heard a second explosion, this one of a deeper sort. There were sounds of fighting, as well, distant but clear, the bright, sharp clang of blades and sudden cries of injured or dying men. More explosions followed, and then silence.

They waited a long time for something more, but the silence

only deepened. The minutes ticked away, sluggish footfalls leading nowhere. Ahren grew steadily more impatient. He had the Elf-stones tucked in his tunic and his broadsword belted at his waist. If he had to fight, he was ready. But there would be no fighting so long as he stayed here.

"I think we should go look for them," he said finally.

Kian shook his head, his dark face expressionless. "Someone has to stay with the airship, Elven Prince. We can't leave her unguarded."

Ahren knew Kian was right, but it didn't make him feel any better. If anything, it made him feel worse. His obligation to the company required him to stay aboard the *Jerle Shannara* even when it made him feel entirely useless. It wasn't so much that he was anxious to fight, but more that he didn't want to feel as if he wasn't doing his part. It seemed to him that he had failed as a member of this company in every conceivable way. He had failed his friends in the ruins of Castledown when he had run away. He had failed Walker by not being able to recover the Elfstones in time to help him in his battle with Antrax. He had failed Ryer Ord Star by leaving her behind when he escaped *Black Moclips* and the Morgawr.

He was particularly bothered by the death of the seer. Big Red had smoothed out the rough parts, but there was no way to soften the impact. Ahren's sense of guilt went unrelieved. He had been in such a rush to escape that he had let himself believe the lie she told him without questioning it. She had sacrificed herself for him, and to his way of thinking it should have been the other way around.

He sighed with sad resolution. It was too late to change what had happened to her, but not too late to make certain that it didn't happen to someone else. Yet what chance did he have to affect anything stuck back here on the *Jerle Shannara* while everyone else went off to fight his battles for him?

There were more explosions, and then a huge grinding sound that rolled through the ruins like an avalanche. The ground shook so heavily that it rocked the airship and sent both Elves careening into the ship's railing, which they quickly grabbed for support.

Blocks of stone tumbled from the battlements and towers of the old castle, and new cracks appeared in the walls and flooring, opening like hungry mouths.

When the grinding ended, it was silent again. Ahren stared into the ruins, trying to make sense of things, but there was no way to do that from here.

He turned to Kian in exasperation. "I'm going to have a look. Something's happened."

Kian blocked his way, facing him. "No, Elven Prince. It isn't safe for you—"

He gave a sharp grunt, and his eyes went wide in shock. As Ahren watched in confusion, Kian took two quick steps toward him and toppled over, eyes fixed and staring. Ahren caught him as he fell, lowering him to the ship's decking. The haft of a throwing knife protruded from his back, the blade buried to the hilt.

Ahren released him, rushed to the railing and peered over. A Mwellret had hold of the rope ladder and was climbing its rungs. The dark, blunt face lifted into the light, the yellow eyes fixing on Ahren. It was Cree Bega.

"Little Elvess," he purred. "Ssuch foolss."

Unable to believe what was happening, Ahren backed away in horror. He glanced down quickly at Kian, but the Elven Hunter was dead. There was no one else aboard, save Quentin, and the Highlander was too sick to help.

Too late, he thought to cut the ladder away. By then, Cree Bega was climbing onto the deck across from him.

"Musstn't be frightened of me, little Elvess," he hissed. "Doess little Elvess thinkss I mean them harm?"

He stepped over to Kian and pulled out his knife. He held it up as if to examine it, letting the blood run down the smooth, bright blade onto his fingers. His dark tongue slipped out, licking the blood away.

Ahren was frantic. He backed all the way to the pilot box before he stopped, fighting to control his terror. He couldn't use the

Elfstones, his most powerful weapon, because they only worked to defend against creatures of magic. Nor could he run, because if he ran, Quentin was a dead man. He swallowed hard. He couldn't run anyway, not if he wanted to retain even a shred of self-respect. It was better that he died here and now than flee again, than fail still another time to do what was needed.

"Givess me what I wantss, little Elvess, and perhapss I will let you live," Cree Bega said softly. "The bookss of magic. Hidess them where, Elven Prince?"

Ahren drew his broadsword. He was shaking so badly he almost dropped it, but he breathed in deeply to steady himself. "Get off the ship," he said. "The others will be back in minutes."

"Otherss are too far away, foolissh little Elvess. They won't come thiss way in time to ssave you."

"I don't need them to save me." He made himself take a step toward the other, away from the pilot box, away from the almost overpowering temptation to run. "You're the one who's alone."

The Mwellret started toward him, coming slowly, dark face expressionless, movements almost languid. *Don't look into his eyes*, Ahren reminded himself quickly. *If you look into a Mwellret's eyes, he will freeze you in place and cut your throat before you know what is happening.*

"Doess ssomething sseem wrong, little Elvess?" Cree Bega whispered. "Afraid to look at me?"

Ahren glanced at the ret in spite of himself, looking into his eyes, almost as if the question required it of him, and in an instant Cree Bega sprang. Ahren slashed at the other in desperation to ward him off, but the Mwellret blocked the blow. The throwing knife sliced across Ahren's chest, cutting through skin and muscle as if they were made of paper. Burning pain flooded through the Elven Prince as he pushed the other away, dropping into a crouch and whipping the sword back and forth to clear a space between them.

Cree Bega slid clear, watching him. "Esscapess uss once perhapss, little Elvess, but not twice. Little sseer made that misstake. Sshall I tell you what we did to her? After the Morgawr gave her to uss? How sshe sscreamed and begged for uss to kill her? Doess that make you ssad?"

Ahren felt a roaring in his ears, a tremendous pressure from the rage he felt building inside, but he would not give way to it because he knew that if he did, he was a dead man. He hated Cree Bega. He hated all the rets, but their leader in particular. Cree Bega was a weight around his neck that would drag him to his death if he didn't cut it loose. The Elven Prince was not the boy he had been even a few weeks ago, and he was not going to let the Mwellret win this contest of wills. He was not going to panic. He was not going to be baited into foolish acts. He was not going to run. If he died, he would do so fighting to defend himself in the way that Ard Patrinell had taught him.

He went into a defensive stance, calling on his training skills, his concentration steady and absolute. He kept his eyes averted from the ret's, kept himself fluid and relaxed, knowing that Cree Bega would want to make this next pass his last, that the ret would try to kill him quickly and move on. Ahren wondered suddenly why the ret was alone. Others had come into the ruins. Where were they? Where was the Morgawr?

He edged to his left, trying to put the Mwellret in a position that hemmed him between the railing and the mainmast. Blood ran down Ahren's chest and stomach in a thin sheet and his body burned from the wound he had received, but he forced himself to ignore both. He dropped his blade slightly, suggesting he might not quite know what to do with it, inviting the other to find out. But Cree Bega stayed where he was, turning to follow Ahren's movements without moving away.

"Sshe died sslowly, little Elvess," he hissed at Ahren. "Sso sslowly, it sseemed sshe would take forever. Doess it bother you that you weren't there to ssave her?"

Ahren went deep inside himself, back in time, back to where he practiced his defensive skills with Patrinell on this very deck, all those long, hot days in the boiling sun. Ahren could see his friend

372

and teacher still, big and rawboned and hard as iron, making the boy repeat over and over the lessons of survival he would one day need to call upon.

That day had arrived, just as Patrinell had forecast. Fate had chosen this time and place.

Cree Bega lunged for him, a smooth, effortless attack that took him to Ahren's left, away from his sword arm and toward his vulnerable side. But Ahren had anticipated that this was how the ret would come at him. Guided by the voice of his mentor whispering in his mind, buttressed by the hours of practice he had endured, and sustained by his determination to acquit himself well, he was ready. He kept his eyes on Cree Bega's knife, squared his body away, angled his sword further down, as if to drop his guard completely, then brought it up again when the other was too far committed to pull back, his blade slipping under Cree Bega's extended arm, cutting through to the bone, and continuing to slide up across his chest and into his neck.

The Mwellret staggered back, the knife dropping away from his nerveless fingers, clattering uselessly on the wooden deck. A gasp escaped his open mouth, and his blank features tightened in surprise. Ahren followed up instantly, thrusting with his sword, catching Cree Bega in the chest and running him through.

He yanked his weapon free and stepped away as the other staggered backwards to the railing and hung there. No words came out of his open mouth, but there was such hatred in his eyes that Ahren shrank from them in spite of himself.

He was still struggling to look away when the other sagged into a sitting position and quit breathing.

THIRTY-TWO

If she hadn't already been using the magic of the wishsong to conceal her presence, Grianne Ohsmford would not have survived. The Morgawr was right on top of her when she turned, and his hand shot out to grip and hold her fast. But her defenses were already up, and her magic deflected his effort just enough that it was turned aside. As she jerked away, his blunt nails scraped across her neck, tearing open her skin. She threw up a wall of sound between them, shrieking at him in anger and shock, but his own magic was in place, as well, his black-cloaked form shielded by it, just as it must have been shielded all along. She had thought to catch him off guard when she separated him from the Mwellrets, but he was too experienced. He had created an illusion of himself for her to attack, and she had almost paid the price for her carelessness.

Spinning away from him in a haze of sound and movement, she dropped into a crouch by the far wall, breathing hard. He made no effort to come after her, remaining in place by the chamber entry, watching her, measuring the effect of his appearance.

"Did you think I wouldn't be expecting you, my little Ilse Witch?" he asked softly, the words smooth and almost gentle. "I know you too well for that. I trained you too well to think that you wouldn't come looking for me."

"You lied to me," she replied, barely able to contain her rage. "About the Druid, about my parents and Bek, about my whole life."

"Lies are sometimes necessary to achieve our purposes. Lies make possible what we would otherwise be denied. Do you feel yourself ill-used?"

"I feel myself made into something loathsome." She took a tentative step left, looking to find an opening in his defenses. She could feel his power building, swirling all around him like heat off a fire. He would come at her shortly. She had been too slow, too confident, and she had lost the advantage of surprise.

"You made yourself what you are," he told her. "I merely gave you the opportunity to do so. You were wasting your life anyway. Your father chose to keep you from the Druid, and for that I was grateful. Trying to keep you from me, as well, was a mistake."

"He knew nothing of you! You killed him and my mother for no reason! You stole me away to make me your tool! You used me for your own purposes, and you would have done so forever if I had not discovered the truth!"

He gave a small lift of his shoulders as if to disclaim his guilt for anything of which she had accused him. His tall frame bent toward her as if to throw its shadow across her like a net. "How did the Druid persuade you of the truth, little witch? You never would have believed him before. Or was it your brother who told you?"

She did not care to explain anything to him, did not want even to speak with him. She wanted him gone from her life, from the earth she walked, and from her memory as well, were it possible. She hated him with such passion that it seemed to her that in the closeness of their shared space she could smell the stench of him—not the rankness of body odor, but the putrefaction of evil. Everything about him was so revolting to her that it was impossible to think of doing anything other than distancing herself in any way she could.

"You shouldn't have come after me," she told him, taking another sideways step, building her own magic in response to his.

"You shouldn't have betrayed me," he replied.

The power of her wishsong was born of earth magic, absorbed from the Elfstones by her ancestor, Wil Ohmsford, and passed on to his descendants. It could do almost anything once mastered by its wielder, from taking life to restoring it. But the Morgawr possessed magic very like it and every bit as powerful. His was rooted in the essence of his being, rather than extracted from the earth. Conceived at his birth in the dark reaches of the Wilderun, he the warlock brother of the witch sisters, Mallenroh and Morag, it had been fueled by his hunger for power and honed by his experiments with living creatures. Twisted by a special form of madness, he had sought for a way to increase the power of his birthright, and by so doing, the years of his life.

He found that way early on, when he was still quite young, discovering that feeding on the lives of others invested him with their life force. Stealing away their souls increased his vitality and strength; it fed his hunger in a way that nothing else could. It was easy enough, he had told the Ilse Witch long ago, once you got over your revulsion for what it required.

All those years she had tolerated this madness because she thought him her ally in achieving her greatest goal—the destruction of the Druid Walker. She had known what he was, and still she had allowed herself to be his creature. She had subverted herself for him when reason told her she should not. She had done so in the beginning because it seemed her only choice; she was homeless and still a child. But she had matured quickly, and that excuse had long since ceased to be a reasonable one for why she had stayed so long with him, or would be with him still if not for Bek. Nor could she claim that because she was a child, she'd had no other choice but to be what he made her. In truth, she had embraced his efforts freely, adopted his thinking and his ways, and hungered to be a part of his madness, his coveted power. That made her as guilty as he was.

"I am taking back my life." The tension she felt caused her to shiver. "I am taking back what you stole."

"I let no one take anything from me," he replied. "Your life is mine, and I will give it up when I choose to do so and not before."

"This time the choice is not yours to make."

He laughed softly, a swirl of dark cloth as he gestured disdainfully at her. "The choice is always mine. Laying claim to your life was good for you, little witch, until you sought power that wasn't yours. You would pretend that you are better than I am, but you are not. You are no freer of guilt, no nobler of purpose, no higher of mind. You are a monster. You are as cold and dark as I. If you think otherwise, you are a fool."

"The difference between us, Morgawr, is not that I think I am better than you. The difference is that I recognize what I am, and I understand how terrible that is. You would go on as you are and not regret it. Even if I am able to change myself, I will look back at what I was and regret it always."

"Your time for regret will be short, then. Your life is almost over."

There was a fresh edge to his voice, one infused with anticipation. He was getting ready to attack. She could feel it in the movement of the air, in its crackle and hiss as the magic he summoned began to break free of its restraints.

As a result, she wasn't where he expected her to be when he lashed out. She had eased to the side, leaving just a shadow of herself behind to draw him out. Feeling the backwash of the magic's power, watching the whipsaw effect of his fury cause the wall behind her to rupture, she struck back at him with shards that would have ripped him apart had he not already made his own warding motion in response.

Trading ferocious assaults, they quickly turned the chamber into a smoking, debris-clogged furnace, the heat and sound intense and suffocating. But they were more evenly matched than either had expected, and neither could gain the upper hand

Then the Morgawr simply disappeared. One moment he was there, his great form shadowy and fluid behind a screen of smoke and heat, and the next he was gone. Grianne slid back to her right, not wanting to give him a chance to come at her from another direction. She tested the air, searching for him, but the trail of his body heat told her he had fled from the room.

She went after him at once. If he was running, his confidence was breaking down. She did not want to give him a chance to recover. A fierce anticipation flooded through her. Maybe now she could put an end to him.

Black Moclips was closing on the Morgawr's fleet when Redden Alt Mer decided to take a look for something he was already pretty certain wasn't still aboard. He did it on a whim, having not even thought of it until now, remembering it because of something Ahren Elessedil had told him when they had talked about Ryer Ord Star, wanting suddenly to discover if it was true.

So he climbed down out of the pilot box, the controls locked, the airship on course, and walked past the living dead of the Federation and climbed down into the aft fighting station in the port-side pontoon. He walked back to where the ram began its upward curve, removed a panel on the side of the hull, and peered inside.

There it was, against all odds, in spite of his certainty it wouldn't be, still in the same condition in which it had been installed, neatly wrapped and ready for use. *You never know,* he mused.

He carried it out and laid it on the deck, piecing it together in moments, wondering why he bothered. Because it was there, he supposed. Because he lived in a world where a man's fate was often determined by chance, and he had believed in the importance of chance all his life.

Back in the pilot box, he saw the sail-stripped masts of the Morgawr's fleet begin to loom ahead of him like trees in a winter forest.

A few sails were still unfurled to permit the airships to hover, but most were rolled and cinched. Mwellrets clustered against the railings, peering intently at him as he neared, trying to figure out why *Black Moclips* was coming back and why they couldn't see the Morgawr or their fellow rets. They were not yet concerned, however. He didn't seem to pose a threat. He wasn't flying directly at them, instead pointing off to their port side and slightly away, as if intending to fly out to sea.

Black Moclips was traveling very fast now and still picking up speed. She was doing better than thirty knots, flying through the clear morning sky like a missile launched from a catapult, skimming the back of a gentle southerly wind, the ride smooth and easy. Sea birds flew at him and banked away, as if sensing that trouble rode his shoulder, but he only smiled at the thought.

When his speed reached forty knots and he was less than a quarter of a mile off the fleet's port side, he went back down to the main deck and threw the heavy ropes and grappling hooks over the side. They swung out and away, trailing the vessel like monstrous fishing hooks. *An apt analogy*, he thought wryly. He sprinted to the pilot box, seized the controls, opened the starboard tubes, and raked the sails hard to port. *Black Moclips* swung sharply left, the sudden movement throwing most of the crew sprawling across the deck, where they remained, staring at nothing. Alt Mer ignored them, straightening out the airship and picking up new speed, heading directly for the Morgawr's fleet, the barbed ends of the grappling hooks glinting in the sunlight as they swung back and forth like lures. Aware that they were being attacked, the Mwellrets were racing about like frightened ants now. Sails were being run up, lines fastened in place, and anchors weighed. The Mwellret guards were trying frantically to get their dead-eyed crews to their stations. But in stealing their lives, the Morgawr had also stolen their ability to respond quickly. They weren't going to get under way in time.

Black Moclips was a brute among Federation warships, not particularly large, but blocky and powerful. She went through the Morgawr's fleet as if it were a stack of kindling, her battering rams and hull snapping off masts like pieces of kindling, the grappling hooks tearing apart sails and shredding lines. Half of the airships lost power immediately and plummeted into the ocean. The rest spun away, damaged and fighting to stay aloft. If they hadn't been so stupid about it, the rets would have put their ships down in the water right away, but they lacked the experience that would have taught them to do so.

The shock of multiple collisions rattled *Black Moclips* to her mastheads, tearing huge holes in her hull and collapsing her forward rams. Both grappling hooks had torn free somewhere along the way, leaving entire sections of decking and railing in splinters. Alt Mer was thrown to the back of the pilot box and lost control of the craft completely. He struck his head on the retaining wall, bright splashes of color clouding his vision. But he scrambled up again anyway, hands groping for the steering levers.

In seconds, he had *Black Moclips* swinging back around for a second pass. He could see clearly now the damage he had inflicted on the Morgawr's fleet. Airships lay in pieces in the water, some of them burning. Debris and bodies were scattered everywhere. A few survivors clung to the wreckage, but not many. Most were gone. He tried not to think of it. He tried to think instead of the lives he was saving, concentrating on his friends and shipmates and his promise to protect them.

Back toward the remainder of the fleet he sailed, picking up speed as he approached. One or two airships were under way now, and he made for them. His purpose was clear. By the time he was finished, not one of them would be left. He intended to sink them all and leave the Morgawr and whoever was with him stranded on Mephitic.

He couldn't do this, of course, if there was any chance at all that the ships he was attacking might be repaired. He had to destroy them utterly. He had to decimate them.

There was only one way to do that.

He wished Little Red could be here to see this. She would appreciate the simplicity of it. He glanced over his shoulder at the island, but he was too far away now to make out anything clearly. Smoke and ash rose off the damaged fleet in waves, obscuring his view. A dingy gray haze masked the clear blue of the morning sky, and the fresh salt air smelled of burning wood and metal.

His speed was back up to better than thirty knots as he bore down on the ships still flying. He corrected his course to allow for what he intended, a pass that would take him directly into their midst, but lower down this time. Only one of those remaining had managed to get all her sails up and her anchor weighed, but she was floundering in dead air and smoke. Smoke roiled off the decks of three others.

Alt Mer threw off his cloak and unsnapped his safety line. Mobility was his best ally at this point. He closed down the parse tube exhausts, but locked the thrusters all the way forward to keep drawing down power from the light sheaths. No airship Captain would do this unless he wanted to blow his vessel to pieces. The power generated by the radian draws had to be expelled from the tube exhausts or they would explode and take the airship with them.

Not to mention everything within shouting distance.

He held *Black Moclips* on course, letting the power build inside the parse tubes until he could see smoke and fire breaking through the seams. *They just need to hold together a little longer*, he thought. He took a deep breath to steady himself. The Morgawr's airships loomed right ahead.

"Time to move on," he whispered.

Moments later, *Black Moclips* tore through the hulls of the remaining airships like an enraged bull through stalks of corn in an autumn field, and exploded in a ball of fire.

* * *

Bek Ohmsford raced through the ruins after his sister, heedless of the noise he was making because no one could hear him anyway over the sounds of the battle being fought somewhere just ahead. Sharp cracklings and deep booms echoed through the stone corridors of the ancient castle, breaking down centuries-old silence and walls alike, the exchanges of magic powerful enough to cause the earth itself to vibrate beneath his feet. Grianne had found the Morgawr, or it might be the other way around, but the battle between them had begun in either case, and he needed to be a part of it.

Except that he had no idea what to do once he was, and it was a problem he couldn't afford to delay solving for long. After he found his sister, he was going to have to do something to help her. But what sort of help could he offer? His mastery of the wishsong's power was a poor second to her own. She had already warned him that he stood no chance against the Morgawr, that the warlock's experience and skill were so vast that Bek would be swiftly overwhelmed.

So what was he going to do that would make a difference? How was he going to avoid being the distraction she had told him she could not afford to have him be?

He didn't know. He knew only that he couldn't stay behind and let her face the Morgawr alone. He had gone through too much to find and heal her to let something bad happen to her now.

The sounds ahead quieted, and he slowed in response, listening carefully. He was in a gloom-shrouded part of the castle, its walls towering over him, corridors narrow and high and rooms cavernous. The ceilings were vaulted and multitiered, and the dark shadows they cast were alive with unexplained movement. He eased along one wall, walking softly, once again trying to hide his approach. Smoke rolled through the chambers, and the air had a burnt smell to it.

He quieted his breathing. Everything was still. What if it was over? What if the Morgawr had won and Grianne was dead? He went cold at the prospect, casting it away from him as he would a poisonous snake, not wanting to touch it. That was not what had happened, he told himself firmly. Grianne was all right.

Nevertheless, he moved ahead more quickly, anxious to make certain. He was surprised that the enormity of the struggle hadn't roused the castle's dweller. With so much sound and fury invading its privacy and so much damage inflicted upon its keep, Bek would have thought the spirit furious enough to retaliate. But there was no indication of that happening, nothing in the air to trigger a warning, nothing in the feel of the stone to suggest danger. For whatever reason, the spirit was not responding. Bek found it puzzling. Maybe it was because the spirit reacted only to attempts to take things away, as it had with Bek and Truls. Maybe that was all it cared about—keeping possession of its treasures. Maybe the fact that the walls and towers that made up its domain were collapsing didn't mean anything to it, no more so than when they crumbled as a result of time's passage.

He had an idea then, sudden and unexpected, of how he might use his magic against the Morgawr. But he had to find him first, and he sensed that time was running out.

But finding the warlock did not take him as long as he had expected. The silence was shattered moments later by a rough-edged sound that reverberated through the stone walls, a quick and sudden rending. He went toward it at once, following its echoes as they died away, hearing voices. He reached a break in the walls, and through it saw his sister and the Morgawr locked in combat. The warlock had trapped her and was holding her fast by the sheer force of his magic. She was fighting to break free—Bek could see the strain on her smooth face—but she could not seem to bring her magic to bear in a way that would allow her to do so. The Morgawr was squeezing her, crushing her, closing off air and space and light, the darkness he wielded a visible presence as it closed.

Bek saw the Morgawr's hand reach for Grianne, stretching the fabric of her protective magic to touch her face. Grianne's head snapped away, and she wrenched at the shackles that had trapped her. The Morgawr was too strong, Bek saw. Even for her, for the Ilse Witch, he was too powerful. His fingers extended, and Bek could see the sudden hunching of his shoulders as he forced his way closer. His intent was unmistakable. He meant to feed on her.

Grianne!

There was no time left for Bek to think about what he wanted to do, no time for anything but doing it. He threw out the magic of his wishsong in an enveloping cloak that settled over the Morgawr like spiderwebbing, a faint tickling that the warlock barely noticed. But deep within the heart of the ruins, where even the Morgawr could not penetrate, the castle's dweller stirred in recognition. Up from its slumber it surged, fully awake in seconds, sensing all at once that something it had thought lost for good was again within reach. It roared through its crumbling walls, down its debris-strewn corridors, and across its empty courtyards. It paid no heed to the *Jerle Shannara* or to the living or the dead men who surrounded her or to what was taking place just offshore over the Blue Divide. It paid no heed to anything but the creature that had roused it.

The Morgawr.

Except that it didn't see the warlock for what he was. It saw him for what Bek had used the magic of the wishsong to make him appear. It saw him as the boy who had stolen its key weeks earlier, who had teased it with boldness and tricked it with magic.

Mostly, it saw him as a thief who still had that key.

The Morgawr had only a moment to look up from Grianne, to realize that something was terribly wrong, and then the spirit was upon him. It swept into the Morgawr like a whirlwind, ripping him away from his victim, bearing him backwards into the closest wall and pinning him there. The Morgawr shrieked in fury and fought back with his own magic, tearing at the wind, at the air, at the magic of the dweller, mad with rage. Bek screamed through the thunderous roar for Grianne to run, and she gathered herself and started toward him.

Then, almost inexplicably, she turned back.

Bracing herself, she threw her own magic at the Morgawr, lending strength to the castle dweller's efforts to crush him. The sound was so terrifying, so wrenchingly invasive, that Bek put his hands over his ears and scrunched up his face in pain. Reptilian face twisting with shock and fury, arms windmilling to gain purchase where there was none to be had, the Morgawr jerked upright as the combined magics ripped through him. For a moment, he held them at bay, girl and spirit both, his dark heart long since turned to stone, his mind to iron. He would not be beaten by such as these, the bright glare of his green eyes seemed to say. Not on this day.

Then the stone behind him cracked wide, and he was thrust inside the fissure. The opening ran deep and long, through multiple tiers of blocks set by its builders centuries ago to form a support wall for towers and ramparts now mostly gone. Thrashing against his imprisonment, the Morgawr fought to escape, but the pressure of the magics that held him fast was enormous.

He could not break free. Bek could see it on his face and in his eyes. He was trapped.

Slowly, the stone began to seal again. The Morgawr shrieked, striking at it with his magic, chunks of it falling away beneath the sharp edges of his power. But not enough stone could be shredded or slowed, and the gap narrowed. Bit by bit, he was squeezed as he had sought to squeeze Grianne. Little by little, he was crushed more tightly by the dwindling space. Now he could no longer move his arms to gesture, to invoke his spells, to trigger his magic's release. His body twisted frantically, and his shrieking rose to inhuman levels.

When the walls closed all the way, the fingers of one hand were still protruding from a tiny crack. They twitched momentarily in the fresh silence that settled over the ruins. When they finally went still, the crack had disappeared and the wall was leaking blood.

* * *

The explosions from land and sea had brought the Wing Riders out of hiding on the distant atoll. They flew their Rocs into the clear morning air and banked toward the dark smudges of smoke rising off the ruins of the ancient castle, then turned again at the sight of more smoke rolling over the waters of the Blue Divide. They caught a glimpse of the Morgawr's freshly smoldering airships and watched in shock as *Black Moclips* flew into them. Then everything disappeared in a massive explosion that filled the air with fire and smoke and created a shock wave so strong it could be felt miles away.

Hunter Predd could not tell what had transpired beyond the obvious. Hiding from the Morgawr had clearly not worked, but the nature of the battle being fought now was hard to judge. Catching sight of Spanner Frew and two of the Rover crew standing at the shore's edge, he banked Obsidian toward them, with Po Kelles and Niciannon following right behind. More explosions sounded, parse tubes giving way to the pressure of overheated diapson crystals as the destruction of the Morgawr's fleet continued. The Wing Riders swept downward to the island, landed close to the Rovers, jumped from their birds, and rushed over.

"What's happened?" Hunter Predd asked the shipwright. Seeing the other's dazed look, he took hold of his arm and turned him about forcibly. "Talk to me!"

Spanner Frew shook his head in disbelief. "He flew right into them, Wing Rider. He hooded the crystals, drew down enough power to destroy a dozen airships, and he flew right into them. All by himself, he destroyed them. I can't believe it!"

Hunter Predd knew without having to ask that the shipwright was talking about Redden Alt Mer. He looked out over the Blue Divide into the billowing clouds of smoke. Pieces of airships floated on the water, twisted and blackened. The water itself was on fire. There was no sign of an airship aloft and no sign of life in the water.

He stood with Po Kelles and the Rovers and stared in silence at the carnage. Big Red had found a way to stop them after all, he thought with a mix of admiration and sadness.

"Maybe he got out in time," he said quietly.

None of the others replied or even looked at him. They knew the truth of it. No one could survive an explosion like that. Even if you somehow managed to jump clear, the fall would kill you; the fire and the debris would finish you if it didn't.

They stared out into the heavy clouds of smoke, transfixed. None of them wanted to believe that Redden Alt Mer was really gone. None of them wanted to believe it could end like this.

It was quiet now, the morning gone still and peaceful. The explosions had stopped, even from the castle behind them. Whatever battles had been fought, they were over. Hunter Predd found himself wondering who had won. Or maybe if anyone had.

"We'd better see what's happened to the others," he said.

They were just turning away, when something appeared out of the roiling clouds of black smoke. At first, the Wing Rider thought it was a Roc or a War Shrike and wondered where it had come from. But it wasn't the right size and it wasn't flying in the right way. It was something else altogether.

"Black Beard," he whispered softly.

The flying object began to take shape as it emerged from the haze, slowly becoming recognizable for what it was, floundering badly, but staying aloft.

It was a single wing.

"Shades!" Spanner Frew hissed.

The man who flew it still had the luck.

THIRTY-THREE

A little more than five months later, the man with the luck and those he had sworn to protect were safely home again. Redden Alt Mer stood at the rail of the *Jerle Shannara* and stared out into the misty twilight of the Dragon's Teeth, thinking for the first time in weeks of his harrowing escape from the destruction of the Morgawr's fleet, reminded of it suddenly by a hunting bird winging its way in slow spirals through the mist that drifted down out of the mountains. His thinking lasted only a moment. That he had found a way through the fire and smoke and explosive debris still amazed him and didn't bear looking at too closely. Life was a gift you accepted without questioning its generosity or reason.

Still, he would not want to risk his luck like that again. When he returned to the coast and March Brume, he would still fly airships, but he would fly them in safer places.

"What do you suppose they are talking about?" Rue asked, leaning close so that her words would not carry.

Some distance off in the gloom, Bek Ohmsford stood with his sister, two solitary figures engaged in a taut, intense discussion. Their argument, pure and simple, transcended the parting that was taking place. Those who watched from the airship, those few who still remained—Ahren Elessedil, Quentin Leah, Spanner Frew, Kelson Riat, and Britt Rill—waited patiently to see how it would end.

"They're talking about the choice she has made," he answered quietly. "The choice Bek can't accept."

They had flown in from the coast yesterday, the Wing Riders Hunter Predd and Po Kelles leaving them there to return home to the Wing Hove, their mission complete, their pledge to provide scouting and foraging for the expedition fulfilled. How invaluable their help had been. It was hard to watch them make that final departure, hard to know they wouldn't still be warding the ship. Some things he got so used to he couldn't imagine life without them. It was like that for Alt Mer with the Wing Riders.

Still, he would see them again. Out along the coast, over the Blue Divide, on calmer days and under better circumstances.

They would have returned Ahren Elessedil and the Blue Elfstones to Arborlon and the Elves, then flown the Elven Prince home to face his brother, but for the insistence of Grianne Ohmsford that they come first to the Dragon's Teeth, to the Valley of Shale and the Hadeshorn. She would hear no arguments against it. She owed something to Walker, she told them. She must come to where the dead could be summoned and spoken with, to where the shade of the Druid could tell her the rest of what she must know.

When she had told them why, they were stunned into silence. Not even Bek could believe it. Not then and clearly not now.

"She might be mistaken about this," Rue continued obstinately. "She might be taking on more than was ever intended of her."

Alt Mer nodded. "She might. But none of us thinks so, not even Bek. She was saved for this, made whole by the Sword of Shannara and her brother's love." He grimaced. "I sound almost poetic."

She smiled. "Almost."

They watched in silence again. Bek was gesturing furiously, but

Grianne was only standing there, weathering the storm of his anger, calm resolution reflected in her stance and lack of movement. She had made up her mind, Alt Mer knew, and she was not someone who could be persuaded to change it easily. It was more than stubbornness, of course. It was her certainty of her destiny, of what was needed of her, of what was expected. It was her understanding of what it would take for her to gain redemption for the damage she had done to so many lives in so many places for all those years that she had been the Ilse Witch.

When this is done, he thought, *nothing will be the same again for any of us; our lives will be changed forever. Perhaps the lives of everyone in the Four Lands will be changed, as well.* What waited in the days ahead was that compelling—a new order, a fresh beginning, a reaching into the past to find hope for the future. All these would come about because of what happened here, on this night, in the mountains of the Dragon's Teeth, in the Valley of Shale, at the edge of the Hadeshorn, when Grianne Ohmsford summoned the shade of Walker.

So she had promised them.

He found it hard to argue with someone who believed she was meant to be Walker Boh's successor and the next Druid to serve the Four Lands.

Bek was having none of it. He had gone through too much in bringing his sister safely home again to let her wander off now, to place herself at risk once more—at greater risk perhaps than ever.

"You assume that you are meant to achieve something that even Walker could not!" he snapped, willing her to flinch in the face of his wrath. "He could not return for this, could not save himself to make the Druid order come alive. Why do you think it will be any different for you? At least he was not universally despised!"

He threw out the last few words in desperation and regretted them as soon as they were spoken. But Grianne did not seem bothered, and she reached out to touch his face gently.

"Don't be so angry, Bek. Your life does not lie with me in any case. It lies with her."

She glanced toward the *Jerle Shannara* and Rue Meridian. Stubbornly denying what he knew was true, Bek refused to look. "My life is not the subject of this discussion," he insisted. "Yours is the one that's likely to be thrown away if you go through with this. Why can't you just come home with me, find a little peace and comfort for a change, not go out and try to do something impossible!"

"I don't know yet exactly what it is I am expected to do," she answered calmly. "I only know what was revealed to me through the magic of the Sword of Shannara—that I am to become the next Druid and will atone for my wrongs by accepting that trust. If through my efforts a Druid Council is formed, as Walker intended that it should be, then the Druids will have a strong presence again in the Four Lands. That was why I was saved, Bek. That was what Walker gave his life for, so that I could make possible the goals he had set for himself but knew he would not live to see fulfilled."

She stepped close to him and placed her slender hands on his shoulders. "I don't do this out of foolish expectation or selfish need. I do this out of an obligation to make something worthwhile of a wasted life. Look at me, Bek. Look at what I have done. I can't ignore who I am. I can't walk away from a chance to redeem myself. Walker was counting on that. He knew me well enough to understand how I would feel, once the truth was revealed to me. He trusted that I would do what was needed to atone for the harm I have visited on others. How wrong it would be for me to betray him now."

"You wouldn't betray him by becoming who you should have been in the first place if none of this had happened!"

She smiled sadly. "But it did happen. It did, and we can't change that. We have to live with it. I have to live with it."

She put her arms around him and hugged him. He stood rigid in her embrace for a few moments, then little by little, the tension and the anger drained away until at last he hugged her back.

"I love you, Bek," she said. "My little brother. I love you for what you did for me, for believing in me when no one else would, for seeing who I could be if I was free of the Morgawr and his lies. That won't change, even if everything else in the world does."

"I don't want you to go." His words were bitter with disappointment. "It isn't fair."

She sighed softly, her breath a whisper in his ear. "I was never meant to come home with you, Bek. That isn't my life; it isn't the life I was meant to live. I wouldn't be happy, not after what I have been through. Coran and Liria are your parents, not mine. Their home is yours. Mine lies elsewhere. You have to accept this. If I am to find peace, I have to make amends for the damage I have done and the hurt I have caused. I can do this by following the destiny Walker has set for me. A Druid can make a difference in the lives of so many. Perhaps becoming one will make a difference in mine, as well."

He hugged her tighter to him. He sensed the inevitability of what she was saying, the certainty that no matter how hard he argued against it, no matter what obstacles he presented, she was not going to change her mind. He hated what that meant, the loss of any real chance at a life as brother and sister, as family. But he understood that he had lost most of that years ago, and he couldn't have it back the way it was or even the way it would have been. Life didn't allow for that.

"I just don't want to lose you again," he said.

She released him and stepped away, her strange blue eyes almost merry. "You couldn't do that, little brother. I wouldn't allow it. Whatever I do, however this business tonight turns out, I won't ever be far away from you."

He nodded, feeling suddenly as if he were just a boy again, still small and in his sister's care. "Go on, then. Do what you need to do." He gave her a quick smile. "I'm all argued out. All worn out." He looked off into the sunset, which had become a faint silver glow in the gathering dark, and fought back his tears. "I'm going home, now. I need to go home. I need for this to be over."

She came close once more, so small and frail it seemed impossible that she could possess the kind of strength a Druid would need. "Then go, Bek. But know that a part of me goes with you. I will not forget you, nor my promise not ever to be too far away."

She kissed him. "Will you wish me luck?"

"Good luck," he muttered.

She smiled. "Don't be sad, Bek. Be happy for me. This is what I want."

She tightened her dark robes about her and turned away. "Wait!" he said impulsively. He unstrapped the Sword of Shannara from where he wore it across his back and handed it to her. "You'll know what to do with this better than I will."

She looked uncertain. "It was given to you. It belongs to you."

He shook his head. "It belongs to the Druids. Take it back to them."

She accepted the talisman, cradling it in her arms like a baby at rest. "Good-bye, Bek."

In moments, she had started her climb into the mountains. He stood watching until he could no longer see her, all the while unable to overcome the feeling that he was losing her again.

Rue Meridian watched him return to the airship across the broken rock of the barren flats on which they had landed, his head lowered into shadow, fists clenched. Clearly, he was not happy about how things had turned out with his sister. Anger and disappointment radiated from him. Rue knew what he had asked of Grianne and knew, as well, that he had been refused. She could have saved him the trouble, but she supposed he had to find it out for himself. Bek was nothing if not a believer in impossibilities.

"He looks like a whipped puppy," Big Red mused.

She nodded.

"At least we can go home now," he continued. "We're finished here."

She watched Bek approach for a moment longer, then left her brother's side, climbed down the rope ladder, and walked out onto the flats. She didn't think Bek even saw her until she moved to block his way and he looked up to find her standing right in his path.

"I've been thinking," she said. "About your home, the one you were born in. It wasn't too far from here, was it?"

He stared at her.

"Do you think we could find where it was, if we went looking?"

His puzzlement was clear. "I don't know."

"Want to try?"

"It's only ruins."

"It's your past. You need to see it."

He glanced toward the airship doubtfully.

"No," she said. "Not them. They don't have time for such things. It would be just you and me. On foot." She let him consider for a moment. "Think of it as an adventure, a small one, but one for just the two of us. After we find it, we can keep going, walk south through the Borderlands along the Rainbow Lake down to the Silver River, then home to the Highlands. Big Red can fly Quentin to Leah on the *Jerle Shannara*, then take Ahren on to Arborlon."

She stepped closer, put her arms around him and her face next to his. "I don't know about you, but I've had enough of airships for a while. I want to walk."

He looked stunned, as if he had been handed a gift he hadn't expected and didn't deserve. "You're coming with me? To the Highlands?"

She smiled and kissed him softly on the mouth. "Bek," she whispered, "I was never going anywhere else."

* * *

Grianne Ohmsford spent the larger part of the night climbing into the foothills below the Dragon's Teeth, seeking to reach the Valley of Shale before dawn. She might have had Alt Mer fly her in on the airship, but she wanted time alone before summoning the shade of Walker. Besides, it was easier to say her good-byes now rather than later, particularly to Bek. She knew it would be hard to tell him she wasn't going with him, and it had been. His expectations for her had always been his own and never hers, and it was difficult for him to give them up. He would come to understand, but only in time.

She found the darkness familiar and comforting, still an old friend after all these years. Wrapped in its protective concealment, given peace by its unbroken solitude, she could think about what she was doing and where she was going; she could reflect on the events that had led her to this place and time. The destruction of the Morgawr had not given her the satisfaction she had hoped for. She would need more than revenge to heal. Her Druid life might provide her with that healing, though she knew it would not do so in the traditional way. It would not soothe and comfort her. It would not erase the past or allow her to forget she had been the Ilse Witch. She was not even assured of the nurturing rest of a good night's sleep. Instead, she would be given an opportunity to balance the scales. She would be given a chance at redemption for an otherwise unbearable past. She would be given a reason for living out the rest of her life.

She did not know if that would be enough to salvage her damaged psyche, her wounded soul, but it was worth a try.

By midnight, she was approaching her destination. She had never been here before and did not know the way, but her instincts told her where she needed to go. Or perhaps it was Walker who guided her, reaching out from the dead. Either way, she proceeded without slowing, and found in the simple act of moving forward a kind of peace. She should have been frightened of what waited; she knew one day the fear she could not seem to put a name to would catch up to her, would make itself known. But her feelings now were all of resolution and commitment, of finding a new place in the world and making a new beginning.

When she reached the rim of the Valley of Shale, coming upon it quite suddenly through a cluster of massive boulders, she stopped and gazed down into its bowl. The valley was littered with chips of glistening black rock, their shiny surfaces reflecting the moonlight like animal eyes. At the valley's center, the Hadeshorn was a smooth, flat mirror, its waters undisturbed. It was an unsettling place, all silence and empty space, nothing living, nothing but herself. She thought it a perfect place for a meeting with a shade.

She sat down to wait.

Everyone despises you, Bek had told her. The words had been spoken with the intent of changing her mind, but also to hurt her. They had not succeeded in the former, but had in the latter. Did still.

With dawn an hour away, she went down into the valley and stood at the edge of the lake. From what she had been shown by the magic of the Sword of Shannara, she understood what had happened to Walker in this place and would happen now to her. There was a power in the presence of the dead that was disconcerting even to her. Shades were beyond the living and yet still held sway over them because of what they knew.

The future. Its possibilities. Her fate, with all of its complex permutations.

Walker would see what she could not. He would know the choices that awaited her, but would not be able to tell her of their meaning. Knowledge of the future was forbidden to the living because the living must always determine what that future would be. The best the dead could do was to share glimpses of its possibilities and let the living make of them what they would.

She stared off into the distance, thinking that she didn't care to know the future in any case. She was here to discover if what the magic had shown her was real—if she was meant to be a Druid, to be Walker's successor, to carry on his work. She had told Bek and the others that she was, but she could not be sure until she heard it from the Druid's shade. She wanted it to be so; she wanted to be given a chance at doing something that would matter in a good way, that would help secure the work Walker had begun. She wanted to give him back something for the pain she had caused him. Mostly, she wanted to think that she was useful again, that she could find purpose in life, that things did not begin and end with her time as the Ilse Witch.

She glanced down at the waters of the Hadeshorn. *Poison*, the magic of the Sword of Shannara had whispered. But she was poison, too. She bent impulsively to dip her hand into the dark mirror of moonlight and stars but snatched it back as the waters began to stir. At the center of the lake, steam hissed like dragon's breath. It was time. Walker was coming.

She straightened within the dark folds of her cloak and waited for him.

"I did not think to see you again, little brother," Kylen Elessedil declared, sweeping into the room with his customary brusqueness, not bothering with formalities or greetings, not wasting unnecessary time.

"Your surprise is no greater than my own," Ahren allowed. "But here I am anyway."

It had been two days since he had said good-bye to Quentin Leah in the Highlands and three since Grianne Ohmsford had walked into the Dragon's Teeth. Afterwards, Ahren had flown west with the Rovers aboard the *Jerle Shannara* to Arborlon, thinking the whole time of what he would say when this moment came. He knew what was expected of him—not only by those with whom he had traveled, but also by himself. His was arguably the most important task of all, certainly the most tricky, given the way his brother felt about him. The boy he had been when he had left to follow the tracings of Kael Eles-sedil's map would not have been able to handle it. It remained to be seen if the man he had become could.

That he had been met by Elven Home Guard and brought to this small room at the back of the palace, quietly and without fan-fare, testified to the fact that his brother still regarded him mostly as a nuisance. Kylen would tolerate his return just long enough to de-termine if anything more was necessary. The reappearance of Ahren was no cause for celebration absent a recovery of the Elfstones.

"Where is the Druid?" his brother asked, getting right to the point. He walked to the curtained windows at the back of the room and looked out through the folds. "Still aboard ship?"

"Gone back into the Dragon's Teeth," Ahren answered. It was not a lie exactly, just a shading of the truth. Kylen didn't need to know everything just yet. In particular, he didn't need to know how things stood with the Druids.

"Were you successful in your efforts on this expedition, brother?"

"Mostly, yes."

Kylen arched an eyebrow. "I am told you return with less than a quarter of those who went."

"More than that. Some have gone on to their homes. There was no need for them to come here. But, yes, many were lost, Ard Pa-trinell and his Elven Hunters among them."

"So that of all the Elves who went, you alone survived?"

Ahren nodded. He could hear the accusation in the other's words, but he refused to dignify it with a response. He did not need to justify himself to anyone now, least of all to his brother, whose only disappointment was that even a single Elf had survived.

Kylen Elessedil moved away from the window and came over to stand in front of him. "Tell me, then. Did you find the Elfstones? Do you have them with you?"

He could not quite hide the eagerness in his voice or the flush that colored his fair skin. Kylen saw himself empowered by the

Elfstones. He did not understand their demands. He might not even realize that they were useless in most of the situations in which he would think to use them. It was the lure of their power that drew him, and the thought of it obscured his thinking.

Still, it was not Ahren's problem. "I have them. I will give them to you as soon as I am certain we are clear on the terms of the agreement Father and Walker reached."

Anger flooded his brother's face. "It is not your place to remind me of my obligations! I know what my father promised! If the Druid has fulfilled his part of the bargain—if you have the Elfstones and a share of the Elven magic to give to me—then it shall be done as Father wished!"

His brother made no attempt to hide the fact that he thought everything was intended just for him rather than for the Elven people. Kylen was a brave man and a strong fighter, but too ambitious for his own good and not much of a politician. He would be causing problems with the Elven High Council by now. He would have already angered certain segments of his people.

"The Elfstones will be yours by the time I leave," Ahren said. "The magic Walker sought to find requires translation and interpretation in order to comprehend its origins and worth. Those Elves who go to become Druids in the forming of the new council can help with that work. Two dozen would be an adequate number to start."

"A dozen will do," his brother said. "You may choose them yourself."

Ahren shook his head. "Two dozen are necessary."

"You test my patience, Ahren." Kylen glared at him, then nodded. "Very well, they are yours."

"A full share of the money promised to each of the men and women who went on this expedition must be paid out to the survivors or to the families of the dead."

His brother nodded grudgingly. He was looking at Ahren with something that approached respect, clearly impressed, if not pleased, by his younger brother's poise and determination. "Anything else? You'll want to keep the airship, I expect."

Ahren didn't bother answering. Instead, he reached into his pocket, withdrew the pouch containing the Elfstones, and handed it to his brother. Kylen took only a moment to release the drawstrings and dump the Stones into his hand. He stared down wordlessly into their depthless blue facets, an unmistakable hunger in his eyes.

"Do you need me to tell you how to make the magic work?" Ahren asked cautiously.

His brother looked over at him. "I know more about them than you think, little brother. I made a point of finding out."

Ahren nodded, not quite understanding, not sure if he wanted to. "I'll be going, then," he said. "After I gather supplies and talk with those I think might come to Paranor." He waited for Kylen to respond, and when he didn't, said, "Good-bye, Kylen."

Kylen was already moving toward the door, the Elfstones clutched in his hand. He stopped as he opened it, and looked back. "Take whatever you need, little brother. Go wherever you want. But, Ahren?" A broad smile wreathed his handsome face. "Don't ever come back."

He went out through the door and closed it softly behind him.

It was dawn off the coast of the Blue Divide, and Hunter Predd was flying on patrol aboard Obsidian. He had slept almost continuously for several days after his return, but because he was restless by nature, he required no more time than that to recover from the hardships of his journey and so was back in the air. He never felt at home anywhere else, even in the Wing Hove; he was always anxious to be airborne, always impatient to be flying.

The day was bright and clear, and he breathed deeply of the sea air, the taste and smell familiar and welcome. The voyage of the *Jerle*

Shannara seemed a long time ago, and his memories of its places and people were beginning to fade. Hunter Predd did not like living in the past, and thus discarded it pretty much out of hand. It was the present that mattered, the here and now of his life as a Wing Rider, of his time in the air. He supposed that was in the nature of his occupation. If you let your mind wander, you couldn't do what was needed.

He searched the skyline briefly for airships, thinking to spot one somewhere in the distance along the coast, perhaps even one captained by Redden Alt Mer. He thought that of all those he had sailed with, the Rover was the most remarkable. Lacking magic or knowledge or even special skills, he was the most resilient, the one nothing seemed to touch. The man with the luck. Hunter Predd could still see him flying, miraculously unscathed, out of the smoky wreckage of the Morgawr's fleet aboard his single wing. He thought that when nothing else could save you in this world, luck would always do.

Seagulls flew across his path, white-winged darts against the blue of the water. Obsidian gave a warning cry, then wheeled left. He had seen something floating in the water, something his rider had missed. Hunter Predd's attention snapped back to the job at hand. He saw it now, bobbing in the surf, a splash of bright color.

Perhaps it was a piece of clothing.

Perhaps it was a body.

He felt a catch in his throat, remembering a time that suddenly did not seem so long ago after all.

Using his hands and knees to guide the Roc, he flew down for a closer look.